The Gormenghast Novels

The Gormenghast Novels

TITUS GROAN   GORMENGHAST   TITUS ALONE

Mervyn Peake

The Overlook Press
Woodstock · New York .

This paperback edition published in 1995 by

The Overlook Press, Peter Mayer Publishers, Inc.
Woodstock & New York

WOODSTOCK:
One Overlook Drive
Woodstock, NY 12498
www.overlookpress.com
[for individual orders, bulk and special sales, contact our Woodstock office]

NEW YORK:
141 Wooster Street
New York, NY 10012

Library of Congress Cataloging-in-Publication Data

Peake, Mervyn Lawrence, 1911–1968
    The gormenghast novels / Mervyn Peake.
—1st collected paperback edition.
    p. cm.
Contents: Titus Groan—Gormenghast—Titus Alone.   1. Fantastic fiction,
English   I. Title.
                                                                95-16431
PR6031.E183G64 1995   CIP
823'.912—dc20

20 19 18 17 16 15 14 13 12 11   ISBN: 0-87951-628-3

For information about the Mervyn Peake Society, write to Secretary Frank H.
Surry, 2 Mount Park Road, Ealing, London, W5 2RP England

For information about *Peake Studies,* write to Peter Winnington, Les 3 Chasseurs,
1413 Orzens, Switzerland

ACKNOWLEDGMENTS

"The Critical Reception of Mervyn Peake's Titus Books" © 1991 G. Peter Winnington

"Memories of Mervyn Peake" © 1986 Louise Collis. Reprinted from *Art and Artists*, August 1986.

"The Gutters of Gormenghast" © 1973 Hugh Brogan. Reprinted from *The Cambridge Review*, vol. 95, no. 2217, 23 Nov. 1973.

"Situating *Gormenghast*" © 1979 Ronald Binns. Reprinted from *Critical Quarterly*, vol. 21. no. 1, 1979.

"'The Passions in their Clay': Mervyn Peake's Titus Stories by Joseph L. Sanders. Reprinted from *Voices for the Future*, vol. 3, 1984, Popular Press, Bowling Green, OH, © 1984 Popular Press

"Titus and the Thing in *Gormenghast*" © 1976 Christiano Rafanelli. Reprinted from *The Mervyn Peake Review*, Autumn 1976, no. 3.

"Fuschia and Steerpike: Mood and Form" © 1977 G. Peter Winnington. Reprinted from *The Mervyn Peake Review*, Autumn 1977, no. 5.

"Psychology of the *Bildungsroman*" © 1978 Bruce Hunt. Reprinted from *The Mervyn Peake Review*, Spring 1978, no. 6.

"*Gormenghast*: Fairytale Gone Wrong?" © 1982 Margaret Ochocki. Reprinted from *The Mervyn Peake Review*, Autumn 1982, no. 15.

"The Cry of a Fighting Cock: Notes on Steerpike and Ritual in *Gormenghast*" © 1991 Ann Yeoman.

"Beowulf to Kafka: Mervyn Peake's *Titus Alone* © 1981 Colin Greenland. Reprinted from *Foundation*, no. 21, 1981.

"A Critical Conclusion: The End of *Titus Alone*" © 1981 Laurence Bristow-Smith. Reprinted from *The Mervyn Peake Review*, Spring 1981, no. 12.

"'A Barrier of Foolery': The Depiction of Women in *Titus Alone*" © 1988 Tanya Gardiner-Scott. Reprinted from *Peake Studies*, vol 1. no. 1, Autumn 1988.

Introduction to *Titus Awakes* © 1990 John Watney. Reprinted from *The Mervyn Peake Review*, no. 23 1990.

TITUS AWAKES © The Mervyn Peake Estate. Reprinted from *The Mervyn Peake Review*, no. 23, 1990, with the kind permission of The Mervyn Peake Estate and The Mervyn Peake Society.

Drawing from Robert Louis Stevenson's *Treasure Island* (London: Eyre & Spottiswoode, 1949, the Octopus Publishing Group), reproduced with kind permisison of The Mervyn Peake Estate.

We have made every effort to contact the copyright holders for the above essays; in cases where we have been unable to do so, we would welcome hearing from the authors or their representatives.

Contents

THE GENIUS OF MERVYN PEAKE

by Quentin Crisp

STYLE is a terrible thing to happen to anybody. As Miss Stein has already remarked, "the way to say it is to say it." Any attempt to devise a way of "saying it" that will tinge the subject with the writer's personality results in obscurity, mannerism, originality; and Mr. Eliot tells us that whatever is original is under suspicion. In particular it is what might be called "comparative originality" that is so awful. If a man were to look over the fence on one side of his garden and observe that the neighbor on his left had laid his garden path round a central lawn; and were to look over the fence on the other side of his garden and observe that the neighbor on his right had laid his path down the middle of the lawn, and were then to lay his own garden path diagonally from one corner to the other, that man's soul would be lost. Originality is only to be praised when not prefaced by the look to right and left.

The uniqueness of Mervyn Peake is of this order. Suspicion is allayed. Ages ago now Peake mentioned to me that he thought of writing a book many thousands of pages long, at the end of which the hero would probably only be a few months old; and when I expressed some doubts about the way in which such work would be received by the publishers, he replied, "I believe in doing what I like. I set about selling it afterwards." The work of which he was speaking was *Titus Groan*. His attitude has been justified—if justification were needed.

Perhaps the truest measure of Peake's originality is that there is something "old-world" about his work. He has done nothing to avoid comparison with Cruikshank and Tenniel, between whose illustrations and his own there are superficial likenesses. The resemblance is more technical than anything else. Only with one artist can he be compared with any degree of elaboration, and that is William Blake, who also was both an artist and a writer. Of the two, Peake is infinitely the greater draughtsman, infinitely less a mystic. Blake revelled in the fantastic; Peake dwells on the dreadful. In this respect he has taken another risk, for horror is a fashion at the present time, and it might be possible for historians to say that Peake has brought to book-illustration the qualities already introduced into painting and literature. This would not be true. Peake's "horror" is quite unlike that of his contemporaries in painting—probably because it is not directly psycho-analytical. The discovery of the unconscious and "all that" has affected modern life as deeply as the rediscovery of the pagan ideal affected the world of the 14th and 15th centuries, or as deeply as the properties of light affected the world of the Impressionists. But, while Peake cannot be unaware of this new stimulus to artistic activity, he is not, I think, greatly moved by it. Surrealism in its glibbest sense is concerned with dreams rather than with fancy; the horror of the scenes it depicts is symbolic, lying not in the objects themselves but in the conflicts, repressions and whatnot that the objects represent. Peake, on the other hand, seems to me concerned more with fancy than with dream, and he is not exegetical. At least, the working is not shown in the margin. He does not use the far horizon suggestive of infinity, not the incongruously grouped objects suggestive of individuality without context, which are the two most effective tricks of the Surrealists. Peake's distortions are the distortions common to all painters from the primitives onward. One kind is purely "aesthetic," an expression of a more intense and more continuous rhythm than is present in real life. This is Peake's strongest point and would be enough to draw attention to his work even if no other quality were evident. It appears to best advantage in his pure line work—the illustrations to *Quest for Sita* by Maurice Collis, for instance. Another kind is for purposes of caricature in its simplest sense, as in *Captain Slaughterboard Drops Anchor*, of which there is a new, colored edition. But there is this third kind; distortion for the sake of distortion, the power of which seems magical and is very hard to define.

Let us take as an example an illustration for *Ride a Cock-Horse*, one of his earliest books. It is called, "Three Men in a Tub..." and is in a closely hatched pen-and-ink technique with fairly strong washes of color added. It is interesting to note that it shows the tub and a candlestick most carefully drawn and with no distortion. This marks another difference between Peake and the surrealists, whose deliquescent watch-faces are merely things. Peake is not interested in things but in people. His horror is, therefore, more critical—one might say, more moral and less pure. Also, of course, the lack of distortion in the drawing of the objects increases the grotesqueness of the people—all of whom in this particular picture are stupid and brutish. But more than this there is a distortion of the subject matter, for the Butcher is depicted caressing the Baker's chin with one hand while in the other he holds out of sight of the Baker (poor fool)—a chopper. We are forced to conclude therefore that there is something about butchers that the artist doesn't like.

In an article on Peake's illustrations which appeared in *Alphabet and Image*, Frances Sarzano describes *Ride a Cock-Horse* as one of Peake's best books. From a technical standpoint it is. The drawing is tremendously vital and the composition of every picture is ingenious and at the same time inevitable. But as illustration it is shameless. The text throughout is traditional and of little emotional content, but the horror of the pictures that accompany it (said to be "subdued"), seems to me devastating. Take the case of poor Mr. and Mrs. Spratt.

They were a harmless couple, so far as we know, who very wisely pooled their gastronomic differences in order to maintain a life of domestic contentment. But the contempt that Peake has poured upon them has transfixed them into positions of bloated idiocy. On one side of the table in a blousy torpor sprawls Mrs. Spratt; half asleep (and doubtless belching), her figure completely ruined by her foolishly unvaried diet; on the other side sits her husband with his face in total shadow so that there shall be no limit to the suggestion of debauched greed. The plate in the middle of the table is empty and the bone which they have gluttonously stripped of everything has been thrown to the cat. But what a cat! The highest tribute to Peake's genius that I can find is to say that I cannot bring myself to describe that cat! Did he blame it for remaining in the Spratt household? Surely if Peake is to illustrate any more nursery rhymes they should run something like this...

> Ride a Cock-Horse
> to Banbury Cross
> to see a bad actress
> obtain a divorce...

All this suggests that the ideal book for Peake to illustrate would be one written by himself. Such is *Captain Slaughterboard*, which I personally find absorbing, though I am told by an assistant in a book shop in Liverpool Street that the children for whom it is intended always pick it up (as they do all of Peake's books), but seldom buy it. The explanation offered is that they are put off by the horror. I cannot think of any other reason, but I am disinclined to believe it. I think it is parents who wish their children didn't like dreadful tales and pictures!

Another book, both the text and the pictures of which are by Mervyn Peake, is *Rhymes without Reason*, but this is an unsatisfac-

with best wishes from
C'n Slaughterboard

A pen-and-ink drawing on the front endpaper of a copy of
Captain Slaughterboard Drops Anchor, sold recently at Sotheby's

tory little publication in which the text is vastly superior to the illustrations...

> The very nastiest grimace
> you make upon the sly
> is "choice" beside the hippo's face
> who doesn't even try...

I quote from memory but I think it goes like that. This and *Witchcraft in England* are the only books of Peake's which it is possible to criticise unfavorably, though it is easy to express very distinct preferences for some rather than for others because all of them are so different. With the new edition of *Alice in Wonderland* and *Through the Looking-Glass* (published in Sweden), *Bleak House* (not yet out), and *Letters from a Lost Uncle* (still unfinished) Mervyn Peake will have done at least a dozen books— and, though a slight majority of these is in cross-hatched pen and ink, all are different and include work in charcoal, pencil, lithographic chalk and color.

This variety of technique is a very good sign in an artist. In Peake it is just that he does what he likes; but it also expresses indirectly a wonderful scorn for easy success. Though it may mean work still in an experimental stage being put before the critics, who will doubtless take the opportunity to find fault, it must be remembered that an artist as vigorous as Peake may easily fulfil himself in all these media.

* * * * * *

Over and above the admiration felt for Peake the artist, is the promise of Peake the writer. For an illustrator is very much like an actor. If he lends himself utterly to every book he illustrates he is involved in shifting his whole outlook on life, to say nothing of varying his technique incessantly. (Dulac saw this difficulty; Rackham ignored it). And if he doesn't he is not really an illustrator except when he can find a kindred spirit in the world of literature. And who is to be a kindred spirit to Mervyn Peake? Not even Dickens, for though, like Peake, he dwelt only on physical ugliness and saw it always as the outward and visible sign of inward and spiritual disgrace, he was a moralist of an extremely crude order. Of course there must be some kindred spirits and Frances Sarzano gives a small list of possible books for Peake to illustrate. It includes naturally *Don Quixote and Gulliver's Travels*, and—astonishingly— Pope's "The Rape of the Lock." To my mind this list has the disadvantage of including so many books that have been illustrated so well before, a dilemma that forces Peake into looking over the fence at the gardens of his neighbours and might tempt him to "comparative originality," whereas there are modern works which present no such handicaps—Kafka's *Trial*, the Telephone Book, or some serious work of Peake's own; for oddly enough *Titus Groan* has no illustrations and only an indifferent cover.

And, when we come back to *Titus Groan* and Peake the writer, we come back to the comparison with Blake; for just as Blake's drawings never quite equal his *Songs of Innocence and Experience* and come nowhere near the *Marriage of Heaven and Hell*, so there is more enchantment in a little poem like "Maeve" than in the most suggestive of Peake's illustrations. (This poem appeared in his book of verse called *Shapes and Sounds* and was afterwards included in Walter De la Mare's anthology *Love*). What a canvas would be needed to be the pictorial equal of *Titus Groan*! The merits and faults of this book have been discussed by a number of critics including Charles Morgan, and it seems to be agreed that it doesn't fulfil its promise. But how could it? In this work Peake succeeds in building a whole new world, but he was asked also to govern it. This he could not do.

Nevertheless it is in writing that Peake must ultimately seek his fulfillment, for literature is an ampler medium than painting—certainly than the illustrating which is always interpretive. Also Peake's most personal quality is a strangeness verging on dreadfulness and, if this is expressed in painting, a certain ludicrous quality is always liable to creep in; the eye begins to vomit sooner than the ear—far sooner than the mind. Am I prophesying about Peake's future? It is certainly a temptation when writing of a man of only thirty-four, who has in seven years established himself both as a writer and as an artist; but it would be difficult, for Mervyn Peake does what he likes.

Besides it is unnecessary to say what he will be.

Mervyn Peake is.

Acknowledgment is made to Quentin Crisp and Paul Britten Austin for permission to reprint this article from *Facet*, 1946, Vol. 1, pages 8-13.

RHYMES WITHOUT REASON

INTRODUCTION

by Anthony Burgess

THE middle and late nineteen-forties saw the appearance of a number of British works of literature which were quick to assume the status of 'classics' – meaning eloquent, authoritative, definitive statements begotten by an epoch but speaking for more than that epoch. All who beguiled the bad days of the end of the war and the start of the peace by reading *Four Quartets*, *The Unquiet Grave*, *Brideshead Revisited*, *The Loved One*, *Animal Farm* and *Nineteen Eighty-Four*, were aware that these books were only able to say what they did about the human permanencies because of the urgency enforced by the times. They all have in common the concise presentation of a world – Connolly's France, Waugh's alternatives of Catholic order and necropolitan despair, Orwell's two dystopias, Eliot's mystical 'still point' where history is redeemed by eternity. These worlds are built round a separable idea, which may be summed up as man's impotence to be good or happy without cherishing the values the war nearly quelled for ever. One book, however, resisted and still resists the shelling-out of a central sermon or warning. The world created in *Titus Groan* is neither better nor worse than this one: it is merely different. It has absorbed our history, culture and rituals and then stopped dead, refusing to move, self-feeding, self-motivating, self-enclosed. This is the world of Gormenghast.

Titus Groan, the first novel in a trilogy, appeared in 1946. Its author, Mervyn Peake, was then thirty-five. Critical response to the book was

very favourable, in some instances ecstatic. Peake continued the fortunes of his hero and the elaboration of his hero's world in *Gormenghast*
(1950) and *Titus Alone* (1959). Fine though these sequels are, they could
not repeat the impact of the first book: 1946, year of austerity, was
very ready for imaginative feasts. But, despite the praise of critics, *Titus
Groan* never reached the widest possible public; it was destined to be
something of a coterie obsession. Peake makes few appearances in
histories of modern fiction, and one can see why. Unlike the vaunted
post-war names, he does not seek – in his subject-matter – to probe
topical themes like race, class and homosexuality or advance the frontiers of what we call the contemporary consciousness; in technique, he
appears to look back rather than forward. His books nourish the private
imagination; they do not exemplify the development of an art.

Peake has been praised, but he has also been mistrusted. His prose
works are not easily classifiable; they are unique as, say, the books of
Peacock or Lovecraft are unique. Moreover, he has too many talents:
he is a fine poet and a highly original draughtsman. The Peake style
in book illustration is inimitable, and it has been greatly imitated. He
has, in his total mastery of the literary as well as the pictorial art, only
one peer – Wyndham Lewis. Their aims in both arts could not be more
dissimilar, but Peake and Lewis come together in an approach to descriptive writing which owes a great deal to the draughtsman's trade.
If their books seem slow-moving, that is because of the immense solidity
of their visual contents, the lack of interest in time and the compensatory obsession with filling up space. *Titus Groan* is aggressively three-
dimensional. Look at the opening description of Gormenghast, where
the term 'a certain ponderous architectural quality' exactly conveys
what we are in for. But around the solidity is an extra dimension, one
of magic, showing the poet as well as the draughtsman: 'This tower,
patched unevenly with black ivy, arose like a mutilated finger from
among the fists of knuckled masonry and pointed blasphemously at
heaven.'

This sounds like 'Gothic' writing, but the term is inadequate. As we
read *Titus Groan*, we seem to be given clues directing us towards the
daylight of a literary category, but all the keys change into red herrings.
Take the names of the characters, for instance – Nettel ('the octogenarian who lived in the tower above the rusting armoury'); Rottcodd,
curator of the Hall of the Bright Carvings; Flay, Swelter, Steerpike,
Mrs Slagg, Prunesquallor. These are fitting for a Peacock novel, for
Dickens or for a comic children's story. They are farcical, but the mood
is not one of easy laughter or even of airy fantasy: the ponderous
architectural quality holds everything down, and we have to take the
characters very seriously, despite their names. Nor is it appropriate to
think in terms of a gallery of glorious eccentrics (a very British concept).

Nobody flies away from a centre of normality; everybody belongs to a system built on very rigid rules.

The estate of Gormenghast is sustained by tradition and ritual. Lord Sepulchrave, the father of Titus, is instructed daily by Sourdust, lord of the library, in the acts he must perform. These are laid down in ancient books: 'the exact times; the garments to be worn for each occasion and the symbolic gestures to be used'. The whole ritualistic system is only properly understood by Sourdust — 'the technicalities demanding the devotion of a lifetime, though the sacred spirit of tradition implied by the daily manifestations was understood by all.' This same sacred spirit operates at all levels. Thus, the Great Kitchen is kept clean by eighteen men called the Grey Scrubbers, automata whose calling is predestined and hereditary. But it is out of this kitchen that a revolutionary force emerges — the youth Steerpike who, on his own admission, has 'a disrespectful nature'. He calls the Countess of Groan, that great lady who lives in a sea of white cats, 'the old Bunch of Rags'; he even calls the sun 'the old treacle bun'. Pulling the legs off a stag-beetle, slowly, one by one, he says: 'Equality is the great thing, equality is *everything*.' The worn-out radical arguments sound fresh and sinister in this closed world: 'Don't you think it's wrong if some people have to work all their lives for a little money to exist on while others never do any work and live in luxury?' Steerpike is one of the destroyers. He burns the library, killing its lord and sending Titus's father mad. There is a season of violence and murder. But Gormenghast remains, and the Warden of the Immemorial Rites proclaims Titus its seventy-seventh earl.

The book ends with its titular hero not yet two years old, but there is plenty of time for him: we have finished a mere third of the tripartite epic. And it is as we near the end of *Titus Groan* that we realize the propriety of applying the term 'epic' in an exact sense. The book is closer to ancient pagan romance than to traditional British fiction. The doomed ritual lord, the emergent hero, the castle, the hall of retainers, the mountain, the lake, the twisted trees, the strange creatures, the violent knives, the dark and the foreboding belong (however qualified by tea, muffins, tobacco and sherry wine) to a prehistoric England. And the magnificence of the language denotes an epic concept.

It is difficult, in post-war English writing, to get away with big rhetorical gestures. Peake manages it because, with him, grandiloquence never means diffuseness; there is no musical emptiness in the most romantic of his descriptions; he is always exact.

The roof of the Twisted Woods reflected the staring circle in a phosphorescent network of branches that undulated in the lower slopes of Gormenghast Mountain . . . . Every blade of the grass was of consequence,

and the few scattered stones held an authority that made their solid, separate marks upon the brain – each one with its own unduplicated shape:
each rising brightly from the ink of its own spilling.

Occasionally, as in the book's peroration, he seems to go too far:

Through honeycombs of stone would now be wandering the passions
in their clay. There would be tears and there would be strange laughter.
Fierce births and deaths beneath umbrageous ceilings . . . And there shall
be a flame-green daybreak soon. And love itself will cry for insurrection!

But context is everything. The whole book is a gesture only too well
aware that it goes too far; there is a certain built-in self-mockery, most
evidently proclaimed in the grotesque names and titles. We are asked
to accept conventions that it is impossible to take seriously, but within
those conventions the blood is genuinely moved or chilled. The husky
purr of the Countess, her heavy body decked, thick as foliage, with
birds, conveys a shudder authentic enough: 'In Titus it's all centred.
Stone and mountain – the Blood and the Observance. Let them touch
him. For every hair that's hurt I'll stop a heart. If grace I have when
turbulence is over – so be it; and if not – what then?'
It is a complex book in that it evokes many layers of response: the
sophisticated pleasure in consummate artifice, the more naive enjoyment proper to a rather archaic romance, horror which is qualified by
disbelief, a kind of 'camp' titillation, self-indulgence in 'Gothic' atmosphere, a genuine aesthetic elation induced by language finely used. It
is an intellectual book, in which wit – in the old sense of cerebral play
– operates at times when we expect only the nerves to be engaged:
'The Thing scraped the ceiling with its head and moved forward noiselessly in one piece. Having no human possibility of height, it had *no*
height. It was not a tall ghost – it was immeasurable; Death walking
like an element.' One is always aware of the cool control of the author's
intelligence, even in the most romantic flights, maintaining, like an
estate generator, the imagined world and excluding the real one. But
is the real one totally excluded?
We have to go back to the year of the book's first appearance, the
first year after a long and horrifying war, before we can answer that
question. The attaching of a calf's skull to dead Sourdust's vertebrae,
the cat's claws ripping a 'crimson wedge' from Steerpike's cheek below
the right eye, the fight between Flay and Swelter in the Hall of Spiders
– these are not gratuitous Gothicisms so much as reflections out of an
era of horrors. The burning of hundreds of years of tradition and the
madness of an earl deprived of his sustaining props of ritual – these
seem to be symbols of the end of true, historical, centuries of order.

But it would be dangerous to search too earnestly for the allegorical in *Titus Groan*. It remains essentially a work of the closed imagination, in which a world parallel to our own is presented in almost paranoiac denseness of detail. But the madness is illusory, and control never falters. It is, if you like, a rich wine of fancy chilled by the intellect to just the right temperature. There is no really close relative to it in all our prose literature. It is uniquely brilliant, and we are right to call it a modern classic.

TITUS GROAN

Dost thou love picking meat? Or would'st thou see
A man in the clouds, and have him speak to thee?

BUNYAN

THE HALL OF THE BRIGHT CARVINGS

GORMENGHAST, that is, the main massing of the original stone, taken by itself would have displayed a certain ponderous architectural quality were it possible to have ignored the circumfusion of those mean dwellings that swarmed like an epidemic around its outer walls. They sprawled over the sloping earth, each one half way over its neighbour until, held back by the castle ramparts, the innermost of these hovels laid hold on the great walls, clamping themselves thereto like limpets to a rock. These dwellings, by ancient law, were granted this chill intimacy with the stronghold that loomed above them. Over their irregular roofs would fall throughout the seasons, the shadows of time-eaten buttresses, of broken and lofty turrets, and, most enormous of all, the shadow of the Tower of Flints. This tower, patched unevenly with black ivy, arose like a mutilated finger from among the fists of knuckled masonry and pointed blasphemously at heaven. At night the owls made of it an echoing throat; by day it stood voiceless and cast its long shadow.

Very little communication passed between the denizens of these outer quarters and those who lived *within* the walls, save when, on the first June morning of each year, the entire population of the clay dwellings had sanction to enter the Grounds in order to display the wooden carvings on which they had been working during the year. These carvings, blazoned in strange colour, were generally of animals or figures and were treated in a highly stylized manner peculiar to themselves. The competition among them to display the finest object of the year was bitter and rabid. Their sole passion was directed, once their days of love had guttered, on the production of this wooden sculpture, and among the muddle of huts at the foot of the outer wall, existed a score of creative craftsmen whose position as leading carvers gave them pride of place among the shadows.

At one point *within* the Outer Wall, a few feet from the earth, the great stones of which the wall itself was constructed, jutted forward in the form of a massive shelf stretching from east to west for about two hundred to three hundred feet. These protruding stones were painted white, and it was upon this shelf that on the first morning of June the carvings were ranged every year for judgement by the Earl of Groan.

Those works judged to be the most consummate, and there were never more than three chosen, were subsequently relegated to the Hall of the Bright Carvings.

Standing immobile throughout the day, these vivid objects, with their fantastic shadows on the wall behind them shifting and elongating hour by hour with the sun's rotation, exuded a kind of darkness for all their colour. The air between them was turgid with contempt and jealousy. The craftsmen stood about like beggars, their families clustered in silent groups. They were uncouth and prematurely aged. All radiance gone.

The carvings that were left unselected were burned the same evening in the courtyard below Lord Groan's western balcony, and it was customary for him to stand there at the time of the burning and to bow his head silently as if in pain, and then as a gong beat thrice from within, the three carvings to escape the flames would be brought forth in the moonlight. They were stood upon the balustrade of the balcony in full view of the crowd below, and the Earl of Groan would call for their authors to come forward. When they had stationed themselves immediately beneath where he was standing, the Earl would throw down to them the traditional scrolls of vellum, which, as the writings upon them verified, permitted these men to walk the battlements above their cantonment at the full moon of each alternate month. On these particular nights, from a window in the southern wall of Gormenghast, an observer might watch the minute moonlit figures whose skill had won for them this honour which they so coveted, moving to and fro along the battlements.

Saving this exception of the day of carvings, and the latitude permitted to the most peerless, there was no other opportunity for those who lived within the walls to know of these 'outer' folk, nor in fact were they of interest to the 'inner' world, being submerged within the shadows of the great walls.

They were all-but forgotten people: the breed that was remembered with a start, or with the unreality of a recrudescent dream. The day of carvings alone brought them into the sunlight and reawakened the memory of former times. For as far back as even Nettel, the octogenarian who lived in the tower above the rusting armoury, could remember, the ceremony had been held. Innumerable carvings had smouldered to ashes in obedience to the law, but the choicest were still housed in the Hall of the Bright Carvings.

This hall which ran along the top storey of the north wing was presided over by the curator, Rottcodd, who, as no one ever visited the room, slept during most of his life in the hammock he had erected at the far end. For all his dozing, he had never been known to relinquish the feather duster from his grasp; the duster with which he would perform one of the only two regular tasks which appeared to be necessary in that long and silent hall, namely to flick the dust from the Bright Carvings.

As objects of beauty, these works held little interest to him and yet in spite of himself he had become attached in a propinquital way to a few of the carvings. He would be more than thorough when dusting the Emerald Horse. The black-and-olive Head which faced it across the boards and the Piebald Shark were also his especial care. Not that there were any on which the dust was allowed to settle.

Entering at seven o'clock, winter and summer, year in and year out, Rottcodd would disengage himself of his jacket and draw over his head a long grey overall which descended shapelessly to his ankles. With his feather duster tucked beneath his arm, it was his habit to peer sagaciously over his glasses down the length of the hall. His skull was dark and small like a corroded musket bullet and his eyes behind the gleaming of his glasses were the twin miniatures of his head. All three were constantly on the move, as though to make up for the time they spent asleep, the head wobbling in a mechanical way from side to side when Mr Rottcodd walked, and the eyes, as though taking their cue from the parent sphere to which they were attached, peering here, there, and everywhere at nothing in particular. Having peered quickly over his glasses on entering and having repeated the performance along the length of the north wing after enveloping himself in his overall, it was the custom of Rottcodd to relieve his left armpit of the feather duster, and with that weapon raised, to advance towards the first of the carvings on his right hand side, without more ado. Being at the top floor of the north wing, this hall was not in any real sense a hall at all, but was more in the nature of a loft. The only window was at its far end, and opposite the door through which Rottcodd would enter from the upper body of the building. It gave little light. The shutters were invariably lowered. The Hall of the Bright Carvings was illuminated night and day by seven great candelabra suspended from the ceiling at intervals of nine feet. The candles were never allowed to fail or even to gutter, Rottcodd himself seeing to their replenishment before retiring at nine o'clock in the evening. There was a stock of white candles in the small dark ante-room beyond the door of the hall, where also were kept ready for use Rottcodd's overall, a huge visitors' book, white with dust, and a stepladder. There were no chairs or tables, nor indeed any furniture save the hammock at the window end where Mr Rottcodd slept. The boarded floor was white with dust which, so assiduously kept from the carvings, had no alternative resting place and had collected deep and ash-like, accumulating especially in the four corners of the hall.

Having flicked at the first carving on his right, Rottcodd would move mechanically down the long phalanx of colour standing a moment before each carving, his eyes running up and down it and all over it, and his head wobbling knowingly on his neck before he introduced his feather duster. Rottcodd was unmarried. An aloofness and even a nervousness was apparent on first acquaintance and the ladies held a peculiar horror for him. His, then, was an ideal existence, living alone day and night in a long loft. Yet occasionally, for one reason or another, a servant or a member of the household would make an unexpected appearance and startle him with some question appertaining to ritual, and then the dust would settle once more in the hall and on the soul of Mr Rottcodd.

What were his reveries as he lay in his hammock with his dark bullet head tucked in the crook of his arm? What would he be dreaming of, hour after hour, year after year? It is not easy to feel that any great thoughts haunted his mind nor – in spite of the sculpture whose bright files surged over the dust in narrowing perspective like the highway for an emperor – that Rottcodd made any attempt to avail himself of his isolation, but rather that he was enjoying the solitude for its Own Sake, with, at the back of his mind, the dread of an intruder.

One humid afternoon a visitor *did* arrive to disturb Rottcodd as he lay deeply hammocked, for his siesta was broken sharply by a rattling of the door handle which was apparently performed in lieu of the more popular practice of knocking at the panels. The sound echoed down the long room and then settled into the fine dust on the boarded floor. The sunlight squeezed itself between the thin cracks of the window blind. Even on a hot, stifling, unhealthy afternoon such as this, the blinds were down and the candlelight filled the room with an incongruous radiance. At the sound of the door handle being rattled Rottcodd sat up suddenly. The thin bands of moted light edging their way through the shutters barred his dark head with the brilliance of the outer world. As he lowered himself over the hammock, it wobbled on his shoulders, and his eyes darted up and down the door returning again and again after their rapid and precipitous journeys to the agitations of the door handle. Gripping his feather duster in his right hand, Rottcodd began to advance down the bright avenue, his feet giving rise at each step to little clouds of dust. When he had at last reached the door the handle had ceased to vibrate. Lowering himself suddenly to his knees he placed his right eye at the keyhole, and controlling the oscillation of his head and the vagaries of his left eye (which was for ever trying to dash up and down the vertical surface of the door), he was able by dint of concentration to observe, within three inches of his keyholed eye, an eye which was *not* his, being not only of a different colour to his own iron marble but being, which is more convincing, on the other side of the door. This third eye which was going through the same performance as the one belonging to Rottcodd, belonged to Flay, the taciturn servant of Sepulchrave, Earl of Gormenghast. For Flay to be four rooms horizontally or one floor vertically away from his lordship was a rare enough thing in the castle. For him to be absent at all from his master's side was abnormal, yet here apparently on this stifling summer afternoon was the eye of Mr Flay at the outer keyhole of the Hall of the Bright Carvings, and presumably the rest of Mr Flay was joined on behind it. On mutual recognition the eyes withdrew simultaneously and the brass doorknob rattled again in the grip of the visitor's hand. Rottcodd turned the key in the lock and the door opened slowly.

Mr Flay appeared to clutter up the doorway as he stood revealed, his arms folded, surveying the smaller man before him in an expressionless way. It did not look as though such a bony face as his could give normal utterance, but rather that instead of sounds, something more brittle, more ancient, something dryer would emerge, something perhaps more in the nature of a splinter or a fragment of stone. Nevertheless, the harsh lips parted. 'It's me,' he said, and took a step forward into the room, his knee joints cracking as he did so. His passage across a room – in fact his passage through life – was accompanied by these cracking sounds, one per step, which might be likened·to the breaking of dry twigs.

Rottcodd, seeing that it was indeed he, motioned him to advance by an irritable gesture of the hand, and closed the door behind him.

Conversation was never one of Mr Flay's accomplishments and for some time he gazed mirthlessly ahead of him, and then, after what seemed an eternity to Rottcodd he raised a bony hand and scratched himself behind the ear. Then he made his second remark, 'Still here, eh?' he said, his voice forcing its way out of his face.

Rottcodd, feeling presumably that there was little need to answer such a question, shrugged his shoulders and gave his eyes the run of the ceiling.

Mr Flay pulled himself together and continued: 'I said still here, eh, Rottcodd?' He stared bitterly at the carving of the Emerald Horse. 'You're still here, eh?'

'I'm invariably here,' said Rottcodd, lowering his gleaming glasses and running his eyes all over Mr Flay's visage. 'Day in, day out, invariably. Very hot weather. Extremely stifling. Did you want anything?'

'Nothing,' said Flay and he turned towards Rottcodd with something menacing in his attitude. 'I want *nothing*.' He wiped the palms of his hands on his hips where the dark cloth shone like silk.

Rottcodd flicked ash from his shoes with the feather duster and tilted his bullet head. 'Ah,' he said in a non-committal way.

'You say "ah",' said Flay, turning his back on Rottcodd and

beginning to walk down the coloured avenue, 'but I tell you, it is more than "ah".'

'Of course,' said Rottcodd. 'Much more, I dare say. But I fail to understand. I am a Curator.' At this he drew his body up to full height and stood on the tips of his toes in the dust.

'A what?' said Flay, straggling above him for he had returned. 'A curator?'

'That is so,' said Rottcodd, shaking his head.

Flay made a hard noise in his throat. To Rottcodd it signified a complete lack of understanding and it annoyed him that the man should invade his province.

'Curator,' said Flay, after a ghastly silence, 'I will tell you something. I know something. Eh?'

'Well?' said Rottcodd.

'I'll tell you,' said Flay. 'But first, what day is it? What month, and what year is it? Answer me.'

Rottcodd was puzzled at this question, but he was becoming a little intrigued. It was so obvious that the bony man had something on his mind, and he replied, 'It is the eighth day of the eighth month, I am uncertain about the year. But why?'

In a voice almost inaudible Flay repeated 'The eighth day of the eighth month.' His eyes were almost transparent as though in a country of ugly hills one were to find among the harsh rocks two sky-reflecting lakes. 'Come here,' he said, 'come closer, Rottcodd, I will tell you. You don't understand Gormenghast, what happens in Gormenghast – the things that happen – no, no. Below you, that's where it all is, under this north wing. What are these things up here? These wooden things? No use now. Keep them, but no use now. Everything is moving. The castle is moving. Today, first time for years he's alone, his Lordship. Not in my sight.' Flay bit at his knuckle. 'Bedchamber of Ladyship, that's where he is. Lordship is beside himself: won't have me, won't let me in to see the New One. The New One. He's come. He's downstairs. I haven't seen him.' Flay bit at the corresponding knuckle on the other hand as though to balance the sensation. 'No one's been in. Of course not. I'll be next. The birds are lined along the bedrail. Ravens, starlings, all the perishers, and the white rook. There's a kestrel; claws through the pillow. My lady feeds them with crusts. Grain and crusts. Hardly seen her new-born. Heir to Gormenghast. Doesn't look at him. But my lord keeps staring. Seen him through the grating. Needs me. Won't let me in. Are you listening?'

Mr Rottcodd certainly was listening. In the first place he had never heard Mr Flay talk so much in his life before, and in the second place the news that a son had been born at long last to the ancient and historic house of Groan was, after all, an interesting tit-bit for a curator living alone on the upper storey of the desolate north wing. Here was something with which he could occupy his mind for some time to come. It was true, as Mr Flay pointed out, that he, Rottcodd, could not possibly feel the pulse of the castle as he lay in his hammock, for in point of fact Rottcodd had not even suspected that an heir was on its way. His meals came up in a miniature lift through darkness from the servants' quarters many floors below and he slept in the ante-room at night and consequently he was completely cut off from the world and all its happenings. Flay had brought him real news. All the same he disliked being disturbed even when information of this magnitude was brought. What was passing through the bullet-shaped head was a question concerning Mr Flay's entry. Why had Flay, who never in the normal course of events would have raised an eyebrow to acknowledge his presence – why had he now gone to the trouble of climbing to a part of the castle so foreign to him? And to force a conversation on a personality as unexpansive as his own. He ran his eyes over Mr Flay in his own peculiarly rapid way and surprised himself by saying suddenly, 'To what may I attribute your presence, Mr Flay?'

'What?' said Flay. 'What's that?' He looked down on Rottcodd and his eyes became glassy.

In truth Mr Flay had surprised himself. Why, indeed, he thought to himself, had he troubled to tell Rottcodd the news which meant so much to him? Why Rottcodd, of all people? He continued staring at the curator for some while, and the more he stood and pondered the clearer it became to him that the question he had been asked was, to say the very least, uncomfortably pertinent.

The little man in front of him had asked a simple and forthright question. It had been rather a poser. He took a couple of shambling steps towards Mr Rottcodd and then, forcing his hands into his trouser pockets, turned round very slowly on one heel.

'Ah,' he said at last, 'I see what you mean, Rottcodd – I see what you mean.'

Rottcodd was longing to get back to his hammock and enjoy the luxury of being quite alone again, but his eye travelled even more speedily towards the visitor's face when he heard the remark. Mr Flay had said that he saw what Rottcodd had meant. Had he really? Very interesting. What, by the way, *had* he meant? What precisely was it that Mr Flay had seen? He flicked an imaginary speck of dust from the gilded head of a dryad.

'You are interested in the birth below?' he inquired.

Flay stood for a while as though he had heard nothing, but after a few minutes it became obvious he was thunderstruck. 'Interested!' he cried in a deep, husky voice, 'Interested! The child is a Groan. An authentic male Groan. Challenge to Change! No *Change*, Rottcodd. No Change!'

'Ah,' said Rottcodd. 'I see your point, Mr Flay. But his lordship was not dying?'

'No,' said Mr Flay, 'he was not dying, but *teeth lengthen!*' and he strode to the wooden shutters with long, slow heron-like paces, and the dust rose behind him. When it had settled Rottcodd could see his angular parchment-coloured head leaning itself against the lintel of the window.

Mr Flay could not feel entirely satisfied with his answer to Rottcodd's question covering the reason for his appearance in the Hall of the Bright Carvings. As he stood there by the window the question repeated itself to him again and again. Why Rottcodd? Why on earth Rottcodd? And yet he knew that directly he heard of the birth of the heir, when his dour nature had been stirred so violently that he had found himself itching to communicate his enthusiasm to another being – from that moment Rottcodd had leapt to his mind. Never of a communicative or enthusiastic nature he had found it difficult even under the emotional stress of the advent to inform Rottcodd of the facts. And, as has been remarked, he had surprised even himself not only for having unburdened himself at all, but for having done so in so short a time.

He turned, and saw that the Curator was standing wearily by the Piebald Shark, his small cropped round head moving to and fro like a bird's, and his hands clasped before him with the feather duster between his fingers. He could see that Rottcodd was politely waiting for him to go. Altogether Mr Flay was in a peculiar state of mind. He was surprised at Mr Rottcodd for being so unimpressed at the news, and he was surprised at himself for having brought it. He took from his pocket a vast watch of silver and held it horizontally on the flat of his palm. 'Must go,' he said awkwardly. 'Do you hear me, Rottcodd, I must go?'

'Good of you to call,' said Rottcodd. 'Will you sign your name in the visitors' book as you go out?'

'No! Not a visitor.' Flay brought his shoulders up to his ears. 'Been with lordship thirty-seven years. Sign a *book*,' he added contemptuously, and he spat into a far corner of the room.

'As you wish,' said Mr Rottcodd. 'It was to the section of the visitors' book devoted to the staff that I was referring.'

'No!' said Flay.

As he passed the curator on his way to the door he looked carefully at him as he came abreast, and the question rankled. Why? The castle was filled with the excitement of the nativity. All was alive with conjecture. There was no control. Rumour swept through the strong-hold. Everywhere, in passage, archway, cloister, refectory, kitchen, dormitory, and hall it was the same. Why had he chosen the unenthusiastic Rottcodd? And then, in a flash he realized. He must have subconsciously known that the news would be new to no one else;

that Rottcodd was virgin soil for his message, Rottcodd the curator who lived alone among the Bright Carvings was the only one on whom he could vent the tidings without jeopardizing his sullen dignity, and to whom although the knowledge would give rise to but little enthusiasm it would at least be new.

Having solved the problem in his mind and having realized in a dullish way that the conclusion was particularly mundane and uninspired, and that there was no question of his soul calling along the corridors and up the stairs to the soul of Rottcodd, Mr Flay in a thin straddling manner moved along the passages of the north wing and down the curve of stone steps that led to the stone quadrangle, feeling the while a curious disillusion, a sense of having suffered a loss of dignity, and a feeling of being thankful that his visit to Rottcodd had been unobserved and that Rottcodd himself was well hidden from the world in the Hall of the Bright Carvings.

THE GREAT KITCHEN

As Flay passed through the servants' archway and descended the twelve steps that led into the main corridor of the kitchen quarters, he became aware of an acute transformation of mood. The solitude of Mr Rottcodd's sanctum, which had been lingering in his mind, was violated. Here among the stone passages were all the symptoms of ribald excitement. Mr Flay hunched his bony shoulders and with his hands in his jacket pockets dragged them to the front so that only the black cloth divided his clenched fists. The material was stretched as though it would split at the small of his back. He stared mirthlessly to right and left and then advanced, his long spidery legs cracking as he shouldered his way through a heaving group of menials. They were guffawing to each other coarsely and one of them, evidently the wit, was contorting his face, as pliable as putty, into shapes that appeared to be independent of the skull, if indeed he had a skull beneath that elastic flesh. Mr Flay pushed past.

The corridor was alive. Clusters of aproned figures mixed and disengaged. Some were singing. Some were arguing and some were draped against the wall, quite silent from exhaustion, their hands dangling from their wrists or flapping stupidly to the beat of some kitchen catch-song. The clamour was pitiless. Technically this was more the spirit which Flay liked to see, or at all events thought to be more appropriate to the occasion. Rottcodd's lack of enthusiasm had shocked him and here, at any rate, the traditional observance of felicity at the birth of an heir to Gormenghast was being observed. But it would have been impossible for him to show any signs of enthusiasm himself when surrounded by it in others. As he moved along the crowded corridor and passed in turn the dark passages that led to the slaughter-house with its stench of fresh blood, the bakeries with their sweet loaves and the stairs that led down to the wine vaults and the underground network of the castle cellars, he felt a certain satisfaction at seing how many of the roysterers staggered aside to let him pass, for his station as retainer-in-chief to his Lordship was commanding and his sour mouth and the frown that had made a permanent nest upon his jutting forehead were a warning.

It was not often that Flay approved of happiness in others. He saw in happiness the seeds of independence, and in independence the seeds of revolt. But on an occasion such as this it was different, for the spirit of convention was being rigorously adhered to, and in between his ribs Mr Flay experienced twinges of pleasure.

He had come to where, on his left, and halfway along the servants' corridor, the heavy wooden doors of the Great Kitchen stood ajar. Ahead of him, narrowing in dark perspective, for there were no windows, the rest of the corridor stretched silently away. It had no doors on either side and at the far end it was terminated by a wall of flints. This useless passage was, as might be supposed, usually deserted, but Mr Flay noticed that several figures were lying stretched in the shadows. At the same time he was momentarily deafened by a great bellowing and clattering and stamping.

As Mr Flay entered the Great Kitchen the steaming, airless concentration of a ghastly heat struck him. He felt that his body had received a blow. Not only was the normal sickening atmosphere of the kitchen augmented by the sun's rays streaming into the room at various points through the high windows, but, in the riot of the festivities, the fires had been banked dangerously. But Mr Flay realized that it was *right* that this should be as insufferable as it was. He even realized that the four grillers who were forcing joint after joint between the metal doors with their clumsy boots, until the oven began to give under the immoderate strain, were in key with the legitimate temper of the occasion. The fact that they had no idea what they were doing nor why they were doing it was irrelevant. The Countess had given birth; was this a moment for rational behaviour?

The walls of the vast room which were streaming with calid moisture, were built with grey slabs of stone and were the personal concern of a company of eighteen men known as the 'Grey Scrubbers'. It had been their privilege on reaching adolescence to discover that, being the sons of their fathers, their careers had been arranged for them and that stretching ahead of them lay their identical lives consisting of an unimaginative if praiseworthy duty. This was to restore, each morning, to the great grey floor and the lofty walls of the kitchen a stainless complexion. On every day of the year from three hours before daybreak until about eleven o'clock, when the scaffolding and ladders became a hindrance to the cooks, the Grey Scrubbers fulfilled their hereditary calling. Through the character of their trade, their arms had become unusually powerful, and when they let their huge hands hang loosely at their sides, there was more than an echo of the simian. Coarse as these men appeared, they were an integral part of the Great Kitchen. Without the Grey Scrubbers something very earthy, very heavy, very real would be missing to any sociologist searching in that steaming room, for the completion of a circle of temperaments, a gamut of the lower human values.

Through daily proximity to the great slabs of stone, the faces of the Grey Scrubbers had become like slabs themselves. There was no expression whatever upon the eighteen faces, unless the lack of expression is in itself an expression. They were simply slabs that the Grey Scrubbers spoke from occasionally, stared from incessantly, heard with, hardly ever. They were traditionally deaf. The eyes were there, small and flat as coins, and the colour of the walls themselves, as though during the long hours of professional staring the grey stone had at last reflected itself indelibly once and for all. Yes, the eyes were there, thirty-six of them and the eighteen noses were there, and the lines of the mouths that resembled the harsh cracks that divided the stone slabs, they were there too. Although nothing physical was missing from any one of their eighteen faces yet it would be impossible to perceive the faintest sign of animation and, even if a basinful of their features had been shaken together and if each feature had been picked out at random and stuck upon some dummy-head of wax at any capricious spot or angle, it would have made no difference, for even the most fantastic, the most ingenious of arrangements could not have tempted into life a design whose component parts were dead. In all, counting the ears, which on occasion may be monstrously expressive, the one hundred and eight features were unable, at the best of times, to muster between them, individually or taken *en masse*, the faintest shadow of anything that might hint at the workings of what lay beneath.

Having watched the excitement developing around them in the Great Kitchen, and being unable to comprehend what it was all about for lack of hearing, they had up to the last hour or two been unable to enter into that festive spirit which had attacked the very heart and bowels of the kitchen staff.

But here and now, on this day of days, cognizant at last of the arrival of the new Lord, the eighteen Grey Scrubbers were lying side by side upon the flagstones beneath a great table, dead drunk to a man. They had done honour to the occasion and were out of the picture, having been rolled under the table one by one like so many barrels of ale, as indeed they were.

Through the clamour of the voices in the Great Kitchen that rose and fell, that changed tempo, and lingered, until a strident rush or a wheezy slide of sound came to a new pause, only to be shattered by a hideous croak of laughter or a thrilled whisper, or a clearing of some coarse throat – through all this thick and interwoven skein of bedlam, the ponderous snoring of the Grey Scrubbers had continued as a recognizable theme of dolorous persistence.

In favour of the Grey Scrubbers it must be said that it was not until the walls and floor of the kitchen were shining from their exertions that they attacked the bungs as though unweaned. But it was not only they who had succumbed. The same unquestionable proof of loyalty could be observed in no less than forty members of the kitchen, who, like the Grey Scrubbers, recognizing the bottle as the true medium through which to externalize their affection for the family of Groan, were seeing visions and dreaming dreams.

Mr Flay, wiping away with the back of his claw-like hand the perspiration that had already gathered on his brow, allowed his eyes to remain a moment on the inert and foreshortened bodies of the inebriate Grey Scrubbers. Their heads were towards him, and were cropped to a gun-grey stubble. Beneath the table a shadow had roosted, and the rest of their bodies, receding in parallel lines, were soon devoured in the darkness. At first glance he had been reminded of nothing so much as a row of curled-up hedgehogs, and it was some time before he realized that he was regarding a line of prickly skulls. When he had satisfied himself on this point his eyes travelled sourly around the Great Kitchen. Everything was confusion, but behind the flux of the shifting figures and the temporary chaos of overturned mixing tables, of the floor littered with stock-pots, basting pans, broken bowls and dishes, and oddments of food, Mr Flay could see the main fixtures in the room and keep them in his mind as a means of reference, for the kitchen swam before his eyes in a clammy mist. Divided by the heavy stone wall in which was situated a hatch of strong timber, was the *garde-manger* with its stacks of cold meat and hanging carcases and on the inside of the wall the spit. On a fixed table running along a length of the wall were huge bowls capable of holding fifty portions. The stock-pots were perpetually simmering, having boiled over, and the floor about them was a mess of sepia fluid and egg-shells that had been floating in the pots for the purpose of clearing the soup. The sawdust that was spread neatly over the floor each morning was by now kicked into heaps and soaked in the splashings of wine. And where scattered about the floor little blobs of fat had been rolled or trodden in, the sawdust stuck to them giving them the appearance of rissoles. Hanging along the dripping walls were rows of sticking knives and steels, boning knives, skinning knives and two-handed cleavers, and beneath them a twelve-foot by nine-foot chopping block, cross-hatched and hollowed by decades of long wounds.

On the other side of the room, to Mr Flay's left, a capacious enormous copper, a row of ovens and a narrow doorway acted as his landmarks. The doors of the ovens were flying wide and acid flames were leaping dangerously, as the fat that had been thrown into the fires bubbled and stank.

Mr Flay was in two minds. He hated what he saw, for of all the rooms in the castle, it was the kitchen he detested most, and for a very real reason; and yet a thrill in his scarecrow body made him aware of how right it all was. He could not, of course, analyse his feelings nor would the idea have occurred to him, but he was so much a part and parcel of Gormenghast that he could instinctively tell when the essence of its tradition was running in a true channel, powerfully and with no deviation.

But the fact that Mr Flay appreciated, as from the profoundest of motives, the vulgarity of the Great Kitchen in no way mitigated his contempt for the figures he saw before him as individuals. As he looked from one to another the satisfaction which he had at first experienced in seeing them collectively gave way to a detestation as he observed them piecemeal.

A prodigious twisted beam, warped into a spiral, floated, or so it seemed in the haze, across the breadth of the Great Kitchen. Here and there along its undersurface, iron hooks were screwed into its grain. Slung over it like sacks half filled with sawdust, so absolutely lifeless they appeared, were two pastry-cooks, an ancient *poissonnier*, a *rôtier* with legs so bandy as to describe a rugged circle, a red-headed *légumier*, and five *sauciers* with their green scarves around their necks. One of them near the far end from where Flay stood twitched a little, but apart from this all was stillness. They were very happy.

Mr Flay took a few paces and the atmosphere closed around him. He had stood by the door unobserved, but now as he came forward a roysterer leaping suddenly into the air caught hold of one of the hooks in the dark beam above them. He was suspended by one arm, a cretinous little man with a face of concentrated impudence. He must have possessed a strength out of all proportions to his size, for with the weight of his body hanging on the end of one arm he yet drew himself up so that his head reached the level of the iron hook. As Mr Flay passed beneath, the dwarf, twisting himself upside down with incredible speed, coiled his legs around the twisted beam and dropping the rest of himself vertically with his face a few inches from that of Mr Flay, grinned at him grotesquely with his head upside down, before Flay could do anything save come to an abrupt halt. The dwarf had then swung himself on to the beam again and was running along it on all fours with an agility more likely to be found in jungles than in kitchens.

A prodigious bellow outvoicing all cacophony caused him to turn his head away from the dwarf. Away to his left in the shade of a supporting pillar he could make out the vague unmistakable shape of what had really been at the back of his brain like a tumour, ever since he had entered the great kitchen.

SWELTER

THE chef of Gormenghast, balancing his body with difficulty upon a cask of wine, was addressing a group of apprentices in their striped and sodden jackets and small white caps. They clasped each other's shoulders for their support. Their adolescent faces steaming with the heat of the adjacent ovens were quite stupefied, and when they laughed or applauded the enormity above them, it was with a crazed and sycophantic fervour. As Mr Flay approached to within a few yards of the cluster, another roar, such as he had heard a moment or two earlier, rolled into the heat above the wine-barrel.

The young scullions had heard this roar many times before but had never associated it with anything other than anger. At first, consequently, it had frightened them, but they had soon perceived that there was no irritation in its note today.

The chef, as he loomed over them, drunken, arrogant and pedantic, was enjoying himself.

As the apprentices swayed tipsily around the wine cask, their faces catching and losing the light that streamed through a high window, they also, in a delirious fashion – were enjoying themselves. The echoes died from the apparently reasonless bellow of the chief chef and the sagging circle about the barrel stamped its feet feverishly and gave high shrill cries of delight, for they had seen an inane smile evolving from the blur of the huge head above them. Never before had they enjoyed such latitude in the presence of the chef. They struggled to outdo one another in the taking of liberties unheard of hitherto. They vied for favours, screaming his name at the tops of their voices. They tried to catch his eye. They were very tired, very heavy and sick with the drink and the heat, but were living fiercely on their fuddled reserves of nervous energy. All saving one high-shouldered boy, who throughout the scene had preserved a moody silence. He loathed the figure above him and he despised his fellow-apprentices. He leaned against the shadowy side of the pillar, out of the chef's line of vision.

Mr Flay was annoyed, even on such a day, by the scene. Although approving in theory, in practice it seemed to him that the spectacle was unpleasant. He remembered, when he had first come across Swelter, how he and the chef had instantaneously entertained a mutual dislike, and how this antipathy festered. To Swelter it was irksome to see the bony straggly figure of Lord Sepulchrave's first servant in his kitchen at all, the only palliative to this annoyance being the opportunity which if afforded for the display of his superior wit at Mr Flay's expense.

Mr Flay entered Swelter's steaming province for one purpose only. To prove to himself as much as to others, that he, as Lord Groan's personal attendant, would on no account be intimidated by any member of the staff.

To keep this fact well in front of his own mind, he made a tour of the servants' quarters every so often, never entering the kitchen, however, without a queasiness of stomach, never departing from it without a renewal of spleen.

The long beams of sunlight, which were reflected from the moist walls in a shimmering haze, had pranked the chef's body with blotches of ghost-light. The effect from below was that of a dappled volume of warm vague whiteness and of a grey that dissolved into swamps of midnight – of a volume that towered and dissolved among the rafters. As occasion merited he supported himself against the stone pillar at his side and as he did so the patches of light shifted across the degraded whiteness of the stretched uniform he wore. When Mr Flay had first eyed him, the cook's head had been entirely in shadow. Upon it the tall cap of office rose coldly, a vague topsail half lost in a fitful sky. In the total effect there was indeed something of the galleon.

One of the blotches of reflected sunlight swayed to and fro across the paunch. This particular pool of light moving in a mesmeric manner backwards and forwards picked out from time to time a long red island of spilt wine. It seemed to leap forward from the mottled cloth when the light fastened upon it in startling contrast to the chiaroscuro and to defy the laws of tone. This ungarnished sign of Swelter's debauche, taking the swollen curve of linen, had somehow, to Mr Flay's surprise, a fascination. For a minute he watched it appear, and disappear to reappear again – a lozenge of crimson, as the body behind it swayed.

Another senseless bout of foot-stamping and screaming broke the spell, and lifting his eyes he scowled about him. Suddenly, for a moment, the memory of Mr Rottcodd in his dusty deserted hall stole into his consciousness and he was shocked to realize how much he had really preferred – to this inferno of time-hallowed revelry – the limp and seemingly disloyal self-sufficiency of the curator. He straddled his way to a vantage point, from where he could see and remain unseen, and from there he noticed that Swelter was steadying himself on his legs and with a huge soft hand making signs to the adolescents below him to hold their voices. Flay noticed how the habitual truculence of his tone and manner had today altered to something mealy, to a conviviality weighted with lead and sugar, a ghastly intimacy more dreadful than his most dreaded rages. His voice came down from the shadows in huge wads of sound, or like the warm, sick notes of some prodigious mouldering bell of felt.

His soft hand had silenced the seething of the apprentices and he allowed his thick voice to drop out of his face.

'Gallstones!' and in the dimness he flung his arms apart so that the buttons of his tunic were torn away, one of them whizzing across the room and stunning a cockroach on the opposite wall. 'Close your ranks and close your ranks and listen mosht attentivesome. Come closer then, my little sea of faces, come ever closer in, my little ones.'

The apprentices edged themselves forward, tripping and treading upon each other's feet, the foremost of them being wedged against the wine-barrel itself.

'Thatsh the way. Thatsh jusht the way,' said Swelter, leering down at them. 'Now we're quite a happly little family. Mosht shelect and advanced.'

He then slid a fat hand through a slit in his white garment of office and removed from a deep pocket a bottle. Plucking out the cork with his lips, that had gripped it with an uncanny muscularity, he poured half a pint down his throat without displacing the cork, for he laid a finger at the mouth of the bottle, so dividing the rush of wine into two separate spurts that shot adroitly into either cheek, and so, making contact at the back of his mouth, down his throat in one dull gurgle to those unmentionable gulches that lay below.

The apprentices screamed and stamped and tore at each other in an access of delight and of admiration.

The chef removed the cork and twisted it around between his thumb and forefinger and satisfying himself that it had remained perfectly dry during the operation, recorked the bottle and returned it through the slit into his pocket.

Again he put up his hand and silence was restored save for the heavy, excited breathing.

'Now tell me thish, my stenching cherubs. Tell me thish and tell me exshtra quickly, who am *I*? Now tell me exshtra quickly.'

'Swelter,' they cried, 'Swelter, sir! Swelter!'

'Is that *all* you know?' came the voice. 'Is that *all* you know, my little sea of faces? Silence now! and lishen well to me, chief chef of Gormenghast, man and boy forty years, fair and foul, rain or shine, sand and sawdust, hags and stags and all the resht of them done to a turn and spread with sauce of aloes and a dash of prickling pepper.'

'With a dash of prickling pepper,' yelled the apprentices hugging themselves and each other in turn. 'Shall we cook it, sir? We'll do it now, sir, and slosh it in the copper, sir, and stir it up. Oh! what a tasty dish, sir, oh! what a tasty dish!'

'Shilence,' roared the chef. 'Silensh, my fairy boys. Silence, my belching angels. Come closer here, come closer with your little creamy faces and I'll tell you who I am.'

The high-shouldered boy, who had taken no part in the excitement, pulled out a small pipe of knotted worm-wood and filled it deliberately. His mouth was quite expressionless, curving neither up nor down, but his eyes were dark and hot with a mature hatred. They were half closed but their eloquence smouldered through the lashes as he watched the figure on the barrel lean forward precariously.

'Now lishen well,' continued the voice, 'and I'll tell you exactly who I am and then I'll shing to you a shong and you will know who's shinging to you, my ghastly little ineffectual fillets.'

'A song! A song!' came the shrill chorus.

'Firshtly,' said the chef leaning forward and dropping each confidential word like a cannon ball smeared with syrup. 'Firshtly, I am none other than Abiatha Swelter, which meansh, for you would not know, that I am the shymbol of both excellence and plenty. I am the *father* of exchellence and plenty. Who did I shay I was?'

'Abafer Swelter,' came the scream.

The chef leaned back on his swollen legs and drew the corners of his mouth down until they lost themselves among the shadows of his hot dewlaps.

'Abi*a*tha,' he repeated slowly, stressing the central 'A'. 'Abi*a*tha. What did I shay my name wash?'

'Abi*a*tha,' came the scream again.

'Thatsh right, thatsh right. Abi*a*tha. Are you lishening, my pretty vermin, are you lishening?'

The apprentices gave him to understand that they were listening very hard.

Before the chef continued he applied himself to the bottle once again. This time he held the glass neck between his teeth and tilting his head back until the bottle was vertical, drained it and spat it out over the heads of the fascinated throng. The sound of black glass smashing on the flagstones was drowned in screams of approval.

'Food,' said Swelter, 'is shelestial and drink is mosht entrancing – such flowers of flatulence. Sush gaseous buds. Come closer in, *steal* in, and I will shing. I will lift my sweetest heart into the rafters, and will shing to you a shong. An old shong of great shadness, a most dolorous piece. Come closer in.'

It was impossible for the apprentices to force themselves any closer to the chef, but they struggled and shouted for the song, and turned their glistening faces upwards.

'Oh what a pleasant lot of little joints you are,' said Swelter, peering at them and wiping his hands up and down his fat hips. 'What a very drippy lot of little joints. Oh yesh you are, but *so* underdone. Lishen cocks, I'll twisht your grandma's so shweetly in their graves. We'll make them turn, my dears, we'll make them turn – and what a turn for them, my own, and for the worms that nibble. Where's Steerpike?'

'Steerpike! Steerpike!' yelled the youths, the ones in front twisting their heads and standing upon their toes, the ones in the rear craning forward and peering about them. 'Steerpike! Steerpike! He's somewhere here, sir! Oh there he is sir! There he is sir! Behind the pillar sir!'

'Silence,' bellowed the chef, turning his gourd of a head in the direction of the pointed hands as the high-shouldered boy was pushed forward.

'Here he is, sir! Here he is, sir!'

The boy Steerpike looked impossibly small as he stood beneath the monstrous monument.

'I shall shing to *you*, Steerpike, to *you*,' whispered the cook, reeling and supporting himself with one hand against the stone pillar that was glistening with condensed heat, little trickles of moisture moving down its fluted sides. 'To you, the newcomer, the blue mummer and the slug of summer – to you the hideous, and insidious, and appallingly cretinous goat in a house of stenches.'

The apprentices rocked with joy.

'To you, only to *you*, my core of curdled cat-bile. To you alone, sho hearken diligentiums. Are you sharkening? Are you all lishening for this his how's it goesh. My shong of a hundred yearsh ago, my plaintively mosht melancholic shong.'

Swelter seemed to forget he was about to sing, and after wiping the sweat from his hands on the head of a youth below him, peered for Steerpike again.

'And why to you, my ray of addled sunshine? Why to you aslone? Shtaking it for granted, my dear little Steerpike – taking it for more than for mosht granted, that you, a creature of lesh consequence than stoat's-blood, are sho far removal'd from anything approaching nature – yet tell me, more rather, don't tell me why your ears which musht originally have been deshigned for fly-papers, are, for shome reason butter known to yourself, kept imodeshtly unfurled. What do you proposhe to do next in thish batter? You move here and there on your little measly legs. I have sheen you at it. You breathe all over my kitchen. You look at thingsh with your insholent animal eyes. I've sheen you doing it. I have sheen you look at me. Your looking at me now. Shteerpike, my impatient love-bird, what doesh it all mean, and why should I shing for you?'

Swelter leaned back and seemed to be considering his own question a moment as he wiped his forehead with the sleeve of his forearm. But he waited for no reply and flung his pendulent arms out sideways and somewhere on the orbit of an immense arc something or other gave way.

Steerpike was not drunk. As he stood below Mr Swelter, he had nothing but contempt for the man who had but yesterday struck him across the head. He could do nothing, however, except stay where he was, prodded and nudged from behind by the excited minions, and wait.

The voice recurred from above. 'It is a shong, my Steerpike, to an imaginawary monshter, jusht like yourshelf if only you were a twifle bigger and more monshtrous shtill. It is a shong to a hard-hearted monshter sho lishen mosht shfixedly, my pretty wart. Closher, closher! Can't you come a little closher to a dirgeous mashterpeesh?'

The wine was beginning to redouble its subversive activity in the chef's brain. He was now supporting himself almost the whole of the while against the sweating pillar and was sagging hideously.

Steerpike stared up at him from under his high bony brow. The cook's eyes were protruding like bloodshot bubbles. One arm hung, a dead-weight, down the fluted surface of the support. The enormous area of the face had fallen loose. It glistened like a jelly.

A hole appeared in the face. Out of it came a voice that had suddenly become weaker.

'I am Shwelter,' it repeated, 'the great chef Abiatha Shwelter, scook to hish Lordshipsh, boardshipsh and all shorts of ships that shail on shlippery sheas. Abiafa Shwelter, man and boy and girls and ribbonsh, lots of kittensh, forty year of cold and shunny, where'sh the money, thick and hairy, I'm a fairy! I'm a shongster! Lishen well, lishen well!'

Mr Swelter lowered his head downwards over his wine-raddled breast without moving his shoulders and made an effort to see whether his audience was sufficiently keyed up for his opening chords. But he could make out nothing below him saving the 'little sea of faces' which he had alluded to, but the little sea had now become practically obliterated from him by a swimming mist.

'Are you lishening?'

'Yes, yes! The song, the song!'

Swelter lowered his head yet again into the hot spindrift and then held up his right hand weakly. He made one feeble effort to heave himself away from the pillar and to deliver his verses at a more imposing angle, but, incapable of mustering the strength he sank back, and then, as a vast inane smile opened up the lower half of his face, and as Mr Flay watched him, his hard little mouth twisted downwards, the chef began gradually to curl in upon himself, as though folding himself up for death. The kitchen had become as silent as a hot tomb. At last, through the silence, a weak gurgling sound began to percolate but whether it was the first verse of the long awaited poem, none could tell for the chef, like a galleon, lurched in his anchorage. The great ship's canvas sagged and crumpled and then suddenly an enormousness foundered and sank. There was a sound of something spreading as an area of seven flagstones became hidden from view beneath a catalyptic mass of wine-drenched blubber.

THE STONE LANES

Mr Flay's gorge had risen steadily and, as the dreadful minutes passed, he had been filled with a revulsion so consuming that but for the fact that the chef was surrounded by the youths he would have attacked the drunkard. As it was he bared his sand-coloured teeth, and fixed his eyes for a last moment on the cook with an expression of unbelievable menace. He had turned his head away at last and spat, and then brushing aside whoever stood in his path, had made his way with great skeleton strides, to a narrow doorway in the wall opposite that through which he had entered. By the time Swelter's monologue was dragging to its crapulous close, Mr Flay was pacing onwards, every step taking him another five feet further from the reek and horror of the Great Kitchen.

His black suit, patched on the elbows and near the collar with a greasy sepia-coloured cloth, fitted him badly but belonged to him as inevitably as the head of a tortoise emerging from its shell or the vulture's from a rubble of feathers belong to that reptile or that bird. His head, parchment-coloured and bony, was indigenous to that greasy fabric. It stuck out from the top window of its high black building as though it had known no other residence.

While Mr Flay was pacing along the passages to that part of the castle where Lord Sepulchrave had been left alone for the first time for many weeks, the curator, sleeping peacefully in the Hall of the Bright Carvings, snored beneath the venetian blind. The hammock was still swinging a little, a very little, from the movement caused by Mr

Rottcodd's depositing himself therein directly he had turned the key on
Mr Flay. The sun burned through the shutters, made bands of gold
around the pedestals that supported the sculpture and laid its tiger
stripes across the dusty floor boarding.

The sunlight, as Mr Flay strolled on, still had one finger through the
kitchen window, lighting the perspiring stone pillar which was now
relieved of its office of supporting the chef for the soak had fallen from
the wine-barrel a moment after the disappearance of Mr Flay and lay
stretched at the foot of his rostrum.

Around him lay scattered a few small flattened lumps of meat, coated
with sawdust. There was a strong smell of burning fat, but apart from
the prone bulk of the chef, the Grey Scrubbers under the table, and the
gentlemen who were suspended from the beam, there was no one left in
the huge, hot, empty hall. Every man and boy who had been able to
move his legs had made his way to cooler quarters.

Steerpike had viewed with a mixture of amazement, relief and
malignant amusement the dramatic cessation of Mr Swelter's oratory.
For a few moments he had gazed at the wine-spattered form of his
overlord spread below him, then glancing around and finding that he

was alone he had made for the door through which Mr Flay had passed and was soon racing down the passages turning left and right as he ran in a mad effort to reach the fresh air.

He had never before been through that particular door, but he imagined that he would soon find his way into the open and to some spot where he could be on his own. Turning this way and that he found that he was lost in a labyrinth of stone corridors, lit here and there by candles sunk in their own wax and placed in niches in the walls. In desperation he put his hands to his head as he ran, when suddenly, as he rounded the curve of a wall a figure passed rapidly across the passage before him, neither looking to right or left.

As soon as Mr Flay – for it was his lordship's servant on his way to the residential apartments – as soon as he had passed from sight, Steerpike peered round the corner and followed, keeping as much as possible in step to hide the sound of his own feet. This was almost impossible, as Mr Flay's spider-like gait besides being particularly long of stride, had, like the slow-march, a time-lag before the ultimate descent of the foot. However, young Steerpike, feeling that here at any rate was his one chance of escaping from these endless corridors, followed as best he could in the hope that Mr Flay would eventually turn into some cool quadrangle or open space where get-away could be effected. At times, when the candles were thirty or forty feet apart, Mr Flay would be lost to view and only the sound of his feet on the flagstones would guide his follower. Then slowly, as his erratic shape approached the next guttering aura he would begin by degrees to become a silhouette, until immediately before the candle he would for a moment appear like an inky scarecrow, a mantis of pitch-black cardboard worked with strings. Then the progression of the lighting would be reversed and for a moment immediately after passing the flame Steerpike would see him quite clearly as a lit object against the depths of the still-to-be-trodden avenues of stone. The grease at those moments shone from the threadbare cloth across his shoulders, the twin vertical muscles of his neck rose out of the tattered collar nakedly and sharply. As he moved forward the light would dim upon his back and Steerpike would lose him, only hearing the cracking of his knee-joints and his feet striking the stones, until the ensuing candle carved him anew. Practically exhausted, first by the unendurable atmosphere of the Great Kitchen and now with this seemingly endless journey, the boy, for he was barely seventeen, sank suddenly to the ground with exhaustion, striking the flags with a thud, his boots dragging harshly on the stone. The noise brought Flay to a sudden halt and he turned himself slowly about, drawing his shoulders up to his ears as he did so. 'What's that?' he croaked, peering into the darkness behind him.

There was no answer. Mr Flay began to retrace his steps, his head forward, his eyes peering. As he proceeded he came into the light of one of the candles in the wall. He approached it, still keeping his small eyes directed into the darkness beyond, and wrenched the candle, with a great substratum of ancient tallow with it, from the wall and with this to help him he soon came across the boy in the centre of the corridor several yards further on.

He bent forward and lowered the great lump of lambent wax within a few inches of Steerpike, who had fallen face downwards, and peered at the immobile huddle of limbs. The sound of his footsteps and the cracking of his knee-joints had given place to an absolute silence. He drew back his teeth and straightened himself a little. Then he turned the boy over with his foot. This roused Steerpike from his faintness and he raised himself weakly on one elbow.

'Where am I?' he said in a whisper. 'Where am I?'

'One of Swelter's little rats,' thought Flay to himself, taking no notice of the question. 'One of Swelter's, eh? One of his striped rats.' 'Get up,' said Mr Flay aloud. 'What you doing here?' and he put the candle close to the boy's face.

'I don't know where I am,' said young Steerpike. 'I'm lost here. Lost. Give me daylight.'

'What you doing here, I said . . . what you doing here?' said Flay. 'I don't want Swelter's boys here. Curse them!'

'I don't *want* to be here. Give me daylight and I'll go away. Far away.'

'Away? Where?'

Steerpike had recovered control of his mind, although he still felt hot and desperately tired. He had noticed the sneer in Mr Flay's voice as he had said 'I don't want Swelter's boys here,' and so, at Mr Flay's question 'Away where?' Steerpike answered quickly, 'Oh anywhere, anywhere from that dreadful Mr Swelter.'

Flay peered at him for a moment or two, opening his mouth several times to speak, only to close it again.

'New?' said Flay looking expressionlessly through the boy.

'Me?' said young Steerpike.

'*You*,' said Flay, still looking clean through the top of the boy's head, 'New?'

'Seventeen years old, sir,' said young Steerpike, 'but new to that kitchen.'

'When?' said Flay, who left out most of every sentence.

Steerpike, who seemed able to interpret this sort of shorthand talk, answered.

'Last month. I want to leave that dreadful Swelter,' he added, replaying his only possible card and glancing up at the candlelit head.

'Lost, were you?' said Flay after a pause, but with perhaps less darkness in his tone. 'Lost in the Stone Lanes, were you? One of Swelter's little rats, lost in the Stone Lanes, eh?' and Mr Flay raised his gaunt shoulders again.

'Swelter fell like a log,' said Steerpike.

'Quite right,' said Flay, 'doing honours. What have *you* done?'

'Done, sir?' said Steerpike, 'when?'

'What Happiness?' said Flay, looking like a death's-head. The candle was beginning to fail. 'How much Happiness?'

'I haven't any happiness,' said Steerpike.

'What! no Great Happiness? Rebellion. Is it rebellion?'

'No, except against Mr Swelter.'

'Swelter! Swelter! Leave his name in its fat and grease. Don't talk of that name in the Stone Lanes. Swelter, always Swelter! Hold your tongue. Take this candle. Lead the way. Put it in the niche. Rebellion is it? Lead the way, left, left, right, keep to the left, now right . . . I'll teach you to be unhappy when a Groan is born . . . keep on . . . straight on . . .'

Young Steerpike obeyed these instructions from the shadows behind him.

'A Groan is born,' said Steerpike with an inflection of voice which might be interpreted as a question or a statement.

'Born,' said Flay. 'And you mope in the Lanes. With me, Swelter's boy. Show you what it means. A male Groan. New, eh? Seventeen? Ugh! Never understand. Never. Turn right and left again – again . . . through the arch. Ugh! A new body under the old stones – one of Swelter's, too . . . don't like him, eh?'

'No, sir.'

'H'm,' said Flay. 'Wait here.'

Steerpike waited as he was told and Mr Flay, drawing a bunch of keys from his pocket and selecting one with great care as though he were dealing with objects of rarity inserted it into the lock of an invisible door, for the blackness was profound. Steerpike heard the iron grinding in the lock.

'Here!' said Flay out of the darkness. 'Where's that Swelter boy? Come here.'

Steerpike moved forward towards the voice, feeling with his hands along the wall of a low arch. Suddenly he found himself next to the dank smelling garments of Mr Flay and he put forward his hand and held Lord Groan's servant by a loose portion of the long jacket. Mr Flay brought down his bony hand suddenly over the boy's arm, knocking it away and a t'ck, t'ck, t'ck, sounded in the tall creature's throat, warning him against any further attempts at intimacy.

'Cat room,' said Flay, putting his hand to the iron knob of the door.

'Oh,' said Steerpike, thinking hard and repeating 'Cat room' to fill in time, for he saw no reason for the remark. The only interpretation he could give to the ejaculation was that Flay was referring to him as a cat and asking to be given more room. Yet there had been no irritation in the voice.

'Cat room,' said Flay again, ruminatively, and turned the iron door-knob. He opened the door slowly and Steerpike, peering past him, found no longer any need for an explanation.

A room was filled with the late sunbeams. Steerpike stood quite still, a twinge of pleasure running through his body. He grinned. A carpet filled the floor with blue pasture. Thereon were seated in a hundred decorative attitudes, or stood immobile like carvings, or walked superbly across their sapphire setting, inter-weaving with each other like a living arabesque, a swarm of snow-white cats.

As Mr Flay passed down the centre of the room, Steerpike could not but notice the contrast between the dark rambling figure with his ungainly movements and the monotonous cracking of his knees, the contrast between this and the superb elegance and silence of the white cats. They took not the slightest notice of either Mr Flay or of himself save for the sudden cessation of their purring. When they had stood in the darkness, and before Mr Flay had removed the bunch of keys from his pocket, Steerpike had imagined he had heard a heavy, deep throbbing, a monotonous sea-like drumming of sound, and he now knew that it must have been the pullulation of the tribe.

As they passed through a carved archway at the far end of the room and had closed the door behind them he heard the vibration of their throats, for now that the white cats were once more alone it was revived, and the deep unhurried purring was like the voice of an ocean in the throat of a shell.

'THE SPY-HOLE'

'WHOSE are they?' asked Steerpike. They were climbing stone stairs. The wall on their right was draped with hideous papers that were peeling off and showed rotting surfaces of chill plaster behind. A mingling of many weird colours enlivened this nether surface, dark patches of which had a submarine and incredible beauty. In another dryer area, where a great sail of paper hung away from the wall, the plaster had cracked into a network of intricate fissures varying in depth and resembling a bird's-eye view, or map of some fabulous delta. A thousand imaginary journeys might be made along the banks of these rivers of an unexplored world.

Steerpike repeated his question, 'Whose are they?' he said.

'Whose what?' said Flay, stopping on the stairs and turning round. 'Still here are you? Still following me?'

'You suggested that I should,' said Steerpike.

'Ch! Ch!' said Flay, 'what d'you want, Swelter's boy?'

'Nauseating Swelter,' said Steerpike between his teeth but with one eye on Mr Flay, 'vile Swelter.'

There was a pause during which Steerpike tapped the iron banisters with his thumb-nail.

'Name?' said Mr Flay.

'My name?' asked Steerpike.

'Your name, yes, your name. I know what *my* name is.' Mr Flay put a knuckly hand on the banisters preparatory to mounting the stairs again, but waited, frowning over his shoulder, for the reply.

'Steerpike sir,' said the boy.

'Queerpike, eh? eh?' said Flay.

'No, Steerpike.'

'What?'

'Steerpike. Steerpike.'

'What for?' said Flay.

'I beg your pardon?'

'What for, eh? Two Squeertikes, two of you. Twice over. What for? One's enough for a Swelter's boy.'

The youth felt it would be useless to clear up the problem of his name. He concentrated his dark eyes on the gawky figure above him for a few moments and shrugged his shoulders imperceptibly. Then he spoke again, showing no sign of irritation.

'Whose cats were those, sir? May I ask?'

'Cats?' said Flay, 'who said cats?'

'The white cats,' said Steerpike. 'All the white cats in the Cat room. Who do they belong to?'

Mr Flay held up a finger. 'My Lady's,' he said. His hard voice seemed a part of this cold narrow stairway of stone and iron. 'They belong to my Lady. Lady's white cats they are. Swelter's boy. All hers.'

Steerpike pricked his ears up. 'Where does she live?' he said. 'Are we close to where she lives?'

For answer Mr Flay shot his head forward out of his collar and croaked, 'Silence! you kitchen thing. Hold your tongue you greasy fork. Talk too much,' and he straddled up the stairs, passing two landings in his ascent, and then at the third he turned sharply to his left and entered an octagonal apartment where full-length portraits in huge dusty gold frames stared from seven of the eight walls. Steerpike followed him in.

Mr Flay had been longer away from his lordship than he had intended or thought right and it was on his mind that the earl might be needing him. Directly he entered the octagonal room he approached one of the portraits at the far end and pushing the suspended frame a little to one side, revealed a small round hole in the panelling the size of a farthing. He placed his eye to this hole and Steerpike watched the wrinkles of his parchment-coloured skin gather below the protruding bone at the base of the skull, for Mr Flay both had to stoop and then to raise his head in order to apply his eye at the necessary angle. What Mr Flay saw was what he had expected to see.

From his vantage point he was able to get a clear view of three doors in a corridor, the central one belonging to the chamber of her ladyship, the seventy-sixth Countess of Groan. It was stained black and had painted upon it an enormous white cat. The wall of the landing was covered with pictures of birds and there were three engravings of cacti in bloom. This door was shut, but as Mr Flay watched the doors on either side were being constantly opened and closed and figures moved quickly in and out or up and down the landing, or conversed with many gesticulations or stood with their chins in the curled palms of their hands as though in profound meditation.

'Here,' said Flay without turning round.

Steerpike was immediately at Flay's elbow. 'Yes?' he said.

'Cat door's hers,' said Flay removing his eye, and then, stretching his arms out he spread his long fingers to their tips and yawned cavernously.

Young Steerpike glued his eye to the hole, keeping the heavy gold frame from swinging back with his shoulder. All at once he found himself contemplating a narrow-chested man with a shock of grey hair and glasses which magnified his eyes so that they filled the lenses up to their gold rims, when the central door opened, and a dark figure stole forth, closing the door behind him quietly, and with an air of the deepest dejection. Steerpike watched him turn his eyes to the shock-headed man, who inclined his body forward clasping his hands before him. No notice was taken of this by the other, who began to pace up and down the landing, his dark cloak clasped around him and trailing on the floor at his heels. Each time he passed the doctor, for such it was, that gentleman inclined his body, but as before there was no response, until suddenly, stopping immediately before the physician in attendance, he drew from his cape a slender rod of silver mounted at the end with a rough globe of black jade that burned around its edges with emerald fire. With this unusual weapon the mournful figure beat sadly at the doctor's chest as though to inquire whether there was anyone at home. The doctor coughed. The silver and jade implement was pointed to the floor, and Steerpike was amazed to see the doctor, after hitching his exquisitely creased trousers to a few inches above his ankle, squat down. His great vague eyes swam about beneath the magnifying lenses like a pair of jellyfish seen through a fathom of water. His dark grey hair was brushed out over his eyes like thatch. For all the indignity of his position it was with a great sense of style that he became seated following with his eyes the gentleman who had begun to walk around him slowly. Eventually the figure with the silver rod came to a halt.

'Prunesquallor,' he said.

'My Lord?' said the doctor, inclining his grey hayrick to the left.

'Satisfactory, Prunesquallor?'

The doctor placed the tips of his fingers together. 'I am exceptionally gratified my lord, exceptionally. Indeed I am. Very, very much so; ha, ha, ha. Very, very much so.'

'Professionally you mean, I imagine?' said Lord Sepulchrave, for as Steerpike had begun to realize to his amazement, the tragic-looking man was none other than the seventy-sixth Earl of Groan and the owner of, as Steerpike put it to himself, the whole caboodle, bricks, guns and glory.

'Professionally . . .' queried the doctor to himself, '. . . what does he mean?' Aloud he said, 'professionally, my lord, I am unspeakably satisfied, ha, ha, ha, ha, and socially, that is to say, er, as a gesture, ha, ha, I am over-awed. I am a proud fellow, my lord, ha, ha, ha, ha, a very proud fellow.'

The laugh of Doctor Prunesquallor was part of his conversation and quite alarming when heard for the first time. It appeared to be out of control as though it were a part of his voice, a top-storey of his vocal range that only came into its own when the doctor laughed. There was something about it of wind whistling through high rafters and there was a good deal of the horse's whinny, with a touch of the curlew. When giving vent to it, the doctor's mouth would be practically immobile like the door of a cabinet left ajar. Between the laughs he would speak very rapidly, which made the sudden stillness of his beautifully shaven jaws at the time of laughter all the more extraordinary. The laugh was not necessarily connected with humour at all. It was simply a part of his conversation.

'Technically, I am so satisfied as to be unbearable even to myself, ha, ha, ha, he, he, ha. Oh very, very satisfactory it all was. Very much so.'

'I am glad,' said his lordship, gazing down at him for a moment. 'Did you notice anything?' (Lord Sepulchrave glanced up and down the corridor.) 'Strange? Anything unusual about him?'

'Unusual?' said Prunesquallor. 'Did you say unusual, my lord?'

'I did,' said Lord Sepulchrave, biting his lower lip. 'Anything wrong with him? You need not be afraid to speak out.'

Again his lordship glanced up and down the landing but there was no one to be seen.

'Structurally, a sound child, sound as a bell, tinkle, tinkle, structurally, ha, ha, ha,' said the doctor.

'Damn the structure!' said Lord Groan.

'I am at a loss, my lord, ha, ha. Completely at a loss, sir. If not structurally, then how, my lord?'

'His face,' said the earl. 'Didn't you see his face?'

Here the doctor frowned profoundly to himself and rubbed his chin with his hand. Out of the corner of his eyes he looked up to find his lordship scrutinizing him. 'Ah!' he said lamely, 'the face. The face of his little lordship. Aha!'

'Did you notice it, I say?' continued Lord Groan. 'Speak man!'

'I noticed his face, sir. Oh yes, definitely I noticed it.' This time the doctor did not laugh but drew a deep breath from his narrow chest.

'Did you or did you not think it was strange? Did you or did you not?'

'Speaking professionally,' said Doctor Prunesquallor, 'I should say the face was irregular.'

'Do you mean it's ugly?' said Lord Groan.

'It is unnatural,' said Prunesquallor.

'What is the difference, man,' said Lord Groan.

'Sir?' questioned the doctor.

'I asked if it was ugly, sir, and you answer that it is unnatural. Why must you hedge?'

'Sir!' said Prunesquallor, but as he gave no colour to the utterance, very little could be made of it.

'When I say "ugly" have the goodness to use the word. Do you understand?' Lord Groan spoke quietly.

'I comprehend, sir. I comprehend.'

'Is the boy hideous,' persisted Lord Groan as though he wished to thrash the matter out. 'Have you ever delivered a more hideous child? Be honest.'

'Never,' said the doctor. 'Never, ha, ha, ha, ha. Never. And never a boy with such – er, ha, ha, ha, never a boy with such extraordinary eyes.'

'Eyes?' said Lord Groan, 'what's wrong with them?'

'Wrong?' cried Prunesquallor. 'Did you say "wrong" your lordship? Have you not seen them?'

'No, quick, man. Hurry yourself. What is it? What is the matter with my son's eyes?'

'They are violet.'

FUCHSIA

As his lordship stared at the doctor another figure appeared, a girl of about fifteen with long, rather wild black hair. She was gauche in movement and in a sense, ugly of face, but with how small a twist might she not suddenly have become beautiful. Her sullen mouth was full and rich – her eyes smouldered.

A yellow scarf hung loosely around her neck. Her shapeless dress was a flaming red.

For all the straightness of her back she walked with a slouch.

'Come here,' said Lord Groan as she was about to pass him and the doctor.

'Yes father,' she said huskily.

'Where have you been for the last fortnight, Fuchsia?'

'Oh, here and there, father,' she said, staring at her shoes. She tossed her long hair and it flapped down her back like a pirate's flag. She stood in about as awkward a manner as could be conceived. Utterly unfeminine – no man could have invented it.

'Here and there?' echoed her father in a weary voice. 'What does "here and there" mean? You've been in hiding. Where, girl?'

' 'N the libr'y and 'n the armoury, 'n walking about a lot,' said Lady Fuchsia, and her sullen eyes narrowed. 'I just heard silly rumours about mother. They said I've got a brother – idiots! idiots! I hate them. I haven't, have I? Have I?'

'A little brother,' broke in Doctor Prunesquallor. 'Yes, ha, ha, ha, ha, ha, ha, ha, a minute, infinitesimal, microscopic addition to the famous line is now behind this bedroom door. Ha, ha, ha, ha, ha, ha, he, he, he! Oh yes! Ha, ha! Oh yes indeed! Very much so.'

'No!' said Fuchsia so loudly that the doctor coughed crisply and his lordship took a step forward with his eyebrows drawn together and a sad curl at the corner of his mouth.

'It's not true!' shouted Fuchsia, turning from them and twirling a great lock of black hair round and round her wrist. 'I don't believe it! Let me go! Let me go!'

As no one was touching her, her cry was unnecessary and she turned and ran with strange bounds along the corridor that led from the landing. Before she was lost to view, Steerpike could hear her voice shouting from the distance, 'Oh how I hate! hate! hate! How I *hate* people! Oh how I *hate* people!'

All this while Mr Flay had been gazing out of a narrow window in the octagonal room and was preoccupied with certain matters relating to how he could best let Lord Groan know that he, Flay, his servant for over forty years, disapproved of having been put aside as it were at the one moment when a son had been born – at the one moment when he, Flay, would have been invaluable as an ally. Mr Flay was rather hurt about the whole business, and he very much wanted Lord Groan to know this, and yet at the same time it was very difficult to think of a way in which he could tactfully communicate his chagrin to a man quite as sullen as himself. Mr Flay bit his nails sourly. He had been at the window for a much longer time than he had intended and he turned with his shoulders raised, an attitude typical of him and saw young Steerpike, whose presence he had forgotten. He strode over to the boy and catching him by his coat-tails jerked him backwards into the centre of the room. The great picture swung back across the spy-hole.

'Now,' he said, 'back! You've seen her door, Swelter's boy.'

Steerpike, who had been lost in the world beyond the oak partition, was dazed, and took a moment to come to.

'Back to that loathsome chef?' he cried at last, 'oh no! couldn't!'

'Too busy to have you here,' said Flay, 'too busy, can't wait.'

'He's ugly,' said Steerpike fiercely.

'Who?' said Flay. 'Don't stop here talking.'

'Oh so ugly, he is. Lord Groan said so. The doctor said so. Ugh! So hideous.'

'Who's hideous, you kitchen thing,' said Flay, jerking his head forward grotesquely.

'Who?' said Steerpike. 'The baby. The new baby. They both said so. Most terrible he is.'

'What's this?' cried Flay. 'What's these lies all about? Who've you heard talking? Who've you been listening to? I'll tear your little ears off, you snippet thing! Where've you been? Come here!'

Steerpike, who had determined to escape from the Great Kitchen, was now bent on finding an occupation among those apartments where he might pry into the affairs of those above him.

'If I go back to Swelter I'll tell him and all of them what I heard his lordship say and then . . .'

'Come here!' said Flay between his teeth, 'come here or I'll break your bones. Been agaping, have you? I'll fix you.' Flay propelled Steerpike through the entrance at a great pace and halted halfway down a narrow passage before a door. This he unlocked with one of his many keys and thrusting Steerpike inside turned it upon the boy.

'TALLOW AND BIRDSEED'

LIKE a vast spider suspended by a metal chord, a candelabrum presided over the room nine feet above the floor boards. From its sweeping arms of iron, long stalactites of wax lowered their pale spilths drip by drip, drip by drip. A rough table with a drawer half open, which appeared to be full of birdseed, was in such a position below the iron spider that a cone of tallow was mounting by degrees at one corner into a lambent pyramid the size of a hat.

The room was untidy to the extent of being a shambles. Everything had the appearance of being put aside for the moment. Even the bed was at an angle, slanting away from the wall and crying out to be pushed back flush against the red wallpaper. As the candles guttered or flared, so the shadows moved from side to side, or up and down the wall, and with those movements behind the bed there swayed the shadows of four birds. Between them vacillated an enormous head. This umbrage was cast by her ladyship, the seventy-sixth Countess of Groan. She was propped against several pillows and a black shawl was draped around her shoulders. Her hair, a very dark red colour of great lustre, appeared to have been left suddenly while being woven into a knotted structure on the top of her head. Thick coils still fell about her shoulders, or clustered upon the pillows like burning snakes.

Her eyes were of the pale green that is common among cats. They were large eyes, yet seemed, in proportion to the pale area of her face, to be small. The nose was big enough to appear so in spite of the expanse that surrounded it. The effect which she produced was one of bulk, although only her head, neck, shoulders and arms could be seen above the bedclothes.

A magpie moving sideways up and down her left forearm, which lay supine upon the bedclothes, pecked intermittently at a heap of grain which lay in the palm of her hand. On her shoulders sat a stonechat, and a huge raven which was asleep. The bed-rail boasted two starlings, a missel-thrush and a small owl. Every now and then a bird would appear between the bars of a small high window which let in less than no light. The ivy had climbed through it from the outside and had begun to send its tendrils down the inner wall itself and over the crimson wallpaper. Although this ivy had choked out what little light might have trickled into the room, it was not strong enough to prevent the birds from finding a way through and from visiting Lady Gertrude at any hour of night or day.

'That's enough, that's enough, that's enough!' said the Countess in a deep husky voice, to the magpie. 'That's enough for you today, my dear.' The magpie jumped a few inches into the air and landed again on her wrist and shook his feathers; his long tail tapped on the eiderdown.

Lady Groan flung what remained of the grain across the room and the stonechat hopping from the bed-rail to her head, took off again from that rabous landing ground with a flutter, circled twice around the room steering during his second circuit through the stalactites of shining wax, and landed on the floor beside the grain.

The Countess of Groan dug her elbows into the pillows behind her, which had become flattened and uncomfortable and levered her bulk up with her strong, heavy arms. Then she relaxed again, and spread out her arms to left and right along the bed-rail behind her and her hands drooped from the wrists at either extremity, overhanging the edges of the bed. The line of her mouth was neither sad nor amused, as she gazed abstractedly at the pyramid of wax that was mounting upon the table. She watched each slow drip as it descended upon the blunt apex of the mound, move sluggishly down the uneven side and solidify into a long pulpy petal.

Whether the Countess was thinking deeply or was lost in vacant reverie it would have been impossible to guess. She reclined hugely and motionlessly, her arms extended along the iron rail, when suddenly a great fluttering and scrambling broke into the wax-smelling silence of the room and turning her eyes to the ivy-filled window, fourteen feet from the ground, the Countess without moving her head, could see the leaves part and the white head and shoulders of an albino rook emerge guiltily.

'Ah-ha,' she said slowly, as though she had come to a conclusion, 'so it is you, is it? So it is the truant back again. Where has he been? What has he been doing? What trees has he been sitting in? What clouds has he been flying through? What a boy he is! What a bunch of feathered whiteness. What a bunch of wickedness!'

The rook had been sitting fringed on all sides with the ivy leaves, with his head now on one side, now on the other; listening or appearing to listen with great interest and a certain show of embarrassment, for from the movement that showed itself in the ivy leaves from time to time, the white rook was evidently shifting from foot to foot.

'Three weeks it is,' continued the Countess, 'three weeks I've been without him; I wasn't good enough for *him*, oh no, not for Master Chalk, and here he is back again, wants to be forgiven! Oh yes! Wants a great treeful of forgiveness, for his heavy old beak and months of absolution for his plumage.'

Then the Countess hoisted herself up in bed again, twisted a strand of her dark hair round a long forefinger, and with her face directed at the doorway, but her eyes still on the bird, said as though to herself and almost inaudibly, 'Come on then.' The ivy rustled again, and before that sound was over the bed itself vibrated with the sudden arrival of the white rook.

He stood on the foot-rail, his claws curled around it, and stared at Lady Groan. After a moment or two of stillness the white rook moved his feet up and down on the rail in a treading motion and then, flopping on to the bedclothes at her ladyship's feet, twisted his head around and pecked at his own tail, the feathers of his neck standing out as he did so, crisply like a ruff. The pecking over he made his way over the undulating terrain of the bed, until within a few inches of her ladyship's face, when he tilted his big head in a characteristic manner and cawed.

'So you beg my pardon, do you?' said Lady Groan, 'and you think that's the end of it? No more questions about where you've been or where you've flown these three long weeks? So that's it, is it, Master Chalk? You want me to forgive you for old sakes' sake? Come here with your old beak and rub it on my arm. Come along my whitest one, come along, then. Come along.' The raven on Lady Groan's shoulder awoke from his sleep and raised his ethiopian wing an inch or two, sleepily. Then his eyes focused upon the rook in a hard stare. He sat there wide awake, a lock of dark red hair between his feet. The small owl as though to take the place of the raven fell asleep. One of the starlings turned about in three slow paces and faced the wall. The missel-thrush made no motion, and as a candle guttered, a ghoul of shadow from under a tall cupboard dislodged itself and moved across the floorboards, climbed the bed, and crawled half way across the eiderdown before it returned by the same route, to curl up and roost beneath the cupboard again.

Lady Groan's gaze had returned to the mounting pyramid of tallow. Her pale eyes would either concentrate upon an object in a remorseless way or would appear to be without sight, vacant, with the merest suggestion of something childish. It was in this abstracted manner that she gazed through the pale pyramid, while her hands, as though working on their own account, moved gently over the breast, head and throat of the white rook.

For some time there was complete silence in the room and it was with something of a shock that a rapping at the panels of her bedroom door awakened Lady Groan from her reverie.

Her eyes now took on the concentrated, loveless, cat-like look.

The birds coming to life at once, flapped simultaneously to the end rail of the bed, where they stood balancing in a long uneven line, each one on the alert, their heads turned towards the door.

'Who's that?' said Lady Groan heavily.

'It's me, my lady,' cried a quavering voice.

'Who's that hitting my door?'

'It's me with his lordship,' replied the voice.

'What?' shouted Lady Groan. 'What d'you want? What are you hitting my door for?'

Whoever it was raised her voice nervously and cried, 'Nannie Slagg, it is. It's me, my lady; Nannie Slagg.'

'What d'you want?' repeated her ladyship, settling herself more comfortably.

'I've brought his Lordship for you to see,' shouted Nannie Slagg, a little less nervously.

'Oh, you have, have you? You've brought his lordship. So you want to come in, do you? With his lordship.' There was a moment's silence. 'What for? What have you brought him to me for?'

'For you to see, if you please, my lady,' replied Nannie Slagg. 'He's had his bath.'

Lady Groan relaxed still further into the pillows. 'Oh, you mean the *new* one, do you?' she muttered.

'Can I come in?' cried Nannie Slagg.

'Hurry up then! Hurry up then! Stop scratching at my door. What are you waiting for?'

A rattling at the door handle froze the birds along the iron bed-rail and as the door opened they were all at once in the air, and were forcing their way, one after another through the bitter leaves of the small window.

A GOLD RING FOR TITUS

NANNIE SLAGG entered, bearing in her arms the heir to the miles of rambling stone and mortar; to the Tower of Flints and the stagnant moat; to the angular mountains and the lime-green river where twelve years later he would be angling for the hideous fishes of his inheritance.

She carried the child towards the bed and turned the little face to the mother, who gazed right through it and said:

'Where's that doctor? Where's Prunesquallor? Put the child down and open the door.'

Mrs Slagg obeyed, and as her back was turned Lady Groan bent forward and peered at the child. The little eyes were glazed with sleep and the candlelight played upon the bald head, moulding the structure of the skull with shifting shade.

'H'm,' said Lady Groan, 'what d'you want me to do with him?'

Nannie Slagg, who was very grey and old, with red rims around her eyes and whose intelligence was limited, gazed vacantly at her ladyship.

'He's had his bath,' she said. 'He's just had his bath, bless his little lordship's heart.'

'What about it?' said Lady Groan.

The old nurse picked the baby up dexterously and began to rock him gently by way of an answer.

'Is Prunesquallor there?' repeated Lady Groan.

'Down,' whispered Nannie, pointing a little wrinkled finger at the floor, 'd-downstairs; oh yes, I think he is still downstairs taking punch in the Coldroom. Oh dear, yes, bless the little thing.'

Her last remark presumably referred to Titus and not to Doctor Prunesquallor. Lady Groan raised herself in bed and looking fiercely at the open door, bellowed in the deepest and loudest voice, 'SQUALLOR!'

The word echoed along the corridors and down the stairs, and creeping under the door and along the black rug in the Coldroom, just managed, after climbing the doctor's body, to find its way into both his ears simultaneously, in a peremptory if modified condition. Modified though it was, it brought Doctor Prunesquallor to his feet at once. His fish eyes swam all round his glasses before finishing at the top, where they gave him an expression of fantastic martyrdom. Running his long, exquisitely formed fingers through his mop of grey hair, he drained his glass of punch at a draught and started for the door, flicking small globules of the drink from his waistcoat.

Before he had reached her room he had begun a rehearsal of the conversation he expected, his insufferable laughter punctuating every other sentence whatever its gist.

'My lady,' he said, when he had reached her door and was showing the Countess and Mrs Slagg nothing except his head around the doorpost in a decapitated manner, before entering. 'My lady, ha, ha, he, he. I heard your voice downstairs as I er – was –'

'Tippling,' said Lady Groan.

'Ha, ha – how very right you are, how very very right you are, ha, ha, ha, he, as I was, as you so graphically put it, ha, ha, tippling. Down it came, ha, ha – down it came.'

'What came?' interrupted the Countess loudly.

'Your voice,' said Prunesquallor, raising his right hand and deliberately placing the tips of his thumb and little finger together, 'your voice located me in the Coldroom. Oh yes, it did!'

The Countess stared at him heavily and then dug her elbows into the pillow.

Mrs Slagg had rocked the baby to sleep.

Doctor Prunesquallor was running a long tapering forefinger up and down a stalactite of wax and smiling horribly.

'I called you,' said the Countess, 'to tell you, Prunesquallor, that tomorrow I get up.'

'Oh, he, ha, ha, oh ha, ha, my ladyship, oh, ha, ha, my ladyship – *tomorrow?*'

'Tomorrow,' said the Countess, 'why not?'

'Professionally speaking –' began Doctor Prunesquallor.

'Why not?' repeated the Countess interrupting him.

'Ha, ha, most abnormal, most unusual, ha, ha, ha, most unique, so *very* soon.'

'So you would docket me, would you, Prunesquallor? I thought you would; I guessed it. I get up tomorrow – tomorrow *at dawn.*'

Doctor Prunesquallor shrugged his narrow shoulders and raised his eyes. Then placing the tips of his fingers together and addressing the dark ceiling above him, 'I *advise*, but never order,' he said, in a tone which implied that he could have done any amount of ordering had he thought it necessary. 'Ha ha, ha, oh no! I only advise.'

'Rubbish,' said the Countess.

'I do not think so,' replied Prunesquallor, still gazing upwards. 'Ha, ha, ha, ha, oh no! not at all.' As he finished speaking his eyes for a second travelled downwards at great speed and took in the image of the Countess in bed and then even more rapidly swam up the glasses. What he had seen disquieted him, for he had found in her expression such a concentration of distaste that as he deflected his gaze away from her he found that his feet were moving backwards one after the other and that he was at the door before he knew that he had decided what to do. Bowing quickly he withdrew his body from the bedroom.

'Isn't he sweet, oh isn't he the sweetest drop of sugar that ever was?' said Mrs Slagg.

'Who?' shouted the Countess so loudly that a string of tallow wavered in the shifting light.

The baby awoke at the sound and moaned, and Nannie Slagg retreated.

'His little lordship,' she whimpered weakly, 'his pretty little lordship.'

'Slagg,' said the Countess, 'go away! I would like to see the boy when he is six. Find a wet nurse from the Outer Dwellings. Make him green dresses from the velvet curtains. Take this gold ring of mine. Fix a chain to it. Let him wear it around his wry little neck. Call him Titus. Go away and leave the door six inches open.'

The Countess put her hand under the pillow and drew forth a small reed, placed it in her vast mouth and gave it breath. Two long sweet notes sang out through the dark air. At the sound, Mrs Slagg, grabbing the gold ring from the bedclothes, where the Countess had thrown it, hurried as fast as her old legs could carry her from the room as though a werewolf were at her heels. Lady Groan was leaning forward in bed, her eyes were like a child's; wide, sweet and excited. They were fixed upon the door. Her hands were gripping the edges of her pillow. She became rigid.

In the distance, a vibration was becoming louder and louder until the volume seemed to have filled the chamber itself, when suddenly there slid through the narrow opening of the door and moved into the fumid atmosphere of the room an undulation of whiteness, so that, within a breath, there was no shadow in all the room that was not blanched with cats.

SEPULCHRAVE

EVERY morning of the year, between the hours of nine and ten, he may be found, seated in the Stone Hall. It is there, at the long table that he takes his breakfast. The table is raised upon a dais, and from where he sits he can gaze down the length of the grey refectory. On either side and running the entire length, great pillars prop the painted ceiling where cherubs pursue each other across a waste of flaking sky. There must be about a thousand of them all told, interweaving among the clouds, their fat limbs for ever on the move and yet never moving, for they are imperfectly articulated. The colours, once garish, have faded and peeled away and the ceiling is now a very subtle shade of grey and lichen green, old rose and silver.

Lord Sepulchrave may have noticed the cherubs long ago. Probably when a child he had attempted more than once to count them, as his father had done, and as young Titus in his turn will try to do; but however that might be, Lord Groan had not cast up his eyes to the old welkin for many years. Nor did he ever stare about him now. How could he *love* this place? He was a part of it. He could not imagine a world outside it; and the idea of loving Gormenghast would have shocked him. To have asked him of his feelings for his hereditary home would be like asking a man what his feelings were towards his own hand or his own throat. But his lordship remembered the cherubs in the ceiling. His great grandfather had painted them with the help of an enthusiastic servant who had fallen seventy feet from the scaffolding and had been killed instantly. But it seemed that Lord Sepulchrave found his only interest in these days among the volumes in his library and in a knob of jade on his silver rod, which he would scrutinize for hours on end.

Arriving, as was his consistent habit, at exactly nine o'clock every morning, he would enter the long hall and move with a most melancholy air between rows of long tables, where servants of every grade would be awaiting him, standing at their places, their heads bowed.

Mounting the dais he would move around to the far side of the table where hung a heavy brass bell. He would strike it. The servants sitting down at once, would begin their meal of bread, rice wine and cake.

Lord Groan's menu was otherwise. As he sat, this morning, in his high-backed chair, he saw before him – through a haze of melancholia that filmed his brain and sickened his heart, robbing it of power and his limbs of health – he saw before him a snow-white tablecloth. It was set for two. The silver shone and the napkins were folded into the shapes of peacocks and were perched decoratively on the two plates. There was a delicious scent of bread, sweet and wholesome. There were eggs painted in gay colours, toast piled up pagoda-wise, tier upon tier and each as frail as a dead leaf; and fish with their tails in their mouths lay coiled in sea-blue saucers. There was coffee in an urn shaped like a lion, the spout protruding from that animal's silver jaws. There were all varieties of coloured fruits that looked strangely tropical in that dark hall. There were honeys and jams, jellies, nuts and spices and the ancestral breakfast plate was spread out to the greatest advantage amid the golden cutlery of the Groans. In the centre of the table was a small tin bowl of dandelions and nettles.

Lord Sepulchrave sat silently. He did not seem to notice the delicacies spread before him, nor when for a moment or two at a time his head was raised, did he appear to see the long cold dining-hall nor the servants at their tables. To his right, at the adjacent corner of the board, was arranged the cutlery and earthenware crockery that implied the imminent arrival of his lordship's breakfast companion. Lord Groan, his eyes upon the jade knob of the rod which he was twisting slowly upon its ferrule, again rang the brass bell and a door opened in the wall behind him. Sourdust entered with great books under his arm. He was arrayed in crimson sacking. His beard was knotted and the hairs that composed it were black and white. His face was very lined, as though it had been made of brown paper that had been crunched by some savage hand before being hastily smoothed out and spread over the tissues. His eyes were deep-set and almost lost in the shadows cast by his fine brow, which for all its wrinkles, retained a sweeping breadth of bone.

The old man seated himself at the end of the table, and stacked the four volumes beside a porcelain decanter, and raising his sunken eyes to Lord Groan, murmured these words in a weak and shaking voice and yet with a certain dignity as though it were not simply a case of having to get through the ritual, but that it was now, as always, well worth getting through.

'I, Sourdust, lord of the library, personal adviser to your lordship, nonagenarian, and student of the Groan lore, proffer to your lordship the salutations of a dark morning, robed as I am in rags, student as I am of the tomes, and nonagenarian as I happen to be in the matter of years.'

This was delivered in one breath and then he coughed unpleasantly several times, his hand at his chest.

Lord Groan propped his chin on the knuckles of his hands that were cupping the jade knob. His face was very long and was olive coloured. The eyes were large, and of an eloquence, withdrawn. His nostrils were mobile and sensitive. His mouth, a narrow line. On his head was the iron crown of the Groans that fastens with a strap under the chin. It had four prongs that were shaped like arrow heads. Between these barbs small chains hung in loops. The prerogative of precedent on his side, he was wrapped in his dark grey dressing-gown.

He did not seem to have heard Sourdust's salutations, but focusing his eyes for the first time upon the table, he broke a corner off a piece of toast, and placed it mechanically in his mouth. This he muzzled in his cheek for the major part of the meal. The fish became cold on the plate. Sourdust had helped himself to one of them, a slice of watermelon and a fire-green egg, but all else lost its freshness or its heat upon the ritualistic table.

Below in the long basement of the hall the clattering of the knives had ceased. The rice wine had been passed up and down the table, and the jugs were empty. They were waiting for the sign to go about their duties.

Sourdust, having wiped his old mouth with the napkin, turned his eyes to his lordship, who was now leaning back in the chair and sipping at a glass of black tea, his eyes un-focused as usual. The Librarian was watching the left eyebrow of his lordship. It was twenty-one minutes to ten by the clock at the far end of the hall. Lord Groan appeared to be looking through this clock. Three-quarters of a minute went by, it was ten seconds – five seconds – three seconds – one second – to twenty to ten. It was twenty minutes to ten. Lord Groan's left eyebrow rose up his forehead mechanically and stayed suspended beneath three wrinkles. Then it slowly lowered itself. At the movement, Sourdust arose and stamped upon the ground with an old thin leg. The crimson sacking about his body shook as he did so and his beard of black and white knots swung madly to and fro.

The tables were at once emptied and within half a minute the last of the retainers had vanished from the hall, and the servants' door at the far end had been closed and bolted.

Sourdust re-seated himself, panting a little and coughing in an ugly way. Then he leaned across the table and scratched the white cloth in front of Lord Groan with a fork.

His lordship turned his black and liquid eyes towards the old librarian and adviser. 'Well?' he said, in a far-away voice, 'what is it, Sourdust?'

'It is the ninth day of the month,' said Sourdust.

'Ah,' said his lordship.

There was a period of silence, Sourdust making use of the interim by re-knotting several tassels of his beard.

'The ninth,' repeated his lordship.

'The ninth,' muttered Sourdust.

'A heavy day,' mused his lordship, 'very heavy.'

Sourdust, bending his deep-set eyes upon his master, echoed him: 'A heavy day, the ninth . . . always a heavy day.'

A great tear rolled down Sourdust's cheek threading its way over the crumpled surface. The eyes were too deeply set in their sockets of shadow to be seen. By not so much as the faintest sign or movement had Sourdust suggested that he was in a state of emotional stress. Nor was he, ever, save that at moments of reflection upon matters connected with the traditions of the Castle, it so happened that great tears emerged from the shadows beneath his brow. He fingered the great tomes beside his plate. His lordship, as though making the resolve after long deliberation, leaned forward, placed his rod on the table and adjusted his iron crown. Then, supporting his long olive chin with his hands, he turned his head to the old man: 'Proceed,' he whispered.

Sourdust gathered the sacking about himself in a quick shaky way, and getting to his feet moved round to the back of his own chair which he pushed a few inches closer to the table, and squeezing between the table and the chair he re-seated himself carefully and was apparently more comfortable than before. Then with great deliberation, bending his corrugated brow upon each in turn he pushed the varied assortment of dishes, cruets, glasses, cutlery and by now tepid delicacies away from before him, clearing a semi-circle of white cloth. Only then did he remove the three tomes from beside his elbow. He opened them one after the other by balancing them carefully on their vellum spines and allowing them to break open at pages indicated by embroidered book-markers.

The left hand pages were headed with the date and in the first of the three books this was followed by a list of the activities to be performed hour by hour during the day by his lordship. The exact times; the garments to be worn for each occasion and the symbolic gestures to be used. Diagrams facing the left hand page gave particulars of the routes by which his lordship should approach the various scenes of operation. The diagrams were hand tinted.

The second tome was full of blank pages and was entirely symbolic, while the third was a mass of cross references. If, for instance, his lordship, Sepulchrave, the present Earl of Groan, had been three inches shorter, the costumes, gestures and even the routes would have differed from the ones described in the first tome, and from the enormous library, another volume would have had to have been chosen which would have applied. Had he been of a fair skin, or had he been heavier than he was, had his eyes been green, blue or brown instead of black, then, automatically another set of archaic regulations would have appeared this morning on the breakfast table. This complex system was understood in its entirety only by Sourdust – the technicalities demanding the devotion of a lifetime, though the sacred spirit of tradition implied by the daily manifestations was understood by all.

For the next twenty minutes Sourdust instructed his lordship in the less obvious details of the day's work that lay ahead, in a high cracked old voice, the cross-hatching of the skin at the corners of his mouth twitching between the sentences. His lordship nodded silently. Occasionally the routes marked down for the 'ninth' in the diagrams of the first tome are obsolete, as for instance, where at 2.37 in the afternoon Lord Groan was to have moved down the iron stairway in the grey vestibule that led to the pool of carp. That stairway had been warped and twisted out of shape seventy years ago when the vestibule had been razed to the ground in the great fire. An alternative route had to be planned. A plan approaching as far as possible to the spirit of the original conception, and taking the same amount of time. Sourdust scored the new route shakily on the tablecloth with the point of a fork. His lordship nodded.

The day's duties being clear, and with only a minute to run before ten, Sourdust relaxed in his chair and dribbled into his black-and-white beard. Every few seconds he glanced at the clock.

A long sigh came from his lordship. For a moment a light appeared in his eyes and then dulled. The line of his mouth seemed for a moment to have softened.

'Sourdust,' he said, 'have you heard about my son?'

Sourdust, with his eyes on the clock, had not heard his lordship's question. He was making noises in his throat and chest, his mouth working at the corners.

Lord Groan looked at him quickly and his face whitened under the olive. Taking a spoon he bent it into three-quarters of a circle.

The door opened suddenly in the wall behind the dais and Flay entered.

'T's time,' he said, when he reached the table.

Lord Sepulchrave rose and moved to the door.

Flay nodded sullenly at the man in crimson sacking, and after filling his pockets with peaches followed his lordship between the pillars of the Stone Hall.

PRUNESQUALLOR'S KNEE-CAP

FUCHSIA's bedroom was stacked at its four corners with her discarded toys, books and lengths of coloured cloth. It lay in the centre of the western wing and upon the second floor. A walnut bed monopolized the inner wall in which stood the doorway. The two triangular windows in the opposite wall gave upon the battlements where the master sculptors from the mud huts moved in silhouette across the sunset at the full moon of alternate months. Beyond the battlements the flat pastures spread and beyond the pastures were the Twisted Woods of thorn that climbed the ever steepening sides of Gormenghast mountain.

Fuchsia had covered the walls of her room with impetuous drawings in charcoal. There had been no attempt to create a design of any kind upon the coral plaster at either end of the bedroom. The drawings had been done at many an odd moment of loathing or excitement and although lacking in subtlety or proportion were filled with an extraordinary energy. These violent devices gave the two walls of her bedroom such an appearance of riot that the huddled heaps of toys and books in the four corners looked, by comparison, compact.

The attic, her kingdom, could be approached only through this bed-chamber. The door of the spiral staircase that ascended into the darkness was immediately behind the bedstead, so that to open this door which resembled the door of a cupboard, the bed had to be pulled forward into the room.

Fuchsia never failed to return the bed to its position as a precaution against her sanctum being invaded. It was unnecessary, for no one saving Mrs Slagg ever entered her bedroom and the old nurse in any case could never have manoeuvred herself up the hundred or so narrow, darkened steps that gave eventually on the attic, which since the earliest days Fuchsia could remember had been for her a world undesecrate.

Through succeeding generations a portion of the lumber of Gormenghast had found its way into this zone of moted half-light, this warm, breathless, timeless region where the great rafters moved across the air, clouded with moths. Where the dust was like pollen and lay softly on all things.

The attic was composed of two main galleries and a cock loft, the second gallery leading at right angles from the first after a descent of three rickety steps. At its far end a wooden ladder rose to a balcony resembling a narrow verandah. At the left extremity of this balcony a doorway, with its door hanging mutely by one hinge, led to the third of the three rooms that composed the attic. This was the loft which was for Fuchsia a very secret place, a kind of pagan chapel, an eyrie, a citadel, a kingdom never mentioned, for that would have been a breach of faith – a kind of blasphemy.

On the day of her brother's birth, while the castle beneath her, reaching in room below room, gallery below gallery, down, down to the very cellars, was alive with rumour, Fuchsia, like Rottcodd, in his Hall of the Bright Carvings was unaware of the excitement that filled it.

She had pulled at the long black pigtail of a chord which hung from the ceiling in one corner of her bedroom and had set a bell jangling in the remote apartment which Mrs Slagg had inhabited for two decades.

The sunlight was streaming through the eastern turrets and was lighting the Carvers' Battlement and touching the sides of the mountain beyond. As the sun rose, thorn tree after thorn tree on Gormenghast mountain emerged in the pale light and became a spectre, one following another, now here, now there, over the huge mass until the whole shape was flattened into a radiant jagged triangle against the darkness. Seven clouds like a group of naked cherubs or sucking-pigs, floated their plump pink bodies across a sky of slate. Fuchsia watched them through her window sullenly. Then she thrust her lower lip forward. Her hands were on her hips. Her bare feet were quite still on the floorboards.

'Seven,' she said, scowling at each. 'There's seven of them. One, two, three, four, five, six, seven. Seven clouds.'

She drew a yellow shawl more tightly around her shoulders for she was shivering in her nightdress, and pulled the pigtail again for Mrs Slagg. Rummaging in a drawer, she found a stick of black chalk and approaching an area of wall that was comparatively vacant she chalked a vicious 7 and drew a circle round it with the word 'CLOWDS' written beneath in heavy, uncompromising letters.

As Fuchsia turned away from the wall she took an awkward shuffling step towards the bed. Her jet black hair hung loosely across her shoulders. Her eyes, that were always smouldering, were fixed on the door. Thus she remained with one foot forward as the door knob turned and Mrs Slagg entered.

Seeing her, Fuchsia continued her walk from where she had left off, but instead of going towards the bed, she approached Mrs Slagg with five strides, and putting her arms quickly around the old woman's neck, kissed her savagely, broke away, and then beckoning her to the window, pointed towards the sky. Mrs Slagg peered along Fuchsia's outstretched arm and finger and inquired what there was to look at.

'Fat clouds,' said Fuchsia. 'There's seven of them.'

The old woman screwed up her eyes and peered once more but only for a moment. Then she made a little noise which seemed to indicate that she was not impressed.

'Why seven?' said Fuchsia. 'Seven is for something. What's seven for? One for a glorious golden grave – two for a terrible torch of tin; three for a hundred hollow horses; four for a knight with a spur of speargrass; five for a fish with fortunate fins, six – I've forgotten six, and seven – what's seven for? Eight for a frog with eyes like marbles, nine, what's nine? Nine for a – nine, nine – ten for a tower of turbulent toast – but what is seven. What is seven?'

Fuchsia stamped her foot and peered into the poor old nurse's face.

Nannie Slagg made little noises in her throat which was her way of filling in time and then said, 'Would you like some hot milk, my precious? Tell me now because I'm busy, and must feed your mother's white cats, dear. Just because I'm of the energetic system, my dearheart, they give me everything to do. What did you ring for? Quickly, quickly my caution. What did you ring for?'

Fuchsia bit her big red lower lip, tossed a mop of midnight from her brow and gazed out of the window, her hands grasping her elbows behind her. Very stiff she had become and angular.

'I want a big breakfast,' said Fuchsia at last. 'I want a lot to eat, I'm going to think today.'

Nannie Slagg was scrutinizing a wart on her left forearm.

'You don't know where I'm going, but I'm going somewhere where I can think.'

'Yes, dear,' said the old nurse.

'I want hot milk and eggs and lots of toast done only on one side.' Fuchsia frowned as she paused; 'and I want a bag of apples to take along with me for the whole of the day, for I get hungry when I think.'

'Yes, dear,' said Mrs Slagg again, pulling a loose thread from the hem of Fuchsia's skirt. 'Put some more on the fire, my caution, and I'll bring your breakfast and make your bed for you, though I'm not very well.'

Fuchsia descended suddenly upon her old nurse again and kissing her cheek, released her from the room, closing the door on her retreating figure with a crash that echoed down the gloomy corridors.

As soon as the door had closed, Fuchsia leaped at her bed and diving between the blankets head first, wriggled her way to the far end, where from all appearances, she became engaged in a life and death struggle with some ambushed monster. The heavings of the bedclothes ended as suddenly as they had begun and she emerged with a pair of long woollen stockings which she must have kicked off during the night. Sitting on her pillows she began pulling them on in a series of heaves, twisting with difficulty, at a very late stage, the heel of each from the front to the back.

'I won't see anybody today,' she said to herself – 'no, not anybody at all. I will go to my secret room and think things over.' She smiled a smile to herself. It was sly but it was so childishly sly that it was lovable. Her lips, big and well-formed and extraordinarily mature, curled up like plump petals and showed between them her white teeth.

As soon as she had smiled her face altered again, and the petulant expression peregrine to her features took control. Her black eyebrows were drawn together.

Her dressing became interrupted between the addition of each garment by dance movements of her own invention. There was nothing elegant in these attitudes into which she flung herself, standing sometimes for a dozen of seconds at a time in some extraordinary position of balance. Her eyes would become glazed like her mother's and an expression of abstract calm would for an instant defy the natural concentration of her face. Finally her blood-red dress, absolutely shapeless, was pulled over her head. It fitted nowhere except where a green cord was knotted at her waist. She appeared rather to inhabit, than to wear her clothes.

Meanwhile Mrs Slagg had not only prepared the breakfast for Fuchsia in her own little room, but was on the way back with the loaded tray shaking in her hands. As she turned a corner of the corridor she was brought to a clattering standstill by the sudden appearance of Doctor Prunesquallor, who also halting with great suddenness, avoided a collision.

'Well, well, well, well, well, ha, ha, ha, if it isn't dear Mrs Slagg, ha, ha, ha, how very very, very dramatic,' said the doctor, his long hands clasped before him at his chin, his high-pitched laugh creaking along the timber ceiling of the passage. His spectacles held in either lens the minute reflection of Nannie Slagg.

The old nurse had never really approved of Doctor Prunesquallor. It was true that he belonged to Gormenghast as much as the Tower itself. He was no intruder, but somehow, in Mrs Slagg's eyes he was definitely *wrong*. He was not her idea of a doctor in the first place, although she could never have argued why. Nor could she pin her dislike down to any other cause. Nannie Slagg found it very difficult to marshal her thoughts at the best of times, but when they became tied up with her emotions she became quite helpless. What she felt but had never analysed was that Doctor Prunesquallor rather played down to her and even in an obtuse way made fun of her. She had never thought this, but her bones knew of it.

She gazed up at the shock-headed man before her and wondered why he never brushed his hair, and then she felt guilty for allowing herself such thoughts about a gentleman and her tray shook and her eyes wavered a little.

'Ha, ha, ha, ha, ha, my dear Mrs Slagg, let me take your tray, ha, ha, until you have tasted the fruits of discourse and told me what you have been up to for the last month or more. Why have I not seen you, Nannie Slagg? Why have my ears not heard your footfall on the stairs, and your voice at nightfall, calling . . . calling . . . ?'

'Her ladyship don't want me any more, sir,' said Nannie Slagg, looking up at the doctor reproachfully. 'I am kept in the west wing now, sir.'

'So that's it, is it?' said Doctor Prunesquallor, removing the loaded tray from Nannie Slagg and lowering both it and himself at the same time to the floor of the long passage. He sat there on his heels with the tray at his side and peered up at the old lady, who gazed in a frightened way at his eye swimming hugely beneath his magnifying spectacles.

'You are *kept* in the west wing? So that's it?' Doctor Prunesquallor with his forefinger and thumb stroked his chin in a profound manner and frowned magnificently. 'It is the word "kept", my dear Mrs Slagg, that galls me. Are you an animal, Mrs Slagg? I repeat are you an animal?' As he said this he rose halfway to his feet and with his neck stretched forward repeated his question a third time.

Poor Nannie Slagg was too frightened to be able to give her answer to the query.

The doctor sank back on his heels.

'I will answer my own question, Mrs Slagg. I have known you for some time. For, shall we say, a decade? It is true we have never plumbed the depths of sorcery together nor argued the meaning of existence – but it is enough for me to say that I have known you for a considerable time, and that you are *no animal*. No animal *whatsoever*. Sit upon my knee.'

Nannie Slagg, terrified at this suggestion, raised her little bony hands to her mouth and raised her shoulders to her ears. Then she gave one frightened look down the passage and was about to make a run for it when she was gripped about the knees, not unkindly, but firmly and without knowing how she got there found herself sitting upon the high bony knee-cap of the squatting doctor.

'You are *not* an animal,' repeated Prunesquallor, 'are you?'

The old nurse turned her wrinkled face to the doctor and shook her head in little jerks.

'Of course you're not. Ha, ha, ha, ha, ha, of course you're not. Tell me what you *are*?'

Nannie's fist again came to her mouth and the frightened look in her eyes reappeared.

'I'm . . . I'm an old woman,' she said.

'You're a very unique old woman,' said the doctor, 'and if I am not mistaken, you will very soon prove to be an exceptionally invaluable old woman. Oh yes, ha, ha, ha, oh yes, a very invaluable old woman indeed.' (There was a pause.) 'How long is it since you saw her ladyship, the Countess? It must be a very long time.'

'It is, it is,' said Nannie Slagg, 'a very long time. Months and months and months.'

'As I thought,' said the doctor. 'Ha, ha, ha, as I very much thought. Then you can have no idea of why you will be indispensable?'

'Oh no, sir!' said Nannie Slagg, looking at the breakfast tray whose load was fast becoming cold.

'Do you like babies, my very dear Mrs Slagg?' asked the doctor, shifting the poor woman on to his other acutely bended knee joint and stretching out his former leg as though to ease it. 'Are you fond of the little creatures, taken by and large?'

'Babies?' said Mrs Slagg in the most animated tone that she had so far used. 'I could eat the little darlings, sir, I could eat them up!'

'Quite,' said Doctor Prunesquallor, 'quite so, my good woman. You could eat them up. That will be unnecessary. In fact it would be positively injurious, my dear Mrs Slagg, and especially under the circumstances about which I must now enlighten you. A child will be placed in your keeping. Do not devour him Nannie Slagg. It is for you to bring him up, that is true, but there will be no need for you to swallow him first. You would be, ha, ha, ha, ha – swallowing a Groan.'

This news filtered by degrees through Nannie Slagg's brain and all at once her eyes looked very wide indeed.

'No, oh no, sir!'

'Yes, oh yes, sir!' replied the physician. 'Although the Countess has of late banished you from her presence, yet, Nannie Slagg, you will of necessity be restored, ha, ha, ha, be restored to a very important state. Sometime today, if I am not mistaken, my wide-eyed Nannie Slagg, I shall be delivering a brand new Groan. Do you remember when I delivered the Countess of Lady Fuchsia?'

Nannie Slagg began to shake all over and a tear ran down her cheek as she clasped her hands between her knees, very nearly overbalancing from her precarious perch.

'I can remember every little thing sir – every little thing. Who would have thought?'

'Exactly,' interrupted Doctor Prunesquallor. 'Who would have thought. But I must be going, ha, ha, ha, I must dislodge you, Nannie

Slagg, from my patella – but tell me, did you know nothing of her ladyship's condition?'

'Oh, sir,' said the old lady, biting her knuckle and shifting her gaze. 'Nothing! nothing! No one ever tells me anything.'

'Yet all the duties will devolve on you,' said Doctor Prunesquallor. 'Though you will doubtless enjoy yourself. There is no doubt at all about that. Is there?'

'Oh, sir, another baby, after all this time! Oh, I could smack him already.'

'Him?' queried the doctor. 'Ha, ha, ha, you are very sure of the gender, my dear Mrs Slagg.'

'Oh yes, sir, it's a him, sir. Oh, what a blessing that it is. They *will* let me have him, sir? They will let me won't they?'

'They have no choice,' said the doctor somewhat too briskly for a gentleman and he smiled a wide inane smile, his thin nose pointing straight at Mrs Slagg. His grey hayrick of hair removed itself from the wall. 'What of my Fuchsia? Has she an inkling?'

'Oh, no, not an inkling. Not an inkling, sir, bless her. She hardly ever leaves her room except at night, sir. She don't know nothing, sir, and never talks to no one but me.'

The doctor, removing Nannie Slagg from his knee, rose to his feet. 'The rest of Gormenghast talks of nothing else, but the western wing is in darkness. Very, very, very strange. The child's nurse and the child's sister are in darkness, ha, ha, ha. But not for long, not for long. By all that's enlightened, very much not so!'

'Sir?' queried Nannie Slagg as the doctor was about to move away.

'What?' said Doctor Prunesquallor, scrutinizing his finger nails. 'What is it my dear Mrs Slagg? Be quick.'

'Er – how is *she*, sir? How is her ladyship?'

'Tough as behemoth,' said Prunesquallor, and was around the corner in an instant, and Nannie Slagg, with her mouth and eyes wide open, could, as she lifted up the cold tray, hear his feet in a far passage tapping an elegant tattoo as he moved like a bird towards the bedroom of the Countess of Groan.

As Mrs Slagg knocked at Fuchsia's door, her heart was beating very fast. It was always a long time before she realized the import of whatever she were told, and it was only now that the full measure of what the doctor had divulged was having its effect. To be again, after all these years, the nurse of an heir to the house of Groan – to be able to bathe the helpless limbs, to iron out the little garments and to select the wet nurse from the outer dwellings! To have complete authority in anything connected with the care of the precious mite – all this was now weighing with a great load of painful pride across her heart that was beating rapidly.

So overpowered was she by this emotion that she had knocked twice before she noticed that there was a note pinned upon the outside of the door. Peering at it she at last made out what Fuchsia had scrawled in her invariable charcoal.

Can't wait until the doomsday – you're so SLOW!

Mrs Slagg tried the door handle although she knew that the door would be locked. Leaving the tray and the apples on the mat outside she retreated to her own room where she might indulge herself in halcyon glimpses of the future. Life, it seemed, was not over for her.

THE ATTIC

MEANWHILE Fuchsia had, after waiting impatiently for her breakfast, gone to a cupboard where she kept an emergency supply of eatables – half an old seed cake and some dandelion wine. There was also a box of dates which Flay had purloined and brought up for her several weeks before, and two wrinkled pears. These she wrapped in a piece of cloth. Next she lit a candle and placed it on the floor near the wall, then hollowing her strong young back she laid hold of the foot-rail of her bed and dragged it back sufficiently for her to squeeze herself between the rail and the wall and to unlatch the cupboard door. Stretching over the head-rail she grasped her bundle of food and then picked up the candle from near her feet, and ducking her head crept through the narrow opening and found herself at the lowermost steps of the flight that led upwards in dark spirals. Closing the door behind her, she dragged a bolt into position and the tremors which she always experienced at this moment of locking herself in, took hold of her and for a moment she shook from head to foot.

Then, with her candle lighting her face and the three sliding steps before her as she climbed, she ascended into her region.

As Fuchsia climbed into the winding darkness her body was impregnated and made faint by a qualm as of green April. Her heart beat painfully.

This is a love that equals in its power the love of man for woman and reaches inwards as deeply. It is the love of a man or of a woman for their world. For the world of their centre where their lives burn genuinely and with a free flame.

The love of the diver for his world of wavering light. His world of pearls and tendrils and his breath at his breast. Born as a plunger into the deeps he is at one with every swarm of lime-green fish, with every coloured sponge. As he holds himself to the ocean's faery floor, one hand clasped to a bedded whale's rib, he is complete and infinite. Pulse, power and universe sway in his body. He is in love.

The love of the painter standing alone and staring, staring at the great coloured surface he is making. Standing with him in the room the rearing canvas stares back with tentative shapes halted in their growth, moving in a new rhythm from floor to ceiling. The twisted tubes, the fresh paint squeezed and smeared across the dry upon his palette. The dust beneath the easel. The paint has edged along the brushes' handles. The white light in a northern sky is silent. The window gapes as he inhales his world. His world: a rented room, and turpentine. He moves towards his half-born. He is in love.

The rich soil crumbles through the yeoman's fingers. As the pearl diver murmurs, 'I am home' as he moves dimly in strange water-lights, and as the painter mutters, 'I am me' on his lone raft of floorboards, so the slow landsman on his acre'd marl – says with dark Fuchsia on her twisting staircase, 'I am home.'

It was this feeling of belonging to the winding stair and the attic which Fuchsia experienced as she ran her right hand along the wooden wall as she climbed and encountered after some time the loose board which she expected. She knew that only eighteen steps remained and that after two more turns in the staircase the indescribable grey-gold filtering glow of the attic would greet her.

Reaching the top-most step she stooped and leaned over a three-foot swing door, like the door of a byre, unfastened the latch and entered the first of the three sections of the attic.

An infiltration of the morning's sun gave the various objects a certain vague structure but in no way dispelled the darkness. Here and there a thin beam of light threaded the warm brooding dusk and was filled with slowly moving motes like an attenuate firmament of stars revolving in grave order.

One of these narrow beams lit Fuchsia's forehead and shoulder, and another plucked a note of crimson from her dress. To her right was an enormous crumbling organ. Its pipes were broken and the keyboard shattered. Across its front the labour of a decade of grey spiders had woven their webs into a shawl of lace. It needed but the ghost of an infanta to arise from the dust to gather it about her head and shoulders as the most fabulous of all mantillas.

In the gloom Fuchsia's eyes could barely be seen for the light upon her forehead sank deeper shadows, by contrast, through her face. But they were calm. The excitement that had wakened within them on the stairway had given place to this strange calm. She stood at the stairhead almost another being.

This room was the darkest. In the summer the light seemed to penetrate through the fissures in the warped wood and through the dislodged portions of stone slating in a less direct way than was the case in the larger room or gallery to its right. The third, the smallest attic, with its steps leading upwards from the gallery with the banistered verandah was the best lit, for it boasted a window with shutters which, when opened, gave upon a panorama of roof-tops, towers and battlements that lay in a great half-circle below. Between high bastions might be seen, hundreds of feet beneath, a portion of quadrangle wherein, were a figure to move across, he would appear no taller than a thimble.

Fuchsia took three paces forward in the first of the attics and then paused a moment to re-tie a string above her knee. Over her head vague rafters loomed and while she straightened herself she noticed them and unconsciously loved them. This was the lumber room. Though very long and lofty it looked relatively smaller than it was, for the fantastic piles of every imaginable kind of thing, from the great organ to the lost and painted head of a broken toy lion that must one day have been the plaything of one of Fuchsia's ancestors, spread from every wall until only an avenue was left to the adjacent room. This high, narrow avenue wound down the centre of the first attic before suddenly turning at a sharp angle to the right. The fact that this room was filled with lumber did not mean that she ignored it and used it only as a place of transit. Oh no, for it was here that many long afternoons had been spent as she crawled deep into the recesses and found for herself many a strange cavern among the incongruous relics of the past. She knew of ways through the centre of what appeared to be hills of furniture, boxes, musical instruments and toys, kites, pictures, bamboo armour and helmets, flags and relics of every kind, as an Indian knows his green and secret trail. Within reach of her hand the hide and head of a skinned baboon hung dustily over a broken drum that rose beyond the dim ranges of this attic medley. Huge and impregnable they looked in the warm still half-light, but Fuchsia, had she wished to, could have disappeared awkwardly but very suddenly into these fantastic mountains, reached their centre and lain down upon an ancient couch with a picture book at her elbow and been entirely lost to view within a few moments.

This morning, she was bound for the third of her rooms and moved forward through the canyon, ducking beneath the stuffed leg of a giraffe that caught a thread of the moted sunlight and which, propped across Fuchsia's path, made a kind of low lintel immediately before the passage curved away to the right. As Fuchsia rounded this bend she saw what she expected to see. Twelve feet away were the wooden steps which led down to the second attic. The rafters above the steps were warped into a sagging curve so that it was not possible to obtain more than a restricted view of the room beyond. But the area of empty floor that was visible gave an indication of the whole. She descended the steps. There was a ripping away of clouds; a sky, a desert, a forsaken shore spread through her.

As she stepped forward on the empty board, it was for her like walking into space. Space, such as the condors have shrill inklings of, and the cock-eagle glimpses through his blood.

Silence was there with a loud rhythm. The halls, towers, the rooms of Gormenghast were of another planet. Fuchsia caught at a thick lock of her hair and dragged her own head back as her heart beat loudly and, tingling from head to foot little diamonds appeared at the inner corners of her eyes.

With what characters she had filled this lost stage of emptiness! It was here that she would see the people of her imagination, the fierce figures of her making, as they strolled from corner to corner, brooded like monsters or flew through the air like seraphs with burning wings, or danced, or fought, or laughed, or cried. This was her attic of make-believe, where she would watch her mind's companions advancing or retreating across the dusty floor.

Gripping her eatables tightly in their cloth, her feet echoing dully, she walked onwards towards the fixed ladder that led to the balcony at the far end. She climbed the ladder, both feet coming together on each rung for it was difficult for her to climb with the bottle and her food for the day tucked under her arm. There was no one to see her strong straight back and shoulders and the gauche, indecorous movements of her legs as she climbed in her crimson dress; nor the length of her tangled and inky hair. Half-way up she was able to lift her bundle above her head and push it on to the balcony, and then to swarm after it and find herself standing with the great stage below her as empty as an unremembered heart.

As she looked down, her hands on the wooden banister that ran along the attic verandah, she knew that at a call she could set in motion the five main figures of her making. Those whom she had so often watched below her, almost as though they were really there. At first it had not been easy to understand them nor to tell them what to do. But now it would be easy, at any rate for them to enact the scenes that she had watched them so often perform. Munster, who would crawl along the rafters and drop chuckling into the middle of the floor in a cloud of dust and then bow to Fuchsia before turning and searching for his barrel of bright gold. Or the Rain Man, who moved always with his head lowered and his hands clasped behind him and who had but to lift his eyelid to quell the tiger that followed him on a chain.

These and the dramas in which they took part were now latent in the room below her, but Fuchsia passed the high-backed chair where she would sit at the verandah edge, pulled back the door carefully on its one hinge, and entered into the third of the three rooms.

She put her bundle upon a table in one corner, went to the window and pushed open the two shutters. Her stocking was half-way down her leg again and she knotted the string more firmly round her thigh. It was often her habit in this room to think aloud to herself. To argue with herself. Looking down from her little window upon the roofs of the castle and its adjacent buildings she tasted the pleasure of her isolation. 'I am alone,' she said, her chin in her hands and her elbows on the sill. 'I am quite alone, like I enjoy it. Now I can think for there's no one to provoke me here. Not in my room. No one to tell me what I ought to do because I'm a Lady. Oh no. I do just what I like here. Fuchsia is quite alright here. None of them knows where I go to. Flay doesn't know. Father doesn't know. Mother doesn't know. None of them knows. Even Nannie doesn't know. Only I know. I know where I go. I go here. This is where I go. Up the stairs and into my lumber room. Through my lumber room and into my acting room. All across my acting room and up the ladder and on to my verandah. Through the door and into my secret attic. And here it is I am. I am here now. I have been here lots of times but that is in the past. That is over, but now I'm here it's in the present. This is the present. I'm looking on the roofs of the present and I'm leaning on the present window-sill and later on when I'm older I will lean on this window-sill again. Over and over again.

'Now I'll make myself comfortable and eat my breakfast,' she continued to herself, but as she turned away her quick eyes noticed in the corner of one of the diminished quadrangles far below her an unusually large gathering of what she could just make out to be servants from the kitchen quarters. She was so used to the panorama below her being deserted at that hour in the morning, the menials being at their multifarious duties about the castle that she turned suddenly back to the window and stared down with a sense of suspicion and almost of fear. What was it that quickened her to a sense of something irreparable having been done? To an outsider there would have been nothing untoward or extraordinary in the fact that a group had gathered hundreds of feet below in the corner of a sunny stone quadrangle, but Fuchsia born and bred to the iron ritual of Gormenghast knew that something unprecedented was afoot. She stared, and as she stared the group grew. It was enough to throw Fuchsia out of her mood and to make her uneasy and angry.

'Something has happened,' she said, 'something no one's told me of. They haven't told me. I don't like them. I don't like any of them. What are they all doing like a lot of ants down there? Why aren't they working like they should be?' She turned around and faced her little room.

Everything was changed, she picked up one of the pears and bit a piece out of it abstractedly. She had looked forward to a morning of rumination and perhaps a play or two in the empty attic before she climbed down the stairs again to demand a big tea from Mrs Slagg. There was something portentous in the group far below her. Her day was disrupted.

She looked around at the walls of her room. They were hung with pictures once chosen as her favourites from among the scores that she had unearthed in the lumber room. One wall was filled with a great mountain scene where a road like a snake winding around and around the most impressive of crags was filled with two armies, one in yellow and the other, the invading force battling up from below, in purple. Lit as it were by torch-light the whole scene was a constant source of wonder to Fuchsia, yet this morning she gazed at it blankly. The other walls were less imposingly arranged, fifteen pictures being distributed among the three. The head of a jaguar; a portrait of the twenty-second Earl of Groan with pure white hair and a face the colour of smoke as a result of immoderate tattooing, and a group of children in pink and white muslin dresses playing with a viper were among the works which pleased her most. Hundreds of very dull heads and full-length portraits of her ancestors had been left in the lumber room. What Fuchsia wanted from a picture was something unexpected. It was as though she enjoyed the artist telling her something quite fresh and new. Something she had never thought of before.

A great writhing root, long since dragged from the woods of Gormenghast mountain, stood in the centre of the room. It had been polished to a rare gloss, its every wrinkle gleaming. Fuchsia flung herself down on the most imposing article in the room, a couch of faded splendour and suavity of contour in which the angles of Fuchsia's body as she lay in a half sprawl were thrown out with uncompromising severity. Her eyes which, since she had entered the attic, had taken on the calm expression so alien to her, were now smouldering again. They moved about the room as though they were seeking in vain a resting place, but neither the fantastic root, nor the ingenious patterns in the carpet below her had the power to hold them.

'Everything's wrong. Everything. Everything,' said Fuchsia. Again she went to the window and peered down at the group in the quadrangle. By now it had grown until it filled all that was visible of the stone square. Through a flying buttress to the left of her she could command a view of four distant alleys in a poor district of Gormenghast. These alley-ways were pranked with little knots of folk, and Fuchsia believed that she could hear the far sound of their voices rising through the air. It was not that Fuchsia felt any particular interest in 'occasions' or festivities which might cause excitement below, but that this morning she felt acutely aware that something in which she would become involved was taking place.

On the table lay a big coloured book of verses and pictures. It was

always ready for her to open and devour. Fuchsia would turn over the
pages and read the verses aloud in a deep dramatic voice. This morning
she leaned forward and turned over the pages listlessly. As she came
upon a great favourite she paused and read it through slowly, but her
thoughts were elsewhere.

THE FRIVOLOUS CAKE

A freckled and frivolous cake there was
    That sailed on a pointless sea,
Or any lugubrious lake there was
    In a manner emphatic and free.
How jointlessly, and how jointlessly
    The frivolous cake sailed by
On the waves of the ocean that pointlessly
    Threw fish to the lilac sky.

Oh, plenty and plenty of hake there was
    Of a glory beyond compare,
And every conceivable make there was
    Was tossed through the lilac air.

Up the smooth billows and over the crests
    Of the cumbersome combers flew
The frivolous cake with a knife in the wake
    Of herself and her curranty crew.
Like a swordfish grim it would bounce and skim
    (This dinner knife fierce and blue),
And the frivolous cake was filled to the brim
    With the fun of her curranty crew.

Oh, plenty and plenty of hake there was
    Of a glory beyond compare –
And every conceivable make there was
    Was tossed through the lilac air.

Around the shores of the Elegant Isles
    Where the cat-fish bask and purr
And lick their paws with adhesive smiles
    And wriggle their fins of fur,
They fly and fly 'neath the lilac sky –
    The frivolous cake, and the knife
Who winketh his glamorous indigo eye
    In the wake of his future wife.

The crumbs blow free down the pointless sea
    To the beat of a cakey heart
And the sensitive steel of the knife can feel
    That love is a race apart.

> In the speed of the lingering light are blown
> The crumbs to the hake above,
> And the tropical air vibrates to the drone
> Of a cake in the throes of love.

She ended the final verse with a rush, taking in nothing at all of its meaning. As she ended the last line mechanically, she found herself getting to her feet and making for the door. Her bundle was left behind, open, but, save for the pear, untouched on the table. She found herself on the balcony and lowering herself down the ladder was in the empty attic and within a few moments had reached the head of the stairs in the lumber room. As she descended the spiral staircase her thoughts were turning over and over.

'What have they done? What have they done?' And it was in a precipitous mood that she entered her room and ran to the corner where, catching hold of the pigtail bell-rope she pulled it as though to wrench it from the ceiling.

Within a few moments Mrs Slagg came running up to the door, her slippered feet scraping along unevenly on the floorboards. Fuchsia opened the door to her and as soon as the poor old head appeared around the panels, she shouted at it, 'What's happening Nannie, what's happening down there? Tell me at once, Nannie, or I won't love you. Tell me, tell me.'

'Quiet, my caution, quiet,' said Mrs Slagg. 'What's all the bother, my conscience! oh my poor heart. You'll be the death of me.'

'You must tell me, Nannie. Now! now! or I'll hit you,' said Fuchsia.

From so small a beginning of suspicion Fuchsia's fears had grown until now, convinced by a mounting intuition, she was almost on the point of striking her old nurse, whom she loved so desperately. Nannie Slagg took hold of Fuchsia's hand between eight old fingers and squeezed it.

'A little brother for you, my pretty. Now *there's* a surprise to quieten you; a little *brother*. Just like you, my ugly darling – born in the lap-sury.'

'No!' shouted Fuchsia, the blood rushing to her cheek. 'No! no! I won't have it. Oh no, no, no! I won't! I won't! It *mustn't* be, it *mustn't* be!' And Fuchsia flinging herself to the floor burst into a passion of tears.

'MRS SLAGG BY MOONLIGHT'

THESE then, Lord Sepulchrave, the Countess Gertrude, Fuchsia their eldest child, Doctor Prunesquallor, Mr Rottcodd, Flay, Swelter, Nannie Slagg, Steerpike and Sourdust, have been discovered at their pursuits on the day of the advent, and have perhaps indicated the atmosphere into which it was the lot of Titus to be born.

For his first few years of life, Titus was to be left to the care of Nannie Slagg, who bore this prodigious responsibility proudly upon her thin little sloping shoulders. During the first half of this early period only two major ceremonies befell the child and of these Titus was happily unaware, namely the christening, which took place twelve days after his birth, and a ceremonial breakfast on his first birthday. Needless to say, to Mrs Slagg, every day presented a series of major happenings, so entirely was she involved in the practicalities of his upbringing.

She made her way along the narrow stone path between the acacia trees on this memorable nativity evening and downhill to the gate in the castle wall which led into the heart of the mud dwellings. As she hurried along, the sun was setting behind Gormenghast mountain in a swamp of saffron light and her shadow hurried alongside between the acacia trees. It was seldom that she ventured out of doors and it was with quite a flutter that she had opened with difficulty the heavy lid of a chest in her room and extricated, from beneath a knoll of camphor, her best hat. It was very black indeed, but by way of relief it had upon its high crown a brittle bunch of glass grapes. Four or five of them had been broken but this was not very noticeable.

Nannie Slagg had lifted the hat up to her shoulder level and peered at it obliquely before puffing at the glass grapes to remove any possible dust. Seeing that she had dulled them with her breath she lifted up her petticoat and doubling up over her hat she gave a quick little polish to each fruit in turn.

Then she had approached the door of her room almost furtively and placed her ear at the panel. She had heard nothing, but whenever she found herself doing anything unorthodox, no matter how necessary, she would feel very guilty inside and look around her with her red rimmed eyes opened wide and her head shaking a little, or if alone in a room as at the moment, she would run to the door and listen.

When she felt quite certain that there was no one there she would open the door very quickly and stare out into the empty passage and then go to her task again with renewed confidence. This time, the putting on of her best hat at nine o'clock at night with the idea of sallying forth from the castle, down the long drive and then northwards along the acacia avenue, had been enough to send her to her own doorway as though she suspected someone might be there, someone who was listening to her thoughts. Tiptoeing back to her bed she had added fourteen inches to her stature by climbing into her velvet hat. Then she had left the room, and the stairs had seemed frighteningly empty to her as she descended the two flights.

Remembering, as she turned through the main doorway of the west wing, that the Countess herself had given her the orders to pursue this unusual mission, she had felt a little stronger, but whatever factual authority, it was something much deeper that had worried her, something based upon the unspoken and iron-bound tradition of the place. It had made her feel she was doing wrong. However, a wet nurse had to be found for the infant and the immediate logic of this had jostled her forward. As she had left her own room she had picked up a pair of black woollen gloves. It was a soft, warm, summer evening but Nannie Slagg felt stronger in her gloves.

The acacia trees, silhouetted on her right, cut patterns against the mountain and on her left glowed dimly with a sort of subterranean light. Her path was striped like the dim hide of a zebra from the shadows of the acacia trunks. Mrs Slagg, a midget figure beneath the rearing and overhanging of the aisle of dark foliage, awakened small echoes in the neighbouring rocks as she had moved, for her heels beat a quick uneven measure on the stone path.

This avenue lasted for some considerable distance, and when at last the old nurse found herself at its northern end she was welcomed by the cold light of the rising moon. The outer wall of Gormenghast had suddenly reared above her. She passed through an archway.

Mrs Slagg knew that about this hour the Dwellers would be at their supper. As she pattered onwards the memory of a very similar occasion worked its way into her consciousness: The time when she had been delegated to make a similar choice for Fuchsia. That time it had also been in the evening although an hour or so earlier. The weather had been gusty and she remembered how her voice had failed to carry in the wind, and how they had all misunderstood her and had imagined that Lord Groan had died.

Only three times since that day had she been to this part of the Dwellers' province, and on those occasions it had been to take Fuchsia for the long walks that at one time she had so insisted upon, rain or shine.

Mrs Slagg's days of long walks were over, but she had on one of those occasions passed the mud huts when the Dwellers were having their last meal. She knew that the Dwellers always had their supper in the open, at tables that reached in four long rows over the drab, grey-coloured dust. In this dust, she remembered, a few cactus trees were alone able to take root.

Following the gradual decline of a scarred green that sloped from the arch in the wall and petered out into the dust upon which the hovels were built, she saw suddenly, on raising her eyes from the path, one of these cactus trees.

Fifteen years is a difficult depth of time for an old woman's memory to plumb – more difficult than the waters of her childhood, but when Mrs Slagg saw the cactus tree she remembered clearly and in detail how she had stopped and stared at the great scarred monster on the day of Fuchsia's birth.

Here it was again, its flaking bole dividing into four uprights like the arms of a huge grey candlestick studded with thorns, each one as large and brutal as the horn of a rhinoceros. No flaming flower relieved its black achromatism although that tree had been known long ago to burst open with a three-hour glory. Beyond this tree the ground rose into a little dreary hill, and it was only when she had climbed this hill that Mrs Slagg saw before her the Dwellers at their long tables. Behind them the clay huts were huddled together in a grey swarm, spreading to the foot of the wall. Four or five cacti grew between and reared over the supper tables.

The cacti were similar both in size and in the way they split into high uncouth prongs to the one which Mrs Slagg first saw, and as she approached, were edged with the hot afterglow of the sun.

At the line of tables nearest the outer wall were ranged the elderly, the grandparents, the infirm. To their left, were the married women and their children whom they were tending.

The remaining two tables were filled with men and boys. The girls from the age of twelve to twenty-three had their meals in a low mud building on their own, a few of them being delegated to wait each day upon the ancients at their tables immediately under the battlements.

Beyond, the land dipped into a dry shallow valley which held the dwellings, so that as she came forward step by step the figures at the tables had for their background the rough roofs of mud, the walls of their huts being hidden by the contour of the ground. It was a dreary prospect. From the lush shadows of the acacia drive Mrs Slagg had suddenly broken in upon an arid world. She saw the rough sections of white jarl root and their bowls of sloe wine standing before them. The long tubular jarl root which they dug each day from a wood in the vicinity, stood upon the tables every evening, sliced up into scores of narrow cylinders. This, she remembered, was their traditional diet.

Noting the white roots spreading away in perspective, each piece with its shadow, she remembered with a flutter that her social status was very much in advance of that held by these poor mud-hut dwellers.

It was true that they made pretty carvings, but they were not *within* the walls of Gormenghast, and Nannie Slagg, as she approached the nearest table, pulled on her gloves more tightly still and worked them up around her fingers, pursing her little wrinkled mouth.

The Dwellers had seen her immediately her hat had appeared above the dry brow of the hill, and every head had been turned, and every eye focused upon her. The mothers had paused, some of them with spoons halfway to their children's mouths.

It was unusual for them to have the 'Castles', as they termed any who came from within the walls, approach them at their meals. They stared without moving and without speaking.

Mrs Slagg had stopped. The moonlight flared on the glass grapes.

A very old man like a prophet arose and approached her. When he reached her he stood silently until an elderly woman who had waited until he halted, was helped to her feet and, following his example, had reached Mrs Slagg and stood silently by the old man's side. Thereupon two magnificent urchins of five or six years of age had been sent forward from the table of mothers. These two, when they reached Mrs Slagg stood quietly and then, lifting their arms in imitation of their elders and, placing their wrists together cupped their hands and bowed their heads.

They remained in this attitude for a few moments until the old man lifted his shaggy head and parted the long rough line of his mouth.

'Gormenghast,' he said, and his voice was like the noise of boulders rolling through far valleys, and as he had said 'Gormenghast' the intonation was such as implied reverence. This was the greeting of the Dwellers to any who were of the Castle and once that word had been spoken the person to whom it was addressed replied – 'The Bright Carvers'. Conversation could then proceed. This response, deaf as the Dwellers were to any flattery, holding themselves to be the supreme judges of their work and indifferent to the outside interest, was in its way a palliative in the sense that it put them where they felt in their bones they belonged – on a spiritual if not a worldly or hereditary level. It introduced a certain concord at the outset. It was a master stroke of judgement, a tower of tact, in the seventeenth Earl of Groan, when hundreds of years before he had introduced this tenet into the ritual of the Castle.

Very, very far from bright were the Carvers themselves. They were uniformly dressed in dark grey cloth, tied about the waist with tough thongs which were stripped from the outer surface of the jarl root, whose inner hard white flesh they ate. Nothing was bright about their appearance, save one thing. The light in the eyes of the younger children. Indeed, in the youths and maidens also up to the age of nineteen and sometimes twenty. These young Dwellers were in such contrast to their elders, even to those in their mid-twenties, that it was difficult to imagine that they were of the same stock. The tragic reason was that after they had come to their physical maturity of form their loveliness crumbled away and they became withered as flowers after their few fresh hours of brilliance and strength.

No one looked middle aged. The mothers were, save for the few who had borne their children in their late teens, as ancient in appearance as their own parents.

And yet they did not die as might be imagined, any earlier than is normal. On the contrary, from the long line of ancient faces at the three tables nearest the great wall, it might be imagined that their longevity was abnormal.

Only their children's had radiance, their eyes, the sheen on their hair, and in another way, their movements and their voices. Bright with a kind of *unnatural* brightness. It was not the wholesome lustre of a free flame, but of the hectic radiance that sheet-lightning gives suddenly to limbs of trees at midnight; of sudden flares in the darkness, of a fragment that is lit by torchlight into a spectre.

Even this unnatural emanation died in these youths and girls when they had reached their nineteenth year; along with the beauty of their features, this radiance vanished too. Only *within* the bodies of the adult Dwellers was there a kind of light, or if not light, at least hotness – the hotness of creative restlessness. These were the Bright Carvers.

Mrs Slagg hoisted her little claw of a hand very high in the air. The four who were lined in front of her had taken less formal stances, the children peering up at her with their slim, dusty arms around each others' shoulders.

'I have come,' she said in a voice which, thin as a curlew, carried along the tables, 'I have come – although it is so late – to tell you a wonderful thing.' She readjusted her hat and felt as she did so, with great pleasure, the shining volume of the glass grapes.

The old man turned to the tables and his voice rolled out along them. 'She has come to tell us a wonderful thing,' and the old woman followed him up like a distorted echo and screamed, 'A wonderful thing.'

'Yes, yes, it is wonderful news for you,' the old nurse continued. 'You will all be very proud, I am quite sure.'

Mrs Slagg, now she had started was rather enjoying herself. She clasped her gloved hands together more tightly whenever she felt a qualm of nervousness.

'We are all proud. All of us. The Castle,' (she said this in a rather vain way) 'is very very satisfied and when I tell you what has happened, then, you'll be happy as well; oh yes, I am sure you will. Because I know you are *dependent* on the castle.'

Mrs Slagg was never very tactful. 'You have some food thrown down to you from the battlements every morning, don't you?' She had pursed her mouth and stopped a moment for breath.

A young man lifted his thick black eyebrows and spat.

'So you are very much thought of by the Castle. Every day you are thought of, aren't you? And that's why you'll be so happy when I tell you the wonderful thing that I'm going to tell you.'

Mrs Slagg smiled to herself for a moment, but suddenly felt a little nervous in spite of her superior knowledge and had glanced quickly, like a bird, from one face to another. She had bridled up her wispy head and had peered as sternly as she could at a small boy who answered with a flashing smile. His hair was clustered over his shoulders. Between his teeth as he grinned glistened a white nugget of jarl root.

She shifted her gaze and clapped her hands together sharply two or three times as though for silence, although there was no noise at all. Then she suddenly felt she wanted to be back in the castle and in her own little room and she said before she knew it, 'A new little Groan has been born, a little boy. A little boy of the Blood. I am in charge, of course, and I want a wet nurse for him *at once*. I must have one *at once* to come back with me. There now! I've told you everything.'

The old women had turned to one another and had then walked away to their huts. They returned with little cakes and bottles of sloe wine. Meanwhile the men formed a large circle and repeated the name Gormenghast seventy-seven times. While Mrs Slagg waited and watched the children who had been set playing, a woman had come forward. She told Mrs Slagg that her child had died a few hours after he had been born some days ago but that she was strong enough and would come. She was, perhaps, twenty, and was well-built, but the tragic disintegration of her beauty had begun although her eyes still had the afterglow upon them. She fetched a basket and did not seem to expect any sort of refusal to her offer. And Nannie Slagg was about to ask a few questions, as she felt would be correct, but the Dweller, packing the sloe wine and cakes into a basket, had taken Mrs Slagg quietly by the arm and the old nurse found herself to be making for the Great Wall. She glanced up at the young woman beside her and wondered whether she had chosen correctly, and then, realizing that she hadn't chosen at all, she half stopped and glanced back nervously over her shoulder.

KEDA

THE cactus trees stood hueless between the long tables. The Dwellers were all in their places again. Mrs Slagg ceased to interest them. There were no shadows save immediately below every object. The moon was overhead. It was a picture painted on silver. Mrs Slagg's companion had waited with her quietly. There was a kind of strength in the way she walked and in the way she kept silent. With the dark cloth hanging to her ankles and caught in at her waist with the thong of jarl root; with her bare legs and feet and her head still holding the sunset of her darkened day, she was in strange contrast to little Nannie Slagg, with her quick jerky walk, her dark satin dress, her black gloves, and her monumental hat of glass grapes. Before they descended the dry knoll towards the archway in the wall, a sudden guttural cry as of someone being strangled, froze the old woman's blood and she clutched at the strong arm beside her and clung to it like a child. Then she peered towards the tables. They were too far for her to see clearly with her weak eyes, but she thought she could make out figures standing and there seemed to be someone crouching like a creature about to spring.

Mrs Slagg's companion appeared, after glancing casually in the direction of the sound, to take no more notice of the incident, but keeping a firmer grip this time on the old lady, propelled her forward towards the stone gate.

'It is nothing,' was the sole reply which Mrs Slagg received and by the time the two were in the acacia avenue her blood had quietened.

When they were turning from the long drive into the doorway of Gormenghast through which Nannie had stepped out into the evening air so surreptitiously an hour or so before, she glanced up at her companion and shrugging her shoulders a little, contrived to take on an expression of mock importance.

'Your name? Your name?' she said.

'Keda.'

'Well, Keda, dear, if you will follow me, I will take you to the little boy. I'll show you him myself. He is by the window in *my* room.' Nannie's voice suddenly took on a confidential, almost pathetic note. 'I haven't a very big room,' she said, 'but I've always had the same one, I don't like any of the other ones,' she added rather untruthfully, 'I'm nearer Lady Fuchsia.'

'Perhaps I shall see her,' said the girl, after a pause.

Nannie suddenly stopped on the stairs. 'I don't *know* about that,' she said, 'oh no, I'm not *sure* about that. She is very strange. I never know what she's going to do next.'

'To do?' said Keda. 'How do you mean?'

'About little Titus.' Nannie's eyes began to wander. 'No, I don't know what she'll do. She's such a terror – the naughtiest terror in the castle – she can be.'

'Why are you frightened?' said Keda.

'I know she'll hate him. She likes to be the only one, you know. She likes to dream that she's the queen and that when the rest are dead there'll be no one who can order her to do anything. She said, dear, that she'd burn down the whole place, burn down Gormenghast when she was the ruler and she'd live on her own, and I said she was wicked, and she said that everyone was – everyone and everything except rivers, clouds, and some rabbits. She makes me frightened sometimes.'

They climbed up remaining steps, along a passageway and up the remaining flight to the second floor in silence.

When they had come to the room Mrs Slagg placed her finger at her lips and gave a smile which it would be impossible to describe. It was a mixture of the cunning and the maudlin. Then turning the handle very carefully she opened the door by degrees and putting her high hat of glass grapes through the narrow opening by way of a vanguard, followed it stealthily with all that remained of her.

Keda entered the room. Her bare feet made no noise on the floor. When Mrs Slagg reached the cradle she put her fingers to her mouth and peered over it as though into the deepest recesses of an undiscovered world. There he was. The infant Titus. His eyes were open but he was quite still. The puckered-up face of the newly-born child, old as the world, wise as the roots of trees. Sin was there and goodness, love, pity and horror, and even beauty for his eyes were pure violet. Earth's passions, earth's griefs, earth's incongruous, ridiculous humours – dormant, yet visible in the wry pippin of a face.

Nannie Slagg bending over him waggled a crooked finger before his eyes. 'My little sugar,' she tittered. 'How *could* you? how *could* you?'

Mrs Slagg turned round to Keda with a new look in her face. 'Do you think I should have left him?' she said. 'When I went to fetch you. Do you think I should have left him?'

Keda stared down at Titus. Tears were in her eyes as she watched the child. Then she turned to the window. She could see the great wall that held in Gormenghast. The wall that cut her own people away, as though to keep out a plague; the walls that barred from her view the stretches of arid earth beyond the mud huts where her child had so recently been buried.

To come within the walls was itself something of an excitement to those of the mud huts and something which in the normal course of events was reserved for the day of the Bright Carvings, but to be within the castle itself was something unique. Yet Keda did not seem impressed and had not troubled to ask Mrs Slagg any questions nor even so much as glance about her. Poor Mrs Slagg felt this was something of an impertinence but did not know whether or not she ought to say something about it.

But Titus had stolen the limelight and Keda's indifference was soon forgotten, for he was beginning to cry, and his crying grew and grew in spite of Mrs Slagg's dangling a necklace in front of his screwed up eyes and an attempt at singing a lullaby from her half-forgotten store. She had him over her shoulder, but his shrill cries rose in volume. Keda's eyes were still upon the wall, but of a sudden, breaking herself away from the window, she moved up behind Nannie Slagg and, as she did so, parted the dark brown material from her throat and freeing her left breast, took the child from the shoulders of the old woman. Within a few moments the little face was pressed against her and struggles and sobs were over. Then as she turned and sat at the window a calm came upon her as from her very centre, the milk of her body and the riches of her frustrated love welled up and succoured the infant creature in her keeping.

'FIRST BLOOD'

TITUS, under the care of Nannie Slagg and Keda, developed hourly in the western wing. His weird little head had changed shape, from day to day as the heads of infants do, and at last settled to its own proportion. It was both long and of a bulk that promised to develop into something approaching the unique.

His violet eyes made up, in the opinion of Mrs Slagg, for any strangeness in the shape of his head and features which were, after all, nothing extraordinary for a member of his family.

Even from the very first there was something lovable about Titus. It is true that his thin crying could be almost unbearable, and Mrs Slagg, who insisted upon having the whole charge of him between his meals, was driven at times to a kind of fluttering despair.

On the fourth day the preparations for his christening were well in hand.

This ceremony was always held in the afternoon of the twelfth day, in a pleasant open room on the ground level, which, with its bay windows, gave upon the cedar trees and shaven lawns that sloped away to the Gormenghast terraces where the Countess walked at dawn with her snow-white cats.

The room was perhaps the most homely and at the same time the most elegant in the castle. There were no shadows lurking in the corners. The whole feeling was of quiet and pleasing distinction, and when the afternoon sun lit up the lawns beyond the bay windows into a green-gold carpet, the room with its cooler tints became a place to linger in. It was seldom used.

The Countess never entered it, preferring those parts of the castle where the lights and the shadows were on the move and where there was no such clarity. Lord Sepulchrave was known to walk up and down its length on rare occasions and to stop and stare at the cedars on the lawn as he passed the window, and then to leave the room again for a month or two until the next whim moved him.

Nannie Slagg had on a few occasions sat there, furtively knitting with her paper bag of wool on the long refectory table in the centre, and the high back of the carved chair towering over her. Around her the spaciousness of the temperate room. The tables with their vases of garden flowers, plucked by Pentecost, the head gardener. But for the most part the room was left empty week after week, saving for an hour in the morning of each day when Pentecost would arrange the flowers. Deserted as the room was, Pentecost would never permit a day to pass in which he had not changed the water in the vases and refilled them again with taste and artistry, for he had been born in the mud huts and had in his marrow the love and understanding of colour that was the hall-mark of the Bright Carvers.

On the morning of the christening he had been out to cut the flowers for the room. The towers of Gormenghast rose into the morning mists and blocked away a commotion of raw cloud in the eastern sky. As he stood for a moment on the lawns he looked up at the enormous piles of masonry and could vaguely discern among the shadows the corroded carvings and broken heads of grey stone.

The lawns beneath the west wall where he stood were black with dew, but where, at the foot of one of the seven cedars, a grazing shaft of sun fell in a little pool of light, the wet grass blazed with diamonds of every colour. The dawn air was cold, and he drew more closely about him the leather cape which he wore over his head like a monk. It was strong and supple and had been stained and darkened by many storms and by the dripping of the rain from moss-gloved trees. From a cord hanging at his side hung his gardening knife.

Above the turrets, like a wing ripped from the body of an eagle, a solitary cloud moved northwards through the awakening air quilled with blood.

Above Pentecost the cedars, like great charcoal drawings, suddenly began to expose their structure, the layers of flat foliage rising tier above tier, their edges ribbed with sunrise.

Pentecost turned his back upon the castle and made his way through the cedars, leaving in his wake upon the glittering blotches of the dew, black imprints of feet that turned inwards. As he walked it seemed that he was moving into the earth. Each stride was a gesture, a probing. It was a kind of downward, inward search, as though he knew that what was important for him, what he really understood and cared for, was below him, beneath his slowly moving feet. It was in the earth – it was the earth.

Pentecost, with his leather cowl, was not of impressive dimensions, and his walk, although filled with meaning, had nevertheless something ridiculous about it. His legs were too short in proportion to his body, but his head, ancient and lined, was nobly formed and majestic with its big-boned, wrinkled brow and straight nose.

Of flowers he had a knowledge beyond that of the botanist, or the artist, being moved by the growth rather than the fulfilment, the organic surge that found its climax in the gold or the blue rather than in the colours, the patterns or anything visible.

As the mother who would not love the child the less were its face to be mutilated, so was he with flowers. To all growing things he brought this knowledge and love, but to the apple tree he gave himself up wholly.

Upon the northern slope of a low hill that dropped gradually to a stream, his orchard trees arose clearly, each one to Pentecost a personality in its own right.

On August days Fuchsia from her window in the attic could see him far below standing at times upon a short ladder, and sometimes when the boughs were low enough, upon the grass, his long body and little legs foreshortened and his cowl over his fine head hiding his features; and diminutive as he appeared from that immense height, she could make out that he was polishing the apples into a mirror-like gloss as they hung from the boughs, bending forward to breathe upon them and then with silk cloth rubbing them until she could see the glint upon their crimson skins – even from the height of her eyrie in the shadowy loft.

Then he would move away from the tree that he had burnished and pace around it slowly, enjoying the varied grouping of its apples and the twisted stem of the supporting bole.

Pentecost spent some time in the walled-in garden, where he cut the flowers for the christening room. He moved from one part to another until he knew and could visualize the vases filled in the room and had decided upon the colour for the day.

The sun was by now clear of the mists, and like a bright plate in the sky, rose as though drawn up by an invisible string. In the Christening Room there was still no light, but Pentecost entered by the bay-window, a dark mis-proportioned figure with the flowers smouldering in his arms.

Meanwhile the castle was either awaking or awakened. Lord Sepulchrave was having his breakfast with Sourdust in the refectory. Mrs Slagg was pushing and prodding at a heap of blankets beneath which Fuchsia lay curled up in darkness. Swelter was having a glass of wine in bed, which one of the apprentices had brought him, and was only half awake, his huge bulk wrinkled in upon itself in a ghastly manner. Flay was muttering to himself as he walked up and down an endless grey passage, his knee joints, like a clock, ticking off his every step. Rottcodd was dusting the third of the carvings, and sending up little clouds with his feet as he moved; and Doctor Prunesquallor was singing to himself in his morning bath. The walls of the bathroom were hung with anatomical diagrams painted on long scrolls. Even in his bath he was wearing his glasses and as he peered over the side to recover a piece of scented soap, he sang to his external oblique as though it were his love.

Steerpike was looking at himself in a mirror and examining an insipid moustache, and Keda in her room in the northern wing was watching the sunlight as it moved across the Twisted Woods.

Lord Titus Groan, innocent that the breaking day heralded the hour of his christening, was fast asleep. His head was lolling over on one side, and his face was nearly obscured by the pillow, one of his little fists rammed in his mouth. He wore a yellow silk nightdress, covered with blue stars, and the light through the half-drawn blinds crept over his face.

The morning moved on. There was a great deal of coming and going. Nannie was practically insane with excitement and without Keda's silent help would have been incapable of coping with the situation.

The christening dress had to be ironed, the christening rings and the little jewelled crown to be procured from the iron case in the armoury, and only Shrattle had the key and he was stone deaf.

The bath and dressing of Titus had to be especially perfect, and with everything to do the hours slipped away all too quickly for Mrs Slagg and it was two o'clock in the afternoon before she knew where she was.

Keda had found Shrattle at last and had persuaded him by ingenious signs that there was a christening that afternoon and that the crown was necessary and that she would return it as soon as the ceremony was over, and had in fact smoothed over, or solved all the difficulties that made Nannie Slagg wring her hands together and shake her old head in despair.

The afternoon was perfect. The great cedars basked magnificently in the still air. The lawns had been cut and were like dull emerald glass. The carvings upon the walls that had been engulfed in the night and had faltered through the dawn were now chiselled and free in the brightness.

The Christening Room itself looked cool and clear and unperturbed. With space and dignity it awaited the entrance of the characters. The flowers in their vases were incredibly gracious. Pentecost had chosen lavender as the dominant note for the room, but here and there a white flower spoke coolly to a white flower across the green carpet spaces and one gold orchid was echoed by another.

Great activity might have been observed in many of the rooms of Gormenghast as the hour of three approached, but the cool room waited in a serene silence. The only life in the room lay in the throats of the flowers.

Suddenly the door opened and Flay came in. He was wearing his long black moth-eaten suit, but there had been some attempt on his part at getting rid of the major stains and clipping the more ragged edges of cuff and trouser into straight raw lines. Over and above these improvements he wore around his neck a heavy chain of brass. In one hand he balanced, on a tray, a bowl of water. The negative dignity of the room threw him out in relief as a positive scarecrow. Of this he was quite unconscious. He had been helping to dress Lord Sepulchrave, and had made a rapid journey with the christening bowl as his lordship stood polishing his nails at the window of his bedroom, his toilet completed. The filling of the bowl and placing it on the central table in the cool room was his only duty, until the actual ceremony took place. Putting the bowl down unceremoniously on the table he scratched the back of his head and then drove his hands deep into his trouser pockets. It was some time since he was last in the Cool Room. It was not a room that he cared for. To his mind it was not a part of Gormenghast at all. With a gesture of defiance he shot his chin forward like a piece of machinery and began to pace around the room glancing malevolently at the flowers, when he heard a voice beyond the door, a thick, murderously unctuous voice.

'Woah, back there, woah! back there; watch your feet, my little rats' eyes! To the *side*. To the *side*, or I'll fillet you! Stand still! stand *still*! Merciful flesh that I should have to deal with puts!'

The door knob moved and then the door began to open and Flay's physical opposite began to appear around the opening. For some time, so it seemed to Flay, taut areas of cloth evolved in a great arc and then at last above them a head around the panels and the eyes embedded in that head concentrated their gaze upon Mr Flay.

Flay stiffened – if it is possible for something already as stiff as a piece of teak to stiffen still further – and he lowered his head to the level of his clavicles and brought his shoulders up like a vulture. His arms were absolutely straight from the high shoulders to where the fists were clenched in his trouser pockets.

Swelter, as soon as he saw who it was, stopped dead, and across his face little billows of flesh ran swiftly here and there until, as though they had determined to adhere to the same impulse, they swept up into both oceans of soft cheek, leaving between them a vacuum, a gaping segment like a slice cut from a melon. It was horrible. It was as though nature had lost control. As though the smile, as a concept, as a manifestation of pleasure, had been a mistake, for here on the face of Swelter the idea had been abused.

A voice came out of the face: 'Well, well, well,' it said, 'may I be boiled to a frazzle if it isn't Mr Flee. The one and only Flee. Well, well, well. Here before me in the Cool Room. Dived through the keyhole, I do believe. Oh, my adorable lights and liver, if it isn't the Flee itself.'

The line of Mr Flay's mouth, always thin and hard, became even thinner as though scored with a needle. His eyes looked up and down the white mountain, crowned with its snowy, high cloth hat of office, for even the slovenly Swelter had dressed himself up for the occasion.

Although Mr Flay had avoided the cook whenever possible, an occasional accidental meeting such as today's was unavoidable, and from their chance meetings in the past Mr Flay had learned that the huge house of flesh before him, whatever its faults, had certainly a gift for sarcasm beyond the limits of his own taciturn nature. It had therefore been Mr Flay's practice, whenever possible, to ignore the chef as one ignores a cesspool by the side of a road, and although his pride was wounded by Swelter's mis-pronunciation of his name and the reference to his thinness, Flay held his spiky passions in control, merely striding to the doorway after his examination of the other's bulk and spitting out of the bay window as though to clear his whole system of something noxious. Silent though he had learned by experience to be, each galling word from Swelter did not fail to add to the growing core of hatred that burned beneath his ribs.

Swelter, as Mr Flay spat, had leaned back in his traces as though in mock alarm, his head folded back on his shoulders, and with an expression of comic concentration, had gazed alternately at Mr Flay and then out of the window several times. 'Well, well, well,' he said in his most provoking voice that seemed to seep out of dough – 'well, well, well – your accomplishments will never end. Baste me! Never. One lives and learns. By the little eel I skinned last Friday night, one lives and one learns.' Wheeling round he presented his back to Mr Flay and bellowed, 'Advance and make it sprightly! Advance the triumvirate, the little creatures who have wound themselves around my heart. Advance and be recognized.'

Into the room filed three boys of about twelve years of age. They each carried a large tray stacked with delicacies.

'Mr Flee, I will introduce you,' said Swelter, as the boys approached, glueing their frightened eyes on their precarious cargoes. 'Mr Flee – Master Springers – Master Springers – Mr Flee. Mr Flee – Master Wrattle, Master Wrattle – Mr Flee. Mr Flee – Master Spurter, Master Spurter – Mr Flee. Flee – Springers – Flee – Wrattle – Flee – Spurter – Flee!'

This was brought out with such a mixture of eloquence and impertinence that it was too much for Mr Flay. That he, the first servant of Gormenghast – Lord Sepulchrave's confidant – should be introduced to Swelter's ten-a-penny kitchen boys was trying him too hard, and as he suddenly strode past the chef towards the door (for he was in any event due back with his lordship), he pulled the chain over his head and slashed the heavy brass links across the face of his taunter. Before Swelter had recovered, Mr Flay was well on his way along the passages. The chef's face had suffered a transformation. All the vast *media* of his head became, as clay becomes under the hand of the modeller, bent to the externalization of a passion. Upon it, written in letters of pulp, was spelt the word *revenge*. The eyes had almost instantly ceased to blaze and had become like little pieces of glass.

The three boys had spread the delicacies upon the table, and, leaving in the centre the simple christening bowl, they now cowered in the bay window, longing in their hearts to run, to run as they had never run before, out into the sunshine and across the lawns and over streams and fields, until they were far, far away from the white presence with the hectic red marks of the chain-links across its face.

The chef, with his hatred so riveted upon the person of Flay, had forgotten them and did not vent his spleen upon them. His was not the hatred that rises suddenly like a storm and as suddenly abates. It was, once the initial shock of anger and pain was over, a calculated thing that grew in a bloodless way. The fact that three minions had seen their dreaded overlord suffer an indignity was nothing to Swelter at this moment, for he could see the situation in proportion and in it these children had no part.

Without a word he walked to the centre of the room. His fat hands rearranged a few of the dishes nimbly upon the table. Then he advanced to a mirror that hung above a vase of flowers and examined his wounds critically. They hurt him. Catching sight of the three boys as he shifted his head in order to peer again more closely at himself, for he was only able to see portions of his face at one and the same time, he signalled to them to be gone. He followed shortly afterwards and made his way to his room above the bakeries.

By this time the hour was practically at hand for the gathering and

from their various apartments the persons concerned were sallying
forth. Each one with his or her particular stride. His or her particular
eyes, nose, mouth, hair, thoughts and feelings. Self-contained, carrying
their whole selves with them as they moved, as a vessel that holds its
own distinctive wine, bitter or sweet. These seven closed their doors
behind them, terrifyingly *themselves*, as they set out for the Cool Room.

There were, in the Castle, two ladies, who, though very seldom
encountered, were of the Groan blood, and so, when it came to a family
ceremony such as this, were of course invited. They were their ladyships
Cora and Clarice, sisters-in-law to Gertrude, sisters of Sepulchrave,
and twins in their own right. They lived in a set of rooms in the southern
wing and shared with each other an all-absorbing passion for brooding
upon an irony of fate which decreed that they should have no say in the
affairs of Gormenghast. These two along with the others were on their
way to the Cool Room.

Tradition playing its remorseless part had forced Swelter and Flay to
return to the Cool Room to await the first arrival, but luckily someone
was there before them – Sourdust, in his sacking garment. He stood
behind the table, his book open before him. In front of him the bowl of
water, around which the examples of Swelter's art sat, perched on
golden salvers and goblets that twinkled in the reflected sunlight.

Swelter, who had managed to conceal the welts on his face by an
admixture of flour and white honey, took up his place to the left of the
ancient librarian, over whom he towered as a galleon above a tooth of
rock. Around his neck he also wore a ceremonial chain similar to that
of Flay, who appeared a few moments later. He stalked across the room
without glancing at the chef, and stood upon the other side of Sourdust,
balancing from the artist's point of view if not the rationalist's, the
components of the picture.

All was ready. The participants in the ceremony would be arriving
one by one, the less important entering first, until the penultimate
entrance of the Countess harbingered a necessary piece of walking
furniture, Nannie Slagg, who would be carrying in her arms a shawl-
full of destiny – the Future of the Blood Line. A tiny weight that was
Gormenghast, a Groan of the strict lineage – Titus, the Seventy-
Seventh.

'ASSEMBLAGE'

FIRST to arrive was the outsider – the commoner – who through his service to the family was honoured by a certain artificial equality of status, liable at any moment to be undermined – Doctor Prunesquallor.

He entered fluttering his perfect hands, and, mincing to the table, rubbed them together at the level of his chin in a quick, animated way as his eyes travelled over the spread that lay before him.

'My very dear Swelter, ha, ha, may I offer you my congratulations, ha, ha, as a doctor who knows something of stomachs, my dear Swelter, something indeed of stomachs? Not only of stomachs but of palates, of tongues, and of the membrane, my dear man, that covers the roof of the mouth, and not only of the membrane that covers the roof of the mouth but of the sensitized nerve endings that I can positively assure you are tingling, my dear and very excellent Swelter, at the very thought of coming into contact with these delicious-looking oddments that you've no doubt tossed off at an odd moment, ha, ha, very, very likely I should say, oh yes, very, very likely.'

Doctor Prunesquallor smiled and exhibited two brand new rows of gravestones between his lips, and darting his beautiful white hand forward with the little finger crooked to a right angle, he lifted a small emerald cake with a blob of cream atop of it, as neatly off the top of a plate of such trifles as though he were at home in his dissecting room and were removing some organ from a frog. But before he had got it to his mouth, a hissing note stopped him short. It came from Sourdust, and it caused the doctor to replace the green cake on the top of the pile even more swiftly than he had removed it. He had forgotten for the moment, or had pretended to forget, what a stickler for etiquette old Sourdust was. Until the Countess herself was in the room no eating could begin.

'Ha, ha, ha, ha, very very right and proper Mr Sourdust, very right and proper indeed,' said the doctor, winking at Swelter. The magnified appearance of his eyes gave this familiarity a peculiar unpleasantness. 'Very, very right indeed. But that's what this man Swelter does to one, with his irresistible little lumps of paradise – ha, ha, he makes one quite barbarian he does, don't you Swelter? You barbarize one, ha, ha, don't you? You positively barbarize one.'

Swelter, who was in no mood for this sort of badinage, and in any case preferred to hold the floor if there was to be any eloquence, merely gave a mirthless twitch to his mouth and continued to stare out of the window. Sourdust was running his finger along a line in his book which he was re-reading, and Flay was a wooden effigy.

Nothing, however, seemed to be able to keep the mercury out of Doctor Prunesquallor, and after looking quickly from face to face, he examined his finger nails, one by one, with a ridiculous interest; and then turning suddenly from his task as he completed the scrutiny of the tenth nail, he skipped to the window, a performance grotesquely incongruous in one of his years, and leaning in an over-elegant posture against the window frame, he made that peculiarly effeminate gesture of the left hand that he was so fond of, the placing of the tips of thumb and index finger together, and thus forming an O, while the remaining three fingers were strained back and curled into letter C's of dwindling sizes. His left elbow, bent acutely, brought his hand about a foot away from him and on a level with the flower in his buttonhole. His narrow chest, like a black tube, for he was dressed in a cloth of death's colour, gave forth a series of those irritating laughs that can only be symbolized by '*ha, ha, ha*', but whose pitch scraped at the inner wall of the skull.

'Cedars,' said Doctor Prunesquallor, squinting at the trees before him with his head tilted and his eyes half closed, 'are excellent trees. Very, very excellent. I positively enjoy cedars, but do cedars positively enjoy me? Ha, ha – do they, my dear Mr Flay, do they? – or is this rather above you, my man, is my philosophy a trifle above you? For if I enjoy a cedar but a cedar does not, ha, ha, enjoy me, then surely I am at once in a position of compromise, being, as it were, ignored by the vegetable world, which would think twice, mark you, my dear fellow, would think twice about ignoring a cartload of mulch, ha, ha, or to put it another way . . .'

But here Doctor Prunesquallor's reflections were interrupted by the first of the family arrivals, the twin sisters, their ladyships Cora and Clarice. They opened the door very slowly and peered around it before advancing. It had been several months since they had ventured from their apartments and they were suspicious of everyone and of everything.

Doctor Prunesquallor advanced at once from the window. 'Your ladyships will forgive me, ha, ha, the presumption of receiving you into what is, ha, ha, after all more your own room than mine, ha, ha, ha, but which is nevertheless, I have reason to suspect, a little strange to you if I may be so extraordinarily flagrant; so ludicrously indiscreet, in fact . . .'

'It's the doctor, my dear,' the lady Cora whispered flatly to her twin sister, interrupting Prunesquallor.

Lady Clarice merely stared at the thin gentleman in question until anyone but the doctor would have turned and fled.

'I know it is,' she said at last. 'What's wrong with his eyes?'

'He's got some disease of course, I suppose. Didn't you know?' replied Lady Cora.

She and her sister were dressed in purple, with gold buckles at their throats by way of brooches, and another gold buckle each at the end of hatpins which they wore through their grey hair in order apparently to match their brooches. Their faces, identical to the point of indecency, were quite expressionless, as though they were the preliminary lay-outs for faces and were waiting for sentience to be injected.

'What are you doing here?' said Cora, staring remorselessly.

Doctor Prunesquallor bent forward towards her and showed her his teeth. Then he clasped his hands together. 'I am privileged,' he said, 'very, very much so, oh yes, very, very much.'

'Why?' said Lady Clarice. Her voice was so perfect a replica of her sister's as might lead one to suppose that her vocal cords had been snipped from the same line of gut in those obscure regions where such creatures are compounded.

The sisters were now standing, one on either side of the doctor, and they stared up at him with an emptiness of expression that caused him to turn his eyes hurriedly to the ceiling, for he had switched them from one to the other for respite from either, but had found no relief. The white ceiling by contrast teemed with interest and he kept his eyes on it.

'Your ladyships,' he said, 'can it be that you are ignorant of the part I play in the social life of Gormenghast? I say the social life, but who, ha, ha, ha, who could gainsay me if I boast that it is more than the *social* life, ha, ha, ha, and is, my very dear ladyships, positively the organic life of the castle that I foster, and control, ha, ha, in the sense that, trained as I undoubtedly am in the science of this, that, and the other, ha, ha, ha, in connection with the whole anomatical caboodle from head to foot. I, as part of my work here, deliver the new generations to the old – the sinless to the sinful, ha, ha, ha, the stainless to the tarnished – oh dear me, the white to the black, the healthy to the diseased. And this ceremony today, my very dear ladyships, is a result of my professional adroitness, ha, ha, ha, on the occasion of a brand new Groan.'

'What did you say?' said Lady Clarice, who had been staring at him the whole time without moving a muscle.

Doctor Prunesquallor closed his eyes and kept them closed for a very long time. Then opening them he took a pace forward and breathed in as much as his narrow chest would allow. Then turning suddenly he wagged his finger at the two in purple.

'Your ladyships,' he said. 'You must *listen*, you will never get on in life unless you *listen*.'

'Get *on* in life?' said Lady Cora at once, 'get *on* in life. I like that. What chance have we, when Gertrude has what we ought to have?'

'Yes, yes,' said the other, like a continuation of her sister's voice in another part of the room. 'We ought to have what she has.'

'And what is *that*, my very dear ladyships?' queried Doctor Prunesquallor, tilting his head at them.

'Power,' they replied blankly and both together, as though they had rehearsed the scene. The utter tonelessness of their voices contrasted so incongruously with the gist of the subject that even Doctor Prunesquallor was for a moment taken aback and loosened his stiff white collar around his throat with his forefinger.

'It's power we want,' Lady Clarice repeated. 'We'd like to have that.'

'Yes, it's that we want,' echoed Cora, 'lots of power. Then we could make people do things,' said the voice.

'But Gertrude has all the power,' came the echo, 'which we ought to have but which we haven't got.'

Then they stared at Swelter, Sourdust and Flay in turn.

'*They* have to be here, I suppose?' said Cora, pointing at them before returning her gaze to Doctor Prunesquallor, who had reverted to examining the ceiling. But before he could reply the door opened and Fuchsia came in, dressed in white.

Twelve days had elapsed since she had discovered that she was no longer the only child. She had steadily refused to see her brother and today for the first time she would be obliged to be with him. Her first anguish, inexplicable to herself, had dulled to a grudging acceptance. For what reason she did not know, but her grief had been very real. She did not know what it was that she resented.

Mrs Slagg had had no time to help Fuchsia to look presentable, only telling her to comb her hair and to put her white dress on at the *last* minute so that it should not be creased, and then to appear in the Cool Room at two minutes past three.

The sunlight on the lawns and the flowers in the vases and the room itself had seemed pleasant auguries for the afternoon before the entrance of the two servants, and the unfortunate incident that occurred. This violence had set a bitter keynote to the ensuing hours.

Fuchsia came in with her eyes red from crying. She curtseyed awkwardly to her mother's cousins and then sat down in a far corner, but she was almost at once forced to regain her feet, for her father, followed closely by the Countess, entered and walked slowly to the centre of the room.

Without a word of warning Sourdust rapped his knuckles on the table and cried out with his old voice: 'All are gathered save only him, for whom this gathering is gathered. All are here save only he for whom we all are here. Form now before the table of his baptism in the array of waiting, while I pronounce the entrance of Life's enterer and of the Groan inheritor, of Gormenghast's untarnished child-shaped mirror.'

Sourdust coughed in a very ill way and put his hand to his chest. He glanced down at the book and ran his finger along a new line. Then he tottered around the table, his knotted grey-and-white beard swinging a little from side to side, and ushered the five into a semi-circle around the table, with their backs to the window. In the centre were the Countess and Lord Sepulchrave, Fuchsia was to her father's left and Doctor Prunesquallor on the right of Lady Groan, but a little behind the semi-circle. The twin sisters were separated, one standing at either extremity of the arc. Flay and Swelter had retreated a few paces backwards and stood quite still. Flay bit at his knuckles.

Sourdust returned to his position behind the table which he held alone, and was relatively more impressive now that the crag of Flay and the mound of Swelter no longer dwarfed him. His lifted his voice again, but it was hard for him to speak, for there were tears in his throat and the magnitude of his office weighed heavily on him. As a savant in the Groan lore he knew himself to be spiritually responsible for the correct procedure. Moments such as this were the highlights in the ritualistic cycle of his life.

'Suns and the changing of the seasonal moons; the leaves from trees that cannot keep their leaves, and the fish from olive waters have their voices!'

His hands were held before him as though in prayer, and his wrinkled head was startlingly apparent in the clear light of the room. His voice grew stronger.

'Stones have their voices and the quills of birds; the anger of the thorns, the wounded spirits, the antlers, ribs that curve, bread, tears and needles. Blunt boulders and the silence of cold marshes – these have their voices – the insurgent clouds, the cockerel and the worm.'

Sourdust bent down over his book and found the place with his finger and then turned the page.

'Voices that grind at night from lungs of granite. Lungs of blue air and the white lungs of rivers. All voices haunt all moments of all days; all voices fill the crannies of all regions. Voices that he shall hear when he has listened, and when his ear is tuned to Gormenghast; whose voice is endlessness of endlessness. This is the ancient sound that he must follow. The voice of stones heaped up into grey towers, until he dies across the Groan's death-turret. And banners are ripped down from wall and buttress and he is carried to the Tower of Towers and laid among the moulderings of his fathers.'

'How much more is there?' said the Countess. She had been listening less attentively than the occasion merited and was feeding with crumbs from a pocket in her dress a grey bird on her shoulder.

Sourdust looked up from his book at Lady Groan's question. His eyes grew misty for he was pained by the irritation in her voice.

'The ancient word of the twelfth lord is complete, your ladyship,' he said, his eyes on the book.

'Good,' said Lady Groan. 'What now?'

'We turn about, I think, and look out on the garden,' said Clarice vaguely, 'don't we, Cora? You remember just before baby Fuchsia was carried in, we all turned round and looked at the garden through the window. I'm sure we did – long ago.'

'Where have you been since then?' said Lady Groan, suddenly addressing her sisters-in-law and staring at them one after the other. Her dark-red hair was beginning to come loose over her neck, and the bird had scarred with its feet the soft inky-black pile of her velvet dress so that it looked ragged and grey at her shoulder.

'We've been in the south wing all the time, Gertrude,' replied Cora.

'That's where we've been,' said Clarice. 'In the south wing all the time.'

Lady Groan emptied a look of love across her left shoulder, and the grey bird that stood there with its head beneath its wing moved three quick steps nearer to her throat. Then she turned her eyes upon her sisters-in-law: 'Doing what?' she said.

'Thinking,' said the twins together, 'that's what we've been doing – thinking a lot.'

A high uncontrolled laugh broke out from slightly behind the Countess. Doctor Prunesquallor had disgraced himself. It was no time for him to emphasize his presence. He was there on sufferance, but a violent rapping on the table saved him and all attention was turned to Sourdust.

'Your lordship,' said Sourdust slowly, 'as the seventy-sixth Earl of Groan and Lord of Gormenghast, it is written in the laws that you do now proceed to the doorway of the Christening Room and call for your son along the empty passage.'

Lord Sepulchrave, who up to this moment, had, like his daughter beside him, remained perfectly still and silent, his melancholy eyes fixed upon the dirty vest of his servant Flay which he could just see over the table, turned towards the door, and on reaching it, coughed to clear his throat.

The Countess followed with her eyes, but her expression was too vague to understand. The twins followed him with their faces – two areas of identical flesh. Fuchsia was sucking her knuckles and seemed to be the only one in the room uninterested in the progress of her father. Flay and Swelter had their eyes fixed upon him, for although their thoughts were still engaged with the violence of half an hour earlier, they were so much a part of the Groan ritual that they followed his lordship's every movement with a kind of surly fascination.

Sourdust, in his anxiety to witness a perfect piece of traditional procedure, was twisting his black-and-white beard into what must surely have been inextricable knots. He leaned forward over the christening bowl, his hands on the refectory table.

Meanwhile, hiding behind a turn in the passage, Nannie Slagg, with Titus in her arms, was being soothed by Keda as she waited for her call.

'Now, now be quiet, Mrs Slagg, be quiet and it will be over soon,' said Keda to the little shaking thing that was dressed up in the shiniest of dark-green satin and upon whose head the grape hat arose in magnificent misproportion to her tiny face.

'Be quiet, indeed,' said Nannie Slagg in a thin animated voice. 'If you only knew what it means to be in such a position of honour – oh, my poor heart! You would not dare to try to make me quiet indeed! I have never heard such ignorance. Why is he so long? Isn't it time for him to call me? And the precious thing so quiet and good and ready to cry any minute – oh, my poor heart! Why is he so long? Brush my dress again.'

Keda, who had been commanded to bring a soft brush with her, would have been brushing Nannie's satin dress for practically the whole morning had the old nurse had her way. She was now instructed by an irritable gesture of Mrs Slagg's hand to brush her anew and to soothe the old woman she complied with a few strokes.

Titus watched Keda's face with his violet eyes, his grotesque little features modified by the dull light at the corner of the passage. There was the history of man in his face. A fragment from the enormous rock of mankind. A leaf from the forest of man's passion and man's knowledge and man's pain. That was the ancientness of Titus.

Nannie's head was old with lines and sunken skin, with the red rims of her eyes and the puckers of her mouth. A vacant anatomical ancientry.

Keda's oldness was the work of fate, alchemy. An occult agedness. A transparent darkness. A broken and mysterious grove. A tragedy, a glory, a decay.

These three sere beings at the shadowy corner waited on. Nannie was sixty-nine, Keda was twenty-two, Titus was twelve days old.

Lord Sepulchrave had cleared his throat. Then he called:

'My Son.'

'TITUS IS CHRISTENED'

His voice moved down the corridor and turned about the stone corner, and when he first heard the sound of Mrs Slagg's excited footsteps he continued with that part of the procedure which Sourdust had recited to him over their breakfast for the last three mornings.

Ideally, the length of time which it took him to complete the speech should have coincided with the time it took Nannie Slagg to reach the door of the Cool Room from the darkened corner.

'Inheritor of the powers I hold,' came his brooding voice from the doorway, 'continuer of the blood-stock of the stones, freshet of the unending river, approach me now. I, a mere link in the dynastic chain, adjure you to advance, as a white bird on iron skies through walls of solemn cloud. Approach now to the bowl, where, named and fêted, you shall be consecrate in Gormenghast. Child! Welcome!'

Unfortunately Nannie, having tripped over a loose flagstone, was ten feet away at the word 'Welcome' and Sourdust, upon whose massive forehead a few beads of perspiration had suddenly appeared, felt the three long seconds pass with a ghastly slowness before she appeared at the door of the room. Immediately before she had left the corner Keda had placed the little iron crown gently on the infant's head to Nannie's satisfaction, and the two of them as they appeared before the assembly made up for their three seconds' tardiness by a preposterous quality that was in perfect harmony with the situation.

Sourdust felt satisfied as he saw them, and their delay that had rankled was forgotten. He approached Mrs Slagg carrying his great book with him, and when he had reached them he opened the volume so that it fell apart in two equal halves and then, extending it forward towards Nannie Slagg, he said:

'It is written, and the writing is adhered to, that between these pages where the flax is grey with wisdom, the first-born male-child of the House of Groan shall be lowered and laid lengthways, his head directed to the christening bowl, and that the pages that are heavy with words shall be bent in and over him, so that he is engulfed in the sere Text encircled with the Profound, and is as one with the inviolable Law.'

Nannie Slagg, an inane expression of importance on her face, lowered Titus within the obtuse V shape of the half-opened book so that the crown of his head just overlapped the spine of the volume at Sourdust's end and his feet at Mrs Slagg's.

Then Lord Sepulchrave folded the two pages over the helpless body and joined the tube of thick parchment at its centre with a safety-pin.

Resting upon the spine of the volume, his minute feet protruding from one end of the paper trunk and the iron spikes of the little crown protruding from the other, he was, to Sourdust, the very quintessential of traditional propriety. So much so that as he carried the loaded book towards the refectory table his eyes became so blurred with tears of satisfaction, that it was difficult for him to make his way between the small tables that lay in his path, and the two vases of flowers that stood so still and clear in the cool air of the room were each in his eyes a fume of lilac, and a blurr of snow.

He could not rub his eyes, and free his vision, for his hands were occupied, so he waited until they were at last clear of the moisture that filmed them.

Fuchsia, in spite of knowing that she should remain where she was, had joined Nannie Slagg. She had been irritated by an attempt that Clarice had made to nudge her in a furtive way whenever she thought that no one was watching.

'You never come to see me although you're a relation, but that's because I don't want you to come and never ask you,' her aunt had said, and had then peered round to see whether she was being watched, and noticing that Gertrude was in a kind of enormous trance, she continued:

'You see, my poor child, I and my sister Cora are a good deal older than you and we both had convulsions when we were about your age. You may have noticed that our left arms are rather stiff and our left legs, too. That's not our fault.'

Her sister's voice came from the other side of the semi-circle of figures in a hoarse flat whisper, as though it was trying to reach the ears of Fuchsia without making contact with the row of ears that lay between. 'Not our fault at all,' she said, 'not a bit our fault. Not any of it.'

'The epileptic fits, my poor child,' continued Cora, after nodding at her sister's interruption, 'have left us practically starved all down the right side. Practically starved. We had these fits you see.'

'When we were about your age,' came the empty echo.

'Yes, just about your age,' said Cora, 'and being practically starved all down the right side we have to do our embroidered tapestries with one hand.'

'Only one hand,' said Clarice. 'It's very clever of us. But no one sees us.'

She leaned forward as she wedged in this remark, forcing it upon Fuchsia as though the whole future of Gormenghast hung upon it.

Fuchsia fiddled and wound her hair round her fingers savagely.

'Don't do that,' said Cora. 'Your hair is too black. Don't do that.'

'Much too black,' came the flat echo.

'Especially when your dress is so white.'

Cora bent forward from her hips so that her face was within a foot of Fuchsia's. Then with only her eyes turned away, but her face broadside on to her niece, 'We don't *like* your mother,' she said.

Fuchsia was startled. Then she heard the same voice from the other side, 'That's true,' said the voice, 'we don't.'

Fuchsia turned suddenly, swinging her inky bulk of hair. Cora had disobeyed all the rules and unable to be so far from the conversation had moved like a sleep-walker round the back of the group, keeping an eye on the black-velvet mass of the Countess.

But she was doomed to disappointment, for as soon as she arrived, Fuchsia, glancing around wildly, caught sight of Mrs Slagg and she mooched away from her cousins and watched the ceremony at the table where Sourdust held her brother in the leaves of the book. As soon as Nannie was unburdened of Titus Fuchsia went to her side, and held her thin green-satin arm. Sourdust had reached the table with Lord Sepulchrave behind him. He re-instated himself. But his pleasure at the way things were proceeding was suddenly disrupted when his eyes, having cleared themselves of the haze, encountered no ceremonial curve of the select, but a room of scattered individuals. He was shocked. The only persons in alignment were the Countess, who through no sense of obedience, but rather from a kind of coma, was in the same position in which she had first anchored herself, and her husband who had returned to her side. Sourdust hobbled round the table with the tome-full. Cora and Clarice were standing close together, their bodies facing each other but their heads staring in Fuchsia's direction. Mrs Slagg and Fuchsia were together and Prunesquallor, on tip-toe, was peering at the stamen of a white flower in a vase through a magnifying lens he had whipped from his pocket. There was no need for him to be on tip-toe for it was neither a tall table nor a tall vase nor indeed a tall flower. But the attitude which pleased him most when peering at flowers was one in which the body was bent over the petals in an elegant curve.

Sourdust was shocked. His mouth worked at the corners. His old, fissured face became a fantastic area of cross-hatching and his weak eyes grew desperate. Attempting to lower the heavy volume to the table before the christening bowl where a space had been left for it, his fingers grew numb and lost their grip on the leather and the book slid from his hands, Titus slipping through the pages to the ground and tearing as he did so a corner from the leaf in which he had lain sheathed, for his little hand had clutched at it as he had fallen. This was his first recorded act of blasphemy. He had violated the Book of Baptism. The metal crown fell from his head. Nannie Slagg clutched Fuchsia's arm, and then with a scream of 'Oh my poor heart!' stumbled to where the baby lay crying piteously on the floor.

Sourdust was trying to tear the sacking of his clothes and moaning with impotence as he strained with his old fingers. He was in torture. Doctor Prunesquallor's white knuckles had travelled to his mouth with amazing speed, and he stood swaying a little. He had turned a moment later to Lady Groan.

'They resemble rubber, your ladyship, ha, ha, ha, ha. Just a core of india-rubber, with an elastic centre. Oh yes, they are. Very, very much so. Resilience is no word for it. Ha, ha, ha, absolutely no word for it – oh dear me, no. Every ounce, a bounce, ha, ha, ha! Every ounce a bounce.'

'What are you talking about man!' said the Countess.

'I was referring to your child, who has just fallen on the floor.'

'Fallen?' queried the Countess in a gruff voice. 'Where?'

'To earth, your ladyship, ha, ha, ha. Fallen positively to earth. Earth, that is, with a veneer or two of stone, wood and carpet, in between its barbaric self and his minute lordship whom you can no doubt hear screaming.'

'So that's what it is,' said Lady Groan, from whose mouth, which was shaped as though she were whistling, the grey bird was picking a morsel of dry cake.

'Yes,' said Cora on her right, who had run up to her directly the baby had fallen and was staring up at her sister-in-law's face. 'Yes, that's what it is.'

Clarice, who had appeared on the other side in a reverse of her sister's position, confirmed her sister's interpretation, 'that's just what it is.'

Then they both peered around the edge of the Countess and caught each other's eyes knowingly.

When the grey bird had removed the piece of cake from her ladyship's big pursed-up mouth it fluttered from her shoulder to perch upon her crooked finger where it clung as still as a carving, while she, leaving the twins (who, as though her departure had left a vacuum between them came together at once to fill it) proceeded to the site of the tragedy. There she saw Sourdust recovering his dignity, but shaking in his crimson sacking while he did so. Her husband, who knew that it was no situation for a man to deal with, stood aside from the scene, but looked nervously at his son. He was biting the ferrule of his jade-headed rod and his sad eyes moved here and there but constantly returned to the crying infant in the nurse's arms.

The Countess took Titus from Mrs Slagg and walked to the bay window.

Fuchsia, watching her mother, felt in spite of herself a quickening of something akin to pity for the little burden she carried. Almost a qualm of nearness, of fondness, for since she had seen her brother tear at the leaves that encased him, she had known that there was another being in the room for whom the whole fustian of Gormenghast was a thing to flee from. She had imagined in a hot blurr of jealousy that her brother would be a beautiful baby, but when she saw him and found that he was anything but beautiful, she warmed to him, her smouldering eyes taking on, for a second, something of that look which her mother kept exclusively for her birds and the white cats.

The Countess held Titus up into the sunlight of the window and examined his face, making noises in her cheek to the grey bird as she did so. Then she turned him around and examined the back of his head for some considerable time.

'Bring the crown,' she said.

Doctor Prunesquallor came up with his elbows raised and the fingers of both hands splayed out, the metal crown poised between them. His eyes rolled behind his lenses.

'Shall I crown him in the sunlight? ha, he, ha. Positively crown him,' he said, and showed the Countess the same series of uncompromising teeth that he had honoured Cora with several minutes before.

Titus had stopped crying and in his mother's prodigious arms looked unbelievably tiny. He had not been hurt, but frightened by his fall. Only a sob or two survived and shook him every few seconds.

'Put it on his head,' said the Countess. Doctor Prunesquallor bent forward from the hips in a straight oblique line. His legs looked so thin in their black casing that when a small breath of wind blew from the garden it seemed that the material was blown inwards beyond that part where his shin bones should have been. He lowered the crown upon the little white potato of a head.

'Sourdust,' she said without turning round, 'come here.'

Sourdust lifted his head. He had recovered the book from the floor and was fitting the torn piece of paper into position on the corner of the torn page, and smoothing it out shakily with his forefinger.

'Come along, come along now!' said the Countess.

He came around the corner of the table and stood before her.

'We'll go for a walk, Sourdust, on the lawn and then you can finish the christening. Hold yourself still, man,' she said. 'Stop rattling.'

Sourdust bowed, and feeling that to interrupt a christening of the direct heir in this way was sacrilege, followed her out of the window, while she called out over her shoulder, 'all of you! all of you! servants as well!'

They all came out and each choosing their parallel shades of the mown grass that converged in the distance in perfectly straight lines of green, walked abreast and silently thus, up and down, for forty minutes.

They took their pace from the slowest of them, which was Sourdust. The cedars spread over them from the northern side as they began their journey. Their figures dwindling as they moved away on the striped emerald of the shaven lawn. Like toys; detachable, painted toys, they moved each one on his mown stripe.

Lord Sepulchrave walked with slow strides, his head bowed. Fuchsia mouched. Doctor Prunesquallor minced. The twins propelled themselves forward vacantly. Flay spidered his path. Swelter wallowed his.

All the time the Countess held Titus in her arms and whistled varying notes that brought through gilded air strange fowl to her from unrecorded forests.

When at last they had re-gathered in the Cool Room, Sourdust was more composed, although tired from the walk.

Signalling them to their stations he placed his hands upon the torn volume with a qualm and addressed the semi-circle before him.

Titus had been replaced in the Book and Sourdust lowered him carefully to the table.

'I place thee, Child-Inheritor,' he said, continuing from where he had been interrupted by the age of his fingers, 'Child-Inheritor of the rivers, of the Tower of Flints and the dark recesses beneath cold stairways and the sunny summer lawns. Child-Inheritor of the spring breezes that blow in from the jarl forests and of the autumn misery in petal, scale, and wing. Winter's white brilliance on a thousand turrets and summer's torpor among walls that crumble – listen. Listen with the humility of princes and understand with the understanding of the ants. Listen, Child-Inheritor, and wonder. Digest what I now say.'

Sourdust then handed Titus over the table to his mother, and cupping his hand, dipped it in the christening bowl. Then, his hand and wrist dripping, he let the water trickle through his fingers and on to the baby's head where the crown left, between its prongs, an oval area of bone-forced skin.

'Your name is TITUS,' said Sourdust very simply, 'TITUS the seventy-seventh Earl of Groan and Lord of Gormenghast. I do adjure you hold each cold stone sacred that clings to these, your grey ancestral walls. I do adjure you hold the dark soil sacred that nourishes your high leaf-burdened trees. I do adjure you hold the tenets sacred that ramify the creeds of Gormenghast. I dedicate you to your father's castle. Titus, be true.'

Titus was handed back to Sourdust, who passed him to Nannie Slagg. The room was delicious with the cool scent of flowers. As Sourdust gave the sign, after a few minutes of meditation, that feeding might begin, Swelter came forward balancing four plates of delicacies on each of his forearms and with a plate in either hand went the rounds. Then he poured out glasses of wine, while Flay followed Lord Sepulchrave around like a shadow. None of the company attempted to make conversation, but stood silently eating or drinking in different parts of the room, or stood at the bay window, munching or sipping as they stared across the spreading lawns. Only the twins sat in a corner of the room and made signs to Swelter when they had finished what was on their plates. The afternoon would be for them the theme for excited reminiscence for many a long day. Lord Sepulchrave touched nothing as the delicacies were passed round, and when Swelter approached him with a salver of toasted larks, Flay motioned him away peremptorily, and noticing as he did so the evil expression in the chef's pig-like eyes, he drew his bony shoulders up to his ears.

As the time moved on Sourdust began to grow more and more conscious of his responsibilities as the master of ritual, and eventually, having registered the time by the sun, which was split in half by the slim branch of a maple, he clapped his hands and shambled towards the door.

It was then for the assembled company to gather in the centre of the room and for one after another to pass Sourdust and Mrs Slagg, who, with Titus on her lap, was to be stationed at his side.

These positions were duly taken up, and the first to walk forward to the door was Lord Sepulchrave, who lifted his melancholy head in the air, and, as he passed his son spoke the one word 'Titus' in a solemn, abstracted voice. The Countess shambled after him voluminously and bellowed 'TITUS' at the wrinkled infant.

Each in turn followed: the twins confusing each other in their efforts to get the first word in, the doctor brandishing his teeth at the word 'Titus' as though it were the signal for some romantic advance of sabred cavalry. Fuchsia felt embarrassed and stared at the prongs of her little brother's crown.

At last they had all passed by, delivering with their own peculiar intonations the final word 'Titus' as they reared their heads up, and Mrs Slagg was left alone, for even Sourdust had left her and followed in the wake of Mr Flay.

Now that she was left by herself in the Cool Room Mrs Slagg stared about her nervously at the emptiness and at the sunlight pouring through the great bay window.

Suddenly she began to cry with fatigue and excitement and from the shock she had received when the Countess had bellowed at his little lordship and herself. A shrunken, pathetic creature she looked in the high chair with the crowned doll in her arms. Her green satin gleamed mockingly in the afternoon light. 'Oh, my weak heart,' she sobbed, the tears crawling down the dry, pear-skin wrinkles of her miniature face – 'my poor, poor heart – as though it were a crime to love him.' She pressed the baby's face against her wet cheek. Her eyes were clenched and the moisture clung to her lashes, and as her lips quivered, Fuchsia stole back and knelt down, putting her strong arms around her old nurse and her brother.

Mrs Slagg opened her bloodshot eyes and leaned forward, the three of them coming together into a compact volume of sympathy.

'I *love* you –' whispered Fuchsia, lifting her sullen eyes. 'I love you, I love you,' then turning her head to the door – 'you've made her cry,' she shouted, as though addressing the string of figures who had so recently passed through – 'you've made her cry, you beasts!'

MEANS OF ESCAPE

MR FLAY was possessed by two major vexations. The first of these lay in the feud which had arisen between himself and the mountain of pale meat; the feud that had flared up and fructified in his assault upon the chef. He avoided even more scrupulously than before any corridor, quadrangle or cloister where the unmistakable proportions of his enemy might have loomed in sight. As he performed his duties, Mr Flay was perpetually aware that his enemy was in the castle and was haunted by the realization that some devilish plot was being devised, momently, in that dropsical head – some infernal hatching, in a word – *revenge*. What opportunities the chef would find or make, Flay could not imagine, but he was constantly on the alert and was for ever turning over in his dark skull any possibilities that occurred to him. If Flay was not actually frightened he was at least apprehensive to a point this side of fear.

The second of his two anxieties hinged upon the disappearance of Steerpike. Fourteen days ago he had locked the urchin up and had returned twelve hours later with a jug of water and a dish of potatoes only to find the room empty. Since then there had been no sign of him, and Mr Flay, although uninterested in the boy for his own sake, was nevertheless disturbed by so phenomenal a disappearance and also by the fact that he had been one of Swelter's kitchen hands and might, were he to return to the foetid regions from which he had strayed, disclose the fact they had met, and probably, in a garbled version of the affair, put it to the chef that he had been lured away from his province and incarcerated for some sinister reason of his own invention. Not only this, for Mr Flay remembered how the boy had overheard the remarks which Lord Groan had made about his son, remarks which would be detrimental to the dignity of Gormenghast if they were to be noised abroad to the riff-raff of the castle. It would not do if at the very beginning of the new Lord Groan's career it were common knowledge that the child was ugly, and that Lord Sepulchrave was distressed about it. What could be done to ensure the boy's silence Flay had not

yet determined, but it was obvious that to find him was the prime
necessity. He had, during his off moments, searched room after room,
balcony after balcony, and had found no clue as to his whereabouts.

At night as he lay before his master's door he would twitch and
awake and then sit bolt upright on the cold floor-boards. At first the
face of Swelter would appear before his eyes, huge and indistinct, with
those beady eyes in their folds of flesh, cold and remorseless. He would
shoot his hard, cropped head forward, and wipe the sweat from his
palms upon his clothes. Then, as the foul phantom dissolved in the
darkness, his mind would lure him into the empty room where he had
last seen Steerpike and in his imagination he would make a circuit of
the walls, feeling the panels with his hands and come at last to the
window, where he would stare down the hundreds of feet of sheer wall
to the yard below.

Straightening out his legs again his knee joints would crack in the
darkness as he stretched himself out, the iron-tasting key between his
teeth.

What had actually happened in the Octagonal Room and the subsequent events that befell Steerpike are as follows:

When the boy heard the key turn in the lock he half-ran to the door
and glued his eye to the keyhole and watched the seat of Mr Flay's
trousers receding down the passage. He had heard him turn a corner,
and then a door was shut in the distance with a far bang, and thereafter
there had been silence. Most people would have tried the handle of the
door. The instinct, however irrational, would have been too strong; the
first impulse of one who wishes to escape. Steerpike looked at the knob
of the door for a moment. He had heard the key turn. He did not
disobey the simple logic of his mind. He turned from the only door in
the room and, leaning out of the window, glanced at the drop below.

His body gave the appearance of being malformed, but it would be
difficult to say exactly what gave it this gibbous quality. Limb by limb
it appeared that he was sound enough, but the sum of these several
members accrued to an unexpectedly twisted total. His face was pale
like clay and save for his eyes, masklike. These eyes were set very close
together, and were small, dark red, and of startling concentration.

The striped kitchen tunic which he wore fitted him tightly. On the
back of his head was pushed a small white skull cap.

As he gazed downward quietly at the precipitous drop he pursed his
mouth and his eyes roved quickly over the quadrangle below him. Then
suddenly he left the window and with his peculiar half-run, half-walk,
he hurried around the room, as though it were necessary for him to
have his limbs moving concurrently with his brain. Then he returned

to the window. Everywhere was stillness. The afternoon light was beginning to wane in the sky although the picture of turrets and rooftops enclosed by the window frame was still warmly tinted. He took one last comprehensive glance over his shoulder at the walls and ceiling of the prison room, and then, clasping his hands behind his back, returned his attention to the casement.

This time, leaning precariously out over the sill and with his face to the sky, he scrutinized the rough stones of the wall *above* the lintel and noticed that after twenty feet they ended at a sloping roof of slates. This roof terminated in a long horizontal spine like a buttress, which, in turn, led in great sweeping curves towards the main rooftops of Gormenghast. The twenty feet above him, although seeming at first to be unscalable, were, he noticed, precarious only for the first twelve feet, where only an occasional jutting of irregular stone offered dizzy purchase. Above this height a gaunt, half-dead creeper that was matted greyly over the slates, lowered a hairy arm which, unless it snapped at his weight, would prove comparatively easy climbing.

Steerpike reflected that once astride the cornice he could, with relatively little difficulty, make his way over the whole outer shell of central Gormenghast.

Again he fastened his gaze upon the first dozen feet of vertical stone, choosing and scrutinizing the grips that he would use. His survey left him uneasy. It would be unpleasant. The more he searched the wall with his intense eyes the less he liked the prospect, but he could see that it *was* feasible if he concentrated every thought and fibre upon the attempt. He hoisted himself back into the room that had suddenly added an atmosphere of safety to its silence. Two courses were open to him. He could either wait and, in due course presumably Flay would reappear and would, he suspected, attempt to return him to the kitchens – or he could make the hazardous trial.

Suddenly, sitting on the floor, he removed his boots and tied them by their laces about his neck. Then he rammed his socks into his pockets and stood up. Standing on tiptoe in the middle of the room he splayed his toes out and felt them tingle with awareness, and then he pulled his fingers sideways cruelly, awakening his hands. There was nothing to wait for. He knelt on the windowsill and then, turning around, slowly raised himself to his feet and stood outside the window, the hollow twilight at his shoulder-blades.

'A FIELD OF FLAGSTONES'

HE refused to allow himself to think of the sickening drop and glued his eyes upon the first of the grips. His left hand clasped the lintel as he felt out with his right foot and curled his toes around a rough corner of stone. Almost at once he began to sweat. His fingers crept up and found a cranny he had scrutinized at leisure. Biting his underlip until it bled freely over his chin, he moved his left knee up the surface of the wall. It took him perhaps seventeen minutes by the clock, but by the time of his beating heart he was all evening upon the swaying wall. At moments he would make up his mind to have done with the whole thing, life and all, and to drop back into space, where his straining and sickness would end. At other moments, as he clung desperately, working his way upwards in a sick haze, he found himself repeating a line or two from some long forgotten rhyme.

His fingers were almost dead and his hands and knees shaking wildly when he found that his face was being tickled by the ragged fibres that hung upon the end of the dead creeper. Gripping it with his right hand, his toes lost purchase and for a moment or two he swung over the empty air. But his hands could bring into play unused muscles and although his arms were cracking he scraped his way up the remaining fifteen feet, the thick, brittle wood holding true, small pieces only breaking away from the sides. As soon as he had edged himself over the guttering, he lay, face downwards, weak and shaking fantastically. He lay there for an hour. Then, as he raised his head and found himself in an empty world of rooftops, he smiled. It was a young smile, a smile in keeping with his seventeen years, that suddenly transformed the emptiness of the lower part of his face and as suddenly disappeared; from where he lay at an angle along the sun-warmed slates, only sections of this new rooftop world were visible and the vastness of the failing sky. He raised himself upon his elbows, and suddenly noticed that where his feet had been prized against the guttering, the support was on the point of giving way. The corroded metal was all that lay between the weight of his body as he lay slanting steeply on the slates and the long drop to the quadrangle. Without a moment's delay he began to edge his way up the incline, levering with his bare feet, his shoulder blades rubbing the moss-patched roof.

Although his limbs felt much stronger after their rest he retched as he moved up the slate incline. The slope was longer than it had appeared from below. Indeed, all the various roof structures – parapet, turret and cornice – proved themselves to be of greater dimensions than he had anticipated.

Steerpike, when he had reached the spine of the roof, sat astride it and regained his breath for the second time. He was surrounded by lakes of fading daylight.

He could see how the ridge on which he sat led in a wide curve to where in the west it was broken by the first of four towers. Beyond them the sweep of roof continued to complete a half circle far to his right. This was ended by a high lateral wall. Stone steps led from the ridge to the top of the wall, from which might be approached, along a cat-walk, an area the size of a field, surrounding which, though at a lower level, were the heavy, rotting structures of adjacent roofs and towers, and between these could be seen other roofs far away, and other towers.

Steerpike's eyes, following the rooftops, came at last to the parapet surrounding this area. He could not, of course, from where he was guess at the stone sky-field itself, lying as it did a league away and well above his eye level, but as the main massing of Gormenghast arose to the west, he began to crawl in that direction along the sweep of the ridge.

It was over an hour before Steerpike came to where only the surrounding parapet obstructed his view of the stone sky-field. As he climbed this parapet with tired, tenacious limbs he was unaware that only a few seconds of time and a few blocks of vertical stone divided him from seeing what had not been seen for over four hundred years. Scrabbling one knee over the topmost stones he heaved himself over the rough wall. When he lifted his head wearily to see what his next obstacle might be, he saw before him, spreading over an area of four square acres, a desert of grey stone slabs. The parapet on which he was now sitting bolt upright surrounded the whole area, and swinging his legs over he dropped the four odd feet to the ground. As he dropped and then leaned back to support himself against the wall, a crane arose at a far corner of the stone field and, with a slow beating of its wings, drifted over the distant battlements and dropped out of sight. The sun was beginning to set in a violet haze and the stone field, save for the tiny figure of Steerpike, spread out emptily, the cold slabs catching the prevailing tint of the sky. Between the slabs there was dark moss and the long coarse necks of seeding grasses. Steerpike's greedy eyes had devoured the arena. What use could it be put to? Since his escape this surely was the strongest card for the pack that he intended to collect. Why, or how, or when he would use his hoarded scraps of knowledge he could not tell. That was for the future. Now he knew only that by risking his life he had come across an enormous quadrangle as secret as it was naked, as hidden as it was open to the wrath or tenderness of the elements. As he gave at the knees and collapsed into a half-sleeping, half-fainting huddle by the wall, the stone field wavered in a purple blush, and the sun withdrew.

'OVER THE ROOFSCAPE'

THE darkness came down over the castle and the Twisted Woods and over Gormenghast Mountain. The long tables of the Dwellers were hidden in the thickness of a starless night. The cactus trees and the acacias where Nannie Slagg had walked, and the ancient thorn in the servants' quadrangle were as one in their shrouding. Darkness over the four wings of Gormenghast. Darkness lying against the glass doors of the Christening Room and pressing its impalpable body through the ivy leaves of Lady Groan's choked window. Pressing itself against the walls, hiding them to all save touch alone; hiding them and hiding everything; swallowing everything in its insatiable omnipresence. Darkness over the stone sky-field where clouds moved through it invisibly. Darkness over Steerpike, who slept, woke and slept fitfully and then woke again – with only his scanty clothing, suitable more to the stifling atmosphere of the kitchens than to this nakedness of night air. Shivering he stared out into a wall of night, relieved by not so much as one faint star. Then he remembered his pipe. A little tobacco was left in a tin box in his hip pocket.

He filled the bowl in the darkness, ramming it down with his thin, grimed forefinger, and with difficulty lit the strong coarse tobacco. Unable to see the smoke as it left the bowl of the pipe and drifted out of his mouth, yet the glow of the leaf and the increasing warmth of the bowl were of comfort. He wrapped both his thin hands around it and with his knees drawn up to his chin, tasted the hot weed on his tongue as the long minutes dragged by. When the pipe was at last finished he found himself too wide awake to sleep, and too cold, and he conceived the idea of making a blind circuit of the stone field, keeping one hand upon the low wall at his side until he had returned to where he now stood. Taking his cap off his head he laid it on the parapet and began to feel his way along to the right, his hand rubbing the rough stone surface just below the level of his shoulder. At first he began to count his steps so that on his return he might while away a portion more of the night by working out the area of the quadrangle, but he had soon lost count in the labours of his slow progress.

As far as he could remember there were no obstacles to be expected

nor any break in the parapet, but his memories of the climb and his first
view of the sky-field were jumbled up together, and he could not in the
inky darkness rely on his memory. Therefore he felt for every step,
sometimes certain that he was about to be impeded by a wall or a break
in the stone flags, and he would stop and move forward inch by inch
only to find that his intuition had been wrong and that the monotonous,
endless, even course of his dark circuit was empty before him. Long
before he was halfway along the first of the four sides, he was feeling for
his cap on the balustrade, only to remember that he had not yet reached
the first corner.

He seemed to have been walking for hours when he felt his hand
stopped, as though it had been struck, by the sudden right angle of the
parapet. Three times more he would have to experience the sudden
change of direction in the darkness, and then he would, as he groped
forward, find his cap.

Feeling desperate at the stretch of time since he had started his
sightless journey he became what seemed to him in the darkness to be
almost reckless in his pace, stepping forward jerkily foot by foot. Once

or twice, along the second wall, he stopped and leaned over the parapet. A wind was beginning to blow and he hugged himself.

As he neared unknowingly the third corner a kind of weight seemed to lift from the air, and although he could see nothing, the atmosphere about him appeared thinner and he stopped as though his eyes had been partially relieved of a bandage. He stopped, leaned against the wall, and stared above him. Blackness was there, but it was not the opaque blackness he had known.

Then he felt, rather than saw, above him a movement of volumes. Nothing could be discerned, but that there were forces that travelled across the darkness he could not doubt; and then suddenly, as though another layer of stifling cloth had been dragged from before his eyes, Steerpike made out above him the enormous, indistinct shapes of clouds following one another in grave order as though bound on some portentous mission.

It was not, as Steerpike at first suspected, the hint of dawn. Long as the time had seemed to him since he clambered over the parapet, it was still an hour before the new day. Within a few moments he saw for himself that his hopes were ill founded, for as he watched, the vague clouds began to thin as they moved overhead, and between them yet others, beyond, gave way in their turn to even more distant regions. The three distances of cloud moved over, the nearest – the blackest – moving the fastest. The stone field was still invisible, but Steerpike could make out his hand before his face.

Then came the crumbling away of a grey veil from the face of the night, and beyond the furthermost film of the terraced clouds there burst of a sudden a swarm of burning crystals, and, afloat in their centre, a splinter of curved fire.

Noting the angle of the moon and judging the time, to his own annoyance, to be hours earlier than he had hoped, Steerpike, glancing above him, could not help but notice how it seemed as though the clouds had ceased to move, and how, instead, the cluster of the stars and the thin moon had been set in motion and were skidding obliquely across the sky.

Swiftly they ran, those bright marvels, and, like the clouds, with a purpose most immediate. Here and there over the wide world of tattered sky, points of fire broke free and ran, until the last dark tag of cloud had slid away from the firmament and all at once the high, swift beauty of the floating suns ceased in their surging and a night of stationary stars shone down upon the ghostly field of flags.

Now that heaven was alive with yellow stones it was possible for Steerpike to continue his walk without fear, and he stumbled along preferring to complete his detour than to make his way across the flags to his cloth cap. When he reached his starting point he crammed the cap on his head, for anything was precious in those hours that might mitigate the cold. By now he was fatigued beyond the point of endurance.

The ordeal of the last twelve to fifteen hours had sapped his strength. The stifling inferno of Swelter's drunken province, the horror of the Stone Lanes where he had fainted and had been found by Flay, and then the nightmare of his climb up the wall and the slate roof, and thence by the less perilous but by no means easy stages to the great stone field where he now stood, and where when he had arrived he had swooned for the second time that day: all this had taken its toll. Now, even the cold could not keep him awake and he lay down suddenly, and with his head upon his folded arms, slept until he was awakened by a hammering of hunger in his stomach and by the sun shining strongly in the morning sky.

But for the aching of his limbs, which gave him painful proof of the reality of what he had endured, the trials of the day before had about them the unreality of a dream. This morning as he stood up in the sunlight it was as though he found himself transplanted into a new day, almost a new life in a new world. Only his hunger prevented him from leaning contentedly over the warming parapet and, with a hundred towers below him, planning for himself an incredible future.

The hours ahead held no promise of relaxation. Yesterday had exhausted him, yet the day that he was now entering upon was to prove itself equally rigorous, and though no part of the climbing entailed would be as desperate as the worst of yesterday's adventures, his hunger and faintness augured for the hours ahead a nightmare in sunshine.

Within the first hour from the time when he had awakened, he had descended a long sloping roof, after dropping nine feet from the parapet, and had then come upon a small, winding stone staircase which led him across a gap between two high walls to where a cluster of conical roofs forced him to make a long and hazardous circuit. Arriving at last at the opposite side of the cluster, faint and dizzy with fatigue and emptiness and with the heat of the strengthening sun, he saw spread out before him in mountainous façades a crumbling panorama, a roofscape of Gormenghast, its crags and its stark walls of cliff pocked with nameless windows. Steerpike for a moment lost heart, finding himself in a region as barren as the moon, and he became suddenly desperate in his weakness, and falling on his knees retched violently.

His sparse tow-coloured hair was plastered over his big forehead as though with glue, and was darkened to sepia. His mouth was drawn down very slightly at the corners. Any change in his masklike features was more than noticeable in him. As he knelt he swayed. Then he very deliberately sat himself down on his haunches and, pushing back some of the sticky hair from his brow so that it stuck out from his head in a stiff dank manner, rested his chin on his folded arms and then, very slowly, moved his eyes across the craggy canvas spread below him, with the same methodical thoroughness that he had shown when scanning the wall above the window of the prison room.

Famished as he was, he never for a moment faltered in his scrutiny, although it was an hour later when having covered every angle, every surface, he relaxed and released his eyes from the panorama, and after shutting them for a while fixed them again upon a certain window that he had found several minutes earlier in a distant precipice of grey stone.

'NEAR AND FAR'

WHO can say how long the eye of the vulture or the lynx requires to grasp the totality of a landscape, or whether in a comprehensive instant the seemingly inexhaustible confusion of detail falls upon their eyes in an ordered and intelligible series of distances and shapes, where the last detail is perceived in relation to the corporate mass?

It may be that the hawk sees nothing but those grassy uplands, and among the coarse grasses, more plainly than the field itself, the rabbit or the rat, and that the landscape in its entirety is never seen, but only those areas lit, as it were with a torch, where the quarry slinks, the surrounding regions thickening into cloud and darkness on the yellow eyes.

Whether the scouring, sexless eye of the bird or beast of prey disperses and sees all or concentrates and evades all saving that for which it searches, it is certain that the less powerful eye of the human cannot grasp, even after a life of training, a scene in its entirety. No eye may see dispassionately. There is no comprehension at a glance. Only the recognition of damsel, horse or fly and the assumption of damsel, horse or fly; and so with dreams and beyond, for what haunts the heart will, when it is found, leap foremost, blinding the eye and leaving the main of Life in darkness.

When Steerpike began his scrutiny the roofscape was neither more nor less than a conglomeration of stone structures spreading to right and left and away from him. It was a mist of masonry. As he peered, taking each structure individually, he found that he was a spectator of a stationary gathering of stone personalities. During the hour of his concentration he had seen, growing from three-quarters the way up a sheer, windowless face of otherwise arid wall, a tree that curved out and upwards, dividing and subdividing until a labyrinth of twigs gave to its contour a blur of sunlit smoke. The tree was dead, but having grown from the south side of the wall it was shielded from the violence of the winds, and, judging by the harmonious fanlike beauty of its shape, it had not suffered the loss of a single sapless limb. Upon the lit wall its perfect shadow lay as though engraved with superhuman skill. Brittle and dry, and so old that its first tendril must surely have begun to thrust itself forth before the wall itself had been completed, yet this tree had the grace of a young girl, and it was the intricate lace-like shadow upon the wall that Steerpike had seen first. He had been baffled until all at once the old tree itself, whose brightness melted into the bright wall behind it, materialized.

Upon the main stem that grew out laterally from the wall, Steerpike had seen two figures walking. They appeared about the size of those stub ends of pencil that are thrown away as too awkward to hold. He guessed them to be women for as far as he could judge they were wearing identical dresses of purple, and at first sight it appeared that they were taking their lives in their hands as they trod that horizontal stem above a drop of several hundred feet, but by the relative sizes of the figures and the tree trunk it was obvious that they were as safe as though they had been walking along a bridge.

He had watched them reach a point where the branch divided into three and where as he shaded his eyes he could see them seat themselves upon chairs and face one another across a table. One of them lifted her elbow in the position of one pouring out tea. The other had then arisen and hurried back along the main stem until she had reached the face of wall into which she suddenly disappeared; and Steerpike, straining his eyes, could make out an irregularity in the stonework and presumed that there must have been a window or doorway immediately above where the tree grew from the wall. Shutting his eyes to rest them, it was a minute before he could locate the tree again, lost as it was among a score of roofs and very far away; but when he did find it he saw that there were two figures once again seated at the table. Beneath them swam the pellucid volumes of the morning air. Above them spread the withered elegance of the dead tree, and to their left its lace-like shadow.

Steerpike had seen at a glance that it would be impossible for him to reach the tree or the window and his eyes had continued their endless searching.

He had seen a tower with a stone hollow in its summit. This shallow basin sloped down from the copestones that surrounded the tower and was half filled with rainwater. In this circle of water whose glittering had caught his eye, for to him it appeared about the size of a coin, he could see that something white was swimming. As far as he could guess it was a horse. As he watched he noticed that there was something swimming by its side, something smaller, which must have been the foal, white like its parent. Around the rim of the tower stood swarms of crows, which he had identified only when one of them, having flapped away from the rest, grew from the size of a gnat to that of a black moth as it circled and approached him before turning in its flight and gliding without the least tremor of its outspread wings back to the stone basin, where it landed with a flutter among its kind.

He had seen, thirty feet below him and frighteningly close, after his eyes had accustomed themselves to the minutiae of distances a head suddenly appear at the base of what was more like a vertical black gash in the sunny wall than a window. It had no window-frame, no curtains, no window-sill. It was as though it waited for twelve stone blocks to fill it in, one above the other. Between Steerpike and this wall was a gap of eighteen to twenty feet. As Steerpike saw the head appear he lowered himself gradually behind an adjacent turret so as not to attract attention and watched it with one eye around the masonry.

It was a long head.

It was a wedge, a sliver, a grotesque slice in which it seemed the features had been forced to stake their claims, and it appeared that they had done so in a great hurry and with no attempt to form any kind of symmetrical pattern for their mutual advantage. The nose had evidently been the first upon the scene and had spread itself down the entire length of the wedge, beginning among the grey stubble of the hair and ending among the grey stubble of the beard, and spreading on both sides with a ruthless disregard for the eyes and mouth which found precarious purchase. The mouth was forced by the lie of the terrain left to it, to slant at an angle which gave to its right-hand side an expression of grim amusement and to its left, which dipped downwards across the chin, a remorseless twist. It was forced by not only the unfriendly monopoly of the nose, but also by the tapering character of the head to be a short mouth; but it was obvious by its very nature that, under normal conditions, it would have covered twice the area. The eyes in whose expression might be read the unending grudge they bore against the nose were as small as marbles and peered out between the grey grass of the hair.

This head, set at a long incline upon a neck as wry as a turtle's cut across the narrow vertical black strip of the window.

Steerpike watched it turn upon the neck slowly. It would not have surprised him if it had dropped off, so toylike was its angle.

As he watched, fascinated, the mouth opened and a voice as strange and deep as the echo of a lugubrious ocean stole out into the morning. Never was a face so belied by its voice.

The accent was of so weird a lilt that at first Steerpike could not recognize more than one sentence in three, but he had quickly attuned himself to the original cadence and as the words fell into place Steerpike realized that he was staring at a poet.

For some time after the long head had emptied itself of a slow, ruminative soliloquy it stared motionlessly into the sky. Then it turned as though it were scanning the dark interior of whatever sort of room it was that lay behind that narrow window.

In the long light and shade the protruding vertebrae of his neck, as he twisted his head, stood out like little solid parchment-covered knobs. All at once the head was facing the warm sunlight again, and the eyes travelled rapidly in every direction before they came to rest. One hand propped up the stubbly peg of a chin. The other, hanging listlessly over the rough sill-less edge of the aperture swung sideways slowly to the simple rhythm of the verses he then delivered.

> Linger now with me, thou Beauty,
>   On the sharp archaic shore.
> Surely 'tis a wastrel's duty
>   And the gods could ask no more.
> If you lingerest when I linger,
>   If thou tread'st the stones I tread,
> Thou wilt stay my spirit's hunger
>   And dispel the dreams I dread.
>
> Come thou, love, my own, my only,
>   Through the battlements of Groan;
> Lingering becomes so lonely
>   When one lingers on one's own.
>
> I have lingered in the cloisters
>   Of the Northern Wing at night,
> As the sky unclasped its oysters
>   On the midnight pearls of light.
> For the long remorseless shadows
>   Chilled me with exquisite fear.
> I have lingered in cold meadows
>   Through a month of rain, my dear.
>
> Come, my Love, my sweet, my Only,
>   Through the parapets of Groan.
> Lingering can be very lonely
>   When one lingers on one's own.
>
> In dark alcoves I have lingered
>   Conscious of dead dynasties.
> I have lingered in blue cellars
>   And in hollow trunks of trees.
> Many a traveller through moonlight
>   Passing by a winding stair

Or a cold and crumbling archway
  Has been shocked to see me there.

I have longed for thee, my Only,
  Hark! the footsteps of the Groan!
Lingering is so very lonely
  When one lingers all alone.

Will you come with me, and linger?
  And discourse with me of those
Secret things the mystic finger
  Points to, but will not disclose?
When I'm all alone, my glory,
  Always fades, because I find
Being lonely drives the splendour
  Of my vision from my mind.

Come, oh, come, my own! my Only!
  Through the Gormenghast of Groan.
Lingering has become so lonely
  As I linger all alone!

Steerpike, after the end of the second verse ceased to pay any attention
to the words, for he conceived the idea, now that he realized that the
dreadful head was no index to the character, of making his presence
known to the poet, and of craving from him at least some food and
water if not more. As the voice swayed on he realized that to appear
suddenly would be a great shock to the poet, who was so obviously
under the impression that he was alone. Yet what else was there to do?
To make some sort of preparatory noise of warning before he showed
himself occurred to him, and when the last chorus had ended he
coughed gently. The effect was electric. The face reverted instantaneously to the soulless and grotesque mask which Steerpike had first
seen and which during the recitation had been transformed by a sort of
inner beauty. It had coloured, the parchment of the dry skin reddening
from the neck upwards like a piece of blotting-paper whose corner has
been dipped into red ink.

Out of the black window Steerpike saw, as a result of his cough, the
small gimlety eyes peer coldly from a crimson wedge.

He raised himself and bowed to the face across the gully.

One moment it was there, but the next, before he could open his
mouth, it was gone. In the place of the poet's face was, suddenly, an
inconceivable commotion. Every sort of object suddenly began to
appear at the window, starting at the base and working up like an
idiotic growth, climbing erratically as one thing after another was
crammed between the walls.

Feverishly the tower of objects grew to the top of the window, hemmed in on both sides by the coarse stones. Steerpike could not see the hands that raised the mad assortment so rapidly. He could only see that out of the darkness object after object was scrammed one upon the other, each one lit by the sun as it took its place in the fantastic pagoda. Many toppled over, and fell, during the hectic filling of the frame. A dark gold carpet slipped and floated down the abyss, the pattern upon its back showing plainly until it drifted into the last few fathoms of shadow. Three heavy books fell together, their pages fluttering, and an old high-backed chair, which the boy heard faintly as it crashed far below.

Steerpike had dug his nails into the palms of his hands partly from self-reproach for his failure, and partly to keep himself from relaxing in his roofscape scrutiny in spite of his disappointment. He turned his head from the near object and continued to comb the roofs and the walls and the towers.

He had seen away to his right a dome covered with black moss. He had seen the high façade of a wall that had been painted in green-and-black checks. It was faded and partly overgrown with clinging weeds and had cracked from top to bottom in a gigantic saw-toothed curve.

He had seen smoke pouring through a hole between the slabs of a long terrace. He had seen the favourite nesting grounds of the storks and a wall that was emerald with lizards.

'DUST AND IVY'

ALL this while he had been searching for one thing and one thing only – a means of entering the castle. He had made a hundred imaginary journeys, taking into account his own weakness, but one after another they had led to blank unscalable walls and to the edges of the roofs. Window after window he took as his objective and attempted to trace his progress only to find that he was thwarted. It was not until the end of the hour approached that a journey he was unravelling in his eye culminated with his entry at a high window in the Western Wing. He went over the whole journey again, from where he sat, to the tiny window in the far wall and realized that it could be done, if luck was on his side and if his strength lasted.

It was now two o'clock in the afternoon and the sun was merciless. He removed his jacket and, leaving it behind him, set forth shakily.

The next three hours made him repent that he had ever left the kitchens. Had it been possible for him to have suddenly been conjured back to Swelter's enormous side he would have accepted the offer in his weakness. As the light began to wane, twenty-four hours after he had lain above the prison room on the sloping roof of slates, he came to the foot of that high wall, near the summit of which was the window he had seen three hours previously. There he rested. He was about midway between the ground two hundred feet below him and the window. He had been accurate in his observation when he had guessed that the face of the wall was covered over its entire area with a thick, ancient growth of ivy. As he sat against the wall, his back against the enormous hairy stem of the creeper as thick as the bole of a tree, the ivy leaves hung far out and over him and, turning his head upwards, he found that he was gazing into a profound and dusty labyrinth. He knew that he would have to climb through darkness, so thick was the skein of the coarse, monotonous foliage; but the limbs of the straggling weed were thick and strong, so that he could rest at times in his climb and lean heavily upon them. Knowing that with every minute that passed his weakness was growing, he did not wait longer than to regain his breath, and then, with a twist of his mouth he forced himself as close as he could to the wall, and engulfed in the dust-smelling darkness of the ivy he began, yet again, to climb.

For how long Steerpike clambered upwards in the acrid darkness, for how long he breathed in the rotten, dry, dust-filled air, is of no consequence compared to the endlessness of the nightmare in his brain. That was the reality, and all he knew, as he neared the window, was that he had been among black leaves for as far back as he could recall – that the ivy stem was dry and coarse and hairy to hold, and that the bitter leaves exuded a pungent and insidious smell.

At times he could see glimpses of the hot evening reflected through the leaves, but for the most part he struggled up in darkness, his knees and knuckles bleeding and his arms weary beyond weariness from the forcing back of the fibrous growth and from tearing the tendrils from his face and clothing.

He could not know that he was nearing the window. Distance, even more than time, had ceased to have any meaning for him, but all at once he found that the leaves were thinning and that blotches of light lay pranked about him. He remembered having observed from below how the ivy had appeared to be less profuse and to lie closer to the wall as it neared the window. The hirsute branches were less dependable now and several had snapped at his weight, so that he was forced to keep to one of the main stems that clung dustily to the wall. Only a foot or two in depth, the ivy lay at his back partially shielding him from the sun. A moment later and he was alone in the sunshine. It was difficult for his fingers to find purchase. Fighting to wedge them between the clinging branches and the wall he moved, inch by inch, upwards. It seemed to him that all his life he had been climbing. All his life he had been ill and tortured. All his life he had been terrified, and red shapes rolled. Hammers were beating and the sweat poured into his eyes.

The questionable gods who had lowered for him from the roof above the prison room that branch of creeper when he was in similar peril were with him again, for as he felt upwards his hand struck a protruding layer of stone. It was the base of a rough window-sill. Steerpike sobbed and forced his body upwards and loosing his hands for a moment from the creeper, he flung his hands over the sill. There he hung, his arms outstretched stiffly before him like a wooden figure, his legs dangling. Then, wriggling feebly, he rolled himself at length over the stone slab, overbalanced, and in a whirl of blackness fell with a crash upon the boarded floor of Fuchsia's secret attic.

'THE BODY BY THE WINDOW'

ON the afternoon following her brother's birth, Fuchsia stood silently at the window of her bedroom. She was crying, the tears following one another down her flushed cheeks as she stared through a smarting film at Gormenghast Mountain. Mrs Slagg, unable to comprehend, made abortive efforts to console her. This time there had been no mutual hugging and weeping, and Mrs Slagg's eyes were filled with a querulous, defeated expression. She clasped her little wrinkled hands together.

'What is it, then, my caution dear? What is it, my own ugliness? Tell me! Tell me at once. Tell your old Nannie about your little sorrows. Oh, my poor heart! you must tell me all about it. Come, inkling, come.'

But Fuchsia might as well have been carved from dark marble. Only her tears moved.

At last the old lady pattered out of the room, saying she would bring in a currant cake for her caution, that no one ever answered her, and that her back was aching.

Fuchsia heard the tapping of her feet in the corridor. Within a moment she was racing along the passage after her old nurse, whom she hugged violently before running back and floundering with a whirl of her blood-red dress down long flights of stairs and through a series of gloomy halls, until she found herself in the open, and beyond the shadows of the castle walls. She ran on in the evening sunshine. At last, after skirting Pentecost's orchard and climbing to the edge of a small pine wood she stopped running and in a quick, stumbling manner forced a path through a low decline of ferns to where a lake lay motionless. There were no swans. There were no wild waders. From the reflected trees there came no cries from birds.

Fuchsia fell at full length and began to chew at the grass in front of her. Her eyes as they gazed upon the lake were still inflamed.

'I hate things! I hate all things! I hate and hate every single tiniest thing. I hate the *world*,' said Fuchsia aloud, raising herself on her elbows, her face to the sky.

'I shall live *alone*. Always alone. In a house, or in a tree.'

Fuchsia started to chew at a fresh grass blade.

'Someone will come then, if I live alone. Someone from another kind of world – a new world – not from this world, but someone who is *different*, and he will fall in love with me at once because I live alone and aren't like the other beastly things in this world, and he'll enjoy having me because of my pride.'

Another flood of tears came with a rush . . .

'He will be tall, taller than Mr Flay and strong like a lion and with yellow hair like a lion's, only more curly; and he will have big, strong feet because mine are big, too, but won't look so big if his are bigger; and he will be cleverer than the Doctor, and he'll wear a long black cape so that my clothes will look brighter still; and he will say: "Lady Fuchsia", and I shall say: "What is it?" '

She sat up and wiped her nose on the back of her hand.

The lake darkened, and while she sat and stared at the motionless water, Steerpike was beginning his climb of the ivy.

Mrs Slagg was telling her troubles to Keda and trying to preserve the dignity which she thought she ought to show as the head nurse of the direct and only heir to Gormenghast, and at the same time longing to unburden herself in a more natural way. Flay was polishing an ornate helmet which Lord Groan had to wear, that evening being the first after the advent, and Swelter was whetting a long meat-knife on a grindstone. He was doubled over it like a crammed bolster, and was evidently taking great pains to bring the blade to an uncommonly keen edge. The grindstone, dwarfed ridiculously by the white mass above it, wheeled to the working of a foot-treadle. As the steel whisked obliquely across the flat of the whirling stone, the harsh, sandy whistling of the sound apparently gave pleasure to Mr Swelter, for a wodge of flesh kept shifting its position on his face.

As Fuchsia got to her feet and began to push her way up the hill of ferns, Steerpike was forty feet from her window and clawing away at the dry, dirty bunches of old sparrows' nests that were blocking his upward climb.

When Fuchsia reached the castle she made straight for her room, and when she had closed the door behind her, drew a bolt across it and going to an old cardboard box in a corner found, after some rummaging, a piece of soft charcoal. She approached a space on the wall and stood staring at the plaster. Then she drew a heart and around it she wrote: *I am Fuchsia. I must always be. I am me. Don't be frightened. Wait and see.*

Then she felt a great yearning for her picture-book with the poems. She lit a candle and, pulling back her bed, crept through the stairway door and began to climb spirally upwards to her dim sanctum.

It was not very often that she climbed to the attic in the late afternoon, and the darkness of the front room as she entered stopped her on the last stair for a moment. Her candle as she passed through the narrow gully illumined fitfully the weird assortment that comprised its walls, and when she came to the emptiness of her acting room she moved forward slowly, treading in the pale aura of light cast by the candle-flame.

In her third especial attic she knew that she had left, some weeks before, a supply of red-and-green wax tapers that she had unearthed, put aside, and forgotten. She had rediscovered them. Three of these would light the room up beautifully for she wanted the window to be shut. She climbed the ladder to the balcony, pushed open the door with one hinge and entered, with a gush of dark love.

Her long coloured candles were by the door and she lit one of them immediately from the little white one in her hand. Turning to place it on the table, her heart stopped beating, for she found that she was staring across the room at a body lying huddled beneath her window.

Steerpike had lain in a dead faint for some considerable time when consciousness began to seep through him. Twilight had fallen over Gormenghast. Out of the blackness of his brain far shapes that surrounded him in the room had begun to approach him growing in definition and in bulk as they did so until they became recognizable.

For several minutes he lay there. The comparative coolness of the room and the stillness of his body at length restored in his mind a state of inquiry. He could not remember the room, as was natural, nor could he remember how he had arrived there. He only knew that his throat was parched and beneath his belt a tiger was clawing in his stomach. For a long time he stared at a drunken and grotesque shape that arose from the centre of the floor. Had he been awakened from sleep to see it looming up before him it would no doubt have startled him considerably, but recovering from his faint, he was drained of apprehension; he was only weak. It would have been strange for him to have recognized in the dim light of the twilit room Fuchsia's fantastic Root from the Twisted Woods.

His eyes travelled away from it at length and noticed the darkened pictures on the walls, but the light was too dim for him to be able to discern what they contained.

His eyes moved here and there, recovering their strength; but his body lay inert, until at length he raised himself upon one elbow.

Above him was a table, and with an effort he struggled on to his knees and, gripping its edge raised himself by degrees. The room began to swim before his eyes and the pictures on the walls dwindled away to the size of stamps and swayed wildly across the walls. His hands were not his hands as he gripped the table edge. They were another's hands in which he could vaguely, and in an occult way, feel the shadows of sentiency. But the fingers held on, independently of his brain or body, and he waited until his eyes cleared and he saw below him the stale oddments of food that Fuchsia had brought up to the attic on the morning of the previous day.

They were littered on the table, each object remorseless in its actuality.

The nebulous incoherence of things had changed in his brain, as he stared down upon the still-life group on the table, to a frightening *proximity*.

Two wrinkled pears; half a seed cake; nine dates in a battered white cardboard box, and a jug of dandelion wine. Beside these a large hand-painted book that lay open where a few verses were opposed by a picture in purple and grey. It was to Steerpike in his unusual physical state as though that picture were the world, and that he, in some shadowy adjacent province, were glimpsing the reality.

He was the ghost, the purple-and-grey page was truth and actual fact.

Below him stood three men. They were dressed in grey, and purple flowers were in their dark confused locks. The landscape beyond them was desolate and was filled with old metal bridges, and they stood before it together upon the melancholy brow of a small hill. Their hands were exquisitely shaped and their bare feet also, and it seemed that they were listening to a strange music, for their eyes gazed out beyond the page and beyond the reach of Steerpike, and on and on beyond the hill of Gormenghast and the Twisted Woods.

Equally real to the boy at that moment were the grey-black simple letters that made up the words and the meaning of the verses on the opposite side of the page. The uncompromising visual starkness of all that lay on the table had for a moment caused him to forget his hunger, and although uninterested in poetry or pictures, Steerpike, in spite of himself, read with a curiously slow and deliberate concentration upon the white page of the three old men in their grey and purple world.

Simple, seldom and sad
　　We are;
Alone on the Halibut Hills
　　Afar,
With sweet mad Expressions
　　Of old
Strangely beautiful,
　　So we're told
By the Creatures that Move
　　In the sky
　　And Die
On the night when the Dead Trees
　　Prance and Cry.

Sensitive, seldom and sad –
Sensitive, seldom and sad –

Simple, seldom and sad
　　Are we
When we take our path
　　To the purple sea –
With mad, sweet Expressions
　　Of Yore,
Strangely beautiful,
　　Yea, and More
On the Night of all Nights
　　When the sky
　　Streams by
In rags, while the Dead Trees
　　Prance and Cry.

Sensitive, seldom, and sad –
Sensitive, seldom, and sad.

Steerpike noticed small thumb-marks on the margin of the page. They
were as important to him as the poems or the picture. Everything was
equally important because all had become so real now where all had
been so blurred. His hand as it lay on the table was now his own. He
had forgotten at once what the words had meant, but the script was
there, black and rounded.

He put out his hand and secured one of the wrinkled pears. Lifting it to
his mouth he noticed that a bite had already been taken from its side.

Making use of the miniature and fluted precipice of hard, white
discoloured flesh, where Fuchsia's teeth had left their parallel grooves,
he bit greedily, his top teeth severing the wrinkled skin of the pear, and
the teeth of his lower jaw entering the pale cliff about halfway up its
face; they met in the secret and dark centre of the fruit – in that

abactinal region where, since the petals of the pear flower had been scattered in some far June breeze, a stealthy and profound maturing had progressed by day and night.

As he bit, for the second time, into the fruit his weakness filled him again as with a thin atmosphere, and he carefully lowered himself face down over the table until he had recovered strength to continue his clandestine meal. As he lifted his head, he noticed the long couch with its elegant lines. Taking hold of the seed cake in one hand and the jug of dandelion wine in the other, after tipping the dates out of their cardboard box into his pocket, he felt his way along the edge of the table and stumbled across the few paces that divided him from the couch, where he seated himself suddenly and put his dusty feet up, one after the other, upon the wine-red leather of the upholstery.

He had supposed the jug to contain water, for he had not looked inside when he lifted it and felt its weight in his wrist, and when he tasted the wine on his tongue he sat up with a sudden revival of strength, as though the very thought of it had resuscitated him. Indeed, the wine worked wonders with him, and within a few minutes, with the cake, the dates and the rest of the second pear to support its tonic properties, Steerpike was revived, and getting to his feet he shuffled around the room in his own peculiar way. Drawing his lips back from his closed teeth, he whistled in a thin, penetrating, tuneless manner, breaking off every now and then as his eyes rested with more than a casual glance on some picture or another.

The light was fading very rapidly, and he was about to try the handle of the door to see whether, dark as it was, he could find a still more comfortable room in which to spend the night before he finally stretched himself on the long couch, when he heard the distinct sound of a footstep.

With a hand still outstretched towards the door, he stood motionless for a moment, and then his head inclined itself to the left as he listened. There was no doubt that someone was moving either in the next room or in the next room but one.

Moving one step nearer to the door as silently as a ghost, he turned the handle and drew it back the merest fraction, but sufficiently for him to place one eye at the aperture and to command a view of something which made him suck at his breath.

There was no reason why, because the room he had been in for the last hour or more was small, he should have presumed that the door out of it would lead to an apartment of roughly the same size. But when on peering through the chink between the door and the lintel he saw how mistaken had been his intuition regarding the size of the room beyond, he received a shock second only to that of seeing the figure that was approaching him.

Nor was it only the *size*. It was perhaps even more of a shock to realize that he had been *above* the adjacent room. Through the gloom he watched the figure of a girl, holding in her hand a lighted candle that lit the bodice of her dress to crimson. The floor across which she walked slowly but firmly appeared to stretch endlessly behind her and to her right and to her left. That she was below him and that within a few feet a balcony divided him from her, as she approached, was so unexpected that a sense of unreality such as he had experienced during his recovery from his faint again pervaded him. But the sound of her footsteps was very real and the light of the candle flame upon her lower lip awoke him to the actuality. Even in his predicament he could not help wondering where he had seen her before. A sudden movement of the shadows on her face had awakened a memory. Thoughts moved swiftly through his mind. No doubt there were steps leading up to the balcony. She would enter the room in which he stood. She walked with certainty. She did not hesitate. She was unafraid. These must be her rooms, he had entered. Why was she here at this hour? Who was she? He closed the door softly.

Where had he seen that red dress before? Where? Where? Very recently. The crimson. He heard her climbing the stairs. He glanced around the room. There was no hiding place. As his eyes moved he saw the Book on the table. Her book. He saw a few crumbs where the seed cake had been standing on the cloth. He half ran on tip-toe to the window and glanced down. The emptiness of the dark air falling to the tops of towers sickened him as memories of his climb were reawakened. He turned away. Even as he heard her feet on the balcony he was saying: 'Where? Where? Where did I see the red dress?' and as the feet stopped at the door he remembered, and at the same moment dropped softly to his hands and knees beneath the window. Then, huddling himself into an awkward position, and with one arm outstretched limply, he closed his eyes in emulation of the faint from which he had not so long ago recovered.

He had seen her through the circular spyhole in the wall of the Octagonal Room. She was the Lady Fuchsia Groan, the daughter of Gormenghast. His thoughts pursued each other through his head. She had been distraught. She had been enraged that a brother had been born for her; she had escaped down the passage from her father. There could be no sympathy *there*. She was, like her father, ill at ease. She was opening the door. The air wavered in the candlelight. Steerpike, watching from between his lashes, saw the air grow yet brighter as she lit two long candles. He heard her turn upon her heel and take a pace forward and then there was an absolute silence.

He lay motionless, his head thrown back upon the carpet and twisted slightly on his neck.

It seemed that the girl was as motionless as he, and in the protracted and deathly stillness he could hear a heart beating. It was not his own.

'ULLAGE OF SUNFLOWER'

FOR the first few moments Fuchsia had remained inert, her spirit dead to what she saw before her. As with those who on hearing of the death of their lover are numb to the agony that must later wrack them, so she for those first few moments stood incomprehensive and stared with empty eyes.

Then, indeed, was her mind split into differing passions, the paramount being agony that her secret had been discovered – her casket of wonder rifled – her soul, it seemed, thrown naked to a world that could never understand.

Behind this passion lay a fear. And behind her fear was curiosity – curiosity as to who the figure was. Whether he was recovering or dying; how he had got there, and a long way behind the practical question of what she should do. As she stood there it was as though within her a bonfire had been lighted. It grew until it reached the zenith of its power and died away, but undestroyable among the ashes lay the ache of a wound for which there was no balm.

She moved a little nearer in a slow, suspicious way, holding the candle stiffly at arm's length. A blob of the hot wax fell across her wrist and she started as though she had been struck. Another two cautious paces brought her to the side of the figure and she bent down and peered at the tilted face. The light lay upon the large forehead and the cheekbones and throat. As she watched, her heart beating, she noticed a movement in the stretched gullet. He was alive. The melting wax was hurting her hand as it ran down the coloured side of the candle. A candlestick was kept behind the couch on a rickety shelf and she raised herself from her stooping with the idea of finding it, and began to retreat from Steerpike. Not daring to take her eyes off him, she placed one leg behind the other with a grotesque deliberation and so moved backwards. Before reaching the wall, however, the calf of her leg came into unexpected contact with the edge of the couch, and she sat down very suddenly upon it as though she had been tapped behind the knees. The candle shook in her hand and the light flickered across the face of the figure on the floor. Although it seemed to her that the head started a little at the noise she had made, she put it down to the fickle play of the light upon his features, but peered at him for a long time nevertheless to convince herself. Eventually she curled her legs under her on the couch and raised herself to her knees and, reaching her free hand out behind her, she felt her fingers grip the shelf and after some fumbling close upon the iron candlestick.

She forced the candle at once into one of the three iron arms and, getting up, placed it on the table by her book.

It had come into her mind that some effort might be made to reinvigorate the crumpled thing. She approached it again. Horrible as the thought was, that if she were the means of a recovery she would be compelled to talk to a stranger in *her* room, yet the idea of him lying there indefinitely, and perhaps dying there, was even more appalling.

Forgetting for a moment her fear, she knelt loudly on the floor beside him and shook him by the shoulder, her lower lip sticking out plumply and her black hair falling across her cheeks. She stopped to scrape some tallow from her fingers and then continued shaking him. Steerpike let himself be pushed about and remained perfectly limp; he had decided to delay his recovery.

Fuchsia suddenly remembered that when she had seen her Aunt Cora faint, a very long time ago, in the central hall of the East Wing, her father had ordered a servant in attendance to get a glass of water, and that when they had been unable to get the drink down the poor white creature's throat, they had thrown it in her face and she had recovered immediately.

Fuchsia looked about her to see whether she had any water in the room. Steerpike had left the jug of dandelion wine by the side of the couch, but it was out of her range of vision and she had forgotten it. As her eyes travelled around her room they came at last to rest upon an old vase of semi-opaque dark-blue glass, which a week or so ago Fuchsia had filled with water, for she had found among the wild grass and the nettles near the moat, a tall, heavy-necked sunflower with an enormous Ethiopian eye of seeds and petals as big as her hand and as yellow as even she could wish for. But its long, rough neck had been broken and its head hung in a deadweight of fire among the tares. She had feverishly bitten through those fibres that she could not tear apart where the neck was fractured and had run all the way with her wounded treasure through the castle and up the flights of stairs and into her room, and then up again, around and around as she climbed the spiral staircase, and had found the dark-blue glass vase and filled it with water and then, quite exhausted, had lowered the dry, hairy neck into the depths of the vase and, sitting upon the couch, had stared at it and said to herself aloud:

'Sunflower who's broken, I found you, so drink some water up, and then you won't die – not so quickly, anyway. If you do, I'll bury you, anyway. I'll dig a long grave and bury you. Pentecost will give me a spade. If you don't die, you can stay. I'm going now,' she had finished by saying, and had gone to her room below and had found her nurse, but had made no mention of her sunflower.

It had died. Indeed she had only changed the water once, and with its petals decaying it still leaned stiffly out of the blue glass vase. Directly Fuchsia saw it she thought of the water in the vase. She had filled it full of clear white water. That it might have evaporated never entered her head. Such things were not part of her world of knowledge.

Steerpike's vision, for he would peer cunningly through his eyelashes whenever occasion favoured, was obtruded by the table and he could not see what the Lady Fuchsia was doing. He heard her approaching and kept his eyelids together, thinking it was just about time for him to groan, and begin to recover, for he was feeling cramped, when he realized that she was bending directly over him.

Fuchsia had removed the sunflower and laid it on the floor, noticing at the same time an unpleasant and sickly smell. There was something pungent in it, something disgusting. Tipping the vase suddenly upside down, she was amazed to see, instead of a rush of refreshing water, a sluggish and stenching trickle of slime descend like a green soup over the upturned face of the youth.

She had tipped something wet over the face of someone who was ill and that to Fuchsia was the whole principle, so she was not surprised when she found that its cogency was immediate.

Steerpike, indeed, had received a nasty shock. The stench of the stagnant slime filled his nostrils. He spluttered and spat the slough from his mouth, and rubbing his sleeve across his face smeared it more thinly but more evenly and completely than before. Only his dark-red concentrated eyes stared out from the filthy green mask, unpolluted.

SOAP FOR GREASEPAINT

Fuchsia squatted back on her heels in surprise as he sat bolt upright and glared at her. She could not hear what he muttered through his teeth. His dignity had been impaired, or perhaps not so much his dignity as his vanity. Passions he most certainly had, but he was more wily than passionate, and so even at this moment, with the sudden wrath and shock within him, he yet held himself in check and his brain overpowered his anger, and he smiled hideously through the putrid scum. He got to his feet painfully.

His hands were the dull sepia-red of dry blood for he had been bruised and cut in his long hours of climbing. His clothes were torn; his hair dishevelled and matted with dust and twigs and filth from his climb in the ivy.

Standing as straight as he could, he inclined himself slightly towards Fuchsia, who had risen at the same time.

'The Lady Fuchsia Groan,' said Steerpike, as he bowed.

Fuchsia stared at him and clenched her hands at her sides. She stood stiffly, her toes were turned slightly inwards towards each other, and she leaned a little forwards as her eyes took in the bedraggled creature in front of her. He was not much bigger than she was, but much more clever; she could see that at once.

Now that he had recovered, her mind was filled with horror at the idea of this alien at large in her room.

Suddenly, before she had known what she was doing, before she had decided to speak, before she knew of what to speak, her voice escaped from her hoarsely:

'What do you want? Oh, what do you want? This is *my* room. *My* room.'

Fuchsia clasped her hands at the curve of her breasts in the attitude of prayer. But she was not praying. Her nails were digging into the flesh of either hand. Her eyes were wide open.

'Go away,' she said. 'Go away from my room.' And then her whole mood changed as her feelings arose like a tempest.

'I hate you!' she shouted, and stamped her foot upon the ground. 'I hate you for coming here. I hate you in my room.' She seized the table edge with both her hands behind her and rattled it on its legs.

Steerpike watched her carefully.

His mind had been working away behind his high forehead. Unimaginative himself he could recognize imagination in her: he had come upon one whose whole nature was the contradiction of his own. He knew that behind her simplicity was something he could never have. Something he despised as impractical. Something which would never carry her to power nor riches, but would retard her progress and keep her apart in a world of her own make-believe. To win her favour he must talk in her own language.

As she stood breathless beside the table and as he saw her cast her eyes about the room as though to find a weapon, he struck an attitude, raising one hand, and in an even, flat, hard voice that contrasted, even to Fuchsia in her agony, with her own passionate outcry said:

'Today I saw a great pavement among the clouds made of grey stones, bigger than a meadow. No one goes there. Only a heron.

'Today I saw a tree growing out of a high wall, and people walking on it far above the ground. Today I saw a poet look out of a narrow window. But the stone field that is lost in the clouds is what you'd like best. Nobody goes there. It's a good place to play games and to' (he took the plunge cunningly) '– and to *dream* of things.' Without stopping, for he felt that it would be hazardous to stop:

'I saw today,' he said, 'a horse swimming in the top of a tower: I saw a million towers today. I saw clouds last night. I was cold. I was colder than ice. I have had no food. I have had no sleep.' He curled his lip in an effort at a smile. 'And then you pour green filth on me,' he said.

'And now I'm here where you hate me being. I'm here because there was nowhere else to go. I have seen so much. I have been out all night. I have escaped' (he whispered the word dramatically) 'and, best of all, I found the field in the clouds, the field of stones.'

He stopped for breath and lowered his hand from its posturing and peered at Fuchsia.

She was leaning against the table, her hands gripping its sides. It may have been the darkness that deceived him, but to his immense satisfaction he imagined she was staring *through* him.

Realizing that if this were so, and his words were beginning to work upon her imagination, he must proceed without a pause sweeping her thoughts along, allowing her only to think of what he was saying. He was clever enough to know what would appeal to her. Her crimson dress was enough for him to go on. She was romantic. She was a simpleton; a dreaming girl of fifteen years.

'Lady Fuchsia,' he said, and clenched his hand at his forehead, 'I come for sanctuary. I am a rebel. I am at your service as a dreamer and a man of action. I have climbed for hours, and am hungry and thirsty. I stood on the field of stones and longed to fly into the clouds, but I could only feel the pain in my feet.'

'Go away,' said Fuchsia in a distant voice. 'Go away from me.' But Steerpike was not to be stopped, for he noticed that her violence had died and he was tenacious as a ferret.

'Where can I go to?' he said. 'I would go this instant if I knew where to escape to. I have already been lost for hours in long corridors. Give me first some water so that I can wash this horrible slime from my face, and give me a little time to rest and then I will go, far away, and I will never come again, but will live alone in the stone sky-field where the herons build.'

Fuchsia's voice was so vague and distant that it appeared to Steerpike that she had not been listening, but she said slowly: 'Where is it? Who are you?'

Steerpike answered immediately.

'My name is Steerpike,' he said, leaning back against the window in the darkness, 'but I cannot tell you now where the field of stones lies all cold in the clouds. No, I couldn't tell you that – not yet.'

'Who are you?' said Fuchsia again. 'Who are you in my room?'

'I have told you,' he said. 'I am Steerpike. I have climbed to your lovely room. I like your pictures on the walls and your book and your horrible root.'

'My root is beautiful. Beautiful!' shouted Fuchsia. 'Do not talk about my things. I hate you for talking about my things. Don't look at them.' She ran to the twisted and candle-lit root of smooth wood in the wavering darkness and stood between it and the window where he was.

Steerpike took out his little pipe from his pocket and sucked the stem. She was a strange fish, he thought, and needed carefully selected bait.

'How did you get to my room?' said Fuchsia huskily.

'I climbed,' said Steerpike. 'I climbed up the ivy to your room. I have been climbing all day.'

'Go away from the window,' said Fuchsia. 'Go away to the door.'

Steerpike, surprised, obeyed her. But his hands were in his pockets. He felt more sure of his ground.

Fuchsia moved gauchely to the window taking up the candle as she passed the table, and peering over the sill, held the shaking flame above the abyss. The drop, which she remembered so well by daylight, looked even more terrifying now.

She turned towards the room. 'You must be a good climber,' she said sullenly but with a touch of admiration in her voice which Steerpike did not fail to detect.

'I am,' said Steerpike. 'But I can't bear my face like this any longer. Let me have some water. Let me wash my face, your Ladyship; and then if I can't stay here, tell me where I can go and sleep. I haven't had a cat's nap. I am tired; but the stone field haunts me. I must go there again after I've rested.'

There was a silence.

'You've got kitchen clothes on,' said Fuchsia flatly.

'Yes,' said Steerpike. 'But I'm going to change them. It's the kitchen I escaped from. I detested it. I want to be free. I shall never go back.'

'Are you an *adventurer*?' said Fuchsia, who, although she did not think he looked like one, had been more than impressed by his climb and by the flow of his words.

'I am,' said Steerpike. 'That's just what I am. But at the moment I want some water and soap.'

There was no water in the attic, but the idea of taking him down to her bedroom where he could wash and then go away for food, rankled in her, for he would pass through her other attic rooms. Then she realized that he had, in any event, to leave her sanctum and, saving for a return climb down the ivy the only path lay through the attics and down the spiral staircase to her bedroom. Added to this was the thought that if she took him down now he would see very little of her rooms in the darkness, whereas tomorrow her attic would be exposed.

'Lady Fuchsia,' said Steerpike, 'what work is there that I can do? Will you introduce me to someone who can employ me? I am not a kitchen lackey, my Ladyship, I am a man of purpose. Hide me tonight, Lady Fuchsia, and let me meet someone tomorrow who may employ me. All I want is one interview. My brains will do the rest.'

Fuchsia stared at him, open mouthed. Then she thrust her full lower lip forward and said:

'What's the awful smell?'

'It's the filthy dregs you drowned me in,' said Steerpike. 'It's my face you're smelling.'

'Oh,' said Fuchsia. She took up the candle again. 'You'd better follow.'

Steerpike did so, out of the door, along the balcony, and then down the ladder. Fuchsia did not think of helping him in the ill-lit darkness, though she heard him stumble. Steerpike kept as close to her as he could and the little patch of faint candlelight on the floor which preceded her, but as she threaded her way dexterously between the oddments that lay banked up in the first attic, he was more than once struck across the face, by a hanging rope of spiked seashells, by the giraffe's leg which Fuchsia ducked beneath, and once he was brought to a gasping halt by the brass hilt of a sword.

When he had reached the head of the spiral staircase Fuchsia was already halfway down and he wound after her, cursing.

After a long time he felt the close air of the staircase lighten about him and a few moments later he had come to the last of the descending circles and had stepped down into a bedroom. Fuchsia lit a lamp on the wall. The blinds were not drawn and the black night filled up the triangles of her window.

She was pouring from a jug the water which Steerpike so urgently needed. The smell was beginning to affect him, for as he had stepped down into the room he had retched incontinently, with his thin, bony hands at his stomach.

At the gurgling sound of the water as it slopped into the bowl on Fuchsia's washstand he drew a deep breath through his teeth. Fuchsia, hearing his foot descend upon the boards of her room, turned, jug in hand, and as she did so she overflooded the bowl with a rush of water which in the lamplight made bright pools on the dark ground. 'Water,' she said, 'if you want it.'

Steerpike advanced rapidly to the basin and plucked off his coat and vest, and stood beside Fuchsia in the darkness very thin, very bunched at the shoulders, and with an extraordinary perkiness in the poise of his body.

'What about soap?' said Steerpike, lowering his arms into the basin. The water was cold, and he shivered. His shoulder blades stood out sharply from his back as he bent over and shrugged his shoulders together. 'I can't get this muck off without soap and a scrubbing-brush, your Ladyship.'

'There's some things in that drawer,' said Fuchsia slowly. 'Hurry up and finish, and then go away. You're not in your own room. You're in my room where no one's allowed to come, only my old nurse. So hurry up and go away.'

'I will,' said Steerpike, opening the drawer and rummaging among the contents until he had found a piece of soap. 'But don't forget you promised to introduce me to someone who might employ me.'

'I didn't,' said Fuchsia. 'How do you dare to tell such lies to me? How do you dare!'

Then came Steerpike's stroke of genius. He saw that there was no object in pressing his falsehood any further and, making a bold move into the unknown he leapt with great agility away from the basin, his face now thick in lather. Wiping away the white froth from his lips, he channelled a huge dark mouth with his forefinger and posturing in the attitude of a clown listening he remained immobile for seven long seconds with his hand to his ear. Where the idea had come from he did not know, but he had felt since he first met Fuchsia that if anything were to win her favour it was something tinged with the theatre, the bizarre, and yet something quite simple and guileless, and it was this that Steerpike found difficult. Fuchsia stared hard. She forgot to hate him. She did not see him. She saw a clown, a living limb of nonsense. She saw something she loved as she loved her root, her giraffe leg, her crimson dress.

'Good!' she shouted, clenching her hands. 'Good! good! good! good!' All at once she was on her bed, landing upon both her knees at once. Her hands clasped the footrail.

A snake writhed suddenly under the ribs of Steerpike. He had succeeded. What he doubted for the moment was whether he could live up to the standard he had set himself.

He saw, out of the corner of his eye, which like the rest of his face was practically smothered in soap-suds, the dim shape of Lady Fuchsia looming a little above him on the bed. It was up to him. He didn't know much about clowns, but he knew that they did irrational things very seriously, and it had occurred to him that Fuchsia would enjoy them. Steerpike had an unusual gift. It was to understand a subject without appreciating it. He was almost entirely cerebral in his approach. But this could not easily be perceived; so shrewdly, so surely he seemed to enter into the heart of whatever he wished, in his words or his deeds, to mimic.

From the ludicrous listening posture he straightened himself slowly, and with his toes turned outwards extravagantly he ran a few steps towards a corner of Fuchsia's room, and then stopped to listen again, his hand at his ear. Continuing his run he reached the corner and picked up, after several efforts at getting his hand to reach as far down as the floor, a piece of green cloth which he hobbled back with, his feet as before turned out so far as to produce between them a continuous line.

Fuchsia, in a transport, watched him, the knuckles of her right hand in her mouth, as he began a thorough examination of the bed rail immediately below her. Every now and then he would find something very wrong with the iron surface of the rail and would rub it vigorously with his rag, stand back from it for a longer view, with his head on one side, the dark of the soapless mouth drooping at each corner in anguish, and then polish the spot again, breathing upon it and rubbing it with an inhuman concentration of purpose. All the time he was thinking, 'What a fool I am, but it will work.' He could not sink himself. He was not the artist. He was the exact imitation of one.

All at once he removed with his forefinger a plump sud of soap from the centre of his forehead, leaving a rough, dark circle of skin where it had been, and tapped his frothy finger along the footrail three times at equal intervals, leaving about a third of the soap behind at each tap. Waddling up and down at the end of the bed, he examined each of these blobs in turn and, as though trying to decide which was the most imposing specimen, removed one after the other until, with only the central sud remaining, he came to a halt before it, and then, kicking away one of his feet in an extraordinarily nimble way, he landed himself flat on his face in a posture of obedience.

Fuchsia was too thrilled to speak. She only stared, happy beyond happiness. Steerpike got to his feet and grinned at her, the lamplight glinting upon his uneven teeth. He went at once to the basin and renewed his ablutions more vigorously than ever.

While Fuchsia knelt on her bed and Steerpike rubbed his head and face with an ancient and grubby towel, there came a knock upon the door and Nannie Slagg's voice piped out thinly:

'Is my conscience there? Is my sweet piece of trouble there? Are you there, my dear heart, then? Are you there?'

'No, Nannie, no, I'm not! Not *now*. Go away and come back again soon, and I'll be here,' shouted Fuchsia thickly, scrambling to the door. And then with her mouth to the keyhole: 'What d'you want? What d'you want?'

'Oh, my poor heart! what's the matter, then? What's the matter, then? What is it, my conscience?'

'Nothing, Nannie. Nothing. What d'you want?' said Fuchsia, breathing hard.

Nannie was used to Fuchsia's sudden and strange changes of mood;

so after a pause in which Fuchsia could hear her sucking her wrinkled lower lip, the old nurse answered:

'It's the Doctor, dear. He says he's got a present for you, my baby. He wants you to go to his house, my only, and I'm to take you.'

Fuchsia, hearing a 'Tck! tck!' behind her, turned and saw a very clean-looking Steerpike gesturing to her. He nodded his head rapidly and jerked his thumb at the door, and then, with his index and longest finger strutting along the washstand, indicated, as far as she could read, that she should accept the offer to walk to the Doctor's with Nannie Slagg.

'All right!' shouted Fuchsia, 'but I'll come to *your* room. Go there and wait.'

'Hurry, then, my love!' wailed the thin, perplexed voice from the passage. 'Don't keep him waiting.'

As Mrs Slagg's feet receded, Fuchsia shouted: 'What's he giving me?'

But the old nurse was beyond earshot.

Steerpike was dusting his clothes as well as he could. He had brushed his sparse hair and it looked like dank grass as it lay flatly over his big forehead.

'Can I come, too?' he said.

Fuchsia turned her eyes to him quickly.

'Why?' she said at last.

'I have a reason,' said Steerpike. 'You can't keep me here all night, anyway, can you?'

This argument seemed good to Fuchsia and, 'Oh, yes, you can come, too,' she said at once. 'But what about Nannie,' she added slowly. 'What about my nurse?'

'Leave her to me,' said Steerpike. 'Leave her to me.'

Fuchsia hated him suddenly and deeply for saying this, but she made no answer.

'Come on, then,' she said. 'Don't stay in my room any more. What are you waiting for?' And unbolting the door she led the way, Steerpike following her like a shadow to Mrs Slagg's bedroom.

AT THE PRUNESQUALLORS

MRS SLAGG was so agitated at the sight of an outlandish youth in the company of her Fuchsia that it was several minutes before she had recovered sufficiently to listen to anything in the way of an explanation. Her eyes would dart to and fro from Fuchsia to the features of the intruder. She stood for so long a time, plucking nervously at her lower lip, that Fuchsia realized it was useless to continue with her explanation and was wondering what to do next when Steerpike's voice broke in.

'Madam,' he said, addressing Mrs Slagg, 'my name is Steerpike, and I ask you to forgive my sudden appearance at the door of your room.' And he bowed very low indeed, his eyes squinting up through his eyebrows as he did so.

Mrs Slagg took three uncertain steps towards Fuchsia and clutched her arm. 'What is he saying? What is he saying? Oh, my poor heart, who is he, then? What has he done to you, my only?'

'He's coming, too,' said Fuchsia, by way of an answer. 'Wants to see Dr Prune as well. What's his present? What's he giving me a present for? Come on. Let's go to his house. I'm tired. Be quick, I want to go to bed.'

Mrs Slagg suddenly became very active when Fuchsia mentioned her tiredness and started for the door, holding the girl by her forearm. 'You'll be into your bed in no time. I'll put you there myself and tuck you in, and turn your lamp out for you as I always did, my wickedness, and you can go to sleep until I wake you, my only, and can give you breakfast by the fire; so don't you mind, my tired thing. Only a few minutes with the Doctor – only a few minutes.'

They passed through the door, Mrs Slagg peering suspiciously around Fuchsia's arm at the quick movements of the high-shouldered boy.

Without another word between them they began to descend several flights of stairs until they reached a hall where armour hung coldly upon the walls and the corners were stacked with old weapons that were as rich with rust as a hedge of winter beech. It was no place to linger in, for a chill cut upwards from the stone floor and cold beads of moisture stood like sweat upon the tarnished surface of iron and steel.

Steerpike arched his nostrils at the dank air and his eyes travelled swiftly over the medley of corroding trophies, of hanging panoplies, smouldering with rust; and the stack of small arms, and noted a slim length of steel whose far end seemed to be embedded in some sort of tube, but it was impossible to make it out clearly in the dim light. A sword-stick leapt to his mind, and his acquisitive instincts were sharpened at the thought. There was no time, however, for him to rummage among the heaps of metal at the moment, for he was conscious of the old woman's eyes upon him, and he followed her and Fuchsia out of the hall vowing to himself that at the first opportunity he would visit the chill place again.

The door by which they made their exit lay opposite the flight that led down to the centre of the unhealthy hall. On passing through it they found themselves at the beginning of an ill-lit corridor, the walls of which were covered with small prints in faded colours. A few of them were in frames, but of these only a small proportion had their glass unbroken. Nannie and Fuchsia, being familiar with the corridor, had no thought for its desolate condition nor for the mellowed prints that depicted in elaborate but unimaginative detail the more obviously pictorial aspects of Gormenghast. Steerpike rubbed his sleeve across one or two as he followed, removing a quantity of dust, and glanced at them critically, for it was unlike him to let any kind of information slip from him unawares.

This corridor ended abruptly at a heavy doorway, which Fuchsia opened with an effort, letting in upon the passage a less oppressive darkness for it was late evening, and beyond the door a flock of clouds were moving swiftly across a slate-coloured sky in which one star rode alone.

'Oh, my poor heart, how late it's getting!' said Nannie, peering anxiously at the sky, and confiding her thoughts to Fuchsia in such a surreptitious way that it might be supposed she was anxious that the firmament should not overhear her. 'How late it *is* getting, my only, and I must be back with your Mother very soon. I must take her something to drink, the poor huge thing. Oh, no, we mustn't be long!'

Before them was a large courtyard and at the opposite corner was a three-storied building attached to the main bulk of the castle by a flying buttress. By day it stood out strangely from the ubiquitous grey stone of Gormenghast, for it was built with a hard red sandstone from a quarry that had never since been located.

Fuchsia was very tired. The day had been overcharged with happenings. Now, as the last of the daylight surrendered in the west, she was still awake and beginning, not ending, another experience.

Mrs Slagg was clasping her arm, and as they approached the main doorway, she stopped suddenly and, as was her usual habit when flustered, brought her hand up to her mouth and pulled at her little lower lip, her old watery eyes peering weakly at Fuchsia. She was about to say something, when the sound of footsteps caused her and her two companions to turn and to stare at a figure approaching in the darkness. A faint sound as of something brittle being broken over and over again accompanied his progress towards them.

'Who is it?' said Mrs Slagg. 'Who is it, my only? Oh, how dark it is!'

'It's only Flay,' said Fuchsia. 'Come on. I'm tired.' But they were hailed from the gloom.

'Who?' cried the hard, awkward voice. Mr Flay's idiom, if at times unintelligible, was anything but prolix.

'What do you want, Mr Flay?' shouted Nannie, much to her own and to Fuchsia's surprise.

'Slagg?' queried the hard voice again. 'Wanted,' it added.

'Who's wanted?' Nannie shrilled back, for she felt that Mr Flay was always too brusque with her.

'Who's with you?' barked Flay, who was now within a few yards. 'Three just now.'

Fuchsia, who had long ago acquired the knack of interpreting the ejaculations of her father's servant, turned her head around at once and was both surprised and relieved to find that Steerpike had disappeared. And yet, was there a tinge of disappointment as well? She put out her arm and pressed the old nurse against her side.

'Three just now,' repeated Flay, who had come up.

Mrs Slagg also noticed that the boy was missing. 'Where is he?' she queried. 'Where's the ugly youth?'

Fuchsia shook her head glumly and then turned suddenly on Flay, whose limbs seemed to straggle away into the night. Her weariness made her irritable and now she vented her pent-up emotion upon the dour servant.

'Go away! go away!' she sobbed. 'Who wants you here, you stupid, spiky thing? Who wants you – shouting out "Who's there?" and thinking yourself so important when you're only an old thin thing? Go away to my father where you belong, but leave us alone.' And Fuchsia, bursting into a great exhausted cry, ran up to the emaciated Flay and, throwing her arms about his waist, drenched his waistcoat in her tears.

His hands hung at his sides, for it would not have been right for him to touch the Lady Fuchsia however benevolent his motive, for he was, after all, only a servant although a most important one.

'Please go now,' said Fuchsia at last, backing away from him.

'Ladyship,' said the servant, after scratching the back of his head, 'Lordship wants her.' He jerked his head at the old nurse.

'Me?' cried Nannie Slagg, who had been sucking her teeth.

'You,' said Flay.

'Oh, my poor heart! When? When does he want me? Oh, my dear body! What can he want?'

'Wants you tomorrow,' replied Flay and, turning about, began to walk away and was soon lost to sight, and a short time afterwards even the sound of his knee joints was out of hearing.

They did not wait any longer, but walked as swiftly as they could to the main door of the house of sandstone, and Fuchsia gave a heavy rap with a door knocker, rubbing with her sleeve at the moisture in her eyes.

As they waited they could hear the sound of a violin.

Fuchsia knocked at the door again, and a few seconds later the music ceased and footsteps approached and stopped. A bolt was drawn back, the door opened upon a strong light, and the Doctor waved them in. Then he closed the door behind them, but not before a thin youth had squeezed himself past the doorpost and into the hall where he stood between Fuchsia and Mrs Slagg.

'Well! well! well! well!' said the Doctor, flicking a hair from the sleeve of his coat, and flashing his teeth. 'So you have brought a friend with you, my dear little Ladyship, so you have brought a friend with you – or' (and he raised his eyebrows) 'haven't you?'

For the second time Mrs Slagg and Fuchsia turned about to discover the object of the Doctor's inquiry, and found that Steerpike was immediately behind them.

He bowed, and with his eye on the Doctor, 'At your service,' he said.

'Ha, ha, ha! but I don't want *anyone* at my service,' said Dr Prunesquallor, folding his long white hands around each other as though they were silk scarves. 'I'd rather have somebody "in" my service perhaps. But not *at* it. Oh, no. I wouldn't have any service left if every young gentleman who arrived through my door was suddenly *at* it. It would soon be in shreds. Ha, ha, ha! absolutely in shreds.'

'He's come,' said Fuchsia in her slow voice, 'because he wants to work because he's clever, so I brought him.'

'Indeed,' said Prunesquallor. 'I have always been fascinated by those who want to work, ha, ha. Most absorbing to observe them. Ha, ha, ha! most absorbing and uncanny. Walk along, dear ladies, walk along. My very dear Mrs Slagg, you look a hundred years younger every day. This way, this way. Mind the corner of that chair, my very dear Mrs Slagg, and oh! my dear woman, you *must* look where you're going, by all that's circumspect, you really must. Now, just allow me to open this door and then we can make ourselves comfortable. Ha, ha, ha! that's right, Fuchsia, my dear, prop her up! prop her up!'

So saying, and shepherding them in front of him and at the same time rolling his magnified eyes all over Steerpike's extraordinary costume, the Doctor at last arrived within his own room and closed the door behind himself sharply with a click. Mrs Slagg was ushered into a chair with soft wine-coloured upholstery, where she looked particularly minute, and Fuchsia into another of the same pattern. Steerpike was waved to a high-backed piece of oak, and the Doctor himself set about bringing bottles and glasses from a cupboard let into the wall.

'What is it to be? What is it to be? Fuchsia, my dear child! what do you fancy?'

'I don't want anything, thank you,' said Fuchsia. 'I feel like going to sleep, Dr Prune.'

'Aha! aha! A little stimulant, perhaps. Something to sharpen your faculties, my dear. Something to tide you over until – ha, ha, ha! you are snug within your little bed. What do you think? what do you think?'

'I don't know,' said Fuchsia.

'Aha! but *I* do. *I* do,' said the Doctor, and whinnied like a horse;

then, pulling back his sleeves so that his wrists were bare, he advanced like some sort of fastidious bird towards the door, where he pulled a cord in the wall. Lowering his sleeves again neatly over his cuffs, he waited, on tip-toe, until he heard a sound without, at which he flung open the door, uncovering, as it were, a swarthy-skinned creature in white livery whose hand was raised as though to knock upon the panels. Before the Doctor had said a word Nannie leaned forward in her chair. Her legs, unable to reach the floor, were dangling helplessly.

'It's elderberry wine that you love best, isn't it?' she queried in a nervous, penetrating whisper to Fuchsia. 'Tell the Doctor that. Tell him that, at once. You don't want any stimulant, do you?'

The Doctor tilted his head slightly at the sound but did not turn, merely raising his forefinger in front of the servant's eyes and wagging it, and his thin, rasping voice gave an order, for a powder to be mixed and for a bottle of elderberry wine to be procured. He closed the door, and, dancing up to Fuchsia,

'Relax, my dear, relax,' he said. 'Let your limbs wander wherever they like, ha, ha, ha, as long as they do not stray *too* far, ha, ha, ha! as long as they don't stray *too* far. Think of each of them in turn until they're all as limp as jellyfish, and you'll be ready to run to the Twisted Woods and back before you know where you are.'

He smiled and his teeth flashed. His mop of grey hair glistened like twine in the strong lamplight. 'And what for you, Mrs Slagg? What for Fuchsia's Nannie? A little port?'

Mrs Slagg ran her tongue between her wrinkled lips and nodded as her fingers went to her mouth on which a silly little smile hovered. She watched the Doctor's every movement as he filled up the wineglass and brought it over to her.

She bowed in an old-fashioned way from her hips as she took the glass, her legs pointing out stiffly in front of her for she had edged herself further back in the chair and might as well have been sitting on a bed.

Then all at once the Doctor was back at Fuchsia's chair, and bending over her. His hands, wrapped about each other in a characteristic manner, were knotted beneath his chin.

'I've got something for you, my dear; did your nurse tell you?' His eyes rolled to the side of his glasses giving him an expression of fantastic roguery which on his face would have been, for one who had never met him, to say the least, unsettling.

Fuchsia bent forward, her hands on the red bolster-like arms of the chair.

'Yes, Dr Prune. What is it, thank you, what is it?'

'Aha! ha, ha, ha, ha! Aha, ha, ha! It is something for you to wear, ha, ha! If you like it and if it's not too heavy. I don't want to fracture your cervical vertebrae, my little lady. Oh no, by all that's most healthy I wouldn't care to do that; but I'll trust you to be careful. You will, won't you? Ha, ha.'

'Yes, yes, I will,' said Fuchsia.

He bent even closer to Fuchsia. 'Your baby brother has hurt you. *I* know, ha, ha. *I* know,' the Doctor whispered, and the sound edged between his rows of big teeth, very faintly, but not so faintly as to escape Steerpike's hearing. 'I have a stone for your bosom, my dear child, for I saw the diamonds within your tearducts when you ran from your mother's door. These, if they come again, must be balanced by a heavier if less brilliant stone, lying upon your bosom.'

Prunesquallor's eyes remained quite still for a moment. His hands were still clasped at his chin.

Fuchsia stared. 'Thank you, Dr Prune,' she said at last.

The physician relaxed and straightened himself. 'Ha, ha, ha! Ha, ha, ha!' he trilled, and then bent forward to whisper again. 'So I have decided to give you a stone from another land.'

He put his hand into his pocket, but kept it there as he glanced over his shoulder.

'Who is your friend of the fiery eyes, my Fuchsia? Do you know him well?'

Fuchsia shook her head and stuck her lower lip out as though with instinctive distaste.

The Doctor winked at her, his magnified right eye closing enormously. 'A little later, perhaps,' said Prunesquallor, opening his eyelid again like some sort of sea creature, 'when the night is a little further advanced, a little longer in the molar, ha, ha, ha!' He straightened himself. 'When the world has swung through space a further hundred miles or so, ha, ha! then – ah, yes . . . then –' and for the second time he looked knowing and winked. Then he swung round upon his heel.

'And now,' he said, 'what will *you* have? And what, in the name of hosiery, are you wearing?'

Steerpike got to his feet. 'I am wearing what I am forced to wear until clothes can be found which are more appropriate,' he said. 'These rags, although an official uniform, are as absurd upon me as they are insulting. Sir,' he continued, 'you asked me what I would take. Brandy, I thank you, sir, Brandy.' Mrs Slagg, staring her poor old eyes practically out of their hot sockets, peered at the Doctor as the speech ended, to hear what he could possibly say after so many words. Fuchsia had not been listening. Something to wear, he had said. Something to lie heavily on her bosom. A stone. Tired as she was she was all excitement to know what it could be. Dr Prunesquallor had always been kind to her, if rather above her, but he had never given her a present before. What colour would the heavy stone be? What would it be? What would it be?

The Doctor was for a moment nonplussed at the youth's self-assurance, but he did not show it. He simply smiled like a crocodile. 'Am I mistaken, dear boy, or is that a kitchen jacket you're wearing?'

'Not only is this a kitchen jacket, but these are kitchen trousers and kitchen socks and kitchen shoes and everything is kitchen about me, sir, except myself, if you don't mind me saying so, Doctor.'

'And what,' said Prunesquallor, placing the tips of his fingers together, 'are you? Beneath your foetid jacket, which I must say looks amazingly unhygienic even for Swelter's kitchen. What *are* you? Are you a problem case, my dear boy, or are you a clear-cut young gentleman with no ideas at all, ha, ha, ha?'

'With your permission, Doctor, I am neither. I have plenty of ideas, though at the moment plenty of problems, too.'

'Is that so?' said the Doctor. 'Is that so? How very unique! Have your brandy first, and perhaps some of them will fade gently away upon the fumes of that very excellent narcotic. Ha, ha, ha! Fade gently and imperceptibly away . . .' And he fluttered his long fingers in the air.

At this moment a knock upon the door panels caused the Doctor to cry out in his extraordinary falsetto:

'Make entry! Come along, come along, my dear fellow! Make entry! What in the name of all that's rapid are you waiting for?'

The door opened and the servant entered, balancing a tray upon which stood a bottle of elderberry wine and a small white cardboard box. He deposited the bottle and the box upon the table and retired. There was something sullen about his manner. The bottle had been placed upon the table with perhaps too casual a movement. The door had clicked behind him with rather too sharp a report. Steerpike noticed this, and when he saw the Doctor's gaze return to his face, he raised his eyebrows quizzically and shrugged his shoulders the merest fraction.

Prunesquallor brought a brandy bottle to the table in the centre of the room, but first poured out a glass of elderberry wine which he gave to Fuchsia with a bow.

'Drink, my Fuchsia dear,' he said. 'Drink to all those things that you love best. *I* know. *I* know,' he added with his hands folded at his chin again. 'Drink to everything that's bright and glossy. Drink to the Coloured Things.'

Fuchsia nodded her head unsmilingly at the toast and took a gulp. She looked up at the Doctor very seriously. 'It's nice,' she said. 'I like elderberry wine. Do you like your drink, Nannie?'

Mrs Slagg very nearly spilt her port over the arm of the chair when she heard herself addressed. She nodded her head violently.

'And now for the brandy,' said the Doctor. 'The brandy for Master . . . Master . . .'

'Steerpike,' said the youth. 'My name is Steerpike, sir.'

'Steerpike of the Many Problems,' said the Doctor. 'What did you say they were? My memory is so very untrustworthy. It's as fickle as a fox. Ask me to name the third lateral bloodvessel from the extremity of my index finger that runs east to west when I lie on my face at sundown, or the percentage of chalk to be found in the knuckles of an average spinster in her fifty-seventh year, ha, ha, ha! – or even ask me, my dear boy, to give details of the pulse rate of frogs two minutes before they die of scabies – these things are no tax upon my memory, ha, ha, ha! but ask me to remember exactly what you said your problems were, a minute ago, and you will find that my memory has forsaken me utterly. Now why is that, my dear Master Steerpike, why is that?'

'Because I never mentioned them,' said Steerpike.

'That accounts for it,' said Prunesquallor. 'That, no doubt, accounts for it.'

'I think so, sir,' said Steerpike.

'But you *have* problems,' said the Doctor.

Steerpike took the glass of brandy which the Doctor had poured out.

'My problems are varied,' he said. 'The most immediate is to impress you with my potentialities. To be able to make such an unorthodox remark is in itself a sign of some originality. I am not indispensable to you at the moment, sir, because you have never made use of my services; but after a week's employment under your roof, sir, I could become so. I would be invaluable. I am purposely precipitous in my remarks. Either you reject me here and now or you have already at the back of your mind a desire to know me further. I am seventeen, sir. Do I sound like seventeen? Do I act like seventeen? I am clever enough to know I am clever. You will forgive my undiplomatic approach, sir, because you are a gentleman of imagination. That then, sir, is my immediate problem. To impress you with my talent, which would be put to your service in any and every form.' Steerpike raised his glass. 'To you, sir, if you will allow my presumption.'

The Doctor all this while had had his glass of cognac raised, but it had remained motionless an inch from his lips, until now, as Steerpike ended and took a sip at his brandy, he sat down suddenly in a chair beside the table and set down his own glass untasted.

'Well, well, well, well,' he said at last. 'Well, well, well, well, well! By all that's intriguing this is really the quintessential. What maladdress, by all that's impudent! What an enormity of surface! What a very rare frenzy indeed!' And he began to whinny, gently at first, but after a little while his high-pitched laughter increased in volume and in *tempo*, and within a few minutes he was helpless with the shrill gale of his own merriment. How so great a quantity of breath and noise managed to come from lungs that must have been, in that tube of a chest, wedged uncomfortably close together, it is difficult to imagine. Keeping, even at the height of his paroxysms, an extraordinary theatrical elegance, he rocked to and fro in his chair, helpless for the best part of nine minutes after which with difficulty he drew breath thinly through his teeth with a noise like the whistling of steam; and eventually, still shaking a little, he was able to focus his eyes upon the source of his enjoyment.

'Well, Prodigy, my dear boy! you have done me a lot of good. My lungs have needed something like that for a long time.'

'I have done something for you already, then,' said Steerpike with the clever imitation of a smile on his face. During the major part of the Doctor's helplessness he had been taking stock of the room and had poured himself out another glass of brandy. He had noted the *objets d'art*, the expensive carpets and mirrors, and the bookcase of calf-bound volumes. He had poured out some more port for Mrs Slagg and had ventured to wink at Fuchsia, who had stared emptily back, and he had turned the wink into an affection of his eye.

He had examined the labels on the bottles and their year of vintage. He had noticed that the table was of walnut and that the ring upon the Doctor's right hand was in the form of a silver serpent holding between his gaping jaw a nugget of red gold. At first the Doctor's laughter had caused him a shock, and a certain mortification, but he was soon his cold, calculating self, with his ordered mind like a bureau with tabulated shelves and pigeon-holes of reference, and he knew that at all costs he must be pleasant. He had taken a risky turning in playing such a boastful card, and at the moment it could not be proved either a failure or a success; but this he did know, that to be able to take risks was the keynote of the successful man.

Prunesquallor, when his strength and muscular control were restored sufficiently, sipped at his cognac in what seemed a delicate manner, but Steerpike was surprised to see that he had soon emptied the glass.

This seemed to do the Doctor a lot of good. He stared at the youth.

'You *do* interest me, I must admit that much, Master Steerpike,' he said. 'Oh yes, I'll go that far, ha, ha, ha! You interest me, or rather you tantalize me in a pleasant sort of way. But whether I want to have you hanging around my house is, as you with your enormous brain will readily admit, quite a different kettle of fish.'

'I don't hang about, sir. It is one of those things I never do.'

Fuchsia's voice came slowly across the room.

'You hung about in my room,' she said. And then, bending forward, she looked up at the Doctor with an almost imploring expression. 'He *climbed* there,' she said. 'He's clever.' Then she leaned back in her chair.

'I am tired; and he saw my own room that nobody ever saw before he saw it, and it is worrying me. Oh, Dr Prune.'

There was a pause.

'He climbed there,' she said again.

'I had to go somewhere,' said Steerpike. 'I didn't know it was your room. How could I have known? I am sorry, your Ladyship.'

She did not answer.

Prunesquallor had looked from one to the other.

'Aha! aha! Take a little of this powder, Fuchsia dear,' he said, bringing across to her the white cardboard box. He removed the lid and tilted a little into her glass which he filled again with elderberry wine. 'You won't taste anything at all, my dear girl; just sip it up and you will feel as strong as a mountain tiger, ha, ha! Mrs Slagg, you will take this box away with you. Four times a day, with whatever the dear child happens to be drinking. It is tasteless. It is harmless, and it is extremely efficacious. Do not forget, my good woman, will you? She needs something and this is the very something she needs, ha, ha, ha! this is the very something!'

Nannie received the box on which was written '*Fuchsia. One teaspoonful to be taken 4 times a day.*'

'Master Steerpike,' said the Doctor, 'is that the reason you wanted to see me, to beard me in my den, and to melt my heart like tallow upon my own hearth-rug?' He tilted his head at the youth.

'That is so, sir,' said Steerpike. 'With Lady Fuchsia's permission I accompanied her. I said to her: "Just let me see the Doctor, and put my case to him, and I am confident he will be impressed".'

There was a pause. Then in a confidential voice Steerpike added: 'In my less ambitious moments it is as a research scientist that I see myself, sir, and in my still less ambitious, as a dispenser.'

'What knowledge of chemicals have you, if I may venture to remark?' said the Doctor.

'Under your initial guidance my powers would develop as rapidly as you could wish,' said Steerpike.

'You are a clever little monster,' said the Doctor, tossing off another cognac and placing the glass upon the table with a click. 'A diabolically clever little monster.'

'That is what I hoped you would realize, Doctor,' said Steerpike. 'But haven't all ambitious people something of the monstrous about them? You, sir, for instance, if you will forgive me, are a little bit monstrous.'

'But, my poor youth,' said Prunesquallor, beginning to pace the room, 'there is not the minutest molecule of ambition in my anatomy, monstrous though it may appear to you, ha, ha, ha!'

His laughter had not the spontaneous, uncontrollable quality that it usually possessed.

'But, sir,' said Steerpike, 'there *has* been.'

'And why do you think so?'

'Because of this room. Because of the exquisite furnishings you possess; because of your calf-bound books; your glassware; your violin. You could not have collected together such things without ambition.'

'That is not ambition, my poor confused boy,' said the Doctor: 'it is a union between those erstwhile incompatibles, ha, ha, ha! – taste and a hereditary income.'

'Is not taste a cultivated luxury?' said Steerpike.

'But yes,' said the Doctor. 'But yes. One has the potentialities for taste; on finding this out about oneself, ha, ha! – after a little self-probing, it is a cultivated thing, as you remark.'

'Which needs assiduous concentration and diligence, no doubt,' said the youth.

'But yes; but yes,' answered the Doctor smiling, with a note in his voice that suggested it was only common politeness in him to keep amused.

'Surely such diligence is the same thing as ambitiousness. Ambitiousness to perfect your taste. That is what I mean by "ambition", Doctor, I believe you have it. I do not mean ambition for success, for "success" is a meaningless word – the successful, so I hear, being very often, to themselves, failures of the first water.'

'You interest me,' said Prunesquallor. 'I would like to speak to Lady Fuchsia alone. We haven't been paying very much attention to her, I am afraid. We have deserted her. She is alone in a desert of her own. Only watch her.'

Fuchsia's eyes were shut as she leaned back in the chair, her knees curled up under her.

'While I speak with her you will be so very, very good as to leave the room. There's a chair in the hall, Master Steerpike. Thank you, dear youth. It would be a handsome gesture.'

Steerpike disappeared at once, taking his brandy with him.

Prunesquallor looked at the old woman and the girl. Mrs Slagg, with her little mouth wide open, was fast asleep. Fuchsia had opened her eyes at the sound of the door shutting behind Steerpike.

The Doctor immediately beckoned her to approach. She came to him at once, her eyes wide.

'I've waited so long, Dr Prune,' she said. 'Can I have my stone now?'

'This very moment,' said the Doctor. 'This very second. You will not know very much about the nature of this stone, but you will treasure it more than anyone I could possibly think of. Fuchsia dear, you were so distraught as you ran like a wild pony away from your father and me;

so distraught with your black mane and your big hungry eyes – that I said to myself: "It's for Fuchsia", although ponies don't usually care much about such things, ha, ha, ha! But you will, won't you?'

The Doctor took from his pocket a small pouch of softest leather.

'Take it out yourself,' he said. 'Draw it out with this slender chain.'

Fuchsia took the pouch from the Doctor's hand and from it drew forth into the lamplight a ruby like a lump of anger.

It burned in her palm.

She did not know what to do. She did not wonder what she ought to say. There was nothing at all to say. Dr Prunesquallor knew something of what she felt. At last, clutching the solid fire between her fingers, she shook Nannie Slagg, who screamed a little as she awoke. Fuchsia got to her feet and dragged her to the door. A moment before the Doctor opened it for them, Fuchsia turned her face up to his and parted her lips in a smile of such dark, sweet loveliness, so subtly blended with her brooding strangeness, that the Doctor's hand clenched the handle of the door. He had never seen her look like this before. He had always thought of her as an ugly girl of whom he was strangely fond. But now, what was it he had seen? She was no longer a small girl for all her slowness of speech and almost irritating simplicity.

In the hall they passed the figure of Steerpike sitting comfortably on the floor beneath a large carved clock. They did not speak, and when they parted with the Doctor Nannie said: 'Thank you' in a sleepy voice and bowed slightly, one of her hands in Fuchsia's. Fuchsia's fingers clenched the blood-red stone and the Doctor only said: 'Goodbye, and take care, my dears, take care. Happy dreams. Happy dreams,' before he closed the door.

A GIFT OF THE GAB

As he returned through the hall his mind was so engrossed with his new vision of Fuchsia that he had forgotten Steerpike and was startled at the sound of steps behind him. A moment or two earlier Steerpike had himself been startled by footsteps descending the staircase immediately above where he had been sitting in the shadowy, tiger stripes of the bannisters.

He moved swiftly up to the Doctor. 'I am afraid I am still here,' he said, and then glanced over his shoulder following the Doctor's eyes. Steerpike turned and saw, descending the last three steps of the staircase, a lady whose similarity to Dr Prunesquallor was unmistakable, but whose whole deportment was more rigid. She, also, suffered from faulty eyesight, but in her case the glasses were darkly tinted so that it was impossible to tell at whom she was looking save by the general direction of the head, which was no sure indication.

The lady approached them. 'Who is this?' she said directing her face at Steerpike.

'This,' said her brother, 'is none other than Master Steerpike, who was brought to see me on account of his talents. He is anxious for me to make use of his brain, ha, ha! – not, as you might suppose, as a floating specimen in one of my jam jars, ha, ha, ha! but in its functional capacity as a vortex of dazzling thought.'

'Did he go upstairs just now?' said Miss Irma Prunesquallor. 'I said did he go upstairs just now?'

The tall lady had the habit of speaking at great speed and of repeating her questions irritably before there had been a moment's pause in which they might be answered. Prunesquallor had in moments of whimsy often amused himself by trying to wedge an answer to her less complex queries between the initial question and its sharp echo.

'Upstairs, my dear?' repeated her brother.

'I said "upstairs", I think,' said Irma Prunesquallor sharply. 'I think I said "upstairs". Have you, or he, or anyone been upstairs a quarter of an hour ago? Have you? Have you?'

'Surely not! surely not!' said the Doctor. 'We have all been downstairs, I think. Don't you?' he said, turning to Steerpike.

'I do,' said Steerpike. The Doctor began to like the way the youth answered quietly and neatly.

Irma Prunesquallor drew herself together. Her long tightly fitting black dress gave peculiar emphasis to such major bone formations as the iliac crest, and indeed the entire pelvis; the shoulder blades, and in certain angles, as she stood in the lamplight, to the ribs themselves. Her neck was long and the Prunesquallors' head sat upon it surrounded by the same grey thatch-like hair as that adopted by her brother, but in her case knotted in a low bun at the neck.

'The servant is out. OUT,' she said. 'It is his evening *out*. Isn't it? Isn't it?'

She seemed to be addressing Steerpike, so he answered: 'I have no knowledge of the arrangements you have made, madam. But he was in the Doctor's room a few minutes ago, so I expect it was he whom you heard outside your door.'

'Who said I heard anything outside *my* door?' said Irma Prunesquallor, a trifle less rapidly than usual. 'Who?'

'Were you not within your room, madam?'

'What of it? what of it?'

'I gathered from what you said that you thought that there was someone walking about upstairs,' answered Steerpike obliquely; 'and if, as you say, you were *inside* your room, then you must have heard the footsteps *outside* your room. That is what I attempted to make clear, madam.'

'You seem to know too much about it. Don't you? don't you?' She bent forward and her opaque-looking glasses stared flatly at Steerpike.

'I know nothing, madam,' said Steerpike.

'What, Irma dear, *is* all this? What in the name of all that's circuitous *is* all this?'

'I heard feet. That is all. Feet,' said his sister; and then, after a pause she added with renewed emphasis: 'Feet.'

'Irma, my dear sister,' said Prunesquallor, 'I have two things to say. Firstly, why in the name of discomfort are we hanging around in the hall and probably dying of a draught that as far as I am concerned runs up my right trouser leg and sets my gluteous maximus twitching; and secondly, what is wrong, when you boil the matter down – with feet? I have always found mine singularly useful, especially for walking with. In fact, ha, ha, ha, one might almost imagine that they had been designed for that very purpose.'

'As usual,' said his sister, 'you are drunk with your own levity. You have a brain, Alfred. I have never denied it. Never. But it is undermined by your insufferable levity. I tell you that someone has been prowling about upstairs and you take no notice. There has been no one to prowl. Do you not see the point?'

'I heard something, too,' said Steerpike, breaking in. 'I was sitting in the hall where the Doctor suggested I should remain while he decided in what capacity he would employ me, when I heard what sounded like footsteps upstairs. I crept to the top of the stairs silently, but there was no one there, so I returned.'

Steerpike, thinking the upstairs to be empty, had in reality been making a rough survey of the first floor, until he heard what must have been Irma moving to the door of her room, at which sound he had slid down the bannisters.

'You hear what he says,' said the lady, following her brother with a stiff irritation in every line of her progress. 'You hear what he says.'

'Very much so!' said the Doctor. 'Very much so, indeed. Most indigestible.'

Steerpike moved a chair up for Irma Prunesquallor with such a show of consideration for her comfort and such adroitness that she stared at him and her hard mouth relaxed at one corner.

'Steerpike,' she said, wrinkling her black dress above her hips as she reclined a little into her chair.

'I am at your service, madam,' said Steerpike. 'What may I do for you?'

'What on earth are you wearing? What are you wearing, boy?'

'It is with great regret that at my introduction to you I should be in clothes that so belie my fastidious nature, madam,' he said. 'If you will advise me where I may procure the cloth I will endeavour to have myself fitted tomorrow. Standing beside you, madam, in your exquisite gown of darkness –'

' "Gown of darkness" is good,' interrupted Prunesquallor, raising his hand to his head, where he spread his snow-white fingers across his brow. ' "Gown of darkness". A phrase, ha, ha! Definitely a phrase.'

'You have broken in, Alfred!' said his sister. 'Haven't you? haven't you? I will have a suit cut for you tomorrow, Steerpike,' she continued. 'You will live here, I suppose? Where are you sleeping? Is he sleeping here? Where do you live? Where does he live, Alfred? What have you arranged? Nothing, I expect. Have you done anything? Have you? have you?'

'What sort of thing, Irma, my dear? What sort of thing are you referring to? I have done all sorts of things. I have removed a gallstone the size of a potato. I have played delicately upon my violin while a rainbow shone through the dispensary window; I have plunged so deeply into the poets of grief that save for my foresight in attaching fish-hooks to my clothes I might never again have been drawn earthwards, ha, ha! from those excruciating depths!'

Irma could tell exactly when her brother would veer off into soliloquy and had developed the power to pay no attention at all to what he said. The footsteps upstairs seemed forgotten. She watched Steerpike as he poured her out a glass of port with a gallantry quite remarkable in its technical perfection of movement and timing.

'You wish to be employed. Is that it? Is that it?' she said.

'It is my ardent desire to be in your service,' he said.

'Why? Tell me why,' said Miss Prunesquallor.

'I endeavour to keep my mind in an equipoise between the intuitive, and rational reasoning, madam,' he said. 'But with you I cannot, for my intuitive desire to be of service overshadows my reasons, though they are many. I can only say I feel a desire to fulfil myself by finding employment under your roof. And so,' he added, turning up the corners of his mouth in a quizzical smile, 'that is the reason *why* I cannot exactly say *why*.'

'Mixed up with this metaphysical impulse, this fulfilment that you speak of so smoothly,' said the Doctor, 'is no doubt a desire to snatch the first opportunity of getting away from Swelter and the unpleasant duties which you have no doubt had to perform. Is that not so?'

'It is,' said Steerpike.

This forthright answer so pleased the Doctor that he got up from his chair and, smiling toothily, poured himself yet another glass. What pleased him especially was the mixture of cunning and honesty which he did not yet perceive to be a still deeper strata of Steerpike's cleverness.

Prunesquallor and his sister both felt a certain delight in making the acquaintance of a young gentleman with brains, however twisted those brains might be. It was true that in Gormenghast there were several cultivated persons, but they very seldom came in contact with them these days. The Countess was no conversationalist. The Earl was usually too depressed to be drawn upon subjects which had he so wished he could have discussed at length and with a dreamy penetration. The twin sisters could never have kept to the point of any conversation.

There were many others apart from the servants with whom Prunesquallor came into almost daily contact in the course of his social or professional duties, but seeing them overmuch had dulled his interest in their conversation and he was agreeably surprised to find that Steerpike, although very young, had a talent for words and a ready mind. Miss Prunesquallor saw less of people than her brother. She was pleased by the reference to her dress and was flattered by the manner in which he saw to her comforts. To be sure, he was rather a small creature. His clothes, of course, she would see to. His eyes at first she found rather monkey-like in their closeness and concentration, but as she got used to them she found there was something exciting in the way they looked at her. It made her feel he realized she was not only a lady, but a woman.

Her own brain was sharp and quick, but unlike her brother's it was superficial, and she instinctively recognized in the youth a streak of cleverness akin to her own, although stronger. She had passed the age when a husband might be looked for. Had any man ever gazed at her in this light, the coincidence of his also having the courage to broach such a subject would have been too much to credit. Irma Prunesquallor had never met such a person, her admirers confining themselves to purely verbal approach.

As it happened Miss Prunesquallor, before her thoughts were interrupted by the sound of Steerpike's feet padding past her bedroom door, had been in a state of dejection. Most people have periods of retrospection in which their thoughts are centred upon the less attractive elements in their past. Irma Prunesquallor was no exception, but today there had been something wild about her dejection. After readjusting her glasses irritably upon the bridge of her nose, she had wrung her hands before sitting at her mirror. She ignored the fact that her neck was too long, that her mouth was thin and hard, that her nose was far too sharp, and that her eyes were quite hidden, and concentrated on the profusion of coarse grey hair which swept back from her brow in one wave to where, low down on her neck, it gathered itself into a great hard knot – and on the quality of her skin, which was, indeed, unblemished. These two things alone in her eyes made her an object destined for admiration. And yet, what admiration had she received? Who was there to admire her or to compliment her upon her soft and peerless skin and on her sweep of hair?

Steerpike's gallantry had for a moment taken the chill off her heart.

By now all three of them were seated. The Doctor had drunk rather more than he would have ever prescribed to a patient. His arms were moving freely whenever he spoke and he seemed to enjoy watching his fingers as they emphasized, in dumb show, whatever he happened to be talking about.

Even his sister had felt the effect of more than her usual quota of port. Whenever Steerpike spoke she nodded her head sharply as though in total agreement.

'Alfred,' she said. 'Alfred, I'm speaking to you. Can you hear me? Can you? Can you?'

'Very distinctly, Irma, my very dear, dear sister. Your voice is ringing in my middle ear. In fact, it's ringing in both of them. Right in the very middle of them both, or rather, in both their very middles. What is it, flesh of my flesh?'

'We shall dress him in pale grey,' she said.

'Who, blood of my blood?' cried Prunesquallor. 'Who is to be apparisoned in the hue of doves?'

'Who? How can you say "Who?"! This youth, Alfred, this youth. He is taking Pellet's place. I am discharging Pellet tomorrow. He has always been too slow and clumsy. Don't you think so? Don't you think so?'

'I am far beyond thinking, bone of my bone. Far, far beyond thinking. I hand over the reins to you, Irma. Mount and begone. The world awaits you.'

Steerpike saw that the time was ripe.

'I am confident I shall give satisfaction, dear lady,' he said. 'My reward will be to see you, perhaps, once more, perhaps twice more, if you will allow me, in this dark gown that so becomes you. The slight stain which I noticed upon the hem I will remove tomorrow, with your permission. Madam,' he said, with that startling simplicity with which he interlarded his remarks, 'where can I sleep?'

Rising to her feet stiffly, but with more self-conscious dignity than she had found it necessary to assume for some while past, she motioned him to follow her with a singularly wooden gesture, and led the way through the door.

Somewhere in the vaults of her bosom a tiny imprisoned bird had begun to sing.

'Are you going forever and a day?' shouted the Doctor from his chair in which he was spread out like a length of rope. 'Am I to be marooned forever, ha, ha, ha! for evermore and evermore?'

'For tonight, yes,' replied his sister's voice. 'Mister Steerpike will see you in the morning.'

The Doctor yawned with a final flash of his teeth, and fell fast asleep.

Miss Prunesquallor led Steerpike to the door of a room on the second floor. Steerpike noticed that it was simple, spacious and comfortable.

'I will have you called in the morning, after which I will instruct you in your duties. Do you hear me? Do you hear me?'

'With great pleasure, madam.'

Her passage to the door was more stilted than ever, for she had not for a very long while made such an effort to walk attractively. The black silk of her dress gleamed in the candlelight and rustled at the knees. She turned her head at the door and Steerpike bowed, keeping his head down until the door was closed and she had gone.

Moving quickly to the window he opened it. Across the courtyard the mountainous outline of Gormenghast Castle rose darkly into the night. The cool air fanned his big protruding forehead. His face remained like a mask, but deep down in his stomach he grinned.

WHILE THE OLD NURSE DOZES

FOR the time being Steerpike must be left at the Prunesquallors, where in the somewhat elastic capacity of odd-job man, medical assistant, lady's help and conversationalist, he managed to wedge himself firmly into the structure of the household. His ingratiating manner had, day by day, a more insidious effect, until he was looked upon as part of the *ménage*, being an alien only with the cook who, as an old retainer, felt no love for an upstart and treated him with undisguised suspicion.

The Doctor found him extremely quick to learn and within a few weeks Steerpike was in control of all the dispensary work. Indeed, the chemicals and drugs had a strong fascination for the youth and he would often be found compiling mixtures of his own invention.

Of the compromising and tragic circumstances that were the outcome of all this, is not yet time to speak.

Within the castle the time-honoured rituals were performed daily. The excitement following upon the birth of Titus had in some degree subsided. The Countess, against the warnings of her medical adviser was, as she had declared she would be, up and about. She was, it is true, very weak at first, but so violent was her irritation at not being able to greet the dawn as was her habit, accompanied by a white tide of cats, that she defied the lassitude of her body.

She had heard the cats crying to her from the lawn sixty feet below her room as she lay in bed those three mornings after little Titus had been delivered, and lying there hugely in her candlelit room she had yearned to be with them, and beads of sweat had stood out upon her skin as in her agony she hankered for strength.

Had not her birds been with her, the frustration of her spirit must surely have done her more than the physical harm of getting up. The constantly changing population of her feathered children were the solace of those few days that seemed to her like months.

The white rook was the most constant in his re-appearances at the ivy-choked window, although up to the moment of her confinement he had been the most fickle of visitors.

In her deep voice she would hold converse with him for an hour at a time, referring to him as 'Master Chalk' or her 'wicked one'. All her companions came. Sometimes the room was alive with song. Sometimes, feeling the need to exercise their pinions in the sky, a crowd of them would follow one another through the window of ivy, around which in the shadowy air as they waited their turn to scramble through, a dozen birds at a time would hover, fall and rise, rattling their many-coloured wings.

Thus it might be that from time to time she would be almost deserted. On one occasion only a stonechat and a bedraggled owl were with her.

Now she was strong enough to walk and watch them circling in the sky or to sit in her arbour at the end of the long lawn, and with the sunlight smouldering in the dark red hair and lying wanly over the area of her face and neck, watch the multiform and snow-white convolutions of her malkins.

Mrs Slagg had found herself becoming more and more dependent upon Keda's help. She did not like to admit this to herself. There was something so still about Keda which she could not understand. Every now and again she made an effort to impress the girl with an authority which she did not possess, keeping on the alert to try and find some fault in her. This was so obvious and pathetic that it did not annoy the girl from the Mud Dwellings. She knew that an hour or so afterwards when Mrs Slagg felt that her position was once again established, the old nurse would run up to her, nearly in tears for some petty reason or other and bury her shaking head in Keda's side.

Fond as Keda had become of Titus whom she had suckled and cared for tenderly, she had begun to realize that she must return to the Mud Dwellings. She had left them suddenly as a being who, feeling that Providence has called him, leaves the old life suddenly for the new. But now she realized that she had made a mistake and knew that she would be false to remain any longer in the castle than was necessary for the child. Not so much a mistake as a crime against her conscience, for it was with a very real reason that she had accompanied Mrs Slagg at such short notice.

Day after day from the window in the small room she had been given next to Mrs Slagg's she gazed to where the high surrounding wall of the castle grounds hid from her sight the Dwellings that she had known since her infancy, and where during the last year her passions had been so cruelly stirred.

Her baby, whom she had buried so recently, had been the son of an old carver of matchless reputation among the Dwellers. The marriage had been forced upon her by the iron laws. Those sculptors who were unanimously classed as pre-eminent were, after the fiftieth year, allowed to choose a bride from among the damsels, and against their choice no shadow of objection could be raised. This immemorial custom had left Keda no option but to become the wife of this man, who, though a sour and uncouth old creature, burned with a vitality that defied his years.

From the morning until the light failed him he would be with his carvings. He would peer at it from all angles, or crouch grotesquely at some distance, his eyes narrowed in the sunlight. Then, stealing up upon it, it would seem that he was preparing to strike like a beast attacking its paralysed quarry; but on reaching the wooden form he would run his great hand over the surfaces as a lover will fondle the breasts of his mistress.

Within three months from the time when he and Keda had performed the marriage ceremony, standing alone upon the marriage hill, to the south of the Twisted Woods, while an ancient voice called to them through the half-lit distances, their hands joined, her feet upon his – within the three months that followed he had died. Suddenly letting the chisel and the hammer fall to the ground, his hands had clutched at his heart, his lips had drawn themselves away from his teeth, and he had crumpled up, his energy passing out of him and leaving only the old dry sack of his body. Keda was alone. She had not loved him but had admired him and the passion that consumed him as an artist. Once more she was free save that, on the day that he died, she felt within her the movement of another life than her own and now, nearly a year later, her firstborn was lying near the father, lifeless, in the dry earth.

The dreadful and premature age that descended so suddenly upon the faces of the Dwellers had not yet completely fallen over her features. It was as though it was so close upon her that the beauty of her face cried out against it, defying it, as a stag at bay turns upon the hounds with a pride of stance and a shaking of antlers.

A hectic beauty came upon the maidens of the Mud buildings a month or so before the ravages to which they were predestined attacked them. From infancy until this tragic interim of beauty their loveliness was of a strange innocence, a crystal-like tranquillity that held no prescience of the future. When in this clearness the dark seeds began to root and smoke was mixed with the flame, then, as with Keda now, a thorny splendour struck outward from their features.

One warm afternoon, sitting in Mrs Slagg's room with Titus at her breast, she turned to the old nurse and said quietly: 'At the end of the month I shall return to my home. Titus is strong and well and he will be able to do without me.'

Nannie, whose head had been nodding a little, for she was always either dropping off for a nap or waking up from one, opened her eyes when Keda's words had soaked into her brain. Then she sat up very suddenly and in a frightened voice called out: 'No! no! you mustn't go. You mustn't! You mustn't! Oh, Keda, you know how old I am.' And she ran across the room to hold Keda's arm. Then for the sake of her dignity: 'I've told you not to call him Titus,' she cried in a rush. ' "Lord Titus" or "his Lordship," is what you *should* say.' And then, as though with relief, she fell back upon her trouble. 'Oh, you can't go! you can't go!'

'I must go,' said Keda. 'There are reasons why I must go.'

'Why? why? why?' Nannie cried out through the tears that were beginning to run jerkily down her foolish wrinkled face. 'Why must you go?' Then she stamped a tiny slippered foot that made very little noise. 'You must answer me! You must! Why are you going away from me?' Then, clenching her hands – 'I'll tell the Countess,' she said, 'I'll tell her.'

Keda took no notice at all, but lifted Titus from one shoulder to another where his crying ceased.

'He will be safe in your care,' said Keda. 'You must find another helper when he grows older for he will be too much for you.'

'But they won't be like you,' shrilled Nannie Slagg, as though she were abusing Keda for her suitability. 'They won't be like *you*. They'll bully me. Some of them bully old women when they are like me. Oh, my weak heart! my poor weak heart! what can I do?'

'Come,' said Keda. 'It is not as difficult as that.'

'It *is*. It *is*!' cried Mrs Slagg, renewing her authority. 'It's worse than that, much worse. Everyone deserts me, because I'm old.'

'You must find someone you can trust. I will try and help you,' said Keda.

'*Will* you? *will* you?' cried Nannie, bringing her fingers up to her mouth and staring at Keda through the red rims of her eyelids. 'Oh, *will* you? They make me do everything. Fuchsia's mother leaves everything to me. She has hardly seen his little Lordship, has she? Has she?'

'No,' said Keda. 'Not once. But he is happy.'

She lifted the infant away from her and laid him between the blankets in his cot, where after a spell of whimpering he sucked contentedly at his fist.

Nannie Slagg suddenly gripped Keda's arm again. 'You haven't told me why; you haven't told me why,' she said. 'I want to know why you're going away from me. You never tell me anything. Never. I suppose I'm not worth telling. I suppose you think I don't matter. Why don't you tell me things? Oh, my poor heart, I suppose I'm too old to be told anything.'

'I will tell you why I have to go,' said Keda. 'Sit down and listen.' Nannie sat upon a low chair and clasped her wrinkled hands together. 'Tell me everything,' she said.

Why Keda broke the long silence that was so much a part of her nature she could not afterwards imagine, feeling only that in talking to one who would hardly understand her she was virtually talking to herself. There had come to her a sense of relief in unburdening her heart.

Keda sat upon Mrs Slagg's bed near the wall. She sat very upright and her hands lay in her lap. For a moment or two she gazed out of the window at a cloud that had meandered lazily into view. Then she turned to the old woman.

'When I returned with you on that first evening,' said Keda quietly, 'I was troubled. I was troubled and I am still unhappy because of love. I feared my future; and my past was sorrow, and in my present you had need of me and I had need of refuge, so I came.' She paused.

'Two men from our Mud Dwellings loved me. They loved me too much and too violently.' Her eyes returned to Nannie Slagg, but they hardly saw her, nor noticed that her withered lips were pursed and her head tilted like a sparrow's. She continued quietly:

'My husband had died. He was a Bright Carver, and died struggling. I would sit down in the long shadows by our dwellings and watch a dryad's head from day to day finding its hidden outline. To me it seemed he carved the child of leaves. He would not rest, but fight; and stare – and stare. Always he would stare, cutting the wood away to give his dryad breath. One evening when I felt my unborn moving within me my husband's heart stopped beating and his weapons fell. I ran to him and knelt beside his body. His chisel lay in the dust. Above us his unfinished dryad gazed over the Twisted Woods, an acorn between its teeth.

'They buried him, my rough husband, in the long sandy valley, the valley of graves where we are always buried. The two dark men who loved and love me carried his body for me and they lowered it into the sandy hollow that they had scooped. A hundred men were there and a hundred women; for he had been the rarest of the carvers. The sand was heaped upon him and there was only another dusty mound among the mounds of the Valley and all was very silent. They held me in their eyes while he was buried – the two who love me. And I could not think of him whom we were mourning. I could not think of death. Only of life. I could not think of stillness, only of movement. I could not understand the burying, nor that life could cease to be. It was all a dream. I was alive, *alive*, and two men watched me standing. They stood beyond the grave, on the other side. I saw only their shadows for I dared not lift up my eyes to show my gladness. But I knew that they were watching me and I knew that I was young. They were strong men, their faces still unbroken by the cruel bane we suffer. They were strong and young. While yet my husband lived I had not seen them. Though one brought white flowers from the Twisted Woods and one a dim stone from the Gormen Mountain, yet I saw nothing of them, for I knew temptation.

'That was long ago. All is changed. My baby has been buried and my lovers are filled with hatred for one another. When you came for me I was in torment. From day to day their jealousy had grown until, to save the shedding of blood, I came to the castle. Oh, long ago with you, that dreadful night.'

She stopped and moved a lock of hair back from her forehead. She did not look at Mrs Slagg, who blinked her eyes as Keda paused and nodded her head wisely.

'Where are they now? How many, many times have I dreamed of them! How many, many times have I, into my pillow, cried: "Rantel!" whom I first saw gathering the Root, his coarse hair in his eyes . . . cried "Braigon!" who stood brooding in the grove. Yet not with all of me am I in love. Too much of my own quietness is with me. I am not drowned with them in Love's unkindness. I am unable to do aught but watch them, and fear them and the hunger in their eyes. The rapture that possessed me by the grave has passed. I am tired now, with a love I do not quite possess. Tired with the hatreds I have woken. Tired that I am the cause and have no power. My beauty will soon leave me, soon, soon, and peace will come. But ah! too soon.'

Keda raised her hand and wiped away the slow tears from her cheeks. 'I must have love,' she whispered.

Startled at her own outburst she stood up beside the bed rigidly. Then her eyes turned to the nurse. Keda had been so much alone in her reverie that it seemed natural to her to find that the old woman was asleep. She moved to the window. The afternoon light lay over the towers. In the straggling ivy beneath her a bird rustled. From far below a voice cried faintly to some unseen figure and stillness settled again. She breathed deeply, and leaned forward into the light. Her hands grasped the frame of the window on her either side and her eyes from wandering across the towers were drawn inexorably to that high encircling wall that hid from her the houses of her people, her childhood, and the substance of her passion.

FLAY BRINGS A MESSAGE

Autumn returned to Gormenghast like a dark spirit re-entering its stronghold. Its breath could be felt in forgotten corridors, – Gormenghast had itself *become* autumn. Even the denizens of this fastness were its shadows.

The crumbling castle, looming among the mists, exhaled the season, and every cold stone breathed it out. The tortured trees by the dark lake burned and dripped, and their leaves snatched by the wind were whirled in wild circles through the towers. The clouds mouldered as they lay coiled, or shifted themselves uneasily upon the stone skyfield, sending up wreaths that drifted through the turrets and swarmed up the hidden walls.

From high in the Tower of Flints the owls inviolate in their stone galleries cried inhumanly, or falling into the windy darkness set sail on muffled courses for their hunting grounds. Fuchsia was less and less to be found in the castle. As, with every day that passed, the weather became increasingly menacing, so she seemed to protract the long walks that had now become her chief pleasure. She had captured anew the excitement that had once filled her when with Mrs Slagg, several years before, she had insisted on dragging her nurse on circuitous marches which had seemed to the old lady both hazardous and unnecessary. But Fuchsia neither needed nor wanted a companion now.

Revisiting those wilder parts of the environs that she had almost forgotten, she experienced both exaltation and loneliness. This mixture of the sweet and bitter became necessary to her, as her attic had been necessary. She watched with frowning eyes the colour changing on the trees and loaded her pockets with long golden leaves and fire-coloured ferns and, indeed, with every kind of object which she found among the woods and rocky places. Her room became filled with stones of curious shapes that had appealed to her, fungi resembling hands or plates: queer-shaped flints and contorted branches; and Mrs Slagg, knowing it would be fruitless to reproach her, gazed each evening, with her fingers clutching her lower lip, at Fuchsia emptying her pockets of fresh treasures and at the ever-growing hoard that had begun to make the room a tortuous place to move about in.

Among Fuchsia's hieroglyphics on the wall great leaves had begun to take residence, pinned or pasted between her drawings, and areas of the floor were piled with trophies.

'Haven't you got enough, dear?' said Nannie, as Fuchsia entered late one evening and deposited a moss-covered boulder on her bed. Tiny fronds of fern emerged here and there from the moss, and white flowers the size of gnats.

Fuchsia had not heard Nannie's question, so the little old creature advanced to the side of the bed.

'You've got enough now, haven't you, my caution? Oh, yes, yes, I think so. Quite enough for your room now, dear. How dirty you are, my . . . Oh, my poor heart, how unappetizing you are.'

Fuchsia tossed back her dripping hair from her eyes and neck, so that it hung in a heavy clump like black seaweed over the collar of her cape. Then after undoing a button at her throat with a desperate struggle, and letting the corded velvet fall to her feet, she pushed it under her bed with her foot. Then she seemed to see Mrs Slagg for the first time. Bending forward she kissed her savagely on the forehead and the rain dripped from her on to the nurse's clothes.

'Oh, you dirty thoughtless thing! you naughty nuisance. Oh, my poor heart, how could you?' said Mrs Slagg, suddenly losing her temper and stamping her foot. 'All over my black satin, you dirty thing. You nasty wet thing. Oh, my poor dress! Why can't you stay in when the weather is muddy and blowy? You always were unkind to me! Always, always.'

'That's not true,' said Fuchsia, clenching her hands.

The poor old nurse began to cry.

'Well, *is* it, *is* it?' said Fuchsia.

'I don't know. I don't know at all,' said Nannie. 'Everyone's unkind to me; how should I know?'

'Then I'm going away,' said Fuchsia.

Nannie gulped and jerked her head up. 'Going away?' she cried in a querulous voice. 'No, no! you mustn't go away.' And then with an inquisitive look struggling with the fear in her eyes, 'Where to?' she said. 'Where could you go to, dear?'

'I'd go far away from here – to another kind of land,' said Fuchsia, 'where people who didn't know that I was the Lady Fuchsia would be surprised when I told them that I *was*; and they would treat me better and be more polite and do some homage sometimes. But I wouldn't stop bringing home my leaves and shining pebbles and fugnesses from the woods, whatever they thought.'

'You'd go away from me?' said Nannie in such a melancholy voice that Fuchsia held her in her strong arms.

'Don't cry,' she said. 'It isn't any good.'

Nannie turned her eyes up again and this time they were filled with the love she felt for her 'child'. But even in the weakness of her compassion she felt that she should preserve her station and repeated: '*Must* you go into the dirty water, my own one, and tear your clothes just like you've always done, caution dear? Aren't you big enough to go out only on nice days?'

'I like the autumn weather,' said Fuchsia very slowly. 'So that's why I go out to look at it.'

'Can't you see it from out of your window, precious?' said Mrs Slagg. 'Then you would keep warm at the same time, though what there is to stare at *I* don't know; but there, I'm only a silly old thing.'

'I know what I want to do, so don't you think about it any more,' said Fuchsia. 'I'm finding things out.'

'You're a wilful thing,' said Mrs Slagg a little peevishly, 'but I know much more than you think about all sorts of things. I do; yes, I do; but I'll get you your tea at once. And you can have it by the fire, and I will bring the little boy in because he ought to be awake by now. Oh dear! there is so much to do. Oh, my weak heart, I wonder how long I will last.'

Her eyes, following Fuchsia's, turned to the boulder around which a wet mark was spreading on the patchwork quilt.

'You're the dirtiest terror in the world,' she said. 'What's that stone for? What is it *for*, dear? What's the *use* of it? You never listen. Never. Nor grow any older like I told you to. There's no one to help me now. Keda's gone, and I do everything.' Mrs Slagg wiped her eyes with the back of her hand. 'Change your wet clothes or I won't bring you anything, and your dirty wet shoes at once!' . . . Mrs Slagg fumbled at the door-handle, opened the door and shuffled away down the corridor, one hand clasped at her chest.

Fuchsia removed her shoes without untying the laces by treading on the heels and working her feet loose. Mrs Slagg had made up a glowing fire and Fuchsia, pulling off her dress, rubbed her wet hair with it. Then, wrapping a warm blanket about her, she fell back into a low armchair that had been drawn up to the fire and, sinking into its familiar softness, gazed absently at the leaping flames with half-closed eyes.

When Mrs Slagg returned with a tray of tea and toasted scones, currant bread, butter and eggs and a jar of honey, she found Fuchsia asleep.

Placing the tray on the hearth she tiptoed to the door and disappeared, to return within the minute with Titus in her arms. He was dressed in a white garment which accentuated what warmth of colour there was in his face. At birth he had been practically bald, but now, though it was only two months later, he was blessed with a mop of hair as dark as his sister's.

Mrs Slagg sat down with Titus in a chair opposite Fuchsia and peered weakly at the girl, wondering whether to wake her at once or whether to let her finish her sleep and then to make another pot of tea. 'But the scones will be cold, too,' she said to herself. 'Oh, how tiresome she is.' But her problem was solved by a loud single knuckle-rap at the door, which caused her to start violently and clutch Titus to her shoulder, and Fuchsia to wake from her doze.

'Who is it?' cried Mrs Slagg. 'Who is it?'

'Flay,' said the voice of Lord Sepulchrave's servant. The door opened a few inches and a bony face looked in from near the top of the door.

'Well?' said Nannie, jerking her head about. 'Well? Well? What is it?'

Fuchsia turned her head and her eyes moved up the fissure between the door and the wall until they came at last to settle on the cadaverous features.

'Why don't you come inside?' she said.

'No invitation,' said Flay flatly. He came forward, his knees cracking at each step. His eyes shifted from Fuchsia to Mrs Slagg and from Mrs Slagg to Titus, and then to the loaded tea-tray by the fire, on which they lingered before they returned to Fuchsia wrapped in her blanket. When he saw she was still looking at him his right hand raised itself like a bunch of blunt talons and began to scratch at a prominent lump of bone at the back of his head.

'Message from his Lordship, my Lady,' he said; and then his eyes returned to the tea-tray.

'Does he want me?' said Fuchsia.

'Lord Titus,' said Flay, his eyes retaining upon their lenses the pot of tea, toasted scones, currant bread, butter, eggs and a jar of honey.

'He wants little Titus, did you say?' cried Mrs Slagg, trying to make her feet reach the ground.

Flay gave a mechanical nod. 'Got to meet me, quadrangle-arch, half-past eight,' added Flay, wiping his hands on his clothes.

'He wants my little Lordship,' whispered the old nurse to Fuchsia, who although her first antipathy to her brother had worn off had not acquired the same excited devotion which Nannie lavished upon the infant. 'He wants my little wonder.'

'Why not?' said Flay and then relapsed into his habitual silence after adding: 'Nine o'clock – library.'

'Oh, my poor heart, he ought to be in bed by then,' gulped the nurse; and clutched Titus even closer to her.

Fuchsia had been looking at the tea-tray as well.

'Flay,' she said, 'do you want to eat anything?'

By way of reply the spidery servant made his way at once across the room to a chair which he had kept in the corner of his eye, and returned with it to seat himself between the two. Then he took out a tarnished watch, scowled at it as though it were his mortal enemy, and returned it to a secret recess among his greasy black clothes.

Nannie edged herself out of the chair and found a cushion for Titus to lie on in front of the fire, and then began to pour out the tea. Another cup was found for Flay, and then for a long while the three of them sat silently munching or sipping, and reaching down to the floor for whatever they needed but making no effort to look after each other. The firelight danced in the room, and the warmth was welcome, for outside or in the corridors the wet earthy draughts of the season struck to the marrow.

Flay took out his watch again and, wiping his mouth with the back of his hand, arose to his feet. As he did so, he upset a plate at the side of his chair and it fell and broke on the floor. At the sound he started and clutched the back of the chair and his hand shook. Titus screwed his face up at the noise as though about to cry, but changed his mind.

Fuchsia was surprised at so obvious a sign of agitation in Flay whom she had known since her childhood and on whom she had never before noticed any sign of nerves.

'Why are you shaking?' she said. 'You never used to shake.'

Flay pulled himself together and then sat down suddenly again, and turned his expressionless face to Fuchsia. 'It's the night,' he said tonelessly. 'No sleep, Lady Fuchsia.' And he gave a ghastly mirthless laugh like something rusty being scraped by a knife.

Suddenly he had regained his feet again and was standing by the door. He opened it very gradually and peered through the aperture before he began to disappear inch by inch, and the door clicked finally upon him.

'Nine o'clock,' said Nannie tremulously. 'What does your father want with my little Lordship at nine o'clock? Oh, my poor heart, what does he want him for?'

But Fuchsia, tired out from her long day among the dripping woods was once more fast asleep, the red firelight flickering to and fro across her lolling head.

THE LIBRARY

THE library of Gormenghast was situated in the castle's Eastern wing which protruded like a narrow peninsula for a distance out of all proportion to the grey hinterland of buildings from which it grew. It was from about midway along this attenuated East wing that the Tower of Flints arose in scarred and lofty sovereignty over all the towers of Gormenghast.

At one time this Tower had formed the termination of the Eastern wing, but succeeding generations had added to it. On its further side the additions had begun a tradition and had created the precedent for Experiment, for many an ancestor of Lord Groan had given way to an architectural whim and made an incongruous addition. Some of these additions had not even continued the Easterly direction in which the original wing had started, for at several points the buildings veered off into curves or shot out at right angles before returning to continue the main trend of stone.

Most of these buildings had about them the rough-hewn and oppressive weight of masonry that characterized the main volume of Gormenghast, although they varied considerably in every other way, one having at its summit an enormous stone carving of a lion's head, which held between its jaws the limp corpse of a man on whose body was chiselled the words: '*He was an enemy of Groan*'; alongside this structure was a rectangular area of some length entirely filled with pillars set so closely together that it was difficult for a man to squeeze between them. Over them, at the height of about forty feet, was a perfectly flat roof of stone slabs blanketed with ivy. This structure could never have served any practical purpose, the closely packed forest of pillars with which it was entirely filled being of service only as an excellent place in which to enjoy a fantastic game of hide-and-seek.

There were many examples of an eccentric notion translated into architecture in the spine of buildings that spread eastwards over the undulating ground between the heavy walls of conifer, but for the most part they were built for some especial purpose, as a pavilion for entertainments, or as an observatory, or a museum. Some in the form of halls with galleries round three sides had been intended for concerts or dancing. One had obviously been an aviary, for though derelict, the branches that had long ago been fastened across the high central hall of the building were still hanging by rusty chains, and about the floor were strewn the broken remains of drinking cups for the birds; wire netting, red with rust, straggled across the floor among rank weeds that had taken root.

Except for the library, the eastern wing, from the Tower of Flints onwards, was now but a procession of forgotten and desolate relics, an Ichabod of masonry that filed silently along an avenue of dreary pines whose needles hid the sky.

The library stood between a building with a grey dome and one with a façade that had once been plastered. Most of the plaster had fallen away, but scraps had remained scattered over the surface, sticking to the stones. Patches of faded colour showed that a fresco had once covered the entire face of the building. Neither doors nor windows broke the stone surface. On one of the larger pieces of plaster that had braved a hundred storms and still clung to the stone, it was possible to make out the lower part of a face, but nothing else was recognizable among the fragments.

The library, though a lower building than these two to which it was joined at either end, was of a far greater length than either. The track that ran alongside the eastern wing, now in the forest, and now within a few feet of the kaleidoscopic walls shadowed by the branches of the evergreens, ended as it curved suddenly inwards towards the carved door. Here it ceased among the nettles at the top of the three deep steps that led down to the less imposing of the two entrances to the library, but the one through which Lord Sepulchrave always entered his realm. It was not possible for him to visit his library as often as he wished, for the calls made upon him by the endless ceremonials which were his exacting duty to perform robbed him for many hours each day of his only pleasure – books.

Despite his duties, it was Lord Sepulchrave's habit to resort each evening, however late the hour, to his retreat and to remain there until the small hours of the following day.

The evening on which he sent Flay to have Titus brought to him found Lord Sepulchrave free at seven in the evening, and sitting in the corner of his library, sunk in a deep reverie.

The room was lit by a chandelier whose light, unable to reach the extremities of the room lit only the spines of those volumes on the central shelves of the long walls. A stone gallery ran round the library at about fifteen feet above the floor, and the books that lined the walls of the main hall fifteen feet below were continued upon the high shelves of the gallery.

In the middle of the room, immediately under the light, stood a long table. It was carved from a single piece of the blackest marble, which reflected upon its surface three of the rarest volumes in his Lordship's collection.

Upon his knees, drawn up together, was balanced a book of his grandfather's essays, but it had remained unopened. His arms lay limply at his side, and his head rested against the velvet of the chair back. He was dressed in the grey habit which it was his custom to wear in the library. From full sleeves his sensitive hands emerged with the shadowy transparency of alabaster. For an hour he had remained thus; the deepest melancholy manifested itself in every line of his body.

The library appeared to spread outwards from him as from a core. His dejection infected the air about him and diffused its illness upon every side. All things in the long room absorbed his melancholia. The shadowing galleries brooded with slow anguish; the books receding into the deep corners, tier upon tier, seemed each a separate tragic note in a monumental fugue of volumes.

It was only on those occasions now, when the ritual of Gormenghast dictated, that he saw the Countess. They had never found in each other's company a sympathy of mind or body, and their marriage, necessary as it was from the lineal standpoint, had never been happy. In spite of his intellect, which he knew to be far and away above hers, he felt and was suspicious of the heavy, forceful vitality of his wife, not so much a physical vitality as a blind passion for aspects of life in which he could find no cause for interest. Their love had been passionless, and save for the knowledge that a male heir to the house of Groan was imperative, they would have gladly forgone their embarrassing yet fertile union. During her pregnancy he had only seen her at long intervals. No doubt the unsatisfactory marriage had added to his native depression, but compared with the dull forest of his inherent melancholy it was but a tree from a foreign region that had been transplanted and absorbed.

It was never this estrangement that grieved him, nor anything tangible but a constant and indigenous sorrow.

Of companions with whom he could talk upon the level of his own thought there were few, and of these only one gave him any satisfaction, the Poet. On occasion he would visit that long, wedge-headed man and find in the abstract language with which they communicated their dizzy stratas of conjecture a temporary stir of interest. But in the Poet there was an element of the idealist, a certain enthusiasm which was a source of irritation to Lord Sepulchrave, so that they met only at long intervals.

The many duties, which to another might have become irksome and appeared fatuous, were to his Lordship a relief and a relative escape from himself. He knew that he was past all hope a victim of chronic melancholia, and were he to have had each day to himself he would have had to resort constantly to those drugs that even now were undermining his constitution.

This evening, as he sat silently in the velvet-backed chair, his mind had turned to many subjects like a black craft, that though it steers through many waters has always beneath it a deathly image reflected among the waves. Philosophers and the poetry of Death – the meaning of the stars and the nature of these dreams that haunted him when in those chloral hours before the dawn the laudanum built for him within his skull a tallow-coloured world of ghastly beauty.

He had brooded long and was about to take a candle that stood ready on a table at his elbow and search for a book more in keeping with his mood than were the essays on his knee, when he felt the presence of another thought that had been tempering his former cogitations, but which now stood boldly in his mind. It had begun to make itself felt as something that clouded and disturbed the clarity of his reflections when he had pondered on the purpose and significance of tradition and ancestry, and now with the thought detached from its erudite encumbrances he watched it advance across his brain and appear naked, as when he had first seen his son, Titus.

His depression did not lift; it only moved a little to one side. He rose to his feet and, moving without a sound, replaced the book in a shelf of essays. He returned as silently to the table.

'Where are you?' he said.

Flay appeared at once from the darkness of one of the corners.

'What hour is it?'

Flay brought out his heavy watch. 'Eight, your Lordship.'

Lord Sepulchrave, with his head hanging forward on his breast, walked up and down the length of the library for a few minutes. Flay watched him as he moved, until his master stopped opposite his servant.

'I wish to have my son brought to me by his nurse. I shall expect them at nine. You will conduct them through the woods. You may go.'

Flay turned and, accompanied by the reports of his knee-joints, disappeared into the shadows of the room. Pulling back the curtain from before the door at the far end, he unlatched the heavy oak and climbed the three steps into the night. Above him the great branches of the pines rubbed against one another and grated in his ears. The sky was overcast and had he not made this same journey through the darkness a thousand times he must surely have lost himself in the night. To his right he could sense the spine of the Western Wing although he could not see it. He walked on and in his mind he said: 'Why now? Had the summer to see his son in. Thought he'd forgotten him. Should have seen the child long ago. What's the game? Heir to Gormenghast to come through woods on cold night. Wrong. Dangerous. Catch a cold. But Lordship knows. He knows. I am only his servant. First servant. No one else *that*. Chose me; ME, Flay, because he trusts me. Well may he trust me. Ha, ha, ha! And why? they wonder. Ha ha! Silent as a corpse. That's why.'

As he neared the Tower of Flints the trees thinned and a few stars appeared in the blackness above him. By the time the body of the castle was reached only half the sky was hidden by the night clouds and he could make out vague shapes in the darkness. Suddenly he stopped, his heart attacking his ribs, and drew up his shoulders to his ears; but a moment later he realized that the vague obese patch of blackness a few feet from him was a shrub of clipped box and not that figure of evil who now obsessed him.

He straddled onwards, and came at last to an entrance beneath the sweep of an archway. Why he did not enter it at once and climb the stairs to find Nannie Slagg he did not know. That he could see through the archway and across the darkness of the servants' quadrangle a dim light in a high window of one of the kitchen buildings was in itself nothing unusual. There was generally a light showing somewhere in the kitchen quarters although most of the staff would have resorted to their underground dormitories by that time of night. An apprentice given some fatigue duty to perform after his normal hours might be scrubbing a floor, or an especial dish for the morrow might necessitate a few cooks working late into the evening.

Tonight, however, a dull greenish light from a small window held his eye, and before he realized that he was even intrigued, he found that his feet had forestalled his brain and were carrying him across the quadrangle.

On his way across he stopped twice to tell himself that it was a pointless excursion and that he was in any case feeling extremely cold; but he went on nevertheless with an illogical and inquisitive itch overriding his better judgement.

He could not tell which room it was that gave forth this square, greenish, glow. There was something unhealthy about its colour. No one was about in the quadrangle; there were no other footsteps but his own. The window was too high for even him to peer into, although he could easily reach it with his hands. Once again he said to himself: 'What are you doing? Wasting your time. Told by Lordship to fetch Nannie Slagg and child. Why are you here? What are you doing?'

But again his thin body had anticipated him and he had begun to roll away an empty cask from against the cloister walls.

In the darkness it was no easy matter to steer the barrel and to keep it balanced upon the tilted rim as he rolled it towards the square of light; but he managed with very little sound to bring it eventually immediately under the window.

He straightened his back and turned his face up to the light that escaped like a kind of gas and hovered about the window in the haze of the autumn night.

He had lifted his right foot onto the barrel, but realized that to raise himself into the centre of the window would cause his face to catch the light from the room. Why, he did not know, but the curiosity which he had felt beneath the low arch was now so intense, that after lowering his foot and pulling the barrel to the right of the small window, he scrambled upon it with a haste that startled him. His arms were outstretched on either side along the viewless walls and his fingers, spread out like the ribs of a bone fan, began to sweat as he moved his head gradually to the left. He could already see through the glass (in spite of a sweep of old cobwebs, like a fly-filled hammock) the smooth stone walls of the room beneath him; but he had still to move his head further into the light in order to obtain a clear view of the floor of the room.

The light that seeped in a dull haze through the window dragged out as from a black canvas the main bone formation of Mr Flay's head, leaving the eye sockets, the hair, an area beneath the nose and lower lip, and everything that lay beneath the chin, as part of the night itself. It was a mask that hung in the darkness.

Mr Flay moved it upwards inch by inch until he saw what he had by some prophetic qualm known all along that it was his destiny to see. In the room below him the air was filled with an intensification of that ghastly green which he had noticed from across the quadrangle. The lamp that hung from the centre of the room by a chain was enclosed in a bowl of lime-green glass. The ghoulish light which it spewed forth gave to every object in the room a theatrical significance.

But Flay had no eyes for the few scattered objects in the nightmare below him, but only for an enormous and sinister *presence*, the sight of which had caused him to sicken and sway upon the cask and to remove his head from the window while he cooled his brow on the cold stones of the wall.

IN A LIME-GREEN LIGHT

EVEN in his nausea he could not help wondering what it was that Abiatha Swelter was doing. He raised his head from the wall and brought it by degrees to its former position.

This time Flay was surprised to find that the room appeared empty, but, with a start at its dreadful nearness, he found that the chef was sitting on a bench against the wall and immediately below him. It was not easy to see him clearly through the filth and cobwebs of the window, but the great pasty dome of his head surrounded by the lamp-tinted whiteness of his swollen clothes, seemed, when Flay located them, almost at arm's length. This proximity injected into Mr Flay's bones a sensation of exquisite horror. He stood fascinated at the pulpy baldness of the chef's cranium and as he stared a portion of its pale plush contracted in a spasm, dislodging an October fly. Nothing else moved. Mr Flay's eyes shifted for a moment and he saw a grindstone against the wall opposite. Beside it was a wooden stool. To his right, he saw two boxes placed about four feet apart. On either side of these wooden boxes two chalk lines ran roughly parallel to each other, and passed laterally along the room below Mr Flay. Nearing the left hand wall of the room they turned to the right, keeping the same space between them, but in their new direction they could not proceed for more than a few feet before being obstructed by the wall. At this point something had been written between them in chalk, and an arrow pointed towards the wall. The writing was hard to read, but after a moment Flay deciphered it as: '*To the Ninth stairs.*' This reading of the chalk came as a shock to Mr Flay, if only for the reason that the Ninth stairs were those by which Lord Sepulchrave's bedroom was reached from the floor below. His eyes returned swiftly to the rough globe of a head beneath him, but there was still no movement except perhaps the slight vibration of the chef's breathing.

Flay turned his eyes again to the right where the two boxes were standing, and he now realized that they represented either a door or an entrance of some sort from which led this chalked passageway before it turned to the right in the direction of the Ninth stairs. But it was upon a long sack which had at first failed to attract his attention that he now focused his eyes. It lay as though curled up immediately between and a little in advance of the two boxes. As he scrutinized it, something terrified him, something nameless, and which he had not yet had time to comprehend, but something from which he recoiled.

A movement below him plucked his eyes from the sack and a huge shape arose. It moved across the room, the whiteness of the enveloping clothes tinctured by the lime-green lamp above. It sat beside the grindstone. It held in its hand what seemed, in proportion to its bulk, a small weapon, but which was in reality a two-handed cleaver.

Swelter's feet began to move the treadles of the grindstone, and it began to spin in its circles. He spat upon it rapidly three or four times in succession, and with a quick movement slid the already razor-keen edge of the cleaver across the whirr of the stone. Doubling himself over the grindstone he peered at the shivering edge of the blade, and every now and then lifted it to his ear as though to listen for a thin and singing note to take flight from the unspeakable sharpness of the steel.

Then again he bent to his task and continued whetting the blade for several minutes before listening once more to the invisible edge. Flay began to lose contact with the reality of what he saw and his brain to drift into a dream, when he found that the chef was drawing himself upwards and travelling to that part of the wall where the chalk lines ended and where the arrow pointed to the Ninth staircase. Then he removed his shoes, and lifted his face for the first time so that Mr Flay could see the expression that seeped from it. His eyes were metallic and murderous, but the mouth hung open in a wide, fatuous smile.

Then followed what appeared to Flay an extraordinary dance, a grotesque ritual of the legs, and it was some time before he realized, as the cook advanced by slow, elaborate steps between the chalk lines, that he was practising tip-toeing with absolute silence. 'What's he practising that for?' thought Flay, watching the intense and painful concentration with which Swelter moved forward step by step, the cleaver shining in his right hand. Flay glanced again at the chalk arrow. 'He's come from the ninth staircase: he's turned left down the worn passage. There's no rooms right or left in the worn passage. I ought to know. *He's approaching the Room.*' In the darkness Flay turned as white as death.

The two boxes could represent only one thing – the doorposts of Lord Sepulchrave's bedroom. And the sack . . .

He watched the chef approach the symbol of himself asleep outside his master's room, curled up as he always was. By now the tardiness of the approach was unendingly slow. The feet in their thick soles would descend an inch at a time, and as they touched the ground the figure cocked his head of lard upon one side and his eyes rolled upwards as he listened for his own footfall. When within three feet of the sack the chef raised the cleaver in both hands and with his legs wide apart to give him a broader area of balance, edged his feet forward, one after the other, in little, noiseless shiftings. He had now judged the distance between himself and the sleeping emblem of his hate. Flay shut his eyes as he saw the cleaver rise in the air above the cumulous shoulder and the steel flared in the green light.

When he opened his eyes again, Abiatha Swelter was no longer by the sack, which appeared to be exactly as he had last seen it. He was at the chalk arrow again and was creeping forward as before. The horror that had filled Flay was aggravated by a question that had entered his mind. How did Swelter know that he slept with his chin at his knees? How did Swelter know his head always pointed to the east? Had he been observed during his sleeping hours? Flay pressed his face to the window for the last time. The dreadful repetition of the same murderous tip-toeing journey towards the sack, struck such a blow at the very centre of his nervous control that his knees gave way and he sank to his haunches on the barrel and wiped the back of his hand across his forehead. Suddenly his only thought was of escape – of escape from a region of the castle that could house such a fiend; to escape from that window of green light; and, scrambling from the cask, he stumbled into the mist-filled darkness and, never turning his head again to the scene of horror, made tracks for the archway from whence he had deviated so portentously from his course.

Once within the building he made directly for the main stairs and with gigantic paces climbed like a mantis to the floor in which Nannie Slagg's room was situated. It was some time before he came to her door, for the west wing in which she lived was on the opposite side of the building and necessitated a *détour* through many halls and corridors.

She was not in her room, and so he went at once to Lady Fuchsia's, where, as he had surmised, he found her sitting by the fire with little of the deference which he felt she should display in front of his Lordship's daughter.

It was when he had knocked at the door of the room with the knuckly single rap, that he had wakened Fuchsia from her sleep and startled the old nurse. Before he had knocked on the panels he had stood several minutes recovering his composure as best he could. In his mind emerged the picture of himself striking Swelter across the face with the chain, long ago as it seemed to him now in the Cool Room. For a moment he started sweating again and he wiped his hands down his sides before he entered. His throat felt very dry, and even before noticing Lady Fuchsia and the nurse he had seen the tray. That was what he wanted. Something to drink.

He left the room with a steadier step and, saying that he would await Mrs Slagg and Titus under the archway and escort her to the library, he left them.

REINTRODUCING THE TWINS

AT the same moment that Flay was leaving Fuchsia's bedroom, Steerpike was pushing back his chair from the supper table at the Prunesquallors', where he had enjoyed, along with the Doctor and his sister Irma, a very tender chicken, a salad and a flask of red wine; and now, the black coffee awaiting them on a little table by the fire, they were preparing to take up warmer and more permanent stations. Steerpike was the first to rise and he sidled around the table in time to remove the chair from behind Miss Prunesquallor and to assist her to her feet. She was perfectly able to take care of herself, in fact she had been doing it for years, but she leaned on his arm as she slowly assumed the vertical.

She was swathed to her ankles in maroon-coloured lace. That her gowns should cling to her as though they were an extra layer of skin was to her a salient point, in spite of the fact that of all people it was for her to hide those angular outcrops of bone with which Nature had endowed her and which in the case of the majority of women are modified by a considerate layer of fat.

Her hair was drawn back from her brow with an even finer regard for symmetry than on the night when Steerpike had first seen her, and the knot of grey twine which formed a culmination as hard as a boulder, a long way down the back of her neck, had not a single hair out of place.

The Doctor had himself noticed that she was spending more and more time upon her toilette, although it had at all times proved one of her most absorbing occupations; a paradox to the Doctor's mind which delighted him, for his sister was, even in his fraternal eyes, cruelly laden with the family features. As she approached her chair to the left of the fire, Steerpike removed his hand from her elbow, and, shifting back the Doctor's chair with his foot while Prunesquallor was drawing the blinds, pulled forward the sofa into a more favourable position in front of the fire.

'They don't meet – I said "They don't *meet*",' said Irma Prunesquallor, pouring out the coffee.

How she could see anything at all, let alone whether they met or not, through her dark glasses was a mystery.

Dr Prunesquallor, already on his way back to his chair, on the padded arms of which his coffee was balancing, stopped and folded his hands at his chin.

'To what are you alluding, my dear? Are you speaking of a brace of spirits? ha ha ha! – twin souls searching for consummation, each in the other? Ha ha! ha ha ha! Or are you making reference to matters more terrestrial? Enlighten me, my love.'

'Nonsense,' said his sister. 'Look at the curtains. I said: "Look at the curtains".'

Dr Prunesquallor swung about.

'To me,' he said, 'they look exactly like curtains. In fact, they *are* curtains. Both of them. A curtain on the left, my love, and a curtain on the right. Ha ha! I'm absolutely certain they are!'

Irma, hoping that Steerpike was looking at her, laid down her coffee-cup.

'What happens in the *middle*, I said: what happens right down the *middle*?' Her pointed nose warmed, for she sensed victory.

'There is a great yearning one for the other. A fissure of impalpable night divides them. Irma, my dear sister, there is a lacuna.'

'Then *kill* it,' said Irma, and sank back into her chair. She glanced at Steerpike, but he had apparently taken no notice of the conversation and she was disappointed. He was leaning back into one corner of the couch, his legs crossed, his hands curled around the coffee-cup as though to feel its warmth, and his eyes were peering into the fire. He was evidently far away.

When the Doctor had joined the curtains together with great deliberation and stood back to assure himself that the Night was satisfactorily excluded from the room, he seated himself, but no sooner had he done so than there was a jangling at the door-bell which continued until the cook had scraped the pastry from his hands, removed his apron and made his way to the front door.

Two female voices were speaking at the same time.

'Only for a moment, only for a moment,' they said. 'Just passing – On our way home – Only for a moment – Tell him we won't stay – No, of course not; we won't stay. Of course not. Oh no – Yes, yes. Just a twinkling – only a twinkling.'

But for the fact that it would have been impossible for one voice to wedge so many words into so short a space of time and to speak so many of them simultaneously, it would have been difficult to believe that it was not the voice of a single individual, so continuous and uniform appeared the flat colour of the sound.

Prunesquallor cast up his hands to the ceiling and behind the convex lenses of his spectacles his eyes revolved in their orbits.

The voices that Steerpike now heard in the passage were unfamiliar to his quick ear. Since he had been with the Prunesquallors he had taken advantage of all his spare time and had, he thought, run to earth all the main figures of Gormenghast. There were few secrets hidden from him, for he had that scavenger-like faculty of acquiring unashamedly and from an infinite variety of sources, snatches of knowledge which he kept neatly at the back of his brain and used to his own advantage as opportunity offered.

When the twins, Cora and Clarice, entered the room together, he wondered whether the red wine had gone to his head. He had neither seen them before nor anything like them. They were dressed in their inevitable purple.

Dr Prunesquallor bowed elegantly. 'Your Ladyships,' he said, 'we are more than honoured. We are really very much more than honoured, ha ha ha!' He whinnied his appreciation. 'Come right along, my dear ladies, come right the way in. Irma, my dear, we have been doubly lucky in our privileges. Why "doubly" you say to yourself, why "doubly"? Because, O sister, they have *both* come, ha ha ha! Very much so, very much so.'

Prunesquallor, who knew from experience that only a fraction of what anyone said ever entered the brains of the twins, permitted himself a good deal of latitude in his conversation, mixing with a certain sycophancy remarks for his own amusement which could never have been made to persons more astute than the twins.

Irma had come forward, her iliac crest reflecting a streak of light.

'Very charmed, your Ladyships; I said "very, very charmed".'

She attempted to curtsey, but her dress was too tight.

'You know my sister, of course, of course, of course. Will you have coffee? Of course you will, and a little wine? Naturally – or what would you prefer?'

But both the Doctor and his sister found that the Ladies Cora and Clarice had not been paying the slightest attention but had been staring at Steerpike more in the manner of a wall staring at a man than a man staring at a wall.

Steerpike in a well-cut uniform of black cloth, advanced to the sisters and bowed. 'Your Ladyships,' he said, 'I am delighted to have the honour of being beneath the same roof. It is an intimacy that I shall never forget.' And then, as though he were ending a letter – 'I am your very humble servant,' he added.

Clarice turned herself to Cora, but kept her eyes on Steerpike.

'He says he's glad he's under the same roof as us,' she said.

'Under the same roof,' echoed Cora. 'He's very glad of it.'

'Why?' said Clarice emptily. 'What difference does it make about the roof?'

'It couldn't make any difference whatever the roof's like,' said her sister.

'I like roofs,' said Clarice; 'they are something I like more than most things because they are on top of the houses they cover, and Cora and I like being over the tops of things because we love power, and that's why we are both fond of roofs.'

'That's why,' Cora continued. 'That's the reason. Anything that's on top of something else is what we like, unless it is someone we don't like who's on top of something we are pleased with like ourselves. We're not allowed to be on top, except that our own room is high, oh, so high up in the castle wall, with our Tree – our own Tree that grows from the wall, that is so much more important than anything Gertrude has.'

'Oh yes,' said Clarice; 'she hasn't anything as important as that. But she steals our birds.'

She turned her expressionless eyes to Cora, who met them as though she were her sister's reflection. It may be that between them they recognized shades of expression in each other's faces, but it is certain that no one else, however keen his eyesight, could have detected the slightest change in the muscles that presumably governed the lack of expressions of their faces. Evidently this reference to stolen birds was the reason why they came nearer to each other so that their shoulders touched. It was obvious that their sorrow was conjoined.

Dr Prunesquallor had, during all this, been trying to shepherd them into the chairs by the fire, but to no avail. They had no thought for others when their minds were occupied. The room, the persons around them ceased to exist. They had only enough room for one thought at a time.

But now that there was a sudden lull the Doctor, reinforced this time by Irma, managed to shift the twins by means of a mixture of deference and force and to get them established by the fire. Steerpike, who had vanished from the room, now returned with another pot of coffee and two more cups. It was this sort of thing that pleased Irma, and she tilted her head on its neck and turned up the corners of her mouth into something approaching the coy.

But when the coffee was passed to the twins they did not want it. One, taking her cue from the other, decided that she, or the other one, or possibly both, or neither, did not want it.

Would they have anything to drink? Cognac, sherry, brandy, a liqueur, cherry wine . . . ?

They shook their heads profoundly.

'We only came for a moment,' said Cora.

'Because we were passing,' said Clarice. 'That's the only reason.'

But although they refused on those grounds to indulge in a drink of any sort, yet they gave no indication of being in a hurry to go, nor had they for a long time anything to say, but were quite content to sit and stare at Steerpike.

But after a long interval, halfway through which the Doctor and his sister had given up all attempts to make conversation, Cora turned her face to Steerpike.

'Boy,' she said, 'what are you here for?'

'Yes,' echoed Clarice, 'that's what we want to know.'

'I want,' said Steerpike, choosing his words, 'only your gracious patronage, your Ladyships. Only your favour.'

The twins turned their faces towards each other and then at the same moment they returned them to Steerpike.

'Say that again,' said Cora.

'All of it,' said Clarice.

'Only your gracious patronage, your Ladyships. Only your favour. That is what I want.'

'Well, we'll give it you,' said Clarice. But for the first time the sisters were at variance for a moment.

'Not yet,' said Cora. 'It's too soon for that.'

'Much too soon,' agreed Clarice. 'It's not time yet to give him any favour at all. What's his name?'

This was addressed to Steerpike.

'His name is Steerpike,' was the youth's reply.

Clarice leaned forward in her chair and whispered to Cora across the hearthrug: 'His name is Steerpike.'

'Why not?' said her sister flatly. 'It will do.'

Steerpike was, of course, alive with ideas and projects. These two half-witted women were a gift. That they should be the sisters of Lord Sepulchrave was of tremendous strategic value. They would prove an advance on the Prunesquallors, if not intellectually at any rate socially, and that at the moment was what mattered. And in any case, the lower the mentality of his employers the more scope for his own projects.

That one of them had said his name 'Steerpike' would 'do' had interested him. Did it imply that they wished to see more of him? That would simplify matters considerably.

His old trick of shameless flattery seemed to him the best line to take at this critical stage. Later on, he would see. But it was another remark that had appealed to his opportunist sense even more keenly, and that was the reference to Lady Groan.

These ridiculous twins had apparently a grievance, and the object of it was the Countess. This when examined further might lead in many directions. Steerpike was beginning to enjoy himself in his own dry, bloodless way.

Suddenly as in a flash he remembered two tiny figures the size of halma players, dressed in the same crude purple. Directly he had seen them enter the room an echo was awakened somewhere in his subconscious, and although he had put it aside as irrelevant to the present requirements, it now came back with redoubled force and he recalled where he had seen the two minute replicas of the twins.

He had seen them across a great space of air and across a distance of towers and high walls. He had seen them upon the lateral trunk of a dead tree in the summer, a tree that grew out at right angles from a high and windowless wall.

Now he realized why they had said 'Our Tree that grows from the wall that is so much more important than anything Gertrude has.' But then Clarice had added: 'But she steals our birds.' What did that imply? He had, of course, often watched the Countess from points of vantage with her birds or her white cats. That was something he must investigate further. Nothing must be let fall from his mind unless it were first turned to and fro and proved to be useless.

Steerpike bent forward, the tips of his fingers together. 'Your Ladyships,' he said, 'are you enamoured of the feathered tribe? – Their beaks, their feathers, and the way they fly?'

'What?' said Cora.

'Are you in love with birds, your Ladyships?' repeated Steerpike, more simply.

'What?' said Clarice.

Steerpike hugged himself inside. If they could be as stupid as this, he could surely do anything he liked with them.

'Birds,' he said more loudly; 'do you like them?'

'What birds?' said Cora. 'What do you want to know for?'

'We weren't talking about birds,' said Clarice unexpectedly. 'We hate them.'

'They're such silly things,' Cora ended.

'Silly and stupid; we hate them,' said Clarice.

'*Avis, avis*, you are undone, undone!' came Prunesquallor's voice. 'Your day is over. Oh, ye hordes of heaven! the treetops shall be emptied of their chorus and only clouds ride over the blue heaven.'

Prunesquallor leaned forward and tapped Irma on the knee.

'Pretty pleasing,' he said, and showed her all his brilliant teeth together. 'What did *you* think, my riotous one?'

'Nonsense!' said Irma, who was sitting on the couch with Steerpike. Feeling that as the hostess she had so far this evening had very little opportunity of exhibiting what she, and she alone, felt was her outstanding talent in that direction, she bent her dark glasses upon Cora and then upon Clarice and tried to speak to both of them at once.

'Birds,' she said, with something arch in her voice and manner, 'birds *depend* – don't you think, my dear Ladyships – I said birds *depend* a lot upon their eggs. Do you not agree with me? I said do you not agree with me?'

'We're going now,' said Cora, getting up.

'Yes, we've been here too long. Much too long. We've got a lot of sewing to do. We sew beautifully, both of us.'

'I am sure you do,' said Steerpike. 'May I have the privilege of appreciating your craft at some future date when it is convenient for you?'

'We do embroidery as well,' said Cora, who had risen and had approached Steerpike.

Clarice came up to her sister's side and they both looked at him. 'We do a lot of needlework, but nobody sees it. Nobody is interested in us, you see. We only have two servants. We used –'

'That's all,' said Cora. 'We used to have hundreds when we were younger. Our father gave us hundreds of servants. We were of great – of great –'

'Consequence,' volunteered her sister. 'Yes, that's exactly what it was that we were. Sepulchrave was always so dreamy and miserable, but he did play with us sometimes; so we did what we liked. But now he doesn't ever want to see us.'

'He thinks he's so wise,' said Cora. 'But he's no cleverer than we are.'

'He's not as clever,' said Clarice.

'Nor is Gertrude,' they said almost at the same moment.

'She stole your birds, didn't she?' said Steerpike, winking at Prune-squallor.

'How did you know?' they said, advancing on him a step further.

'Everyone knows, your Ladyships. Everyone in the castle knows,' replied Steerpike, winking this time at Irma.

The twins held hands at once and drew close together. What Steerpike had said had sunk in and was making a serious impression on them. They had thought it was only a private grievance, that Gertrude had lured away their birds from the Room of Roots which they had taken so long preparing. But everyone knew! Everyone knew!

They turned to leave the room, and the Doctor opened his eyes, for he had almost fallen asleep with one elbow on the central table and his hand propping his head. He arose to his feet but could do nothing more elegant than to crook a finger, for he was too tired. His sister stood beside him creaking a little, and it was Steerpike who opened the door for them and offered to accompany them to their room. As they passed through the hall he removed his cape from a hook. Flinging it over his shoulders with a flourish he buttoned it at the neck. The cloak accentuated the highness of his shoulders, and as he drew its folds about him, the spareness of his body.

The aunts seemed to accept the fact that he was leaving the house with them, although they had not replied when he had asked their permission to escort them to their rooms.

With an extraordinary gallantry he shepherded them across the quadrangle.

'Everybody knows, you said.' Cora's voice was so empty of feeling and yet so plaintive that it must have awakened a sympathetic response in anyone with a more kindly heart than Steerpike's.

'That's what you said,' repeated Clarice.

'But what can we do? We can't do anything to show what we could do if only we had the power we haven't got,' said Clarice lucidly. 'We used to have hundreds of servants.'

'You shall have them back,' said Steerpike. 'You shall have them all back. New ones. Better ones. Obedient ones. I shall arrange it. They shall work for you, *through* me. Your floor of the castle shall be alive again. You shall be supreme. Give me the administration to handle, your Ladyships, and I will have them dancing to your tune – whatever it is – they'll dance to it.'

'But what about Gertrude?'

'Yes, what about Gertrude,' came their flat voices.

'Leave everything to me. I will secure your rights for you. You are Lady Cora and Lady Clarice, Lady Clarice and Lady Cora. You must not forget that. No one must be allowed to forget it.'

'Yes, that's what must happen,' said Cora.

'Everyone must think of who we are,' said Clarice.

'And never stop thinking about it,' said Cora.

'Or we will use our power,' said Clarice.

'Meanwhile, I will take you to your rooms, dear ladies. You must trust me. You must not tell anyone what we've said. Do you both understand?'

'And we'll get our birds back from Gertrude.'

Steerpike took them by the elbows as they climbed the stairs.

'Lady Cora,' he said, 'you must try to concentrate on what I am saying to you. If you pay attention to me I will restore you to your places of eminence in Gormenghast from which Lady Gertrude has dethroned you.'

'Yes.'

'Yes.'

The voices showed no animation, but Steerpike realized that only by *what* they said, not by *how* they said it, could he judge whether their brains reacted to his probing.

He also knew when to stop. In the fine art of deceit and personal advancement as in any other calling this is the hallmark of the master. He knew that when he reached their door he would itch to get inside and to see what sort of appointments they had and what on earth they meant by their Room of Roots. But he also knew to a nicety the time to slacken the rein. Such creatures as the aunts for all their slowness of intellect had within them the Groan blood which might at any moment, were a false step to be made, flare up and undo a month of strategy. So Steerpike left them at the door of their apartments and bowed almost to the ground. Then as he retired along the oak passage, and was turning a corner to the left he glanced back at the door where he had left the twins. They were still looking after him, as motionless as a pair of waxen images.

He would not visit them tomorrow, for it would do them good to spend a day of apprehension and of silly discussion between themselves. In the evening they would begin to get nervous and need consoling, but he would not knock at the door until the following morning. Meanwhile he would pick up as much information as he could about them and their tendencies.

Instead of crossing over to the Doctor's house when he had reached the quadrangle he decided he would take a stroll across the lawns and perhaps around by the terraces to the moat, for the sky had emptied itself of cloud and was glittering fiercely with a hundred thousand stars.

'THE FIR-CONES'

THE wind had dropped, but the air was bitterly cold and Steerpike was glad of his cape. He had turned the collar up and it stood stiffly above the level of his ears. He seemed to be bound for somewhere in particular, and was not simply out for a nocturnal stroll. That peculiar half-walking, half-running gait was always with him. It appeared that he was eternally upon some secret mission, as indeed from his own viewpoint he generally was.

He passed into deep shadows beneath the arch, and then as though he were a portion of that inky darkness that had awakened and disengaged itself from the main body, he reappeared beyond the archway in the half light.

For a long time he kept close to the castle walls, moving eastwards continually. His first project of making a *détour* by way of the lawns and the terraces where the Countess walked before breakfast had been put aside, for now that he had started walking he felt an enjoyment in moving alone, absolutely alone, under the starlight. The Prunesquallors would not wait up for him. He had his own key to the front door and, as on previous nights, after late wanderings he would pour himself out a nightcap and perhaps enjoy some of the Doctor's tobacco in his little stubby pipe before he retired.

Or he might, as he had so often done before during the night, resort to the dispensary and amuse himself by compounding potions with lethal possibilities. It was always to the shelf of poisons that he turned at once when he entered and to the dangerous powders.

He had filled four small glass tubes with the most virulent of these concoctions, and had removed them to his own room. He had soon absorbed all that the Doctor, whose knowledge was considerable, had divulged on the subject. Under his initial guidance he had, from poisonous weeds found in the vicinity, distilled a number of original and death-dealing pastes. To the Doctor these experiments were academically amusing.

Or on retiring to the Prunesquallors' he might take down one of the Doctor's many books and read, for these days a passion to accumulate knowledge of any and every kind consumed him; but only as a means to an end. He must know all things, for only so might he have, when situations arose in the future, a full pack of cards to play from. He imagined to himself occasions when the conversation of one from whom he foresaw advancement might turn to astronomy, metaphysics, history, chemistry, or literature, and he realized that to be able to drop into the argument a lucid and exact thought, an opinion based on what might *appear* to be a life-time study, would instantaneously gain more for him than an hour of beating about the bush and waiting until the conversation turned upon what lay within his scope of experience.

He foresaw himself in control of men. He had, along with his faculty of making swift and bold decisions, an unending patience. As he read in the evenings after the Doctor and Irma had retired for the night, he would polish the long, narrow steel of the swordstick blade which he had glimpsed and which he had, a week later, retrieved from the pile of ancient weapons in the chill hall. When he had first drawn it from the pile it had been badly tarnished, but with the skilful industry and patience with which he applied himself to whatever he undertook, it had now become a slim length of white steel. He had after an hour's hunting found the hollow stick which was screwed into the innocent-looking hilt by a single turn of the wrist.

Whether on his return he would apply himself to the steel of his swordstick, and to the book on heraldry which he had nearly completed, or whether in the dispensary he would grind in the mortar, with the red oil, that feathery green powder with which he was experimenting, or whether he would be too tired to do anything but empty a glass of cognac and climb the stairs to his bedroom, he did not know, nor, for that matter, was he looking so short a way ahead. He was turning over in his mind as he walked briskly onwards not only every remark which he could remember the twins having let fall during the evening, but the trend of the questions which he proposed to put to them on the evening of the day after tomorrow.

With his mind working like an efficient machine, he thought out probable moves and parries, although he knew that in any dealings with the aunts the illogical condition of their brains made any surmise or scheming on his part extraordinarily difficult. He was working with a low-grade material, but one which contained an element which natures more elevated lack – the incalculable.

By now he had reached the most eastern corner of the central body of the castle. Away to his left he could distinguish the high walls of the west wing as they emerged from the ivy-blackened, sunset-facing precipice of masonry that shut off the northern halls of Gormenghast from the evening's light. The Tower of Flints could only be recognized as a narrow section of the sky the shape of a long black ruler standing upon its end, the sky about it was crowded with the stars.

It occurred to him as he saw the Tower that he had never investigated the buildings which were, he had heard, continued on its further side. It was too late now for such an expedition and he was thinking of making a wide circle on the withered lawns which made good walking at this corner of the castle, when he saw a dim light approaching him.

Glancing about, he saw within a few yards the black shapes of stunted bushes. Behind one of these he squatted and watched the light, which he recognized now as a lantern, coming nearer and nearer. It seemed that the figure would pass within a few feet of him, and peering over his shoulder to see in what direction the lantern was moving, he realized that he was immediately between the light and the Tower of Flints. What on earth could anyone want at the Tower of Flints on a cold night? Steerpike was intrigued. He dragged his cape well over himself so that only his eyes were exposed to the night air. Then, remaining as still as a crouching cat, he listened to the feet approaching.

As yet the body of whoever it was that carried the lantern had not detached itself from the darkness, but Steerpike, listening intently, heard now not only the long footsteps but the regular sound of a dry stick being broken. 'Flay,' said Steerpike to himself. But what was that other noise? Between the regular sounds of the paces and the click of the knee joints a third, a quicker, less positive sound, came to his ears.

Almost at the same moment as he recognized it to be the pattering of tiny feet, he saw, emerging from the night, the unmistakable silhouettes of Flay and Mrs Slagg.

Soon the crunching of Flay's footsteps appeared to be almost on top of him, and Steerpike, motionless as the shrub he crouched beneath, saw the straggling height of Lord Sepulchrave's servant hastily pass above him, and as he did so a cry broke out. A tremor ran down Steerpike's spine, for if there was anything that worried him it was the supernatural. The cry, it seemed, was that of some bird, perhaps of a seagull, but was so close as to disprove that explanation. There were no birds about that night nor, indeed, were they ever to be heard at that hour, and it was with some relief that he heard Nannie Slagg whisper nervously in the darkness:

'There, there, my only . . . It won't be long, my little Lordship dear . . . it won't be long now. Oh, my poor heart! why must it be at night?' She seemed to raise her head from the little burden she carried and to gaze up at the lofty figure who strode mechanically beside her; but there was no answer.

'Things become interesting,' said Steerpike to himself. 'Lordships, Flays and Slaggs, all heading for the Tower of Flints.'

When they were almost swallowed into the darkness, Steerpike rose to his feet and flexed his cape-shrouded legs to get the stiffness from them, and then, keeping the sound of Mr Flay's knees safely within earshot, he followed them silently.

Poor Mrs Slagg was utterly exhausted by the time they arrived at the library, for she had consistently refused to allow Flay to carry Titus, for he had, much against his better judgement, offered to do so when he saw how she was continually stumbling over the irregularities of the ground, and when, among the conifers how she caught her feet in the pine roots and ground creepers.

The cold air had thoroughly wakened Titus, and although he did not cry it was obvious that he was disconcerted by this unusual adventure in the dark. When Flay knocked at the door and they entered the library, he began to whimper and struggle in the nurse's arms.

Flay retired to the darkness of his corner, where there was presumably some chair for him to sit on. All he said was: 'I've brought them, Lordship.' He usually left out the 'your' as being unnecessary for him as Lord Sepulchrave's primary attendant.

'So I see,' said the Earl of Groan, advancing down the room, 'I have disturbed you, nurse, have I not? It is cold outside. I have just been out to get these for him.'

He led Nannie to the far side of the table. On the carpet in the lamplight lay scattered a score of fir-cones, each one with its wooden petals undercut with the cast shadow of the petal above it.

Mrs Slagg turned her tired face to Lord Sepulchrave. For once she said the right thing. 'Are they for his little Lordship, sir?' she queried. 'Oh, he will love them, won't you, my only?'

'Put him among them. I want to talk to you,' said the Earl. 'Sit down.'

Mrs Slagg looked around for a chair and seeing none turned her eyes pathetically towards his Lordship, who was now pointing at the floor in a tired way. Titus, whom she had placed amongst the cones, was alternately turning them over in his fingers and sucking them.

'It's all right, I've washed them in rainwater,' said Lord Groan. 'Sit on the floor, nurse, sit on the floor.' Without waiting, he himself sat upon the edge of the table, his feet crossed before him, his hands upon the marble surface at his side.

'Firstly,' he said, 'I have had you come this way to tell you that I have decided upon a family gathering here in a week's time. I want you to inform those concerned. They will be surprised. That does not matter. They will come. You will tell the Countess. You will tell Fuchsia. You will also inform their Ladyships Cora and Clarice.'

Steerpike, who had opened the door inch by inch, had crept up a stairway he had found immediately to his left. He had shut the door quietly behind him and tiptoed up to a stone gallery which ran around the building. Conveniently for him it was in the darkest shadow, and as he leaned against the bookshelves which lined the walls and watched the proceedings below, he rubbed the palms of his hands together silently.

He wondered where Flay had got to, for as far as he could see there was no other way out save by the main doorway, which was barred and bolted. It seemed to him that he must, like himself, be standing or sitting quietly in the shadows, and not knowing in what part of the building that might be, he kept absolute silence.

'At eight o'clock in the evening, I shall be awaiting him and them, for you must tell them I have in my mind a breakfast that shall be in honour of my son.'

As he said these words, in his rich, melancholy voice, poor Mrs Slagg, unable to bear the insufferable depression of his spirit, began to clutch her wrinkled hands together. Even Titus seemed to sense the sadness which flowed through the slow, precise words of his father. He forgot the fir-cones and began to cry.

'You will bring my son Titus in his christening robes and will have with you the crown of the direct heir to Gormenghast. Without Titus the castle would have no future when I am gone. As his nurse, I must ask you to remember to instil into his veins, from the very first, a love for his birthplace and his heritage, and a respect for all of the written and unwritten laws of the place of his fathers.

'I will speak to them, much against my own peace of spirit: I will speak to them of this and of much more that is in my mind. At the Breakfast, of which the details will be discussed on this same evening of next week, he shall be honoured and toasted. It shall be held in the Refectory.'

'But he is only two months old, the little thing,' broke in Nannie in a tear-choked voice. 'There is no time to lose, nevertheless,' answered the Earl. 'And now, my poor old woman, why are you crying so bitterly? It is autumn. The leaves are falling from the trees like burning tears – the wind howls. Why must you mimic them?'

Her old eyes gazed at him and were filmed. Her mouth quivered. 'I am so tired, sir,' she said.

'Then lie down, good woman, lie down,' said Lord Sepulchrave. 'It has been a long walk for you. Lie down.'

Mrs Slagg found no comfort in lying upon her back on the huge library floor with the Earl of Groan talking to her from above in phrases that meant nothing to her.

She gathered Titus to her side and stared at the ceiling, her tears running into her dry mouth. Titus was very cold and had begun to shiver.

'Now, let me see my son,' said his Lordship slowly. 'My son Titus. Is it true that he is ugly?'

Nannie scrambled to her feet and lifted Titus in her arms.

'He is not ugly, your Lordship,' she said, her voice quavering. 'My little one is lovely.'

'Let me see him. Hold him up, nurse; hold him up to the light. Ah! that is better. He has improved,' said Lord Sepulchrave. 'How old is he?'

'Nearly three months,' said Nannie Slagg. 'Oh, my weak heart! he is nearly three months old.'

'Well, well, good woman, that is all. I have talked too much tonight. That is all that I wanted – to see my son, and to tell you to inform the Family of my desire to have them here at eight o'clock today week. The Prunesquallors had better come as well. I will inform Sourdust myself. Do you understand?'

'Yes, sir,' said Nannie, already making for the door. 'I will tell them, sir. Oh, my poor heart, how tired I am!'

'Flay!' said Lord Sepulchrave, 'take the nurse back to her room. You need not return tonight. I shall have left in four hours' time. Have my room prepared and the lanthorn on my bedside table. You may go.'

Flay, who had emerged into the lamplight, nodded his head, relit the wick of the lamp, and then followed Nannie Slagg out of the door and up the steps to the starlight. This time he took no heed of her expostulations, but taking Titus from her, placed him carefully into one of his capacious jacket pockets, and then, lifting the tiny struggling woman in his arms, marched solemnly through the woods to the castle.

Steerpike followed, deep in thought, and did not even trouble to keep them in sight.

Lord Sepulchrave, lighting a candle, climbed the staircase by the door and, moving along the wooden balcony, came at last to a shelf of dusty volumes. He blew the grey pollen from the vellum spine of one which he tilted forward from the rest with his index finger and then, turning over a page or two, near the beginning, made his way around the balcony again and down the stairs.

When he had reached his seat he leaned back and his head fell forward on his chest. The book was still in his hand. His sorrowful eyes wandered about the room from under the proud bone of his brow, until they fell at last upon the scattered fir-cones.

A sudden uncontrollable gust of anger seized him. He had been childish in gathering them. Titus had not in any case derived any amusement from them.

It is strange that even in men of much learning and wisdom there can be an element of the infantile. It may be that it was not the cones themselves that angered him, but that they acted in some way as a reminder of his failures. He flung the book from him, and then immediately retrieved it, smoothing its sides with his shaking hands. He was too proud and too melancholy to unbend and be the father of the boy in anything but fact; he would not cease to isolate himself. He had done more than he expected himself to do. At the breakfast which he had envisaged he would toast the heir to Gormenghast. He would drink to the Future, to Titus, his only son. That was all.

He sat back again in the chair, but he could not read.

KEDA AND RANTEL

WHEN Keda came back to her people the cacti were dripping with the rain. The wind was westerly, and above the blurred outline of the Twisted Woods the sky was choked with crumpled rags. Keda stood for a moment and watched the dark rulers of the rain slanting steadily from the ragged edge of the clouds to the ragged edge of the woods. Behind the opaque formations the sun was hidden as it sank, so that but little light was reflected from the empty sky above her.

This was the darkness she knew of. She breathed it in. It was the late autumn darkness of her memories. There was here no taint of those shadows which had oppressed her spirit within the walls of Gormenghast. Here, once again an Outer dweller, she stretched her arms above her head in her liberation.

'I am free,' she said. 'I am home again.' But directly she had said these words she knew that it was not so. She was home, yes, among the dwellings where she was born. Here beside her, like an ancient friend, stood the gaunt cactus, but of the friends of her childhood who were left? Who was there to whom she could go? She did not ask for someone in whom she could confide. She only wished that she might go unhesitatingly to one who would ask no questions, and to whom she need not speak.

Who was there? And against this question arose the answer which she feared: There were the two men.

Suddenly the fear that had swept her died and her heart leapt with inexplicable joy and as the clouds above her in the sky had rolled away from their zenith, those that had choked her heart broke apart and left her with an earthless elation and a courage that she could not understand. She walked on in the gathering dusk and, passing by the empty tables and benches that shone unnaturally in the darkness with the film of the rain still upon them, she came at last to the periphery of the mud dwellings.

It seemed at first as though the narrow lanes were deserted. The mud dwellings, rising usually to a height of about eight feet, faced each other across dark lanes like gullies, and all but met overhead. At this hour in the lanes it would have been pitch dark if it had not been for the dwellers' custom of hanging lamps above the doors of all their houses, and lighting them at sunset.

Keda had turned several corners before she came upon the first sign of life. A dwarf dog, of that ubiquitous breed that was so often to be seen slinking along the mud lanes, ran past Keda on little mangy legs, hugging the wall as he ran. She smiled a little. Since childhood she had been taught to despise these scavenging and stunted curs, but as she watched it slink past her she did not despise it, but in the sudden gladness that had filled her heart she knew of it only as a part of her own being, her all-embracing love and harmony. The dog-urchin had stopped a few yards after passing her and was sitting up on its mangy haunches and scratching with one of its hind legs at an itch beneath its ear. Keda felt her heart was breaking with a love so universal that it drew into its fiery atmosphere all things because they *were*; the evil, the good, the rich, the poor, the ugly, the beautiful, and the scratching of this little yellowish hound.

She knew these lanes so well that the darkness did not hinder her progress. The desertion of the mud lanes was, she knew, natural to that hour of evening when the majority of the dwellers would be huddled over their root fires. It was for this reason that she had left the castle so late on her homeward journey. There was a custom among the dwellers that when passing each other at night they should move their heads into the light of the nearest door-lamp and then, as soon as they had observed one another, continue upon their journeys. There was no need for them to show any expression; the chances were that the mutual recognition of friends would be infrequent. The rivalry between the families and the various schools of carving was relentless and bitter, and it would often happen that enemies would find each other's features in this way within a few feet of their own, lit by these hanging lamps; but this custom was rigorously observed – to stare for a moment and pass on.

It had been Keda's hope that she would be able to reach her house, the house which was hers through the death of her old husband, without having to move into the lamplight and be recognized by a passing Dweller, but now she did not mind. It seemed to her that the beauty that filled her was keener than the edge of a sword and as sure a protection against calumny and gossip, the jealousies and underground hatreds which she had once feared.

What was it that had come over her? she wondered. A recklessness alien to the whole quietness of her nature startled but fascinated her. This, the very moment which she had anticipated would fill her with anxiety – when the problems, to escape which she had taken refuge in the castle, would lower themselves over her like an impenetrable fog and frighten her – was now an evening of leaves and flame, a night of ripples.

She walked on. From behind the rough wooden doors of many of the dwellings she could hear the heavy voices of those within. She now came to the long lane that led directly up to the sheer outer wall of Gormenghast. This lane was a little broader than most, being about nine feet wide and broadening at times to almost twelve. It was the highway of the Dwellers, and the daily rendezvous for groups of the Bright Carvers. Old women and men would sit at the doors, or hobble on their errands, and the children play in the dust in the shifting shadow of the great Wall that edged by degrees along the street until by evening it had swallowed the long highway and the lamps were lit. Upon the flat roof of many of the dwellings a carving would be placed, and on evenings of sunset the easterly line of those wooden forms would smoulder and burn and the westerly line against the light in the sky would stand in jet-black silhouette, showing the sweeping outlines and the harsh angles which the Dwellers delighted in contrasting.

These carvings were now lost in the upper darkness above the door lamps, and Keda, remembering them as she walked, peered in vain for a glimpse of them against the sky.

Her home did not lie in this highway but at the corner of a little mud square where only the most venerable and revered of the Bright Carvers were permitted to settle. In the centre of this square stood the pride of the mud dwellers – a carving, some fourteen feet high, which had been hewn several hundred years before. It was the only one of that carver's works which the dwellers possessed although several pieces from his hand were within the castle walls, in the Hall of the Bright Carvings. There were diverse opinions as to who he may have been, but that he was the finest of all the carvers was never disputed. This work, which was repainted each year in its original colours, was of a horse and rider. Hugely stylized and very simple, the bulk of rhythmic wood dominated the dark square. The horse was of the purest grey and its neck was flung backwards in a converse arch so that its head faced the sky, and the coils of its white mane were gathered like frozen foam about the nape of its strained neck and over the knees of the rider, who sat draped in a black cape. On this cape were painted dark crimson stars. He was very upright, but his arms and hands, in contrast to the vitality of the grey and muscular neck of the horse, hung limply at his sides. His head was very sharply cut with the chisel and was as white as the mane, only the lips and the hair relieving the deathlike mask, the former a pale coral and the latter a dark chestnut brown. Rebellious children were sometimes brought by their mothers to see this sinister figure and were threatened with his disfavour should they continue in their wrong-doing. This carving had a terror for them, but to their parents it was a work of extraordinary vitality and beauty of form, and with a richness of mysterious mood the power of which in a work was one of their criteria of excellence.

This carving had come into Keda's mind as she approached that turning from the highway which led to the mud square, when she heard the sound of feet behind her. Ahead, the road lay silent, the door lamps lighting faintly small areas of the earth below them, but giving no intimation of any passing figure. Away to the left, beyond the mud square, the sudden barking of a dog sounded in her ears, and she became conscious of her own footsteps as she listened to those that were overtaking her.

She was within a few yards of one of the door lamps and knowing that were she to pass it before the approaching figure had done so, then both she and the unknown man would have to walk together in the darkness until the next lamp was reached, when the ritual of scanning each other's features would be observed, Keda slackened her pace, so that the observance might be more rapidly disposed of and the follower, whoever he was, might proceed on his way.

She stopped as she came to the light, nor in doing so and waiting was there anything unusual, for such was the not infrequent habit of those who were nearing the lamps and was, in fact, considered an act of politeness. She moved through the glow of the lamp so that on turning about the rays would illumine her face, and the approaching figure would then both see her and be seen the more easily.

In passing under the lamp the light wavered on her dark brown hair lighting its highest strands almost to the colour of barley, and her body, though full and rounded, was upright and lithe, and this evening, under the impact of her new emotion had in it a buoyancy, an excitement, that through the eyes attacked the one who followed.

The evening was electric and unreal, and yet perhaps, thought Keda, this *is* reality and my past life has been a meaningless dream. She knew that the footsteps in the darkness which were now only a few yards away were a part of an evening she would not forget and which she seemed to have enacted long ago, or had foreseen. She knew that when the footsteps ceased and she turned to face the one who followed she would find that he was Rantel, the more fiery, the more awkward of the two who loved her.

She turned and he was standing there.

For a long time they stood. About them the impenetrable blackness of the night shut them in as though they were in a confined space, like a hall, with the lamp overhead.

She smiled, her mature, compassionate lips hardly parting. Her eyes moved over his face – over the dark mop of his hair, his powerful jutting brow, and the shadows of his eyes that stared as though fixed in their sockets, at her own. She saw his high cheekbones and the sides of his face that tapered to his chin. His mouth was drawn finely and his shoulders were powerful. Her breast rose and fell, and she was both weak and strong. She could feel the blood flowing within her and she felt that she must die or break forth into leaves and flowers. It was not passion that she felt: not the passion of the body, though that was there, but rather an exultation, a reaching for life, for the whole of the life of which she was capable, and in that life which she but dimly divined was centred love, the love for a man. She was not in love with Rantel: she was in love with what he meant to her as someone she *could* love.

He moved forward in the light so that his face was darkened to her and only the top of his ruffled hair shone like wire.

'Keda,' he whispered.

She took his hand. 'I have come back.'

He felt her nearness; he held her shoulders in his hands.

'You have come back,' he said as though repeating a lesson. 'Ah, Keda – is this you? You went away. Every night I have watched for you.' His hands shook on her shoulders. 'You went away,' he said.

'You have followed me?' said Keda. 'Why did you not speak to me by the rocks?'

'I wanted to,' he said, 'but I could not.'

'Oh, why not?'

'We will move from the lamp and then I will tell you,' he said at last. 'Where are we going?'

'Where? To where should I go but to where I lived – to my house?'

They walked slowly. 'I will tell you,' he said suddenly. 'I followed you to know where you would go. When I knew it was not to Braigon I overtook you.'

'To Braigon?' she said. 'Oh Rantel, you are still as unhappy.'

'I cannot alter, Keda; I cannot change.'

They had reached the square.

'We have come here for nothing,' said Rantel, coming to a halt in the darkness. 'For nothing, do you hear me, Keda? I must tell you now. Oh, it is bitterness to tell you.'

Nothing that he might say could stop a voice within her that kept crying: '*I* am with you, Keda! I am *life*! I am *life*! Oh, Keda, Keda, *I* am with you!' But her voice asked him as though something separate from her real self were speaking:

'Why have we come for nothing?'

'I followed you and then I let you continue here with me, but your house, Keda, where your husband carved, has been taken from you. You can do nothing. When you left us the Ancients met, the Old

Carvers, and they have given your house to one who is of their company, for they say that now that your husband is dead you are not worthy to live in the Square of the Black Rider.'

'And my husband's carvings,' said Keda, 'what has become of them?'

While she waited for him to answer she heard his breathing quicken and could dimly see him dragging his forearm over his brow.

'I will tell you,' he said. 'O fire! why was I so slow – so *slow*! While I was watching for you, watching from the rocks, as I have done every night since you left, Braigon broke into your house and found the Ancients dividing up your own carvings among themselves. "She will not come back," they said of you. "She is worthless. The carvings will be left untended," they said, "and the grain-worm will attack them." But Braigon drew his knife and sent them into a room below the stairs and made twelve journeys and carried the carvings to his own house, where he has hidden them, he says, until you come.

'Keda, Keda, what can *I* do for you? Oh Keda, what can *I* do?'

'Hold me close to you,' she said. 'Where is that music?'

In the silence they could hear the voice of an instrument.

'Keda . . .'

His arms were about her body and his face was deep in her hair.

She could hear the beating of his heart, for her head was lying close to him. The music had suddenly ended and silence, as unbroken as the darkness about them, returned.

Rantel spoke at last. 'I will not live until I take you, Keda. Then I will live. I am a Sculptor. I will create a glory out of wood. I will hack for you a symbol of my love. It will curve in flight. It will leap. It shall be of crimson and have hands as tender as flowers and feet that merge into the roughness of earth, for it shall be its body that leaps. And it shall have eyes that see all things and be violet like the edge of the spring lightning, and upon the breast I shall carve your name – Keda, Keda, Keda – three times, for I am ill with love.'

She put up her hand and her cool fingers felt the bones of his brow and his high cheekbones, and came to his mouth where they touched his lips.

After a little while Rantel said softly: 'You have been crying?'

'With joy,' she said.

'Keda . . .'

'Yes . . .'

'Can you bear cruel news?'

'Nothing can pain me any more,' said Keda. 'I am no longer the one you knew. I am alive.'

'The law that forced you in your marriage, Keda, may bind you again. There is another. I have been told he has been waiting for you, Keda, waiting for you to return. But I could slay him, Keda, if you wish.' His body toughened in her arms and his voice grew harsher. 'Shall I slay him?'

'You shall not speak of death,' said Keda. 'He shall not have me. Take me with you to your house.' Keda heard her own voice sounding like that of another woman, it was so different and clear. 'Take me with you – he will not take me after we have loved. They have my house, where else should I sleep tonight but with you? For I am happy for the first time. All things are clear to me. The right and the wrong, the true and the untrue. I have lost my fear. Are you afraid?'

'I am not afraid!' cried Rantel into the darkness, 'if we love one another.'

'I love all, all,' said Keda. 'Let us not talk.'

Dazed, he took her with him away from the square, and threading their way through the less frequented lanes found themselves at last at the door of a dwelling at the base of the castle wall.

The room they entered was cold, but within a minute Rantel had sent the light from an open fire on the earth dancing across the walls. On the mud floor was the usual grass matting common to all the dwellings.

'Our youth will pass from us soon,' said Keda. 'But we are young this moment and tonight we are together. The bane of our people will fall on us, next year or the year after, but now – NOW, Rantel; it is NOW that fills us. How quickly you have made the fire! Oh, Rantel, how beautifully you have made it! Hold me again.'

As he held her there was a tapping at the window; they did not move, but only listened as it increased until the coarse slab of glass sunk in the mud walls vibrated with an incessant drumming. The increasing volume of the sudden rain was joined by the first howls of a young wind.

The hours moved on. On the low wooden boards, Rantel and Keda lay in the warmth of the fire, defenceless before each other's love.

When Keda wakened she lay for some while motionless. Rantel's arm was flung over her body and his hand was at her breast like a child's. Lifting his arm she moved slowly from him, lowered his hand again softly to the floor. Then she rose and walked to the door. And as she took the first steps, there flashed through her the joyous realization that the mood of invulnerability before the world was still with her. She unlatched the door and flung it open. She had known that the outer wall of Gormenghast would face her as she did so. Its rough base within a stone's throw would rise like a sheer cliff. And there it was, but there was more. Ever since she could remember anything the face of the outer wall had been like the symbol of endlessness, of changelessness, of

power, of austerity and of protection. She had known it in so many moods. Baked to dusty whiteness, and alive with basking lizards, she could remember how it flaked in the sun. She had seen it flowering with the tiny pink and blue creeper flowers that spread like fields of coloured smoke in April across acres of its temperate surface. She had seen its every protruding ledge of stone, its every jutting irregularity furred with frost, or hanging with icicles. She had seen the snow sitting plumply on those juttings, so that in the darkness when the wall had vanished into the night these patches of snow had seemed to her like huge stars suspended.

And now this sunlit morning of late autumn gave to it a mood which she responded to. But as she watched its sunny surface sparkling after a night of heavy rain, she saw at the same moment a man sitting at its base, his shadow on the wall behind him. He was whittling at a branch in his hand. But although it was Braigon who was sat there and who lifted his eyes as she opened the door, she did not cry in alarm or feel afraid or ashamed, but only looked at him quietly, happily, and saw him as a figure beneath a sparkling wall, a man whittling at a branch; someone she had longed to see again.

He did not get to his feet, so she walked over to him and sat down at his side. His head was massive and his body also; squarely built, he gave the impression of compact energy and strength. His hair covered his head closely with tangled curls.

'How long have you been here, Braigon, sitting in the sun carving?'

'Not long.'

'Why did you come?'

'To see you.'

'How did you know that I had come back?'

'Because I could carve no more.'

'You stopped carving?' said Keda.

'I could not see what I was doing. I could only see your face where my carving had been.'

Keda gave vent to a sigh of such tremulous depth that she clasped her hands at her breast with the pain that it engendered.

'And so you came here?'

'I did not come at once. I knew that Rantel would find you as you left the gate in the Outer Wall, for he hides each night among the rocks waiting for you. I knew that he would be with you. But this morning I came here to ask him where he had found you a dwelling for the night, and where you were, for I knew your house had been taken away from you by the law of the Mud Square. But when I arrived here an hour ago I saw the ghost of your face on the door, and you were happy; so I waited here. You are happy, Keda?'

'Yes,' she said.

'You were afraid in the castle to come back; but now you are here you are not afraid. I can see what it is,' he said. 'You have found that you are in love. Do you love him?'

'I do not know. I do not understand. I am walking on air, Braigon. I cannot tell whether I love him or no, or whether it is the world I love so much and the air and the rain last night, and the passions that opened like flowers from their tight buds. Oh, Braigon, I do not know. If I love Rantel, then I love you also. As I watch you now, your hand at your forehead and your lips moving such a little, it is you I love. I love the way you have not wept with anger and torn yourself to shreds to find me here. The way you have sat here all by yourself, oh Braigon, whittling a branch, and waiting, unafraid and understanding everything, I do not know how, for I have not told you of what has transformed me, suddenly.'

She leaned back against the wall and the morning sun lay whitely upon her face. 'Have I changed *so* much?' she said.

'You have broken free,' he said.

'Braigon,' she cried, 'it is you – it is *you* whom I love.' And she clenched her hands together. 'I am in pain because of you and him, but my pain makes me happy. I must tell you the truth, Braigon. I am in love with all things – pain and all things, because I can now watch them from above, for something has happened and I am clear – clear. But I love you, Braigon, more than all things. It is *you* I love.'

He turned the branch over in his hand as though he had not heard, and then he turned to her.

His heavy head had been reclining upon the wall and now he turned it slightly towards her, his eyes half closed.

'Keda,' he said, 'I will meet you tonight. The grass hollow where the Twisted Woods descend. Do you remember?'

'I will meet you there,' she said. While she spoke the air became shrill between their heads and the steel point of a long knife struck the stones between them and snapped with the impact.

Rantel stood before them, he was shaking.

'I have another knife,' he said in a whisper which they could only just hear. 'It is a little longer. It will be sharper by this evening when I meet you at the hollow. There is a full moon tonight. Keda! Oh Keda! Have you forgotten?'

Braigon got to his feet. He had moved only to place himself before Keda's body. She had closed her eyes and she was quite expressionless.

'I cannot help it,' she said, 'I cannot help it. I am happy.'

Braigon stood immediately before his rival. He spoke over his shoulder, but kept his eyes on his enemy.

'He is right,' he said. 'I shall meet him at sunset. One of us will come back to you.'

Then Keda raised her hands to her head. 'No, no, no, no!' she cried. But she knew that it must be so, and became calm, leaning back against the wall, her head bowed and the locks of her hair falling over her face.

The two men left her, for they knew that they could never be with her that unhappy day. They must prepare their weapons. Rantel re-entered his hut and a few moments later returned with a cape drawn about him. He approached Keda.

'I do not understand your love,' he said.

She looked up and saw his head upright upon his neck. His hair was like a bush of blackness.

She did not answer. She only saw his strength and his high cheekbones and fiery eyes. She only saw his youth.

'I am the cause,' she said. 'It is I who should die. And I *will* die,' she said quickly. 'Before very long – but now, now what is it? I cannot enter into fear or hate, or even agony and death. Forgive me. Forgive me.'

She turned and held his hand with the dagger in it.

'I do not know. I do not understand,' she said. 'I do not think that we have any power.'

She released his hand and he moved away along the base of the high wall until it curved to the right and she lost him.

Braigon was already gone. Her eyes clouded.

'Keda,' she said to herself, 'Keda, this is tragedy.' But as her words hung emptily in the morning air, she clenched her hands for she could feel no anguish and the bright bird that had filled her breast was still singing . . . was still singing.

THE ROOM OF ROOTS

'THAT's quite enough for today,' said Lady Cora, laying down her embroidery on a table beside her chair.

'But you've only sewn three stitches, Cora,' said Lady Clarice, drawing out a thread to arm's length.

Cora turned her eyes suspiciously. 'You have been watching me,' she said. 'Haven't you?'

'It wasn't private,' replied her sister. 'Sewing isn't private.' She tossed her head.

Cora was not convinced and sat rubbing her knees together, sullenly.

'And now I've finished as well,' said Clarice, breaking the silence. 'Half a petal, and quite enough, too, for a day like this. Is it tea time?'

'Why do you always want to know the time?' said Cora. ' "Is it breakfast time, Cora?" . . . "Is it dinner time, Cora?" . . . "Is it tea time, Cora?" – on and on and on. You know that it doesn't make any difference *what* the time is.'

'It does if you're hungry,' said Clarice.

'No, it doesn't. Nothing matters very much; even if you're hungry.'

'Yes, it does,' her sister contested. 'I *know* it does.'

'Clarice Groan,' said Cora sternly, rising from her chair, 'you know *too* much.'

Clarice did not answer, but bit her thin, loose lower lip.

'We usually go on much longer with our sewing, don't we, Cora?' she said at last. 'We sometimes go on for hours and hours, and we nearly always talk a lot, but we haven't today, have we, Cora?'

'No,' said Cora.

'Why haven't we?'

'I don't know. Because we haven't needed to, I suppose, you silly thing.'

Clarice got up from her chair and smoothed her purple satin, and then looked archly at her sister. '*I* know why we haven't been talking,' she said.

'Oh no, you don't.'

'Yes, I do,' said Clarice. '*I* know.'

Cora sniffed, and after walking to a long mirror in the wall with a swishing of her skirts, she readjusted a pin in her hair. When she felt she had been silent long enough:

'Oh no, you don't,' she said, and peered at her sister in the mirror over the reflection of her own shoulder. Had she not had forty-nine years in which to get accustomed to the phenomenon she must surely have been frightened to behold in the glass, next to her own face, another, smaller, it is true, for her sister was some distance behind her, but of such startling similarity.

She saw her sister's mouth opening in the mirror.

'I *do*,' came the voice from behind her, 'because I know what *you've* been thinking. It's easy.'

'You *think* you do,' said Cora, 'but I know you *don't*, because I know exactly what you've been thinking all day that I've been thinking and that's why.'

The logic of this answer made no lasting impression upon Clarice, for although it silenced her for a moment she continued: 'Shall I tell you what you've been brooding on?' she asked.

'You can if you like, I suppose. *I* don't mind. What, then? I might as well incline my ear. Go on.'

'I don't know that I want to now,' said Clarice. 'I think I'll keep it to myself, although it's *obvious*.' Clarice gave great emphasis to this word 'obvious'. 'Isn't it tea time yet? Shall I ring the bell, Cora? What a pity it's too windy for the tree.'

'You were thinking of that Steerpike boy,' said Cora, who had sidled up to her sister and was staring at her from very close quarters. She felt she had rather turned the tables on poor Clarice by her sudden renewal of the subject.

'So were you,' said Clarice. 'I knew that long ago. Didn't you?'

'Yes, I did,' said Cora. 'Very long ago. Now we both know.'

A freshly burning fire flung their shadows disrespectfully to and fro across the ceiling and over the walls where samples of their embroidery were hung. The room was a fair size, some thirty feet by twenty. Opposite the entrance from the corridor was a small door. This gave upon the Room of Roots, in the shape of a half circle. On either side of this smaller opening were two large windows with diamond panes of thick glass and on the two end walls of the room, in one of which was the small fireplace, were narrow doorways, one leading to the kitchen and the rooms of the two servants, and the other to the dining-room and the dark yellow bedroom of the twins.

'He said he would exalt us,' said Clarice. 'You heard him, didn't you?'

'I'm not deaf,' said Cora.

'He said we weren't being honoured enough and we must remember who we are. We're Lady Clarice and Cora Groan; that's who we are.'

'Cora and Clarice,' her sister corrected her, 'of Gormenghast.'

'But no one is awed when they see us. He said he'd make them be.'

'Make them be what, dear?' Cora had begun to unbend now that she found their thoughts had been identical.

'Make them be awed,' said Clarice. 'That's what they ought to be. Oughtn't they, Cora?'

'Yes; but they won't do it.'

'No. That's what it is,' said Clarice, 'although I tried this morning.'

'What, dear?' said Cora.

'I tried this morning, though,' repeated Clarice.

'Tried what?' asked Cora in a rather patronizing voice.

'You know when I said "I'll go for a saunter"?'

'Yes.' Cora sat down and produced a minute but heavily scented handkerchief from her flat bosom. 'What about it?'

'I didn't go to the bathroom at all.' Clarice sat down suddenly and stiffly. 'I took some ink instead – *black* ink.'

'What for?'

'I won't tell you yet, for the time isn't ripe,' said Clarice importantly; and her nostrils quivered like a mustang's. 'I took the black ink, and I poured it into a jug. There was lots of it. Then I said to myself, what you tell me such a lot, and what I tell you as well, which is that Gertrude is no better than us – in fact, she's not as good because she hasn't got a speck of Groan blood in her veins like we have, but only the common sort that's no use. So I took the ink and I knew what I would do. I didn't tell you because you might have told me not to, and I don't know why I'm telling you now because you may think I was wrong to do it; but it's all over now so it doesn't matter what you think, dear, does it?'

'I don't know yet,' said Cora rather peevishly.

'Well, I knew that Gertrude had to be in the Central Hall to receive the seven most hideous beggars of the Outer Dwellings and pour a lot of oil on them at nine o'clock, so I went through the door of the Central Hall at nine o'clock with my jug full of ink, and I walked up to her at nine o'clock, but it was not what I wanted because she had a black dress on.'

'What do you mean?' said Cora.

'Well, I was going to pour the ink all over her dress.'

'That would be good, *very* good,' said Cora. 'Did you?'

'Yes,' said Clarice, 'but it didn't show because her dress was black, and she didn't see me pouring it, anyway, because she was talking to a starling.'

'One of *our* birds,' said Cora.

'Yes,' said Clarice. 'One of the stolen birds. But the others saw me. They had their mouths open. They saw my decision. But Gertrude didn't, so my decision was no use. I hadn't anything else to do and I felt frightened, so I ran all the way back; and now I think I'll wash out the jug.'

She got up to put her idea into operation when there was a discreet tapping at their door. Visitors were very few and far between and they were too excited for a moment to say 'Come in.'

Cora was the first to open her mouth and her blank voice was raised more loudly than she had intended:

'Come in.'

Clarice was at her side. Their shoulders touched. Their heads were thrust forward as though they were peering out of a window.

The door opened and Steerpike entered, an elegant stick with a shiny metal handle under his arm. Now that he had renovated and polished the pilfered sword-stick to his satisfaction, he carried it about with him wherever he went. He was dressed in his habitual black and had acquired a gold chain which he wore about his neck. His meagre quota of sandy-coloured hair was darkened with grease, and had been brushed down over his pale forehead in a wide curve.

When he had closed the door behind him he tucked his stick smartly under his arm and bowed.

'Your Ladyships,' he said, 'my unwarranted intrusion upon your privacy, with but the summary knock at the panels of your door as my mediator, must be considered the acme of impertinence were it not that I come upon a serious errand.'

'Who's died?' said Cora.

'Is it Gertrude?' echoed Clarice.

'No one has died,' said Steerpike, approaching them. 'I will tell you the facts in a few minutes; but first, my dear Ladyships, I would be most honoured if I were permitted to appreciate your embroideries. Will you allow me to see them?' He looked at them both in turn inquiringly.

'He said something about them before; at the Prunesquallors' it was,' whispered Clarice to her sister. 'He said he wanted to see them before. Our embroideries.'

Clarice had a firm belief that as long as she whispered, no matter how loudly, no one would hear a word of what she said, except her sister.

'I heard him,' said her sister. 'I'm not blind, am I?'

'Which do you want to see first?' said Clarice. 'Our needlework or the Room of Roots or the Tree?'

'If I am not mistaken,' said Steerpike by way of an answer, 'the creations of your needle are upon the walls around us, and having seen them, as it were, in a flash, I have no choice but to say that I would first of all prefer to examine them more closely, and then if I may, I would be delighted to visit your Room of Roots.'

' "Creations of our needle", he said,' whispered Clarice in her loud, flat manner that filled the room.

'Naturally,' said her sister, and shrugged her shoulders again, and turning her face to Steerpike gave to the right-hand corner of her inexpressive mouth a slight twitch upwards, which although it was as mirthless as the curve between the lips of a dead haddock, was taken by Steerpike to imply that she and he were above making such *obvious* comments.

'Before I begin,' said Steerpike, placing his innocent-looking swordstick on a table, 'may I inquire out of my innocence why you ladies were put to the inconvenience of bidding me to enter your room? Surely your footman has forgotten himself. Why was he not at the door to inquire who wished to see you and to give you particulars before you allowed yourselves to be invaded? Forgive my curiosity, my dear Ladyships, but where was your footman? Would you wish me to speak to him?'

The sisters stared at each other and then at the youth. At last Clarice said:

'We haven't got a footman.'

Steerpike, who had turned away for this very purpose, wheeled about, and then took a step backwards as though struck.

'No footman!' he said, and directed his gaze at Cora.

She shook her head. 'Only an old lady who smells,' she said. 'No footman at all.'

Steerpike walked to the table and, leaning his hands upon it, gazed into space.

'Their Ladyships Cora and Clarice Groan of Gormenghast have no footman – have no one save an old lady who smells. Where are their servants? Where are their retinues, their swarms of attendants?' And then in a voice little above a whisper: 'This must be seen to. This must end.' With a clicking of his tongue he straightened his back. 'And now,' he continued in a livelier voice, 'the needlework is waiting.'

What Steerpike had said, as they toured the walls, began to re-fertilize those seeds of revolt which he had sown at the Prunesquallors'. He watched them out of the corner of his eyes as he flattered their handiwork, and he could see that although it was a great pleasure for them to show their craft, yet their minds were continually returning to the question he had raised. 'We do it all with our left hands, don't we, Cora?' Clarice said, as she pointed to an ugly green-and-red rabbit of intricate needlework.

'Yes,' said Cora, 'it takes a long time because it's all done like that

– with our left hands. Our right arms are starved, you know,' she said, turning to Steerpike. 'They're quite, quite starved.'

'Indeed, your Ladyship,' said Steerpike. 'How is that?'

'Not only our left arms,' Clarice broke in, 'but all down our left-hand sides and our right-hand legs, too. That's why they're rather stiff. It was the epileptic fits which we had. That's what did it, and that's what makes our needlework all the more clever.'

'And beautiful,' said Cora.

'I cannot but agree,' said Steerpike.

'But nobody sees them,' said Clarice. 'We are left alone. Nobody wants our advice on anything. Gertrude doesn't take any notice of us, nor does Sepulchrave. You know what we ought to have, don't you, Cora?'

'Yes,' said her sister, 'I know.'

'What, then?' said Clarice. 'Tell me. Tell me.'

'Power,' said Cora.

'That's right. Power. That's the very thing we want.' Clarice turned her eyes to Steerpike. Then she smoothed the shiny purple of her dress.

'I rather liked them,' she said.

Steerpike, wondering where on earth her thoughts had taken her, tilted his head on one side as though reflecting upon the truth in her remark, when Cora's voice (like the body of a plaice translated into sound) asked:

'You rather liked *what?*'

'My convulsions,' said Clarice earnestly. 'When my left arm became starved for the first time. *You* remember, Cora, don't you? When we had our *first* fits? I rather liked them.'

Cora rustled up to her and raised a forefinger in front of her sister's face. 'Clarice Groan,' she said, 'we finished talking about *that* long ago. We're talking about Power now. Why can't you follow what we're talking about? You are always losing your place. I've noticed that.'

'What about the Room of Roots?' asked Steerpike with affected gaiety. 'Why is it called the Room of Roots? I am most intrigued.'

'Don't you *know?*' came their voices.

'He doesn't know,' said Clarice. 'You see how we've been forgotten. He didn't know about our Room of Roots.'

Steerpike was not kept long in ignorance. He followed the two purple ninepins through the door, and after passing down a short passage, Cora opened a massive door at the far end whose hinges could have done with a gill of oil apiece, and followed by her sister entered the Room of Roots. Steerpike in his turn stepped over the threshold and his curiosity was more than assuaged.

If the name of the room was unusual there was no doubt about its being apt. It was certainly a room of roots. Not of a few simple, separate formations, but of a thousand branching, writhing, coiling, intertwining, diverging, converging, interlacing limbs whose origin even Steerpike's quick eyes were unable for some time to discover.

He found eventually that the thickening stems converged at a tall, narrow aperture on the far side of the room, through the upper half of which the sky was pouring a grey, amorphous light. It seemed at first as though it would be impossible to stir at all in this convoluting meshwork, but Steerpike was amazed to see that the twins were moving about freely in the labyrinth. Years of experience had taught them the possible approaches to the window. They had already reached it and were looking out into the evening. Steerpike made an attempt at following them, but was soon inextricably lost in the writhing maze. Wherever he turned he was faced with a network of weird arms that rose and fell, dipped and clawed, motionless yet alive with serpentine rhythms.

Yet the roots were dead. Once the room must have been filled with earth, but now, suspended for the most part in the higher reaches of the chamber, the thread-like extremities clawed impotently in the air. Nor was it enough that Steerpike should find a room so incongruously monopolized, but that every one of these twisting terminals should be *hand-painted* was even more astonishing. The various main limbs and their wooden tributaries, even down to the minutest rivulet of root, were painted in their own especial colours, so that it appeared as though seven coloured boles had forced their leafless branches through the window, yellow, red and green, violet and pale blue, coral pink and orange. The concentration of effort needed for the execution of this work must have been considerable, let alone the almost superhuman difficulties and vexations that must have resulted from the efforts to establish, among the labyrinthic entanglements of the finer roots, which tendril belonged to which branch, which branch to which limb, and which limb to which trunk, for only after discovering its source could its correct colour be applied.

The idea had been that the birds on entering should choose those roots whose colours most nearly approximated to their own plumage, or if they had preferred it to nest among roots whose hue was complementary to their own.

The work had taken the sisters well over three years, and yet when all had been completed the project for which all this work had been designed had proved to be empty, the Room of Roots a failure, their hopes frozen. From this mortification the twins had never fully recovered. It is true that the room, as a room, gave them pleasure, but that the birds never approached it, let alone settled and nested there, was a festering sore at the back of what minds they had.

Against this nagging disappointment was the positive pride which they felt in having a room of roots at all. And not only the Roots but logically enough the Tree whose branches had once drawn sustenance into its highest twigs, and, long ago, burst forth each April with its emerald jets. It was this Tree that was their chief source of satisfaction, giving them some sense of that distinction which they were now denied.

They turned their eyes from its branches and looked around for Steerpike. He was still not unravelled. 'Can you assist me, my dear Ladyships?' he called, peering through a skein of purple fibres.

'Why don't you come to this window?' said Clarice.

'He can't find the way,' said Cora.

'Can't he? I don't see why not,' said Clarice.

'Because he can't,' said Cora. 'Go and show him.'

'All right. But he must be very stupid,' said Clarice, walking through the dense walls of roots which seemed to open up before her and close again behind her back. When she reached Steerpike, she walked past him and it was only by practically treading on her heels that he was able to thread his way towards the window. At the window there was a little more space, for the seven stems which wedged their way through its lower half protruded some four feet into the room before beginning to divide and subdivide. Alongside the window there were steps that led up to a small platform which rested on the thick horizontal stems.

'Look outside,' said Cora directly Steerpike arrived, 'and you'll see It.'

Steerpike climbed the few steps and saw the main trunk of the tree floating out horizontally into space and then running up to a great height, and as he saw it he recognized it as the tree he had studied from the roof tops, half a mile away near the stone sky-field.

He saw how, what had then seemed a perilous balancing act on the part of the distant figures, was in reality a safe enough exercise, for the bole was conveniently flat on its upper surface. When it reached that point where it began to ascend and branch out, the wooden highway spread into an area that could easily have accommodated ten or twelve people standing in a close group.

'Definitely a *tree*,' he said. 'I am all in favour of it. Has it been dead as long as you can remember it?'

'Of course,' said Clarice.

'We're not as old as *that*,' said Cora, and as this was the first joke she had made for over a year, she tried to smile, but her facial muscles had become, through long neglect, unusable.

'Not so old as what?' said Clarice.

'You don't understand,' said Cora. 'You are much slower than I am. I've noticed that.'

'I WANT some tea,' said Clarice; and leading the way she performed the miraculous journey through the room once more, Steerpike at her heels like a shadow and Cora taking an alternative path.

Once more in the comparatively sane living room where the tapers had been lit by the old woman, they sat before the fire and Steerpike asked if he might smoke. Cora and Clarice after glancing at each other nodded slowly, and Steerpike filled his pipe and lit it with a small red coal.

Clarice had pulled at a bell-rope that hung by the wall, and now as they sat in a semi-circle about the blaze, Steerpike in the centre chair, a door opened to their right and an old dark-skinned lady, with very short legs and bushy eyebrows, entered the room.

'Tea, I suppose,' she said in a subterranean voice that seemed to have worked its way up from somewhere in the room beneath them. She then caught sight of Steerpike and wiped her unpleasant nose with the back of her hand before retiring and closing the door behind her like an explosion. The embroideries flapped outwards in the draught this occasioned, and sank again limply against the walls.

'This is too much,' said Steerpike. 'How can you bear it?'

'Bear what?' said Clarice.

'Do you mean, your Ladyships, that you have become used to being treated in this offhand and insolent manner? Do you not mind whether your natural and hereditary dignities are flouted and abused – when an old commoner slams the doors upon you and speaks to you as though you were on her own degraded level? How can the Groan blood that courses so proudly and in such an undiluted stream, through your veins, remain so quiet? Why in its purple wrath is it not boiling at this moment?' He paused a moment and leant further forward.

'Your birds have been stolen by Gertrude, the wife of your brother. Your labour of love among the roots, which but for that woman would now be bearing fruit, is a fiasco. Even your Tree is forgotten. I had not *heard* of it. Why had I not heard of it? Because you and all you possess have been put aside, forgotten, neglected. There are few enough of your noble and ancient family in Gormenghast to carry on the immemorial rites, and yet you two who could uphold them more scrupulously than any, are slighted at every turn.'

The twins were staring at him very hard. As he paused they turned their eyes to one another. His words, though sometimes a little too swift for them, communicated nevertheless their subversive gist. Here, from the mouth of a stranger, their old sores and grievances were being aired and formulated.

The old lady with the short legs returned with a tray which she set before them with a minimum of deference. Then inelegantly waddling away, she turned at the door and stared again at their visitor, wiping, as before, the back of her large hand across her nose.

When she had finally disappeared, Steerpike leaned forward and, turning to Cora and Clarice in turn, and fixing them with close and concentrated eyes, he said:

'Do you believe in honour? Your Ladyships, answer me, do you believe in honour?'

They nodded mechanically.

'Do you believe that injustice should dominate the castle?'

They shook their heads.

'Do you believe it should go unchecked – that it should flourish without just retribution?'

Clarice, who had rather lost track of the last question, waited until she saw Cora shaking her head before she followed suit.

'In other words,' said Steerpike, 'you think that something must be *done*. Something to crush this tyranny.'

They nodded their heads again, and Clarice could not help feeling a little satisfied that she had so far made no mistake with her shakes and nods.

'Have you any ideas?' said Steerpike. 'Have you any plans to suggest?'

They shook their heads at once.

'In that case,' said Steerpike, stretching his legs out before him and crossing his ankles, 'may I make a suggestion, your Ladyships?'

Again, most flatteringly, he faced each one in turn to obtain her consent. One after the other they nodded heavily, sitting bolt upright in their chairs.

Meanwhile, the tea and the scones were getting cold, but they had all three forgotten them.

Steerpike got up and stood with his back to the fire so that he might observe them both at the same time.

'Your gracious Ladyships,' he began, 'I have received information which is of the highest moment. It is information which hinges upon the unsavoury topic with which we have been forced to deal. I beg your undivided concentration; but I will first of all ask you a question: who has the undisputed control over Gormenghast? Who is it who, having this authority, makes no use of it but allows the great traditions of the castle to drift, forgetting that even his own sisters are of his blood and lineage and are entitled to homage and – shall I say it? – yes, to adulation, too? Who is that man?'

'Gertrude,' they replied.

'Come, come,' said Steerpike, raising his eyebrows, 'who is it who forgets even his own sisters? Who is it, your Ladyships?'

'Sepulchrave,' said Cora.

'Sepulchrave,' echoed Clarice.

They had become agitated and excited by now although they did not show it, and had lost control over what little circumspection they had ever possessed. Every word that Steerpike uttered they swallowed whole.

'Lord Sepulchrave,' said Steerpike. After a pause, he continued. 'If it were not that you were his sisters, and of the Family, how could I dare to speak in this way of the Lord of Gormenghast? But it is my duty to be honest. Lady Gertrude has slighted you, but who could make amends? Who has the final power but your brother? In my efforts to re-establish you, and to make this South Wing once again alive with your servants, it must be remembered that it is your selfish brother who must be reckoned with.'

'He *is* selfish, you know,' said Clarice.

'Of course he is,' said Cora. 'Thoroughly selfish. What shall we do? Tell us! Tell us!'

'In all battles, whether of wits or of war,' said Steerpike, 'the first thing to do is to take the initiative and to strike hard.'

'Yes,' said Cora, who had reached the edge of the chair and was stroking her smooth heliotrope knees in quick, continual movements which Clarice emulated.

'One must choose *where* to strike,' said Steerpike, 'and it is obvious that to strike at the most vulnerable nerve centre of the opponent is the shrewdest preliminary measure. But there must be no half-heartedness. It is all or nothing.'

'All or nothing,' echoed Clarice.

'And now you must tell me, dear ladies, what is your brother's main interest?'

They went on smoothing their knees.

'Is it not literature?' said Steerpike. 'Is he not a great lover of books?'

They nodded.

'He's very clever,' said Cora.

'But he reads it all in books,' said Clarice.

'Exactly.' Steerpike followed quickly upon this. 'Then if he lost his books, he would be all but defeated. If the centre of his life were destroyed he would be but a shell. As I see it, your Ladyships, it is at his library that our first thrust must be directed. You must have your rights,' he added hotly. 'It is only fair that you should have your rights.' He took a dramatic step towards the Lady Cora Groan; he raised his voice: 'My Lady Cora Groan, do you not agree?'

Cora, who had been sitting on the extreme edge of her chair in her excitement, now rose and nodded her head so violently as to throw her hair into confusion.

Clarice, on being asked, followed her sister's example, and Steerpike relit his pipe from the fire and leaned against the mantelpiece for a few moments, sending out wreaths of smoke from between his thin lips.

'You have helped me a great deal, your Ladyships,' he said at last, drawing at his stubby pipe and watching a smoke-ring float to the ceiling. 'You are prepared, I am sure, for the sake of your own honour, to assist me further in my struggle for your deliverance.' He understood from the movements of their perched bodies that they agreed that this was so.

'The question that arises in that case,' said Steerpike, 'is how are we to dispose of your brother's books and thereby bring home to him his responsibilities? What do you feel is the obvious method of destroying a library full of books? Have you been to his library lately, your Ladyships?'

They shook their heads.

'How would you proceed, Lady Cora? What method would you use to destroy a hundred thousand books?'

Steerpike removed his pipe from his lips and gazed intently at her.

'I'd burn them,' said Cora.

This was exactly what Steerpike had wanted her to say; but he shook his head. 'That would be difficult. What could we burn it with?'

'With fire,' said Clarice.

'But how would we start the fire, Lady Clarice?' said Steerpike pretending to look perplexed.

'Straw,' said Cora.

'That is a possibility,' said Steerpike, stroking his chin. 'I wonder if *your* idea would work swiftly enough. Do you think it would?'

'Yes, yes!' said Clarice. 'Straw is lovely to burn.'

'But would it catch the books,' persisted Steerpike, 'all on its own? There would have to be a great deal of it. Would it be quick enough?'

'What's the hurry?' said Cora.

'It must be done swiftly,' said Steerpike, 'otherwise the flames might be put out by busybodies.'

'I love fires,' said Clarice.

'But we oughtn't to burn down Sepulchrave's library, ought we?'

Steerpike had expected, sooner or later, that one of them would feel conscience-stricken and he had retained his trump card.

'Lady Cora,' he said, 'sometimes one has to do things which are unpalatable. When great issues are involved one can't toy with the situation in silk gloves. No. We are making history and we must be stalwart. Do you recall how when I first came in I told you that I had

received information? You do? Well, I will now divulge what has come
to my ears. Keep calm and steady; remember who you are. I shall look
after your interests, have no fear, but at this moment sit down, will you,
and attend?

'You tell me you have been treated badly for this and for that, but
only listen now to the latest scandal that is being repeated below stairs.
"*They* aren't being asked," everyone is saying. "*They* haven't been
asked." '

'Asked what?' said Clarice.

'Or where?' said Cora.

'To the Great Gathering which your brother is calling. At this Great
Gathering the details for a party for the New Heir to Gormenghast,
your nephew Titus, will be discussed. Everyone of importance is going.
Even the Prunesquallors are going. It is the first time for many years
that your brother has become so worldly as to call the members of his
family together. He has, it is said, many things which he wishes to talk
of in connection with Titus, and in my opinion this Great Gathering in
a week's time will be of prime importance. No one knows exactly what
Lord Sepulchrave has in mind, but the general idea is that preparations
must be begun even now for a party on his son's first Birthday.

'Whether you will even be invited to that Party I would not like to
say, but judging from the remarks I have heard about how you two
have been thrust aside and forgotten like old shoes, I should say it was
very unlikely.

'You see,' said Steerpike, 'I have not been idle. I have been listening
and taking stock of the situation, and one day my labours will prove
themselves to have been justified – when I see you, my dear Ladyships,
sitting at either end of a table of distinguished guests, and when I hear
the glasses clinking and the rounds of applause that greet your every
remark I shall congratulate myself that I had long ago enough
imagination and ruthless realism to proceed with the dangerous work
of raising you to the level to which you belong.

'Why should you not have been invited to the party? Why? Why?
Who are you to be spurned thus and derided by the lowest menials in
Swelter's kitchen?'

Steerpike paused and saw that his words had produced a great effect.
Clarice had gone over to Cora's chair where now they both sat bolt
upright and very close together.

'When you suggested so perspicaciously just now that the solution to
this insufferable state of affairs lay in the destruction of your brother's
cumbersome library, I felt that you were right and that only through a
brave action of that kind might you be able to lift up your heads once
more and feel the slur removed from your escutcheon. That idea of
yours spelt genius. I appeal to your Ladyships to do what you feel to be

consistent with your honour and your pride. You are not old, your Ladyships, oh no, you are not old. But are you young? I should like to feel that what years you have left will be filled with glamorous days and romantic nights. Shall it be so? Shall we take the step towards justice? Yes or no, my dear ladies, yes or no.'

They got up together. 'Yes,' they said, 'we want Power back.'

'We want our servants back and justice back and everything back,' Cora said slowly, a counterpoint of intense excitement weaving through the flat foreground of her voice.

'And romantic nights,' said Clarice. 'I'd like that. Yes, yes. Burn! Burn,' she continued loudly, her flat bosom beginning to heave up and down like a machine. 'Burn! burn! burn!'

'When?' said Cora. 'When can we burn it up?'

Steerpike held up his hand to quieten them. But they took no notice, only leaning forward, holding each other's hands and crying in their dreadful emotionless voices:

'Burn! Burn! Burn! Burn! Burn!' until they had exhausted themselves.

Steerpike had not flinched under this ordeal. He now realized more completely than before why they were ostracized from the normal activities of the castle. He had known they were slow, but he had not known that they could behave like this.

He changed his tone.

'Sit down!' he rapped out. 'Both of you. Sit down!'

They complied at once, and although they were taken aback at the peremptory nature of his order, he could see that he now had complete control over them, and though his inclination was to show his authority and to taste for the first time the sinister delights of his power, yet he spoke to them gently – for, first of all, the library must be burned for a reason of his own. After that, with such a dreadful hold over them, he could relax for a time and enjoy a delicious dictatorship in the South Wing.

'In six days' time, your Ladyships,' he said, fingering his gold chain – 'on the evening before the Great Gathering to which you have not been invited – the library will be empty and you may burn it to the ground. I shall prepare the incendiaries and will school you in all the details later; but on the great night itself when you see me give the signal you will set fire at once to the fuel and will make your way immediately to this room.'

'Can't we watch it burn?' said Cora.

'Yes,' said Clarice, 'can't we?'

'From your Tree,' said Steerpike. 'Do you want to be found out?'

'No!' they said. 'No! No!'

'Then you can watch it from your Tree and be quite safe. I will remain in the woods so that I can see that nothing goes wrong. Do you understand?'

'Yes,' they said. 'Then we'll have Power, won't we?'

The unconscious irony of this caused Steerpike's lip to lift, but he said:

'Your Ladyships will then have Power.' And approaching them in turn he kissed the tips of their fingers. Picking up his sword-stick from the table he walked swiftly to the door, where he bowed.

Before he opened it he said: 'We are the only ones who know. The only ones who will ever know, aren't we?'

'Yes,' they said. 'Only us.'

'I will return within a day or two,' said Steerpike, 'and give you the details. Your honour must be saved.'

He did not say good night, but opened the door and disappeared into the darkness.

'PREPARATIONS FOR ARSON'

ON one excuse or another Steerpike absented himself from the Prunesquallors' during the major part of the next two days. Although he accomplished many things during this short period, the three stealthy expeditions which he made to the library were the core of his activities. The difficulty lay in crossing, unobserved, the open ground to the conifer wood. Once in the wood and among the pines there was less danger. He realized how fatal it might prove to be seen in the neighbourhood of the library, so shortly before the burning. On the first of the reconnaissances, after waiting in the shadows of the Southern wing before scudding across the overgrown gardens to the fields that bordered the conifers, he gathered the information which he needed. He had managed after an hour's patient concentration to work the lock of the library door with a piece of wire, and then he had entered the silent room, to investigate the structure of the building. There was a remoteness about the deserted room. Shadowy and sinister though it was by night, it was free of the vacancy which haunted its daylight hours. Steerpike felt the insistent silence of the place as he moved to and fro, glancing over his high shoulder more than once as he took note of the possibilities for conflagration.

His survey was exhaustive, and when he finally left the building he appreciated to a nicety the nature of the problem. Lengths of oil-soaked material would have to be procured and laid behind the books where they could stretch unobserved from one end of the room to the other. After leading around the library they could be taken up the stairs and along the balcony. To lay these twisted lengths (no easy matter to procure without awakening speculation) was patently a job for those hours of the early morning, after Lord Sepulchrave had left for the castle. He had staggered, on his second visit, under an enormous bundle of rags and a tin of oil to the pine wood at midnight, and had occupied himself during the hours while he waited for Lord Sepulchrave to leave the building in knotting together the odd assortment of pilfered cloth into lengths of not less than forty feet.

When at last he saw his Lordship leave the side door and heard his slow, melancholy footsteps die away on the pathway leading to the Tower of Flints, he rose and stretched himself.

Much to his annoyance the probing of the lock occupied even more time than on the last occasion, and it was four o'clock in the morning before he pushed the door open before him.

Luckily, the dark autumn mornings were on his side, and he had a clear three hours. He had noticed that from without no light could be observed and he lit the lamp in the centre of the room.

Steerpike was nothing if not systematic, and two hours later, taking a tour of the library, he was well satisfied. Not a trace of his handiwork could be seen save only where four extremities of the cloth hung limply beside the main, unused, door of the building. These strips were the terminals of the four lengths that circumscribed the library and would be dealt with.

The only thing that caused him a moment's reflection was the faint smell of the oil in which he had soaked the tightly twisted cloth.

He now concentrated his attention upon the four strips and twining them together into a single cord, he knotted it at its end. Somehow or other this cord must find its way through the door to the outside world. He had on his last visit eventually arrived at the only solution apart from that of chiselling a way through the solid wall and the oak that formed the backs of the bookshelves. This was obviously too laborious. The alternative, which he had decided on, was to bore a neat hole through the door immediately under the large handle in the shadow of which it would be invisible save to scrutiny. Luckily for him there was a reading-stand in the form of a carven upright with three short, bulbous legs. This upright supported a tilted surface the size of a very small table. This piece stood unused in front of the main door. By moving it a fraction to the right, the twisted cord of cloth was lost in darkness and although its discovery was not impossible, both this risk and that of the faint aroma of oil being noticed, were justifiable.

He had brought the necessary tools with him and although the oak was tough had bored his way through it within half an hour. He wriggled the cord through the hole and swept up the sawdust that had gathered on the floor.

By this time he was really tired, but he took another walk about the library before turning down the lamp and leaving by the side door. Once in the open he bore to his right, and skirting the adjacent wall, arrived at the main door of the building. As this entrance had not been used for many years, the steps that led to it were invisible beneath a cold sea of nettles and giant weeds. He waded his way through them and saw the loose end of the cord hanging through the raw hole he had chiselled. It glimmered whitely and was hooked like a dead finger. Opening the blade of a small sharp knife he cut through the twisted cloth so that only about two inches protruded, and to prevent this stub end slipping back through the hole, drove a small nail through the cloth with the butt of his knife.

His work for the night now seemed to be complete and, only stopping to hide the can of oil in the wood, he retraced his steps to the Prunesquallors', where climbing at once to his room he curled up in bed, dressed as he was, and incontinently fell asleep.

The third of his expeditions to the library, the second during the daylight, was on other business. As might be supposed, the childishness of burning down Lord Sepulchrave's sanctum did not appeal to him. In a way it appalled him. Not through any prickings of conscience, but because destruction in any form annoyed him. That is, the destruction of anything inanimate that was well constructed. For living creatures he had not this same concern, but in a well-made object, whatever its nature, a sword or a watch or a book, he felt an excited interest. He enjoyed a thing that was cleverly conceived and skilfully wrought, and this notion, of destroying so many beautifully bound and printed volumes, had angered him against himself, and it was only when his plot had so ripened that he could neither retract nor resist it, that he went forward with a single mind. That it should be the Twins who would actually set light to the building with their own hands was, of course, the lynch-pin of the manoeuvre. The advantages to himself which would accrue from being the only witness to the act were too absorbing for him to ponder at this juncture.

The aunts would, of course, not realize that they were setting fire to a library filled with people: nor that it would be the night of the Great Gathering to which, as Steerpike had told them, they were not to be invited. The youth had waylaid Nannie Slagg on her way to the aunts and had inquired whether he could save her feet by delivering her message to them. At first she had been disinclined to divulge the nature of her mission, but when she at last furbished him with what he had already suspected, he promised he would inform them at once of the Gathering, and after a pretence of going in their direction, he had returned to the Prunesquallors' in time for his midday meal. It was on the following morning that he told the Twins that they had *not* been invited.

Once Cora and Clarice had ignited the cord at the main door of the library and the fire was beginning to blossom, it would be up to him to be as active as an eel on a line.

It seemed to Steerpike that to save two generations of the House of Groan from death by fire should stand him in very good stead, and moreover, his headquarters would be well established in the South Wing with their Ladyships Cora and Clarice who after such an episode would, if only through fear of their guilt being uncovered, eat out of his hand.

The question of how the fire started would follow close upon the rescue. On this he would have as little knowledge as anyone, only having seen the glow in the sky as he was walking along the South Wing for exercise. The Prunesquallors would bear out that it was his habit to take a stroll at sundown. The twins would be back in their room before news of the burning could ever reach the castle.

Steerpike's third visit to the library was to plan how the rescues were to be effected. One of the first things was, of course, to turn and remove the key from the door when the party had entered the building, and as Lord Sepulchrave had the convenient habit of leaving it in the lock until he removed it on retiring in the small hours, there should be no difficulty about this. That such questions as 'Who turned the key?' and 'how did it disappear?' would be asked at a later date was inevitable, but with a well-rehearsed alibi for himself and the twins, and with the Prunesquallors' cognizance of his having gone out for a stroll on that particular evening, he felt sure the suspicion would no more centre upon himself than on anyone else. Such minor problems as might arise in the future could be dealt with in the future.

This was of more immediate consequence: How was he to rescue the family of Groan in a manner reasonably free of danger to himself and yet sufficiently dramatic to cause the maximum admiration and indebtedness?

His survey of the building had shown him that he had no wide range of choice – in fact, that apart from forcing one of the doors open by some apparently superhuman effort at the last moment, or by smashing an opening in the large skylight in the roof through which it would be both too difficult and dangerous to rescue the prisoners, the remaining possibility lay in the only window, fifteen feet from the ground.

Once he had decided on this window as his focus he turned over in his mind alternative methods of rescue. It must appear, above all else, that the deliverance was the result of a spontaneous decision, translated at once into action. It did not matter so much if he were suspected,

although he did not imagine that he *would* be; what mattered was that
nothing could later be proved as *prearranged*.

The window, about four feet square, was above the main door and
was heavily glazed. The difficulty naturally centred on how the
prisoners were to reach the window from the inside, and how Steerpike
was to scale the outer wall in order to smash the pane and show himself.

Obviously he must not be armed with anything which he would not
normally be carrying. Whatever he used to force an entrance must be
something he had picked up on the spur of the moment outside the
library or among the pines. A ladder, for instance, would at once arouse
suspicions, and yet something of that nature was needed. It occurred to
him that a small tree was the obvious solution, and he began to search
for one of the approximate length, already felled, for many of the pines
which were cleared for the erection of the library and adjacent buildings
were still to be seen lying half buried in the thick needle-covered
ground. It did not take him long to come upon an almost perfect
specimen of what he wanted. It was about twelve to fifteen feet long,
and most of its lateral branches were broken off close to the bole, leaving
stumps varying from three inches to a foot in length. 'Here,' said
Steerpike to himself, 'is *the* thing.'

It was less easy for him to find another, but eventually he discovered
some distance from the library what he was searching for. It lay in a
dank hollow of ferns. Dragging it to the library wall, he propped both
the pines upright against the main door and under the only window.
Wiping the sweat from his bulging forehead he began to climb them,
stamping off those branches that would be too weak to support Lady
Groan, who would be the heaviest of the prisoners. Dragging them
away from the wall, when he had completed these minor adjustments,
and feeling satisfied that his 'ladders' were now both serviceable yet
natural, he left them at the edge of the trees where a number of felled
pines were littered, and next cast about for something with which he
could smash the window. At the base of the adjacent building, a
number of moss-covered lumps of masonry had fallen away from the
walls. He carried several of these to within a few yards of the 'ladders'.
Were there any question of his being suspected later, and if questions
were raised as to how he came across the ladders and the piece of
masonry so conveniently, he could point to the heap of half-hidden
stones and the litter of trees. Steerpike closed his eyes and attempted to
visualize the scene. He could see himself making frantic efforts to open
the doors, rattling the handles and banging the panels. He could hear
himself shouting 'Is there anybody in there?' and the muffled cries from
within. Perhaps he would yell: 'Where's the key? Where's the key?' or
a few gallant encouragements, such as 'I'll get you out somehow.' Then
he would leap to the main door and beating on it a few times, deliver

a few more yells before dragging up the 'ladders', for the fire by that time should be going very well. Or perhaps he would do none of these things, simply appearing to them like the answer to a prayer, in the nick of time. He grinned.

The only reason why he could not spare himself both time and energy by propping the 'ladders' against the wall after the last guest had entered the library was that the Twins would see them as they performed their task. It was imperative that they should not suspect the library to be inhabited, let alone gain an inkling of Steerpike's preparations.

On this, the last occasion of his three visits to the library, he once again worked the lock of the side door and overhauled his handiwork. Lord Sepulchrave had been there on the previous night as usual, but apparently had suspected nothing. The tall bookstand was as he had left it, obstructing a view of and throwing a deep shadow over the handle of the main door from beneath which the twisted cloth stretched like a tight rope across the two foot span to the end of the long bookshelves. He could now detect no smell of oil, and although that meant that it was evaporating, he knew that it would still be more inflammable than the dry cloth.

Before he left he selected half a dozen volumes from the less conspicuous shelves, which he hid in the pine wood on his return journey, and which he collected on the following night from their rainproof nest of needles in the decayed bole of a dead larch. Three of the volumes had vellum bindings and were exquisitely chased with gold, and the others were of equally rare craftsmanship, and it was with annoyance, on returning to the Prunesquallors' that night, that he found it necessary to fashion for them their neat jackets of brown paper and to obliterate the Groan crest on the fly-leaves.

It was only when these nefarious doings were satisfactorily completed that Steerpike visited the aunts for the second time and re-primed them in their very simple rôles as arsonists. He had decided that rather than tell the Prunesquallors that he was going out for a stroll he would say instead that he was paying a visit to the aunts, and then with them to prove his alibi (for somehow or other they must be got to and from the library without the knowledge of their short-legged servant); their story and that of the Doctor's would coincide.

He had made them repeat a dozen or so times: 'We've been indoors *all* the time. We've been indoors *all* the time,' until they were themselves as convinced of it as though they were reliving the Future!

THE GROTTO

It happened on the day of Steerpike's second daylight visit to the Library. He was on his return journey and had reached the edge of the pine woods and was awaiting an opportunity to run unobserved across the open ground, when, away to his left, he saw a figure moving in the direction of Gormenghast Mountain.

The invigorating air, coupled with his recognition of the distant figure, prompted him to change his course, and with quick, birdlike steps he moved rapidly along the edge of the wood. In the rough landscape away to his left, the tiny figure in its crimson dress sang out against the sombre background like a ruby on a slate. The midsummer sun, and how much less this autumn light, had no power to mitigate the dreary character of the region that surrounded Gormenghast. It was like a continuation of the castle, rough and shadowy, and though vast and often windswept, oppressive too, with a kind of raw weight.

Ahead lay Gormenghast Mountain in all its permanence, a sinister thing as though drawn out of the earth by sorcery as a curse on all who viewed it. Although its base appeared to struggle from a blanket of trees within a few miles of the castle, it was in reality a day's journey on horseback. Clouds were generally to be seen clustering about its summit even on the finest days when the sky was elsewhere empty, and it was common to see the storms raging across its heights and the sheets of dark rain slanting mistily over the blurred crown and obscuring half the mountain's hideous body, while, at the same time, sunlight was playing across the landscape all about it and even on its own lower slopes. Today, however, not even a single cloud hung above the peak, and when Fuchsia had looked out of her bedroom window after her midday meal she had stared at the Mountain and said: 'Where are the clouds?'

'What clouds?' said the old nurse, who was standing behind her, rocking Titus in her arms. 'What is it, my caution?'

'There's nearly always clouds on top of the Mountain,' said Fuchsia. 'Aren't there any, dear?'

'No,' said Fuchsia. 'Why aren't there?'

Fuchsia realized that Mrs Slagg knew virtually nothing, but the long custom of asking her questions was a hard one to break down. This realization that grown-ups did not necessarily know any more than children was something against which she had fought. She wanted Mrs Slagg to remain the wise recipient of all her troubles and the comforter that she had always seemed, but Fuchsia was growing up and she was now realizing how weak and ineffectual was her old guardian. Not that she was losing her loyalty or affection. She would have defended the wrinkled midget to her last breath if necessary; but she was isolated within herself with no one to whom she could run with that unquestioning confidence – that outpouring of her newest enthusiasms – her sudden terrors – her projects – her stories.

'I think I'll go out,' she said, 'for a walk.'

'Again?' said Mrs Slagg, stopping for a moment the rocking of her arms. 'You go out such a lot now, don't you? Why are you always going away from me?'

'It's not from you,' said Fuchsia; 'it's because I want to walk and think. It isn't going away from *you*. You know it isn't.'

'I don't know anything,' said Nannie Slagg, her face puckered up, 'but I know you never went out all the summer, did you dear? And now that it is so tempersome and cold you are always going out into the nastiness and getting wet or frozen every day. Oh, my poor heart. Why? Why *every* day?'

Fuchsia pushed her hands into the depths of the big pockets of her red dress.

It was true she had deserted her attic for the dreary moors and the rocky tracts of country about Gormenghast. Why was this? Had she suddenly outgrown her attic that had once been all in all to her? Oh no; she had not outgrown it, but something had changed ever since that dreadful night when she saw Steerpike lying by the window in the darkness. It was no longer inviolate – secret – mysterious. It was no longer another world, but a part of the castle. Its magnetism had weakened – its silent, shadowy drama had died and she could no longer bear to revisit it. When last she had ventured up the spiral stairs and entered the musty and familiar atmosphere, Fuchsia had experienced a pang of such sharp nostalgia for what it had once been to her that she had turned from the swaying motes that filled the air and the shadowy shapes of all that she had known as her friends; the cobwebbed organ, the crazy avenue of a hundred loves – turned away, and stumbled down the dark staircase with a sense of such desolation as seemed would never lift. Her eyes grew dim as she remembered these things; her hands clenched in her deep pockets.

'Yes,' she said, 'I have been out a lot. Do you get lonely? If you do, you needn't, because you know I love you, don't you? You *know* that, don't you?'

She thrust her lower lip forward and frowned at Mrs Slagg, but this was only to keep her tears back, for nowadays Fuchsia had so lonely a feeling that tears were never far distant. Never having had either positive cruelty or kindness shown to her by her parents, but only an indifference, she was not conscious of what it was that she missed – affection.

It had always been so and she had compensated herself by weaving stories of her own Future, or by lavishing her own love upon such things as the objects in her attics, or more recently upon what she found or saw among the woods and wastelands.

'You know that, don't you?' Fuchsia repeated.

Nannie rocked Titus more vigorously than was necessary and by the pursing of her lips indicated that his Lordship was asleep and that she was speaking too loudly.

Then Fuchsia came up to her old nurse and stared at her brother. The feeling of aversion for him had disappeared, and though as yet the lilac-eyed creature had not affected her with any sensation of sisterly love, nevertheless she had got used to his presence in the Castle and would sometimes play with him solemnly for half an hour or so at a time.

Nannie's eyes followed Fuchsia's.

'His little Lordship,' she said, wagging her head, 'it's his little Lordship.'

'Why do you love him?'

'Why do I love him! oh, my poor, weak heart! Why do I love him, stupid? How could you say such a thing?' cried Nannie Slagg. 'Oh my little Lordship *thing*. How could I *help* it – the innocent notion that he is! The very next of Gormenghast, aren't you, my only? The very next of all. What did your cruel sister say, then, what did she say?

'He must go to his cot now, for his sleep, he must, and to dream his golden dreams.'

'Did you talk to me like that when I was a baby?' asked Fuchsia.

'Of course I did,' said Mrs Slagg. 'Don't be silly. Oh, the ignorance of you! Are you going to tidy your room for me now?'

She hobbled to the door with her precious bundle. Every day she asked this same question, but never waited for an answer, knowing that whatever it was, it was *she* who would have to make some sort of order out of the chaos.

Fuchsia again turned to the window and stared at the Mountain whose shape down to the last outcrop had long since scored its outline in her mind.

Between the castle and Gormenghast Mountain the land was desolate, for the main part empty wasteland, with large areas of swamp where undisturbed among the reedy tracts the waders moved. Curlews and peewits sent their thin cries along the wind. Moorhens reared their young and paddled blackly in and out of the rushes. To the east of Gormenghast Mountain, but detached from the trees at its base, spread the undulating darkness of the Twisted Woods. To the west the unkempt acres, broken here and there with low stunted trees bent by the winds into the shape of hunchbacks.

Between this dreary province and the pine wood that surrounded the West Wing of the castle, a dark, shelving plateau rose to a height of about a hundred to two hundred feet – an irregular tableland of greeny-black rock, broken and scarred and empty. It was beyond these cold escarpments that the river wound its way about the base of the Mountain and fed the swamps where the wild fowl lived.

Fuchsia could see three short stretches of the river from her window. This afternoon the central portion and that to its right were black with the reflection of the Mountain, and the third, away to the west beyond the rocky plateau, was a shadowy white strip that neither glanced nor sparkled, but, mirroring the opaque sky, lay lifeless and inert, like a dead arm.

Fuchsia left the window abruptly and closing the door after her with a crash, ran all the way down the stairs, almost falling as she slipped clumsily on the last flight, before threading a maze of corridors to emerge panting in the chilly sunlight.

Breathing in the sharp air she gulped and clenched her hands together until her nails bit at her palms. Then she began to walk. She had been walking for over an hour when she heard footsteps behind her and, turning, saw Steerpike. She had not seen him since the night at the Prunesquallors' and never as clearly as now, as he approached her through the naked autumn. He stopped when he noticed that he was observed and called:

'Lady Fuchsia! May I join you?'

Behind him she saw something which by contrast with the alien, incalculable figure before her, was close and real. It was something which she understood, something which she could never do without, or be without, for it seemed as though it were her own self, her own body, at which she gazed and which lay so intimately upon the skyline. Gormenghast. The long, notched outline of her home. It was now his background. It was a screen of walls and towers pocked with windows. He stood against it, an intruder, imposing himself so vividly, so solidly, against her world, his head overtopping the loftiest of its towers.

'What do you want?' she said.

A breeze had lifted from beyond the Twisted Woods and her dress was blown across her so that down her right side it clung to her showing the strength of her young body and thighs.

'Lady Fuchsia!' shouted Steerpike across the strengthening wind. 'I'll tell you.' He took a few quick paces towards her and reached the sloping rock on which she stood. 'I want you to explain this region to me – the marshes and Gormenghast Mountain. Nobody has ever told me about it. You know the country – you understand it,' (he filled his lungs again) 'and though I love the district I'm very ignorant.' He had almost reached her. 'Can I share your walks, occasionally? Would you consider the idea? Are you returning?' Fuchsia had moved away. 'If so, may I accompany you back?'

'That's not what you've come to ask me,' said Fuchsia slowly. She was beginning to shake in the cold wind.

'Yes, it is,' said Steerpike, 'it is just what I've come to ask you. And whether you will tell me about Nature.'

'I don't know anything about Nature,' said Fuchsia, beginning to walk down the sloping rock. 'I don't understand it. I only look at it. Who told you I knew about it? Who makes up these things?'

'No one,' said Steerpike. 'I thought you must know and understand what you love so much. I've seen you very often returning to the castle laden with the things you have discovered. And also, you *look* as though you understand.'

'I *do*?' said Fuchsia, surprised. 'No, I can't do. I don't understand wise things at all.'

'Your knowledge is intuitive,' said the youth. 'You have no need of book learning and such like. You only have to gaze at a thing to *know* it. The wind is getting stronger, your Ladyship, and colder. We had better return.'

Steerpike turned up his high collar, and gaining her permission to accompany her back to the castle, he began with her the descent of the grey rocks. Before they were halfway down, the rain was falling and the autumn sunlight had given way to a fast, tattered sky.

'Tread carefully, Lady Fuchsia,' said Steerpike suddenly; and Fuchsia stopped and stared quickly over her shoulder at him as though she had forgotten he was there. She opened her mouth as though to speak when a far rattle of thunder reverberated among the rocks and she turned her head to the sky. A black cloud was approaching and from its pendulous body the rain fell in a mass of darkness.

Soon it would be above them and Fuchsia's thoughts leapt backwards through the years to a certain afternoon when, as today, she had been caught in a sudden rainstorm. She had been with her mother on one of those rare occasions, still rarer now, when the Countess for some reason or other decided to take her daughter for a walk. Those occasional outings had been silent affairs, and Fuchsia could remember how she had longed to be free of the presence that moved at her side and above her, and yet she recalled how she had envied her huge mother when the wild birds came to her at her long, shrill, sweet whistle and settled upon her head and arms and shoulders. But what she chiefly remembered was how, on that day, when the storm broke above them, her mother instead of turning back to the castle, continued onwards towards these same layers of dark rock which she and Steerpike were now descending. Her mother had turned down a rough, narrow gully and had disappeared behind a high slab of dislodged stone that was leaning against

a face of rock. Fuchsia had followed. But instead of finding her mother
sheltering from the downpour against the cliff and behind the slab, to
her surprise she found herself confronted with the entrance to a grotto.
She had peered inside, and there, deep in its chilly throat, was her
mother sitting upon the ground and leaning against the sloping wall,
very still and silent and enormous.

They had waited there until the storm had tired of its own anger and
a slow rain descended like remorse from the sky. No word had passed
between them, and Fuchsia, as she remembered the grotto, felt a shiver
run through her body. But she turned to Steerpike. 'Follow me, if you
want to,' she said. 'I know a cave.'

The rain was by now thronging across the escarpment, and she began
to run over the slippery grey rock surfaces with Steerpike at her heels.

As she began the short, steep descent she turned for an instant to see
whether Steerpike had kept pace with her, and as she turned, her feet
slipped away from under her on the slithery surface of an oblique slab,
and she came crashing to the ground, striking the side of her face, her
shoulders and shin with a force that for the moment stunned her. But
only for a moment. As she made an effort to rise and felt the pain
growing at her cheekbone, Steerpike was beside her. He had been some
twelve yards away as she fell, but he slithered like a snake among the
rocks and was kneeling beside her almost immediately. He saw at once
that the wound upon her face was superficial. He felt her shoulder and
shinbone with his thin fingers and found them sound. He removed his
cape, covered her and glanced down the gully. The rain swam over his
face and thrashed on the rocks. At the base of the steep decline he could
see, looming vaguely through the downpour, a huge propped rock, and
he guessed that it was towards this that Fuchsia had been running, for
the gully ended within forty feet in a high, unscalable wall of granite.

Fuchsia was trying to sit up, but the pain in her shoulder had drained
her of strength.

'Lie still!' shouted Steerpike through the screen of rain that divided
them. Then he pointed to the propped rock.

'Is that where we were going?' he asked.

'There's a cave behind it,' she whispered. 'Help me up. I can get
there all right.'

'Oh no,' said Steerpike. He knelt down beside her, and then with
great care he lifted her inch by inch from the rocks. His wiry muscles
toughened in his slim arms, and along his spine, as by degrees he raised
her to the level of his chest, getting to his feet as he did so. Then, step
by tentative step over the splashing boulders he approached the cave.
A hundred rain-thrashed pools had collected among the rocks.

Fuchsia had made no remonstrance, knowing that she could never
have made this difficult descent; but as she felt his arms around her and

the proximity of his body, something deep within her tried to hide itself. Through the thick, tousled strands of her drenched hair she could see his sharp, pale, crafty face, his powerful dark-red eyes focused upon the rocks below them, his high protruding forehead, his cheekbones glistening, his mouth an emotionless line.

This was Steerpike. He was holding her; she was in his arms; in his power. His hard arms and fingers were taking the weight at her thighs and shoulders. She could feel his muscles like bars of metal. This was the figure whom she had found in her attic, and who had climbed up the sheer and enormous wall. He had said that he had found a stone sky-field. He had said that she understood Nature. He wanted to learn from her. How could he with his wonderful long sentences learn anything from her? She must be careful. He was clever. But there was nothing wrong in being clever. Dr Prune was clever and she liked him. She wished she was clever herself.

He was edging between the wall of rock and the slanting slab, and suddenly they were in the dim light of the grotto. The floor was dry and the thunder of the rain beyond the entrance seemed to come from another world.

Steerpike lowered her carefully to the ground and propped her against a flat, slanting portion of the wall. Then he pulled off his shirt and began, after wringing as much moisture from it as he could, to tear it into long narrow pieces. She watched him, fascinated in spite of the pain she was suffering. It was like watching someone from another world who was worked by another kind of machinery, by something smoother, colder, harder, swifter. Her heart rebelled against the bloodlessness of his precision, but she had begun to watch him with a grudging admiration for a quality so alien to her own temperament.

The grotto was about fifteen feet in depth, the roof dipping to the earth, so that in only the first nine feet from the entrance was it possible to stand upright. Close to the arching roof, areas of the rock-face were broken and fretted into dim convolutions of stone, and a fanciful eye could with a little difficulty beguile any length of time by finding among the inter-woven patterns an inexhaustible army of ghoulish or seraphic heads according to the temper of the moment.

The recesses of the grotto were in deep darkness, but it was easy enough for Fuchsia and Steerpike to see each other in the dull light near the shielded entrance.

Steerpike had torn his shirt into neat strips and had knelt down beside Fuchsia and bandaged her head and staunched the bleeding which, especially from her leg, where the injury was not so deep, was difficult to check. Her upper arm was less easy, and it was necessary for her to allow Steerpike to bare her shoulder before he could wash it clean.

She watched him as he carefully dabbed the wound. The sudden pain and shock had changed to a raw aching and she bit her lip to stop her tears. In the half light she saw his eyes smouldering in the shadowy whiteness of his face. Above the waist he was naked. What was it that made his shoulders look deformed? They were high, but were sound, though like the rest of his body, strangely taut and contracted. His chest was narrow and firm.

He removed a swab of cloth from her shoulder slowly and peered to see whether the blood would continue to flow.

'Keep still,' he said. 'Keep your arm as still as you can. How's the pain?'

'I'm all right,' said Fuchsia.

'Don't be heroic,' he said, sitting back on his heels. 'We're not playing a game. I want to know *exactly* how much you're in pain – not whether you are brave or not. I know that already. Which hurts you most?'

'My leg,' said Fuchsia. 'It makes me want to be ill. And I'm cold. Now you know.'

Their eyes met in the half light.

Steerpike straightened himself. 'I'm going to leave you,' he said. 'Otherwise the cold will gnaw you to bits. I can't get you back to the castle alone. I'll fetch the Prune and a stretcher. You'll be all right here. I'll go now, at once. We'll be back within half an hour. I can move when I want to.'

'Steerpike,' said Fuchsia.

He knelt down at once. 'What is it?' he said, speaking very softly.

'You've done quite a lot to help,' she said.

'Nothing much,' he replied. His hand was close to hers.

The silence which followed became ludicrous and he got to his feet.

'Mustn't stay.' He had sensed the beginning of something less frigid. He would leave things as they were. 'You'll be shaking like a leaf if I don't hurry. Keep absolutely still.'

He laid his coat over her and then walked the few paces to the opening.

Fuchsia watched his hunched yet slender outline as he stood for a moment before plunging into the rain-swept gully. Then he had gone, and she remained quite still, as he had told her, and listened to the pounding of the rain.

Steerpike's boast as to his fleetness was not an idle one. With incredible agility he leapt from boulder to boulder until he had reached the head of the gully and from there, down the long slopes of the escarpment, he sped like a Dervish. But he was not reckless. Every one of his steps was a calculated result of a decision taken at a swifter speed than his feet could travel.

At length the rocks were left behind and the castle emerged through a dull blanket.

His entrance into the Prunesquallors' was dramatic. Irma, who had never before seen any male skin other than that which protrudes beyond the collar and the cuffs, gave a piercing cry and fell into her brother's arms only to recover at once and to dash from the room in a typhoon of black silk. Prunesquallor and Steerpike could hear the stair rods rattling as she whirled her way up the staircase and the crashing of her bedroom door set the pictures swaying on the walls of all the downstairs rooms.

Dr Prunesquallor had circled around Steerpike with his head drawn back so that his cervical vertebrae rested against the rear wall of his high collar, and a plumbless abysm yawned between his Adam's apple and his pearl stud. With his head bridled backwards thus, somewhat in the position of a cobra about to strike, and with his eyebrows raised quizzically, he was yet able at the same time to flash both tiers of his startling teeth which caught and reflected the lamplight with an unnatural brilliancy.

He was in an ecstasy of astonishment. The spectacle of a half-nude, dripping Steerpike both repelled and delighted him. Every now and again Steerpike and the Doctor could hear an extraordinary moaning from the floor above.

When, however, the Doctor heard the cause of the boy's appearance, he was at once on the move. It had not taken Steerpike long to explain what had happened. Within a few moments the Doctor had packed up a small bag and rung for the cook to fetch both a stretcher and a couple of young men as bearers.

Meanwhile, Steerpike had dived into another suit and run across to Mrs Slagg in the castle, whom he instructed to replenish the fire and to have Fuchsia's bed ready and some hot drink brewing, leaving her in a state of querulous collapse, which was not remedied by his tickling her rudely in the ribs as he skipped past her to the door.

Coming into the quadrangle he caught sight of the Doctor as he was emerging from his garden gate with the two men and the stretcher. Prunesquallor was holding his umbrella over a bundle of rugs under which he had placed his medical bag.

When he had caught them up, he gave them their directions saying that he would run on ahead, but would reappear on the escarpment to direct them in the final stage of their journey. Tucking one of the blankets under his cape he disappeared into the thinning rain. As he ran on alone, he made jumps into the air. Life was amusing. *So* amusing. Even the rain had played into his hand and made the rock slippery. Everything, he thought to himself, can be of use. Everything. And he clicked his fingers as he ran grinning through the rain.

*

When Fuchsia awoke in her bed and saw the firelight flickering on the ceiling and Nannie Slagg sitting beside her, she said:

'Where is Steerpike?'

'Who, my precious? Oh, my poor pretty one!' And Mrs Slagg fidgeted with Fuchsia's hand which she had been holding for over an hour. 'What is it you need, my only? What is it, my caution dear? Oh, my poor heart, you've nearly killed me, dear. Very nearly. Yes, very nearly, then. There, there. Stay still, and the Doctor will be here again soon. Oh, my poor, weak heart!' The tears were streaming down her little, old terrified face.

'Nannie,' said Fuchsia, 'where's Steerpike?'

'That horrid boy?' asked Nannie. 'What about him, precious? You don't want to see him, do you? Oh no, you couldn't want that boy. What is it, my only? Do you want to see him?'

'Oh, no! no!' said Fuchsia. 'I don't want to. I feel so tired. Are you there?'

'What is it, my only?'

'Nothing; nothing. I wonder where he is.'

KNIVES IN THE MOON

THE moon slid inexorably into its zenith, the shadows shrivelling to the feet of all that cast them, and as Rantel approached the hollow at the hem of the Twisted Woods he was treading in a pool of his own midnight.

The roof of the Twisted Woods reflected the staring circle in a phosphorescent network of branches that undulated to the lower slopes of Gormenghast Mountain. Rising from the ground and circumscribing this baleful canopy the wood was walled with impenetrable shadow. Nothing of what supported the chilly haze of the topmost branches was discernible – only a winding façade of blackness.

The crags of the mountain were ruthless in the moon; cold, deadly and shining. Distance had no meaning. The tangled glittering of the forest roof rolled away, but its furthermost reaches were brought suddenly nearer in a bound by the terrifying effect of proximity in the mountain that they swarmed. The mountain was neither far away nor was it close at hand. It arose starkly, enormously, across the lens of the eye. The hollow itself was a cup of light. Every blade of the grass was of consequence, and the few scattered stones held an authority that made their solid, separate marks upon the brain – each one with its

own unduplicated shape: each rising brightly from the ink of its own
spilling.

When Rantel had come to the verge of the chosen hollow he stood
still. His head and body were a mosaic of black and ghastly silver as he
gazed into the basin of grass below him. His cloak was drawn tightly
about his spare body and the rhythmic folds of the drapery held the
moonlight along their upper ridges. He was sculpted, but his head
moved suddenly at a sound, and lifting his eyes he saw Braigon arise
from beyond the rim across the hollow.

They descended together, and when they had come to the level
ground they unfastened their cloaks, removed their heavy shoes and
stripped themselves naked. Rantel flung his clothes away to the sloping
grass. Braigon folded his coarse garments and laid them across a
boulder. He saw that Rantel was feeling the edge of his blade which
danced in the moonlight like a splinter of glass.

They said nothing. They tested the slippery grass with their naked feet.

Then they turned to one another. Braigon eased his fingers around the short bone hilt. Neither could see the expression in the other's face for their features were lost in the shadows of their brows and only their tangled hair held the light. They crouched and began to move, the distance closing between them, the muscles winding across their backs.

With Keda for hearts' reason, they circled, they closed, they feinted, their blades parrying the thrusts of the knife by sudden cross movements of their forearms.

When Rantel carved it was onslaught. It was as though the wood were his enemy. He fought it with rasp and chisel, hacking its flesh away until the shape that he held in his mind began to surrender to his violence. It was in this way that he fought. Body and brain were fused into one impulse – to kill the man who crouched before him. Not even Keda was in his mind now.

His eyes embraced the slightest movement of the other's body, of his moving feet, of his leaping knife. He saw that around Braigon's left arm a line of blood was winding from a gash in the shoulder. Rantel had the longer reach, but swiftly as his knife shot forward to the throat or breast, Braigon's forearm would swing across behind it and smack his arm away from its target. Then at the impact Rantel would spin out of range, and again they would circle and close in upon one another, their shoulders and arms gleaming in the unearthly brilliance.

As Braigon fought he wondered where Keda was. He wondered whether there could ever be happiness for her after himself or Rantel had been killed; whether she could forget that she was the wife of a murderer; whether to fight were not to escape from some limpid truth. Keda came vividly before his eyes, and yet his body worked with mechanical brilliance, warding off the savage blade and attacking his assailant with a series of quick thrusts, drawing blood from Rantel's side.

As the figure moved before him he followed the muscles as they wove beneath the skin. He was not only fighting with an assailant who was awaiting for that split second in which to strike him dead, but he was stabbing at a masterpiece – at sculpture that leapt and heaved, at a marvel of inky shadow and silver light. A great wave of nausea surged through him and his knife felt putrid in his hand. His body went on fighting.

The grass was blotched with the impression of their feet. They had scattered and crushed the dew and a dark irregular patch filled the centre of the hollow showing where their game with death had led them. Even this bruised darkness of crushed grass was pale in comparison with the intensity of their shadows which, moving as they moved, sliding beneath them, springing when they sprang, were never still.

Their hair was sticking to the sweat on their brows. The wounds in their bodies were weakening them, but neither could afford to pause.

About them the stillness of the pale night was complete. The moonlight lay like rime along the ridges of the distant castle. The reedy marshlands far to the east lay inert – a region of gauze. Their bodies were raddled now with the blood from many wounds. The merciless light gleamed on the wet, warm streams that slid ceaselessly over their tired flesh. A haze of ghostly weakness was filling their nakedness and they were fighting like characters in a dream.

Keda's trance had fallen from her in a sudden brutal moment and she had started to run towards the Twisted Woods. Through the great phosphorescent night, cloakless, her hair unfastening as she climbed, she came at last to the incline that led to the lip of the hollow. Her pain mounted as she ran. The strange, unworldly strength had died in her, the glory was gone – only an agony of fear was with her now.

As she climbed to the ridge of the hollow she could hear – so small a sound in the enormous night – the panting of the men, and her heart for a moment lifted, for they were alive.

With a bound she reached the brow of the slope and saw them crouching and moving in moonlight below her. The cry in her throat was choked as she saw the blood upon them, and she sank to her knees.

Braigon had seen her and his tired arms rang with a sudden strength. With a flash of his left arm he whirled Rantel's daggered hand away, and springing after him as swiftly as though he were a part of his foe, he plunged his knife into the shadowy breast.

As he struck he withdrew the dagger, and as Rantel sank to the ground, Braigon flung his weapon away.

He did not turn to Keda. He stood motionless, his hands at his head. Keda could feel no grief. The corners of her mouth lifted. The time for horror was not yet. This was not *real* – yet. She saw Rantel raise himself upon his left arm. He groped for his dagger and felt it beside him in the dew. His life was pouring from the wound in his breast. Keda watched him as, summoning into his right arm what strength remained in his whole body, he sent the dagger running through the air with a sudden awkward movement of his arm. It found its mark in a statue's throat. Braigon's arms fell to his sides like dead weights. He tottered forward, swayed for a little, the bone hilt at his gullet, and then collapsed lifeless across the body of his destroyer.

'Equality,' said Steerpike, 'is the thing. It is the only true and central premise from which constructive ideas can radiate freely and be operated without prejudice. Absolute equality of status. Equality of wealth. Equality of power.'

He tapped at a stone that lay among the wet leaves with his swordstick and sent it scurrying through the undergrowth.

He had waylaid Fuchsia with a great show of surprise in the pine woods as she was returning from an evening among the trees. It was the last evening before the fateful day of the burning. There would be no time tomorrow for any dallying of this kind. His plans were laid and the details completed. The Twins were rehearsed in their rôles and Steerpike was reasonably satisfied that he could rely on them. This evening, after having enjoyed a long bath at the Prunesquallors', he had spent more time than usual dressing himself. He had plastered his sparse tow-coloured hair over his bulging forehead with unusual care, viewing himself as he did so from every angle in the three mirrors he had erected on a table by the window.

As he left the house, he spun the slim swordstick through his fingers. It circled in his hand like the spokes of a wheel. Should he, or should he not pay a quick call on the Twins? On the one hand he must not excite them, for it was as though they had been primed for an examination and might suddenly forget everything they had been taught. On the other hand, if he made no direct reference to tomorrow's enterprise but encouraged them obliquely it might keep them going through the night. It was essential that they should have a good night's sleep. He did not want them sitting bolt upright on the edge of their beds all night staring at each other, with their eyes and mouths wide open.

He decided to pay a very short visit and then to take a stroll to the woods, where he thought he might find Fuchsia, for she had made a habit of lying for hours beneath a certain pine in what she fondly imagined was a secret glade.

Steerpike decided he would see them for a few moments, and at once he moved rapidly across the quadrangle. A fitful light was breaking through the clouds, and the arches circumscribing the quadrangle cast pale shadows that weakened or intensified as the clouds stole across the sun. Steerpike shuddered as he entered the sunless castle.

When he came to the door of the aunts' apartments he knocked, and entered at once. There was a fire burning in the grate and he walked towards it, noticing as he did so the twin heads of Cora and Clarice twisted on their long powdered necks. Their eyes were staring at him over the embroidered back of their couch, which had been pulled up to the fire. They followed him with their heads, their necks unwinding as he took up a position before them with his back to the fire, his legs astride, his hands behind him.

'My dears,' he said, fixing them in turn with his magnetic eyes; 'my *dears*, how are you? But what need is there to ask? You both look radiant. Lady Clarice, I have seldom seen you look lovelier; and your sister refuses to let you have it all your own way. You refuse utterly, Lady Cora, don't you? You are about as bridal as I ever remember you. It is a delight to be with you again.' The twins stared at him and wriggled, but no expression appeared in their faces.

After a long silence during which Steerpike had been warming his hands at the blaze Cora said, 'Do you mean that I'm glorious?'

'That's not what he said,' came Clarice's flat voice.

'Glorious,' said Steerpike, 'is a dictionary word. We are all imprisoned by the dictionary. We choose out of that vast, paper-walled prison our convicts, the little black printed words, when in truth we need fresh sounds to utter, new enfranchised noises which would produce a new effect. In dead and shackled language, my dears, you *are* glorious, but oh, to give vent to a brand new sound that might convince you of what I really think of you, as you sit there in your purple splendour, side by side! But no, it is impossible. Life is too fleet for onomatopoeia. Dead words defy me. I can make no sound, dear ladies, that is apt.'

'You could try,' said Clarice. 'We aren't busy.'

She smoothed the shining fabric of her dress with her long, lifeless fingers.

'Impossible,' replied the youth, rubbing his chin. 'Quite impossible. Only believe in my admiration for your beauty that will one day be recognized by the whole castle. Meanwhile, preserve all dignity and silent power in your twin bosoms.'

'Yes, yes,' said Cora, 'we'll preserve it. We'll preserve it in our bosoms, won't we, Clarice? Our silent power.'

'Yes, all the power we've got,' said Clarice. 'But we haven't got much.'

'It is coming to you,' said Steerpike. 'It is on its way. You are of the blood; who else but you should wield the sceptre? But alone you cannot succeed. For years you have smarted from the insults you have been forced to endure. Ah, how patiently, you have smarted! How patiently! Those days have gone. Who is it that can help you?' He took a pace towards them and bent forward. 'Who is it that can restore you: and who will set you on your glittering thrones?'

The aunts put their arms about one another so that their faces were cheek to cheek, and from this doublehead they gazed up at Steerpike with a row of four equidistant eyes. There was no reason why there should not have been forty, or four hundred of them. It so happened that only four had been removed from a dead and endless frieze whose inexhaustible and repetitive theme was forever, eyes, eyes, eyes.

'Stand up,' said Steerpike. He had raised his voice.

They got to their feet awkwardly and stood before him evil. A sense of power filled Steerpike with an acute enjoyment.

'Take a step forward,' he said.

They did so, still holding one another.

Steerpike watched them for some time, his shoulders hunched against the mantelpiece. 'You heard me speak,' he said. 'You heard my question. Who is it that will raise you to your thrones?'

'Thrones,' said Cora in a whisper; 'our thrones.'

'Golden ones,' said Clarice. 'That is what we want.'

'That is what you shall have. Golden thrones for Lady Cora and Lady Clarice. Who will give them to you?'

He stretched forward his hands and, holding each of them firmly by an elbow, brought them forward in one piece to within a foot of himself. He had never gone so far before, but he could see that they were clay in his hands and the familiarity was safe. The dreadful proximity of the identical faces caused him to draw his own head back.

'Who will give you the thrones, the glory and the power?' he said. 'Who?'

Their mouths opened together. 'You,' they said. 'It's *you* who'll give them to us. Steerpike will give them to us.'

Then Clarice craned her head forward from beside her sister's and she whispered as though she were telling Steerpike a secret for the first time.

'We're burning Sepulchrave's books up,' she said, 'the whole of his silly library. We're doing it – Cora and I. Everything is ready.'

'Yes,' said Steerpike. 'Everything is ready.'

Clarice's head regained its normal position immediately above her neck, where it balanced itself, a dead thing, on a column, but Cora's came forward as though to take the place of its counterpart and to keep the machinery working. In the same flat whisper she continued from where her sister had left off:

'All we do is to do what we've been told to do.' Her head came forward another two inches. 'There isn't anything difficult. It's easy to do. We go to the big door and then we find two little pieces of cloth sticking through from the inside, and then –'

'We set them on fire!' broke in her sister in so loud a voice that Steerpike closed his eyes. Then with a profound emptiness: 'We'll do it *now*,' said Clarice. 'It's easy.'

'Now?' said Steerpike. 'Oh no, not now. We decided it should be tomorrow, didn't we? Tomorrow evening.'

'I want to do it *now*,' said Clarice. 'Don't you, Cora?'

'No,' said Cora.

Clarice bit solemnly at her knuckles. 'You're frightened,' she said; 'frightened of a little bit of fire. You ought to have more pride than that, Cora. I have, although I'm gently manured.'

'Mannered, you mean,' said her sister. 'You *stupid*. How ignorant you are. With our blood, too. I am ashamed of our likenesses and always will be, so *there*!'

Steerpike brushed an elegant green vase from the mantel with his elbow, which had the effect he had anticipated. The four eyes moved towards the fragments on the floor – the thread of their dialogue was as shattered as the vase.

'A sign!' he muttered in a low, vibrant voice. 'A portent! A symbol! The circle is complete. An angel has spoken.'

The twins stared open-mouthed.

'Do you see the broken porcelain, dear ladies?' he said. 'Do you *see* it?'

They nodded.

'What else is that but the *Régime*, broken for ever – the bullydom of Gertrude – the stony heart of Sepulchrave – the ignorance, malice and brutality of the House of Groan as it now stands – smashed for ever? It is a signal that your hour is at hand. Give praise, my dears; you shall come unto your splendour.'

'When?' said Cora. 'Will it be soon?'

'What about tonight?' said Clarice. She raised her flat voice to its second floor, where there was more ventilation. 'What about tonight?'

'There is a little matter to be settled first,' said Steerpike. 'One little job to be done. Very simple; very, very simple; but it needs clever people to do it.' He struck a match.

In the four lenses of the four flat eyes, the four reflections of a single flame, danced – danced.

'Fire!' they said. 'We know all about it. All, all, all.'

'Oh, then, to bed,' said the youth, speaking rapidly. 'To bed, to bed, to bed.'

Clarice lifted a limp hand like a slab of putty to her breast and scratched herself abstractedly. 'All right,' she said. 'Good night.' And as she moved towards the bedroom door she began to unfasten her dress.

'I'm going too,' said Cora. 'Good night.' She also, as she retired, could be seen unclasping and unhooking herself. Before the door closed behind her she was half unravelled of imperial purple.

Steerpike filled his pocket with nuts from a china bowl and letting himself out of the room began the descent to the quadrangle. He had had no intention of broaching the subject of the burning, but the aunts had happily proved less excitable than he had anticipated and his confidence in their playing their elementary rôles effectively on the following evening was strengthened.

As he descended the stone stairs he filled his pipe, and on coming into the mild evening light, his tobacco smouldering in the bowl, he felt in an amiable mood, and spinning his swordstick he made for the pine woods, humming to himself as he went.

He had found Fuchsia, and had built up some kind of conversation, although he always found it more difficult to speak to her than to anyone else. First he inquired with a certain sincerity whether she had recovered from the shock. Her cheek was inflamed, and she limped badly from the severe pain in her leg. The Doctor had bandaged her up carefully and had left instructions with Nannie that she must not go out for several days, but she had slipped away when her nurse was out of the room, leaving a scribble on the wall to the effect that she loved her; but as the creature never looked at the wall the message was abortive.

By the time they had come to the edge of the woods Steerpike was talking airily of any subject that came into his head, mainly for the purpose of building up in her mind a picture of himself as someone profoundly brilliant, but also for the enjoyment of talking for its own sake, for he was in a sprightly mood.

She limped beside him as they passed through the outermost trees and into the light of the sinking sun. Steerpike paused to remove a stag-beetle from where it clung to the soft bark of a pine.

Fuchsia went on slowly, wishing she were alone.

'There should be no rich, no poor, no strong, no weak,' said Steerpike, methodically pulling the legs off the stag-beetle, one by one, as he spoke. 'Equality is the great thing, equality is *everything*.' He flung the mutilated insect away. 'Do you agree, Lady Fuchsia?' he said.

'I don't know anything about it, and I don't care much,' said Fuchsia.

'But don't you think it's wrong if some people have nothing to eat and others have so much they throw most of it away? Don't you think it's wrong if some people have to work all their lives for a little money to exist on while others never do any work and live in luxury? Don't you think brave men should be recognized and rewarded, and not just treated the same as cowards? The men who climb mountains, or dive under the sea, or explore jungles full of fever, or save people from fires?'

'I don't know,' said Fuchsia again. 'Things ought to be fair, I suppose. But I don't know anything about it.'

'Yes, you do,' said Steerpike. 'When you say "Things ought to be fair" it is exactly what I mean. Things *ought* to be fair. Why aren't they fair? Because of greed and cruelty and lust for power. All that sort of thing must be stopped.'

'Well, why don't you stop it, then?' said Fuchsia in a distant voice. She was watching the sun's blood on the Tower of Flints, and a cloud like a drenched swab, descending, inch by inch, behind the blackening tower.

'I am going to,' said Steerpike with such an air of simple confidence that Fuchsia turned her eyes to him.

'You're going to stop cruelty?' she asked. 'And greediness, and all those things? I don't think you could. You're very clever, but, oh no, you couldn't do anything like that.'

Steerpike was taken aback for a moment by this reply. He had meant his remark to stand on its own – a limpid statement of fact – something that he imagined Fuchsia might often turn over in her mind and cogitate upon.

'It's nearly gone,' said Fuchsia as Steerpike was wondering how to reassert himself. 'Nearly gone.'

'What's nearly gone?' He followed her eyes to where the circle of the sun was notched with turrets. 'Oh, you mean the old treacle bun,' he said. 'Yes, it will get cold very quickly now.'

'Treacle bun?' said Fuchsia. 'Is that what you call it?' She stopped walking. 'I don't think you ought to call it that. It's not respectful.' She gazed. As the death-throes weakened in the sky, she watched with big, perplexed eyes. Then she smiled for the first time. 'Do you give names to other things like that?'

'Sometimes,' said Steerpike. 'I have a disrespectful nature.'

'Do you give people names?'

'I have done.'

'Have you got one for me?'

Steerpike sucked the end of his swordstick and raised his straw-coloured eyebrows. 'I don't think I have,' he said. 'I usually think of you as Lady Fuchsia.'

'Do you call my mother anything?'

'Your mother? Yes.'

'What do you call my mother?'

'I call her the old Bunch of Rags,' said Steerpike.

Fuchsia's eyes opened wide and she stood still again. 'Go away,' she said.

'That's not very fair,' said Steerpike. 'After all, you *asked* me.'

'What do you call my father, then? But I don't want to know. I think you're cruel,' said Fuchsia breathlessly, 'you who said you'd stop cruelty altogether. Tell me some more names. Are they *all* unkind – and funny?'

'Some other time,' said Steerpike, who had begun to feel chilly. 'The cold won't do your injuries any good. You shouldn't be out walking at all. Prunesquallor thinks you're in bed. He sounded very worried about you.'

They walked on in silence, and by the time they had reached the castle night had descended.

'MEANWHILE'

THE morning of the next day opened drearily, the sun appearing only after protracted periods of half-light, and then only as a pale paper disc, more like the moon than itself, as, for a few moments at a time it floated across some corridor of cloud. Slow, lack-lustre veils descended with almost imperceptible motion over Gormenghast, blurring its countless windows, as with a dripping smoke. The mountain appeared and disappeared a score of times during the morning as the drifts obscured it or lifted from its sides. As the day advanced the gauzes thinned, and it was in the late afternoon that the clouds finally dispersed to leave in their place an expanse of translucence, that stain, chill and secret, in the throat of a lily, a sky so peerless, that as Fuchsia stared into its glacid depths she began unwittingly to break and re-break the flower-stem in her hands.

When she turned her head away it was to find Mrs Slagg watching her with such a piteous expression that Fuchsia put her arms about her old nurse and hugged her less tenderly than was her wish, for she hurt the wrinkled midget as she squeezed.

Nannie gasped for breath, her body bruised from the excess of Fuchsia's burst of affection, and a gust of temper shook her as she climbed excitedly onto the seat of a chair.

'How *dare* you! How *dare* you!' she gasped at last after shaking and wriggling a miniature fist all around Fuchsia's surprised face. 'How *dare* you bully me and hurt me and crush me into so much pain, you wicked thing, you vicious, naughty thing! *You*, whom I've always done everything for. *You*, whom I washed and brushed and dressed and spoiled and cooked for since you were the size of a slipper. You . . . you . . .' The old woman began to cry, her body shaking underneath her black dress like some sort of jerking toy. She let go of the rail of the chair, crushed her fists into her tearful, bloodshot eyes, and, forgetting where she was, was about to run to the door, when Fuchsia jumped forward and caught her from falling. Fuchsia carried her to the bed and laid her down.

'Did I hurt you very much?'

Her old nurse, lying on the coverlet like a withered doll in black satin, pursed her lips together and waited until Fuchsia, seating herself on the side of the bed, had placed one of her hands within range. Then her fingers crept forward, inch by inch, over the eiderdown, and with a sudden grimace of concentrated naughtiness she smacked Fuchsia's hand as hard as she was able. Relaxing against the pillow after this puny revenge, she peered at Fuchsia, a triumphant gleam in her watery eyes.

Fuchsia, hardly noticing the malicious little blow, leant over and suffered herself to be hugged for a few moments.

'Now you must start getting dressed,' said Nannie Slagg. 'You must be getting ready for your father's Gathering, mustn't you? It's always one thing or another. "Do this. Do that." And my heart in the state it is. Where will it all end? And what will you wear today? What dress will look the noblest for the wicked, tempestable thing?'

'You're coming, too, aren't you?' Fuchsia said.

'Why, what a *thing* you are,' squeaked Nannie Slagg, climbing down over the edge of the bed. 'Fancy such an ignorous question! I am taking his little LORDSHIP, you big stupid!'

'What! is Titus going, too?'

'Oh, your *ignorance*,' said Nannie. ' "Is Titus going, *too*?" she says.' Mrs Slagg smiled pityingly. 'Poor, poor, wicked thing! what a querail!' The old woman gave forth a series of pathetically unconvincing laughs and then put her hands on Fuchsia's knees excitedly. 'Of *course* he's going,' she said. 'The Gathering is *for* him. It's about his Birthday Breakfast.'

'Who else is going, Nannie?'

Her old nurse began to count on her fingers.

'Well, there's your father,' she began, placing the tips of her forefingers together and raising her eyes to the ceiling. 'First of all there's him, your father . . .'

As she spoke Lord Sepulchrave was returning to his room after performing the bi-annual ritual of opening the iron cupboard in the armoury, and, with the traditional dagger which Sourdust had brought for the occasion, of scratching on the metal back of the cupboard another half moon, which, added to the long line of similar half moons, made the seven hundred and thirty-seventh to be scored into the iron. According to the temperaments of the deceased Earls of Gormenghast the half moons were executed with precision or with carelessness. It was not certain what significance the ceremony held, for unfortunately the records were lost, but the formality was no less sacred for being unintelligible.

Old Sourdust had closed the iron door of the ugly, empty cupboard with great care, turning the key in the lock, and but for the fact that while inserting the key a few strands of his beard had gone in with it and been turned and caught, he would have felt the keen professional pleasure that all ritual gave him. It was in vain for him to pull, for not only was he held fast, but the pain to his chin brought tears to his eyes. To bring the key out and the hairs of his beard with it would ruin the ceremony, for it was laid down that the key must remain in the lock for twenty-three hours, a retainer in yellow being posted to guard the cupboard for that period. The only thing to do was to sever the strands with the knife, and this is eventually what the old man did, after which he set fire to the grey tufts of his alienated hairs that protruded from the keyhole like a fringe around the key. These flamed a little, and when the sizzling had ceased Sourdust turned apologetically to find that his Lordship had gone.

When Lord Sepulchrave reached his bedroom he found Flay laying out the black costume that he habitually wore. The Earl had it in his mind to dress more elaborately this evening. There had been a slight but perceptible lifting of his spirit ever since he had conceived this Breakfast for his son. He had become aware of a dim pleasure in having a son. Titus had been born during one of his blackest moods, and although he was still shrouded in melancholia, his introspection had, during the last few days, become tempered by a growing interest in his heir, not as a personality, but as the symbol of the Future. He had some vague presentiment that his own tenure was drawing to a close and it gave him both pleasure when he remembered his son, and a sense of stability amid the miasma of his waking dreams.

Now that he knew he had a son he realized how great had been the unspoken nightmare which had lurked in his mind. The terror that with *him* the line of Groan should perish. That he had failed the castle of his forebears, and that rotting in his sepulchre the future generations would point at his, the last of the long line of discoloured monuments and whisper: 'He was the last. He had no son.'

As Flay helped him dress, neither of them speaking a word, Lord Sepulchrave thought of all this, and fastening a jewelled pin at his collar he sighed, and within the doomed and dark sea-murmur of that sigh was the plashing sound of a less mournful billow. And then, as he gazed absently past himself in the mirror at Flay, another comber of far pleasure followed the first, for his books came suddenly before his eyes, row upon row of volumes, row upon priceless row of calf-bound Thought, of philosophy and fiction, of travel and fantasy; the stern and the ornate, the moods of gold or green, of sepia, rose, or black; the picaresque, the arabesque, the scientific – the essays, the poetry and the drama.

All this, he felt, he would now re-enter. He could inhabit the world of words, with, at the back of his melancholy, a solace he had not known before.

'Then *next*,' said Mrs Slagg, counting on her fingers, 'there's your mother, of course. Your father and your mother – that makes Two.'

Lady Gertrude had not thought of changing her dress. Nor had it occurred to her to prepare for the gathering.

She was seated in her bedroom. Her feet were planted widely apart as though for all time. Her elbows weighed on her knees, from between which the draperies of her skirt sagged in heavy U-shaped folds. In her hands was a paper-covered book, with a coffee-stain across its cover and with as many dogs' ears as it had pages. She was reading aloud in a deep voice that rose above the steady drone of a hundred cats. They filled the room. Whiter than the tallow that hung from the candelabra or lay broken on the table of birdseed. Whiter than the pillows on the bed. They sat everywhere. The counterpane was hidden with them. The table, the cupboards, the couch, all was luxuriant with harvest, white as death, but the richest crop was all about her feet where a cluster of white faces stared up into her own. Every luminous, slit-pupilled eye was upon her. The only movement lay in the vibration in their throats. The voice of the Countess moved on like a laden ship upon a purring tide.

As she came to the end of every right-hand page and was turning it over her eyes would move around the room with an expression of the deepest tenderness, her pupils filling with the minute white reflections of her cats.

Then her eyes would turn again to the printed page. Her enormous face had about it the wonderment of a child as she read. She was re-living the story, the old story which she had so often read to them.

'And the door closed, and the latch clicked, but the prince with stars for his eyes and a new-moon for his mouth didn't mind, for he was young and strong, and though he wasn't handsome, he had heard lots of doors close and click before this one, and didn't feel at all frightened. But he would have been if he had known who had closed the door. It was the Dwarf with brass teeth, who was more dreadful than the most spotted of all things, and whose ears were fixed on backwards.

'Now when the prince had finished brushing his hair . . .'

*

While the Countess was turning the page Mrs Slagg was ticking off the third and fourth fingers of her left hand.

'Dr Prunesquallor and Miss Irma will come as well, dear: they always come to nearly everything – don't they, though I can't see *why* – they aren't ancestral. But they always come. Oh, my poor conscience! it's always I who have to bear with them, and do everything, and I'll have to go in a moment, my caution, to remind your mother, and she'll shout at me and make me so nervous; but I'll have to go for she won't remember, but that's just how it *always* happens. And the Doctor and Miss Irma make another two people, and that makes four altogether.' Mrs Slagg gasped for breath. 'I don't like Dr Prunesquallor, my baby; I don't like his proud habits,' said Nannie. 'He makes me feel so silly and small when I'm not. But he's always asked, even when his vain and ugly sister isn't; but she's been asked this time so they'll both be there, and you must stay next to me, won't you? Won't you? Because I've got his little Lordship to care for. Oh, my dear heart! I'm not well – I'm not; I'm *not*. And nobody cares – not even you.' Her wrinkled hand gripped at Fuchsia's. 'You will look after me?'

'Yes,' said Fuchsia. 'But I like the Doctor.'

Fuchsia lifted up the end of her mattress and burrowed beneath the feather-filled weight until she found a small box. She turned her back on her nurse for a moment and fastened something around her neck, and when she turned again Mrs Slagg saw the solid fire of a great ruby hung beneath her throat.

'You must wear it *today*!' Mrs Slagg almost screamed. 'Today, today, you naughty thing, when everyone's there. You will look as pretty as a flowering lamb, my big, untidy thing.'

'No, Nannie, I won't wear it like that. not when it's a day like today. I shall wear it only when I'm alone or when I meet a man who reverences me.'

The Doctor, meanwhile, lay in a state of perfect contentment in a hot bath filled with blue crystals. The bath was veined marble and was long enough to allow the Doctor to lie at full length. Only his quill-like face emerged above the perfumed surface of the water. His hair was filled with winking lather-bubbles; and his eyes were indescribably roguish. His face and neck were bright pink as though direct from a celluloid factory.

At the far end of the bath one of his feet emerged from the depths. He watched it quizzically with his head cocked so far upon one side that his left ear filled with water. 'Sweet foot,' he cried. 'Five toes to boot and what-not in the beetroot shoot!' He raised himself and shook the hot water gaily from his ear and began swishing the water on either side of his body.

The eyes closed and the mouth opened and all the teeth were there shining through the steam. Taking a great breath, or rather, a deep breath, for his chest was too narrow for a great one, and with a smile of dreadful bliss irradiating his pink face, the Doctor emitted a whinny of so piercing a quality, that Irma, seated at her boudoir table, shot to her feet, scattering hairpins across the carpet. She had been at her toilet for the last three hours, excluding the preliminary hour and a half spent in her bath – and now, as she swished her way to the bedroom door, a frown disturbing the powder on her brow, she had, in common with her brother, more the appearance of having been plucked or peeled, than of cleanliness, though *clean* she was, scrupulously clean, in the sense of a rasher of bacon.

'What on earth is the matter with you; I said, what on earth is the matter with you, Bernard?' she shouted through the bathroom keyhole.

'Is that you my love? Is that you?' her brother's voice came thinly from behind the door.

'Who *else* would it be; I said, who *else* would it be,' she yelled back, bending herself into a stiff satin right angle in order to get her mouth to the keyhole.

'Ha, ha, ha, ha, ha,' came her brother's shrill, unbearable laughter. 'Who else indeed? Well, well, let us think, let us *think*. It might be the moon-goddess, but that's improbable, ha, ha, ha; or it might be a sword swallower approaching me in my professional capacity, ha, ha, that is *less* improbable – in fact, my dear tap-root, have you by any chance been swallowing swords for years on end without ever telling me, ha, ha? Or haven't you?' His voice rose: 'Years on end, and swords on end – where will it end, if our ears unbend – what shall I spend on a wrinkled friend in a pair of tights like a bunch of lights?'

Irma who had been straining her ears cried out at last in her irritation: 'I suppose you know you'll be late – I said: "I suppose you –" '

'A merry plague upon you, O blood of my blood,' the shrill voice broke in. 'What is Time, O sister of similar features, that you speak of it so subserviently? Are we to be the slaves of the sun, that second-hand, overrated knob of gilt, or of his sister, that fatuous circle of silver paper? A curse upon their ridiculous dictatorship! What say you, Irma, my Irma, wrapped in rumour, Irma, of the incandescent tumour?' he trilled happily. And his sister rose rustling to her full height, arching her nostrils as she did so, as though they itched with pedigree. Her brother annoyed her, and as she seated herself again before the mirror in her boudoir she made noises like a lady as she applied the powder-puff for the hundredth time to her spotless length of neck.

*

'Sourdust will be there, too,' said Mrs Slagg, 'because he knows all about things. He knows what order you do things in, precious, and when you must *start* doing them, and when you ought to *stop*.'

'Is that everyone?' asked Fuchsia.

'Don't hurry me,' replied the old nurse, pursing her lips into a prune of wrinkles. 'Can't you wait a minute? Yes, that makes five, and you make six, and his little Lordship makes seven . . .'

'And you make eight,' said Fuchsia. 'So you make the most.'

'Make the most what, my caution?'

'It doesn't matter,' said Fuchsia.

While, in various parts of the Castle, these eight persons were getting ready for the Gathering the twins were sitting bolt upright on the couch watching Steerpike drawing the cork out of a slim, dusty bottle. He held it securely between his feet and bending over with the corkscrew firmly embedded was easing the cork from the long black cormorant throat.

Having unwound the corkscrew and placed the undamaged cork on the mantelpiece, he emptied a little of the wine into a glass and tasted it with a critical expression on his pale face.

The aunts leaned forward, their hands on their knees, watching every movement.

Steerpike took one of the Doctor's silk handkerchiefs from his pocket and wiped his mouth. Then he held the wineglass up to the light for a long time and studied its translucence.

'What's wrong with it?' said Clarice slowly.

'Is it poisoned?' said Cora.

'Who poisoned it?' echoed Clarice.

'Gertrude,' said Cora. 'She'd kill us if she could.'

'But she can't,' said Clarice.

'And that's why we're going to be powerful.'

'And proud,' added Clarice.

'Yes, because of today.'

'Because of *today*.'

They joined their hands.

'It is good vintage, your Ladyship. A very adequate vintage. I selected it myself. You will, I know, appreciate it fully. It is not poisoned, my dear women. Gertrude, though she has poisoned your lives, has not, as it so happens, poisoned this particular bottle of wine. May I pour you out a glassful each, and we will drink a toast to the business of the day?'

'Yes, yes,' said Cora. 'Do it now.'

Steerpike filled their glasses.

'Stand up,' he said.

The purple twins arose together, and as Steerpike was about to propose the toast, his right hand holding the glass on the level of his chin and his left hand in his pocket, Cora's flat voice broke in:

'Let's drink it on our Tree,' she said. 'It's lovely outside. On our Tree.'

Clarice turned to her sister with her mouth open. Her eyes were as expressionless as mushrooms.

'That's what we'll do,' she said.

Steerpike, instead of being annoyed, was amused at the idea. After all, this was an important day for him. He had worked hard to get all in readiness and he knew that his future hung upon the smooth working of his plan, and although he would not congratulate himself until the library was in ashes, he felt that it was up to him and the aunts to relax for a few minutes before the work that lay ahead.

To drink a toast to the Day upon the boughs of the dead Tree appealed to his sense of the dramatic, the appropriate and the ridiculous.

A few minutes later the three of them had passed through the Room of Roots, filed along the horizontal stem and sat down at the table.

As they sat, Steerpike in the middle and the twins at either side, the evening air was motionless beneath them and around. The aunts had apparently no fear of the dizzy drop. They never thought of it. Steerpike, although he was enjoying the situation to the full, nevertheless averted his eyes as far as possible from the sickening space below him. He decided to deal gently with the bottle. On the wooden table their three glasses glowed in the warm light. Thirty feet away the sunny south wall towered above and fell below them featureless from its base to its summit save for the lateral offshoot of this dead tree, halfway up its surface, on which they sat, and the exquisitely pencilled shadows of its branches.

'Firstly, dear Ladyships,' said Steerpike, rising to his feet and fixing his eyes upon the shadow of a coiling bough, 'firstly I propose a health to *you*. To your steadfast purpose and the faith you have in your own destinies. To your courage. Your intelligence. Your beauty.' He raised his glass. 'I drink,' he said, and took a sip.

Clarice began to drink at the same moment, but Cora nudged her elbow. 'Not yet,' she said.

'Next I must propose a toast to the future. Primarily to the Immediate Future. To the task we have resolved to carry through today. To its success. And also to the Great Days that will result from it. The days of your reinstatement. The days of your Power and Glory. Ladies, to the Future!'

Cora, Clarice and Steerpike lifted their elbows to drink. The warm air hung about them, and as Cora's raised elbow struck her sister's and jogged the wineglass from her hand, and as it rolled from the table to the tree and from the tree out into the hollow air, the western sunlight caught it as it fell, glittering, through the void.

'THE BURNING'

ALTHOUGH it was Lord Sepulchrave who had summoned the Gathering, it was to Sourdust that the party turned when they had all arrived in the library, for his encyclopaedic knowledge of ritual gave authority to whatever proceedings were to follow. He stood by the marble table and, as the oldest, and in his opinion, the wisest person present, had about him a quite understandable air of his own importance. To wear rich and becoming apparel no doubt engenders a sense of well-being in the wearer, but to be draped, as was Sourdust, in a sacrosanct habit of crimson rags is to be in a world above such consideration as the price and fit of clothes and to experience a sense of propriety that no wealth could buy. Sourdust knew that were he to demand it the wardrobes of Gormenghast would be flung open to him. He did not want it. His mottled beard of alternate black and white hairs was freshly knotted. The crumpled parchment of his ancestral face glimmered in the evening light that swam through the high window.

Flay had managed to find five chairs, which he placed in a line before the table. Nannie, with Titus on her lap, took up the central position. On her right Lord Sepulchrave and on her left the Countess Gertrude sat in attitudes peculiar to them, the former with his right elbow on the arm of the chair and his chin lost in the palm of his hand, and the Countess obliterating the furniture she sat in. On her right sat the Doctor, his long legs crossed and a footling smile of anticipation on his face. At the other end of the row his sister sat with her pelvis at least a foot to the rear of an excited perpendicular – her thorax, neck and head. Fuchsia, for whom, much to her relief, no chair was to be found, stood behind them, her hands behind her back. Between her fingers a small green handkerchief was being twisted round and round. She watched the ancient Sourdust take a step forward and wondered what it must feel like to be so old and wrinkled. 'I wonder if I'll ever be as old as that,' she thought; 'an old wrinkled woman, older than my mother, older than Nannie Slagg even.' She gazed at the black mass of her mother's back. 'Who is there anyway who isn't old? There isn't anybody. Only that boy who hasn't any lineage. I wouldn't mind much, but he's different from me and too clever for me. And even he's not young. Not like I'd like my friends to be.'

Her eyes moved along the line of heads. One after the other: old heads that didn't understand.

Her eyes rested at last on Irma.

'She hasn't any lineage, either,' said Fuchsia to herself, 'and her neck is much too clean and it's the longest and thinnest and funniest I've ever seen. I wonder if she's really a white giraffe all the time, and pretending she isn't.' Fuchsia's mind flew to the stuffed giraffe's leg in the attic. 'Perhaps it belongs to *her*,' she thought. And the idea so appealed to Fuchsia that she lost control of herself and spluttered.

Sourdust, who was about to begin and had raised his old hand for the purpose, started and peered across at her. Mrs Slagg clutched Titus a little tighter and listened very hard for anything further. Lord Sepulchrave did not move his body an inch, but opened one eye slowly. Lady Gertrude, as though Fuchsia's splutter had been a signal, shouted to Flay, who was behind the library door:

'Open the door and let that bird in! What are you waiting for, man?' Then she whistled with a peculiar ventriloquism, and a wood warbler sped, undulating through the long, dark hollow of library air, to land on her finger.

Irma simply twitched but was too refined to look round, and it was left to the Doctor to make contact with Fuchsia by means of an exquisitely timed wink with his left eye behind its convex lens, like an oyster shutting and opening itself beneath a pool of water.

Sourdust, disturbed by this unseemly interjection and also by the presence of the wood warbler, which kept distracting his eye by running up and down Lady Gertrude's arm, lifted his head again, fingering a running bowline in his beard.

His hoarse and quavering voice wandered through the library like something lost.

The long shelves surrounded them, tier upon tier, circumscribing their world with a wall of other worlds imprisoned yet breathing among the network of a million commas, semi-colons, full stops, hyphens and every other sort of printed symbol.

'We are gathered together,' said Sourdust, 'in this ancient library at the instigation of Sepulchrave, 76th Earl to the house of Gormenghast and lord of those tracts of country that stretch on every hand, in the North to the wastelands, in the South to the grey salt marshes, in the East to the quicksands and the tideless sea, and in the West to knuckles of endless rock.'

This was delivered in one weak, monotonous stream. Sourdust coughed for some time and then, regaining his breath, continued mechanically: 'We are gathered on this seventeenth day of October to give ear to his Lordship. These nights the moon is in the ascendant and the river is full of fish. The owls in the Tower of Flints seek their prey as heretofore and it is appropriate that his Lordship should, on the seventeenth day of an autumn month, bring forward the matter that is in his mind. The sacred duties which he has never wavered to perform are over for the hour. It is appropriate that it should be now – now, at the sixth hour of the daylight clock.

'I as master of Ritual, as Guardian of the Documents and as Confidant to the Family, am able to say that for his Lordship to speak to you in no way contravenes the tenets of Gormenghast.

'But, your Lordship, and your revered Ladyship,' said Sourdust in his old sing-song, 'it is no secret to those here gathered that it is towards the child who now occupies pride of place, it is towards Lord Titus that our thoughts will converge this afternoon. That is no secret.'

Sourdust gave vent to a dreadful chesty cough. 'It is to Lord Titus,' he said, gazing mistily at the child and then, raising his voice, 'it is to Lord Titus,' he repeated irritably.

Nannie suddenly realized that the old man was making signs at her, and understood that she was to lift the infant up in the air as though he were a specimen, or something to be auctioned. She lifted him, but no one looked at the exhibit except Prunesquallor, who nearly engulfed Nannie, baby and all with a smile so devouring, so dental, as to cause Nannie to raise her shoulder against it and to snatch Titus back to her little flat chest.

'I will turn my back on you and strike the table four times,' said Sourdust. 'Slagg will bring the child to the table and Lord Sepulchrave will –' here he suffered a more violent fit of coughing than ever, and at the same moment Irma's neck quivered a little and she in her own way followed suit with five little ladylike barks. She turned her head apologetically in the direction of the Countess and wrinkled her forehead in self-deprecation. She could see that the Countess had taken no notice of her mute apology. She arched her nostrils. It had not crossed her mind there was a smell in the room other than the prevalent smell of musty leather: it was just that her nostrils with their hyper-sensitive nerve-endings were acting on their own accord.

Sourdust took some time to recover from his bout, but eventually he straightened himself and repeated:

'Slagg will bring the child to the table, and Lord Sepulchrave will graciously advance, following his menial, and on arriving at a point immediately behind me will touch the back of my neck with the forefinger of his left hand.

'At this signal I and Slagg will retire, and Slagg, having left the infant on the table, Lord Sepulchrave will pass behind the table and stand facing us across its surface.'

'Are you hungry, my little love? Is there no grain inside you? Is that it? Is that it?'

The voice came forth so suddenly and heavily and so closely upon the quavering accents of Sourdust that everyone felt for the first few moments that the remark was addressed to them personally; but on turning their heads they could see that the Countess was addressing herself exclusively to the wood warbler. Whether the warbler made any reply was never ascertained for not only was Irma seized with a new and less ladylike bout of short dry coughs, but her brother and Nannie Slagg, joining her, filled the room with noise.

The bird rose into the air, startled, and Lord Sepulchrave stopped on his passage to the table and turned irritably to the line of noisy figures; but as he did so a faint smell of smoke making itself perceptible for the first time caused him to raise his head and sniff the air in a slow, melancholy way. At the same time Fuchsia felt a roughness in her throat. She glanced about the room and wrinkled her nose, for smoke though still invisible was infiltrating steadily through the library.

Prunesquallor had risen from beside the Countess and with his white hands wound about each other and with his mouth twisted into a quizzical line he permitted his eyes to move rapidly around the room. His head was cocked on one side.

'What's the matter, man?' asked the Countess heavily from immediately below him. She was still seated.

'The matter?' queried the Doctor, smiling more emphatically but still keeping his eyes on the move. 'It is a case of atmosphere, as far as I can dare to judge at such very, very short notice, your Ladyship, as far as I *dare* to judge, ha, ha, ha! It is a case of thickening atmosphere, ha, ha!'

'Smoke,' said the Countess heavily and bluntly. 'What is the matter with smoke? Haven't you ever smelt it before?'

'Many and many a time, your Ladyship,' answered the Doctor. 'But never, if I may say so, never in *here*.'

The Countess grunted to herself and settled deeper into the chair.

'There never *is* smoke in here,' said Lord Sepulchrave. He turned his head to the door and raised his voice a little:

'Flay.'

The long servant emerged out of the shadows like a spider.

'Open the door,' said Lord Sepulchrave sharply; and as the spider turned and began its return journey his Lordship took a step towards old Sourdust, who was by now doubled over the table in a paroxysm of coughing. His Lordship taking one of Sourdust's elbows beckoned to Fuchsia, who came across the room and supported the old man on the other side, and the three of them began to make their way to the door in Flay's wake.

Lady Groan simply sat like a mountain and watched the little bird.

Dr Prunesquallor was wiping his eyes, his thick glasses pushed for the moment above his eyebrows. But he was very much on the alert and as soon as his spectacles were again in place he grinned at everyone in turn. His eye lingered for a moment on his sister Irma, who was systematically tearing an expensively embroidered cream-coloured silk handkerchief into small pieces. Behind the dark lenses of her glasses her eyes were hidden from view, but to judge from the thin, wet, drooping line of her mouth and the twitching of the skin on her pointed nose it might be safely assumed that they were making contact with, and covering the inner side of, the lenses of her spectacles with the moisture with which the smoke had filmed them.

The Doctor placed the tips of his fingers and thumbs together and then, separating the tapering extremities of the index fingers, he watched them for a few seconds as they gyrated around one another. Then his eyes turned to the far end of the room where he could see the Earl and his daughter, with the old man between them, approaching the library door. Someone, presumably Flay, seemed to be making a great deal of noise in wrestling with the heavy iron door-handle.

The smoke was spreading, and the Doctor, wondering why in the devil's name the door had not been thrown open, began to peer about the room in an effort to locate the source of the ever-thickening wreaths. As he took a step past Nannie Slagg he saw that she was standing by the table from whose marble surface she had plucked Titus. She was holding him very closely to herself and had wrapped him in layers of cloth which had completely hidden him from view. A sound of muffled crying could be heard coming from the bundle. Nannie's little wrinkled mouth was hanging open. Her streaming eyes were redder than usual with the stinging smoke. But she stood quite still.

'My very dear good woman,' said Dr Prunesquallor, turning on his heel as he was about to float past her, 'my very dear Slagg, convey his minute Lordship to the door that for some reason that is too subtle for me to appreciate remains shut. Why, in the name of Ventilation, *I* don't know. But it *does*. It remains shut. Take him nevertheless, my dear Slagg, to the aforesaid door and place his infinitesimal head at the keyhole (surely *THAT'S* still open!), and even if you cannot squeeze the child right through it you can at least give his Lordship's lungs something to get on with.'

Nannie Slagg was never very good at interpreting the Doctor's long sentences, especially when coming through a haze of smoke, and all that she could gather was that she should attempt to squeeze her tiny Lordship through the keyhole. Clutching the baby even tighter in her thin arms, 'No! no! no!' she cried, retreating from the doctor.

Dr Prunesquallor rolled his eyes at the Countess. She was apparently aware of the state of the room at last and was gathering together great swathes of drapery in a slow, deliberate manner preparatory to rising to her feet.

The rattling at the library door became more violent, but the indigenous shadows and the smoke combined to make it impossible to see what was going on.

'Slagg,' said the Doctor, advancing on her, 'go to the door immediately, like the intelligent woman you are!'

'No! no!' shrieked the midget, in so silly a voice that Doctor Prunesquallor after taking a handkerchief from his pocket lifted her from her feet and tucked her under his arm. The handkerchief enveloping Nannie Slagg's waist prevented the nurse's garments from coming in contact with the Doctor's clothes. Her legs, like black twigs blown in the wind, gesticulated for a few moments and then were still.

Before they had reached the door, however, they were met by Lord Sepulchrave, who emerged darkly from the smoke. 'The door has been locked from the outside,' he whispered between fits of coughing.

'Locked?' queried Prunesquallor. 'Locked, your Lordship? By all that's perfidious! This is becoming intriguing. Most intriguing. Perhaps a bit too intriguing. What do *you* think, Fuchsia, my dear little lady? Eh? ha, ha! Well, well, we must become positively cerebral, mustn't we? By all that's enlightened we really must! Can it be smashed?' He turned to Lord Sepulchrave. 'Can we breach it, your Lordship, battery and assault and all that delicious sort of thing?'

'Too thick, Prunesquallor,' said Lord Sepulchrave: 'four-inch oak.'

He spoke slowly in strange contrast to Prunesquallor's rapid, ejaculatory chirping.

Sourdust had been propped near the door, where he sat coughing as though to shake his old body to bits.

'No key for the other door,' continued Lord Sepulchrave slowly. 'It is never used. What about the window?' For the first time a look of alarm appeared on his ascetic face. He walked quickly to the nearest bookshelves and ran his fingers along the spines of calf. Then he turned with a quickness unusual for him. 'Where is the smoke thickest?'

'I've been searching for its origin, your Lordship,' came Prunesquallor's voice out of the haze. 'It's everywhere so thick that it's very difficult to say. By all the pits of darkness it most damnably is. But I'm looking, ha, ha! I'm looking.' He trilled for a moment like a bird. Then his voice came again. 'Fuchsia, dear!' he shouted. 'Are you all right?'

'Yes!' Fuchsia had to swallow hard before she could shout back, for she was very frightened. 'Yes, Dr Prune.'

'Slagg!' shouted the Doctor, 'keep Titus near the keyhole. See that she does, Fuchsia.'

'Yes,' whispered Fuchsia; and went in search of Mrs Slagg.

It was just then that an uncontrolled scream rang through the room.

Irma, who had been tearing her cream-coloured handkerchief, now found that she had ripped it into such minute particles that with nothing left to tear, and with her hands in forced idleness, she could control herself no longer. Her knuckles had tried to stifle the cry, but her terror had grown too strong for such expedients, and at the final moment she forgot all she had learnt about decorum and about how to be a lady, and clenching her hands at her thighs she had stood on tiptoe and screamed from her swanlike throat with an effect calculated to freeze the blood of a macaw.

An enormous figure had loomed out of the smoke a few feet from Lord Sepulchrave, and as he watched the vague head take shape and recognized it as that belonging to the top half of his wife's body, his limbs had stiffened, for Irma's scream had rung out simultaneously with the appearance of the head, the untoward proximity of which conjoined with the scream giving ventriloquistic horror to the moment. Added to the frightfulness of a head and a voice, attacking his ear and eye simultaneously though from different distances, was the dreadful conception of Gertrude losing control in that way and giving vent to a scream of such a shrill pitch as to be incompatible with the slack 'cello string that reverberated so heavily in her throat. He knew at once that it was *not* Gertrude who had screamed, but the very idea that it might have been, filled him with sickness, and there raced through his mind the thought that for all his wife's uncompromising, loveless weight of character it would be a grim and evil thing were she to change.

The flat blur of his wife's head turned itself towards the scream upon a blurred neck, and he could see the vast wavering profile begin to move away from him, inch by inch, and steer into the thickness beyond, charting its course by the shrill shooting-star of Irma's cry.

Lord Sepulchrave gripped his hands together convulsively until his knuckles were bloodless and their ten staring crests wavered whitely through the smoke which lay between his hands and his head.

The blood began to beat a tattoo at his temples, and upon his high white brow a few big beads gathered.

He was biting at his lower lip, and his eyebrows were drawn down over his eyes as though he were cogitating upon some academic problem. He knew that no one could see him, for by now the smoke was all but opaque, but he was watching himself. He could see that the position of his arms, and the whole attitude of his body was exaggerated and stiffened. He discovered that his fingers were splayed out in a histrionic gesture of alarm. It was for him to control his members before he could hope to organize the activities in the smoke-filled room. And so he watched and waited for the moment to assert himself, and as he watched he found himself struggling. There was blood on his tongue.

He had bitten his wrist. His hands were now grappling with one another and it seemed an eternity before the fingers ceased their deadly, interlocked and fratricidal strangling. Yet his panic could have taken no longer than a few moments, for the echo of Irma's scream was still in his ears when he began to loosen his hands.

Meanwhile Prunesquallor had reached his sister's side and had found her bridling her body up in preparation for another scream. Prunesquallor, as urbane as ever, had nevertheless something in his fish-like eyes that might almost be described as determination. One glance at his sister was sufficient to make him realize that to attempt to reason with her would be about as fruitful as to try to christianize a vulture. She was on tip-toe and her lungs were expanded when he struck her across her long white face with his long white hand, the pent breath from her lungs issuing from her mouth, ears and nostrils. There was something of shingle in the sound – of shingle dragged seawards on a dark night.

Dragging her across the room swiftly, her heels scraping the floor, he found a chair, after probing around in the smoke with his delicate feet, and sat his sister in it.

'Irma!' he shouted into her ear, 'my humiliating and entirely unfortunate old string of whitewash, sit where you are! Alfred will do the rest. Can you hear me? Be good now! blood of my blood, be good now, damn you!'

Irma sat quite still as though dead, save for a look of profound wonder in her eyes.

Prunesquallor was on the point of making another effort to locate the origin of the smoke when he heard Fuchsia's voice high above the coughing that by now was a constant background of noise in the library.

'Dr Prune! Dr Prune! quickly! Quickly, Dr Prune!'

The Doctor pulled down his cuffs smartly over his wrists, tried to square his shoulders, but met with no success, and then began to pick his way, half running, half walking, towards the door where Fuchsia, Mrs Slagg and Titus had been last seen. When he judged he was about half way to the door and was clear of the furniture, Prunesquallor began to accelerate his speed. This he did by increasing not only the length of his stride but the height also, so that he was, as it were, prancing through the air, when he was brought to a sudden ruthless halt by a collision with something that felt like an enormous bolster on end.

When he had drawn his face away from the tallow-smelling draperies that seemed to hang about him like curtains, he stretched out his hand tentatively and shuddered to feel it come in contact with large fingers.

' 'Squallor?' came the enormous voice. 'Is that 'Squallor?' The mouth of the Countess was opening and shutting within an inch of his left ear.

The Doctor gesticulated eloquently, but his artistry was wasted in the smoke.

'It *is*. Or rather,' he continued, speaking even more rapidly than usual – 'it is *Prunesquallor*, which is, if I may say so, more strictly correct, ha, ha, ha! even in the dark.'

'Where's Fuchsia?' said the Countess. Prunesquallor found that his shoulder was being gripped.

'By the door,' said the Doctor, longing to free himself from the weight of her Ladyship's hand, and wondering, even in the middle of the coughing and the darkness, what on earth the material that fitted around his shoulders so elegantly would look like when the Countess had finished with it. 'I was on the point of finding her when we met, ha, ha! met, as it were, so palpably, so inevitably.'

'Quiet, man! quiet!' said Lady Gertrude, loosening her grasp. 'Find her for me. Bring her here – and smash a window, 'Squallor, smash a window.'

The Doctor was gone from her in a flash and when he judged himself to be a few feet from the door – 'Are you there, Fuchsia?' he trilled.

Fuchsia was just below him, and he was startled to hear her voice come up jerkily through the smoke.

'She's ill. Very ill. Quick, Dr Prune, quick! Do something for her.' The Doctor felt his knees being clutched. 'She's down here, Dr Prune. I'm holding her.'

Prunesquallor hitched up his trousers and knelt down at once.

There seemed to be more vibration in the atmosphere in this part of the room, more than could be accounted for by any modicum of air that might have been entering through the keyhole. The coughing was dreadful to hear; Fuchsia's was heavy and breathless; but the thin, weak, and ceaseless coughing of Mrs Slagg gave the Doctor the more concern. He felt for the old nurse and found her in Fuchsia's lap. Slipping his hand across her little chicken-bosom he found that her heart was the merest flutter. To his left in the darkness there was a mouldy smell, and then the driest series of brick-dust coughs he had ever heard revealed the proximity of Flay, who was fanning the air mechanically with a large book he had clawed out of a nearby shelf. The fissure left in the row of hidden books had filled immediately with the coiling smoke – a tall, narrow niche of choking darkness, a ghastly gap in a row of leather wisdom teeth.

'Flay,' said the Doctor, 'can you hear me, Flay? Where's the largest window in the room, my man? Quickly now, where is it?'

'North wall,' said Flay. 'High up.'

'Go and shatter it at once. At once.'

'No balcony there,' said Flay. 'Can't reach.'

'Don't argue! Use what you've got in that head of yours. You know the room. Find a missile, my good Flay – find a missile, and break a window. Some oxygen for Mrs Slagg. Don't you think so? By all the zephyrs, yes! Go and help him, Fuchsia. Find where the window is and break it, even if you have to throw Irma at it, ha, ha, ha! And don't be alarmed. Smoke, you know, is only smoke: it's not composed of crocodiles, oh dear no, nothing so tropical. Hurry now. Break the window somehow and let the evening pour itself in – and I will see to dear Mrs Slagg and Titus, ha, ha, ha! Oh dear, yes!'

Flay gripped Fuchsia's arm, and they moved away into the darkness.

Prunesquallor did what he could to help Mrs Slagg, more by way of assuring her that it would be over in a brace of shakes than through anything scientific. He saw that Titus was able to breathe although wrapped up very tightly. Then he sat back on his heels and turned his head, for an idea had struck him.

'Fuchsia!' he shouted, 'find your father and ask him to sling his jade-cane at the window.'

Lord Sepulchrave, who had just fought down another panic, and had nearly bitten his lower lip in half, spoke in a wonderfully controlled voice immediately after the Doctor had finished piping his message.

'Where are you, Flay?' he said.

'I'm here,' said Flay from a few feet behind him.

'Come to the table.'

Flay and Fuchsia moved to the table, feeling for it with their hands.

'Are you at the table?'

'Yes, Father,' said Fuchsia, 'we're both here.'

'Is that you, Fuchsia?' said a new voice. It was the Countess.

'Yes,' said Fuchsia. 'Are you all right?'

'Have you seen the warbler?' answered her mother. 'Have you seen him?'

'No,' said Fuchsia. The smoke was stinging her eyes and the darkness was terror. Like her father, she had choked a score of cries in her throat.

Prunesquallor's voice rang out again from the far end of the room: 'Damn the warbler and all its feathered friends! Have you got the missiles, Flay?'

'Come here, you 'Squallor,' began the Countess; but she could not continue, for her lungs had filled with black wreaths.

For a few moments there was no one in the room who was capable of speaking and their breathing was becoming momently more difficult. At last Sepulchrave's voice could be distinguished.

'On the table,' he whispered – 'paper-weight – brass – on the table. Quick – Flay – Fuchsia – feel for it. Have you found it? – Paper-weight – brass.'

Fuchsia's hands came across the heavy object almost at once, and as they did so the room was lit up with a tongue of flame that sprang into the air among the books on the right of the unused door. It died almost at once, withdrawing itself like the tongue of an adder, but a moment later it shot forth again and climbed in a crimson spiral, curling from left to right as it licked its way across the gilded and studded spines of Sepulchrave's volumes. This time it did not die away, but gripped the leather with its myriad flickering tentacles while the names of the books shone out in ephemeral glory. They were never forgotten by Fuchsia, those first few vivid titles that seemed to be advertising their own deaths.

For a few moments there was a deadly silence, and then, with a hoarse cry, Flay began to run towards the shelves on the left of the main door. The firelight had lit up a bundle on the floor, and it was not until Flay had picked it up and carried it to the table that the others were reminded with horror of the forgotten octogenarian – for the bundle was Sourdust. For some time it was difficult for the Doctor to decide whether he were alive or not.

While Prunesquallor was attempting to revive the old man's breathing as he lay in his crimson rags upon the marble table, Sepulchrave, Fuchsia and Flay took up positions beneath the window, which could be seen with ever growing clarity. Sepulchrave was the first to fling the brass paper-weight, but his effort was pitiable, final proof (if any were needed) that he was no man of action, and that his life had not been mis-spent among his books. Flay was the next to try his skill. Although having the advantage of his height, he was no more successful than his Lordship, on account of a superabundance of calcium deposit in his elbow joints.

While this was going on, Fuchsia had begun to climb up the bookshelves, which reached upwards to within about five feet of the window. As she climbed laboriously, her eyes streaming and her heart beating wildly, she scooped the books to the ground in order to find purchase for her hands and feet. It was a difficult climb, the ascent being vertical and the polished shelves too slippery to grip with any certainty.

The Countess had climbed to the balcony, where she had found the wood-warbler fluttering wildly in a dark corner. Plucking out a strand of her dark-red hair she had bound the bird's wings carefully to its sides, and then after laying its pulsing breast against her cheek, had slipped it between her own neck and the neck of her dress, and allowed it to slide into the capacious midnight regions of her bosom, where it lay quiescent between great breasts, thinking, no doubt, when it had recovered from the terror of the flames, that here, if anywhere, was the nest of nests, softer than moss, inviolate, and warm with drowsy blood.

When Prunesquallor had ascertained beyond doubt that Sourdust was dead, he lifted one of the loose ends of crimson sacking that straggled across the marble table from the ancient shoulders and laid it across the old man's eyes.

Then he peered over his shoulders at the flames. They had spread in area and now covered about a quarter of the east wall. The heat was fast becoming insufferable. His next glance was directed to the door that had so mysteriously become locked, and he saw that Nannie Slagg, with Titus in her arms, was crouching immediately before the keyhole, the only possible place for them. If the only window could be broken and some form of erection constructed below it, it was just possible that they could climb out in time, though how, in heaven's name, they were to descend on the far side was another matter. A rope, perhaps. But where was a rope to be found – and for that matter what could the erection be constructed with?

Prunesquallor peered around the room in an effort to catch sight of anything that might be used. He noticed that Irma was full length on the floor, and twitching like a section of conger-eel that has been chopped off but which still has ideas of its own. Her beautiful, tightly fitting skirt had become rucked up around her thighs. Her manicured nails were scratching convulsively at the floor boards. 'Let her twitch,' he said to himself quickly. 'We can deal with her later, poor thing.' Then he turned his eyes again to Fuchsia, who was by now very near the top of the bookcase and was reaching precariously for her father's rod with the knob of black jade.

'Keep steady, my Fuchsia-child.'

Fuchsia dimly heard the Doctor's voice come up to her from below. For a moment everything swam before her eyes, and her right hand which gripped the slippery shelf was shaking. Slowly her eyes cleared. It was not easy for her to swing the rod with her left hand, but she drew her arm back stiffly preparatory to swinging at the window with a single rigid movement.

The Countess, leaning over the balcony, watched her as she coughed heavily, and shifting her gaze between her seismic bouts whistled through her teeth to the bird in her bosom, pulling the neck of her dress forward with a forefinger as she did so.

Sepulchrave was gazing upwards at his daughter half way up the wall among the books that danced in the crimson light. His hands were fighting each other again, but his delicate chin was jutting forward, and there was mixed with the melancholy of his eyes not more of panic than would be considered reasonable in any normal man under similar conditions. His home of books was on fire. His life was threatened, and he stood quite still. His sensitive mind had ceased to function, for it had played so long in a world of abstract philosophies that this other world of practical and sudden action had deranged its structure. The ritual which his body had had to perform for fifty years had been no preparation for the unexpected. He watched Fuchsia with a dream-like fascination, while his locked hands fought on.

Flay and Prunesquallor stood immediately below Fuchsia, for she had been swaying above them. Now, with her arm extended and ready to strike they moved a little to the right in order to escape any glass that might fly inwards.

As Fuchsia began to swing her arm at the high window she focused her eyes upon it and found herself staring at a face – a face framed with darkness within a few feet of her own. It sweated firelight, the crimson shadows shifting across it as the flames leapt in the room below. Only the eyes repelled the lurid air. Close-set as nostrils they were not so much eyes as narrow tunnels through which the Night was pouring.

AND HORSES TOOK THEM HOME

As Fuchsia recognized the head of Steerpike the rod fell from her outstretched arm, her weakened hand loosed its grasp upon the shelf and she fell backwards into space, the dark hair of her head reaching below her as she fell, her body curving backwards as though she had been struck.

The Doctor and Flay, leaping forward, half caught her. A moment later and the glass above them came splintering into the room, and Steerpike's voice from overhead cried:

'Hold your horses! I'm letting down a ladder. Don't panic there. Don't panic!'

Every eye was turned from Fuchsia to the window, but Prunesquallor as he had heard the glass break above him had shielded the girl by swinging her behind him. It had fallen all about them, one large piece skimming the Doctor's head and splintering on the floor at his feet. The only one to sustain any injury was Flay, who had a small piece of flesh nicked from his wrist.

'Hang on there!' continued Steerpike in an animated voice which sounded singularly unrehearsed. 'Don't stand so near, I'm going to crack some more glass out.'

The company below the window drew back and watched him strike off the jagged corners of glass from the sides of the window with a piece of flint. The room behind them was now well ablaze, and the sweat was pouring from their upturned faces, their clothes scorching dangerously, and their flesh smarting with the intense heat.

Steerpike, on the outside of the wall, standing on the short protruding branches of the pine-ladder began to struggle with the other length of pine which he had propped beside him. This was no easy job, and the muscles of his arms and back were strained almost to failing point as he levered the long pole upwards and over his shoulder by degrees, keeping his balance all the while with the greatest difficulty. As well as he could judge the library ought by now to be in perfect condition for a really theatrical piece of rescue work. Slowly but surely he edged and eased the pole across his shoulder and through the broken window. It was not only a heavy and dangerous feat, standing as he was, balanced upon the stubby six-inch off-shoots of pine and hauling the resinous thing over his shoulder, but what added to his difficulty was these lateral stubs themselves which caught in his clothes and on the window ledge at each attempt he made to slide the long monster through the opening and down into the bright library.

At last both difficulties were overcome and the gathering on the inner side of the wall below the window found the fifteen-foot bole of a pine edging its way through the smoky air above them, swaying over their heads and then landing with a crash at their feet. Steerpike had held fast to the upper end of the pole and it would have been possible for one of the lighter members of the party to have climbed it at once, but Prunesquallor moved the base of the tree a little to the left and swivelled it until the most powerful of the stubby, lateral 'rungs' were more conveniently situated.

Steerpike's head and shoulders now appeared fully in view through the broken window. He peered into the crimson smoke. 'Nice work,' he said to himself, and then shouted, 'Glad I found you! I'm just coming!'

Nothing could have gone more deliciously according to plan. But there was no time to waste. No time to crow. He could see that the floor-boards had caught and there was a snake of fire slithering its way beneath the table.

Steerpike lifted his voice. 'The Heir of Gormenghast!' he shouted. 'Where is Lord Titus? Where is Lord Titus?'

Prunesquallor had already reached Mrs Slagg, who had collapsed over the child, and he lifted them both together in his arms and ran swiftly back to the ladder. The Countess was there; they were all there at the foot of the pine; all except Sourdust, whose sacking had begun to smoulder. Fuchsia had dragged Irma across the floor by her heels and she lay as though she had been washed ashore by a tempest. Steerpike had crawled through the window and was a third of the way down the bole. Prunesquallor, climbing to the third rung, was able to pass Titus to the youth, who retreated through the window backwards and was down the outer ladder in a flash.

He left the infant among the ferns under the library wall and swarmed up the ladder for the old nurse. The tiny, limp midget was almost as easy to deal with as Titus, and Prunesquallor passed her through the window as though he were handling a doll.

Steerpike laid her next to Titus, and was suddenly back at the window. It was obvious that Irma was the next on the list, but it was with her that the difficulties began. The moment she was touched she began to thrash about with her arms and legs. Thirty years of repression were finding vent. She was no longer a lady. She could never be a lady again. Her pure white feet were indeed composed of clay and now with all the advantages of a long throat she renewed her screaming, but it was weaker than before, for the smoke which had coiled around her vocal cords had taken their edge away, and they were now more in the nature of wool than gut. Something had to be done with her, and quickly. Steerpike swarmed down the top half of the pole and dropped to the library floor. Then, at his suggestion, he and the Doctor began to strip away lengths of her dress with which they bound her arms and legs, stuffing the remainder in her mouth. Together, with the help of Flay and Fuchsia, they heaved the writhing Irma by degrees up the ladder, until Steerpike, climbing through the window, was able to drag her through into the night air. Once through, she was treated with still less decorum, and her descent of the wall was abrupt, the boy with the high shoulders merely seeing to it that she should not break more bones than was necessary. In point of fact she broke none, her peerless flesh sustaining only a few purple bruises.

Steerpike had now three figures in a row among the cold ferns. While he was swarming back, Fuchsia was saying, 'No, I don't want to. *You* go now. Please, *you* go now.'

'Silence, you child,' answered the Countess. 'Don't waste time. As I tell you, girl! as I tell you! At once.'

'No, Mother, no –'

'Fuchsia dear,' said Prunesquallor, 'you will be out in a brace of shakes and ladders! ha, ha, ha! It will save time, gipsy! Hurry now.'

'Don't stand there gawping, girl!'

Fuchsia glanced at the Doctor. How unlike himself he looked, the sweat pouring from his forehead and running between his eyes.

'Up you go! up you go,' said Prunesquallor.

Fuchsia turned to the ladder and after missing her foothold once or twice disappeared above them.

'Good girl!' shouted the Doctor. 'Find your Nannie Slagg! Now, then, now, then, your Ladyship, up you go.'

The Countess began to climb, and although the sound of the wooden stubs being broken on either side of the pole accompanied her, yet her progress towards the window held a prodigious inevitability in every step she took and in every heave of her body. Like something far larger than life, her dark dress shot with the red of the fire, she ploughed her way upwards to the window. There was no one on the other side to help her, for Steerpike was in the library, and yet for all the contortions of her great frame, for all the ungainliness of her egress, a slow dignity pervaded her which gave even to the penultimate view – that of her rear disappearing hugely into the night – a feeling rather of the awesome than the ludicrous.

There remained only Lord Sepulchrave, Prunesquallor, Flay and Steerpike.

Prunesquallor and Steerpike turned to Sepulchrave quickly in order to motion him to follow his wife, but he had disappeared. There was not a moment to lose. The flames were crackling around them. Mixed with the smell of the smoke was the smell of burning leather. There were few places where he could be, unless he had walked into the flames. They found him in an alcove a few feet from the ladder, a recess still hidden to some extent from the enveloping heat. He was smoothing the backs of a set of the Martrovian dramatists bound in gold fibre and there was a smile upon his face that sent a sick pang through the bodies of the three who found him. Even Steerpike watched that smile uneasily from beneath his sandy eyebrows. Saliva was beginning to dribble from the corner of his Lordship's sensitive mouth as the corners curved upwards and the teeth were bared. It was the smile one sees in the mouth of a dead animal when the loose lips are drawn back and the teeth are discovered curving towards the ears.

'Take them, take your books, your Lordship, and come, come quickly!' said Steerpike fiercely. 'Which do you want?'

Sepulchrave turned about sharply and with a superhuman effort forced his hands stiffly to his sides and walked at once to the pine ladder. 'I am sorry to have kept you,' he said, and began to climb swiftly.

As he was lowering himself on the far side of the window they heard him repeat as though to himself: 'I am sorry to have kept you.' And then there was a thin laugh like the laugh of a ghost.

There was no longer any time for deciding who was to follow whom; no time for chivalry. The hot breath of the fire was upon them. The room was rising around them, and yet Steerpike managed to keep himself back.

Directly Flay and the Doctor had disappeared he ran up the pine-bole like a cat, and sat astride the window ledge a moment before he descended on the far side. With the black autumn night behind him he crouched there, a lurid carving, his eyes no longer black holes in his head but glittering in the blood-red light like garnets.

'Nice work,' he said to himself for the second time that night. 'Very nice work.' And then he swung his other leg over the high sill.

'There is no one left,' he shouted down into the darkness.

'Sourdust,' said Prunesquallor, his thin voice sounding singularly flat. 'Sourdust has been left.'

Steerpike slid down the pole.

'Dead?' he queried.

'He is,' said Prunesquallor.

No one spoke.

As Steerpike's eyes became accustomed to the darkness he noticed that the earth surrounding the Countess was a dusky white, and that it was moving, and it was a few moments before he realized that white cats were interweaving about her feet.

Fuchsia, directly her mother had followed her down the ladder, began to run, stumbling and falling over the roots of trees and moaning with exhaustion as she staggered on. When after an eternity she had reached the main body of the Castle she made her way to the stables, and at last had found and ordered three grooms to saddle the horses and proceed to the library. Each groom led a horse by the side of the one he rode. On one of these, Fuchsia was seated, her body doubled forward. Broken by the shock she was weeping, her tears threading their brackish paths over the coarse mane of her mount.

By the time they had reached the library the party had covered some distance of the return journey. Flay was carrying Irma over his shoulder. Prunesquallor had Mrs Slagg in his arms and Titus was sharing the warbler's nest in the Countess's bosom. Steerpike, watching Lord Sepulchrave very closely, was guiding him in the wake of the others, deferentially holding his Lordship's elbow.

When the horses arrived the procession had practically come to a standstill. The beasts were mounted, the grooms walking at their sides holding the bridles, and staring over their shoulders with wide, startled eyes at the raw patch of light that danced in the darkness like a pulsating wound between the straight black bones of the pine trees.

During their slow progress they were met by indistinguishable crowds of servants who stood to the side of the track in horrified silence. The fire had not been visible from the Castle, for the roof had not fallen and the only window was shielded by the trees, but the news had spread with Fuchsia's arrival. The night which had so dreadful a birth continued to heave and sweat until the slow dawn opened like an icy flower in the east, and showed the smoking shell of Sepulchrave's only home. The shelves that still stood were wrinkled charcoal, and the books were standing side by side upon them, black, grey, and ash-white, the corpses of thought. In the centre of the room the discoloured marble table still stood among a heap of charred timber and ashes, and upon the table was the skeleton of Sourdust. The flesh was gone, with all its wrinkles. The coughing had ceased for ever.

SWELTER LEAVES HIS CARD

The winds of the drear interim that lies between the last of autumn and the first of winter had torn the few remaining leaves from even the most sheltered of the branches that swung in the Twisted Woods. Elsewhere the trees had been skeletons for many weeks. The melancholy of decay had given place to a less mournful humour. In dying, the chill season had ceased to weep, and arising from its pyre of coloured leaves had cried out with such a voice as had no hint of tears – and something fierce began to move the air and pace across the tracts of Gormenghast. From the death of the sap, of the bird-song, of the sun, this other life-in-death arose to fill the vacuum of Nature.

The whine was yet in the wind; the November whine. But as night followed night its long trailing note became less and less a part of the mounting music which among the battlements was by now an almost nightly background to those who slept or tried to sleep in the castle of the Groans. More and more in the darkness the notes of grimmer passions could be discerned. Hatred and anger and pain and the hounding voices of vengeance.

One evening, several weeks after the burning, at about an hour before midnight, Flay lowered himself to the ground outside Lord Sepulchrave's bedroom door. Inured though he was to the cold floor boards, for they had been his only bed for many years, yet on this November evening they struck a chill into his flinty bones and his shanks began to ache. The wind whistled and screamed about the Castle and gelid draughts skidded along the landing, and Flay heard the sound of doors opening and shutting at varying distances from him. He was able to follow the course of a draught as it approached from the northern fastnesses of the Castle, for he recognized the sound that was peculiar to each distant door as it creaked and slammed, the noises becoming louder and louder until the heavy mildewy curtains which hung at the end of the passage, forty feet away, lifted and muttered and the door which lay immediately beyond them grated and strained at its only hinge, and Flay knew that the icy spearhead of a fresh draught was close upon him.

'Getting old,' he muttered to himself, rubbing his thighs and folding himself up like a stick-insect at the foot of the door.

He had slept soundly enough last winter when the snow had lain deeply over Gormenghast. He remembered with distaste how it had coated the windows, clinging to the panes, and how when the sun sank over the Mountain the snow had appeared to bulge inwards through the window panes in a lather of blood.

This memory disturbed him, and he dimly knew that the reason why the cold was affecting him more and more during these desolate nights had nothing to do with his age. For his body was hardened to the point of being more like some inanimate substance than flesh and blood. It was true that it was a particularly bad night, rough and loud, but he remembered that four nights ago there had been no wind and yet he had shivered as he was shivering now.

'Getting old,' he muttered grittily to himself again between his long discoloured teeth; but he knew that he lied. No cold on earth could make his hairs stand up like tiny wires, stiffly, almost painfully along his thighs and forearms, and at the nape of his neck. Was he afraid? Yes, as any reasonable man would be. He was very afraid, although the sensation was rather different in him from that which would have been experienced in other men. He was not afraid of the darkness, of the opening and shutting of distant doors, of the screaming wind. He had lived all his life in a forbidding, half-lit world.

He turned over, so as to command a view of the stairhead, although it was almost too dark to see it. He cracked the five knuckles of his left hand, one by one, but he could hardly hear the reports for a new wave of the gale rattled every window and the darkness was alive with the slamming of doors. He was afraid; he had been afraid for weeks. But Flay was not a coward. There was something tenacious and hard in his centre; something obstinate which precluded panic.

All of a sudden the gale seemed to hurl itself to a climax and then to cease utterly, but the interim of dead silence was over as soon as it had started, for a few seconds later, as though from a different quarter, the storm unleashed another of its armies of solid rain and hail, pouring its broadsides against the Castle from the belly of a yet more riotous tempest.

During the few moments of what seemed to be an absolute silence between the two storms, Flay had jerked his body forward from the ground, and had sat bolt upright, every muscle frozen. He had forced a knuckle between his teeth to stop them from chattering, and with his eyes focused upon the dark stairhead he had heard, quite plainly, a sound that was both near and far away, a sound hideously distinct. In that lacuna of stillness the stray sounds of the Castle had become wayward, ungaugeable. A mouse nibbling beneath floor boards might equally have been within a few feet or several halls away.

The sound that Flay heard was of a knife being deliberately whetted. How far away he had no means of telling. It was a sound in vacuo, an abstract thing, yet so enormously it sounded, it might well have been within an inch of his craning ear.

The number of times the blade moved across the hone had no relation to the actual length of time which Flay experienced as he listened. To him the mechanical forward and backward movement of steel against stone lasted the night itself. Had the dawn broken as he listened he would not have been surprised. In reality it was but a few moments, and when the second tempest flung itself roaring against the Castle walls, Flay was on his hands and knees with his head thrust forward towards the sound, his lips drawn back from his teeth.

For the rest of the night the storm was unabated. He crouched there at his master's door, hour after hour, but he heard no more of that hideous scraping.

The dawn, when it came, powdering with slow and inexorable purpose the earthy blackness with grey seeds, found the servant open-eyed, his hands hanging like dead weights over his drawn-up knees, his defiant chin between his wrists. Slowly the air cleared, and stretching his cramped limbs one by one he reared up stiffly to his feet, shrugging his shoulders to his ears. Then he took the iron key from between his teeth and dropped it into his jacket pocket.

In seven slow paces he had reached the stairhead and was staring down into a well of cold. The stairs descended as though for ever. As his eyes moved from step to step they noticed a small object in the centre of one of the landings about forty feet below. It was in the shape of a rough oval. Flay turned his head to Lord Sepulchrave's door.

The sky was drained of its fury and there was silence.

He descended, his hand on the banisters. Each step awoke echoes from below him, and fainter echoes from above him, away to the east.

As he reached the landing a ray of light ran like a slender spear through an eastern window and quivered in a little patch on the wall, a few feet from where he stood. This thread of light intensified the shadows below and above it, and it was only after some groping that Flay came across the object. In his harsh hands it felt disgustingly soft. He brought it close to his eyes and became aware of a sickly, penetrating smell; but he could not see what it was that he held. Then, lifting it into the sunbeam so that his hand cast a shadow over the lozenge of light upon the wall, he saw, as though it were something supernaturally illuminated, a very small, richly and exquisitely sculpted gateau. At the perimeter of this delicacy, a frail coral-like substance had been worked into the links of a chain, leaving in the centre a minute arena of jade-green icing, across whose glacid surface the letter 'S' lay coiled like a worm of cream.

THE UN-EARTHING OF BARQUENTINE

THE Earl, tired from a day of ritual (during part of which it was required of him to ascend and descend the Tower of Flints three times by the stone staircase, leaving on each occasion a glass of wine on a box of wormwood placed there for the purpose on a blue turret) had retired to his room as soon as he was able to get away from the last performance of the day and had taken a more powerful dose of laudanum than he had previously needed. It was noticed that he now brought to his work during the day a fervour quite unprecedented. His concentration upon detail and his thoroughness in the execution and understanding of the minutiae involved in the monotonous ceremonies were evidence of a new phase in his life.

The loss of his library had been a blow so pulverizing that he had not yet begun to suffer the torment that was later to come to him. He was still dazed and bewildered, but he sensed instinctively that his only hope lay in turning his mind as often as possible from the tragedy and in applying himself unstintingly to the routine of the day. As the weeks passed by, however, he found it more and more difficult to keep the horror of that night from his mind. Books which he loved not only for their burden, but intrinsically, for varying qualities of paper and print, kept reminding him that they were no longer to be fingered and read. Not only were the books lost and the thoughts in the books, but what was to him, perhaps, the most searching loss of all, the hours of rumination which lifted him above himself and bore him upon their muffled and enormous wings. Not a day passed but he was reminded of some single volume, or of a series of works, whose very positions on the walls was so clearly indented in his mind. He had taken refuge from this raw emptiness in a superhuman effort to concentrate his mind exclusively upon the string of ceremonies which he had daily to perform. He had not tried to rescue a single volume from the shelves, for even while the flames leapt around him he knew that every sentence that escaped the fire would be unreadable and bitter as gall, something to taunt him endlessly. It was better to have the cavity in his heart yawning and completely empty than mocked by a single volume. Yet not a day passed but he knew his grip had weakened.

Shortly after the death of Sourdust in the library it was remembered that the old librarian had had a son, and a search was made at once. It was a long time before they discovered a figure asleep in the corner of a room with a very low ceiling. It was necessary to stoop, in order to enter the apartment through the filthy walnut door. After having stooped under the decaying lintel there was no relief from the cramped position and no straightening of the back, for the ceiling sagged across the room for the most part at the level of the door-head, but at the centre, like a mouldering belly, it bulged still further earthwards, black with flies. Ill lit by a long horizontal strip of window near the floor-boards, it was difficult for the servants who had been sent on this mission to see at first whether there was anyone in the room or not. A table near the centre with its legs sawn off halfway down, into which they stumbled, had, as they soon discovered, been obscuring from their view Barquentine, old Sourdust's son. He lay upon a straw-filled mattress. At first sight the servants were appalled at a similarity between the son and the dead father, but when they saw that the old man lying on his back with his eyes closed had only one leg, and that a withered one, they were relieved, and straightening themselves were dazed by striking their heads against the ceiling.

When they had recovered they found that they were kneeling, side by side, on all fours. Barquentine was watching them. Lifting the stump of his withered leg he rapped it irritably on the mattress, sending up a cloud of dust.

'What do you want?' he said. His voice was dry like his father's, but stronger than the mere twenty years that lay between their ages could have accounted for. Barquentine was seventy-four.

The servant nearest him rose to a stooping position, rubbed his shoulder-blades on the ceiling and with his head forced down to the

level of his nipples stared at Barquentine with his loose mouth hanging open. The companion, a squat, indelicate creature, replied obtusely from the shadows behind his loose-lipped friend:

'He's dead.'

'Whom are you talking of, you oaf?' said the septuagenarian irritably, levering himself on his elbow and raising another cloud of dust with his stump.

'Your father,' said the loose-mouthed man in the eager tone of one bringing good tidings.

'How?' shouted Barquentine, who was becoming more and more irritable. 'How? When? Don't stand there staring at me like stenching mules.'

'Yesterday,' they replied. 'Burned in the library. Only bones left.'

'Details!' yelled Barquentine, thrashing about with his stump and knotting his beard furiously as his father had done. 'Details, you bladder heads! Out! Out of my way! Out of the room, curse you!'

Foraging about in the darkness he found his crutch and struggled onto his withered leg. Such was the shortness of this leg that when he was on his foot it was possible for him to move grotesquely to the door without having to lower his head to avoid the ceiling. He was about half the height of the crouching servants, but he passed between their bulks like a small, savage cloud of material, ragged to the extent of being filigree, and swept them to either side.

He passed through the low door in the way that infants will walk clean under a table, head in air, and emerge triumphantly on the other side.

The servants heard his crutch striking the floor of the passage and the alternate stamp of the withered leg. Of the many things that Barquentine had to do during the next few hours, the most immediate were to take command of his father's apartments: to procure the many keys: to find, and don, the crimson sacking that had always been in readiness for him against the day of his father's death: and to acquaint the Earl that he was cognizant of his duties, for he had studied them, with and without his father, for the last fifty-four years, in between his alternative relaxations of sleep and of staring at a patch of mildew on the bulge-bellied ceiling of his room.

From the outset he proved himself to be uncompromisingly efficient. The sound of his approaching crutch became a sign for feverish activity, and trepidation. It was as though a hard, intractible letter of the Groan law were approaching – the iron letter of tradition.

This was, for the Earl, a great blessing, for with a man of so strict and unswerving a discipline it was impossible to carry through the day's work without a thorough rehearsal every morning – Barquentine insisting upon his Lordship learning by heart whatever speeches were to be made during the day and all the minutiae that pertained to the involved ceremonies.

This took up a great deal of the Earl's time, and kept his mind, to a certain degree, from introspection; nevertheless, the shock he had sustained was, as the weeks drew on, beginning to have its effect. His sleeplessness was making of each night a hell more dreadful than the last.

His narcotics were powerless to aid him, for when after a prodigious dose he sank into a grey slumber, it was filled with shapes that haunted him when he awoke, and waved enormous sickly-smelling wings above his head, and filled his room with the hot breath of rotting plumes. His habitual melancholy was changing day by day into something more sinister. There were moments when he would desecrate the crumbling and mournful mask of his face with a smile more horrible than the darkest lineaments of pain.

Across the stoniness of his eyes a strange light would pass for a moment, as though the moon were flaring on the gristle, and his lips would open and the gash of his mouth would widen in a dead, climbing, curve.

Steerpike had foreseen that madness would sooner or later come to the Earl, and it was with a shock of annoyance that he heard of Barquentine and of his ruthless efficiency. It had been part of his plan to take over the duties of old Sourdust, for he felt himself to be the only person in the Castle capable of dealing with the multifarious details that the work would involve – and he knew that, with the authority which could hardly have been denied him had there been no one already versed in the laws of the Castle, he would have been brought not only into direct and potent contact with Sepulchrave, but would have had opened up to him by degrees the innermost secrets of Gormenghast. His power would have been multiplied a hundred-fold; but he had not reckoned with the ancientry of the tenets that bound the anatomy of the place together. For every key position in the Castle there was the apprentice, either the son or the student, bound to secrecy. Centuries of experience had seen to it that there should be no gap in the steady, intricate stream of immemorial behaviour.

No one had thought or heard of Barquentine for over sixty years, but when old Sourdust died Barquentine appeared like a well-versed actor on the mouldering stage, and the slow drama of Gormenghast continued among shadows.

Despite this setback in his plans, Steerpike had managed to make even more capital out of his rescue work than he had anticipated. Flay was inclined to treat him with a kind of taciturn respect. He had never quite known what he ought to do about Steerpike. When they had coincided a month previously at the garden gate of the Prunesquallors',

Flay had retired as from a ghost, sullenly, glancing over his shoulder at the dapper enigma, losing his chance of castigating the urchin. In Mr Flay's mind the boy Steerpike was something of an apparition. Most fathomless of all, the lives of the Earl, the Countess, Titus and Fuchsia had been saved by the whelp, and there was a kind of awe, not to say admiration, mixed with his distaste.

Not that Flay unbent to the boy, for he felt it a grievance that he should in any way admit equality with someone who had come originally from Swelter's kitchen.

Barquentine, also, was a bitter pill to swallow, but Flay realized at once the traditional rightness and integrity of the old man.

Fuchsia, for whom the fine art of procedure held less lure, found in old Barquentine a creature to hide from and to hate – not for any specific reason, but with the hatred of the young for the authority vested in age.

She found that as the days went on she began to listen for the sound of his crutch striking on the floor, like the blows of a weapon.

FIRST REPERCUSSIONS

UNABLE to reconcile the heroism of Steerpike's rescue with his face as she had seen it beyond the window before she fell, Fuchsia began to treat the youth with less and less assurance. She began to admire his ingenuity, his devilry, his gift of speech which she found so difficult but which was for him so simple. She admired his cold efficiency and she hated it. She wondered at his quickness, his self-assurance. The more she saw of him the more she felt impelled to recognize in him a nature at once more astute and swift than her own. At night his pale face with its closely-set eyes would keep appearing before her. And when she awoke she would remember with a start how he had saved their lives.

Fuchsia could not make him out. She watched him carefully. Somehow he had become one of the personalities of the Castle's central life. He had been insinuating his presence on all who mattered with such subtlety, that when he leapt dramatically to the fore by rescuing the family from the burning library, it was as though that deed of valour were all that had been needed to propel him to the forefront of the picture.

He still lived at the Prunesquallors' but was making secret plans for moving into a long, spacious room with a window that let in the morning sun. It lay on the same floor as the aunts in the South Wing.

There was really very little reason for him to stay with the Doctor, who did not seem sufficiently aware of the new status he had acquired and whose questions regarding the way he (Steerpike) had found the pine tree, already felled and lopped for the Rescue, and various other details, though not difficult to answer – for he had prepared his replies to any of the possible questions he might be faced with – were, nevertheless, pertinent. The Doctor had had his uses. He had proved a valuable stepping-stone, but it was time to take up a room, or a suite of rooms, in the Castle proper, where knowledge of what was going on would come more easily.

Prunesquallor, ever since the burning, had been, for him, strangely voiceless. When he spoke it was in the same high, thin, rapid way, but for a great part of each day he would lie back in his chair in the sitting-room, smiling incessantly at everyone who caught his eye, his teeth displayed as uncompromisingly as ever before, but with something more cogitative about the great magnified eyes that swam beneath the thick lenses of his spectacles. Irma, who since the fire had been strapped in her bed, and who was having about half a pint of blood removed on alternate Tuesdays, was now allowed downstairs in the afternoons, where she sat dejectedly and tore up sheets of calico which were brought to her chair-side every morning. For hours on end she would continue with this noisy, wasteful and monotonous soporific, brooding the while upon the fact that she was no lady.

Mrs Slagg was still very ill. Fuchsia did all she could for her, moving the nurse's bed into her own room, for the old woman had become very frightened of the dark, which she now associated with smoke.

Titus seemed to be the one least affected by the burning. His eyes remained bloodshot for some time afterwards, but the only other result was a severe cold, and Prunesquallor took the infant over to his own house for its duration.

Old Sourdust's bones had been removed from the marble table among the charred remains of the woodwork and books.

Flay, who had been assigned the mission of collecting the dead librarian's remains and of returning with them to the servants' quadrangle, where a coffin was being constructed from old boxes, found it difficult to handle the charred skeleton. The head had become a bit loose, and Flay after scratching his own skull for a long while at last decided that the only thing to do would be to carry the rattling relics in his arms as though he were carrying a baby. This was both more respectful and lessened the danger of disarticulation or breakage.

On that particular evening as he returned through the woods the rain had fallen heavily before he reached the fringe of the trees, and by the time he was half way across the wasteland which divided the pines from Gormenghast, the rain was streaming over the bones and skull in his arms and bubbling in the eye sockets. Flay's clothes were soaking, and the water squelched in his boots. As he neared the Castle the light had become so obscured by the downpour that he could not see more than a few paces ahead. Suddenly a sound immediately behind him caused him to start, but before he was able to turn, a sharp pain at the back of his head filled him with sickness, and sinking gradually to his knees he loosed the skeleton from his arms and sank in a stupor upon the bubbling ground. How many hours or minutes he had been lying there he could not know, but when he recovered consciousness the rain was still falling heavily. He raised his great rough hand to the back of his head where he discovered a swelling the size of a duck's egg. Swift jabs of pain darted through his brain from side to side.

All at once he remembered the skeleton and got dizzily to his knees. His eyes were still misted, but he saw the wavering outline of the bones; but when a few moments later his eyes had cleared, he found that the head was missing.

SOURDUST IS BURIED

BARQUENTINE officiated at his father's funeral. To his way of thinking it was impossible for the bones to be buried without a skull. It was a pity that the skull could not be the one which belonged, but that there should be some sort of termination to the body before it was delivered to the earth was apparently imperative. Flay had recounted his story and the bruise above his left ear testified to its veracity. There seemed to be no clue to who the cowardly assailant might be, nor could any motive be imagined that could prompt so callous, so purposeless an action. Two days were spent in a fruitless search for the missing ornament, Steerpike leading a gang of stable hands on a tour of the wine vaults which according to his own theory would afford, so he argued, many an ideal niche or corner in which the criminal might hide the skull. He had always had a desire to discover the extent of the vaults. The candle-lit search through a damp labyrinth of cellars and passages, lined with dusty bottles, disproved his theory, however; and when on the same evening the search parties, one and all, reported that their quests had been abortive, it was decided that on the following evening the bones were to be buried whether the head were found or not.

It being considered a desecration to unearth any bodies from the servants' graveyard, Barquentine decided that the skull of a small calf would prove equally effective. One was procured from Swelter, and after it had been boiled and was free of the last vestige of flesh, it was dried and varnished, and as the hour of the burial approached and there was no sign of the original skull being found, Barquentine sent Flay to Mrs Slagg's room to procure some blue ribbon. The calf's skull was all but perfect, it being on the small side and dwarfing the rest of the remains far less than might have been feared. At all events, the old man would be complete if not homogeneous. He would not be headless, and his funeral would be no slipshod, bury-as-you-please affair.

It was only when the coffin stood near the graveside in the Cemetery of the Esteemed, and only when the crowd was standing silently about the small, rectangular trench, that Barquentine motioned Sepulchrave forward, and indicated that the moment had come for the Earl to attach the calf skull to the last of old Sourdust's vertebrae with the aid of the blue ribbon which Mrs Slagg had found at the bottom of one of her shuttered baskets of material. Here was honour for the old man. Barquentine knotted his beard ruminatively and was well pleased. Whether it were some obscure tenet of the Groan lore which Barquentine was rigorously adhering to, or whether it was that he found comfort of some kind in ribbons, it is impossible to say, but whatever the reason might be, Barquentine had procured from somewhere or other several extra lengths of varying colours and his father's skeleton boasted a variety of silk bows which were neatly tied about such bones as seemed to offer themselves to this decorative treatment.

When the Earl had finished with the calf-skull, Barquentine bent over the coffin and peered at the effect. He was, on the whole, satisfied. The calf's head was rather too big, but it was adequate. The late evening light lit it admirably and the grain of the bone was particularly effective.

The Earl was standing silently a little in front of the crowd, and Barquentine, digging his crutch into the earth, hopped around it until he was facing the men who had carried the coffin. One glint of his cold eyes brought them to the graveside.

'Nail the lid on,' he shouted, and hopped around his crutch again on his withered leg, the ferrule of his support swivelling in the soft ground and raising the mud in gurgling wedges as it twisted.

Fuchsia, standing at her mother's mountainous side, loathed him with her whole body. She was beginning to hate everything that was old. What was that word which Steerpike kept denouncing whenever he met her? He was always saying it was dreadful – 'Authority': that was it. She looked away from the one-legged man and her eyes moved absently along the line of gaping faces. They were staring at the coffin-men who were nailing down the planks. Everyone seemed horrible to

Fuchsia. Her mother was gazing over the heads of the crowd with her characteristic sightlessness. Upon her father's face a smile was beginning to appear, as though it were something inevitable, uncontrollable – something Fuchsia had never seen before on his face. She covered her eyes with her hands for a moment and felt a surge of unreality rising in her. Perhaps the whole thing was a dream. Perhaps everyone was really kind and beautiful, and she had seen them only through the black net of a dream she was suffering. She lowered her hands and found herself gazing into Steerpike's eyes. He was on the other side of the grave and his arms were folded. As he stared at her, with his head a little on one side, like a bird's, he raised his eyebrows to her, quizzically, his mouth twisted up on one side. Fuchsia involuntarily made a little gesture with her hand, a motion of recognition, of friendliness, but there was about the gesture something so subtle, so tender, as to be indescribable. For herself, she did not know that her hand had moved – she only knew that the figure across the grave was young.

He was strange and unappealing, with his high shoulders and his large swollen forehead; but he was slender, and young. Oh, that was what it was! He did not belong to the old, heavy, intolerant world of Barquentine: he belonged to the lightness of life. There was nothing about him that drew her, nothing she loved except his youth and his bravery. He had saved Nannie Slagg from the fire. He had saved Dr Prune from the fire – and oh! he had saved her, too. Where was his swordstick? What had he done with it? He was so silly about it, carrying it with him wherever he went.

The earth was being shovelled into the grave for the ramshackle coffin had been lowered. When the cavity was filled, Barquentine inspected the rectangular patch of disturbed earth. The shovelling had been messy work, the mud clinging to the spades, and Barquentine had shouted at the grave-hands irritably. Now, he scraped some of the unevenly distributed earth into the shallower patches with his foot, balancing at an angle upon his crutch. The mourners were dispersing, and Fuchsia, shambling away from her parents, found herself to the extreme right of the crowd as it moved towards the castle.

'May I walk with you?' said Steerpike, sidling up.

'Yes,' said Fuchsia. 'Oh, yes; why shouldn't you?' She had never wanted him before, and was surprised at her own words.

Steerpike shot a glance at her as he pulled out his small pipe. When he had lit it, he said:

'Not much in my line, Lady Fuchsia.'

'What isn't?'

'Earth to earth; ashes to ashes, and all that sort of excitement.'

'Not much in anyone's line, I shouldn't think,' she replied. 'I don't like the idea of dying.'

'Not when one's young, anyway,' said the youth. 'It's all right for our friend rattle-ribs: not much life left inside him, anyway.'

'I like you being disrespectful, sometimes,' said Fuchsia in a rush. 'Why must one try and be respectful to old people when they aren't considerate?'

'It's their idea,' said Steerpike. 'They like to keep this reverence business going. Without it where'd they be? Sunk. Forgotten. Over the side: for they've nothing except their age, and they're jealous of our youth.'

'Is that what it is?' said Fuchsia, her eyes widening. 'Is it because they are jealous? Do you really think it's that?'

'Undoubtedly,' said Steerpike. 'They want to imprison us and make us fit into their schemes, and taunt us, and make us work for them. All the old are like that.'

'Mrs Slagg isn't like that,' said Fuchsia.

'She is the exception,' said Steerpike, coughing in a strange way with his hand over his mouth. 'She is the exception that proves the rule.'

They walked on in silence for a few paces. The Castle was looming overhead and they were treading into the shadow of a tower.

'Where's your swordstick?' said Fuchsia. 'How can you be without it? You don't know what to do with your hands.'

Steerpike grinned. This was a new Fuchsia. More animated – yet was it animation, or a nervous, tired excitement which gave the unusual lift to her voice?

'My swordstick,' said Steerpike, rubbing his chin, 'my dear little swordstick. I must have left it behind in the rack.'

'Why?' said Fuchsia. 'Don't you adore it any more?'

'I *do*, oh yes! I *do*,' Steerpike replied in a comically emphatic voice. 'I adore it just as much, but I felt it would be safer to leave it behind, because do you know what I should probably have *done* with it?'

'What would you have done?' said Fuchsia.

'I would have pricked Barquentine's guts with it,' said Steerpike; 'most delicately, here and there, and everywhere, until the old scarecrow was yelling like a cat; and when he had yelled all the breath from his black lungs, I'd have tied him by his one leg to a branch and set fire to his beard. So you see what a good thing it was that I didn't have my swordstick, don't you?'

But when he turned to her Fuchsia was gone from his side.

He could see her running through the misty air in a strange, bounding manner; but whether she was running for enjoyment, or in order to rid herself of him, he could not know.

THE TWINS ARE RESTIVE

ABOUT a week after Sourdust's burial, or to be precise, about a week after the burial of all that was left of what had once been Sourdust, along with the calf skull and the ribbons, Steerpike revisited the Aunts for the purpose of selecting a set of rooms on the same floor as their own apartments in the south wing. Since the burning they had become not only very vain, but troublesome. They wished to know when, now that they had carried out the task according to plan, they were to come into their own. Why was not the south wing already alive with pageantry and splendour? Why were its corridors still so dusty and deserted? Had they set fire to their brother's library for nothing? Where were the thrones they had been promised? Where were the crowns of gold? At each fresh appearance of Steerpike in their apartments these questions were renewed, and on every occasion it became more difficult to leave them mollified and convinced that their days of grievance were drawing to a close.

They were as outwardly impassive, their faces showing no sign at all of what was going on inside their identical bodies, but Steerpike had learned to descry from the almost imperceptible movements which they made with their limp fingers, roughly what was happening in their minds, or to what height their emotions were aroused. There was an uncanniness about the way their white fingers would move simultaneously, indicating that their brains were at that precise moment travelling along the same narrow strip of thought, at the same pace, with the same gait.

The glittering promises with which Steerpike had baited his cruel hook had produced an effect upon them more fundamental than he had anticipated. This concept of themselves as rulers of the south wing, was now uppermost in their minds, and in fact it filled their minds leaving no room for any other notion. Outwardly it showed itself in their conversation which harped upon nothing else. With the flush of success upon them, their fingers became looser, although their faces remained as expressionless as powdered slabs. Steerpike was now reaping the consequences of having persuaded them of their bravery and ingenuity, and of the masterly way in which they, and they alone, could set the library alight. It had been necessary at the time to blow them into tumours of conceit and self-assurance, but now, their usefulness for the moment at an end, it was becoming more and more difficult to deal with their inflation. However, with one excuse or another he managed to persuade them of the inadvisability of rushing a matter of such magnitude as that of raising them to their twin summits. Such things must be achieved with deliberation, cunning and foresight. Their position must improve progressively through a sequence of minor victories, which although each in itself attracted no notice, would build up insidiously, until before the castle was aware of it the South wing would blazon forth in rightful glory. The twins, who had expected the change in their status to be brought about overnight, were bitterly disappointed, and although Steerpike's arguments to the effect that their power when it came must be something of sure foundation convinced them as he spoke, yet no sooner were they alone than they reverted at once to a condition of chagrin, and Steerpike's every appearance was the sign for them to air their grievances anew.

On this particular afternoon, as soon as he had entered their room and their childish clamour had started, he cut them short by crying: 'We shall begin!'

He had lifted his left hand high into the air to silence them, as he shouted. In his right hand he held a scroll of paper. They were standing with their shoulders and hips touching, side by side, their heads forced a little forward. When their loud, flat voices ceased, he continued:

'I have ordered your thrones. They are being made in secret, but as I have insisted that they are to be beaten from the purest gold they will take some time to complete. I have been sent these designs by the goldsmith, a craftsman without a peer. It is for you, my Ladyships, to choose. I have no doubt which you will choose, for although they are all three the most consummate works of art, yet with your taste, your flair for proportion, your grasp of minutiae, I feel confident you will select the one which I believe has no rival among the thrones of the world.'

Steerpike had, of course, made the drawings himself, spending several hours longer on them than he had intended, for once he had started he had become interested, and had the Doctor or his sister opened his door in the small hours of this same morning they would have found the high-shouldered boy bending over a table in his room, absorbed; the compasses, protractors and set square neatly placed in a row at the side of the table, the beautifully sharpened pencil travelling along the ruler with cold precision.

Now, as he unrolled the drawings before the wide eyes of the Aunts he handled them deftly, for it pleased him to take care of the fruits of his labours. His hands were clean, the fingers being curiously pointed, and the nails rather longer than is normal.

Cora and Clarice were at his side in an instant. There was no expression in their faces at all. All that could be found there was uncompromisingly anatomical. The thrones stared at the Aunts and the Aunts stared back at the thrones.

'I have no doubt which one you will prefer, for it is unique in the history of golden thrones. Choose, your Ladyships – choose!' said Steerpike.

Cora and Clarice pointed simultaneously at the biggest of the three drawings. It almost filled the page.

'How *right* you are!' said Steerpike. 'How *right* you are! It was the only choice. I shall be seeing the goldsmith tomorrow and shall advise him of your selection.'

'I want mine soon,' said Clarice.

'So do I,' said Cora, 'very soon.'

'I thought I had explained to you,' said Steerpike, taking them by their elbows and bringing them towards him – 'I thought I had explained to you that a throne of hammered gold is not a thing which can be wrought overnight. This man is a craftsman, an artist. Do you want your glory ruined by a makeshift and ridiculous pair of bright yellow sit-upons? Do you want to be the laughing-stock of the Castle, all over again, because you were too impatient? Or are you anxious for Gertrude and the rest of them to stare, open-mouthed with jealousy, at you as you sit aloft like the two purple queens you undoubtedly are? . . . Everything must be of the best. You have entrusted me to raise you to the status that is your due and right. You must leave it to me. When the hour comes, we shall strike. In the meanwhile it is for us to make of these apartments something unknown to Gormenghast.'

'Yes,' said Cora. 'That's what I think. They must be wondrous. The rooms must be wondrous.'

'Yes,' said Clarice. 'Because *we* are. The rooms must be just like us.' Her mouth fell open, as though the lower jaw had died.

'But we are the only ones who *are* worthy. No one must forget that, must they, Cora?'

'No one,' said Cora. 'No one at all.'

'Exactly,' said Steerpike, 'and your first duty will be to recondition the Room of Roots.' He had glanced at them shrewdly. 'The roots must be repainted. Even the smallest must be repainted, because there is no other room in Gormenghast that is so wonderful as to be full of roots. *Your* roots. The roots of *your* tree.'

To his surprise the twins were not listening to him. They were holding each other about their long barrel-like chests.

'He made us do it,' they were saying. 'He made us burn dear Sepulchrave's books. Dear Sepulchrave's books.'

'HALF-LIGHT'

MEANWHILE, the Earl and Fuchsia were sitting together two hundred feet below and over a mile away from Steerpike and the Aunts. His lordship, with his back to a pine tree and his knees drawn up to his chin, was gazing at his daughter with a slithery smile upon his mouth that had once been so finely drawn. Covering his feet and heaped about his slender body on all sides was a cold, dark, undulating palliasse of pine needles, broken here and there with heavy, weary-headed ferns and grey fungi, their ashen surfaces exuding a winter sweat.

A kind of lambent darkness filled the dell. The roof was skyproof, the branches interlacing so thickly that even the heaviest downpour was stayed from striking through; the methodical drip . . . drip . . . drip of the branch-captured rain only fell to the floor of needles several hours after the start of the heaviest storm. And yet a certain amount of reflected daylight filtered through into the clearing, mainly from the East, in which direction lay the shell of the library. Between the clearing and the path that ran in front of the ruin, the trees, although as thick, were not more than thirty to forty yards in depth.

'How many shelves have you built for your father?' said the Earl to his daughter with a ghastly smile.

'Seven shelves, father,' said Fuchsia. Her eyes were very wide and her hands trembled as they hung at her sides.

'Three more shelves, my daughter – three more shelves, and then we will put the volumes back.'

'Yes, father.'

Fuchsia, picking up a short branch, scored across the needled ground three long lines, adding them to the seven which already lay between her father and herself.

'That's it, that's it,' came the melancholy voice. 'Now we have space for the Sonian Poets. Have you the books ready – little daughter?'

Fuchsia swung her head up, and her eyes fastened upon her father. He had never spoken to her in that way – she had never before heard that tone of love in his voice. Chilled by the horror of his growing madness, she had yet been filled with a compassion she had never known, but now there was more than compassion within her, there was released, of a sudden, a warm jet of love for the huddled figure whose long pale hand rested upon his knees, whose voice sounded so quiet and so thoughtful. 'Yes, father, I've got the books ready,' she replied; 'do you want me to put them on the shelves?'

She turned to a heap of pine cones which had been gathered.

'Yes, I am ready,' he replied after a pause that was filled with the silence of the wood. 'But one by one. One by one. We shall stock three shelves tonight. Three of my long, rare shelves.'

'Yes, father.'

The silence of the high pines drugged the air.

'Fuchsia.'

'What, father?'

'You are my daughter.'

'Yes.'

'And there is Titus. He will be the Earl of Gormenghast. Is that so?'

'Yes, father.'

'When I am dead. But do I know you, Fuchsia? Do I know you?'

'I don't know – very well,' she replied; but her voice became more certain now that she perceived his weakness. 'I suppose we don't know each other very much.'

Again she was affected by an uprising of love. The mad smile making incongruous every remark which the Earl ventured, for he spoke with tenderness and moderation, had for the moment ceased to frighten her. In her short life she had been brought face to face with so many forms of weirdness that although the uncanny horror of the sliding smile distressed her, yet the sudden breaking of the barriers that had lain between them for so long as she could remember overpowered her fear. For the first time in her life she felt that she was a daughter – that she had a father – of her own. What did she care if he was going mad – saving for his own dear sake? He was hers.

'My books . . .' he said.

'I have them here, father. Shall I fill up the first long shelf for you?'

'With the Sonian Poets, Fuchsia.'

'Yes.'

She picked up a cone from the heap at her side and placed it on the end of the line she had scored in the ground. The Earl watched her very carefully.

'That is Andrema, the lyricist – the lover – he whose quill would pulse as he wrote and fill with a blush of blue, like a bruised nail. His verses, Fuchsia, his verses open out like flowers of glass, and at their centre, between the brittle petals lies a pool of indigo, translucent and as huge as doom. His voice is unmuffled – it is like a bell, clearly ringing in the night of our confusion; but the clarity is the clarity of imponderable depth – depth – so that his lines float on for evermore, Fuchsia – on and on and on, for evermore. That is Andrema . . . Andrema.'

The Earl, with his eyes on the cone which Fuchsia had placed at the end of the first line, opened his mouth more widely, and suddenly the pines vibrated with the echoes of a dreadful cry, half scream, half laughter.

Fuchsia stiffened, the blood draining from her face. Her father, his mouth still open, even after the scream had died out of the forest, was now upon his hands and knees. Fuchsia tried to force her voice from the dryness of her throat. Her father's eyes were on her as she struggled, and at last his lips came together and his eyes recovered the melancholy sweetness that she had so lately discovered in them. She was able to say, as she picked up another cone and made as if to place it at the side of 'Andrema': 'Shall I go on with the library, father?'

But the Earl could not hear her. His eyes had lost focus. Fuchsia dropped the cone from her hand and came to his side.

'What is it,' she said. 'Oh father! father! what is it?'

'I am not your father,' he replied. 'Have you no knowledge of me?' And as he grinned his black eyes widened and in either eye there burned a star, and as the stars grew greater his fingers curled. 'I live in the Tower of Flints,' he cried. 'I am the death-owl.'

A ROOF OF REEDS

To her left, as she moved slowly along the broken and overgrown track, Keda was conscious the while of that blasphemous finger of rock which had dominated the western skyline for seven weary days. It had been like a presence, something which, however the sunlight or moonlight played upon it, was always sinister; in essence, wicked.

Between the path she walked and the range of mountains was a region of marshland which reflected the voluptuous sky in rich pools, or with a duller glow where choked swamps sucked at the colour and breathed it out again in sluggish vapour. A tract of rushes glimmered, for each long sword-shaped leaf was edged with a thread of crimson. One of the larger pools of almost unbroken surface not only reflected the burning sky, but the gruesome, pointing finger of the rock, which plunged through breathless water.

On her right the land sloped upwards and was forested with mis-shapen trees. Although their outermost branches were still lit, the violence of the sunset was failing, and the light was crumbling momently from the boughs.

Keda's shadow stretched to her right, growing, as she proceeded, less and less intense as the raddled ground dulled from a reddish tint to a nondescript ochre, and then from ochre to a warm grey which moment by moment grew more chill, until she found herself moving down a track of ash-grey light.

For the last two days the great shoulder of hill with the dreadful monotony of its squat, fibrous trees which covered it, had lain on Keda's right hand, breathing, as it were, over her shoulder; groping for her with stunted arms. It seemed that for all her life the oppressive presence of trees, of stultified trees, had been with her, leering at her, breathing over her right shoulder, each one gesticulating with its hairy hands, each one with a peculiar menace of its own, and yet every one monotonously the same in the endlessness of her journey.

For the monotony began to have the quality of a dream, both uneventful and yet terrifying, and it seemed that her body and her brain were flanked by a wall of growth that would never end. But the last two days had at least opened up to her the wintry flats upon her left, where for so long her eyes had been attested and wearied by a canyon face of herbless rock upon whose high grey surface the only sign of life had been when an occasional ledge afforded purchase for the carrion crow. But Keda, stumbling exhaustedly in the ravine, had no thought for them as they peered at her, following her with their eyes, their naked necks protruding from the level of their scraggy bellies, their shoulders hunched above their heads, their murderous claws curled about their scant supports.

Snow had lain before her like a long grey carpet, for the winter sun was never to be seen from that canyon's track, and when at last the path had veered to the right and the daylight had rushed in upon her, she had stumbled forward for a few paces and dropped upon her knees in a kind of thanksgiving. As she raised her head the blonde light had been like a benison.

But she was indescribably weary, dropping her aching feet before her as she continued on her way without knowledge of what she was doing. Her hair fell across her face raggedly; her heavy cloak was flecked with mud and matted with burrs and clinging brambles.

Her right hand clung on mechanically to a strap over her shoulder which supported a satchel, now empty of food, but weighted with a stranger cargo.

Before she had left the Mud Dwellings on the night when her lovers had killed each other beneath the all-seeing circle of that never-to-be-forgotten, spawning moon, she had, as in a trance, found her way back to her dwelling, collected together what food she could find, and then, like a somnambulist, made her way first to Braigon's and then to Rantel's workshop and taken from each a small carving. Then, moving out into the emptiness of the morning, three hours before the dawn, she had walked, her brain dilated with a blank and zoneless pain, until, as the dawn like a wound in the sky welled into her consciousness, she fell among the salt grasses where the meres began, and with the carvings in her arms, slept unseen throughout a day of sunshine.

That was very long ago. How long ago? Keda had lost all sense of time. She had journeyed through many regions – had received her meals from many hands in return for many kinds of labour. For a long while she tended the flocks of one whose shepherd had been taken ill with fold-fever and had died with a lamb in his arms. She had worked on a long barge with a woman who, at night, would mew like an otter as she swam among the reeds. She had woven the hazel hurdles and had made great nets for the fresh-water fish. She had moved from province to province.

But a weariness had come, and the sickness at dawn; and yet she was forced to be continually moving. But always with her were her burning trophies, her white eagle; her yellow stag.

And now it was beyond her strength to work, and a power she did not question was inexorably driving her back towards the Dwellings.

Under the high, ragged and horrible bosom of the hill, she stumbled on. All colour was stifled from the sky and the profane finger of rock was no longer visible save as a narrow hint of dark on dark. The sunset had flamed and faded – every moment seeming permanent – and yet the crumbling from crimson to ash had taken no longer than a few demoniac moments.

Keda was now walking through darkness, all but the few yards immediately in front of her feet, obscured. She knew that she must sleep: that what strength remained in her was fast ebbing, and it was not because she was unused to spending the night hours alone among unfriendly shapes that she was stayed from coiling herself at the foot of the hill. The last few nights had been pain, for there was no mercy in the air that pressed its frozen hands to her body; but it was not for this reason that her feet still fell heavily before her, one after the other, the forward tilt of her body forcing them onwards.

It was not even that the trees that sucked at her right shoulder had filled her with horror, for now she was too tired for her imagination to fill her mind with the macabre. She moved on because a voice had spoken to her that morning as she walked. She had not realized that it was her own voice crying out to her, for she was too exhausted to know that her lips were giving vent to the occult.

She had turned, for the voice had seemed to be immediately beside her. 'Do not stop,' it had said; 'not tonight, for you shall have a roof of reeds.' Startled, she had continued for not more than a few paces when the voice within her said: 'The old man, Keda, the old brown man. You must not stay your feet.'

She had not been frightened, for the reality of the supernatural was taken for granted among the Dwellers. And as she staggered, ten hours later, through the night the words wavered in her mind, and when a torch flared suddenly in the road ahead of her, scattering its red embers, she moaned with exhaustion and relief to have been found, and fell forward into the arms of the brown father.

What happened to her from that moment she did not know; but when she awoke she was lying upon a mattress of pine-needles, smelling of a hot, dry sweetness, and around her were the wooden walls of a cabin. For a moment she did not lift her eyes, although the words which she had heard upon the road were in her ears: for she knew what she would see, and when she at last lifted her head to see the thatching of the river-reeds above her she remembered the old man, and her eyes turned to a door in the wall. It opened softly as she lay, half drowsed with the perfume of the pine, and she saw a figure. It was as though Autumn was standing beside her, or an oak, heavy with its crisp, tenacious leaves. He was of brown, but lambent, as of sepia-black glass held before a flame. His shaggy hair and beard were like pampas grass; his skin the colour of sand; his clothes festooned about him like foliage along a hanging branch. All was brown, a symphony of brown, a brown tree, a brown landscape, a brown man.

He came across the room to her, his naked feet making no sound upon the earth of the cabin floor, where the creepers sent green tributaries questing.

Keda raised herself upon her elbow.

The rough summit of the oak tree moved, and then one of its branches motioned her back, so that she lay still again upon the pine-needles. Peace like a cloud enveloped her as she gazed at him and she knew that she was in the presence of a strange selflessness.

He left her side and, moving across the earth floor with that slow, drifting tread, unfastened some shutters and the rayless light of the north sky poured through a square window. He left the room, and she lay quietly, her mind becoming clearer as the minutes passed. The trestle bed that she lay upon was wide and low, being raised only a foot from the ground by two logs which supported the long planks. Her tired body seemed to float with every muscle relaxed among the billowing needles. Even the pain in her feet, the bruises she had sustained in her wanderings, were floating – a kind of floating pain, impersonal, and almost pleasurable. Across her the brown father had spread three rough blankets, and her right hand moving under them, as though to test the pleasure of moving itself independently from the tired mass of her body, struck upon something hard. She was too weary to wonder what it was; but sometime later she drew it forth – the white eagle. 'Braigon', she murmured, and with the word a hundred haunting thoughts returned. Again she felt about her and found the wooden stag. She brought them against her warm sides, and after the pain of memory a new emotion, kindred to that which she had felt on the night she had lain with Rantel, suffused her, and her heart, faintly at first and then more loud, and louder still, began to sing like a wild bird; and though her body heaved suddenly with sickness, the wild bird went on singing.

'FEVER'

WHITE and cool as was the light of the north window, Keda could tell that the sun was alone in the sky and that the winter day was cloudless and temperate. She could not tell how late it was, nor whether it was morning or evening. The old man brought a bowl of soup to her bedside. She wished to speak to him, but not yet, for the spell of silence was still so richly about her and so eloquent that she knew that with him there was no need to say anything at all. Her floating body felt strangely clear and sweet, lying as though it were a lily of pain.

She lay now holding the carvings at her side, her fingers spread over their smooth wooden contours, while she experienced the slow ebbing of fatigue from her limbs. Minute after minute passed, the steady light filling the room with whiteness. Every now and again she would raise herself up and dip the earthenware spoon into the pottage; and as she drank her strength came back in little thick leaps. When she had at last emptied the bowl she turned over upon her side, and a tingling of strength rose in her with every moment that passed.

Again she was conscious of the cleanness of her body. For some time the effort was too great to be made, but when at last she pulled away the blankets she found that she was washed free of all the dust of her last days of wandering. She was unstained, and there was no trace of the nightmare upon her – only the sweet bruises, the long threads where thorns had torn her.

She tried to stand, and nearly fell; but drawing in a deep breath steadied herself and moved slowly to the window. Before her was a clearing, where greyish grass grew thickly, the shadow of a tree falling across it. Half in this shadow and half out of it a white goat was standing, and moving its sensitive narrow head side to side. A little beyond, to the left, was the mouth of a well. The clearing ended where a derelict stone building, roofless and black with spreading moss, held back a grove of leafless elms, where a murmuration of starlings was gathered. Beyond this grove Keda could catch a glimpse of a stony field, and beyond this field a forest climbing to a rounded summit of boulders. She turned her eyes again. There stood the white goat. It had moved out of the shadow and was like an exquisite toy, so white it was,

with such curls of hair, such a beard of snow, such horns, such great
and yellow eyes.

Keda stood for a long while gazing upon the scene, and although she
saw with perfect clarity – the roofless house, the pine-shadow, the
hillocks, the trellis-work vine, yet these were no part of her immediate
consciousness, but figments of the half-dream languor of her awakening.
More real to her was the bird-song at her breast, defying the memory
of her lovers and the weight of her womb.

The age that was her heritage and the inexorable fate of the Dwellers
had already begun to ravage her head, a despoliation which had begun
before the birth of her first little child who was buried beyond the great
wall, and her face had now lost all but the shadow of her beauty.

Keda left the window and, taking a blanket, wrapped it about her,
and then opened the door of the room. She found herself facing another
of roughly the same size but with a great table monopolizing the centre
of the floor, a table with a dark-red cloth drawn across it. Beyond the
table the earth descended by three steps, and in the further and lower
portion of the floor were the old man's garden tools, flower pots and
pieces of painted and unpainted wood. The room was empty and Keda
passed slowly through a doorway into the clearing of sunlight.

The white goat watched her as she approached and took a few
slender-legged steps towards her, lifting its head high into the air. She
moved onwards and became conscious of the sound of water. The sun
was about halfway between the zenith and the horizon, but Keda could
not at first tell whether it was morning or afternoon, for there was no
way of knowing whether the sun were climbing through the high east
or sinking in the high west. All was stillness; the sun seemed to be fixed
for ever as though it were a disc of yellow paper pasted against the pale-
blue wintry sky.

She went forward slowly through the unknown time of day towards
the sound of water. She passed the long roofless building on her left and
for a moment was chilled by the shadow it cast.

Descending a steep bank of ferns, she came across the brook
almost immediately. It ran between dark, leafless brambles. A little
to Keda's left, where she stood among the thorny bushes at the
water's edge, there was a crossing of boulders – old and smooth and
hollowed into shallow basins by the passage of what must have been
centuries of footfall. Beyond the ford a grey mare drank from the
stream. Her mane fell over her eyes and floated on the surface of the
water as she drank. Beyond the grey mare stood another of dappled
skin, and beyond the dappled mare, at a point where the brook
changed direction and bore to the right under a wall of evergreens,
was a third – a horse whose coat was like black velvet. The three
were quite still and absorbed, their manes trailing the water, their

legs knee-deep in the sounding stream. Keda knew that if she walked
a little way along the bank to her left until she gained a view of the
next reach of the river, she would see the drinking horses one after
another receding across the flats, each one an echo of the one before
it – echoes of changing colour, but all knee-deep in water, all with
their hanging manes, their drinking throats.

Suddenly she began to feel cold. The horses all lifted their heads and
stared at her. The stream seemed to stand still; and then she heard
herself talking.

'Keda,' she was saying, 'your life is over. Your lovers have died. Your
child and her father are buried. And you also are dead. Only your bird
sings on. What is the bright bird saying? That all is complete? Beauty
will die away suddenly and at any time. At any time now – from sky
and earth and limb and eye and breast and the strength of men and the
seed and the sap and the bud and the foam and the flower – all will
crumble for you, Keda, for all is over – only the child to be born, and
then you will know what to do.'

She stood upon the boulders of the ford and saw below her the image
of her face in the clear water. It had become very old; the scourge of the
Dwellers had descended; only the eyes, like the eyes of a gazelle, defied
the bane which now gave to her face the quality of a ruin. She stared;
and then she put her hands below her heart, for the bird was crying,
crying with joy. 'It is over!' screamed the beaked voice. 'It is only for
the child that you are waiting. All else fulfilled, and then there is no
longer any need.'

Keda lifted her head, and her eyes opened to the sky where a kestrel
hung. Her heart beat and beat, and the air thickened until darkness
muffled her eyes, while the gay cry of the bird went on and on: '*It is over!*
it is over! it is over!'

The sky cleared before her. Beside her stood the brown father. When
she turned to him he raised his head and then led her back to the cabin,
where she lay exhausted upon her bed.

The sun and the moon had forced themselves behind her eyes and
filled her head. A crowd of images circled about them; the cactus trees
of the Mud Dwellings revolved about the towers of Gormenghast,
which swam about the moon. Heads ran forward towards her, starting
as mere pin points on an infinitely far horizon, enlarging unbearably as
they approached, they burst over her face – her dead husband's face,
Mrs Slagg's and Fuchsia's, Braigon's, Flay's, the Countess's, Rantel's
and the Doctor's with his devouring smile. Something was being put
into her mouth. It was the lip of a cup. She was being told to drink.

'Oh, father!' she cried.

He pressed her gently back against the pillow.

'There is a bird crying,' she said.

'What does it cry?' said the old man.

'It cries with joy, for me. It is happy for me, for soon it will all be over – when I am light again – and I can do it, oh, father, when I am light again.'

'What is it you will do?'

Keda stared at the reeds above her. 'That is what shall happen,' she murmured, 'with a rope, or with deep water, or a blade . . . or with a blade.'

FAREWELL

IT was a long while before Keda was well enough to set forth on horseback for the Mud Dwellings. Her fever had raged, and but for the care with which the old man watched over her she must surely have died. For many long nights in her delirium she unburdened herself of a torrent of words, her natural reticence shattered by the power of her heightened imaginings.

The old man sat by her, his bearded chin resting on a gnarled fist, his brown eyes upon her vibrant face. He listened to her words and pieced together the story of her loves and fears from the wrack of her outpouring. Removing a great damp leaf from her forehead he would replace it with another, ice-cold and shoe-shaped, from the store he had collected for her brow. Within a few minutes it would be warm from her burning forehead. Whenever he could leave her he prepared the herbs with which he fed her and concocted the potions which eventually stilled the nightmare in her brain, and quietened her blood.

As the days passed he began to know her better, in the great, inarticulate way of guardian trees. No word was spoken. Whatever passed between them of any significance travelled in silence, and taking his hand she would lie and receive great joy from gazing at his august and heavy head, his beard and his brown eyes, and the rustic bulk of his body beside her.

Yet in spite of the peace that filled her in his presence, the feeling she should be among her own people began to grow more powerful with every day that passed.

It was a long while after her fever had abated that the old man allowed Keda to get to her feet, although he could see that she was fretting. At last she was strong enough to go for short walks in the enclosure, and he led her, supporting her with his arm to the hillocks of pale hair, or among the elms.

From the beginning, their relationship had been baptized with silence, and even now, several months after that first afternoon when she had awakened beneath his roof, whatever words they spoke were only to facilitate the domestic tasks of the day. Their communion of silence which from the first they had recognized to be a common language was with them perpetually flowering in a kind of absolute trust in the other's receptivity.

Keda knew that the brown father realized she must go, and the old man knew that Keda understood why he could not let her go, for she was still too weak, and they moved together through the spring days, Keda watching him milking his white goat, and the brown father leaning like an oak against the wall of the cabin while Keda stirred the broth above the stone range, or scraped the loam from the spade and placed it among the few crude garden tools when daylight failed.

One evening when they were returning home after the longest walk which Keda had managed, they stopped for a moment upon the brow of one of the hillocks, and turned to the west before descending into the shadows that lay about the cabin.

There was a greenish light in the sky with a surface like alabaster. As they watched, the evening star sang out in a sudden point of light.

The ragged horizon of trees brought back to Keda's mind the long and agonizing journey that had brought her to this haven, to the cabin of the hermit, to this evening walk, to this moment of light, and she remembered the clawing of the branches at her right shoulder and how, upon her left, all the while there had stood the blasphemous finger of rock. Her eyes seemed to be drawn along the line of the dark trees until they rested upon a minute area of sky framed by the black and distant foliage. This fragment of sky was so small that it could never have been pointed out or even located again by Keda had she taken her eyes from it for a second.

The skyline of trees was, near its outline, perforated with a myriad of microscopic glints of light, and it was beyond coincidence that Keda's eyes were drawn towards the particular opening in the foliage that was divided into two equal parts by a vertical splinter of green fire. Even at that distance, fringed and imprisoned with blackness, Keda recognized instantaneously the finger of rock.

'What does it mean, father, that thin and dreadful crag?'

'If it is dreadful to you, Keda, it means that your death is near; which is as you wish and what you have foreseen. For me it is not yet dreadful, although it has changed. When I was young it was for me the steeple of all love. As the days die, it alters.'

'But I am not afraid,' said Keda.

They turned and began to descend among the hillocks towards the cabin. Darkness had settled before they opened the door. When Keda had lit the lamp they sat at the table opposite one another, conversing for a long while before her lips moved and she began to speak aloud:

'No, I am not afraid,' she said. 'It is I who am choosing what I shall do.'

The old man lifted his rough head. His eyes in the lamplight appeared as wells of brown light.

'The child will come to me when she is ready,' he said. 'I will always be here.'

'It is the Dwellers,' said Keda. 'It is they.' Her left hand drew involuntarily to beneath her heart, and her fingers wavered there a moment as though lost. 'Two men have died for me; and I bring back to the Bright Carvers their blood, on my hands, and the unlawful child. They will reject me – but I shall not mind, for still . . . still . . . my bird is singing – and in the graveyard of the outcasts I will have my reward – oh father – my reward, the deep, deep silence which they cannot break.'

The lamp trembled and shadows moved across the room, returning stealthily as the flame steadied.

'It will not be long,' he said. 'In a few days' time you shall begin your journey.'

'Your dark-grey mare,' said Keda, 'how shall I return her to you, father?'

'She will return,' he replied, 'alone. When you are near to the Dwellings, set her free and she will turn and leave you.'

She took her hand from his arm and walked to her room. All night long the voice of a little wind among the reeds cried: '*Soon, soon, soon.*'

On the fifth day he helped her to the rough blanket saddle. Upon the mare's broad back were slung two baskets of loaves and other provender. Her path lay to the north of the cabin, and she turned for a moment before the mare moved away to take a last look at the scene before her. The stony field beyond the high trees. The roofless house, and to her west, the hillocks of pale hair, and beyond the hillocks the distant woods. She looked her last upon the rough grass enclosure; the well, and the tree which cast its long shadow. She looked her last at the white goat with its head of snow. It was sitting with one frail white foreleg curled to its heart.

'No harm will come to you. You are beyond the power of harm. You will not hear their voices. You will bear your child, and when the time has come you will make an end of all things.'

Keda turned her eyes to him. 'I am happy, father. I am happy. I know what to do.'

The grey mare stepped forward into darkness beneath trees, and

pacing with a strange deliberation turned eastwards along a green path
between banks of fern. Keda sat very still and very upright with her
hands in her lap while they drew nearer with every pace to Gormenghast
and the homes of the Bright Carvers.

EARLY ONE MORNING

SPRING has come and gone, and the summer is at its height.

It is the morning of the Breakfast, of the ceremonial Breakfast.
Prepared in honour of Titus, who is one year old today, it piles itself
magnificently across the surface of a table at the northern end of the
refectory. The servants' tables and benches have been removed so that
a cold stone desert spreads southwards unbroken save by the regular
pillars on either side which lead away in dwindling perspective. It is the
same dining-hall in which the Earl nibbles his frail toast at eight o'clock
every morning – the hall whose ceiling is riotous with flaking cherubs,
trumpets and clouds, whose high walls trickle with the damp, whose
flagstones sigh at every step.

At the northern extremity of this chill province the gold plate of the
Groans, pranked across the shining black of the long table, smoulders
as though it contains fire; the cutlery glitters with a bluish note; the
napkins, twisted into the shape of doves, detach themselves from their
surroundings for very whiteness, and appear to be unsupported. The
great hall is empty and there is no sound save the regular dripping of
rainwater from a dark patch in the cavernous ceiling. It has been
raining since the early hours of the morning and by now a small lake is
gathered halfway down the long stone avenue between the pillars,
reflecting dimly an irregular section of the welkin where a faded cluster
of cherubs lie asleep in the bosom of a mildew'd cloud. It is to this
cloud, darkened with *real* rain, that the drops cling sluggishly and fall
at intervals through the half-lit air to the glaze of water below.

Swelter has just retired to his clammy quarters after casting his
professional eye for the last time over the breakfast table. He is pleased
with his work and as he arrives at the kitchen there is a certain
satisfaction in the twist of his fat lips. There are still two hours to run
before the dawn.

Before he pushes open the door of the main kitchen he pauses and
listens with his ear to the panels. He is hoping to hear the voice of one
of his apprentices, of *any* one of his apprentices – it would not matter
which – for he has ordered silence until his return. The little uniformed

creatures had been lined up in two rows. Two of them are squabbling in thin, high whispers.

Swelter is in his best uniform, a habit of exceptional splendour, the high cap and tunic being of virgin silk. Doubling his body he opens the door the merest fraction of an inch and applies his eye to the fissure. As he bends, the shimmering folds of the silk about his belly hiss and whisper like the voice of far and sinister waters or like some vast, earthless ghost-cat sucking its own breath. His eye, moving around the panel of the door, is like something detached, self-sufficient, and having no need of the voluminous head that follows it nor for that matter of the mountainous masses undulating to the crutch, and the soft, trunk-like legs. So alive is it, this eye, quick as an adder, veined like a blood-alley. What need is there for all the cumulus of dull, surrounding clay – the slow white hinterland that weighs behind it as it swivels among the doughy, circumscribing wodges like a marble of raddled ice? As the eye rounds the corner of the door it devours the long double line of skinny apprentices as a squid might engulf and devour some long-shaped creature of the depths. As it sucks in the line of boys through the pupil, the knowledge of his power over them spreads sensuously across his trunk like a delicious gooseflesh. He has seen and heard the two shrill-whispering youths, now threatening one another with little raw fists. They have disobeyed him. He wipes his hot hands together, and his tongue travels along his lips. The eye watches them, Flycrake and Wrenpatch. They would do very nicely. So they were annoyed with one another, were they, the little dung-flies? How diverting! And how thoughtful of them! They will save him the trouble of having to invent some reason or another for punishing a brace of their ridiculous little brothers.

The chef opens the door and the double line freezes.

He approaches them, wiping his hands upon his silken buttocks as he moves forward. He impends above them like a dome of cloud.

'Flycrake,' he says, and the word issues from his lips as though it were drawn through a filter of sedge, 'there is room for you, Flycrake, in the shadow of my paunch, and bring your hairy friend with you – there is room for him as well I shouldn't wonder.'

The two boys creep forward, their eyes very wide, their teeth chattering.

'You were talking, were you not? You were talking even more garrulously than your teeth are now chattering. Am I wrong? No? Then come a little nearer; I should hate to have any trouble in reaching you. You wouldn't like to cause me any trouble, would you? Am I right in saying that you would not like to give me trouble, Master Flycrake? Master Wrenpatch?' He does not listen for an answer, but yawns, his face opening lewdly upon regions compared with which nudity becomes a milliner's invention. As the yawn ends and without a suspicion of warning, his two hands swing forward simultaneously and he catches the two little wretches by their ears and lifts them high into the air. What he would have done with them will never be known, for at the very moment when the hanging apprentices are lifted about the level of Swelter's throat, a bell begins to jangle discordantly through the steamy air. It is very seldom that this bell is heard, for the rope from which it is suspended, after disappearing through a hole in the ceiling of the Great Kitchen, moves secretly among rafters, winding to and fro in the obscure, dust-smelling regions that brood between the ceiling of the ground rooms and the floor boards of the first storey. After having been re-knotted many times, it finally emerges through a wall in Lord Sepulchrave's bedroom. It is very rarely that his Lordship has any need to interview his chef, and the bell as it swings wildly above the heads of the apprentices can be seen throwing from off its iron body the dust of four seasons.

Swelter's face changes at the first iron clang of the forgotten bell. The gloating and self-indulgent folds of face-fat redistribute themselves and a sycophantism oozes from his every pore. But only for a moment is he thus, his ears gulping at the sound of iron; for all at once he drops Flycrake and Wrenpatch to the stone slabs, surges from the room, his flat feet sucking at the stones like porridge.

Without abating the speed of his succulent paces, and sweeping with his hands whoever appears in his path as though he were doing breast-stroke, he pursues his way to Lord Sepulchrave's bedroom, the sweat beginning to stand out more and more on his cheeks and forehead as he nears the sacred door.

Before he knocks he wipes the sweat from his face with his sleeve, and then listens with his ear at the panels. He can hear nothing. He lifts his hand and strikes his folded fingers against the door with great force. He does this because he knows from experience that it is only with great difficulty that his knuckles can make any sound, the bones lying so deeply embedded within their stalls of pulp. As he half expected, all to be heard is a soft *plop*, and he resorts unwillingly to the expedient of extracting a coin from a pocket and striking it tentatively on the panel. To his horror, instead of the slow, sad, authoritative voice of his master ordering him to enter, he hears the hooting of an owl. After a few moments, during which he is forced to dab at his face, for he has been unnerved by the melancholy cry, he strikes again with the coin. This time there is no question that the high, long-drawn hoot which answers the tapping is an order for him to enter.

Swelter glances about him, turning his head this way and that, and he is on the point of making away from the door, for fear has made his body as cold as jelly, when he hears the regular crk, crk, crk, crk, of Flay's knee-joints approaching him from the shadows to his rear. And then he hears another sound. It is of someone running heavily, impetuously. As the sound approaches it drowns the regular *staccato* of Mr Flay's knee-joints. A moment later as Swelter turns his head the shadows break apart and the sultry crimson of Fuchsia's dress burns as it rushes forward. Her hand is on the handle of the door at once and she flings it open without a moment's hesitation or a glance at Swelter. The chef, a mixture of emotions competing within him as might a group of worms make battle for sovereignty in the belly of an ox, peers over Fuchsia's shoulder. Not until he has recoiled from what meets his eye can the secondary, yet impelling impulse to watch for the approach of Flay appease itself. Dragging his eyes from the spectacle before him he is in time to shift his bulk a little to the right and so to impede the thin man's progress, for Flay is now immediately behind him. Swelter's hatred of Lord Sepulchrave's servant has now ripened into a fester-patch, and his one desire is to stop the breathing for once and for all of a creature so fleshless, and of one who raised the welts upon his face on the Christening day.

Mr Flay, presented with the doming back and the splay-acred rear of the chef, is on edge to see his master who has rung his bell for him, and is in no mood to be thwarted, nor to be terrified at the white mass before him, and although for many a long stony night he has been unable to rest – for he is well aware of the chef's determination to kill him during his sleep – yet now, presented with the materialization of his nocturnal horror, he finds himself as hard as ironwood, and he jerks his dark, sour, osseous head forward out of his collar like a turtle and hisses from between his sand-coloured teeth.

Swelter's eyes meet those of his enemy, and never was there held between four globes of gristle so sinister a hell of hatred. Had the flesh, the fibres, and the bones of the chef and those of Mr Flay been conjured away and away down that dark corridor leaving only their four eyes suspended in mid-air outside the Earl's door, then, surely, they must have reddened to the hue of Mars, reddened and smouldered, and at last broken into flame, so intense was their hatred – broken into flame and circled about one another in ever-narrowing gyres and in swifter and yet swifter flight until, merged into one sizzling globe of ire they must surely have fled, the four in one, leaving a trail of blood behind them in the cold grey air of the corridor, until, screaming as they fly beneath innumerable arches and down the endless passageways of Gormenghast, they found their eyeless bodies once again, and re-entrenched themselves in startled sockets.

For a moment the two men are quite still, for Flay has not yet drawn breath after hissing through his teeth. Then, itching to get to his master he brings his sharp, splintery knee up suddenly beneath the balloon-like overhang of the chef's abdomen. Swelter, his face contracting with pain and whitening so that his blanched uniform becomes grey against his neck, raises his great arms in a clawing motion as his body doubles involuntarily for relief. As he straightens himself, and as Flay makes an effort to get past him to the door, with a jabbing movement of his shoulder, they are both frozen to the spot with a cry more dreadful than before, the long, dolorous cry of the death-owl, and the voice of Fuchsia, a voice that seems to be fighting through tears and terror, cries loudly:

'My father! My father! Be silent and it will be better, and I will take care of you. Look at me, father! Oh, look at me! I know what you want because I *do* know, father – I *do* know, and I will take you there when it is dark and then you will be better. – But look at me, father – look at me.'

But the Earl will not look at her. He is sitting huddled in the centre of the broad carven mantelpiece, his head below the level of his shoulders. Fuchsia, standing below him with her hands shaking as they grip the marble of the mantel, tilts herself towards him. Her strong back is hollowed, her head is thrown back and her throat taut. Yet she dare not touch him. The austerity of the many years that lay behind them – the chill of the mutual reserve they had always shown to one another, is like a wall between them even now. It seemed as though that wall were crumbling and that their frozen love was beginning to thaw and percolate through the crevices, but now, when it is most needed and most felt, the wall has closed again and Fuchsia dares not touch him. Nor dare she admit to herself that her father has become possessed.

He makes no answer, and Fuchsia, sinking to her knees, begins to cry, but there are no tears. Her body heaves as she crouches below Lord Sepulchrave as he squats on the mantelpiece, and her throat croaks, but no tears relieve her. It is dry anguish and she becomes older during these long moments, older than many a man or woman could ever understand.

Flay, clenching his hands, moves into the room, the hair standing out rigidly like little wires all over his scanty flesh. Something had crumpled up inside him. His undeviating loyalty to the House of Groan and to his Lordship is fighting with the horror of what he sees. Something of the same feeling must have been going on inside Swelter for as he and Flay gaze at the Earl there is upon their faces the same emotion translated, as it were, into two very different languages.

His Lordship is dressed in black. His knees are drawn up almost to his chin. His long, fine white hands are curled slightly inwards as they hang over his knees, between which, and his supported chin, the wrists are wedged. But it is the eyes which strike a chill to the centre of those who watch, for they have become circular. The smile which played across his lips when Fuchsia had been with him in the pine wood is gone forever. His mouth is entirely expressionless.

Suddenly a voice comes from the mouth. It is very quiet:
'Chef.'

'Your Lordship?' says Swelter trembling.

'How many traps have you in the Great Kitchen?'

Swelter's eyes shift to left and right and his mouth opens, but he can make no sound.

'Come, Chef, you must know how many traps are set every night – or have you become slovenly?'

Swelter holds his podgy hands together. They tremble before him as he works his fingers between one another.

'Sir,' says Swelter . . . 'there must be forty traps in the Great Kitchen . . . forty traps, your gracious Lordship.'

'How many were found in the traps at five o'clock today? Answer me.'

'They were all full, your Lordship – all except one, sir.'

'Have the cats had them?'

'The . . . the cats, your –'

'I said, have the cats had them?' repeats Lord Sepulchrave sadly.

'Not yet,' says the Chef. 'Not yet.'

'Then bring me one . . . bring me a plump one . . . immediately. What are you waiting for, Mr Chef? . . . What are you waiting for?'

Swelter's lips move wetly. 'A plump one,' he says. 'Yes, my Lord . . . a . . . plump . . . one.'

As soon as he has disappeared the voice goes on: 'Some twigs, Mr Flay, some twigs at once. Twigs of all sizes, do you understand? From small branches downwards in size – every kind of shape, Flay, every kind of shape, for I shall study each in turn and understand the twigs I build with, for I must be as clever as the others with my twigs, though we are careless workmen. What are you waiting for, Mr Flay? . . .'

Flay looks up. He has been unable to keep his eyes on the transformed aspect of his master, but now he lifts them again. He can recognize no expression. The mouth might as well not be there. The fine aquiline nose appears to be more forceful and the saucerlike shape of the eyes hold within either sky a vacant moon.

With a sudden awkward movement Flay plucks Fuchsia from the floor and flings her over his high shoulder and, turning, he staggers to the door and is soon among the passages.

'I must go back, I must go back to him!' Fuchsia gasps.

Flay only makes a noise in his throat and strides on.

At first Fuchsia begins to struggle, but she has no strength left for the dreadful scene has unnerved her and she subsides over his shoulder, not knowing where she is being taken. Nor does Flay know where he is taking her. They have reached the east quadrangle and have come out into the early morning when Fuchsia lifts her head.

'Flay,' she says, 'we must find Doctor Prune at once. I can walk, please, now. Thank you, Flay, but be quick. Be quick. Put me down.'

Flay eases her off his shoulder and she drops to the ground. Fuchsia has seen the Doctor's house in the corner of the quadrangle and she cannot understand why she had not thought of him before. Fuchsia begins to run, and directly she is at the Doctor's front door she beats it violently with the knocker. The sun is beginning to rise above the marshes and picks out a long gutter and a cornice of the Doctor's house, and presently, after Fuchsia has slammed at the door again, it picks out the extraordinary headpiece of Prunesquallor himself as it emerges sleepily through a high window. He cannot see what is below him in the shadows, but calls out:

'In the name of modesty and of all who slumber, go easy with that knocker! What in the world is it? . . . Answer me. What is it, I repeat? . . . Is it the plague that has descended on Gormenghast – or a forceps case? Is it a return of midnight-mange, or merely flesh-death? Does the patient rave? . . . Is he fat or thin? . . . Is he drunk or mad? . . . Is he . . .' The Doctor yawns and it is then that Fuchsia has her first chance to speak:

'Yes, oh yes! Come quickly, Doctor Prune! Let me tell you. Oh, please, let me tell you!'

The high voice at the sill cries: 'Fuchsia!' as though to itself. 'Fuchsia!' And the window comes down with a crash.

Flay moves to the girl and almost before he has done so the front door is flung open and Doctor Prunesquallor in his flowered pyjamas is facing them.

Taking Fuchsia by the hand and motioning Flay to follow he minces rapidly to the living room.

'Sit down, sit down, my frantic one!' cries Prunesquallor. 'What the devil is it? Tell the old Prune all about it.'

'It's father,' says Fuchsia, the tears finding release at long last. 'Father's become wrong, Doctor Prune; Father's become all wrong . . . Oh, Doctor Prune, he is a black owl now . . . Oh, Doctor, help him! Help him!'

The Doctor does not speak. He turns his pink, over-sensitive, intelligent head sharply in the direction of Flay, who nods and comes forward a step, with the report of a knee-joint. Then he nods again, his jaw working. 'Owl,' he says. 'Wants mice! . . . Wants twigs: on mantelpiece! Hooting! Lordship's mad.'

'No!' shouts Fuchsia. 'He's ill, Doctor Prune. That's all. His library's been burned. His beautiful library; and he's become ill. But he's not mad. He talks so quietly. Oh, Doctor Prune, what are you going to do?'

'Did you leave him in his room?' says the Doctor, and it does not seem to be the same man speaking.

Fuchsia nods her tear-wet head.

'Stay here,' says the Doctor quietly; as he speaks he is away and within a few moments has returned in a lime-green dressing gown with lime-green slippers to match, and in his hand, a bag.

'Fuchsia dear, send Steerpike to me, in your father's room. He is quick-witted and may be of help. Flay, get about your duties. The Breakfast must proceed, as you know. Now then, my gipsy-child; death or glory.' And with the highest and most irresponsible of trills he vanishes through the door.

A CHANGE OF COLOUR

THE morning light is strengthening, and the hour of the Great Breakfast approaches. Flay, utterly distraught, is wandering up and down the candle-lit stone lanes where he knows he will be alone. He had gathered the twigs and he had flung them away in disgust only to re-gather them, for the very thought of disobeying his master is almost as dreadful to him as the memory of the creature he has seen on the mantelpiece. Finally, and in despair, he has crunched the twigs between his own stick-like fingers, the simultaneous crackling of the twigs and of his knuckles creating for a moment a miniature storm of brittle thunder in the shadow of the trees. Then, striding back to the Castle he has descended uneasily to the Stone Lanes. It is very cold, yet there are great pearls upon his forehead, and in each pearl is the reflection of a candle flame.

Mrs Slagg is in the bedroom of the Countess, who is piling her rust-coloured hair above her head as though she were building a castle. Every now and again Mrs Slagg peers furtively at the bulk before the mirror, but her attention is chiefly centred upon an object on the bed. It is wrapped in a length of lavender-coloured velvet, and little porcelain bells are pinned here and there all over it. One end of a golden chain is attached to the velvet near the centre of what has become, through process of winding, a small velvet cylinder, or mummy, measuring some three and a half feet in length and with a diameter of about eighteen inches. At the other end of the chain and lying on the bed beside the lavender roll is a sword with a heavy blade of blue-black steel and a hilt embossed with the letter 'G'. This sword is attached to the gold chain with a piece of string.

Mrs Slagg dabs a little powder upon something that moves in the shadow at one end of the roll, and then peers about her, for it is hard for her to see what she is doing, the shadows in the bedroom of the Countess are of so dark a breed. Between their red rims her eyes wander here and there before she bends over Titus and plucks at her underlip. Again her eyes peer up at the Countess, who seems to have grown tired of her hair, the edifice being left unfinished as though some fitful architect had died before the completion of a bizarre edifice which no one else knew how to complete. Mrs Slagg moves from the bedside in little half-running, half-walking steps, and from the table beneath the candelabra plucks a candle that is waxed to the wood among the birdseed, and, lighting it from a guttering torso of tallow that stands by, she returns to the lavender cylinder which has begun to twist and turn.

Her hand is unsteady as she lifts the wax above the head of Titus, and the wavering flame makes it leap. His eyes are very wide open. As he sees the light his mouth puckers and works, and the heart of the earth contracts with love as he totters at the wellhead of tears. His little body writhes in its dreadful bolster and one of the porcelain bells chimes sweetly.

'Slagg,' said the Countess in a voice of husk.

Nannie, who is as light as a feather, starts into the air an inch or two at the sudden sound, and comes to earth again with a painful jarring of her little arid ankles; but she does not cry out, for she is biting her lower lip while her eyes cloud over. She does not know what she has done wrong and she has done nothing wrong, but there is always a feeling of guilt about her when she shares a room with the Countess. This is partly due to the fact that she irritates the Countess, and the nurse can sense this all the while. So it is in a thin and tremulous voice that she stammers:

'Yes, oh yes, Ladyship? Yes . . . yes, your Ladyship?'

The Countess does not turn her head to speak, but stares past herself in the cracked mirror, her elbows resting on the table, her head supported in the cups of her hands.

'Is the child ready?'

'Yes, yes, just ready, just ready. Ready now, your Ladyship, bless his little smallness . . . yes . . . yes . . .'

'Is the sword fixed?'

'Yes, yes, the sword, the –'

She is about to say 'the horrid, black sword', but she checks herself nervously, for who is she to express her feeling when ritual is involved? 'But it's so *hot* for him,' she continues hurriedly, 'so hot for his little body in all this velvet – though, of course,' she adds, a stupid little smile working in and out of the wrinkles of her lips, 'it's very pretty.'

The Countess turns slowly in her chair. 'Slagg,' she says, 'come over here, Slagg.'

The old woman, her heart beating wildly, patters her way around the bed and stands by the dressing-table. She clasps her hands together on her flat chest and her eyes are wide open.

'Have you still no idea of how to answer even simple questions?' asks the Countess very slowly.

Nannie shakes her head, but suddenly a red spot appears in either cheek. 'I *can* answer questions, I *can!*' she cries, startling herself with her own ineffectual vehemence.

The Countess does not seem to have heard her. 'Try and answer *this* one,' she murmurs.

Mrs Slagg cocks her head on one side and listens like a grey bird.

'Are you attending, Slagg?'

Nannie nods her head as though suffering from palsy.

'Where did you meet that youth?' There is a moment's silence.

'That Steerpike?' the Countess adds.

'Long ago,' says Nannie, and closes her eyes as she waits for the next question. She feels pleased with herself.

'*Where* is what I said: *where*, not *when*,' booms the voice.

Mrs Slagg tries to gather her thoughts together. Where? Oh, where was it? she wondered. It was long ago . . . And then she recalled how he had appeared with Fuchsia suddenly at the door of her room.

'With Fuchsia . . . Oh, yis . . . yis, it was with my Fuchsia, your Ladyship.'

'Where does he come from? Answer me, Slagg, and then finish my hair.'

'I never do know . . . No, not ever . . . I have never been told. Oh, my poor heart, no. Where *could* the boy come from?' She peers at the dark bulk above her.

Lady Gertrude wipes the palm of her hand slowly across her brow. 'You are the same Slagg,' she says, 'the same brilliant Slagg.'

Nannie begins to cry, wishing desperately that she were clever.

'No use crying,' says the Countess. 'No use. No use. My birds don't cry. Not very often. Were you at the fire?'

The word 'fire' is terrible to Mrs Slagg. She clutches her hands together. Her bleary eyes grow wild. Her lips tremble, for in her imagination she can see the great flames rising about her.

'Finish my hair, Nannie Slagg. Stand on a chair and do it.'

Nannie turns to find a chair. The room is like a shipwreck. The red walls glower in the candle-light. The old woman patters her way between stalactites of tallow, boxes and old sofas. The Countess whistles and a moment later the room is alive with wings. By the time Mrs Slagg has dragged a chair to the dressing-table and climbed upon it, the

Countess is deep in conversation with a magpie. Nannie disapproves of birds altogether and cannot reconcile the habits of the Countess with the House of Groan, but she is used to such things, not being over seventy years old for nothing. Bending a little over her ladyship's locks she works with difficulty to complete the hirsute cornice, for the light is bad.

'Now then, darling, now then,' says the heavy voice below her, and her old body thrills, for she has never known the Countess speak to her in such a way before; but glancing over the mountainous shoulder she sees that the Countess is talking to a bedraggled finch and Nannie Slagg is desolate.

'So Fuchsia was the first to find him, was she?' says the Countess, rubbing her finger along the finch's throat.

Mrs Slagg, startled, as she always is when anyone speaks, fumbles with the red hank in her hand. 'Who? Oh, who do you mean . . . your Ladyship? . . . Oh, she's always a good girl, Fuchsia is, yis, yis, *always*.'

The Countess gets to her feet in a monumental way, brushing several objects from the dressing-table to the floor with her elbow. As she rises she hears the sound of sobbing and turns her head to the lavender roll. 'Go away, Slagg – go away, and take him with you. Is Fuchsia dressed?'

'Yis . . . oh, my poor heart, yis . . . Fuchsia is all ready, yis, quite ready, and waiting in her room. Oh yis, she is . . .'

'His Breakfast will soon be beginning,' says the Countess, turning her eyes from a brass clock to her infant son. 'Very soon.'

Nannie, who has recovered Titus from the fastnesses of the bed, stops at the door before pattering out into the dawn-lit corridor. Her eyes stare back almost triumphantly and a little pathetic smile works at the crinkled corners of her mouth. '*His* Breakfast,' she whispers. 'Oh, my weak heart, his *first* Breakfast.'

Steerpike has been found at last, Fuchsia colliding with him as he rounds a corner of the staircase on his way down from the aunts. He is very sprucely dressed, his high shoulders without a speck of dust upon them, his finger-nails pared, his hair smoothed down over his pasty-coloured forehead. He is surprised to see Fuchsia, but he does not show it, merely raising his eyebrows in an expression both inquiring and deferential at the same time.

'You are up very early, Lady Fuchsia.'

Fuchsia, her breast heaving from her long run up the stairs, cannot speak for a moment or two; then she says: 'Doctor Prune wants you.'

'Why me?' says the youth to himself; but aloud he said: 'Where is he?'

'In my father's room.'

Steerpike licks his lips slowly. 'Is your father ill?'

'Yes, oh yes, very ill.'

Steerpike turns his head away from Fuchsia, for the muscles of his face cry out to relax. He gives them a free rein and then, straightening his face and turning to Fuchsia, he says: 'Everything I can do I will do.' Suddenly, with the utmost nimbleness, he skips past her, jumping the first four steps together, and races down the stone flight on his way to the Earl's bedroom.

He has not seen the Doctor for some time. Having left his service their relationship is a little strained, but this morning as he enters at the Earl's door he can see there will be neither space nor time for reminiscences in his own or the Doctor's brain.

Prunesquallor, in his lime-green dressing-gown, is pacing to and fro before the mantelpiece with the stealth of some kind of vertical cat. Not for a moment does he take his eyes off the Earl, who, still upon the mantelpiece, watches the physician with great eyes.

At the sound of Steerpike at the door the round eyes move for a moment and stare over the Doctor's shoulder. But Prunesquallor has not shifted his steady, magnified gaze. The roguish look is quite absent from his long, bizarre face.

The Doctor has been waiting for this moment. Prancing forward he reaches up with his white hands and pins the Earl's arms to his sides, dragging him from his perch. Steerpike is at the Doctor's side in a moment and together they carry the sacrosanct body to the bed and turn it over upon its face. Sepulchrave has not struggled, only emitting a short stifled cry.

Steerpike holds the dark figure down with one hand, for there is no attempt to escape, and the Doctor flicks a slim needle into his Lordship's wrist and injects a drug of such weird potency that when they turn the patient over Steerpike is startled to see that the face has changed to a kind of chalky green. But the eyes have altered also and are once more the sober, thoughtful, human eyes which the Castle knew so well. His fingers have uncurled; the claws are gone.

'Be so good as to draw the blind,' says the Doctor, raising himself to his full height beside the bed, and returning his needle to its little silver case. This done, he taps the points of his long white fingers together thoughtfully. With the blinds drawn across the sunrise the colour of his lordship's face is mercifully modified.

'That was quick work, Doctor.'

Steerpike is balancing upon his heels. 'What happens next?' He clicks his tongue ruminatively as he waits for Prunesquallor's answer. 'What was the drug you used, Doctor?'

'I am not in the mood to answer questions, dear boy,' replies

Prunesquallor, showing Steerpike the whole range of his teeth, but in a mirthless way. 'Not at all in the mood.'

'What about the Breakfast?' says Steerpike, unabashed.

'His Lordship will *be* at the Breakfast.'

'Will he, though?' says the youth, peering at the face. 'What about his colour?'

'In half an hour his skin will have returned to normal. He will be there . . . Now, fetch me Flay and some boiling water, a towel. He must be washed and dressed. Quickly now.'

Before Steerpike leaves the room he bends over Lord Sepulchrave, whistling tunelessly between his teeth. The Earl's eyes are closed and there is a tranquillity about his face which has been absent for many years.

A BLOODY CHEEKBONE

STEERPIKE has some difficulty in finding Flay, but he comes across him at last in the blue-carpeted Room of Cats, whose sunlit pile they had trodden together under very different circumstances a year ago. Flay has just reappeared from the Stone Lanes and looks very bedraggled, a long dirty hank of cobweb hanging over his shoulder. When he sees Steerpike his lips curl back like a wolf's.

'What you want?' he says.

'How's Flay?' says Steerpike.

The cats are crowded upon one enormous ottoman with its carven head and footpiece rising into the air in a tangle of gilded tracery as though two toppling waves at sunset were suspended in mid-air, the hollow between them filled with foam. There is no sound from them and they do not move.

'The Earl wants you,' continues Steerpike, enjoying Flay's discomfort. He does not know whether Flay has any knowledge of what is happening to his master.

Flay involuntarily propels his gawky body forwards as he hears that his Lordship wants him, but he pulls himself up at the end of his first long step towards the door, and peers even more suspiciously and acidly at the youth in his immaculate black cloth.

Steerpike on a sudden, without considering the consequences of his action with the same thoroughness that is typical of him, forces his eyes open with the forefinger and thumb of either hand. He wishes to see whether the thin creature before him has seen the Earl during his madness. He is really banking on the assumption that Flay will not have done so, in which case the forcing of his eyes into owlish circles will have no meaning. But he has made this early morning one of his rare mistakes.

With a hoarse, broken cry, Flay, his head reddening with wrath at this insult to his master, staggers to the divan and, shooting out a gaunt hand, plucks a cat by its head from the snowy hill and hurls it at his tormentor. As this happens a cloaked and heavy woman enters the room. The living missile, hurtling at Steerpike's face, reaches out one of its white legs and as the youth jerks his head to one side, five claws rip out a crimson wedge from his cheek immediately below the right eye.

The air is filled at once with the screaming of a hundred cats which, swarming the walls and furniture, leaping and circling the blue carpet with the speed of light, give the room the appearance of a white maelstrom. The blood, streaming down Steerpike's neck, feels as warm as tea as it slides to his belly. His hand, which he has raised automatically to his face in a vain attempt to ward off the blow, moves to his cheek as he drops back a pace, and the tips of his fingers become wet. The cat itself has ended its flight against the wall, near the door through which the third figure has just entered. As it falls in a huddle to the floor, half stunned, and with the wedge of Steerpike's sallow skin between the claws of its left forefoot, it sees the figure above it; it crawls with a moan to within a pace of the visitor, and then, with a superfeline effort, springs to the height of her great breasts where it lies coiled with its eyes like yellow moons appearing above the whiteness of its haunches.

Flay turns his eyes from Steerpike. It has done him good to watch the red blood bubbling from the upstart's cheek, but now his satisfaction is at an end, for he is gazing stupefied into the hard eyes of the Countess of Groan.

Her big head has coloured to a dim and dreadful madder. Her eyes are completely remorseless. She has no interest in the cause of the quarrel between Flay and the Steerpike youth. All she knows is that one of her white cats had been dashed against the wall and has suffered pain.

Flay waits as she approaches. His bony head is quite still. His loose hands hang gawkily at his sides. He realizes the crime he has committed, and as he waits his world of Gormenghast – his security, his love, his faith in the House, his devotion – is all crumbling into fragments.

She is standing within a foot of him. The air is heavy with her presence.

Her voice is very husky when she speaks. 'I was going to strike him down,' she says heavily. 'That is what I intended to do with him. To break him.'

He lifts his eyes. The white cat is within a few inches of him. He watches the hairs of its back; each one has become a bristle and the back is a hummock of sharp white grass.

The Countess begins to talk again in a louder voice, but it has become so choked that Flay cannot understand what she is saying. At last he can make out the words: 'You are no more, no more at all. You are ended.'

Her hand, as it moves gently over the body of the white cat, is trembling uncontrollably. 'I have finished with you,' she says. 'Gormenghast has finished with you.' It is hard for her to draw the words from her great throat. 'You are over . . . over.' Suddenly she raises her voice. 'Crude fool!' she cries. 'Crude, broken fool and brute! Out! Out! The Castle throws you. *Go!*' she roars, her hands upon the cat's breast. 'Your long bones sicken me.'

Flay lifts his small bony head higher into the air. He cannot comprehend what has happened. All he knows is that it is more dreadful than he can feel, for a kind of numbness is closing in on his horror like a padding. There is a greenish sheen across the shoulders of his greasy black suit, for the morning light has of a sudden begun to dance through the bay window. Steerpike, with a blood-drenched handkerchief wound about his face, is staring at him and tapping the top of a table with his nails. He cannot help but feel that there is something very fine about the old creature's head. And he had been very quick. Very quick indeed. Something to remember, that: cats for missiles.

Flay moved his little eyes around the room. The floor is alive and white behind the Countess, around whose feet lies the stilled froth of a tropic tide, the azure carpet showing now here and now there. He feels he is looking at it for the last time and turns to go, but as he turns he thinks of the Breakfast. He is surprised to hear his own mirthless voice saying: 'Breakfast.'

The Countess knows that her husband's first servant must be at the Breakfast. Had he killed every white cat in the world he must still be at the Breakfast in honour of Titus, the 77th Earl of Gormenghast, to be. Such things are cardinal.

The Countess turns herself about and moves to the bay window after making a slow detour of the room and picking up from a rack near the fireplace a heavy iron poker. As she reaches the window her right arm swings slowly back and forward with the deliberation of a shire-mare's bearded hoof as it falls into a rainpool. There is a startling split and crash, a loud cascading of glass upon the flagstones outside the window, and then silence.

With her back to the room she stares through the star-shaped gap in the glass. Before her spreads the green lawn. She is watching the sun breaking through the distant cedars. It is the day of her son's Breakfast. She turns her head. 'You have a week,' she says, 'and then you leave these walls. A servant shall be found for the Earl.'

Steerpike lifts his head, and for a moment he ceases to drum on the woodwork with his finger-nails. As he starts tapping again, a kestrel, sweeping through the star of the shattered pane, alights on the shoulder of the Countess. She winces as its talons for a moment close, but her eyes soften.

Flay approaches a door in three slow, spidery slides. It is the door that opens into the Stone Lanes. He fumbles for his key, and turns it in the lock. He must rest in his own region before he returns to the Earl, and he lets himself into the long darkness.

The Countess, for the first time, remembers Steerpike. She moves her eyes slowly in the direction where she had last seen him, but he is no longer there nor in any part of the room.

A bell chimes from the corridor beyond the Room of Cats and she knows that there is but a short while before the Breakfast.

She feels a splash of water on her hand, and, turning, sees that the sky has become overcast with a blanket of ominous dark rose-coloured cloud, and of a sudden the light fades from the lawn and the cedars.

Steerpike, who is on his way back to the Earl's bedroom, stops a moment at a staircase window to see the first descent of the rain. It is falling from the sky in long, upright and seemingly motionless lines of rosy silver that stand rigidly upon the ground as though there were a million harp strings strung vertically between the solids of earth and sky. As he leaves the window he hears the first roar of the summer thunder.

The Countess hears it as she stares through the jagged star in the bay window. Prunesquallor hears it as he balances the Earl upon his feet at the side of the bed. The Earl must have heard it, too, for he takes a step of his own volition towards the centre of the room. His own face has returned.

'Was that thunder, Doctor?' he says.

The Doctor watches him very carefully, watches his every movement, though few would have guessed how intently he was studying his patient had they seen his long ingenious mouth open with customary gaiety.

'Thunder it was, your Lordship. A most prodigious peal. I am waiting for the martial chords which must surely follow such an opening, what? Ha, ha, ha, ha, ha!'

'What has brought you to my bedroom, Doctor? I do not remember sending for you.'

'That is not unnatural, your Lordship. You did not send for me. I was summoned a few minutes ago, to find that you had fainted, an unfortunate, but by no means rare thing to happen to anyone. Now, I wonder why you should have fainted?' The Doctor stroked his chin. 'Why? Was the room very hot?'

The Earl comes across to the Doctor. 'Prunesquallor,' he says, 'I don't faint.'

'Your Lordship,' says the Doctor, 'when I arrived in this bedroom you were in a faint.'

'Why should I have fainted? I do not faint, Prunesquallor.'

'Can you remember what you were doing before you lost consciousness?'

The Earl moves his eyes from the Doctor. All at once he feels very tired and sits down on the edge of the bed.

'I can remember nothing, Prunesquallor. Absolutely nothing. I can only recall that I was hankering for something, but for what I do not know. It seems a month ago.'

'I can tell you,' says Prunesquallor. 'You are making ready to go to your son's Breakfast Gathering. You were pressed for time and were anxious not to be late. You are, in any event, overstrained, and in your anticipation of the occasion you became overwrought. Your "hankering" was to be with your one-year-old son. That is what you vaguely remember.'

'When is my son's Breakfast?'

'It is in half an hour's time, or to be precise, it is in twenty-eight minutes' time.'

'Do you mean *this morning*?' A look of alarm has appeared on Lord Sepulchrave's face.

'This morning as ever was, as ever is, and as ever will or won't be, bless its thunderous heart. No, no, my lord, do not get up yet.' (Lord Sepulchrave has made an attempt to stand.) 'In a moment or two and you will be as fit as the most expensive of fiddles. The Breakfast will not be delayed. No, no, not at all – You have twenty-seven long, sixty-second-apiece minutes, and Flay should be on his way to get your garments laid out for you – yes, indeed.'

Flay is not only on his way, but he is at the door, having been unable to remain in the Stone Lanes any longer than it took him to tear his way through them and up to his master's room by an obscure passage which he alone knew. Even so he is only a moment or two in advance of Steerpike, who slides under Flay's arm and through the bedroom door as Flay opens it.

Steerpike and the servant are amazed to find that Lord Sepulchrave is seemingly his own melancholy self again, and Flay shambles towards his master and drops upon his knees before him with a sudden, uncontrollable, clumsy movement, his knees striking the floor with a crash. The Earl's sensitive pale hand rests for a moment on the shoulders of the scarecrow, but all he says is: 'My ceremonial velvet, Flay. Be as quick as you can. My velvet and the bird-brooch of opals.'

Flay scrambles to his feet. He is his master's first servant. He is to lay out his master's clothes and to prepare him for the Great Breakfast in honour of his only son. This is no time or place for the wretched youth to be in his Lordship's bedroom. Nor for that matter need the Doctor stay.

With his hand on the wardrobe door he turns his head creakily. '*I* manage, Doctor,' he says. His eyes move from Prunesquallor to Steerpike, and he draws back his lips in an expression of contempt and disgust.

The Doctor notices this expression. 'Quite right. Quite, quite right! His Lordship will improve with every minute that passes, and there is no need for us any longer, most assuredly not, by all that's tactful I should definitely think not, ha, ha, ha! Oh, dear me, no. Come along, Steerpike. Come along. And, by the way, what's all that blood on your face? Are you playing at being a pirate or have you had a tiger in bed with you? Ha, ha, ha! But tell me afterwards, dear boy, tell me afterwards.' And the Doctor proceeds to shepherd Steerpike out of the room.

But Steerpike dislikes being shepherded and 'After you, Doctor,' he says, and insists on Prunesquallor's preceding him through the door. Before he closes it he turns and, speaking to the Earl in a confidential tone: 'I will see that everything is in readiness,' he says. 'Leave it to me, your Lordship. I will see you later, Flay. Now then, Doctor, let us be on our way.'

The door closes.

THE TWINS AGAIN

THE Aunts have been sitting opposite one another for well over an hour with hardly a movement. Surely only vanity could account for so long a scrutiny of a human face, and as it so happens it *is* Vanity and nothing but Vanity, for knowing that their features are identical and that they have administered the identical amount of powder and have spent the identical length of time in brushing their hair, they have no doubt at all that in scrutinizing one another they are virtually gazing at themselves. They are garbed in their best purple, a hue so violent as to give physical discomfort to any normally sensitive eye.

'Now, Clarice,' says Cora at last, 'you turn your lovely head to the
right, so that I can see what I look like from the *side*.'

'Why?' says Clarice. 'Why should I?'

'Why shouldn't you? I've got a right to *know*.'

'So have I, if it comes to that.'

'Well, it will come to that, won't it? Stupid!'

'Yes, but . . .'

'You do what I say and then I'll do it for you.'

'Then I'll see what my profile's like, won't I?'

'We both will, not just you.'

'I *said* we both will.'

'Well? What's the matter, then?'

'Nothing.'

'Well?'

'Well, what?'

'Well, go on, then – turn your lovely head.'

'Shall I do it now?'

'Yes. There's nothing to wait for, is there?'

'Only the Breakfast. It won't be just yet.'

'Why not?'

'Because I heard the bell go in the corridor.'

'So did I. That means there's a lot of time.'

'I want to look at my profile, Cora. Turn it now.'

'All right. How long shall I be, Clarice?'

'Be a long time.'

'Only if I have a long time, too.'

'We can't both have a long time, silly.'

'Why not?'

'Because there isn't one.'

'Isn't one what, dear?'

'Isn't one long time, is there?'

'No, there's lots of them.'

'Yes, lots and lots of beautiful long times.'

'Ahead of us, you mean, Clarice?'

'Yes, ahead of us.'

'After we're on our thrones, isn't it?'

'How do you know?'

'Well, that's what you were thinking. Why do you try to deceive me?'

'I wasn't. I only wanted to know.'

'Well, now you *do* know.'

'Do know what?'

'You *do* know, that's all. I'm not going any deeper for you.'

'Why not?'

'Because you can't go as deep as I can. You never could.'

'I've never *tried*, I don't suppose. It's not worth it, I shouldn't think. I know when things are worth it.'

'Well, when *are* they, then?'

'When are they what?'

'When are they worth something?'

'When you've bought something wonderful with your wealth, then it's always worth it.'

'Unless you don't *want* it, Clarice, you always forget that. Why can't you be less forgetful?'

There is a long silence while they study each other's faces.

'They'll look at us, you know,' says Cora flatly. 'We're going to be looked at at the Breakfast.'

'Because we're of the original blood,' says Clarice. 'That's why.'

'And that's why we're important, too.'

'Two what?'

'To everyone, of course.'

'Well, we're not yet, not to everyone.'

'But we will be soon.'

'When the clever boy makes us. He can do anything.'

'Anything. Anything at all. He told me so.'

'Me, too. Don't think he only tells you, because he doesn't.'

'I didn't say he did, did I?'

'You were going to.'

'Two what?'

'To exalt yourself.'

'Oh, yes, yes. We will be exalted when the time is ripe.'

'Ripe and rich.'

'Yes, of course.'

'Of course.'

There is another silence. Their voices have been so flat and expressionless that when they cease talking the silence seems no new thing in the room, but rather a continuation of flatness in another colour.

'Turn your head now, Cora. When I'm looked at at the Breakfast I want to know how they see me from the side and what exactly they are looking at; so turn your head for me and I will for you afterwards.'

Cora twists her white neck to the left.

'More,' says Clarice.

'More what?'

'I can still see your other eye.'

Cora twists her head a fraction more, dislodging some of the powder from her neck.

'That's right, Cora. Stay like that. Just like that. Oh, Cora!' (the voice is still as flat), 'I am *perfect*.'

She claps her hands mirthlessly, and even her palms meet with a dead sound.

Almost as though this noise were a summons the door opens and Steerpike moves rapidly across the room. There is a fresh piece of plaster across his cheek. The twins rise and edge towards him, their shoulders touching as they advance.

He runs his eyes over them, takes his pipe out of his pocket and strikes a light. For a moment he holds the flame in his hand, but only for a moment, for Cora has raised her arm with the slow gesture of a somnambulist and has let it fall upon the flame, extinguishing it.

'What in plague's name are you up to?' shouts Steerpike, for once losing his control. Seeing an Earl as an owl on a mantelpiece, and having part of one's face removed by a cat, both on the same morning, can temporarily undermine the self-control of any man.

'No fire,' says Cora. 'We don't have fires any more.'

'We don't like them any more. No. Not any more.'

'Not after we –'

Steerpike breaks in, for he knows how their minds have turned, and this is no moment just before the Breakfast for them to start reminiscing. 'You are awaited! Breakfast table is agog for you. They all want to know where you are. Come along, my lovely brace of ladies. Let me escort you some of the way, at least. You are looking most alluring – but what can have been keeping you? Are you ready?'

The twins nod their heads.

'May I be so honoured as to give you my right arm, Lady Cora? And, Lady Clarice, my dear, if you will take my left . . . ?'

Steerpike, bending his elbows, waits for the Aunts to split apart to take his either arm.

'The right's more important than the left,' says Clarice. 'Why should you have it?'

'Why shouldn't I?'

'Because I'm as good as you.'

'But not as clever, are you, dear?'

'Yes, I am, only you're favoured.'

'That's because I'm alluring, like he says I am.'

'He said we both were.'

'That was just to please you. Didn't you know?'

'Dear ladies,' says Steerpike, breaking in, 'will you please be quiet! Who is in command of your destinies? Who is it you promised you would trust and obey?'

'You.' They speak together.

'I think of you as co-equals, and I want you to think of yourselves as of similar status, for when your thrones arrive they will be of equal glory. Now, will you take my arms, if you please?'

Cora and Clarice take an arm each. The door of their room had been left open and the three of them make their exit, the youth's thin black figure walking between the stiff purple bodies of the Aunts, who are gazing over his head at each other, so that as they recede down the half-lit corridor and diminish in size as they move into the long perspective, the last that can be seen, long after Steerpike in his black and the purple of the twins has become swallowed in the depths, are the tiny, pallid patterns of the two identical profiles facing one another and floating, as it were, in the mid-air shadows, diminishing and diminishing as they drift away, until the last mote of light has crumbled from them.

THE DARK BREAKFAST

BARQUENTINE is unaware that there have been grave and sinister happenings in the Castle on this historic morning. He knows, of course, that the Earl has, since the burning of the library, been in a critical state of health, but of his dreadful transformation upon the mantelpiece he is ignorant. Since the early hours he has been studying the finer points of ritual to be observed at the Breakfast. Now, as he stumps his way to the dining-hall, his crutch clanking ominously on the flagstones, he sucks at a hank of his beard, which curls up and into his mouth through long training, and mutters irritably.

He still lives in the dusty, low-ceilinged room which he has had for over sixty years. With his new responsibilities bringing with them the necessity for interviewing numerous servants and officials has come no desire to establish himself in any of the numerous suites of rooms which are his to occupy if he so desires. The fact that those who are obliged to come either to consult him or for orders are forced to contort themselves painfully in order to negotiate a passage through his rabbit hutch doorway, and when inside to move about in a doubled-up condition, has no effect on him at all. Barquentine is not interested in the comfort of others.

Fuchsia, approaching the dining-hall in company with Mrs Slagg, who is carrying Titus, hears the rattle of Barquentine's crutch following them down the corridor. At a normal time she would have shuddered at the sound, but the horrifying and tragic minutes which she had spent with her father have filled her with so violent an alarm and so nameless a foreboding as to expel all other fears. She has on the immemorial crimson which is worn by the first daughter of the House of Groan at the christening of a brother, and around her neck are the so-called

Daughter's Doves, a necklace of white sandstone doves carved by
the 17th Earl of Gormenghast, strung together on a cord of plaited
grass.

There is no sound from the infant, who is encased in the lilac roll.
Fuchsia carries the black sword at one side, although the golden chain
is still attached to Titus. Nannie Slagg, beside herself with trepidation
and excitement, peers now at her bundle and now at Fuchsia, sucking
at her wrinkled lips as her little feet shuffle along below her best sepia-
coloured skirt.

'We won't be late, my caution, will we? Oh no, because we mustn't,
must we?' She peers into one end of the lilac roll. 'Bless him that he's so
good, with all this horrible thunder; yis, he's been as good as good.'

Fuchsia does not hear; she is moving in a nightmare world of her
own. Who can she turn to? Who can she ask? 'Doctor Prune, Doctor
Prune,' she says to herself, '. . . he will tell me; he will know that I can
make him well again. Only I can make him well again.'

Before them, as they turn a corner, the door of the dining-hall looms
up and, obliterating most of it, with his hand on the brass handle, is
Swelter. He swings open the door for them and they enter the Dining
Hall. They are the last to arrive and more through coincidence than
design this is as it should be – Titus being the guest of honour, or
perhaps the *host* of honour, for it is today that, as the Heir of
Gormenghast, he Enters upon the Realms, having braved the cycle of
four seasons.

Fuchsia climbs the seven wooden steps which lead up to the rostrum
and the long table. Away to her right spreads the cold, echoing hall,
with the pool of rain-drips spreading on the stone floor. The drumming
of the thick vertical rain on the roof is a background to everything that
happens. Reaching down with her right hand Fuchsia helps Mrs Slagg
up the last two steps. The assemblage, perfectly silent at the long table,
have turned their heads towards Nannie with her momentous bundle,
and when both her feet are well established upon the level of the
rostrum the company rises and there is a scraping of chair-legs on the
boards. It seems to Fuchsia that high, impenetrable forests have risen
before her, great half-lit forms of a nature foreign to her own – belonging
to some other kingdom. But though for a moment she thinks of this, she
is not feeling it, for she is subjugated beneath the weight of her fear for
her father.

It is with a shock of indefinable emotion that she sees him as she lifts
her head. She had never for a moment contemplated his being able to
attend the Breakfast, imagining that the Doctor would be with him in
his bedroom. So vivid in her mind is the picture of her father in his
room as she had last seen him, that to find him in this so different
atmosphere gives her for a moment a gush of hope – hope that she had

been dreaming – that she had not been to his room – that he had not been upon the mantelpiece with his round, loveless eyes; for now as she stares at him he is so gentle and sad and thin and she can see that there is a weak smile of welcome upon his lips.

Swelter, who has followed them in, is now ushering Mrs Slagg into a chair on whose back-rest is painted the words: 'FOR A SERVANT'. There is a space cleared before her on the table in the shape of a half-circle, in which has been laid a long cushion. When Mrs Slagg sits down she finds that her chin is on a level with the table-edge, and it is with difficulty that she lifts the lilac bundle high enough to place it on the cushion. On her left is Gertrude Groan. Mrs Slagg glances at her apprehensively. She is gazing at an expanse of darkness, for the black clothes of the Countess seem to have no ending. She lifts her eyes a little and there is still darkness. She lifts them more, and still the darkness climbs. Raising her whole head and staring almost vertically above her she imagines that, near the zenith of her vision, she can descry a warmth of colour in the night. To think that an hour earlier she had been helping to plait those locks that now appear to be brushing the flaking cherubs of the ceiling.

On her right is the Earl. He leans back in his chair, very listless and weak, but he still smiles wanly at his daughter, who is on the opposite side of the table and facing her mother. On Fuchsia's right and left sit Irma Prunesquallor and her brother respectively. The Doctor and Fuchsia have their little fingers interlocked under the table. Cora is sitting opposite to the Earl her brother, and on the left of the Countess, and facing Irma, is Clarice. A fine, succulent ham, lit by a candle, takes up most of the space at the Earl's and Cora's end of the table, where Swelter presides and has now taken up his official duties armed with carving-knife and steel. At the other end of the table Barquentine smoulders on a high chair.

The eating is done spasmodically whenever a gap of time appears between the endless formalities and ornate procedures which Barquentine sets in motion at the correct time-honoured moments. Tiresome in the extreme for all those present, it would be hardly less tedious for the reader to be obliged to suffer the long catalogue of Breakfast ritual, starting with the smashing of the central Vase, whose shattered fragments are gathered together in two heaps, one at the head and the other at the feet of Titus, and ending with the extraordinary spectacle of Barquentine trampling (apparently as a symbol of the power invested in his hands as warder of the unbroken laws of Gormenghast), up and down the length of the Breakfast table seven times amidst the *débris* of the meal, his wooden leg striking at the dark oak.

Unknown to any who sit there at the long table there are not nine of them upon the daïs – but ten. All through the meal there have been ten.

The tenth is Steerpike. In the late afternoon of the previous day, when the dining-hall had swum in a warm haze of motes and every movement had bred its hollow echo through the silence, he had moved swiftly up to the platform from the doorway with a black, stumpy roll of cloth and what appeared to be a bundle of netting under his arm. After satisfying himself that he was quite alone, he half unrolled the cloth, slipped up the wooden steps of the daïs, and in a flash has slithered under the table

For a few moments there were only some scrabbling sounds and the occasional clinking of metal, but the noise mounted, and for two minutes there was intense activity. Steerpike believed in working fast, especially in nefarious matters. When at last he emerged he dusted himself carefully and it might have been noticed, had there been anyone there to notice it, that although he still carried the lumpy roll of cloth, the netting was no longer with him. Had this same hypothetical watcher glanced under the table from any part of the room he would have noticed nothing extraordinary, for there would have been nothing to see; but had he taken the trouble to have crawled between the table legs and then gazed upwards, he would have noticed that, stretching down the centre of the low 'roof' was a very comfortable hammock.

And it is in this hammock that Steerpike is now reclining at full length, in semi-darkness, hedged in with a close-up panorama of seventeen legs and one wooden stump, or to be exact with sixteen, for Fuchsia is sitting with one of hers curled up under her. He had left the Twins hurriedly on his way down with them and had managed to be the first to slip into the hall. The oak of the table is within a few inches of his face. He has had very little satisfaction, so much of the time having been spent above him in fantastic dumb shows invisible to him. There is, in fact, no conversation and all he has heard during the seemingly interminable meal is the loveless, didactic voice of Barquentine, reeling out the time-worn, legendary phrases; the irritating, and apologetic coughing of Irma, and the slight creaking of Fuchsia's chair every time she moves. Occasionally the Countess mutters something which no one can hear, which is invariably followed by Nannie rubbing her ankles nervously together. Her feet are at least twenty inches from the floor and it is a great temptation to Steerpike to give them a twitch.

Finding he is going to gain no advantage at all by having secreted himself so cunningly, and yet seeing also that it is impossible to get away, he begins to think like a machine, overhauling in his mind his position in the Castle.

Saving Sepulchrave and Titus, whose cardinal interests are still limited to the worlds of whiteness and blackness – of milk and sleep –

there is very little for the remainder of the company to do other than to brood, for there is no conversation, and there is very little chance of eating the breakfast so lavishly spread before them, for no one passes anything along the table. And so the company brood through the wasted meal. The dry, ancient voice at the end of the table has had an almost hypnotic effect, even at this early hour, and as their minds move to and fro and in and out the rain continues to beat upon the high roof overhead, and to drip, drip, drip, into the pool in the far centre of the long dining-hall.

No one is listening to Barquentine. The rain has drummed for ever. His voice is in the darkness – and the darkness in his voice, and there is no end at all.

THE REVERIES

THE REVERIE OF CORA

. . . and it's so cold, hands and cold feet but nice ones mine are nicer than Clarice's which she pricks with her embroidery clumsy thing but hers are also cold I hope but I want Gertrude's to be colder than the ice in dreadful places she's so fat and proud and far too big and I desire her frozen with her stupid bosom and when we're stronger in power we will tell her so Clarice and I when he lets us with his cleverness which is more clever than all the Castle and our thrones will make us regal but I'm the one to sit highest and I wonder where he is and stupid Gertrude thinks I'm frightened and I am but she doesn't know and I wish she would die and I'd see her big ugly body in a coffin because I'm of the blood and poor Sepulchrave looks different which she's done to him ugly woman with fat bosom and carrots hair the vegetable thing so cold here cold and my hands and feet which is what Clarice is feeling like I suppose she's so slow compared with me she looks so silly with her mouth open not like me my mouth isn't open yes it is I've left it open but now I've shut it and it's closed up and my face must be perfect like I'll be when I get my power and the West Wing is raging with glory why was the fire so big when I don't understand and we are made to be in darkness and one day perhaps I will banish Steerpike when he's done everything for us and perhaps I won't for it's not time to know yet and I'll wait and see because he isn't really of good stock like us and ought to be a servant but he's so clever and sometimes treats me with reverence which is due to me of course for I'm Lady Cora of

Gormenghast I am and there's only me and my sister who are like that and she's not got the character I have and must take advice from me it is so cold and Barquentine is so long and he is so nasty but I will bow a little to him not too much but about an inch to show that he's done his work adequately not well but adequately with his voice and his wooden crutch which is so unnecessarily stupid to have instead of a leg and perhaps I'll look at it so that he sees me while I look just for a little moment to show him I am me and he mustn't forget my blood and what is poor Sepulchrave looking like that for with his mouth slipping down on one side and upon the other while he looks at her and she looks so frightened poor stupid Fuchsia who is still too young to understand anything yet she never comes to visit us when she could be taught but her cruel mother has turned her against us with her evil I feel hungry but nobody will pass me anything for the narrow squeaky Doctor is asleep or very nearly and Swelter never notices nor does anyone except the clever boy.

There is a thud on the table beyond the Doctor, to her right.

REVERIE OF ALFRED PRUNESQUALLOR

. . . and although it is patent that he hasn't very long I can't keep pumping hydrophondoramischromatica of ash into him every five hours or so and he'll need it even more frequently than that his mouth is slipping already devil take it which is too near the mark by all that's gruesome it is but the stuff will wipe him out unless I go easy and what will happen god knows if the owl crops up again but we or rather I must be prepared for anything and make tentative plans to meet contingencies for the others have no responsibilities except to the ritual of the place and never have had a case of this transference kind so unpleasantly actual for though the depersonalization has set in for good that is the lesser thing for the hooting is outside the range of science yet what started the whole thing was the burning undoubtedly oh yes undoubtedly for it was only melancholia up till then but thanks and praise be to all the bottle gods and powder princes that I had the drugs and that I guessed the strength well enough for the moment but he must go back to bed immediately the breakfast is over and have someone in the room with him whenever I have to go for meals but they might be brought to me in his room better idea still and perhaps Fuchsia might do it though the sight of her father might be too much for her but we cannot tell yet and must be careful bless her dear heart poor girl she looks so mournful and she is holding my finger so sadly I would rather she gripped it desperately it would be more symptomatic of an honest panic in her. I must comfort her if I can though what in the name of tact can I say to calm an intelligent and sensitive child who has seen her father hooting from a mantelpiece but care must be taken great care and perhaps Irma will get a room ready for her in the house but the next few hours will tell and I must be on the alert for the Countess is no help with her mind in the clouds, and Irma is of course Irma and nothing but undiluted Irma for now and ever and must be left where she is, and Steerpike remains who is an enigma to me and of whom I have doubts very definitely and in whose presence I find less and less amusement and more and more a sense of evil which I can base upon no power of rational reasoning save that he is obviously out for himself and himself alone but who isn't? and I will bear him in mind and dispense with him if I can but a brain is a brain and he has one and it may be necessary to borrow it at short notice but no no I will not by all that's instinctive I will not and that settles it I'll handle whatever needs to be handled myself well well I don't remember quite such a strong presentiment in my old carcase for a long time we must wait and see and the waiting won't be long and we'll hope the seeing won't be long either for there is something very unhealthy about all this by all that's bursting into flower in an April dell there most undeniably is and my languorous days seem to be over for the time being but bless me the gipsy girl is squeezing a bit harder and what on earth is she staring at his mouth is slipping and it's coming on again . . .

There is a thud on the table beside him . . .

REVERIE OF FUCHSIA

. . . what can I do oh what can I do he is so ill and pale like the thin face that he has got that is broken all alone but he is better better than he was oh no the sickness in me no I mustn't think of eyes oh who will help me who will you must look now Fuchsia be brave you must look Fuchsia look how he is better now while he is here at table he is quite close to me my father and so sad why does he smile smile oh who will save him who will save me who will be the power to help us father who will not let me be near and let me understand which I could and he is better remember he is better than oh Fuchsia be brave for the roundness of his eyes is gone gone but oh no I mustn't why were they round round and yellow I do not understand oh tell me my trees and rocks for Nannie won't know oh doctor dear you must tell me and I will ask you when we're alone oh quick quick this horrible breakfast quickly go and I will take care of him for I understand because the tower was there the tower was over his long lines of books his books and its shadow fell across his library at morning always always father dear the Tower of Flints that the owls live in oh no I do not understand but I know dear father let me comfort you and you must never be like that again never never never and I will be your sentry for always always your sentry and will never talk to other people never only you my dear pale man and none will come near you only perhaps the doctor when you want him but only when you do and I will bring you flowers of every kind of colour and shape and speckled stones that look like frogs and ferns and all the beautiful things I can find and I will find books for you and will read to you all day and all night and never let you know I'm tired and we shall go for walks when you are better and you will become happy happy if only you could be if only sad thin broken face so pale and none else would be there not my mother nor anyone not Steerpike no no not him, he is too hard and clever not like you who are more clever but with kindness and not quick with clever words. I can see his mouth his mouth oh Dr Prune quick quick the blackness and he's going far away and the voice Dr Prune quick the voice is going far away of Barquentine is going far away I cannot see no no oh black my Dr Prune the black is swaying . . . swaying . . .

A darkness is closing its midnight curtains across her mind and the shapes before her of her mother, Nannie, Clarice and the Earl recede into floating fragments, while like the echo of an echo the voice of Barquentine stammers on and on. Fuchsia cannot feel the Doctor's finger any longer in her palm except as an infinitely far away sensation, as though she were holding a thin tube of air. In a final wave the blackness descends once and for all, and her dark head, falling forward, strikes the table with a thud.

REVERIE OF IRMA PRUNESQUALLOR

. . . and I'd very much like to know what advantage I am getting out of having spent so long a time in the bath and preparing myself for them so exquisitely for my swan-white throat is the most perfect one in Gormenghast though I wish my nose weren't quite so pointed, but it is velvet white like the rest of my skin and it's a pity I wear spectacles with black lenses too I suppose but I am positive my skin is snow white not only because I can see it dimly in the mirror when I take my spectacles off although it hurts my eyes but also because my writing paper is perfectly white when I've got my glasses on and look at my face and throat in the mirror and then hold a piece of my white writing paper next to my face I can see that my skin and the stationery are exactly the same tone of grey and everything else in the mirror all around me is darker and very often black but what's the use of writing-paper with crinkled edges to me for there's no one to write to us there used to be when I was younger not that I was more attractive then for after all I am still a virgin but there was Spogfrawne who had had so many beautiful adventures among the people he redeemed from sin and he appreciated me and wrote me three letters on tissue paper although it was a pity that his pen-nib used to go right through it so often and make it difficult for me to read the passionate parts where he told me of his love in fact I couldn't read them at all and when I wrote and asked him to try and remember them and write me a fourth letter just putting in only the passionate sentences which I couldn't read in the first three of his beautiful letters he wouldn't answer me and I think it was because I asked him in my last message to him to either write more carefully on the tissue paper or to use ordinary paper that he became shy poor silly stupid glamorous Mr Spogfrawne who I will always remember but he hasn't been heard of since and I am still a virgin and who is there to make love to me tenderly and to touch the tip of my snowy hands and perhaps just a tiny touch on my hip bone which juts out so magnificently as Steerpike mentioned that evening when Alfred was called away to get a fly out of that Slagg woman's eye for Steerpike bless the boy has always been most observant and I know how it broke my heart to see him so miserable on the day he left us and now I never see him and it is a pity that he is not a little older and taller but once he speaks to me and fastens his eye on me in that respectful way he has noticing the beauty of my skin and hair and the way my hips come out so excitingly then I do not wish him any different but feel a little queer and realize how impelling he is for what is age anyway but years and years are nothing if not silly and ridiculous man made things which do not understand the way of delicate women with the years coming so unkindly and how could they be so many in my case all forty of them that have never had their due or why I am unmarried I do not know when I take so much care over my cleanliness but who is there who is there oh my emptiness is all alone and with Alfred who can be so silly though he's really clever but doesn't listen to me and falls asleep like he is doing now and I wish he wouldn't keep looking at the Earl who after all isn't someone to be stared at although there is something very strange about him tonight and how chilly it is in this big and empty and horrible hall which is so famous but what use is it if we don't talk to each other and there are no men to watch every gracious movement of my throat and I will be glad to be back in my house again where I will go on reading my book, and it won't be so cold and perhaps I can write

a note to Steerpike and ask him to supper yes I will do that Alfred said
he won't be in tomorrow evening and . . .

Her thoughts are broken by a thud to her left.

THE REVERIE OF LADY CLARICE

Her thoughts have been identical with those of her sister in every way
save only in one respect, and this cleavage can best be appreciated by
the simple process of substituting Cora's name for her own wherever it
appears in the reverie of the former.

REVERIE OF GERTRUDE THE COUNTESS OF GORMENGHAST

. . . at any rate the old Sourdust would have taken longer over this job
than this one and it won't be long before I can have my white cat who
is crying at my heart again may the fiends wrack the long servant's
bones and I've left enough water in the basin for the ravens' bath and
can see to the sandpipers' wing directly I get away from here and my
white cat is comforted but the stupid man has about fourteen pages to
get through yet thank heaven I don't have many of these things to
attend and there won't be another child if I know anything about it but
now here is a son for Gormenghast which is what the Castle needed and
when he is older I will teach him how he can take care of himself and
how to live his own life as far as it is possible for one who will find the
grey stones across his heart from day to day and the secret is to be able
to freeze the outsider off completely and then he will be able to live
within himself which Sepulchrave does in the wrong way for what use
are books to anyone whose days are like a rook's nest with every twig a
duty and I shall teach the boy to whistle birds out of the sky to his wrist
which I have never taught Fuchsia because I have kept my knowledge
for the boy and if I have the time before he is twelve years old and if it's
a pleasant evening I might take him to the pool that is as green as my
malachite ring with the silver setting and let him watch the lesser-fly-
spotted-wag-catchers building their soft grey nests out of moth-wings
and dew-twine but how do I know he will be observant and careful with
birds for Fuchsia disappointed me before she was five with her
clumsiness for she used to ram the flowers into the glass vases and
bruise the stalks although she loved them but it is my son I wish to
teach for there is no use in my revealing my secrets to a girl but he will
be so useless for a long time and must be kept away from my room until
he is about five at least when he will be able to absorb what I tell him
about the skies' birds and how he can keep his head quite clear of the

duties he must perform day after day until he dies here as his fathers have done and be buried in the sepulchre of the Groans and he must learn the secret of silence and go his own way among the birds and the white cats and all the animals so that he is not aware of men but performs his legendary duties faithfully as his father has always done whose library was burned away along with old Sourdust and how it started I have very little idea except that the Steerpike youth was very quickly upon the scene and though he was the means of our escape I do not like him and never shall with his ridiculous little body and slimy manners he must be sent away for I have a feeling he will do harm and Fuchsia must not be with him for she is not to mix with so cheap and ignoble a thing as that sharp youth she converses too often with Prunesquallor with whom I saw her talking twice last month for he is not of the blood and as for the murderous and devilish Flay who has hurt my poor defenceless cat so much that all the other white glories will be uneasy through the black hours of night and feel the pains which he feels as he is curled in my arms for Flay has broken himself with his ghastly folly and shall be banished whatever Sepulchrave may say whose face has changed tonight and has been changed on the three occasions on which I have seen him since the burning of his books and I will tell the Doctor to attend him constantly for I have a presentiment of his death and it is good that Titus is born for the line of the Groans must never be broken through me and there must be no ending at all and no ending and I shall tell him of his heritage and honour and of how to keep his head above the interwoven nest and watch the seasons move by and the sounds of the feathered throats . . .

A thud upon the table immediately opposite her causes the Countess to lift her eyes slowly from the table cloth.

REVERIE OF NANNIE SLAGG

. . . yees yees yees it's all so big and wonderful I suppose it is oh my poor heart this lovely rich breakfast which nobody eats and the little precious boy in the middle of the cutlery bless his little heart for he hasn't cried once not once the tiny morsel and with everybody around him too and thinking about him for it's his breakfast my pretty precious and Nannie will tell you all about it when you're a big boy oh my poor heart how old I'll be by then and how cold it is a good thing I wrapped the little boy in his wrap which is under all the lilac windings yees yees and he mustn't sneeze oh no but be still though I am so cold and his great heavy mother beside me so that I feel I don't matter at all and I suppose I don't matter at all for nobody takes any notice of me and nobody loves me except my darling caution but even she sometimes forgets but not the others who never think of me except when they want me to do something for them for I have to do everything and oh my poor heart I'm not young any more and strong and I get tired and even Fuchsia never remembers how tired I get even now I'm tired for having to sit so long in the cold so far beneath the huge Countess who doesn't even look at her little boy who's being so good and I don't think she could ever love him like I love him but oh my poor heart it's a good thing the Countess can't hear me thinking about her like this though sometimes I think she can tell when I think against her because she's so silent and when she looks at me I don't know what to do or where to go and I feel so little and weak and I feel like that now but how cold it is and I'd rather have my own simple kind of breakfast by the fire in my own small room than look at all this food on the table getting cold although it's all here for the little boy bless him and I will look after him as long as I have any strength in my poor bones and make him a good boy and teach Fuchsia to take care of him and she is loving him more than ever she did before though she doesn't like to hold him like I do and I am glad because she might drop him the clumsy caution and oh my poor heart if he should ever fall and be killed oh no no never she must never hold him for she is so ignorant of how to be careful of a little baby she doesn't look at him now in the middle of the table any more than her mother or any of the others do but just stares at her father with her naughty dark face so sad what can it be for she must tell me and tell me everything leaving nothing out about why she looks so mournful the silly girl who can have no trouble at her age and hasn't got all the work to do and the trials which I have on my old shoulders all the time and it is silly for her to be so sad when she is only a child and doesn't know anything bless her.

Nannie is startled by a thud upon the table nearly opposite her.

REVERIE OF SEPULCHRAVE, 76th EARL OF GORMENGHAST

. . . and there will be a darkness always and no other colour and the lights will be stifled away and the noises of my mind strangled among the thick soft plumes which deaden all my thoughts in a shroud of numberless feathers for they have been there so long and so long in the cold hollow throat of the Tower and they will be there for ever for there can be no ending to the owls whose child I am to the great owls whose infant and disciple I shall be so that I am forgetting all things and will be taken into the immemorial darkness far away among the shadows of the Groans and my heartache will be no more and my dreams and thoughts no more and even memory will be no longer so that my volumes will die away from me and the poets be gone for I know the great tower stood above my cogitations day and night through all the hours and they will all go the great writers and all that lay between the fingered covers all that slept or walked between the vellum lids where for the centuries they haunted and no longer are and my remorse is over now and forever for desire and dream has gone and I am complete and longing only for the talons of the tower and suddenness and clangour among the plumes and an end and a death and the sweet oblivion for the last tides are mounting momently and my throat is growing taut and round round like the Tower of Flints and my fingers curl and I crave the dusk and sharpness like a needle in the velvet and I shall be claimed by the powers and the fretting ended ... ended ... and in my annihilation there shall be a consummation for he has come into the long line and is moving forward and the long dead branch of the Groans has broken into the bright leaf of Titus who is the fruit of me and there shall be no ending and the grey stones will stand for always and the high towers for always where the raindrifts weave and the laws of my own people will go on for ever while among my great dusk haunters in the tower my ghost will hover and my blood-stream ebb for ever and the striding fever over who are these and these so far from me and yet so vast and so remote and vast my Fuchsia dusky daughter bring me branches and a fieldmouse from an acre of grey pastures ...

HERE AND THERE

SWELTER's thoughts were glued upon Flay's death at his own hand. The time was ripe. He had practised the art of silent and stealthy movement until he could no longer hear even the breath-note of his own footstep which over the stretch of the last fortnight he had striven to stifle. He now moved his bulk across the earth as silently as the passing of a cloud through the dusk. His two-handed cleaver had an edge to it which sang with the voice of a gnat when he held it to his fungus of an ear. Tonight he would leave a small pink wafer at the top of the last flight of stairs, within a bare twenty feet of the thin man. It would be a dark night. He listened to the thrumming rain and his eyes turned to the lake on the cold floor, far down the dining hall. He stared at but did not see the bleared reflection of the flanking cherubs a hundred feet above the steel-grey veneer of water. His eyes were unfocused. He would do the work he had waited to do tomorrow night. Tomorrow night. As his tongue emerged from between his lips like a carrot and moved from side to side, his eyes moved from the water to

Flay, and the vagueness was at once gone from them. In his stare was the whole story; and Flay, lifting his eyes from the top of his master's head, interpreted the vile expression.

He had known that the attack upon his life was imminent. The coloured cakes when he had found them on the three preceding occasions had been successively closer to him. Swelter was trying to wreck him by torturing his mind and twisting his nerves and he had not slept for many nights but he was ready. He had not forgotten the two-handed cleaver in the green light and had found in the armoury an old sword, from which he had removed the rust and had sharpened to a point and an edge in the stone lanes. Compared to the edge which Swelter had given to the cleaver the sword was blunt but it was murderous enough. In Swelter's expression he could read the nearness of the night encounter. It would be within a week. He could not tell which day. It might be this very night. It might be any night of the next seven.

He knew that Swelter could not see him until he was practically upon him at his Master's door. He knew that the Chef could not know that he had read his eyes so clearly. He also knew that he was banished from the Castle grounds. Swelter must not know this. Gertrude would see that he, Flay, was not at Lord Sepulchrave's door from now onwards, but he could return in the night and follow the monster as he crept upwards to the passageway on his lethal mission.

That is what he would do. He would wait every night in the cloisters until the huge body stole by him and up the stairs. Not till then would he decide where and when to strike. He only knew that he must lead his foe away from his sick master's door and that the death must take place in some remote part of the castle, perhaps in the room of spiders . . . or under the attic arches, or even among the battlements themselves. His thoughts were broken by the thud of Fuchsia falling forward and he saw the Doctor rise to his feet and stretch across the table for a glass, his left hand moving around Fuchsia's shoulder as he did so.

On the table itself young Titus began to kick and struggle and then with a high thin cry poor Mrs Slagg watches him kick the vase of flowers over, and tear at the lilac-coloured velvet with his hands.

Steerpike hears the thud above him and taking his cue from the varying contortions of the legs which hem him in is able to guess pretty accurately what is happening. There are only two legs which do not move at all and they are both Gertrude's. Fuchsia's only visible leg (for her right is still curled beneath her) has slipped sideways on the boards as she slumps forward. Nannie's are struggling frantically to reach the floor. Lord Sepulchrave's are swinging idly to and fro and are close together like a single pendulum. Cora and Clarice are going through the motions of treading water. The Doctor's have straightened out into unbroken lengths and his sister's have entered upon the last stages of a suicide pact, each one strangling the other in an ivy-like embrace.

Swelter is shifting the soft, dace-like areas of his feet backwards and forwards, a deliberate and stroking motion, as of something succulent wiping itself on a mat.

Flay is rubbing the cracked toe-cap of one of his boots rapidly up and down his shin bone immediately above the ankle, and, this done, Steerpike notices that his legs begin to make their way round the long table towards Fuchsia's chair detonating as they go.

During this short space of time while the screaming of Titus is drowning the barking of Barquentine, Prunesquallor has dabbed a quantity of water over Fuchsia's face with a napkin and has then placed her head gently between her knees.

Barquentine has not ceased a moment in the administration of his duties as the occasional lulls in Titus's howling testify, for during the short intervals of what might have been rain-filled silence the dry, acid tongue of the Librarian stutters on and on.

But it is nearly over. He is laying his tomes aside. His withered stump which, since Fuchsia's faint and the howling of Titus has been scratching at the boards with an irritability such as might suggest that its ugly termination was possessed of teeth instead of toes and was doing its best to gnaw its way through the oak boarding below it – this stump is now setting about another business, that of getting itself and the rest of Barquentine upon the seat of the chair.

Once aboard the long, narrow table it is for him to march up and down it from end to end seven times regardless of the china and golden cutlery, regardless of the glassware, the wine and the repast in general, regardless of everything in fact save that he must be regardless. Mrs Slagg snatches the year-old baby from before the approaching crutch and withered leg, for Barquentine has lost no time in complying with tradition and the ferrule of his crutch strikes jarringly upon the polished oak, or cracks among the china plates or splinters the cut glass. A dull soggy note followed by a squelch betrays the fact that his withered leg has descended ankle deep in a tureen of tepid porridge, but it was not for him to turn aside in the promulgation of his duty.

Doctor Prunesquallor has staggered away with Fuchsia in his arms, having instructed Flay to escort Lord Sepulchrave to his room. The Countess strangely enough has taken Titus from Nannie Slagg and having descended from the platform to the stone slabs below is walking heavily to and fro with the little boy half over her shoulder. 'Now then, now then,' she says. 'No use crying; no use at all; not when you're two; wait till you're three. Now then, now then, wait till you're bigger and

I'll show you where the birds live, there's a good child, there's a . . . Slagg . . . Slagg,' she bellows suddenly, interrupting herself. 'Take it away.' The Earl and Flay have gone and so has Swelter after casting a baffled eye over the table and at the wizened Barquentine as he stamps into the exquisitely prepared and despoiled breakfast.

Cora and Clarice are left watching Barquentine with their mouths and the pupils of their eyes so wide open as to cause these caverns to monopolize their faces to the extent of giving to their countenances an appearance of darkness or of absence. They are still seated and their bodies beneath their straight dresses are perfectly rigid while their eyes follow the ancient's every movement, leaving him only momently when a louder sound than usual forces them to turn their eyes to the table to observe what the latest ornament to be broken may be.

The darkness in the great hall has deepened in defiance of the climbing of the sun. It can afford to be defiant with such a pall of inky cloud lying over the castle, over the cracked toothed mountain, over the entire and drenching regions of Gormenghast from horizon to horizon.

Barquentine and the Twins trapped in the shadows of the hall which is itself trapped within the shadows of the passing clouds are lit by one lone candle, the others having guttered away. In this vast, over-arching refectory these three – the vitriolic marionette in his crimson rags and the two stiff purple puppets, one at either end of the table – look incredibly minute, tiny fierce ribs of colour glinting on their clothes as the candleflame moves. The broken glass on the long table darting forth a sudden diamond from time to time. From the far end of the Hall near the servants' door, and looking down the inky perspective of stone pillars, the spectacle of the three at the table would seem to be taking place in an area the size of a domino.

As Barquentine completes his seventh journey, the flame of the last candle stumbles, recovers, and then sinks suddenly into a swamp of tallow and the Hall is plunged into a complete obscurity, save where the lake in the middle of the Hall is a pattern of darkness surrounded by depths of another nature. Near the margin of this inner rain-fed darkness an ant is swimming for its life, its strength failing momently for there are a merciless two inches of water beneath it. From far away near the high table comes a scream, and then another and the sound of a chair falling to the stone slabs seven feet below the platform, and the sound of Barquentine cursing.

Steerpike, having observed the legs disappearing out of the door, and to whom they belonged, has wriggled from his hammock under the table. He is groping his way to the door. When he reaches it, and has found the handle, he slams it violently and then, as though he has just *entered* the room he shouts:

'Hello there; what's happening there? What's the trouble?'

On hearing his voice the twins begin to scream for help, while Barquentine yells, 'Light! light! fetch a light you dotard. What are you waiting for?' His strident voice rises to a shriek and his crutch grinds itself on the table. 'Light! scumcat! light! curse and split you!'

Steerpike, whose last hour and a half has been a dire disappointment and boring in the extreme, hugs himself for joy at their shouts.

'Right away, sir. Right away,' he dances out of the door and down the passage. He is back in less than a minute with a lantern and helps Barquentine off the table who, once on the ground, batters his way without a word of thanks down the steps and to the door, cursing as he goes, his red rags glowing dully in the lantern light. Steerpike watches his horrid body disappear and then raising his high sharp shoulders still higher he yawns and grins at the same time. Cora and Clarice are on either side of him and are both breathing very loudly, their flat bosoms rising and falling rapidly like hatchways. Their eyes are glued upon him as he escorts them through the door, down the corridor and all the way to their apartments, which he enters. The windows are streaming with the rain. The roof is loud with it.

'My dear ladies,' says Steerpike, 'I feel that some hot coffee is indicated, but what do *you* feel?'

PRESAGE

TOWARDS evening the heavy sky began to disintegrate and a short time before sundown a wind from the west carried the clouds away in dense and shambly masses and the rain with them. Most of the day had been spent in ceremonial observance of multifarious kinds, both in the castle and in the downpour culminating in the pilgrim-like procession of the forty-three Gardeners headed by Pentecost, to Gormenghast mountain and back, during which time it was their duty to meditate upon the glory of the House of Groan and especially on the fact that its latest member was twelve months old, a subject (however momentous) they must surely have exhausted after the first mile or so of the soaking and rock-strewn paths that led them over the foothills.

Be that as it may, Barquentine, lying exhausted on his dirty mattress at eight o'clock in the evening and coughing horribly as his father had done so convincingly before him, was able to look back with sour satisfaction on a day of almost undiluted ritual. It had been an irritating thing that Lord Sepulchrave had been unable to attend the last three ceremonies, but there was a tenet in the law which exonerated his absence in the case of dire illness. He sucked his beard and his withered leg lay quite still. A few feet above his head a spider scrawled itself across the ceiling. He disliked it, but it did not anger him.

Fuchsia had regained consciousness within a short while and with Mrs Slagg had bravely taken her part in the day's observances, carrying her small brother whenever the old nurse grew weary. Prunesquallor, until late in the evening when he left Flay with his Lordship, had kept a strict watch upon his patient.

An indescribable atmosphere of expectancy filled Gormenghast. Instead of Titus's birthday bringing with it a feeling of completion or climax as it should have done, there was, conversely, a sense of something beginning. Obscure forces were, through the media of the inhabitants of the castle, coming to a head. For some, this sensation was extremely acute although unrecognizable and was no doubt sharpened and conditioned by their own personal problems. Flay and Swelter were on the edge of violence. Sepulchrave was moving at the margin of climax and Fuchsia hardly less so, being consumed with fear and anguish at the parental tragedy. She also was waiting; they were all waiting. Prunesquallor was suffering no little strain and was eternally on the watch and the Countess having held interview with him and having heard as much as Prunesquallor dared tell her, and having guessed a good deal more, was remaining in her room and receiving hourly bulletins as to her husband's condition. Even Cora and Clarice could tell that the normal monotonous life of the castle was not as heretofore and in their room they sat silently – waiting also. Irma spent most of her time in her bath and her thoughts were constantly returning to a notion new to her and shocking to her, and even terrifying. It was that the House of Groan was different. Different. Yet, how could it be different? 'Impossible! I said Impossible!' she repeated to herself, through a lather of fragrant suds, but she could not convince herself. This idea of hers was creeping about Gormenghast insidiously, remaining for the most part unrecognized save as a sensation of uneasiness.

It was only Irma who put her finger on the spot. The others were involved with counting the portentous minutes before their own particular clouds broke over them, yet at the back of their personal troubles, hopes and fears, this less immediate trepidation grew, this intangible suggestion of *change*, that most unforgivable of all heresies.

A few minutes before sunset the sky over the castle was a flood of light and the wind having dropped, and the clouds vanished, it was difficult to believe that the mild and gilded atmosphere could ever have hallowed such a day as began so darkly and continued with such consistent violence. But it was still Titus's birthday. The crags of the mountain for all their jaggedness were draped in so innocent a veil of milk and rose as to wholly belie their nature. The marshlands spread to the North in tranquil stretches of rush-pricked water. The castle had become a great pallid carving, swarmed here and there by acres of glittering ivy whose leaves dripped diamonds.

Beyond the great walls of Gormenghast the mud-huts were gradually regaining the whitish colour of their natural earth as the late sunlight drew out the moisture. The old cactus trees steamed imperceptibly and beneath the greatest of these and lit by the slanting rays of the sun was a woman on horseback.

For a long while there seemed to be no movement either in her or her mount. Her face was dark and her hair had fallen about her shoulders. The pale light was on her face, and there was a mournful triumph and an extreme loneliness. She bent forward a little and whispered to the horse who raised his forefoot on hearing her and beat it back into the soft earth. Then she began to dismount and it was not easy for her, but she lowered herself carefully down the wet grey flank. Then she took the basket from where it had been fastened to the rope bridle and stepped slowly forward to the horse's head. Running her fingers through the tangled and dripping forelock, she moved them over the hard brow beneath. 'You must go back now,' she said slowly, 'to the Brown Father, so that he may know that I am safe.' Then she pushed the long wet, grey head away from her with a slow and deliberate movement. The horse turned itself away, the rain bubbling up in the hoofmarks and forming little gold pools of sky. It turned back to her once, after a few paces. Then lifting its head very high it shook its long mane from side to side and the air became filled with a swarm of pearls. Then suddenly it began to pace along the track of its own hoofmarks and without a moment's abatement in its pace or the least deviation from its homeward course, it sped from her. She watched it as it appeared, disappeared, only to reappear again, as the undulations of the region gave cause, until it was almost too small to observe. At last she saw that it was about to reach the ridge of the last stretch of upland before its descent to the invisible plain. As she watched, it suddenly came to a dead halt, and her heart beat rapidly, for it turned about and stood for a moment motionless. Then lifting its head very high as it had done before, it began to move backwards step by step. They were facing one another over that vast distance as the grey horse was at last swallowed beneath the horizon.

She turned towards the mud-huts lying below her in a rose red light. A crowd had begun to gather and she saw that she was being pointed out.

With the warm glow of the dying light upon them, the mud dwellings for all their meanness and congestion had something ethereal about them, and her heart went out to them as a hundred re-awakened memories flew to her mind. She knew that bitterness was harboured in the narrow streets, that pride and jealousy leaned like ghosts against the posts of every carver's doorway, but for a fleeting moment she saw only the evening light falling across the scenes of her childhood, and it was with a start that she awakened from this momentary reverie to notice how the crowd had grown. She had known that this moment would be like this. She had foreseen such an evening of soft light. She had foreseen that the earth would be glassed with rain and she had the overpowering sensation of living through a scene she had already enacted. She had no fear although she knew she would be met by hostility, prejudice and perhaps violence. Whatever they did with her it would not matter. She had suffered it already. All this was far wan history and an archaism.

Her hand moved to her brow and pushed away a cold lock of hair that clung blackly to her cheek. 'I must bear my child,' she said to herself, her lips framing the soundless words, 'and then I shall be complete and only myself and all will be over.' Her pupils grew vast. 'You shall be free. From the very beginning you shall be free of me, as I shall be free of you; and I shall follow my knowledge – ah, so soon, so soon into the julip darkness.'

She folded her hands and moved slowly towards the dwellings. High on her right hand the great outer wall had become colder; its inner face was draped with shadow and in the depths of the castle Titus sending forth a great tear-filled cry began to struggle with an unnatural strength in the old nurse's arms. All at once an eyelid of the rich dusk lifted and Hesper burned over Gormenghast as under Keda's heart her burden struggled.

IN PREPARATION FOR VIOLENCE

THE twelve-month cycle was ended. Titus had begun his second year – a year which, though hardly fledged, was so soon to bring forth violence. There was a sickness in the atmosphere.

Of all this suspicion and restlessness, he knew nothing, and he will have no memories of these days. Yet the aftermath of all that was happening in his infancy will soon be upon him.

Mrs Slagg watched him querulously as he tottered in his efforts to keep balance, for Titus had almost learned to walk. 'Why won't he smile?' she whimpered. 'Why won't his little Lordship ever smile?'

The sound of Barquentine's crutch echoed down the hollow corridors.

His withered leg padded beside it and the red sacking flapped its tatters in hot gusts. His edicts went forth like oaths.

Drear ritual turned its wheel. The ferment of the heart, within these walls, was mocked by every length of sleeping shadow. The passions, no greater than candle flames, flickered in Time's yawn, for Gormenghast, huge and adumbrate, out-crumbles all. The summer was heavy with a kind of soft grey-blue weight in the sky – yet not *in* the sky, for it was as though there were no sky, but only air, an impalpable grey-blue substance, drugged with the weight of its own heat and hue. The sun, however brilliantly the earth reflected it from stone or field or water, was never more than a rayless disc this summer – in the thick, hot air – a sick circle, unrefreshing and aloof.

The autumn and winter winds and the lashing rain storms and the very cold of those seasons, for all their barbarism, were of a spleen that voiced the heart. Their passions were allied to human passions – their cries to human cries.

But it was otherwise with this slow pulp of summer, this drag of heat, with the incurious yellow eye within it, floating monotonously, day after day.

At the river's edge the shallow water stank and mists of insects drifted over the scum, spinning their cry of far forgotten worlds, thinner than needles.

Toads in the green ooze belched. In the river's bosom the reflection of the topmost crags of Gormenghast Mountain hung like stalactites, and in the scarcely perceptible motion of the water appeared to crumble momently – yet never to diminish or to disintegrate for all their crumbling. Across the river a long field of sparse grey-green grasses and dove-grey dust lay stretched as though stunned between its low flint walls.

Little clouds of the fine dust were rising at the every footfall of a small mottled horse, on whose back sat a man in a cape.

At every fifth step forward of his mount's left leg the rider stood up in his stirrups and placed his head between the horse's ears. The river wound beside them, the fields undulating and fading in a blur of heat. The mottled horse and the caped rider moved on. They were very small. In the haze to the extreme north the tower of Flints arose like a celluloid ruler set floating upon its end, or like a water-colour drawing of a tower that has been left in the open and whose pigment has been all but washed away by a flirt of rain.

Distance was everywhere – the sense of far-away – of detachment. What might have been touched with an outstretched arm was equally removed, withdrawn in the grey-blue polliniferous body of the air, while overhead the inhuman circle swam. Summer was on the roofs of Gormenghast. It lay inert, like a sick thing. Its limbs spread. It took the shape of what it smothered. The masonry sweated and was horribly silent. The chestnuts whitened with dust and hung their myriads of great hands with every wrist broken.

What was left of the water in the moat was like soup. A rat floundered across it, part swimming, part walking. Thick sepia patches of water were left in the unhealthy scum where its legs had broken through the green surface.

The quadrangles were soft with dust. It had settled along the branches of the nearby trees. Footmarks were left deeply until the dry gusts came again. The varying lengths of stride – the Doctor's, Fuchsia's, the Countess's, Swelter's, could all be measured here, crossing and recrossing one another as though at the same time, yet hours, days and weeks divided them.

In the evening the bats, those fabulous winged mice, veered, tacked and slid through the hot gloom.

Titus was growing older.

It was four days since the Dark Breakfast. It was one year and four days since he was born in the room of wax and birdseed. The Countess would see no one. From daybreak to sunset she turned her thoughts, like boulders, over. She set them in long lines. She rearranged their order as she cogitated upon the Burning. She watched from her window as figures passed below. She turned her impressions over heavily. She was pondering all who passed by. From time to time Steerpike passed, as she sat at her window. Her husband was going mad. She had never loved him and she did not love him now, her heart being awakened to tenderness only by her birds and her white cats. But though she did not love him for himself, her unthinking and rooted respect for the heritage which he personified and her dumb pride in the line of his descent had filled her since her discovery of his illness.

Flay had gone, at her orders, to what lay beyond the great walls. He had gone, and though she would no more have thought of recalling him than of ceasing to tend the cat which he had bruised, yet she was aware of having uprooted a part of Gormenghast, as though from an accustomed skyline of towers one had been broken down. He had gone – but not altogether. Not for a little while, completely.

On the five nights following the day of his banishment – Titus's first birthday – he had returned unobserved when light had fallen.

He had moved like a stick-insect through the grey star-pricked, summer night, and knowing every bay, inlet and headland of the great stone island of the Groans, of its sheer cliffs, of its crumbling outcrops, he had pursued his way without hesitation on a zig-zag course. He had only to lean against the cliff face and he was absorbed. For the five last nights he had come, after long, sultry days of waiting among the skirting trees of the twisted woods, through a gap in the castle walls to the western wing. In his banishment he had felt the isolation of a severed hand, which realizes that it is no more part of the arm and body it was formed to serve and where the heart still beats. As yet, for him, the horror of his ostracization was too close for him to grasp – only the crater-like emptiness. The stinging-nettles had not had time to fill the yawning hollow. It was loneliness without pain.

His loyalty to the castle, too deep for him to question, was his heart's background: to all that was implied by the broken line of the towers. With his knees drawn up to his chin he pored upon that skyline as he sat at the base of an outcrop of rock among the trees. At his side lay the long sword he had sharpened. The sun was going down. In another three hours he would be on his way, for the sixth time since his banishment, to the cloisters he had known since his youth. To the cloisters in whose northern shadows was an entrance to the stairhead of the wine vaults and the Kitchens. A thousand recollections attached themselves to these cloisters alone. Sudden happenings – the awakening of ideas that had borne fruit or had withered at his touch – the memories of his youth – of his infancy even, for a brightly coloured vignette at the back of his dark skull recurred from time to time, a vignette of crimson, gold and grey. He had had no recollection of who it was who led him by the hand, but he recalled how, between two of the southerly arches, he and his guardian were stopped – how the air had been filled with sunshine – how a giant, for so he must then have appeared to the child, a giant in gold had given him an apple – the globe of crimson which he had never released from his mind's empyric grasp, nor the grey of the long hair that fell across the brow and over the shoulders of his first memory.

Few of Flay's memories were as colourful. His early years had been hard, grinding and monotonous. His recollections were associated with fears and troubles and hardships. He could remember how beneath the very cloister arches to which he was so soon to make his way he had received in grim silence, insult and even violence, no less than twinges of pleasure. He had leaned there, against the fourth pillar, on the afternoon following his unexpected summons to Lord Sepulchrave's study, where he had been told of his advancement – of his being chosen as the Earl's first servant; of how the Earl had noticed and approved of his silent and taciturn bearing, and of his reward. He had leaned there, his heart thumping; and he recalled how he had for a moment weakened, wishing he had a friend to whom he might speak of his happiness. But that was long ago. Clicking his tongue he dismissed recollections from his mind.

A gibbous moon was rising and the earth and the trees about him were dappled and striped with slowly shifting blotches of black and pearlish white. Radiance, in the shape of an oyster, moved across his head. He turned his eye to the moon among the trees and scowled at it. This was no night for a moon. He cursed it, but in a childlike way for all the grim formation of his bones, stretching out his legs, on whose knees his chin had been supported.

He moved his thumb along the edge of his sword, and then unrolled a misshapen parcel at his side. He had not forgotten to bring some food with him from the castle, and now, five nights later, he made a meal upon all that was left of it. The bread had gone dry, but it tasted sweet to him after a day's abstinence, with the cheese and the wild blackberries he had gathered in the woods. He left nothing but a few crumbs on his black trousers. There was no rational reason why he should feel, as he finished the berries, that horror lay between his last mouthful and his next meal – whenever it might be, and however he might acquire it.

Perhaps it was the moon. On his five previous nocturnal journeys to the castle there had been no light. Thick rainless clouds had provided a perfect cover. Schooled to adversity he took it as a sign that the hour was approaching. Indeed, it seemed more natural that Nature should be his enemy.

He rose slowly, and from beneath a heap of ferns he drew forth into the moonlight great lengths of cloth – and then began a most peculiar operation. Squatting down, he began, with the concentration of a child, to bind the cloth about his knees, around and around endlessly, until they were swathed to a depth of five thick inches, loosely at the joint and more tightly as they wound below and above it and as the binding thickened. This business took him the best part of an hour, for he was very scrupulous and had several times to unwind long swathes to adjust and ease the genuflexions of his knees.

Finally, however, all was ready and he got to his feet. He took a step

forward; then another, and it seemed as though he was listening for something. Was there no sound? He took three more paces, his head lowered and the muscles behind his ears working. What was that that he heard? It was like a muffled clock that ticked three times, and stopped. It sounded very far away. There were a few lengths of cloth left over and he bound his knees to another half inch of thickness. When he next stepped forward the silence was absolute.

It was still possible for him to move with comparative freedom. His legs were so long that he had become accustomed to use them as stilts, and it was only with the slightest bending of the knee that they were wont to detonate.

The moonlight lay in a gauze-like sheet of whiteness over the roof of the Twisted Woods. The air was hot and thick, and the hour was late when he began to move towards the castle. To reach the cloisters would take him an hour of rapid walking. The long sword gleamed in his hand. At the corners of his lipless mouth was the red stain of blackberries.

The trees were left behind and the long slopes where the juniper bushes crouched like animals or deformed figures in the darkness. He had skirted the river and had found a clammy mist lying like a lover along its length, taking its curves and hugging its croaking body, for the bull-frogs had made the night air loud. The moon behind the miasmic wreaths swam and bulged as though in a distorting mirror. The air was sickly with an aftermath of the day's heat, as lifeless as though it had been breathed before, thrice exhaled and stale. Only his feet felt cold as they sank ankle-deep in the dew. It was as though he trod through his own sweat.

With every step he became more conscious that he was narrowing the distance between himself and something horrible. With every step the cloisters leapt forward to meet him and his heart pounded. The skin was puckered between his eyes. He strode on.

The outer wall of the castle was above him. It mouldered in the moon. Where colonies of lizards clung to its flaking surfaces it shone.

He passed through an arch. The unchecked growth of ivy which clung about it had almost met at the centre of the aperture, and Flay, bending his head, forced his way through a mere fissure. Once through and the grounds of Gormenghast opened balefully out with an alien intimacy as though an accustomed face should, after confining itself for years to a score of cardinal expressions, take on an aspect never known before.

Keeping as much in the shadows as he could, Flay made rapid progress over the uneven ground towards the servants' wing. He was treading on forbidden ground. Excommunicated by the Countess, each footfall was a crime committed.

During the final stages of his progress to the cloisters he moved with a kind of angular stealth. At times he would come to a halt and genuflect in rapid succession, but he could hear no sound; then he would move on again, the sword in his hand. And then, suddenly, before he realized it, he was in the servants' quadrangle and skirting the wall to the cloisters. Within a minute and he was part of the charcoaled shadow of the third pillar where he had waited so patiently for the last five moonless nights.

BLOOD AT MIDNIGHT

TONIGHT the atmosphere was alive – a kind of life made even more palpable by the torpor of the air – the ghastly summer air of Gormenghast. By day, the heat of the dead light; by darkness, the vomitings of the sick room. There was no escaping. The season had come down.

As Mr Flay waited, his shoulder-blades against the stone pillars, his thoughts flowed back to the day of the Christening when he had slashed at the great soft face – to the night when he had watched the rehearsal of his murder – to that horrible sack that had been *he* – to the day of the debauchery of the Great Kitchens – to the horrors of the hooting Earl – to a hundred memories of his tormentor, whose face in his imagination opened out before him in the darkness like something septic.

His ears were strained with listening and his muscles ached. He had not moved for over an hour, save to turn his head upon his neck. And then, suddenly, what was it that had changed? He had shut his eyes for a moment and on opening them the air had altered. Was the heat even more horrible? His torn shirt was stuck to his shoulders and belly. It was more than that – it was that the darkness was omnipresent. The quadrangle was as inky as the shadows in which he had been shrouded. Clouds had moved over the moon. Not even the bright sword in his hand could be seen as he moved it out into what had been moonlight.

And then it came. A light more brilliant than the sun's – a light like razors. It not only showed to the least minutiae the anatomy of masonry, pillars and towers, trees, grass-blades and pebbles, it conjured these things, it constructed them from nothing. They were not there before – only the void, the abactinal absences of all things – and then a creation reigned in a blinding and ghastly glory as a torrent of electric fire coursed across heaven.

To Flay it seemed an eternity of nakedness; but the hot black eyelid of the entire sky closed down again and the stifling atmosphere rocked uncontrollably to such a yell of thunder as lifted the hairs on his neck. From the belly of a mammoth it broke and regurgitated, dying finally with a long-drawn growl of spleen. And then the enormous midnight gave up all control, opening out her cumulous body from horizon to horizon, so that the air became solid with so great a weight of falling water that Flay could hear the limbs of trees breaking through a roar of foam.

There was no longer any necessity for Flay, shielded from the rain by the roof of the cloisters, to hold his body in so cramped a manner. What little sound he made would be inaudible now that the falling rain hissed and drummed, beat across the massive back of Gormenghast and swarmed down its sides, bubbling and spurting in every cranny of stone, and swilling every niche where had lain for so long the white dust.

Even more so now had he to listen for the sound of approaching paces, and it is doubtful whether he would have been able to disengage the sound of the chef's feet from the drumming background. What he had never expected happened and his heart broke into an erratic hammering, for the impalpable darkness to his left was disturbed by a faint light, and, immediately after, the source of this hazy aura moved through the midnight. It was a strip of vertical light that appeared to float on end of its own volition. The invisible bearer of the octagonal lantern had closed all but one of the shutters.

As Flay edged his fingers more firmly along the butt of his sword, the glow of the lantern came abreast of him and a moment later had passed, and at this same moment, against the pale yellow glow could be distinguished the silhouette of Swelter's upper volume. It was quite simple. It curved up and over in one black dome. There seemed to be no head. It must have been thrust down and forward, an attitude that might have been imagined impossible in one whose rolls of lard-coloured fat filled in the space between the chin and the clavicles.

When Flay judged the silhouette a good twelve paces distant he began to follow, and then there began the first of the episodes – that of the stalk. If ever man stalked man, Flay stalked Swelter. It is to be doubted whether, when compared with the angular motions of Mr Flay, any man on earth could claim to stalk at all. He would have to do it with another word.

The very length and shape of his limbs and joints, the very formation of his head, and hands and feet were constructed as though for this process alone. Quite unconscious of the stick-insect action, which his frame was undergoing, he followed the creeping dome. For Mr Swelter was himself – at all events in his own opinion – on the tail of his victim. The tail did not happen to be where he supposed it, two floors above, but he was moving with all possible stealth, nevertheless. At the top of the first flight he would place his lantern carefully by the wall, for it was then that the candles began and continued at roughly equal distances, to cast their pale circles of light from niches in the walls. He began to climb.

If Mr Flay stalked, Mr Swelter *insinuated*. He insinuated himself through space. His body encroached, sleuth-like, from air-volume to air-volume, entering, filling and edging out of each in turn, the slow and vile belly preceding the horribly deliberate and potentially nimble progress of his fallen arches.

Flay could not see Swelter's feet, only the silhouetted dome, but by the way it ascended he could tell that the chef was moving one step at a time, his right foot always preceding his left, which he brought to the side of its dace-like companion. He went up in slow, silent jerks in the way of children, invalids or obese women. Flay waited until he had rounded the curve of the stairs and was on the first landing before he followed, taking five stone steps at a time.

On reaching the top of the first flight he moved his head around the corner of the wall and he no longer saw the silhouette of his enemy. He saw the whole thing glowing by the light of two candles. The passageway was narrow at this point, broadening about forty to fifty feet further down the corridor to the dimensions of a hall, whence the second flight led up to Lord Sepulchrave's corridor.

Swelter was standing quite still, but his arms were moving and he appeared to be talking to someone. It was difficult for Flay to see exactly what he was doing until, a moment after he had heard the voice saying: 'And I'll make you red and wet, my pretty thing,' he saw the dim bulk half turn with difficulty in the constricted space of the passageway and he caught the gleam of steel, and a moment later a portion of the shaft and the entire murderous head of the double-handed cleaver. Mr Swelter was nursing it in his arms as though he was suckling it.

'Oh, so red and wet,' came the moss-soft voice again, 'and then we'll wipe you dry with a nice clean handkerchief. Would you like a silk one, my pretty? Would you? Before we polish you and tuck you up? What, no answer? But you know what Papa's saying, don't you now? Of course, you do – after all that he has taught you. And why? Because you're such a quick, sharp baby – oh, such a sharp baby.'

And then Mr Flay was forced to hear the most disgusting sound – as of some kind of low animal with gastric trouble. Mr Swelter was laughing.

Flay, with a fair knowledge of low life, was nevertheless unable to withhold himself and, kneeling down quickly upon the great pads at his knees, he was silently sick.

Wiping the sweat from his brow as he rose to his feet he peered again about the angle of wall and saw that Swelter had reached the foot of the second staircase where the corridor widened. The sound of the rain, though less intense, was perpetually there. In the very sound of it, though distant, could be felt an unnatural weight. It was as though the castle were but the size of a skull over which a cistern of water was being rapidly emptied. Already the depressions and valley-like hollows in the castle grounds were filled with dark lakes that mounted momently, doubling and trebling their areas as their creeping edges met. The terrain was awash.

A closer degree of intimacy had been established in the castle between whatever stood, lay, knelt, was propped, shelved, hidden or exposed, or left ready for use, animate or inanimate, within the castle walls. A kind of unwilling knowledge of the nearness of one thing to another – of one human, to another, though great walls might divide them – of *nearness* to a clock, or a banister, or a pillar or a book, or a sleeve. For Flay the horrible nearness to *himself* – to his own shoulder and hand. The outpouring of a continent of sky had incarcerated and given a weird hyper-reality of *closeness* to those who were shielded from all but the sound of the storm.

Lying awake, for none could hope to sleep, there was not one in all the dark and rattling place who had not cogitated, if only for a moment, on the fact that the entire castle was awake also. In every bed there lay, with his or her lids apart, a figure. They saw each other. This consciousness of each other's solid and individual presences had not only been engendered by the imprisoning downpour but by the general atmosphere of suspicion that had been mounting – a suspicion of they knew not exactly what – only that something was changing – changing in a world where change was crime.

It was lucky for Flay that what he had relied on, the uncommunicative character of the Countess, held true, for she had not mentioned his banishment to a soul, although its cause still smarted in her prodigious bosom.

Hence Swelter's ignorance of the fact that, as he made his first few porridge-like paces along Lord Sepulchrave's ill-lit corridor, he was approaching a Flay-less darkness, for immediately before the door there was impenetrable shadow. A high window on the left had been blown in and glass lay scattered and, at the stairhead, glittered faintly by the light of a candle.

Mr Flay, in spite of the almost unbearable tension, experienced a twinge of ironic pleasure when, having mounted the second flight, he watched the rear of his enemy wavering into the darkness, in search of his own stalker.

There was a shallow alcove across the passageway from the top of the stairs – and with two strides Mr Flay had reached it. From there he could watch the darkness to his left. It was purposeless to follow his enemy to the door of his master's room. He would wait for his return. How would the chef be able to aim his blow in the darkness? He would prod forward with the cleaver until it touched the panels of the door. He would take a soft pace backwards. Then, as he raised the great instrument above his head, a worm, wriggling its bliss through his brain, would bring the double-handed cleaver down, like a guillotine, the great blade whetted to a screaming edge. And as this picture of Mr Swelter's methods illumined the inside of Mr Flay's darkened skull, those very movements were proceeding. Concurrently with Flay's visualization of the cleaver falling – the cleaver fell.

The floorboard beneath Mr Flay's feet lifted, and a wooden ripple ran from one end of the passageway to the other, where it broke upon a cliff of plaster. Curiously enough, it was only through the movement of the boards beneath his feet that Mr Flay knew that the chef had struck, for at the same moment a peal of thunder killed all other sound.

Swelter had brought the cold edge downwards with such a concentration of relish that the excruciating sense of consummation had dulled his wits for a moment, and it was only when he attempted to work the steel away from what gripped its edge that he realized that something was amiss. It is true that he had expected the blade to slide through the 'prostrate' beneath him as through butter, for all the thin man's osseous character – but not, surely – not with *such* ease – such *liquid* ease. Could it be that he had given to the double-handed cleaver such an edge as set up a new sensation – that of killing, as it were, without knowing it – as lazes through long grass the lethal scythe. He had not prodded forward with his toe to make doubly sure – for it had never occurred to him that he who had lain there, night after night, for over twelve years, could be elsewhere. In any event he might have wakened the long scrag by so doing. What had gone wrong? The orgasmic moment he had so long awaited was over. The cleaver was difficult to shift. Perhaps it was caught among the ribs. He began to run his hands down the shaft inch by inch, bending his knees and trunk as he did so, hot tracts of hairless clay redistributing their undulations the while. Inexorably downwards moved his fingers until they itched for contact with the corpse. Surely his hands must by now be almost at the boards themselves, yet he knew how deceptive the sense of distances can be when darkness is complete. And then he came upon the steel. Sliding his palms greedily along either edge he gave a sudden loud, murderous hiss, and loosing his fingers from the edge of the cleaver he swung his bulk about as though his foe were close behind him – and he peered back along the passage at the faint light at the stairhead. There seemed to be no one there, and after a few moments of scrutiny he wiped his hands across his thighs, and turning to the cleaver, wrenched it from the boards.

For a short while he stood fingering his misused weapon, and during this space Mr Flay had conceived and acted, moving a few yards further down the corridor where an even more favourable ambush presented itself in the shape of a sagging tapestry. As he moved out into the darkness, for he was beyond the orbit of the candles' influence, the lightning struck again and flared bluishly through the broken window so that at one and the same moment both Swelter and Flay caught sight of one another. The bluish light had flattened them out like cardboard figures which had, in the case of the chef, an extraordinary effect. Someone with an unpleasant mind had cut him out of an enormous area of electric-blue paper the size of a sheet. For the few moments that the lightning lasted his fingers and thumbs were like bright blue sausages clasped about the cleaver's handle.

Flay, presenting no less the illusion of having no bulk, struck not so much a sense of horror into Mr Swelter as a fresh surge of malice. That he should have dulled the exquisite edge of his cleaver upon Flay-less boards, and that he who should now be lying in two pieces was standing there in *one*, standing there insolently in a kind of stage lighting as a tangible criticism of his error, affected him to the extreme of control, and a horrid sweat broke from his pores.

No sooner had they seen one another than the darkness closed again. It was as though the curtain had come down on the first act. All was altered. Stealth was no longer enough. Cunning was paramount and their wits were under test. Both had felt that theirs was the initiative and the power to surprise – but now, for a few moments at least, they were equated.

Flay had, from the beginning, planned to draw the chef from Lord Sepulchrave's doorway and passage, and if possible to lure him to the storey above, where, interspaced with wooden supports, for the roof was rotten, and with many a fallen beam, mouldered the Hall of Spiders, at whose far end a window lay open to a great area of roof, terraced with stone and turreted about its sheer edges. It had occurred to him that if he were to snatch the candle from the stairhead he might lure his enemy there, and as the darkness fell he was about to put this idea into operation when the door of Lord Sepulchrave's bedroom opened and the Earl, with a lamp in his hand, moved out into the corridor. He moved as though floating. A long cloak, reaching to his ankles, gave no hint of legs beneath it. Turning his head neither to left nor right, he moved like the symbol of sorrow.

Swelter, flattening himself as much as he was able against the wall, could see that his lordship was asleep. For a moment Mr Flay had the advantage of seeing both the Earl and the chef without being seen himself. Where was his master going? Swelter was for a few moments at a loss to know what to do and by that time the Earl was almost abreast of Mr Flay. Here was an opportunity of drawing the chef after him without the fear of being overtaken or slashed at from behind, and Flay, stepping in front of the Earl, began to precede him down the passage, walking backwards all the while so that he could see the chef over his Lordship's shoulder as the dim figure followed. Mr Flay was well aware that his own head would be lit by the Earl's lamp whereas Swelter would be in semi-darkness, but there was no great advantage to the chef in that – for the creature could not get *at* him for fear of waking the Earl of Gormenghast.

As Flay receded step by step he could not, though he tried to, keep his eyes continually upon the great cook. The proximity of his Lordship's lamp-lit face left him no option but to turn his eyes to it, rapidly, from time to time. The round, open eyes were glazed. At the corners of the mouth there was a little blood, and the skin was deadly white.

Meanwhile, Swelter had narrowed the distance between the Earl and himself. Flay and the chef were staring at one another over their master's shoulder. The three of them seemed to be moving as one piece. Individually so much at variance, they were, collectively, so compact.

Darting an eye over his shoulder, as though without reference to the head that held it, Flay could see that he was within a few feet of the stairway, and the procession began the slow ascent of the third flight. The leader, his body facing down the stairs, the while, kept his left hand on the iron banister. In his right the sword glimmered – for, as with all the stairways of Gormenghast, there were candles burning at every landing.

As Flay reached the last step he saw that the Earl had stopped and that inevitably the great volume of snail-flesh had come to a halt behind him.

It was so gentle that it seemed as though a voice were evolving from the half-light – a voice of unutterable mournfulness. The lamp in the shadowy hand was failing for lack of oil. The eyes stared through Mr Flay and through the dark wall beyond and on and on through a world of endless rain.

'Good-bye,' said the voice. 'It is all one. Why break the heart that never beat from love? We do not know, sweet girl; the arras hangs: it is so far; so far away, dark daughter. Ah no – not that long shelf – not that long shelf: it is his lifework that the fires are eating. All's one. Good-bye . . . good-bye.'

The Earl climbed a further step upwards. His eyes had become more circular.

'But they will take me in. Their home is cold; but they will take me in. And it may be their tower is lined with love – each flint a cold blue stanza of delight, each feather, terrible; quills, ink and flax, each talon, glory!' His accents were infinitely melancholy as he whispered: 'Blood,

blood, and blood and blood, for you, the muffled, all, all for you and I am on my way, with broken branches. She was not mine. Her hair as red as ferns. She was not mine. Mice, mice; the towers crumble – flames are swarmers. There is no swarmer like the nimble flame; and all is over. Good-bye . . . Good-bye. It is all one, for ever, ice and fever. Oh, weariest lover – it will not come again. Be quiet now. Hush, then, and do your will. The moon is always; and you will find them at the mouths of warrens. Great wings shall come, great silent, silent wings . . . Good-bye. All's one. All's one. All's one.'

He was now on the landing, and for a moment Mr Flay imagined he was about to move across the corridor to a room opposite, where a door was swinging, but he turned to the left. It would have been possible, indeed it would have been easier and more to Flay's advantage to have turned about and sped to the Hall of Spiders, for Lord Sepulchrave, floating like a slow dream, barred Swelter's way; but at the very idea Mr Flay recoiled. To leave his sleeping master with a prowling chef at his shoulder horrified him, and he continued his fantastic retreat as before.

They were about half way to the Hall of Spiders when, to both Flay's and Swelter's surprise, the Earl moved off to the left down a narrow artery of midnight stone. He was immediately lost, for the defile wound to the left after the first few paces and the guttering of the lamp was quenched. His disappearance had been so sudden and unexpected that neither party was prepared to leap into the vacuum left between them and to strike out in the faint light. It was in this region that the Grey Scrubbers slept and some distance down there was suspended from the ceiling a broken chandelier. Towards this light Mr Flay suddenly turned and ran, while Swelter, whose frustrated blood-lust was ripe as a persimmon, thinking the thin man to have panicked, pursued him with horribly nimble steps for all the archless suction of his soles.

Covering the flagstones with a raking stride, Mr Flay was for all his speed little more than nine feet in advance of Swelter as he broke his way into the Hall of Spiders. Without losing a moment, he scrambled over three fallen beams, his long limbs jerking out fantastically as he did so, and turned when he had reached the centre of the room to discover that the door he had entered by was already filled with his enemy. So intent had they been on their game of wits and death that it had not occurred to them to wonder how it was that they were able to see one another in what was normally a lightless hall. They found no time for surprise. They did not even realize that the fury had died out of the storm and that the only sound was of a heavy, lugubrious droning. A third of the sky was clear of cloud and in this third was the humpbacked moon, very close and very white. Its radiance poured through the open wall at the far end of the Hall of Spiders. Beyond the opening it danced and glittered on the hissing water that had formed great walled-in lakes among the roofs. The rain slanted its silver threads and raised spurts of quicksilver on striking water. The Hall itself had the effect of a drawing in black, dove-grey and silver ink. It had long been derelict. Fallen and half-fallen beams were leaning or lying at all angles and between these beams, joining one to another, hanging from the ceiling of the floor above (for most of the immediate welkin had fallen in), spreading in every direction taut or sagging, plunged in black shadow, glimmering in half-light, or flaming exquisitely with a kind of filigree and leprous brilliance where the moon fell unopposed upon them, the innumerable webs of the spiders filled the air.

Flay had broken through a liana of shadowy webs, and now, in the centre of the room – watching the cook in the doorway, he clawed away the misty threads from his eyes and mouth with his left hand. Even in those areas of the hall where the moonbeams could not penetrate and where the great glooms brooded, the darkness was intersected here and there by glittering strands that seemed to shift their position momently. The slightest deflection of the head drew forth against the darkness a new phenomenon of glittering twine, detached from its web, disarticulated, miraculous and transient.

What eyes had they for such ephemera? Those webs to them were screens to aid or hinder. To snare with or be snared by. These were the features of Death's battleground. Swelter's shadowy moonless body at the door was intersected by the brilliant radii and jerking perimeters of a web that hung about halfway between himself and Mr Flay. The centre of the web coincided with his left nipple. The spacial depths between the glittering threads of the web and the chef seemed abysmic and prodigious. He might have belonged to another realm. The Hall of Spiders yawned and shrank, the threads deceiving the eye, the distances, shifting, surging forward or crumbling away, to the illusory reflectings of the moon.

Swelter did not stay by the door longer than it took him to gain a general impression of the kind of hovel in which the thin man chose to protect his long bones. Seeping with malice, yet the chef was not inclined to under-rate the guile of his antagonist. He had been lured here for some reason. The arena had not been of his choosing. He swivelled his eyes to left and right, his cleaver poised before him. He noted the encumbrances – the haphazard beams, dusty and half-decayed, and the omnipresent awnings of the spiders. He could not see why these should be more to his disadvantage than to the man he intended to sever.

Flay had never had a concrete reason for his choice of the Hall of Spiders. Perhaps it was because he imagined that he would prove more agile among the webs and beams; but this he now doubted, having found how swiftly the chef had followed him. But that he had fulfilled his intention of inveigling his enemy to the place of his own choosing must surely infer that the initiative once again lay with him. He felt himself to be a *thought* ahead of the cook.

He held the long sword ahead of him as he watched the great creature approach. Swelter was sweeping aside the webs that impeded him with his cleaver, keeping his eyes upon Mr Flay and shifting his head on his neck from side to side in order to improve his view. He came to a halt and with his eyes perpetually fixed on Mr Flay began to drag away the clinging cobwebs from the blade and handle of his weapon.

He came forward again, sweeping the cleaver in great arcs before him and treading gingerly over the slanting timbers, and then seemed about to halt once more in order to repeat the unwebbing process when, with an obvious change of purpose, he moved forward as though no obstacles were in his path. He seemed to have decided that to be continually reconditioning himself and his weapon during the blood-encounter was ill-advised and untimely, not to say an insult to the occasion.

As pirates in the hot brine-shallows wading, make, face to face, their comber-hindered lunges, sun-blind, fly-agonied, and browed with pearls, so here the timbers leaned, moonlight misled and the rank webs impeded. It was necessary to ignore them – to ignore them as they tickled the face and fastened themselves about the mouth and eyes. To realize that although between the sword and the hand, the hand and the elbow, the elbow and the body, the silvery threads hung like tropical festoons, and although the naked steel was as though delivered in its caul, that the limbs were free to move, as free as ever before. The speed of the swung cleaver would in no way be retarded. The secret was to *ignore*.

So Swelter moved forward, growing at each soft, deft pace more and more like something from the deeps where the grey twine-weed coils the sidling sea-cow. Suddenly stepping into a shaft of moonlight he flamed in a network of threads. He peered through a shimmering mesh. He was gossamer.

He concentrated his entire sentience on the killing. He banished all irrelevancies from his canalized mind. His great ham of a face was tickling as though aswarm with insects, but there was no room left in his brain to receive the messages which his nerve endings were presumably delivering – his brain was full. It was full of death.

Flay watched his every step. His long back was inclined forwards like the bole of a sloping conifer. His head was lowered as though he was about to use it as a battering ram. His padded knees were slightly bent. The yards of cloth were now redundant, but there was no opportunity for him to unwind them. The cook was within seven feet of him.

Between them lay a fallen beam. About two yards to Swelter's left its extremity had settled into the dust, but to the right, the relic of an old iron box supporting it roughly at its centre, it terminated about three feet up in the air, spilth'd with fly-choked webs.

It was towards the support of this beam that Swelter made his way, beating the filigreed moonlight to his knees where it sagged and flared. His path could be traced. He had left behind him from the door, to where he stood, the web-walled canyon of a dream. Standing now, immediately behind the broken box, he had narrowed the distance between them to just over the measure of his arm and cleaver. The air between them was a little clearer. They were closer now than they had ever been this raining night. That dreadful, palpable closeness that can only be felt when there is mutual hatred. Their separate and immediate purposes were identical. What else had they in common? Nothing but the Spider's Hall about them, the webs, the beams, the by-play of the spangling moon and the drumming of the rain in their ears.

At any other time the chef would have made play with his superior wit. He would have taunted the long, half-crouching figure before him. But now, with blood to be spilt, what did it matter whether or not he incensed his foe? His wit would fall in a more concrete way. It would flash – but in steel. And let his final insult be that Flay could no longer tell an insult from a lamb-chop – unless with his body in two pieces he were still able to differentiate.

For a moment they stood, moving a little up and down on their toes. With his sword before him Mr Flay began to move along his side of the fallen beam, to the left, in order presumably to come to closer grips. As Swelter moved his little eyes to the right following every movement of the other's body, he found that his vision was being impeded by so heavy an interfusion of ancient webbing that it would be unwise for him to remain where he was. In a flash he had both taken a sideways pace to his left and switched his eyes in the same direction. Flay at once crept in upon him, his face half shrouded by the thick webs through which he peered. His head was immediately above the lower end of the beam. Swelter's rapid glance to his left had been fruitful. He had seen the lifted end of the beam as his first true friend in a hall of hindrances, and when his eyes returned to his thin foe his fat lips twisted. Whether such a muscular obscenity could be termed a 'smile' he neither knew nor cared. Mr Flay was crouching exactly where he had hoped that he might lure him. His chin was, characteristically, jutting forwards – as though this habit had been formed for Mr Swelter's convenience alone. There was no time to lose. Swelter was three feet from the raised terminal of the long beam when he sprang. For a moment there was so much flesh and blood in the air that a star changed colour under Saturn's shoulder. He did not land on his feet. He had not intended to.

To bring the entire weight of his body down upon the beam-head was all that mattered. He brought it down; and as his under-belly struck, the far end of the beam leapt like a living thing, and, striking Mr Flay beneath his outstretched jaw, lifted him to his full height before he collapsed, a dead weight, to the floor.

The chef, heaving himself grotesquely to his feet, could hardly get to the body of his victim quickly enough. There he lay, his coat rucked up at the level of his arm-pits, his lean flank exposed. Mr Swelter raised the cleaver. He had waited so long for this. Many, many months. He turned his eyes to the web-shrouded weapon in his hands, and as he did so Mr Flay's left eyelid fluttered, and a moment later he had focused the chef and was watching him through his lashes. He had not the strength to move at that horrifying moment. He could only watch. The cleaver was lifted, but he now saw that Swelter was peering quizzically at the blade, his eyebrows raised. And then he heard the sponge-like voice for the second time that night.

'Would you like to be wiped, my pretty one?' it said, as though certain that a reply would be forthcoming from the brutal head of steel. 'You would, wouldn't you – before you have your supper? Of course. And how could you ever enjoy a nice warm bath with all your clothes on, eh? But I'll soon be washing you, little blossom. And I must wipe your face, dear; wipe it blue as ink, then you can start drinking, can't you?' He held the lean metal head at his bosom. 'It's just the thing for thirsty ones, my darling. Just the very nightcap.' There followed a few moments of low gastric chuckling before he began to drag the webbing from the cleaver's blade. He was standing about two feet away from the prostrate figure of Flay, who was half in and half out of moonlight. The demarcation line lay across his bare flank. Luckily for him it was his upper half that was in shadow and his head was all but lost. As he watched the overhang above him and noted that the chef had all but cleared the blade of cobwebs, his attention became focused upon the upper segment of the face of his foe. It was veiled, as indeed was the rest of the face and body, with the ubiquitous webs, but it seemed that above the left ear there was something additional. So accustomed had Swelter become to the tickling of the webs across his face and to the hundred minor irritations of the skin, that he had not noticed that upon his right eye there sat a spider. So thickly had his head been draped that he had accepted this impediment to his vision as being part of the general nuisance. Flay could see the spider quite clearly from where he lay, but what he now saw was something fateful. It was the spider's mate. She had emerged from the grey muddle above the left ear and was taking, leg by leg, the long, thin paces. Was she in search of her husband? If so, her sense of direction was sound, for she made towards him.

Swelter was running the flat of his hand along the steel face of his weapon. It was naked for use. Putting his blubber lips to the moonlit steel he kissed it, and then, falling a short step back, he lifted the cleaver with both hands, grasping the long handle high above his lowered head. He stood upon tip-toe, and, poised for a moment thus, went suddenly blind. His left eye had become involved with a female spider. She sat upon it squarely, enjoying the rolling movement of the orb she covered. It was for this precise instant that Flay had been waiting ever since he had caught sight of the insect a few seconds previously. It seemed that he had lain there stretched vulnerably beneath the murderous cleaver for an hour at least. Now was his moment, and gripping his sword which had fallen beside him when he fell, he rolled himself with great rapidity from beneath the belly of the cook and from the cleaver's range.

Swelter, sweating with irritation at being baulked for the second time in this business of climax, imagined nevertheless that Flay was still below him. Had he struck downwards in spite of the spiders on his eyes it may be that Flay could not have escaped. But Mr Swelter would have considered it a very sorry ending after all his pains to find he had made slaughter without having been able to see the effect. Outside Lord Sepulchrave's door it was different. There was no light, anyway. But here with a beautiful moon to illumine the work it was surely neither the time nor the place to be at the mercy of a spider's whim.

And so he lowered the cleaver to his bosom and, freeing his right hand, plucked the insects from his eyes, and he had started to raise the weapon again before he saw that his victim had gone. He wheeled about, and as he did so he experienced a white-hot pain in his left buttock and a searing sensation at the side of his head. Screaming like a pig, he wheeled about, raising his finger to where his ear should have been. It had gone. Flay had swiped it off, and it swung to and fro in a spider-made hammock a foot above the floor-boards at the far end of the room. And what voluptuary ever lolled with half the languor of that boneless thing!

A moonbeam, falling on the raddled lobe, withdrew itself discreetly and the ear disappeared into tactful darkness. Flay had, in rapid succession, jabbed and struck. The second blow had missed the skull, but he had drawn first blood; in fact, first and second, for Swelter's left rump bled magnificently. There was, in point of fact, an island growing gradually – a red island that had seeped through to the white vastness of his cloth rear. This island was changing its contours momentarily, but as the echo of Swelter's scream subsided, it very much resembled in its main outline the inverted wing of an angel.

The blows had no more than gored him. Of Swelter's acreage, only a perch or two here and there might, if broken, prove vulnerable loam. That he bled profusely could prove little. There was blood in him to revitalize an anaemic army, with enough left over to cool the guns. Placed end to end his blood vessels might have coiled up the Tower of Flints and half way down again like a Virginia creeper – a vampire's home from home.

Be that as it may, he was blooded, and the cold, calculating malice had given way to a convulsive hatred that had no relation to the past. It was on the boil of *now*, and heading into the webs that divided them, he let loose a long scything blow at Mr Flay. He had moved very rapidly and but for the fact that the moonlit webs deceived him as to the distance between them, so that he struck too soon, it is probable that all would have been over bar the disposal of the body. As it was, the wind of the blow and the hiss of the steel were enough to lift the hairs on Mr Flay's head and to set up a horrible vibration in his ears. Recovering almost at once from the surprise, however, Flay struck in return at the cook, who was for a moment off his balance, catching him across the bolster-like swelling of his shoulder.

And then things happened very rapidly, as though all that had gone before was a mere preamble. Recovering from the flounder of his abortive blow, and with the fresh pain at his shoulder, Swelter, knowing he had, with his cleaver extended, the longer reach, gripped the weapon at the extreme end of the handle and began to gyrate, his feet moving with horrifying rapidity beneath his belly, not only with the kind of complicated dance movement which swivels the body around and around at great speed, but in a manner which brought him nearer every moment to Mr Flay. Meanwhile, his cleaver, outstretched before him, sang on its circular path. What remained of the webs in the centre of the room fell away before this gross, moon-dappled cyclone. Flay, nonplussed for the moment, watched in fascinated horror the rapid succession of faces which the swivelling of Swelter conduced; faces of which he had hundreds; appearing and reappearing at high speed (with an equal number of rear-views of the huge head, interlarded, in all literalness). The whirr of steel was approaching rapidly. The rotation was too speedy for him to strike between the cycles, nor was his reach long enough were he to stand his ground.

Moving backwards he found that he was being forced gradually into a corner at the far end of the room. Swelter was bearing down on him with a kind of nightmare quality. His mind was working, but the physical perfection of his footwork and the revolving of the steel had something of the trance about them – something that had become through their very perfection detached and on their own. It was difficult to imagine how the great white top could stop itself.

And then Mr Flay had an idea. As though cowering from the oncoming steel, he moved back further and further into the corner until his bent backbone came into contact with the junction of the two walls.

Cornered of his own choosing, for he would have had time to leap for
the rain-filled opening of moonlight had he wished, he raised himself to
his full height, prising his spine into the right-angle of the walls, his
sword lowered to his feet – and waited.

The scything cleaver spun nearer momently. At every glimpse of the
chef's rotating head he could see the little blood-shot eyes focused upon
him. They were like lumps of loathing, so concentrated was his every
thought and fibre upon the death of Flay that, as he whirred closer and
closer, his normal wits were in abeyance, and what Flay had hoped for
happened. The arc of the long weapon was of such amplitude that at its
left and right extremes it became all of a sudden within a few inches of
the adjacent walls and at the next revolution had nicked away the
plaster before, finally, as the walls – so it seemed to Swelter – leapt
forward to meet him, the chef discovered the palms of his hands and
forearms stinging with the shock of having taken a great section of the
mouldering wall away. Flay, with his sword still held along his leg, its
point beside his toe-cap, was in no position to receive the impact of
Swelter's body as it fell forward upon him. So sudden and so jarring
had been the stoppage of his murderous spinning, that, like a broken
engine, its rhythm and motivation lost, its body out of control, Swelter
collapsed, as it were, within his own skin, as he slumped forwards. If
Flay had not been so thin and had not forced himself so far into the
corner, he would have been asphyxiated. As it was, the clammy, web-
bedraggled pressure of Swelter's garments over his face forced him to
take short, painful breaths. He could do nothing, his arms pinned at his
sides, his visage crushed. But the effects of the shock were passing, and
Swelter, as though suddenly regaining his memory, heaved himself
partially from the corner in a tipsy way, and although Mr Flay at such
close range was unable to use his sword, he edged rapidly along the left-
hand wall and, turning, was within an ace of darting a thrust at
Swelter's ribs when his foe staggered out of range in a series of great
drunken curves. The giddiness with which his gyrations had filled him
were for the moment standing him in good stead, for reeling as he did
about the Hall of Spiders he was an impossible target for all but mere
blood-letting.

And so Flay waited. He was acutely aware of a sickening pain at the
back of his neck. It had grown as the immediate shock of the blow to his
jaw had subsided. He longed desperately for all to be over. A terrible
fatigue had entered him.

Swelter, once the room no longer span around him and his sense
of balance was restored, moved with horrible purpose across the
Hall, the cleaver trembling with frustration in his hand. The sound
of his feet on the boards was quite distinct, and startled Flay into
glancing over his shoulder into the moonlight. The rain had ceased

and, save for the dolorous whispering of Gormenghast a-drip, there
was a great hush.

Flay had felt all of a sudden that there could be no finality, no
decision, no death-blow in the Hall of Spiders. Save for this conviction
he would have attacked Swelter as he leaned, recovering from his
giddiness, by the door at the far end of the room. But he only stood by
the moon-filled opening, a gaunt silhouette, the great cloth rolls like
malformations at his knees, and waited for the chef's advance, while he
worked at the vertebrae of his aching neck with his long bony fingers.
And then had come the onrush. Swelter was upon him, his cleaver
raised, the left side of his head and his left shoulder shiny with blood,
and a trail of it behind him as he came. Immediately before the opening
to the outer air was a six-inch step upwards which terminated the
flooring. Beyond this there was normally a three-foot drop to a
rectangular walled-in area of roof. Tonight there was no such drop, for
a great lake of rain-water lapped at the dusty boards of the Hall. To a
stranger the lake gave the appearance of profound depth as it basked in
the moon. Flay, stepping backwards over the raised strip of boarding,
sent up a fountain of lemon-yellow spray as his foot descended. In a
moment he was spidering his legs backwards through water as warm as
tea. The air, for all the downpour, was as oppressive as ever. The
horrible weight of heat was undispersed.

And then the horror happened. Swelter, following at high speed, had
caught his toe at the raised lip of the opening, and unable to check his
momentum, had avalanched himself into warm water. The cleaver
sailed from his grasp and, circling in the moonlight, fell with a fluke of
flame in the far, golden silence of the lake. As Swelter, face down and
floundering like a sea-monster, struggled to find his feet, Flay reached
him. As he did so, with a primeval effort the cook, twisting his trunk
about, found, and then lost again, a temporary foothold and, writhing,
fell back again, this time upon his back, where he floated, lashing, great
washes of water spreading on all sides to the furthermost reaches. For
a moment he was able to breathe, but whether this advantage was
outbalanced by his having to see, towering above him, the dark,
unpreaching body of his foe – with the hilt of the sword raised high over
his head, both hands grasping it and the point directed at the base of
his ribs, only he could know. The water about him was reddening and
his eyes, like marbles of gristle, rolled in the moonlight as the sword
plunged steeply. Flay did not trouble to withdraw it. It remained like
a mast of steel whose sails had fallen to the decks where, as though with
a life of their own, unconnected with wind or tide, they leapt and shook
in ghastly turbulence. At the masthead, the circular sword hilt, like a
crow's nest, boasted no inch-high pirate. Flay, leaning against the outer
wall of the Hall of Spiders, the water up to his knees and watching with

his eyes half-closed, the last death throes, heard a sound above him, and in a shudder of gooseflesh turned his eyes and found them staring into a face – a face that smiled in silver light from the depths of the Hall beyond. Its eyes were circular and its mouth was opening, and as the lunar silence came down as though for ever in a vast white sheet, the long-drawn screech of a death-owl tore it, as though it had been calico, from end to end.

GONE

IN after years Mr Flay was almost daily startled to remembrance of what now ensued. It returned in the way that dreams recur, suddenly and unsolicited. The memory was always unearthly, but no less so than the hours themselves which followed upon Swelter's death – hours as it were from a monstrous clock across whose face, like the face of a drum, was stretched the skin of the dead chef – a clock whose hands trailed blood across and through the long minutes as they moved in a circular trance. Mr Flay moved with them.

He would remember how the Earl at the window was awake; how he had held his rod with the jade knob in his hand, and how he had stepped down in the lake of rain. He had prodded the body and it had twisted for a minute and then righted itself, as though it were alive and had a positive wish to remain staring at the moon. The Earl then closed the cook's eyes, moving the two petals of pulp over their respective blood-alleys.

'Mr Flay,' Lord Sepulchrave had said.

'Lordship?' queried his servant, hoarsely.

'You did not reply to me when I saluted you.'

Flay did not know what his master could mean. Saluted him? He had not been spoken to. And then he remembered the cry of the owl. He shuddered.

Lord Sepulchrave tapped the hilt of the sword-mast with his rod. 'Do you think that they will enjoy him?' he said. He parted his lips slowly. 'We can but proffer him. That is the least we can do.'

Of the nightmare that followed it is needful to say only that the long hours of toil which followed culminated at the Tower of Flints to which they had dragged the body, after having steered it between a gap in the battlements through which the lake was emptying itself. Swelter had descended in the two-hundred-foot cascade of moon-sparkling water and they had found his body, spread to the size of a sheet and bubbling on the drenched gravel. A rope had been procured and a hook attached and the long drag had at last been effected.

The white silence was terrible. The moonlight like a hoar frost on the Tower of Flints. The shell of the library glimmered in the distance far down the long line of halls and pavilions, and of domed, forsaken structures. To their right the lit pinewoods were split with lines of midnight. About their feet a few cones, like ivory carvings, were scattered, anchored to the pale earth by their shadows.

What was once Swelter glistened.

And the Earl had said: 'This is my hour, Flay. You must go from here, Mr Flay. You must go away. This is the hour of my reincarnation. I must be alone with him. That you killed him is your glory. That I can take him to *them* is mine. Good-bye, for my life is beginning. Good-bye . . . good-bye.' And he had turned away, one hand still holding the rope, and Flay half ran and half walked for a short distance towards the Castle, his head turned over his shoulder, his body shuddering. When he stopped, the Earl was dragging the glistening thing behind him and was at the time-eaten opening at the base of the Tower.

A moment later and he was gone, the flattened weight undulating as it slithered up and over the three steps that led into the corroded entrance, the form of the steps showing in blurred contour.

Everything was moving round and round – the Tower, the pines, the corpse, the moon, and even the inhuman cry of pain that leapt from the Tower's throat into the night – the cry, not of an owl, but of a man about to die. As it echoed and echoed, the lank and exhausted servant fell fainting in his tracks, while the sky about the Tower became white with the lit bodies of circling owls, and the entrance to the Tower filled with a great weight of feathers, beaks and talons as the devouring of the two incongruous remains proceeded.

THE ROSES WERE STONES

ALONE among the Twisted Woods – like a branch himself, restless among the rooted trees, he moved rapidly, the sound of his knees becoming day by day familiar to the birds, and hares.

Ribbed with the sunlight where the woodlands thinned, dark as shadows themselves where no sun came, he moved as though pursued. For so long a time had he slept in the cold, lightless corridor that waking, as it were, with no protection from the dawn, or stretching himself for sleep, defenceless before the twilight and sundown, he was at first unable to feel other than nakedness and awe. Nature, it seemed, was huge as Gormenghast. But as time went on he learned to find the shortest and most secret ways of hill and woodland, of escarpment and marshland, to trace the winding of the river and its weed-bound tributaries.

He realized that though the raw ache for the life he had lost was no less with him, yet the exertions he was obliged to make for his own preservation and the call that such a life made upon his ingenuity, had their compensations. He learned, day by day, the ways of this new world. He felt proud of the two caves which he had found in the slopes of Gormenghast mountain. He had cleared them of rocks and hanging weeds. He had built the stone ovens and the rock tables, the hurdling across their walls to discourage the foxes, and the beds of foliage. One lay to the south at the fringe of the unexplored country. It was remote and very thrilling to his bones – for the mountain lay between him and the far Castle. The second cave was in the northern slope, smaller, but one which on rainy nights was more likely to prove accessible. In a glade of the Twisted Woods he had constructed a shack as his primary and especial home. He was proud of his growing skill at snaring rabbits: and of his successes with the net he had so patiently knotted with lengths of tough root fibre; and it was sweet to taste the fish he prepared and ate alone in the shadow of his shack. The long evenings were like blond eternities – stifling and silent save for the occasional flutter of a wing or the scream of a passing bird. A stream which had all but dried moved past his doorway and disappeared in the shadows of the undergrowth to the south. His love of this lost glade he had selected grew with the development of a woodland instinct which must have been latent in his blood, and with the feeling that he possessed something of his own – a hut he had made with his own hands. Was this rebellion? He did not know. The day over, he would sit at the door of his cabin, his knees beneath his chin, his bony hands clasping his elbows, and stare ruminatively (a stranger would have thought sullenly) before him as the shadows lengthened inch by inch. He had started to turn over in his mind the whole story of Gormenghast as it had affected him. Of Fuchsia, now that he could see her no longer, he found it painful to reminisce, for he missed her more than he could have imagined possible.

The weeks went by and his skill grew, so that he had no longer to lie in wait for half a day at a time at the mouths of warrens, a club in his hand; nor waste long hours by the river, fishing the less hopeful reaches for lack of lore. He could devote more and more of his time to conditioning his shack against the approaching autumn and inevitable winter; to exploring further afield, and to brooding in the evening sunlight. It was then that the vile, nightmare memory would most often return. The shape of a cloud in the sky – the sight of a red beetle – anything might suddenly awake the horror; and he would dig his nails into the palms of his hands as the recollection of the murder and of the subsequent death of his master discoloured his brain.

There were few days in which he did not climb the foothills of the Mountain, or pick his way to the edge of the Twisted Woods, in order to see the long broken line of Gormenghast's backbone. Hours of solitude in the woods were apt to detach him from the reality of any other life, and he would at times find that he was running gawkily through the boles in a sudden fear that there was no Gormenghast: that he had dreamed it all: that he belonged to nowhere, to nothing: that he was the only man alive in a dream of endless branches.

The sight of that broken skyline so interwoven with his earliest recollections reassured him that though he was himself ejected and abandoned, yet all that had given him purpose and pride in life was there, and was no dream or fable, but as real as the hand which shielded his eyes, a reality of immemorial stone, where lived, where died, and where was born again the lit line of the Groans.

On one such evening, after scanning the Castle for some while, and moving his eyes at last across the corruscation of the mud huts, he rose to his feet and began his return journey to the glade, when suddenly changing his mind, he retraced a hundred or so of his steps and set off to his left, penetrating with astonishing speed a seemingly impenetrable valley of thorns. These stunted trees gave way at length to sparser shrub, the leaves, which had all but fallen with drought, hanging to the brittled branches only by reason of the belated refreshment which the sudden storm had given to their roots on the night of the murder. The incline on either side could now be seen more clearly, and as Flay picked his way through the last barrier of shrubs, ash-coloured slopes lifted unbroken on his either hand, the grass as sleek and limp as hair, with not a pale blade upright. There was not a breath of wind. He rested himself, lying out upon his back on a hot slope to his right. His knees were drawn up (for angles were intrinsic to his frame in action or repose) and he gazed abstractedly over the small of his outstretched arm at the sheen on the grasses.

He did not rest for long, for he wished to arrive at his northern cave before dusk. He had not been there for some while, and it was with a kind of swart enjoyment that he surrendered to the sudden whim. The sun was already a far cry from its zenith, hanging in haze, a few degrees above the horizon.

The prospect from the northern cave was unusual. It gave Mr Flay what he imagined must be pleasure. He was discovering more and more in this new and strange existence, this vastness so far removed from corridors and halls, burned libraries and humid kitchens, that gave rise in him to a new sensation, this interest in phenomena beyond ritual and obedience – something which he hoped was not heretical in him – the multiformity of the plants and the varying textures in the barks of trees, the varieties of fish and bird and stone. It was not in his temperament to react excitedly to beauty, for, as such, it had never occurred to him. It was not in him to think in terms. His pleasure was of a dour and practical breed; and yet, not altogether. When a shaft of light fell across a dark area his eyes would turn to the sky to discover the rift through which the rays had broken. Then they would return with a sense of accomplishment to the play of the beams. But he would keep his eye upon them. Not that he supposed them to be worth looking at – imagining there was something wrong in himself for wasting his time in such a fruitless way. As the days went by he had found that he was moving to and fro through the region in order to be at one place or another in time to watch the squirrels among the oaks at noon, the homecoming of the rooks, or the death of the day from some vantage point of his finding.

And so it was this night that he wished to watch the crags as they blackened against the falling sun.

It took him another hour of walking to reach the northern cave, and he was tired when he stripped himself of his ragged shirt and rested his back against the cool outer wall. He was only just in time, for the circle, like a golden plate, was balancing upon its rim on the point of the northernmost of the main crags of Gormenghast Mountain. The sky about it was old-rose, translucent as alabaster, yet sumptuous as flesh. And mature. Mature as a soft skin or heavy fruit, for this was no callow experiment in zoneless splendour – this impalpable sundown was consummate and the child of all the globes' archaic sundowns since first the red eye winked.

As the thin man's gaze travelled down the steep sides of this crag to the great heart-shaped gulch beneath it where what vegetation there was lay sunk in a sea of shade, he felt rather than saw, for his thoughts were still in the darkness, a quickening of the air about him and lifting his head he noticed how, with a deepening of the rose in the sky, all things were tinted, as though they had awaited the particular concentration of hue which the sky now held, before admitting the opinions of their separate colours to be altered or modified. As at the stroke of a warlock's wand the world was suffused – all things saving the sun, which, in contradiction to the colour of the vapours and the forms that it had raddled, remained golden.

Flay began to untie his boots. Behind him his swept cave yawned, a million prawn-coloured motes swaying against the darkness at the entrance. He noticed, as he worked his heel free of the leather, that the crag was biting its way into the sun and had all but reached its centre. He leant his bony head backwards against the stone, and his face became lit and the stubble of his first beard shone, its every hair a thread of copper wire, as he followed the course of the crag's crest in its seemingly upward and arrow-headed journey, its black barbs eating outwards as it climbed.

Inexorable as was its course, there was, that summer evening, more destiny in the progress of another moving form, so infinitesimal in the capacious mountain dusk, than in the vast sun's ample, spellbound cycle.

Through her, in microcosm, the wide earth sobbed. The starglobe sank in her; the colours faded. The death-dew rose and the wild birds in her breast climbed to her throat and gathered songless, hovering, all tumult, wing to wing, so ardent for those climes where all things end.

To Flay, it was as though the silence of his solitude had been broken, the senses invading each other's provinces, for on seeing the movement of something the size of the letter 'i', that moved in silhouette against the gigantic yellow plate, he had the sensation of waking from a dream which took hold of him. Distant as it was, he could tell it for a human form. That it was Keda it was not in his power to realize. He knew himself for witness. He could not stop himself. He knelt forward on his knees, while the moments melted, one into the next. He grew more rigid. The tiny, infinitely remote figure was moving across the sun towards the crag's black edge. Impotently, he watched, his jaw thrust forwards and a cold sweat broke across his bony brow, for he knew himself to be in the presence of Sorrow – and an interloper upon something more personal and secret than he had the right to watch. And yet impersonal. For in the figurette was the personification of all pain, taking, through sliding time, its final paces.

She moved slowly, for the climb had tired her and it had not been long since she had borne the child of clay, like alabaster, the earthless daughter who had startled all. It was as though Keda was detached from the world, exalted and magnificently alone in the rose-red haze of the upper air. At the edge of the naked drop to the shades below she came to a standstill, and, after a little while, turned her head to Gormenghast and the Dwellings, afloat in the warm haze. They were unreal. They were so far, so remote. No longer *of* her, they were over. Yet she turned her head for the child's sake.

Her head, turning, was dimensionless. A thong about her neck supported the proud carvings of her lovers. They hung across her breasts. At the edge of age, there was a perilous beauty in her face as of the crag's edge that she stood upon. The last of footholds; such a little space. The colour fading on the seven-foot strip. It lay behind her like a carpet of dark roses. The roses were stones. There was one fern

growing. It was beside her feet. How tall? . . . A thousand feet? Then
she must have her head among far stars. How far all was! Too far for
Flay to see her head had turned – a speck of life against that falling sun.

Upon his knees he knew that he was witness.

About her and below lay the world. All things were ebbing. A moon
that climbed suddenly above the eastern skyline, chilling the rose,
waned through her as it waxed, and she was ready.

She moved her hair from her eyes and cheekbones. It hung deep and
still as the shadow in a well; it hung down her straight back like
midnight. Her brown hands pressed the carvings inwards to her breast,
and as a smile began to grow, the eyebrows raised a little, she stepped
outwards into the dim atmosphere, and falling, was most fabulously lit
by the moon and the sun.

'BARQUENTINE AND STEERPIKE'

THE inexplicable disappearance of both Lord Sepulchrave and Swelter
was, of course, the burden of Gormenghast – its thoughts' fibre – from
the meanest of the latter's scullions to the former's mate. The enigma
was absolute, for the whereabouts of Flay was equally obscure.

There was no end to the problem. The long corridors were susurrous
with rumour. It was unthinkable that so ill-matched a pair should have
gone together. Gone? Gone where? There was nowhere to go. It was
equally unthinkable that they should have gone singly, and for the
same reason.

The illness of the Earl had, of course, been uppermost in the minds
of the Countess, Fuchsia and the Doctor, and an exhaustive search had
been organized under the direction of Steerpike. It revealed no vestige
of a clue, although from Steerpike's point of view it had been well worth
while, for it gave him occasion to force an entry into rooms and halls
which he had for a long while hoped to investigate with a view to his
own re-establishment.

It was on the ninth day of the search that Barquentine decided to call
a halt to exertions which were going not only against his grain, but the
grain of every rooted denizen of the stone forest – that terraced labyrinth
of broken rides.

The idea of the head of the House being away from his duties for an
hour was sufficiently blasphemous: that he should have *disappeared* was
beyond speech. It was beyond anger. Whatever had happened to him,

whatever had been the cause of his desertion, there could be no two ways about it – his Lordship was a renegade, not only in the eyes of Barquentine, but (dimly or acutely perceived) in the eyes of all.

That a search had to be made was obvious, but it was also in everyone's thoughts that to find the Earl would cause so painful, so frantically delicate a situation that there would be advantages were his disappearance to remain a mystery.

The horror with which Barquentine had received the news had now, at the end of the ninth day, given place to a stony and intractable loathing for all that he associated with the personality of his former master, his veneration for the Earl (as a descendant of the original line) disassociating itself from his feelings about the man himself. Sepulchrave had behaved as a traitor. There could be no excuses. His illness? What was that to him? Even in illness he was of the Groans.

During those first days after the fateful news he had become a monster as he scoured the building, cursing all who crossed his path, probing into room after room, and thrashing out with his crutch at any whom he considered tardy.

That Titus should from the very beginning be under his control and tutelage was his only sop. He turned it over on his withered tongue.

He had been impressed by Steerpike's arrangements for the search, during which he had been forced to come into closer contact with the youth than formerly. There was no love lost between them, but the ancient began to have a grudging respect for the methodical and quickly moving youth. Steerpike was not slow to observe the obscurest signs of this and he played upon them. On the day when, at Barquentine's orders, the searchings ceased, the youth was ordered to the Room of Documents. There he found the ragged Barquentine seated on a high-backed chair, a variety of books and papers on a stone table before him. It was as though his knotted beard was sitting on the stone between his wrinkled hands. His chin was thrust forward, so that his stretched throat appeared to be composed of a couple of lengths of rope, several cords and a quantity of string. Like his father's, his head was wrinkled to the brink of belief, his eyes and mouth when closed disappearing altogether. Propped against the stone table was his crutch.

'You called for me?' queried Steerpike from the door.

Barquentine raised his hot-looking, irritable eyes and dropped the cross-hatched corners of his mouth.

'Come here, you,' he rasped.

Steerpike moved to the table, approaching in a curious, swift and sideways manner. There was no carpet on the floor and his footsteps sounded crisply.

When he reached the table and stood opposite the old man, he inclined his head to one side.

'Search over,' said Barquentine. 'Call the dogs off. Do you hear?'

He spat over his shoulder.

Steerpike bowed.

'No more nonsense!' barked the old voice. 'Body of me, we've seen enough of it.'

He started to scratch himself through a horrible-looking tear in his scarlet rags. There was a period of silence while this operation proceeded. Steerpike began to shift the weight of his body to his other leg.

'Where do you think you're going to? Stand still, you rat-damned misery, will you? By the lights of the mother I buried rump-end up, hold your clod, boy, hold your clod.' The hairs about his mouth were stuck with spittle as he fingered his crutch on the stone table.

Steerpike sucked at his teeth. He watched every move of the old man in front of him, and waited for a loophole in the armour.

Sitting at the table, Barquentine might have been mistaken for a normally constructed elder, but it came as a shock even to Steerpike to see him clamber off the seat of the high-backed chair, raise his arm for the crutch and strike a path of wood and leather around the circumference of the table, his chin on a level with its surface.

Steerpike, who was himself on the small side, even for his seventeen years, found that the Master of Ritual, were he to have brought his head forward for a few inches, would have buried his bristling nose a hand's breadth above the navel, that pivot for a draughtsman's eye, that relic whose potentiality appears to have been appreciated only by the dead Swelter, who saw in it a reliable salt-cellar, when that gentleman decided upon eggs for his breakfast in bed.

Be that as it irrelevantly may, Steerpike found himself staring down into an upturned patch of wrinkles. In this corrugated terrain two eyes burned. In contrast to the dry sand-coloured skin they appeared grotesquely liquid, and to watch them was ordeal by water; all innocence was drowned. They lapped at the dry rims of the infected well-heads. There were no lashes.

He had made so rapid and nimble a detour of the stone table that he surprised Steerpike, appearing with such inexpectation beneath the boy's nose. The alternate thud, and crack of sole and crutch came suddenly to silence. Into this silence a small belated sound, all upon its own, was enormous and disconnected. It was Barquentine's foot, shifting its position as the crutch remained in place. He had improved his balance. The concentration in the ancient's face was too naked to be studied for more than a moment at a time. Steerpike, after a rapid survey, could only think that either the flesh and the passion of the head below him was fused into a substance of the old man's compounding; or that all the other heads he had ever seen were masks – masks of matter *per se*, with no admixture of the incorporeal. This old tyrant's head *was* his feeling. It was modelled from it, and of it.

Steerpike was too near it – the nakedness of it. Naked and dry with those wet well-heads under the time-raked brow.

But he could not move away – not without calling down, or rather calling *up*, the wrath of his wizened god. He shut his eyes and worked his tongue into a tooth-crater. Then there was a sound, for Barquentine, having exhausted, apparently, what diversion there was to be found in the youth's face as seen from below, had spat twice and very rapidly, each expectoration finding a temporary lodging on the bulges of Steerpike's lowered lids.

'Open them!' cried the cracked voice. 'Open them up, bastard whelp of a whore-rat!'

Steerpike with wonder beheld the septuagenarian balancing upon his only leg with the crutch raised above his head. It was not directed at himself, however, but with its grasper swivelled in the direction of the table, seemed about to descend. It did, and a thick dusty mist arose from the books on which it landed. A moth flapped through the dust.

When it had settled, the youth, his head turned over his shoulder, his small dark-red eyes half closed, heard Barquentine say:

'So you can call the dogs off! Body of me, if it isn't time! Time and enough. Nine days wasted! Wasted! – by the stones, wasted! Do you hear me, stoat's lug? Do you hear me?'

Steerpike began to bow, with his eyebrows raised by way of indicating that his ear drums had proved themselves equal to the call made upon them. If the art of gesture had been more acutely develoed in him he might have implied by some hyper-subtle inclination of his body that what aural inconvenience he experienced lay not so much in his having to strain his ears, as in having them strained for him.

As it was, it proved unnecessary for him to ever complete the bow he had begun, for Barquentine was delivering yet another blow to the books and papers on the table, and a fresh cloud of dust had arisen. His eyes had left the youth – and Steerpike was stranded – in one sense only – in that the flood-water of the eyes no longer engulfed him, the stone table as though it were a moon, drawing away the dangerous tide.

He wiped the spittle from his eyelids with one of Dr Prunesquallor's handkerchiefs.

'What are those books, boy?' shouted Barquentine, returning the handle of his crutch to his armpit. 'By my head of skin, boy, what are they?'

'They are the Law,' said Steerpike.

With four stumps of the crutch the old man was below him again and sluicing him with his hot wet eyes.

'By the blind powers, it's the truth,' he said. He cleared his throat. 'Don't stand there staring. What is Law? Answer me, curse you!'

Steerpike replied without a moment's consideration but with the worm of his guile like a bait on the hook of his brain: 'Destiny, sir. Destiny.'

Vacant, trite and nebulous as was the reply, it was of the right *kind*. Steerpike knew this. The old man was aware of only one virtue – Obedience to Tradition. The destiny of the Groans. The law of Gormenghast.

No individual Groan of flesh and blood could awake in him this loyalty he felt for '*Groan*' the abstraction – the symbol. That the course of this great dark family river should flow on and on, obeying the contours of hallowed ground, was his sole regard.

The seventy-sixth Earl should be ever be found, dead or alive, had forfeited his right to burial among the Tombs. Barquentine had spent the day among volumes of ritual and precedent. So exhaustive was the compilation of relevant and tabulated procedure to be adopted in unorthodox and unforeseen circumstances that a parallel to Lord Sepulchrave's disappearance was at last rooted out by the old man – the fourteenth Earl of Groan having disappeared leaving an infant heir. Nine days only had been allowed for the search, after which the child was to be proclaimed the rightful Earl, standing the while upon a raft of chestnut boughs afloat on the lake, a stone in the right hand, an ivy-branch in the left, and a necklace of snail-shells about the neck; while shrouded in foliage the next of kin and all who were invited to the 'Earling' stood, sat, crouched or lay among the branches of the marginal trees.

All this had now, once again, hundreds of years later, to be put in hand, for the nine days were over and it was in Barquentine that all power in matters of procedure was vested. It was for him to give the orders. In his little old body was Gormenghast in microcosm.

'Ferret,' he said, still staring up at Steerpike, 'your answer's good. Body of me, Destiny it is. What is your bastard name, child?'

'Steerpike, sir.'

'Age?'

'Seventeen.'

'Buds and fledglings? So they still spawn 'em so! Seventeen.' He put a withered tongue between his dry, wrinkled lips. It might have been the tongue of a boot. 'Seventeen,' he repeated in a voice of such ruminative incredulity as startled the youth, for he had never before heard any such intonation emerge from that old throat. 'Bloody wrinkles! say it again, chicken.'

'Seventeen,' said Steerpike.

Barquentine went off into a form of trance, the well-heads of his eyes appearing to cloud over and become opaque like miniature sargassos, of dull chalky-blue – the cataract veil – for it seemed that he was trying to remember the daedal days of his adolescence. The birth of the world; of spring on the rim of Time.

Suddenly he came-to, and cursed; and as though to shake off something noxious he worked his shoulder-blades to and fro, as he pad-hopped irritably around his crutch, the ferrule squeaking as it swivelled on the carpetless floor.

'See here, boy,' he said, when he had come to a halt, 'there is work to do. There is a raft to be built, body of me, a raft of chestnut boughs and no other. The procession. The bareback racing for the bagful. The barbecue in the Stone Hall. Hell slice me up, boy! call the hounds off.'

'Yes, sir,' said Steerpike. 'Shall I send them back to their quarters?'

'Eh?' muttered Barquentine, 'what's that?'

'I said shall I return them to their quarters?' said Steerpike. An affirmative noise from the throat of strings was the reply.

But as Steerpike began to move off, 'Not yet, you dotard! Not yet!' And then: 'Who's your master?'

Steerpike reflected a moment. 'I have no immediate master,' he said. 'I attempt to make myself useful – here and there.'

'You do, do you, my sprig? "Here and there," do you? I can see through you. Right the way through you, suckling, bones and brain. You can't fool me, by the stones you can't. You're a neat little rat but there'll be no more "here and there" for you. It will be only "here", do you understand?' The old man ground his crutch into the floor. '*Here*,' he added, with an access of vehemence; 'beside *me*. You may be useful. Very useful.' He scratched himself through a tear at his armpit.

'What will my salary amount to?' said Steerpike, putting his hands in his pockets.

'Your *keep*, you insolent bastard! your *keep*! What more do you want? Hell fire child! have you no pride? A roof, your food, and the honour of studying the Ritual. Your *keep*, curse you, and the secrets of the Groans. How else could you serve me but by learning the iron Trade? Body of me – I have no son. Are you ready?'

'I have never been more so,' said the high-shouldered boy.

BY GORMENGHAST LAKE

LITTLE gusts of fresh, white air blew fitfully through the high trees that surrounded the lake. In the dense heat of the season it seemed they had no part; so distinct they were from the sterile body of the air. How could such thick air open to shafts so foreign and so aqueous? The humid season was split open for their every gush. It closed as they died like a hot blanket, only to be torn again by a blue quill, only to close again; only to open.

The sickness was relieved, the sickness and the staleness of the summer day. The scorched leaves pattered one against the next, and the tares screaked thinly together, the tufted heads nodding, and upon the lake was the stippled commotion of a million pin-pricks and the sliding of gooseflesh shadows that released or shrouded momently the dancing of diamonds.

Through the trees of the southern hanger that sloped steeply to the water could be seen, through an open cradle of high branches, a portion of Gormenghast Castle, sun-blistered and pale in its dark frame of leaves; a remote façade.

A bird swept down across the water, brushing it with her breast-feathers and leaving a trail as of glow-worms across the still lake. A spilth of water fell from the bird as it climbed through the hot air to clear the lakeside trees, and a drop of lake water clung for a moment to the leaf of an ilex. And as it clung its body was titanic. It burgeoned the vast summer. Leaves, lake and sky reflected. The hanger was stretched across it and the heat swayed in the pendant. Each bough, each leaf – and as the blue quills ran, the motion of minutiae shivered, hanging. Plumply it slid and gathered, and as it lengthened, the distorted reflection of high crumbling acres of masonry beyond them, pocked with nameless windows, and of the ivy that lay across the face of that southern wing like a black hand, trembled in the long pearl as it began to lose its grip on the edge of the ilex leaf.

Yet even as it fell the leaves of the far ivy lay fluttering in the belly of the tear, and, microscopic, from a thorn-prick window a face gazed out into the summer.

In the lake the reflections of the trees wavered with a concertina motion when the waters ruffled and between the gusts slowed themselves into a crisp stillness. But there was one small area of lake to which the gusts could not penetrate, for a high crumbling wall, backed by a coppice, shielded a shallow creek where the water steamed and was blotched with swarms of tadpoles.

It lay at the opposite end of the lake to the steep hanger and the castle, from which direction the little breeze blew. It basked in the northerly corner of the lake's eastern extremity. From west to east (from the hanger to the creek) stretched the lake's attenuate length, but the north and south shores were comparatively close to one another, the southern being for the main part embattled with dark ranks of conifers, some of the cedars and pines growing out of the water itself. Along the north shore there was fine grey sand which petered out among the spinneys of birch and elder.

On the sand, at the water's edge, and roughly in the centre of the northern shore, was spread an enormous rust-coloured rug, and in the centre of the rug sat Nannie Slagg. Fuchsia lay upon her back, close by her, with her head upon one side and her forearm across her eyes to protect them from the sun. Tottering to and fro across the hot drab sand was Titus in a yellow shift. His hair had grown and darkened. It was quite straight, but made up for its lack of curls by its thickness and weight. It reached his shoulders, a dark umber, and over his forehead it hung in a heavy fringe.

Stopping for a moment (as though something very important had occurred to him) in the middle of a tiny, drunken totter, he turned his head to Mrs Slagg. His eyebrows were drawn down over the unique violet of his eyes, and there was a mixture of the pathetic, the ludicrous, and the sage in the expression of his pippin face. Even a suspicion of the pompous for a moment as he swayed and sat down suddenly having lost his balance – and then, having collapsed, a touch of the august. But, suddenly, in a sideways crawl, one leg thrusting him forward, his arms paddling wrist-deep through the sand and his other leg making no effort to play its part, content only to trail itself beneath and behind its energetic counterpart, he forsook the phlegmatic and was all impetuousness; but not a smile crossed his lips.

When he had reached the rust-coloured rug he sat quite still a few feet from Mrs Slagg and scrutinized the old lady's shoe, his elbow on his knee and his chin sunk in his hand, an attitude startlingly adult and inappropriate in a child of less than eighteen months.

'Oh, my poor heart! how he *does* look,' came Mrs Slagg's thin voice. 'As though I haven't loved him and toiled to make him joyous. Worn myself out to the marrow for his little Lordship, I have, day after day, night after night, with this after this and that after that piling ag'ny on ag'ny until you'd think he would be glad of love; but he just goes on as though he's wiser than his old Nannie, who knows all about the vacancies of babies' ('vagaries', she must have meant), 'and all I get is naughtiness from his sister – oh, my weak heart, naughtiness and spleen.'

Fuchsia raised herself on her elbow and gazed at the brooding conifers on the far side of the lake. Her eyes were not red from crying: she had cried so much lately that she had drained herself of salt for a little. They had the look of eyes in which hosts of tears had been fought back and had triumphed.

'What did you say?'

'That's it! that's it!' Mrs Slagg became petulant. 'Never listens. Too wise now to listen, I suppose, to an old woman who hasn't long to live.'

'I didn't hear you,' said Fuchsia.

'You never *try*,' replied Nannie. 'That's what it is – you never *try*. I might as well not be here.'

Fuchsia had grown tired of the old nurse's querulous and tearful admonishments. She shifted her gaze from the pines to her brother, who had begun to struggle with the buckle of one of her shoes. 'Well, there's a lovely breeze, anyway,' she said.

The old nurse, who had forgotten she was in the middle of chastening Fuchsia, jerked her wizened face towards the girl in a startled way.

'What, my caution dear?' she said. And then remembering that her 'caution' had been in her disfavour for some reason which she had forgotten, she pursed her face up with a ridiculous and puny haughtiness, as much as to say: 'I may have called you "my caution dear", but that doesn't mean that we're on speaking terms.'

Fuchsia gazed at her in a sullen sadness. 'I said there's a lovely breeze,' she repeated.

Mrs Slagg could never keep up her sham dignity for long, and she smacked out at Fuchsia, as a final gesture, and misjudging the distance, her blow fell short and she toppled over on her side. Fuchsia, leaning across the rug, re-established the midget as though she were setting an ornament and left her arm purposely within range, for she knew her old nurse. Sure enough, once Nannie Slagg had recovered and had smoothed out her skirt in front of her and reset her hat with the glass-grapes, she delivered a weak blow at Fuchsia's arm.

'What did you say about the breezes, dear? Nothing worth hearing, I expect, as usual.'

'I said they were lovely,' said Fuchsia.

'Yes, they *are*,' said Nannie, after reflection. 'Yes, they *are*, my only – but they don't make me any younger. They just go round the edge of me and make my skin feel nicer.'

'Well, that's better than nothing, I suppose,' said Fuchsia.

'But it's not *enough*, you argumentary *thing*. It's not *enough* when there's so much to do. What with your big mother being so cross with me as though I could help your poor father's disappearance and all the trouble of the food in the kitchen; as though *I* could help.'

At the mention of her father Fuchsia closed her eyes.

She had herself searched – searched. She had grown far older during the last few weeks – older in that her heart had been taxed by greater strains of passion than it had ever felt before. Fear of the unearthly, the ghastly – for she had been face to face with it – the fear of madness and of a violence she suspected. It had made her older, stiller, more apprehensive. She had known pain – the pain of desolation – of having been forsaken and of losing what little love there was. She had begun to fight back within herself and had stiffened, and she began to be conscious of a vague pride; of an awakening realization of her heritage. Her father in disappearing had completed a link in the immemorial chain. She grieved his loss, her breast heavy and aching with the pain of it; but beyond it and at her back she felt for the first time the mountain-range of the Groans, and that she was no longer free, no longer just Fuchsia, but of the blood. All this was cloud in her. Ominous, magnificent and indeterminate. Something she did not understand. Something which she recoiled from – so incomprehensible in her were its workings. Suddenly she had ceased to be a girl in all save in habits of speech and action. Her mind and heart were older and all things, once so clear, were filled with mist – all was tangled. Nannie repeated again, her dim eyes gazing over the lake: 'As though *I* could help all the troubles and the badness of people here and there doing what they shouldn't. Oh, my weak heart! as though it were all *my* fault.'

'No one says it's your fault,' said Fuchsia. 'You think people are thinking what they don't. It hasn't been anything to do with you.'

'It hasn't, *has* it – oh, my caution dear, it hasn't, *has* it?' Then her eyes became focused again (as far as they were able). '*What* hasn't, darling?'

'Never mind,' said Fuchsia. 'Look at Titus.'

Nannie turned her head, disapproving of Fuchsia's answer as she did so, and saw the little creature in his yellow shift rise to his feet and walk solemnly away, from the great rust-coloured rug and over the hot drab sand, his hands clasped before him.

'Don't *you* go and leave us, too!' cried Nannie Slagg. 'We can do without that horrid, fat Mr Swelter, but we can't do without our little Lordship. We can do without Mr Flay and –'

Fuchsia rose to her knees, 'We can't! we can't! Don't talk like that – so horribly. Don't talk of it – you never must. Dear Flay and – but you don't understand; it's no good. Oh, what has happened to them?' She sank back on her heels, her lower lip quivering, knowing that she must not let the old nurse's thoughtless remarks touch on her open wounds.

As Mrs Slagg stared open-eyed, both she and Fuchsia were startled by a voice, and, turning, they saw two tall figures approaching them through the trees – a man – and, could it be? – yes, it was – a woman. It had a parasol. Not that there would have been anything masculine about this second figure, even were it to have left the parasol at home. Far from it. The swaying motion was prodigiously feminine. Her long neck was similar to her brother's, tactlessly so, as would have been her face had not a fair portion of it been mercifully obscured by her black glasses: but their major dissimilarity was manifest in their pelvic zone. The Doctor (for it was Prunesquallor) showed about as much sign of having a pair of hips as an eel set upon its end, while Irma, in white silk, had gone out of her way, it appeared, to exhibit to their worst advantage (her waist being ridiculously tight) a pair of hips capable of balancing upon their osseous shelves enough bric-a-brac to clutter up a kleptomaniac's cupboard.

'The top of the morning to you, my dears,' trilled the Doctor; 'and when I say "top" I mean the last cubic inch of it that sits, all limpid-like on a crest of ether, ha, ha, ha.'

Fuchsia was glad to see the Doctor. She liked him, for all his windy verbiage.

Irma, who had hardly been out of doors since that dreadful day when she disgraced herself at the Burning, was making every effort to re-establish herself as a lady – a lady, it is true, who had lapsed, but a lady nevertheless, and this effort at re-establishment was pathetically ostentatious. Her dresses were cut still lower across her bosom; her peerless, milky skin appearing to cover a couple of perches at least. She made even more play with her hips which swayed when she talked as though, like a great bell, they were regulated and motivated by a desire to *sound*, for they did all but chime as her sharp, unpleasant voice (so contrasted to the knell her pelvis might have uttered) dictated their figure-of-eight (bird's-eye view, cross section) patternations.

Her long, sharp nose was directed at Fuchsia.

'Dear child,' said Irma, 'are you enjoying the delicious breeze, then, dear child? I said are you enjoying the delicious breeze? Of course. Irrefutably and more so, I have no doubt whatever.' She smiled, but there was no mirth in her smile, the muscles of her face complying only so far as to move in the directions dictated, but refusing to enter into the spirit of the thing – not that there was any.

'Tut tut!' said her brother in a tone which implied that it was unnecessary to answer his sister's conventional openings; and he sat down at Fuchsia's side and flashed her a crocodile smile with gold stoppings.

'I'm glad you've come,' said Fuchsia.

He patted her on the knee in a friendly staccato way, and then turned to Nannie.

'*Mrs* Slagg,' he said, laying great emphasis upon the 'Mrs' as though it was some unique prefix, 'and how are *you*? How's the blood-stream, my dear, invaluable little woman? How's the blood-stream? Come, come, let your doctor know.'

Nannie edged a little closer to Fuchsia, who sat between them, and peered at the Doctor around her shoulder.

'It's quite comfortable, sir . . . I think, sir, thank you,' she said.

'Aha!' said Prunesquallor, stroking his smooth chin, 'a comfortable stream, is it? Aha! v-e-r-y good. V-e-r-y good. Dawdling lazily 'twixt hill and hill, no doubt. Meandering through groves of bone, threading the tissues and giving what sustenance it can to your dear old body. Mrs Slagg, I am *so* glad. But in your*self* – right deep down in your*self* – how do you feel? Carnally speaking, are you at peace – from the dear grey hairs of your head to the patter of your little feet – are you at peace?'

'What does he mean, dear?' said poor Mrs Slagg, clutching Fuchsia's arm. 'Oh, my poor heart, what does the Doctor mean?'

'He wants to know if you feel well or not,' said Fuchsia.

Nannie turned her red-rimmed eyes to the shock-headed, smooth-skinned man, whose eyes behind their magnifying spectacles swam and bulged.

'Come, come, my dear Mrs Slagg, I'm not going to eat you. Oh, dear no. Not even with some toast to pop you on, and a little pepper and salt. Not a bit of it. You have been unwell, oh dear, yes – since the conflagration. My dear woman, you have been unwell – most unwell, and most naturally. But are you *better* – that's what your doctor wants to know – are you *better*?'

Nannie opened her puckered little mouth. 'I ebbs and I flows, sir,' she said, 'and I falls away like.' Then she turned her head to Fuchsia very quickly as though to make sure she was still there, the glass grapes tinkling on her hat.

Doctor Prunesquallor brought forth a large silk handkerchief and began to dab his forehead. Irma, after a good deal of difficulty, presumably with whalebones and such like, had managed to sit down on the rug amid a good deal of creaking as of pulleys, cranks, hawsers and fish-hooks. She did not approve of sitting on the ground, but she was tired of looking down on their heads and decided to risk a brief interlude of unladyness. She was staring at Titus and saying to herself: 'If that were my child I should cut his hair, especially with his position to keep up.'

'And what does your "ebbing" consist of?' said the Doctor, returning his silk handkerchief to his pocket. 'Is it your heart that's tidal – or your nerves – or your liver, bless you – or a general weariness of the flesh?'

'I get tired,' said Mrs Slagg. 'I get so tired, sir. I have *everything* to do.' The poor old lady began to tremble.

'Fuchsia,' said the Doctor, 'come along this evening and I'll give you a tonic which you must make her take every day. By all that's amaranthine you really must. Balsam and swansdown, Fuchsia dear, cygnets and the eider bird, she must take it every day – syrup on the nerves, dear, and fingers cool as tombs for her old, old brow.'

'Nonsense,' said his sister. 'I said nonsense, Bernard.'

'And here,' continued Doctor Prunesquallor, taking no notice of his sister's interjection, 'is Titus. Apparisoned in a rag torn from the sun itself, ha, ha, ha! How vast he is getting! But how solemn.' He made clucking noises in his cheek. 'The great day draws near, doesn't it?'

'Do you mean the "Earling"?' said Fuchsia.

'No less,' said Prunesquallor, his head on one side.

'Yes,' she answered, 'it is in four days' time. They are making the raft.' Then suddenly, as though she could hold back the burden of her thoughts no longer: 'Oh, Doctor Prune, I must talk to you! May I see you soon? Soon? Don't use long words with me when we're alone, dear Doctor, like you sometimes do, because I'm so . . . well . . . because I've got – I've got worries. Doctor Prune.'

Prunesquallor languidly began to make marks in the sand with his long white forefinger. Fuchsia, wondering why he did not reply, dropped her eyes and saw that he had written:

'9 o'clock tonight Cool Room.'

Then the long hand brushed away the message and at the same moment they were conscious of presences behind them and, turning, they saw the twins, Fuchsia's identical aunts, standing like purple carvings in the heat.

The Doctor sprang nimbly to his feet and inclined his reedy body in their direction.

They took no notice of his gallantry, staring past him in the direction of Titus, who was sitting quietly at the lake's edge.

From the sky's zenith to where he sat upon the strip of sand it seemed that a great backcloth had been let down, for the heat had flattened out the lake, lifted it upright on its sandy rim; lifted the sloping bank where the conifers, with their shadows, made patterns in three shades of green, sun-struck and enormous; and balanced in a jig-saw way upon the ragged edge of this painted wood was a heavy, dead, blue sky, towering to the proscenium arch of the vision's limit – the curved eyelid. At the base of this staring drop-cloth of raw phenomena he sat, incredibly minute; Titus in a yellow shift, his chin once more in his hand.

Fuchsia felt uncomfortable with her aunts standing immediately behind her. She looked up sideways at them and it was hard to conceive that they would ever be able to move again. Effigies, white-faced, white-handed, and hung with imperial purple. Mrs Slagg was still unaware of their presence, and in the silence a silly impulse to chatter gripped her, and, forgetting her nervousness, she perked her head up at the standing Doctor.

'You see, excuse me, Doctor sir,' she said, startling herself by her own bravery, 'you see, I've always been of the energetic system, sir. That's how I always was since I was a little girl, doing this and that by turns. "What *will* she do next?" they always said. Always.'

'I am sure they did,' answered the Doctor, reseating himself on the rug and turning to Nannie Slagg, his eyebrows raised, and a look of incredulous absorption on his pink face.

Mrs Slagg was encouraged. No one had ever before appeared to be so interested in anything she said. Prunesquallor had decided that there was a fair chance of the twins remaining transfixed as they were, for a good half-hour yet, and that to hang around on his elegant legs was neither in his interests, physically, nor in accord with his self-respect, which, although of peculiar brand was nevertheless deep-rooted. They had not acknowledged his gesture. It is true they had not noticed it – but that was not his fault.

'To hell with the old trouts,' he trilled to himself. 'Breastless as wallpaper. By all that's sentient, my last post-mortem had more go in it than the pair of 'em, turning somersaults.'

As he held forth, inwardly, he was paying, outwardly, the most passionate attention to Mrs Slagg's every syllable.

'And it's always been the same,' she was quavering, 'always the same. Responserverity all the time, Doctor; and I'm not a little thing any more.'

'Of course not, of course not, tut, tut; by all that's shrewd you speak nobly, Mrs Slagg – very nobly,' said Prunesquallor, considering at the same time whether there would have been enough room for her in his black bag, without removing the bottles.

'Because we're not as young as we *were*, are we, sir?'

Prunesquallor considered this point very carefully. Then he shook his head. 'What you say has the ring of truth in it,' he said. 'In fact, it has every possible kind of ring in it. Ring-ting, my heart's on the wing, as it were. But tell me, Mrs Slagg – tell me in your own concise way – of Mr Slagg – or am I being indelicate? No – no – it couldn't be. Do *you* know, Fuchsia? Do you? For myself, I am at sea over Mr Slagg. He is under my keel – utterly under. That's queer! Utterly under. Or isn't it? No matter. To put it brutally: was there a – No, no! Finesse, *please*. Who was – No, no! Crude; crude. Forgive me. Of Mr Slagg, dear lady, have you any . . . kind of – Good gracious me! and I've known you all this long while and then *this* teaser comes – crops up like a dove on tenderhooks. There's a "ring" in that – ha, ha, ha! And what a teaser! Don't you think so, dear?'

He turned to Fuchsia.

She could not help smiling, but held the old nurse's hand.

'When did you marry Mr Slagg, Nannie?' she asked.

Prunesquallor heaved a sigh. 'The direct approach,' he murmured. 'The apt angle. God bless my circuitous soul, we learn . . . we learn.'

Mrs Slagg became very proud and rigid from the glass grapes on her hat to her little seat.

'Mr Slagg,' she said in a thin, high voice, 'married *me*.' She paused, having delivered, as it seemed to her, the main blow; and then, as an afterthought: 'He died the same night – and no wonder.'

'Good heavens – alive and dead and half way between. By all that's enigmatic, my dear, dear Mrs Slagg, what can you possibly *mean*?' cried the Doctor, in so high a treble that a bird rattled its way through the leaves of a tree behind them and sped to the west.

'He had a stroke,' said Mrs Slagg.

'We've – had – strokes – too,' said a voice.

They had forgotten the twins and all three turned their startled heads, but they were not in time to see which mouth had opened.

But as they stared Clarice intoned: 'Both of us, at the same time. It was lovely.'

'No, it wasn't,' said Cora. 'You forget what a nuisance it became.'

'Oh, *that*!' replied her sister. 'I didn't mind *that*. It's when we couldn't do things with the left side of us that I didn't like it much.'

'That's what I said, didn't I?'

'Oh no, you didn't.'

'Clarice Groan,' said Cora, 'don't be above yourself.'

'How do you mean?' said Clarice, raising her eyes nervously.

Cora turned to the Doctor for the first time. 'She's ignorant,' she said blankly. 'She doesn't understand figures of eight.'

Nannie could not resist correcting the Lady Cora, for the Doctor's attention had infected her with an eagerness to go on talking. A little nervous smile appeared on her lips, however, when she said: 'You don't mean "figures of eight", Lady Cora; you mean "figures of speech".'

Nannie was so pleased at knowing the expression that the smile remained shuddering in the wrinkles of her lips until she realized that she was being stared at by the aunts.

'Servant,' said Cora. 'Servant . . .'

'Yes, my lady. Yes, yes, my lady,' said Nannie Slagg, struggling to her feet.

'Servant,' echoed Clarice, who had rather enjoyed what had happened.

Cora turned to her sister. 'There's no need for *you* to say anything.'

'Why not?' said Clarice.

'Because it wasn't you that she was disobedient with, stupid.'

'But I want to give her some punishment, too,' said Clarice.

'Why?'

'Because I haven't given any for such a long time. . . . Have you?'

'You've *never* given any at all,' said Cora.

'Oh yes, I have.'

'Who to?'

'It doesn't matter *who* it was. I've given it, and that's that.'

'That's what?'

'That's the punishment.'

'Do you mean like our brother's?'

'I don't know. But we mustn't burn *her*, must we?'

Fuchsia had risen to her feet. To strike her aunts, or even to touch them, would have made her quite ill and it is difficult to know what she was about to do. Her hands were shaking at her sides.

The phrase, 'But we mustn't burn *her*, must we?' had found itself a long shelf at the back of Doctor Prunesquallor's brain that was nearly empty, and the ridiculous little phrase found squatting drowsily at one end was soon thrown out by the lanky newcomer, which stretched its body along the shelf from the 'B' of its head to the 'e' of its tail, and turning over had twenty-four winks (in defiance of the usual convention) – deciding upon one per letter and two over for luck; for there was not much time for slumber, the owner of this shelf – of the whole bone house, in fact – being liable to pluck from the most obscure of his grey-cell caves and crannies, let alone the shelves, the drowsy phrases at any odd moment. There was no real peace. Nannie Slagg, with her knuckles between her teeth, was trying to keep her tears back.

Irma was staring in the opposite direction. Ladies did not participate in 'situations'. They did not *apprehend* them. She remembered that perfectly. It was Lesson Seven. She arched her nostrils until they were positively triumphal and convinced herself that she was not listening very hard.

Dr Prunesquallor, imagining the time to be ripe, leapt to his feet and, swaying like a willow wand that had been stuck in the ground and twanged at its so exquisitely peeled head – uttered a strangely bizarre cry, followed by a series of trills, which can only be stylized by the 'Ha-ha-ha-ha-ha-ha-ha-ha-ha-ha-ha-ha-ha-ha-ha-ha-ha-ha-ha-ha-ha-ha-ha, of literary convention, and wound up with:

'Titus! By all that's infinitesimal. Lord-bless-my-soul, if he hasn't been eaten by a shark!'

Which of the five heads turned itself the most rapidly would be difficult to assess. Possibly Nannie was a fraction of a second behind the others, for the double reason that the condition of her neck was far from plastic and because any ejaculation, however dramatic and however much it touched on her immediate concerns, took time to percolate to the correct area of her confused little brain.

However, the word 'Titus' was different in that it had before now discovered a short cut through the cells. Her heart had leapt more quickly than her brain and, obeying it involuntarily, before her body knew that it had received any orders through the usual channels, she was upon her feet and had begun to totter to the shore.

She did not trouble to consider whether there could possibly *be* a shark in the fresh water that stretched before her; nor whether the Doctor would have spoken so flippantly about the death of the only male heir; nor whether, if he *had* been swallowed she could do anything about it. All she knew was that she must run to where he used to be.

With her weak old eyes it was only after she had travelled half the distance that she saw him. But this in no way retarded what speed she had. He was still *about* to be eaten by a shark, if he hadn't already been; and when at last she had him in her arms, Titus was subjected to a bath of tears.

Tottering with her burden, she cast a last apprehensive glance at the glittering reach of water, her heart pounding.

Prunesquallor had begun to take a few loping, toe-pointed paces after her, not having realized how shattering his little joke would be. He had stopped, however, reflecting that since there *was* to be a shark, it would be best for Mrs Slagg to frustrate its evil plans for the sake of her future satisfaction. His only anxiety was that her heart would not be overtaxed. What he had hoped to achieve by his fanciful outcry had materialized, namely the cessation of the ridiculous quarrel and the freeing of Nannie Slagg from further mortification.

The twins were quite at a loss for some while. 'I saw it,' said Cora.

Clarice, not to be outdone, had seen it as well. Neither of them was very interested.

Fuchsia turned to the Doctor as Nannie sat down, breathless, on the rust-coloured rug, Titus sliding from her arms.

'You shouldn't have done that, Doctor Prune,' she said. 'But, oh, Lord, how funny! Did you see Miss Prunesquallor's face?' She began to giggle, without mirth in her eyes. And then: 'Oh, Doctor Prune, I shouldn't have said that – she's your sister.'

'Only just,' said the Doctor; and putting his teeth near Fuchsia's ear he whispered: 'She thinks she's a lady.' And then he grinned until the very lake seemed to be in danger of engulfment. 'Oh, dear! the poor thing. Tries *so* hard, and the more she tries the less she *is*. Ha! ha! ha! Take it from me, Fuchsia dear, the only ladies are those to whom the idea of whether they are or not never occurs. Her blood's all right – Irma's – same as mine, ha, ha, ha! but it doesn't go by blood. It's equipoise, my Gipsy, equipoise that does it – with a bucketful of tolerance thrown in. Why, bless my inappropriate soul, if I'm not treading on the skirts of the serious. Tut, tut, if I'm not.'

By now they were all sitting upon the rug and between them creating a monumental group of unusual grandeur. The little gusts of air were still leaping through the wood and ruffling the lake. The branches of the trees behind them chafed one another, and their leaves, like a million conspiring tongues, were husky with heresy.

Fuchsia was about to ask what 'equipoise' meant when her eye was caught by a movement among the trees on the farther side of the lake, and a moment later she was surprised to see a column of figures threading their way down to the shore, along which they began to move to the north, appearing and disappearing as the great water-growing cedars shrouded or revealed them.

Saving for the foremost figure, they carried loops of rope and the boughs of trees across their shoulders, and excepting the leader they appeared to be oldish men, for they moved heavily.

They were the Raft-makers, and were on their way by the traditional footpath, on the traditional day, to the traditional creek – that heat-hazy indentation of water backed by the crumbling wall and the coppice where the minnows and the tadpoles and the myriad microscopic small-fry of the warm, shallow water were so soon to be disturbed.

It was quite obvious who the leading figure was. There could be no mistaking that nimble, yet shuffling and edgeways-on – that horribly deliberate motivation that was neither walking nor running – both close to the ground as though on the scent, and yet loosely and nimbly above it.

Fuchsia watched him, fascinated. It was not often that Steerpike was to be seen without his knowing it. The Doctor, following Fuchsia's eyes, was equally able to recognize the youth. His pink brow clouded. He had been cogitating a great deal lately on this and that – *this* being in the main the inscrutable and somehow 'foreign' youth, and *that* centring for the most part on the mysterious Burning. There had been so strange a crop of enigmas of late. If they had not been of so serious a character Doctor Prunesquallor would have found in them nothing but diversion. The unexpected did so much to relieve the monotony of the Castle's endless rounds of unwavering procedure; but Death and Disappearance were no tit-bits for a jaded palate. They were too huge to be swallowed, and tasted like bile.

Although the Doctor, with a mind of his own, had positively heterodox opinions regarding certain aspects of the Castle's life – opinions too free to be expressed in an atmosphere where the woof and warp of the dark place and its past were synonymous with the mesh of veins in the bodies of its denizens – yet he was *of* the place and was a freak only in that his mind worked in a wide way, relating and correlating his thoughts so that his conclusions were often clear and accurate and nothing short of heresy. But this did not mean that he considered himself to be superior. Oh no. He was not. The blind faith was the pure faith, however muddy the brain. His gem-like conclusions may have been of the first water, but his essence and his spirit were warped in proportion to his disbelief in the value of even the most footling observance. He was no outsider – and the tragedies that had occurred touched him upon the raw. His airy and fatuous manner was deceptive. As he trilled, as he prattled, as he indulged in his spontaneous 'conceits', as he gestured, fop-like and grotesque, his magnified eyes skidding to and fro behind the lenses of his glasses, like soap at the bottom of a bath, his brain was often other-where, and these days it was well occupied. He was marshalling the facts at his disposal – his odds and ends of information, and peering at them with the eye of his brain, now from this direction, now from that; now from below, now from above, as he talked, or seemed to listen, by day and by night, or in the evening with his feet on the mantelpiece, a liqueur at his elbow and his sister in the opposite chair.

He glanced at Fuchsia to make sure that she had recognized the distant boy, and was surprised to see a look of puzzled absorption on her dark face, her lips parted a little as though from a faint excitement. By now the crocodile of figures was rounding the bend of the lake away to their left. And then it stopped. Steerpike was moving away from the retainers, to the shore. He had apparently given them an order, for they all sat down among the shore-side pines and watched him as he stripped himself of his clothes and thrust his sword-stick, point down, into the muddy bank. Even from so great a distance it could be seen that his shoulders were very hunched and high.

'By all that's public,' said Prunesquallor, 'so we have a new official, have we? The lakeside augury of things to come – fresh blood in summertime with forty years to go. The curtains part – precocity advances, ha, ha, ha! And what's he doing now?'

Fuchsia had given a little gasp of surprise, for Steerpike had dived into the lake. A moment before he dived he had waved to them, although as far as they had been able to judge he had not so much as moved his eyes in their direction.

'What was *that*?' said Irma, swivelling her neck about in a most lubricated way. 'I said, "what was *that*?", Bernard. It sounded like a splash; do you hear me, Bernard? I say it sounded like a *splash*.'

'That's why,' said her brother.

' "That's why?" What do you mean, Bernard, by "that's why"? You are so tiresome. I said, you are so tiresome. That's why *what*?'

'That's why it was like a splash, my butterfly.'

'But *why*? Oh, my conscience for a normal brother! Why, Bernard, was-it-like-a-splash?'

'Only because it happened to be one, peahen,' he said. 'It was an authentic, undiluted splash. Ha! ha! ha! An undiluted splash.'

'Oh!' cried Mrs Slagg, her fingers plucking at her nether lip, 'it wasn't the shark, was it, Doctor sir? Oh, my weak heart, sir! Was it the shark?'

'Nonsense!' said Irma. 'Nonsense, you silly woman! Sharks in Gormenghast Lake! The very idea!'

Fuchsia's eyes were on Steerpike. He was a strong swimmer and was by now halfway across the lake, the thin white arms obtusely angled at the elbows methodically dipping and emerging.

Cora's voice said: 'I can see somebody.'

'Where?' said Clarice.

'In the water.'

'What? In the lake?'

'Yes, that's the only water there is, stupid.'

'No, it isn't.'

'Well, it's the only water there is that's near us now.'

'Oh yes, it's the only water of *that* sort.'

'Can you see him?'

'I haven't looked yet.'

'Well, look now.'

'Shall I?'

'Yes. Now.'

'Oh . . . I see a man. Do you see a man?'

'I told *you* about him. Of course I do.'

'He's swimming to me.'

'Why to you? It might as well be to me.'

'Why?'

'Because we're just the same.'

'That's our glory.'

'*And* our pride. Don't forget that.'

'No, I won't.'

They stared at the approaching swimmer. His face was most of the time either under water or lying sideways along it to draw breath, and they had no idea that it was Steerpike.

'Clarice,' said Cora.

'Yes.'

'We are the only ladies present, aren't we?'

'Yes. What about it?'

'Well, we'll go down to the shore, so that when he arrives we can unbend to him.'

'Will it hurt?' said Clarice.

'Why are you so ignorant of phrases?' Cora turned her face to her sister's profile.

'I don't know what you mean,' muttered Clarice.

'I haven't time to explain about language,' said Cora. 'It doesn't matter.'

'Doesn't it?'

'No. But this is what does.'

'Oh.'

'We are being swum to.'

'Yes.'

'So we must receive his homage on the shore.'

'Yes . . . yes.'

'So we must go and patronize him now.'

'Now?'

'Yes, now. Are you ready?'

'When I get up I'll be.'

'Have you finished?'

'Nearly. Have you?'

'Yes.'

'Come on, then.'

'Where?'

'Don't bother me with ignorance. Just walk where I do.'

'Yes.'

'Look!'

'Look!'

Steerpike had found himself in his depth and was standing upright. The water lapped at the base of his ribs, the mud of the lake's floor oozing between his toes, while he waved his arms over his head to the group, the bright drops falling from them in sparkling strings.

Fuchsia was excited. She loved what he had done. To suddenly see them, to throw off his clothes, to plunge into the deep water and to strike out across the lake to them, and then finally to stand, panting, with the water curling at his narrow wiry waist – was fine; all upon the spur of the moment.

Irma Prunesquallor, who had not seen her 'admirer' for several weeks, gave a shriek as she saw his naked body rising from the lake, and covering her face with her hands she peered between her fingers.

Nannie still couldn't make out who it was, and months afterwards was still in doubt.

Steerpike's voice sounded over the shallow water.

'Well met!' he shouted. 'Only just saw you! Lady Fuchsia! good day. It's delightful to see you again. How is your health? Miss Irma? Excuse my skin. And, Doctor, how's yours?'

Then he gazed with his dark-red, close-together eyes at the twins, who were paddling out to meet him, quite unconscious of the water up to their ankles.

'You're getting your legs wet, your ladyships. Be careful! Go back!' cried the youth, in mock alarm. 'You do me too much honour. For God's sake, go back!'

It was necessary for him to shout in such a manner as gave no indication that he held authority over them. Indeed, he did not care two straws whether they marched on until they were up to their necks. It was a quaint situation. In the interests of modesty he could move no farther shorewards.

As he intended, they were unable to recognize the authority in his voice which they had learned to obey. The twins moved deeper in the water, and the Doctor, Fuchsia, and Nannie Slagg were amazed to see that they were up to their hips in the lake, the voluminous skirts of their purple dresses floating out magnificently.

Steerpike stared past them for a moment and indicated by a helpless shrugging of his shoulders and a display of the palms of his hands that he was powerless to cope with the situation. They had become very near him. Near enough for him to speak to them without being heard by the group which had by now gathered at the fringe of the lake.

In a low, quick voice, and one which he knew by experience would find an immediate response, he said: 'Stand where you are. Not one more step, do you hear me? I have something to tell you. Unless you stand still and listen to me you will forfeit the golden thrones which are now complete and are on their way to your apartment. Go back now. Go back to the Castle – to your room, or there will be trouble.'

While he spoke he made signs to those on the shore; he shrugged his shoulders impotently. The while, his quick voice ran on, mesmerizing the twins, hip-deep among the sparkling ripples.

'You will not speak of the Fire – and you will keep to yourselves and not go out and meet people as you are doing today against my orders. You have disobeyed. I shall arrive at your rooms at ten o'clock tonight. I am displeased, for you have broken your promise. Yet you shall have your glory; but only if you never speak of the Fire. Sit down at once!' This peremptory order was one which Steerpike could not resist. Their eyes had been fixed on him as he spoke, and he wished to convince himself that they were powerless to disobey him at such moments as this – that they were unable to think of anything save what he was driving into their consciousness by the peculiar low voice which he adopted and by the constant repetition of a few simple maxims. A twist of his lips suggested the vile, overweening satisfaction he experienced as he watched the two purple creatures sink upon their rears in the lukewarm lake. Only their long necks and saucer-like faces remained above the surface. Surrounding each of them was the wavering fringe of a purple skirt.

Directly he had seen, tasted and absorbed the delicious essence of the situation, his voice rapped out: 'Go back! Back to your rooms and wait for me. Back at once – no talking on the shore.'

As they sank into the lake, automatically, at his orders, he had, for the benefit of the watchers, clasped his head in his hands as though in desperation.

Then the aunts arose, all stuck about with purple and made their way, hand in hand, to the amazed gathering on the sands.

Steerpike's lesson had been well digested, and they walked solemnly past the Doctor, Fuchsia, Irma and Nannie Slagg and into the trees; and, turning to their left along a hazel ride, proceeded, in a kind of sodden trance, in the direction of the Castle.

'It beats me, Doctor! Beats me completely!' shouted the youth in the water.

'You surprise me, dear boy!' cried the Doctor. 'By all that's amphibious, you surprise me. Have a heart, dear child, have a heart, and swim away – we're so tired of the sight of your stomach.'

'Forgive its magnetism!' replied Steerpike, who dived back under water and was next to be seen some distance off, swimming steadily in the direction of the Raft-makers.

Fuchsia, watching the sunlight flashing on the wet arms of the now distant boy, found that her heart was pounding. She mistrusted his eyes. She was repelled by his high, round forehead and the height of his shoulders. He did not belong to the Castle as she knew it. But her heart beat, for he was alive – oh, so alive! and adventurous; and no one seemed to be able to make him feel humble. As he had answered the Doctor his eyes had been on her. She did not understand. Her melancholy was like a darkness in her; but when she thought of him it seemed that through the darkness a forked lightning ran.

'I'm going back now,' she said to the Doctor. 'Tonight we will meet, thank you. Come on, Nannie. Good-bye, Miss Prunesquallor.'

Irma made a kind of curling movement with her body and smiled woodenly.

'Good day,' she said. 'It has been delightful. Most. Bernard, your arm. I said – your *arm*.'

'You did, and there's no doubt about it, snow-blossom. I heard you,' said her brother. 'Ha! ha! ha! And here it is. An arm of trembling beauty, its every pore agog for the touch of your limp fingers. You wish to take it? You shall. You shall take it – but seriously, ha! ha! ha! Take it seriously, I pray you, sweet frog; but do let me have it back some time. Let us away. Fuchsia, for now, good-bye. We part, only to meet.'

Ostentatiously he raised his left elbow and Irma, lifting her parasol over her head, her hips gyrating and her nose like a needle pointing the way, took his arm and they moved into the shadows of the trees.

Fuchsia lifted Titus and placed him over her shoulder, while Nannie folded up the rust-coloured rug, and they in their turn began the homeward journey.

Steerpike had reached the further shore and the party of men had resumed their *détour* of the lake, the chestnut boughs across their shoulders. The youth moved jauntily ahead of them, spinning the sword-stick.

COUNTESS GERTRUDE

LONG after the drop of lake water had fallen from the ilex leaf and the myriad reflections that had floated on its surface had become a part of the abactina of what had gone for ever, the head at the thorn-prick window had remained gazing out into the summer.

It belonged to the Countess. She was standing on a ladder, for only in such a way could she obtain a view through that high, ivy-cluttered opening. Behind her the shadowy room was full of birds.

Blobs of flame on the dark crimson wallpaper smouldered, for a few sunbeams shredded their way past her head and struck the wall with silent violence. They were entirely motionless in the half light and burned without a flicker, forcing the rest of the room into still deeper shade, and into a kind of subjugated motion, a counter-play of volumes of many shades between the hues of deep ash-grey and black.

It was difficult to see the birds, for there were no candles lighted. The summer burned beyond the small high window.

At last the Countess descended the ladder, step after mammoth step, until both feet on the ground she turned about, and began to move to the shadowy bed. When she reached its head she ignited the wick of a half-melted candle and, seating herself at the base of the pillows, emitted a peculiarly sweet, low, whistling note from between her great lips.

For all her bulk it was as though she had, from a great winter tree, become a summer one. Not with leaves was she decked, but, thick as foliage, with birds. Their hundred eyes twinkled like glass beads in the candlelight.

'Listen,' she said. 'We're alone. Things are bad. Things are going wrong. There's evil afoot. I know it.'

Her eyes narrowed. 'But let 'em try. We can bide our time. We'll hold our horses. Let them rear their ugly hands, and by the Doom, we'll crack 'em chine-ways. Within four days the Earling – and then I'll take him, babe and boy – Titus the Seventy-seventh.'

She rose to her feet. 'God shrive my soul, for it'll need it!' she boomed, as the wings fluttered about her and the little claws shifted for balance. 'God shrive it when I find the evil thing! For absolution, or no absolution – there'll be *satisfaction* found.' She gathered some cake crumbs from a nearby crate, and placed them between her lips. At the trotting sound of her tongue a warbler pecked from her mouth, but her eyes had remained half closed, and what could be seen of her iris was as hard and glittering as a wet flint.

'Satisfaction,' she repeated huskily, with something purr-like in the heavy-sounding syllables. 'In Titus it's all centred. Stone and mountain – the Blood and the Observance. Let them touch him. For every hair that's hurt I'll stop a heart. If grace I have when turbulence is over – so be it; and if not – what then?'

THE APPARITION

SOMETHING in a white shroud was moving towards the door of the twins' apartment. The Castle was asleep. The silence like space. The Thing was inhumanly tall and appeared to have no arms.

In their room the aunts sat holding each other by the empty grate. They had been waiting so long for the handle of the door to turn. This is now what it began to do. The twins had their eyes on it. They had been watching it for over an hour – the room ill lit – their brass clock ticking. And then, suddenly, through the gradually yawning fissure of the door the Thing entered, its head scraping the lintel – its head grinning and frozen, was the head of a skull.

They could not scream. The twins could not scream. Their throats were contracted; their limbs had stiffened. The bulging of their four identical eyes was ghastly to see, and as they stood there, paralysed, a voice from just below the grinning skull cried:

'Terror! terror! terror! pure; naked; and bloody!'

And the nine-foot length of sheet moved into the room.

Old Sourdust's skull had come in useful. Balanced on the end of the sword-stick, and dusted with phosphorus, the sheet hanging vertically down its either side, and kept in place by a tack through the top of the cranium, Steerpike was able to hold it three feet above his own head and peer through a slit he had made in the sheet at his eye level. The white linen fell in long sculptural folds to the floor of the room.

The twins were the colour of the sheet. Their mouths were wide open and their screams tore inwards at their bowels for lack of natural vent. They had become congealed with an icy horror, their hair, disentangling from knot and coil, had risen like pampas grass that lifts in a dark light when gusts prowl shuddering and presage storm. They could not even cling more closely together, for their limbs were weighted with cold stone. It was the end. The Thing scraped the ceiling with its head and moved forward noiselessly in one piece. Having no human possibility of height, it had *no* height. It was not a tall ghost – it was immeasurable; Death walking like an element.

Steerpike had realized that unless something was done it would be only a matter of time before the twins, through the loose meshwork of their vacant brains, divulged the secret of the Burning. However much they were in his power he could not feel sure that the obedience which had become automatic in his presence would necessarily hold when they were among others. As he now saw it, it seemed that he had been at the mercy of their tongues ever since the Fire – and he could only feel relief that he had escaped detection – for until now he had had hopes that, vacuous as they were, they would be able to understand the peril in which, were any suspicion to be attached to them, they would stand. But he now realized that through terrorism and victimization alone could loose lips be sealed. And so he had lain awake and planned a little episode. Phosphorus, which along with the poisons he had concocted in Prunesquallor's dispensary, and which as yet he had found no use for – his sword-stick, as yet unsheathed, save when alone he polished the slim blade, and a sheet. These were his media for the concoction of a walking death.

And now he was in their room. He could watch them perfectly through the slit in the sheet. If he did not speak now, before the hysterics began, then they would hear nothing, let alone grasp his meaning. He lifted his voice to a weird and horrible pitch.

'I am Death!' he cried. 'I am all who have died. I am the death of Twins. Behold! Look at my face. It is naked. It is bone. It is Revenge. *Listen.* I am the One who strangles.'

He took a further pace towards them. Their mouths were still open and their throats strained to loose the clawing cry.

'I come as Warning! Warning! Your throats are long and white and ripe for strangling. My bony hands can squeeze all breath away . . . I come as Warning! *Listen!*'

There was no alternative for them. They had no power.

'I am Death – and I will talk to you – the Burners. Upon that night you lit a crimson fire. You burned your brother's heart away! Oh, horror!'

Steerpike drew breath. The eyes of the twins were well nigh upon their cheekbones. He must speak very simply.

'But there is yet a still more bloody crime. The crime of speech. The crime of Mentioning, Mentioning. For this, I murder in a darkened room. *I* shall be watching. Each time you move your mouths *I* shall be watching. Watching. Watching with my enormous eyes of bone. I shall be listening. Listening, with my fleshless ears: and my long fingers will be itching . . . itching. Not even to each other shall you speak. Not of your crime. Oh, horror! Not of the crimson Fire.

'My cold grave calls me back, but shall I answer it? No! For I shall be beside *you* for ever. Listening, listening; with my fingers itching. You will not see me . . . but I shall be here . . . there . . . and wherever you go . . . for evermore. Speak not of Fire . . . or Steerpike . . . Fire – or Steerpike, your protector, for the sake of your long throats . . . Your long white throats.'

Steerpike turned majestically. The skull had tilted a little on the point of the sword-stick, but it did not matter. The twins were icebound in an arctic sea.

As he moved solemnly through the doorway, something grotesque, terrifying, ludicrous in the slanting angle of the skull – as though it were listening . . . gave emphasis to all that had gone before.

As soon as he had closed the door behind him he shed himself of the sheet, and, wrapping the skull in its folds, hid it from view among some lumber that lay along the wall of the passage.

There was still no sound from the room. He knew that it would be fruitless to appear the same evening. Whatever he said would be lost. He waited a few moments, however, expecting the hysteria to find a voice, but at length began his return journey. As he turned the corner of a distant passageway, he suddenly stopped dead. It had begun. Dulled as it was by the distance and the closed doors, it was yet horrifying enough – the remote, flat, endless screaming of naked panic.

When, on the evening of the next day, he visited them he found them in bed. The old woman who smelt so badly had brought them their meals. They lay close together and were obviously very ill. They were so white that it was difficult to tell where their faces ended and the long pillow began.

The room was brightly lit. Steerpike was glad to notice this. He remembered that, as 'Death', he had mentioned his preference for 'strangling in a *darkened* room'. The strong lights indicated that the twins were able to remember at least a part of what he had said that night.

But even now he was taking no chances.

'Your Ladyships,' he said, 'you look seedy. Very seedy. But believe me, you don't look as bad as I feel. I have come for your advice and perhaps for your help. I must tell you. Be prepared.' He coughed. 'I have had a visitor. A visitor from Beyond. Do not be startled, ladies. But his name was Death. He came to me and he said: "Their Ladyships have done foul murder. I shall go to them now and squeeze the breath from their old bodies." But I said: "No! hold back, I pray you. For they have promised never to divulge a word." And Death said: "How can I be sure? How can I have proof?" I answered: "I am your witness. If their Ladyships so much as mention the word FIRE or STEERPIKE, you shall take them with you under wormy ground." '

Cora and Clarice were trying to speak, but they were very weak. At last Cora said:

'He . . . came . . . here . . . too. He's still here. Oh, save us! save us!'

'He came here!' said Steerpike, jumping to his feet. 'Death came here, too?'

'Yes.'

'How strange that you are still alive! Did he give you orders?'

'Yes,' said Clarice.

'And you remember them all?'

'Yes . . . yes!' said Cora, fingering her throat. 'We can remember everything. Oh, save us.'

'It is for you to save yourselves with silence. You wish to live?'

They nodded pathetically.

'Then never a word.'

'Never a word,' echoed Clarice in the hush of the bright room.

Steerpike bowed and retired, and returned by an alternative staircase flanked by a long, steep curve of banister, down which he slid at high speed, landing nimbly at the foot of the stairs with a kind of pounce.

He had commandeered a fresh suite of rooms whose windows gave upon the cedar lawns. It was more in keeping with the position which his present duties commanded.

Glancing along the corridor before he entered his apartments, he could see in the distance – too far for the sound of their footsteps – the figures of Fuchsia and the Doctor.

He entered his room. The window was a smoke-blue rectangle, intersected by black branches. He lit a lamp. The walls flared, and the window became black. The branches had disappeared. He drew the blinds. He kicked off his shoes and, springing on the bed, twisted himself onto his back and, for a moment, discarded his dignity and became, at least physically, a little more in keeping with his seventeen years; for he wriggled, arched his spine and stretched out his arms and legs with a terrible glee. Then he began to laugh and laugh, the tears pouring from his dark-red eyes until, utterly exhausted and helpless, he fell back upon the pillows and slept, his thin lips twisted.

An hour earlier, Fuchsia had met the Doctor at their rendezvous, the Cool Room. He had not been flippant. He had helped her with words well chosen and thoughts simple and direct that touched deftly on the areas of her sorrow. Together they had covered in their conversation, the whole range of lamentable and melancholy experiences which it had been their lot to encounter. They had spoken of all connected with them, of Fuchsia's brooding mother; of the uncanny disappearance of her father, and whether he was dead or alive; of the Doctor's sister and of the Twins: of the enigma of Swelter and Flay and of little Nannie Slagg; of Barquentine and of Steerpike.

'Be careful of him, Fuchsia,' said the Doctor. 'Will you remember that?'

'I will,' said Fuchsia. 'Yes, I will, Doctor Prune.'

Dusk was beyond the bay window . . . a great, crumbling dusk that wavered and descended like a fog of ashes.

Fuchsia unfastened the two top buttons of her blouse and folded the corners back. She had turned away from the Doctor as she did so. Then she held her hands cupped over her breast bone. It seemed as though she were hiding something.

'Yes, I *will* be careful, Doctor Prune,' she repeated, 'and I'll remember all you have said – and tonight I had to wear it – I had to.'

'You had to wear what, my little mushroom?' said Prunesquallor, lightening his voice for the first time, for the serious session was over and they could relax. 'Bless my dull wits if I haven't lost the thread – if there *was* one! Say it again, my Swarthy-sweet.'

'Look! – look! – for you and for me, because I wanted to.'

She dropped her hands to her side, where they hung heavily. Her eyes shone. She was a mixture of the clumsy and the magnificent – her head bridled up – her throat gleaming, her feet apart and the toes turned in a little. 'LOOK!'

The Doctor at her command looked very hard indeed. The ruby he had given her that night, when for the first time he had met Steerpike, burned against her breast.

And then, suddenly, unexpectedly, she had fled, her feet pounding on the stone floors, while the door of the Cool Room swung to and fro . . . to and fro.

THE EARLING

THE day of the 'Earling' was a day of rain. Monotonous, sullen, grey rain with no life in it. It had not even the power to stop. There were always a hundred heads at the windows of the North wing that stared into the sky, into the rain. A hundred figures leant across the sills of the Southern wall, and stared. They would disappear back into the darkness, one by one, but others would have appeared at other windows. There would always be about a hundred starers. Rain. The slow rain. The East and the West of the Castle watched the rain. It was to be a day of rain . . . There could be no stopping it.

Even before the dawn, hours before, when the Grey Scrubbers were polishing the walls of the stone kitchen, and the Raft-Makers were putting the finishing touches to the raft of chestnut boughs, and the stable boys, by the light of lanterns, were grooming the horses, it was obvious that there was a change in the Castle. It was the Greatest Day. And it rained. It was obvious, this change, in many ways, most superficially of all, in the visual realm, for all wore sacking. Every mortal one. Sacking dyed in the hot blood of eagles. On this day there could be no one, no one save Titus, exempted from the immemorial decree – '*That the Castle shall wear sacking on the Earling day.*'

Steerpike had officiated at the distribution of the garments under the direction of Barquentine. He was getting to know a great deal about the more obscure and legendary rites. It was in his mind to find himself on Barquentine's decease the leading, if not the sole authority in matters of ritual and observance. In any event, the subject fascinated him. It was potential.

'Curse!' he muttered, as he woke to the sound of rain. But still, what did it matter? It was the future that he had his eyes on. A year ahead. Five years ahead. In the meantime, 'all aboard for glory!'

Mrs Slagg was up early and had put her sacking garment on at once in deference to the sacrosanct convention. It was a pity that she could not wear her hat with the glass grapes, but of course, on the day of the Earling, no one wore hats. A servant had brought in, the night before, the stone which Titus was to hold in his left hand, the ivy branch which he was to carry in his right, and the necklace of snail-shells for his little neck. He was still asleep, and Nannie was ironing the white linen smock which would reach his ankles. It was blanched to a quality as of white light. Nannie fingered it as though it were gossamer.

'So it's come to this.' Nannie was talking to herself. 'So it's come to this. The tiniest thing in the world to be an Earl today. *Today!* Oh, my weak heart, how cruel they are to make a tiny thing have such responsiverity! Cruel. Cruel. It isn't righteousness! No, it isn't. But he *is*. He *is* the Earl, the naughty mite. The only one – and no one can say he isn't. Oh, my poor heart! they've never been to see him. It's only *now* they want to see him because the day has come.'

Her miniature screwed-up face was skirmishing with tears. Her mouth worked itself in and out of its own dry wrinkles between every sentence. 'They expect him to come, the new little Earl, for their homage and everything, but it's me who baths him and gets him ready, and irons out his white smock, and gives him his breakfast. But they won't think of all that – and then . . . and then . . .' (Nannie suddenly sat down on the edge of a chair and began to cry) 'they'll take him away from me. Oh, justlessness – and I'll be all alone – all alone to die . . . and –'

'I'll be with you,' said Fuchsia from the door. 'And they won't take him away from you. Of course, they won't.'

Nannie Slagg ran up to her and clung to her arm. 'They *will*!' she cried. 'Your huge mother said she would. She *said* she would.'

'Well, they haven't taken *me* away, have they?' said Fuchsia.

'But you're only a girl!' cried Nannie Slagg louder than ever. 'You don't matter. You're not going to be anything.'

Fuchsia dislodged the old woman's hand and walked heavily to the window. The rain poured down. It poured down.

The voice behind her went on: 'As though I haven't poured my love out every day – every day. I've poured it all away until I'm hollowed out. It's always me. It always has been. Toil after toil. Moil after moil; with no one to say "God bless you". No one to understand.'

Fuchsia could stand it no longer. Much as she loved her nurse, she could not hear that melancholy, peevish voice and watch the doleful rain and keep herself calm. Unless she left the room she would break something – the nearest breakable thing. She turned and ran, and in her own room once more, fell upon her bed, the skirt of a sacking costume rucked up about her thighs.

Of the Castle's countless breakfasts that dark morning there were few that tasted well. The steady monotone of the pattering rain was depressing enough, but for it to descend on such a day was sheer gloom. It was as though it defied the Castle's inmost faith; taunted it with a dull, ignorant descent of blasphemy, as though the undrainable clouds were muttering: 'What is an Earling to us? It is immaterial.'

It was well that there was much to do before the hour of twelve, and there were few who were not occupied with some task or another relevant to the Day. The great kitchen was in an uproar of activity before eight o'clock had struck.

The new chef was in great contrast to the old; a bow-legged, mule-faced veteran of the ovens, with a mouthful of brass teeth and tough, dirty grey hair. His head appeared to sprout the stuff rather than grow it. There was something ferocious about it. In the kitchen it was said that he had his head cropped every other day – indeed, there were some who held that they had seen it on the move at the speed of the minute hand of a great clock.

Out of his mule face and from between the glintings of his teeth a slow, resonant voice would make its way from time to time. But he was not communicative, and for the most part gave his orders by means of gesturing with his heavy hands.

The activities in the great kitchen, where everything relating to the preparation of food in all its aspects seemed to be going on at the same moment, and where the heat was beginning to make the stone hall sweat, were not, in fact, being pursued in readiness for this Day of Earling, but for the morrow; for, alongside the sartorial beggary went a mendicant's diet, the figures of sacking having only crusts to eat until the next day dawned, when, once more in their own clothes, the symbolic humility in the presence of the new Earl of Gormenghast over, they were able to indulge in a barbecue that rivalled that on the day of Titus's birth.

The kitchen staff, man and boy, and the entire servantage in all its forms and both its sexes, were to be ready at half-past eleven to troop down to Gormenghast Lake, where the trees would be in readiness for them.

The carpenters had been working at the lakeside and among the branches for the last three days. In the cedars had been erected the wooden platforms which had for twenty-two years been leaning against a midnight wall in the depths of the ale vaults. Strangely shaped areas of battened planking, like fragments from an immense jig-saw pattern. They had had to be strengthened, for twenty-two years in the unhealthy cellars had not improved them, and they had, of course, to be repainted – white. Each weirdly outlined platform was so shaped that it might fit perfectly in place among the cedar branches. The varying eccentricities of the trees had many hundreds of years ago been the subject of careful study, so that at all the future Earlings the stages, so ingeniously devised, might be slipped into place with the minimum of difficulty. On the back of each wooden stage was written the name of the tree for which it was constructed and the height of the platform from the ground, so that there would be no confusion.

There were four of these wooden inventions, and they were now in place. The four cedars to which they belonged were all thigh deep in the lake, and against the great boles of these trees ladders were erected which sloped across the shallow water from the shore to a foot or so below the level of the platforms. Similar but ruder structures were wedged in among the branches of ash and beech, and where possible among the closely growing larches and pines. On the opposite side of the lake, where the aunts had paddled from the sand to the dripping Steerpike, the trees were set too far back from the water's edge to afford the necessary vantage; but in the densely wooded hanger were a thousand boughs among the convolutions of which the menials could find themselves some kind of purchase or another.

A yew tree in a clearing, rather farther back from the water than the rest of the inhabited trees, had the wedge-faced poet as its guest. A great piece had been torn from its side, and in the cleft the rain bubbled and the naked flesh of the tree was crimson. The rain fell almost vertically in the breathless air, stippling the grey lake. It was as though its white, glass texture of yesterday was now composed of a different substance – of grey sandpaper – a vast granulated sheet of it. The platforms ran with films of the rain. The leaves dripped and splashed in the films. The sand on the opposite shore was sodden. The Castle was too far to be seen through the veil of endless water. There was no individual cloud to be seen. It was a grey sky, unbroken, from which the melancholy strings descended.

The day drew on, minute after raining minute; hour after raining hour, until the trees of the steep hanger were filled with figures. They were to be found on practically every branch that was strong enough to support them. A great oak was filled with the kitchen staff. A beech, with the gardeners, Pentecost sitting majestically in the main dividing fork of the slippery trunk. The stable lads were perching themselves precariously among the branches of a dead walnut and, cat-calling and whistling, were pulling each other's hair at every opportunity or kicking out with their feet. For every tree or group of trees, its trade or status.

Only a few officials moved about at the water's edge, awaiting the arrival of the principal figures. Only a few *officials* among the trees, but on the further shore, and along the strip of dark sand, there was gathered a great congregation. It stood in complete silence. Old men, old women, and clusters of strange striplings. There was about them a complete silence. They were apart. They were the Mud Dwellers – the denizens of the Outer Wall – the forgotten people – the Bright Carvers.

There was a woman by the shore. She stood a little apart from a group. Her face was young and it was old: the structure youthful, the expression, broken by time – the bane of the Dwellers. In her arms was an infant with flesh like alabaster.

The rain came down on all. It was warm rain. Warm, melancholy and perpetual. It laved the little alabaster body of the child and still it laved it. There was no ending, and the great lake swelled. In the high branches of the dead walnut tree the whistling and scuffling had ceased, for horses were moving through the conifers of the adjacent shore. They had reached the water's edge and were being tethered to the low sweeping arms of the cedars.

On the first horse, a great grey hunter by any normal standard, was seated, side-saddle, the Countess. She had been hidden among leaves, only the horse showing itself; but immediately she became exposed to view her mount became a pony.

The symbolic sacking hung about her in vast, dripping folds. Behind her, a roan bore Fuchsia, with her legs astride. She was patting its neck as she came through the trees. It was like patting soaked velvet. Its black mane was like a repetition of Fuchsia's hair. Lank with the rain, it clung to the forehead and the throat.

The aunts were in a pony trap. That they were not in purple seemed extraordinary. Their dresses had always been as indigenous and inevitable a part of them as their faces. They seemed uncomfortable in the sacking and kept plucking at it with their limp hands. The thin man who led the pony brought it to a halt at the lake side, and at the same moment another trap, of similar design but painted a dark and unpleasant orange, trundled through the pines, and there was Mrs Slagg, sitting as upright as she could, her proud attitude (as she supposed it) nullified by the terrified look of her face, which protruded like some kind of wizened fruit from the coarse folds of the garment. She could remember the Earling of Sepulchrave. He had been in his teens. He had swum out to the raft, and there had been no rain. But – oh, her poor heart! – this was so different. It would never have rained at an 'Earling' when she was a young girl. Things were so different then.

On her lap was Titus – drenched. Even so the smock she had been so carefully ironing looked miraculously white, as though it gave forth light instead of receiving it. He sucked his thumb as he stared about him. He saw the figures peering down at him from the trees. He did not smile: he simply stared, turning his face from one to another. Then he became interested in a golden bangle which the Countess had sent him the same morning, pulling it as far up his arm as he could, then down to his plump, wrinkled wrist, studying it seriously all the while.

The Doctor and his sister had a sycamore to themselves. Irma took some time being hoisted, and was not at all happy about the whole business. She disliked having her hips wedged between rough branches even in the cause of symbolism. The Doctor, seated a little above her, looked like some form of bird, possibly a plucked crane.

Steerpike had followed Nannie Slagg in order to impress the crowd. Although he should have been in a pine-for-four, he now selected a small ash, where he could both be seen and could see with equal advantage to himself and the rest of Gormenghast.

The Twins were keeping their mouths tightly shut. They repeated to themselves every thought as it occurred to them, to find whether the word 'fire' could possibly have crept into it, and when they found it hadn't, they decided in any event to keep it to themselves, in order to be on the safe side. Thus it was that they had not spoken a word since Steerpike left them in their bedroom. They were still white, but not so horribly so. The breath of a yellow reflection had infiltrated itself into their skin and this was nasty enough. Nothing could have been more truly spoke than when Steerpike (as Death) had cried that he would be forever with them. They held each other tightly as they waited to be helped from the trap, for Death had not left them since that curdling night and his livid skull was before their eyes.

By well-proportioned mixtures of brute-strength and obsequious delicacy the officials had at last established the Countess Gertrude upon her stage in the enormous swarthy boughs of the cedar tree. A red carpet had been spread over the woodwork of the platform. The waders and lakeside birds of many breeds which had been disturbed by the activities of the Day, after flying distractedly hither and thither over the forest in swarms, had, as soon as the Countess was seated in the enormous wickerwork chair, flocked to her tree, in which they settled. Angling and disputing for positions at her feet and over various parts of her accommodating body were a whitethroat, a fieldfare, a willow-wren, a nuthatch, a tree-pipit, a sand martin, a red-backed shrike, a goldfinch, a yellow bunting, two jays, a greater spotted woodpecker, three moorhens (on her lap with a mallard, a woodcock, and a curlew), a wagtail, four missel thrushes, six blackbirds, a nightingale and twenty-seven sparrows.

They fluttered themselves, sending sprays of varying dimensions according to their wing-spans through the dripping air. There was more shelter beneath the cedars with their great out-stretched hands spread one above the other in dark-green, dripping terraces, than was the case for those in alternative vegetation.

At this extreme the stable boys in the top branches of the walnut might as well have been sitting in the lake, they could not have been wetter.

It was the same for the Dwellers on the shore – that proud, inpoverished congregation. They cast no reflection in the water at their feet – it was too triturated by the pricking of the rain.

Getting Barquentine established on his stage was the trickiest and most unpleasant task which fell to the lot of the officials. It took place to the accompaniment of such hideous swearing as caused his withered leg to blush beneath the sacking. It must have been hardened by many years of oaths, but this morning an awakened sense of shame at what the upper part of the body could *descend* to, raddled it from hip to toe. Its only consolation was that the contaminating influence had not descended lower than the lungs, and what diseases the withered leg experienced were entirely physical.

When he was seated on the high-backed 'Earling' chair he pushed his crutch irritably beneath it and then began to wring out his beard. Fuchsia was by now in her cedar. She had one to herself and it was comparatively dry, a thick foliage spreading immediately above the stage – and she was gazing across the water at the Dwellers. What was it about them that quickened her – those people of the Outer Wall? Why did she feel ill at ease? It was as though they held a dark secret of which, one day, they would make use; something which would jeopardize the security of the Castle. But they were powerless. They depended upon the grace of Gormenghast. What could they do? Fuchsia noticed a woman standing a little apart from a group. Her feet were in the lake. In her arms she held a child. It seemed, as Fuchsia watched, that she could see for a quick moment the dark strands of rain through the limbs of the child. She rubbed her eyes and again she stared. It was so far. She could not tell.

Even the officials had climbed into the ivy-throttled elm with its broken limb that hung by a sapless tendon.

The Aunts, on the fourth of the cedar stages, shivered, their mouths tightly closed. Death sat with them and they could not concentrate on the procedure.

Barquentine had started, his old voice grating its way through the warm downpour. It could be heard everywhere, for no one noticed the sound of the rain any more. It had been so monotonous for so long that it had become inaudible. Had it stopped suddenly the silence would have been like a blow.

Steerpike was watching Fuchsia through the branches. She would be difficult, but it was only a matter of careful planning. He must not hurry it. Step by step. He knew her temperament. Simple – painfully simple; inclined to be passionate over ridiculous things; headstrong – but a girl, nevertheless, and easy to frighten or to flatter; absurdly loyal to the few friends she had; but mistrust could always be sown quite easily. Oh, so painfully simple! That was the crux of it. There was Titus, of course – but what were problems for if not to be solved. He sucked at his hollow tooth.

Prunesquallor had wiped his glasses for the twentieth time and was watching Steerpike watching Fuchsia. He was not listening to Barquentine, who was rattling off the catechismic monody as fast as he could, for he was suffering the first twinges of rheumatism.

'. . . and will forever hold in sacred trust the castle of his fathers and the domain adhering thereto. That he will in letter and in spirit defend it in every way against the incursions of alien worlds. That he will observe its sacred rites, honour its crest, and in due time instil into the first male of his loins, reverence for its every stone until among his fathers he has added, in the tomb, his link to the unending chain of Groans. So be it.'

Barquentine wiped the water from his face with the flat of his hand and wrung out his beard again. Then he fumbled for his crutch and hoisted himself on to his leg. With his free arm he pushed aside a branch and screamed down through the branches:

'Are you skulks ready?'

The two Raftmen were ready. They had taken Titus from Nannie Slagg and were standing on the raft of chestnut boughs at the lake's edge. Titus was sitting at their feet in the middle of the raft, the size of a doll. His sepia hair was stuck to his face and neck. His violet eyes were a little startled. His white smock clung to him so that the form of his little body was divulged.

The clinging cloth was luminous.

'Push off, curse you! Push off!' yelled Barquentine. His voice raked the water's surface east to west.

With a long, gradual shoving of their poles the two men propelled the raft into deeper water. Moving up either side of the raft and plunging their poles a dozen or so times brought them near the centre of the lake. In a leather bag hung at his waist the older of the two Raftmen had the symbolic stone, ivy branch and necklace of snail-shells. The water was now too deep for them to strike bottom and they dived over the side and, turning, clasped the edge of the raft. Then, striking out, frog-like with their legs, they had soon brought the raft to the approximate position.

'More to the west!' screamed Barquentine from the shore. 'More to the west, idiots!'

The swimmers splashed themselves around to the adjacent edge of the raft and once more began to kick out. Then they lifted their heads from the rain-prodded water and stared in the direction of Barquentine's voice.

'Hold!' yelled the unpleasant voice. 'And hide your damned selves!'

The two men worked their way around until their heads were very nearly obscured by the thick chestnut rim of the raft on the far side from the trees.

With only their faces bobbing above the surface they trod water. Titus was alone. He stared about him, bewildered. Where was everybody? The rain streamed over him. His features began to pucker and his lips to tremble, and he was about to burst into tears when he changed his mind and decided to stand up instead. The raft had become quite still and he kept his balance.

Barquentine grunted to himself. This was good. Ideally speaking, the prospective Earl should be on his feet while being named. In the case of Titus this tenet would naturally have had to be waived if the infant had decided to keep seated or to crawl about.

'Titus Groan,' cried the ancient voice from the shore, 'the Day has come! The Castle awaits your sovereignty. From horizon to horizon all is yours, to hold in trust – animal, vegetable and mineral, time without end, save for your single death that cannot stem a tide of such illustrious Blood.'

This was the Raftmen's cue, and clambering over the side they placed the necklace of snails around the little wet neck, and as the voice from the shore cried, 'Now!' attempted to place in Titus's hands the stone and the ivy branch.

But he would not hold them.

'Hell's blood and gallstones!' screamed Barquentine, 'what's the matter? Rot your hides! what's the matter? Give him his stone and ivy, curse you!'

They opened his little fingers with difficulty and placed the symbols against his palms, but he snatched his hands away from them. He would not hold the things.

Barquentine was beside himself. It was as though the child had a mind of its own. He smote the stage with his crutch and spat with fury. There was not one, either, among the dripping trees or along the strip of bubbling sand – not one whose eyes were not fixed on Titus.

The men on the raft were helpless.

'Fools! fools! fools!' came the hideous voice through the rain. 'Leave them at his feet, curse your black guts! Leave them at his feet! Oh, body of me, take your damned heads away!'

The two men slipped back into the water, cursing the old man. They had left the stone and the ivy branch on the raft at the child's feet.

Barquentine knew that the Earling was to be completed by noon: it was decreed in the old tomes and was Law. There was barely a minute to go.

He swung his bearded head to left and right. 'Your Ladyship, the Countess Gertrude of Gormenghast! Your Ladyship Fuchsia of Gormenghast! Their Ladyships Cora and Clarice Groan of Gormenghast! Arise!'

Barquentine crutched himself forward on the slippery stage until he was within a few inches of the edge. There was no time to lose.

'Gormenghast will now watch! And listen! It is the Moment!'

He cleared his throat and began and could not stop, for there was no time left. But as he cried the traditional words, his finger-nails were splintering into the oakwood of his crutch and his face had become purple. The huge beads of sweat on his brow were lilac, for the colour of his congested head burned through them.

'In the sight of all! In the sight of the Castle's Southern wing, in the sight of Gormenghast mountain, and in the sacred sight of your forefathers of the Blood, I, Warden of the Immemorial Rites proclaim you, on this day of Earling, to be the Earl, the only legitimate Earl between heaven and earth, from skyline to skyline – Titus, the Seventy-seventh Lord of Gormenghast.'

A hush most terrible and unearthly had spread and settled over the lake, over the woods and towers and over the world. Stillness had come like a shock, and now that the shock was dying, only the white emptiness of silence remained. For while the concluding words were being cried in a black anger, two things had occurred. The rain had ceased and Titus had sunk to his knees and had begun to crawl to the raft's edge with a stone in one hand and an ivy branch in the other. And then, to the horror of all, had dropped the sacrosanct symbols into the depths of the lake.

In the brittle, pricking silence that followed, a section of delicate blue sky broke free from the murk of the clouds above him, and he rose to his feet and, turning to the dark multitude of the Dwellers, approached in little careful paces to the edge of the raft that faced the side of the lake where they were gathered. His back was turned to Barquentine, to the Countess his mother, and to all who stared transfixed at the only moving thing in the porcelain silence.

Had a branch broken in any one of the thousand trees that surrounded the water, or had a cone fallen from a pine, the excruciating tension would have snapped. Not a branch broke. Not a cone fell.

In the arms of the woman by the shore the strange child she held began to struggle with a strength that she could not understand. It had reached outward from her breast, outward, over the lake; and as it did so the sky began to blossom in azure and Titus, at the edge of the raft, tore at his necklace with such force that he found it loose in his hands. Then he lifted his head and his single cry froze the multitude that watched him on every side, for it was neither a cry of tears nor of joy; nor was it fear, or even pain – it was a cry that for all its shrillness was unlike the voice of a child. And as he cried he swung the necklace across the sparkling water; and as it sank a rainbow curved over Gormenghast and a voice answered him.

A tiny voice. In the absolute stillness it filled the universe – a cry like the single note of a bird. It floated over the water from the Dwellers, from where the woman stood apart from her kind; from the throat of the little child of Keda's womb – the bastard babe, and Titus's foster-sister, lambent with ghost-light.

MR ROTTCODD AGAIN

THE while, beneath the downpour and the sunbeams, the Castle hollow as a tongueless bell, its corroded shell dripping or gleaming with the ephemeral weather, arose in immemorial defiance of the changing airs, and skies. These were but films of altering light and hue: sunbeam shifting into moonbeam; the wafted leaf into the wafted snow; the musk into a tooth of icicle. These but the transient changes on its skin: each hour a pulse the more – a shade the less: a lizard basking and a robin frozen.

Stone after grey stone climbed. Windows yawned: shields, scrolls and legendary mottoes, melancholy in their ruin, protruded in worn relief over arches or doorways; along the sills of casements, in the walls of towers or carved in buttresses. Storm-nibbled heads, their shallow faces striated with bad green and draped with creepers, stared blindly through the four quarters, from between broken eyelids.

Stone after grey stone; and a sense of the heaving skywards of great blocks, one upon another in a climbing weight, ponderous and yet alive with the labour of dead days. Yet, at the same time, *still*; while sparrows, like insects, flickered in wastes of ivy. Still, as though paralysed by its own weight, while about it the momentary motions fluttered and died: a leaf falling: a bull frog croaking from the moat, or an owl on wings of wool floating earthwards in slow gyres.

Was there something about these vertical acres of stone that mouthed of a stillness that was more complete, a silence that lay *within*, and drummed? Small winds rustled on the castle's outer shell; leaves dropped away or were brushed by a bird's wing; the rain ceased and creepers dripped – but *within* the walls not even the light changed, save when the sun broke through in a series of dusty halls in the southern wing. Remoteness.

For *all* were at the 'Earling'. Around the lakeside was the Castle's breath. Only the old stone lung remained. Not a footfall. Not a voice. Only wood, and stone, and doorway, bannister, corridor and alcove, room after room, hall after hall, province after province.

It was as though, at any moment some inanimate Thing must surely move; a door open upon its own, or a clock start whirling its hands: the stillness was too vast and charged to be content to remain in this titanic atrophy – the tension must surely find a vent – and burst suddenly, violently, like a reservoir of water from a smashed dam – and the shields fall from their rusty hooks, the mirrors crack, the boards lift and open and the very castle tremble, shake its walls like wings; yawn, split and crumble with a roar.

But nothing happened. Each hall a mouth that gaped and could not close. The stone jaws prised and aching. The doors like eye-teeth missing from the bone! There was no sound and nothing human happened.

What moved in these great caves? A shifting shadow? Only where sunlight through the south wing wandered. What else? No other movement?

Only the deathly padding of the cats. Only the soundlessness of the dazed cats – the line of them – the undulating line as blanched as linen, and lorn as the long gesture of a hand.

Where, in the wastes of the forsaken castle, spellbound with stone lacunas – where could they find their way? From hush to hush. All was unrooted. Life, bone and breath; echo and movement gone . . .

They flowed. Noiselessly and deliberately they flowed. Through doors ajar they flowed on little feet. The stream of them. The cats.

Under the welkin of the flaking cherubs doming through shade, they ran. The pillars narrowing in chill perspective formed them their mammoth highway. The refectory opened up its tracts of silence. Over the stones they ran. Along a corridor of fissured plaster. Room after hollow room – hall after hall, gallery after gallery, depth after depth, until the acres of grey kitchen opened. The chopping blocks, the ovens and grills, stood motionless as altars to the dead. Far below the warped beams they flowed in a white band. There was no hesitation in their drift. The tail of the white line had disappeared, and the kitchen was as barren as a cave in a lunar hillside. They were swarming up cold stairs to other lands.

Where has she gone? Through the drear sub-light of a thousand yawns, they ran, their eyes like moons. Up winding stairs to other worlds again, threading the noonday dusk. And they could find no pulse and she was gone.

Yet there was no cessation. League after league, the swift, unhurried padding. The pewter room slid by, the bronze room and the iron. The armoury slid by on either side – the passageways slid by – on either side – and they could find no breath in Gormenghast.

The doorway in the Hall of the Bright Carvings was ajar. As they slid through the opening it was as though a long, snow-soft serpent had appeared, its rippling body sown with yellow eyes. Without a pause it streamed among the carvings lifting hundreds of little dust clouds from the floor. It reached the hammock at the shuttered end, where, like a continuation of silence and stillness in a physical form, dozed the curator, the only living thing in the castle apart from the feline snake that was flooding past him and was even now on its way back to the door. Above it, the coloured carvings smouldered. The golden mule – the storm-grey child – the wounded head with locks of chasmic purple.

Rottcodd dozed on, entirely unaware, not only that his sanctum had been invaded by her ladyship's cats, but unaware also that the castle was empty below him and that it was the day of the Earling. No one had told him of the Earl's disappearance for no one had climbed to the dusty Hall since Mr Flay's last visit.

When he awoke, he felt hungry. Hauling up the shutters of the window he noticed that the rain had stopped, and as far as he could judge from the position of the sun it was well into the afternoon. Yet nothing had been sent up for him in the miniature lift from the Kitchen, forty fathoms below. This was unheard of. It was so new an idea that his food should not be awaiting him that for the moment he could not be certain that he was awake. Perhaps he was dreaming that he had left his hammock.

He shook the cord that disappeared into the black well. Faintly he could hear the bell jangling far beneath. Remote as was the thin, metal sound, it seemed that it was much clearer today, than he ever remembered it to have been before. It was as though it were the only thing in motion. As though it had no other sound to contend with, not so much as the buzzing of a fly upon a pane – it jangled in so solitary a way, so distinct and so infinitely far. He waited, but nothing happened. He lifted the end of the cord for the second time and let it fall. Once more, as though from a city of forsaken tombs, a bell rang. Again he waited. Again nothing happened.

In deep and agitated thought he returned to the window which was so seldom open, passing beneath the glimmering chandeliers. Accustomed as he was to silence, there was something unique today about the emptiness. Something both close and insistent. And as he pondered he became aware of a sense of instability – a sensation almost of fear – as though some ethic he had never questioned, something on which whatever he believed was founded and through which his every concept filtered was now threatened. As though, somewhere, there was *treason*. Something unhallowed, menacing, and ruthless in its disregard for the fundamental premises of *loyalty* itself. What could be thought to count, or have even the meanest kind of value in action or thought if the foundations on which his house of belief was erected was found to be sinking and imperilling the sacrosanct structure it supported.

It could not be. For what *could* change? He fingered his chin and shot a hard, beady glance out of the window. Behind him the long, adumbrate Hall of the Bright Carvings glimmered beneath the suspended chandeliers. Here and there, a shoulder or a cheek bone or a fin or a hoof burned green or indigo, crimson or lemon in the gloom. His hammock swung a little.

Something had gone wrong. Even had his dinner been sent up the shaft to him in the normal way he must still have felt that there was something wrong. This silence was of another kind. It was portentous.

He turned his thoughts over, tortuously and his eyes, losing for a moment their beady look, wandered over the scene below him. A little to his left and about fifty feet beneath his window was a table-land of drab roof around the margin of which were turrets grey with moss, set about three feet apart from one another. There were many scores of them, and as his eyes meandered over the monotonous outline he jerked his head forwards and his focus was no longer blurred, for he had suddenly realized that every turret was surmounted by a cat, and every cat had its head thrust forwards, and that every cat, as white as a plume, was peering through slit eyes at something moving – something moving far below on the narrow, sand-coloured path which led from the castle's outhouses to the northern woods.

Mr Rottcodd, gauging by the converging stares of the turreted cats, what area of distant earth to scan, for with such motionless and avid concentration in every snow-lit form and yellow eye, there must surely be a spectacle of peculiar interest below them, he was able within a few moments to discover, moving toy-like, from the woods, a cavalcade of the stone castle's core.

Toy horses led. Mr Rottcodd, who had long sight but who could hardly tell how many fingers he held up before his own face save by the apprehension of the digits themselves, removed his glasses. The blurred figures, so far below his window, threading their way through sunlight, no longer swam, but, starting into focus, startled him. What had happened? As he asked himself the question, he knew the answer. That no one had thought fit to tell him! No one! It was a bitter pill for him to swallow. He had been forgotten. Yet he had always wished to be forgotten. He could not have it both ways.

He stared: and there was no mistaking. Each figure was tiny but crystal clear in the rain-washed atmosphere. The cradle-saddled horse that led the throng: the child whom he had never glimpsed before, asleep, one arm along the cradle's rim. Asleep on the day of his 'Earling'. Rottcodd winced. It was Titus. So Sepulchrave had died and he had never known. They had been to the lake; to the lake; and there below him on a slow grey mare was borne along the path – the Seventy-seventh.

Leading the mare by a bridle was a youth he had not seen before. His shoulders were high and the sun shone on a rounded forehead. Over the back of the mare, beneath the saddle-cradle, and hanging almost to the ground, there was hung a gold embroidered carpet riddled with moth holes.

With Titus in the cradle was tied a cardboard crown, a short sword in a sky-blue scabbard and a book, the parchment leaves of which he was creasing with his little sprawling thighs. He was fast asleep.

Behind him, riding side-saddle, came the Countess, her hair like a pin-head of fire. She made no movement as her mount paced on. Then Mr Rottcodd noticed Fuchsia. Her back very straight and her hands loose upon the rein. Then the Aunts in their trap, whom Mr Rottcodd found it difficult to recognize for all the uniqueness of their posture, shed as they were of their purple. He noticed Barquentine, whom he took for Sourdust, his dead father, jabbing his crutch into his horse's flank, and then Nannie Slagg alone in her conveyance, her hands at her mouth and a stable boy at the pony's. As vanguard to the pedestrians came the Prunesquallors, Irma's arm through her brother's followed by Pentecost and the wedge-faced poet. But who was that mule-headed and stocky man who slouched between them, and where was Swelter the chef, and where was Flay? Following Pentecost, but at a respectful distance, ambled the rank and file – the innumerable menials which the far forest momently disgorged.

To see, after so long a while, the figureheads of the castle pass below him – distant as they were – was, to Rottcodd in his Hall of the Bright Carvings, a thing both of satisfaction and of pain. Satisfaction because the ritual of Gormenghast was proceeding as sacredly and deliberately as ever before, and pain because of his new sense of flux, which, inexplicable and irrational as it appeared on the surface, was, nevertheless, something which poisoned his mind and quickened his heartbeat. An intuitive sense of danger which, although in its varying forms and to varying degrees had made itself felt among those who lived below – had not, until this morning disturbed the dusty and sequestered atmosphere in which it had been Mr Rottcodd's lot to doze away his life.

Sepulchrave dead? And a new Earl – a child not two years. Surely the very stones of the castle would have passed the message up, or the Bright Carvings have mouthed the secret to him. From the toyland of figures and horses and paths and trees and rocks and from the glimpse of a green reflection in the lake the size of a stamp, arose, of a sudden, the cry of an old voice, cruel, even in its remoteness, and then the silence of the figures moving on, broken by an occasional minutiae of sound as of a tin-tack falling on a brick, as a hoof struck a stone; a bridle creaked with the voice of a gnat, and Rottcodd stared from his eyrie as the figures moved on and on towards the base of the Castle, each with a short black shadow sewn to its heels. The terrain about them was as though freshly painted, or rather, as though like an old landscape that had grown dead and dull it had been varnished and now shone out anew, each fragment of the enormous canvas, pristine, the whole, a glory.

The leading mare with Titus on her back, still fast asleep in the wickerwork saddle, was by now approaching that vaster shadow, cast by the Castle itself, which fanned itself out prodigiously, like a lake of morose water from the base of the stone walls.

The line of figures was stretched out in an attenuate sweep, for even now with the head of the procession beneath the walls, the far copses by the lake were still being emptied. Rottcodd switched his eyes back for a moment to the white cats – each on its grey-moss turret. He could see now that they were not merely staring at the group, as before, but towards a certain section of the line, towards the head of the line, where rode the silent Countess. Their bodies were no longer motionless. They were shuddering in the sun; and as Mr Rottcodd turned his pebbly eyes away, and peered at the figurettes below (the three largest of whom might have been fitted into the paw of the most distant of the cats, who were themselves a good fifty feet below Rottcodd), he was forced to return his gaze at once to the heraldic malkins, for they had sent forth in unison from their quivering bodies a siren-like, and most unearthly cry.

The long, dusty hall behind Mr Rottcodd seemed to stretch away into the middle distance, for with its lethal silence reaffirmed by that cry from the outer world, its area appeared to expand and a desert land was at his shoulder blades; and beyond the far door, and under the boards in the halls below, and beneath them stretching on either hand where mute stairs climbed or wound, the brooding castle yawned.

The Countess had reined in her horse and lifted her head. For a moment she moved her eyes across the face of the precipice that overhung her. And then she pursed her mouth and a note like the note of a reed, shrill and forlorn, escaped her.

The turrets of grey moss were suddenly tenantless. Like white streams of water, like cascades, the cats sped earthwards down the mountainous and sickening face of stone. Rottcodd, unable to realize how they had so suddenly melted into nothing like snow in the sun, was amazed to see, when he transferred his eyes from the empty tableland of roof, to the landscape below him, a small cloud moving rapidly across a field of tares. The cloud slowed its speed and swarmed, and as the Countess jogged her slow mount forwards, it was as though it paddled in a white mist, fetlock deep, that clung about the progress of the hooves.

Titus awoke as the mare which bore him entered the Castle's shadow. He knelt in his basket, his hair black with the morning's rain and clinging snake-like about his neck and shoulders. His hands clasped the edge of the saddle-cradle before him. His drenched and glittering smock had become grey as he passed into the deep, water-like darkness where the mare was wading. One by one the tiny figures lost their toy-like brilliance and were swallowed. The hair of the Countess was quenched like an ember in that sullen bay. The feline cloud at her feet was now a smoke-grey mist. One by one, the bright shapes moved into the shadow and were drowned.

Rottcodd turned from the window. The carvings were there. The dust was there. The chandeliers threw their weak light. The carvings smouldered. But everything had changed. Was this the hall that Rottcodd had known for so long? It was ominous.

And then, as he stood quite still, his hands clasped about the handle of the feather duster, the air about him quickened, and there was *another* change, *another* presence in the atmosphere. Somewhere, something had been shattered – something heavy as a great globe and brittle like glass; and it had been shattered, for the air swam freely and the tense, aching weight of the emptiness with its insistent drumming had lifted. He had heard nothing but he knew that he was no longer alone. The castle had drawn breath.

He returned to his hammock – strangely glad and strangely perplexed. He lay down, one hand behind his head, the other trailing over the side of the hammock in the cords of which he could feel the purring of a sentient Castle. He closed his eyes. How, he wondered, had Lord Sepulchrave died? Mr Flay had said nothing about his being ill. But that was long ago. How long ago? With a start, which caused him to open his eyes he realized that it was over a year since the thin man had brought the news of Titus's birth. He could remember it all so clearly. The way his knees had clicked. His eye at the keyhole. His nervousness. For Mr Flay had been his most recent visitor. Could it be that, for more than a year he had seen no living soul?

Mr Rottcodd ran his eyes along the wooden back of a dappled otter. Anything might have happened during that year. And again he experienced an acute uneasiness. He shifted his body in the hammock. But what *could* have happened? What could have happened? He clicked his tongue.

The Castle was breathing, and far below the Hall of the Bright Carvings all that was Gormenghast revolved. After the emptiness it was like tumult through him; though he had heard no sound. And yet, by now there would be doors flung open; there would be echoes in the passageways, and quick lights flickering along the walls.

Through honeycombs of stone would now be wandering the passions in their clay. There would be tears and there would be strange laughter. Fierce births and deaths beneath umbrageous ceilings. And dreams, and violence, and disenchantment.

And there shall be a flame-green daybreak soon. And love itself will cry for insurrection! For tomorrow is also a day – and Titus has entered his stronghold.

GORMENGHAST

FOR MAEVE

ONE

TITUS is seven. His confines, Gormenghast. Suckled on shadows; weaned, as it were, on webs of ritual: for his ears, echoes, for his eyes, a labyrinth of stone: and yet within his body something other – other than this umbrageous legacy. For first and ever foremost he is *child*.

A ritual, more compelling than ever man devised, is fighting anchored darkness. A ritual of the blood; of the jumping blood. These quicks of sentience owe nothing to his forbears, but to those feckless hosts, a trillion deep, of the globe's childhood.

The gift of the bright blood. Of blood that laughs when the tenets mutter 'Weep'. Of blood that mourns when the sere laws croak 'Rejoice!' O little revolution in great shades!

Titus the seventy-seventh. Heir to a crumbling summit: to a sea of nettles: to an empire of red rust: to rituals' footprints ankle-deep in stone.

Gormenghast.

Withdrawn and ruinous it broods in umbra: the immemorial masonry: the towers, the tracts. Is all corroding? No. Through an avenue of spires a zephyr floats; a bird whistles; a freshet bears away from a choked river. Deep in a fist of stone a doll's hand wriggles, warm rebellious on the frozen palm. A shadow shifts its length. A spider stirs . . .

And darkness winds between the characters.

Who are the characters? And what has he learned of them and of his home since that far day when he was born to the Countess of Groan in a room alive with birds?

He has learned an alphabet of arch and aisle: the language of dim stairs and moth-hung rafters. Great halls are his dim playgrounds: his fields are quadrangles: his trees are pillars.

And he has learned that there are always eyes. Eyes that watch. Feet that follow, and hands to hold him when he struggles, to lift him when he falls. Upon his feet again he stares unsmiling. Tall figures bow. Some in jewellery; some in rags.

The characters.

The quick and the dead. The shapes, the voices that throng his mind, for there are days when the living have no substance and the dead are active.

Who are these dead – these victims of violence who no longer influence the tenor of Gormenghast save by a deathless repercussion? For ripples are still widening in the dark rings and a movement runs over the gooseflesh waters though the drowned stones lie still. The characters who are but names to Titus, though one of them his father, and all of them alive when he was born. Who are they? For the child will hear of them.

III

Let them appear for a quick, earthless moment, as ghosts, separate, dissimilar and complete. They are even now moving, as before death, on their own ground. Is Time's cold scroll recoiling on itself until the dead years speak, or is it in the throb of *now* that the spectres wake and wander through the walls?

There was a library and it is ashes. Let its long length assemble. Than its stone walls its paper walls are thicker; armoured with learning, with philosophy, with poetry that drifts or dances clamped though it is in midnight. Shielded with flax and calfskin and a cold weight of ink, there broods the ghost of Sepulchrave, the melancholy Earl, seventy-sixth lord of half-light.

It is five years ago. Witless of how his death by owls approaches he mourns through each languid gesture, each fine-boned feature, as though his body were glass and at its centre his inverted heart like a pendant tear.

His every breath a kind of ebb that leaves him further from himself, he floats rather than steers to the island of the mad – beyond all trade-routes, in a doldrum sea, its high crags burning.

Of how he died Titus has no idea. For as yet he has not so much as seen, let alone spoken to the long Man of the Woods, Flay, who was his father's servant and the only witness of Sepulchrave's death when, climbing demented into the Tower of Flints, the Earl gave himself up to the hunger of the owls.

Flay, the cadaverous and taciturn, his knee joints reporting his progress at every spider-like step, he alone among these marshalled ghosts is still alive, though banished from the castle. But so inextricably has Flay been woven into the skein of the castle's central life, that if ever a man was destined to fill in the gap of his own absence with his own ghost it is he.

For excommunication is a kind of death, and it is a different man who moves in the woods from the Earl's first servant of seven years ago. Simultaneously, then, as ragged and bearded he lays his rabbit snares in a gully of ferns, his ghost is sitting in the high corridor, beardless, and long ago, outside his master's door. How can he know that it will not be long before he adds, by his own hand, a name to the roll of the murdered? All that he knows is that his life is in immediate peril: that he is crying with every nerve in his long, tense, awkward body for an end to this insufferable rivalry, hatred and apprehension. And he knows that this cannot be unless either he or the gross and pendulous horror in question be destroyed.

And so it happened. The pendulous horror, the chef of Gormenghast, floating like a moon-bathed sea-cow, a long sword bristling like a mast from his huge breast, had been struck down but an hour before the death of the earl. And here he comes again in a province he has made peculiarly his own in soft and ruthless ways. Of all ponderous volumes, surely the most illusory, if there's no weight or substance in a ghost, is Abiatha Swelter, who wades in a slug-like illness of fat through the humid ground mists of the Great Kitchen. From hazy progs and flesh-pots half afloat, from bowls as big as baths, there rises and drifts like a miasmic tide the all but palpable odour of the day's belly-timber. Sailing, his canvas stretched and spread, through the hot mists the ghost of Swelter is still further rarefied by the veiling fumes; he has become the ghost of a ghost, only his swede-like head retaining the solidity of nature. The arrogance of this fat head exudes itself like an evil sweat.

Vicious and vain as it is, the enormous ghost retreats a step to make way for the phantom Sourdust on a tour of inspection. Master of Ritual, perhaps the most indispensable figure of all, corner-stone and guardian of the Groan law, his weak and horny hands are working at the knots of his tangled beard. As he shambles forward, the red rags of his office fall about his bleak old body in dirty festoons. He is in the worst of health, even for a ghost, coughing incessantly in a dry, horrible manner, the black-and-white strands of his beard jerking to and fro. Theoretically he is rejoicing that in Titus an heir has been born to the house, but his responsibilities have become too heavy to allow him any lightness of heart, even supposing he could ever have lured into that stuttering organ so trivial a sensation. Shuffling from ceremony to ceremony, his sere head raised against its natural desire to drop forward on his chest and covered with as many pits and fissures as a cracked cheese, he personifies the ancientry of his high office.

It was for his real body to die in the same fated library which now, in spectre form, is housing the wraith of Sepulchrave. As the old master of Ritual moves away and fades through the feverish air of Swelter's kitchen, he cannot foresee or remember (for who can tell in which direction the minds of phantoms move?) that filled to his wrinkled mouth with the acrid smoke he shall die, or has already died, by fire and suffocation, the great flames licking at his wrinkled hide with red and golden tongues.

He cannot know that Steerpike burned him up: that his lordship's sisters, Cora and Clarice, lit the fuse, and that from that hour on, his overlord, the sacrosanct earl, should find the road to lunacy so clear before him.

And lastly, Keda, Titus' foster-mother, moving quietly along a dappled corridor of light and pearl-grey shadow. That she should be a ghost seems natural, for even when alive there was something intangible, distant and occult about her. To have died leaping into a great well of twilight air was pitiless enough, but less horrible than the last moments of the Earl, the chef and the decrepit master of ritual – and a swifter ending to life's gall than the banishment of the long man of the woods. As in those days, before she fled from the castle to her death, she is caring for Titus as though all the mothers who have ever lived advise her through her blood. Dark, almost lambent like a topaz, she is still young, her sole disfigurement the universal bane of the Outer Dwellers, the premature erosion of an exceptional beauty – a deterioration that follows with merciless speed upon an adolescence almost spectral. She alone among these fate-struck figures is of that poverty-stricken and intolerable realm of the ostracized, whose drear cantonment, like a growth of mud and limpets, clamps itself to Gormenghast's outer wall.

The sun's rays searing a skein of cloud, burn with unhampered radiance through a hundred windows of the Southern walls. It is a light too violent for ghosts, and Keda, Sourdust, Flay, Swelter and Sepulchrave dissolve in sunbeams.

*

These, then, in thumbnail, the Lost Characters. The initial few, who, dying, deserted the hub of the castle's life before Titus was three. The future hung on their activities. Titus himself is meaningless without them, for in his infancy he fed on footsteps, on the patterns that figures made against high ceilings, their hazy outlines, their slow or rapid movements, their varying odours and voices.

Nothing that stirs but has its repercussions, and it may well be that Titus will hear the echoes, when a man, of what was whispered then. For it was no static assembly of personalities into which Titus was launched – no mere pattern, but an arabesque in motion whose thoughts were actions, or if not, hung like bats from an attic rafter or veered between towers on leaf-like wings.

TWO

WHAT of the living?

His mother, half asleep and half aware: with the awareness of anger, the detachment of trance. She saw him seven times in seven years. Then she forgot the halls that harboured him. But now she watches him from hidden windows, Her love for him is as heavy and as formless as loam. A furlong of white cats trails after her. A bullfinch has a nest in her red hair. She is the Countess Gertrude of huge clay.

Less formidable, yet sullen as her mother and as incalculable, is Titus' sister. Sensitive as was her father without his intellect, Fuchsia tosses her black flag of hair, bites at her childish underlip, scowls, laughs, broods, is tender, is intemperate, suspicious, and credulous all in a day. Her crimson dress inflames grey corridors, or flaring in a sunshaft through high branches makes of the deep green shadows a greenness darker yet, and a darkness greener.

Who else is there of the direct blood-line? Only the vacant Aunts, Cora and Clarice, the identical twins and sisters of Sepulchrave. So limp of brain that for them to conceive an idea is to risk a haemorrhage. So limp of body that their purple dresses appear no more indicative of housing nerves and sinews than when they hang suspended from their hooks.

Of the others? The lesser breed? In order of social precedence, possibly the Prunesquallors first, that is, the Doctor and his closely-swathed and bone-protruding sister. The doctor with his hyena laugh, his bizarre and elegant body, his celluloid face.

His main defects? The unsufferable pitch of his voice; his maddening laughter and his affected gestures. His cardinal virtue? An undamaged brain.

His sister Irma. Vain as a child; thin as a stork's leg, and, in her black glasses, as blind as an owl in daylight. She misses her footing on the social ladder at least three times a week, only to start climbing again, wriggling her pelvis the while. She clasps her dead, white hands beneath her chin in the high hope of hiding the flatness of her chest.

Who next? Socially, there is no one else. That is to say no one who, during the first few years of Titus' life, plays any part that bears upon the child's future: unless it be the Poet, a wedgeheaded and uncomfortable figure little known to the hierophants of Gormenghast, though reputed to be the only man capable of holding the earl's attention in conversation. An all-but-forgotten figure in his room above a precipice of stone. No one reads his poems, but he holds a remote status – a gentleman, as it were, by rumour.

Blue blood aside, however, and a shoal of names floats forward. The lynch-pin son of the dead Sourdust, by name Barquentine, Master of Ritual, is a stunted and cantankerous pedant of seventy, who stepped into his father's shoes (or, to be exact, into his *shoe*, for this Barquentine is a one-legged thing who smites his way through ill-lit corridors on a grim and echoing crutch).

Flay, who has already appeared as his own ghost, is very much alive in Gormenghast forest. Taciturn and cadaverous, he is no less than Barquentine a traditionalist of the old school. But, unlike Barquentine, his angers when the Law is flouted are uprisings of a hot loyalty that blinds him, and not the merciless and stony intolerance of the cripple.

To speak of Mrs Slagg at this late juncture seems unfair. That Titus himself, heir to Gormenghast, is her charge, as was Fuchsia in *her* childhood, is surely enough to place her at the head of any register. But she is so minute, so frightened, so old, so querulous, she neither could, nor would, head any procession, even on paper. Her peevish cry goes out: 'Oh, my weak heart! how *could* they?' and she hurries to Fuchsia either to smack the abstracted girl in order to ease herself, or to bury the wrinkled prune of her face in Fuchsia's side. Alone in her small room again, she lies upon her bed and bites her minute knuckles.

There is nothing frightened or querulous about young Steerpike. If ever he had harboured a conscience in his tough narrow breast he had by now dug out and flung away the awkward thing – flung it so far away that were he ever to need it again he could never find it.

The day of Titus' birth had seen the commencement of his climb across the roofs of Gormenghast and the end of his servitude in Swelter's kitchen – that steaming province which was both too unpleasant and too small to allow for his flexuous talents and expanding ambition.

High-shouldered to a degree little short of malformation, slender and adroit of limb and frame, his eyes close-set and the colour of dried blood, he is still climbing, not now across the back of Gormenghast but up the spiral staircase of its soul, bound for some pinnacle of the itching fancy – some wild, invulnerable eyrie best known to himself; where he can watch the world spread out below him, and shake exultantly his clotted wings.

Rottcodd is fast asleep in his hammock at the far end of the hall of the Bright Carvings, that long attic room that houses the finest examples of the Mud Dwellers' art. It is seven years since he watched from the attic window the procession far below him wind back from Gormenghast lake, where Titus had come into his Earldom, but nothing has happened to him during the long years apart from the annual arrival of fresh works to be added to the coloured carvings in the long room.

His small cannon-ball of a head is asleep on his arm and the hammock is swaying gently to the drone of a vinegar-fly.

THREE

ABOUT the rough margins of the castle life – margins irregular as the coastline of a squall-rent island, there were characters that stood or moved gradually to the central hub. They were wading out of the tides of limitless negation – the timeless, opaque waters. Yet what are these that set foot on the cold beach? Surely so portentous an expanse should unburden itself of gods at least; scaled kings, or creatures whose outstretched wings might darken two horizons. Or dappled Satan with his brow of brass.

But no. There were no scales or wings at all.

It was too dark to see them where they waded; although a blotch of shadow, too big for a single figure, augured the approach of that hoary band of Professors, through whose hands for a while Titus will have to wriggle.

But there was no veil of half-light over the high-shouldered young man who was entering a small room rather like a cell that opened from a passage-way of stones as dry and grey and rough as an elephant's hide. As he turned at the doorway to glance back along the corridor, the cold light shone on the high white lump of his brow.

As soon as entered he closed the door behind him and slid the bolt. Surrounded by the whiteness of the walls he appeared, as he moved across the room, weirdly detached from the small world surrounding him. It was more like the shadow of a young man, a shadow with high shoulders, that moved across whiteness, than an actual body moving in space.

In the centre of the room was a simple stone table. Upon it, and grouped roughly at its centre, were a whorl-necked decanter of wine, a few sheafs of paper, a pen, a few books, a moth pinned to a cork, and half an apple.

As he moved past the table he removed the apple, took a bite and replaced it without slackening his pace, and then suddenly looked for all the world as though his legs were shrinking from the ground up, but the floor of the room sloped curiously and he was on his way down a decline in the floor that sank to a curtain-hung opening in the wall.

He was through this in a moment, and the darkness that lay beyond took him, as it were, to herself, muffling the edges of his sharp body.

He had entered a disused chimney at the ground level. It was very dark, and this darkness was not so much mitigated as intensified by a series of little shining mirrors that held the terminal reflections of what was going on in those rooms which, one above the other, flanked the high chimney-like funnel that rose from where the young man stood in the darkness to where the high air meandered over the weather-broken roofs, which, rough and cracked as stale bread, blushed horribly in the prying rays of sundown.

Over the course of the last year, he had managed to gain entrance to these particular rooms and halls, one above the other, which flanked the chimney, and had drilled holes through the stone-work, wood and plaster – no easy work when the knees and back are strained against the opposite walls of a lightless funnel – so that the light pierced through to him in his funnel'd darkness from apertures no wider than coins. These drilling operations had, of course, to be carried out at carefully chosen times, so that no suspicion should be aroused. Moreover, the holes had as nearly as possible to be drilled at selected points, so·as to coincide with whatever natural advantages the rooms might hold.

Not only had he carefully selected the rooms which he felt it would be worth his while watching from time to time either for the mere amusement of eavesdropping for its own sake – or for the furtherance of his own designs.

His methods of disguising the holes which might so easily have been detected if badly positioned, were varied and ingenious, as for example in the chamber of the ancient Barquentine, Master of Ritual. This room, filthy as a fox's earth, had upon its right-hand wall a blistered portrait in oils of a rider on a piebald horse, and the young man had not only cut a couple of holes in the canvas immediately beneath the frame where its shadow lay like a long black ruler, but he had cut away the rider's buttons, the pupils of his eyes as well as those of the horse's. These circular openings at their various heights and latitudes afforded him alternative views of the room according to where Barquentine chose to propel his miserable body on that dreaded crutch of his. The horse's eye, the most frequently used of the apertures, offered a magnificent view of a mattress on the floor on which Barquentine spent most of his leisure moments, knotting and re-knotting his beard, or sending up clouds of dust every time he raised and let fall his only leg, a withered one at that, in bouts of irritation. In the chimney itself, and immediately behind the holes, a complicated series of wires and mirrors reflected the occupants of the de-privatized rooms and sent them down the black funnel, mirror glancing to mirror, and carrying the secrets of each action that fell within their deadly orbit – passing them from one to another, until at the base a constellation of glass provided the young man with constant entertainment and information.

In the darkness he would turn his eyes, for instance, from Craggmire, the acrobat, who crossing his apartment upon his hands might frequently be seen tossing from the sole of one foot to the sole of the other a small pig in a green nightdress – would turn his eyes from this diversion to the next mirror which might disclose the Poet, tearing at a loaf of bread with his small mouth, his long wedge of a head tilted at an angle, and flushed with the exertion, for he could not use both hands – one being engaged in writing; while his eyes (so completely out of focus that they looked as though they'd never get in again) were more spirit than anything corporeal.

But from the young man's point of view there were bigger fish than these – which were, with the exception of Barquentine, no more than the shrimps of Gormenghast – and he turned to mirrors more deadly, more thrilling: mirrors that reflected the daughter of the Groans herself – the strange raven-haired Fuchsia and her mother, the Countess, her shoulders thronged with birds.

FOUR

I

ONE summer morning of bland air, the huge, corroding bell-like heart of Gormenghast was half asleep and there appeared to be no reverberation from its muffled thudding. In a hall of plaster walls the silence yawned.

Nailed above a doorway of this hall a helmet or casque, red with rust, gave forth into the stillness a sandy and fluttering sound, and a moment later the beak of a jackdaw was thrust through an eye-slit and withdrawn. The plaster walls arose on every side into a dusky and apparently ceilingless gloom, lit only by a high, solitary window. The warm light that found its way through the web-choked glass of this window gave hint of galleries yet further above but no suggestion of doors beyond, nor any indication of how these galleries could be reached. From this high window a few rays of sunlight, like copper wires, were strung steeply and diagonally across the hall, each one terminating in its amber pool of dust on the floorboards. A spider lowered itself, fathom by fathom, on a perilous length of thread and was suddenly transfixed in the path of a sunbeam and, for an instant, was a thing of radiant gold.

There was no sound, and then – as though timed to break the tension, the high window was swung open and the sunbeams were blotted out, for a hand was thrust through and a bell was shaken. Almost at once there was a sound of footsteps, and moment later a dozen doors were opening and shutting, and the hall was thronged with the criss-crossing of figures.

The bell ceased clanging. The hand was withdrawn and the figures were gone. There was no sign that any living thing had ever moved or breathed between the plaster walls, or that the many doors had ever opened, save that a small whitish flower lay in the dust beneath the rusting helmet, and that a door was swinging gently to and fro.

II

As it swung, broken glimpses were obtained of a whitewashed corridor that wound in so slow and ample a curve that by the time the right-hand wall had disappeared from view the roof of the passageway appeared no more than the height of an ankle from the ground.

This long, narrowing, ash-white perspective, curving with the effortless ease of a gull in air, was suddenly the setting for action. For something, hardly distinguishable as a horse and rider until it had cantered a full third of the long curve to the deserted hall, was rapidly approaching. The sharp clacking of hooves was all at once immediately behind the swinging door, which was pushed wide by the nose of a small grey pony.

Titus sat astride.

He was dressed in the coarse, loosely fitting garments that were worn by the castle children. For the first nine years of his life the heir to the Earldom was made to mix with, and attempt to understand the ways of, the lower orders. On his fifteenth birthday such friendships as he had struck would have to cease. His demeanour would have to change and a more austere and selective relationship with the personnel of the castle would take its place. But it was a tradition that in the early years, the child of the Family must, for certain hours, at least, of every day, be as the less exalted children, feed with them, sleep in their dormitories, attend with them the classes of the Professors, and join in the various time-honoured games and observances like any other minor. Yet for all that, Titus was conscious of always being watched: of a discrepancy in the attitude of the officials and even at times of the boys. He was too young to understand the implications of his status, but old enough to sense his uniqueness.

Once a week, before the morning classes, he was allowed to ride his grey horse for an hour beneath the high southern walls, where the early sun would send his fantastic shadow careering along the tall stones at his side. And when he waved his arm, his shadow-self on a shadow-horse would wave its huge shadow-arm as they galloped together.

But today, instead of trotting away to his beloved southern wall he had, in a moment of devilment, turned his horse through a moss-black arch and into the castle itself. In the still silence his heart beat rapidly as he clattered along stone corridors he had never seen before.

He knew that it would not be worth his while to take French leave of the morning classes, for he had been locked up more than once during the long summer evenings for such acts of disobedience. But he tasted the sharp fruits of the quick bridle-wrench which had freed him from the ostler. It was only for a few minutes that he was alone, but when he came to a halt in the high plaster-walled hall, with the rusting helmet above him, and far above the helmet the dim mysterious balconies, he had already dulled his sudden itch for rebellion.

Small though he looked on the grey, there was something command-ing in the confident air with which he sat the saddle – something impressive in his childish frame, as though there was a kind of weight there, or strength – a compound of spirit and matter; something solid that underlay the whims, terrors, tears and laughter and vitality of his seven years.

By no means good-looking, he had, nevertheless, this presence. Like his mother, there was a certain *scale* about him, as though his height and breadth bore no relation to the logic of feet and inches.

The ostler entered the hall, slow, shuffling, hissing gently, a perpetual habit of his whether grooming a horse or not, and the grey pony was at once led away in the direction of the school-rooms to the west.

Titus watched the back of the ostler's head as he was led along but said nothing. It was as though what had just occurred was something they had rehearsed many times before, and that there was no need for comment. The child had known this man and his hissing, which were as inseparable as a rough sea from the sound that it makes, for little more than a year, when the grey was given him at a ceremony known as 'The Pony Giving', a ceremony that took place without fail on the third Friday after the sixth birthday of any son of the Line who was also, by reason of his father's death, an earl in his minority. But for all this length of time – and fifteen months was a considerable span for a child who could only remember with any distinctness his last four years – the ostler and Titus had exchanged not more than a dozen sentences. It was not that they disliked one another, the ostler merely preferring to give the boy pieces of stolen seed-cake to making any effort at conversation, and Titus quite content to have it so, for the ostler was to him simply the shuffling figure who took care of his pony, and it was enough to know his mannerisms, the way his feet shuffled, the white scar above his eye, and to hear him hissing.

Within an hour the morning classes were under way. At an ink-stained desk, with his chin cupped in his hands, Titus was contemplating, as in a dream, the chalk-marks on the blackboard. They represented a sum in short division, but might as well have been some hieroglyphic message from a moonstruck prophet to his lost tribe a thousand years ago. His mind, and the minds of his small companions in that leather-walled schoolroom, was far away, but in a world, not of prophets, but of swopped marbles, birds' eggs, wooden daggers, secrets and catapults, midnight feasts, heroes, deadly rivalries and desperate friendships.

FIVE

FUCHSIA was leaning on her window-sill and staring out over the rough roofs below her. Her crimson dress burned with the peculiar red more often found in paintings than in Nature. The window-frame, surrounding not only her but the impalpable dusk behind her, enclosed a masterpiece. Her stillness accentuated the hallucinatory effect, but even if she were to have moved it would have seemed ·that a picture had come to life rather than that a movement had taken place in Nature. But the pattern did not alter. The inky black of her hair fell motionlessly and gave infinite subtlety to the porous shadow-land beyond her, showing it for what it was, not so much a darkness in itself as something starved for sunbeams. Her face, throat and arms were warm and tawny, yet seemed pale against her red dress. She stared down, out of this picture, at the world below her – at the north cloisters, at Barquentine, heaving his miserable and vicious body forwards on his crutch, and cursing the flies that followed him as he passed across a gap between two roofs and disappeared from sight.

Then she moved, suddenly turning about at a sound behind her and found Mrs Slagg looking up at her. In her hands the midget held a tray weighted with a tumbler of milk and a bunch of grapes.

She was peeved and irritable, for she had spent the last hour searching for Titus, who had outgrown the fussings of her love. 'Where is he? Oh, where *is* he?' she had whimpered, her face puckered up with anxiety and her weak legs, like twigs, that were forever tottering from one duty to another, aching. 'Where is his wickedness, that naughty Earl of mine? God help my poor weak heart! Where can he be?'

Her peevish voice raised thin echoes far above her as though, in hall after hall, she had awakened nests of fledgelings from their sleep.

'Oh, it's you,' said Fuchsia, throwing a lock of hair from her face with a quick jerk of her hand. 'I didn't know who it was.'

'Of course it's me! Who else could it be, you *stupid*? Who else ever comes in your room? You ought to know that by *now*, oughtn't you? Oughtn't you?'

'I didn't see you,' said Fuchsia.

'But I saw *you* – leaning out of the window like a great heavy thing – and never listening though I called you and called you and called you to open the door. Oh, my weak heart! – it's always the same – call, call, call, with no one to answer. Why do I trouble to live?' She peered at Fuchsia. 'Why should I live for *you*? Perhaps I'll die tonight,' she added maliciously, squinting at Fuchsia again. 'Why don't you take your milk?'

'Put it on the chair,' said Fuchsia, 'I'll have it later – and the grapes. Thank you. Goodbye.'

At Fuchsia's peremptory dismissal, which had not been meant unkindly, abrupt as it had sounded, Mrs Slagg's eyes filled with tears. But ancient, tiny and hurt though she was, her anger rose again like a miniature tempest, and instead of her usual peevish cry of 'Oh, my weak heart! how *could* you?' she caught hold of Fuchsia's hand and tried to bend back the girl's fingers and, failing, was about to try and bite her ladyship's arm when she found herself being carried to the bed. Denied of her little revenge, she closed her eyes for a few moments, her chicken bosom rising and falling with fantastic rapidity. When she opened her eyes, the first thing she saw was Fuchsia's hand spread out before her and, rising on one elbow, she smacked at it again and again until exhausted, when she buried her wrinkled face in Fuchsia's side.

'I'm sorry,' said the girl. 'I didn't mean Goodbye in that way. I only meant that I wanted to be left alone.'

'Why?' (Mrs Slagg's voice was hardly audible, so closely was her face pressed into Fuchsia's dress.) 'Why? why? why? Anyone would think I got in your way. Anyone would think I didn't know you inside out. Haven't I taught you everything since you were a baby? Didn't I rock you to sleep, you beastly thing? Didn't I?' She raised her old tearful face to Fuchsia. 'Didn't I?'

'You did,' said Fuchsia.

'*Well*, then!' said Nanny Slagg. '*Well*, then!' And she crawled off the bed and made her descent to the ground.

'Get off the counterpane at *once*, you *thing*, and don't stare at me! Perhaps I'll come and see you tonight. Perhaps. I don't know. Perhaps I don't want to.' She made for the door, reached for the handle and was within a few moments alone once more in her small room, where with her red-rimmed eyes wide open, she lay upon her bed like a discarded doll.

Fuchsia, with the room to herself, sat down in front of a mirror that had smallpox so badly at its centre that in order to see herself properly she was forced to peer into a comparatively unblemished corner. Her comb, with a number of its teeth missing, was eventually found in a drawer below the mirror when, just as she was about to start combing her hair – a performance she had but lately taken to – the room darkened, for half the light from her window was suddenly obscured by the miraculous appearance of the young man with high shoulders.

Before Fuchsia had had a moment to ponder how any human being could appear on her window-sill a hundred feet above the ground – let alone recognize the silhouette – she snatched a hair brush from the table before her and brandished it behind her head in readiness for she knew not what. At a moment when others might have screamed or shrunk away, she had showed fight – with what at that startling moment might have been a bat-winged monster for all she knew. But in the instant before she flung the brush she recognized Steerpike.

He knocked with his knuckle on the lintel of the window.

'Good afternoon, madam,' he said. 'May I present my card?' And he handed Fuchsia a slip of paper bearing the words:

'His Infernal Slyness, the Arch-fluke Steerpike.'

But before Fuchsia had read it she had begun to laugh in her short, breathless way, at the mock-solemn tone of his 'Good afternoon, madam.' It had been so perfectly ponderous.

But until she had motioned him to descend to the floor of the room – and she had no alternative – he had not moved an inch in that direction, but stood, with his hands clasped and his head cocked on one side. At her gesture he suddenly came to life again, as though a trigger had been touched, and within a moment had unknotted a rope from his belt and flung the loose end out of the window, where it dangled. Fuchsia, leaning out of the window, gazed upwards and saw the rest of the rope ascending the seven remaining storeys to a ragged roof, where presumably it was attached to some turret or chimney.

'All ready for my return,' said Steerpike. 'Nothing like rope, madam. Better than a horse. Climbs down a wall whenever you ask it, and never needs feeding.'

'You can leave off "Madaming" me,' said Fuchsia, somewhat loudly, and to Steerpike's surprise. 'You know my name.'

Steerpike, rapidly swallowing, digesting and purging his irritation, for he never wasted his time by mouthing his setbacks, seated himself on a chair in the reverse direction and placed his chin on the chair back.

'I will never forget,' he said, 'to always call you by your proper name, and in a very proper tone of voice, Lady Fuchsia.'

Fuchsia smiled vaguely, but she was thinking of something else.

'You are certainly one for climbing,' she said at last. 'You climbed to my attic – do you remember?'

Steerpike nodded.

'And you climbed up the library wall when it was burning. It seems very long ago.'

'And the time, if I may say so, Lady Fuchsia, when I climbed through the thunderstorm and over the rocks with you in my arms.'

It was as though all the air had been suddenly drawn from the room, so deathly silent and thin had the atmosphere become. Steerpike thought he could detect the faintest tinge of colour on Fuchsia's cheekbones.

At last he said: 'One day, Lady Fuchsia, will you explore with me the roofs of this great house of yours? I would like to show you what I have found, away to the south, your Ladyship, where the granite domes are elbow-deep in moss.'

'Yes,' she replied, 'yes . . .' His sharp, pallid face repelled her, but she was attracted by his vitality and air of secrecy.

She was about to ask him to leave, but he was on his feet before she could speak and had jumped through the window without touching its frame, and was swinging to and fro on the jerking rope before he started swarming it, hand over hand, on his long, upward climb to the ragged roof above.

When Fuchsia turned from the window she found upon her rough dressing-table a single rosebud.

As he climbed Steerpike remembered how the day of Titus' birth seven years previously had seen the commencement of his climb across the roofs of Gormenghast and the end of his servitude in Swelter's kitchen. The muscular effort required accentuated the hunching of his shoulders. But he was preternaturally nimble and revelled no less in physical than in mental tenacity and daring. His penetrating close-set eyes were fixed upon that point to which his rope was knotted as though it were the zenith of his fancy.

The sky had darkened, and with the rising of a swift wind came the driven rain. It hissed and spouted in the masonry. It found a hundred natural conduits where it slid. Air-shafts, flues and blowholes coughed with echoes, and huge flumes muttered. Lakes formed among the roofs, where they reflected the sky as though they had been there forever like waters in the mountains.

With the rope neatly coiled about his waist, Steerpike ran like a shadow across an acre of sloping slates. His collar was turned up. His white face was bearded with the rain.

High, sinister walls, like the falls of wharves, or dungeons for the damned, lifted into the watery air or swept in prodigious arcs of ruthless stone. Lost in the flying clouds the craggy summits of Gormenghast were wild with straining hair – the hanks of the drenched rock-weed. Buttresses and outcrops of unrecognizable masonry loomed over Steerpike's head like the hulks of mouldering ships, or stranded monsters whose streaming mouths and brows were the sardonic work of a thousand tempests. Roof after roof of every gradient rose or slid away before his eyes: terrace after terrace shone dimly below him through the rain, their long-forgotten flagstones dancing and hissing with the downpour.

A world of shapes fled past him, for he was as fleet as a cat and he ran without pause, turning now this way, now that, and only slackening his pace when some more than normally hazardous cat-walk compelled. From time to time as he ran he leaped into the air as though from excess of vitality. Suddenly, as he rounded a chimney-stack, black with dripping ivy, he dropped to walking-pace and then, ducking his head beneath an arch, he fell to his knees and hauled up, with a grating of hinges, a long-forgotten skylight. In a moment he was through and had dropped into a small empty room twelve feet beneath. It was very dark. Steerpike uncoiled himself of the rope and looped it over a nail in the wall. Then he glanced around the dark room. The walls were covered with glass-fronted showcases, filled with every kind of moth. Long thin pins impaled these insects to the cork lining of each box, but careful as the original collector must have been in his handling and mounting of the delicate things, yet time had told, and there was not a case without its damaged moth, and the floors of most of the little boxes smouldered with fallen wings.

Steerpike turned to the door, listening a moment, and then opened it. He had before him a dusty landing, and immediately on his left a ladder leading down to yet another empty room, as forlorn as the one he had just left. There was nothing in it except a great pyramidal stack of nibbled books, its dark interstices alive with the nests of mice. There was no door to this room, but a length of sacking hung limply over a fissure in the wall, which was broad enough for Steerpike to negotiate, moving sideways. Again there were stairs, and again there was a room, but longer this time, a kind of gallery. At its far end stood a stuffed stag, its shoulders white with dust.

As he crossed the room he saw through the corner of his eye, and framed by a glass-less window, the sinister outline of Gormenghast mountain, its high crags gleaming against a flying sky. The rain streamed through the window and splashed on the boards, so that little beads of dust ran to and fro on the floor like globules of mercury.

Reaching the double door, he ran his hands through his dripping hair and turned down the collar of his coat; and then, passing through and veering to the left, followed a corridor for some way before he reached a stairhead.

No sooner had he peered over the banisters than he started back, for the Countess of Groan was passing through the lamplit room below. She seemed to be wading in white froth, and the hollow rooms behind Steerpike reverberated with a dull throbbing, a multitudinous sound, the echo of the genuine ululation which he could not hear, the droning of the cats. They passed from the hall below like the ebbing of a white tide through the mouth of a cave, at its centre, a rock that moved with them crowned with red seaweed.

The echoes died. The silence was like a stretched sheet. Steerpike descended rapidly to the room below and made to the east.

The Countess walked with her head bowed a little and her arms akimbo. There was a frown on her brow. She was not satisfied that the immemorial sense of duty and observance was universally held sacrosanct in the wide network of the castle. Heavy and abstracted as she seemed, yet she was as quick as a snake to detect danger, and though she could not put a finger, as it were, on the exact area of her doubts, she was nevertheless suspicious, wary and revengeful of she knew not exactly what.

She was turning over all the fragments of knowledge which might relate to the mysterious burning of her late husband's library, to his disappearance and to the disappearance of his chef. She was using, almost for the first time, a naturally powerful brain – a brain that had been purred to sleep for so long by her white cats that it was difficult at first for her to awaken it.

She was on her way to the Doctor's house. She had not visited him for several years, and on the last occasion it was only to have him attend to the broken wing of a wild swan. He had always irritated her, but against her own inclination she had always felt a certain peculiar confidence in him.

As she descended a long flight of stone stairs, the undulating tide at her feet had become a cascade in slow motion. At the foot of the stairs she stopped.

'Keep . . . close . . . keep . . . close . . . together,' she said aloud, using her words like stepping-stones – a noticeable gap between each, which in spite of the depth and huskiness of her voice had something childlike in its effect.

The cats were gone. She stood on solid earth again. The rain thrummed outside a leaded window. She walked slowly to the door that opened upon a line of cloisters. Through the arches she saw the Doctor's house on the far side of a quadrangle. Walking out into the rain as though it were not there, she moved through the downpour with a monumental and unhurried measure, her big head lifted.

SIX

PRUNESQUALLOR was in his study. He called it his 'study'. To his sister, Irma, it was a room in which her brother barricaded himself whenever she wished to talk to him about anything important. Once within and the door locked, the chain up and the windows bolted, there was very little she could do save beat upon the door.

This evening Irma had been more tiresome than ever. What was it, she had inquired, over and over again, which prevented her from meeting someone who could appreciate and admire her? She did not want him, this hypothetical admirer, necessarily to dedicate his *whole* life to her, for a man must have his work – (as long as it didn't take too long) – mustn't he? But if he was wealthy and *wished* to dedicate his life to her – well, she wouldn't make promises, but would give the proposal a fair hearing. She had her long, unblemished neck. Her bosom was flat, it was true, and so were her feet, but after all a woman can't have everything. 'I *move* well, don't I, Alfred?' she had cried in a sudden passion. 'I say, I *move* well?'

Her brother, whose long pink face had been propped on his long white hand, raised his eyes from the tablecloth on which he had been drawing the skeleton of an ostrich. His mouth opened automatically into something that had more of a yawn than a smile about it, but a great many teeth were flashed. His smooth jaws came together again, and as he looked at his sister he pondered for the thousandth time upon the maddening coincidence of being saddled with such a sister. It being the thousandth time, he was well practised, and his ponder lasted no more than a couple of rueful seconds. But in those seconds he saw again the stark idiocy of her thin, lipless mouth, the twitching fatuity of the skin under her eyes, the roaring repression that could do no more than bleat through her voice; the smooth, blank forehead (from which the coarse, luxuriant masses of her iron-grey hair were strained back over her cranium, to meet in the compact huddle of a bun as hard as a boulder) – that forehead which was like the smoothly plastered front of an empty house, deserted save by the ghost of a bird-like tenant which hopped about in the dust and preened its feathers in front of tarnished mirrors.

'Lord! Lord!' he thought, 'why, out of all the globe's creatures, should I, innocent of murder, be punished in this way?'

He grinned again. This time there was nothing of the yawn left in the process. His jaws opened out like a crocodile's. How could any human head contain such terrible and dazzling teeth? It was a brand-new graveyard. But oh! how anonymous it was. Not a headstone chiselled with the owner's name. Had they died in battle, these nameless, dateless, dental dead, whose memorials, when the jaws opened, gleamed in the sunlight, and when the jaws met again rubbed shoulders in the night, scraping an ever closer acquaintance as the years rolled by? Prunesquallor had smiled. For he had found relief in the notion that there were several worse things imaginable than being saddled with his sister metaphorically, and one of them was that he should have been saddled with her in all its literal horror. For his imagination had caught a startlingly vivid glimpse of her upon his back, her flat feet in the stirrups, her heels digging into his flanks as, careering round the table on all fours with the bit in his mouth and with his haunches being cross-hatched with the flicks of her whip, he galloped his miserable life away.

'When I ask you a question, Alfred – I say when I ask you a question, Alfred, I like to think that you can be civil enough, even if you *are* my brother, to answer me instead of smirking to yourself.'

Now if there was one thing that the doctor could never do it was to smirk. His face was the wrong shape. His muscles moved in another way altogether.

'Sister mine,' he said, 'since thus you are, forgive, if you can, your brother. He waits breathlessly your answer to his question. It is this, my turtle-dove. *What did you say to him?* For he has forgotten so utterly that were his death dependent on it, he would be forced to live – with you, his fruit-drop, with you alone.'

Irma never listened beyond the first five words of her brother's somewhat involved periods, and so a great many insults passed over her head. Insults, not vicious in themselves, they provided the Doctor with a form of verbal self-amusement without which he would have to remain locked in his study the entire time. And, in any case, it wasn't a study, for although its walls were lined with books, it held nothing else beyond a very comfortable arm-chair and a very beautiful carpet. There was no writing-desk. No paper or ink. Not even a wastepaper basket.

'What was it you asked me, flesh of my flesh? I will do what I can for you.'

'I have been saying, Alfred, that I am not without charm. Nor without grace, or intellect. Why is it I am never approached? Why do I never have advances made to me?'

'Are you speaking financially?' asked the doctor.

'I am speaking spiritually, Alfred, and you know it. What have others got that I haven't?'

'Or conversely,' said Prunesquallor, 'what haven't they got that you already have?'

'I don't follow, Alfred. I said I don't follow you.'

'That's just what you do do,' said her brother, reaching out his arms and fluttering his fingers. 'And I wish you'd stop it.'

'But my deportment, Alfred. Haven't you noticed it? What's wrong with your sex – can't they see I *move* well?'

'Perhaps we're too spiritual,' said Doctor Prunesquallor.

'But my carriage! Alfred, my carriage!'

'Too powerful, sweet white-of-egg, far too powerful; you lurch from side to side of life's drear highway: those hips of yours rotating as you go. Oh, no, my dear one, your carriage scares them off, that's what it does. You terrify them, Irma.'

This was too much for her.

'You've never *believed* in me!' she cried, rising from the table, and a dreadful blush suffusing her perfect skin. 'But I can tell you' – her voice rose to a shrill scream – '*that I'm a lady!* What do you think I want with *men*? The beasts! I hate them. Blind, stupid, clumsy, horrible, heavy, vulgar things they are. And you're *one* of them!' she screamed, pointing at her brother, who, with his eyebrows raised a little, was continuing with his drawing of the ostrich from where he had left off. 'And *you* are one of them! Do you hear me, Alfred, one of *them*!'

The pitch of her voice had brought a servant to the door. Unwisely, he had opened it, ostensibly to ask whether she had rung for him, but in reality to see what was going on.

Irma's throat was quivering like a bowstring.

'What have ladies to do with men?' she screamed; and then, catching sight of the face of the servant at the door, she plucked a knife from the table and flung it at the face. But her aim was not all it might have been, possibly because she was so involved in being a lady, and the knife impaled itself on the ceiling immediately above her own head, where it gave a perfect imitation of the shuddering of her throat.

The doctor, adding with deliberation the last vertebra to the tail of the skeleton ostrich, turned his face firstly to the door, where the servant, his mouth hanging open, was gazing spellbound at the shuddering knife.

'Would you be so kind as to remove your redundant carcass from the door of this room, my man,' he said, in his high, abstracted voice, 'and keep it in the kitchen, where it is paid to do this and that among the saucepans, I believe . . . would you? No one rang for you. Your mistress' voice, though high, is nothing like the ringing of a bell . . . nothing at all.'

The face withdrew.

'And what's more,' came a desperate cry from immediately below the knife, 'he never comes to see me any more! Never! Never!'

The doctor rose from the table. He knew she was referring to Steerpike, but for whom she would probably never have experienced the recrudescence of this thwarted passion which had grown upon her since the youth had first dispatched his flattering arrows at her all too sensitive heart.

Her brother wiped his mouth with a napkin, brushed a crumb from his trousers, and straightened his long, narrow back.

'I'll sing you a little song,' he said. 'I made it up in the bath last night, ha! ha! ha! ha! – a whimsy little jangle, I tell myself – a whimsy little jangle.'

He began to move round the table, his elegant white hands folded about one another. 'It went like this, I fancy . . .' But as he knew she would probably be deaf to what he recited, he took her glass from beside her plate and – 'A little wine is just what you need, Irma dear, before you go to bed – for you are going straight away, aren't you, my spasmic one, to Dreamland – ha, ha, ha! – where you can be a lady all night long.'

With the speed of a professional conjurer he whipped a small packet from his pocket and, extracting a tablet, dropped it into Irma's glass. He decanted a little wine into the glass and handed it to her with the exaggerated graciousness which seldom left him. 'And I will take some myself,' he said, 'and we will drink to each other.'

Irma had collapsed into a chair, and her long marmoreal face was buried in her hands. Her black glasses, which she wore to protect her eyes from the light, were at a rakish slant across her cheek.

'Come, come, I am forgetting my promise!' cried the doctor, standing before her, very tall, slender and upright, with that celluloid head of his, all sentience and nervous intelligence, tilted to one side like a bird's.

'First a quaff of this delicious wine from a vineyard beneath a brooding hill – I can see it so clearly – and you, O Irma, can you see it, too? The peasants toiling and sweating in the sun – and why? Because they have no option, Irma. They are desperately poor, and their bowed necks are wry. And the husband-men, like every good husband, tending his love – stroking the vines with his horny hand, whispering to them, coaxing them, "O little grapes," he whispers, "give up your wine. Irma is waiting." And here it is; here it is, ha, ha, ha, ha! Delicious and cold and white, in a cut-glass goblet. Toss back your coif and quaff, my querulous queen!

Irma roused herself a little. She had not heard a word. She had been in her own private hell of humiliation. Her eyes turned to the knife in the ceiling. The thin line of her mouth twitched, but she took the glass from her brother's outstretched hand.

Her brother clinked his glass against hers and, duplicating the movement of his arm, she raised her own automatically and drank.

'And now for the little jingle which I threw off in that nonchalant way of mine. How did it go? How did it go?'

Prunesquallor knew that by the third verse the strong, tasteless soporific which had dissolved in her wine would begin to take effect. He sat on the floor at her knees and, quelling a revulsion, he patted her hand.

'Queen bee,' he said, 'look at me, if you can. Through your midnight spectacles. It shouldn't be too dreadful – for one who had fed on horrors. Now, listen . . .' Irma's eyes were already beginning to close.

'It goes like this, I think. I called it *The Osseous 'Orse.*'

> Come, flick the ulna juggler-wise
>   And twang the tibia for me!
> O Osseous 'orse, the future lies
>   Like serum on the sea.
>
> Green fields and buttercups no more
>   Regale you with delight, no, no!
> The tonic tempests leap and pour
>   Through your white pelvis ever so.

'Are you enjoying it, Irma?' She nodded sleepily.

> Come, clap your scapulae and twitch
>   The pale pagoda of your spine,
> Removed from life's eternal itch
>   What need for iodine?
>
> The Osseous 'orse sat up at once
>   And clanged his ribs in biblic pride.
> I fear I looked at him askance
>   Though he had naught to hide . . .
>
>   No hide at all . . . just . . .

At this point the doctor, having forgotten what came next, turned his eyes once more to his sister Irma; she was fast asleep. The doctor rang the bell.

'Your mistress's maid; a stretcher; and a couple of men to handle it.' (A face had appeared in the doorway.) '*And* be rapid.' The face withdrew.

When Irma had been put to bed and her lamp had been turned low and silence swam through the house, the doctor unlocked the door of his study, entered and sank back into his arm-chair. His friable-looking elbows rested upon the padded arms. His fingers were twined together into a delicate bunch, and on this bunch he supported his long and sunken jaw. After a few moments he removed his glasses and laid them on the arm of his chair. Then, with his fingers clasped together once again beneath his chin, he shut his eyes and sighed gently.

SEVEN

BUT he was not destined to more than a few moments of relaxation, for feet were soon to be heard outside his window. Only two of them, it was true, but there was something in the weight and deliberation of the tread that reminded him of an army moving in perfect unison, a dread and measured sound. The rain had quietened and the sound of each foot as it struck the ground was alarmingly clear.

Prunesquallor could recognize that portentous gait among a million. But in the silence of the evening his mind flew to the phantom army it awakened in his leap-frogging brain. What was there in the clockwork stepping of an upright host to contract the throat and bring, as does the thought of a sliced lemon, that sharp astringency to throat and jaw? Why do the tears begin to gather? And the heart to thud?

He had no time to ponder the matter now, so at one and the same time he tossed a mop of grey thatch from his brow and an army-on-the-march from his mind.

Reaching the door before his bell could clang the servants into redundance he opened it, and to the massive figure who was about to whack the door with her fist –

'I welcome your Ladyship,' he said. His body inclined itself a little from the hips and his teeth flashed, while he wondered what, in the name of all that was heterodox, the Countess thought she was doing in visiting her physician at this time of night. She visited nobody, by day or night. That was one of the things about her. Nevertheless, here she was.

'Hold your horses.' Her voice was heavy, but not loud.

One of Doctor Prunesquallor's eyebrows shot to the top of his forehead. It was a peculiar remark to be greeted with. It might have been supposed that he was about to embrace her. The very notion appalled him.

But when she said: 'You can come in now,' not only did his other eyebrow fly up his forehead, but it set its counterpart a-tremble with the speed of its uprush.

To be told he could 'come in now' when he was already inside was weird enough; but the idea of being given permission to enter his own house by a guest was grotesque.

The slow, heavy, quiet authority in the voice made the situation even more embarrassing. She had entered his hall. 'I wish to see you,' she said, but her eyes were on the door which Prunesquallor was closing. When it had barely six inches to go before the night was locked out and the latch had clicked – 'Hold!' she said, in a rather deeper tone, 'hold hard!' And then, with her big lips pursed like a child's, she gave breath to a long whistle of peculiar sweetness. A tender and forlorn note to escape from so ponderous a being.

The doctor, as he turned to her, was a picture of perplexed inquiry, though his teeth were still shining gaily. But as he turned something caught the corner of his eye. Something white. Something that moved.

Between the space left by the all-but-closed door, and very close to the ground, Doctor Prunesquallor saw a face as round as a hunter's moon, as soft as fur. And this was no wonder, for it was a face of fur, peculiarly blanched in the dim light of the hall. No sooner had the Doctor reacted to this face than another took its place, and close upon it, silent as death, came a third, a fourth, a fifth . . . In single file there slid into the hall, so close upon each other's tails that they might have been a continuous entity, her ladyship's white clowder.

Prunesquallor, feeling a little dizzy, watched the undulating stream flow past his feet as he stood with his hand on the door-knob. Would they never end? He had watched them for over two minutes.

He turned to the Countess. She stood in coiling froth like a lighthouse. By the dim glow of the hall lamp her red hair threw out a sullen light.

Prunesquallor was perfectly happy again. For what had irked him was not the cats, but the obscure commands of the Countess. Their meaning was now self-evident. And yet, how peculiar to have enjoined a swarm of cats to hold their horses!

The very thought of it got hold of his eyebrows again, which had lowered themselves reluctantly while he waited for his chance to close the door, and they had leapt up his forehead as though a pistol had been cracked and a prize awaited the fastest.

'We're . . . all . . . here,' said the Countess. Prunesquallor turned to the door and saw that the stream had, indeed, run dry. He shut the door.

'Well, well, well, well!' he trilled, standing on his toes and fluttering his hands, as though he were about to take off like a fairy. 'How *delightful!* how very, very *delightful* that you should call, your Ladyship. God bless my ascetic soul! if you haven't whipped the old hermit out of his introspection. Ha, ha, ha, ha, ha! And here, as you put it, you all are. There's no doubt about that, is there? What a party we will have! *Mew*sical chairs and all! ha ha ha ha ha ha ha.'

The almost unbearable pitch of his laughter created an absolute stillness in the hall. The cats, sitting bolt upright, had their round eyes fixed on him.

'But I keep you waiting!' he cried. 'Waiting in my outer rooms! Are you a mere valetudinarian, my dear Ladyship, or some prolific mendicant whose bewitched offspring she hopes I can return to human shape? Of course you are not, by all that's evident, so why should you be left in this cold – this damp – this obnoxious hell of a hall, with the rain pouring off you in positive waterfalls . . . and so . . . and so, *if* you'll allow me to lead on . . .' – he waved a long, thin, delicate arm with as white a hand on the end of it, which fluttered like a silk flag – '. . . I'll throw a few doors open, light a lamp or two, flick away a few crumbs in readiness for . . . What wine shall it be?'

He began to tread his way to the sitting-room with a curious flicking movement of the feet.

The Countess followed him. The servants had cleared the table of the supper dishes and the room had been left with so serene a composure about it that it was hard to believe that it was but a short while ago in this same room that Irma had disgraced herself.

Prunesquallor flung wide the door of the sitting-room for the Countess to pass through. He flung it with a spectacular abandon: it seemed to imply that if the door broke, or the hinges snapped, or a picture was jerked off the wall, what of it? This was his house; he could do what he liked with it. If he chose to jeopardize his belongings, that was his affair. This was an occasion when such meagre considerations would only enter the minds of the vulgar.

The Countess advanced down the centre of the room and then stopped. She stared about her abstractedly – at the long lemon-yellow curtain, the carved furniture, the deep green rug, the silver, the ceramics, the pale grey-and-white stripes of the wallpaper. Perhaps her mind reverted to her own candle-smelling, bird-filled, half-lit chaos of a bedroom, but there was no expression on her face.

'Are . . . all . . . your . . . rooms . . . like . . . this . . .?' she muttered. She had just seated herself in a chair.

'Well, let me see,' said Prunesquallor. 'No, not exactly, your Ladyship . . . not *exactly*.'

'I . . . suppose . . . they're . . . spotless. Is . . . that it . . . eh?'

'I believe they are; yes, yes, I quite believe they are. Not that I see more than five or six of them during the course of a year; but what with the servants flitting here and there with dusters and brooms, and clanking their buckets and wringing things out – and what with my sister Irma flitting after them to see that the right things are wrung and the wrung things are right, I have no doubt that we are all but sterilized to extinction: no tartar on the banisters: not a microbe left to live its life in peace.'

'I see,' said the Countess. It was extraordinary how damning those two words sounded. 'But I have come to talk to you.'

For a moment she stared about her ruminatively. The cats, with not a whisker moving, were everywhere in the room. The mantelpiece was heraldic with them. The table was a solid block of whiteness. The couch was a snowdrift. The carpet was sewn with eyes.

Her ladyship's head, which always seemed far bigger than any human head had a right to be, was turned away from the doctor and down a little, so that her powerful throat was tautened: yet ample along the near side. Her profile was nearly hidden by her cheek. Her hair was built up, for the most part, into a series of red nests and for the rest smouldered as it fell in snakelike coils to her shoulders, where it all but hissed.

The doctor twirled about on his narrow feet and flung open a silkwood cabinet door with a grandiose flourish, bringing his long white hands together beneath his chin and tossing a mop of grey hair from his forehead. He flashed his brilliant teeth at the Countess (who was still presenting him with her shoulder and about an eighth of her face), and then with eyebrows raised –

'Your Ladyship,' he said, 'that you should decide to visit me, and to discuss some subject with me, is an honour. But first, *what* will you drink?'

The doctor in flinging open the door of his cabinet had revealed as rare and delicately chosen a group of wines as he had ever selected from his cellar.

The Countess moved her great head through the air.

'A jug of goat's milk, Prunesquallor, if you please,' she said.

What there was in the doctor that loved beauty, selectivity, delicacy and excellence – and there was a good deal in him that responded to these abstractions – shrank up like the horn of a snail and all but died. But his hand, which was poised in the air and was half-way to the trapped sunlight of a long-lost vineyard, merely fluttered to and fro as though it was conducting some gnomic orchestra, while he turned about, apparently in full control of himself. He bowed, and his teeth flashed. Then he rang the bell, and when a face appeared at the door –

'Have we a goat?' he said. 'Come, come, my man – yes or no. Have we, or haven't we, a goat?'

The man was positive that they had no such thing.

'Then you will find one, if you please. You will find one immediately. It is wanted. That will do.'

The Countess had seated herself. Her feet were planted apart and her heavy freckled arms were along the sides of her chair. In the silence that followed even Prunesquallor could think of nothing to say. The stillness was eventually broken by the voice of the Countess.

'Why do you have knives sticking in your ceiling?'

The doctor recrossed his legs and followed her impassive gaze which was fixed on the long bread-knife that suddenly appeared to fill the room. A knife in the fender, on a pillow, or under a chair is one thing, but a knife surrounded by the blank white wasteland of a ceiling has no shred of covering – is as naked and blatant as a pig in a cathedral.

But any subject was fruitful to the doctor. It was only a lack of material, a rare enough contingency in him, that he found appalling.

'That knife, your ladyship,' he said, giving the implement a glance of the deepest respect, 'bread-knife though it be, has a history. A history, madam! It has indeed.'

He turned his eyes to his guest. She waited impassively.

'Humble, unromantic, ill-proportioned, crude as it looks, yet it means much to me. Indeed, madam, it is so, and I am no sentimentalist. And *why?* you will be asking yourself. Why? Let me tell you all.'

He clasped his hands together and raised his narrow and elegant shoulders.

'It was with that knife, your ladyship, that I performed my first successful operation. I was among mountains. Huge tufted things. Full of character; but no charm. I was alone with my faithful mule. We were lost. A meteor flew overhead. What use was that to us? No use at all. It merely irritated us. For a moment it showed a track through the fever-dripping ferns. It was obviously the wrong one. It would only have taken us back to a morass we had just spent half a day struggling out of. What a sentence! What a vile sentence, your Ladyship, ha, ha, ha, ha, ha! Where was I? Ah, yes! Plunged in darkness. Miles from anywhere. What happened next? The strangest thing. Prodding my mule forward with my walking-cane – I was riding the brute at the time – it suddenly gave a cry like a child and began to collapse under me. As it subsided it turned its huge hairy head and what little light there was showed me its eyes were positively imploring me to free it from some agony or other. Now agony is an agonizing thing to happen to anyone, your Ladyship, but to locate the seat of the agony in a mule in the darkness of a mountainous and fever-dripping night is – er . . . not easy (Lytotis), ha, ha, ha! But *do* something I must. It was already upon its side in the darkness – the great thing. I had leapt from its collapsing spine and at once my faculties began to do their damndest. The brute's eyes, still fixed on mine, were like lamps that were running out of oil. I put a couple of questions to myself – pertinent ones, I felt at the time – and still do; and the first was: IS the agony spiritual or physical? If the former, the darkness wouldn't matter, but the treatment would be tricky. If the latter, the darkness would be hell; but the problem was in

my province – or very nearly. I plumped for the latter, and more by
good fortune or that curious sixth sense one has when alone with a
mule, among tufted mountains, I found almost at once it to have been
a happy guess: for directly I had decided to work on a carnal basis I got
hold of the mule's head, heaved it up, and swivelled it to such an angle
that by the glow of its eyes I was able to illumine – faintly, of course,
but to illumine, none the less – with a dull glow, the *rest* of its body. At
once I was rewarded. It was a pure case of "foreign body". Coiled – I
couldn't tell you how many times – round the beast's hind leg, was a
python! Even at that ghastly and critical moment I could see what a
beautiful thing it was. Far more beautiful than my old brute of a mule.
But did it enter my head that I should transfer my allegiance to the
reptile? No. After all, there is such a thing as loyalty as well as beauty.
Besides, I hate walking, and the python would have taken some riding,
your Ladyship: the very saddling would tax a man's patience. And
besides . . .'

The doctor glanced at his guest and immediately wished he hadn't.
Taking out his silk handkerchief, he wiped his brow. Then he flashed
his teeth, and with somewhat less ebullience in his voice . . . 'It was
then that I thought of my bread-knife,' he added.

For a moment there was silence. And then, as the doctor filled his
lungs and was ready to continue –

'How old are you?' said the Countess. But before Doctor Prunesquallor could readjust himself there was a knock at the door and the
servant entered with a goat.

'Wrong sex, you idiot!' As the Countess spoke she rose heavily from
her chair and, approaching the goat, she fondled its head with her big
hands. It strained towards her on the rope leash and licked her arm.

'You amaze me,' said the doctor to the servant. 'No wonder you cook
badly. Away, my man, away! Unearth yet another, and get the gender
right, for the love of mammals! Sometimes one wonders what kind of
a world one is living in – by all things fundamental, one really
does.'

The servant disappeared.

'Prunesquallor,' said the Countess, who had moved to the window
and was staring out across the quadrangle.

'Madam?' queried the doctor.

'I am not easy in my heart, Prunesquallor.'

'Your heart, madam?'

'My heart and my mind.'

She returned to her chair, where she seated herself again and laid her
arms along the padded sides as before.

'In what way, your Ladyship?' Prunesquallor's voice had lost its
facetious vapidity.

'There is mischief in the castle,' she replied. 'Where it is I do not know. But there is mischief.' She stared at the doctor.

'Mischief?' he said at last. 'Some influence, do you mean – some bad influence, madam?'

'I do not know for sure. But something has changed. My bones know it. There is someone.'

'Someone?'

'An enemy. Whether ghost or human I do not know. But an enemy. Do you understand?'

'I understand,' said the doctor. Every vestige of his waggery had disappeared. He leaned forward. 'It is not a ghost,' he said. 'Ghosts have no itch for rebellion.'

'Rebellion!' said the Countess loudly. 'By whom?'

'I do not know. But what else can it be you sense, as you say, in your bones, madam?'

'Who would *dare* to rebel?' she whispered, as though to herself. 'Who would dare? . . .' And then, after a pause: 'Have you *your* suspicions?'

'I have no proof. But I will watch for you. For, by the holy angels, since you have brought the matter up there is evil abroad and no mistake.'

'Worse,' she replied, 'worse than that. There is perfidy.'

She drew a deep breath and then, very slowly: '. . . and I will crush its life out: I will break it: not only for Titus' sake and for his dead father's, but more – for Gormenghast.'

'You speak of your late husband, madam, the revered Lord Sepulchrave. Where are his remains, madam, if he is truly dead?'

'And more than that, man, more than that! What of the fire that warped his brilliant brain? What of that fire in which, but for that youth Steerpike . . .' She lapsed into a thick silence.

'And what of the suicide of his sisters; and the disappearance of the chef on the same night as his Lordship your husband – and all within a year, or little more: and since then a hundred irregularities and strange affairs? What lies at the back of all this? By all that's visionary, madam, your heart has reason to be uneasy.'

'And there is Titus,' said the Countess.

'There is Titus,' the doctor repeated as quick as an echo.

'How old is he now?'

'He is nearly eight.' Prunesquallor raised his eyebrows. 'Have you not seen him?'

'From my window,' said the Countess, 'when he rides along the South Wall.'

'You should be with him, your Ladyship, now and then,' said the doctor. 'By all that's maternal, you really should see more of your son.'

The Countess stared at the doctor, but what she might have replied was stunned for ever by a rap at the door and the reappearance of the servant with a nannygoat.

'Let her go!' said the Countess.

The little white goat ran to her as though she were a magnet. She turned to Prunesquallor. 'Have you a jug?'

The doctor turned his head to the door. 'Fetch a jug,' he said to the disappearing face.

'Prunesquallor,' she said, as she knelt down, a prodigious bulk in the lamplight, and stroked the sleek ears of the goat, 'I will not ask you on whom your suspicions lie. No. Not yet. But I expect you to watch, Prunesquallor – to watch everything, as I do. You must be all aware, Prunesquallor, every moment of the day. I expect to be informed of heterodoxy, wherever it may be found. I have a kind of faith in you, man. A kind of faith in you. I don't know why . . .' she added.

'Madam,' said Prunesquallor, 'I will be on tip-toe.'

The servant came in with a jug, and retired.

The elegant curtains fluttered a little in the night air. The light of the lamp was golden in the room, glimmering on the porcelain bowls, on the squat cut-glass vases and the tall cloisonné ware: on the vellum backs of books and the glazed drawings that hung upon the walls. But

its light was reflected most vividly from the countless small white faces
of the motionless cats. Their whiteness blanched the room and chilled
the mellow light. It was a scene that Prunesquallor never forgot. The
Countess on her knees by the dying fire: the goat standing quietly while
she milked it with an authority in the deft movement of her fingers that
affected him strangely. Was this heavy, brusque, uncompromising
Countess, whose maternal instincts were so shockingly absent: who had
not spoken to Titus for a year: who was held in awe, and even in fear,
by the populace: who was more a legend than a woman – was this
indeed *she*, with the half-smile of extraordinary tenderness on her wide
lips?

And then he remembered her voice again, when she had whispered:
'Who would dare to rebel? Who would *dare*?' and then the full, ruthless
organ-chord of her throat: 'And I will crush its life out! I will break it!
Not only for Titus' sake . . .'

EIGHT

CORA and Clarice, although they did not know it, were imprisoned
in their apartments. Steerpike had nailed and bolted from the outside
all their means of exit. They had been incarcerated for two years,
their tongues having loosened to the brink of Steerpike's undoing.
Cunning and patient as he was with them, the young man could find
no other foolproof way of ensuring their permanent silence on the
subject of the library fire. No other way – but one. They believed
that they alone among the inhabitants of the castle were free of a
hideous disease of Steerpike's invention, and which he referred to as
'Weasel plague'.

The twins were like water. He could turn on or off at will the taps of
their terror. They were pathetically grateful that through his superior
wisdom they were able to remain in relative health. If a flat refusal to
die in the face of a hundred reasons why they should, could be called
health. They were obsessed by the fear of coming into contact with the
carriers. He brought them daily news of the dead and dying.

Their quarters were no longer those spacious apartments where
Steerpike first paid them his respects seven years ago. Far from them
having a Room of Roots and a great tree leaning over space hundreds
of feet above the earth, they were now on the ground level in an obscure
precinct of the castle, a dead end, a promontory of dank stone, removed
from even the less frequented routes. Not only was there no way through

it, but it was shunned also for reason of its evil reputation. Unhealthy with noxious moisture, its very breath was double pneumonia.

Ironically enough, it was in such a place as this that the aunts rejoiced in the erroneous belief that they alone could escape the virulent and ghastly disease that was in their imaginations prostrating Gormenghast. They had by now become so self-centred under Steerpike's guidance as to be looking forward to the day when they, as sole survivors, would be able (after due precautions) to pace forth and be at last, after all these long years of frustration, the unopposed claimants to the Groan crown, that massive and lofty symbol of sovereignty, with its central sapphire the size of a hen's egg.

It was one of their hottest topics: whether the crown should be sawn in half and the sapphire split, so that they could always be wearing at least part of it, or whether it should be left intact and they should wear it on alternate days.

Hot and contested though this subject was, it stirred no visible animation. Not even their lips were seen to move, for they had acquired the habit of keeping them slightly parted and projecting their toneless voices without a tremor of the mouth. But for most of the time their long, solitary days were passed in silence. Steerpike's spasmodic appearances – and they had become less and less frequent – were, apart from their wild, bizarre and paranoiac glimpses of a future of thrones and crowns, their sole excitement.

How was it that their Ladyships Cora and Clarice could be hidden away in this manner and the iniquity condoned?

It was not condoned; for two years previously they had been as far as Gormenghast was concerned buried with a wealth of symbolism in the tombs of the Groans, a couple of wax replicas having been modelled by Steerpike for the dread occasion. A week before these effigies were lowered into the sarcophagus, a letter, as from the twins, but in reality forged by the youth, had been discovered in their apartments. It divulged the dreadful information that the sisters of the seventy-sixth Earl, who had himself disappeared from the castle without a trace, bent upon their self-destruction, had stolen by night from the castle grounds to make an end of themselves among the ravines of Gormenghast mountain.

Search parties, organized by Steerpike, had found no trace.

On the night previous to the discovery of the note, Steerpike had conveyed the Twins to the rooms which they now occupied upon some pretext connected with an inspection of a couple of sceptres he had found and regilded.

All this seemed a long time ago. Titus had been a mere infant. Flay but lately banished. Sepulchrave and Swelter had melted into air. Like teeth missing from the jaw of Gormenghast, the disappearance of the

Twins, added to those others, gave to the Castle for a time an unfamiliar visage and an aching bone. To some extent the wounds had healed and the change of face had been accepted. Titus was, after all, alive and well – and the continuation of the Family assured.

The Twins were sitting in their room, after a day of more than usual silence. A lamp, set on an iron table (it burnt all day), gave them sufficient light to do their embroidery; but for some while neither of them applied herself to her work.

'What a long time life takes!' said Clarice at last. 'Sometimes I think it's hardly worth encroaching on.'

'I don't know anything about *encroaching*,' replied Cora; 'but since you have spoken I might as well tell you that you've forgotten something, as usual.'

'What have I forgotten?'

'You've forgotten that I did it yesterday and it is your turn today – thus.'

'My turn to what?'

'To *comfort* me,' said Cora, looking hard at a leg of the iron table. 'You can go on doing it until half-past seven, and then it will be your turn to be depressed.'

'Very well,' said Clarice; and she began at once to stroke her sister's arm.

'No, no, no!' said Cora, 'don't be so obvious. Do things without any mention – like getting tea, for instance, and laying it quietly before me.'

'All right,' answered Clarice, rather sullenly. 'But you've spoilt it now – haven't you? – telling me what to do. It won't be so thoughtful of me, will it? But perhaps I could get coffee instead.'

'Never mind all that,' Cora replied, 'you talk too much. I don't want to suddenly find it's your turn.'

'What! For *my* depression?'

'Yes, yes,' her sister said irritably; and she scratched the back of her round head.

'Not that I think you deserve one.'

Their conversation was disturbed, for a curtain parted behind them and Steerpike approached, a sword-stick in his hand.

The Twins rose together and faced him, their shoulders touching.

'How are my lovebirds?' he said. He lifted his slender stick and, with ghastly impudence, tickled their ladyships' ribs with its narrow ferruled end. No expression appeared on their faces, but they went through the slow, wriggling motions of Eastern dancers. A clock chimed from above the mantelpiece, and as it ceased the monotonous sound of the rain appeared to redouble its volume. The light had become very bad.

'You haven't been here for a long while,' said Cora.

'How true,' said Steerpike.

'Had you forgotten us?'

'Not a bit of it,' he said, 'not a bit of it.'

'What happened, then?' asked Clarice.

'Sit down!' said Steerpike harshly, 'and listen to me.' He stared them out of countenance until their heads dropped, abashed, and they found themselves staring at their own clavicles. 'Do you think it is easy for me to keep the plague from your door and to be at your beck and call at the same time? Do you?'

They shook their heads slowly like pendulums.

'Then have the grace not to interrogate me!' he cried in mock anger. 'How dare you snap at the hand that feeds you! How dare you!'

The Twins, acting together, rose from their chairs and started moving across the room. They paused a moment and turned their eyes to Steerpike in order to make sure that they were doing what was expected of them. Yes. The stern finger of the young man was pointing to the heavy damp carpet that covered the floor of the room.

Steerpike derived as much pleasure in watching these anile and pitiful creatures, dressed in their purple finery, as they crawled beneath the carpet as he got from anything. He had led them gradually, and by easy and cunning steps, from humiliation to humiliation, until the distorted satisfaction he experienced in this way had become little short of a necessity to him. Were it not that he found this grotesque pleasure in the exercise of his power over them, it is to be doubted whether he would have gone to all the trouble which was involved in keeping them alive.

As he stared at the twin hummocks under the carpet he did not realize that something very peculiar and unprecedented was happening. Cora, in her warren-like seclusion, crouched in the ignominious darkness, had conceived an idea. Where it came from she did not trouble to inquire of herself, nor *why* it should have come, for Steerpike, their benefactor, was a kind of god to her, as he was to Clarice. But the idea had suddenly flowered in her brain unbidden. It was that she would very much like to kill him. Directly she had conceived the idea she felt frightened, and her fear was hardly lessened by a flat voice in the darkness saying with empty deliberation: 'So . . . would . . . I. We could do it together, couldn't we? We could do it together.'

NINE

THERE was an all but forgotten landing high in the southern wing, a landing taken over for many a decade by succeeding generations of dove-grey mice, peculiarly small creatures, little larger than the joint of a finger and indigenous to this southern wing, for they were never seen elsewhere.

In years gone by this unfrequented stretch of floor, walled off on one side with high banisters, must have been of lively interest to some person or persons; for though the colours had to a large extent faded, yet the floor-boards must once have been a deep and glowing crimson, and the three walls the most brilliant of yellows. The banisters were alternately apple-green and azure, the frames of the doorless doorways being also this last colour. The corridors that led away in dwindling perspective, continued the crimson of the floor and the yellow of the walls, but were cast in a deep shade.

The balcony banisters were on the southern side, and, in the sloping roof above them, a window let in the light and, sometimes, the sun itself, whose beams made of this silent, forgotten landing a cosmos, a firmament of moving motes, brilliantly illumined, an astral and at the same time a solar province; for the sun would come through with its long rays and the rays would be dancing with stars. Where the sunbeams struck, the floor would flower like a rose, a wall break out in crocus-light, and the banisters would flame like rings of coloured snakes.

But even on the most cloudless of summer days, with the sunlight striking through, the colours had in their brilliance the pigment of decay. It was a red that had lost its flame that smouldered from the floor-boards.

And across this old circus-ground of bygone colours the families of the grey mice moved.

When Titus first came upon the coloured banisters of the staircase it was at a point two floors below the yellow-walled balcony. He had been exploring on that lower floor, and finding himself lost he had taken fright, for room after room was cavernous with shadow or vacant and afloat with sunlight that lit the dust on the wide floors – somehow more frightening to the child in its golden dereliction than the deepest shadows. Had he not clenched his hands he would have screamed, for the very lack of ghosts in the deserted halls and chambers was in itself unnerving; for there was a sense that something had either just left each corridor, or each hall as he came upon it, or else that the stages were set and ready for its appearance.

It was with his imagination dilated and his heart hammering aloud that Titus, suddenly turning a corner, came upon a section of the staircase two floors below the haunt of the grey mice.

Directly Titus saw the stairway he ran to it, as though every banister were a friend. Even in the access of his relief, and even while the hollow echo of his footsteps was in his ears, his eyes widened at the apple-green – the azure of the banisters, each one a tall plinth of defiance. Only the rail which these bright things supported was hueless, being of a smooth, hand-worn ivory whiteness. Titus gripped the banisters and then peered through them and downward. There seemed little life in the fathoms beneath him. A bird flew slowly past a far landing; a section of plaster fell from a shadowy wall three floors below the bird, but that was all.

Titus glanced above him and saw how close he stood to the head of the stairway. Anxious as he was to escape from the atmosphere of these upper regions, yet he could not resist running to the top of the stairs, where he could see the colours burning. The small grey mice squeaked and scampered away down the passageways or into their holes. A few remained against the walls and watched Titus for a short while before returning to their sleeping or nibbling.

The atmosphere was indescribably golden and friendly to the boy: so friendly that his proximity to the hollow room below him did little to disturb his delight. He sat down, his back against a yellow wall, and watched the white motes manoeuvring in the long sunbeams.

'This is *mine! mine!*' he said aloud. 'I found it.'

TEN

THROUGH the vile subterranean light that filled the Professors' Common-room three figures appeared to float as the brown billows shifted. Tobacco smoke had made of the place a kind of umber tomb. These three were the vanguard of a daily foregathering, as sacrosanct and inevitable as the elm-top meeting place of rooks in March. But how much less healthy! A foregathering of the Professors, for it was eleven o'clock and the short recreation had begun.

Their pupils – the sparrows, as it were – of Gormenghast were racing to the vast red-sandstone yard – a yard surrounded on all sides by high ivy-covered walls of the same stone. Innumerable knife blades had snapped upon its harsh surface, for there must surely be a thousand spidery initials scored into the stone! A hundred painfully incised valedictions and observations whose significance had long since lost its edges. Deeper incisions into the red stone had mapped out patterns for some or other game of local invention. Many a boy had sobbed against these walls; many a knuckle been bruised as a head flicked sideways from the blow. Many a child had fought his way back into the open yard with bloody mouth, and a thousand swaying pyramids of boys had tottered and collapsed as the topmost clung to the ivy.

The yard was approached by a tunnel which commenced immediately beneath the long south classroom, where steps led down through a trapdoor. The tunnel, old and thick with ferns, was at this moment echoing barbarically to the cat-calls of a horde of boys as they made pell-mell for the red-stone yard, their immemorial playground.

But in the Professors' Common-room the three gentlemen were finding relaxation through an abatement rather than an increase of energy.

To enter the room from the Professors' corridor was to suffer an extraordinary change of atmosphere, no less sudden than if a swimmer in clear white water were suddenly to find himself struggling to keep afloat in a bay of soup. Not only was the air fuscous with a mixture of smells, including stale tobacco, dry chalk, rotten wood, ink, alcohol and, above all, imperfectly cured leather, but the general colour of the room was a transcription of the smells, for the walls were of horsehide, the dreariest of browns, relieved only by the scattered and dully twinkling heads of drawing-pins.

On the right of the door hung the black gowns of office in various stages of decomposition.

Of the three Professors, the first to have reached the room that morning in order to establish himself securely in the only arm-chair (it was his habit to leave the class he was teaching – or pretending to teach – at least twenty minutes before its official conclusion, in order to be certain that the chair was free) was Opus Fluke. He lay rather than sat in what was known among the staff as 'Fluke's Cradle'. Indeed he had worn that piece of furniture – or symbol of bone-laziness – into such a shape as made the descent of any other body than his own into that crater of undulating horsehair a hazardous enterprise.

Those daily indulgences before the mid-morning break and their renewal before the dinner-bell were much prized by Mr Opus Fluke, who during these periods augmented the pall of tobacco smoke already obscuring the ceiling of the Common-room with enough of his own exhaling to argue not only that the floor-boards were alight, but also that the core of the conflagration was Mr Fluke himself, lying, as he was, at an angle of five degrees with the floor, in a position that might, in any case, argue asphyxiation. But there was nothing on fire except the tobacco in his pipe and as he lay supine, the white wreaths billowing from his wide, muscular and lipless mouth (rather like the mouth of a huge and friendly lizard), he evinced so brutal a disregard for his own and other people's windpipes as made one wonder how this man could share the selfsame world with hyacinths and damsels.

His head was well back. His long, bulging chin pointed to the ceiling like a loaf of bread. His eyes followed lugubriously the wavering ascent of a fresh smoke-ring until it was absorbed into the upper billows. There was a kind of ripeness in his indolence, in his dreadful equability.

Of Opus Fluke's two companions in the Common-room the younger, Perch-Prism, was squatting jauntily on the edge of a long ink-stained table. This ancient span of furniture was littered with textbooks, blue pencils, pipes filled to various depths with white ash and dottle, pieces of chalk, a sock, several bottles of ink, a bamboo walking-cane, a pool of white glue, a chart of the solar system, burned away over a large portion of its surface through some past accident with a bottle of acid, a stuffed cormorant with tin-tacks through its feet, which had no effect in keeping the bird upright; a faded globe, with the words '*Cane Slypate Thursday*' scrawled in yellow chalk across it from just below the equator to well into the Arctic Circle; any number of lists, notices, instructions; a novel called '*The Amazing Adventures of Cupid Catt*', and at least a dozen high ragged pagodas of buff-coloured copybooks.

Perch-Prism had cleared a small space at the far end of this table, and there he squatted, his arms folded. He was a smallish, plumpish man, with self-assertion redolent in every movement he made, every word he uttered. His nose was pig-like, his eyes button-black and horribly alert, with enough rings about them to lasso and strangle at birth any idea that he was under fifty. But his nose, which appeared to be no more than a few hours of age, did a great deal in its own porcine way to offset the effect of the rings around the eyes, and to give Perch-Prism, on the balance, an air of youth.

Opus Fluke in his favourite chair: Perch-Prism perched on the table's edge: but the third of these gentlemen in the Common-room, in contrast to his colleagues, appeared to have something to do. Gazing into a small shaving-mirror on the mantelpiece, with his head on one side to catch what light could force its way through the smoke, Bellgrove was examining his teeth.

He was a fine-looking man in his way. Big of head, his brow and the bridge of his nose descended in a single line of undeniable nobility. His jaw was as long as his brow and nose together and lay exactly parallel in profile to those features. With his leonine shock of snow-white hair there was something of the major prophet about him. But his eyes were disappointing. They made no effort to bear out the promise of the other features, which would have formed the ideal setting for the kind of eye that flashes with visionary fire. Mr Bellgrove's eyes didn't flash at all. They were rather small, a dreary grey-green in colour, and were quite expressionless. Having seen them it was difficult not to bear a grudge against his splendid profile as something fraudulent. His teeth were both carious and uneven and were his worst feature.

With great rapidity Perch-Prism stretched out his arms and legs simultaneously and then withdrew them. At the same time he closed his bright black eyes and yawned as widely as his small, rather prim mouth could manage. Then he clapped his hands beside him on the table, as much as to say: 'One can't sit here dreaming all day!' Puckering his brow, he took out a small, elegant and well-kept pipe (he had long since discovered it as his only defence against the smoke of others) and filled it with quick, deft fingers.

He half-closed his eyes as he lit up, his pig-like nose catching the flare of the light on its underside. With his black and cerebral eyes hidden for a moment behind his eyelids, he was less like a man than a ravaged suckling.

He drew quickly three or four times at his pipe. Then, after removing it from his neat little mouth –

'*Must* you?' he said, his eyebrows raised.

Opus Fluke, lying along his chair like a stretcher-case, moved nothing except his lazy eyes, which he turned slowly until they were semi-focusing bemusedly upon Perch-Prism's interrogatory face. But he saw that Perch-Prism had evidently addressed himself to someone else, and Mr Fluke, rolling his eyes languidly back, was able to obtain an indistinct view of Bellgrove behind him. That august gentleman, who had been examining his teeth with such minute care, frowned magnificently and turned his head.

'Must I *what*? Explain yourself, dear boy. If there's anything I abominate it's sentences of two words. You talk like a fall of crockery, dear boy.'

'You're a damned old pedant, Bellgrove, and much overdue for burial,' said Perch-Prism, 'and as quick off the mark as a pregnant turtle. For pity's sake stop playing with your teeth!'

Opus Fluke in his battered chair, dropped his eyes and, by parting his long leather-lipped mouth in a slight upward curve, might have been supposed to be registering a certain sardonic amusement had not a formidable volume of smoke arisen from his lungs and lifted itself out of his mouth and into the air in the shape of a snow-white elm.

Bellgrove turned his back to the mirror and lost sight of himself and his troublesome teeth.

'Perch-Prism,' he said, 'you're an insufferable upstart. What the hell have my teeth got to do with you? Be good enough to leave them to me, sir.'

'Gladly,' said Perch-Prism.

'I happen to be in pain, my dear fellow.' There was something weaker in Bellgrove's tone.

'You're a hoarder,' said Perch-Prism. 'You cling to bygone things. They don't suit you, anyway. Get them extracted.'

Bellgrove rose into the ponderous prophet category once more. 'Never!' he cried, but ruined the majesty of his utterance by clasping at his jaw and moaning pathetically.

'I've no sympathy at all,' said Perch-Prism, swinging his legs. 'You're a stupid old man, and if you were in my class I would cane you twice a day until you had conquered (one) your crass neglect, (two) your morbid grasp upon putrefaction. I have no sympathy with you.'

This time as Opus Fluke threw out his acrid cloud there was an unmistakable grin.

'Poor old bloody Bellgrove,' he said. 'Poor old Fangs!' And then he began to laugh in a peculiar way of his own which was both violent and soundless. His heavy reclining body, draped in its black gown, heaved to and fro. His knees drew themselves up to his chin. His arms dangled over the sides of the chair and were helpless. His head rolled from side to side. It was as though he were in the last stages of strychnine poisoning. But no sound came, nor did his mouth even open. Gradually the spasm grew weaker, and when the natural sand colour of his face had returned (for his corked-up laughter had turned it dark red) he began his smoking again in earnest.

Bellgrove took a dignified and ponderous step into the centre of the room.

'So I am "Bloody Bellgrove" to you, am I, Mr Fluke? That is what you think of me, is it? That is how your crude thoughts run. Aha! . . . aha! . . .' (His attempt to sound as though he were musing philosophically upon Fluke's character was a pathetic failure. He shook his venerable head.) 'What a coarse type you are, my friend. You are like an animal – or even a vegetable. Perhaps you have forgotten that as long as fifteen years ago I was considered for Headship. Yes, Mr Fluke, "*considered*". It was then, I believe, that the tragic mistake was made of your appointment to the staff. H'm . . . Since then you have been a disgrace, sir – a disgrace for fifteen years – a disgrace to our calling. As for me, unworthy as I am, yet I would have you know that I have more experience behind me than I would care to mention. You're a slacker, sir, a damned slacker! And by your lack of respect for an old scholar you only . . .'

But a fresh twinge of pain caused Bellgrove to grab at his jaw.

'Oh, my *teeth*!' he moaned.

During this harangue Mr Opus Fluke's mind had wandered. Had he been asked he would have been unable to repeat a single word of what had been addressed to him.

But Perch-Prism's voice cut a path through the thick of his reverie.

'My dear Fluke,' it said, 'did you, or didn't you, on one of those rare occasions when you saw fit to put in an appearance in a classroom – on this occasion with the gamma Fifth, I believe – refer to me as a "bladder-headed cock"? It has come to my hearing that you referred to me as exactly that. Do tell me: it sounds so like you.'

Opus Fluke stroked his long, bulging chin with his hand.

'Probably,' he said at last, 'but I wouldn't know. I never listen.' The extraordinary paroxysm began again – the heaving, rolling, helpless, noiseless body-laughter.

'A convenient memory,' said Perch-Prism, with a trace of irritability in his clipped, incisive voice. 'But what's that?'

He had heard something in the corridor outside. It was like the high, thin, mewing note of a gull. Opus Fluke raised himself on one elbow. The high-pitched noise grew louder. All at once the door was flung open from without and there before them, framed in the doorway, was the Headmaster.

ELEVEN

IF ever there was a primogenital figure-head or cipher, that archetype had been resurrected in the shape of Deadyawn. He was pure symbol. By comparison, even Mr Fluke was a busy man. It was thought that he had genius, if only because he had been able to delegate his duties in so intricate a way that there was never any need for him to do anything at all. His signature, which was necessary from time to time at the end of long notices which no one read, was always faked, and even the ingenious system of delegation whereon his greatness rested was itself worked out by another.

Entering the room immediately behind the Head a tiny freckled man was seen to be propelling Deadyawn forward in a high rickety chair, with wheels attached to its legs. This piece of furniture, which had rather the proportions of an infant's high chair, and was similarly fitted with a tray above which Deadyawn's head could partially be seen, gave fair warning to the scholars and staff of its approach, being in sore need of lubrication. Its wheels screamed.

Deadyawn and the freckled man formed a compelling contrast. There was no reason why they should *both* be human beings. There seemed no common denominator. It was true that they had two legs each, two eyes each, one mouth apiece, and so on, but this did not seem to argue any similarity of *kind*, or if it did only in the way that giraffes and stoats are classified for convenience sake under the commodious head of 'fauna'.

Wrapped up like an untidy parcel in a gun-grey gown emblazoned with the signs of the zodiac in two shades of green, none of which signs could be seen very clearly for reason of the folds and creases, save for Cancer the crab on his left shoulder, was Deadyawn himself, and all but asleep. His feet were tucked beneath him. In his lap was a hot-water bottle.

His face wore the resigned expression of one who knew that the only difference between one day and the next lies in the pages of a calendar.

His hands rested limply on the tray in front of him at the height of his chin. As he entered the room he opened one eye and gazed absently into the smoke. He did not hurry his vision and was quite content when, after several minutes, he made out the three indistinct shapes below him. Those three shapes – Opus Fluke, Perch-Prism and Bellgrove – were standing in a line, Opus Fluke having fought himself free of his cradle as though struggling against suction. The three gazed up at Deadyawn in his chair.

His face was as soft and round as a dumpling. There seemed to be no structure in it: no indication of a skull beneath the skin.

This unpleasant effect might have argued an equally unpleasant temperament. Luckily this was not so. But it exemplified a parallel boneless-ness of outlook. There was no fibre to be found in him, and yet no weakness as such; only a negation of character. For his flaccidity was not a positive thing, unless jelly-fish are consciously indolent.

This extreme air of abstraction, of empty and bland removedness, was almost terrifying. It was that kind of unconcern that humbled the ardent, the passionate of nature, and made them wonder why they were expend-ing so much energy of body and spirit when every day but led them to the worms. Deadyawn, by temperament or lack of it, achieved unwittingly what wise men crave: equipoise. In his case an equipoise between two poles which did not exist: but nevertheless there he was, balanced on an imaginary fulcrum.

The freckled man had rolled the high chair to the centre of the room. His skin stretched so tightly over his small bony and rather insect-like face that the freckles were twice the size they would normally have been. He was minute, and as he peered perkily from behind the legs of the high chair, his carrot-coloured hair shone with hair-oil. It was brushed flat across the top of his little bony insect-head. On all sides the walls of horse-hide rose into the smoke and smelt perceptibly. A few drawing-pins glimmered against the murky brown leather.

Deadyawn dropped one of his arms over the side of the high chair and wriggled a languid forefinger. 'The Fly' (as the freckled midget was called) pulled a piece of paper out of his pocket, but instead of passing it up to the Headmaster he climbed, with extraordinary agility, up a dozen rungs of the chair and cried into Deadyawn's ear: 'Not yet! not yet! Only three of them here!'

'What's that?' said Deadyawn, in a voice of emptiness.

'Only three of them here!'

'Which ones,' said Deadyawn, after a long silence.

'Bellgrove, Perch-Prism and Fluke,' said The Fly in his penetrating, fly-like voice. He winked at the three gentlemen through the smoke.

'Won't *they* do?' murmured Deadyawn, his eyes shut. 'They're on my staff, aren't . . . they . . .?'

'Very much so,' said The Fly, 'very much so. But your Edict, sir, is addressed to the whole staff.'

'I've forgotten what it's all about. Remind . . . me . . .'

'It's all written down,' said The Fly. 'I have it here, sir. All you have to do is to read it, sir.' And again the small red-headed man honoured the three masters with a particularly intimate wink. There was something lewd in the way the wax-coloured petal of his eyelid dropped suggestively over his bright eye and lifted itself again without a flutter.

'You can give it to Bellgrove. He will read it when the time comes,' said Deadyawn, lifting his hanging hand on to the tray before him and languidly stroking the hot-water bottle . . . 'Find out what's keeping them.'

The Fly pattered down the rungs of the chair and emerged from its shadow. He crossed the room with quick, impudent steps, his head and rump well back. But before he reached the door it had opened and two Professors entered – one of them, Flannelcat, with his arms full of exercise-books and his mouth full of seedcake, and his companion, Shred, with nothing in his arms, but with his head full of theories about everyone's sub-conscious except his own. He had a friend, by name Shrivell, due to arrive at any moment, who, in contrast to Shred, was stiff with theories about his own sub-conscious and no one else's.

Flannelcat took his work seriously and was always worried. He had a poor time from the boys and a poor time from his colleagues. A high proportion of the work he did was never noticed, but do it he must. He had a sense of duty that was rapidly turning him into a sick man. The pitiful expression of reproach which never left his face testified to his zeal. He was always too late to find a vacant chair in the Common-room, and always too early to find his class assembled. He was continually finding the arms of his gown tied into knots when he was in a hurry, and that pieces of soap were substituted for his cheese at the masters' table. He had no idea who did these things, nor any idea how they could be circumvented. Today, as he entered the Common-room, with his arms full of books and the seedcake in his mouth, he was in as much of a fluster as usual. His state of mind was not improved by finding the Headmaster looming above him like Jove among the clouds. In his confusion the seedcake got into his windpipe, the concertina of school books in his arms began to slip and, with a loud crash, cascaded to the floor. In the silence that followed there was a moan of pain, but it was only Bellgrove with his hands at his jaw. His noble head was rolling from side to side.

Shred ambled forward from the door and, after bowing slightly in Deadyawn's direction, he buttonholed Bellgrove.

'In pain, my dear Bellgrove? In pain?' he inquired, but in a hard, irritating, inquisitive voice – with as much sympathy in it as might be found in a vampire's breast.

Bellgrove bridled up his lordly head, but did not deign to reply.

'Let us take it that you *are* in pain,' continued Shred. 'Let us work on that hypothesis as a basis: that Bellgrove, a man of somewhere between sixty and eighty, is in pain. Or rather, that he *thinks* he is. One must be exact. As a man of science, I insist on exactitude. Well, then, what next? Why, to take into account that Bellgrove, supposedly in pain, also thinks that the pain has something to do with his teeth. This is absurd, of course, but must, I say, be taken into account. For what reason? Because they are symbolic. Everything is symbolic. There is no such thing as a "thing" *per se*. It is only a symbol of something else that is itself, and so on. To my way of thinking his teeth, though apparently rotten, are merely the symbol of a diseased mind.'

Bellgrove snarled.

'And why is the mind diseased?' He took hold of Bellgrove's gown just below that gentleman's left shoulder and, with his face raised, scrutinized the big head above him.

'Your mouth is twitching,' he said. 'Interesting . . . very . . . interesting. You probably do not know it, but there was bad blood in your mother. Very bad blood. Or alternatively, you dream of stoats. But no matter, no matter. To return. Where were we? Yes, yes, your teeth – the symbols, we have said – haven't we? of a diseased mind. Now what *kind* of disease? That is the point. What *kind* of disease of the mind would affect your teeth like this? Open your mouth, sir . . .'

But Bellgrove, a fresh twinge undermining his scant reserves of patience and decorum, lifted his huge boot the size of a tray and brought it down with a blind relish upon Mr Shred's feet. It covered them both and must have been excruciatingly painful, for Mr Shred's brow coloured and contracted; but he made no sound save to remark, 'Interesting, very interesting . . . probably your mother.'

Opus Fluke's body-laughter did everything except break him in half or find vent in a sound.

By now several other Professors had infiltrated through the smoke from the direction of the door. There was Shrivell, Shred's friend, or follower, for he held all Shred's opinions in the reverse direction. But for sheer discipleship Mr Shrivell was a rebel compared to the three gentlemen who, moving in a solid huddle, their three mortar-boards forming between them a practically unbroken surface, had seated themselves in a far corner, like conspirators. They owed allegiance, those three, to no member of the staff, or to any such abstraction as the 'staff' itself, but to an ancient savant, a bearded figure of no specific occupation, but whose view of Death, Eternity, Pain (and its non-existence), Truth, or, indeed, anything of a philosophic nature, was like fire in their ears.

In holding the views of their Master on such enormous themes they had developed a fear of their colleagues and a prickliness of disposition which, as Perch-Prism had cruelly pointed out to them more than once, was inconsistent with their theory of non-existence. 'Why are you so prickly,' he used to say, 'when there ain't no pain or prickles?' At which the three, Spiregrain, Splint and Throd, would all at once become a single black tent as they shot into conference with the speed of suction. How they longed at times for their bearded Leader to be with them! He knew all the answers to impertinent questions.

They were unhappy men, these three. Not with native melancholy, but in views of their theories. And there they sat: the smoke wreaths coiling round them, their eyes moving suspiciously from one face to another of their heretic brethren, in jealous fear of a challenge to their faith.

Who else had entered? Only Cutflower, the dandy; Crust, the sponger; and the choleric Mulefire.

Meanwhile The Fly had been standing in the corridor with his knuckles between his teeth, and had been emitting the shrillest of whistles. Whether they caused the sudden appearance of the few stragglers at the end of the corridor or whether these characters were in any case on their way to the Common-room, there was no doubt that The Fly's shrill music added speed to their steps.

Smoke hung above them as they approached the door, for they had no desire to enter Fluke's fug, as they called it, with virgin lungs.

'The "Yawner's" here,' said The Fly as the Professors came abreast, their gowns fluttering. A dozen eyebrows were raised. It was seldom that they saw the Headmaster.

When the door was closed upon the last of them the leather room was, indeed, no place for anyone with asthma. No flowers could flourish there unless, indeed, some gaunt and horny thing – some cactus long inured to dust and thirst. No singing birds could thrive – no, not the raven, even; for smoke would fill their thin, sweet windpipes. It knew nothing, this atmosphere, of fragrant pastures – of dawn among the dew-bright hazel woods – or rivulets or starlight. It was a leather cave of sepia fog.

The Fly, his sharp insect face hardly visible through the smoke, swarmed up the high chair, hand over hand, and found Deadyawn asleep and his water-bottle stone cold. He prodded the Headmaster in the ribs with his little bony thumb just where Taurus and Scorpio were overlapping. Deadyawn's head had sunk even lower during his sleep and was barely above the tray. His feet were still tucked under him. He was like some creature that had lost its shell, for his face was disgustingly naked. Naked not only physically, but naked in its vacancy.

At The Fly's prod he did not wake with a start, as is the normal thing: that would have been tantamount to a kind of interest in life. He merely opened one eye. Moving it from The Fly's face, he let it wander over the miscellany of gownsmen below him.

He closed his eye again. 'What . . . are . . . all . . . these . . . people . . . for?' His voice floated out of his soft head like a paper streamer. 'And why am I?' he added.

'It's all very necessary,' answered The Fly. 'Shall I remind you, sir, yet again of Barquentine's Notice?'

'Why not?' said Deadyawn. 'But not too loudly.'

'Or shall Bellgrove read it out, sir?'

'Why not?' said the Headmaster. 'But get my bottle filled first.'

The Fly climbed down the chair-rungs with the cold bottle and threaded his perky way through the group of masters to the door. Before he reached it he had, aided by the poor visibility in the room but mainly by the exceptional agility of his small thin fingers, relieved Flannelcat of an old gold watch and chain, Mr Shred of several coins, and Cutflower of an embroidered handkerchief.

When he returned with the hot-water bottle, Deadyawn was asleep again, but The Fly handed Bellgrove a roll of paper before he climbed up the wheeled chair to waken the Headmaster.

'Read it,' said The Fly. 'It's from Barquentine.'

'Why *me*?' said Bellgrove, his hand at his jaw. 'Damn Barquentine with his notices! Damn him, I say!'

He untied the roll of paper and took a few heavy paces to the window, where he held it up to what light there was.

The Professors were by then sitting on the floor, in groups or singly, like Flannelcat among the cold ashes under the mantelpiece. But for a lack of wigwams, squaws, feathers and tomahawks there might have been a tribe encamped beneath the hanging smoke.

'Come along, Bellgrove! Come along, man!' said Perch-Prism. 'Get those teeth of yours into it.'

'For a classical scholar,' said the irritating Shred, 'for a classical scholar, I have always felt that Bellgrove must be handicapped, grievously handicapped, firstly by the difficulty he finds in understanding sentences of more than seven words, and secondly by the stultifying effect on his mind of a frustrated-power complex.'

A snarl was heard through the smoke.

'Is *that* what it is? Is *that* what it is? La!'

This was Cutflower's voice. It came from the near end of the long table on which he sat, dangling his thin, elegant legs. There was so high a polish upon his narrow, pointed shoes that the high-lights of the toe caps were visible through the smoke, like torches through a fog. No other sign of feet had been seen in the room for half an hour.

'Bellgrove,' he continued, taking up where Perch-Prism had left off, 'stab away, man! Stab away! Give us the gist of it, la! Give us the gist of it. Can't he *read*, la, the old fraud?'

'Is that you, Cutflower?' said another voice. 'I've been looking for you all morning. Bless my heart! what a fine polish on your shoes, Cutflower! I wondered what the devil those lights were! But seriously, I'm very embarrassed, Cutflower. Indeed I am. It's my wife in exile, you know – ragingly ill. But what can I do, spendthrift that I am, with my bar of chocolate once a week? You see how it is, my dear chap; it's the end: or almost: unless . . . I half wondered – er – *could* you . . .? Something until Tuesday . . . Confidential, you know, ha . . . ha . . . ha . . .! How one hates asking . . . squalor, and so on . . . But seriously, Cutflower (what a dazzling pair of hoofs, old man!) but seriously, if you could manage . . .'

'Silence!' shouted The Fly, interrupting Crust, who had not realized he had been sitting so close to a colleague until he heard Cutflower's affected accents beside him. Everyone knew that Crust had no wife in exile, ill or otherwise. They also knew that his endless requests were not so much because he was poverty-stricken but were made in the desire to cut a dashing figure. To have a wife in exile who was dying in unthinkable pain appeared to Crust to give him a kind of romantic status. It was not sympathy he wanted but envy. Without an exiled and guttering mate what was he? Just Crust. That was all. Crust to his colleagues and Crust to himself. Something of five letters that walked on two legs.

But Cutflower, taking advantage of the smoke, had slipped from the table. He took a few dainty steps to his left and tripped over Mulefire's outstretched leg.

'May Satan thrash you purple!' roared an ugly voice from the floor. 'Curse your stinking feet, whoever you bloody are!'

'Poor old Mulefire! Poor old hog!' It was yet another voice, a more familiar one; and then there was the sense of something rocking uncontrollably, but there was no accompanying sound.

Flannelcat was biting at his underlip. He was overdue for his class. They were all overdue. But none save Flannelcat was perturbed on that score. Flannel knew that by now the classroom ceiling would be blue with ink: that the small bow-legged boy, Smattering, would be rolling beneath his desk in a convulsion of excited ribaldry: that catapults would be twanging freely from every wooden ambush, and stink-bombs making of his room a nauseous hell. He knew all this and he could do nothing. The rest of the staff knew all this also, but had no desire to do anything.

A voice out of the pall cried: 'Silence, gentlemen, for Mr Bellgrove!' and another . . . 'Oh, hell, my teeth! my teeth!' . . . and another . . . 'If only he didn't dream of stoats!' . . . and another: 'Where's my gold watch gone to?' and then The Fly again: 'Silence, gentlemen! Silence for Bellgrove! Are you ready, sir?' The Fly peered into Deadyawn's vacant face.

In reply Deadyawn answered: 'Why . . . not?' with a peculiarly long interval between the 'Why' and the 'not'.

Bellgrove read:

Edict 1597577361544329621707193

To Deadyawn, Headmaster, and to the Gentlemen of the Professorial Staff: to all Ushers, Curators and others in authority –

This — day of the —th month in the eighth year of the Seventy-seventh Earl, to wit: Titus, Lord of Gormenghast – notice and warning is given in regard to their attitude, treatment and methods of behaviour and approach in respect of the aforementioned Earl, who now at the threshold of the age of reason, may impress Headmaster, gentlemen of the professorial staff, ushers, curators, and the like, with the implications of his lineage to the extent of diverting these persons from their duty in regard to the immemorial law which governs the attitude which Deadyawn, etc., are strictly bound to show, inasmuch that they treat the seventy-seventh Earl in every particular and on every occasion as they would treat any other minor in their hands without let or favour: that a sense of the customs, traditions and observances – and above all, a sense of the duties attached to every branch of the Castle's life – be instilled and an indelible sense of the responsibilities which will become his when he attains his majority, at which time, with his formative years spent among the riff-raff of the Castle's youth, it is to be supposed that the 77th Earl will not only have developed an adroitness of mind, a knowledge of human nature, a certain stamina, but in addition a degree of learning dependent upon the exertions which you, Sir, Headmaster, and you, Sirs, gentlemen of the professorial staff, bring to bear, which is your bounden duty, to say nothing of the privilege and honour which it represents.

All this, Sirs, is, or should be common knowledge to you, but the 77th Earl now being in his eighth year, I have seen fit to reawaken you to your responsibilities, in my capacity as Master of Ritual, etc., in which capacity I have the authority to make appearances at any moment in any classroom I choose in order to acquaint myself with the way in which your various knowledge is inculcated, and with particular regard to its effect upon the progress of the young Earl.

Deadyawn, Sir, I would have you impress your Staff with the magnitude of their office, and in particular . . .

But Bellgrove, his jaw suddenly hammering away as upon a white-hot anvil, flung the parchment from him and sank to his knees with a howl of pain which awoke Deadyawn to such a degree that he opened both his eyes.

'What was that?' said Deadyawn to The Fly.

'Bellgrove in pain,' said the midget. 'Shall I finish the notice?'

'Why not?' said Deadyawn.

The paper was passed up to The Fly by Flannelcat, who had scrambled nervously out of the ashes, and was already imagining Barquentine in his classroom and the dirty liquid eyes of that one-legged creature fixed upon the ink that was even now trickling down the leather walls.

The Fly plucked the paper from Flannelcat's hand and continued after a preparatory whistle effected through a collusion of the knuckles, lips and windpipe. So shrill was the sound of it that the recumbent staff were jolted upright on their haunches as one man.

The Fly read quickly, one word running into the next, and finished Barquentine's edict almost at a single breath.

. . . would have you impress your Staff with the magnitude of their office, and in particular those members who confuse the ritual of their calling with mere habit, making of themselves obnoxious limpets upon the living rock; or, like vile bindweed round a breathing stem, stifle the Castle's breath.

Signed (as for) Barquentine, Master of Ritual, Keeper of the Observances, and hereditary overlord of the manuscripts by

Steerpike (Amanuensis).

Someone had lit a lantern. It did very little, as it stood on the table, but illumine with a dusky glow the breast of the stuffed cormorant. There was something disgraceful about its necessity at noon in summer-time.

'If ever there was an obnoxious limpet swaddled in bindweed you are that limpet, my friend,' said Perch-Prism to Bellgrove. 'Do you realize that the whole thing was addressed to you? You've gone too far for an old man. Far too far. What will you do when they remove you, friend? Where will you go? Have you anyone that loves you?'

'Oh, rotten hell!' shouted Bellgrove, in so loud and uncontrolled a voice that even Deadyawn smiled. It was perhaps the faintest, wannest smile that ever agitated for a moment the lower half of a human face. The eyes took no part in it. They were as vacant as saucers of milk; but one end of the mouth lifted as might the cold lip of a trout.

'Mr . . . Fly . . .' said the Headmaster in a voice as far away as the ghost of his vanished smile. 'Mr . . . Fly . . . you . . . virus, where . . . are . . . you?'

'Sir?' said The Fly.

'Was . . . that . . . Bellgrove?'

'It was, sir,' said The Fly.

'And . . . how . . . is . . . he . . . these . . . days?'

'He is in pain,' said The Fly.

'Deep . . . pain . . .?'

'Shall I inquire, sir?' said The Fly.

'Why . . . not . . .?'

'Bellgrove!' shouted The Fly.

'What is it, damn you?' said Bellgrove.

'The Head is inquiring about your health.'

'About mine?' said Bellgrove.

'About *yours*,' said the Fly.

'Sir?' queried Bellgrove, peering in the direction of the voice.

'Come . . . nearer . . .' said Deadyawn. 'I . . . can't . . . see . . . you . . . my . . . poor . . . friend.'

'Nor I you, sir.'

'Put . . . out . . . your . . . hand, . . . Bellgrove. Can . . . you . . . feel . . . anything?'

'Is this your foot, sir?'

'It . . . is . . . indeed, . . . my . . . poor . . . friend.'

'Quite so, sir,' said Bellgrove.

'Now . . . tell . . . me . . . Bellgrove, . . . tell . . . me . . .'

'Yes, sir?'

'Are . . . you . . . unwell . . . my . . . poor . . . friend?'

'Localized pain, sir.'

'Would . . . it . . . be . . . the . . . mandibles . . . ?'

'That is so, sir.'

'As . . . in . . . the . . . old . . . days . . . when . . . you . . . were . . . ambitious . . . When . . . you . . . had . . . ideals, . . . Bellgrove . . . We . . . all . . . had . . . hopes . . . of . . . you, . . . I . . . seem . . . to . . . remember.' (There was a horrible sound of laughter like porridge.)

'Indeed, sir.'

'Does . . . anyone . . . still . . . believe . . . in . . . you, . . . my . . . poor . . . poor . . . friend?'

There was no answer.

'Come . . . come. It is not for you to resent your destiny. To . . . cavil . . . at . . . the . . . sere . . . and . . . yellow . . . leaf. Oh . . . no, . . . my . . . poor . . . Bellgrove, . . . you . . . have . . . ripened. Perhaps . . . you . . . have . . . over-ripened. Who . . . knows? We . . . all . . . go . . . bad . . . in . . . time. Do . . . you . . . look . . . about . . . the . . . same, . . . my . . . friend?'

'I don't know,' said Bellgrove.

'I . . . am . . . tired,' said Deadyawn. 'What . . . am . . . I . . . doing . . . here? Where's . . . that . . . virus . . . Mr . . . Fly?'

'Sir!' came the musket shot.

'Get . . . me . . . out . . . of . . . this. Wheel . . . me . . . out . . . of . . . it . . . into stillness . . . Mr . . . Fly . . . Wheel . . . me . . . into . . . the . . . soft . . . darkness . . .' (His voice lifted into a ghastly treble, which though it was still empty and flat had in it the seeds of life.) 'Wheel . . . me . . .' (it cried) 'into . . . the . . . golden . . . void.'

'Right away, sir,' said The Fly.

All at once it seemed as though the professors' Common-room was full of ravenous seagulls, but the screaming came from the unoiled wheels of the high chair, which were slowly turning. The door-handle was located by Flannelcat after a few moments' fumbling and the door was pushed wide. A glow of light could be seen in the passage outside. Against this light the smoke-wreaths coiled, and a little later the high, fantastic silhouette of Deadyawn, like a sack at the apex of the rickety high chair made its creaking departure from the room like some high, black form of scaffolding with a life of its own.

The scream of the wheels grew fainter and fainter.

It was some while before the silence was broken. None present had heard that high note in the Headmaster's voice before. It had chilled them. Nor had they ever heard him at such length, or in so mystical a vein. It was horrible to think that there was more to him than the nullity which they had so long accepted. However, a voice did at last break the pensive silence.

'A very dry "do" indeed,' said Crust.

'Some kind of light, for grief's sake!' shouted Perch-Prism.

'What *can* the time be?' whimpered Flannelcat.

Someone had started a fire in the grate, using for tinder a number of Flannelcat's copybooks, which he had been unable to collect from the floor. The globe of the world was put on top, which, being of some light wood, gave within a few minutes an excellent light, great continents peeling off and oceans bubbling. The memorandum that Slypate was to be caned, which had been chalked across the coloured face, was purged away and with it the boy's punishment, for Mulefire never remembered and Slypate never reminded him.

'My, my!' said Cutflower, 'if the Head's sub-conscious ain't self-conscious call me purblind, la! . . . call me purblind! What goings-on, la!'

'What is the time, gentlemen? What can it be, if you please?' said Flannelcat, groping for his exercise-books on the floor. The scene had unnerved him, and what books he had recovered from the floor kept falling out of his arms.

Mr Shrivell pulled one of them out of the fire and, holding it by a flameless corner, waved it for a moment before the clock.

'Forty minutes to go,' he said. 'Hardly worth it . . . or is it? Personally, I think I'll just . . .'

'So will I, la!' cried Cutflower. 'If my class isn't either on fire by now or flooded out, call me witless, la!'

The same idea must have been at the back of most of their minds, for there was a general movement towards the door, only Opus Fluke remaining in his decrepit arm-chair, his loaf-like chin directed at the ceiling, his eyes closed and his leathery mouth describing a line as fatuous as it was indolent. A few moments later the husky, whispering sound of a score of flying gowns as they whisked along the walls of corridors presaged the turning of a score of door-handles and the entry into their respective classrooms of the Professors of Gormenghast.

TWELVE

A ROOF of cloud stretching to every horizon held the air motionless beneath it, as though the earth and sky, pressing towards one another, had squeezed away its breath. Below the cruddled underside of the unbroken cloud-roof, the air, through some peculiar trick of light, which had something of an underwater feeling about it, reflected enough of itself from the gaunt back of Gormenghast to make the herons restive as they stood and shivered on a long-abandoned pavement half in and half out of the clouds.

The stone stairway which led up to this pavement was lost beneath a hundred seasons of obliterating ivy, creepers and strangling weeds. No one alive had ever struck their heels into the great cushions of black moss that pranked the pavement or wandered along its turreted verge, where the herons were and the jackdaws fought, and the sun's rays, and the rain, the frost, the snow and the winds took their despoiling turns.

There had once been a great casement facing upon this terrace. It was gone. Neither broken glass nor iron nor rotten wood was anywhere to be seen. Beneath the moss and ground creepers it may be that there were other and deeper layers, rotten with antiquity; but where the long window had stood the hollow darkness of a hall remained. It opened its unprotected mouth midway along the pavement's inner verge. On either side of this cavernous opening, widely separated, were the raw holes in the stonework that were once the supporting windows. The hall itself was solemn with herons. It was there they bred and tended their young. Preponderately a heronry, yet there were recesses and niches in which by sacredness of custom the egrets and bitterns congregated.

This hall, where once the lovers of a bygone time paced and paused and turned one about another in forgotten measures to the sound of forgotten music, this hall was carpeted with lime-white sticks. Sometimes the setting sun as it neared the horizon slanted its rays into the hall, and as they skimmed the rough nests the white network of the branches flared on the floor like leprous corals, and here and there (if it were spring) a pale blue-green egg shone like a precious stone, or a nest of young, craning their long necks towards the window, their thin bodies covered with powder-down, seemed stage-lit in the beams of the westering sun.

The late sunbeams shifted across the ragged floor and picked out the long, lustrous feathers that hung from the throat of a heron that stood by a rotten mantelpiece; and then a whiteness once more as the forehead of an adjacent bird flamed in the shadows . . . and then, as the light traversed the hall, an alcove was suddenly dancing with the varied bars and blotches and the reddish-yellow of the bitterns.

As dusk fell, the greenish light intensified in the masonry. Far away, over the roofs, over the outer wall of Gormenghast, over the marches, the wasteland, the river and the foothills with their woods and spinneys, and over the distant hazes of indeterminate terrain, the claw-shaped head of Gormenghast Mountain shone like a jade carving. In the green air the herons awoke from their trances and from within the hall there came the peculiar chattering and clanking sound of the young as they saw the darkness deepening and knew that it would soon be time for their parents to go hunting.

Crowded as they had been in their heronry with its domed roof, once golden and green with a painting, but now a dark, disintegrating surface where flakes of paint hung like the wings of moths – yet each bird appeared as a solitary figure as it stepped from the hall to the terrace: each heron, each bittern, a recluse, pacing solemnly forwards on its thin, stiltlike legs.

Of a sudden in the dusk, knocking as it were a certain hollow note to which their sweet ribs echoed, they were in air – a group of herons, their necks arched back, their ample and rounded wings rising and falling in leisurely flight: and then another and another: and then a night-heron with a ghastly and hair-raising croak, more terrible than the unearthly booming note of a pair of bitterns, who soaring and spiralling upwards and through the clouds to great heights above Gormenghast, boomed like bulls as they ascended.

The pavement stretched away in greenish darkness. The windows gaped, but nothing moved that was not feathered. And nothing had moved there, save the winds, the hailstones, the clouds, the rain-water and the birds for a hundred years.

Under the high green clawhead of Gormenghast Mountain the wide stretches of marshland had suddenly become stretches of tension, of watchfulness.

Each in its own hereditary tract of water the birds stood motionless, with glistening eyes and heads drawn back for the fatal stroke of the dagger-like beak. Suddenly and all in a breath, a beak was plunged and withdrawn from the dark water, and at its lethal point there struggled a fish. In another moment the heron was mounted aloft in august and solemn flight.

From time to time during the long night these birds returned, sometimes with frogs or water-mice in their beaks or newts or lily buds.

But now the terrace was empty. On the marshlands every heron was in its place, immobile, ready to plunge its knife. In the hall the nestlings were, for the moment, strangely still.

The dead quality of the air between the clouds and the earth was strangely portentous. The green, penumbral light played over all things. It had crept into the open mouth of the hall where the silence was.

It was then that a child appeared. Whether a boy or a girl or an elf there was not time to tell. But the delicate proportions were a child's and the vitality was a child's alone. For one short moment it had stood on a turret at the far end of the terrace and then it was gone, leaving only the impression of something overcharged with life – of something slight as a hazel switch. It had hopped (for the movement was more a hop than a leap or a step) from the turret into the darkness beyond and was gone almost as soon as it had appeared, but at the same moment that the phantom child appeared, a zephyr had broken through the wall of moribund air and run like a gay and tameless thing over the gaunt, harsh spine of Gormenghast's body. It played with sere flags, dodged through arches, spiralled with impish whistles up hollow towers and chimneys, until, diving down a saw-toothed fissure in a pentagonal roof, it found itself surrounded by stern portraits – a hundred sepia faces cracked with spiders' webs; found itself being drawn towards a grid in the stone floor and, giving way to itself, to the law of gravity and to the blue thrill of a down-draught, it sang its way past seven storeys and was, all at once, in a hall of dove-grey light and was clasping Titus in a noose of air.

THIRTEEN

The old, old man in whose metaphysical net the three disciples, Spiregrain, Throd and Splint were so irrevocably tangled, leaned forward in space as though weighing on the phantom handle of an invisible stick. It was a wonder he did not fall on his face.

'Always draughty in this reach of the corridor,' he said, his white hair hanging forward over his shoulders. He struck his thighs with his hands before replacing them at a point in space where a stick would have been. 'Breaks a man up – wrecks him – makes a shadow of him – throws him to the wolves and screws his coffin down.'

Reaching down with his long arms he drew his thick socks over the ends of his trousers and then stamped his feet, straightened his back, doubled it forward again, and then threw a look of antagonism along the corridor.

'A dirty, draughty reach. No reason for it. Scuppers a man,' he said. 'And yet' – he shook his white locks – 'it isn't true, you know. I don't

believe in draughts. I don't believe I'm cold. I don't believe in anything!
ha, ha, ha, ha, ha! I can't agree with you for instance.'

His companion, a younger man, with long, hollow cheeks, cocked his
head as though it were the breech of a gun. Then he raised his eyebrow
as much as to say, 'Carry on . . . ,' but the old man remained silent.
Then the young man raised his voice as though he were raising the
dead, for it was a singularly flat and colourless affair . . .

'How do you mean, sir, that you can't agree?'

'I just can't,' said the old man, bending forward, his hands gripped
before him, 'that's all.'

The young man righted his head and dropped his eyebrow.

'But I haven't *said* anything yet: we've only just met, you know.'

'You may be right,' replied the old man, stroking his beard. 'You
may very well be right; I can't say.'

'But I tell you I haven't *spoken!*' The colourless voice was raised, and
the young man's eyes made a tremendous effort to flash; but either the
tinder was wet or the updraught insufficient, for they remained
peculiarly sparkless.

'I haven't *spoken,*' he repeated.

'Oh, *that!*' said the old man. 'I don't need to depend on that.' He
gave a low, horribly knowledgeable laugh. 'I can't agree, that's all.
With your face, for instance. It's wrong – like everything else. Life is so
simple when you see it that way – ha, ha, ha, ha!' The low, intestinal
enjoyment which he got out of his attitude to life was frightful to the
young man, who, ignoring his own nature, his melancholy, ineffectual
face, his white voice, his lightless eyes, became angry.

'And *I* don't agree with *you!*' he shouted. 'I don't agree with the way
you bend your ghastly old knacker's-yard of a body at such an absurd
angle. I don't agree with the way your white beard hangs from your
chin like dirty seaweed . . . I don't agree with your broken teeth . . .
I . . .'

The old man was delighted; his stomach laughter cackled on and
on . . . 'But nor do *I*, young man,' he wheezed . . . 'nor do I. I don't
agree with it, either. You see, I don't even agree that I'm here; and
even if I did I wouldn't agree that I ought to be. The whole thing is
ridiculously simple.'

'You're being cynical!' cried the young man; 'so you are!'

'Oh no,' said the old man with short legs, 'I don't believe in being
anything. If only people would stop trying to *be* things! What *can* they
be, after all, beyond what they already are – or would be if I believed
that they were anything?'

'Vile! vile! VILE!' shouted the young man with hollow cheeks. His
thwarted passions had found vent after thirty years of indecision.
'Surely we have long enough in the grave, you old beast, in which to be

nothing – in which to be cold and finished with! Must life be like that, too? No, no! let us burn!' he cried. 'Let us burn our blood away in life's high bonfire!'

But the old philosopher replied: 'The grave, young man, is not what you imagine. You insult the dead, young man. With every reckless word, you smirch a tomb, deface a sepulchre, disturb with clumsy boots the humble death-mound. For death is life. It is only living that is lifeless. Have you not seen them coming over the hills at dusk, the angels of eternity? Have you not?'

'No,' said the young man, 'I haven't!'

The bearded figure leaned even further forward and fixed the young man with his gaze.

'What! you have never seen the angels of eternity, with their wings as big as blankets?'

'No,' said the young man. 'And I don't want to.'

'To the ignorant nothing is profound,' said the bearded ancient. 'You called me a cynic. How can I be? I am nothing. The greater contains the less. But this I will tell you: though the Castle is a barren image – though green trees, bursting with life, are in reality bursting for lack of it – when the April lamb is realized to be nothing more nor less than a lamb in April – when these things are known and accepted, then, oh, it is then' – he was stroking his beard very fast by this time – 'that you are on the borderland of Death's amazing kingdom, where everything moves twice as fast, and the colours are twice as bright, and love is twice as gorgeous, and sin is twice as spicy. Who but the doubly purblind can fail to see that it is only on the Other Side that one can begin to Agree? But here, here . . .' he motioned with his hands as though to dismiss the terrestrial world – 'what is there to agree *with*? There is no sensation here, no sensation at all.'

'There is joy and pain,' said the young man.

'No, no, no. Pure illusion,' said the ancient. 'But in Death's amazing kingdom Joy is unconfined. It will be nothing to dance for a month on end in the celestial pastures . . . nothing at all. Or to sing as one flies astride a burning eagle . . . to sing out of the gladness of one's breast.'

'And what of pain?' said the youth.

'We have invented the idea of pain in order to indulge ourselves in self-pity,' was the reply. 'But Real Pain, as we have it on the Other Side, that *will* be worth having. It will be an experience to burn one's finger in the Kingdom.'

'What if *I* set fire to your white beard, you old fraud!' shouted the young man, who had stubbed his toes during the day and knew the validity of the earthly discomforts.

'What if you did, my child?'

'It would sting your jaw, and you know it!' cried the youth.

The supercilious smile which played across the lips of the theorist was unbearable, and his companion had no strength to stop himself as he stretched out his arm for the nearest candle and lit the beard that hung there like a challenge. It flared up quickly and gave to the horrified and astonished expression of the old man an unreal and theatrical quality which belied the very real pain, terrestrial though it was, which he felt, first of all, against his jaw and then along the sides of his head.

A shrill and terrible scream from his old throat, and the corridor was at once filled with figures, as though they had been awaiting their entrance cues. Coats were thrown over his head and shoulders and the flames stifled, but not before the excited youth with the hollow cheeks had made his escape, never to be heard of again.

SPIREGRAIN, THROD AND SPLINT

The old man was carried to his room, a small dark-red box of a place, with no carpet on the floor, but a picture over the mantelpiece of a fairy sitting in a buttercup against a very blue sky. After three days he recovered consciousness only to die of shock a moment later when he remembered what had happened.

Among those present at the death-bed in the small red room were the three friends of the old fire-blackened pedagogue.

They stood in a line, stooping a little, for the room was very low. They were standing unnecessarily close to one another for, with the slightest movement of their heads, their old black leather mortar-boards struck against one another and were tilted indecorously.

And yet it was a moving moment. They could feel the exodus of a great source of inspiration. Their master lay dying below them. Disciples to the end, they believed in the absence of physical emotion so implicitly, that when the master died what could they do but weep that the origin of their faith was gone for ever from them?

Under their black leather mortar-boards their heads dislodged the innocent air, remorselessly as though their brows, noses and jaws, like the features of a figurehead, were cleaving paths for them through viewless water. Only in their hanging gowns, their flat leather mortar-boards and the tassels that hung like the grizzly spilths that swing from turkeys' beaks, had they anything in common.

Flanking the death-bed was a low table. On it stood a small prism and a brandy bottle which held a lighted candle. This was the only illumination in the room, yet the red walls burned with a sombre effulgence. The three heads of the Professors, which were roughly at the same height from the ground, were so different as to make one wonder whether they were of the same genus. In running the eye from one face to the next, a similar sensation was experienced as when the hand is run from glass to sandpaper, from sandpaper to porridge. The sandpaper face was neither more nor less interesting than the glass one, but the eyes were forced to move slowly over a surface so roughened with undergrowth, so dangerous with its potholes and bony outcrops, its silted gullies and thorny wastes, that it was a wonder that any eye ever reached the other side.

Conversely, with the glassy face, it was all that an eye could do to keep from sliding off it.

As for the third visage, it was neither maddeningly slippery, nor rough with broken ravines and clinging ground weed. To traverse it with a sweep of the eye was as impossible as to move gradually across the glazed face.

It was a case of slow wading. The face was wet. It was always wet. It was a face seen under water. And so for an eye to take an innocent run across these *three*, there lay ahead this strange ordeal, by rock and undergrowth, by slippery ice and by a patient paddling.

Behind them on the red wall their shadows lay, about half as big again as the professors themselves.

The glassy one (Professor Spiregrain) bent his head over the body of his dead master. His face seemed to be lit from within by a murky light. There was nothing spiritual about its lambency. The hard glass nose was long and exceptionally sharp. To have said he was well shaved would give no idea of a surface that no hair could penetrate, any more than a glacier could sprout grass.

Following his example, Professor Throd lowered *his* head likewise: its features were blurred into the main mass of the head. Eyes, nose and mouth were mere irregularities beneath the moisture.

As for the third professor, Splint, when he, following the example of his colleagues, bent his head over the candle-lit corpse, it was as though a rocky and barbarous landscape had suddenly changed its angle in space. Had a cloud of snakes and parrots been flung out thereby on to the candle-bright sheets of the death-bed, it would have seemed natural enough.

It was not long before Spiregrain, Throd and the jungle-headed Mr Splint became tired of bending mutely over their master, who was, in any case, no pleasant sight even for the most zealous of disciples, and they straightened themselves.

The small red room had become oppressive. The candle was getting very low in the brandy bottle. The fairy in the buttercup over the mantelpiece smirked in the flickering light, and it was time to go.

There was nothing they could do. Their master was dead.

Said Throd of the wet face: 'It is grief's gravy, Spiregrain.'

Said Spiregrain of the slippery head: 'You are too crude, my friend. Have you no poetry in you? It is Death's icicle impales him now.'

'Nonsense,' whispered Splint, in a fierce, surly voice. He was really very gentle, in spite of his tropical face – but he became angry when he felt his more brilliant colleagues were simply indulging themselves. 'Nonsense. Neither icicle nor gravy it was. Straightforward fire, it was. Cruel enough, in all faith. But . . .' and his eyes became wild with a kind of sudden excitement more in keeping with his visage than they had been for years . . . 'but look you! He's the one who wouldn't believe in pain, you know – he didn't *acknowledge* fire. And now he's dead I'll tell you something . . . (He *is* dead, isn't he?)' . . .

Splint turned his eyes quickly to the stiff figure below him. It would be a dreadful thing if the old man was listening all the time. The other two bent over also. There could be no doubt about it, although the candlelight flickering over the fire-bitten face gave an uncanny semblance of movement to the features. Professor Splint pulled a sheet over the corpse's head before he turned to his companions.

'What *is* it?' said Spiregrain. 'Be quick!' His glass nose sliced the gloomy air as he turned his head quickly to the rugged Splint.

'It's *this*, Spiregrain. It's *this*,' said Splint, his eyes still on fire. He scratched at his jaw with a gravelly sound and took a step back from the bed. Then he held up his arms. 'Listen, my friends. When I fell down those nine steps three weeks ago, and pretended that I felt no pain, I confess to you now that I was in agony. And now! And now that *he* is dead I glory in my confession, for I am afraid of him no more; and I tell you – I tell you both, openly and with pride, that I look forward to my next accident, however serious it may be, because I will have nothing to hide. I will cry out to all Gormenghast, "I am in agony!" – and when my eyes fill with tears, they will be tears of joy and relief and not of pain. Oh, brothers! colleagues! do you not understand?'

Mr Splint took a step forward in his excitement, dropping his hands, which he had kept raised all this time (and at once they were gripped on either side). Oh, what friendship, what an access of honest friendship, rushed like electricity through their six hands.

There was no need to talk. They had turned their backs on their faith. Professor Splint had spoken for the three of them. Their cowardice (for they had never dared to express a doubt when the old man was alive) was something that bound them together now more tightly than a common valour could ever have done.

'Grief's gravy was an overstatement,' said Throd. 'I only said it because, after all, he *is* dead, and we *did* admire him in a way – and I like saying the right thing at the right time. I always have. But it was excessive.'

'So was "Death's icicle" I suppose,' said Spiregrain, rather loftily; 'but it was a neat phrase.'

'Not when he was *burned* to death,' said Throd, who saw no reason why Spiregrain should not recant as fully as himself.

'Nevertheless,' said Splint, who found himself the centre of the stage, which was usually monopolized by Spiregrain, 'we are free. Our ideals are gone. We believe in pain. In life. In all those things which he told us didn't exist.'

Spiregrain, with the guttering candle reflected in his glassy nose, drew himself up and, in a haughty tone, inquired of the others whether they didn't think it would be more tactful to discuss their dismissal of their dead master's Beliefs somewhat further from his relics. Though he was doubtless out of earshot he certainly didn't look it.

They left at once, and directly the door had shut behind them the candle flame, after a short, abortive leap into the red air, grovelled for a moment in its cup of liquid wax and expired. The little red box of a room had become, according to one's fancy, either a little black box or a tract of dread imponderable space.

Once away from the death-chamber and a peculiar lightness sang in their bones.

'You were right, Splint, my dear fellow . . . quite right. We are free, and no mistake.' Spiregrain's voice, thin, sharp, academic, had a buoyancy in it that caused his confederates to turn to him.

'I knew you had a heart under it all,' wheezed Throd. 'I feel the same.'

'No more Angels to look forward to!' yelled Splint, in a great voice.

'No more longing for Life's End,' boomed Throd.

'Come, friends,' screamed the glass-faced Spiregrain, forgetting his dignity, 'let us begin to live again!' and catching hold of their shoulders, he walked them rapidly along the corridor, his head held high, his mortar-board at a rakish angle. Their three gowns streamed behind them, the tassels of their headgear also, as they increased their pace. Turning this way and that, almost skimming the ground as they went, they threaded the arteries of cold stone until, suddenly, bursting out into the sunshine on the southern side of Gormenghast, they found ahead of them the wide sun-washed spaces, the tall trees fringing the foothills, and the mountain itself shining against the deep blue sky. For a moment the memory of the picture in their late master's room flashed through their minds.

'Oh, lush!' they cried. 'Oh, lush it is, for ever!' And, breaking into a run and then a gallop, the three enfranchised professors, hand in hand, their black gowns floating on the air, bounded across the golden landscape, their shadows leaping beside them.

FOURTEEN

It was in Bellgrove's class, one late afternoon, that Titus first thought consciously about the idea of colour: of things having colours: of everything having its own *particular* colour, and of the way in which every particular colour kept changing according to where it was, what the light was like, and what it was next to.

Bellgrove was half asleep, and so were most of the boys. The room was hot and full of golden motes. A great clock ticked away monotonously. A bluebottle buzzed slowly over the surfaces of the hot window-panes or from time to time zithered its languid way from desk to desk. Every time it passed certain desks, small inky hands would grab at it, or rulers would smack out through the tired air. Sometimes it would perch, for a moment, on an inkpot or on the back of a boy's collar and scythe its front legs together, and then its back legs, rubbing them, scything them, honing them, or as though it were a lady dressing for a ball drawing on a pair of long, invisible gloves.

Oh, bluebottle, you would fare ill at a ball! There would be none who could dance better than you; but you would be shunned: you would be too original: you would be before your time. They would not know your steps, the other ladies. None would throw out that indigo light from brow or flank – but, bluebottle, they wouldn't *want* to. There lies the agony. Their buzz of converse is not yours, bluebottle. You know no scandal, no small talk, no flattery, no jargon: you would be hopeless, for all that you can pull the long gloves on. After all, your splendour is a kind of horror-splendour. Keep to your inkpots and the hot glass panes of schoolrooms and buzz your way through the long summer terms. Let the great clock-ticks play counterpoint. Let the swish of a birch, the detonation of a paper pellet, the whispered conspiracy be your everlasting pards.

Down generations of boys, buzz, bluebottle, buzz in the summer prisons – for the boys are bored. Tick, clock, tick! Young Scarabee's on edge to fight the 'Slogger' – young Dogseye hankers for his silkworms' weaving – Jupiter minor knows a plover's nest. Tick, clock, tick!

Sixty seconds in a minute; sixty minutes in an hour; sixty times sixty.

Multiply the sixes and add how many noughts? Two, I suppose. Six sixes are thirty-six. Thirty-six and two noughts is 3,600. Three thousand and six hundred seconds in an hour. Quarter of an hour is left before the silkworms – before the 'Slogger' – before the plover's nest. Buzz-fly, buzz! Tick, clock, tick! Divide 3,600 by four and then subtract a bit because of the time taken to work it all out.

$$4 \overline{\smash)3{,}600}$$
$$900$$

Nine hundred seconds! Oh, marvellous! marvellous! Seconds are so small. One – two – three – four – seconds are so huge.

The inky fingers scrubble through the forelock – the blackboard is a grey smear. The last three lessons can be seen faintly one behind the other – like aerial perspective. A fog of forgotten figures – forgotten maps – forgotten languages.

But while Bellgrove was sleeping – while Dogseye was carving – while the clock ticked – while the fly buzzed – while the room swam in a honey-coloured milky-way of motes – young Titus (inky as the rest, sleepy as the rest, leaning his head against the warm wall, for his desk was flush with the leather) had begun to follow a train of thought, at first lazily, abstractedly, without undue interest – for it was the first train of thought that he had ever troubled to follow very far. How lazily the images separated themselves from one another or adhered for a moment to the tissue of his mind!

Titus became dreamily interested, not in their sequence but in the fact that thoughts and pictures could follow one upon the other so effortlessly. And it had been the colour of the ink, the peculiar dark and musty blue of the ink in its sunken bowl in the corner of his desk, which had induced his eyes to wander over the few objects grouped below him. The ink was blue, dark, musty, dirtyish, deep as cruel water at night: what were the other colours? Titus was surprised at the richness, the variety. He had only seen his thumb-marked books as things to read or to avoid reading: as things that got lost: things full of figures or maps. Now he saw them as coloured rectangles of pale, washed-out blue or laurel green, with the small windows cut out of them where, on the naked whiteness of the first page, he had scripted his name.

The lid of the desk itself was sepia, with golden browns and even yellows where the surface had been cut or broken. His pen, with its end chewed into a subdividing tail of wet fronds, shimmered like a fish, the indigo ink creeping up the handle from the nib, the green paint that was once so pristine blurred with the blue of the ink at the pen's belly, and then the whitish mutilated tail.

He even saw his own hand as a coloured thing before he realized it was part of him; the ochre colour of his wrist, the black of his sleeve; and then . . . and then he saw the marble, the glass marble beside the inkpot, with its swirling spirals of rainbow colours twisted within the clear, cold white glass: it was wealth. Titus fingered it and counted the coloured threads that spiralled within – red, yellow, green, violet, blue . . . and their white and crystal world, so perfect, all about them, clear and cold and smooth, heavy and slippery. How it could clink and crack like a gunshot when it struck another! When it skidded the floor and struck! Crack like a gunshot on the round and brilliant forehead of his foe! Oh, beautiful marbles! Oh, blood-alleys! Oh, clouded ones, a-swim in blood and milk! Oh, crystal worlds, that make the pockets jangle – that make the pockets heavy!

How pleasant it was to hold that cold and glittering grape on a hot summer afternoon, with the Professor asleep at his high carved desk! How lovely it was to feel the cold slipping thing in the hot palm of his sticky hand! Titus clenched it and then held it against the light. As he rolled it between his thumb and forefinger the coloured threads began to circle each other: to spiral themselves round and round and in and out in endless convolutions. Red: yellow: green: violet: blue . . . Red – yellow – green – red . . . yellow . . . red . . . *red*. Alone in his mind the red became a thought – a colour-thought – and Titus slipped away into an earlier afternoon. The ceiling, the walls, the floor of his thought were red: he was enveloped in it; but soon the walls contracted and all the surfaces dwindled together and came at last to a focus; the blur, the abstraction had gone, and in its place was a small drop of blood, warm and wet. The light caught it as it shone. It was on his knuckle, for he had fought a boy in this same classroom a year ago – in that earlier afternoon. A melancholy anger crept over Titus at this memory. This image that shone out so redly, this small brilliant drop of blood – and other sensations, flitted across this underlying anger and brought on a sense of exhilaration, of self-confidence, and fear also at having spilled this red liquid – this stream of legendary yet so real crimson. And the bead of blood lost focus, became blurred, and then, changing its hazy contour, became a heart . . . a heart. Titus put his hands against his small chest. At first he could feel nothing, but moving his finger-tips he felt the double-thud, and the drumming rushed in from another region of his memory: the sound of the river on a night when he had been alone by the high bulrushes and had seen between their inky, rope-thick columns a sky like a battle.

And the battle-clouds changed their shapes momently, now crawling across the firmament of his imagination like redskins, now whipping like red fish over the mountains, their heads like the heads of the ancient carp in Gormenghast moat, but their bodies trailing behind in festoons like rags or autumn foliage. And the sky, through which these creatures swam, endlessly, in multitudes, became the ocean and the mountains below them were under-water corals, and the sun became the eye of a subaqueous god, glowering across the sea bed. But the great eye lost its menace, for it became no bigger than the marble in Titus' hand: for, wading towards him hip deep through the waters, dilating as they neared until they pressed out and broke the frame of fancy, was a posse of pirates.

They were as tall as towers, their great brows beetling over their sunken eyes, like shelves of overhanging rocks. In their ears were hoops of red gold, and in their mouths scythe-edged cutlasses a-drip. Out of the red darkness they emerged, their eyes half closed against the sun, the water at their waists circling and bubbling with the hot light reflected from their bodies, their dimensions blotted out all else: and still they came on, until their wire-glinting breasts and rocky heads filled out the boy's brain. And still they came on, until there was only room enough for the smouldering head of the central buccaneer, a great salt-water lord, every inch of whose face was scabbed and scarred like a boy's knee, whose teeth were carved into the shapes of skulls, whose throat was circled by the tattooing of a scaled snake. And as the head enlarged, an eye became visible in the darkness of its sockets, and in a moment nothing else but this wild and sinister organ could be seen. For a short while it stayed there, motionless. There was nothing else in the great world but this – globe. It *was* the world, and suddenly like the world it rolled. And as it rolled it grew yet again, until there was nothing but the pupil, filling the consciousness; and in that midnight pupil Titus saw the reflection of himself peering forward. And someone approached him out of the darkness of the pirate's pupil, and a rust-red pinpoint of light above the figure's brow became the coiled locks of his mother's wealth of hair. But before she could reach him her face and body had faded and in the place of the hair was Fuchsia's ruby; and the ruby danced about in the darkness as though it were being jerked on the end of a string. And then it, also, was gone and the marble shone in his hand with all its spiralled colours – yellow, green, violet, blue, red . . . yellow . . . green . . . violet . . . blue . . . yellow . . . green . . . violet . . . yellow . . . green . . . yellow . . . *yellow*.

And Titus saw quite clearly not only the great sunflower with its tired prickly neck which he had seen Fuchsia carrying about for the last two days, but a hand holding it, a hand that was not Fuchsia's. It held the heavy plant aloft between the thumb and forefinger as though it was the most delicate thing in the world. Every finger of the hand was aflame with gold rings, so that it looked like a gauntlet of flaming metal – an armoured thing.

And then, all at once, blotting it out, a swarm of leaves were swirling through him, a host of yellow leaves, coiling, diving, rising, as they swept forward across a treeless desert, while overhead, like a bonfire in the sky, the sun shone down on the rushing leaves. It was a yellow world: a restless, yellow world: and Titus was beginning to drift into a yet deeper maw of the colour when Bellgrove wakened with a jerk, gathered his gown about him like God gathering a whirlwind, and brought his hand down with a dull, impotent thud on the lid of his desk. His absurdly noble head raised itself. His proud and vacant gaze settled at last on young Dogseye.

'Would it be too much to ask you,' he said at last, with a yawn which exposed his carious teeth, 'whether a young man – a not very studious young man, by name Dogseye – lies behind that mask of dirt and ink? Whether there is a human body within that sordid bunch of rags, and whether that body is Dogseye's, also.' He yawned again. One of his eyes was on the clock, the other remained bemusedly on the young pupil. 'I will put it more simply: Is that really *you*, Dogseye? Are you sitting in the second row from the front? Are you occupying the third desk from the left? And were you – if, indeed, it is you, behind that dark-blue muzzle – were you carving something indescribably fascinating on to the lid of your desk? Did I wake to catch you at it, young man?'

Dogseye, a nondescript little figure, wriggled.

'Answer me, Dogseye. Were you carving away when you thought your old master was asleep?'

'Yes, sir,' said Dogseye, surprisingly loudly; so loudly that he startled himself and glanced about him as though for the voice.

'What were you carving, my boy?'

'My name, sir.'

'What, the whole thing, my boy?'

'I'd only done the first three letters, sir.'

Bellgrove rose swathed. He moved, a benign, august figure, down the dusty aisle between the desks until he reached Dogseye.

'You haven't finished the "G",' he said in a far-away, lugubrious voice. 'Finish the "G" and leave it at that. And leave the "EYE" for other things . . .' – an inane smirk began to flit across the lower part of his face – 'such as your grammar-book,' he said brightly, his voice horribly out of character. He began to laugh in such a way as might develop into something beyond control, but he was brought up short with a twinge of pain and he clutched at his jaw, where his teeth cried out for extraction.

After a few moments – 'Get up,' he said. Seating himself at Dogseye's desk he picked up the penknife before him and worked away at the 'G' of 'DOG' until a bell rang and the room was transformed into a stampeding torrent of boys making for the classroom door as though they expected to find upon the other side the embodiment of their separate dreams – the talons of adventure, the antlers of romance.

IRMA WANTS A PARTY

'Very well, then, and so you *shall!*' cried Alfred Prunesquallor. 'So you shall, indeed.'

There was a wild and happy desperation in his voice. Happy, in that a decision had been made at all, however unwisely. Desperate, because life with Irma was a desperate affair in any case; but especially in regard to this passion of hers to have a party.

'Alfred! Alfred! are you serious? Will you pull your weight, Alfred? I say, will you pull your weight?'

'What weight I have I'll pull to pieces for you, Irma.'

'You are resolved, Alfred – I say, you are *resolved*,' she asked breathlessly.

'It is you who are resolved, sweet Perturbation. It is I who have submitted. But there it is. I am weak. I am ductile. You *will* have your way – a way, I fear, that is fraught with the possibility of monstrous repercussions – but your own, Irma, your own. And a party we will throw. Ha, ha, ha, ha, ha, ha, ha!'

There was something that did not altogether ring true in his shrill laughter. Was there a touch of bitterness in it somewhere?

'After all,' he continued, perching himself on the back of a chair (and with his feet on the seat and his chin on his knees he looked remarkably like a grasshopper) . . . 'After all, you have waited a long time. A long time. But, as you know, I would never advise such a thing. You're not the type to give a party. You're not even the type to go to a party. You have nothing of the flippancy about you that makes a party *go*, sister mine; but you are determined.'

'Unutterably,' said Irma.

'And have you confidence in your brother as a host?'

'Oh, Alfred, I *could* have!' she whispered grimly. 'I *would* have, if you wouldn't try to make everything sound clever. I get so tired of the way you say things. And I don't really like the things you say.'

'Irma,' said her brother, 'nor do I. They always sound stale by the time I hear them. The brain and the tongue are so far apart.'

'That's the sort of nonsense I *loathe!*' cried Irma, suddenly becoming passionate. 'Are we going to talk about the party, or are we going to listen to your silly soufflés? Answer me, Alfred. Answer me at once.'

'I will talk like bread and water. What shall I say?'

He descended from the chairback and sat on the seat. Then he leant forward a little and, with his hands folded between his knees, he gazed expectantly at Irma through the magnifying lenses of his spectacles. Staring back at him through the darkened glass of her own lenses, the enlargement of his eyes was hardly noticeable.

Irma felt that for the moment she had a certain moral ascendancy over her brother. The air of submission which he had about him gave her strength to divulge to him the real reason for her hankering for this party she had in mind . . . for she needed his help.

'Did you know, Alfred,' she said, 'that I am thinking of getting married?'

'Irma!' cried her brother. 'You aren't!'

'Oh, yes, I am,' muttered Irma. 'Oh yes, I am.'

Prunesquallor was about to inquire who the lucky man was when a peculiar twinge of sympathy for her, poor white thing that she was, sitting so upright in the chair before him, caught at his heart. He knew how few her chances of meeting men had been in the past: he knew that she knew nothing of love's gambits save what she had read in books. He knew that she would lose her head. He also knew that she had no one in view. So he said:

'We will find *just* the man for you. You deserve a thoroughbred: something that can cock his ears and whisk his tail. By all that's unimpeachable, you do indeed. Why . . .'

The Doctor stopped himself: he had been about to take verbal flight when he remembered his promise: so he leant forward again to hear what his sister had to say.

'I don't know about cocking his ears and frisking his tail,' said Irma, with the suggestion of a twitch at one corner of her thin mouth; 'but I would like you to know, Alfred – I said I would like you to know, that I am glad you understand the position. I am being wasted, Alfred. You realize that, don't you – don't you?'

'I do, indeed.'

'My skin is the whitest in Gormenghast.'

'And your feet are the flattest,' thought her brother: but he said:

'Yes, yes, but what we must *do*, sweet huntress – (O virgin through wild sex's thickets prowling)' (he could not resist this image of his sister) 'what we must *do* is to decide whom to ask. To the Party, I mean. That is fundamental.'

'Yes, yes!' said Irma.

'And when we will ask them.'

'That's easier,' said Irma.

'And at what time of the day.'

'The evening, of course,' said Irma.

'And what they shall wear.'

'Oh, their evening clothes, obviously,' said Irma.

'It depends on whom we ask, don't you think? What ladies, my dear, have dresses as resplendent as yours, for instance? There's a certain cruelty about evening dress.'

'Oh, that is of no avail.'

'Do you mean "of no account"?'

'Yes, yes,' said Irma.

'But how embarrassing! Won't they feel it keenly, my dear – or will you put on rags, in an overflow of love and sympathy?'

'There will be no women.'

'No women!' cried her brother, genuinely startled.

'I must be alone,' his sister murmured, pushing her black glasses further up the bridge of her long, pointed nose . . . 'with *them* – the males.'

'But what of the entertainment for your guests?'

'I shall be there,' said Irma.

'Yes, yes; and no doubt you will prove ravishing and ubiquitous; but, my love, my love, think again.'

'Alfred,' said Irma, standing up and lowering one of her iliac crests and raising its counterpart so high that her pelvis looked thoroughly dangerous – 'Alfred,' she said, 'how can you be so perverse? What use could women be? You haven't forgotten what we have in mind, have you? Have you?'

Her brother was beginning to admire her. Had she all this long while been hiding beneath her neuroticism, her vanity, her childishness, an iron will?

He rose and, cupping his hands over her hips, corrected their angle with the quick jerk of a bonesetter. Then, sitting back in his chair and fastidiously crossing his long, elegant, cranelike legs while going through the movements of washing his hands: 'Irma, my revelation, tell me but this . . .' he raised his eyes quizzically – 'who are these males – these stags – these rams – these tom cats – these cocks, stoats and ganders that you have in mind? And on what scale is this carousal to be?'

'You know very well, Alfred, that we have no choice. Among the gentry, who are there? I ask you, Alfred, who are there?'

'Who, indeed?' mused the Doctor, who could think of no one. The idea of a party in his house was so novel that the effort of trying to people it was beyond him. It was as though he were trying to assemble a cast for an unwritten drama.

'As for the size of the party, Alfred – are you listening? – I have in mind a gathering of some forty men.'

'No! no!' shouted her brother, clutching at the arms of his chair, 'not in *this* room, surely? It would be worse than the white cats. It would be a dog fight.'

Was that a blush that stole across his sister's face?

'Alfred,' she said after a while, 'it is my last chance. In a year my glamour may be tarnished. Is it a time to think of your own personal comfort?'

'Listen to me.' Prunesquallor spoke very slowly. His high voice was strangely meditative. 'I will be as concise as I can. Only you must listen, Irma.'

She nodded.

'You will have more success if your party is not too large. At a large party the hostess has to flutter from guest to guest and can never enjoy a protracted conversation with anyone. What is more, the guests continually flutter towards the hostess in a manner calculated to show her how much they are enjoying themselves.

'But at a smaller party where everyone can easily be seen the introductions and general posturing can be speedily completed. You will then have time to size up the persons present and decide on those worth giving your attention to.'

'I see,' said Irma. 'I am going to have lanterns hanging in the garden, too, so that I can lure those whom I think fit out into the apple orchard.'

'Good heavens!' said Prunesquallor, half to himself. 'Well, I hope it won't be raining.'

'It won't,' said Irma.

He had never known her like this. There was something frightening in seeing a second side of a sister whom he had always assumed had only one.

'Well, some of them must be left out, then.'

'But who *are* they? Who *are* they?' he cried. 'I can't bear this frightful tension. What are these males that you seem to think of *en bloc*? This doglike horde who at, as it were, a whistle will be ready to stream across the quadrangle and through the hall, through this door and to take up a score of masculine postures? In the name of fundamental mercy, Irma, tell me who they are.'

'The Professors.'

As Irma uttered the words her hands grappled with one another behind her back. Her flat bosom heaved. Her sharp nose twitched and a terrible smile came over her face.

'They are gentlemen!' she cried in a loud voice. 'Gentlemen! And worthy of my love.'

'What! All forty of them.' Her brother was on his feet again. He was shocked.

But at the same time he could see the logic of Irma's choice. Who else was there for a party with this hidden end in view? As for their being 'gentlemen' – perhaps they were. But only just. If their blood was bluish, so for the most part were their jaws and finger-nails. If their backgrounds bore scrutiny, the same could hardly be said for their foregrounds.

'What a vista opens out before us! How old are you, Irma?'

'You know very well, Alfred.'

'Not without thinking,' said the Doctor. 'But leave it. It's what you

look like that matters. God knows you're clean! It's a good start. I am trying to put myself in your place. It takes an effort – ha ha – I can't do it.'

'Alfred.'

'My love?'

'How many do you think would be ideal?'

'If we chose well, Irma, I should say a dozen.'

'No, no, Alfred, it's a party! It's a *party*! Things *happen* at parties – not at friends' gatherings. I've read about it. Twenty at least, to make the atmosphere pregnant.'

'Very well, my dear. Very *well*. Not that we will include a mildewed and wheezy beast with broken antlers because he comes twentieth on the list when the other nineteen are stags, are virile and eligible. But come, let us go into this matter more closely. Let us say, for sake of argument, that we have whittled the probable down to fifteen. Now, of this fifteen, Irma, my sweet co-strategist, surely we could not hope for more than six as possible husbands for you. – No, no, do not wince; let us be honest, though it is brutal work. The whole thing is very subtle, for the six you might prefer are not necessarily the six that would care to share the rest of their lives with *you*; oh no. It might be another six altogether whom you don't care about one little bit. And over and above these interchangeables we must have the floating background of those whom I have no doubt you would spurn with your elegantly cloven hooves were they to make the least advance. You would bridle up, Irma: I'm sure you would. But nevertheless they are needful, these untouchables, for we must have a hinterland. They are the ones who will make the party florid, the atmosphere potential.'

'Do you think we could call it a *soirée*, Alfred?'

'There is no law against it that I know of,' answered Prunesquallor, a little irritably perhaps, for she had obviously not been listening. 'But the Professors, as I remember them, are hardly the types I would associate with the term. Who, by the way, *do* comprise the Staff these latter days? It is a long time since I last saw the flapping of a gown.'

'I know that you are cynical, Alfred, BUT I would have you know that they are my choice. I have always wished for a man of learning to be my own. I would understand him. I would administer to him. I would protect him and darn his socks.'

'And a more dexterous darner never protected the tendo achilles with a double skein!'

'Alfred!'

'Forgive me, my own. By all that's unforeseeable I am getting to like the idea. For my part, Irma, I will see to the wines and liqueurs, the barrels and the punch-bowl. For your part the eatables, the invitations, the schooling of the staff – our staff, not the luminaries'. And now, my dear, *when*? This is the question – *when*?'

'My gown of a thousand frills, with its corsage of hand-painted parrots will be ready within ten days, and . . .'

'Parrots!' cried the Doctor in consternation.

'Why not?' said Irma, sharply.

'But,' wavered her brother, 'how many of them?'

'What on earth does it matter to you, Alfred? They are brightly coloured birds.'

'But will they chime in with the frills, my sweet one? I would have thought – if you must have hand-painted creatures on your corsage, as you call it – that something calculated to turn the thoughts of the Professors to your femininity, your desirability, something less aggressive than parrots might be wise . . . Mind you, Irma, I'm only . . .'

'Alfred!' Her voice jerked him back to his chair.

'My province, I *think*,' she said, with heavy sarcasm. 'I imagine when it comes to parrots you can leave them to me.'

'I will,' said her brother.

'Will ten days give us time, Alfred?' she said, as she rose from her chair and approached her brother, smoothing back her iron-grey hair with her long, pale fingers. Her tone had softened. To the Doctor's horror she sat on the arm of his chair.

Then, with a sudden kittenish abandon, she flung back her head so that her over-long yet pearl-white neck was tautened in a backward curve and her chignon tapped her between her shoulder-blades in so peremptory a way as to make her cough. But directly she had ascertained that it was not her brother being wilful, the ecstatic and kittenish expression came back to her powdered face, and she clapped her hands together at her breast.

Prunesquallor, staring up, horrified at yet another facet of her character coming to light, noticed that one of her molars needed filling, but decided it was not the moment to mention it.

'Oh Alfred! Alfred!' she cried. 'I *am* a woman, aren't I?' The hands were shaking with excitement as they gripped one another. 'I'll *show* them I am!' she screamed, her voice losing all control. And then, calming herself with a visible effort, she turned to her brother and, smiling at him with a coyness that was worse than any scream – 'I'll send their cards to them tomorrow, Alfred,' she whispered.

FIFTEEN

THREE shafts of the rising sun, splintering through the murk, appeared to set fire to the earth where they struck it. The bright impact of the nearest beam exposed a tangle of branches which clawed in a craze of radiance, microscopically perfect and adrift in darkness.

The second of these floodlit islands appeared to float immediately *above* the first, for the sky and the earth were a single curtain of darkness. In reality it was as far away again, but hanging as it did gave no sense of distance.

At its northern extremity there grew from the wasp-gold earth certain forms like eruptions of masonry rather than spires and buttresses of natural rock. The sunshaft had uncovered a mere finger of some habitation which, widening as it entered the surrounding darkness to the North, became a fist of stones, which, in its turn, heaving through wrist and forearm to an elbow like a smashed honeycomb, climbed through darkness to a gaunt, time-eaten shoulder only to expand again and again into a mountainous body of timeless towers.

But of all this nothing was visible but the bright and splintered tip of a stone finger.

The third 'island' was the shape of a heart. A coruscating heart of tares on fire.

To the dark edge of this third light a horse was moving. It appeared no bigger than a fly. Astride its back was Titus.

As he entered the curtain of darkness which divided him from his citylike home he frowned. One of his hands gripped the mane of his mount. His heart beat loudly in the absolute hush. But the horse moved without hesitation, and he was quietened by the regular movement beneath him.

All at once a new 'island' of light, undulating as it ran from the east, enlarging its mercurial margins all the while as though to push away the darkness, created in the gloom a fantastic kaleidoscope of fleeting rocks and trees and valleys and ridges – the fluctuating 'coastline' flaring in sharp and minute tracery. This flow of radiance was followed by another and another. Great saffron gaps had appeared in the sky – and then, from skyline to skyline, the world was naked light.

Titus shouted. The horse shook its head; and then, over the land of his ancestors, he galloped for home.

But in the excitement of the gallop Titus turned his head from the castle towers, which lifted themselves momently higher above the horizon, turned it to where, away in the cold haze of the dawn Gormenghast Mountain with its clawlike peak threw out its challenge across the thrilling air – '*Do you dare?*' it seemed to cry. '*Do you dare?*'

Titus leaned back in the stirrups and tugged his horse to a standstill, for a rare confusion of voices and images had made a cockpit of his panting body. Forests as wet and green as romance itself heaved their thorned branches through him as he sat there shuddering, half turned on the saddle. Swathes of wet foliage shuffled beneath his ribs. In his mouth he tasted the bitterness of leaves. The smell of the forest earth, black with rotted ferns and pungent with fermentation, burned for a moment in his nostrils.

His eyes had travelled down from the high, bare summit of Gormenghast Mountain to the shadowy woods, and then again had turned to the sky. He stared at the sun as it climbed. He felt the day beginning. He turned his horse about. His back was towards Gormenghast.

The mountain's head shone in a great vacancy of light. It held within its ugly contour either everything or nothing at all. It awakened the imagination by its peculiar emptiness.

And from it came the voice again.

'Do you dare? Do you dare?'

And a host of voices joined. Voices from the sun-blotched glades. From the marshes and the gravel beds. From the birds of the green river reaches. From where the squirrels are and the foxes move and the woodpeckers thicken the drowsy stillness of the day with their far arcadian tapping: from where the rotten hollow of some tree, mellow with richness, glows as though lit from within by the sweet and secret cache of the wild bees.

Titus had risen an hour before the bell. He had hurried into his clothes without a sound, and had then tiptoed through silent halls to a southern gateway; and then, running across a walled-in courtyard, had arrived at the Castle stables. The morning was black and murky, but he was restless for a world without Walls. He had paused at Fuchsia's door on his way and had tapped at it.

'Who's there?' Her voice had sounded strangely husky from the other side.

'It's me,' said Titus.

'What do you want?'

'Nothing,' said Titus. 'I'm going for a ride.'

'It's beastly weather,' said Fuchsia. 'Good-bye.'

'Good-bye,' said Titus; and had resumed his tiptoeing along the corridor when he heard the sound of a handle being rattled. He turned and saw, not only Fuchsia disappearing back into her bedroom, but at the same moment something which was travelling very fast through the air and at his head. To protect his face he threw up his arm and, more by accident than adroitness, found he had caught in his hand a large and sticky slice of cake.

Titus knew that he was not allowed out of the Castle before breakfast. He knew that it was doubly disobedient to venture beyond the Outer Walls. As the only survivor of a famous line he had to take more than ordinary care of himself. It was for him to give particulars of when and where he was going, so that should he be late in returning it would be known at once. But, dark as was the day, it had no power to suppress the craving which had been mounting for weeks – the craving to ride and ride when the rest of the world lay in bed: to drink the spring air in giant gulps as his horse galloped beneath him over the April fields, beyond the Outer Dwellings. To pretend, as he galloped, that he was free.

Free . . . !

What could such a conception mean to Titus, who hardly knew what it was to move from one part of his home to another without being watched, guided or followed and who had never known the matchless privacy of the obscure? To be without a famous name? To have no lineage? To be something of no interest to the veiled eye of the grown-up world? To be a creature that grew, as a redskin creeps: through childhood and youth, from one year to the next, as though from thicket to thicket, from ambush to ambush, peering from Youth's tree-top vantages?

Because of the wild vista that surrounded Gormenghast and spread to every horizon as though the castle were an island of maroons set in desolate water beyond all trade-routes: because of this sense of space, how could Titus know that the vague, unfocused dissatisfaction which he had begun to feel from time to time was the fretting of something caged?

He knew no other world. Here all about him the raw material burned: the properties and settings of romance. Romance that is passionate; obscure and sexless: that is dangerous and arrogant.

The future lay before him with its endless ritual and pedantry, but something beat in his throat and he rebelled.

To be a truant! A Truant! It was like being a Conqueror – or a Demon.

And so he had saddled his small grey horse and ridden out into the dark April morning. No sooner had he passed through one of the arches in the Outer Wall and cantered in the direction of Gormenghast forest than he became suddenly, hopelessly lost. All in a moment the clouds seemed to have cut out all possible light from the sky, and he had found himself among branches which switched back and struck him in the darkness. At another time, his horse had found itself up to the knees in a cold and sucking mire. It had shuddered beneath him as it backed with difficulty to find firmer purchase for its hooves. As the sun had climbed, Titus was able to make out where he was. And then, suddenly, the long sunshafts had broken through the gloom and he had seen away in the distance – far further than he would ever have guessed possible – the shining stone of one of the Castle's western capes.

And then the flooding of the sun, until not a rag was left in the sky, and the thrill of fear became the thrill of anticipation – of adventure.

Titus knew that already he would be missed. Breakfast would be over; but long before breakfast an alarm must have been raised in the dormitory. Titus could see the raised eyebrow of his professor in the schoolroom as he eyed the empty desk, and could hear the chatter and speculation of the pupils. And then he felt something more thrilling than the warm kiss of the sun on the back of his neck: it was a reedy flight of cold April air across his face – something perilous and horribly exciting – something very shrill, that whistled through his qualmy stomach and down his thighs. It was as though it was the herald of adventure that whistled to him to turn his horse's head, while the soft gold sunlight murmured the same message in a drowsier voice.

For a moment so huge a sense of himself swam inside Titus as to make the figures in the castle like puppets in his imagination. He would pull them up in one hand and drop them into the moat when he returned – *if* he returned. He would not be their slave any more! Who was he to be told to go to school: to attend this and to attend that? He was not only the 77th Earl of Gormenghast, he was Titus Groan in his own right.

'All right, then!' he shouted to himself, 'I'll show them!' And, digging his heels into his horse's flanks, he headed for the Mountain.

But the cold drift of spring air across his face was not only a prelude to Titus' truancy. It foretold yet another alternation in the weather, as rapid and as unexpected as the coming of the sun. For although there were no clouds in the upper air, yet the sun seemed now to have a haze upon it and the warmth on his neck was weaker.

It was not until he had covered over three miles of his rebellious expedition and was in the hazel woods that led to the foothills of Gormenghast Mountain, that he positively noticed a mistiness in the atmosphere. From then onwards a whiteness seemed to grow above him, to arise out of the earth and gather together on every side. The sun ceased to be more than a pale disc, and then, was gone altogether.

There was no turning back now: Titus knew that he would be lost immediately if he turned his horse about. As it was, he could see nothing but a lambent glow, gradually growing dimmer – a glow immediately before and above him. It was the upper half of Gormenghast Mountain shining through the thickening mists.

To climb out of the white vapour was his only hope and, jogging the horse into a dangerous trot, for visibility was but a yard or two, he made (with the pale shimmer above him for a guide) for the high slopes; and at last he found the air begin to thin. When the sun shone down again unhindered and the highest wisps of the mist were coiling some distance below, Titus realized in full what it was to be alone. The solitude was of a kind he had never experienced before. The silence of a motionless altitude with a world of fantastic vapour spread below.

Away to the west the roofscape of his heavy home floated, as lightly as though every stone were a petal. Strung across the capstone jaws of its great head a hundred windows, the size of teeth, reflected the dawn. There was less the nature of glass about them than of bone, or of the stones which locked them in. In contrast to the torpor of these glazes, punctuating the remote masonry with so cold a catenation, acres of ivy spread themselves like dark water over the roofs and appeared restless, the millions of heart-shaped eyelids winking wetly.

The mountain's head shone above him. Was there no living thing on those stark slopes but the truant child? It seemed that the heart of the world had ceased to beat.

The ivy leaves fluttered a little and a flag here and there stirred against its pole, but there was no vitality in these movements, no purpose, any more than the long hair of some corpse, tossing this way and that in a wind, can deny the death of the body it flatters.

Not a head appeared at any of those topmost, teeth-like windows that ran along the castle's brow. Had anyone stood there he might have seen the sun hanging a hand's-breadth above the margins of the ground mist.

From horizon to horizon it spread, this mist, supporting the massives of the mountains on its foaming back, like a floating load of ugly crags and shale. It laid its fumes along the flanks of the mountain. It laid them along the walls of the castle, fold upon baleful fold, a great tide. Soundless, motionless, beneath some exorcism more potent than the moon, it had no power to ebb.

Not a breath from the mountain. Not a sigh from the swathed Castle, nor from the hollow hush of the mists. Was there no pulse beneath the vapour? Not a heart beating? For surely the weakest heart would reverberate in such white silence and thud its double drum-note in far gullies.

The sunlight gave no stain to the chalky pall. It was a white sun, as though reflecting the mists below it – brittle as a disc of glass.

Was it that Nature was restless and was experimenting with her various elements? For no sooner had the white mist settled itself as though for ever, lying heavily in the ravine like a river of cold smoke – lying over the flats like a quilt, feeling into every rabbit burrow with its cold fingers – than a chill and scouring wind shipped out of the north, and sweeping the land bare again, dropped as suddenly as it had risen, as though it had been sent specifically to clear the mist away. And the sun was a globe of gold again. The wind was gone and the mists were gone and the clouds were gone and the day was warm and young, and Titus was on the slopes of Gormenghast Mountain.

SIXTEEN

FAR below Titus, like a gathering of people, stood a dozen spinneys. Between them the rough land glittered here and there where threads of water reflected the sky.

Out of this confusion of glinting water, brambles and squat thorn bushes, the clumps of trees arose with a peculiar authority.

To Titus they seemed curiously alive, these copses. For each copse appeared singularly *unlike* any other one, though they were about equal in size and were exclusively a blend of ash and sycamore.

But it was plain to see that whereas the nearest of these groups to Titus was in an irritable state, not one of the trees having anything to do with his neighbour, their heads turned away from one another, their shoulders shrugged, yet not a hundred feet away another spinney was in a condition of suspended excitement, as with the heads of its trees bowed together above some green and susurrous secret. Only one of the trees had raised its head a little. It was tilted on one side as though loth to miss any of the fluttering conversation at its shoulder. Titus shifted his gaze and noticed a copse where, drawn back, and turned away a little on their hips, twelve trees looked sideways at one who stood aloof. Its back was to them. There could be no doubt that, with its gaze directed from them it despised the group behind it.

There were the trees that huddled together as though they were cold or in fear. There were trees that gesticulated. There were those that seemed to support one of their number who appeared wounded. There were the arrogant groups, and the mournful, with their heads bowed: the exultant copses and those where every tree appeared to be asleep.

The landscape was alive, but so was Titus. They were only trees, after all: branches, roots and leaves. This was his day; there was no time to waste.

He had given the slip to that grey line of towers. Here about him were the rocks and ferns of the mountain, with the morning sunbeams dancing over them in hazes of ground-light.

A dragonfly hovered above a rockface at his elbow, and at the same moment he became aware of a great shouting of birds from beyond the copses.

To the north of the copses lay the shining flats, but it was from further to the west, and closer to the foot of the mountain where he stood, that the voices of the birds floated, so thinly and clearly; it was there that the wide forests lay basking. Fold after green fold, clump after clump of foliage undulating to the notched skyline.

His yearnings became focused. His truancy no longer nagged him. His curiosity burned.

What brooded within those high and leafy walls? Those green and sunny walls? What of the inner shadows? What of the acorn'd terraces, and the hollow aisles of leaves? His truant conscience lay stunned beneath the hammers of his excitement.

He wanted to gallop, but the slopes of shale and loose stone were too dangerous. But as he picked his way to lower levels the ground became correspondingly easier, and he was able to move more rapidly over considerable stretches.

The green wall of the forest rose higher into the sunny sky as he neared, until he had to raise his head to see the highest branches.

Gormenghast was hidden behind a rise in the ground to the west. To the east and behind him the slopes of the mountain climbed in ugly shelves. He drew in the reins and slid from the horse's back.

The ground about him was of silky and rather ashen grass, which shone with a peculiar white light. Rough rocks lay scattered about, in the shadow of whose hot brows and thrust-out jaws a variety of ferns grew luxuriously.

Lizards ran across the hot upper surfaces, and with Titus' first step towards the forest wall a snake slid down a rockface like a stream of water and whipped across his path with a rattling of its loosely-jointed tail.

What was this shock of love? A rattle-snake; a dell of silky grass; some great rocks with lizards and ferns, and the green forest wall. Why should these add up to so thrilling, so breathtaking a total?

He knotted the reins loosely about the pony's neck and gave it a long push in the direction of Gormenghast. 'Go home,' he said. The pony turned her head to him at once and then, tossing it to and fro, began to move away. In a few moments she had disappeared over the rise in the ground, and Titus was truly alone.

SEVENTEEN

THE morning classes had begun. In the schoolrooms a hundred things were happening at the same time. But beyond their doors there was drama of another kind: a drama of scholastic silence, for in the deserted halls and corridors that divided the classes it surged like a palpable thing and lapped against the very doors of the classrooms.

In an hour's time the usher would rattle the brass bell in the Central

Hall and the silence would be shaken to bits as, erupting from their various prisons, a world of boys poured through the halls like locusts.

In the classrooms of Gormenghast, as in the Masters' Common-room, the walls were of horse hide. But this was the only thing they had in common, for the moods of the various rooms and their shapes could not be more various.

Fluke's room, for instance, was long, narrow and badly lit from a small top-window at the far end. Opus Fluke lay in an arm-chair, draped with a red rug. He was in almost total shadow. Although he could hardly make out the boys in front of him, he was in a better position than they were, for they could not see him at all. He had no desk in front of him, but sat there; as it were, in the open darkness. One or two text-books were littered about the floor beneath his chair for the sake of form. The dust lay over them so thickly that they were like grey swellings. Mr Fluke had not yet discovered that they had been nailed into the floorboards for over a year.

Perch-Prism's room was deadly square and far too well lit to please the neophytes. Only the leather walls were musty and ancient, and even they were scrubbed and oiled from time to time. The desks, the benches and the floorboards were scoured with soda and boiling water every morning, so that apart from the walls there was a naked whiteness about the room which made it quite the most unpopular. Cribbing was almost impossible in that cruel light.

Flannelcat's room was a short tunnel with a semi-circular glass window which filled in the whole of the near end. In contrast to Fluke, sitting in the shadows, Mr Flannelcat perched aloft at a very high desk presented a different picture. As the only light in the room poured in from behind him, Mr Flannelcat might as well, in the eyes of his pupils, have been cut out of black paper. There he sat against the bright semi-circular window at the end of the tunnel, his silhouetted gestures jerking to and fro against the light. Through the window could be seen the top of Gormenghast Mountain, and this morning, floating lazily over its shining head, were three small clouds like dandelion seeds.

But of the numerous classrooms of Gormenghast, each one with its unique character, there was, that morning, one in particular. It lay upon one of the upper floors, a great, dreamy hall of a place with far more desks than were ever used and far more space than was ever (academically) needed. Great strips of its horsehide hung away from the walls.

The window of the classroom faced to the south, so that the floor which had never been stained was bleached, and the ink that had been spilt, term after term, had faded to so beautiful and wan a blue that the floor-boards had an almost faery colouring. Certainly there was nothing else particularly faery about the place.

What, for instance, was that sacklike monster, that snoring hummock, that deadweight of disjointed horror? Vile and brutish it looked as it lay curled like a black dog on the Professor's desk; but what was it? One would say it was dead, for it was as heavy as death and as motionless; but there was a sound of stifled snoring coming from it, with an occasional whistle as of wind through jagged glass.

Whatever it was it held no terror, nor even interest for the score or so boys who, in that dreaming and timeless hall in the almost forgotten regions of the Upper School, appeared to have something very different to think about. The sunbeams poured through the high window. The room was in a haze of motes. But there was nothing dreamy about the pupils.

What was happening? There was hardly any noise, but the tension in the air had a loudness of its own.

For there was in progress a game of high and dangerous hazards. It was peculiar to this classroom. The air was breathless. Those not taking part in the peculiar battle squatted on desks or cupboards. A fresh phase was about to begin. Their ingenuous faces were turned to the window. Seasoned creatures they looked, these wiry children of chance. The veterans moved into position.

Everything was ready. The two loose floor-boards had been taken up and the first of them was propped against the window-sill so that it slanted across and towards the floor of the classroom at a shallow angle. Its secret underside had been scraped and waxed with candle-stubs for as long as could be remembered, and it was that underside which was facing the ceiling. The second of the long floor-boards, equally polished, was placed end to end with the first, so that a stretch of narrow and slippery wood extended some thirty feet across the schoolroom from the window to the opposite wall.

The team which was standing close by the open window was the first to make a move, and one of its number – a black-haired boy with a birthmark on his forehead – jumped on to the window-sill, apparently without giving a thought to the hundred-foot drop on the other side.

At this movement, members of the enemy team who were crouching behind a row of desks at the back of the schoolroom, marshalled their paper pellets, as hard as walnuts, which they proposed to let loose from small naked catapults, worn to a silky finish by ceaseless handling. There has been a time when clay – and even glass marbles were used; but after the third death and a deal of confusion in the hiding of the bodies, it was decided to be content with paper bullets. Those were by no means gentle substitutes, the paper having been chewed, kneaded, mixed with white gum, and then compressed between the hinges of desks. Travelling as they did with deadly speed, they struck like the lash of a whip.

But what were they to fire at? Their enemies stood by the window and were obviously not expecting anything to fly in their direction. The firing party were not even looking at them – they stared fixedly ahead, but at the same time were beginning to close their left eyes and stretch their strands of grim elastic. And then, suddenly, the significance of the game unfolded itself in a sharp and rhythmic whirl. Too rapid, too vital, too dangerous for any dance or ballet. Yet as traditional and as filled with subtleties. What was happening?

The black-haired boy with the birthmark had flexed his knees, hollowed his back, clapped his inky hands and leaped from the window-sill out into the morning sunlight, where the branches of a giant plane tree were like lattice-work against the sun. For a moment he was a creature of the air, his head thrown back, his teeth bared, his fingers outstretched, his eyes fixed upon a white branch of the tree. A hundred feet below him the dusty quadrangle shone in the morning sun. From the schoolroom it looked as though the boy was gone for ever. But his pards by the window had flattened themselves against the flanking wall, and their enemies, crouched behind the desks, had their eyes fixed on the slippery floor-boards that ran across the classroom like a strip of ice.

The boy in mid-air had clawed at the branch, had gripped its end, and was swinging out on a long and breath-taking curve through the foliaged air. At the extremity and height of this outward-going arc, he wriggled himself in a peculiar manner which gave an added downlash to the branch and swung him high on the up-swing of his return journey – high into the air and out of the leaves, so that for a moment he was well above the level of the window from which he had leapt. And it was now that his nerves must be like iron – now, with but a fraction of time to spare before his volition failed him, that he let go the branch. He was in mid-air again. He was falling – falling at speed, and at such an angle as to both clear the lintel of the window and the sill below it – and to land on his small tense buttocks – to land like a bolt from heaven on the slanting floor-board; and a fraction of a second later to thump into the leather wall at the far end of the schoolroom, having whirled down the boards with the speed of a slung stone.

But he had not reached the wall unscathed for all the suddenness of his reappearance and velocity of flight. His ear buzzed like a nest of wasps. A withering crossfire from the six catapults had resulted in one superlative hit, three blows on the body and two misses. But there had been no cessation in the game, for even as he crashed into the dented leather wall another of his team was already in mid-air, his hands stretched for the branch and his eyes bright with excitement, while the firing party, no less on the move, were recharging their weapons with fresh ammunition and were beginning to close their left eyes again and stretch the elastic.

By the time the birthmark boy had trotted back to the window, with his ear on fire, another apparition had fallen from the sunny sky, had whizzed down the sloping board and skidded across the schoolroom to crash into the wall where the leather was grimed and torn with years of collision. There was a schoolroom silence over everything – a silence filled with the pale sunshine. The floor was patterned with the golden shadow of the desks, of the benches, of the enormous broken blackboard. It was the stillness of a summer term – self-absorbed, unhurried, dreamlike, punctuated by the quick, inky handclap of each boy as he leapt into space, the whizz of the pellets through the air, the caught breath of the victim, the thud of a body as it collided with the leather wall, and then the scuffling sound of catapults being recharged; and then again the clap of the boy at the window, and the far rustle of leaves as he swung through a green arc above the quadrangle. The teams changed. The swingers took out their catapults. The firing party moved to the window. It had a rhythm of its own, this hazardous, barbaric, yet ceremonial game – a ritual as unquestioned and sacrosanct as anything could be in the soul of a boy.

Devilry and stoicism bound them together. Their secrets were blacker, deeper, more terrible or more hilarious through mutual knowledge of the throat-contracting thrill of a lightning skid across a mellow schoolroom: through mutual knowledge of the long leaf-shrouded flights through space: of their knowledge of the sound as the stinging bullet spins past the head or the pain as it strikes.

But what of all this? This rhythm of stung boys? Or boys as filled with life as fish or birds. Only that it was taking place that morning.

What of the ghastly black huddle on the Professor's desk? The sunlight streaming through the leaves of the plane tree had begun to dapple it with shimmering lozenges of light. It snored – a disgraceful sound to hear during the first lesson of a summer morning.

But the moments of its indulgence were numbered, for there was, all of a sudden, a cry from near the ceiling and above the schoolroom door. It was the voice of an urchin, a freckled wisp of a thing, who was perched on a high cupboard. The glass of the fanlight above the door was at his shoulder. It was dark with grime, but a small circle the size of a coin was kept transparent and through this spy-hole he could command a view of the corridor outside. He could thus give warning not only to the whole class but to the Professor, at the first sign of danger.

It was rarely that either Barquentine or Deadyawn made a tour of the schoolrooms, but it was as well to have the freckled urchin stationed on the cupboard from first thing in the morning onwards, for there was nothing more irritating than for the class to be disturbed.

That morning, lying there like a toy on the cupboard top, he had become so intrigued by the changing fortunes of the 'game' below him that it had been over a minute since he had last put his eye to the spy-hole. When he did so it was to see, not twenty feet from the door, a solid phalanx of Professors, like a black tide, with Deadyawn himself at the fore, out-topping the others, in his high chair on wheels.

Deadyawn, who headed the phalanx, was head and shoulders above the rest of the staff, although he was by no means sitting up straight in his high, narrow chair. With its small wheels squeaking at the feet of the four legs, it rocked to and fro as it was propelled rapidly forwards by the usher, who was as yet invisible to the wisp at the spy-hole, being hidden by the high, ugly piece of furniture – ugly beyond belief – with its disproportionate feeding-tray at the height of Deadyawn's heart and the raw little shelf for his feet.

What was visible of Deadyawn's face above the tray appeared to be awake – a sure sign that something of particular urgency was in the air.

Behind him the rustling darkness was solid with the professors. What had happened to their various classes, and what on earth they could want on this lazy floor of the castle at any time, let alone at the beginning of the day, was unguessable. But here, nevertheless, they were, their gowns whisking and whispering along the walls on either side. There was an intentness in their gait, a kind of mass seriousness, quite frightening.

The midget boy on the cupboard-top cried his warning with a shriller note in his voice than his schoolfellows had ever heard before.

'The "Yawner"!' he screamed. 'Quick! quick! quick! The Yawner'n all of 'em! Let me down! let me down!'

The rhythm of the hazardous game was broken. Not a single pellet whizzed past the head of the last boy to burst out of the sunlight and crash into the leather wall. In a moment the room was suspiciously quiet. Four rows of boys sat half turned at their desks, their heads cocked on one side, as they listened to the squeaking of Deadyawn's chair on its small wheels as it rolled towards them through the silence.

The wisp had been caught, having dropped from what must have seemed to him a great height into the arms of a big straw-headed youth.

The two floor-boards had been grabbed and shot back into their long, narrow cavities immediately below the professor's desk. But a mistake had been made, and when it was noticed it was too late for anything to be done about it. One of the boards in the whirl of the moment had been put back *upside down*.

On the desk itself the heavy black dog-like weight was still snoring.

Even the shrill cry of the 'look-out' had done no more than send a twitch through the jointed huddle.

Any boy in the first row, had he thought it possible to reach the professor's desk and get back to his own place before the entry of Deadyawn and the staff, would have thrown the folds of Bellgrove's gown off Bellgrove's sleeping head, where it lay sunk between his arms on the desk top, and would have shaken Bellgrove into some sort of awareness; for the black and shapeless thing was indeed the old master himself, lost beneath the awning of his gown. For his pupils had draped it over his reverend head, as they always did when he fell asleep.

But there was no time. The squeaking of the wheels had stopped. There was a great trampling and scuffling of feet as the professors closed their ranks behind their chief. The doorhandle was beginning to turn.

As the door opened, thirty or so boys, doubled over their desks, could be seen scribbling furiously, their brows knit in concentration.

There was for the moment an unholy silence.

And then the voice of the usher, Mr Fly, cried out from behind Deadyawn's chair:

'The Headmaster!' And the classroom scrambled to its feet. All except Bellgrove.

The wheels began to squeak again as the high chair was steered up one of the inkstained aisles between the rows of desks.

By this time the mortar-boards had followed the Headmaster into the room, and under these mortar-boards the faces of Opus Fluke, Spiregrain, Perch-Prism, Throd, Flannelcat, Shred and Shimmer, Cutflower and the rest were easily recognizable. Deadyawn, who was on a tour of the classrooms, had, after inspecting each in turn, sent the boys to their red-stone yard and kept their masters with him – so that he now had practically the whole staff at his heels. The boys would shortly be spread out in great fans and sent off on a day-long hunt for Titus. For it was his disappearance which was causing this unprecedented activity.

How merciful a thing is man's ignorance of his immediate future! What a ghastly, paralysing thing it would have been if all those present could have known what was about to happen within a matter of seconds! For nothing short of pre-knowledge could have stopped the occurrence, so suddenly it sprang upon them.

The scholars were still standing, and Mr Fly, the usher, who had reached the end of the passage between the desks, was about to turn the high chair to the left and to run it up under Bellgrove's desk where Deadyawn could speak to his oldest professor, when the calamity occurred, and even the dreadful fact of Titus' disappearance was forgotten. For The Fly had slipped! His feet had fled from under his perky body. His cocky little walk was suddenly a splayed confusion of legs. They shot to and fro like a frog's. But for all their lashing they could get no grip on the slippery floor, for he had trodden on that deadly board which had been returned – upside down – to its place below Bellgrove's desk.

The Fly had no time to let go his grip of the High Chair. It swayed above him like a tower – and then while the long line of the staff peered over one another's shoulders and the boys stood at their desks transfixed, something more appalling than they had ever contemplated took place before them.

For as The Fly came down in a crash on the boards, the wheels of the high chair whirled like tops and gave their final screech and the rickety piece of furniture leapt like a mad thing and from its summit something was hurled high into the air! It was Deadyawn!

He descended from somewhere near the ceiling like a visitor from another planet, or from the cosmic realms of Outer Space, as with all the signs of the Zodiac fluttering about him he plunged earthwards.

Had he but had a long brass trumpet at his lips and the power of arching his back and curling upwards as he neared the floorboards, and of swooping across the room over the heads of the scholars in a riot of draperies, to float away and out through the leaves of the plane tree and over the back of Gormenghast, to disappear for ever from the rational world – then, if only he had had the power to do this, that dreadful sound would have been avoided: that most dreadful and sickening sound which not a single boy or professor who heard it that morning was ever able to forget. It darkened the heart and brain. It darkened the very sunlight itself in that summer classroom.

But it was not enough that their hearing was appalled by the sound of a skull being crushed like an egg – for, as though everything was working together to produce the maximum horror, Fate had it that the Headmaster, in descending absolutely vertically, struck the floor with the top of his cranium, and remained upside down, in a horrible state of balance, having stiffened with a form of premature *rigor mortis*.

The soft, imponderable, flaccid Deadyawn, that arch-symbol of delegated duties, of negation and apathy, appeared now that he was upside down to have more life in him than he had ever had before. His limbs, stiffened in the death-spasm, were positively muscular. His crushed skull appeared to balance a body that had suddenly perceived its reason for living.

The first movement, after the gasp of horror that ran across the sunny schoolroom, came from among the débris of what was once the high chair.

The usher emerged, his red hair ruffled, quick eyes bulging, his teeth chattering with terror. At the sight of his master upside down he made for the window, all trace of cockiness gone from his carriage, his sense of propriety so outraged that there was nothing he wanted so much as to make a quick end to himself. Climbing on the window-sill, The Fly swung his legs over and then dropped to the quadrangle a hundred feet below.

Perch-Prism stepped forward from the ranks of the professors.

'All boys will make their way immediately to the red-stone yard,' he said in a crisp, high staccato. 'All boys will wait there quietly until they are given instructions. Parsley!'

A youth, with his jaw hanging wide and his eyes glazed, started as though he had been struck. He wrenched his eyes from the inverted Deadyawn, but could not find his voice.

'Parsley,' said Perch-Prism again, 'you will lead the class out – and Chives, you will take up the rear. Hurry now! hurry! Turn your heads to the door, there. You! yes, you, Sage Minor! And you there, Mint or whatever your name is – wake your ideas up. Hustle! hustle! hustle!'

Stupefied, the scholars began to file out of the door, their heads still turned over their shoulders at their late Headmaster.

Three or four other professors had to some extent recovered from the first horrible shock and were helping Perch-Prism to hustle the remnants of the class from the room.

At last the place was clear of boys. The sunlight played across the empty desks: it lit up the faces of the professors, but seemed to leave their gowns and mortar-boards as black as though they alone were in shadow. It lit the soles of Deadyawn's boots as they pointed stiffly to the ceiling.

Perch-Prism, glancing at the professors, saw that it was up to him to make the next move. His beady black eyes shone. What he had of a jaw he thrust forward. His round, babyish, pig-like face was set for action.

He opened his prim, rather savage little mouth and was about to call for help in righting the corpse, when a muffled voice came from an unexpected quarter. It sounded both near and far. It was difficult to make out a word, but for a moment or two the voice became less blurred. 'No, I don't think so, l'l man,' it said, 'for 't's love long lost, my queen, while Bellgrove guards you . . .' (the drowsy voice continued in its sleep) '. . . when lion . . . sprowl I'll tear their manes . . . awf . . . yoo. When serpents hiss at you I'll tread on dem . . . probably . . . and scatter birds of prey to left an' right.'

A long whistle from under the draperies and then, all of sudden, with a shudder, the invertebrate mass began to uncoil itself as Bellgrove's shrouded head raised itself slowly from his arms. Before he freed himself of the last layer of gown he sat back in his tutorial chair, and while he worked with his hands to free his head, his voice came out of the cloth darkness: '. . . Name an isthmus!' it boomed. 'Tinepott? . . .

Quagfire? . . . Sparrowmarsh? . . . Hagg? . . . Dankle? . . . What! Can no one tell his old master the name of an isthmus?'

With a wrench he unravelled his head of the last vestment of gown, and there was his long, weak, noble face as naked and venerable as any deep sea monster's.

It was a few moments before his pale-blue eyes had accustomed themselves to the light. He lifted his sculptured brow and blinked. 'Name an isthmus,' he repeated, but in a less interested voice, for he was beginning to be conscious of the silence in the room.

'Name . . . an . . . isthmus!'

His eyes had accustomed themselves sufficiently for him to see, immediately ahead of him, the body of the Headmaster balanced upon his head.

In the peculiar silence his attention was so riveted upon the apparition in front of him that he hardly realized the absence of his class.

He got to his feet and bit at his knuckle, his head thrust forward. He withdrew his head and shook himself like a great dog; and then he leaned forward and stared once more. He had prayed that he was still asleep. But no, this was no dream. He had no idea that the Headmaster was dead, and so, with a great effort (thinking that a fundamental change had taken in Deadyawn's psyche, and that he was showing Bellgrove this balancing feat in an access of self-revelation) he (Bell-grove) began to clap his big, finely-constructed hands together in a succession of deferential thuds, and to wear upon his face an expression of someone both intrigued and surprised, his shoulders drawn back, his head at a slant, his eyebrows raised, and the big forefinger of his right hand at his lips. The line of his mouth rose at either end, but his upward curve might as well have been downwards for all the power it had to disguise his consternation.

The heavy thuds of his hand-clapping sounded solitary. They echoed fully about the room. He turned his eyes to his class as though for support or explanation. He found neither. Only the infinite emptiness of deserted desks, with the broad, hazy shafts of the sun slanting across them.

He put his hand to his head and sat down suddenly.

'Bellgrove!' A crisp, sharp voice from behind him caused him to swing around. There, in a double line, silent as Deadyawn or the empty desks, stood the Professors of Gormenghast, like a male chorus or a travesty of Judgement Day.

Bellgrove stumbled to his feet and passed his hand across his brow.

'Life itself is an isthmus,' said a voice beside him.

Bellgrove turned his head. His mouth was ajar. His carious teeth were bared in a nervous smile.

'What's that?' he said, catching hold of the speaker's gown near the shoulder and pulling it forwards.

'Get a grip on yourself,' said the voice, and it was Shred's. 'This is a new gown. Thank you. Life is an isthmus, I said.'

'Why?' said Bellgrove, but with one eye still on Deadyawn. He was not really listening.

'You ask me *why*!' said Shred. 'Only think! Our Headmaster there,' he said (bowing slightly to the corpse) 'is even now in the second continent. Death's continent. But long before he was even . . .'

Mr Shred was interrupted by Perch-Prism. 'Mr Fluke,' he shouted, 'will you give me a hand?' But for all their efforts they could do little with Deadyawn except reverse him. To seat him in Bellgrove's chair, prior to his removal to the Professors' mortuary, was in a way accomplished, though it was more a case of leaning the headmaster *against* the chair than seating him *in* it, for he was as stiff as a star-fish.

But his gown was draped carefully about him. His face was covered with the blackboard duster, and when at last his mortar-board had been found under the débris of the high chair, it was placed with due decorum on his head.

'Gentlemen,' said Perch-Prism, when they had returned to the Common-room after a junior member had been dispatched to the doctor's, the undertaker's and to the red-stone yard to inform the scholars that the rest of the day was to be spent in an organized search for their school-fellow Titus – 'Gentlemen,' said Perch-Prism, 'two things are paramount. One, that the search for the young Earl shall be pushed forward immediately in spite of interruption; and two, the appointment of the new Headmaster must be immediately made, to avoid anarchy. In my opinion,' said Perch-Prism, his hands grasping the shoulder-tags of his gown while he rocked to and fro on his heels, 'in my opinion the choice should fall, as usual, upon the senior member of the staff, *whatever his qualifications.*'

There was immediate agreement about this. Like one man they saw an even lazier future open out its indolent vistas before them. Bellgrove alone was irritated. For, mixed with his pride, was resentment at Perch-Prism's handling of the subject. As probable headmaster he should already have been taking the initiative.

'What d'you mean by "whatever his qualifications" . . . damn you, 'Prism?' he snarled.

A terrible convulsion in the centre of the room, where Mr Opus Fluke lay sprawled over one of the desks, revealed how that gentleman was fighting for breath.

He was yelling with laughter, yelling like a hundred hounds; but he could make no sound. He shook and rocked, the tears pouring down his crude, male face, his chin like a long loaf shuddering as it pointed to the ceiling.

Bellgrove, turning from Perch-Prism, surveyed Mr Fluke. His noble head had coloured, but suddenly the blood was driven from it. For a flashing moment Bellgrove saw his destiny. Was he, or was he not, to be a leader of men? Was this, or was this not, one of those crucial moments when authority must be exercised – or withheld for ever? Here they were, in full conclave. Here was he – Bellgrove – within his feet of clay, standing in all his weakness before his colleagues. But there was something in him which was not consistent with the proud cast of his face.

At that moment he knew himself to be of finer marl. He had known what ambition was. True, it was long ago and he was no longer worried by such ideas, but he had known of it.

Quite deliberately, realizing that if he did not act at once he would never act again, he lifted a large stone bottle of red ink from the table at his side and, on reaching Mr Fluke and finding his head thrown back, his eyes closed, and his strong jaws wide open in a paroxysm of seismic laughter, Mr Bellgrove poured the entire contents down the funnel of Fluke's throat in one movement of the wrist. Turning to the staff, 'Perch-Prism,' he said, in a voice of such patriarchal authority as startled the professors almost as much as the ink-pouring, 'you will set about organizing the search for his Lordship. Take the staff with you to the red-stone yard. Flannelcat, you will get Mr Fluke removed to the sick-room. Fetch the doctor for him. Report progress this evening. I shall be found in the Headmaster's study. Good morning, Gentlemen.'

As he swept out of the room with a bellying sweep of his gown and a toss of his silver hair, his old heart was beating madly. Oh, the joy of giving orders! Oh, the joy of it! Once he had closed the door behind him, he ran, with high monstrous bounds, to the Headmaster's study and collapsed into the Headmaster's chair – *his* chair from now onwards. He hugged his knees against his chin, flopped over on his side, and wept with the first real sense of happiness he had known for many years.

EIGHTEEN

LIKE rooks hovering in a black cloud over their nests, a posse of professors in a whirl of gowns and a shuffling roofage of mortar-boards, flapped and sidled their individual way towards, and eventually *through*, a narrow opening in a flank of the Masters' Hall.

This opening was less like a doorway than a fissure, though the remains of a lintel were visible and a few boards swung aimlessly near the head of the opening to show that there had once been a door. Faintly discernible on these upper boards were these words: *To the Professorial Quarters: Strictly Private* – and above them some irreverent hand had sketched the lively outline of a stoat in gown and mortar-board. Whether or not the professors had ever noticed this drawing, it is certain that it held no interest for them today. It was enough for them to work their way through the fissure in the wall where the darkness engulfed them, one by one.

Doorless as the opening was, yet there was no question about the Professors' Quarters being 'strictly private'. What lay beyond that cleft in the heavy wall had been a secret for many generations, a secret known only to the succeeding staff – those hoary and impossible bands with whom, by ancient tradition, there was no interference. There had once been talk of *progress* by a young member of a bygone staff, but he had been instantly banished.

It was for the professors to suffer no change. To eye the scaling paint, the rusting pen-nib, the sculpted desk lid, with understanding and approval.

They had by now, one and all, negotiated the narrow opening. Not a soul was left in the Masters' Hall. It was as though no one had been there. A wasp zoomed across the empty floor-boards with a roar; and then the silence filled the hall once again, as though with a substance.

Where were the professors now? What were they doing? They were half-way along the third curve of a domed passageway which ended in a descending flight of steps at the base of which stood an enormous turnstile.

As the professors moved like a black, hydra-headed dragon with a hundred flapping wings, it might have been noticed that for all the sinister quality of the monster's upper half, yet in its numerous legs there was a certain gaiety. The little legs of blackness almost twinkled, almost hopped. The great legs let fall their echoing feet in a jocular and carefree fashion as though they were smacking a friend on the back.

And yet it was not wholly gay, this great composite dragon. For there were two of its feet which moved less happily than the others. They belonged to Bellgrove.

Delighted as he was to be the Headmaster, yet the alteration which this was making in his way of life was beginning to gall him. And yet was there not something about him more imposing than before? Had he taken some kind of grip on himself? His face was stern and melancholy. He led his staff like a prophet to their quarters. *Their* quarters, for they were no longer *his*. With his accession to Headmasterdom he had forfeited his room above the Professors' Quadrangle which he had occupied for three-quarters of his life. Alone among the professors it was for him to turn back after he had escorted his staff a certain distance of the way, and to return alone to the headmaster's bedroom above the Masters' Hall.

It had been a difficult time for him since he first put on the Zodiac gown of high office. Was he winning or losing his fight for authority? He longed for respect, but he loved indolence also. Time would tell whether the nobility of his august head could become the symbol of his leadership. To tread the corridors of Gormenghast the acknowledged master of staff and pupil alike! He must be wise, stern, yet generous. He must be revered. That was it . . . *revered*. But did this mean that he would be involved in extra work . . . ? Surely, at his age . . . ?

The excitement in the multiform legs of the dragon had only begun to operate since the professors had left the Masters' Hall behind them, and with the Hall their duties also. For their day in the classrooms of Gormenghast was over, and if there was one thing above others that the professors looked forward to, it was this thrill, this five o'clock thrill of returning to their quarters.

They breathed in the secret air of their demesne. Over their faces a series of private smiles began to play. They were nearing a world they understood – not with their brains, but with the dumb, happy, ancestral understanding of their marrow bones.

The long evening was ahead. Not one ink-faced boy would they see for fifteen hours.

Taking deep breaths into its many lungs the hydra-headed dragon approached the stone flight of steps. In its wake, along the domed ceiling of the long corridor, an impalpable serpent of exhaled pipe-smoke hovered and coiled.

An almost imperceptible widening of the corridor was now apparent. The professors became less cramped in their movements as the dragon began to come to bits. The widening of the corridor had become something quite unique, for a great vista of wooden floor-boards was spread before them until the walls (now about forty feet apart) turned abruptly away on either side to flank the wide wooden terrace which overlooked the flight of stairs. Although this flight was exceptionally broad and the professors as they descended had plenty of space in which to indulge themselves (if the whim should take them) in a general loosening of their deportment, a more vigorous smacking or a fiercer twinkling of their feet – yet at the base of the stairs there was, once again, a bottleneck; for although there was plenty of room on each side of the ancient turnstile for them to stream past and into the great crumbling chamber beyond, yet the custom was that the turnstile should be the only means of access to the chamber.

Above the stone flight the sloping roof was in so advanced a state of disintegration that a great deal of light found its way through the holes in the roof, to lie in golden pools all over the great flight of stairs with their low treads and wide terrace-like shelves of shallow stone.

As with their difficult egress from the Masters' Hall, the professors were now being held up at the Great Turnstile.

But here it was a more leisurely affair. There was neither the scuffling nor the agitation. They were in their own realms again. Their apartments that surrounded the small quadrangle would be waiting for them. What did it matter if they waited a little longer than they could have wished? The long, bland, archaic, nostalgic, almond-smelling evening lay ahead of them, and then the long, sequestered night before the clanging bell aroused them, and a day of ink- and thumb-marks, cribbing and broken spectacles, flies and figures, coastlines, prepositions, isthmuses and essays, paper darts, test tubes, catapults, chemicals and prisms, dates, battles and tame white mice, and hundred half-formed, ingenious and quizzical faces, with their chapped red ears that never listened, renewed itself.

Deliberately, almost *augustly*, the gowned and mortar-boarded figures followed one another through the great red turnstile and filed into the chamber beyond.

But for the most part, the professors stood in groups, or were seated on the lower steps of the stone flights, where they waited to take their turn at the 'stile'. They were in no hurry. Here and there a savant could be seen lying stretched at full length along one of the steps or shelves of the stone stairs. Here and there a group would be squatting like aboriginals upon their haunches, their gowns gathered about them. Some were in shadow, and very dark they looked – like bandits in a bad light; some were silhouetted against the hazy, golden swathes of the sun shafts; and some stood transfixed in the last rays as they streamed through the honeycombed roof.

A small muscular gentleman with a spade-shaped beard was balancing himself upside down and was working his way down the wide steps on his hands. His head was, for the most part, hidden because his gown fell over and obliterated it, so that, apart from balancing, he had to feel for the edge of each step with his hidden hands. But occasionally his head would appear out of the folds of his gown and the beard could be seen for a quick moment, its harsh black spade a few inches from the ground.

Of the few who watched him bemusedly there were none who had not seen it all a hundred times before. A long-limbed figure, with his knees drawn up to his blue jaw, which they supported, stared abstractedly at a group which stood out in silhouette against a swarm of golden motes. Had he been a little closer and a little less abstracted he might have heard some very peculiar ejaculations.

But he could see quite clearly that at the centre of this distant group a short precise figure was handing out to his colleagues what looked like small stiff pieces of paper.

And so it was. The sprightly Perch-Prism was dispensing the invitation cards which he had received that same afternoon by special messenger:

IRMA and ALFRED PRUNESQUALLOR
hope to have the
pleasure of ....'s company
on
.... (etc.)

One by one the invited parties were handed their invitations, and there was not a single professor who could withhold either a gasp or grunt of surprise or a twitch of the eyebrow.

Some were so stupefied that they were forced to sit down on the steps for a short while until their pulse rate slackened.

Shred and Shrivell tapped their teeth with the gilded edges of their cards, and were already making guesses at the psychological implications.

Fluke, his wide lipless mouth disgorging endless formations of dense and cumulous smoke, was gradually allowing a giant grin to spread itself across his gaunt face.

Flannelcat was embarrassingly excited, and was already trying to rub a thumb-mark from the corner of his card, which he had every intention of framing.

Bellgrove had his great prophet's jaw hanging wide.

There were sixteen invitations altogether. The entire staff of the Leather Room had been invited.

They had arrived, these invitation cards, at a time when Perch-Prism had been the only master present in the Common-room and he had taken over the responsibility of delivering them personally to the others.

Suddenly Opus Fluke's long leather mouth opened like a horse's and a howl of insensitive laughter reverberated through the sun-blotched place.

A score of mortar-boards swivelled.

'Really!' said the sharp, precise voice of Perch-Prism. 'Really, my dear Fluke! What a way to receive an invitation from a lady! Come, come.'

But Fluke could hear nothing. The idea of being invited to a party by Irma Prunesquallor had somehow broken through to the most sensitized area of his diaphragm, and he yelled and yelled again until he was breathless. As he panted hoarsely to a standstill, he did not even look about him: he was still in his own world of amusement; but he *did* hold the Invitation Card up before his wet and pebbly eyes once more, only to open his wide mouth again in a fresh spasm; but there was no laughter left in him.

Perch-Prism's pug-baby features expressed a certain condescension, as though he *understood* how Mr Fluke felt, but was nevertheless surprised and mildly irritated by the coarseness in his colleague's make-up.

It was Perch-Prism's saving grace that in spite of his old-maidishness, his clipped and irritatingly academic delivery and his general aura of omniscience, yet he had a strongly developed sense of the ridiculous and was often forced to laugh when his brain and pride wished otherwise.

'And the Headmaster,' he said, turning to the noble figure at his side, whose jaw still hung open like the mouth of a sepulchre, 'what does *he* think, I wonder? What does our Headmaster think about it all?'

Bellgrove came to with a start. He looked about him with the melancholy grandeur of a sick lion. Then he found his mouth was open, so he closed it gradually, for he would not have them think that he would hurry himself for anyone.

He turned his vacant lion's eye to Perch-Prism, who stood there perkily looking up at him and tapping his shiny invitation card against his polished thumbnail.

'My dear Perch-Prism,' said Bellgrove, 'why on earth should you be interested in my reaction to what is, after all, not a very extraordinary thing in my life? It is possible, you know,' he continued laboriously, 'it is just possible that when I was a young man I received more invitations to various kinds of functions than you have ever received, or can ever hope to receive, during the course of your life.'

'But *exactly*!' said Perch-Prism. 'And that is why we want his opinion. That is why our Headmaster alone can help us. What could be more enlightening than to have it straight from the horse's mouth?'

For neatness' sake he could not help wishing that he were addressing Opus Fluke, for Bellgrove's mouth, though hardly hyper-human, was nothing like a horse's.

'Prism,' he said, 'compared with me you are a young man. But you are not so young as to be ignorant of the elements of decent conduct. Be good enough in your puff-adder attitude to life to find room for one delicacy at least; and that is to address me, if you must, in a manner less calculated to offend. I will *not* be talked *across*. My staff must realize this from the outset. I will *not* be the third person singular. I am old, I admit it. But I am nevertheless here. *Here*,' he roared; 'and standing on the selfsame pavement with you, Master 'Prism; and I *exist*, by hell! in my full conversational and vocative rights.'

He coughed and shook his leonine head. 'Change your idiom, my young friend, or change your tense, and lend me a handkerchief to put over my head – these sunbeams are giving me a headache.'

Perch-Prism produced a blue silk handkerchief at once and draped it over the peeved and noble head.

'Poor old "prickles" Bellgrove, poor old fangs,' he mused, whispering the words into the old man's ears as he tied the corners of the blue handkerchief into little knots, where it hung over the elder's head. 'It'll be just the thing for him, so it will – a *wild* party at the Doctor's, ha, ha, ha, ha, ha!'

Bellgrove opened his rather weak mouth and grinned. He could never keep his sham dignity up for long; but then he remembered his position again and in a voice of sepulchral authority –

'Watch your step, sir,' he said. 'You have twisted my tail for long enough.'

'What a peculiar business this Prunesquallor affair *is*, my dear Flannelcat,' said Mr Crust. 'I rather doubt whether I can afford to go. I wonder whether you could possibly – er – lend me . . .'

But Flannelcat interrupted. 'They've asked me, too,' he said, his invitation card shaking in his hand. 'It is a long time since . . .'

'It is a long time since our evenings were disturbed from the Outside like this,' interrupted Perch-Prism. 'You gentlemen will have to brush yourselves up a bit. How long is it since you have seen a lady, Mr Fluke?'

'Not half long enough,' said Opus Fluke, drawing noisily at his pipe. 'Never care for hens. Irritated me. May be wrong – quite possible – that's another point. But for me – no. Spoilt the day completely.'

'But you will accept, of course, won't you, my dear fellow?' said Perch-Prism, inclining his shiny round head to one side.

Opus Fluke yawned and then stretched himself before he replied.

'When is it, friend?' he asked (as though it made any difference to him when his every evening was an identical yawn).

'Next Friday evening, at seven o'clock – R.S.V.P. it is,' panted Flannelcat.

'If dear old bloody Bellgrove goes,' said Mr Fluke, after a long pause,

'I couldn't stay away – not if I was paid. It'll be as good as a play to watch him.'

Bellgrove bared his irregular teeth in a leonine snarl and then he took out a small notebook, with his eyes on Mr Fluke, made a note. Approaching his taunter, 'Red Ink', he whispered, and then began to laugh uncontrollably. Mr Fluke was stupefied.

'Well . . . well . . . well . . .' he said at last.

'It is far from "well", Mr Fluke,' said Bellgrove, recovering his composure; 'and it will not be well until you learn to speak to your Headmaster like a gentleman.'

Said Shrivell to Shred: 'As for Irma Prunesquallor, it's a plain case of mirror-madness, brought on by enlargement of the terror-duct – but not altogether.'

Said Shred to Shrivell: 'I disagree. It is the Doctor's shadow cast upon the shorn and naked soul of his sister, which shadow she takes to be destiny – and *here* I agree with you that the terror-duct comes into play, for the length of her neck and the general frustration have driven her subconscious into a general craving for males – a substitute, of course, for gollywogs.'

Said Shrivell to Shred: 'Perhaps we are both right in our different ways.' He beamed at his friend. 'Let us leave it at that, shall we? We will know more when we see her.'

'Oh, shut up! you bloody old woman,' said Mulefire, with a deadly scowl.

'Oh come, come, la!' said Cutflower. 'Let us be terribly gay, la! My, my! If it isn't getting chilly, la – call me feverish.'

It was true, for looking up they found they were plunged in deep shade, the sun-blotch having moved on; and they saw also, as they raised their heads, that they were the last of the professors to be left on the stone steps.

Motioning the others to follow, Bellgrove led them through the red turnstile, where a moment or two after, they had all passed through its creaking arms and into the dark and crumbling hall beyond; he turned and climbed the staircase alone and eventually found himself in the Masters' Hall once more.

But the staff, after passing through the crumbling chamber, indian-filed its way along a peculiarly high and narrow passage; and at last, after descending yet another flight of stairs – this time of ancient walnut – they passed through a doorway on the far side of which lay their quadrangle.

It was here, in the communal privacy of their quarters, that the excitement which they had felt mounting within them once they had passed out of the Masters' Hall, lessened; but another kind of excitement quickened. On reaching their quadrangle they had digested the fact that they were free for another evening. The sense of 'escape' had gone, but an even lighter sensation freed their hearts and feet. Their bowels felt like water. Great lumps arose in their throats. There were tears in the corners of their eyes.

All about their quadrangle the pillars of the cloisters glowed (although they were in shadow) with the dark rose-gold of the brick. Above the arches of the cloisters a terrace of rose-coloured brickwork circumscribed the quadrangle at about twenty feet above the ground; and punctuating the wall at the rear of this high terrace were the doors of the Professors' apartment. On each door, according to custom, the owner's name was added to the long list of former occupants. These names were carefully printed on the black wood of each door, their vertical columns of small and exact lettering all but filling the available space. The rooms themselves were small and uniform in shape, but were as various in character as their occupants.

The first thing that the professors did on returning to their quarters was to go to their several rooms and change their black gowns of office for the dark-red variety issued for their evening hours.

Their mortar-boards were hung up behind their doors or sent skimming across their rooms to some convenient ledge or corner. The dog's-eared condition of most of their boards was due to this 'skimming'. When thrown in the right way, out of doors and against a slight breeze, they could be made to climb into the air, the black cup uppermost, the tassels floating below like the black tails of donkeys. When thirty at a time soared at the sun above the quadrangle, then was a schoolboy's nightmare made palpable.

Once in their wine-red gowns it was the usual custom to step out of their rooms on to the terrace of rose-red brick, where, leaning on its balustrade, the professors would spend one of the pleasantest hours of the day, conversing or ruminating until the sound of the supper-gong called them to the refectory.

To the old Quadman, sweeping the leaves from the mellow brickwork of the quadrangle floor, it was a sight that never failed to please as, surrounded on every side by the glowing cloisters and above them by the long wine-red line of the professors as they leaned with their elbows on the terrace wall, he shepherded the fluttering leaves together with his ragged broom.

On this particular night, although not a single mortar-board was sent skimming, the staff became very flighty indeed towards the end of their evening meal in the Long Hall, when innumerable suggestions were propounded as to the inner reason for the Prunesquallors' invitations. The most fantastic of all was put forward by Cutflower, to wit that Irma, in need of a husband, was turning to them as a possible source. At this suggestion the crude Opus Fluke, in an

excess of ribald mirth, crashed his great, raw ham of a hand down
on the long table so heavily as to cause a *corps de ballet* of knives,
forks and spoons to sail into the air and for a pair of table legs to do
the splits; so that the nine professors at his table found the remains
of their supper lying at every angle below the level of their knees.
Those who were holding their glasses in their hands were happy
enough, but for those whose wine was spilt among the débris, a
moment or two of reflection was occasioned before they could regain
the spirit of the evening.

The idea that any one of them should get married seemed to them
ludicrously funny. It was not that they felt themselves unworthy, far
from it. It was that such a thing belonged to another world.

'But yes, but yes, indeed, Cutflower, you are right,' said Shrivell at
the first opportunity of making himself heard. 'Shred and I were saying
much the same thing.'

'Quite so,' said Shred.

'In my case,' said Shrivell, 'sublimation is simple enough, for what
with the crags and eagles that find their way into every confounded
dream I have – and I dream every night, not to speak of my automatic
writing, which puts my absurd love for Nature in its place – for in
reading what I have written, as it were in a trance, I can see how foolish
it is to give a thought to natural phenomena, which are, after all,
nothing but an accretion of accidents . . . er . . . where was I?'

'It doesn't matter,' said Perch-Prism. 'The point is that we have been
invited: that we shall be guests, and that above all we shall do the right
thing. Good grief!' he said, looking about him at the faces of the staff,
'I wish I was going alone.'

A bell rang.

The Professors rose at once to their feet. A moment of traditional
observance had arrived. Turning the long tables upside down – and
there were twelve of them – they seated themselves, one behind another,
within the upturned table tops as though they were boats and were
about to oar their way into some fabulous ocean.

For a moment there was a pause, and then the bell rang again. Before
its echo had died in the long refectory, the twelve crews of the motionless
flotilla had raised their voices in an obscure chant of former days when,
presumably, it held some kind of significance. Tonight it was bayed
forth into the half-light with a slow, knocking rhythm, but there was no
disguising the boredom in their voices. They had intoned those lines,
night after night, for as long as they had been professors, and it might
well have been taken for a dirge so empty were their voices:

Hold fast
To the law
Of the last
Cold tome,
Where the earth
Of the truth
Lies thick
On the page,
And the loam
Of faith
In the ink
Long fled
From the drone
Of the nib
Flows on
Through the breath
Of the bone
Reborn
In a dawn
Of doom
Where blooms
The rose
For the winds
The Child
For the tomb
The thrush.
For the hush
Of song,
The corn
For the scythe
And the thorn
In wait
For the heart
Till the last
Of the first
Depart,
And the least
Of the past
Is dust
And the dust
Is lost.
Hold fast!

NINETEEN

THE margin of the forest under whose high branches Titus was standing was an interwoven screen of foliage, more like a green wall constructed for some histrionic purpose than a natural growth. Was it to hide away some drama that it arose there, so sheer and so thick? Or was it the backcloth of some immortal mime? Which was the stage and which the audience? There was not a sound.

Titus, wrenching two boughs apart, thrust himself forward and wriggled into the green darkness; thrust again, prising his feet against a great lateral root. The leaves and the moss were cold with the dew. Working forwards on his elbows, he found his way almost completely barred by a tough network of boughs; but the edge of his eagerness to break his way through was whetted, for a branch had swung back and switched him across his cheek, and in the pain of the moment he fought the muscled branches, until the upper part of his body had forced a gap which he kept from re-closing with his aching shoulders. His arms were forward of his body and he was able to free his face of the leaves, and, as he panted to regain his breath, to see ahead of him, spreading into the clear distances, the forest floor like a sea of golden moss. From its heaving expanses, arose, as through the chimera of a daydream, a phantasmic gathering of ancient oaks. Like dappled gods they stood, each on his own preserve, the wide glades of moss flowing between them in swathes of gold and green and away into the clear, dwindling distances.

When his breath came more easily, Titus realized the silence of the picture that hung there before him. Like a canvas of gold with its hundreds of majestic oaks, their winding branches dividing and sub-dividing into gilded fingertips – the solid acorns and the deep clusters of the legendary leaves.

His heart beat loudly as the warm breath of the silence flowed about him and drew him in.

In his last wrench and thrust to escape from the marginal boughs, his coat was torn off bodily by a thorn-tree with a hand of hideous fingers. He left it there, hanging from the branch, the long thorns of the tree impaling it like the finger-nails of a ghoul.

Once the noise of his fight with the branches had subsided and the warm everlasting silence had come down again, he stepped forward upon the moss. It was resilient and springy, its golden surface exquisitely compact. He moved again with a higher tread and found that on landing it was the easiest thing in the world to float off into the next

movement. The ground was made for running on, for every step lifted
the body into the next. Titus leapt to his right and began to lope off
down the dark-green verge of the forest in giant bounds. The exhilaration of these 'flights' through the air were for some while all-
absorbing, but as their novelty staled so there came a mounting terror,
for the thick screen of the forest's verge on his right appeared endless,
stretching away, as it did, to the limit of his vision; and the motionless,
soundless glow of the oaks and the great spaces of moss on his left
seemed never to change, though tree after tree swam by him as he fled.

Not a bird called. Not a squirrel moved among the branches. Not a
leaf fell. Even his feet when they struck the moss were soundless; only
a faint sigh passed his ears as he floated, reminding him that there was
such a thing as sound.

And now, what he had loved he loathed. He loathed this deathly,
terrible silence. He loathed the gold light among the trees, the endless
vistas of the moss – even the gliding flight from footmark to footmark.
For it was as though he were being drawn towards some dangerous
place or person, and that he had no power to hold himself back. The
mid-air thrill was now the thrill of Fear.

He had been afraid of leaving the dark margin on his right, for it was
his only hold upon his location; but now he felt it as part of some
devilish plan, and that to cling to its tangled skirt would be to deliver
himself to some ambushed horror; and so he turned suddenly to his left
and, although the vistas of oakland were now a sickening and phantom
land, he bounded into its gold heart with all the speed he could.

Fear grew upon him as he careered. He had become more an antelope
than a boy, but for all his speed he must have been a novice in the art
of travel – through moss-leaping – for suddenly, while he was in mid-
air, his arms held out on either side for balance, he caught sight, for the
merest fraction of an instant, of a living creature.

Like himself, it was in mid-air, but there was no other resemblance.
Titus was heavily if sparsely built. This creature was exquisitely
slender. It floated through the golden air like a feather, the slender
arms along the sides of the gracile body, the head turned slightly away
and inclined a little as though on a pillow of air.

Titus was by now convinced that he was asleep: that he was running
through the deep of a dream: that his fear was nightmare: that what he
had just seen was no more than an apparition, and that though it
haunted him he knew the hopeless absurdity of following so fleeting a
wisp of the night.

Had he thought himself awake he must surely have pursued, however
faint his hope of overtaking the slender creature. For the conscious
mind can be set aside and subdued by the emotions, but in a dream
world all is logic. And so, in fear of the gold oakwood of his dream, he

continued in his loping, effortless, soundless, dream-like bounds, deeper and deeper into the forest and over the elastic velvet of the moss.

For all his conviction that he was asleep, and in spite of the resilience and apparent ease of his flight-running, he had become very tired. The gilded and encrusted trunks of the great oak trees swam by him one after another. The emptiness seemed even more complete and terrible since that will-o'-the-wisp had floated across his path.

All of a sudden he became sharply aware of his fatigue and of hunger, and at the same time a weakening of his conviction that he was dreaming. 'If I am dreaming,' he thought, 'then why should I need to spring from the ground? Why shouldn't I just be carried along?' And to test his idea he made no further effort, merely keeping his balance in the air each time his drop to earth lifted him again into those long and fantastic cruises; but the impetus weakened with every dwindling flight and the volitant boy came gradually to a standstill.

With the rhythm of his progress broken, his belief that he was in a state of dream was finally dispelled. For his hunger had become insistent.

He looked about him. The same scene enclosed him with its mellow cyclorama – its hateful dream of gold.

But for all this horror (it had laid hold of him again now that he no longer believed himself asleep), his fear was in some way lessened by a peculiar thrill which seemed to grow in intensity rather than quieten until it had become a trembling globe of ice under his ribs. Something for which he had unconsciously pined had shown either itself or its emblem in the gold oak woods. Realizing that he had been wide awake ever since he had crept (how long ago!) to the stables of Gormenghast, he knew that slender spectre – that reed-like, feather-like thing with its head turned half way as it rose in slanting volitation across a glade as wide as a lawn, was true, was here in the oak forest with him at that very moment: was perhaps watching him.

It was not only the uncanniness of such a phasma which haunted him now. It was his craving to see again that essence so far removed from what was Gormenghast.

And yet, what had he seen? Nothing that he could describe. It had been so rapid – that flight across his vision: gone, as it were, before his eyes were ready. The head turned away . . . turned away. What was it that cried to him? What was it that this shred, this floating shred of life, expressed? For in the air with which it had moved through space was a quality for which Titus unknowingly hungered. On the long glissade of the wasp-gold flight, like a figment from a rarer and more curious climate than Titus had ever breathed, it had expressed as it rose across the glade the quintessence of detachment: the sense of something intrinsically tameless, and of a distilled and thin-air beauty.

All this in a flash. All this, a confusion in Titus' heart and brain.

What he had felt when he had halted his horse that same morning and heard the voices of the mountain and the woods crying, 'Do you dare!' was redoubled within him. He had seen something which lived a life of its own: which had no respect for the ancient lords of Gormenghast, for ritual among the footworn flagstones: for the sacredness of the immemorial House. Something that would no more think of bowing to the seventy-seventh Earl than would a bird, or the branch of a tree.

He beat his fist into the palm of his other hand. He was frightened. He was excited. His teeth chattered. The glimpse of a world, of an unformulated world, where human life could be lived by other rules than those of Gormenghast, had shaken him; but for all the newness, all the vague hugeness of the mutinous sensations that were thronging in him, yet under the pain of his hunger, even they began to give way to the consuming need for food.

Was there a slightly different feeling about the light as it slanted through the oak leaves and lay along the glades? Was there a less deathly stillness in the air? For a moment Titus thought he heard a sigh among the leaves above him. Was there a quickening in the torpor of the midday stillness?

There was no way for Titus to know which way to turn. He only knew that he could not return in the direction from which he had come. And so he began to walk as quickly, yet as lightly, as he could (to avoid the nightmare sensation that those loping and unbridled flights through the air had bred in him) in the direction in which the mysterious and floating creature had disappeared.

It was not long before the peerless lawns of moss that stretched between the oaks became pranked by clumps of ferns which, ignoring the sun's rays, appeared silhouetted, so dark was the viridian of their hanging fronds, so luminous their golden background. The relief to the boy's spirit was instantaneous, and when the sumptuous floor gave place to coarse grasses and the rank profusion of flowering weeds, and when, most refreshing of all to Titus' eyes, the oaks no longer cast their ancestral spell across the vistas, but were challenged by a variety of trees and shrubs, until the last of those gnarled monarchs had withdrawn and Titus found himself in a fresher atmosphere, then, at last he was clear of the nightmare and, with his hunger for redundant proof, was once again in the clear, sharp, actual world that he knew. The ground began to drop away before him at a lively gradient. As on the far side of the oak forest, here also were scattered rocks and groups of ferns; and then all of a sudden Titus gave a shout of happiness to see a living thing after the emptiness and nervelessness of the golden glades – a dog fox that, disturbed by his footsteps, had woken out of its midday sleep in a quiet nest of ferns, had got to its feet with extraordinary self-possession and trotted away at an even pace across the slant of the falling ground.

At the base of the slope a hazel wood began. Here and there a silver birch lifted its feathery head above the thicker foliage; or a dark-green ilex seemed like a green shadow in the sunlight. Titus began to hear the voices of birds. How could he quieten his hunger? It was too early in the year for wild fruit or berries. He was utterly lost, and the exhilaration he had felt at escaping from the oak woods was beginning to dwindle and to turn into depression when, after threading his way for little more than a quarter of a mile through the hazel trees he heard the sound of water; faint but distinct, away to the west. At once he began to run in the direction of the cool sound, but was forced to relapse into a walking pace, for his legs were heavy and tired, and the ground was uneven and patched with ground ivies. But as the sound of the water grew momently louder, so the ilex trees began to grow more thickly among the hazels, so that there was a rich, dark, blackish greenness about the shadows of the trees both overhead and at Titus' feet. The water now sounded loud in his ears, but so dense had the trees become that it was with a sudden shock that the dazzling breadth of a fast foam-streaked river appeared before him, and at that very instant, from out of the shadows of the wood on the opposite bank, there stepped a figure.

He was a gaunt and marcid creature, very tall and thin; his high scrawny shoulders twisted forwards, his cadaverous head lowered, with the thinly bearded jaw protruding as though in defiance. He was clothed in what had once been a suit of black material, but was now so bleached by sun and soaked in a hundred dews that it had become a threadbare blotchwork of olive-and-grey rags indistinguishable among the leaves of the forest.

As this gaunt figure stepped down to the water's edge a sound of clicking that Titus could in no way account for floated over the bright waters. It appeared to break out at his every step like a distant musket shot or the breaking of a dry twig, and to cease whenever he stopped moving. But Titus soon forgot about this peculiar noise, for the man on the opposite bank had reached the river and waded out to where a flat, sun-baked rock the size of a table basked in the midstream.

As he extracted from among his rags a length of line and a hook, and as he began to fix the bait, he glanced about him, comparatively carelessly at first and then with a dawning apprehension, until finally he dropped his line upon the rock beside him and, sweeping the opposite shore with his eyes, he focused them on Titus.

Partially shielded behind a heavy branch of leaves, Titus, who had made no sound, was horrified at being so suddenly discovered and the blood rushed into his face. But he could not take his eyes from those of the emaciated man. He was now crouching on the rock. His small eyes, which had burned beneath his rocklike brows, now glittered with a peculiar light and all at once his hoarse voice sounded across the river:

'My Lord!' It was a sharp, rough cry, with a catch in the throat as though the voice had not been sounded for a long while.

Titus, whose instincts had been torn between flying from those hot wild eyes and his excitement at finding another human being, however emaciated and uncouth, stepped forward into the sunlight at the river's edge. He was frightened and his heart beat loudly, but he was famished also and deadly weary.

'Who are you?' he cried. The figure stood up on the hot rock. His head was thrust forward towards Titus; his tall body trembled.

'Flay,' he said at last, his voice hardly audible.

'Flay!' cried Titus. 'I've heard of you.'

'Aye,' said Flay, his hands gripped together . . . 'likely enough, my lord.'

'They told me you were dead, Mr Flay.'

'No doubt of it.' (He looked about him again, taking his eyes from Titus for the first time.) 'Alone?' His interrogation sounded hoarsely across the water.

'Yes,' said Titus. 'Are you ill?'

Titus had never seen so gaunt a man before.

'Ill, lordship? No, boy, no . . . but banished.'

'Banished!' cried Titus.

'Banished, boy. When you were only a . . . when your father . . . my lord . . .' He ended suddenly. 'Your sister Fuchsia?'

'She's all right.'

'Ah!' said the thin man, 'no doubt of it.' (There was a note almost of happiness in his voice, but then, with a new note): 'You're done, my lord, 'n windless. What brought you?'

'I escaped, Mr Flay – ran away. I'm hungry, Mr Flay.'

'Escaped!' whispered the long man to himself with horror; but he gathered and pocketed his hook and line and withheld a hundred burning questions.

'Water's too deep – too fast here. Made crossing – boulders – half mile up stream – not far, lordship, not far. Follow your edge with me, follow your river edge, boy – we'll have a rabbit'; (he seemed to be talking to himself as he waded back to the bank on his side of the river) 'rabbit and pigeon and a long cabin-sleep . . . Blown he is . . . son of Lord Sepulchrave . . . ready to drop . . . Tell him anywhere . . . eyes like her ladyship's . . . Escaped from the Castle! . . . No . . . no . . . mustn't do that . . . No, no . . . must send him back, seventy-seventh Earl . . . Had him in my pocket . . . size of a monkey . . . long ago . . .'

And so Flay rambled on as he strode along the bank, with Titus following him on the opposite shore, until after what seemed an endless journey by the water's edge they came to the crossing of boulders. The river ran shallowly at this point, but it had been no easy work for Flay to shift and set the heavy boulders in place. For five years they had stood firm in the rushing water. Flay had made a perfect ford, and Titus crossed at once to him. For a moment or two they stood awkwardly staring at each other; and then, all of a sudden, the cumulative effects of his physical excitement, the shocks and privations of the day, told upon Titus and he collapsed at the knees. The gaunt man caught him up in an instant and, putting the boy carefully over his shoulder, set off through the trees. For all his apparent emaciation there was no question as to Mr Flay's stamina. The river was soon left far behind. His long, sinewy arms held Titus firmly in place across his shoulder; his lank legs covered the ground with a long, thin, muscular stride and, save for the clicking of his knee-joints, with peculiar silence. He had learned during his exile among the woods and rocks the value of silence, and it was second nature for him to pick his way over the ground like a man born to the woods.

The pace and certainty of his progress testified to his intimate knowledge of every twist and turn of the terrain.

Now he was waist deep in a valley of bracken. Now he was climbing a slope of reddish sandstone; now he was skirting a rock-face whose crown overhung its base and whose extensive surface was knuckly with the clay nests of innumerable martins; now he had below him a drop into a sunless valley; and now the walnut-covered slopes from where, each evening, with hideous regularity a horde of owls set sail on bloody missions.

When Flay, topping the brow of a sandy hill, stood for a moment breathing heavily and stared down into the little valley, Titus, who had insisted upon walking by himself for some while past – for even Flay had not been able to sustain his weight during the uphill climbs – stopped also, and with his hands on his knees, his tired legs rigid, he leaned forward in a position of rest.

The little valley, or dell, beneath them was shut in by tree-covered slopes, save to the south where walls of rock overgrown with lichen and mosses shone brightly in the rays of the declining sun.

At the far end of this grey-green wall were three deep holes in the rock – two of them several feet above the ground and one at the level of the valley's sandy floor.

Along the valley ran a small stream, broadening out into an extensive pool of clear water in the centre, for at the far end of the lake where it had narrowed to a tongue was a rough dam. Long evenings had been spent in its making, simple as it was. Flay had hauled a couple of the heaviest logs he could manage and laid them close to one another across the stream. Titus could see them plainly from where he stood and the thin stream of the overflow at the dam's centre. The sound of this overflow trilled and splashed in the silence of the evening light, and the little valley was filled with its glass-like voice.

They descended to the patchwork valley of grass and sand and skirted the stream until they reached the dam and the broad expanse of the trapped water. Not a breath of air disturbed the tender blue of its glass-like surface in which the hillside trees were minutely reflected. Rows of stakes had been driven into and against the inner sides of the logs to form a crib. This space had been filled with mud and stones until a wall had risen and the lake had formed, and a new sound had come to the valley – the tinkling sound of the glittering overflow.

A few moments later they were at the mouth of the lowest of the openings into the rock. It was but a cleft, about the width of an ordinary door, but it widened into a cave, a spacious and fern-hung place. This inner cave was lit by the reflected light thrown from the sides of the wide natural chimneys whose vents were those mouth-like openings in the rock face a dozen feet above the entrance. Titus followed Flay through this fissure-like doorway and when he had reached the cool and roughly circular floor of the inner cave he marvelled at its lightness, although it was not possible for a single ray of the sun to pierce unhindered, for the wide rocky chimneys wound this way and that before they reached the sunlight. Yet the sunbeams reflected from the sides of the winding chimneys flooded the floor with cool light. It was a high domed place, this cave, with several massive shelves of rock and a number of natural ledges and niches. On the left-hand side the most impressive of these natural outcrops stood out from the wall in the form of a five-sided table with a smooth shelving top.

These few things Titus was able to take in automatically, but he was too exhausted and sick with hunger to do more than nod his head and smile faintly at the long man, who had lowered his tilted head at Titus as though to see whether the boy was pleased. A moment later Titus was lying on a rough couch of deep dry ferns. He closed his eyes and, in spite of his hunger, fell asleep.

TWENTY

When Titus awoke the walls of the cave were leaping to and fro in a red light, their outcrops and shelves of stone flinging out their disproportionate shadows and withdrawing them with a concertina motion. The ferns, like tongues of fire, burned as they hung from the darkness of the dome-ing roof, and the stones of the crude oven in which an hour or more ago Flay had lit a great fire of wood and fir-cones, glowed like liquid gold.

Titus raised himself on his elbow and saw the scare-crow silhouette of the almost legendary Mr Flay (for Titus had heard many stories of his father's servant) as he knelt against the glow with his twelve-foot shadow reaching along the gleaming floor and climbing the wall of the cave.

'I am in the middle of an adventure,' Titus repeated to himself, several times, as though the words themselves were significant.

His mind raced over the happenings of the day which had just ended. He had no sense of confusion when he woke. He recollected everything instantaneously. But his recollections were interrupted by the sudden teasing excitement of the rich odour of something being roasted – it may have been this that had awakened him. The long man was twisting something round and round, slowly, on the flames. The ache of his hunger became unbearable, and Titus got to his feet, and as he did so Mr Flay said, 'It's ready, lordship – stay where you are.'

Breaking pieces from the flesh of the pheasant, and pouring over them a rich gravy, he brought them over to Titus on a wooden plate which he had made himself. It was the cross section of what had been a dead tree, four inches thick, its centre scooped into a shallow basin. In his other hand, as he approached the boy, was a mug of spring water.

Titus lay down again on the bracken bed, resting himself on one elbow. He was too ravenous to speak but gave the straggling figure that towered over him a gesture of the hand – as though of recognition – and then, without a moment wasted, he devoured the rich meal like a young animal.

Flay had returned to the stone oven, where he busied himself with various tasks, feeding himself intermittently as he proceeded. Then he sat down on a ledge of rock near the fire on which he fixed his eyes. Titus had been too preoccupied to watch him, but now, with his wooden plate scraped to the grain, he drank deeply of the cold spring water and glanced over the lip of the mug at the old exile, the man whom his mother had banished – the faithful servant of his dead father.

'Mr Flay,' he said.

'Lordship?'

'How far away am I?'

'Twelve miles, lordship.'

'And it's very late. It's night-time, isn't it?'

'Aye. Take you at dawn. Time for sleep. Time for sleep.'

'It's like a dream, Mr Flay. This cave. You. The fire. Is it true?'

'Aye.'

'I like it,' said Titus. 'But I'm afraid, I think.'

'Not proper, lordship – you being here – in my south cave.'

'Have you other caves?'

'Yes, two others – to the west.'

'I will come and see them – if I can escape, one day, eh, Mr Flay?'

'Not proper, lordship.'

'I don't care,' said Titus. 'What else have you got?'

'A shanty.'

'Where?'

'Gormenghast forest – river-bank – salmon – sometimes.'

Titus got up and walked to the fire where he sat down, his legs crossed. The flames lit his young face.

'I'm a bit frightened, you know,' he said. 'It's my first night away from the castle. I suppose they are all looking for me . . . I expect.'

'Ah . . .' said Flay. 'Mostly likely.'

'Do you ever get frightened, all on your own?'

'Not frightened, boy – exiled.'

'What does it mean – *exiled*?'

Flay shifted himself on the ledge of rock, and shrugged his high, bony shoulders up to his ears; like a vulture. There was a kind of tickling in his throat. He turned his small, sunken eyes at last to the young Earl as he sat by the flames, his head raised, a puzzled frown on his brows. Then the tall man lowered himself to the floor, as though he were a kind of mechanism, his knee joints cracking like musket shots as he bent and then straightened his legs.

'Exiled?' he repeated at last, in a curiously low and husky voice. 'Banished, it means. Forbidden, lordship, forbidden service, sacred service. To have your heart dug out; to have it dug out with its long roots, lordship – that's what exiled means. It means, this cave and emptiness while I am needed. *Needed*,' he repeated hotly. 'What watchmen are there now?'

'Watchmen?'

'How do I know? How do I know?' he continued, ignoring Titus' query. Years of silence were finding vent. 'How do I know what devilry goes on? Is all well, lordship? Is the castle well?'

'I don't know,' said Titus. 'I suppose so.'

'You wouldn't know, would you, boy,' he muttered. 'Not yet.'

'Is it true that my mother sent you away?' asked Titus.

'Aye. The Countess of Groan. She exiled me. How is she, my lordship?'

'I don't know,' said Titus. 'I don't see her very often.'

'Ah . . .' said Flay. 'A fine, proud woman, boy. She understands the evil and the glory. Follow her, my lord, and Gormenghast will be well; and you will do your ancient duty, as your father did.'

'But I want to be free, Mr Flay. I don't want any duties.'

Mr Flay jerked himself forward. His head was lowered. In the deep shadows of their sockets his eyes glowed. His hand that supported his weight shook on the ground below him.

'A *wicked* thing to say, my lord, a *wicked* thing,' he said at last. 'You are a Groan of the blood – and the last of the line. You must not fail the Stones. No, though the nettles hide them, and the blackweeds, my lord – you must not fail them.'

Titus stared up at him, surprised at this outburst in the taciturn man; but even as he stared his eyes began to droop for he was weary.

Flay arose to his feet, and as he did so a hare loped through the entrance of the cave where it was lit up against the intense darkness like a thing of gold. It stopped for a moment sitting bolt upright and stared at Titus, and then leapt upon a fern-hung shelf of moss and lay as still as a carving, its long ears laid like sheaths along its back.

Flay lifted Titus and laid him along the bracken-bed. But something had happened, suddenly, in the boy's brain. He sat bolt upright the moment after his head had touched the floor, and his eyes had closed, as it seemed in that quick moment, in a long sleep.

'Mr Flay,' he whispered with a passionate urgency. 'Oh, Mr Flay.'

The man of the woods knelt down at once.

'Lordship? What is it?'

'Am I dreaming?'

'No, boy.'

'Have I slept?'

'Not yet.'

'Then I saw it.'

'Saw what, lordship? Lie quiet now – lie quiet.'

'That thing in the oakwoods, that flying thing.'

Mr Flay's body tautened and there was an absolute silence in the cave.

'What kind of a thing?' he muttered at last.

'A thing of the air, a flying thing . . . sort of . . . delicate . . . but I

couldn't see its face . . . it floated, you know, across the trees. Was it
real? Have you *seen* it, Mr Flay? What was it, Mr Flay? Tell me, please
because . . . because . . .'

But there was no need for an answer to the boy's question, for he had
fallen into a deep sleep and Mr Flay rose to his feet, and, moving across
the cave where the light was dying as the fire smouldered into ashes,
made his way to the entrance of his cavern. Then he leaned against the
outer wall. There was no moon but a sprinkling of stars were reflected
dimly in the dammed-up lake of water. Faint as an echo in the silence
of the night came the bark of a fox from Gormenghast forest.

TWENTY-ONE

I

TITUS was to be kept in the Lichen Fort for a week. It was a round,
squat edifice, its rough square stones obliterated by the unbroken
blanket of the parasitic lichen which gave it its name. This covering
was so thick that a variety of birds were able to make their nests in the
pale green fur. The two chambers, one above the other of this fort, were
kept comparatively clean by a caretaker who slept there and kept the
key.

Titus had been held prisoner in this fort on two previous occasions
for flagrant offences against the hierarch – although he never knew
exactly what he had done wrong. But this time it was for a longer
period. He did not particularly mind. It was a relief to know what his
punishment was, for when Flay had left him at the hem of the woods
that showed them the castle but a couple of miles away, his anxiety had
grown to such a pitch that he had visions of the most frightful
punishments ahead. He had arrived in the early morning and found
three fresh search parties marshalled in the red-stone yard and about
to set out. Horses were drawn up at the stables and their riders were
being given instructions. He had taken a deep breath and entered the
yard, and staring straight ahead of him all the time, had marched across
it, his heart beating wildly, his face perspiring, his shirt and trousers
torn almost to shreds. At that moment he was glad he was heir to the
mountainous bulks of masonry that rose above him, of the towers, and
of the tracts he had crossed that morning in the low rays of the sun. He
held his head up and clenched his hands, but when within a dozen
yards of the cloisters, he ran, the tears gathering in his eyes, until he

came to Fuchsia's room into which he rushed, his eyes burning, a dishevelled urchin, and falling upon his startled sister, clung to her like a child.

She returned his embrace, and for the first time in her life, kissed, and held him passionately in her arms; loved him as she had never loved a soul, and was so filled with pride to have been the one to whom he had fled, that she lifted her young, strident voice and shouted in barbaric triumph, and then breaking away from him, jumped to her window and spat into the morning sun. 'That's what I think of them, Titus,' she shouted, and he ran after her, and spat himself, and then they both began to laugh until they were weak and fell upon the floor where they fought in a dizzy ecstasy until, exhausted, they lay side by side, their hands joined, and sobbed with the love they had found in one another.

Hungry for affection, yet not knowing what it was that made them restless, not even knowing that they *were* restless, the truth had sprung upon them at the same instant with a shock which found no outlet for its expression save in this physical tumult. In a flash they had found faith in one another. They dared, simultaneously, to uncover their hearts. A truth had come, empiric, irrational and appallingly exciting. The truth that she, this extraordinary girl, ridiculously immature for all her twenty years, yet rich as harvest, and he, a boy on the brink of wild discoveries, were bound by more than their blood, and the loneliness of their hereditary status, and the lack of a mother in any ordinary sense, yes, more than this – were bound all at once in the cocoon of a compassion and an integration one with another as deep, it seemed, as the line of their ancestors; as inchoate, imponderable, and uncharted as the realms that were their darkened legacy.

For Fuchsia to have, not just a brother, but a boy who had run to her in tears because *she, she* out of all Gormenghast, was the one he trusted – oh, that made up for everything. Let the world do what it might, she would dare death to protect him. She would tell lies for him! Giant lies! She would steal for him! She would kill for him! She rose to her knees and lifted her strong rounded arms, and as she sent forth a loud, incoherent shout of defiance, the door opened, and Mrs Slagg stood there. Her hand which was still on the door handle above her head trembled, as with amazement she stared at the kneeling girl and heard the unrestrained cry.

Behind her stood a man, with raised eyebrows, a lantern-jawed figure, in grey livery with a kind of seaweed belt which by some obscure edict of many a decade ago, it was his business, holding the position he did, to wear. A festoon of the golden weed trailed down his right leg to the region of his knee. The weather being dry, it crackled as he moved.

Titus was the first to see them and jumped to his feet. But it was Mrs Slagg who spoke first –

'Look at your hands!' she panted. 'Your legs, your face! Oh, my weak heart! Look at the grime, and the cuts and bruises, and, and, oh my wicked, *wicked* lordship, look at the rags of you! Oh, I could smack you I could when I think of all I've mended, and washed and ironed and bandaged. Oh yes, I could, I could smack you and hurt you, you cruel, dirty, lordship-thing. How *could* you. How could you? And me with my heart almost stopped – but *you* wouldn't care, oh no, not though . . .'

Her pitiful tirade was broken into by the man with the lantern jaw.

'I have to take you to Barquentine,' he said simply, to Titus. 'Get washed, my lord, and don't be long.'

'What does *he* want?' said Fuchsia in a low voice.

'I know nothing of that, your ladyship,' said lantern-jaw. 'But for your brother's sake, get him clean, and help him with a good excuse. Perhaps he has one. I don't know. I know nothing.' His seaweed rattled dryly as he turned away from the door with his tongue in his cheek and his eyes on the ceiling.

II

The week that followed was the longest Titus ever spent, in spite of Fuchsia's illicit visits to the Lichen Fort. She had found an obscure and narrow window through which she passed what cakes and fruit she could, to vary the adequate but uninteresting diet which the warder, luckily a deaf old man, prepared for his fledgeling-prisoner. Through this opening she was able to whisper to her brother.

Barquentine had lectured him at length: had stressed the responsibility that would become his; but as Titus held to the story that he had, from the outset, lost himself and could not find his way home, the only crime was in having set out on the expedition in the first place. For such a misdemeanour several heavy tomes were fetched down from high shelves, the dust was blown and shaken from their leaves and eventually the appropriate verses were found which gave precedent for the sentence of seven days in the Lichen Fort.

During that week the wrinkled and altogether beastly face of Barquentine, the 'Lord of the Documents', came before him in the darkness of the night. No fewer than four times he dreamed of the wet-eyed, harsh-mouthed cripple, pursuing him with his greasy crutch; of how it struck the flagstones like a hammer; and of the crimson rags of his high office that streamed behind the pursuer, as they hurried down unending corridors.

And when he awoke he remembered Steerpike who had stood behind

Barquentine's chair, or climbed the ladder to find the relevant tomes, and how the pale man, for so he was to Titus, had *winked* at him.

Beyond his knowledge, beyond his power of reason, a revulsion took hold of him and he recoiled from that wink like flesh from the touch of a toad.

One afternoon of his imprisonment he was interrupted at his hundredth attempt at impaling his jack-knife in the wooden door, at which he flung the weapon in what he imagined was a method peculiar to brigands. He had cried himself to a stop during the morning, for the sun shone through the narrow window-slits and he longed for the wild woods that were so fresh in his mind and for Mr Flay and for Fuchsia.

He was interrupted by a low whistle at one of the narrow windows, and then as he reached it, Fuchsia's husky whisper:

'Titus.'

'Yes.'

'It's me.'

'O, good!'

'I can't stay.'

'Can't you?'

'No.'

'Not for a little, Fuchsia?'

'No. Got to take your place. Beastly tradition business. Dragging the moat for the Lost Pearls or something. I should be there now.'

'Oh!'

'But I'll come after dark.'

'O, good!'

'Can't you see my hand? I'm reaching as far as I can.'

Titus thrust his arm as far as he could through the window slit of the five-foot wall, and could just touch the tip of her fingers.

'I must go.'

'Oh!'

'You'll soon be out, Titus.'

The silence of the Lichen Fort was about them like deep water, and their fingers touching might have been the prows of foundered vessels which grazed one another in the subaqueous depths, so huge and vivid and yet unreal was the contact that they made with one another.

'Fuchsia.'

'Yes?'

'I have things to tell you.'

'Have you?'

'Yes. Secrets.'

'Secrets?'

'Yes, and adventure.'

'I won't tell! I won't ever tell. Nothing you tell me I'll tell. When I come tonight, or if you like when you're free, tell me then. It won't be long.'

Her finger tips left his. He was alone in space.

'Don't take your hand away,' she said after a moment's pause. 'Can you feel anything?'

He worked his fingers even further into the darkness and touched a paper object which with difficulty he tipped over towards himself and then withdrew. It was a paper bag of barley sugar.

'Fuchsia,' he whispered. But there was no reply. She had gone.

III

On the last day but one he had an official visitor. The caretaker of the Lichen Fort had unbolted the heavy door and the grotesquely broad, flat feet of the Headmaster, Bellgrove, complete in his zodiac gown, and dog-eared mortar-board, entered with a slow and ponderous tread. He took five or more paces across the weed-scattered earthen floor before he noticed the boy sitting at a table in a corner of the fort.

'Ah. There you are. There you are, indeed. How are you, my friend?'

'All right. Thank you, sir.'

'H'm. Not much light in here, eh, young man? What have you been doing to pass the time away?'

Bellgrove approached the table behind which Titus was standing. His noble, leonine head was weak with sympathy for the child, but he was doing his best to play the rôle of headmaster. He had to inspire confidence. That was one of the things that headmasters had to do. He must be Dignified and Strong. He must evoke Respect. What else had he to be? He couldn't remember.

'Give me your chair, young fellow,' he said in a deep and solemn voice. 'You can sit on the table, can't you? Of course you can. I seem to remember being able to do things like that when I was a boy!'

Had he been at all amusing? He gave Titus a sidelong glance in the faint hope that he *had* been, but the boy's face showed no sign of a smile, as he placed the chair for his headmaster and then sat with his knees crossed on the table. Yet his expression was anything but sullen.

Bellgrove, holding his gown at the height of his shoulders and at the same time leaning backwards from the hips and thrusting his head forward and downwards so that the blunt end of his long chin rested in the capacious pit of his neck like an egg in an egg-cup, raised his eyes to the ceiling.

'As your headmaster,' he said, 'I felt it my bounden duty, *in loco parentis*, to have a word with you, my boy.'

'Yes, sir.'

'And to see how you were getting along. H'm.'

'Thank you, sir,' said Titus.

'H'm,' said Bellgrove. There were a few moments of rather awkward silence and then the headmaster, finding that the attitude which he had struck was putting too great a strain upon those muscles employed for its maintenance, sat down upon the chair and began unconsciously to work his long, proud jawbone to and fro, as though to test it for the toothache that had been so strangely absent for over five hours. Perhaps it was the unwonted relief of his long spell of normal health that caused a sudden relaxing of Bellgrove's body and brain. Or perhaps it was Bellgrove's innate simplicity, which *sensed* that in this particular situation (where a boy and a Headmaster equally ill at ease with the Adult Mind, sat opposite one another in the stillness) there was a reality, a world apart, a secret place to which they alone had access. Whatever it was, a sudden relaxing of the tension he had felt made itself manifest in a long, wheezing, horse-like sigh, and he stared across at Titus contemplatively, without wondering in the least whether his relaxed, almost *slumped* position in the chair, was of the kind that headmasters adopt. But when he spoke, he had, of course, to frame his sentences in that threadbare, empty way to which he was now a slave. Whatever is felt in the heart or the pit of the stomach, the old habits remain rooted. Words and gestures obey their own dictatorial, unimaginative laws; the ghastly ritual, that denies the spirit.

'So your old headmaster has come to see you, my boy . . .'

'Yes, sir,' said Titus.

'. . . Leaving his classes and his duties to cast his eye on a rebellious pupil. A very naughty pupil. A terrible child who, from what I can remember of his scholastic progress, has little cause to absent himself from the seats of learning.'

Bellgrove scratched his long chin ruminatively.

'As your headmaster, Titus, I can only say that you make things a little difficult. What am I to do with you? H'm. What indeed? You have been punished. You are *being* punished: so I am glad to say that there is no need for us to trouble any more about *that* side of it; but what am I to say to you *in loco parentis*. I am an old man, you would say, wouldn't you, my small friend? You would say I was an old man, wouldn't you?'

'I suppose so, sir.'

'And as an old man, I *should* by now be very wise and deep, shouldn't I, my boy? After all I have long white hair and a long black gown, and that's a good start, isn't it?'

'I don't know, sir.'

'Oh, well it *is*, my boy. You can take it from me. The first thing you must procure if you are anxious to be wise and sagacious is a long black gown, and long white hair, and if possible a long jaw-bone, like your old headmaster's.'

Titus didn't think that the Professor was being very funny, but he threw his head back and laughed very loudly indeed, and thumped his hands on the side of his table.

A flush of light illumined the old man's face. His anxiety fled from his eyes and hid itself where the deep creases and pits that honeycomb the skin of ancient men provided caves and gullies for its withdrawal.

It was so long since anyone had really laughed at anything he had said, and laughed honestly and spontaneously. He turned his big lion head away from the boy so that he could relax his old face in a wide and gentle smile. His lips were drawn apart in the most tender of snarls, and it was some while before he could turn his head about and return his gaze to the boy.

But at once the habit returned, unconsciously, and his decades of schoolmastering drew his hands behind his back, beneath his gown, as though there were a magnet in the small of his back: his long chin couched itself in the pit of his neck; the irises of his eyes floated up to the top of the whites, so that in his expression there was something both of the drug-addict and the caricature of a sanctimonious bishop – a peculiar combination and one which generations of urchins had mimicked as the seasons moved through Gormenghast, so that there was hardly a spot in dormitory, corridor, classroom, hall or yard where at one time or another some child had not stood for a moment with his inky hands behind his back, his chin lowered, his eyes cast up to the sky, and, perhaps, an exercise book on top of his head by way of mortar-board.

Titus watched his headmaster. He had no fear of him. But he had no love for him either. That was the sad thing. Bellgrove, eminently lovable, because of his individual weakness, his incompetence, his failure as a man, a scholar, a leader or even as a companion, was nevertheless utterly alone. For the weak, above all, have their friends. Yet his gentleness, his pretence at authority, his palpable humanity were unable, for some reason or other, to function. He was demonstrably the type of venerable and absent-minded professor about whom all the sharp-beaked boys of the world should swarm like starlings in wheeling murmurations – loving him all unconsciously, while they twitted and cried their primordial jests, flung their honey-centred, prickle-covered verbiage to and fro, pulled at the long black thunder-coloured gown, undid with fingers as quick as adders' tongues the buttons of his braces; pleaded to hear the ticking of his enormous watch of brass and rust red iron, with the verdigris like lichen on the chain; fought between those legs like the trousered stilts of the father of all storks; while the great, corded, limpish hands of the fallen monarch flapped out from time to time, to clip the ears of some more than venturesome child, while far above, the long, pale lion's head turned its eyes to and fro in a slow, ceremonious rhythm, as though he were a lighthouse whose slowly swivelling beams were diffused and deadened in the sea-mists; and all the while, with the tassel of the mortar-board swinging high above them like the tail of a mule, with the trousers loosening at the venerable haunches, with the cat-calls and the thousand quirks and oddities that grow like brilliant weeds from the no-man's-land of urchins' brains – all the while there would be this love like a sub-soil, showing itself in the very fact that they trusted his lovable weakness, wished to be with him because he was like them irresponsible, magnificent with his locks of hair as white as the first page of a new copy-book, and with his neglected teeth, his jaw of pain, his completeness, ripeness, false-nobility, childish temper and childish patience; in a word, that he *belonged* to them; to tease and adore, to hurt and to worship for his very weakness' sake. For what is more lovable than failure?

But no. None of this happened. None of it. Bellgrove was all this. There was no gap in the long tally of his spineless faults. He was constructed as though expressly for the starlings of Gormenghast. There he was, but no one approached him. His hair was white as snow, but it might as well have been grey or brown or have moulted in the dank of faithless seasons. There seemed to be a blind spot in the mass-vision of the swarming youths.

They looked this great gift-lion in the mouth. It snarled in its weakness, for its teeth were aching. It trod the immemorial corridors. It dozed fitfully at its desk through the terms of sun and ice. And now, it was a Headmaster and lonelier than ever. But there was pride. The claws were blunt, but they were ready. But not so, now. For at the moment his vulnerable heart was swollen with love.

'My young friend,' he said, his eyes still on the ceiling of the fort and his chin tucked into the pit of his neck. 'I propose to talk to you as man to man. Now the thing *is* . . .' (he lingered over the last word) . . . 'the thing . . . *is* . . . what shall we talk *about*?' He lowered his rather dull eyes and saw that Titus was frowning at him thoughtfully.

'We *could*, you see, young man, talk of so many things, could we not, as man to man. Or even as boy to boy. H'm. Quite so. But what? That is the paramount consideration – isn't it?'

'Yes, sir. I suppose so,' said Titus.

'Now, if you are twelve, my boy, and I am eighty-six, let us say, for I think that ought to cover me, then let us take twelve from eighty-six and halve the result. No, no. I won't make *you* do it because that would be most unfair. Ah yes, indeed it would – for what's the good of being a prisoner and then being made to do lessons too? Eh? Eh? Might as well not be punished, eh? . . . Let me see, where were we, where were we? Yes, yes, yes, twelve from eighty-six, that's about seventy-four, isn't it? Well, what is half seventy-four? I wonder . . . h'm, yes, twice three are six, carry one, and twice seven are fourteen . . . thirty-seven, I do believe. Thirty-seven. And what *is* thirty-seven? Why, it's just exactly the half-way age between us. So if I tried to be thirty-seven years young – and you tried to be thirty-seven years old – but that would be *very* difficult, wouldn't it? Because you've never been thirty-seven, have you? But then, although your old headmaster has *been* thirty-seven, long ago, he can't remember a thing about it except that it was somewhere about that time that he bought a bag of glass marbles. O yes he did. And why? Because he became tired of teaching grammar and spelling and arithmetic. O yes, and because he saw how much happier the people were who played marbles than the people were who didn't. That's a bad sentence, my boy. So I used to play in the dark after the other young professors were asleep. We had one of the old Gormenghast tapestry-carpets in the room and I used to light a candle and place my marbles on the corners of patterns in the carpet, and in the middle of crimson and yellow flowers. I can remember the carpet perfectly as though it was here in this old fort, and there, every night, by the glow of a candle, I would practise until I could flick a marble along the floor so that when it struck another it spun round and round but stayed exactly where it was, my boy, while the one it had struck shot off like a rocket to land at the other end of the room in the centre of a crimson carpet flower (if I was successful), or if not, near enough to couch itself at the next flick. And the sounds of the glass marbles in the still of the night when they struck was like the sound of tiny crystal vases breaking on stone floors – but I am getting too poetic, my boy, aren't I? And boys don't like poetry, do they?'

Bellgrove took off his mortar-board, placed it on the floor and wiped his brow with the biggest and grubbiest handkerchief Titus had ever seen come out of a grown-up's pocket.

'Ah me, my young friend, the sound of those marbles . . . the sound of those silly marbles. Forlorn, it is, my boy, to remember the little glass notes – forlorn as the tapping of a woodpecker in a summer forest.'

'I've got some marbles, sir,' said Titus, sliding off the table and diving his hand into his trouser pocket.

Bellgrove dropped his hands to his sides where they hung like dead weights. It was as though his joy at finding his little plan maturing so successfully was so all-absorbing that he had no faculties left over to control his limbs. His wide, uneven mouth was ajar with delight. He rose to his feet and turning his back on Titus made his way to the far end of the small fort. He was sure that his joy was written all over his face and that it was not for headmasters to show that sort of thing to any but their wives, and he had no wife . . . no wife at all.

Titus watched him. What a funny way he put his big flat feet on the ground, as though he were smacking it slowly with the soles of his boots – not so much to hurt it, as to wake it up.

'My boy,' said Bellgrove at last when he had returned to Titus, having fought the smile away from his face – 'this is an extraordinary coincidence, you know. Not only do you like marbles, but I . . .' and he drew from the decaying darkness of a pocket like a raw-lipped gulch, exactly six globes.

'O sir!' said Titus. 'I never thought *you'd* have marbles.'

'My boy,' said Bellgrove. 'Let it be a lesson to you. Now where shall we play. Eh? Eh? Good grief, my young friend, what a long way down it is to the floor and how my poor old muscles creak . . .'

Bellgrove was lowering himself by degrees to the dusty ground.

'We must examine the terrain for irregularities, h'm, yes, that's what

we must do, isn't it, my boy? Examine the terrain, like generals, eh?
And find our battle ground.'

'Yes, sir,' said Titus, dropping to the knees and crawling alongside
the old, pale lion. 'But it looks flat enough to me, sir, I'll make one of
the squares here, and . . .'

But at this moment the door of the fort opened again and Doctor
Prunesquallor stepped out of the sunlight and into the grey gloom of
the small fort.

'Well! well! well! well! well!' he trilled, peering into the shadows.
'Well, well, well! What a dreadful place to gaol an earl in, by all that's
merciless. And where is he, this fabulous little wrong-doer – this breaker
of bounds, this flouter of unwritten laws, this thoroughly naughty boy?
God bless my shocked spirit if I don't see two of them – and one much
bigger than the other – or is there someone with you, Titus, and if so,
who can it be, and what in the name of dust and ashes can you find so
absorbing on the earth's bosom, that you must crawl about on it, belly
to stubble, like beasts that stalk their prey?'

Bellgrove rose, creaking, to his knees and then catching his feet in the
swathes of his gown, tore a great rent in its threadbare material as he
struggled into an upright position. He straightened his back and stuck
the attitude of a headmaster, but his old face had coloured.

'Hullo, Doctor Prune,' said Titus. 'We were just going to play
marbles.'

'Marbles! eh? By all that's erudite, and a very fine invention too, God
bless my spherical soul,' cried the physician. 'But, if your accomplice
isn't Professor Bellgrove, your headmaster, then my eyes are behaving
in a very peculiar manner.'

'My dear Doctor,' said Bellgrove, his hands clasping his gown near
the shoulders, its torn portion trailing the floor at his feet like a fallen
sail – 'It is indeed I. My pupil, the young earl, having misbehaved
himself, I felt it my bounden duty, *in loco parentis*, to bring what wisdom
I have at my command to bear upon his predicament. To help him, if
I can, for, who knows, even the old may have experience; to succour
him, for, who knows, even the old may have mercy in their bones; and
to lead him back into the current of wise living – for, who knows, even
the old may . . .'

'I don't like "current of wise living", Bellgrove – a beastly phrase for
a headmaster, if I may make so damnably bold,' said Prunesquallor.
'But I see what you mean. By all that smacks of insight, I most probably
do. But what a place for incarcerating a child! Let's have a look at you,
Titus. How are you, my little bantam?'

'All right, thank you, sir,' said Titus. 'I'll be free tomorrow.'

'Oh God, it breaks my heart,' cried Prunesquallor. ' "I'll be free
tomorrow" indeed! Come here, boy.'

There was a catch in the Doctor's voice. Free tomorrow, he thought. Free tomorrow. Would the child ever be free tomorrow?

'So your headmaster has come to see you and is going to play marbles with you,' he said. 'Do you know that you are greatly honoured? Have you thanked him for coming to see you?'

'Not yet, sir,' said Titus.

'Well, you must, you know, before he leaves you.'

'He's a good boy,' said Bellgrove. 'A very good boy.' After a pause he added, as though to get back to firm, authoritarian ground again, 'and a very wicked one at that.'

'But I'm delaying the game – by all that's thoughtless, I am indeed!' cried the Doctor, giving Titus a pat on the back of the head.

'Why don't you play, too, Doctor Prune?' inquired Titus. 'Then we could have "threecorners".'

'And how do you play "threecorners"?' said Prunesquallor, hitching up his elegant trousers and squatting on the floor, his pink, ingenious face directed at the tousle-haired child. 'Do *you* know, my friend?' he inquired, turning to Bellgrove.

'Indeed, indeed,' said Bellgrove, his face lighting up. 'It is a noble game.' He lowered himself to the ground again.

'By the way,' said the Doctor, turning his head quickly to the Professor, 'you're coming to our party, aren't you? You will be our chief guest, as you know, sir.'

Bellgrove, with a great grinding and creaking of joints and fibres, got all the way to his feet again, stood for a moment magnificently and precariously upright and bowed to the squatting doctor, a lock of white hair falling across his blank blue eyes as he did so.

'Sir,' he said, 'I *am* sir – and my staff with me. We are deeply honoured.' Then he sank to his knees again with extraordinary rapidity.

For the next hour, the old prison warder, peering through a keyhole the size of a table-spoon, in the inner door, was astounded to see the three figures crawling to and fro across the floor of the prison fort, to hear the high trill of the Doctor develop and strengthen into the cry of a hyena, the deep and wavering voice of the Professor bell forth like an old and happy hound, as his inhibitions waned, and the shrill cries of the child reverberate about the room, splintering like glass on the stone walls while the marbles crashed against one another, spun in their tracks, lodged shuddering in their squares, or skimmed the prison floor like shooting stars.

TWENTY-TWO

THERE was no sound in all Gormenghast that could strike so chill against the heart as the sound of that small and greasy crutch on which Barquentine propelled his dwarfish body.

The harsh and rapid impact of its iron-like stub upon the hollow stones was, at each stroke, like a whip-crack, an oath, a slash across the face of mercy.

Not a hierophant but had heard at one time or another the sound of that sinister shaft mounting in loudness as the Master of Ritual thrust himself forwards, his withered leg and his crutch between them negotiating the tortuous corridors of stone, at a pace that it was difficult to believe.

There were few who had not, on hearing the crack of that stub of a crutch on distant flag-stones, altered their directions to avoid the small smouldering symbol of the law, as, in its crimson rags, it stamped its brimstone path along the centre of every corridor, altering its course for no man.

Something of the wasp, and something of the scraggy bird of prey, there was, about this Barquentine. There was something of the gale-twisted thorn tree also, and something of the gnome in his blistered face. The eyes, horribly liquid, shot their malice through veils of water. They seemed to be brimming, those eyes of his, as though old, cracked, sandy saucers were filled so full of topaz-coloured tea as to be swollen at their centres.

Endless, interwoven and numberless as were the halls and corridors of the castle, yet even in the remotest of these, in the obscure fastnesses, where, infinitely removed from the main arteries, the dank and mouldering silence was broken only by the occasional fall of rotten wood or the hoot of an owl – even in such tracts as these a wanderer would be haunted and apprehensive for fear of those ubiquitous tappings – faint it may be, as faint as the clicking of fingernails, but a sound for all its faintness that brought with it a sense of horror. There seemed no refuge from the sound. For the crutch, ancient, filthy and hard as iron, was the man himself. There was no good blood, no good red blood in Barquentine any more than there was in his support, that ghastly fulcrum. It grew from him like a diseased and nerveless limb – an extra limb. When it struck the stones or the hollow floor-boards below him it was more eloquent of spleen than any word, than any language.

The fanaticism of his loyalty to the House of Groan had far

outstripped his interest or concern for the living – the members of the
Line itself. The Countess, Fuchsia and Titus were mere links to him in
the blood-red, the imperial chain – nothing more. It was the chain that
mattered, not the links. It was not the living metal, but the immeasurable
iron with its patina of sacred dust. It was the Idea that obsessed him
and not the embodiment. He moved in a hot sea of vindication, a lust
of loyalty.

He had risen as usual this morning, at dawn. Through the window
of his filthy room he had peered across the dark flats to Gormenghast
Mountain, not because it shone in a haze of amber and seemed
translucent but in order to get some indication of the kind of day to
expect. The ritual of the hours ahead was to some extent modified by
the weather. Not that a ceremony could be cancelled *because* of adverse
weather, but by reason of the sacred Alternatives, equally valid, which
had been prescribed by leaders of the faith in centuries gone by. If, for
example, there was a thunderstorm in the afternoon and the moat was
churned and spattered with the rain, then the ceremony needed
qualifying in which Titus, wearing a necklace of plaited grass, was to
stand upon the weedy verge and, with the reflection of a particular
tower below him in the water, so sling a golden coil that, skimming the
surface and bounding into the air as it struck the water, it sailed over
the reflection of a particular tower in one leap to sink in the watery
image of a yawning window, where, reflected, his mother stood. There
could be no movement and no sound from Titus or the spectators until
the last of the sparkling ripples had crept from the moat, and the subaqueous head of the Countess no longer trembled against the hollow
darkness of the cave-like window, but was motionless in the moat, with
birds of water on her shoulders like chips of coloured glass and all
about her the infinite, tower-filled depths.

All this would necessitate a windless day and a glass surface to the
moat, and in the Tomes of Ceremony there would, were the day stormy,
be an alternative rendering, an equally honourable way of enriching the
afternoon to the glory of the House and the fulfilment of the participants.

And so, it was Barquentine's habit to push open his window at dawn
and stare out across the roofs and the marshes beyond, to where the
Mountain, blurred, or edged like a knife gave indication of the day
ahead.

Leaning forward, thus, on his crutch, in the cold light of yet another
day, Barquentine scratched savagely at his ribs, at his belly, under his
arms, here, there, everywhere with his claw of a hand.

There was no need for him to dress. He slept in his clothes on a lice-
infested mattress. There was no bed; just the crawling mattress on the
carpetless floor-boards where cockroaches and beetles burrowed and
insects of all kinds lived, bred and died, and where the midnight rat sat

upright in the silver dust and bared its long teeth to the pale beams, when in its fullness the moon filled up the midnight window like an abstract of itself in a picture frame.

It was in such a hovel as this that the Master of Ritual had woken every morning for the last sixty years. Swivelling about on his crutch, he stumped his way from the window and was almost immediately at the rough wall by the doorway. Turning his back to this irregular wall he leaned against it and worked his ancient shoulder-blades to and fro, disturbing in the process a colony of ants which (having just received news from its scouts that the rival colony near the ceiling was on the march and was even now constructing bridges across the plaster crack) was busily preparing its defences.

Barquentine had no notion that in easing the itch between his blades he was incapacitating an army. He worked his back against the rough wall, to and fro, to and fro in a way quite horrible in so old and stunted a man. High above him the door rose, like the door of a barn.

Then, at last, he leaned forward on his crutch and hopped across the room to where a rusted iron ring protruded from the floor. It was like the mouth of a funnel, and indeed a metal pipe led down from this terminal opening to where, several stories below, it ended in a similar metal ring, or mouthpiece, which protruded several inches from the ceiling of an eating-room. Immediately *beneath* this termination and a score of feet below it, a hollow, disused cauldron awaited the heavy stone which morning after morning rumbled its way down the winding pipe to end its journey with a wild clang in the belly of the reverberating bowl, murmuring to itself in an undertone for minutes on end with the boulder in its maw.

Every evening it was taken up and placed outside Barquentine's door, this boulder, and every morning the old man lifted it up above the iron ring in the floor-boards of his room, spat on it, and sent it hurtling down the crooked funnel, its hoarse clanging growing fainter and fainter as it approached the eating-room. It was a warning to the servants that he was on his way down, that his breakfast and a number of other preliminaries were to be ready.

To the clank of the boulder a score of hearts made echo. On this particular morning as Barquentine spat upon the heavy stone, the size of a melon, and sent it netherward on its resounding journey past many a darkened floor of bedded inmates (who, waking as it leapt behind their couches in the hollow of the walls, cursed him, the dawn and this cock-crow of a boulder) – on this particular morning there was more than the normal light of lust for ritual in the wreckage of the ancient's face – there was something more, as though his greed for the observances to take place in the shadow of his aegis was filling him with a passion hardly bearable in so sere a frame.

There was one picture on the wall of his verminous hovel; an engraving, yellow with age and smirched with dust, for it had no glass across it, save the small ice-like splinter at one corner that was all that remained of the original glazing. This engraving, a large and meticulous affair, was of the Tower of Flints. The artist must have stood to the south of the tower as he worked or as he studied the edifice, for beyond the irregularity of turrets and buttresses that backed it and spread almost to the sky like a seascape of stormy roofage, could be seen the lower slopes of Gormenghast Mountain, mottled with clumps of shrub and conifer.

What Barquentine had not noticed was that the doorway of the Tower of Flints had been cut away. A small area of paper, the size of a stamp, was missing. Behind this hole the wall had been laboriously pierced so that a little tunnel of empty darkness ran laterally from Barquentine's chamber to the hollow and capacious shaft of a vertical chimney, whose extremity was blocked from the light by a landslide of fallen slates long sealed and cushioned with gold moss, and whose round base, like the base of a well of black air, gave upon the small cell-like room so favoured by Steerpike that even at this early and chilly hour he was sitting there, at the base of the shaft. All about him were mirrors of his own construction, placed to a nicety, each at its peculiar angle, while above him, punctuating the tubular darkness, a constellation of mirrors twinkled with points of light one about the other.

Every now and again Barquentine would be reflected immediately behind the hollow mouthway of the engraved Tower of Flints where an angled mirror in the shaft sent down his image to another and then another – mirror glancing to mirror – until Steerpike, reclining at the base of the chimney, with a magnifying glass in his hands peered amusedly at the terminal reflection and saw in miniature the crimson rags of the dwarfish pedant as he raised the boulder in his hands and flung it through the ring.

If Barquentine rose early from his hideous couch, Steerpike in a secret room of his own choosing, a room as spotless and bright as a new pin, arose earlier. This was not a habit with him. He had no habits in that sort of way. He did what he wanted to do. He did what furthered his plans. If getting up at five in the morning would lead to something he coveted, then it was the most natural thing in the world for him to rise at that hour. If there was no necessity for action he would lie in bed all morning reading, practising knots with the cord he kept by his bedside, making paper darts of complicated design which he would float across his bedroom, or polishing the steel of the razor-edged blade of his swordstick.

At the moment it was to his advantage to impress Barquentine with his efficiency, indispensability and dispatch. Not that he had not already worked his way beneath the cantankerous crust of the old man's misanthropy. He was in fact the only living creature who had ever gained Barquentine's confidence and grudging approval.

Without fully realizing it, Barquentine, during his daily administrations, was pouring out a hoard of irreplaceable knowledge, pouring it into the predatory and capacious brain of a young man whose ambition it was, when he had gained sufficient knowledge of the observances, to take over the ceremonial side of the castle's life, and, in being the only authority in the minutiae of the law (for Barquentine was to be liquidated), to alter to his own ends such tenets as held him back from ultimate power and to forge such fresh, though apparently archaic documents, as might best serve his evil purposes as the years went by.

Barquentine spoke little. In the pouring out of his knowledge there was no verbal expansiveness. It was largely through action and through access to the Documents that Steerpike learned his 'trade'. The old man had no idea that day after day the accumulating growth of Steerpike's cognizance and the approach of his own death moved towards one another through time, at the same pace. He had no wish to instruct the young man beyond the point of self-advantage. The pale creature was useful to him and that was all, and were he to have known how much had been divulged of Gormenghast's inner secrets through the seemingly casual exchanges and periodical researches in the library, he would have done all in his power to eliminate from the castle's life this upstart, this dangerous, unprecedented upstart, whose pursuit of the doctrines was propelled by a greed for personal power as cold as it was tameless.

The time was almost ripe in Steerpike's judgement for the Master of Ritual to be dispatched. Apart from other motives the wiping out of so ugly a thing as Barquentine seemed to Steerpike, upon aesthetic considerations alone, an act long overdue. Why should such a bundle of hideousness be allowed to crutch its way about, year after year?

Steerpike admired beauty. It did not absorb him. It did not affect him. But he admired it. He was neat, adroit, slick as his own swordstick, sharp as its edge, polished as its blade. Dirt offended him. Untidiness offended him. Barquentine, old, filthy, his face cracked and pitted like stale bread, his beard tangled, dirty and knotted, sickened the young man. It was time for the dirty core of ritual to be plucked out of the enormous mouldering body of the castle's life and for him to take its place, and from that hidden centre – who knew how far his tangent wits might lead him?

It was a wonder to Barquentine how Steerpike was able to meet him with such uncanny precision and punctuality sunrise after sunrise. It was not as though his lieutenant sat there waiting outside the Master's door, or at some landing on the stairs by which Barquentine made his way to the small eating-room. O no. Steerpike, his straw-coloured hair smoothed down across his high globular forehead, his pale face shining, his dark red eyes disconcertingly alive beneath his sandy eyebrows, would walk rapidly out of the shadows and, coming to a smart halt at the old man's side, would incline himself at a slight angle from the hips.

There was no change this morning in the dumb show. Barquentine wondered, for the hundredth time, how Steerpike should coincide so exactly with his arrival at the top of the walnut stairs, and as usual drew his brows down over his eyes and peered suspiciously through the veils of unpleasant moisture that smouldered there, at the pale young man.

'Good morning to you, sir,' said Steerpike.

Barquentine, whose head was on a level with the banisters, put out a tongue like the tongue of a boot and ran it along the wreckage of his dry and wrinkled lips. Then he took a grotesque hop forwards on his withered leg and brought his crutch to his side with a sharp report.

Whether his face was made of age, as though *age* were a stuff, or whether age was the abstract of that face of his, that bearded fossil of a thing that smouldered and decayed upon his shoulders – there was no doubt that archaism was there, as though something had shifted from the past into the current moment where it burned darkly as though through blackened glass in defiance of its own anachronism and the callow present.

He turned this head of his to Steerpike.

'To hell fire with your "good morning", you peeled switch,' he said. 'You shine like a bloody land-eel! What d'you do to yourself, eh? Every poxy sunrise of the year, eh, that you burst out of the decent darkness in that plucked way?'

'I suppose it's this habit of washing I seem to have got into, sir.'

'*Washing*,' hissed Barquentine, as though he was mentioning something pestilent. '*Washing*, you wire-worm. What do you think you *are*, Mister Steerpike? A lily?'

'I'd hardly say that, sir,' said the young man.

'Nor would I,' barked the old man. 'Just skin and bones and hair? That's all you bloody are and nothing more. Dull yourself down. Get the shine off you – and no more of this oiled-paper nonsense, every dawn.'

'Quite so, sir. I am too visible.'

'Not when you're wanted!' snapped Barquentine, as he began to hobble downstairs. 'You can be invisible enough when you want to be, eh? Hags-hell, boy, you can be nowhere when it suits you, eh? By the guts of the great auk! I see through *you* – my pretty whelp! I see through *you*!'

'What, when I'm invisible, sir?' asked Steerpike, raising his eyebrows as he trod lightly behind the cripple who was raising echoes on all sides with the stamping of his crutch on the wooden stairs.

'By the piss of Satan, pug, your sauce is dangerous!' shouted Barquentine hoarsely, turning precariously in his tracks, with his withered leg two steps above his crutch.

'Are the north-cloisters done?' He shot the question at Steerpike, in a changed tone of voice – a tone no less vicious, cantankerous, but pleasanter to the young man's ear, being less personally vituperative.

'They were completed last night, sir.'

'Under your guidance, for what it's worth?'

'Under my guidance.'

They were approaching the first landing of the walnut stairs. Steerpike, as he trod behind Barquentine, took a pair of dividers from his pocket, and using them as though they were tongs, lifted up a hank of the old man's hair from the back of his head, to reveal a neck as wry as a turtle's. Amused by his success at being able to raise so thick a bunch of dirty grey hair without the cripple's knowledge, he repeated the performance while the harsh voice continued and the crutch clack-clack-clacked down the long flight.

'I shall inspect them immediately after breakfast.'

'Quite so,' said Steerpike.

'Has it occurred to your suckling-brain that this day is hallowed by the very dirt of the castle. Eh? Eh? That it is only once a year, boy, once a year, that the Poet is honoured? Eh? Why, the lice in my beard alone know, but there it is, by the black souls of the unbelievers, there it is, a law of laws, a rite of the first water, *dear* child. The cloisters are ready, you say; by the sores on my withered leg, you'll pay for it if they're coloured the wrong red. Eh? Was it the darkest red of all? Eh – the darkest of all the reds?'

'Quite the darkest,' said Steerpike. 'Any darker and it would have been black.'

'By hell, it had better be,' said Barquentine. 'And the rostrum?' he continued after crossing the gnarled landing of black walnut with its handrail missing from the banisters and the banisters themselves leaning in all directions and capped with dust as palings are capped with snow in wintertime.

'And the rostrum?'

'It is set and garnished,' said Steerpike. 'The throne for the Countess has been cleaned and mended, and the high chairs for the gentry polished. The long forms are in place and fill the quadrangle.'

'And the Poet,' cried Barquentine. 'Have you instructed him, as I ordered you? Does he know what is expected of him?'

'His rhetoric is ready, sir.'

'Rhetoric? Cat's teeth! Poetry, you bastard, Poetry.'

'It has been prepared, sir!' Steerpike had re-pocketed his dividers and was now holding a pair of scissors (he seemed to have endless things in his pockets without disturbing the hang of his clothes) and was clipping off strands of Barquentine's hair where it hung below his collar, and was whispering to himself in an absurd undertone, 'Tinker, tailor, soldier, sailor' as the matted wisps fell upon the stairs.

They had reached another landing. Barquentine stopped for a moment to scratch himself. 'He may have prepared his poem,' he said turning his time-wasted visage to the slender, high-shouldered young man, 'but have you told him about the magpie? Eh?'

'I told him that he must rise to his feet and declaim within twelve seconds of the magpie's release from the wire cage. That while declaiming his left hand must be clasping the beaker of moat-water in which the Countess has previously placed the blue pebble from Gormenghast river.'

'That is so, boy. And that he shall be wearing the Poet's Gown, that his feet shall be bare, did you tell him that?'

'I did,' said Steerpike.

'And the yellow benches for the Professors. Were they found?'

'They were. In the south stables. I have had them re-painted.'

'And the seventy-seventh earl, Lord Titus, does the pup know that he is to stand when the rest are seated, and seat himself when the rest are standing? Does the child know that – eh – eh – he is a scatterbrained thing – have you instructed him, you skinned candle? By the gripes of my seventy years, your forehead shines like a bloody iceberg!'

'He has been instructed,' said Steerpike.

Barquentine set out again on his descent to the eating-room. Once the walnut stairs had been negotiated, the Master of Ritual stuttered his way down the level corridors like something possessed. As the dust rose from the floor at each bang of the crutch, Steerpike, following immediately behind his master, amused himself by the invention of a peculiar dance, a kind of counterpoint to Barquentine's jerking progress – a silent and elaborate improvisation, laced, as it were, with lewd and ingenious gestures.

TWENTY-THREE

THE long summer minutes dragged by for Titus as he sat at his desk in the schoolroom where Professor Cutflower (who had once made a point of being at least one mental hour ahead of his class in whatever subject he happened to be taking, but who had long since decided to pursue knowledge on an equal footing with his pupils) was, with the lid of his high desk raised to hide his activity, taking a long pull at a villainous looking bottle with a blue label. The morning seemed endless . . .

But, for Barquentine with a score of preparations still to be completed, and with his rough tongue victimizing the workmen in the south quadrangle, the hours sped by with the speed of minutes.

And so, after what seemed an infinity to Titus and a whisk of time's skirt to Barquentine, the morning that was both fleet and tardy, fructified and like a grape of air, in whose lucent body the earth was for that moment suspended – that phantom ripeness throbbed, that thing called *noon*.

Before it had awoke to die on the instant of its waking, a score of bells and clocks had shouted midday and for a minute after its death, from near and far the clappers in their tents of rusted iron clanged across Gormenghast. It was as though no mechanism on earth could strike or chain that ghost of time. The clocks and the bells stuttered, boomed and rang. They trod with their iron imprint. They beat with their ancient fists and shouted with archaic voices – but the ghost was older.

Noon, ripe as thunder and silent as thought, had fled unfingered.

When every echo had died from even those clocks in the western outcrops, whose posthumous tolling was proverbial, so that the phrase, 'late as a western chime' was common in the castle – when every echo had died, Titus became aware of another sound.

After the languid threnody of the chimes, this fresh sound, so close upon the soft heels of the pendulums, appeared hideously rapid, merciless and impatient.

It had the almost dream-like insistence, for all its actuality, of some hound with feet of stone or iron; or some coursing beast, that, rattling its rapacious and unalterable way in the wake of its prey, was momently closing the gap between evil and innocence.

Titus heard the sound, as though its cause were alongside. Yet the corridor down which he was moving was empty, and the tapping of the crutch was in reality coming from a parallel passageway, and Barquentine, although only a few yards from him, was separated from the boy by a solid wall of stone.

As Titus came to a halt, his heart beating, his eyes narrowed and an expression of hatred came over his childish features – an expression hardly credible in so young a face. To him, Barquentine was the symbol of tyranny, of age, of all that held him back from summer days among the woods, from diving in the moat with his friends, from all he longed for.

As he stood shuddering with his hot uprising of fear and detestation, he listened intently. In which direction, behind that wall of stone, was the crutch travelling?

At either end of Barquentine's corridor subsidiary passages led into the corridor in which Titus now stood. It seemed to him that the Master of Ritual was moving rapidly in a parallel direction to his own. He turned and began to retrace his steps, but the corridor was suddenly darkened by a solid block of Professors who bore down upon him with a fluttering of ethiop draperies and a fleet of mortar-boards. His only hope was to run in the original direction and cross the communicating passage, and away, before Barquentine's possible arrival at that juncture.

He began to run. It was not because of any particular misdeed or rational fear that he ran. It was a compulsion, a necessity for withdrawal. A revolt against anything that was old. Anything that had power. A nebula of terror possessed him and he ran.

Along the right-hand side of the corridor a phalanx of dusty statues loomed in the dim light that gave them the colour of ash. Set, for the most part, on massive plinths they towered above Titus, their silent limbs sawing the dark air, or stabbing it bluntly with broken arms. The heads were almost invisible, matted as they were with cobwebs, and shrouded in perpetual twilight.

He had known these monuments since childhood. But he no more noticed them or remembered them than another child would notice the monotonous pattern of some nursery wallpaper.

But Titus was brought again to a standstill by the tiny yet unmistakable silhouette of the cripple as it rounded the far corner and proceeded towards him out of the distance.

Before Titus had realized what he was doing he had leapt sideways quick as a squirrel, and was all at once in an almost complete darkness that brooded behind the ponderous and muscled carving of a figure without head or arms. The plinth on which this great trunk of stone stood balanced was itself above the level of his head.

Titus stood there trembling as the noise of many feet approached from the west, and a crutch from the east. He fought away the knowledge that he must have been seen by the professors. He clung to the empty hope that they had all had their eyes cast to the ground and had never seen him running ahead of them; had never seen him dive

behind the statue and, more fervent still, the passionate hope that
Barquentine had been too far away to notice any movement in the
corridor. But even as he trembled he knew his hope was based on his
fear and that it was madness for him to stay where he was.

The noise was all about him, the heavy feet, the whisking of the
gowns, the clanging of the iron-like crutch on the slabs.

And then the voice of Barquentine brought everything to a standstill.
'Hold!' it cried. 'Hold there, headmaster! By the pox, you have the
whole spavined staff with you, hell crap me!'

'My very good colleagues are at my back,' said the old and fruity
voice of Bellgrove. And then he added, 'My *very* good colleagues,' as
though to test his own courage in the face of the thing in red rags that
glared up at him.

But Barquentine's mind was elsewhere. 'Which *was* it?' he barked,
taking a fresh hop in Bellgrove's direction. 'Which *was* it, man?'

Bellgrove drew himself up and struck his favourite position as a
headmaster, but his old heart was beating painfully.

'I have no idea,' he said. 'No idea whatsoever, as to what it can be to
which you are referring.' His words could not have sounded heavier or
less honest. He must have felt this himself, for he added, 'Not an
inkling, I assure you.'

'Not an inkling! Not an inkling!' Barquentine cried. 'Black blood on
your inklings!' With another hop and a grind of the crutch he brought
himself immediately below the headmaster.

'By the reek of your lights, there was a boy in this corridor. There
was a boy just now. What? What? There was a slippery pup just now.
Do you deny it?'

'I saw no child,' said Bellgrove. 'Slippery or otherwise.' He lifted the
ends of his mouth in a smirk, where they froze upon his own little joke.

Barquentine stared at him and if Bellgrove's sight had been better
the malice in that stare might have unnerved the old headmaster to the
brink of his undoing. As it was, he clenched his hands under his gown,
and with a picture of Titus in his mind – Titus whose eyes had shone
at the sight of the marbles in the fort – he held on to the lies he was
telling with the grip of a Saint.

Barquentine turned to the staff who were clustered behind their
headmaster like a black chorus. His wet, ruthless eyes moved from face
to face.

For a moment the idea crossed his brain that his sight had played
him false. That he had seen a shadow. He turned his head and stared
along the line of silent monuments.

Suddenly his spleen and frustration found vent and he thrashed out
with his stick at the stone torso at his side. It was a wonder that his
crutch was not broken.

'There was a whelp!' he screamed. 'But enough of that! Time runs away. Is all prepared, what? What? Is all in readiness? You know your time of arrival? You know your orders. By hell, there must be no slips this afternoon.'

'We have the details,' said Bellgrove in so quick and relieved a voice, that it was no wonder that Barquentine darted at him suspiciously.

'And what's your bloody joy in *that*?' he hissed. 'By hell, there's perfidy somewhere!'

'My joy,' said Bellgrove, twice as slowly and ponderously, 'springs from the knowledge which my staff must share with me, as men of culture, that a considerable poem is in store for them this afternoon.'

Barquentine made a noise in his throat.

'And the boy, Titus,' he snapped. 'Does he know what is expected of *him*?'

'The seventy-seventh earl will do his duty,' said Bellgrove.

This last retort of the headmaster's had not been heard by Titus for the boy had found behind him in the darkness that, where he had thought the wall of the corridor would support him as he leaned back in a sudden tiredness – there was no wall at all. In breathless silence he had got to his hands and knees and crawled into emptiness, through a narrow opening, and when he had come to a damp barrier of stones, had found that a tunnel led to his right, a tunnel that descended in a series of shallow stairs. He did not know that a few minutes later, Barquentine was to strike his way down the centre of the corridor of statues, the staff dividing to let him pass, nor that after the staff had disappeared in their original direction, that Bellgrove had returned alone, and had whispered thickly, 'Come out, Titus, come out at once and report to your headmaster,' and receiving no response had himself worked his way behind the stone only to find himself baffled and defeated in the empty darkness.

TWENTY-FOUR

THE floor of the quadrangle was of a pale whitish-yellow brick, a pleasant mellow colour, soothing to the eye. The bricks had been laid so that their narrow surfaces faced upwards, a device which must have called for twice as many as would otherwise have been necessary. But what gave the floor of the quadrangle its peculiar character was the herring-bone pattern which the artificers had followed many hundred years ago.

Blurred and worn as the yellow bricks had become, yet there was a vitality about the surface of the quadrangle, as though the notion of the man who had once, long ago, given orders that the bricks were to be laid in such and such a way, was still alive. The bricks had breath in them. To walk across this quadrangle was to walk across an idea.

The pillars of the cloisters had been painted, a dreadful idea, for the dove grey stone of which they were constructed could not have harmonized more subtly with the pale yellow brickwork from which they seemed to grow. They had, nevertheless, been painted a deep and most oppressive red.

It is true, that on the following day, an army of boys would be set to work in scraping the colour off again, but on the one day of the year when the quadrangle came into its own as the setting for the poet's declamation, it seemed doubly outrageous to smother up the soft grey stone.

The Poet's Rostrum set against the red pillars glowed and darkened only to glow again in the afternoon sunlight. The branch of a tree fluttered across the face of the sun, so that the quadrangle which was filled with benches appeared on the move, for the flickering shadows of the leaves swam to and fro as the high branch swayed in the breeze.

The silent congregation, seated solemnly on their benches, stared over their shoulders at the gate through which the Poet would, at any moment, make his entrance. It was a year since anyone present had caught sight of that tall and awkward man, and then it was at this same ceremony, which, on that previous occasion, had taken place in a thin and depressing drizzle.

The Countess was seated in advance of the front row. Fuchsia's chair was to her mother's left. Standing beside them, with the sweat of irritable anxiety pouring down his face, was Barquentine with his eyes fixed (as were the eyes of the Countess and Fuchsia) not upon the Poet's gate, but upon a small door in the south wall of the quadrangle through which Titus, who was over twenty minutes late, should long ago have come running.

Behind them in a long row, as though their yellow bench was a perch for black turkeys, sat the professors. Bellgrove, at their centre, in his zodiac gown was also staring at the small door in the wall. He took out a big grubby handkerchief and mopped his brow. At that moment the door was pulled open and three boys ran through and came panting up to Barquentine.

'Well?' hissed the old man. 'Well? Have you found him?'

'No, sir!' they panted. 'We can't find him anywhere, sir.'

Barquentine ground the foot of his crutch against the pale bricks as though to ease his anger. Suddenly Steerpike appeared at his side as though out of the mellow ground. He bowed to the Countess while a shadow undulated across the irregular terrain of the scores of heads that filled the quadrangle. The Countess made no response. Steerpike straightened himself.

'I can find no trace of the seventy-seventh earl,' he said, addressing Barquentine.

'Black blood!' The voice of the cripple forced its way between his teeth. 'This is the fourth time that the . . .'

'That . . . the . . . *what*?' The Countess launched the three short words as though they were made of lead. They fell heavily through the afternoon air.

Barquentine gathered his red rags of office about his stunted body, and turned his irritable head to the Countess who stared at him with ice in her eyes. The old man bowed, sucking at his teeth as he did so.

'My lady,' he said. 'This is the fourth time in six months that the seventy-seventh earl has absented himself from a sacred . . .'

'By the least hair of the child's head,' said the Countess, interrupting, in a voice of deadly deliberation – 'if he should absent himself a hundred times an hour I will not have his misdemeanours bandied about in public. I will not have you mouth and blurt his faults. You will keep your observations in your own throat. My son is no chattel that you can discuss, Barquentine, with your pale lieutenant. Leave me. The occasion will proceed. Find a substitute for the boy from the tyros' benches. You will retire.'

At that moment a murmur was heard from the populace behind them, for the Poet, preceded by a man in the skin of a horse, and with that animal's tail trailing the bricks behind him as he paced slowly forwards, was to be seen emerging from the Gate. The Poet in his gown, with a beaker of moat-water in his left hand and his manuscript in his right, followed the figure in the horse's hide, with long awkward paces. His face was like a wedge. His small eyes flickered restlessly. He was pale with embarrassment and apprehension.

Steerpike had found a boy of about Titus' age and height and instructed him in his rôle, which was simple enough. He was to stand when the rest were seated, and to sit when the rest were standing, and that was all, as seventy-seventh earl, by proxy, he had to remember.

When the Countess had placed the pebble from Gormenghast river in the beaker of moat-water, and when the populace had seated themselves again and none save the Poet and the substitute for Titus were left on their feet, then an absolute hush descended over the quadrangle, and the Poet, holding his poem in his hand and raising his head, lifted his hollow voice . . .

'To her ladyship, Gertrude Countess of Groan and to her children, Titus the seventy-seventh lord of the tracts, and Fuchsia sole vessel of the Blood on the distaff side: to all ladies and gentlemen present and to all hereditary officials: to all of varying duties whose observance of the tenets justify their presence at this ceremony, I dedicate this poem which as the laws decree shall be addressed to as many as are here present in all the variance of their receptivity, status and acumen, in so much as poetry is a ritual of the heart, the voice of faith, the core of Gormenghast, the moon when it is red, the trumpet of the Groans.'

The Poet paused to breathe. The words he had just used were invariably declaimed before the poem, and there was nothing left for the Poet to do but to open the door of the wire cage, which Barquentine had passed up to him, and to let loose the magpie as a symbol of something the significance of which had long been lost to the records.

The magpie which was supposed to flap away into the afternoon sunlight, until it was a mere dot in the sky, did no such thing. It hopped from the cage and stood for a moment on the rim of the rostrum before flying with a loud rattle of its wings to the Countess, on whose shoulder it perched for the rest of the proceedings, pecking from time to time at its black wings.

The Poet, raising his manuscript before his eyes, took a deep and shuddering breath, opened his small mouth, took a step backwards, and, losing his balance, all but fell down the steps that descended steeply from his narrow rostrum to the ground seven feet below. An uncontrollable shriek of laughter from the tyros' benches stabbed into the warm afternoon like a needle into a cushion.

The offending youth was led away by an official. The drowsy silence came down again, drowning the shadow-dappled quadrangle as though with an element.

The Poet moved forward on the rostrum, his skin prickly with shame. He raised his manuscript again to read; and as he read the shadows lengthened across the quadrangle. A cloud of starlings moved like migraine across the upper air. The small boys on the tyros' benches, imitating the Poet and nudging one another, fell, one by one, asleep. The Countess yawned. The summer afternoon melted into evening. Steerpike's eyes moved to and fro. Barquentine sucked his teeth irritably.

The voice of the Poet droned on and on. A star came out. And then another. The earth swam on through space. The Countess yawned again and turned her eyes to the west doorway.

Where was Titus?

TWENTY-FIVE

THE glade had been in darkness since the dawn. A strand of almost horizontal light had slid at cockcrow through a multitude of trees and inflamed for a moment an obscure corner of the glade where a herd of giant ferns arched their spines (the long fronds falling like the manes of horses). They had shone with a cold, green, angry radiance. They had been exposed. The long ray had withdrawn as though it had not found what it was looking for.

As the sun climbed, the glade appeared to darken rather than to absorb the strengthening light. The air was domed with foliage; layer after voluminous layer hanging in darkened swathes!

All day long the darkness sat there, muffling the boles of the trees, a terrible day-time dusk, as thick as night.

But all the while the uppermost branches of these same trees and the topmost layers of leaf shone in the cloudless sunlight.

When evening came and the sun was hanging over the western skyline the drowned glade began to lighten. The level beams streamed from the west; the glade shuddered, and then, silent and motionless as a picture of itself, it gave up all its secrets.

Of the trees that grew from this sunken circle of ground there was one which claimed immediate attention. Its girth was such that the trees that surrounded it, though tall and powerful, were made to look like saplings. It was the king. Yet it alone was dead.

And yet its very deadness had given it a life. A life that had no need for the April sap. Its tower-like bulk of a bole mounted into the arboured gloom, and as the light from the west struck it, it shone with the hard, smooth quality of marble, or ivory for it was the colour of a tusk.

It rose out of a sward, sepia in colour, a treacherous basin. This sick and rotting ground was dappled with gold where it was struck by the direct rays, the lozenges of light elongating as the sun sank.

Sixty feet from the ground the trunk of the dead giant was pocked with cavities. They were like entrances, it seemed, or like the portholes of a ship, their raised rims smooth as silk and hard as bone.

And it was here, in these mouths of the great tree, sixty feet above the ground where the girth of the bole was still as ponderous as its sward-lapped base – it was here that the life of the dead tree was centred.

There was no cavern of that high and silky cliff but had its occupant. Save for the bees whose porthole dripped with sweetness, and the birds, there were few of the denizens of this dead-tree-settlement that could get any kind of grip upon the surface of the bole. But there were branches, which swept from the surrounding trees to within leaping range for the wild cat, the flying squirrel, the opossum and for that creature, not always to be found in the moss-lined darkness of its ivory couch, who, separated by a mere membrane of honey-soaked wood from the multitudinous murmur of a hive, was asleep as the evening light stole through the small round opening so high above the ground. As the light quickened the creature moved in its sleep. The eyes opened. They were as clear and green as sea stones and were set in a face that was coloured and freckled like a robin's egg.

The creature slid from its retreat, and paused for a moment as it crouched at the lip of its dizzy cave, and then leaping outwards into space it swung itself from branch to branch like something without weight or substance, while the foliage of the evening forest closed about it, and the far away sound of a bell rang faintly from the distant castle.

TWENTY-SIX

LIKE a child lost in the chasmic mazes of a darkening forest, so was Titus lost in the uncharted wilderness of a region long forgotten. As a child might stare in wonder and apprehension along an avenue of dusk and silence, and then, turning his head along another, and another, each as empty and breathless, so Titus stared in apprehension and with a hammering heart along the rides and avenues of stone.

But here, unlike the child lost in the forest, Titus was surrounded by a fastness without sentience. There was no growth, and no movement. There was no sense here that a sluggish sap was sleeping somewhere; was waiting in the stony tracts for an adamantine April. There was no presence here that shared the moment with him, the exquisitely frightening long-drawn, terror-edged moment of his apprehension. Would nothing stir? Was there no pulse in all these mocking tracts? Nothing that breathed? Nothing among the adumbrate vistas and perspectives of stone that struggled to survive? Empty, silent, forbidding as a lunar landscape, and as uncharted, a tract of Gormenghast lay all about him.

There was no sound, no call of a bird or screech of an insect to break the silence of the stone. No rivulet slid lisping across the flagstones of Great Halls.

He was quite lost. All the sounds of the Castle's life – the clanging of bells; the footsteps striking on the hollow stones; the voices and the echoes of voices; all were gone.

Was this what it was to be an explorer? An adventurer? To gulp this sleeping silence. To be so unutterably alone with it, to wade in it, to find it rising like a tide from the floors, lowering itself from the mouldering caverns of high domes, filling the corridors as though with something palpable?

To feel the lips go dry; the tongue like a leather in the mouth; to feel the knees weaken.

To feel the heart struggling as though to be allowed its freedom, hammering at the walls of his small ribs, hammering for release.

Why had he scrambled through that midnight gap, where his hands had felt and found nothing and then nothing and then again nothing as he edged his way into the gloom? Why had he descended that flight of rusty iron to the deserted corridor and seen how it stretched into how strange a murk of weeds? Why had he not turned back, before it was too late? Turned back and climbed those iron stairs again and waited behind the giant torso for the last echo to disappear from the corridor of carvings. The Headmaster had been on his side – had told lies for him. Had he been ungrateful to steal away? And now he was lost for ever; for ever, and evermore.

Clenching his hands he cried aloud in the hollow wilderness for *help*. Immediately a score of voices answered him, from the four quarters. '*Help, help,*' they cried, again and again, a clamour of voices that were all his own and the last faint echo of his cry, thin, wan, frightened and infinitely far, languished and died and the thick silence crowded back from every side and he was drowned again.

There was nowhere to go and there was everywhere to go. His sense of direction, of where he had come from, had been wiped away by what seemed an age of vacillation.

The silence filled his ears until they ached. He tried to remember what he had read about explorers, but he could recall no story of heroes lost in such a tract as this.

He brought his clenched fist to his mouth and bit his knuckles. For a moment the pain seemed to help him. It gave him a sense of his own reality, and as the pain weakened he bit again; and, in the vain hope of gaining help from yet another scrutiny of the surrounding vistas and avenues of masonry, for he was at a juncture of many ways, he braced himself. His muscles tautened; his head was thrust forward; he peered along the dwindling perspectives. But nothing helped him. Nothing that he saw suggested a course of action, a clue for freedom. There was no ray of light to indicate that there was any outer world. What luminosity there was was uniform, a kind of dusk that had nothing to do with daylight. A self-contained thing, bred in the halls and corridors, something that seeped forth from the walls and floors and ceilings.

Titus moved his dry tongue across his lips and sat down on the flagged floor, but a sense of terror jerked him to his feet again. It seemed that he had begun to be absorbed into the stone. He must be on his feet. He must keep moving. He tiptoed to a wall like the wall of a wharf. For a moment he leaned his small sweating cheek against the mortarless stone. 'I must think . . . think . . . think . . .' He formed the words with his dry tongue. 'Have lost my way. My way? What does that mean?' He began to whisper the words so that he could hear them, but not the castle. There was no echo to this little husky sound. 'It means I don't know where to go. What do I know then? I know that there is a north, south, east and west. But I don't know which is which. Aren't there any other directions?'

His heart gave a leap. 'Yes!' he cried and a hundred affirmatives shouted from throats of stone. He stiffened at the leaping cries, his eyes flickering to left and right, his head motionless. Surely so great a clamour must blast from their retreats the dire ghosts of the place. The centre of his thin chest was sick and bruised with his heart beats.

But nothing appeared and the silence thickened again. What was it he had discovered, that it should have caught him unawares? Another direction? Something that was neither north, south, east or west. What was it? It was skywards. It was roofwards. It was the direction that led to the air.

It was a mere spark, this hope that had ignited. He mouthed his words again. 'There must be stairways,' he said. 'And floor above floor, and then I can see where I am.'

The relief which he felt at having an idea to grip was convulsive, and the tears poured down his face. Then he began to walk, as steadily as he could, along the widest of the grey stone channels. For a considerable distance, it continued in a straight line and then began to take slow curves. The walls on either side were featureless, the ceiling also. Not so much as a cobweb gave interest to the barren surfaces. All at once, after a sharper curve than usual the passage sub-divided into five narrow fingers, and all the child's terrors returned. Was he to return to the hollow silences from which he had come? He could not turn back. He *could* not.

In desperation he leaned against the wall and closed his eyes and it was then that he heard the first sound – that was not of his own making. The first sound since he had slid into the darkness behind the remote statue. He did not jerk at the shock of it but became rigid so that he was unobserved by the raven when it appeared from the darkness of one of the narrow passageways. It walked with a sedate and self-absorbed air to within a few feet of Titus, when it lowered its big head and let fall from its beak a silver bracelet. But only for a moment, for directly it had pecked at the feathers of its breast it lifted up the bracelet and continued for a few paces before hopping, rather clumsily, upon an outcrop of the wall and thence to a larger shelf. Very gradually Titus altered the direction of his head so that he could observe it, this *living* thing. But at the first movement of his head, tentative as it had been, the bird, with a loud and throaty cry and a rattle of black wings, was, all in a moment, in the air, and a fraction of a second later had disappeared down the dark and narrow corridor from which it had so recently paced forth.

Titus at once decided to follow it: not because he wished to see more of the raven, but because the bird was to him a sign of the outer world. There was more than a chance that in returning to this inhospitable corridor, the raven was returning, indirectly, to the open air, and the woods and the wide sky.

As Titus followed, the darkness grew more profound with every step and he began to realize that he was moving under the earth, for the roots of trees grew through the roof and the loam of the walls, and the smell of decay was thick in the air.

Had his fear and horror of the silent halls from which he had so recently escaped been less real he would even now have turned about in the constricted space and made his way back to the hollow nightmare from which he had come. For there seemed no end to this black and stifling tunnel.

At first he had been able to walk upright, but that was long ago. He was now forced, for long periods at a time, to crawl, the smell of the bad earth thick in his face. But for equally long stretches of time the tunnel would widen, and he was able to stumble forwards, his body comparatively upright, until the roof would lower itself again and he would be filled with the fear of suffocation.

There was no light at all. He had all but lost hope that he would ever come out of this horrible experience alive. Had it not been that to keep moving was less frightening than to remain crouched in the darkness Titus would have been tempted to cease forcing his tired body onwards hour after hour, for he had little strength and spirit left.

But at long last when he had no longer the vitality to feel any excitement or relief, so sick he was with fear and exhaustion, he saw ahead of him, as in a dream, a dim, rough-margined opening of light, darkly fringed with coarse weeds and grasses, and he knew, in a flat and colourless way, that he would not die in the dark tunnel; that the hollow halls were a nightmare of the past and that the most he had to fear was the punishment he would receive on returning to the castle.

When he had dragged himself from the tunnel's weedy mouth and had climbed the bank in which the opening gaped, he saw far away to the north and to the west the tower'd outline of his ancient home.

TWENTY-SEVEN

IF the success of a hostess is in any way dependent upon the lavishness of her preparation for the soirée she proposes; upon her outlook, on the almost insane attention which she gives to detail and upon a wealth of forethought, then, theoretically at least, Irma Prunesquallor could look ahead to something that would correspond to those glimpses that came to her in the darkness, when she lay half asleep and saw herself surrounded by a riotous throng of males battling for her hand, which she, the cynosure, swayed coquettishly upon her silk-swaddled pelvis.

If the microscopic overhaul to which she was subjecting her person, her skin, her hair, her dresses and her jewellery gave ground for the belief that so much passionate industry must necessarily wake and rescue a kind of beauty from where it had for so long been immured in her; wake it by a kind of surprise attack; a bombardment of her tall angular clay – then, there was no need for Irma to have any fears upon the score of her attraction. She would be ravishing. She would set a new kind of standard in magnetism. After all she had worked for it.

Having tried on seventeen necklaces and decided upon no necklace at all, so that the full length of her white throat might dip, bridle and sway like a swan's in an absolute freedom of movement, she crossed to the door of her dressing room and, hearing a footstep in the hall below, she could not resist crying out 'Alfred! Alfred! Only three days more, my dear. Only three days more! Alfred! Are you there?'

But there was no reply.

The step she had heard was Steerpike's, who, knowing that the doctor was attending a case in the south kitchen where a rôtier had slipped on a piece of lard and splintered his shoulder-blade, had taken the opportunity which he had for some time been waiting for and climbed through the Doctor's dispensary window, filled a bottle with poison, and, having stowed it away in a deep pocket, decided to leave by the front door with an assortment of explanations in his hand from which to choose were he to be discovered in the hall. Why had there been no answer to his knocking? he would say. Why did they leave the front door open? Where was Dr Prunesquallor? and so on.

But he met no one and took no notice of Irma's cry.

When he got back to his room he poured the poison into a beautiful little cut-glass vessel, placed it against the light of the window where it shone. Then he stood back from it with his head on one side, stepped forward again to move it a little to the left, in the interest of symmetry, and then returning to the centre of the room ran his tongue along his thin lips as he peered with his eyebrows at the little flask of death. Suddenly he stretched his arms out on either side, the fingers splayed like starfish as though he were wakening them to a kind of hypersentience of tingling life.

Then, as though it were the most natural thing in the world, he lowered his hands to the ground, threw up his slender legs and began to perambulate the room on the palms of his hands with the peculiarly stilted, rolling and predatory gait of a starling.

TWENTY-EIGHT

IT was on the following afternoon that Mrs Slagg died. She was found lying upon her bed, towards evening, like a little grubby doll. The black dress was awry as though she had struggled. Her hands were clasped at her shrunken breast. It was hard to imagine that the broken thing had once been new; that those withered, waxen cheeks had been fresh and tinted. That her eyes had long ago glinted with laughter. For she had been sprightly once. A vivacious pert little creature. Bright as a bird.

And here she lay. It was as though the doll-sized body had been thrown aside as too old and decrepit to be of any further use.

Fuchsia, directly she had been told, rushed to the small room that she knew so well.

But the doll on the bed was no longer her nurse. It was not Nannie Slagg, that little motionless bundle. It was something else. Fuchsia closed her eyes and the poignantly familiar image of her old nurse who had been the nearest thing to a mother that Fuchsia had ever known, swam through her mind in a gush of memory.

It was in her to turn again to the bed and to take the beloved relic in her arms in a passion of love, but she could not. She could not. And she did not cry. Something, for all the vividness of her memory, had gone dead in her. She stared again at the shell of all that had nursed her, adored her, smacked her and maddened her.

In her ears, the peevish voice kept crying – 'Oh my weak heart, how *could* they? How *could* they? Anyone would think I didn't know my place.'

Turning suddenly from the bed Fuchsia saw for the first time that she had not been alone in the room. Dr Prunesquallor was standing by the door. Involuntarily she turned to him, raising her eyes to his odd yet strangely compassionate features.

He took a step towards her. 'Fuchsia, my dearest child,' he said. 'Let us go together.'

'O doctor,' she said, 'I don't feel anything. Am I wicked, Doctor Prune? I don't understand.'

The door was suddenly filled by the figure of the Countess who, although she stared at her daughter and at the doctor, did not appear to realize who they were, for no expression appeared on her big pale face. She was carrying over her arm a shawl of rare lace. She moved forward treading heavily on the bare boards. When she reached the bed she gazed for a moment as though transfixed, at the pathetic sight below her, and then, spreading the beautiful black shawl over the body, she turned and left the room.

Prunesquallor, taking Fuchsia's hands, led her through the door which he closed behind them.

'Fuchsia dear,' he said as they began to move together down the corridor, 'have you heard anything of Titus?'

She stopped dead and let go the doctor's hand. 'No,' she said, 'and if nobody finds him I will kill myself.'

'Tut, tut, tut, my little threatener,' said Prunesquallor. 'What a tedious thing to say. And you such an original girl. As though Titus won't reappear like a jack-in-the-box, by all that's typical so he will!'

'He must! He must!' cried Fuchsia, and then she began to weep uncontrollably while the Doctor held her against his side and dabbed her flushed cheeks with his immaculate handkerchief.

TWENTY-NINE

NANNIE SLAGG's funeral was so simple as to appear almost offhand; but this seemingly casual dispatch of the old lady's relics bore no relation to the inherent pathos of the occasion. The gathering at the graveside was out of all proportion to the number of friends on whom, in her lifetime, she would ever have dared to count. For she had become, in her old age, a kind of legend. No one had troubled to see her. She had been deserted in her declining years. But it had been tacitly assumed that she would live for ever. That she would no more pass out of the castle's life than that the Tower of Flints would pass from Gormenghast to leave a gap in the skyline, a gap never again to be filled.

And so, at her funeral, the majority of the mourners were gathered there, to pay their respects to the memory not so much of Mrs Slagg, as to the legend which the tiny creature had, all unwittingly, allowed to grow about her.

It had been impossible for the two bearers to carry the small coffin across their shoulders, for this necessitated so close a formation one behind the other, that they could not walk without tripping one another up. The little box was eventually carried in one hand by the leading mute, while his colleague, with a finger placed on the lid, to prevent it from swaying, walked to one side and a little to the rear.

The bearer, as he strode along, might have been carrying a bird-cage as he paced his way to the Retainers' Graveyard. From time to time the man would turn his eyes with a childish, puzzled expression to the box he carried as though to reassure himself that he was doing what was expected of him. He could not help feeling that something was missing.

The mourners led by Barquentine came behind, followed by the Countess, at some distance. She made no effort to keep pace with the rapid, jerking progress of the cripple. She moved ponderously, her eyes on the ground. Fuchsia and Titus followed, Titus having been released from the Fort for the funeral.

With the nightmare memory of his recent adventure filling his mind he moved in a trance, waking from time to time to wonder at this new manifestation of life's incalculable strangeness – the little box ahead of him, the sunshine playing over the head of Gormenghast Mountain, where it rose, with unbelievable solidity, ahead, like a challenge, on the skyline.

It crowned a region that had become a part of his imaginative being, a region where an exile moved like a stick-insect, through a wilderness of trees, and where, phantom or human, he knew not which, something else was, at this moment, floating again, as he had seen it float before, like a leaf, in the shape of a girl. A girl. Suddenly he broke from his trance at Fuchsia's side.

The word and the idea had fused into something fire-like. Suddenly the slight and floating enigma of the glade had taken on a sex, had become particularized, had woken in him a sensation of excitement that was new to him. Wide awake, all at once, he was at the same time plunged even deeper into a cloudland of symbols to which he had no key. And she was there – there, ahead of him. He could see, far away, the very forest roof that rustled above her.

The figures that moved ahead of him, Barquentine, his mother, and the men with the little box, were less real than the startling confusion of his heart.

He had come to a halt in a valley filled with mounds. Fuchsia was holding his hand. The crowd was all about him. A figure in a hood was scattering red dust into a little trench. A voice was intoning. The words meant nothing to him. He was adrift.

That same evening, Titus lay wide-eyed in the darkness and stared
with unseeing eyes at the enormous shadows of two boys as they fought
a mock battle of grotesque dimensions upon an oblong of light cast
upon the dormitory wall. And while he gazed abstractedly at the cut
and thrust of the shadow-monsters, his sister Fuchsia was crossing to
the Doctor's house.

'Can I talk to you, Doctor?' she asked as he opened the door to her.
'I know it isn't long since you had to bear with me, and . . .' but
Prunesquallor, putting his finger to his lips, silenced her and then drew
her back into a shadow of the hall, for Irma was opening the door of the
sitting-room.

'Alfred,' came the cry, 'what *is* it, Alfred? I said what *is* it?'

'The merest nothing, my love,' trilled the Doctor. 'I must get that
hank of ivy torn up by its very roots in the morning.'

'*What* ivy – I said *what* ivy, you irritating thing,' she answered. 'I
sometimes wish that you could call a spade a spade, I really do.'

'Have we one, sweet nicotine?'

'Have we what?'

'A spade, for the ivy, my love, the ivy that *will* keep tapping at our
front door. By all that's symbolic, it *will* go on doing it!'

'Is that what it was?'

Irma relaxed. 'I don't remember any ivy,' she added. 'But what *are*
you cowering in that corner for? It's not like you, Alfred, to lurk about
in the corner like that. Really, if I didn't know it was you, well really,
I'd be quite . . .'

'But you're *not*, are you, my sweet nerve-ending? Of course you're
not. So upstairs with you. By all that moves in rapid circles, I've had
a seismic sister these last few days, haven't I?'

'O Alfred. It *will* be worth it, won't it? There's so much to think of
and I'm so excited. And so *soon* now. *Our* party! *Our* party!'

'And that's why you must go to bed and fill yourself right up with
sleep. That is what my sister needs, isn't it? Of course it is. Sleep . . . O,
the very treacle of it, Irma! So run away my dear. Away with you! Away
with you! A . . . w . . . a . . . y!' He fluttered his hand like a silk
handkerchief.

'Good night, Alfred.'

'Good night. O thicker-than-water.'

Irma disappeared into the upper darkness.

'And *now*,' said the Doctor, placing his immaculate hands on his
brittle and elegant knees, and rising at the same time on his toes, so
that Fuchsia had the strongest impression that he was about to fall
forwards on his speculative and smiling face . . . 'and now, my Fuchsia,
I think we've had enough of the hall, don't you?' and he led the girl into
his study.

'Now if you'll draw the blinds and if I pull up that green arm-chair, we will be comfortable, affable, incredible and almost insufferable in two shakes of a lamb's tail, won't we?' he said. 'By all that's unanswerable, we will!'

Fuchsia, pulling at the curtain, felt something give way and a loose sail of velvet hung across the glass.

'O Doctor Prune I'm sorry – I'm sorry,' she said, almost in tears.

'Sorry! Sorry!' cried the Doctor. 'How dare you pity me! How dare you humiliate me! You know very well that I can do that sort of thing better than you. I'm an old man; I admit it. Nearly fifty summers have seeped through me. But there's life in me yet. But *you* don't think so. No! By all that's cruel, you don't. But I'll show you. Watch me.' And the Doctor striding like a heron to a further window ripped the long curtain from its runner, and whirling it round himself stood swathed before her like a long green chrysalis, with the pale sharp eager features of his bright face emerging at the top like something from another life.

'There!' he said.

A year ago Fuchsia would have laughed until her sides were sore. Even at the moment it was wonderfully funny. But she couldn't laugh. She knew that he loved doing such a thing. She knew he loved to put her at her ease – and she *had* been put at her ease, for she no longer felt embarrassed, but she also knew that she should be laughing, and she couldn't *feel* the humour, she could only *know* it. For within the last year she had developed, not naturally, but on a zig-zag course. The emotions and the tags of half-knowledge which came to her, fought and jostled, upsetting one another, so that what was natural to her appeared un-natural, and she lived from minute to minute, grappling with each like a lost explorer in a dream who is now in the arctic, now on the equator, now upon rapids, and now alone on endless tracts of sand.

'O Doctor,' she said, 'thank you. That is very, very kind and funny.'

She had turned her head away, but now she looked up and found he had already disengaged himself of the curtain and was pushing a chair towards her.

'What is worrying you, Fuchsia?' he said. They were both sitting down. The dark night stared in at them through the curtainless windows.

She leant forward and as she did so she suddenly looked older. It was as though she had taken a grip of her mind – to have, in a way, grown up to the span of her nineteen years.

'Several important things, Doctor Prune,' she said. 'I want to ask you about them . . . if I may.'

Prunesquallor looked up sharply. This was a new Fuchsia. Her tone had been perfectly level. Perfectly adult.

'Of course you may, Fuchsia. What are they?'

'The first thing is, what happened to my father, Dr Prune?'

The Doctor leaned back in his chair, as she stared at him he put his hand to his forehead.

'Fuchsia,' he said. 'Whatever you ask I will try to answer. I won't evade your questions. And you must believe me. What happened to your father, I do not know. I only know that he was very ill – and you remember that as well as I do – just as you remember his disappearance. If anyone alive knows what happened to him, I do not know who that man might be unless it is either Flay or Swelter who also disappeared at the same time.'

'Mr Flay is alive, Dr Prune.'

'No!' said the Doctor. 'Why do you say that?'

'Titus has seen him, Doctor. More than once.'

'Titus!'

'Yes, Doctor, in the woods. But it's a secret. You won't . . .'

'Is he well? Is he able to keep well? What did Titus say about him?'

'He lives in a cave and hunts for his food. He asked after me. He is very loyal.'

'Poor old Flay!' said the Doctor. 'Poor old faithful Flay. But you mustn't see him, Fuchsia. It would do nothing but harm. I cannot have you getting into trouble.'

'But my father,' cried Fuchsia. 'You said he might know about my father! He may be alive, Dr Prune. He may be *alive*!'

'No. No. I don't believe he is,' said the Doctor. 'I don't believe so, Fuchsia.'

'But Doctor, Doctor! I must see Flay. He loved me. I want to take him something.'

'No Fuchsia. You mustn't go. Perhaps you will see him again – but you will become distressed – more distressed than you are now, if you start escaping from the castle. And Titus also. This is all very wrong. He is not old enough to be so wild and secret. God bless me – what else does he say?'

'This is all in secret, Doctor.'

'Yes – yes, Fuchsia. Of course it is.'

'He has seen something.'

'Seen something? What sort of thing?'

'A flying thing.'

The Doctor froze into a carving of ice.

'A flying thing,' repeated Fuchsia. 'I don't know what he means.' She leaned back in her chair and clasped her hands. 'Before Nannie Slagg died,' she said – her voice falling to a whisper – 'she talked to me. It was only a few days before she died – and she didn't seem as nervy as usual, because she talked like she used to talk when she wasn't worried. She told me about when Titus was born, and when Keda came to nurse him, which I remember myself, and how when Keda went away again to the Outer Dwellings, one of the Carvers made love to her and she had a baby and how the baby wasn't really like other babies, because of Keda not being married, I mean, but different apart from that, and how there were various rumours about it. The Outer Dwellers wouldn't have it, she said, because it wasn't legitimate, and when Keda killed herself the baby was brought up differently as though it was her fault, and when she was a child she lived in a way that made them all hate her and never talked to the other children, but frightened them sometimes and ran across the roofs and down the mud chimneys and began to spend all her time in the woods. And how the mud Dwellers hated her and were frightened of her because she was so rapid and kept disappearing and bared her teeth. And Nannie Slagg told me that she left them altogether and they didn't know where she had gone for a long time, only sometimes they heard her laughing at them at night, and they called her the "Thing", and Nannie Slagg told me all this and said she is still alive and how she is Titus' foster sister and when Titus told her of the flying thing in the air I wondered, Dr Prune, whether . . .'

Fuchsia lifted her eyes and found that the Doctor had risen from his chair and was staring through the window into the darkness where a shooting star was trailing down the sky.

'If Titus knew I had told you,' she said in a loud voice, rising to her feet, 'I would never be forgiven. But I am frightened for him. I don't want anything to happen to him. He is always staring at nothing and doesn't hear half I say. And I love him, Dr Prune. That's what I wanted to tell you.'

'Fuchsia,' said the Doctor. 'It's very late. I will think about all you have told me. A little at a time, you know. If you tell me everything at once I'll lose my place, won't I? But a little at a time. I know there are other things you want to tell me, about this and that and very important things too – but you must wait a day or two and I will try and help you. Don't be frightened. I will do all I can. What with Flay and Titus and the "Thing" I must do some thinking, so run along to bed and come and see me very soon again. Why bless my wits if it isn't hours after your bedtime. Away with you!'

'Good night Doctor.'

'Good night my dear child.'

THIRTY

A FEW days later when Steerpike saw Fuchsia emerge from a door in the west wing and make her way across the stubble of what had once been a great lawn, he eased himself out of the shadows of an arch where he had been lurking for over an hour, and taking a roundabout route began to run with his body half doubled, towards the object of Fuchsia's evening journey.

Across his back, as he ran, was slung a wreath of roses from Pentecost's flower garden. Arriving, unseen, at the servants' burial ground a minute or two before Fuchsia, he had time to strike an attitude of grief as he knelt on one knee, his right hand still on the wreath which he was placing on the little weedy grave.

So Fuchsia came upon him.

'What are *you* doing here?' Her voice was hardly audible. '*You* never loved her.'

Fuchsia turned her eyes to the great wreath of red and yellow roses and then at the few wild flowers which were clasped in her hand.

Steerpike rose to his feet and bowed. The evening was green about them.

'I did not know her as you did, your ladyship,' he said. 'But it struck me as so mean a grave for an old lady to be buried in. I was able to get these roses . . . and . . . well . . .' (his simulation of embarrassment was exact).

'But *your* wildflowers!' he said, removing the wreath from the head of the little mound and placing it at the dusty foot – 'they are the ones that will please her spirit most – wherever she is.'

'I don't know anything about that,' said Fuchsia. She turned from him and flung her flowers away. 'It's all nonsense anyway.' She turned again and faced him. 'But *you*,' she blurted. 'I didn't think *you* were sentimental.'

Steerpike had never expected this. He had imagined that she would feel she had found an ally in the graveyard. But a new idea presented itself. Perhaps he had found an ally in *her*. How far was her phrase 'it's all nonsense anyway' indicative of her nature?

'I have my moods,' he said and with a single action plucked the great wreath of roses from the foot of the grave and hurled it from him. For a moment the rich roses glowed as they careered through the dark green evening to disappear in the darkness of the surrounding mounds.

For a moment she stood motionless, the blood drained from her face, and then she sprang at the young man and buried the nails of her hands in his high cheekbones.

He made no move. Dropping her arms and backing away from him with slow, exhausted steps, she saw him standing perfectly quietly, his face absolutely white save the bright blood on his cheeks that were red like a clown's.

Her heart beat as she saw him. Behind him the green porous evening was hung like a setting for his thin body, his whiteness, and the hectic wounds on his cheeks.

For a moment she forgot her sudden, inconsistent hatred of his act; forgot his high shoulders; forgot her station as a daughter of the Line – forgot everything and saw only a human whom she had hurt, and a tide of remorse filled her, and half blind with confusion she stumbled towards him her arms outstretched. Quick as an adder he was in her arms – but even at that moment they fell, tripping each other up on the rough ground – fell, their arms about one another. Steerpike could feel her heart pounding against his ribs, her cheek against his mouth but he made no movement with his lips. His mind was racing ahead. For a few moments they lay. He waited for her limbs and body to relax, but she was taut as a bowstring in his arms. Not a move did he make, nor she, until lifting her head from his she saw, not the blood on his cheeks but the dark red colour of his eyes, the high bulge of his shining forehead. It was unreal. It was a dream. There was a kind of horrible novelty about it. Her gush of tenderness had ended, and there she was in the arms of the high-shouldered man. She turned her head again and realized with a start of horror that they were using for their pillow the narrow grassy grave-mound of her old nurse.

'Oh horrible!' she screamed. 'Horrible! horrible!' and forcing him aside as she scrambled to her feet she bounded like a wild thing into the darkness.

THIRTY-ONE

Sitting at her bedroom window, Irma Prunesquallor awaited the daybreak as though a clandestine meeting of the most hushed and secret kind had been agreed upon between herself and the first morning ray. And suddenly it came – the dawn – a flush of swallow light above a rim of masonry. The day had arrived. The day of the Party, or of what she now called her Soirée.

In spite of her brother's advice, she had passed a very poor night, her speculative excitement breaking through her sleep over and over again. At last she had lit the long green candles on the table by her bed, and frowning at each in turn had begun to polish yet again the ten long and perfect finger nails, her mouth pursed, her muscles tensed. Then she had slipped on her dressing gown and drawing a chair to the window had waited for the sunrise.

Below her window the quadrangle, as yet untouched by the pale light in the east, was spread like a lake of black water. There was no sound, no movement anywhere. Irma sat motionless, bolt upright, her hands clasped in her lap. Her eyes were fixed upon the sunrise. The candle flames in the room behind her stood balanced upon their wicks like yellow leaves upon tiny black stalks. Not a tremor disturbed their perfect lines – and then, suddenly a cock crew – a barbarous, an imperious sound; primal and unashamed it split the darkness, lifting Irma to her feet as it were on the updraught of its clarion. Her pulses raced. She sprang for the bathroom and within a few moments the hissing, steaming water had filled the bath and Irma, standing in an attitude of excruciating coyness was tossing handfuls of emerald and lilac crystals into the sumptuous depths.

Alfred Prunesquallor, his head thrown back across his pillow, was only half asleep. His brows were drawn together and a strange frown gave to his face an unexpected quality. Had any of his acquaintances seen him lying there they would have wondered whether, after all, they had the slightest inkling as to his real nature. Was this the gay, irrepressible and facetious physician?

He had passed a restless and unhappy night. Confused dreams had kept him turning on his bed, dreams that from time to time gathered themselves into vivid images of terrible clarity.

Struggling for breath and strength, he beat his way through the black moat-water to a drowning Fuchsia no bigger than a child's doll. But every time he reached her and stretched out his hand she sank beneath the surface, and there in her place were floating bottles half filled with coloured poison. And then he would see her again, calling for help, tiny, dark desperate, and he would flounder after her, his heart hammering and he would waken.

At various moments through the night he could see Steerpike running through the air, his body bent forward, his feet a few inches above the ground but never touching it. And keeping pace with him and immediately below him as though it were his shadow a swarm of rats with their fangs bared ran in a compact body like one thing, veering as he veered, pausing as he paused, most horrible and intent, filling the landscape of his midnight brain.

He saw the Countess on a great iron tray far out at sea. The moon shone down like a blue lamp, as she fished, with Flay as her frozen rod,

attenuate and stiff beyond belief. Between the teeth of the petrified
mouth he held a strand of the Countess's dark red hair which shone like
a thread of fire in the blue light.

Effortlessly she held him aloft, her big hand gripping him about both
ankles. His clothes were tight about him and he appeared mummified,
the thin rigid length of him reaching up stiffly into the stars. With
hideous regularity she would pluck at the line and swing aboard another
and yet another of her white and sea-drowned cats, and place it tenderly
upon the mounting heap of whiteness on the tray.

And then he saw Bellgrove galloping like a horse on all fours with
Titus on his back. Through the ravine of terrible darkness and up the
slopes of pine-covered mountains he galloped, his white mane blowing
out behind his head while Titus, plucking arrow after arrow from an
unfailing quiver, let fly at everything in view until, the image dwindling
in the Doctor's brain, he lost them in the dire shade of the night.

And the dead, he saw. Mrs Slagg clutching at her heart as she
pattered along a tight rope, and the tears that coursed down her cheeks
and fell to the earth far below, sounded like gunshots as they struck the
ground.

And Swelter, for an instant, filled the darkness, so that even in his
sleep, the Doctor retched to see so vile a volume forcing its boneless
way, inch by inch, through a keyhole.

And Sepulchrave and Sourdust danced together upon a bed, leaping
and turning in the air, their hands joined, and over their heads were
great crude paper masks, so that over Sourdust's wizened shoulders the
flapping face of a painted kitten put out its tongue at the cardboard
sunflower through the great black centre of which the eyes of the
seventy-sixth earl of Gormenghast glittered like broken glass.

Picture after moving picture all night long until, as dawn approached,
the doctor fell into a dreamless though shallow sleep through which he
could hear the dreamland crowing of a cock and the water roaring into
Irma's bath.

THIRTY-TWO

In a score of schoolrooms all through the day innumerable urchins
wondered what it was that made their masters even less interested than
usual in their existence. Familiar as they were with being neglected
over long periods and with the disinterest that descends on those who
juggle through long decades with sow's ears, yet there was something

very different about the kind of listlessness that made itself so evident at every master's desk.

Not a clock in all the various classrooms but had been stared at at least sixty times an hour: not by the bewildered boys, but by their masters.

The secret had been well kept. Not a child knew of the evening party, and when eventually, with the lessons over for the day, the professors arrived back at their private quadrangle, there was a certain smug and furtive air about the way they moved.

There was no particular reason why the invitation to the Prunesquallors should have been kept secret, but a tacit understanding between the masters had been rigidly honoured. There was a sense, perhaps, unformulated for the most part, in their minds, that there was something rather ridiculous about their having *all* been invited. A sense that the whole thing was somewhat over-simplified. A trifle un-selective. They saw nothing absurd in themselves, individually, and why should they? But a few of them, Perch-Prism in particular, could not visualize his colleagues *en masse*, himself among them, waiting their entrance at the Prunesquallors' door, without a shudder. There is something about a swarm that is damaging to the pride of its individual members.

As was their habit, they leaned this evening over the balustrade of the verandah that surrounded the Masters' Quadrangle. Below them, the small far-away figure of the quadman was sweeping the ground from end to end, leaving behind him the thin strokes of his broom in the fine dust.

They were all there, the evening light upon them; all except Bellgrove, who leaning back in the headmaster's chair in his room above the distant classrooms, was cogitating the extraordinary suggestions which had been made to him during the day. These suggestions, which had been put forward by Perch-Prism, Opus Fluke, Shred, Swivell and other members, were to the effect that they, for one reason or another and on one occasion or another had heard from friends of friends or had half-heard through hollow panels, or in the darkness below stairs, at such times when Irma was talking to herself aloud (a habit which they assured Bellgrove she had no power to master) that she (Irma) had got the very devil of a passion for *him*, their reverend headmaster – and that although it was not *their* affair, they felt he would not be offended to be faced with the reality of the situation – for what could be more obvious than that the party was merely a way for Irma to be near him? It was obvious, was it not, that she could never ask him alone. It would be too blatant, too indelicate, but there it was . . . there it was. They had frowned at him in sympathy and left.

Now Bellgrove was well used to having his leg pulled. He had had it pulled for as long as he had possessed one. He was thus, for all this weakness and vagueness, no simpleton when it came to banter and the kindred arts. He had listened to all they had said, and now as he sat alone he pondered the whole question for the twentieth time. And his conclusions and speculations came forth from him, heavily like this.

1 The whole thing was poppycock.

2 The purpose of the fabrication was no more than that he should provide, unknowingly, an added zest to the party. These wags on his staff looked forward no doubt to seeing him in constant flight with Irma on his tail.

3 As he had not questioned the story, they could have no idea that he had seen through it.

4 So far, very excellent.

5 How were the tables to be turned . . .?

6 What was wrong with Irma Prunesquallor anyway?

A fine, upright woman with a long sharp nose. But what about it? Noses had to be some shape or other. It had character. It wasn't negative. Nor was she. She had no bosom to speak of: that was true enough. But he was rather too old for bosoms anyway. And there was nothing to touch the cool of white pillows in summertime – ('Bless my soul,' he said aloud, 'what *am* I thinking?') . . .

As headmaster he was far more alone than he had ever been before. Bad mixer as he was he preferred to be 'out of it' in a crowd than out of it altogether.

He disliked the sense of isolation, when his staff departed every evening. He had pictured himself as a thwarted hermit – one who could find tranquillity alone with a profound volume on his knee, and a room about him spare, ascetic, the hard chair, the empty grate. But this was not so. He loathed it and bared his teeth at the mean furniture and the dirty muddle of his belongings. This was no way for a headmaster's study to be! He thought of cushions and bedroom slippers. He thought of socks of long ago with heels to their name. He even thought of flowers in a vase.

Then he thought of Irma again. Yes, there was no denying it, a fine young woman. Well set up. Vivacious. Rather silly, perhaps, but an old man couldn't expect all the qualities.

He rose to his feet and plodding to a mirror wiped the dust from its face with his elbow. Then he peered at himself. A slow childish smile spread over his features as though he were pleased with what he saw. Then with his head on one side, he bared his teeth, and frowned for they were terrible. 'I must keep my mouth shut more than I usually do,' he mused, and he began to practise talking with closed lips but could not make out what he was saying. The novelty of the whole situation and the fantastic project that was now consuming him set his old heart beating as he grasped for the first time its tremendous significance. Not less than the personal triumph with which it would fill him, and the innumerable practical advantages that would surely result from such a union, was the delight he was prematurely tasting of hoisting the staff with its own petard. He began to see himself sailing past the miserable bachelors, Irma on his arm, an unquestioned patriarch, a symbol of success and married stability with something of the gay dog about him too – of the light beneath the bushel, the dark horse, the man with an ace up his sleeve. So they thought that they could fool him. That Irma was infatuated with him. He began to laugh in a sick and exaggerated way, but stopped suddenly. *Could* she be? No. They had made the whole thing up. But could she be, all the same? Coincidentally, as it were. No! no! no! Impossible. Why should she be? 'God bless me!' he muttered. 'I must be going mad!'

But the adventure was there. His secret plan was there. It was up to him. A sensation that he imagined was one of youth flooded him. He began to hop laboriously up and down on the floor as though over an invisible skipping rope. He made a jump for the table as though to land on the top, but failed to reach the necessary height, bruised his old leg below the knee.

'Bloody hell!' he muttered and sat down heavily in his chair again.

THIRTY-THREE

As the Professors were changing into their evening gowns, stabbing at startled hanks of hair with broken combs, maligning one another, finding in one another's rooms long lost towels, studs and even major garments that had disappeared in mysterious ways – while this was happening to the accompaniment of much swearing and muttering; and while the coarse jests rumbled along the verandah, and Flannelcat, half sick with excitement, was sitting on the floor of his room with his head between his knees as the heavy hand of Opus Fluke reached hairily through his doorway to steal a towel from a rack – while this and a hundred things were going on around the Masters' Quadrangle, Irma was perambulating the long white room which had been re-opened for the occasion.

It had once been the original salon; a room which the Prunesquallors had never used, being too vast for their requirements. It had been locked up for years, but now, after many days of cleaning and repainting, dusting and polishing, it shone with a terrible newness. A group of skilled men had been kept busy, under Irma's watchful eye. She had a delicate taste, had Irma. She could not bear vulgar colours, or coarse furniture. What she lacked was the power to combine and make a harmony out of the various parts that, though exquisite in themselves, bore no relationship either in style, period, grain, colour or fabric to one another.

Each thing was seen on its own. The walls had to be a most tender shade of washed out coral. And the carpet had to be the kind of green that is almost grey, the flowers were arranged bowl by bowl, vase by vase, and though each was lovely in itself, there was no general beauty in the room.

Unknown to her the 'bittiness' that resulted gave to the salon a certain informality far from her intentions. This was to prove a lubricating thing, for the Professors might well have been frozen into a herd of lock-jawed spectres had Irma made of the place the realm of chill perfection that was at the back of her mind. Peering at everything in turn she moved about this long room like something that had spent all its life in planning to counteract the sharpness of its nose, with such a flaunting splendour of silk and jewellery, powder and scent, as set the teeth on edge like coloured icing.

About three quarters of the way along the southern wall of the salon a very fine double window opened upon a walled-in garden where rockeries, crazy pavement, sun-dials, a small fountain (now playing after a two-day struggle with a gardener), trellis work, arbours, statuettes and a fish pond made of the place something so terrifying to the sensitive eye of the Doctor, that he never crossed the garden with his eyes open. Much practice had given him confidence and he could move across it blindly at high speed. It was Irma's territory; a place of ferns and mosses and little flowers that opened at odd hours during the night. Little miniature grottoes had been made for them to twinkle in.

Only at the far end of the garden was there any sense of nature, and even there it was made manifest by no more than a dozen fine trees whose limbs had grown in roughly the direction they had found most natural. But the grass about their stems was closely mown, and under their boughs a rustic chair or two was artlessly positioned.

On this particular evening there was a hunter's moon. No wonder. Irma had seen to it.

When she reached the french windows she was delighted with the scene before her, the goblin-garden, silver and mysterious, the moonbeams glimmering on the fountain, the sun-dial, the trellis work and the moon itself reflected in the fish pond. It was all a bit blurred to her, and that was a pity, but she could not have it both ways. Either she was to wear her dark glasses and look less attractive, or she must put up with finding everything about her out of focus. It didn't matter much *how* out of focus a garden by moonlight was – in fact in the adding of this supercharge of mystery it became a kind of emotional haze, which was something which Irma, as a spinster, could never have enough of – but how would it be when she had to disengage one professor from another? Would she be able to appreciate the subtlety of their advances, if they made any; those little twitches and twists of the lips, those narrowings and rollings of the eye, those wrinklings of the speculative temple, that shrugging of an eye-brow at play? Would all this be lost to her?

When she had told her brother of her intention to dispense with her glasses, he had advised her, in that case, to leave them off an hour before the guests were due. And he had been right. She was quite sure he had been. For the pain in her forehead had gone and she was moving faster on her swathed legs than she had dared to do at first. But it was all a little confusing, and though her heart beat at the sight of her moon-blur of a garden, yet she clenched her hands at the same time in a gay little temper that she should have been born with bad eyes.

She rang a bell. A head appeared at the door.

'Is that Mollocks?'

'Yes, Madam.'

'Have you got your soft shoes on?'

'Yes, Madam.'

'You may enter.'

Mollocks entered.

'Cast your eye around, Mollocks – I said cast your eye around. No, no! Get the feather duster. No, no. Wait a minute – I said wait a minute.' (Mollocks had made no move.) 'I will ring.' (She rang.) Another head appeared. 'Is that Canvas?' 'Yes, Madam, it is Canvas.' 'Yes Madam is quite enough, Canvas. Quite enough. Your exact name is not so enormously important. Is it? Is it? To the larder with you and fetch a feather brush for Mollocks. Away with you. Where are you, Mollocks?'

'Beside you, Madam.'

'Ah yes. Ah yes. Have you shaved?'

'Definitely, Madam.'

'Quite so, Mollocks. It must be my eyes. You look so dark across the face. Now you are to leave no stone unturned – not one – do you understand me? Move from place to place all over this room, backwards and forwards restlessly – do you understand me, with Canvas at your side – *searching* for those specks of dust that have escaped me – did you say you had your soft shoes on?'

'Yes, Madam.'

'Good. Very good. Is that Canvas who has just come in? Is it? Good. Very good. He is to travel with you. Four eyes are better than two. But *you* can use the brush – *whoever* finds the specks. I don't want anything spoilt or knocked over and Canvas can be very clumsy, can't you, Canvas?'

The old man Canvas who had been sent running about the house since dawn, and who did not feel that as an old retainer he was being appreciated, said that he 'didn't know about that'. It was his only line of defence, a repetitive, stubborn attitude beyond which one could not go.

'Oh yes you are,' repeated Irma. '*Quite* clumsy. Run along now. You are *slow*, Canvas, *slow*.'

Again the old man said he 'didn't know about that' and having said so, turned in a puny fury of temper from his mistress and tripping over his own feet as he turned, grabbed at a small table. A tall alabaster vase swayed on its narrow base like a pendulum while Mollocks and Canvas watched it, their mouths open, their limbs paralysed.

But Irma had surged away from them and was practising a certain slow and languid mode of progress which she felt might be effective. Up and down a little strip of the soft grey carpet she swayed, stopping every now and again to raise a limp hand before her, presumably to be touched by the lips of one or other of the professors.

Her head would be tilted away at these moments of formal intimacy, and there was only a segment of her sidelong glance as it grazed her cheekbones, to reward the imaginary gallant as he mouthed her knuckles.

Knowing Irma's vision to be faulty and that they could not be seen, with the length of the salon between them, Canvas and Mollocks watched her from under their gathered brows, marking time, like soldiers the while, to simulate the sounds of activity.

They had not long, however, in which to watch their mistress for the door opened and the Doctor came in. He was in full evening dress and looked more elegant than ever. Across his immaculate breast was the pick of the few decorations with which Gormenghast had honoured him. The crimson Order of the Vanquished Plague, and the Thirty-fifth Order of the Floating Rib lay side by side upon his narrow, snow-white shirt, and were suspended from wide ribbons. In his buttonhole was an orchid.

'O Alfred,' cried Irma. 'How do I seem to you? How do I seem to you?'

The Doctor glanced over his shoulder and motioned the retainers out of the room with a flick of his hand.

He had hidden himself away all afternoon and sleeping dreamlessly had to a great extent recovered from the nightmares he had suffered. As he stood before his sister he appeared as fresh as a daisy, if less pastoral.

'Now I tell you *what*,' he cried, moving round her, his head cocked on one side, 'I tell you *what*, Irma. You've made something out of yourself,

and if it ain't a work of art, it's as near as makes no matter. By all that
emanates, you've brought it off. Great grief! I hardly know you. Turn
round, my dear, on one heel! La! La! *Significant* form, that's what she is!
And to think the same blood batters in our veins! It's quite embarrassing.'

'What do you mean, Alfred? I thought you were praising me.' (There
was a catch in her voice.)

'And so I was, and so I was! – but tell me sister, what is it, apart from
your luminous, un-sheltered eyes – and your general dalliance – what
is it that's altered you – that has, as it were . . . aha . . . aha . . . H'm . . .
I've got it – O dear me . . . quite so, by all that's pneumatic, how silly
of me – you've got a bosom, my love, or haven't you?'

'Alfred! It is not for you to prove.'

'God forbid, my love.'

'But if you *must* know . . .'

'No, no, Irma, no no! I am content to leave everything to your
judgement.'

'So you won't listen to me . . .' (Irma was almost in tears.)

'O but I will. Tell me all.'

'Alfred dear – you liked the look of me. You *said* you did.'

'And I still do. Enormously. It was only that, well, I've known you
a long time and . . .'

'I'm *told*,' said Irma, breaking in breathlessly, 'that busts are . . .
well . . .'

'. . . that busts are what you make them?' queried her brother
standing on his toes.

'Exactly! Exactly!' his sister shouted. 'And I've *made* one, Alfred, and
it gives me pride of bearing. It's a hot water bottle, Alfred; an expensive
one.'

There was a long and deathly silence. When at last Prunesquallor
had reassembled the fragments of his shattered poise he opened his
eyes.

'When do you expect them, my love?'

'You know as well as I do. At nine o'clock, Alfred. Shall we call in the
Chef?'

'What for?'

'For final instructions, of course.'

'What again?'

'One can't be too final, dear.'

'Irma,' said the Doctor, 'perhaps you have stumbled on a truth of the
first water. And talking of water – is the fountain playing?'

'Darling!' said Irma, fingering her brother's arm. 'It's playing its
heart out,' and she gave him a pinch.

The doctor felt the blushes spreading all over his body, in little rushes like red Indians leaping from ambush, to ambush, now here, now there.

'And *now*, Alfred, since it's nearly nine o'clock, I am going to give you a surprise. You haven't seen *anything* yet. This sumptuous dress. Those jewels at my ears, these flashing stones about my white throat –' (her brother winced) '. . . and the fancy knot-work of my silvery coiff – all this is but a setting, Alfred, a mere setting. Can you bear to wait, Alfred, or shall I tell you? Or still more better – O yes! Yes, still more better, dear, I'll show you N O W –'

And away she went. The Doctor had no idea she could travel so fast. A swish of 'nightmare blue' and she was gone, leaving behind her the faint smell of almond icing.

'I wonder if I'm getting old?' thought the doctor, and he put his hand to his forehead and shut his eyes. When he opened them she was there again – but O creeping hell! what had she done.

What faced him was not merely the fantastically upholstered and bedizened image of his sister to whose temperament and posturing he had long been immune, but something else, which turned her from a vain, nervous, frustrated, outlandish, excitable and prickly spinster which was bearable enough, into an *exhibit*. The crude inner workings of her mind were thrust nakedly before him by reason of the long flower-trimmed veil that she now wore over her face. Only her eyes were to be seen, above the thick black netting, very weak, and rather small. She turned them to left and right to show her brother the principle of the thing. Her nose was hidden, and in itself that was excellent, but in no way could it offset the blatancy, the terrible soul-revealing blatancy of the underlying idea.

For the second time that evening Prunesquallor blushed. He had never seen anything so openly, ridiculously, predatory in his life. Heaven knew she would say the wrong thing at the wrong time, but above all she must not be allowed to expose her intention in that palpable way.

But what he said was 'Aha! H'm. What a flair you have, Irma! What a consummate flair. Who else would have thought of it?'

'O Alfred, I knew you'd love it . . .' she swivelled her eyes again, but her attempt at roguery was heart-breaking.

'Now what *is* it I keep thinking of as I stand and admire you,' her brother trilled, tapping his forehead with his finger – 'tut . . . tut . . . tut, what *is* it . . . something I read in one of your journals, I do believe – ah yes, I've almost got it – there . . . it's slipped away again . . . how irritating . . . wait . . . wait . . . here it comes like a fish to the bait of my poor old memory . . . ah, I almost had it . . . I've *got* it, O yes indeed . . . but, oh dear me, No . . . that wouldn't do at all . . . I mustn't tell you *that* . . .'

'What *is* it, Alfred? . . . what are you frowning about? How irritating you are just when you were studying me – I said how irritating you are.'

'You would be most unhappy if I told you, my dear. It affects you deeply.'

'Affects me! How do you mean?'

'It was the merest snippet, Irma, which I happened to read. What has reminded me of it is that it was all about veils and the modern woman. Now I, as a man, have always responded to the mysterious and provocative wherever it may be found. And if these qualities are evoked by anything on earth they are evoked by a woman's veil. But O dear me, do you know what this creature in the Women's column wrote?'

'What did she write?' said Irma.

'She wrote that "although there may be those who will continue to wear their veils, just as there are those who still crawl through the jungle on all fours because no one has ever told them that it is the custom these days to walk upright, yet she (the writer) would know full well in what grade of society to place any woman who was continuing to wear a veil, after the twenty-second of the month. After all," the writer continued, "some things are 'done' and some things are not done, and as far as the sartorial aristocracy was concerned, veils might as well never have been invented." '

'But what nonsense it all is,' cried the Doctor. 'As though women are so weak that they have to follow one another so closely as all that.' And he gave a high-pitched laugh as though to imply that a mere male could see through all that kind of nonsense.

'Did you say the twenty-second of this month?' said Irma, after a few moments of thick silence.

'That is so,' said her brother.

'And today is the . . .'

'The thirtieth,' said her brother – 'but surely, surely, you wouldn't . . .'

'Alfred,' said Irma. 'Be quiet, please. There are some things which you do not understand and one of them is a woman's mind.' With a deft movement of her hand she freed her face of the veil and there was her nose again as sharp as ever.

'Now I wonder if you'd do something for me, dear.'

'What is it, Irma, my love?'

'I wondered if you'd do something for me, dear?'

'What is it, Irma, my love?'

'I wondered if you'd take – O no, I'll have to do it myself – and you might be shocked – but perhaps if you would shut your eyes, Alfred, I could . . .'

'What in the name of darkness are you driving at?'

'I wondered, dear, at first, whether you would take my bust to the bedroom and fill it with hot water. It has got very cold, Alfred, and I don't want to catch a chill – or perhaps if you'd rather not do that for me, you could bring the kettle down-stairs to my little writing room and I'll do it myself – will you, dear – will you?'

'Irma,' said her brother. 'I will not do it for you. I have done and will continue to do a lot of things for you, pleasant and unpleasant, but I will not start running around, looking for water bottles to fill for my sister's bosom. I will not even bring down the kettle for you. Have you no kind of modesty, my love? I know you are very excited, and really don't know what you are doing or saying, but I must have it quite clear from the start that as far as your rubber bust is concerned, I am unable to help you. If you catch a chill, then I will dose you – but until then, I would be grateful if you would leave the subject alone. But enough of that! Enough of that! The magic hour approaches. Come, come! my tiger lily!'

'Sometimes I despise you, Alfred,' said Irma. 'Who would have thought that *you* were such a prude.'

'Ah no! my dear, you're far too hard on me. Have mercy. Do you think it is easy to bear your scorn when you are looking so radiant?'

'Am I, Alfred! O, am I? Am I?'

THIRTY-FOUR

I⊤ had been arranged that the staff should gather in the quadrangle outside the Doctor's house at a few minutes past nine and wait for Bellgrove, who, as headmaster, had ignored the suggestion that he should be first on the spot and wait for *them*. Perch-Prism's argument that it was a good deal more ludicrous for a horde of men to hang about as though they were hatching some kind of conspiracy than it would be for Bellgrove, even though he *was* headmaster, cut no ice with the old lion.

Bellgrove, in his present mood, was peculiarly dogged. He had glowered over his shoulder at them as though he were at bay. 'Never let it be said in future years . . .' he had ended, 'that a headmaster of Gormenghast had once to wait the pleasure of his staff's arrival – by night, in the South Quadrangle. Never let it be said that so responsible an office had sunk into such disrespect.'

And so it was that a few minutes after nine a great blot formed in the darkness of the quadrangle as though a section of the dusk had coagulated. Bellgrove, who had been hiding behind a pillar of the

cloisters, had decided to keep his staff waiting for at least five minutes. But he was unable to contain his impatience. Not three minutes had passed since their arrival before his excitement propelled him forwards into the open gloom. When he was half way across the quadrangle, and could hear the muttering of their voices, quite plainly, the moon slid out from behind a cloud. In the cold light that now laid bare the rendezvous, the red gowns of the professors burned darkly, the colour of wine. Not so Bellgrove's. *His* ceremonial gown was of the finest white silk, embroidered across the back with a large 'G'. It was a magnificent, voluminous affair, this gown, but the effect was a little startling by moonlight, and more than one of the waiting professors gave a start to see what appeared to be a ghost bearing down upon them.

The Professors had forgotten the ceremonial robe of leadership. Deadyawn had never worn it. For the smaller-minded of the staff there was something irritating about this sartorial discrepancy of their gowns which gave the old man so unique an advantage, both decoratively and socially. They had all been secretly rather pleased to have the opportunity of wearing their red robes in public, although the public consisted solely of the Doctor and his sister (for they didn't count each other) – and now, Bellgrove, of all people, Bellgrove, their decrepit head had stolen with a single peal, as it were, the wealth of their red thunder.

He could feel their discontent, short-lived though it was, and the effect of this recognition was to excite him still further. He tossed his white mane of hair in the moonlight and gathered his arctic gown about him in a great sculptural swathe.

'Gentlemen,' he said. 'Silence if you please. I thank you.'

He dropped his head so that with his face in deep shadow he could relax his features in a smile of delight at finding himself obeyed. When he raised his face it was as solemn and as noble as before.

'Are all who are here gathered present?'

'What the hell does that mean?' said a coarse voice, out of the red gloom of the gowns, and immediately on top of Mulefire's voice, the staccato of Cutflower's laughter broke out in little clanks of sound – 'Oh La! la! la! if that isn't ripeness, la! "Are all who are here gathered present?" La! . . . What a tease the old man is, lord help my lungs!'

'Quite so! Quite so!' broke out a crisper voice. 'What he was trying to ask, presumably' (it was Shrivell speaking) 'was whether everyone here was really here, or whether it was only those who thought themselves here when they weren't really here at all who were here? You see it's quite simple, really, once you have mastered the syntax.'

Somewhere close behind the headmaster there was a sense of strangled body-laughter, a horrible inaudible affair and then the sound of a deep bucketful of breath being drawn out of a well – and then Opus Fluke's mid-stomach voice. 'Poor old Bellgrove,' it said. 'Poor old bloody Bellgrove!' and then the rumbling again, and a chorus of dark and stupid laughter.

Bellgrove was in no mood for this. His old face was flushed and his legs trembled. Fluke's voice had sounded very close. Just behind his left shoulder. Bellgrove took a step to the rear and then turning suddenly with a whirl of his white gown he swung his long arm and at once he was startled at what he at first imagined was a complete triumph. His gnarled old fist had struck a human jaw. A quick, wild, and bitter sense of mastery possessed him and the intoxicating notion that he had been under-rating himself for seventy odd years and that all unwittingly he had discovered in himself the 'man of action'. But his exhilaration was short lived for the figure who lay moaning at his feet was not Opus Fluke at all, but the weedy and dyspeptic Flannelcat, the only member of his staff who held him in any kind of respect.

But Bellgrove's prompt action had a sobering effect.

'Flannelcat!' he said. 'Let that be a warning to them. Get up, my man. You have done nobly. Nobly.' At that moment something whisked through the air and struck an obscure member of the staff on the wrist. At his cry, for he was in real pain, Flannelcat was at once forgotten. A small round stone was found at the feet of the obscure member, and every head was turned at once to the dusky quadrangle, but nothing could be seen.

High up on a northern wall, where the windows appeared no larger than keyholes, Steerpike, sitting with his legs dangling over one of the window-sills, raised his eyebrows at the sound of the cry so far below him, and piously closing his eyes he kissed his catapult.

'Whatever the hell that was, or wherever it came from, it does at least remind us that we are late, my friend,' said Shrivell.

'True enough,' muttered Shred, who almost always trod heavily on the tail of his friend's remarks. 'True enough.'

'Bellgrove,' said Perch-Prism, 'wake your ideas up, old friend, and lead the way in. I see that every light is blazing in the homestead of the Prunes. Lord, what a lot we are! –' he moved his small piglike eyes across the faces of his colleagues – 'what a hideous lot we are – but there it is – there it is.'

'You're not much of a silk-purse yourself,' said a voice.

'In we go, la! In we go!' cried Cutflower. 'Terribly gay now! *Terribly* gay! We must *all* be terribly gay!'

Perch-Prism slid up under Bellgrove's shoulder. 'My old friend,' he said. 'You haven't forgotten what I said about Irma, have you? It may be difficult for you. I have even more recent information. She's dead nuts on you, old man. Dead nuts. Watch your steps, chief. Watch 'em carefully.'

'I – will – watch – my – steps, Perch-Prism, have no fear,' said Bellgrove with a leer that his colleagues could in no way interpret.

Spiregrain, Throd and Splint stood hand in hand. Their spiritual master was dead. They were enormously glad of it. They winked at each other and dug one another in the ribs and then joined hands again in the darkness.

A mass movement towards the gate of the Prunesquallors began. Within this gate there was nothing that could be called a front garden, merely an area of dark red gravel which had been raked by the gardener. The parallel lines formed by his rake were quite visible in the moonlight. He might have saved himself the trouble for within a few moments the neat striated effect was a thing of the past. Not a square red inch escaped the shuffling and stamping of the Professors' feet. Hundreds of footprints of all shapes and sizes, crossing and recrossing, toes and heels superimposed with such freaks of placing that it seemed as though among the professors there were some who boasted feet as long as an arm, and others who must have found it difficult to balance upon shoes that a monkey might have found too tight.

After the bottleneck of the garden gate had been negotiated and the wine-red horde, with Bellgrove at its van, like an oriflamme, were before the front door, the headmaster turned with his hand hovering at the height of the bell pull, and raising his lion-like head, was about to remind his staff that as the guests of Irma Prunesquallor he hoped to find in their deportment and general behaviour that sense of decorum which he had so far had no reason to suppose they possessed or could even simulate, when a butler, dressed up like a Christmas cracker, flung the front door open with a flourish which was obviously the result of many years' experience. The speed of the door as it swung on its hinges was extraordinary, but what was just as dramatic was the silence – a silence so complete that Bellgrove, with his head turned towards his staff and his hand still groping in the air for the bell-pull, could not grasp the reason for the peculiar behaviour of his colleagues. When a man is about to make a speech, however modest, he is glad to have the attention of his audience. To see on every face that stared in his direction an expression of intense interest, but an interest that obviously had nothing to do with *him*, was more than disturbing. What had happened to them? Why were all those eyes so out of focus – or if they were *in* focus why should they skim his own as though there were something absorbing about the woodwork of the high green door behind him? And why was Throd standing on tiptoe in order to look *through* him?

Bellgrove was about to turn – not because he thought there could be anything to see but because he was experiencing that sensation that causes men to turn their heads on deserted roads in order to make sure they are alone. But before he could turn of his own free will he received two sharp yet deferential knuckle-taps on his left shoulder-blade – and leaping about as though at the touch of a ghost he found himself face to face with the tall Christmas-cracker of a butler.

'You will pardon me, sir, for making free with my knuckle, I am sure, sir,' said the glittering figure in the hall. 'But you are impatiently awaited, sir, and no wonder if I may say so.'

'If you *insist*,' said Bellgrove. 'So be it.'

His remark meant nothing at all but it was the only thing he could think of to say.

'And now, sir,' continued the butler, lifting his voice into a higher register which gave quite a new expression to his face – 'if you will be so gracious as to follow me, I will lead the way to madam.'

He moved to one side and cried out into the darkness.

'Forward, gentlemen! if you please,' and turning smartly on his heel he began to lead Bellgrove through the hall and down a number of short passageways until a wider space, at the foot of a flight of stairs, brought him and his followers to a halt.

'I have no doubt, sir,' the butler said, inclining himself reverentially as he spoke – and to Bellgrove's way of thinking the man was speaking overmuch – 'I have no doubt, sir, that you are familiar with the customary procedure.'

'Of course, my man. Of course,' said Bellgrove. 'What is it?'

'O sir!' said the butler. 'You are very humorous,' and he began to titter – an unpleasant sound to come from the top of a cracker.

'There are many "procedures", my man. Which one were you referring to?'

'To the one, sir, that pertains to the order in which the guests are announced – by name, of course, as they file through the doorway of the salon. It is all very cut and dried, sir.'

'What *is* the order, my dear fellow, if it is not the order of seniority?'

'And so it is, sir, in all respects, save that it is customary for the headmaster, which would be you, sir, to bring up the rear.'

'The rear?'

'Quite so sir. As a kind of shepherd, I suppose sir, driving his flock before him, as it were.'

There was a short silence during which Bellgrove began to realize that to be the last to present himself to his hostess, he would be the first to hold any kind of conversation with her.

'Very well,' he said. 'The tradition must, of course, remain inviolate. Ridiculous as it seems in the face of it, I shall, as you put it, bring up the rear. Meanwhile, it is getting late. There is no time to sort out the staff into age-groups, and so on. None of them are chickens. Come along now, gentlemen, come along; and if you will be so kind as to stop combing your hair before the door is opened, Cutflower, I would, as one who is responsible for his staff, be grateful. Thank you.'

Just then, the door which faced the staircase opened and a long rectangle of gold light fell across a section of the embattled masters. Their gowns flamed. Their faces shone like spectres. Turning almost simultaneously after a few minutes of dazzling blankness they shuffled into the surrounding shadow. Around the corner of the open door through which the light was pouring a large face peered out at them.

'Name?' it whispered thickly. An arm crept around the door and drew the nearest figure forwards and into the light by a fistful of wine-red linen.

'Name?' it whispered again.

'The name is Cutflower, *la!*' hissed the gentleman, 'but take your great joint of clod's fist off me, you stupid bastard.' Cutflower, whose gusts of temper were rare and short-lived, was really angry at being pulled forward by his gown and in having it clenched so clumsily into a web of creases. 'Let go!' he repeated hotly. 'By hell, I'll have you whipped, la!'

The crude footman bent down and brought his lip to Cutflower's ear. 'I . . . will . . . kill . . . you . . .' he whispered, but in such an abstracted way as to give Cutflower quite a turn. It was as though the fellow was passing on a scrap of inside information – casually (like a spy) but in confidence. Before Cutflower had recovered he found himself pushed forward, and he was suddenly alone in the long room. Alone, except for a line of servants along the right-hand wall, and away ahead of him, his host and hostess, very still, very upright in the glow of many candles.

Had Bellgrove worked out beforehand the order in which to have his staff announced, it is unlikely that he would have hit upon so happy an idea as that of choosing Cutflower from his pack, and leading off, as it were, with a card so lacking in the solid virtues.

But *chance* had seen to it that of all the gowns it was Cutflower's that should have been within range of the groping hand. And Cutflower, the volatile and fatuous Cutflower, as he stepped lightly like a wagtail across the grey-green roods of carpet was, in spite of the shocking start he had been given, injecting the air, the cold expectant air, with something no other member of the staff possessed in the same way – a warmth or a gaiety of a kind, but not a *human* gaiety; rather, it was glass-like; a sparkling, twinkling quality.

It was as though Cutflower was so glad to be alive that he had never lived. Every moment was vivid, a coloured thing, a trill or a crackle of words in the air. Who could imagine, while Cutflower was around, that there were such vulgar monsters as death, birth, love, art and pain around the corner? It was too embarrassing to contemplate. If Cutflower knew of them he kept it secret. Over their gaping and sepulchral deeps he skimmed now here, now there, in his private canoe, changing his course with a flick of his paddle when death's black whale, or the red squid of passion, lifted for a moment its body from the brine.

He was not more than a third of the way to his hosts, and the echo of the stentorian voice, which had flung his name across the room, was hardly dead, and yet (with his wagtail walk, his spruceness, his perky ductile features so ready to be amused and so ready to amuse as long as no one took life seriously) he had already broken the ice for the Prunesquallors. There was a certain charm in his fatuity, his perkiness. His toecaps shone like mirrors. His feet came down tap-tap-tap-tap in a way all their own.

The Professors craning their necks as they watched his progress breathed more freely. They knew now that they could never accomplish that long carpet-journey with anything like Cutflower's air, but he reminded them at every footstep, every inclination of the head, that the whole point of life was to be happy.

And O, the charm of it! The artless charm of it! When Cutflower, with but a few feet to go, broke into a little dancing run, and putting forward both his hands cupped them over the limp white fingers which Irma had extended.

'Oh, la! la!' he had cried, his voice running all the way back down the salon. 'This *is*, my dear Miss Prunesquallor, this positively *is* . . .' and turning to the Doctor, 'Isn't it?' he added as he clasped the outstretched hand, squaring his shoulders and shaking his head happily as he did so.

'Well, I hope it will *become* so, my friend,' cried Prunesquallor. 'How good to see you! And bye the bye, Cutflower, you give me heart you do . . . by all that re-vivifies I thank you from its bottom. Don't disappear now, for the whole evening, will you?'

Irma leaned across her brother and drew her lips apart in a dead, wide and calculated smile.

It was meant to express many things, and among them the sense of how unconditionally she associated herself with her brother's sentiment. It also tried to imply that for all her qualities as a *femme fatale*, she was little more than a wide-eyed girl at heart and terribly vulnerable. But it was early in the evening and she knew she must make many mistakes before her smiles came out right.

Cutflower, whose eyes were still on the doctor, was fortunate enough to be unaware of Irma's blandishment. He was about to say something, when the loud and common voice from the other end of the room brayed forth, 'Professor Mulefire', and Cutflower turned his head gaily from his hosts and shielded his eyes in imitation of a look-out man scanning some distant horizon. With a quick, delighted smile and a twirl of his dapper body, he was away to the side tables, where with his elbows raised very high, he worked his ten fingers together into a knot, as he passed his eye along the wines and delicacies. Self-absorbed, he rocked to and fro on the sides of his shoes.

How different was Mulefire with his long clumsy irritable strides! And indeed how disparate were all who followed one another that evening with only the colour of their gowns in common.

Flannelcat, like a lost soul for whom the journey was a mile at least; the heavy, sloppy, untidy Fluke, who looked as though, for all his strength and for all the forward thrust of his loaf-like jaw, he might at any moment fold up at the knees and go to sleep on the carpet. Perch-Prism, horribly alert, his porcine features shining white in the glow of the candles, his button-black eyes darting to and fro as he moved crisply with short aggressive steps.

With this shape and that shape, with this walk and that walk, they emerged from the hall to the tocsin-bray of their names, until Bellgrove found himself alone in the semi-darkness.

As one after another of the professional guests had made their carpet-journey towards her, Irma had had a world of time in which to ruminate on the vulnerability of each to the charm she would so soon be unleashing. Some, of course, were quite impossible – but even as she dismissed them she began to brood with favour upon such phrases as 'rough diamond', 'heart of gold', 'still waters' . . .

While the sides of the room filled with those who had presented themselves and their conversation became louder and louder as their numbers increased, Irma, standing rigid by her brother, speculating upon the pros and cons of those she had received, was wakened out of a more than usually sanguine speculation by her brother's voice.

'And how is Irma, that sister of mine, that sweet throb? Is she cooing? Is she weary of the flesh – or isn't she? Great spearheads, Irma! How determined, how martial you look! Relax a little, melt within yourself. Think of milk and honey. Think of jelly-fish.'

'Be quiet,' she hissed out of the corner of a smile she was concocting, a smile more ambitious than she had so far dared to invent. Every muscle in her face was pulling its weight. Not all of them knew in which direction to pull, but their common enthusiasm was formidable. It was as though all her previous contortions were mere rehearsals. Something in white was approaching.

The 'something in white' was moving slowly but with more purpose than for over forty years. While he had waited, sitting quietly by himself on the lowest step of the Prunesquallors' staircase, Bellgrove had repeated to himself, his lips moving to the slow rhythm of his thoughts, those conclusions he had come to.

He had decided, intellectually, that Irma Prunesquallor, dwarfed by lack of outlet for her feminine instincts, could find fruition in a life devoted to *his* comforts. That not only he, but she, in years to come would bless the day when he, Bellgrove, was man enough, was sapient enough, to lift her from stagnation and set her marching through matrimony towards that equipoise of spirit that only wives can know. There were a hundred rational reasons why she should leap at the chance in spite of his advanced years. But what weight had all these arguments for a fine and haughty lady, sensitive as a blood horse and gowned like a queen, if at the same time there was no love? And Bellgrove remembered as he had crossed the quadrangle an hour ago how it was this point that irked him. But now, it was not the rightness of his reasoning that set his old knees trembling, it was something more. For, from a wise and practical project the whole conception had been shifted into another light. His ideas had suddenly been overlaid with stars. What was precise was now enormous, unsubstant, diaphanous, for he had seen her. And tonight it was not merely the Doctor's sister that awaited him, but a daughter of Eve, a living focus, a cosmos, a pulse of the great abstraction, Woman. Was her name Irma? Her name was Irma. But what was the name Irma but four absurd little letters in a certain order? To hell with symbols, cried Bellgrove to himself. She is there, by God, from head to foot and matchless!

It was true that he had only seen her from a distance and it is possible that the distance lent an enchantment self-engendered. No doubt, his sight was not as sharp as it used to be – and the fact that he could not remember having seen any other woman for many years gave Irma a flying start.

But he had obtained a general picture, as he peered through a narrow chasm of light that shone between Throd's and Spiregrain's bodies.

And he had seen how proudly she held herself. Stiff as a soldier, and yet how feminine! That is what he would like to have about him in the evening. A stately type. He could imagine her, sitting bolt upright, at his side, her face twitching a little from gentle breeding, her snow-white hands darning away at his socks while he pondered on this and that, turning his eyes from time to time to see whether it was really true, that she was really there, his *wife, his* wife, on the chocolate-coloured couch.

And then suddenly he had found himself alone. The big face was peering for him from the door. 'Name?' it whispered hoarsely, for its voice was almost gone.

'I'm the headmaster, you idiot,' barked Bellgrove. He was in no mood for fools. Something was in his blood. Whether it was love or not he must find out soon. There was an impatient streak in him – and this was no moment in which to suffer the man gladly.

The creature with the big face, seeing that Bellgrove was the last to be announced, took a deep breath and to get rid of his pent-up irritability (for he was an hour late for his appointment with a blacksmith's wife) gathered all the forces of his throat together and yelled – but his voice collapsed after the first syllable and only Bellgrove heard the guttering sound that was intended for 'master'.

But there was something rather fine, rather impressive in the abbreviation. Something less formal, it is true, but more penetrating in the first simple syllable.

'The Head –!'

The short hammer blow of the monosyllable reverberated along the room like a challenge.

It struck like a drumstick on the membranes of Irma's ear and Bellgrove, peering forward as he took his first paces into the room, had the impression of his hostess rearing herself up on her hips, tossing her head before it froze into a motionless carving.

His heart, that was already beating wildly, had leapt at the sight. Her attention was riveted upon him. Of that there was no doubt. Not only her attention, but the attention of all those present. He became aware of a lethal hush. Soft as the carpet was, his feet could be heard as they lowered themselves one after another into the grey-green of the pile.

For a moment, as he moved with that fantastic solemnity which the urchins of Gormenghast were so fond of mimicking, he gave his eyes the run of his staff. There they stood, three deep, a solid wine-red phalanx that completely obscured the side-tables. Yes, he could see Perch-Prism, his eyebrows raised, and Opus Fluke with his horse's mouth half open in a grin so inane that for a moment it was difficult for Bellgrove to regain that composure necessary to the advancement of his immediate interests. So they were waiting to see in what way he would try to evade the 'predatory' Irma, were they? So they expected him to back away from her immediately after he had received his formal reception, did they? So they looked for an evening of hide and seek between their hostess and their headmaster, the low curs! By the light of a militant heaven, he would show the dogs! He would show them. And, by the powers, he would surprise them too.

By now he was about half way along the carpet, already trodden into a recognizable highway, the pile of the carpet throwing out a greener sheen than elsewhere, the pile pressed forward by a hundred feet.

Irma, her eyes weak with peering, could just see him. As he approached and the blurred edges of his swan white gown, and the contours of his leonine head, grew sharper, she marvelled at his god-like quality. She had received so many half-men that she had tired, not of numbers, but of waiting for the kind of male she could reverence. There had been the perky ones, and the stolid ones and the sharp ones and the blunt ones – all *males* she supposed, but although she had a few of them at the back of her mind for further consideration, yet she had been sadly disappointed. There had been that irritating bachelor quality about them, a kind of dead self-sufficiency, a terrible thing in a man, who is, as every woman knows, a mere tag-end of a thing before the distaff side has stitched him together.

But here was something different. Something *old* it is true, but something noble. She manoeuvred with her mouth. It had had a good deal of practice by this time and the smile she prepared for Bellgrove reflected to a great extent what she had in mind for it. Above all, it was winsome, devastatingly winsome. For a pretty face to be winsome is normal enough and very winsome it can be, but it is a tepid thing, a negative thing compared with the winsomeness to which Irma could subject her features. With her it was as startling as any foreground symbol set against an incongruous background. Irma's weak and eager eyes, Irma's pinnacle of a nose, Irma's length of powdered face; these were the incongruous background on which the smile deployed its artful self. She played with it for a moment or two, as an angler with a fish, and then she let it set like concrete.

Her body had simultaneously rhythmed itself into a stance both statuesque and snakelike, her thorax, amplified with its hot-water bottle bosom, positioned in air so far to the left of her pelvis as to have no visible means of support. Her snow-white hands were clasped at her throat where her jewellery sparkled.

Bellgrove was almost upon her. 'This,' he said to himself, breathing deeply, 'is one of those moments in a man's life when valour is tested.'

The years ahead hung on his every move. His staff had shaken hands with her as though a woman was merely another kind of man. Fools! The seeds of Eve were in this radiant creature. The lullabyes of half a million years throbbed in her throat. Had they no sense of wonder, no reverence, no pride? He, an old man (but a not unhandsome one), would show the dogs the way of it – and there she was, before him, the maddeningly feminine bouquet of her pineapple perfume swimming about his head. He inhaled. He trembled, and then, lion-like, he tossed his venerable mane from his eyes, and raising his shoulders as he took her hand in his, he bowed his head above their milky limpness and planted in the damp of her palms, the first two kisses he had given for over fifty years.

To say that the frozen silence contracted itself into a yet higher globe of ice were to under-rate the exquisite tension and to shroud it in words. The atmosphere had become a physical sensation. As when, before a masterpiece, the acid throat contracts, and words are millstones, so when the supernaturally outlandish happens and a masterpiece is launched through the medium of human gesture, then all human volition is withered at the source and the heart of action stops beating.

Such a moment was this. Irma, a stalagmite of crimson stone, knew, for all the riot of her veins, that a page had turned over. At chapter forty? O no! At chapter one, for she had never lived before save in a pulseless preface.

How long did they remain thus? How many times had the earth moved round the sun? How many times had the great blue whales of the northern waters risen to spurt their fountains at the sky? How many reed-bucks had fallen to the claws of how many leopards, while that sublime unit of two-figure statuary remained motionless? It is fruitless to ask. The clocks of the world stood still or should have done.

But at last the arctic stillness broke. A professor at the side tables gave forth a sharp scream, whether of laughter or nerves was never established.

The Doctor glanced across at the wine red gowns, his eyebrows raised, his teeth glinting. There were a few beads of moisture on his forehead. He was going through a lot.

Irma had not consciously heard the sharp cry of laughter nor knew what had broken her from a trance, but she found herself inclining her head graciously above the white locks of the headmaster's reverential poll.

This was *it*. Something within her was laughing wildly, like cowbells.

It was a pity that the headmaster could not appreciate the amplitude of her graciousness as she hung above him – but, there it was – she couldn't have it both ways – but wait – what was this?

O sweetest mercy! And the wild thorn-throbs of it! What was he doing, the great, gentle, august, brilliant lion? He was raising his eyes to hers with his lips still pressed against her fingers. It was as though he had divined her most secret thoughts.

She lowered her lids and found that his dead-pebble eyes were upon hers. With their gaze directed upwards and through the white tangle of the eyebrows they appeared to be caged.

She knew the moment to be enormous – enormous in its implications – in its future – but she knew also as a woman that she must draw her hand away. As the first suspicion of a movement crept through her flaccid fingers, Bellgrove lifted his head, withdrew his big hands from hers and at that moment Irma's bosom began to slip. In the complex arrangement of strings, safety pins and tape which held the hot water bottle in place, Time had found a weakness.

But Irma, tingling with excitement, was in so elevated a frame of body and mind that, beyond her capacity as it were, her brain was planning for her in advance, those things she should do, and say, in or out of any emergency. And this was one of those moments when the cells of Irma's brain marched in solid ranks to her rescue.

Her bosom was slipping. She clasped her hands together at her throat so that her forearms might keep the hot water bottle in place, and then with every eye upon her she lifted her head high and began to pace towards the doorway at the far end of the salon. She had not even glanced at her brother, but with a quite overweening confidence had started away, the folds of her evening gown trailing behind her.

The bottle had become horribly cold across her chest. But she revelled in its cruel temperature. Why should she care about such little things? Something on an altogether vaster scale was bearing her on its flood.

The barb had struck. She was naked. She was proud. Had love's arrow not been metaphorical she would have held it high in the air for all to see. And all this she was making plain, by the very movement of her pacing body, and by the volcanic blush which had turned her marmoreal head into something that might have been found among the blood-red ruins of some remote civilization.

Her jewellery took on another tint. Her blush burned through it.

But her expression bore no relation to the blush. It was strangely articulate, and thus, frighteningly simple.

There was no need for words. Her face was saying, 'I am in his power; he has awakened me; I, a mere woman, have been blasted into sentience. Whatever the future holds it will not be through me that love goes hungry. I am aware; not only that history is being made, but of my duty, even at this pinnacled moment, and so, I am leaving the room, to re-adjust myself – to compose myself, and to bring back into the salon the kind of woman that the headmaster may admire – no quivering love-struck damsel, but a dame in all the high sensuousness of her sex, a dame, composed and glorious!'

Irma, directly she had reached the door and had swept out into the hall, flew, a silken spinster, up the flight of stairs to her room. Slamming the door behind her she gave vent to the primeval jungle in her veins and screamed like a macaw, and then, prancing forward towards the bed, tripped over a small embroidered foot-stool and fell spreadeagled across the carpet.

What did it matter? What did anything ridiculous or shaming matter so long as *he* was not there to see it?

THIRTY-FIVE

THERE are times when the emotions are so clamorous and the rational working of the mind so perfunctory that there is no telling where the *actual* leaves off and the images of fantasy begin.

Irma, in her room, could picture Bellgrove at her side as though he were there, but she could also see clean through him, so that his body was pranked with the pattern of the wallpaper beyond. She could see a great host of professors, thousands of them, and all the size of hatpins. They stood upon her bed, a massed and solemn congregation, and bowed to her; but she also saw that her pillow-slip needed changing. She looked out of the window, her eyes wide and un-focused. The moonlight lay in a haze upon the high foliage of an elm, and the elm became Mr Bellgrove again with his distinguished and lordly mane. She saw a figure, no doubt some figment, as it slid over the wall of her grotto'd garden and ran like a shadow to beneath the window of the dispensary. Far away at the back of her mind, there was something that said 'you have seen that movement before; crouching, rapid movement' – yet she had, in her transport, no clue as to what was real and what was fantasy.

And so, when she saw a figure steal across the garden below her she had no conception that it was a real, breathing creature, far less that it was Steerpike. The young man who had forced open the window in the room below that in which Irma was standing moonstruck, had, by the light of a candle, wasted no time in finding the drug for which he was looking. The bottles on the packed shelves shone blue and crimson and deadly green as the small flame moved. Within a few moments he had decanted a few thimblefuls of a sluggish liquid into the flask he carried, and returned the doctor's bottle to the shelf. He corked his own container and within a moment was half-way out of the window.

Above the walls of the garden the upper massives of Gormenghast castle shone in the baleful moonlight. As he paused for a moment before dropping from the window-sill to the ground, he shuddered. The night was warm and there was no cause to shudder save that a twinge of joy, of dark joy can shake the body, when a man is alone, under the moon, on a secret mission, with hunger in his heart and ice in his brain.

THIRTY-SIX

WHEN Irma returned to her guests she paused before she opened the doors of the salon, for a loud and confused noise came from within. It was of a kind that she had never heard before, so happy it was, so multitudinous, so abandoned – the sound of voices at play. She had, of course, in her small way, at gatherings, heard, from time to time, the play of many voices. But what she was hearing now was *not* the play of voices; it was voices at play; and as such it was novel and peculiar to her ears, in the way that shadow at play (as against the play of shadows) would have been to her eyes. She had, on rare occasions, enjoyed the play of her brother's brain – but in her salon there was something very different going on and from the few remarks that she could distinguish through the panels of the door it was obvious that here there was no play of language, no play of thought, but language playing on its own; enfranchised notions playing by themselves, the truants of the brain.

Gathering the long wreaths of her gown about her she crouched for a moment with her eyes to the keyhole but could see no more than the smoky midnight of the gowns.

What had happened, she wondered, while she had been upstairs? When she had left, in the motionless silence, like a queen, the room had throbbed with her single personality, the silence, the flattering and significant silence, had been her setting, as the great sky is the setting for the white flight of a gull. But now, the stretched drum-skin of the atmosphere had split – and the professors, exultant that this was so, had, each in his own way, erected within himself the romantic image of what he fondly imagined himself to be. For the long lost glories, that never in fact existed save in the wishfulness of their brains, were being remembered with a reality as vivid, if not more so, as truth itself. False memories flowered within them. The days of brilliance when their lances shone, when they leapt into the gold saddle quick as thought and galloped through the white rays of the dawn; when they ran like stags, swam like fish and, laughing like thunder, woke the swaddled towers. Ah Lord, the callow days; the cocky days, the days of sinew and the madcap evenings – the darkness at their elbows, co-conspirator, muffling their firetipped follies.

That but few of the Professors had ever tasted the heady mead of youth in no way dulled the contours of their self-portraits which they were now painting of themselves. And it had all happened so rapidly, this resurgence; this hark-back. It was as though some bell had been struck, some mountain-bell to which their guts responded. They had for so long a time made their evening way to their sacred, musty, airless quadrangle, that to be, for a whole evening in a new atmosphere was like sunrise. True, there was only Irma on the female side, but she was a symbol of all femininity, she was Eve, she was Medusa, she was terrible and she was peerless; she was hideous and she was the lily of the prairies; she was that alien thing from another world – that thing called woman.

Directly she had left the room a thousand imaginary memories had beset them of women they had never known. Their tongues loosened, and their limbs also, and the Doctor found there was no need to launch the evening. For the flame was alight and the professorial torpor had been burned away, and they were back, all at once in a time when they were brilliant, omniscient and devastating and as dazzlingly attractive as the Devil himself.

With their brains illumined by these spurious and flattering images, the swarming gownsmen trod on air, and bridled up their hot and monstrous heads, flashed their teeth, or if toothless, grinned darkly, their mouths slung across their faces like hammocks.

As Irma turned the handle, taking a deep breath which all but destroyed her bust, she straightened herself and stood for a moment motionless, yet vibrant. As she opened the door and the gay thunder of their voices doubled its volume – she raised an eyebrow. Why, she wondered, should such potent happiness coincide with her absence? It was almost as though she had been *forgotten*, or worse, that her departure from the room had been welcomed.

She opened the door a little wider and peered around the corner, but in doing so her powdered head created all unknowingly so graphic a representation of something detached that a professor who happened to be staring in the direction of the door, let fall his lower jaw with a clank, and dropped the plate of delicacies to his feet.

'Ah no, no!' he whispered, the colours draining from his face . . . 'not *now*, dire Death, not *now* . . . I am not ready . . . I . . .'

'Ready for what, sweet trout,' said a voice beside him. 'By hell, these peacock-hearts are excellent. A little pepper please!'

Irma entered. The man who had dropped his jaw swallowed hard and a sick grin appeared on his face. He had cheated death.

As Irma took her first few paces into the room her fear that the gracious authority of her presence had been undermined during her short absence was dispelled, for a score of professors, ceasing their chatter, and whipping their mortar-boards from their heads, cupped them over their hearts.

Swaying slightly as she proceeded towards the centre of the room, she, in her turn, bowed with a superb and icy grandeur now to left, now to right, as the dark festooning draperies of the professorial jungle opened, at her every step, its musty avenues.

Veering to east and west in gradual curves like a ship that has no precise idea as to which port it is making for, she found all about her, wherever she was, a hush, most gratifying. But the avenues closed behind her, and the conversation was resumed with an enthusiasm.

And then, all of a sudden, there was Bellgrove, not a dozen feet away. A long glass of wine was in his hand. He was in profile; and what a profile – 'grandeur' she hissed excitedly! 'That's what it is – grandeur.' And it was then, at her third convulsive stride in the headmaster's direction that something happened which was not only embarrassing but heart-rending in its simplicity, for a hoarse cry, out-topping the general cacophony, silenced the room and brought Irma to a standstill.

It was not the kind of cry that one expects to hear at a party. It had passion in it – and urgency. The very tone and timbre was a smack in the face of propriety, and broke on the instant all those unwritten laws of social behaviour that are the result – the fine flower – of centuries.

As every head was turned in the direction of the sound a movement became apparent in the same quarter where, from a group of professors, something appeared to be making its way towards its rigid hostess. Its face was flushed and its gestures were so convulsive that it was not easy to realize that it was Professor Throd.

On sighting Irma, he had deserted his companions Splint and Spiregrain, and on obtaining a better view of his hostess had suffered a sensation that was in every way too violent, too fundamental, too electric for his small brain and body. A million volts ran through him, a million volts of stark infatuation.

He had seen no woman for thirty-seven years. He gulped her through his eyes as at some green oasis the thirst-tormented nomad gulps the wellhead. Unable to remember any female face, he took Irma's strange proportions and the cast of her features to be characteristic of femininity. And so, his conscious mind blotted out by the intensity of his reaction, he committed the unforgivable crime. He made his feelings public. He lost control. The blood rushed to his head; he cried out hoarsely, and then, little knowing what he was doing, he stumbled forwards, elbowing his colleagues from his path, and fell upon his knees before the lady, and finally, as though in a paroxysm, he collapsed upon his face, his arms and legs spread-eagled like a starfish.

The temperature of the room dropped to zero, and then, as suddenly it rose to an equatorial and burning heat. Five long seconds went by. It would not have been strange in that intense temperature to have found a python hanging from the ceiling – nor, when the icy spell returned again, at the lapse of the third second, to find the carpet white with arctic foxes.

Would no one make a move to crack the glass; the great transparent sheet that spread unbroken from corner to corner of the long room?

And then a stride took place, a stride that brought Bellgrove's gaunt body to within four feet of Irma. With his next step he had halved the distances between himself and her – and then, all at once, he was above her and had found himself gazing down into eyes that pleaded. It was as though he had been injected with lion's blood. Power rushed into him as though from a tap.

'Most dear Madam,' he said. 'Have no fear, I pray you. That one of my staff should be lying below you is shameful, yes, shameful, madam, but lo! is it not a symbol of what we all feel? What shame there is lies in his weakness, madam, not in his passion. Some, dear lady, would have his name expunged from all registers – but no. But no. For he has *warmth*, madam; warmth above all! In this case it has led to something distasteful, dammit' (he relapsed into his common tongue) 'and so, dear hostess, allow me, as headmaster, to have him removed from your presence. Yet forgive him, I implore you, for he recognized quality when he saw it, and his only sin is that in recognizing it too violently he had not the strength to hold his passion captive.'

Bellgrove paused and wiped his forearm across his wet forehead and tossed back his white mane. He had spoken with his eyes shut. A sense of dreamlike strength had filled him. He knew in the self-imposed darkness that Irma's eyes were upon him; he could feel the intensity of her close presence. He could hear the feet of his staff, as his words continued, shuffling away in tactful pairs, and he could even hear himself talking as though the voice was another's.

What a deep and resonant organ the man has, he thought to himself, pretending for the moment that it was not his own voice he was hearing, for there was something humble in his nature which, every once in a while, found outlet.

But such thoughts were no more than momentary. What was paramount in him was the realization that here he was again, within a few inches of the lady whom he now intended to pursue with all the cunning of old age and all the steeple-swarming, torrent-leaping, barnstorming impetus of recaptured youth.

'By the Lord!' he cried, voicelessly, and to himself yet very loud it sounded, in his own brains – 'by the Lord, if I don't show 'em how it's done! Two arms, two legs, two eyes, one mouth, ears, trunk and buttocks, belly and skeleton, lungs, tripes and backbone, feet and hands, brains, eyes and testicles. I've got 'em all – so help me, rightside up.'

His eyes had remained closed, but now he lifted the heavy lids and, peering between his pale eyelashes, he found in the eyes of his hostess so hot and wet a succubus of love as threatened to undermine her marble temple and send its structure toppling.

He glanced about him. His staff, tactful to the point of tactlessness, were gathered in groups and were talking together like those gentlemen of the stage who, in an effort to appear normal, yet with nothing to say, repeat in simulated languor or animation – 'one . . . two . . . three . . . four' and so on. But in the case of the professors they mouthed their fatuities with all the over-emphasis of un-rehearsal. In a far corner of the room a scrum of gownsmen were becoming restive.

'Talk about a wax giraffe, Cor slice me edgeways!' muttered Mulefire between his teeth.

'Certainly not, you hulk of flesh unhallowed,' said Perch-Prism. 'I'm ashamed of you!'

'And so indeed, la! Am I a beetroot? What it is, la, to have known better days and better ways, Heaven shrive me – Am I a beetroot?' It was the gay Cutflower talking, but there was something ruffled about his tone.

'As Theoreticus says in his diatribe against the use of the vernacular,' whispered Flannelcat, who had waited for a long while for the moment when by coincidence he would both have the courage to say something and have something to say.

'Well, what did the old bleeder say?' said Opus Fluke.

But no one was interested and Flannelcat knew that his opportunity was gone, for several voices broke in and cut across his nervous reply.

'Tell me, Cutflower, is the Head still staring at her and why can't you pass the wine, by the clay of which we're made, it's given me the thirst of cactusland,' said Perch-Prism, his flat nose turned to the ceiling. 'But for my breeding I'd turn round and see for myself.'

'Not a twitch,' said Cutflower. 'Statues, la! Most uncanny.'

'Once upon a time,' broke in the mournful voice of Flannelcat, 'I used to collect butterflies. It was long ago – in a swallow country full of dry river-beds. Well, one damp afternoon when . . .'

'Another time, Flannelcat,' said Cutflower. 'You may sit down.'

Flannelcat, saddened, moved away from the group in search of a chair.

Meanwhile Bellgrove had been savouring love's rare aperitif, the ageless language of the eyes.

Pulling himself together with the air of one who is master of every situation, he swept his gown across one shoulder as though it were a toga and stepping back, surveyed the spreadeagled figure at their feet.

In stepping back, however, he had all but trodden upon Doctor Prunesquallor's feet and would have done so but for the agile side-step of his host.

The Doctor had been out of the room for a few minutes and had only just been told of the immobile figure on the floor. He was about to have examined the body when Bellgrove had taken his backward step, and now he was delayed still further by the sound of Bellgrove's voice.

'My dearest lady,' said the old lion-headed man, who had begun to repeat himself, 'warmth is everything. Yet no . . . not everything . . . but a good deal. That you should be caused embarrassment by one of my staff, shall I say one of my colleagues, yea, for so he is, shall always be to me like coals of fire. And why? Because, dearest lady, it was for me to have groomed him, to have schooled him in the niceties or more simply, dammit, to have left him behind. And that is what I must do now. I must have him removed,' and he lifted his voice.

'Gentlemen,' he cried. 'I shall be glad if two of you would remove your colleague and return with him to his quarters. Perhaps Professors . . . Flannelcat . . .'

'But no! but no! I will not have it!'

It was Irma's voice. She took a step forward and brought her hands up to her long chin where she interlocked her fingers.

'Mr Headmaster,' she whispered, 'I have heard what you have had to say. And it was splendid. I said splendid. When you spoke of "warmth", I understood. I, a mere woman, I said a *mere* woman.' She glared about her, darkly, nervously, as though she had gone too far.

'But when, Mr Headmaster, I found you were, in spite of your belief, determined to have this gentleman removed' (she glanced down at the spreadeagled figure at her feet) 'then I knew it was for me, as your hostess, to ask you, as my guest, to think again. I would not have it said, sir, that one of your staff was shamed in my salon – that he was taken away. Let him be put in a chair in a dim corner. Let him be given wine and pasties, whatever he chooses, and when he is well enough, let him join his friends. He has honoured me, I say he has honoured me . . .'

It was then that she saw her brother. In a moment she was at his side. 'O Alfred, I am right, aren't I? Warmth is everything, isn't it?'

Prunesquallor gazed at his sister's twitching face. It was naked with anxiety, naked with excitement and also, to make her expression almost too subtle for credulity, it was naked with the lucence of love's dawn. Pray God it is not a false one, thought Prunesquallor. It would kill her. For a moment, the conception of how much simpler life would be *without* her, flashed through his mind, but he pushed the ugly notion away and rising on his toes he clasped his hands so firmly behind his back that his narrow and immaculate chest came forward like a pigeon's.

'Whether warmth is everything or not, my very dear sister, it is nevertheless a comforting and a cosy thing to have about – although mark you, it can be very stuffy, by all that's oxidized, so it can, but Irma, my sweet one – let that be as it may – for as a physician it has struck me that it is about time that something were done for the warrior at your feet; we must see to him, mustn't we, we must see to him, eh, Mr Bellgrove? By all that's sacred to my weird profession, we most certainly must . . .'

'But he's not to leave the room, Alfred – he's not to leave the room. He's our *guest*, Alfred, remember that.'

Bellgrove broke in before the Doctor could reply.

'You have humbled me, lady,' he said simply, and bowed his lion's head.

'And you,' whispered Irma, a deep blush raddling her neck, 'have elevated me.'

'No, madam . . . ah no!' muttered Bellgrove. 'You are overkind' and then, taking a plunge, 'who can hope to elevate a heart, madam, a heart that is already dancing in the milky way?'

'Why *milky*?' said Irma, who, with no desire to drop the level of conversation, had a habit of breaking out with forthright queries. However engulfed she might be in the major mysteries, yet her brain, detached as it were from the business of the soul, took little flights on its own, like a gnat, asked little questions, played little tricks, only to be jerked back into place and subdued for a while as the voices of her deeper self took over.

Luckily for Bellgrove there was no need for him to reply, for the Doctor had signalled a couple of gownsmen over and the seemingly prostrate suppliant was lifted from the carpet, and carried, like a wooden effigy, to a candle-lit corner, where a comfortable chair with plump green cushions stood ready.

'Seat him in the chair, gentlemen, if you will be so good, and I will have a look at him.'

The two gownsmen lowered the rigid body. It lay straight as a board, supported by no more than its head on the chair-back, and its heels on the ground. Between these extremities were thrust the plump green cushions so that they might, as it were prop the plank – to take the little man's weight, but no weight descended and the cushions remained as plump as ever.

There was something frightful about it all and this frightfulness was in no way mitigated by the radiant smile that was frozen on the face.

With a magnificent gesture, the Doctor stripped himself of his beautiful velvet jacket and flung it away as though he had no further use for it.

Then he began to roll up his silk sleeves like a conjurer.

Irma and Bellgrove were close behind him. By this time the reservoirs of tact on which the professors had been drawing were wellnigh dry and a horde stood watching in absolute silence.

The Doctor was fully conscious of this, but by not so much as a flicker did he reveal his awareness, let alone his delight in being watched.

The incident had changed the whole mood of the party. The hilarity and sense of freedom that had been so spontaneous had received an all but mortal blow. For some while, although certain jests were made, and glasses were filled and emptied, there was a darkness on the spirit of the room, and the jests were forced and the wine was swallowed mechanically.

But now that the first red blush of communal shame had died out of the staff; now that the embarrassment was merely cerebral and now that there was something to absorb them (for there was no resisting such an occasion as was now presented by Prunesquallor as he stood upright in his silken shirt sleeves, as slender as a stork, his skin as pink as a girl's, his glasses gleaming in the light of the candles) – now that there was all this, their equipoise began to return and with it a sense of hope; hope that the evening had not been ruined, that it held in store, once the Doctor had dealt with their seemingly paralysed colleague, a modicum at least of that rare abandon which had begun to set their tongues on fire, and their blood a-jigging – for it was once in a score of years, they told themselves, that they could break the endless rhythm of Gormenghast, the rhythm that steered their feet each evening westward – westward to their quadrangle.

They were absolutely silent as they watched the Doctor's every movement.

Prunesquallor spoke. It seemed that he was talking to himself, although his voice, in reaching those gownsmen who were at the rear of the audience, was certainly a little louder than one would have thought necessary. He took a pace forwards and at the same time raised his hands before him to the height of his shoulders where he worked his fingers to and fro in the air with the speed of a professional pianist.

Then he brought his hands together and began to draw them to and fro one across the other, palm to palm. His eyes were closed.

'Rarer than Bluggs Disease,' he mused, 'or the spiral spine! No doubt of it . . . by all that's convulsive . . . no doubt of it at all. There *was* a case, quite fascinating – now where was it and when was it . . . very similar – a man if I remember rightly had seen a ghost . . . yes, yes . . . and the shock had all but finished him . . .'

Irma shifted her feet . . .

'Now *shock* is the operative word,' went on the Doctor rocking himself gently on his heels, his eyes still closed – 'and shock must be answered with shock. But how, and where . . . how and where . . . Let me see . . . let me see . . .'

Irma could wait no longer. 'Alfred,' she cried, '*do* something! *Do* something!'

The Doctor did not seem to hear her, so deep was he in his reverie.

'Now, perhaps if one knew the nature of the shock, its scale, the area of the brain that received it – the *kind* of unpleasantness . . .'

'Unpleasantness!' came Irma's voice again. 'Unpleasantness! How dare you, Alfred! You *know* that it was I who turned his head, poor creature, that it was for me he fell headlong, for me that he is rigid and dreadful.'

'Aha!' cried the Doctor. It was obvious he had not heard a word that his sister had said. 'Aha!' If he had appeared animated and vital before, he was trebly so now. His every gesture was as rapid and fluid as mercury. He took a prancing step towards his patient.

'By all that's pragmatical, it's this or nothing.' He slid his hand into one of his waistcoat pockets and withdrew a small silver hammer. This he swivelled between his thumb and index finger for a few moments, his eyebrows raised.

In the meanwhile Bellgrove had begun to grow impatient. The situation had taken a queer turn. It was not in circumstances like these that he had hoped to present himself to Irma nor was this the kind of atmosphere in which his tenderness could flourish. For one thing he was no longer the centre of attraction. His immediate desire was to be alone with her. The very words 'alone with her' made him blush. His hair shone more whitely than ever against his dark red brow. He glanced at her and immediately knew what to do. It was crystal clear that she was uncomfortable. The figure on the chair was not a pleasant sight for anyone, let alone a lady of distinction, a lady of delicate tastes.

He tossed the shaggy splendour of his mane. 'Madam,' he said. 'This is no place for you.' He drew himself up to his full height, forcing back his shoulders and drawing his long chin into his throat. 'No place at all, madam,' and then apprehensive that Irma might interpret him wrongly and find in his remark some slight upon her party, he shot a glance at her through his eyelashes. But she had found nothing amiss. On the contrary, there was gratitude in her small weak eyes; gratitude in the gleaming incline of her bosom, and in the nervous clasping of her hands.

She no longer heard her brother's voice. She no longer felt the presence of the robed males. Someone had been thoughtful. Someone had realized that she was a woman, and that it was not proper for her to stand with the rest as though there was no difference between herself and her guests. And this someone, this noble and solicitous being was no other than the headmaster – O how splendid it was that there should still be a *gentleman* on the face of the earth: youth had fled from him, ah yes, but not romance.

'Mr Headmaster,' she said, pursing her lips and lifting her eyes to his craggy face with an archness hardly credible, 'it is for *you* to say. It is for me to hearken. Speak on. I am listening . . . I said, I am listening.'

Bellgrove turned his head away from her. The wide, weak smile that had spread itself across his face was not the kind of thing that he would wish Irma to see. A year or so ago, he had once, with no warning, caught sight of himself in a mirror when a smile (an antecedent of the uncontrollable expression that was even now undermining the spurious grandeur of his face) had shocked him. It was to his credit that he had recognized the danger of allowing such a thing to become public – for he was, not without cause, proud of his features. And so he turned his face away. How could he help giving vent to some kind of demonstration of his feelings. For at Irma's words 'It is for you to say' the wide rich panorama of married life suddenly appeared before him, stretched out, it seemed, to the horizon with its vistas of pale gold, its gentle meads. He saw himself as an immemorial oak, its branches spreading godlike, with Irma, a sapling poplar, whose leaves like heart-throbs twinkled in his shade. He saw himself as the proud eagle, landing with a sigh of his wings upon a solitary crag. He saw Irma, waiting for him in the nest, but curiously enough, she was sitting there in a nightdress. And then, suddenly, he saw himself as a very old man, with a toothache, and his memory caught sight of an ancient face in the mirrors of a thousand shaving-rooms.

He crushed this most unwelcome glimpse beneath the heel of his immediate sensations.

He turned back to Irma.

'I offer you my arm, dear madam – such as it is.'

'I will accompany you, Mr Headmaster.'

Irma lowered her little eyelids and then flicked a sideways glance at Mr Bellgrove, who having crooked out his elbow somewhat extrava-

gantly paused a moment before dropping it with a sense of defeat that
was quite intoxicating.

'By hell!' he murmured passionately to himself – 'I am not so old that
I miss the subtleties.'

'Forgive my precipitation, dear madam,' he said, bowing his head.
'But perhaps . . . perhaps you understand . . .'

Clasping her hands together at her bosom Irma turned from the
throng, and swaying strangely, began to pace into the empty regions of
the room. The carpet lit by a hundred candles had lost something of its
glow. It was even brighter but it was not so warm, for the chilly rays of
the moon were now streaming through the open windows.

Bellgrove glanced about him as he turned to follow her. No one
appeared to be interested in their departure. Every eye was fixed upon
the Doctor. For a moment, Bellgrove felt disappointed that he could
not stay, for there was drama in the air. The Doctor was evidently
making an exhaustive overhaul of the stiffened figure whose clothes
were being removed, one by one; no easy work; for the joints were quite
inflexible. Mollock and Canvas, the Prunesquallors' servants, had,
however, a pair of scissors each and, when necessary, were, under the
Doctor's supervision, using them to free the patient.

The Doctor still had the little silver hammer in one hand. With the
other he was running his pianist-fingers over the rigid gentleman as
though he were a keyboard – his eyebrows raised, his head cocked on
one side like a tuner.

Bellgrove could see at a glance that in following Irma he was about
to miss the climax of a considerable drama, but turning on his heel, and
seeing her again he knew that a drama even more considerable was his
for the making.

With his beautiful white gown rippling behind him, he strode in her
wake, and on the eleventh stride he came within the orbit of her
perfume.

Without pausing in the swaying movement of her gait she turned her
head on its swan-white neck. Her emerald ear-ring flashed with light.
Her long, sharp nose, immaculately powdered, would have put most
suitors off, but to Bellgrove it had the proportions of a beak on the
proud head of a bird, exquisitely dangerous and sharp. Something to
admire rather than love. It was almost a weapon, but a weapon which
he felt confident would never be used against him. However that might
be, it was hers – and in that simple fact lay its justification.

As they approached the bay window that was open to the night,
Bellgrove inclined his head to her.

'This,' he said, 'is our first walk together.'

She stopped as they reached the open window. What he had said had
obviously touched her.

'Mr Bellgrove,' she whispered, 'you mustn't say things like that. We hardly know one another.'

'Quite so, dear lady, quite so,' said Bellgrove. He took out a large greyish handkerchief and blew his nose. This is going to be a long business, he thought – unless he were to take some kind of a short cut – some secret path through love's enchanted glades.

Before them, shining balefully in the moonlight lay the walled-in garden. The upper foliage of the trees shone as white as foam. The underside was black as well-water. The whole garden was a lithograph of richest blacks and staring whites. The fishpool with its surrounding carvings appeared to blaze with a kind of lunar vulgarity. A fountain shot its white jets at the night. Under the livid pergolas, under the stone arches, under the garden tubs, under the great rockery, under the fruit trees, under each moon-white thing the shadows lay as black sea-drenched seals. There were no greys at all. There was no transition. It was a picture, terrifyingly simple.

They stared at it together.

'You said just now, Miss Prunesquallor, that we hardly knew each other. And how true this is – when we measure our mutual recognition by the hands of the clock. But can we, madam, *can* we measure our knowledge thus? Is there not something in both of us which contradicts so mean a measure? Or am I flattering myself? Am I laying myself open to your scorn? Am I baring my heart too soon?'

'Your *heart*, sir?'

'My heart.'

Irma struggled with herself.

'What were you saying about it, Mr Headmaster?'

Bellgrove could not quite remember, so he joined his big hands together at the height of the organ in question, and waited a moment or two for inspiration. He seemed to have proceeded rather faster than he had meant and then it struck him that his silence, rather than weakening his position, was enhancing it. It seemed to give an added profundity to the proceedings and to himself. He would keep her waiting. O the magic of it! The power of it! He could feel his throat contracting as though he were biting into a lemon.

This time as he angled his arm he knew she would take it. She did. Her fingers on his forearm set his old heart pounding and then, without a word they stepped forward together into the moonlit garden.

It was not easy for Bellgrove to know in which direction to escort his hostess. Little did he know that it was he who was being steered. And this was natural, for Irma knew every inch of the hideous place.

For some while they stood by the fishpond in which the reflection of the moon shone with a fatuous vacancy. They stared at it. Then they looked up at the original. It was no more interesting than its watery ghost, but they both knew that to ignore the moon on such an evening would be an insensitive, almost a brutish thing to do.

That Irma knew of an arbour in the garden was not her fault. And it was not her fault that Bellgrove knew it not. Yet she blushed inwardly, as casually turning to left and right at the corners of paths, or under flower-loaded trellises, she guided the headmaster circuitously yet firmly in its direction.

Bellgrove, who had in his mind's eye just such a place as he was now unwittingly approaching, had felt it better that they should perambulate together in silence, so that when he had a chance to sit and rest his feet, his deep voice, when he brought it forth again from the depths of his chest, should have its full value.

On rounding a great moon-capped lilac bush and coming suddenly upon the arbour, Irma started, and drew back. Bellgrove came to a halt beside her. Finding her face was turned away from him, he gazed absently at the hard boulder-like bun of iron-grey hair which, with not a hair out of place, shone in the moonlight. It was nothing, however, for a man to dwell upon, and turning from her to the arbour which had caused her trepidation, he straightened himself, and turning his right foot out at a rather more aggressive angle, he struck an attitude, which he knew nothing about, for it was the unconscious equivalent of what was going on in his mind.

He saw himself as the type of man who would never take advantage of a defenceless woman, greathearted, and understanding. Someone a damsel might trust in a lonely wood. But he also saw himself as a buck. His youth had been so long ago that he could remember nothing of it but he presumed, erroneously, that he had tasted the purple fruit, had broken hearts and hymens, had tossed flowers to ladies on balconies, had drunk champagne out of their shoes and generally been irresistible.

He allowed her fingers to fall from his arm. It was at moments like this that he must give her a sense of freedom only to draw her further into the rich purdah of his benevolence.

He held the tabs of his white gown near the shoulders.

'Can you not smell the lilac, madam,' he said – 'the moonlit lilac?'

Irma turned.

'I must be honest with you, mustn't I, Mr Bellgrove?' she said. 'If I said I could smell it, when I couldn't, I would be false to you, and false to myself. Let us not start *that* way. No, Mr Bellgrove, I cannot smell it. I have a bit of a cold.'

Bellgrove had the sense of having to start life all over again.

'You women are delicate creatures,' he said after a long pause. 'You must take care of yourselves.'

'Why are you talking in the plural, Mr Bellgrove?'

'My dear madam,' he replied slowly, and then, after a pause, 'my . . . dear . . . madam,' he said again. As he heard his voice repeat the three words for the second time, it struck him that to leave them as they were – inconsequent, rudderless, without preface or parenthesis, was by far the best thing he could do. He lapsed into silence and the silence was thrilling – the silence which to break with an answer to her question would be to make a commonplace out of what was magic.

He would not answer her. He would play with her with his venerable brain. She must realize from the first that she could not always expect replies to her questions – that his thoughts might be elsewhere, in regions where it would be impossible for her to follow him – or that her questions were (for all his love for her and her for him) not worth answering.

The night poured in upon them from every side – a million million cubic miles of it. O, the glory of standing with one's love, naked, as it were, on a spinning marble, while the spheres ran flaming through the universe!

Involuntarily they moved together into the arbour and sat down on a bench which they found in the darkness. This darkness was intensely rich and velvety. It was as though they were in a cavern, save that the depths were dramatized by a number of small and brilliant pools of moonlight. Pranked for the most part to the rear of the arbour these livid pools were at first a little disturbing, for portions of themselves were lit up with blatant emphasis. This arbitrary illumination had to be accepted, however, for Bellgrove, raising his eyes to where the vents in the roof let through the moonlight, could think of no way by which he could seal them.

From Irma's point of view the dappled condition of the cavernous arbour was both calming and irritating at the same time.

Calming, in that to enter a cave of clotted midnight, with not so much as a flicker of light to gauge her distance from her partner would have been terrifying even with her knowledge of, and confidence in, so reliable and courteous a gentleman as her escort. This dappled arbour was not so fell a place. The pranked lights, more livid, it is true, than gay, removed, nevertheless, that sense of terror only known to fugitives or those benighted in a shire of ghouls.

Strong as was her feeling of gratification that the dark was broken, yet a sense of irritation as strong as her relief fought in her flat bosom for sovereignty. This irritation, hardly understandable to anyone who has neither Irma's figure, nor a vivid picture of the arbour in mind, was caused by the maddening *way* in which the lozenges of radiance fell upon her body.

She had taken out a small mirror in the darkness, more from

nervousness than anything else and in holding it up, saw nothing in the dark air before her but a long sharp segment of light. The mirror itself was quite invisible, as was the hand and arm that held it, but the detached and luminous reflection of her nose hovered before her in the darkness. At first she did not know what it was. She moved her head a little and saw in front of her one of her small weak eyes glittering like quicksilver, a startling thing to observe under any conditions, but infinitely more so when the organ is one's own.

The rest of her was indistinguishable midnight save for a pair of large and spectral feet. She shuffled them, but this blotch of moonlight was the largest in the arbour and to evade it involved a muscular strain quite insufferable.

Bellgrove's entire head was luminous. He was, more than ever before, a major prophet. His white hair positively blossomed.

Irma, knowing that this wonderful and searching light which was transfiguring the head was something that must not be missed – something in fact that she should pore upon – made a great effort to forget herself as a true lover should – but something in her rebelled against so exclusive a concentration upon her admirer, for she knew that it was *she* who should be stared at; *she* who should be poured upon.

Had she spent the best part of a day in titivating herself in order that she might sit plunged in darkness, with nothing but her feet and her nose revealed?

It was insufferable. The visual relationship was wrong; quite, quite wrong.

Bellgrove had suffered a shock when for a moment he had seen ahead of him, in quick succession, a moonlit nose and then a moonlit eye. They were obviously Irma's. There was no other nose in all Gormenghast so knifelike – and no eye so weak and worried – except its colleague. To have seen these features ahead of him when the lady to whom they belonged sat shrouded yet most palpable upon his right hand, unnerved the old man, and it was some while after he had caught sight of the mirror glinting on its return to Irma's reticule that he realized what had happened.

The darkness was as deep and black as water.

'Mr Bellgrove,' said Irma, 'can you hear me, Mr Bellgrove?'

'Perfectly, my dear lady. Your voice is high and clear.'

'I would have you sit upon my right, Mr Headmaster – I would have you exchange places with me.'

'Whatever you would have I am here to have it given,' said Bellgrove. For a moment he winced as the grammatical chaos of his reply wounded what was left of the scholar in him.

'Shall we rise together, Mr Headmaster?'

'Dear lady,' he replied, 'let that be so.'

'I can hardly see you, Mr Headmaster.'

'Nevertheless, dear lady, I am at your side. Would my arm assist you at our interchange? It is an arm that, in earlier days . . .'

'I am quite able to get to my own feet, Mr Bellgrove – *quite* able, thank you.'

Bellgrove rose, but in rising his gown was caught in some rustic contortion of the garden seat, and he found himself squatting in mid-air. 'Hell!' he muttered savagely, and jerking at his gown, tore it badly. A nasty whiff of temper ran through him. His face felt hot and prickly.

'*What* did you say?' said Irma. 'I said, *what* did you say?'

For a moment Bellgrove, in the confusion of his irritation, had unknowingly projected himself back into the Masters' Common room, or into a classroom, or into the life he had led for scores of years . . .

His old lips curled back from his neglected teeth. 'Silence!' he said. 'Am I your headmaster for nothing!'

Directly he had spoken, and had taken in what he had said, his neck and forehead burned.

Irma, transfixed with excitement, could make no move. Had Bellgrove possessed any kind of telepathic instinct he must have known that he had beside him a fruit which, at a touch, might have fallen into his hands, so ripe it was. He had no knowledge of this, but luckily for him, his embarrassment precluded any power on his part to utter a word. And the silence was on his side.

It was Irma who was the first to speak.

'You have mastered me,' she said. Her words, simple and sincere, were more proud than humble. They were proud with surrender.

Bellgrove's brain was not quick – but it was by no means moribund. His mood was now trembling at the opposite pole of his temperament.

This by no means helped to clarify his brain. But he sensed the need for extreme caution. He sensed that his position though delicate was lofty. To find that his act of rudeness in demanding silence from his hostess had raised him rather than lowered him in her eyes, appealed to something in him quite shameless – a kind of glee. Yet this glee, though shameless, was yet innocent. It was the glee of the child who had not been found out.

They were both standing. This time he did not offer Irma his arm. He groped in the darkness and found hers. He found it at the elbow. Elbows are not romantic, but Bellgrove's hand shook as he held the joint, and the joint shook in his grasp. For a moment they stood together. Her pineapple perfume was thick and powerful.

'Be seated,' he said. He spoke a little louder than before. He spoke as one in authority. He had no need to *look* stern, magnetic or masculine. The blessed darkness precluded any exertion in that direction. He made faces in the safety of the night. Putting out his tongue; blowing out his cheeks – there was so much glee in him.

He took a deep breath. It steadied him.

'Are you seated, Miss Prunesquallor?'

'O yes . . . O yes indeed,' came the answering whisper.

'In comfort, madam?'

'In comfort, Mr Headmaster, and in peace.'

'Peace, my dear lady? What kind of peace?'

'The peace, Mr Headmaster, of one who has no fear. Of one who has faith in the strong arm of her loved one. The peace of heart and mind and spirit that belong to those who have found what it is to offer themselves without reserve to something august and tender.'

There was a break in Irma's voice, and then as though to prove what she had said, she cried out into the night, 'Tender! that's what I said. Tender and Unattached!'

Bellgrove shifted himself; they were all but touching.

'Tell me, my dearest lady, is it of me that you speak. If it is not, then humble me – be merciless and break an old man's heart with one small syllable. If you say "no" then, without a word I will leave you and this pregnant arbour, walk out into the night, walk out of your life, and may be, who knows, out of mine also . . .'

Whether or not he was gulling himself it is certain that he was living the very essence of his words. Perhaps the very use of words themselves was as much a stimulus as Irma's presence and his own designs; but that is not to say that the total effect was not sincere. He was infatuated with all that pertained to love. He trod breast-deep through banks of thorn-crazed roses. He breathed the odours of a magic isle. His brain swam on a sea of spices. But he had his own thought too.

'It was of you I spoke,' said Irma. 'You, Mr Bellgrove. Do not touch me. Do not tempt me. Do nothing to me. Just *be* there beside me. I would not have us desecrate this moment.'

'By no means. By no means.' Bellgrove's voice was deep and subterranean. He heard it with pleasure. But he was sensitive enough to know that for all its sepulchral beauty, the phrase he had just used was pathetically inept – and so he added, 'By no means whatsoever . . .' as though he were beginning a sentence.

'By no means whatsoever, ah, definitely not, for who can tell, when, unawares, love's dagger . . .' but he stopped. He was getting nowhere. He must start again.

He must say things that would drive his former remarks out of her mind. He must sweep her along.

'Dear one,' he said, plunging into the rank and feverish margin of love's forest. '*Dear* one!'

'Mr Bellgrove – O, Mr Bellgrove,' came the hardly audible reply.

'It is the headmaster of Gormenghast, your suitor, who is speaking to you, my dear. It is a man, mature and tender – yet a disciplinarian, feared by the wicked, who is sitting beside you in the darkness. I would have you concentrate upon this. When I say to you that I shall call you Irma, I am not asking for permission from my love-light – I am telling her what I shall do.'

'Say it, my male!' cried Irma, forgetting herself. Her strident voice, quite out of key with the secret and muted atmosphere of an arbour'd wooing, splintered the darkness.

Bellgrove shuddered. Her voice had been a shock to him. At a more appropriate moment he would teach her not to do things of that kind.

As he settled again against the rustic back of the seat he found that their shoulders were touching.

'I will say it. Indeed I will say it, my dear. Not as a crude statement with no beginning or ending. Not as a mere reiteration of the most lovely, the most provocative name in Gormenghast, but threaded into my sentences, an integral part of our conversation, Irma, for see, already it has left my tongue.'

'I have no power, Mr Bellgrove, to remove my shoulder from yours.'

'And I have no inclination, my dove.' He lifted his big hand and tapped her on the shoulder she had referred to.

They had been so long in darkness that he had forgotten that she was in evening dress. In touching her naked shoulder he received a sensation that set his heart careering. For a moment he was deeply afraid. What was this creature at his side? and he cried out to some unknown God for delivery from the Unknown, the Serpentine, from all that was shameless, from flesh and the devil.

The tremendous gulf between the sexes yawned – and an abyss, terrifying and thrilling, sheer and black as the arbour in which they sat; a darkness wide, dangerous, imponderable and littered with the wrecks of broken bridges.

But his hand stayed where it was. The muscle of her shoulder was tense as a bowstring, but the skin was like satin. And then his terror fled. Something masterful and even dashing began to possess him.

'Irma,' he whispered huskily. 'Is *this* a desecration. Are we blotting the whitest of all love's copybooks? It is for you to say. For myself I am walking among rainbows – for myself I . . .' But he had to stop speaking for he wished, more than anything else, to lie on his back and to kick his old legs about and to crow like a barn-cock. As he could not do this he had no option but to put his tongue out in the darkness, to squint with his eyes, to make extravagant grimaces of every kind. Excruciating shivers swarmed his spine.

And Irma could not reply. She was weeping with joy. Her only answer was to place her hand upon the headmaster's. They drew together – involuntarily. For a while there was that kind of silence all lovers know. The silence that it is sin to break until of its own volition the moment comes, and the arms relax and the cramped limbs can stretch themselves again, and it is no longer an insensitive thing to inquire what the time might be or to speak of other matters that have no place in Paradise.

At last Irma broke the hush.

'How happy I am,' she said very quietly. 'How very happy, Mister Bellgrove.'

'Ah . . . my dear . . . ah,' said the Headmaster very slowly, very soothingly . . . 'that is as it should be . . . that is as it should be.'

'My wildest, my very *wildest* dreams have become real, have become something I can touch' (she pressed his hand). 'My little fancies, my little visions – they are no longer so, dear master, they are substance, they are you . . . they are You.'

Bellgrove was not sure that he liked being one of Irma's 'little fancies, little visions' but his sense of the inappropriate was swamped in his excitement.

'Irma!' He drew her to him. There was less 'give' in her body than in a cakestand. But he could hear her quick excited breathing.

'You are not the only one whose dreams have become a reality, my dear. We are holding one another's dreams in our very arms.'

'Do you mean it, Mr Bellgrove?'

'Surely, ah, surely,' he said.

Dark as it was Irma could picture him at her side, could see him in detail. She had an excellent memory. She was enjoying what she saw. Her mind's eye had suddenly become a most powerful organ. It was, in point of fact, stronger, clearer and healthier than those real eyes of hers which gave her so much trouble.

And so, as she spoke to him she had no sense of communing with an invisible presence. The darkness was forgotten.

'Mr Bellgrove?'

'My dear lady?'

'Somehow, I knew . . .'

'So did I . . . so did I.'

'It is more than I dare dwell upon – this strange and beautiful fact – that words can be so unnecessary – that when I start a sentence, there is no *need* to finish it – and all this, so very suddenly. I said, so *very* suddenly.'

'What would be sudden to the young is leisurely for us. What would be foolhardy in them is child's-play itself, for you, my dear, and for me. We are mature, my dear. We are ripe. The golden glaze, that patina of time, these are upon us. Hence we are sure and have no callow qualms. Let us admit the length of our teeth, lady. Time, it is true, had flattened our feet, ah yes, but with what purpose? To steady us, to give us balance, to take us safely along the mountain tracks. God bless me . . . ah. God bless me. Do you think that I could have wooed and won you as a youth? Not in a hundred years! And why . . . ah . . . and why? Inexperience. That is the answer. But now, in half an hour or less, I have stormed you; stormed you. But am I breathless? No. I have brought my guns to bear upon you, and yet my dear, have scores of roundshot left . . . ah yes, yes, Irma my ripe one . . . and you can see it all? . . . you can see it all? . . . dammit, we have equipoise and that is what it is.'

Irma's mental sight was frighteningly clear. His voice had sharpened the edges of his image.

'But I'm not very old, Mr Bellgrove, am I,' said Irma, after a pause. To be sure she felt as young as a fledgeling.

'What is age? What is time!' said Bellgrove – and then answering himself in a darker voice. 'They're *hell!*' he said. 'I hate 'em.'

'No, no. I won't have it,' said Irma. 'I won't, Mr Bellgrove. Age and time are what you make them. Let us not speak of them again.'

Bellgrove sat forward on his old buttocks. 'Lady!' he said suddenly, 'I have thought of something that I think you will agree is more than comic.'

'Have you, Mr Bellgrove?'

'Pertaining to what you said about Age and Time. Are you listening, my dear?'

'Yes, Mr Bellgrove . . . eagerly . . . eagerly!'

'What I think would be rather droll would be to say, in a gathering, when the moment became opportune – perhaps during some conversation about clocks – one could work round to it – to say, quite airily . . . "Time is what you make it." '

He turned his head to her in the darkness. He waited.

There was no response from Irma. She was thinking feverishly. She began to panic. Her face was prickling with anxiety. She could make no sound. Then she had an idea. She pressed herself against him a little more closely.

'How delicious!' she said at last, but her voice was very strained.

The silence that followed was no more than a few seconds, but to Irma it was as long as that ghastly hush that awaits all sinners when, at the judgement seat, they wait the Verdict. Her body trembled, for there was so much at stake. Had she said something so stupid, that no headmaster, worthy of his office, could ever consider accepting her? Had she unwittingly lifted some hatchway of her brain and revealed to this brilliant man how cold, black, humourless and sterile was the region that lay within?

No. Ah no! For his voice, rolling from the gloom, had, if possible,

even more tenderness in it than she would have dared to hope for in a man.

'You are cold, my love. You are chilly. The night is not for delicate skins. By hell, it isn't. And I? And what of me? Your suitor? Is he cold also, my dear? Your old gallant? He is. He is indeed. And what is more he is becoming sick of darkness. Darkness that shrouds. That clogs the living lineaments of beauty. That swathes you, Irma. By hell it's maddening and pointless stuff . . .' Bellgrove began to rise . . . 'it's damnable, I tell you, my own, this arbour's damnable.'

He felt the pressure of fingers on his forearm.

'Ah no . . . no . . . I will not have you swear. I will not have strong language in our arbour . . . our sacred arbour.'

For a moment Bellgrove was tempted to play the gay dog. His moods flitted across the basic excitement of the wooing. It was so delicious to be chided by a woman. He wondered whether to shock her – to shock her out of the surplus of his love, would be worth the candle. To taste again the sweetness of being reprimanded, the never-before-experienced gushes of sham remorse – would this be worth the lowering of his moral status. No! He would stick to his pinnacle.

'This arbour,' he said, 'is forever ours. It is the darkness it holds captive; this pitchy stuff that hides your face from me – it is this darkness that I called damnable – and damnable it is. It is your face, Irma, your proud face that I am thirsting for. Can you not understand? By the great moonlight! my love; by the tremendous moonlight! Is it not natural that a man should wish to brood upon his darling's brow?'

The word 'darling' affected Irma as might a bullet wound. She clasped her hands at her breast and pressing them inwards the tepid water in her false bosom gurgled in the darkness.

For a moment Bellgrove, thinking she was laughing at what he had said, stiffened at her side. But the terrible blush of humiliation that was about to climb his neck was quenched by Irma's voice. The gurgle must have been a sign of love, of some strange and aqueous love that was beyond his sounding, for 'O master,' she said, 'take me to where the moon can show you me.'

'Show-you-me?' for a short while Bellgrove was quite unable to decipher what sounded to him like a foreign language. But he did not stand still, as lesser men would have done while pondering, but answering the first part of her command he escorted her from the arbour. Instantaneously, they were floodlit – and at the same instant Irma's syntax clarified in the headmaster's mind.

They moved together, like spectres, like mobile carvings casting their long inky shadows across the little paths, down the slopes of rockeries, up the sides of trellises.

At last they stopped for a little while where a stone cherub squatted upon the rim of a granite bird-bath. To their left they could see the lighted windows of the long reception room. But they could not see that in the midst of a rapt audience the Doctor was raising his silver hammer as though to put all to the test. They could not know that by a supernatural effort of the will, and the martialling of all his deductive faculties, and the freeing of an irrational flair, the Doctor had come to the kind of decision more usually associated with composers than with scientists – and was now on the brink of success or failure.

The 'body' had, to aid the physician in his exhaustive search for the cause of the paralysis, been stripped of all clothing save the mortar-board.

What happened next was something which, however much the stories varied afterwards – for it seemed that every professor present was able to note some minor detail hidden from the rest – was yet consistent in the main. The speed at which it happened was phenomenal, and it must be assumed that the microscopic elaborations of the incident which were to be the main subject of conversation for so long a while afterwards, were no more or less than inventions which were supposed to redound to the advantage of the teller, in some way or other – possibly through the reflected glory which they all felt at having been there at all. However this may be, what was agreed upon by all was that the Doctor, his shirt sleeves rolled well back, rose suddenly on his toes, and lifting his silver hammer into the air, where it flashed with candle-light, let it fall, as it were with a kind of controlled, yet effortless downstroke, upon the nether regions of the spinal column. As the hammer struck, the Doctor leapt back and stood with his arms spread out to his sides, his fingers rigid as he saw before him the instantaneous convulsion of the patient. This gentleman writhing like an expiring eel leapt suddenly high into the air, and on landing upon his feet, was seen to streak across the room and out of the bay windows and over the moonlit lawn at a speed that challenged the credulity of all witnesses.

And those who, standing grouped about the Doctor, had seen the transformation and the remarkable athleticism that followed so swiftly upon it, were not the only ones to be startled by the spectacle.

In the garden, among the livid blotches and the cold wells of shadow a voice was saying . . .

'It is not meet, Irma my dearest, that on this night, this *first* night, we should tire our hearts . . . no, no, it is not meet, sweet bride.'

'*Bride?*' cried Irma, flashing her teeth and tossing her head. 'O Master, not *yet* . . . surely!'

Bellgrove frowned like God considering the state of the world on the Third Day. A knowing smile played across his old mouth but it appeared to have lost its way among the wrinkles.

'Quite so, my delicious helm. Once more you keep me on my course, and for that I revere you, Irma . . . not *bride*, it is true, but . . .'

The old man had jerked like a recoiling firearm, and Irma with him, for she was in his gown-swathed arms. Turning her startled eyes from his she followed his gaze and on the instant clung to him in a desperate embrace, for all at once they saw before them, naked in the dazzling rays of the moon, a flying figure which for all the shortness of the legs, was covering the ground with the speed of a hare. The tassel of the inky mortar-board, sole claim to decency, streamed away behind like a donkey's tail.

No sooner had Irma and the headmaster caught sight of the apparition, than it had reached the high orchard wall of the garden. How it ever climbed the wall was never discovered. It simply went up, its shadow swarming alongside, and the last that was ever seen of Mr Throd, the onetime member of Mr Bellgrove's staff, was a lunar flash of buttocks where the high wall propped the sky.

THIRTY-SEVEN

THERE were at least three hours to be burned. It was unusual for Steerpike to have to think in such terms. There was always something afoot. There were always, in the wide and sinister pattern of his scheduled future, those irregular pieces to find and to fit into the great jig-saw puzzle of his predatory life, and of Gormenghast, on whose body he fed.

But on this particular day, when the clocks had all struck two, and the steel of his swordstick which he had been sharpening was as keen as a razor and as pointed as a needle, he wrinkled his high shining forehead as he returned the blade to the stick. At the end of the three hours that lay before him he had something very important to do.

It would be very simple and it would be absorbing, but it would be very important also; so important that for the first time in his life he was at a loss for a few moments as to how to fill in the hours that remained before the business that lay ahead, for he knew that he could not concentrate upon anything very serious. While he pondered, he moved to the window of his room and looked out across the vistas of roofs and broken towers.

It was a breathless day, a frail mist tempering the warmth. The few flags that could be seen above various turrets hung limply from their mastheads.

This prospect never failed to please the pale young man. His eye ran over it with shrewdity.

Then he turned from the scene, for he had had an idea. Pouncing upon the floor, his arms outstretched, he stood upside-down upon the palms of his hands and began to perambulate the room, one eyebrow raised. His idea was to pay a quick call upon the Twins. He had not visited them for some while. Away across the roofscape he had seen the outskirts of that deserted tract, in one of whose forgotten corridors an archway led to a grey world of empty rooms, in one of which their ladyships Cora and Clarice sat immured. Their presence and the presence of their few belongings seemed to have no effect upon the sense of emptiness. Rather, their presence seemed to reinforce the vacancy of their solitude.

It would take him the best part of an hour's sharp walking to reach that forgotten region, but he was in a restless mood, and the idea appealed to him. Flexing his elbows – for he was still moving about the room on his hands – he pressed, of a sudden, away from the floor and, like an acrobat, was all at once on his feet again.

Within a few moments he was on his way, his room carefully locked behind him. He walked rapidly, his shoulders drawn up and forward a little in that characteristic way that gave to his every movement a quality both purposeful and devilish.

The short cuts he took through the labyrinthian network of the castle led him into strange quarters. There were times when walls would tower above him, sheer and windowless. At other times, naked acres, paved in brick or stone would spread themselves out, wastelands vast and dusty where weeds of all kinds forced their way from between the interstices of the paving stones.

As he moved rapidly from domain to domain, from a world of sunless alleys to the panoramic ruins where the rats held undisputed tenure – from the ruins to that peculiar district where the passageways were all but blocked with undergrowth and the carved façades were cold with sea-green ivy – he exulted. He exulted in it all. In the fact that it was only he who had the initiative to explore these wildernesses. He exulted in his restlessness, in his intelligence, in his passion to hold within his own hands the reins, despotic or otherwise, of supreme authority.

Far above him and to the east the sunlight burned upon a long oval window of blue glass. It blazed like lazuli – like a gem hung aloft against the grey walls. Without changing the speed of his walk he drew from his pocket a small smooth beautifully made catapult, into the pouch of which he fitted a bullet, and then, as though with a single action the elastic was stretched and released and Steerpike returned his catapult to his pocket.

He kept walking, but as he walked his face was turned up to those high grey walls where the blue window blazed.

He saw the small gap in the glass and the momentary impression of a blue powder falling before he heard the distant sound, as of a far gunshot.

A head had appeared at the gap in that splintered window away in the high east.

It was very pale. The body beneath it was swathed in sacking. On the shoulder sat perched a blood red parrot – but Steerpike knew nothing of this and was entering another district and was for a long while in the shadows, moving beneath a continuous roofscape of lichened slates.

When at last he approached the archway which led to the Twins' quarters, he paused and gazed back along the grey perspectives. The air was chill and unhealthy; a smell of rotten wood, or dank masonry filled his lungs. He moved in a climate as of decay – of a decay rank with its own evil authority, a richer, more inexorable quality than freshness; it smothered and drained all vibrancy, all hope.

Where another would have shuddered, the young man merely ran his tongue across his lips. 'This is a *place*,' he said to himself. 'Without any doubt, this is *somewhere*.'

But the hands of the clock kept moving and he had little time for speculation, and so he turned his back on the cold perspectives where the long walls bulged and sagged, where plaster hung and sweated with cold and inanimate fevers, with sicknesses of umber, and illnesses of olive.

When he reached the door behind which the Twins were incarcerated he took a bunch of keys from his pocket and selecting one, which he had cut himself, he turned the lock.

The door opened to his pressure with a stiff and grating sound.

Stiff as were the hinges, it had not taken Steerpike more than a second to throw it wide open. Had he been forced to fight against the swollen wood for an entrance, to struggle with the lock, or to put his shoulder to the damp panelling – or even had his rapid entrance been heralded by the sound of his footsteps, then the spectacle that awaited him, for all its strangeness, would not have had that uncanny and dreamlike horror that now lay hold of him.

He had made no sound. He had given no warning of his visit – but there before him stood the Twins, hand in hand, their faces white as lard. They were positioned immediately before the door; at which they must have been staring. They were like figures of wax, or alabaster or like motionless animals, upright upon their quarters, their gaze fixed, it would seem, upon the face of their master, their mouths half open as though awaiting some tit-bit – some familiar signal.

No expression at all came into their eyes, nor would there have been room for any, for they were separately filled, each one of them, with a foreign body, for in each of the four glazed pupils the image of the young man was exquisitely reflected. Let those who have tried to pass love letters through the eyes of needles or to have written poems on the heads of pins take heart. Crude and heavy handed as they found themselves, yet they will never appreciate the extent of their clumsiness for they will never know how Steerpike's head and shoulders leaned forward through circles the size of beads, whose very equidistance from one another (the Twins were cheek to cheek) was as though to prove by ghastly repetition the nightmare of it all. Minute and exquisite in the microcosm of the pupils, these four worlds, identical and terrible, gleamed between the lids. It would seem they had been painted – these images of Steerpike – with a single hair or with the proboscis of a bee – for the very whites of his eyes were crystalline. And when Steerpike at the door drew back his head – drew it back on a sudden impulse, then the four heads, no bigger than seeds, were drawn back at that same instant, and the eight eyes narrowed as they stared back from the four microscopic mirrors – stared back at their origin, the youth, mountain high in the doorway, the youth on whom their quick and pulseless lives depended – the youth with his eyes narrowed, and whose least movement was theirs.

That the eyes of the Twins should be ignorant of that they reflected was natural enough but it was not natural that in carrying the image of Steerpike to their identical brains, there should be, by not so much as the merest shade, a clue to the excitement in their breasts. For it seemed that they felt nothing, that they saw nothing, that they were dead, and stood upon their feet by some miracle.

Steerpike knew at once that yet another chapter was over in his relationship with Cora and Clarice. They had become clay in his hands, but they were clay no more, unless there is in clay not only something imponderable but something sinister also. Not only this, but something adamantine. From now on he knew that they were no longer ductile – they had changed into another medium – a sister medium – but a harsher one – they were stone.

All this could be seen at a glance. But now, suddenly, there was something which escaped his vigilance. It was this. His reflections were no longer in their eyes. Their ladyships had unwittingly expelled him. Something else had taken place – and as he was unaware that he had ever been reflected so he was equally unaware that he was no longer so – and that in the lenses of their eyes he had exchanged places with the head of an axe.

But what Steerpike *could* see was that they were no longer staring at him – that their gaze was fixed upon something above his head. They had not tilted their heads back although it would have been the normal thing to do for whatever they were looking at was all but out of their line of vision. Their upturned eyes shone white. Save for this movement of their eyeballs they had not so much as stirred.

Fighting down his fear that were he to move his eyes from them, even for a second, he would fall in a peculiar way into some trap, he swung himself about and in a moment had seen a great axe dangling a dozen feet above him, and the complex network of cords and strings which, like a spider's web in the darkness of the upper air, held in position the cold and grizzly weight of the steel head.

With a backward leap the young man was through the doorway. Without a pause he slammed the door and before he had turned the key in the lock he had heard the thud as the head of the axe buried itself in that part of the floor where he had been standing.

THIRTY-EIGHT

STEERPIKE'S return to the castle's heart was rapid and purposeful. A pale sun like a ball of pollen was hung aloft an empty and faded sky, and as he sped below it his shadow sped with him, rippling over the cobbles of great squares, or cruising alongside, upright, where at his elbow the lit and attenuate walls threw back the pallid light. For all that within its boundaries, this shadow held nothing but the uniform blankness of its tone, yet it seemed every whit as predatory and meaningful as the body that cast it – the body, that with so many aids to expressiveness within the moving outline, from the pallor of the young man and the dark red colour of his eyes, to the indefinable expressions of lip and eye, was drawing nearer at every step to a tryst of his own making.

The sun was blocked away. For a few minutes the shadow disappeared like the evil dream of some sleeper who on waking finds the substance of his nightmare standing beside his bed – for *Steerpike* was there, turning the corners, threading the mazes, gliding down slopes of stone or flights of rotten wood. And yet it was strange that with all the vibrancy that lay packed within the margins of his frame, yet his shadow when it reappeared reaffirmed its self-sufficiency and richness as a scabbard for malignity. Why should this be – why with certain slender proportions and certain tricks of movement should a sense of darkness be evoked? Shadows more terrible and grotesque than Steerpike's gave no such feeling. They moved across their walls bloated or spidery with a comparative innocence. It was as though a shadow had a heart – a heart where blood was drawn from the margins of a world of less substance than air. A world of darkness whose very existence depended upon its enemy, the light.

And there it was; there it slid, this particular shadow – from wall to wall, from floor to floor, the shoulders a little high, but not unduly, the head cocked, not to one or other side, but forward. In an open space it paled as it moved over dried earth, for the sun weakened – and then it fainted away altogether as the fringe of a cloud half the size of the sky moved over the sun.

Almost at once the rain began to fall, and the air yet further darkened. Nor was this darkening enough, for beneath, the expanse of the cloud that moved inexorably to the north, dragging behind it miles and miles of what looked like filthy linen, beneath *this* expanse, yet another, of similar hugeness, but swifter, began to overtake it from beneath, and when *this* lower continent of cloud began to pass over that part of the sky where the sun had lately been shining, then something very strange made itself felt at once.

A darkness almost unprecedented had closed down over Gormenghast. Steerpike glancing left and right could see the lights begin to burn in scores of windows. It was too dark to see what was happening above, but judging from a still deepening of the pall, yet further clouds, thick and rain-charged, must have slid across the sky to form the lowest of three viewless and enormous layers.

By now the rain was loud on the roofs, was flooding along the gutterings, gurgling in crannies and brimming the thousand irregular cavities that the centuries had formed among the crumbling stones. The advance of these weltering clouds had been so rapid that Steerpike had not entirely escaped the downpour, but it was not for more than a few moments that the rain beat on his head and shoulders, for, running through the unnatural darkness to the nearest of the lighted windows, he found himself in a part of the castle that he remembered. From here he could make the rest of the journey under cover.

The premature darkness was peculiarly oppressive. As Steerpike made his way through the lighted corridors he noticed how at the main windows there were groups gathered, and how the faces that peered out into the false night wore expressions of perplexity and apprehension. It was a freak of nature, and no more, that the world had been swathed away from the westering sun as though with bandages, layer upon layer, until the air was stifled. Yet it seemed as though the sense of oppression which the darkness had ushered in had more than a material explanation.

As though to fight back against the circumscribing darkness the hierophants had lighted every available lantern, burner, candle and lamp, and had even improvised an extraordinary variety of reflectors, of tin and glass, and even trays of gold and plates of burnished copper. Long before any message could have been couriered across the body of Gormenghast, there was not a limb, not a digit that had not responded to the universal sense of suffocation, not the merest finger joint of stone that had not set itself alight.

Countless candles dribbled with hot wax, and their flames, like little flags, fluttered in the uncharted currents of air. Thousands of lamps, naked, or shuttered behind coloured glass, burned with their glows of purple, amber, grass-green, blue, blood red and even grey. The walls of Gormenghast were like the walls of paradise or the walls of an inferno. The colours were devilish or angelical according to the colour of the mind that watched them. They swam, those walls, with the hues of hell, with the tints of Zion. The breasts of the plumaged seraphim; the scales of Satan.

And Steerpike, moving rapidly through these varying flushes, could hear the loudening of the rain. He had come to something very like an isthmus – a corridor with circular windows on either side that gave upon the outer darkness. This arcade, or cover-way – this isthmus that joined together one great mass of sprawling masonry to another, was illumined along its considerable length at three more or less regular intervals by firstly a great age-green oil lamp with an enormous wick as wide as a sheep's tongue. The glass globe that fitted over it was appallingly ugly; a fluted thing, a piece missing from its lower lip. But its colour was something apart – or rather the colour of the glass when lit from behind, as it now was. To say it was indigo gives no idea of its depth and richness, nor of the underwater or cavernous *glow* that filled that part of the arcade with its aura.

In their different ways the other two lamps, with their globes of sullen crimson and iceberg green, made within the orbits of their influence, arenas no less theatrical. The glazed and circular windows, dark as jet, were yet not featureless. Across the blind blackness of those flanking eyes the strands of rain which appeared not to move but to be stretched across the inky portholes like harp strings – these strands, these strings of water burned blue, beyond the glass, burned crimson, burned green, for the lamplight stained them. And in the stain was something serpentine – something poisonous, exotic, feverish and merciless; the colours were the colours of the sea-snake, and beyond the windows on either hand, was the long-drawn hiss of the reptilian rain.

And while Steerpike sped along this covered-way, the shadow that he cast changed colour. Sometimes it was before him as though eager to arrive at some rendezvous before the body of its caster; and sometimes it followed him, sliding at his heels, dogging him, changing its dark colour as it flowed.

With the isthmus behind him, and a continent of stone once more about him, a continent into whose fastnesses he moved the deeper with every step and with every breath he took, Steerpike banished from his mind every thought of the Twins and of their behaviour. His mind had been largely taken up with conjecture as to the cause of their insurrection, and with tentative plans for their disposal.

But there were matters more pressing and one matter in particular. With enviable ease he emptied his mind of their ladyships and filled it with Barquentine.

His shadow moved upon his right hand. It was climbing a staircase. It crossed a landing. It descended three steps. It followed for a short while at its maker's heels and then overtook him. It was at his elbow when it suddenly deepened its tone and grew up the side of the wall until the shadow-head twelve feet above the ground, pursued its lofty way, the profile undulating from time to time, when it was forced to float across the murky webs that choked the junction of wall and ceiling.

And then the giant shade began to shrivel, and as it descended it moved a little forward of its caster, until finally it was a thick and stunted thing – a malformation, intangible, terrible, that led the way towards those rooms where its immediate journey could, for a little while, be ended.

THIRTY-NINE

BARQUENTINE in his room, sat with his withered leg drawn up to his chin. His hair, dirty as a flyblown web, hung about his face, dry and lifeless. His skin, equally filthy, with its silted fissures, its cheese-like cracks and discolorations, was dry also – an arid terrain, dead it seemed, and waterless as the moon, and yet at its centre those malignant lakes, his vile and brimming eyes.

Outside the broken window at the far end of the room lay stretched the stagnant waters of the moat.

He had been sitting there, his only leg drawn up to his face, his crutch leaning against the back of his chair, his hands clasped about his knee, a hank of his beard between his teeth – he had been sitting there, for over an hour. On the table before him at least a dozen books lay spread; books of ritual and precedence, books of cross-reference, ciphers and secret papers. But his eyes were not on them. No less ruthless for being out of focus and gleaming wetly in their dry sockets, they could not see that a shadow had entered the room – that intangible as air, yet graphic to a degree, it had reared itself against high tiers of books – books of all shapes and in every stage of dilapidation, that glimmered in the bad light save where this shadow lay athwart them, black as a shade from hell.

And while he sat there, what was he thinking of, this wrinkled and filthy dwarf?

He was thinking of how a change had come over the workings of Gormenghast – over the workings of its heart and the temper of its brain. Something so subtle that he could in no way fix upon it. Something that was not to be located in the normal way of his thinking yet something which, nevertheless, was filling his nostrils with its odour. He knew it to be evil, and what was evil in the eyes of Barquentine was anything that smelt of insurrection, anything that challenged, or worked to undo the ancient procedures.

Gormenghast was not what it was. He knew it. There was devilry somewhere among these cold stones. And yet he could not put his finger

upon the spot. He could not say what it was that was now so different.
It was not that he was an old man. He was not sentimental about the
days of his youth. They had been dark and loveless. But he had no pity
for himself. He had only this blind, passionate and cruel love for the
dead letter of the castle's law. He loved it with a love as hot as his hate.
For the members of the Groan line itself he had less regard than for the
meanest and drearest of the rituals that it was their destiny to perform.
Only in so far as they were symbols did he bow his ragged head. He
had no love for Titus – only for his significance as the last of the links
in the great chain. There was something about the way the boy
moved . . . a restlessness, an independence, that galled him. It was
almost as though this heir to a world of towers had learned of other
climes, of warm, clandestine lands, and that the febrile and erratic
movements of the child's limbs were the reflection of what lived and
throve in his imagination. It was as though his brain, in regions remote
and seductive, was sending its unsettling messages to the small bones,
to the tissues of the boy, so that there was, in his movements, something
remote and ominous.

But Barquentine, knowing that the seventy-seventh earl had never
moved as far as a day's journey from his birthplace, spat, as it were,
these reflections from his puzzled brain. And yet the taste lingered. The
taste of something acid; something rebellious. The young earl was too
much himself. It was as though the child imagined he had a life of his
own apart from the life of Gormenghast.

And he was not the only one. There was this Steerpike youth. A
quick, useful disciple no doubt, but a danger, for that very reason.
What was to be done about him? He had learned too much. He had
opened books that were not for him to open and found his way about
too rapidly. There was something about him that set him apart from
the life of the place – something subtly foreign – something ulterior.

Barquentine shifted his body on the chair, growling with irritation
both at the twinge which the altering of his position gave to his
withered leg, and at the frustration of being unable to do more than
gnaw at the fringe of his suspicions. He longed, as master of the
Groan law, to take action, to stamp out, if necessary, a score of
malcontents, but there was nothing clear – no tangible target –
nothing definable upon which he could direct his fire. He only knew
that were he to discover that Steerpike had in the smallest degree
abused the grudging trust he had placed in him, then, bringing all
his authority to bear, he would have the pallid snipe from the Tower
of Flints – he would strike with the merciless venom of the fanatic
for whom the world holds no gradations – only the blind extremes
of black and white. To sin was to sin against Gormenghast. Evil and
doubt were one. To doubt the sacred stones was to profane the

godhead. And there was this evil somewhere – close but invisible. His sense caught a whiff of it – but as soon as he turned his brain as it were over the shoulder of his mind – it was gone – and there was nothing palpable – nothing but the hierophants – moving here and there, upon this business or that, and seemingly absorbed.

Was there no way for him either to snare this wandering evil and turn its face to the light or to quell his suspicions? For they were harmful, keeping him awake through the long night hours, nagging at him, as though the castle's illness were his own.

'By the blood of hell,' he whispered, and his whisper was like grit – 'I will search it out, though it hide like a bat in the vaults or a rat in the southern lofts.'

He scratched himself disgustingly, rumps and crutch, and again he shifted himself on the high chair.

It was then that the shadow that lay across the bookshelves moved a little. The shoulders appeared to rise as the whole silhouette shifted itself further from the door and the impalpable body of the thing rippled across a hundred leather spines.

Barquentine's eyes took focus for a moment or two as they strayed over the documents on the table before him, and, unsolicited at the moment, the recollection of having once been married returned to him. What had happened to his wife he could not remember. He assumed that she had died.

He had no recollection of her face, but could remember – and perhaps it was the sight of the papers before him that had brought back the unwelcome memory – how, as she wept, she would, hardly knowing that she was doing so, make paper boats, which, wet with her tears and grimed from her cracked hands, she sailed across the harbour of her lap or left stranded about the floor or on the rope matting of her bed, in throngs like fallen leaves, wet, grimed and delicate, in scattered squadrons, a navy of grief and madness.

And then, with a start he remembered that she had borne him a son. Or was it she? It was over forty years since he had spoken to his child. He would be hard to find; but found he must be. All he remembered was that a birthmark took up most of the face and that the eyes were crossed.

With his mind cast back to earlier days, a number of pictures floated hesitantly before his eyes, and in all of them he saw himself as someone with his head perpetually raised – as someone on a level with men's knees – as a target for jibes and scorn. He could see in the mind's eye the growth of hatred; he could feel again his crutch being kicked from beneath him, and of the urchins hooting in his wake, 'Rotten leg! rotten spine!' 'Ya! Ya! Barquentine!'

All that was over. He was feared now. Feared and hated.

With his back to the door and to the bookshelves he could not see that the shadow had moved again. He lifted his head and spat.

Picking up a piece of paper he began to make a boat but he did not know what he was doing.

'It has gone on long enough,' he said to himself, – 'too long, by the blood of hags. He must go. He is finished. Dead. Over. Done with. I must be alone, or by the cock of the great Ape, I'll jeopardize the Inner Secrets. He'll have the keys off me with his bloody efficiency.'

And while he muttered in his own throat the shadow of the youth of whom he was speaking slid inexorably over the spines, and came to a stop a dozen feet from Barquentine, but the body of Steerpike was at the same moment immediately behind the cripple's chair.

It had not been easy for the young man to decide in what way he would kill his master. He had many means at his disposal. His nocturnal visits to the Doctor's dispensary had furnished him with a sinister array of poisons. His swordstick was almost too obviously efficacious. His catapult was no toy, but something lethal as a gun and silent as a sword. He knew of ways to break the neck with the edge of the palm, and he knew how to send a pen knife through the air with extraordinary precision. He had not, for nothing, spent an allotted number of minutes every morning and for several years in throwing his knife at the dummy in his bedroom.

But he was not interested merely in dispatching the old man.

He had to kill him in some way which left no trace: to dispose of the body and at the same time to mix pleasure and business in such a compound that neither was the weaker for the union. He had old scores to pay off. He had been spat upon and reviled by the withered cripple. To merely stop his life in the quickest way would be an empty climax – something to be ashamed of.

But what really happened and how Barquentine really died in Steerpike's presence bore no relation to the plan which the young man had made.

For, as he stood immediately behind his victim's chair the old man leaned forward across his books and papers and pulled towards himself a rusty, three-armed candlestick, and after a great deal of scrabbling about among his rags, eventually set a light to the wicks. This had the double effect of sending Steerpike's shadow sidling across the book-filled wall and sucking the strength out of it.

From where Steerpike stood he could see over Barquentine's shoulder the honey-coloured flames of the three candles. They were the shapes of bamboo leaves, attenuate and slender and they trembled against the darkness. Barquentine himself was silhouetted against the glow of the candlelight, and suddenly, as his body shifted, and Steerpike obtained an even clearer view of the candleflame an idea occurred to the young man which made all his carefully prepared plans for the death and disposal of the ancient's body appear amateurish: amateurish through lack of that deceptive simplicity which is the hallmark of all great art; amateurish, for all their ingenuity, and for the very reason of it.

But here – here before him, ready made was a candlestick with three gold flames that licked at the sullen air. And, here within his reach was the old man he wished to kill, but not too quickly; an old man whose rags and skin and beard were as dry and inflammable as the most exacting of fire-raisers could wish. What would be easier than for a man as ancient as Barquentine to lean forward accidentally at his work and for his beard to catch light from the candles? What would be more diverting than to watch the irritable and filthy tyrant caught among flames, his rags blazing, his skin smoking, his beard leaping like a crimson fish? It would only remain, at a later date, for Steerpike to discover the charred corpse and arouse the castle.

The young man glanced about him. The door through which he had entered the room was closed. It was an hour when there was small chance of their being disturbed. The silence in the room was only intensified by the thin grating of Barquentine's breathing.

No sooner had Steerpike realized the advantages of setting fire to the ragged silhouette which squatted like a black gnome immediately before him, than he drew the blade from his swordstick and raised it so that the steel point hovered within an inch of Barquentine's neck, and immediately below his left ear.

Now that Steerpike was so close upon the heels of the gross and bloody deed, a kind of cold and poisonous rage filled him. Perhaps the dry root of some long deadened conscience stirred for a moment in his breast. Perhaps, for that sharp second, he remembered in spite of himself that to kill a man involved a sense of guilt: and perhaps it was because of the momentary distraction of purpose that hatred swept his face, as though a frozen sea were whipped of a sudden into a living riot of tameless water. But the waves subsided as quickly as they had risen. Once again his face was white with a deadly equipoise. The point of his blade had trembled beneath the age-bitten ear. But now it was motionless.

It was then that there was a knock at the door. The old head twisted to the sound, but *away* from the blade so that Steerpike and his weapon were still invisible.

'To black hell with you whoever you are! I will see no son of a bitch today!'

'Very well, sir,' said a door-blocked voice, and then the faint sound of footsteps could be heard, and then silence again.

Barquentine turned his head back, and then scratched himself across the belly.

'Saucy bullprong,' he muttered aloud. 'I'll have his face off him. I'll have his white face off! I'll have the shine off it! By the gall of the great mule he's over-shiny. "Very well, sir" he says, does he? What's well about it? What's *well* about it? The upstart piss-worm!'

Again Barquentine began to scratch, loins, buttocks, belly and ribs.

'O sucking fire!' he cried, 'it gripes my heart! No earl but a brat. The Countess, cat-mad. And for me, no tyro but this upstart of a Steerpike bastard.'

The young man, his swordstick beautifully poised, its cold tip sharp as a needle, pursed his thin lips and clicked his tongue. This time Barquentine turned his head over his left shoulder so that he received half an inch of steel beneath his ear. His body stiffened horribly while his throat swelled into the semblance of a scream, but no scream came. When Steerpike withdrew the blade, and while a trickle of dark blood made its way over the wrinkled terrain of his turtle-neck, the whole frame became all of a sudden convulsively active, each part of him seeming to contort itself without relation to what was happening to the rest of the body. It was a miracle that he remained balanced on the high chair. But these convulsions suddenly ended and Steerpike, standing back with his chin cupped in his hands, was chilled, in spite of the half-smile on his face, by the direst expression of mortal hatred that had ever turned an old man's face into a nest of snakes. The eyes grew, of a sudden, congested, their vile waters taking on, it seemed, the flush of a dangerous sunrise. The mouth and the lines about it appeared to seethe. The dirty brow and neck were wet with venom.

But there was a brain behind it all. A brain which, while Steerpike stood by and smiled, was in spite of the young man's initial advantage, a step ahead of the youth. For the one thing without which he would indeed have been helpless was still in his power to capture. Steerpike had made a mistake at the outset. And he was taken completely by surprise when Barquentine, thrusting himself off the high chair, fell to the floor in a heap. The old man landed upon the object which was his only hope. It had fallen to the ground when he had stiffened at the sword-prick – and now in a flash he had grasped his crutch, prised himself upright, and hopped to the rear of his chair through the bars of which he directed his red gaze upon the face of his armed and agile enemy.

But the spirit in the old tyrant was something so intense that Steerpike in spite of his two legs, his youth and his weapons was taken aback by the realization that so much passion could be housed in so dry and stunted a thing. He was also taken aback at having been outwitted. It was true that even now the duel was ludicrously one-sided – an ancient cripple with a crutch – an athlete with a sword – but nevertheless, had his first action been to remove the crutch he would now have the old man in as helpless a position as a tortoise upon its back.

For a few moments they faced one another, Barquentine expressing everything in his face, Steerpike nothing. Then the young man began to walk slowly backwards to the door, his eyes all the while on his quarry. He was taking no chances. Barquentine had shown how quick he could be.

When he reached the door he opened it and took a rapid glance along the attenuate corridor. It was enough to show him that there was no one in the neighbourhood. He closed the door behind him and then began to advance towards the chair through the bars of which the dwarf was peering.

As Steerpike advanced with his slender steel in his hand, his eyes were upon his prey but his thoughts were centred upon the candlestick.

His foe could have no idea of how he was within reach of what would burn him up. The three little flames trembled above the melting wax. He had brought them to life, those three dead lumps of tallow. And they were to turn upon him. But not yet.

Steerpike continued his lethal advance. What was there that the cripple could do? For the moment he was partially shielded by the back of the chair. And then, in a voice strangely at variance with the demoniac aspect of his face, for it was as cold as ice, he uttered the one word 'Traitor'.

It was not merely his life he was fighting for. That single word, freezing the air, had revealed what Steerpike had forgotten: that in his adversary he was pitting himself against Gormenghast. Before him he had a living pulse of the immemorial castle.

But what of all this? It merely meant that Steerpike must be careful. That he must keep his distance until the moment in which to make his attack. He continued to advance and then, when another step would have taken him within range of Barquentine's crutch, he side-stepped to the right and speeding to the far end of the table, placed his rapier before him across the littered books and taking his knife from his pocket opened it with a single action and then, as Barquentine turned about in his tracks in order to face his assailant, he sent the sharp thing whipping through the candlelight. As Steerpike had intended it pinned the old man's right hand to the shaft of his crutch. In the moment of Barquentine's surprise and pain, Steerpike leapt on the table and sprang along it. Immediately below him the dwarf plucked at the knife in his blind fury. As he did so, Steerpike, all in a breath, had snatched up the candlestick, and lunging forward, swept the tiny flame across the upturned face. In a moment, the lifeless beard had shone out in sizzling fire and it was but a moment before the rotten rags about the shoulders of the old man were ablaze also.

But again, and this time while in the throes of mortal agony, Barquentine's brain had risen instantaneously to the call which was made upon it. He had no moment to lose. The knife was still in his hand though the crutch had fallen away – but all that was forgotten, as with a superhuman effort, one-legged though he was, he flexed his knee and in a spring caught hold of some portion of Steerpike's clothing. No sooner had he made his first grip, than, with his arms straining themselves to breaking point, and his old heart pounding, he made good his purchase and began to swarm the youth like an ape on fire. By now he had a grip of Steerpike's waist and the flames were beginning to catch the clothing of his young enemy. The searing pain across his face and chest but made him cling the tighter. That he must die, he knew. But the traitor must die with him, and in his agony there was something of joy; joy in the 'rightness' of his revenge.

At the same time, Steerpike was fighting to free himself, clawing at the burning leech, striking upwards with his knees, his face transparent with a deadly mixture of rage, astonishment and desperation.

His clothes, less inflammable than Barquentine's threadbare sacking, were nevertheless alight by now, and across his cheek and throat a flame had scorched his skin to crimson. But the more he struggled to wrench himself away the fiercer seemed the arms that gripped his waist.

Had anyone opened the door they would have seen, at that moment, a young man luminous against the darkness, his feet striking and trampling among the sacred books that littered the table, the body writhing and straining as though demented and they would have seen that his vibrating hands were locked upon the turtle throat of a dwarf on fire: and they would have seen the paroxysm that toppled the combatants off the table's edge so that they fell in a smoking heap to the floor.

Even now in his pain and danger there was room in him for the bitter shame of his failure. Steerpike the arch contriver, the cold and perfect organizer, had bungled the affair. He had been out-generalled by a verminous septuagenarian. But his shame took the form of desperate anger. It whipped him to a feverpitch.

In a kind of spasm, quite diabolical in the access of its ferocity and purpose, he struggled to his knees, and then with a jerk, to his feet. He had let go the throat and he stood swaying a moment, his hands free at his sides, and the pain of his burns so intense that, although he did not know it, he was moaning like something lost. It had nothing to do with his merciless nature, this moaning. It was something physical. It was his body crying. His brain knew nothing about it.

The Master of Ritual clung, like a vampire, at his breast. The old arms were clasped about him. Mixed with the pain in the agonized face, there was an unholy glee. He was burning the traitor with his own flame. He was burning an unbeliever.

But the unbeliever was, for all the fiery hugging of his master, by no means ready for sacrifice however right or deserving his death might be. He had paused only to regain strength. He had dropped his arms only through an abnormal degree of control. He knew that he could not free himself from the clutch of the fanatic. And so for a moment he stood there, upright, his coat half burned away, his head thrust back to keep as great a distance as he could between his face and the flames that rose from the blackening creature that clung like a growth. To be able to stand for a moment under so horrific a duress – to be able to stand, to take a deep breath, and to relax the muscles of his arms demanded an almost inhuman control of the will and the passions.

The circumstances having gone so far beyond his control there was no longer any question of choice. It was no longer a case of killing Barquentine. It was a case of saving himself. His plans had gone so wildly astray that there was no recovery. He was ablaze.

There was only one thing he could do. Saddled as he was, his limbs were disencumbered. He knew that he had only a few moments in which to act. His head swam and a darkness filled him, but he began to run, his burned hands spread out like starfish at his sides, to run in a dizzy curve of weakness to the far end of the room – to where the night was a square of darkness. For a moment they were there, against the starless sky, lit like demons with their own conflagration, and then, suddenly they were gone. Steerpike had hurdled the window-sill and had fallen with his virulent burden into the black waters of the moat below. There were no stars but the moon like a nail-paring floated unsubstantially in the low north. It cast no light upon the earth.

Deep in the horrible waters of the moat the protagonists, their consciousness having left them, still moved together as one thing like some foul subaqueous beast of allegory. Above them the surface water through which they had fallen was sizzling and steam drifted up invisible through the darkness.

When after what he could only recall as his death, Steerpike, his head having at last risen above the surface, found that he was not alone but that something clung to him below the water, he vomited and of a sudden, howled. But the nightmare continued and there was no answer to his howl. He did not waken. And then the excruciating pains of his burns racked him, and he knew it was no dream.

And then he realized what he must do. He must keep that charred and hairless head which kept bobbing against his breast, he must keep it below the water. But it was not easy for him to fasten upon the wrinkled throat. The mud had been churned up about them, and the burden he carried was, like his own hands, coated with slime. The vile arms clung about him with the tenacity of tentacles. That he did not sink like a stone was a wonder; perhaps it was the thickness of the water, or the violent stamping of his feet in the stagnant depth which helped him to keep afloat for long enough.

But gradually, inexorably, he fought the old head backwards, his fierce hands clenched on the gullet strings – he fought it downwards, down into the black water, while bubbles rose and the thick and slapping sound of the agitated water filled up the hollow of the listening night.

There was no knowing how long the old man's face remained under water before Steerpike could feel any loosening of the grip at his waist. To the murderer the act of death was endless. But by degrees the lungs had filled with water and the heart had ceased to beat, and the Hereditary Keeper of the Groan lore and Master of Ritual had slid away into the muddy depths of the ancient moat.

The moon was higher in the sky, was surrounded by a sprinkling of stars. It could not be said that they gave light to the walls and towers that flanked the moat, but a kind of dusk was inlaid upon the inky darkness, a dusk in the shape of walls and towers.

Exhausted and in terrible pain, Steerpike had yet to swim on through the scum and duckweed – to swim on until the slimy walls of the moat gave way on the northern side to a muddy bank. It seemed that the walls on his either side were endless. The foul water got into his throat. The vile weeds clung to his face. It was difficult to see more than a few yards ahead; but all at once he realized that the wall upon his right had given way to a steep and muddy bank.

The water had drawn away what clothes the fire had left. He was naked, covered with burns, half drowned, his body shaking with an icy cold, his brow burning with a feverish heat.

Crawling up the bank, not knowing what he was doing, save that he must find some place of neither fire nor water, he came at last to a patch of level mud where a few rank ferns and mud-plants flourished, and there, as though (now that his affairs were concluded) he could afford to faint, he collapsed into darkness.

And there he lay motionless, very small and naked on the mud, like something lifeless that had been discarded, or like a fish thrown up by the sea over whose minute and stranded body the great cliffs tower, for the walls of Gormenghast rose high above the moat, soaring like cliffs themselves into the upper darkness.

FORTY

WHILE the dust that lay upon the gaunt back of the castle became warm in the sun, and the birds grew drowsy in the shadows of the towers, and while there was little to hear but the droning of the bees as they hovered over the wastes of ivy – at the same time, in the green hush of noon, the spirit of Gormenghast forest held its breath like a diver. There was no sound. Hour followed hour and all things were asleep or in a state of trance. The trunks of the great oaks were blotched with honey-coloured shadows and the prodigious boughs were stretched like the arms of bygone kings and appeared to be heavy with the weight of their gold bangles, the bracelets of the sun. There seemed to be no end to the gold afternoon and then something fell from a high branch, and the faint swish of the leaves through which it passed awoke the region. The stillness had been for the moment punctured, but the wound healed over almost at once.

What was it that had fallen through the silence? Even the tree-cat would have hesitated to drop so far through the green gloom. But it was no cat, but something human that stood dappled with leaf-shaped shadows, a child, with its thick hair hacked off close to its head and the face freckled like a bird's egg. The body, slender, indeed thin, appeared, when the child began to move, to be without weight.

The features of her face were quite nondescript – in fact, empty. It was as though she wore a kind of mask, neither pleasant nor unpleasant – something that hid rather than revealed her mind. And yet, at the same time, although by feature there was nothing to remember, nothing distinctive, yet the whole head was so set upon the neck, the neck so perfectly adjusted upon the slender shoulders, and the movements of those three so expressive in their relationship that it seemed that there was not only nothing lacking, but that for the face to have had a life of its own would have ruined the detached and unearthly quality she possessed.

She stood there for a moment, entirely alone in the dreaming oakwoods and began, with strangely rapid movements of her fingers, to pluck the feathers from a missel-thrush which, during her long fall through the foliage, she had snatched from its branch and throttled in her small fierce hand.

FORTY-ONE

SURROUNDING the outer walls of Gormenghast castle the mud city of the Outer Dwellers lay sprawled in the sun, its thousands of hovels hummocking the earth like molehills. These Dwellers, or Bright Carvers as they were sometimes called, had rituals of their own as sacrosanct as those of the castle itself.

Bitter with poverty and prone to those diseases that thrive on squalor, they were yet a proud though bigoted people. Proud of their traditions, of their power of carving – proud of their very misery, it seemed. For one of their number to have left them and to have become wealthy and famous would have been to them a cause for shame and humiliation. But such a possibility was unthinkable. In their obscurity, their anonymity lay their pride. All else was something lower – saving only the family of the Groans to whom they owed allegiance and under whose patronage they were allowed their hold upon the Outer Walls. When the great sacks of crusts were lowered by ropes from the summit of those Walls, over a thousand at a time making their simultaneous descents, they were received (this time-honoured gesture on the part of the castle) with a kind of derision. It was they, the Bright Carvers, who were honouring the castle; it was they who condescended to unhook the ropes every morning of the year, so that the empty sacks might be hoisted up again. And with every mouthful of these dry crusts (which with the jarl-root of the neighbouring forest composed the beginning and end of their diet) they knew themselves to be conferring an honour upon the castle bakeries.

It was perhaps the pride of the subjugated – a compensatory thing – but it was very real to them. Nor was it built on nothing, for in their carvings alone they showed a genius for colour and for ornament that had no kind of counterpart in the life of the Castle.

Taciturn and bitter as they were in their ancient antipathies yet their hottest enmity was directed, not against any that lived *within* the outer walls, but against those of their own kind who in any way made light of their own customs. At the heart of their ragged and unconventional life there was an orthodoxy as hard as iron. Their conventions were ice-bound. To move among them for a day without forewarning of their innumerable conventions would be to invite disaster. Side by side with an outrageous lack of the normal physical decencies was an ingrained prudery, vicious and unswervingly cruel.

For a child to be illegitimate was for that child to be loathed, as though it were a diseased thing. Not only this. A bastard babe was *feared*. There was a strong belief that in some way a love-child was evil. The mother would invariably be ostracized but it was only the babe who was to be feared – it was, in fact, a witch in embryo.

But it was never killed. For to kill, it would be only to kill the body. Its ghost would haunt the killer.

In a lane of flies that wound beneath a curve of the Outer Walls, the dusk began to settle down like pollen. It thickened by degrees until the lane and the irregular roofs of reeds and mud were drowned in it.

Along the wall of the lane or alleyway a line of beggars squatted. It seemed that they were growing out of the dust they sat in. It covered their ankles and their haunches. It was like a dead, grey sea. It was as though the tide were in – a tide of soft dust. It was voluptuously fine and feathery.

And in this common dove-coloured dust, they sat, their backs to the clay walls of a sun-warmed hovel. They had these luxuries, the soft dust and the warm fly-filled air.

As they sat there silently, while the night descended, their eyes were fixed upon those few figures on the other side of the alley, who, their carving over for the day, were gathering up their chisels, rasps and mallets and returning with them to their various huts.

Until a year ago there had been no need for the Bright Carvers to return their sculpture to the safety of their homes. It had remained all night in the open. It was never touched. No, not the meanest vandal of them all would dare to touch or move by an inch the work of another.

But now there was a difference. The carvings were no longer safe. Something horrible had happened. And so the beggars by the wall continued to stare as the removal of the wood sculpture proceeded. It had been going on now for twelve months, evening after evening, but they were not yet used to it. They could not grasp it. All their lives they had known the moonlight on the deserted lanes, and, flanking these lanes the wooden carvings like sentinels at every door. But now, after dark, the heart had gone out of the streets – a vibrancy, a beauty had departed from the alleys.

And so they still watched, at dusk, with a kind of hapless wonder, the younger men as they struggled to return the often massive and weighty horses with their manes like clusters of frozen sea foam – or the dappled gods of Gormenghast forest with their heads so strangely tilted. They watched all this and knew that a blight had come upon the one activity for which the Dwellers lived.

They said nothing, these beggars, but as they sat in the soft dust, there was, at back of each one's mind, the image of a child. Of an illegitimate child, a pariah, a thing of not yet twelve years old, but a raven, a snake, witch, all the same, a menace to them all and to their carvings.

It had happened first about a year ago, that first midnight attack, secret, silent and of a maliciousness quite terrible.

A great piece of sculpture had been found at dawn, its face in the dust, its body scarred with long jagged knife wounds, and a number of small carvings had been stolen. Since that first evil and silent assault a score of works had been defaced and a hundred carvings stolen, carvings no bigger than a hand, but of a rare craftsmanship, rhythm and colour. There was no doubt as to who it was. It was the Thing. Shunned as a bastard ever since the day of her mother's suicide, this child had been a thorn in the flesh of the Dwellers. Running wild, like an animal, and as untameable; a thief as though by nature, she was, even before she ran away, a legend, a thing of evil.

She was always alone. It seemed unthinkable that she could be companioned. There was no soft spot in her self-sufficiency. She stole for her food, moving shadowlike in the night, her face utterly expressionless, her limbs as light and rapid as a switch of hazel. Or she would disappear completely for months on end, but then, suddenly return and darting from roof to roof, blister the evening air with sharp cries of derision.

The Dwellers cursed the day when the Thing was born; the Thing that could not speak but could run, it was rumoured, up the stem of a branchless tree; could float for a score of yards at a time on the wings of a high wind.

They cursed the mother that bore her – Keda, the dark girl, who had been summoned to the castle and who had fed the infant Titus from her breast. They cursed the mother, they cursed the child – but they were afraid – afraid of the supernatural and were oppressed with a sense of awe – that the tameless Thing should be the foster sister of the Earl, Lord Groan of Gormenghast, Titus the Seventy-seventh.

FORTY-TWO

WHEN Steerpike had come out of his faint and when his consciousness of the horrors through which he had passed returned to him, as they did in a flash of pain, for he was raw with the searings of the fire, he got to his feet like a cripple and staggered through the night until he came at last to the Doctor's doorway. There, after beating at the door with his feverish forehead, for his hands were scalded, he fainted again where he stood and knew no more until three days later when he found himself staring at the ceiling of a small room with green walls.

For a long while he could recall nothing, but bit by bit the fragments of that violent evening pieced themselves together until he had the whole picture.

He turned his head with difficulty and saw that the door was to his left. To his right was a fireplace, and ahead of him and near the ceiling was a fair sized window over which the blinds were partially drawn. By the dusky look in the sky he guessed it to be either dawn or evening. Part of a tower could be seen through the gap of the curtains, but he could not recognize it. He had no idea in what part of the castle he was lying.

He dropped his eyes and noticed that he was bandaged from head to foot, and as though he needed this reminder, the pain of his burns became more acute. He shut his eyes and tried to breathe evenly.

Barquentine was dead. He had killed him. But now, at the moment when he, Steerpike, should have been indispensable, being the sole confidant of the old custodian of the law, he was lying here inert, helpless, useless. This must be offset, this derangement of his plans, by quick and authoritative action. His body could do little but his brains were active and resourceful.

But there was a difference. His mind was as acute as ever, it is true, but, unknown to himself, there was something that had been added to his temperament, or perhaps it was that something had left him.

His poise had been so shattered that a change had come about – a change that he knew nothing of, for his logical mind was able to reassure him that whatever the magnitude of his blunder in Barquentine's room, yet the shame was his alone, the mortification was private – he had only lost face to himself for no one had seen the old man's quickness.

To have been so burned was too high a price to pay for glory. But glory would assuredly be his. The graver his condition the rarer his bravery in attempting to save the old man's life from the flames. His prestige had suffered nothing, for Barquentine's mouth was filled with the mud of the moat and could bear no witness.

But there was a *change* all the same, and when he was woken an hour later by a sound in the room, and when on opening his eyes he saw a flame in the fireplace, he started upright with a cry, the sweat pouring down his face, and his bandaged hands trembled at his sides.

For a long while he lay shuddering. A sensation such as he had never experienced before, a kind of fear was near him, if not on him. He fought it away with all his reserves of undoubted courage. At last he fell again into a fitful sleep, and when some while later he awoke he knew before he opened his eyes that he was not alone.

Dr Prunesquallor was standing at the end of his bed. His back was to Steerpike, his head was tilted up and he was staring through the window at the tower that was now mottled with sunlight and the shadows of flying clouds. The morning had come.

Steerpike opened his eyes and on seeing the Doctor, closed them again. In a moment or two he had decided what to do and turning his head to and fro slowly on the pillow, as though in restless sleep –

'I tried to save you,' he whispered, 'O Master, I tried to save you,' and then he moaned.

Prunesquallor turned around on his heel. His bizarre and chiselled face was without that drollery of expression which was so typical of him. His lips were set.

'You tried to save *who*?' said Prunesquallor very sharply as though to elicit some involuntary reply from the sleeping figure.

But Steerpike made a confused sound in his throat, and then in a stronger voice . . .

'I tried . . . I tried.'

He turned again on the pillow and then as though this had awakened him he opened his eyes.

For a few moments he stared quite blankly and then –

'Doctor,' he said, 'I couldn't hold him.'

Prunesquallor made no immediate reply but took the swathed creature's pulse – listened to the heart and then after a while – 'You will tell me about it tomorrow,' he said.

'Doctor,' said Steerpike, 'I would rather tell you now. I am weak and I can only whisper, but I know where Barquentine is. He lies dead in the mud outside the window of his room.'

'And how did he get there, Master Steerpike?'

'I will tell you.' Steerpike lifted his eyes, loathing the bland physician – loathing him with an irrational intensity. It was as though his power of hatred had drawn fresh fuel from the death of Barquentine. But his voice was meek enough.

'I will tell you, Doctor,' he whispered. 'I will tell you all I know.' His head fell back on the pillow and he closed his eyes.

'Yesterday, or last week, or a month ago, for I do not know how long I have been lying here insensible – I entered Barquentine's room about eight o'clock, which was my habit every evening. It was at that hour that he would give me my orders for the next day. He was sitting on his high chair and as I entered he was lighting a candlestick. I do not know why but he started at my entrance, as though I had surprised him, but when he turned his head back again, after cursing me – but he meant no harm to me for all his irritability – he misjudged his distance from the flame, his beard swept across it and a moment later was alight. I rushed to him but his hair and clothing had already caught. There were no rugs or curtains in the room with which to smother the fire. There was no water. But I beat the flames with my hands. But the fire grew fiercer and in his pain and panic he caught hold of me and I began to burn.'

The pupils of the young man's dark eyes dilated as he recounted the partial fabrication, for Barquentine's grip upon him had been no dream, and his brow began to sweat again, and a terrible authenticity appeared to give weight to his words.

'I could not escape, Doctor; I was caught and held against his burning body. Every moment the fire grew fiercer – and my burns more terrible. There was only one thing I could do to get away. I knew I must reach the water that lay below his window. And so I ran. I ran with his arms gripping me. I ran to the window and jumped into the moat – and there in the cold black water, his hands at last gave way. I could not hold him up. It was all I could do to reach the side of the moat, and there, I think I fainted – and when I came round, I found I was naked and I came to your door . . . but the moat must be dragged and the old man must be found . . . in the name of decency he must be found and given a true burial. It is for me to carry on his work. I . . . I . . . cannot tell . . . you more . . . I am . . . not . . .'

He turned his head on the pillow, and in spite of his pains fell asleep. He had played his card and could afford to rest.

FORTY-THREE

'My dear,' said Bellgrove, 'it is surely not for your betrothed to be kept waiting *quite* so long even though he is only the Headmaster of Gormenghast. Why on earth must you always be so late? Good grief, Irma, it isn't as though I'm a green youth who finds it romantic to be drizzled on by the stinking sky. Where have you been for pity's sake?'

'I am inclined not to *answer* you!' cried Irma. 'The humiliation of it! Is it nothing to you that I should take a pride in my appearance – that I should make myself beautiful for you? You *man*, you. It breaks one's heart.'

'I do not complain lightly, my love,' replied Bellgrove. 'As I say, I cannot stand bad weather like a younger man. This was your idea of a place of rendezvous. It could hardly have been worse chosen, with not so much as a shrub to squat under. Rheumatism is on its way. My feet are soaked. And why? Because my fiancée, Irma Prunesquallor, a lady of quite exceptional talents in other directions – they always *are* in *other* directions – who has the entire day in which to pluck at her eyebrows, harvest her sheaves of long grey hair, and so on, cannot organize herself

– or else has grown shall we say *casual* in regard to her suitor? Shall we say *casual*, my dear?'

'Never!' cried Irma. 'O never! my dear one. It is only my longing that you should find me worthy that keeps me at my toilet. O my dearest, you must forgive me. You must forgive me.'

Bellgrove gathered his gown about him in great swathes. He had been staring into the gloomy sky while he had spoken but now, at last he turned his noble face to her. The landscape all about them was hazy with rain. The nearest tree was a grey blur two fields away.

'You ask me to forgive you,' said Bellgrove. He closed his eyes. 'And so I do, and so I do. But remember, Irma, that a punctual wife would please me. Perhaps you could practise a little so that when the time comes I will have nothing to complain of. And now, we will forget about it, shall we?'

He turned his head from her, for he had not yet learned to admonish her without grinning weakly with the joy of it. And so, with his face averted, he bared his rotten teeth at a distant hedgerow.

She took his arm and they began to walk.

'My dear one,' she said.

'My love?' said Bellgrove.

'It is my turn to complain, is it not?'

'It is your turn, my love!' (He lifted his leonine head and shook the rain happily from his mane.)

'You won't be cross, dear?'

He raised his eyebrows and closed his eyes.

'I will not be cross, Irma. What is it that you wish to say?'

'It's your neck, dearest.'

'My neck? What of it!'

'It is very dirty, dear one. It has been for weeks . . . do you think . . .'

But Bellgrove had stiffened at her side. He bared his teeth in a snarl of impotence.

'O stinking hell,' he muttered. 'O stinking, rotten hell.'

FORTY-FOUR

Mr Flay had been sitting for over an hour at the entrance to his cave. The air was breathless and the three small clouds in the soft grey sky had been there all day.

His beard had grown very long and his hair that was once cropped close to the skull was now upon his shoulders. His skin had darkened with the sun and the last few years of hardship had brought new lines to his face.

He was by now a part of the woods, his eyesight sharp as a bird's, and his hearing as quick. His footsteps had become noiseless. The cracking of his knee-joints had disappeared. Perhaps the heat of the summer had baked the trouble out of them for his clothes being as ragged as foliage his knees were for the most part bare to the sun.

He must surely have been made for the woods, so congruously had he become dissolved into a world of branches, ferns and streams. And yet for all his mastery of the woods, for all that he had been absorbed into the wilderness of the endless trees, as though he were but another branch – for all this, his thoughts were never far from that gaunt pile of masonry that, ruinous and forbidding as it was, was nevertheless, the only home he had ever known.

But Flay, for all his longing to return to his birthplace was no sentimentalist in exile. His thoughts when they turned to the castle were by no means in the nature of reveries. They were hard, uneasy, speculative thoughts which far from returning to his early memories of the place were concerned with the nature of things as they were. No less than Barquentine he was a traditionalist to his marrow. He knew in his heart that things were going wrong.

What chance had he had of taking the pulse of the halls and towers? Apart from the marshlight of his intuition and the native gloom of his temperament, on what else was he basing his suspicions? Was it merely his ingrained pessimism and the fear which had understandably grown stronger since his banishment, that, with himself away, the castle was the weaker?

It was this, and very little more. And yet had his fears been mere speculations he would never have made, during the last twenty days, his three unlawful journeys. For he had moved through the midnight corridors of the place – and although as yet he had made no concrete discoveries, he had become aware almost at once of a change. Something had happened, or something was happening which was evil and subversive.

He knew full well that the risks involved in his being found in the castle after his banishment were acute, and that his chances of discovering in the darkness of sleeping halls and corridors, the cause of his apprehension, was remote indeed. Yet he had dared to flaunt the letter of the Groan law in order, in his solitary way, to find whether or not its spirit, as he feared, was sickening.

And now, as he sat half hidden among the ferns that grew at the door of his cave, turning over in his mind those incidents that had in one way or another, over the past years, caused his suspicions of foul play to fructify, he was suddenly aware that he was being watched.

He had heard no sound, but the extra sense he had developed in the woods gave warning. It was as though something had tapped him between his shoulder-blades.

Instantly his eyes swept the scene before him and he saw them at once, standing motionlessly at the edge of a wood away to his right. He recognized them instantaneously although the girl had grown almost out of recognition. Was it possible that they did not recognize him? There was no doubt that they were staring at him. He had forgotten how different he must look, especially to Fuchsia, with his long hair, his beard and ragged clothes.

But now, as they began to run in his direction, he stood up and began to make his way towards them over the rocks.

It was Fuchsia who first recognized the gaunt exile. Just over twenty years old, she stood there before him, a swarthy, strangely melancholy girl, full of love and fear and courage and anger and tenderness. These things were so raw in her breast that it seemed unfair that anyone should be so hotly charged.

To Flay, she was a revelation. Whenever he had thought of her it had always been as a child, and here suddenly she stood before him, a woman, flushed, excited, her eyes upon his face, her hands upon her hips, as she regained her breath.

Mr Flay lowered his head in deference to his visitor.

'Ladyship,' he said – but before Fuchsia could answer Titus came up, his hair in his eyes.

'I told you!' he panted. 'I told you I'd find him! I told you he had a beard and there's the dam he made and there's his cave over there and that's where I slept and where we cooked and . . .' he paused for breath, and then . . . 'Hullo, Mr Flay. You look wonderful and wild!'

'Ah!' said Flay. 'Most likely, lordship, ragged life and no doubt of it. More days than dinners, lordship.'

'Oh, Mr Flay,' said Fuchsia. 'I am so happy to see you again – you were always so kind to me. Are you all right out here, all alone?'

'Of course he's all right!' said Titus. 'He's a sort of savage. Aren't you Mr Flay?'

'Like enough, lordship,' said Flay.

'O, you were too small and you can't remember, Titus,' said Fuchsia. 'I remember it all. Mr Flay was father's first servant – above them all, weren't you, Mr Flay – until he disappeared . . .'

'I know,' said Titus. 'I've heard it all in Bellgrove's class – they told me all about it.'

'They don't know anything,' said Flay. 'They don't know anything, ladyship.' He had turned to Fuchsia and then, dropping his head forward again, 'Humbly invite you to my cave,' he said, 'for rest, for shade and fresh water.'

Mr Flay led the way to his cave, and when they had passed through the entrance and Fuchsia had been shown the double chimney and they had drunk deeply from the spring, for they were hot and thirsty, Titus lay down under the ferny wall of the inner cave and their ragged host sat a little way apart. His arms were folded about his shanks; his bearded chin was on his knees – while his gaze was fixed upon Fuchsia.

She, on her side, while noticing his childlike scrutiny, gave him no cause to feel embarrassed, for she smiled when their eyes met, but kept her gaze wandering about the walls and ceiling, or turning to Titus asked him whether he had noticed this or that on his last visit.

But a time came when a silence fell upon the cave. It was the kind of silence that becomes hard to break. But it was broken in the end, and, strangely enough, by Mr Flay himself, the least forthcoming of the three.

'Ladyship . . . Lordship,' he said.

'Yes, Mr Flay?' said Fuchsia.

'Been away, banished, many years, ladyship,' he opened his hard-lipped mouth as though to continue, but had to close it again for the lack of a phrase. But after a while he commenced again. 'Lost touch, Lady Fuchsia, but forgive me – must ask you questions.'

'Of course, Mr Flay, what sort of questions?'

'I know the sort,' said Titus – 'about what's happened since I was last here and what's been discovered, isn't it, Mr Flay? And about Barquentine's being dead and . . .'

'Barquentine dead?' Flay's voice was sudden and hard.

'Oh yes,' said Titus. 'He was burned to death, you know, wasn't he, Fuchsia?'

'Yes, Mr Flay. Steerpike tried to save him.'

'Steerpike?' muttered the long, ragged, motionless figure.

'Yes,' said Fuchsia. 'He is very ill. I've been to see him.'

'You haven't!' said Titus.

'I certainly have and I shall go again. His burns are terrible.'

'I don't want you to see him,' said Titus.

'Why not?' the blood was beginning to mount to her cheeks.

'Because he's . . .'

But Fuchsia interrupted him.

'What . . . do . . . you . . . know . . . about . . . him?' she said very softly and slowly, but with a shake in her voice – 'Is it a crime for him to be more brilliant than we could ever be? Is it his fault that he is disfigured?' And then in a rush – 'or that he's so brave?'

She turned her eyes to her brother and seeing there, in his features something infinitely close to her, something that seemed to be a reflection of her own heart, or as though she was looking into her own eyes –

'I'm sorry,' she said, 'but don't let's talk about him.'

But this is just what Flay wanted to do. 'Ladyship,' he said. 'Barquentine's son – does he understand – has he been trained – Warden of the Documents – Keeper of the Groan law – is all well?'

'No one can find his son, or whether he ever had a son,' said Fuchsia. 'But all is well. For several years now Barquentine has been training Steerpike.'

Flay rose suddenly to his feet as though some invisible cord had plucked at him from above, and as he rose he turned his head to hide his anger.

'No! No!' he cried to himself, but there was no sound. Then he spoke over his shoulder.

'But Steerpike is ill, ladyship?'

Fuchsia stared up at him. Neither she nor Titus could understand why he had suddenly got to his feet.

'Yes,' said Fuchsia. 'He was burned when he tried to save Barquentine who was on fire – and he's been in bed for months.'

'How much longer, ladyship?'

'The doctor says he can get up in a week.'

'But the Ritual! The instructions; who has given them? Who has directed the Procedure – day by day – interpreted the Documents – O God!' said Flay, suddenly unable to control himself any longer. 'Who has made the symbols come to life? Who has turned the wheels of Gormenghast?'

'It is all right, Mr Flay. It's all right. He does not spare himself. He was not trained for nothing. He is covered in bandages but he directs everything. And all from his sickbed. Every morning. Thirty or forty men are there at a time. He interviews them all. Hundreds of books are at his side – and the walls are covered with maps and diagrams. There is no one else who can do it. He is working all the time, while he lies there. He is working with his brain.'

But Flay struck his hand against the wall of the cave as though to let out his anger.

'No! No!' he said. 'He's no Master of Ritual, ladyship, not for always. No love, ladyship, no love for Gormenghast.'

'I wish there wasn't any Master of Ritual,' said Titus.

'Lordship,' said Flay after a pause, 'you are only a boy. No knowledge. But you will learn from Gormenghast. Sourdust and Barquentine, both burned up,' he continued, hardly knowing that he spoke aloud . . . 'father and son . . . father and son . . .'

'Maybe I'm only a boy,' said Titus hotly, 'but if you know how we've come here today, by the secret passage under the ground (which I found by myself, didn't I, Fuchsia?) then . . .' but Titus had to stop for the sentence was too involved for him.

'But do you know,' he continued, starting afresh, 'we've been in the dark, with candles, sometimes crawling but mostly walking all the way from the castle, except for the last mile where the tunnel comes out, only you'd never know it, under a bank, like the mouth of a badger's set – not too far from here – on the other side of the wood where you first saw us, so it was difficult to find your cave, Mr Flay, because last time I came was mostly on horseback and then through the oakwood – and, O Mr Flay, was it a dream or did I really see a flying thing and did I tell you about it? I sometimes think it was a dream.'

'So it was,' said Flay. 'Nightmare; and no doubt of it.' He seemed to have no desire to talk to Titus about the 'flying thing'.

'Secret tunnel to the castle, lordship?'

'Yes,' said Titus, 'secret and black and smelling of earth and sometimes there are beams of wood to keep the roof up and ants everywhere.'

Flay turned his eyes to Fuchsia as though for confirmation.

'It's true,' said Fuchsia.

'And close by, ladyship?'

'Yes,' said Fuchsia. 'In the woods across the near valley. That's where the tunnel comes out.'

Flay stared at them both in turn. The news of the underground passage seemed to have had a great effect on him, although they could not think why – for although to them it had been a very real and forbidding adventure, yet from bitter experience they knew that what was wonderful to them was usually of little interest to the adult world.

But Mr Flay was hungry for every detail.

'Where did the passage start from within the castle? Had they been seen in the corridor of statues? Could they find their way back to this corridor when the tunnel opened out into that silent and lifeless world of halls and passageways? Could they take him to the bank in the wood where the tunnel ended?'

Of course they could. At once – and thrilled that a grownup, for Fuchsia never thought of herself as one, could be as excited by their discovery as they were themselves – they were soon on their way to the wood.

Flay had almost at once seen more in their discovery than Fuchsia and Titus could have guessed. If it were so, that within a few minutes of his cave, there was, as it were, for Flay, an open door that led into the heart of his ancient home, a road which he could tread, if he wished, when the broad daylight lay upon the woods and fields five feet above his head, then surely his power to root out whatever evil was lurking in Gormenghast, to trace it to its source, was enormously increased. For it had been no easy thing to enter the castle unobserved and to make, sometimes by moonlight, those long journeys above ground from his cave to the Outer Walls, and from them across the quadrangles and open spaces to the inner buildings and the particular rooms and passageways he had in mind.

But if what they said was true, he would, at any time of the day or night, be able to emerge from behind that statue in the corridor of carvings, to find the gaunt anatomy of the place laid bare about him.

FORTY-FIVE

THE days flowed on, and the walls of Gormenghast grew chill to the touch as the summer gave way to autumn, and autumn to a winter both dark and icy. For long periods of time the winds blew night and day, smashing the glass of windows, dislodging masonry, whistling and roaring between towers and chimneys and over the castle's back.

And then, no less awesome, the wind would suddenly drop and silence would grip the domain. A silence that was unbreakable, for the bark of a dog, or the sudden clang of a pail, or the far cry of a boy seemed only *real* in that they accentuated the universal stillness through which, for a moment, they rose, like the heads of fish, from freezing water – only to sink again and to leave no trace.

In January the snow came down in such a way that those who watched it from behind countless windows could no longer believe in the sharper shapes that lay under the blurred pall, or the colours that were sunk in the darkness of that whiteness. The air itself was smothered with flakes the size of a child's fist, and the terrain bulged with the submerged features of a landscape half-remembered.

In the wide, white fields that surrounded the castle, the birds lay dead or leaned sideways stiffening for death. Here and there was the movement of a bird limping, or the last frantic fluttering of a small ice-gummed wing.

From the castle windows it seemed that the dazzling snow had been scattered with small coals, or that the fields had become smallpox'd with the winter-murder'd hosts. There was no clear stretch of snow untriturated by this widespread death; no drift without its graveyard.

Against the blind brilliance of their background, the birds, whatever their natural plumage, appeared as black as jet, and differed only in their silhouette, whose meticulous contours might have been scored with a needle so exquisite was the drawing of their beaks, like thorns, the hairs of their feathers, their delicate claws and heads.

It seemed that, upon the vast funeral linen of the snowscape, each bird of all these hosts had signed, with an exquisite and tragic artistry, the proof of its own death, had signed it in a language at once undecipherable and eloquent – a hieroglyphic of fantastic beauty.

And the snow that had killed them, covered them; covered them with a touch that was the more terrible for its very tenderness. But for all its layer on layer of blinding powder, there were always birds upon the point of death – always this scattered, jet-black multitude. And on every side there were still those that limped, or stood shivering, or pushed their agonizing way, breast deep through the voluminous and lethal pall, leaving behind them their little trenches in the snow to show where they had been.

And yet, for all this mortality, the castle was full of birds. The Countess, her heart heavy in the knowledge of so much thirst and pain, had taken every opportunity to encourage the wildfowl to enter. No sooner had the ice formed in the hundreds of baths and basins set about the castle than it was broken again. Meat, bread crumbs and grain were laid in trails to encourage the birds to enter the warmer air within the castle. And yet, in spite of these enticements (and, fearless with hunger, thousands of birds, including owls, heron and even birds of prey were to be found within the walls), the castle was yet surrounded with the dead and dying. The severity of the weather had made of the castle a focal point. Not only had the bird-life of the immediate region been drawn to Gormenghast, but the forests and moors of far distant places had become empty. The sheer numbers of these migratory birds, descending snow-blind, famished and deadly weary upon the castle – descending hourly, out of the snow-thick sky, was sufficient for so great a death-roll, even though Gormenghast was open sanctuary.

The Countess had proclaimed (to the great inconvenience of those concerned) the dining hall to be their hospital. There, huge, red-haired and solitary, she moved among them, nursing them back to strength. Branches of trees were brought in and propped against the walls. The tables were turned upside down so that those birds that cared to, could perch upon the upturned legs. After some while the place was loud with birdsong, with the strident shouting of crows and jackdaws, and with a hundred various thin or mellow voices.

What birds could be saved from the snow were saved, but it lay too deep and soft for it to be possible for any rescuing beyond the reach of an outstretched hand from a low window.

For a month or more the castle was snowbound. A number of the doors that opened on the outside world had been broken by the piled up weight. Of those that stood the strain, none were usable. Lights burned everywhere within the walls of Gormenghast, for every window was either boarded up or heavily coated.

What Mr Flay would have done had the underground tunnel never been discovered, or had Titus never told him of it, it is hard to say. The drifts about his cave were of such dangerous and voluminous dimensions, that it is doubtful whether he could have escaped being drawn sooner or later out of his depth. Apart from this, his chances of surviving the cruel cold, and of keeping himself from starving, would have been slender, for all his knowledge.

But all these problems were solved by the existence of the tunnel. It was now a commonplace for him to make his way, a candle in his hand, along its earth-smelling length, with its miles of roots and its floor littered with the skulls and bones of small animals. For many parts of the tunnel had been the retreat of foxes, rodents and vermin of all kinds. It had been used both as a refuge from such weather as they were now experiencing and from their foes. His candle, held at arm's length before him, would light up familiar root formations that told him of a spinney overhead, or would disclose the secret cities of the ants.

Free of snow and invaluable as it was as a means of gaining access to the castle, yet the darkness was foul with death and decay, and there was no cause for Flay to linger on those long and friendless journeys below ground.

On the first occasion that he had emerged at the castle end of the tunnel and had followed the passageway and had come upon the outskirts of that region of lifeless halls and corridors, and when he had moved further into the silence, as Titus had done, he had felt something of the awe that had so terrified the boy and he had lifted his bony shoulders up to his ears and thrust his jaw forward as his eyes turned this way and that as though he were being threatened by some invisible foe.

But when after a dozen daylight journeys he had explored a section of the deserted tract to his satisfaction, he retained no vestige of the apprehension that first affected him.

On the contrary, he began to make the silent halls peculiarly his own, in the way that he had unconsciously identified himself with the mood of Gormenghast forest.

It was not in his nature to proceed hot-foot upon his quest for the castle's evil. These things could not be hurried. He must establish his position as he went along.

And so (after he had found the few steps that led up to the rear of the monument in the corridors of carvings), he confined his midnight journeys, for the first few weeks, to discovering what changes had taken place since he was last in Gormenghast, in the nocturnal habits of the populace. His life in the woods had taught him patience and had made even more remarkable that power, which he had always had, of losing himself against his background. Saving for broad daylight he had no need to hide; he had only to stand still and he was absorbed into a wall, into a shadow or into rotten woodwork. When he lowered his head, his hair and beard were but another cobweb in the gloom, and his rags the sunless hart's-tongue that flourished in the dánk grey corridors.

It was a strange experience for him to watch, from one point of vantage or another, the familiar faces he had once known so well. Sometimes they would pass within a few feet of him, some a little older, some a little younger, some a little different from what he remembered; others, who were youths or boys when he was exiled, now hardly recognizable.

But for all his ability to conceal himself, he took no risks, and it was a long time before he made his long midnight journeys of reconnaissance and began to discover where almost everyone of interest to him was likely to be found at various hours of the day or night.

His late master's room had never been opened since his death. Flay had noticed this with grim approval. He had gazed down at the floor outside Sepulchrave's door, where, for over twenty years, he stretched himself for sleep. And he had looked along the corridor and the dreadful night returned to his mind – the night when the earl had walked in his sleep, and had later given himself up to the owls – and the night when he, Flay, had fought the chef of Gormenghast and put him to the sword.

And Flay was forced to turn himself into both a thief and a hoarder. This gave him little pleasure, but was necessary in order that he should keep alive at all. Within a short time he had discovered how to enter the cat-room through the door of a loft, and to arrive at the kitchen by way of the Stone Lanes.

It had become an absurdity for him to make his return journey every morning along the tunnel and to spend the day in his cave. There was little he could do at the cave surrounded as it was with the deep snow-drifts. He could neither hunt for food nor gather enough fuel with which to warm himself. But in the Lifeless Halls there was all that he needed.

He had come across a small room, voluptuously soft with dust; a small, square place with a carved mantelpiece and an open grate. There were several chairs, a bookcase and a walnut table on which, beneath the dust, the silver, glass and crockery were laid out for two.

It was here that Flay established himself. His larder consisted of little more than bread and meat, fresh supplies of which were always plentiful in the Great Kitchen.

He took no advantage of the ample opportunities he had to vary his diet. As for his drinking water, it was only necessary for him to make his way at any hour after midnight and dip his iron can into the rain-water of a near-by cistern.

Judging by the distances he had to cover during his journeys to and fro among the empty halls, and judging in particular by the distance between the room with the fireplace and the opening in the corridor of carvings (the only entrance he had found to the world he had previously known), he knew that lighting fires in his room involved no risk. Had smoke, for sake of argument, been *seen* to rise into the air above a forgotten tract of the castle and were it to have caused any interest, it would have been as easy for the hypothetical observer to have found the chimney and then to have found a way into the compartment, fathoms below, as for a frog to play the fiddle.

There, on the bitter winter evenings, Mr Flay enjoyed a comfort he had never experienced before. Had his exile in the woods not inured him to loneliness, then he must surely have found these long days insupportable. But isolation was now a part of him.

The silence of the Lifeless Halls, like the silence of the snowbound world outside, was limitless. It was a kind of death. The very extent of the hollow expanses, the uncharted labyrinth that made, as it were, the silence visible, was something to raise the hairs upon the neck of any but those long used to loneliness. And Mr Flay, in spite of his numerous expeditions through this dead world, this forgotten realm of Gormenghast, was nevertheless unable to locate its boundaries. It is true that after a long search, guided to some extent by Titus' instructions, he had found the steps that led up the corridor of carvings, but save for this and the few locked doors through which he had heard voices, he had found no other frontier points between his world and theirs.

But in the small hours of one morning, as he returned to his room after a raid upon the kitchen, something happened which turned the rest of his winter into something less isolated but more terrible. He had left the corridor of carvings a mile or more behind, and was deep in his own realm, when he decided that instead of taking his usual path along the narrow and extended passageway to the east, he would explore an alternative corridor which, he imagined, would in its own good time lead to his own district.

As he proceeded he made, upon the wall, following his usual custom, the rough marks with white chalk which had more than once helped him to find his way back to familiar ground.

After about an hour of twisting and turning, of crossing the open junctions of radiating alleyways, of making a hundred arbitrary choices between this entrance and that, this winding descent and that cold incline to a wider passageway – he began to sweat with fear at the very thought of having taken no precautions for his return journey. He knew that he would never have found his way back without the chalk marks. Suddenly he began to feel hungry. At the same time, noticing that his candle was burning low, he drew another from the half-dozen or more that were always in his belt, and sitting down on the floor, placed his freshly lit candle carefully on the ground before him, and opening a long, narrow-bladed knife, began to cut himself a slice of bread.

To his right and left the darkness was as thick as ink. He sat illumined within the aura of candle flame, his face and rags and hands and hair dramatically lit. Behind him on the wall his shadow hovered heavily. He had stretched out his legs before him and was about to sink his teeth for the second time into the bread when he heard the peal of laughter.

Had it not been for its terrible strength and for the fact that it came from *behind* him – from the other side of the wall against which he leaned – he would have had no option but to recognize it as a cry of madness in his own brain – something that he had heard with the ears of his mind.

But there was no question of this. It had nothing to do with him, or his imagination; he was not mad. But he knew that he was in the presence of madness. For the demoniacal cry or howl was something that brought Flay to his feet as though he were drawn upwards on a fish-hook – something that took him, without his knowing that he had moved, to the opposite side of the passage where, flattened against the wall as though at bay, and with his head lowered he stared at the cold bricks against which he had been leaning, as though the wall itself were affected by the lunacy it was hiding and was watching him, its every brick deranged.

Mr Flay could hear his sweat splashing on the stones at his feet. His mouth was leather-dry. His heart was thumping like a drum. And he had nothing to see. Only the candlelight shining steadily at the base of the opposite wall.

And then it came again, with a kind of double note – almost as though, whatever throat it was that was giving vent to this ghastly laughter, was curiously formed – as though it were able to throw out two voices at once.

There was no question of an echo for there was no repetition and no over-lapping – but a kind of duplex horror.

This time, the high pealing note tailed off into a thin whine, but even in this ghostly termination there was the two-fold quality, the terrible, petrifying sense of double madness.

For some while after silence had returned, Mr Flay could not move. He had been struck. His sense of privacy had been shattered; his inability to rationalize and make sense out of the small hours was like an insult, an insult hurled against his narrow but proud mind. And his fear, his naked fear of something he could not see, but something which was within a few yards of him – it was this that froze his limbs.

But the silence continued and there was no repetition, and at last he picked the candle from the floor, and with more than one glance behind him, he moved rapidly back the way he had come, following the chalk marks until at last he arrived at the fateful parting of the ways.

Thereafter he was on his own ground and he strode it without hesitation until he arrived at his room.

It was, of course, impossible to let the matter rest. The enigmatic horror of that laughter was with him all the time, and no sooner had the sun risen on the following day than the grim place drew him. It was not that he wished to indulge himself with the vile thrill of a repetition, but rather that the mystery should be brought forward into the rational daylight, and that whatever it was, beast or human, it must stand revealed, for his deepest interests were those of the one-time first servant of Gormenghast – of a loyalist who could not bear to think that in the ancient castle there were forces or elements at work, happenings that were apart from the ceremonial life, secrets and practices that, for all he knew, were deadly poison in the castle's body.

It was his intention to explore further along the terrifying passage and if possible to double back down some parallel artery when opportunity offered, and so discover if he could some clue to what lay on the other side of the wall.

And this is what he did but with no success. Day after day he threaded his way through the cold brick lanes crossing and re-crossing his own tracks, losing himself a score of times a day – returning over and over again to the original corridor for reference – unable to comprehend the tortuous character of the architecture. Every now and again, on returning to the place where he had heard the wild laughter he listened, but there was never any sound but the beating of his own heart.

There seemed no other way for him but to come again to that dread place, not in the daylight, but at the selfsame time as before, when the small hours of the morning sucked the courage from heart and limb. If he should hear it again, that crazed laughter, and if it was repeated and repeated, then with that sound to guide him it was possible that he could run to earth, in the darkness, what had foiled him by day.

And so, fighting down his terror, he set out in the icy blackness of the early hours. He came eventually to the brick corridor; and when he was still some distance away he heard a sound of crying and shouting. And when he was nearer still, a loud calling to and fro, as if something was calling to itself for it seemed to be the same voice that was answering.

But there was fear in the voice, or voices, and what struck Mr Flay most, as he listened with his ear to the wall, was that the cries were weaker than before. Whatever it was that cried had lost a lot of strength. But it was in vain that he tried to trace the sounds to their source. His questings through those same mazes of masonry that he had searched by daylight were fruitless. Directly he had left the corridor, the silence came down like an impalpable weight and the sharpness of his hearing was of no avail.

Again and again he did all in his power to locate the suffering creature, for Flay had begun to realize that it was nearing the end of its strength. It was not so much terror that he now felt as a blind pity. A pity that drew him to the place night after night. It was as though he had this nameless tragedy upon his conscience; as though his being there to listen to the weakening voice was in some way helpful. He knew that this was not so, but he could not keep away.

The night came when for all his listening there was no sound, and from that time onwards the silence remained unbroken.

He knew that in some way the end had come to some demented thing. What it was that had laughed with that double note, that had cried out and answered itself with the same flat and terrible voice, he never knew. He never knew that he was the last to hear the voices of their ladyships Cora and Clarice, nor that he had been within a few feet of those apartments into which they had once been lured. He never knew that behind the locked doors of this place of incarceration the Twins had languished, their brains losing what grip they had, their madness mounting, until, when their provisions began to fail them, and Steerpike no longer came, they knew that death was on his way.

When weakness overpowered them they lay down side by side and staring at the ceiling, they died at the same moment, on the other side of the wall.

FORTY-SIX

WHILE Flay, in his wilderness of hollow halls, was brooding upon the shock he had sustained, and fretting at its insoluble nature, Steerpike, now up and about once more, was losing no time in establishing his position as Master of Ritual. He was under no illusions as to what the reaction of the castle would be, when it became borne in upon them that he was performing no stop-gap office. To neither be old, nor to be the son of Barquentine, nor one of the accepted school of hierophants, nor indeed to have any claim upon the title, save that of being the only disciple of the drowned cripple's, and of having the brains to perform the onerous office, was an anything but encouraging inception.

Nor was he, physically, any longer personable. His hunched shoulders, his pallor, his dark-red eyes had never encouraged intimacy even supposing he had ever courted it. But now, how much the more so was he likely to be shunned, even in a society that laid no claim to beauty.

The burns upon his face and neck and hands were there to stay. Only the worms could put an end to them. The effect of the face was of something skew-bald; the taut crimson tissue, forming fiery patterns against the wax-like pallor of his skin. His hands were blood-red and silky; their creases and wrinkles like those on the hand of a monkey.

And yet he knew, that although he created a natural revulsion among those about him, the reason for his disfigurement stood in his favour. It was he who had (as far as the castle knew) risked his life to save the hereditary Master. It was he who had suffered delirium and excruciating pain because he had had the courage to try and wrest from death's grip a keystone of the Gormenghast tradition. How, in that case, could his diabolical appearance be held against him?

And what is more he knew, however prejudiced his opponents might be, that in the end they had no option but to accept him, in spite of his burns, his background, and the unproven rumours which he knew were in constant circulation – to accept him, for the simple reason that there was no one else with the necessary knowledge at his finger tips. Barquentine had divulged his secrets to no one else. The very tomes of cross-reference would have been beyond the powers of even the most intelligent of men to comprehend, unless, as a preliminary, he were schooled to the symbols involved. The principle upon which the arrangement of the library was based was, in itself, something which had taken Steerpike a year to unravel, even with Barquentine's irritable guidance.

But cunningly and by slow degrees, as he went about his work, he evoked a grudging acceptance and even a kind of bitter admiration. By not so much as a hair's breadth did he deviate from those thousand letters of the Groan law, that day by day in one form of ritual or another, were made manifest. With every evening he knew himself more deeply entrenched.

His miscalculation over Barquentine's murder had been unforgivable and he did not forgive himself. It was not so much what had happened to his body that galled him, but that he should ever have blundered. His mind, always compassionless, was now an icicle – sharp, lucent and frigid. From now onwards he had no other purpose than to hold the castle ever more tightly in the scalded palm of his hand. He knew that his every step must be taken with the utmost precaution. That although, on the face of it, the life of Gormenghast was, in spite of its rigid tradition, a dark and shambling affair, yet there was always this consciousness beneath the surface; there were those that watched and there were those that listened. He knew that in order to fulfil his dreams he must devote, if necessary, the next ten years to the consolidation of his position, taking no risk, learning all the while, and building up a reputation not only as an authority on all that pertained to the traditions of the place, but as someone who, indefatigable in his zeal, was nevertheless difficult to approach. This would both leave what free time he had for his own purposes, and help to create for himself the legend of a saint, someone removed, someone beyond questioning, for whom, in his early days, the tests of fire and water had not been too terrible to endure when the soul of Gormenghast was in jeopardy.

The years lay spread before him. To the younger generation he would be a kind of god. But it was now in the diligence and exactness of his offices that he must carve for himself the throne that he would one day occupy.

For all the evil of his early years he knew that, though from time to time he had been suspected of insurrection and worse, yet now with his feet well set upon the gold road of advancement, he was (with the darkest of his deeds but a week or two behind him) as free as ever he had been from any question of being unmasked.

He was now close upon twenty-five years old. The fire that had mottled his face had taken no lasting toll of his strength. He was now as wiry and tireless as before the catastrophe. He whistled to himself, between his teeth, tunelessly as he stood at the window of his room and stared out across the snow.

It was mid-day. Against a dark sky, Gormenghast Mountain, for all its ruggedness, was swathed as white as wool. Steerpike stared through it. In a quarter of an hour he would be on his way to the stables, where the horses would be lined up for his inspection. It being the anniversary of the death of a nephew of the fifty-third Countess of Groan, in his day a daring horseman, he would see that the grooms were in mourning and that the traditional equine masks were being worn at the correct angle of dejection.

He held up his hands and placed them before him against the window pane. Then he spread them out like starfish, and examined his nails. Between the scarlet fingers and all about them was the white of the distant snow. It was as though he had placed his hand upon white paper. Then he turned and crossed the room to where his cape was folded over the back of a chair. When he had left the room and had turned the key and was on his way down the stairway, his mind turned for a moment to the Twins. It had been an untidy business in many ways, but perhaps it was as well that circumstances beyond his control had forced the solution. Even at the time of his burns, the re-stocking of their larder had been long overdue. By now they could no longer be alive.

He had gone through his papers, and had refreshed his memory as to exactly what provisions they were likely to have had left on the day of his burning, and from his none too simple calculations, he deduced that they must have died from starvation on about that day when, swathed like a lagged pipe in frosty weather, he first rose from his sick bed. In point of fact they died two days later.

FORTY-SEVEN

I

As the days went by, Titus was becoming more and more difficult to control. In the long dormitories where after dark the boys of his own age would light their shielded candles, squat in groups, perform strange rites or eat their pilfered cakes, Titus was no watcher of the scene. He was no mere watcher from the safety of his bed, when, in fierce and secret grapple, old scores were settled in deathly silence while, in his cubicle by the dormitory door, the formidable janitor slept like a crocodile upon his back. The erratic breathing of this man, his tossings and turnings, his very wheezings and mutterings were an open book to Titus and his confederates. They all conveyed a certain *depth* of sleep, which at its deepest was shallow enough. But it was silence that they feared, for silence meant that his eyes were open in the darkness.

As sacred as the fact that there had always been an Earl of Gormenghast and always would be, and that when the time came he would be virtually unapproachable, a man out of range both socially and for reason of his intrinsic *difference* – as sacred as all this, was the tradition that as a boy the Earl of Gormenghast must be in no way treated as something apart. It was the pride of the Groans that their childhood was no time of cotton-wool.

As for the boys themselves, they found little difficulty in putting this into practice. They knew that there was no difference between themselves and Titus. It was only later that they would think otherwise. And in any case what a child may become in his later years is of little interest to his friends or his foes. It is the world of here and now that matters most. And so Titus fought with the rest in the breathless dormitory – and from time to time was caught out of his bed and was caned by the janitor.

He took the risk and he took the punishment. But he hated it. He hated the ambiguity of it all. Was he a lord or an urchin? He resented a world in which he was neither one thing nor another. That his early trials would fit him for his responsibilities in later life, made no appeal to him. He was not interested in his later life and he was not interested in having responsibilities. Somehow or other the whole thing was unfair.

And so he said to himself: 'All right! So I'm the same as anyone else, am I? Then why do I have to report to Steerpike every evening, in case I'm lost? Why do I have to do extra things after classes – when none of the others have to? Turning keys in rotten old locks. Pouring wine all over turrets – walking here and there until I'm tired! Why should I do all this extra if I'm not any different? It's a rotten trick!'

The professors found him difficult, wayward, and on occasions, insolent. All except Bellgrove, for whom Titus had a fondness and an inexplicable respect.

II

'Are you thinking of doing any work this afternoon, or were you planning to spend it in chewing that end of your pen, dear boy?' asked Bellgrove leaning forward over his desk and addressing Titus.

'Yes, sir!' said Titus with a jerk. He had been far away, in a day dream.

'Do you mean, "Yes, sir, I'm going to work" or "Yes, sir, I'm going to chew my pen", dear boy?'

'O *work*, sir.'

Bellgrove flicked a lock of his mane back over his shoulder with the end of his ruler.

'I *am* so pleased,' he said. 'You know, my young friend, that one day when *I* was about your age, I was suddenly taken with the idea of concentrating upon the paper which my old schoolteacher had set me. I don't know what gave me the idea. I had never thought of doing such a thing before. I had *heard* of people who had tried it, you know – of paying attention, of putting their minds to the work in hand – but I had never thought of doing it *myself*. But – and here you must listen, my dear boy – what happened? I will tell you. I found that the paper which my dear master had set me was quite, quite simple. It was almost an insult. I concentrated more than ever. When I had finished I asked for more. And then more again. All my answers were quite perfect. And what happened? I became so fascinated at finding I was so clever, that I did too much and *became ill*. And so I warn you – and I warn the whole class. Take care of your health. Don't overdo it. Go slow – or you may have a breakdown just as I had, long ago, when I was young, dear boys, and ugly, just as you are, and just as dirty, too, and if you haven't got your work finished by four o'clock, Master Groan, my dear child, I shall be forced to keep you in until five.'

'Yes sir,' said Titus and at that moment he felt a dig in the back. Turning he found that the boy behind him was passing him a note. He could not have chosen a much worse moment for it, but Bellgrove had closed his eyes in a resigned and lordly way. When Titus unfolded the scrap of paper, he found it was no message but a crude caricature of Bellgrove chasing Miss Irma Prunesquallor with a long lasso in his hand. It was very feebly drawn and not particularly funny, and Titus, who was in no mood for it, felt suddenly angry, and screwing it up threw it back over his shoulder. This time Bellgrove's attention was caught by the pellet.

'What was that, dear boy?'

'Just a screwed up bit of paper, sir.'

'Bring it up here, to your old master. It will give him something to do,' said Bellgrove. 'He can work away at it with his old fingers, you know. After all there is nothing much he can do until the class ends.' And then musing aloud, 'O babes and sucklings . . . babes and sucklings . . . how tired of you your old headmaster gets.'

The pellet was retrieved and passed to Titus who got up from his desk. And then suddenly when he had approached to within a few feet of the headmaster's desk he put the screwed-up drawing into his mouth, and with a gulp, swallowed it.

'I've swallowed it, sir.'

Bellgrove frowned, and an expression of pain flitted across his noble face.

'You will stand on your desk,' he said. 'I am ashamed of you, Titus Groan. You will have to be punished.'

When Titus had been standing on his desk for a few minutes he received another tap upon the back. He had already been in trouble through the stupidity of the boy behind and in a flash of anger 'Shut up!' he cried, and swinging around at the same instant found himself staring at Steerpike.

The young Master of Ritual had come silently through the door of the schoolroom. It was his duty to make a periodic round of the classes, and it was an understood thing that in this official capacity it was not for him to knock before he entered – only a few boys had noticed Steerpike's arrival – but the whole class turned at the sound of Titus' voice.

Gradually it dawned upon the class that the reason for the stiff, frozen position that Titus was in, his head turned sharply over his shoulder, his body swivelled around on the narrow pivot of his hips, his hands clenched, his head lowered angrily – that the reason for his tenseness was that his 'shut-up' must have been addressed to none other than the man with the skewbald face, Steerpike himself.

Standing upon the lid of his desk Titus was in the unusual position of looking down at the face of this authority who had suddenly appeared as though out of the floor, like an apparition. The face looked up at him, a wry smile upon the lips, the eyebrows raised a little, and a certain expectancy in the features, as though denoting that although Steerpike realized that it was impossible for the boy to have guessed who it was that had tapped him on the back, and was therefore guiltless of insolence, yet, an apology was called for. It was unthinkable that the

Master of Ritual should be spoken to in this way by anyone – let alone a small boy – whatever his lineage.

But no apology came. For Titus, directly he realized what had happened – that he had cried '*shut-up*' to the arch-symbol of all the authority and repression which he loathed – knew instinctively that this was a moment in which to dare the blackest hell.

To apologize would be to submit.

He knew in the darkness of his heart's blood that he must not climb down. In the face of peril, in the presence of officialdom, age-old and vile, with its scarlet hands, and its hunched shoulders, he must not climb down. He must cling to his dizzy crag until, trembling but triumphant in the enormous knowledge of his victory, he stood once more upon solid ground, secure in the knowledge that as a creature of different clay he had not sold his birthright out of terror.

But he could not move. His face had gone white as the paper on the desk. His brow was sticky with sweat and he was heavy with a ghastly tiredness. To cling to his crag was enough. He had not the courage to stare into the dark red eyes that, with the lids narrowed across them, were fixed upon his face. He had not the courage to do this. He stared over the man's shoulder, and then he closed his eyes. To refuse to say he was sorry was all that his courage could stand.

And then, all at once he felt himself to be standing at a strange angle, and opening his eyes he saw the rows of desks begin to circle in formation through the air and then a far voice shouted as though from miles away as he fell heavily to the floor in a dead faint.

FORTY-EIGHT

'I AM having the most moving time, Alfred. I said I am having the most *moving* time – are you listening or not? O it's *too* galling the way a woman can be courted so splendidly, so nobly by her lover, only to find that her own brother is about as interested as a fly upon the wall. Alfred, I said a fly upon a *wall*!'

'Flesh of my flesh,' said the Doctor after a pause (he had been lost in rumination), 'what is it that you want to know?'

'*Know*,' answered Irma, with superb scorn. 'Why should I want to *know* anything?'

Her fingers smoothed the back of her iron-grey hair, and then of a sudden, pounced upon the bun at the nape of her neck where they fiddled with an uncanny dexterity. It might have been supposed that her long nervous fingers had an eye apiece so effortlessly did they flicker to and fro across the contours of the hirsute knob.

'I was not *asking* you a question, Alfred. I sometimes have thoughts of my own. I sometimes make *statements*. I know you think very little of my intellect. But not everyone is like you – I can assure you. You can have no idea, Alfred, of what is being done to me. I am being drawn out. I am finding treasures in myself. I am like a rich mine, Alfred. I know it, I know it. And I have brains I haven't even used yet.'

'Conversation with you, Irma,' said her brother, 'is peculiarly difficult. You leave no loops, dear one, at the end of your sentences, nothing to help your loving brother, nothing for his ever willing, ever eager, ever shining hook. I always have to start afresh, sweet trout. I have to work my passage. But I will try again. Now, you were saying . . . ?'

'O, Alfred. Just for one moment, do something to please me. Talk *normally*. I am so tired of your way of saying things with all its figures of eight.'

'Figures of *speech!* speech! speech!' cried the Doctor, rising to his feet and wringing his hands, 'why do you always say figure of *eight?* O bless my soul, what is the matter with my nerves? Yes, of course I'll do something to please you. What shall it be?'

But Irma was in tears, her head buried in a soft grey cushion. At last she raised it and taking off her dark glasses, 'It's too *much*,' she sobbed. 'When even one's brother snaps one up. I did trust *you!*' she shouted, 'and now *you're* letting me down too. I only wanted your advice.'

'Who has let you down?' said the Doctor sharply. 'Not the Head-master . . .?'

Irma dabbed her eyes with an embroidered handkerchief the size of a playing card.

'It's because I told him his neck was dirty, the dear, sweet lord . . .'

'*Lord!*' cried Prunesquallor, 'you don't call him *that*, do you?'

'Of course not, Alfred . . . only to myself . . . after all he is my lord, isn't he?'

'If you say so,' said her brother, passing his hand across his brow. 'I suppose he could be anything.'

'O he is. He is. He's anything – or rather, Alfred, he's everything.'

'But you have shamed him, and he feels wounded – proud and wounded, is that it, Irma, my dear?'

'Yes, O yes. It is that exactly. But what can I *do*? What can I *do*?'

The doctor placed the tips of his fingers together.

'You are experiencing already, my dear Irma,' he said, 'the stuff of marriage. And so is he. Be patient, sweet flower. Learn all you can. Use what tact God gave you, and remember your mistakes and what led up to them. Say nothing about his neck. You can only make things worse.

His resentment will fade. His wound will heal in time. If you love him, then simply love him and never fuss about what's dead and gone. After all you love him in spite of all *your* faults, not *his*. Other people's faults can be fascinating. One's own are dreary. Be quiet for a bit. Don't talk too much and can't you walk a little less like a buoy in a swell?'

Irma got up from her chair and moved to the door.

'Thank you, Alfred,' she said and disappeared.

Doctor Prunesquallor sank back on the couch by the window, and with an ease, quite astonishing, dismissed his sister's problem from his mind and was once more in the cogitative reverie from which she had interrupted him.

He had been thinking of Steerpike's accession to the key position that he now occupied. He had also been reflecting upon the way he had behaved as a patient. His fortitude had been matchless and his will to live quite savage. But for the most part, the Doctor was turning over in his mind something that was quite different. It was a phrase, which, at the height of Steerpike's delirium, had broken loose from the chaos of his ravings – '*And the Twins will make it five*,' the young man had shouted – '*and the Twins will make it five*.'

FORTY-NINE

I

ONE dark winter morning, Titus and his sister sat together on the wide window-seat of one of Fuchsia's three rooms that overlooked the South Spinneys. Soon after Nannie Slagg had died Fuchsia had moved, not without much arguing and a sense of dire uprooting, to a more handsome district – and to a set of rooms which, in comparison with her old untidy bedroom of many memories, were full of light and space.

Outside the window the last of the snow lay in patches across the countryside. Fuchsia, with her chin on her hands and her elbows on the window sill, was watching the swaying motion of the thin stream of steel-grey water as it fell a hundred feet from the gutter of a nearby building – for a small, restless wind was blowing erratically and sometimes the stream of melted snow as it fell from the high gutter would descend in a straight and motionless line to a tank in the quadrangle below, and sometimes it would swing to the north and stay outstretched when a gust blew angrily, and sometimes the cascade would fan out in a spray of innumerable leaden drops and fall like rain.

And then the wind would drop again and the steady tubular overflow would fall once more vertically, like a stretched cable, and the water would spurt and thud within the tank.

Titus, who had been turning over the pages of a book, got to his feet.

'I'm glad there's no school today, Few,' he said – it was a name he had started giving her – 'it would have been Perch-Prism with his foul chemistry and Cutflower this afternoon.'

'What's the holiday *for*?' said Fuchsia with her eyes still on the water which was now swaying to and fro across the tank.

'I'm not sure,' said Titus. 'Something to do with Mother, I think. Birthday or something.'

'Oh,' said Fuchsia and then after a pause, 'it's funny how one has to be told everything. I don't remember her having birthdays before. It's all so inhuman.'

'I don't know what you mean,' said Titus.

'No,' said Fuchsia. 'You wouldn't, I suppose. It's not your fault and you're lucky in a way. But I've read quite a lot and I know that most children see a good deal of their parents – more than we do anyway.'

'Well, I don't remember Father at *all*,' said Titus.

'I do,' said Fuchsia. 'But he was difficult too. I hardly ever spoke to him. I think he wanted me to be a boy.'

'Did he?'

'Yes.'

'Oh . . . I wonder why.'

'To be the next Earl of course.'

'Oh . . . but *I* am . . . so it's all right, I suppose.'

'But he didn't know you were going to be born, when *I* was a child, did he? He couldn't have. I was about fourteen when you were born.'

'Were you really . . .'

'Of course I was. And for all that time he wished I was you, I suppose.'

'That's funny, isn't it?' said Titus.

'It wasn't funny at all – and it isn't funny now – is it? Not that it's your fault . . .'

At that moment there was a knock at the door and a messenger entered.

'What do you want?' said Fuchsia.

'I have a message, my lady.'

'What is it?'

'Her ladyship, the Countess, your mother, wishes Lord Titus to accompany me back to her room. She is going to take him for a walk.'

Titus and Fuchsia stared at the messenger and then at one another. Several times they opened their mouths to speak but closed them again. Then Fuchsia turned her eyes back to the melting snow – and Titus

walked out through the half open door, the messenger following him
closely.

II

The Countess was waiting for them on the landing. She gestured the
messenger to be gone with a single, lazy movement to her head.

She gazed at Titus with a curious lack of expression. It was as though
what she saw interested her, but in the way that a stone would interest
a geologist, or a plant, a botanist. Her expression was neither kindly
nor unkindly. It was simply absent. She appeared to be unconscious of
having a face at all. Her features made no effort to communicate
anything.

'I am taking them for a walk,' she said in her heavy, abstracted,
millstone voice.

'Yes, Mother,' said Titus. He supposed she was talking of her cats.

A shadow settled for a moment on her broad brow. The word mother
had perplexed her. But the boy was quite right, of course.

Her massive bulk had always impressed Titus. The hanging draperies
and scollop'd shadows, the swathes of musty darkness – all this he
found most awesome.

He was fascinated by her but he had no point of contact. When she
spoke it was in order to make a statement. She had no conversation.

She turned her head and, pursing her lips, she whistled with a
peculiar ululation. Titus gazed up at the sartorial mass above him.
Why had she wanted him to accompany her? he wondered. Did she
want him to tell her anything? Had she anything to tell *him*? Was it just
a whim?

But she had started to descend the stairs and Titus followed her.

From a hundred dim recesses, from favourite ledges, from shelves
and draught-proof corners, from among the tattered entrails of old
sofas, from the scarred plush of chairs, from under clock-stands, from
immemorial sun-traps, and from nests of claw-torn paper – from the
inside of lost hats, from among rafters, from rusty casques, and from
drawers half-open, the cats poured forth, converged, foamed, and with
a rapid pattering of their milk-white feet filled up the corridors, and a
few moments later had reached the landing and were on their way, in
the wake of their great mistress, down the stairway they obscured.

When they were in the open and had passed through an archway in
the outer wall and were able to see Gormenghast Mountain clear before
them, with dark grey snow on its cruel heights, the Countess waved her
ponderous arm, as though she were scattering grain, and the cats on
the instant, fanning out, sped in every direction, and leapt, twisting in

the air, curvetting for the very joy of their only release from the castle since first the snow came down. And though a number of them sported together, rolling over one another, or sitting up straight with their heads bridled back, tapped at each other sparring like fighters, only to lose all interest of a sudden, their eyes unfocusing, their thoughts turning – yet for the main the white creatures behaved as though each one were utterly alone, utterly content to be alone, conscious only of its own behaviour, its own leap into the air, its own agility, self-possessed, solitary, enviable and legendary in a beauty both heraldic and fluent as water.

Titus walked by his mother's side. For all the interest in the scene before him he could not help turning his eyes to his mother's face. Its vague, almost mask-like character was something which he was beginning to suspect of being no index to her state of mind. For more than once she had gripped his shoulder in her big hand and led him from the path and without a word she had shown him, all but shrouded by the ivy on a tree stem, a cushion of black star-moss. She had turned off a rough track, and then pointed down a small snow-filled gully to where a fox had rested. Every now and again she would pause and gaze at the ground, or into the branches of a tree, but Titus, stare as he would, could see nothing remarkable.

For all that the birds had died in their thousands, yet as Titus and his mother drew near to a strip of woodland where the snow had melted from the boughs, and small streams were running over the stones and snow-flattened grass, they could see that the trees were far from empty.

The Countess paused, and holding Titus by his elbow, they stood motionless. A bird whistled and then another, and then suddenly the small kingfisher, like a blue legend, streaked along a stream.

The cats were leagues away. They breathed the sharp air into their lungs. They roamed to the four quarters. They powdered the horizons.

The Countess whistled with a shrill sweet note, and first one bird and then another flew to her. She examined them, holding them cupped in her hands. They were very thin and weak. She whistled their various calls and they responded as they hopped about her or sat perched upon her shoulders, and then, all at once, a fresh voice from the wood silenced the birds. At every whistle of the Countess, this new answer came, quick as an echo.

Its effect on the Countess seemed out of all reason.

She turned her head. She whistled again and her whistle was answered, quick as an echo. She gave the calls of a dozen birds and a dozen voices echoed her with an insolent precision. The birds about her feet and on her shoulders had stiffened.

Her hand was gripping Titus' shoulder like an iron clamp. It was all he could do not to cry out. He turned his head with difficulty and saw his mother's face – the face that had been so calm as the snow itself. It had darkened.

It was no bird that was answering her; that much she knew. Clever as it was, the mimicry could not deceive her. Nor did it seem that whatever gave vent to the varying calls was anxious to deceive. There had been something taunting about the rapidity with which each whistle of the Countess had been flung back from the wood.

What was it all about? Why was his arm being gripped? Titus, who had been fascinated by his mother's power over the birds, could not understand why the calls from the wood should have so angered her. For she trembled as she held him. It seemed as though she were holding him back from something, as though the wood was hiding something that might hurt him – or draw him away from her.

And then she lifted her face to the tree tops, her eyes blazing.

'Beware!' she cried and a strange voice answered her.

'*Beware!*' it called and the silence came down again.

From a dizzy perch in a tall pine, the Thing peered through the cold needles and watched the big woman and the boy as they returned to the distant castle.

FIFTY

I

IT was not until close upon the Day, that Titus learned how something quite unusual was being prepared for his Tenth birthday. He was by now so used to ceremonies of one kind or another that the idea of having to spend his birthday either performing or watching others perform some time-hardened ritual made no appeal to his imagination. But Fuchsia had told him that there was something quite different about what happened when a child of the line reached the age of ten. She knew, for it had happened to her, although in her case the festivities had been rather spoiled by the rain.

'I won't tell you, Titus,' she had said, 'it will spoil it if I do. O it's so lovely.'

'What kind of lovely?' said Titus, suspiciously.

'Wait and see,' said Fuchsia. 'You'll be glad I haven't told you when the time comes. If only things were always like that.'

When the Day arrived Titus learned to his surprise that he was to be confined for the entire twelve hours in a great playroom quite unknown to him.

The custodian of the Outer Keys, a surly old man with a cast of the left eye, had opened up the room as soon as dawn had broken over the towers. Apart from the occasion of Fuchsia's tenth birthday, the door had been locked since her father, Sepulchrave, was a child. But now, again, the key had turned with a grinding of rust and iron, and the hinges had creaked, and the great playroom opened up again its dusty glories.

This was a strange way to treat a boy on his tenth anniversary; to immure him for the entire day in a strange land, however full of marvels it might be. It was true that there were toys of weird and ingenious mechanism; ropes on which he would swing from wall to wall, and ladders leading to dizzy balconies – but what of all this, if the door was locked and the only window was high in the wall?

And yet, long as the day seemed, Titus was buoyed up by the knowledge that he was there not only because of some obsolete tradition but for the very good reason that he must not be allowed to see what was going on. Had he been abroad he could not fail to have gained some inkling, if not of what lay in store for him that evening, at least of the scale on which the preparations were being conducted.

And the activity of the castle was fantastic. For Titus to have seen a tenth of it must have taken the edge, not off his wonder or speculation, but off the shock of pleasure that he was finally to receive when evening came. For he had no idea what kind of activities were taking place. Fuchsia had refused to be drawn. She remembered her own pleasure too keenly to jeopardize a hundredth part of his.

And so he spent the day alone and save for those times when his meals were brought in on the golden trays of the occasion, he saw no one until an hour before sunset. At that hour four men came in. One of them carried a box, which when it was opened revealed a few garments which Titus was invited to put on. Another carried a light basketwork palanquin, or mountain-chair that rested on two long poles. Of the other two, one carried a long green scarf, and the other a few cakes and a glass of water on a tray.

They retired while Titus got into his ceremonial clothes. They were very simple. A small red velvet skull-cap and a seamless robe of some grey material that reached to his ankles. A fine chain of gold links clasped the garment at his waist. These, with a pair of sandals, were all that had been brought and while he strapped the sandals he called to the men to re-enter.

They came in at once and one of them approached Titus with the scarf in his hand.

'Your lordship,' he said.

'What's *that* for?' said Titus, eyeing the scarf.

'It's part of the ceremony, lordship. You have to be blindfolded.'

'No!' shouted Titus. 'Why should I be?'

'It's nothing to do with me,' said the man. 'It's the law.'

'The law! the law! the law – how I *hate* the law,' cried the boy. 'Why does it want me blindfolded – after keeping me in prison all day? Where are you going to take me? What's it all about? Can't you talk? Can't you talk?'

'Nothing to do with me,' said the man; it was his favourite phrase. 'You see,' he added, 'if we don't blindfold you it won't be such a surprise when you get there and when we undo the scarf. And you see' (he continued as though he had suddenly become interested in what he was talking about) 'you see – with your eyes blindfolded you won't have any idea of where you are going – and then, you know, the crowds are going to be deathly silent and . . .'

'Quiet!' said another voice – it was the man who had the mountain-chair. 'You have overreached yourself! Enough sir, for me to say' (he continued, turning to the boy) 'that it will be for your pleasure and your good.'

'It had *better* be,' said Titus, 'after all *this!*'

His longing to get out of the playroom mitigated his distaste for the blindfolding, and after taking a drink of water and cramming a small cake in his mouth, he took a step forward.

'All right,' he said and standing before the scarf-man, he suffered himself to be bandaged. At the second turn of the scarf he was in total blackness. After the fourth he felt the cloth being knotted at the base of his head.

'We are going to lift you into the chair, your lordship.'

'All right,' said Titus.

Almost immediately after he was seated in the basket-work chair he found himself rising from the ground, and then after a word from one of the men, he felt himself moving forward through black space and the slight swaying of the men beneath him. Without a word, or a pause, each man with an end of the long bamboo poles resting upon his shoulder, they began to move ever more rapidly.

Titus had had no sensation of their leaving the room, although he knew that by now they must have left it far behind. It was obvious that they were still within the walls of the castle for he could both feel the frequent changes of direction which the tortuous corridors made necessary, and also he could hear the hollow echoing of the bearers' feet – an echoing which seemed so loud to Titus in his blindness that he could not help feeling that the castle was empty. There was not a sound, not a whisper in the whole labyrinthine place to compete with the hollow footfalls of the men, with the sound of their breathing or with the regular creaking of the bamboo poles.

It seemed that it would never end – this darkness, and these sounds, but suddenly a breath of fresh air against his face told him that he was in the open. At the same time he could feel that he was being borne down a flight of steps, and when they had reached the level ground he felt for the first time that airborne jogging, as the four men began to trot through an empty landscape.

And it was as utterly deserted as the castle. All the feverish activity of the day had been brought to a close. The gentry, the dignitaries, the officials, the workmen, the performers, the populace, man, woman and child – there was not one who had not arrived at his appointed station.

And the bearers ran on over the darkening ground. Above their heads and reaching down into the west was a great tongue of yellow light.

But with every movement that passed the lustre faded and the moon began to slide up through the darkness of the east so that the light on Titus' upturned face grew sharper and colder.

And the bearers ran on, over the dark ground.

There were no echoes now. Only the isolated sounds of the night – the scurry of some small animal through the undergrowth, or the distant barking of a fox. From time to time Titus could feel the cool sweet gusts of a night breeze blowing across his forehead, lifting the strands of his hair.

'How much further?' he called. It seemed that he had been floating in the basket chair for ever.

'How much further? how much further?' he called again, but there was no reply.

It was impossible to carry so rare a burden as the seventy-seventh earl – to carry him shoulder-high along forest tracks, across precarious fords and over stony slopes of mountains and to have at the same time, while they kept running, any room in their minds for anything else besides. All their awareness was focused upon his safety and the measured smoothness of their rhythmic running. Had he called to them ten times as loudly they would not have heard him.

But Titus was near to the end of his blind journey. He did not know it but the four bearers who had, for the last mile or more, been loping through pinewoods, had come suddenly upon an open shoulder of land. The ground swept downwards and away before them in swathes of moon-chilled ferns and at the base of this slope lay what seemed like a natural amphitheatre, for the land rose on all sides. The floor of this gigantic basin appeared at first sight to be entirely forested and yet the eyes of the bearers had already caught sight of innumerable and microscopic points of light no bigger than pinpricks, that flashed, now here, now there among the branches of the distant trees. And they saw more than this. They saw that in the air above the basin'd forest there was a change of hue. In the darkness that brooded over the branches there was a subtle warmth, a kind of smouldering dusk that in contrast to the cold moon, or to the glints of light among the trees, was almost roseate.

But Titus knew nothing of this swarthy light. Nor that he was being taken down a steep track through the ferns to a district where the great chestnuts far from forming a solid forest, as it falsely appeared from the surrounding slopes, were marshalled a furlong deep about the margin of a wide expanse of water. The points of light that had caught the bearers' attention were all that they had been able to see of the moonlit lake when for a moment they had paused on a high open shoulder.

But what of the glow? It was not long before Titus knew all about it. He was by now among the deep moon-dappled chestnut groves. His exhausted bearers, the sweat pouring down their bodies and running into their eyes, were turning into a ride of ancient trees that led to the centre of the southern bank.

Had his vision been free he would have seen upon his left, and tethered to the low branches of the nearby trees, a hundred or more horses. Their harnessings, bridles, halters and saddles were slung across the higher branches. Here and there the moonlight penetrating the upper foliage set a stirrup dazzling in the gloom or gloated upon the leather of long traces. And then, a little further along the track where the trees were not so numerous, there stood ranged in lines, as though for inspection, a great variety of carriages, carts and traps. Here where there was less covering, the moonlight shone almost unimpeded, and was by now so high and was casting so strong a light that the varying colours of the carriages could be distinguished one from another. The wheels of each were decorated with foliage of young trees whose branches were threaded through the spokes, and with sunflowers also; in the long horse-drawn cavalcade which a few hours previously had made its overland journey to the chestnut woods, there had not been one wheel out of the many hundreds, that, in turning had not set the foliage revolving and the heads of sunflowers circling in the dusk.

All this had been lost to the boy – all this and many another flight of fancy which from hour to hour during the day had been set in motion or enacted according to old customs whose origin or significance was long forgotten.

But the bearers were for the first time slackening their pace. Once again he leaned forward, his hands grasping the basket-work rim of his chair. 'Where are we?' he shouted. 'How much longer will it be? Can't you answer me?'

The silence about him was like something that hummed against his eardrums. This was another kind of silence. This was not the silence of nothing happening – of emptiness, or negation – but was a positive thing – a silence that knew of itself – that was charged, conscious and wide awake.

And now the bearers stopped altogether, and almost at once, across the stillness, Titus heard the sound of approaching footsteps, and then –

'My lord Titus,' said a voice, 'I am here to bid you welcome and to offer you on behalf of your mother, your sister and all who are here gathered, our felicitations on your tenth birthday.

'It is our desire that what has been prepared for your amusement will give you pleasure; and that you will find the tedium of the long and solitary day that now lies at your back has been worth the suffering; in short, my Lord Titus, your mother the Countess Gertrude of Gormenghast, Lady Fuchsia and every one of your subjects are hoping that what is left of your birthday will be very happy.'

'Thank you,' said Titus. 'I would like to get down.'

'At once, your lordship,' said the same voice.

'And I'd like this scarf off my eyes.'

'In one moment. Your sister is on her way to you. She will remove it when she has taken you to the south platform.'

'Fuchsia!' his voice was sharp and strained. 'Fuchsia! Where are you?'

'I'm coming,' she shouted. 'Hold his arm, you man, there! How do you think he can stand in the dark like that – give him to me, give him to me. Oh Titus,' she panted, holding her blind brother tightly in her arms, 'it won't be long now – and O, it's wonderful! wonderful! As wonderful as it was when it was all for me, years ago, and it's a better night than I had, and absolutely calm with a great white moon on top.'

She led him along as she talked, and all at once the marginal trees were behind them and Fuchsia knew that every step they took and every movement they made was watched by a multitude.

As Titus stumbled at her side he tried to imagine in what kind of place he could be. He could form no picture from Fuchsia's disjointed comments. That he was to be taken to a platform of some kind, that there was a moon, and that the whole castle seemed resolved to make amends for the long prefatory day he had spent alone was all that he could gather.

'Twelve steps up,' said Fuchsia, and he felt her placing his foot upon the first of the rough treads. They climbed together, hand in hand, and when they reached the platform she guided him to where a large horse-hair chair bloated with moonlight, an ugly thing if ever there was one – a heavy beast with a purple skin that had tired out the two cart horses by the time they had covered half the journey.

'Sit down,' said Fuchsia, and he sat down gingerly in the darkness, upon the edge of the ugly couch.

Fuchsia stood back from him. Then she raised both her arms above her head. In reply to her signal a voice called out of the darkness. 'It is time! Let the scarf be unwound from his eyes!'

And another voice – quick as an echo –

'It is time! Let his birthday begin!'

And another –

'For his Lordship is ten.'

Titus felt Fuchsia's fingers undoing the knot and then the freeing of the cloth about his eyes. For a moment he remained with his lids closed, and then he slowly opened them and as he did so he rose involuntarily to his feet with a gasp of wonder.

Before him, as he stood, one hand at his mouth, his eyes round as coins, there was stretched, as it were, across the area of his vision, a canvas – a canvas hushed and unearthly. A canvas of great depth; of width that spread from east to the west and of a height that wandered way above the moon. It was painted with the fire and moonlight – upon a dark impalpable surface. The lunar rhythms rose and moved through darkness. A counterpoint of bonfires burned like anchors – anchors that held the sliding woods in check.

And the glaze! The earthless glaze of that midnight lake! And the multitude across the water, motionless in the shadow of the sculptured chestnut trees. And the bonfires burning!

And then a voice out of the paint cried 'Fire!' and a cannon roared, recoiled and smoked upon the bank. 'Fire!' cried the voice again, and then again, until the gun had bellowed ten times over.

It was the sign, and suddenly the picture, as though at the stroke of a warlock's wand, came suddenly to life. The canvas shuddered. Fragments detached themselves and fragments came together. From the height to the depths it was that that Titus saw.

Firstly the moon, by now immediately overhead; a thing as big as a dinner plate and as white, save where the shadows of its mountains lay. The moon whose lustre was over everything like a veil of snow.

And all about the moon, the midnight sky. It came down, this sky, like a curtain, expansive as nemesis and under the sky the hilltops in a haze of ferns that overlapping one another with their fronds, descended the hill, fold after fold until the chestnut forest, luxuriant in its foliage, its upper canopies shining, stretched on Titus' eye-level in a great curve. And under these trees, along the water's edge, as thick upon the ground as nettles in wasteland, was the life of the distant castle, the teeming populace. A hundred at a time would be contained in the cast-shadow of a single tree; a hundred more be lit in a lozenge of moonlight. And then the swarms of faces, thick as bees, illumined and flushed in the red light of the lakeside bonfires. Now that the gun had fired its salute, this long strip of the canvas had begun to seethe. Across the lake it was too far for Titus to be able to make out any single creature, but movements ran through these crowds as a ripple of wind over a field of tares. But this was not all. For these ripples, these trembling blotches of shadow and moonlight, these movements on the shore, were being simultaneously repeated in the lakes. Not the least motion of a head beneath the trees but its ghost had moved beneath it in the water. Not the flicker of a fire was lost in the reflecting water.

And it was this nocturnal glass in whose depths shone the moon-bathed foliage of the chestnut trees that held the eye the longest. For it was nothingness, a sheet of death; and it was everything. Nothing it held was its own although the least leaf was reflected with microscopic accuracy – and, as though to light these aqueous forms with a luminary of their own, a phantom moon lay on the water, as big as a plate and as white, save where the shadow of its mountains lay.

II

And yet this visual richness gave less a sense of satisfaction than of expectancy. This was a setting if ever there were one – but a setting for *what*? The stage was set, the audience was gathered – what next? Titus turned his eyes for the first time to where his sister had been standing, but she was no longer there. He was alone on the platform with the horsehair chair.

And then he saw her seated on a log with her mother beside her. From their feet the land dipped gradually to the water and on this decline was gathered what was pleased to think itself the upper stratum of Gormenghast society. To right and left the ground swarmed with officials of every kind – and over Titus, and over them all were the spreading terraces of the trees.

Finding himself alone, Titus sat down on the purple chair and then, to make himself more comfortable, curled his feet under him, and rested his arm on the bolster-like arm. He lifted his eyes to the lake with its upside-down picture of all that was spread above it.

Fuchsia trembled as she sat beside her mother. She remembered how the chestnut woods had held back their secret until this moment, years ago, and how they would now throw out their startling characters. She turned her head to see whether she could catch her brother's eye, but he was staring straight ahead, and as she watched him his hand went to his mouth again and she saw him sit forward on the couch as rigidly as though he had been turned to stone.

For immediately ahead of him, across the unblemished lake, figures as tall as the chestnut trees themselves were straddling out of the shadows, and to the verge of the opposite bank, where they stood, unbelievably. Before them, their liquescent stage lay spread. The reflections of their fantastically elongated bodies were already deep in the lake.

There were four of them, and they came out one after another from various parts of the forest. They appeared to take no notice of one another although they turned their heads to right and left. The movements of their bodies appeared stiff and exaggerated, but extraordinarily eloquent.

From the high masks that topped them, to the grass on which they balanced could not have measured less than thirty feet.

They were beings of another realm and the crowds that stared up at them from below had not only been shrivelled up into midgets, but were also made to appear grey and prosaic. For these four giants were in every way most beautiful and extraordinary. The woods behind them seemed darker than ever now, for these lofty spectres were tinted under the moon's rays with colours as sharp and barbaric as the plumage of tropical birds.

From one to another, Titus turned his gaze, unable to resist the movements of his eyes, although he longed to dwell on each one separately.

Upon their lofty shoulders they carried their heads like kings – abstracted and inscrutable. Their dignity was something that infused their slightest movement. In the stiff and measured raising of an arm the very humus appeared to be drawn out of the soil below. The tilting of their faces to the sky made the sky naked – made the moon guilty.

The group had stalked out of that part of the forest that faced Titus across the lake. Their four heads were very different. That of the most northerly was crowned with a high conical hat like a dunce's, under which a great white head resembling a lion's turned slowly to left and right, upon the shoulders that supported it. The eyes, perfectly circular, were painted the purest emerald green and when the head was raised they shone to the moon.

But its mane was its glory. From close above the eyes, and from the sides and back of the head it billowed forth luxuriantly and fell as far as the waist in undulations of imperial purple. From the waist downwards – a twenty foot drop to the feet of the stilts – a prodigious skirt descended like a cascade, weighted down by its own length of material. It was quite black, as were those of the other three. This mutual darkness of the lower two thirds of their bodies gave an illusory effect to their upper parts. The skirts could be seen, and their reflections could be seen, but with nothing like the same clarity. It was, at times, almost as though their coloured 'heights' were floating. The arms emerged from halfway down the mane. In either hand the Lion held a dagger.

Next to this figure with its purple mane, stood one as far removed as the Lion from the natural, but more sinister in that the wolfish character of the head was not redeemed by either a noble cast of feature, or lightened by the charade-like nature of the long white dunce's hat.

This vulpine monster was undeniably wicked – but so decoratively wicked! The head was crimson, and the cocked and pointed ears were deepest azure. This azure was repeated in the circles that were scattered over the grey hide of the upper body. In either hand was an enormous cardboard bottle of poison. As with the Lion the black skirt fell like a wall of darkness.

Even now as it stood in what might be thought of as the 'wings', for they had not set foot in the watery stage, their every movement was something awesome. For the Wolf to lift its poison-bottle was for a shudder to run through the swarming populace; for the Lion to shake its mane was for the lake to be circled with gooseflesh.

Next to the Wolf, and separated by half an acre of upturned heads was the Horse – a horse unlike any other travesty of that noble animal that had ever been concocted – and yet it was more a horse than anything else. It was monstrous, in its own way, with an expression of such fatuous melancholy that Titus could neither laugh nor cry for neither expression was true to what he felt.

Upon its head, this giantess wore an enormous basket-work hat whose brim cast a circular shadow upon the moonlit water far beneath. Long powder blue ribbons fell ludicrously from the crown of the hat and clustered about the hairy shoulder ten feet below. All about the lower part of the crown the hat was decorated with grass and livid lilies.

From beneath all this resplendence the loose-lipped head of the Horse protruded with baleful idiocy. Like the Lion, its long maudlin head was white, but red circles were painted on either side between the eyes and the curve of the jaws. The neck was long and absurdly supple, with a stubby fringe of orange hair along the spine.

It was clothed in an apple-green smock from under which the long skirt descended, hiding the tall and perilous stilts that protruded for no more than six inches beneath the black hem. In one hand the Horse carried a parasol and in the other a book of poems. From time to time the Horse would slowly turn its head and incline it, with a sort of sad and smirking deference, to the Lamb upon its left.

This Lamb, a little less in height than its companions, for all its towering stature, was a mass of pale golden curls. Its expression was one of unspeakable sanctity. However it moved its head – whatever the angle, whether it scanned the heavens in search of some beatific vision, or lowered its face as though to muse upon its own unspotted breast –

there was no escape from its purity. Between its ears, and set upon the golden curls was a silver crown. The swathes of a grey shawl were drawn demurely over the shoulders, across the golden breast and fell in sculpturesque folds of some length, so that there was less to be seen of the inevitable skirt. It carried nothing in its hands for they were clasped upon its heart.

These four, with their heads as big as doors, yet appearing almost small in proportion to the awe-inspiring loftiness of the bodies, these four had not stood at the margin of the reflecting lake for more than a minute before, with startling unanimity of purpose, they set forth upon the waters.

Titus, crying with excitement, gripped the rotten upholstery of the chair on either side, his fingers working their way into the ancient horse-hair.

The Four ahead of him appeared to be moving upon the surface across the lake. Their strange, spidery strides took them far from the shore, but the hems of their skirts were still dry! Titus could in no way understand it, until suddenly he realized that in spite of the clear reflections that seemed to plunge into fathomless water, the great lake was in reality but a few inches deep. It was a film.

For a moment he was disappointed. There is danger in deep water, and danger is more real than beauty in a boy's mind. But this disappointment was immediately forgotten for there could have been nothing of all this had the lake not been the merest glaze of water.

The masque of the Four upon the lake was designed, many hundreds of years ago, for this setting among the nocturnal chestnuts. The gestures of the Lion, grandiloquent, absurd yet impressive – the shaking of its purple mane, from which tremendous operation the other three invariably drew back – the terrible, side-long progress of the Wolf with the poison bottle as he manoeuvred himself ever nearer the golden lamb, and the outlandish gait of the Horse with its garnished hat, as it straddled from one end of the lake to the other, reading from its book of poems, while with its parasol it beat time in upper air to the rhythm of the verses – all this was a formula as ancient as the walls of the castle itself.

And all the while this masked drama, played upon stilts as tall as trees and upon a lake that reflected not only the progress of the performers, but the moon over whose liquid image the monstrous Horse would invariably stumble as though he had been tripped – all the while the silence continued unbroken. For although a strong strain of the ridiculous ran through everything, this was not the dominant impression. When the Horse-creature tripped or waved its parasol; when the Wolf was thwarted and its lower jaw fell open like a drawbridge; when the Lamb cast its eyes to the moon, only to be distracted in the throes of its sanctity by the whisking of the Lion's mane – when these things happened there was no laughter but only a kind of relief, for the grandeur of the spectacle, and the godlike rhythms of each sequence were of such a nature that there were few present who were not affected as by some painful memory of childhood.

At last, the time-hallowed ritual drew to its end, and the lofty creatures stepped from the shallow lake, and turning before they disappeared into the deep woods, bowed across the shallows to Titus, as might the gods of Poetry and Battle bow to one another, as equals across enchanted water.

The Four, as they departed, took the silence with them. The rest of the night was by way of being a release from perfection, and was given over to every kind of scattered activity.

Between the bonfires that surrounded the lake and warmed the air above the chestnut forest, fresh fires were being lit, and under the lake-ward boughs hampers and baskets of provisions were being unpacked.

The Countess of Groan, who had remained throughout the masque as immovable as the log on which she sat, now turned her head over her shoulder.

But Titus was no longer on the platform, nor was Fuchsia at her side.

She rose from the log, the traditional place of honour, and moved abstractedly down to the lake's edge between lines of functionaries, who on seeing her rise knew that they were now free for the rest of the night to disport themselves as they wished.

Against the shimmering lake her massive form loomed darkly save for the moonlight on her shoulders and her dark red hair.

She gazed about her but seemed to be unaware of the crowds that thronged the water's edge.

A giant picnic was piecing itself together as the fish and fruit and loaves and pies were laid out beneath the trees, and it was not long before the lake was surrounded by an unbroken feast.

And while all these preparations were going on, shrill packs of urchins raced through the chestnut woods, swarmed among the branches, or streaming out of the trees, pranced or cart-wheeled to the centre of the lake, their reflections flying beneath them, and the film of water spouting from their feet. And when a pack would meet its rival pack, then hand to hand, a hundred watery combats would churn the shallows, as scattered over the aqueous arena the children grappled, the moonlight sliding on their slippery limbs.

And Titus watching longed with his whole being to be anonymous – to be lost within the core of such a breed – to be able to live and run and fight and laugh and if need be, cry, on his own. For to be one of those wild children would have been to be *alone* among companions. As the Earl of Gormenghast he could never be alone. He could only be lonely. Even to lose himself was to be lost with that other child, that symbol, that phantom, the seventy-seventh Earl of Gormenghast who hovered at his elbow.

Fuchsia had signalled him to jump from the platform, and together they had raced into the chestnut woods immediately behind, and for a moment or two, in the darkness, they had held each other in the deep shadows of the trees and had heard one another's hearts beating.

'It was wicked of me,' said Fuchsia at last, 'and dangerous. We are supposed to have our midnight supper at the long table, with Mother. And we must go back soon.'

'You can if you like,' said Titus, who was trembling with a deep hatred of his status. 'But I'm leaving.'

'Leaving?'

'Leaving for ever,' said Titus. 'For ever and ever. I am going into the wild, like . . . Flay . . . and like that . . .'

But he could think of no way to describe that wisp of a creature who had floated through a forest of gold oaks.

'You can't do that,' said Fuchsia. 'You would die and I wouldn't let you.'

'You couldn't stop me,' cried Titus. 'Nobody could stop me –' and he began to tear off the long grey tunic, as though it were in his path.

But Fuchsia, her lips trembling, held his arms to his sides.

'No! no!' she whispered passionately. 'Not now, Titus. You can't . . .'

But with a jerk he freed himself, but immediately tripped in the darkness and fell upon his face. When he raised himself, and saw his sister above him he pulled her down, so that she knelt at his side. In the distance they could hear the cries of the children by the lake, and then, suddenly, the harsh ringing of a bell.

'That is for supper,' whispered Fuchsia, at last, for she had waited in vain for Titus to speak, 'and after supper we will go along the shore together and see the cannon.'

Titus was crying. The long day he had spent alone, the lateness of the hour, the excitement, the sense of his essential isolation – all these things had worked together to weaken him. But he nodded. Whether Fuchsia saw his silent answer to her question or not, she made no further remark, but lifting him from the ground, she dried his eyes with the loose sleeve of her dress.

Together they picked their way to the edge of the wood, and there were the bonfires again and crowds and the lake with the chestnut trees beyond, and there was the platform where he had sat alone, and there was their mother at the long table with her elbows on the moonlit linen, and her chin in her hands, while before her, and seemingly unnoticed, for her gaze was fixed upon the distant hills, the customary banquet lay spread in all its splendour, a rich and crowded masterpiece, the gold plate of the Groans burning with a slow and mellow fire and the crimson goblets smouldering at the moon.

FIFTY-ONE

I

AND all the while the progress of the seasons, those great tides, enveloped and stained with their passing colours, chilled or warmed with their varying exhalations, the tracts of Gormenghast. And so, as Fuchsia wanders across her room in search of a lost book, the south spinneys below her window are misty with a green hesitation, and a few days later the sharp green fires have broken out along the iron boughs.

II

Opus Fluke and Flannelcat are leaning over the verandah railing above the Professors' quadrangle. The old quadman is sweeping the dust thirty feet below them. It is thick and white with heat, for the spring has long since passed.

'Hot work for an old fellow!' shouts Fluke to the old man. The ancient lifts his head and wipes his brow. 'Ah!' he calls up in a voice that could not have been used for weeks. 'Ah, sir, it's a dry do.' Fluke retires and in a few minutes has returned with a bottle which he has stolen from Mulefire's apartment. This he lowers on a length of string to the old man, far below in the dust.

III

In his study, and locked away from the world, Prunesquallor, lying rather than sitting in his elegant arm chair, reads with his crossed feet resting just below the mantelpiece.

The small fire in the grate lights up his keen, absurdly refined, and for all its weirdness of proportion, delicate face. The magnifying lenses of his spectacles, which can give so grotesque an effect to his eyes, gleam in the firelight.

It is no book of medicine that he is so absorbed in. On his knee there is an old exercise book filled with verses. The handwriting is erratic but legible. Sometimes the poems are in a heavy, ponderous and childish hand – sometimes in a quick, excited calligraphy, full of crossings-out and mis-spellings.

That Fuchsia should have ever asked him to read them was the most thrilling thing that he had ever experienced. He loved the girl as though she were his own daughter. But he had never sought her out. Little by little, as the times went by she had taken him into her confidence.

But as he reads, and while the autumn wind whistles in the branches of the garden trees, his brow contracts and he returns his gaze to the four curious lines which Fuchsia had crossed out with a thick pencil –

> How white and scarlet is that face,
> Who knows, in some unusual place
> The coloured heroes are alight
> With faces made of red and white.

IV

It is a cold and dreary winter. Once again Flay, who is now as much at home in the Silent Halls as he had been in the forests, sits at the table in his secret room. His hands are deep in his ragged pockets. Before him is spread a great sail of paper that not only covers the table, but descends in awkward folds and creases to the floor on every side. A portion near its centre is covered with markings, laboriously scripted words, short arrows, dotted lines, and incomprehensible devices. It is a map; a map which Mr Flay has been working upon for over a year. It is a map of the district that surrounds him – the empty world, whose anatomy, little by little, he is piecing together, extending, correcting, classifying. He is, it seems, in a city that has been forsaken and he is making it his own; naming its streets and alleys, its avenues of granite, its winding flights and blackened terraces – exploring ever further its hollow hinterlands, while over all, like a lowering sky, as continuous and as widespread are the endless ceilings and the unbroken roof.

He is no master of graphology. A pen sits awkwardly in his hand. But both while engaged upon his expeditions and when adding with painful slowness to his map, during the long days his life in the pathless woods is standing him in good stead.

With no stars to help him, his sense of orientation has become uncanny.

Tonight he will keep watch upon Steerpike's door as has become his custom in the small hours, and if the opportunity arises, he will follow him upon whatever business he is bent. Until then he has seven hours

in which to push forward with this task of reconnaissance which has now become a passion.

He takes his hands out of his pockets and with a scarred and bony forefinger he traces for himself the path he proposes to follow. It takes a northward course sweeping in a number of arcs before it zig-zags through a veritable cross-hatching of narrow alleys to reappear as a twelve-foot corridor with a worn pavement on its either side. This corridor heads undeviatingly to the north and fades out in a series of small, hesitant dots that part of Mr Flay's paper that has all but overlapped the table. It has reached the margin of his knowledge to the north.

He pulls the chart towards him and the loose paper on the far side of the table slides upwards from the floor, and then, in creeping forwards to beneath his outstretched head, it opens out its wastes of untrodden whiteness with an arctic yawn.

V

And the days move on and the names of the months change and the four seasons bury one another and it is spring again and yet again and the small streams that run over the rough sides of Gormenghast Mountain are big with rain while the days lengthen and summer sprawls across the countryside, sprawls in all the swathes of its green, with its gold and sticky head, with its slumber and the drone of doves and with its butterflies and its lizards and its sunflowers, over and over again, its doves, its butterflies, its lizards, its sunflowers, each one an echo-child while the fruit ripens and the grotesque boles of the ancient apple trees are dappled in the low rays of the sun and the air smells of such rotten sweetness as brings hunger to the breast, and makes of the heart a sea-bed, and a tear, the fruit of salt and water, ripens, fed by a summer sorrow, ripens and falls . . . falls gradually along the cheek-bones, wanders over the wastelands listlessly, the loveliest emblem of the heart's condition.

And the days move on and the names of the months change and the four seasons bury one another and the field-mice draw upon their granaries. The air is murky and the sun is like a raw wound in the grimy flesh of a beggar, and the rags of the clouds are clotted. The sky has been stabbed and has been left to die above the world, filthy, vast and bloody. And then the great winds come and the sky is blown naked, and a wild bird screams across the glittering land. And the Countess stands at the window of her room with the white cats at her feet and stares at the frozen landscape spread below her, and a year later she is standing there again but the cats are abroad in the valleys and a raven sits upon her heavy shoulder.

And every day the myriad happenings. A loosened stone falls from a high tower. A fly drops lifeless from a broken pane. A sparrow twitters in a cave of ivy.

The days wear out the months and the months wear out the years, and a flux of moments, like an unquiet tide, eats at the black coast of futurity.

And Titus Groan is wading through his boyhood.

FIFTY-TWO

A KIND of lull had settled upon the castle. It was not that events were lacking but that even those of major importance had about them a sense of unreality. It was as though some strange wheel of destiny had brought to the earth its pre-ordained lacuna.

Bellgrove was now a husband. Irma had not wasted a moment before she began to raise those formidable earthworks that can so isolate the marital unit from the universe.

She always knew what was best for Bellgrove. She always knew what he most needed. She knew how the headmaster of Gormenghast should behave and she knew how his inferiors should behave in his presence. The staff were terrified of her. There was no difference between them and their pupils where Irma was concerned. It was a case of whispering behind the hand; tip-toeing past the door of Bellgrove's apartment; looking to the condition of their finger nails, and, worst of all, attending their classes at the scheduled time.

She had changed almost out of recognition. Marriage had given her vanity both drive and direction. It had not taken her long to discover the inherent weakness of her husband. She loved him no less for this, but her love became militant. He was her child. Noble, but ah, no longer wise. It was she who was wise and in her loving wisdom it was for her to guide him.

From Bellgrove's point of view it was a sad story. Having had her in the palm of his hand – it was now a bitter business, this reversal. He had been unable to keep it up. Little by little, his lack of will, his native feebleness became apparent. She had found him, one day, practising a series of noble expressions before the mirror. She saw him shake his beautiful white locks, and she had heard him chiding her for some imaginary misdemeanour. 'No, Irma,' he was saying, 'I will not have it. I would be gratified if you would remember your station,' and then he had smirked, as though ashamed, and on looking into the mirror again, had seen her standing behind him.

But he knew himself to be her superior. He knew that there was in him a kind of golden fund, a reserve of strength, but at the same time he knew that this strength was of no avail for he had never drawn upon it. He did not know how to. He didn't even know exactly what kind of strength it was. But it was there, and it was real to him in the way that an ultimate innocence, like a nest egg, awaits its moment in the breasts of sinners.

And yet for all his subjugation it was a relief to be able to be weak again. Gradually he gave himself up to it, bearing in mind, all the time, his own secret superiority – as a man – and as a broken reed. Better, he argued to have been a thing of mystery and music and to have been broken than to have never been a reed, but to have been composed of some prosaic if quite unbreakable material with about as much mystery or music in its blood stream as there is love in a condor's eye.

All these thoughts, of course, he kept strictly to himself. To Irma's mind he was her lord upon a leash. To the staff he was simply on a leash. In his own mind, leash or not, a philosophy was growing. The philosophy of invisible revolution.

He peered at her, not unlovingly, through his white eyelashes. He was glad she was there, mending his ceremonial gown. It was better than being baited by the staff as in the old days. After all, she couldn't tell what he was thinking. He watched her pointed nose. How had he ever admired it?

But oh the glee of thinking to himself. Of dreaming of impossible escapes, or of reversing the status quo, so that once again she would be in his power, as on that magical evening in the dappled arbour. But then – the strain of it, the strain of it. There was no joy in will-power.

He settled back in his chair and revelled in his weakness, his old mouth twisting a little at one corner, his eyes half-closing as he relaxed the leonine features of his magnificent old head.

The sense of unreality which had spread through the castle like some strange malaise had muffled Bellgrove's marriage so that although there was no lack of incident, and no question as to its importance, a sharpness, an awareness was missing and nobody really believed in what was happening. It was as though the castle was recovering from an illness, or was about to have one. It was either lost in a blur of unfocused memory or in the unreality of a disquietening premonition. The immediacy of the castle's life was missing. There were no sharp edges. No crisp sounds. A veil was over all things, a veil that no-one could tear away.

How long it lasted was impossible to say, for although there was this general oppression that weighed on every action, all but annihilating its reality of significance, making, for instance, of Bellgrove's marriage a ceremony of dream, yet the sense of unreality in each individual was different; different in intensity, in quality, and in duration, according to the temperaments of all who were submerged.

There were some who hardly realized that there was a difference. Thick bullet-headed men with mouths like horses, were scarcely aware. They felt that nothing mattered quite as much as it used to do, but that was all.

Others were drowned in it, and walked like ghosts. Their own voices, when they spoke, appeared to be coming to them from far away.

It was the influence of Gormenghast, for what else could it have been? It was as though the labyrinthian place had woken from its sleep of stone and iron and in drawing breath had left a vacuum, and it was in this vacuum that its puppets moved.

And then came a time when, on a late spring evening, the castle exhaled and the distances came forward in a rush, and the far away voices grew sharp and close, and the hands became aware of what they were grasping, and Gormenghast became stone again and returned to its sleep.

But before the weight of emptiness had lifted, a number of things had happened which, although when seen in retrospect appeared vague and shadowy, had nevertheless taken place. However nebulous they had appeared at the time their repercussions were concrete enough.

Titus was no longer a child, and the end of his schooldays was in sight. He had, as the years went by, become more solitary. To all save Fuchsia, the Doctor, Flay and Bellgrove he presented a sullen front. Beneath this dour and unpleasing armour his passionate longing to be free of his hereditary responsibilities smouldered rebelliously. His hatred, not for Gormenghast, for its very dust was in his bloodstream, and he knew no other place, but for the ill fate that had chosen him to be the one upon whose restless shoulders there would rest, in the future, the heavy onus of an ancient trust.

He hated the lack of choice: the assumption on the part of those around him that there were no two ways of thinking: that his desire for a future of his own making was due to ignorance or to a wilful betrayal of his birthright.

But more than all this he hated the confusion in his own heart. For he was proud. He was irrationally proud. He had lost the unself-consciousness of childhood where he was a boy among boys; he was now Lord Titus and conscious of the fact. And while he ached for the anonymity of freedom he moved erect with a solitary pride of bearing, sullen and commanding.

And it was this contradiction within himself that was as much as anything else the cause of his blunt and uncompromising manners. With the youths of his own age he had become more and more unpopular, his schoolmates seeing no cause for the violence of his outbursts. He had ripped the lid off his desk for less than nothing. He could be dangerous and as time went on his isolation grew more complete. The boy who had been ready for any act of mischief, for any midnight venture, in the long dormitories, was now another being!

The tangle of his thoughts and emotions – the confused groping for an outlet for his wayward spirit, his callow lust for revolt, left no room in him for those things that would once have quickened his pulse. He had found that to be alone was more intoxicating. He had changed.

And yet, in spite of the long years that had passed since he, Doctor Prunesquallor and Professor Bellgrove had played marbles in the small fort, he was still as able to delight in the most childish of amusements. He would often be found sitting by the moat, and launching by the hour small wooden boats of his own making. But more abstractedly than in the old days, as though for all his apparent concentration, as he carved with his penknife the tapering bows or the blunt stern of some monarch of the waves – his mind was really far away.

Yet he carved away at these small craft and he named them as he launched them upon their perilous missions to the isles of blood and spices. And he would visit the Doctor and watch him making those peculiar drawings which Irma had never cared for, those drawings of small spidery men, a hundred on a page, engaged now in battle, now in conclave, now in scenes of hunting, now in worship before some spidery god. And for the hour he would be very happy. And he would visit Fuchsia and they would talk and talk until their throats were sore . . . would talk about all there was in Gormenghast for they knew no other place – but neither to his sister nor to Bellgrove who would sometimes, when Irma was engaged elsewhere, shamble down to the moat's edge to launch a ship or two – neither to him, nor to the Doctor did Titus ever unburden himself of his secret fear, the fear that his life would become no more than a round of pre-ordained ritual. For there was no one, not even Fuchsia who, however much she might sympathize, could help him now. There was no one who would dare to encourage him in his longing to free himself of his yoke to escape and to discover what lay beyond the margins of his realm.

FIFTY-THREE

THE unearthly lull that had descended upon Gormenghast had not failed to affect so imaginative and highly strung a nature as Fuchsia's. Steerpike who, although sensitive to atmosphere in a high degree, was less submerged, and moved as it were with his crafty head protruding above the weird water. He could see Fuchsia, as she walked in a transparent world, far below the surface. Acutely aware of this trance-like omnipresence, Steerpike, following the course of his nature, was at once concerned with how best he could use his drug to further his own ends, and it was not long before he had come to a decision.

He must woo the daughter of the House. He must woo her with all the guile and artistry in his power. He must break down her reserve with an approach both simple and candid, with an assumed gentleness, and a concentration upon those things which he could pretend they had in common: and with a charming yet manly deference to her rank. At the same time he would both give the impression of those fires within him that were undoubtedly there, if for the wrong reason, and by devious means, so engineer their assignations and coincidental meetings that she would often come upon him in hazardous situations, for he knew already how much she admired his bravery.

But at the same time he must keep his face hidden as much as possible. He had no illusions about its power to horrify. That she was impregnated with the heavy yet far away atmosphere of the place, was no reason for him to assume that she was impervious to the fearfulness of his ruined face. They would meet after dark, when with no visual distraction she could gradually realize that only in him could she find that complete companionship, that harmony of mind and spirit – that sense of confidence, of which she had been so starved. But she was starved for more than this. He knew her life had been loveless – and he knew of the warmth and vibrancy of her nature. But he had always waited. And now the time had come.

He laid his plans. He made his first advances in the dusky evenings. As Master of Ceremonies, it was not difficult for him to know what parts of the castle would be clear of possible intruders at varying times of the late evening.

Fuchsia, deeply affected by the unearthly atmosphere that had made of her ancient home a place that she could hardly believe in, was led by subtle degrees, through a period of weeks, to a state of mind where she felt it a natural thing to have her advice solicited, as to this point or that, and for Steerpike to tell her of what had happened to him during the day. His voice was quiet and even. His vocabulary, rich and flexible. She was attracted by his grip upon whatever subject they conversed about – it was so far beyond her own powers. Her admiration for his vitality of mind developed, in its turn, into an excited interest in the whole being, this Steerpike, this nimble, fearless confidant of their nocturnal meetings. He was unlike anyone else. He was wide awake and alive to his fingertips. Her old revulsion at the memory of his burned face and red hands became buried under the ever growing structure of this propinquity.

That she, the daughter of the Line, should see so much of an officer of the castle, for unofficial reasons, was, she knew, a crime against her station. But she had been so long a time alone. To be able to feel that she could interest anyone to the extent of their wanting to see her night after night was something so new to her that it was but a short way to the outskirts of that treacherous land whose paths she would so soon be treading.

But she did not look ahead. Unlike this new companion, this man of the dusk, whose every sentence, every thought, every action was ulterior, she lived in the moment of excitement, savouring the taste of an experience that was enough in itself. She had no instinct of self-preservation. She had no apprehension. For Steerpike had moved towards her with a gradual and circuitous cunning until the evening came when their hands met involuntarily in the darkness, and neither hand was withdrawn, and from that moment, it seemed to Steerpike that his road to power was clear before him.

And for a long time everything continued to develop in the way he had foreseen, the intimacy of their secret meetings leading them ever more deeply into, as Fuchsia thought, each other's confidence.

But, with the evil knowledge of the power that was now his, Steerpike, indulging himself in the anticipation of final conquest, made no rash attempt to seduce Fuchsia. He knew that with Fuchsia no longer a virgin, he would have her, if for no other reason than that of simple blackmail, in the palm of his hand. But he was not ready yet. There was a lot to be considered.

As for Fuchsia, it was all so new and tremendous to her that her emotions had enough on which to feed. She was happier than she had ever been in her life.

FIFTY-FOUR

THE disappearance of the Earl, Sepulchrave, Titus' father, and of his sisters, the Twins, and of their terrible and secret ends; the death of Sourdust by burning, and of his son Barquentine by fire and water, what of all this mystery and violence in the eyes of the castle? They had spread themselves, these horrors, over a period of twelve or more years, and although the minds, active in their different ways, of the Countess, the Doctor, and Flay, had, from their different angles, made periodic efforts to discover in the tragedies some common ground, yet no proof of foul play had yet been found which could support their suspicions.

Flay alone knew the grizzly truth about the secret death of his master, Lord Sepulchrave, and of his enemy the gross Swelter whom he had killed. This knowledge he had never divulged.

But his own banishment had been the result of Steerpike's gesture of disloyalty to his mad master, when the skewbald man was a youth of seventeen or eighteen years, and this disloyalty had remained rooted in Flay's mind. But of the incarceration and death of the Twins he knew nothing, although, witless of its origins and significance, he had heard their terrible laughter as they died in the hollow halls.

He had strained his brain and memory, as had the Doctor and the Countess, to draw some significant conclusion from the common deaths by fire of the father and son – Sourdust and Barquentine – and from the fact that Steerpike had been the hero of both occasions. Try as they would they were unable to rationalize their suspicions.

And yet there were, over the course of the years, small concrete although disconnected reasons for apprehension. As yet they fitted into no pattern, but they were there, and they were not forgotten.

The Doctor had always been anxious to discover Steerpike's reason for leaving his service and establishing himself as confidant and retainer of the vacant Twins. His was no mind to find pleasure in such surroundings. His only reason must have been for social advancement or for some darker motive. The identical Twins had disappeared. Their note which Steerpike had found on their table had told of their intention to kill themselves. Prunesquallor had got hold of this note and compared its calligraphy with a letter Irma had once received from them. He compared them in mirrors – he devoted an entire evening to their scrutiny. It seemed that they were by the same hand, the formation of letters big and round and uncertain as a child's.

But the Doctor had known these retarded women for many years and he did not believe, for all the oddness of their thwarted natures, that they would ever take their own lives.

Nor did the Countess believe that they were capable of making an end to themselves. Their puerile ambition and vanity – and their only too obvious longing to assume, one day, the rôles in which they were always seeing themselves, the rôles of ladies, great and splendid, bedecked with jewels, precluded any such idea as suicide. But there was no proof either way.

The Doctor had told the Countess of Steerpike's delirious cry 'And the Twins will make it five!' She had stared out of the window of her room.

'Five what?' she had said.

'Exactly,' said the Doctor. 'Five what?'

'Five enigmas,' she answered heavily, without a change of expression.

'And what are they, your ladyship? Do you mean five . . .?'

She interrupted him heavily. 'The Earl, my husband,' she said. 'Vanished. One. His sisters, vanished: two. Swelter, vanished: three. Sourdust and Barquentine, burned: five . . .'

'But the deaths of Sourdust and Barquentine were hardly enigmatic . . .'

'One wouldn't be. Two would,' said the Countess. 'And the youth at them both.'

'The youth?' queried the Doctor.

'Steerpike,' said the Countess.

'Ah,' said the Doctor, 'we have the same fears.'

'We have,' said the Countess. 'I am waiting.'

The Doctor thought of Fuchsia's poem:

> How white and scarlet is that face!
> Who knows, in some unusual place
> The coloured heroes are alight
> With faces made of red and white.

'But your ladyship,' he said – she was still staring through the window. 'The words "And the Twins will make it five" suggest to me that their ladyships Cora and Clarice would make two of the group he had in his delirious mind. He was making a list of individuals, in his fever, I will stake my brightest penny.'

'And so . . .'

'And so, your ladyship, the deaths and disappearances would be six, not five.'

'Who knows?' said the Countess. 'It is too early. Give him rope. We have no proof. But by the black tap-root of the very castle, if my fear is founded, the towers themselves will sicken at his death: the oldest stones will spew.'

Her heavy face flushed. She lowered her hand into a wide pocket, and drawing forth some grain she extended her arm. A small mottled bird appeared out of nowhere and running along her outstretched arm, perched with its claws about her index finger and with a sideways movement began to peck from her palm.

FIFTY-FIVE

'But he can't help giving you your ritual for each day, can he?' said Fuchsia. 'And instructing you. It's not his fault, it's the law. Father had to do it when he was alive – and *his* father had to – and they've all had to. It isn't possible for him to do any different. He *has* to tell you what's in the books, however trying it is for you.'

'I hate him,' said Titus.

'Why? Why?' cried Fuchsia. 'What's the good of hating him because he's doing what he has to do? You don't expect that he can make an exception, do you, after thousands of years? I suppose you'd rather have Barquentine. Can't you see how bigoted you are? I think he does his work wonderfully.'

'I hate him!' said Titus.

'You're becoming a bore!' said Fuchsia, with heat. 'Can't you say anything except "I hate him"? What's wrong with him? Do you hold his appearance against him? Do you? If so, you're mean and damnable.'

She shook her thick black hair away from her eyes. Her chin trembled.

'Oh God! God! Do you think I want to quarrel with you, Titus, my darling? You know how I love you. But you're unfair. *Unfair.* You know nothing about him.'

'I hate him,' said Titus. 'I hate the cheap and stinking guts of him.'

FIFTY-SIX

As the months passed the tensions increased. Titus and Steerpike were at daggers drawn, although Steerpike, the soul of bland discretion, showed nothing of his feelings, and gave no sign to Titus or the outside world of his loathing of this forward boy – the boy who unconsciously stood between him and the zenith of his ambition.

Titus, who ever since that day when, little more than a child, he had defied Steerpike in the classroom silence, and had fallen fainting from his desk, had held on grimly to the dangerous ascendancy he had gained by that curious and childish victory.

Every day the details of his after-school duties were read out to Titus in the Library, Steerpike flicking through the pages of cross-reference, and explaining the obscurer passages with clarity and precision. Up till now the Master of Ceremonies had kept rigidly to the letter of the Law. But now, in the all but invulnerable position of being the only one who had access to the tomes of reference and procedure, he was making a list of duties which he would insert among the ancient papers. He had been able to unearth some of the original paper, and it was only for him to forge the copper-plate writing, and the archaic spelling and invent a series of duties for Titus which would be both galling and, on occasion, sufficiently hazardous for there to be always the outside chance of the young Earl coming to grief. There were for instance stairways that were no longer safe – there were the rotten beams and crumbling masonry. Beyond this there would always be the possibility of deliberately weakening and undermining certain cat-walks that stretched along the upper walls of the castle, or in some way or another of making sure that in following out the forged procedures, Titus would sooner or later fall *accidentally* to his death.

And with the death of Titus, and with Fuchsia in his power, the Countess alone would stand between him and a virtual dictatorship.

There would yet be enemies. There would be the Doctor whose intelligence was rather more acute than Steerpike would have wished; and there was the Countess herself, the only character for whom he held a puzzled and grudging respect – not for her intelligence, but for the reason of the very fact that she baffled his analysis. What was she? What was she thinking and by what processes? His mind and hers had no point of contact. In her presence he was doubly careful. They were animals of different species. They watched one another with the mutual suspicion of those who have no common tongue.

As for Fuchsia, it was but a step towards mastery. He had surpassed himself. Her heart was now as tender as his overtures had been, with their delicate gradations, their subtle cadences, their superb restraint.

It was no longer a case of their meeting at dusk, now here, now there, at varying rendezvous. For some while, Steerpike had for his own delectation been furnishing yet another secret room for himself. He now had nine, scattered throughout the castle only one of which, a large bedroom-study, was known to the castle. Of the rest five were in obscure quarters of Gormenghast, and three, though in the most populous areas, were as curiously hidden as a wren's nest in a bank of grass and weeds. Their doors, abutting on major arteries of the castle, were never seen to open. They were there for all to see but no one saw them.

In one of these rooms which he had but recently appropriated, and which he only visited at night when thick silence lay along the corridor, he had got together a few pictures, some books, a cabinet of shallow drawers in which he kept his collection of stolen jewellery, of old coins, a range of poisons, and various secret papers. A thick crimson carpet covered the floor. The small table and the two chairs were of elegant design and he had skilfully repaired the damage that long years had worked upon them. How different was this interior to the rough stone corridor without, with its stone pillars on either side of every door and the heavily protruding shelf-like slabs of stone above.

It was to this room that Fuchsia made her nocturnal journeys, her heart beating, her pupils dilated in the darkness. And it was here that she was so courteously received. A shaded lamp threw out a soft golden glow. A book or two, carefully chosen, lay casually here and there. It was always irksome for Steerpike to make those last few changes in the disposition of the objects which were calculated to give an air of informality to the room. He detested untidiness as he detested love. But he knew that Fuchsia would be ill at ease with the kind of formal and perfect arrangement that gave him pleasure.

Even so, she seemed strangely incongruous in that tasteful and orderly trap. For Steerpike could not entirely destroy the reflection of his own coldness. She seemed too much alive – alive in so different a sense from the glittering and icy vitality of her companion – too much alive in the way that love like an earthquake or some natural and sinless force, is incompatible with a neat and formal world. However quietly she sat back in her chair, her black hair about her shoulders, she was potentially disruptive.

But she admired what she saw. She admired all that she was not. It was all so different from Gormenghast. When she remembered her old untidy attic and the rooms she now occupied with the floor littered with poems, and the walls with drawings, she supposed that there must be something wrong with her.

When she remembered her mother, she felt, for the first time, embarrassed.

One night when she tapped upon the door with her fingertips there was no reply. She tapped again, glancing apprehensively along the corridor on either side. The silence was absolute. She had never before had to wait for more than the fraction of a second. And then a voice said, 'Be careful, my lady.'

Fuchsia had started at the sound as at the touch of a red iron. The voice had come from nowhere. There was no sound of a step. In fear and trembling she lit the candle she carried in her hand – a rash and risky thing to do. But there was no one. And then, in the far distance, something began to approach her rapidly. Long before she could see Steerpike she knew it was he. It was but a few moments before his swift, narrow, high-shouldered form was upon her and had snatched the candle from her hand and crushed out the flame. In another moment his key had been turned in the lock and she had been hustled through the door. He locked it from the inside, in the darkness, but he had already whispered fiercely 'Fool.' With that word the world turned over. Everything changed.

The delicate balance of their relationship was set in violent agitation – and a dead weight came down over Fuchsia's heart.

Had the crystalline and dazzling structure which Steerpike had gradually erected, adding ornament to ornament until, balanced before her in all its beauty, it had dazzled the girl – an outward sign of his regard for her – had the exquisite structure been less exquisite, less crystalline, less perfect, then its crash upon the cold stones far beneath would never have been so final. Its substance, brittle as glass, had been scattered in a thousand fragments.

The short, brutal word, and the push which he had given her had turned her on the instant from a dark and eager girl into something more sombre. She was shocked and resentful – but less resentful, for those first moments, than hurt. She had also become, without her knowing it *Lady Fuchsia*. Her blood had risen in her – the blood of her Line. She had forgotten it when love was tender, but now in bitterness she was again the daughter of an Earl.

She had known, of course, that to light a candle outside the very door was against all their strictest rules of care and secrecy. But she had been frightened. Maddening as it would have been for their rendezvous to have been discovered, yet there had been no sin in it, save that of her conducting her affairs in secret, and of allowing herself to be the close friend of a commoner.

But his face had been ugly with anger. She had never known that he could so lose that perfect, that chiselled quietness of pose and feature. She had never known that his clear, neat and persuasive voice could have taken on a tone so savage and cruel.

And to have been pushed! To have been thrust forwards in the darkness. His hands, which once, like those of a musician, had been so thrilling in their delicate strength, had been rough as the claws of an animal. As surely as the change of his voice, as surely as the word '*fool*', this shove in the darkness had woken her to a reality both bitter and galling.

But, as she trembled, there was, mixed with the mortification, the ghostly and exciting memory of that voice out of nowhere. It had evolved out of the darkness and at no more distance from her than a few feet, but there had been no one there. She had no more idea of how it had originated than of the intention or meaning of its warning. She only knew now, that she would not seek assistance from Steerpike; she would not confide her fear of this inexplicable 'voice' in someone who had degraded her. All the Lords of Gormenghast were at her shoulder.

She turned on her heel, in the darkened room, and before he had lit the lamp, 'Let me out of here,' she said. But almost immediately the familiar room was filled with the gold lamplight and she saw upon the table, sitting with its face cupped in its wrinkled hands, a monkey. It was dressed in a little costume of red and yellow diamonds. On its head was a small velvet hat, like a pirate's, with a violet feather curling from the crown.

Steerpike had covered his face with his hands, but he was watching Fuchsia through the slits between his fingers. He had lost command. The sight of a flame, where it had no cause to be, had struck at him like a lash. He had not been burned for nothing and fire was his only fear. Once again he had failed.

But he did not know how seriously. He watched her through his fingers.

She stared at the monkey with an expression quite indefinable. What surprise she felt was not in evidence. The turmoil and the shock of having been so roughly treated was still too strong in her for any other emotion to supplant it, however bizarre the stimulus might be. But when the vivid little animal rose to its feet and took off its hat, and when it replaced it after scratching its head and yawning, then, for an instant, something less sad suffused her face with a fleeting animation.

But it was impossible for her mood to be swung so rapidly from one extreme to another. A part of her mind was fascinated by the oddness of it all, but nothing touched her heart. It was a monkey dressed up and that was all. What would once have inflamed her with excitement, left her now at this paralysing moment, quite frozen.

Steerpike had gained a moment or two but what could he do with them? She had commanded him to let her go from the room when the monkey had caught her eye.

Once again she turned her gaze to him. Her black eyes appeared quite dead, the lustre drained away. Her lips were tightly closed.

She saw him with his hands across his face. And then she heard his voice.

'Fuchsia,' he said. 'Allow me one moment, only one, in which to tell you of the danger from which we have just escaped. There was no time to be lost and though there could never be any excuse, and although I can never ask for forgiveness, yet you must allow me a short moment in which to explain my violence.

'Fuchsia! it was for you. My violence was for you. My roughness was the roughness of love. I had no time to do other than to save you. Have you not heard the footsteps? She has just gone by. One moment later and your light would have brought her to this door. And you know the punishment. Of course you do, the punishment, which by ancient law is meted out to those daughters of the Line who consort with the mere outsiders. It is too awful to think about. And that is why our plans have been so secret, our rules so rigorous. And you know this. And you have been meticulous. But tonight you misjudged the time, did you not? You were four minutes early. O that was risky enough. But to add to such a peril the lighting of your candle. And then, as always happens, it was precisely when all this was happening that your mother should follow me.'

'My mother?' Fuchsia's voice was a whisper.

'Your mother. I had led her away for I knew that she was near. I doubled back. I crossed my tracks. I doubled back again and yet she was there, and moving slowly – I cannot understand it – but I came as I intended to this door with the length of the corridor between us – the length of the corridor and the odd twenty feet that would give me the chance of whipping into our room in time – but no, it wasn't this that I was going to do. No. For what would have been more likely than for you to have met her – and then . . .'

Steerpike dropped his hands from his face where they had been all this time. His voice had been running on with a certain charm for he had managed to vary it with a kind of stutter – not so much nervous in effect as eager and candid.

'But what happened, Fuchsia? Well, you know that as well as I do. I turned the north corner with your mother the length of a corridor behind – and there you were, like a bonfire, the length of the corridor before me. Put yourself in my place. One cannot have all the noble emotions at the same time. One cannot mix up desperation with being a perfect gentleman. At least I can't. Perhaps I should have been given lessons. All I could do was to save the situation. To hide you. To save you. You were there too early; and Fuchsia, it made me angry. I have never been angry with you before as you know. I could never imagine being angry with you. And perhaps even now, it wasn't really *you* I was angry with, but fate, or destiny or whatever it is that might have upset our plans. And it was because our plans have always been so carefully prepared – so that there shall be no risk, and you shall come to no harm – that my rage boiled up. You were no longer Fuchsia to me, at that moment. You were this *thing* that I was to save. After I had got behind the door, then you would be Fuchsia again. Had I waited for a moment before stifling your light or getting you through the door, then our lives might indeed have been ruined. For I love you, Fuchsia. You are all I ever longed for. Can't you see that it was because of this that I had no time to be polite? It was a boiling moment. It was a maelstrom. I called you "fool", yes "fool", out of my love for you – and then, . . . and then . . . here in this room again, it all seemed so unbelievable and it does so still, and I am half ashamed of the gift I had brought you and the writing I have done for you – O Fuchsia – I don't even know if I can show it to you now . . .' he turned abruptly with his hand clenched at his forehead, and then as though to say he would not give way to his despair, 'Come on then, Satan,' he whispered. 'Come on, my wicked boy!' and the monkey leapt on to Steerpike's shoulder.

'What writing?' said Fuchsia.

'I had written you a poem.' He spoke very softly, in a way that had often proved successful but he was a step too far in advance of his progress.

'But perhaps now,' he said, 'you will not wait to see it, Fuchsia.'

'No,' she said after a pause. 'Not now.'

Her inflection was so strange that it was impossible to tell whether she meant 'not now' in the sense of it being no longer possible for her to do anything so intimate as to read a love poem; or not *now*, but some other time.

Steerpike could only cry, 'I understand,' and placed the monkey on the table where it walked rapidly to and fro, on all four legs, and then leapt onto one of his cabinets.

'And I will understand, if you have no wish for Satan.'

'Satan?' her voice was quite expressionless.

'Your monkey,' he said. 'Perhaps you would rather not be bothered. I thought he would please you. I made his clothes myself.'

'I don't know! I don't know!' cried Fuchsia suddenly. 'I don't *know*, I tell you, I don't *know!*'

'Shall I take you to your room?'

'I will go myself.'

'As you please,' said Steerpike. 'But recall what I have said, I implore you. Try and understand; for I love you as the shadows love the castle.'

She turned her eyes to him. For a moment a light came into them, but in the next moment they appeared empty once more; empty and blank.

'I will never understand,' she said. 'It is no good however much you talk. I may have been wrong. I don't know. At any rate everything is changed. I don't feel the same any more. I want to go now.'

'Yes, of course. But will you grant me two small favours?'

'I suppose so,' said Fuchsia. 'What are they? I'm tired.'

'The first one is to ask you from the bottom of my heart to try to understand the strain which was put upon me, and to ask you whether, even if it is for the last time, you will meet me, as we have done for so long, meet me that we can talk for a little while – not about us, not about our trouble, not about my faults, not about this terrible chasm between us, but about all the happy things. Will you meet me tomorrow night, on those conditions?'

'I don't *know!*' said Fuchsia. 'I don't know! But I suppose so. O God, I suppose so.'

'Thank you,' said Steerpike. 'Thank you, Fuchsia.'

'And my other request is only this. To know, whether, if you have no use for Satan, you will let me have him back – because he *is* yours . . . and . . .' Steerpike turned his head from her and moved away a few paces.

'You would like to know, wouldn't you, Satan, to whom you belong . . .' he cried in a voice that was intended to sound gallant.

Fuchsia turned on him suddenly. It seemed that she had now realized the natural edge of her own intellect. She stared at the skewbald man with the monkey on his shoulder and then her words cut into the pale man like knives. 'Steerpike,' she said, '*I think you're going soft.*'

From that moment Steerpike knew that when she came on the following night he would seduce her. With so dark a secret to keep hidden, the daughter of the Countess would indeed be at his mercy. He had waited long enough. Now, upon the heels of his mistake, was the only time for him to strike. He had felt the first intimation of something slipping away beneath his feet. If guile and coercion failed him, then there could be no two ways about it. This was no time for mercy – and though she proved a tigress he would have her – and blackmail would follow as smoothly as a thundercloud.

FIFTY-SEVEN

I

WHEN Flay heard the door open quietly below him he held his breath. For a few moments no one appeared and then a shape still darker than the darkness stepped out into the corridor and began to walk rapidly away to the south. When he heard the door close again he lowered himself from the great stone shelf that stretched above Steerpike's doorway and with his long bony arms outstretched to their full extent he dropped the odd few inches to the ground.

His frustration at being unable to gain any clue as to what had been going on inside the room was only equalled by his horror at finding that it was Fuchsia who had been the clandestine visitor.

He had sensed her danger. He knew it in his bones. But he could not have persuaded her, suddenly, in the night, that she was in peril. He could not have told her what kind of peril. He did not know himself. But he had acted on the spur of the moment and in whispering to her out of the darkness he hoped that she might be put upon her guard, if only for reasons of supernatural fear.

He followed Fuchsia only so far as to be sure that she was safely upon her way to her own rooms. It was all he could do not to call after her, or overtake her, for he was deeply perplexed and frightened. His love for her was something quite alone in his sour life. Fond as he was of Titus, it was the memory of Fuchsia, more than of the boy, or of any other living soul, that gave to the flinty darkness of his mind those touches of warmth which, alone with his worship of Gormenghast, that abstraction of outspread stone, were seemingly so foreign to his nature.

But he knew that he must not speak to her tonight. The distracted way in which she moved, sometimes running and sometimes walking, gave him sufficient evidence of her fatigue and, he feared, of her misery.

He did not know what Steerpike had done or said but he knew he had hurt her, and if it were not that he felt upon the brink of gaining some kind of damning evidence, then he would have returned to that

room from which Fuchsia had emerged, and on the reappearance of
Steerpike, at the doorway, he would have plucked the skewbald face,
barehanded, from the head.

II

As he returned in the direction of the fateful corridor, a heavy pain lay
across his forehead and his thoughts pursued one another in a confusion
of anger and speculation. He could not know that with every step he
was travelling, not nearer to his room but further from it – further in
time, further in space, nor that the night's adventures far from coming
to a close were about to begin in earnest.

By now the night was well advanced. He had returned with a slow
and somewhat dragging pace, lingering here and there to lean his head
against the cold walls while his headache hammered behind his eyes
and across his angular brow. Once he sat down for an hour upon the
lowest step of a flight of age-hollowed stairs, his long beard falling upon
his knee, and taking the sharp curve of them and falling again in a
straggle of string-like hair to within a few inches of the floor.

Fuchsia and Steerpike? What could it mean? The blasphemy of it!
The horror of it! He ground his teeth in the darkness.

The castle was as silent as some pole-axed monster. Inert, breathless,
spread-eagled. It was a night that seemed to prove by the consolidation
of its darkness and its silence the hopelessness of any further dawn.
There was no such thing as dawn. It was an invention of the night's or
of the old-wives of the night – a fable, immemorially old – recounted
century after century in the eternal darkness; retold and retold to the
gnomic children in the tunnels and the caves of Gormenghast – a tale
of another world where such things happened, where stones and bricks
and ivy stems and iron could be seen as well as touched and smelt,
could be lit and coloured, and where at certain times a radiance shone
like honey from the east and the blackness was scaled away, and this
thing they called dawn arose above the woods as though the fable had
materialized, the legend come to life.

It was a night with a bull's mouth. But the mouth was bound and
gagged. It was a night with enormous eyes, but they were hooded.

The only sound that Flay could hear was the tapping of his heart.

III

It was later, and at an indeterminate hour of the same night, or inky morning, that Mr Flay, long after passing the door in the passage, came to an involuntary halt as he was about to cross a small cloistered quadrangle.

There was no reason why he should have been startled by the single band of livid yellow in the sky. He must have known that the dawn could not have been much longer delayed. He was certainly not held by its beauty. He did not think in that way.

In the centre of the quadrangle was a thorn tree, and his eyes turned to the pitchy silhouette of that part of it that cut across the yellow of the sunrise. His familiarity with the shape of the old tree caused him to stare more intently at the rough and branching stem. It seemed thicker than usual. He could only see with any clarity that portion of its bole that crossed the sunrise. It appeared to have changed its outline. It was as though something were leaning against it and adding a little to its bulk. He crouched so that still more of the unfamiliar shape came into view, for the upper part was criss-crossed with branches. As his vision was lowered and he commanded a clearer view beneath the overhanging boughs his muscles became tense for it seemed that against the livid strip of sky – which threw everything else both on the earth and in the air into yet richer blackness – it seemed – that against this livid strip the unfamiliar outline on the left of the stem was narrowing to something the shape of a neck. He got silently to his knees and then, lowering his head and lifting his eyes, he obtained an uninterrupted view of Steerpike's profile. His body and the back of the head were glued together as though he and the tree had grown up as one thing from the ground.

And that was all there was. The universal darkness above and below. The horizontal stream of saffron yellow and, like a rough black bridge that joined the upper darkness to the lower, the silhouette of the ragged thorn stem, with the profile of a face among the stems.

What was he doing there in the darkness alone and motionless?

Flay raised himself and leaned against the nearest of the cloistered pillars. The cut-out face of his enemy was immediately obscured by branches. But what had caught his eye – the unfamiliar outline of the bole – he now recognized as being formed by an angle of the young man's elbow and the line of his hip and thigh.

Without wasting a moment in trying to rationalize his instinctive belief that some fresh act of evil was afoot, Mr Flay prepared himself for, if necessary, a protracted vigil. There was nothing evil in leaning against a thorn tree as the first light broke in a yellow band – even though the leaning form was Steerpike's. There was no reason why he should not return at any moment to his room and sleep or indulge in some other equally innocent occupation.

He knew that he was caught up in one of those stretches of time when for anything to happen normally would be abnormal. The dawn was too tense and highly charged for any common happening to survive.

Steerpike, while he leaned there, rigid with the cold and flexible steel of his own conspirings, eyed the yellow light. He now knew that whatever steps were to be taken for his own advancement should be taken *now*. However much he may have wished to delay his designs there was no gainsaying the sense of urgency – the sense that time was not, for all the logic of his mind, upon his side.

It was true that there was still no evidence of his guilt. But there was something almost as bad. An indescribable sensation that his power was somehow crumbling away; that the earth was slippery beneath his feet; that in spite of his formidable position, there was that in Gormenghast that, with a puff, could blow him into darkness. However much he told himself that he had made no fundamental error – that the few slips he had made had been invariably in minor matters, maddening as they might be, yet this sensation remained. It had come upon him with the shutting of the door – when Fuchsia had left him and he was alone in his room. It was new to him. He had believed in nothing that could not be proven one way or another, in the cells of his agile brain. Apart from the inconvenience that his carelessness would, for a short time, cause him, what else was there for him to rack his brains about in regard to the incident of a few hours earlier? What was there for Fuchsia to hold against him – or even to give as evidence, save that he, the Master of Ceremonies, had been rude to her?

And yet all this was beside the point of his apprehension. If it was Fuchsia's resentment that uncovered, witlessly, the dark pit into which he was now staring, what then was this pit, wherefore was its depth, and why its darkness?

It was the first time that he had ever known that sleep, though he craved it, was beyond him. But his habit of making good use of every moment was deeply rooted – and especially when the time at his disposal was that in which the castle lay abed.

And Flay knew this. He knew that it was hardly a part of Steerpike's nature to lean against a tree for the sake of watching the sun rise. Nor was it characteristic of him to brood. He was no romantic. He lived too much upon the edge of instancy for introspection. No. It was for some other reason that he leaned there, biding his time – for what?

Mister Flay knelt down again and with his chin almost touching the ground and his small eyes swivelled upwards he stared once more at that sharp profile, its edges razor-keen against the yellow band. And then, while on his knees, two things occurred to him almost simultaneously. The first, that it was more than possible that Steerpike was waiting for sufficient light to enable him to make his way to unfamiliar ground. That he wished to go secretly and yet not lose his way, for even now the darkness was intense, the bar of light that lay like a livid ruler across the black east in no way lightening the earth or the sky about it. It kept its brilliance to itself; saffron inlaid on ebony. And this was Flay's guess: that the silhouette was waiting for the first diffusion of the light – that the line of the elbow and the hip would alter – that a profile would detach itself from a thorn tree and that a figure, lithe as a lynx, would steer into the gloom. But not alone. Flay would be following and it was when Flay, still upon his bony knees, his head near the ground, his beard spread, was turning this over in his mind that the need for some confederate, not for reason of companionship or safety, but in order to bear witness, occurred to him. Whatever he was to find, whatever lay ahead, however innocent or however bloody, it would be his word alone against the pale man's. It would be the word of an exile against that of the Master of Ritual. In being within the precincts of the castle at all, he was committing a grievous sin. He had been banished by the Countess and it would ill become him to point his finger at an officer unless his accusation was doubly backed with proof.

No sooner had this notion occurred to him than he was on his feet. He judged that he had, at the most, another quarter of an hour in which to waken – whom? He had no choice. Titus and Fuchsia alone knew of his return to the castle and that he lived in secret among the Hollow Halls.

It was of course grotesquely out of the question either that Fuchsia should be disturbed or allowed within Steerpike's range. As for Titus, he was now almost grown to his full height. But he was of an odd highly strung nature – sullen and excitable by turns. Strong as need be for his years, he was more apt to have his energy sapped by the excess of his imagination than of his body. Flay did not understand him, but he trusted him, and he knew of how the boy's loathing of Steerpike had estranged him from Fuchsia. He had no doubt that Titus would join him, but he doubted for a moment his own courage to do so dangerous a thing as to draw the heir of Gormenghast within the circle of expected danger. Yet he knew that above all else it was his duty to unmask if possible his enemy, for upon so doing hung the safety of the young earl and all he symbolized. And what is more, he swore by the iron of his long muscles, and by the strong teeth in his bony head, that whatever danger might menace his own person, no harm would come to the boy.

And so, without a moment to lose, he turned and re-entered the door in the cloisters and set off upon what in saner moments he would have considered an unthinkable mission. For what could be more iniquitous than to jeopardize the safety of his lordship? But now he saw only that by awakening Titus and launching him at dawn upon so dark a game as that of shadowing a suspect, he was perhaps bringing closer the day when the heart of Gormenghast, purged and loyal, would beat again unthreatened.

With every moment the yellow band in the sky was brightening. He sped with the awkward speed of the predatory spider, his long legs eating up the corridors, four feet at a stride and treading the stairways beneath them as though he were on stilts. But when he came to the dormitory he moved with the circumspection of a thief.

He opened the door by degrees. On his right was the janitor's cubicle. Directly he heard the sound of sand-paper scraping away behind the woodwork he recognized the breathing of the same old man who had held this watch-dog office from the early days and he knew that he was safe enough from that quarter.

But how to recognize the Earl? He had no light. Apart from the breathing of the janitor the dormitory was in absolute silence. There was no time for anything but to put his first notion into operation. There were two rows of beds that stretched away to the south-west. Why he turned to the right hand wall he did not know, but he did so without hesitation. Feeling for the end-rail of the first bed, he leaned over. 'Lordship!' he whispered. 'Lordship!' There was no reply. He turned to the second bed and whispered again. He thought he heard a head turn upon a pillow but that was all. He repeated this quick, harsh whisper at the foot of every bed. 'Lordship . . . lordship! . . .' but nothing happened and the time was slipping by. But at the fourteenth bed he repeated the whisper for a third time, for he could feel rather than hear a restlessness in the darkness below him. 'Lordship! . . .' he whispered again. 'Lord Titus!'

Something sat up in the darkness and he could hear the catch in a boy's breathing.

'Have no fear,' he whispered fiercely and his hand shook on the bedrail. 'Have no fear. Are you Titus, the Earl?'

Immediately there was a reply. 'Mister Flay? What are you doing here?'

'Have you a coat and stockings?'

'Yes.'

'Put them on. Follow me. Explain later, lordship.'

Titus made no reply but slid over the side of his bed and after fumbling for his shoes and garments, clasped them like a bundle in his arms. Together they tiptoed to the dormitory door and, once without, walked rapidly in the darkness, the bearded man with his hand upon the boy's elbow.

At the head of a staircase Titus got into his clothes, his heart beating loudly. Flay stood beside him and when he was ready they descended the stairs in silence.

As they drew nearer to the quadrangle Flay in short broken phrases was able to give Titus a disjointed idea of why he had been woken and whisked out into the night. Much as Titus sympathized with Flay's suspicions and with his hatred of Steerpike, he was becoming afraid that Flay himself had gone mad. He could see that it was a very odd thing for Steerpike to spend the night leaning against a thorn tree, but equally there was nothing criminal in it. What, he wondered, in any event, was Flay doing to be there himself? – and why should the long ragged creature of the woods be so anxious to have him with him? There was no doubt about the excitement of it all and that to be sought out was deeply flattering, but Titus had but a vague idea as to what Flay meant by needing a *witness*. A witness to what, and to prove what? Deeply as Titus suspected Steerpike of being intrinsically foul, yet he had never suspected him of actually doing other than his duty in the castle. He had never hated him for any understandable reason. He had simply hated him for being alive at all.

But when they reached the cloisters and when he peered along Flay's outstretched arm as they lay upon the cold ground, and saw, all at once, after a long and abortive scrutiny of the thorn, the sharp profile, as angular as broken glass save for the doming forehead, then he knew that the gaunt man lying beside him was no more mad than himself, and that for the first time in his life he was tasting upon his tongue the acid of an intoxicating fear, of a fearful elation.

He also knew that to leave Steerpike where he was and to return to bed would be to deliberately turn away from the climate of sharp and dangerous breath.

He put his lips to his companion's ear.

'It's Doctor's quadrangle,' he whispered.

Flay made no reply for several moments, for the remark made little sense to him.

'What of it?' he replied in an almost inaudible voice.

'Very close – on our side,' whispered Titus, 'just across the quadrangle.'

This time there was a longer silence. Flay could see at once the advantage of yet another witness and also of a double bodyguard for the boy. But what would the Doctor think of his reappearance after all these years? Would he countenance this clandestine return to the castle – even in the knowledge that it was for the castle's sake? Would he be prepared, in the future, to deny all knowledge of his, Mr Flay's, return?

Again Titus whispered, 'He is on our side.'

It seemed to Mr Flay that he was now so deeply involved that to argue each problem as it posed itself, to study each move would get him nowhere. Had he behaved in a rational way he would never have left the woods, and he would not now be lying upon his stomach, staring at a man leaning innocently against a tree. That the figure's profile against the saffron dawn was sharp and cruel was no proof of anything.

No. It was for him to obey the impulse of the moment and to have the courage to risk the future. This was no time for anything but action.

The dawn, although fiercer in the east, was yet withheld. There was no light in the air – only a strip of intense colour. But at any moment a diffusion of the sunrise would begin and the sun would heave itself above the broken towers.

There was no time to lose. In a matter of minutes the quadrangle might become impossible to cross without attracting Steerpike's attention, or Steerpike, judging himself to have sufficient light for whatever journey he wished to make, might slip away suddenly into the gloom and be irreparably lost among a thousand ways.

The Doctor's house was on the far side of the quadrangle. To get there would necessitate a detour around the margin of the quadrangle for the thorn tree was at the centre.

Obeying Flay's instructions Titus took off his shoes, and, like Flay with his boots, tied the laces together and slung them around his neck. It was Flay's first idea that they should go together, but they had no sooner taken the first few silent paces than the sudden disappearance of Steerpike reminded Flay that it was only from the particular place where they had been lying that they could keep a check upon his movements. From the Doctor's side of the quadrangle there would be no way of knowing whether or not he were still beneath the tree.

It was a full minute before Flay knew what he ought to do; and then, it was only because one of his hands, thrust deep into a ragged pocket, came upon a piece of chalk that a solution occurred to him. For a piece of white chalk meant only one thing to him. It meant a *trail*. But who was to blaze it? There was only one answer, and for two reasons.

In the first place, if one of them were to remain where he was and keep Steerpike under observation, and in the event of Steerpike's moving away from the thorn tree, of following him and leaving chalk-marks upon the ground or upon walls – then it were best for Flay to perform this none too simple function, not only because of his experience of stalking in the woods and of the danger of being discovered, but because secondly, in learning of what was afoot the Doctor would more readily and speedily accompany the young Earl than Mr Flay, the long lost exile, with whom a certain amount of time-wasting explanation would be a preliminary necessity.

And so Flay explained to Titus what he must do. He must waken the Doctor, silently. How this was to be done he did not know. He must leave this to the boy's ingenuity. He must impress upon the Doctor that there was no time to be lost. It was not the moment in which to warn him that the whole venture was based upon guess-work – that in sober fact there was no cause to rouse the Doctor from his bed. That in the open air, there was not a leaf that was not whispering of treachery, not a stone but muttered its warning, was not the kind of argument to impress anyone wakened of a sudden from their sleep. And yet he must impress the Doctor with a sense of urgency. They must return across the quadrangle to where they were now crouching, for only from this position could they tell whether Steerpike were still beneath the tree, unless, as might have happened, the sun had suddenly risen. Had it not done so, and if Steerpike was still there beneath the thorn, then they would find Mr Flay where Titus had left him; but if Steerpike had gone, then Mr Flay would also have disappeared and it was for them to move swiftly to the thorn tree, and if there were enough light, to follow the chalk trail which Flay would have begun to blaze. If, however, it were still too dark to see the marks, they were to follow them directly there was enough light. It was for them to move sufficiently rapidly to be able to overtake Mr Flay, but absolute silence was the prime essential, for the gap between Flay and Steerpike might, for reasons of darkness, be, of necessity, perilously narrow.

Feeling his way from pillar to pillar, Titus began to make a circuit of the quadrangle. His stocking'd feet made no noise at all. Once a button on the sleeve of his coat clicked against an outcrop of masonry and sounded like the snapping of a twig, so that he stopped dead in his tracks and listened for a moment or two anxiously in the silence, but that was all and a little afterwards he was standing beneath the Doctor's wall.

Meanwhile Flay lay stretched out beneath the pillar on the far side of the square, his bearded chin propped by his bony hands.

Not for a moment did his eyes wander from the silhouette of the head against the dawn. The yellow band had widened and still further intensified so that it was now not so much a thing that might be painted as a radiance beyond the reach of pigment.

As he watched he saw the first movement. The head raised itself and as the face stared up into the branches the mouth opened in a yawn. It was like the yawning of a lizard; the jaws, sharp, soundless, merciless. It was as though all thought was over, and out of some reptilian existence the yawn grew and opened like a reflex. And it was so, for Steerpike, leaning there, had, instead of pitying himself and brooding upon his mistakes, been tabulating and re-grouping in his scheduled brain every aspect of his position, of his plans, of his relationship not only with Fuchsia but with all with whom he had dealings, and making out of the maze of these relationships and projects a working pattern – something that was a masterpiece of cold-blooded systemization. But the plan of action, condensed and crystallized though it was, was nevertheless, for all its ingenuity, somehow less microscopically careful in its every particular than usual. He was prepared for the first time to take risks. The time had come for drawing together the hundred and one threads that had for so long been stretched from one end of the castle to another. This would need action. For the moment he could relax. This dawn would be his own. Tonight he must bewilder Fuchsia; dazzle her, awake her; and if all failed, seduce her so that compromised in the highest degree, he would have her at his mercy. In her present mood she was too dangerous.

But today? He yawned again. His brainwork was done. His plans were complete. And yet there was one loose end. Not in the logic of his brain, but in spite of it – a loose end that he wished to tuck away. What his brain had proved his eyes were witless of. It was his eyes that needed confirmation.

He ran his tongue between his thin, dry lips. Then he turned his face to the east. It shone in the yellow light. It shone like a carbuncle, as, breaking suddenly out of the darkness, the first direct ray of the climbing sun broke upon his bulging brow. His dark red eyes stared back into the heart of the level ray. He cursed the sun and slid out of the beam.

FIFTY-EIGHT

It was lucky for Titus that when the Doctor started from his sleep he immediately recognized the boy's shape against the windowpane.

Titus had climbed the thick creeper below the Doctor's window and had with difficulty forced up the lower sash. There had been no other way to enter. To knock or ring would have been to have lost Steerpike.

Dr Prunesquallor reached for the candle by his bed but Titus bent forward in the darkness.

'No, Dr Prune, don't light it . . . it's Titus . . . and we want your help . . . terribly . . . sorry it's so early . . . can you come? . . . Flay is with me . . .'

'Flay?'

'Yes, he has come from exile – but out of concern for Fuchsia, and me, and the laws . . . but quickly, Doctor, are you coming? We are trailing Steerpike – he's just outside.'

In a moment the Doctor was in his elegant dressing gown – had found and put on his spectacles, a pair of socks and his soft slippers.

'I am flattered,' he said, in his quick, stilted, yet very pleasant voice. 'I am more than flattered – lead on, boy, lead on.'

They descended the dark stairs: on reaching the hall the Doctor vanished but reappeared almost at once with two pokers, one – long, top-heavy brass affair with a murderous club-end and the other a short heavy iron thing with a perfect grip.

The Doctor hid them behind his back. 'Which hand?' he said. Titus chose the left and received the iron. Even with so crude a weapon in his grip the boy's confidence rose at once. Not that his heart beat any less rapidly or that he was any the less aware of danger, but the feeling of acute vulnerability had gone.

The Doctor asked no questions. He knew that this strange business would unfold its meaning as the minutes went by. Titus was in no state to give an explanation now. He had begun breathlessly to tell the Doctor of how Flay would leave a trail of chalk, but had ceased, for there was no time to act and to explain together. Before they opened the front door Dr Prunesquallor drew the blind of the hall window. The quadrangle though still extremely dark was no longer a featureless and inky mass. The buildings on the far side loomed, and a blot of ebony blackness that appeared to float in the gun-grey air showed where the thorn tree grew.

Titus was at the Doctor's side and peered through the pane.

'Can you see him, Doctor?'

'Where ought he to be, my boy?'

'Under the thorn.'

'Hard to say . . . hard to say . . .'

'Easy to tell from the other side, Doctor. Shall we go round by the cloisters . . .? If he's gone there's no time to lose, is there?'

'I take it from you that there isn't, Titus, though what in the name of guilt we are doing only the screech-owl knows. However, away!'

He stood upon his toes in the hall, and lifting his arms, stretched them before him. Between his outstretched finger tips the brass poker was poised as though it were a mace, or some symbolic rod. His dressing gown was corded tightly at his slender waist. His delicate features were set in an extraordinary expression of speculative determination both impressive and bizarre.

He unlatched the door and the two of them set off down the garden path. The Doctor in his slippers, Titus in his socks, with his shoes slung loosely around his neck, they moved rapidly and silently along the skirting cloisters until Titus, gripping the Doctor's arm, brought his companion to a halt. There was the thorn, an inky etching against the rising sun, but the silhouette of Steerpike was missing. This was no surprise for Flay had also vanished. Without loss of time they sped across the quadrangle, and in the early light were able at once to see the

dim sign of a chalk mark on the ground at their feet. Titus went down
on his knees to it at once. That it was a rough arrow pointing to the
north was apparent enough, but there were some words scrawled below
which were not so easy to decipher, but at last Titus was able to
disentangle the roughened phrase '*every twenty paces*'.

' "Every twenty paces" I think it is,' Titus whispered.

Together they counted their steps as they moved gingerly to the
north, the pokers in their hands, their eyes peering into the darkness
ahead of them for the first sign of Flay or of danger.

Sure enough, at roughly the twentieth pace another arrow pointed
them their way and showed Titus' interpretation of Flay's crude
lettering to have been correct. They went forward now with more
confidence. It seemed certain that they must come first upon Mr Flay,
and that so long as they made no sound they could do no harm by
moving swiftly from one arrow to another. There were times when these
arrows were of necessity closer together; when the paths divided, or
there was any kind of choice of direction. At other times, when, with
high flanking walls on either side, or a mile of doorless passageways
ahead, and where there was no alternative direction to confuse his
followers, Flay had not troubled to make his chalk marks for long
stretches. There were times when the length of these stone arteries was
such that, all unknowing, the Doctor and Titus had more than once set
forth along a fresh corridor before Steerpike, at the other end, had
made his exit. Flay alone could hazard the guess that before him and
behind him his friends and his enemy were all at once beneath the same
long ceiling.

Rapid as Titus had been in calling the Doctor yet there was a great
space between them and Mr Flay, for no sooner had Titus left Flay's
side than Steerpike had yawned and sped into the night.

As the light grew it became easier for the Doctor and Titus to
accelerate their pace and to see what part of the castle they were moving
through. The chalk arrows had become short brusque marks upon the
ground. Suddenly, as they turned a corner they came upon the second
of the bearded man's messages. It was scrawled at the foot of some
stone stairs. '*Faster,*' it read. '*He is in a hurry. Catch me but silence.*'

By now the light was strong enough for them both to know that they
were lost. Neither of them could recognize the masonry that rose about
them, the twisting passageways, the shallow flights of stairs and the
long treadless inclines; they were speeding through a new world. A
world unfamiliar in its detail – new to *them*, although unquestionably of
the very stuff of their memories and recognizable in this general and
almost abstract way. They had never been there before, yet it was not
alien – it was all Gormenghast.

But this did not mean it was not dangerous. It was obvious that they were in a deserted province. Early as was the hour yet that was not the reason for the silence. There was an abandoned, empty, voiceless hollow atmosphere that had nothing to do with the dawn or with multitudes abed and asleep.

What beds there were would be broken and empty. What multitudes there were would be the multitudes of the ant and the weevil.

And now began a series of dusky journeys across open squares, with the sky reddening overhead. The Doctor, wildly incongruous in so grim a setting, moved with surprising speed, his brass poker held in both hands at the height of his breast, his head erect, the skirt of his dressing gown flaring behind him.

Titus beside him looked by contrast like a beggar. His socks had worn out, and although they gripped his ankles, the soles had gone, and his feet were cut and bruised. But this he hardly noticed. His hair was across his face. His jacket was bundled over his nightshirt. His trousers were half undone. His shoes jogged at his shoulders.

They had increased their speed, even to the point of running when it seemed safe to do so. But whenever they came to a corner they invariably stopped and peered cautiously about it before proceeding. The chalk marks never failed them, though from the way they had changed from the thick white arrows to the merest flick of chalk on stone or boarding it was plain not only that the speed of Flay's progress had increased but that the stick of chalk itself was wearing out.

There was no longer any difficulty as far as visibility was concerned. They moved in the naked light. It was surely no longer possible for Mr Flay to keep at close range with his quarry. And yet, with all their swiftness they had not yet caught up with him. The Doctor's brow was glistening with perspiration. Both he and Titus were growing increasingly weary. The unfamiliar buildings came and went. One after another, square after square, hall after hall, corridor after corridor, winding and turning to and fro in a maze of dawn-lit stone.

And then, half in a state of disbelief – as though it were all a dream, the Doctor, mechanically stopping at the corner of a high wall, moved his head so that he could command a view of the next expanse or artery that lay ahead. But instead of rounding the corner, his body recoiled a fraction and his arm moved backwards.

When his hand had found Titus and had gripped his elbow he drew the boy to his side. Together they could see him – the gaunt and bearded figure. He was at the far end of a narrow lane, the floor of which was a foot deep in dust and plaster. He was in an almost identical position to their own for he was also stationed at a corner; around which he was peering, and like themselves he had his eyes fixed upon some object of vivid and immediate interest, for even at so considerable a distance the Doctor could see how tense was his scarecrow body.

Had they been a few moments later they would have missed him for
even as they watched he slid around the base of the high, sharp corner
and was lost to them. At once, Titus and the Doctor set off in hot
pursuit until they came to that angle of stone which Flay had so recently
vacated. Cautiously, they moved their heads until once again they were
afforded yet another long perspective with its floor crisp and ashen with
fallen plaster. And there at the end of the corridor was a replica of the
picture they had been witnessing a minute earlier, with Flay at yet
another angle of stone. It was as though they were re-living the incident,
for, visually, it differed in no particular. But this time they did not wait
for Mr Flay to disappear. At a sign from the Doctor they began to run
towards him. Evidently Steerpike was still in view for Mr Flay,
motionless as a stick-insect, made no move until Titus and the Doctor
were within a short way of him. Then suddenly, at the sound of plaster
breaking under Titus' feet, faint though it was, he turned his craggy
face over his shoulder and saw them.

He touched his brow with his hand, and darted a questioning glance
at the Doctor. Then he put his finger to his lips as he bared his irregular
teeth. The Doctor inclined his body, so splendidly sheathed in its
dressing gown, in the gaunt man's direction. Meanwhile Titus crept to
the angle of the wall and peering around the corner saw, at a distance
of about sixty feet, something which set his heart pounding. It was the
Master of Ritual, Steerpike; the man with the red and white face. It was
his foe – long since defied in the summer schoolroom – the pale and
agile officer of the realm – the one who had spoiled his happiness and
weaned his sister from him.

There he sat upon the edge of some kind of low stone basin like a
drinking trough that protruded from the wall at the side of the plaster-
littered passage. Beyond him there was an arch, hung with torn sacking
which obscured whatever lay beyond.

As Titus watched, he saw the sitting figure draw up his knees so that
his feet were beneath him on the rim of the trough. His head and
shoulders were turned a little away so that it was not easy for Titus to
tell what he had taken from his pocket. It seemed that Steerpike's hands
were near his mouth and a little forward of it and then suddenly, as the
first thin reedy note of a bamboo pipe shrilled along the resonant
corridor, all became plain. For some little while, it was impossible to
know how long, the three watchers listened to the solitary figure, to his
nimble fingering of the stops, to the shrill and plaintive improvisations.
Only the Doctor realized how well he played. Only the Doctor knew
how quick and cold it was. How brilliant and empty.

'Is there nothing he can't do?' muttered Prunesquallor to himself.
'By all that's versatile, he frightens me.'

The music had come to an end, and Steerpike stretched out his arms and legs and then slipping his recorder into a pocket, stood up. It was then that Titus gasped, and as he did so was plucked back from the corner by the two men behind him. For a few moments they hardly dared to draw breath. But no footsteps approached them from the adjacent corridor. What was it he had seen? Neither the Doctor nor Flay dared question him, but after a little while the latter, squinting round the corner, could see what it was that had startled the boy. He had himself been puzzled by Steerpike's monkey. For a long while he had been unable to tell what it was that sat hunched upon his quarry's shoulder, or bounded at his side. At other times it disappeared altogether. It had not added, for instance, to the silhouette beneath the thorn tree, and Flay could only think that it clung closely to his side and was lost for long periods at a time beneath the folds of his cape.

But now it bounded beside him, or stood on two legs, its long thin arms hanging loosely, its wrinkled hands trailing among the scraps of plaster.

And so there was a double need for silence. What Steerpike might miss his monkey might easily hear.

But the discovery of what had startled Titus was of small importance compared with the fact that Flay was only just in time to see the man and his monkey pass through the hangings, and under the arch. A moment later and there would have been no knowing whether he had turned to the left or the right. As it was it was not easy to tell save by the indicative rippling of the ragged hangings.

What lay beyond? There was no reason to suppose that there would be any further repetition of this corner-to-corner trailing. Save for the fatigue of the journey and for their constant grip upon the silence, they had as yet encountered neither problem nor peril. But now, as they stared at the hangings, that were yet moving a little in the still air, they knew that they were entering upon a new phase.

Titus gripped the short iron poker in his hand as though to squeeze the life out of it. The Doctor tossed his head, arched his nostrils and tiptoed to the very point where Steerpike had disappeared. Flay, who insisted on leading, had already drawn back, by no more than half an inch, a fold of the drapery, and was peering to his left. What he saw brought the blood to his head and his hand trembled violently.

He found himself staring along a short passage to where the slanting section of yet another and broader corridor slanted darkly. This further corridor was faced with cold bricks; its floor also, and that was all, but it brought the sweat suddenly to his brow and to the palms of his hands. Yet why, for he was looking at no more than the sort of things he had seen a score of times already on this same morning? But there was this difference. He had seen those bricks before. He had come upon the outskirts of his own domain. Unwittingly as he had moved through the

uncharted hinterlands, he had come upon the outskirts of the Hollow
Halls – the world he had made his own. He was no longer lost. Steerpike
had led them by a trail of his own to a domain which Mr Flay had
thought to be impregnable.

What was he doing here? *Here*, where Mr Flay had stood, his blood
running cold, and had heard the grizzly laughter long ago? *Here*, where
night after night and day after day he had sought the screaming nest to
no avail? Here, where ever since those days the silence had come
down like a deadweight – so that he had not dared to return, for the
stillness had become more terrible than the demoniac laughter.

He alone knew of this. He passed the back of his hand across his eyes.

Without waiting to make so much as a sign to the two behind him he
paced out grotesquely, on tiptoe to the juncture and, again to his left he
saw the young man. Had Steerpike turned to the right he might well
have proceeded towards those districts which Mr Flay knew so well.
Turning to the left, however, took him into that labyrinth in which he
had so often lost himself in his search for the haunted room.

Mr Flay knew only too well that to keep Steerpike in sight would be
no easy task. There was the double difficulty of their following him
closely enough to keep him in sight, and yet to remain inaudible and
unseen themselves.

Nothing would be more embarrassing than for them to be discovered
– for Steerpike was committing no crime in moving rapidly through this
deserted place. If there were anything nefarious going on, it was upon
their side, in shadowing the Master of Ritual.

But there was no need for Flay to warn the Doctor and the boy that
the necessity for absolute silence was even more acute. As they slid
along the brickwork corridor they felt a closing in of the world.

And now began the threading of a maze so labyrinthine as to suggest
that the builders of these sunless walls had been ordered to construct a
maze for no other purpose than to torture the mind and freeze the
memory. It was no wonder that Flay had never done more in those past
days, than stumble blindly through so tortuous a region. And yet, in
spite of the confusion, and the necessity for his concentrating upon
keeping Steerpike in view, his instincts were working upon their own
and they told him that they were returning by devious and contradictory
roads to the proximity of the cold brick corridor from which they had
started. Steerpike had slowed his pace. His head hung forward on his
chest, not dejectedly but with an air of abstraction. His feet moved even
slower, until he was virtually loitering. When he came to flights of
shallow stairs he descended with a kind of loose-jointed and collapsing
motion of the legs – as though his body had forgotten its own existence.
He wandered round corners with a dream-like motion, his body at so
strange an angle of relaxation as to be almost dangerous.

When at last he came to a certain door he straightened himself with a jerk – stretched out his fingers and became on the instant all awareness. He made a sound between his teeth and the monkey scrambled from the folds of his cape and sat upon his shoulder, the feather in its hat nodding to and fro. For a moment as the monkey turned his head, and its black eyes peered from that small and wrinkled face, peered back along the way it had come, the Doctor thought he had been seen. But he did not draw back his head or make any movement and the creature with its naked face and its costume of coloured diamonds scratched itself and turned away at last. Only then did the Doctor and his companions withdraw themselves even more deeply into the shadows.

Meanwhile Steerpike sorted out a key from a bunch in his pocket and after pausing a moment or two turned it with difficulty in the lock. But he did not touch the handle of the door. He turned his back upon it and gazed along the way he had come, tapping his teeth with his thumb nail.

It was obvious that for some reason best known to himself he was chary of walking in. The monkey on his shoulder shifted its position and in doing so its long tail tapped lightly across Steerpike's face. But that was seemingly enough to irritate its master, for the little beast was flung to the floor where it crouched and whimpered.

As Steerpike turned his eyes from his bruised plaything his attention was caught by sprawling heaps of rubbish, stones and broken timbers that lay a little way along the side passage. As he stared at them his anger drained from his face, and his features became set again and the corner of his lips lifted into a dead line.

For a moment or two the three watchers feared that they had lost him for he moved suddenly out of their range of vision. It was fortunate for them that the monkey remained where it was, outside the door where it nursed its bruised forearm. Had they followed Steerpike they would at once have met him face to face, for he returned within a minute with a long broken pole.

And now began an operation that completely baffled the hidden spectators. With extreme care Steerpike turned the handle and released the latch. The door was now free but was not yet opened by so much as a quarter of an inch. He stood back from it, and holding the broken pole like a battering ram, pushed gently at the black wooden panel of the mysterious door. It moved upon its hinges with no great difficulty and Steerpike was able to obtain a view of a section of the room beyond. For a little while he held the pole motionless as he stared along its length and through the narrow opening. It was obvious that what he saw concerned him deeply. He rose upon his toes. He cocked his head to one side. Then he withdrew the pole and laid it on the ground at his feet. It was now, at this same moment, as he took a scarf from his pocket and tied it about his face so that only his eyes were visible, that the Doctor, Flay and Titus became conscious of a sickly and musty odour. But the strange performance that was going on before their eyes, so riveted their attention that at first they hardly noticed it. Again Steerpike raised the pole and pushing at the panels with the utmost caution was able momentarily to see more and more of the room which he was evidently so anxious to inspect. When the door was sufficiently ajar to admit the entry of a man, he paused.

As he did so the monkey, whose feathered hat had fallen in the dust, began to make its inquisitive way to the open door. It was evident that its arm was hurting it. Once or twice, in spite of its eagerness to explore the room beyond the door, it glanced apprehensively over its shoulder at Steerpike, baring its teeth in a nervous grimace. But its resilient nature became dominant and springing off its back legs it clung to the door handle with its nervous little hands. Again Steerpike pressed upon the long pole, this time with more force, and as the door swung ajar the monkey, swinging with it, let go and dropped upon the great mouldering carpet that lay within. But it did not drop alone, for no sooner had its four feet touched the ground than with a sickening thud an axe-head fell from high above the door, severing the long tail of the monkey as it buried its murderous edge in the floor. The shrill and appallingly human scream of the little creature rang through the hollow district, echoing and re-echoing the agony of that moment, while, beside itself with pain, surprise and rage, it tore about the huge room that lay spread before it, leaping from chair to chair, from window-sill to mantelpiece, from cupboard to cupboard, scattering vases, lamps and small objects of all kinds to left and right in its wild circuits.

Into this room, now spattered with the monkey's blood, Steerpike advanced at once. There was no longer any caution in his bearing. He gave the careering creature not so much as a single glance. Had he done so he might have noticed that on seeing him the monkey halted its flight and was crouched quivering upon the back of a chair. Its eyes were upon him and in them was a moist and lethal hatred, as though all the spleen and gall of the vile tropics was floating there beneath the small grey eyelids. Its pain and its humiliation were laid at the door of the man who had flung it from his shoulder. As it watched its master it bared its teeth and wrung its hands together. The blood dripped freely from the stump of its tail. What had happened to the monkey – what had caused its harrowing outcry was, of course, unknown to Titus, the Doctor and Mr Flay. But the urgency of that human cry lifted them out of their hiding places, and brought them to the door. They saw at once that Steerpike had left this first room and had presumably descended the three or four steps that led to a second apartment. But the monkey caught sight of them at once and ran towards them. When it reached Titus it rose to its back legs and began a series of grimaces, which in any other circumstances would have been amusing enough, but were at that moment almost heartbreaking. But they had no time for it. Too much was at stake. Their nerves were at full stretch. They were all but exhausted and above all they were still in the invidious position of following a man without any warrant or rational excuse. Nevertheless the last half-hour had intensified their suspicions to a high degree. They knew in their hearts that they had been right to follow him. They were now prepared for anything that might unfold.

Their apprehension had grown so dark, their speculation so fantastic that when they crept to the second door and peered into the apartment below, and when they saw in the centre of the great carpet that filled the room the two skeletons lying side by side in their fast decaying dresses of imperial purple, their pulses beat no faster. Their emotions had been overstrained and had gone limp. But their brains raced.

The Doctor, who had been holding his silk handkerchief across his face, had known for some while that there was death in the air. He was also the first to know that they were looking at all that was left of Cora and Clarice Groan. Titus had no idea that he was staring at his aunts. He was simply looking at skeletons. He had never seen skeletons before.

It was a moment or two before Mr Flay remembered the invariable purple of the Twins. That there had been foul play was immediately apparent to them all.

The remoteness of these rooms from the castle; the double-death; the windowless walls; the possession by Steerpike of a key and his familiarity with the corridors of approach – and more than all this, his present behaviour. For as they watched him the young man, never doubting the security of his solitude, began to behave in a way which could only be interpreted by those who watched him as a form of madness, or if not madness, something so eccentric as to tread its arbitrary borderland.

Steerpike was aware, directly he had entered the terrible room, that he was behaving strangely. He could have stopped himself at any moment. But to have stopped himself would have been to have stopped a valve – to have bottled up something which would have clamoured for release. For Steerpike was anything but inhibited. His control that had so seldom broken had never frustrated him. In one way that this new expression had need of an outlet he gave himself up to whatever his blood dictated. He was watching himself, but only so that he should miss nothing. He was the vehicle through which the gods were working. The dim primordial gods of power and blood.

There at his feet were the decomposing relics, the purple of their dresses hanging over the ribs in clotted folds, the skulls protruding horribly, their sockets staring at the ceiling. No less than had been their vanished faces, these skulls were identical save that across a single socket some spider, fastidious in his craftsmanship, had spun a delicate web. At its centre struggled a fly, so that in a way a kind of animation had come to either Cora or to Clarice.

In some kind of way the Doctor, though he could not understand, was able to gain an inkling as to what was happening in Steerpike's mind, as the skewbald homicide began to strut like a cockerel about the bodies of the women he had imprisoned, humiliated and starved to death. The Doctor could see that Steerpike was by no means mad in any accepted sense for every now and then he would repeat a number of high stepping paces as though to perfect them. It was as though he were identifying himself with some archetypal warrior, or fiend. A fiend, which although it had no sense of humour, had a ghastly gaiety – a kind of lethal lightness that struck at the very heart of the humanities; struck at it, darted at it, played about it, jabbing here and there, as though with a blade of speargrass.

When Flay and the Doctor, in their different ways, saw what was happening in the room they were both aware that Titus should not be with them. He was no child, but this was no scene for a boy. But there was nothing they could do. For them to separate would be criminally unwise. He could never in any event have found his way back alone. That as yet there had been no movement on their part to disturb the criminal was fortunate, but this deathly silence, in which the only sound was that of Steerpike's footsteps, could not last for ever.

The Doctor was appalled, but at the same time, as a man of high intelligence and curiosity he was fascinated by what he saw. Not so Flay. An eccentric himself he despised and abhorred any form of eccentricity in others and what he was now witnessing had the effect of all but blinding him with a kind of bourgeois rage. Only in one thing was he happy – that the upstart had un-masked himself and that from now onwards the battle was joined in earnest.

His small eyes were fixed upon his enemy. His neck was thrust out like a turtle's. His long beard trembled as it hung forward on his chest. His forest knife shook in his hand.

It was not the only weapon that was shaking. The short heavy poker in Titus' clenched fist was far from steady. The young earl was quite frankly terrified by what he saw. An area of solid ground had given way beneath his feet and he had fallen into an underworld of which he had had no conception. A place where a man can pace like a cock about the ribs and skulls of his victims. A place where the air was rank with their corruption.

The Doctor was gripping his arm to steady him, and the grip tightened suddenly. Steerpike had stopped for a moment to re-tie his shoelace. When this was completed he rose from his knee and stood on tiptoe where he remained poised, his head thrown back. Then he dropped his heels and flexed his knees and at the same time turning his toes outwards, he raised his arms to his side, and with his elbows bent at right angles, he began to stamp, his fists clenched at the height of his shoulders. The sound of his feet was very loud and close.

He was in the posture of some earthish dancer, but he soon tired of this strange display – this throw-back to some savage rite of the world's infancy. He had given himself up to it for those few moments, in the way that an artist can be the ignorant agent of something far greater and deeper than his conscious mind could ever understand. But as he strutted, his knees bent, his feet turned outwards, his body and head erect, his elbows crooked, and his hands clenched, he had enjoyed the novelty of what he was doing. He was amused at this peculiar need of his body; that it wished to stamp, to strut, to rear on tiptoes, to sink upon the heels – and all because he was a murderer – all this intrigued him, titillating his brain, so that, now, as he ceased to stamp, and sank into a dusty chair, the muscles of his throat went through the contractions that form laughter – but no sound came.

He shut his eyes, and in the darkness, it seemed to him that he was in peril and he opened them again with a start and sat forward in his chair, glancing about the room. This time as his gaze returned to the skeletons he was revolted. Not with what *he* had done to bring them to this state – but that they should pollute this room; that they should show him their ugly skulls and hollow bones.

He rose from his chair in anger. But he knew in his heart that he was not angry with them. He was enraged with himself. For what had seemed amusing a few moments ago was now a source, almost of fear to him. In looking back and seeing himself strutting like a cock about their bodies, he realized that he had been close to lunacy. This was the first time that any such thought had entered his head, and to dismiss it he crowed like a cock. He was not afraid of strutting; he had known what he was doing; to prove it he would crow and crow again. Not that he wished to do so, but to prove that he could stop whenever he wanted, and start when he wished to, and be all the while in complete control of himself, for there was no madness in him.

What he did not realize was that the death of Barquentine, and the nightmare of the fire and the vile waters of the moat and the long fever that followed had made a difference to him. Whatever he now believed about himself was based on the assumption that he was the same Steerpike as his former self of a few year earlier. But he was no longer that youth. The fire had burned a part of him away. Something of him was drowned for ever in the waters of the moat. His daring was no longer a thing that fanned itself abroad; it had contracted into a fist of brimstone.

He was meaner, more irritable, more impatient for the ultimate power which could only be his through the elimination of all rivals; and if he had ever had any scruples, any love at all for even a monkey, a book, or a sword-hilt, all this, and even this, had been cauterized and drowned away.

As he had entered this second apartment, he had propped the broken pole against the wall on his left. He now felt himself gravitating towards it. He no longer stamped or strutted. He was himself again, or perhaps he had ceased to be himself. At any rate, the three watchers recognized again that familiar walk, with the shoulders hunched and the cat-like footsteps. When he reached the pole he ran his hand along its side. The scarf was still about his face. His dark red eyes were like small circular pits.

As his hand strayed over the surface of the pole, rather as a pianist will fondle a keyboard, his fingers came across a fissure in the wood, and as they played about it they found how easy it would be to tear from the beam a long and narrow splinter. Abstractedly, hardly knowing that he was doing it, a score of disquieting impressions had taken the place of the surety within him, he prised the splinter away, using, at the last, the whole strength of his arm as it arched, in its tension, from the pole. He did not look at it, and he was about to throw it away, for the tearing of it from the pole had been his only interest, when, his gaze having returned to the skeletons, he wandered towards them, and running the long resilient splinter along their ribs, as a child might run a stick along a railing, he heard the bone-notes of an instrument.

For a few minutes he spent his time in this way, creating by a series of taps and runs, a kind of percussive rhythm in key with his mood.

But he was tiring of the place. He had returned in order to satisfy his eyes that the Twins were truly dead, and he had stayed longer than he had intended. Now he flung the splinter away and, kneeling, unclasped the strings of pearls that hung about the vertebrae. Rising, he dropped them into his pocket and made at once for the three steps that led to the upper room and as he did so Mr Flay stepped out from his hiding place.

The effect upon Steerpike was electric. He bounded backwards, with a leap like the leap of a dancer, his cloak swirling about him and his thin lips parted in a murderous snarl of amazement.

There was no longer any case of symbolism. The strutting and the stamping were nothing to the fierce reality of that leap which sent him, as though from a springboard, backwards through the air.

Quick as a reflex, even at the height of his elevation, he felt for his knife. Before he landed he knew that he was unmasked. That from now onwards, unless he slew the bearded figure, on the instant, he would be on the run. In a flash he saw the life of a fugitive spread out before him.

It was only as he landed that he realized at whom he was looking. He had not seen Flay for many years and had supposed him dead. The beard had altered him. But now he knew him, and this knowledge did nothing to stay his hand. Of all men, Flay would have the least sympathy for a rebel.

He had found his knife, had balanced it upon the palm of his hand and had drawn back his right arm when he saw the Doctor and Titus.

The boy was white. The poker shook in his hand but his teeth were gritted. A terrible sickness had hold of him. He was in a nightmare. The last sixty minutes had added more than an hour to his age.

The Doctor was pale also. His face had lost all trace of its habitual drollery. It was a face cut out of marble, strangely proportioned but refined and determined.

The sight of the three of them, blocking the stairs, halted Steerpike's arm as he was about to launch the knife.

And then, in a peculiarly quiet voice clear and precise, a voice that told nothing of the hammering heart . . .

'You will drop your penknife to the ground. You will come forward with your arms raised. You are under arrest,' said the Doctor.

But Steerpike hardly heard him. His future was ruptured. His years of self-advancement and intricate planning were as though they had never been. A red cloud filled his head. His body shuddered with a kind of lust. It was the lust for an unbridled evil. It was the glory of knowing himself to be pitted, openly, against the big battalions. Alone, loveless, vital, diabolic – a creature for whom compromise was no longer necessary, and intrigue was a dead letter. If it was no longer possible for him to wear, one day, the legitimate crown of Gormenghast, there was still the dark and terrible domain – the subterranean labyrinth – the lairs and warrens where, monarch of darkness like Satan himself, he could wear undisputed a crown no less imperial. Poised like an acrobat and vividly aware of the slightest move that was made by the three figures before him, the Doctor's voice for all his sensory acuteness, seemed to come from far away.

'I give you one last chance,' said his ex-patron. 'If you have not dropped your knife within five seconds from now, we will advance upon you!'

But it was not the knife that dropped. It was Flay. The loyal seneschal fell backwards with a grinding cry and was half caught in the arms of Titus and the Doctor, and in that instant, while the blade of Steerpike's knife still quivered in his heart, and while the four hands of Flay's friends were engaged with the weight of the long ragged body, the young man, following the path of the flung knife, as though he were tied behind it, sped over their shoulders and was in the upper room before they could recover.

Now, with the fear of retributory death upon him, and the redoubled cunning that comes to the marked man, Steerpike lost not a second in speeding from the room. But he did not pass through the door alone, for as he slammed it and turned the key in the lock he was bitten savagely in the back of the neck. With a scream he swivelled on his feet and clutched at nothing.

A panic possessed him and he ran as he had never run before, turning left and right like a wild creature as he made his way ever deeper into a nether empire.

Outside the door of what had been the Twins' apartment, the monkey, squatting on a rafter, chattered and wrung its hands.

FIFTY-NINE

A few days after the murder of Mr Flay and the subsequent smashing of the door and escape of the Doctor and Titus from those dread apartments, the relics of the Twins were heaped into a single coffin and were buried, at the orders of the Countess, with all the rites and solemnities that were due to the sisters of an earl.

Mr Flay was buried on the same day in the graveyard of the Elect Retainers, a small space of nettle-covered ground. At evening the long shadow of the Tower of Flints lay across this simple boneyard with its conical heaps of stones to show where not more than a dozen servants of exceptional loyalty lay silently under the tall weeds.

Had Mr Flay been able to foresee his funeral he would have appreciated the honour of joining so small and loyal a company of the dead. And if he had known that the Countess herself, in draperies as black and as intense as the plumage of her own ravens, was to be there at the graveside, then his wounds would indeed have been healed.

The Poet had taken over as Master of Ritual. He had no easy task. Night after night, his long wedge-shaped head was bowed over the manuscripts.

When the Countess had been told by Prunesquallor of the finding of the Twins, the manner of Flay's death, and of Steerpike's escape, she had risen from the upright chair in which she had been sitting, and without any change of expression in her big face had lifted the chair from the floor and had methodically broken its curved legs off one by one, and had then, in what seemed to be a state of abstraction, tossed the chair-legs one after another through the glass-panes of the nearest window.

When she had done this she moved to the smashed window and stared through the jagged hole. There was a white mist in the air and the tops of the towers appeared to be floating.

From where the Doctor stood he saw, for the first time, a picture. He was not looking for one. What pictures he had ever painted had been very delicate and charming. But this was quite different. He saw something dynamic, something quite wonderful in the contrast of the sharp and angular edges of the broken glass, and the smooth and doming line of her ladyship's shoulders that, in the immediate foreground, curved heavily across the jaggedness. And at the same time he saw the deep, copper-beech colour of her hair against the pearl-grey tower-tops that floated in the distance. And the blackness of her dress, and the marble of her neck and the sheen of the glass, and the pollen-like softness of the sky and towers so jaggedly circumscribed. She was a monument against a broken window and beyond the broken window her realm, tremulous and impalpable in the white mist.

But Dr Prunesquallor had only a few moments in which to regret that he had not learned to paint, for the monument turned about.

'Sit down,' she said.

Prunesquallor looked about him. The confusion in the room made it difficult for him to see anything that could possibly be sat on, but he found himself a perch at last in the corner of a window-sill that was scattered with bird seed.

She approached and stood above him. She did not look down, but gazed through a small casement above his head while she spoke. Finding that she never turned her eyes to him and that for him to look up when listening or speaking was neither noticed nor necessary, and what is more that it gave him a pain at the back of his neck, the doctor gazed at the scallops of sartorial immediately ahead of him and within a few inches of his nose, or simply shut his eyes as they conversed.

It was soon obvious to the Doctor that he was in conversation with someone whose thoughts were concentrated upon the capture of Steerpike not only to the exclusion of everything else but with a menacing power and a ruthless simplicity.

Her heavy voice was slower than ever.

'All normal work shall be suspended. Man, woman and child shall be given their orders-of-search. Every known spring and well-head, every cistern, tank and catchment shall have its sentry. No doubt the beast must drink.'

The Doctor suggested a meeting of officers, the drawing up of a plan of campaign, the working out of a time table or rota of sentries and search parties, and the formation of redoubtable bands drawn from the young blood of the castle's lower life where there was no lack of spleen, and where the price which was to be set upon Steerpike's head would encourage their intrepidity.

They agreed that there was no time to waste for with every hour that passed the fugitive would be withdrawing ever more deeply into some forgotten quarter, or constructing some ambuscade or hiding place, even at the heart of the castle's activities. There was no place on earth so terrible and so suited to a game of hide and seek as this gaunt warren.

Leaders were to be chosen. Weapons were to be served out. The castle was to be placed upon a war footing. A curfew was to be imposed, and wherever he might be lurking, from vault to eyrie, the murderer was to have no respite from the sound of feet and the light of torches. Sooner or later he would make his first mistake. Sooner or later, in the corner of some eye, the tail of his shadow would be seen. Sooner or later if there was no relaxation in the search, he would be found at some well-head, drinking like an animal, or flying from some storehouse with his plunder.

The Countess was using her powerful brain as though for the first time. The Doctor had never known her like this. Had her cats entered the room or a bird descended flapping to her shoulder it is doubtful whether, at this moment, she would have noticed them. Her thoughts were so concentrated upon the seizure of Steerpike that she had not moved a muscle since she and the Doctor had started talking. Only her lips had moved. She had talked very slowly and quietly but there was a thickness in her voice.

'I shall outwit him,' she said. 'The ceremonies shall continue.'

'The Day of the Bright Carvings?' queried the Doctor. 'Shall it proceed as usual?'

'As usual.'

'And the Outer Dwellers be allowed within the gates?'

'Naturally,' she said. 'What could stop them?'

What could stop them? It was Gormenghast that spoke. A fiend might be wandering the castle with dripping hands, but the traditional ceremonies were at the back of it all, enormous, immemorial, sacrosanct. In a fortnight's time it was their day, the day of the Mud Dwellers, when all along the white stone shelf at the foot of the long courtyard wall the coloured carvings would be displayed; and at night, when the bonfires roared and all but the three chosen statues were turned to ash in their flames, Titus standing on the balcony with the Outer Dwellers below him in the fire-lit darkness, would hold aloft in turn, each masterpiece. And as each was raised above his head, a gong would clash. And after the echoes of the third reverberation had died away he would order them to be taken to the Hall of Bright Carvings where

Rottcodd slept and the dust collected and the flies crawled over the tall slatted blinds.

Prunesquallor rose to his feet. 'You are right,' he said. 'There must be no difference, your ladyship, save for an eternal vigilance, and unflagging pursuit.'

'There is never any difference,' she replied. 'There is never any difference.' Then she turned her head for the first time and looked at the Doctor. 'We will have him,' she said. Her voice, as soft and heavy and thick as velvet, was in so grim and incongruous a contrast to the merciless pin-head of light that glittered in her narrowed eyes that the doctor made for the door. He was in need of an atmosphere less charged. As he turned the door-handle he caught sight of the smashed window, and saw through the jagged star-shaped opening the towers floating. The white mist seemed lovelier than ever, and the towers more fairy-like.

SIXTY

BELLGROVE and his wife sat opposite one another in their living room. Irma, very upright, as was her habit, her back as straight as a yard of pump-water. There was something irritating in this unnecessary rigidity. It was, perhaps, ladylike, but it was certainly not feminine. It annoyed Bellgrove for it made him feel that there was something wrong in the way that *he* had always used a chair. To his mind an armchair was something to curl up in, or to drape oneself across. It was a thing for human delectation. It was not built to be perched on.

And so he curled his old spine and draped his old legs and lolled his old head, while his wife sat silently and stared at him.

'. . . And why on earth should you think that he would dream of risking his life in order to attack *you*?' the old man was saying. 'You deceive yourself, Irma. Peculiar as he is, there is no reason why he should flatter you to the extent of killing you. To climb in at your bedroom window would be highly hazardous. The entire castle is on the watch for him. Do you really imagine that it matters to him whether you are alive or dead, any more than whether *I* am alive or dead, or that fly up there on the ceiling is alive or dead? Good grief, Irma, be reasonable if you can, if only for the sake of the love that once I bore you.'

'There is no need for you to speak like that,' Irma replied, in a voice as clipped as the sound of castanets. 'Our love has nothing to do with

what we are talking about. Nor is it anything to mock at. It has
changed, that is all. It is no longer green.'

'And nor am I,' murmured Bellgrove.

'What an obvious thing to say!' said Irma, with forced brightness.
'And how very trite – I said how very trite!'

'I heard you, my dear.'

'And this is no time for shallow talk. I have come to you as a wife
should come to her husband. For guidance. Yes, for guidance. You are
old, I know, but . . .'

'What the hell has my age got to do with it?' snarled Bellgrove, lifting
his magnificent head from a cushion. The milk-white locks were
clustered on his shoulders. 'You were never one to ask for advice. You
mean you're terrified.'

'That is so,' said Irma. She said it so simply and so quietly that she
did not recognize her own voice. She had spoken involuntarily.
Bellgrove turned his head sharply in her direction. He could hardly
believe that it was she who had spoken. He rose from his chair and
crossed the ugly carpet to where she sat bolt upright. He squatted on
his heels before her. A sense of pity stirred in him. He took her long
hands in his.

At first she tried to withdraw them but he held them tightly. She had
tried to say 'don't be ridiculous' but no words came.

'Irma,' he said at last. 'Let us try again. We have both changed
– but that is perhaps as it should be. You have shown me sides of
your nature which I never knew existed. Never. How could I ever
have guessed, my dear, that you should for instance have thought
that half my staff were in love with you – or that you could become
so irritated with my innocent habit of falling asleep? We have our
different spirits, our different needs, our different lives. We are fused,
Irma, it is true; we are integrated – but not all that much. Relax
your back, my dear. Relax your backbone. It makes it easier for me
to talk. I've asked you so often – and in all humility – knowing as
I do that your spine is your own.'

'My dearest husband,' said Irma. 'You are talking overmuch. If you
could leave a sentence alone, it would be so much stronger.' She bowed
her head to him. 'But I will tell you something,' she continued, 'it
makes me happy to see you there, crouched at my feet. It makes me feel
young again – or it would do, it *would* do, if they could only lay their
hands on him and end the suspense. It is too much – *too* much . . . night
after night . . . night after night . . . Oh can't you see how it racks a
woman? Can't you? Can't you?'

'My brave one,' said Bellgrove. 'My lady love; pull yourself together.
Sinister as the business is, there is no need for you to take the whole
thing personally. You are nothing to him, Irma, as I have said before.

You are not his foe, my dear, *are* you? Nor yet his accomplice? Or *are* you?'

'Don't be ridiculous.'

'Quite so. I am being ridiculous. Your husband, the headmaster of Gormenghast, is being ridiculous. And why? Because I have caught the germ. I have caught it from my wife.'

'But in the darkness . . . in the darkness . . . I seem to *see* him.'

'Quite so,' said Bellgrove. 'But if you *did* see him you would feel worse still. Except of course that we could claim a reward, you know!'

Bellgrove found that his legs were aching so he rose to his feet.

'My advice, Irma, is to put a little more trust in your husband. He may not be perfect. There may be husbands with finer qualities. With nobler profiles for instance, eh? Or with hair like almond blossom. It is not for me to say. And of course there may be husbands who have even become headmasters, or whose intellect is wider, or whose youth was more dazzling in its gallantry. It is not for me to say. But such as I am I have become yours. And such as you are you have become mine. And such as we both are we have become one another's. And what does this lead to? It leads to this. That if all this is so, and yet you quake at every sound of the night, then I take it that your trust in me has waned since those early days when I had you at my feet. O you have schemed . . . schemed . . . !'

'How *dare* you!' cried Irma. 'How dare you!'

Bellgrove had forgotten himself. He had forgotten what his argument was intended to prove. A little whiff of temper springing from some unformulated thought had caught him unaware. He tried to recover.

'*Schemed*,' he continued, 'for my happiness. And you have very largely succeeded. I like you sitting there, if you weren't so upright. Can't you melt, my dear one . . . just a little. One grows so very tired of straight lines. As for Steerpike, take my advice; make use of *me* when you are frightened. Run to *me*. Fly to *me*. Press yourself against my chest; run your fingers through my locks. Be comforted. If he ever *did* appear before me, you know very well how I would deal with him.'

Irma looked at her venerable husband. 'I certainly do *not*,' she said. 'How would you?'

Bellgrove, who had even less idea than Irma, stroked his long chin, and then a sickly smile appeared on his lips.

'What I would do,' he said, 'is something that no gentleman could possibly divulge. Faith: that is what you need. Faith in me, my dear.'

'There would be nothing you could do,' said Irma, ignoring her husband's suggestion that she should have faith in him. 'Nothing at all. You are too old.'

Bellgrove, who had been about to resume his seat, remained standing. His back was to his wife. A dull pain began to grow beneath his ribs. A sense of the black injustice of bodily decay came over him, but a rebellious voice crying in his heart '*I am young, I am young,*' while the carnal witness of his three score years and ten sank suddenly at the knees.

In a moment Irma was at his side. 'Oh my dear one! What *is* it? What *is* it?'

She lifted his head and put a cushion beneath it. Bellgrove was fully conscious. The shock of finding himself suddenly on the floor had upset him for a moment or two and had taken his breath away, but that was all.

'My legs went,' he said, looking up at the earnest face above him with its wonderfully sharp nose. 'But I am all right again.'

Directly he had made this remark he was sorry for it, for he could have done with an hour of nursing.

'Perhaps you had better get up in that case, my dear,' said Irma. 'The floor is no place for a headmaster.'

'Ah, but I feel very . . .'

'Now, now!' interrupted Irma. 'Let me have no nonsense. I shall go and see whether the doors have been locked. When I return I expect to find you in your chair again.' She left the room.

After kicking his heels irritably on the carpet, the headmaster struggled to his feet, and when he was in his chair again he put out his tongue at the door through which Irma had passed, but immediately he had done so he blushed for shame and blew a kiss in the same direction from the wasted palm of his hand.

SIXTY-ONE

THERE was a part of the outer wall which was so deeply hidden with canopies of creeper that for over a hundred years no eyes had seen the stones of the wall itself but the eyes of insects, mice and birds. These undulating acres of hanging foliage overlooked a certain lane which lay so close to the outer wall of Gormenghast that had the mice or the hidden birds been capable of tossing a twig out of the leafy darkness it would have fallen into this lane that lay below.

It was a narrow way, in deep shadow for most of the day. Only in the late evening, as the sun sank over Gormenghast forest, a quiverful of honey-coloured beams would slant along the alley and there would be pools of amber where all day long the chill, inhospitable shadows had brooded.

And when these amber pools appeared the curs of the district would congregate out of nowhere and would squat in the golden beams and lick their sores.

But it was not in order to watch those half-wild dogs or to marvel at the sunbeams that the Thing had taken to working her way through the dense growth of the wall-draped creepers, threading the vertical foliage with the noiseless ease of a snake until twenty feet above the ground she moved outward from the wall to such a position that she could look down upon certain sections of the lane. It was for a reason more covetous. It was because the solitary carver who shared this evening hour with the dogs and the sunbeams never failed to be at his accustomed place at sundown. It was then that he worked upon the block of jarl-wood. It was then that the image grew under his chisel. It was then that the Thing watched, with her eyes wide as a child's, the evolution of the wooden raven. And it was for this carving that she pined angrily, impatiently. It was so that she might snatch it from its maker, and then away, in a breath, to the hills, that she crouched there evening after evening, watching greedily from the loose ivy, for the completion of so pretty a toy.

SIXTY-TWO

When Fuchsia heard the news of Steerpike's treachery and when she realized how her first and only affair of the heart had been with a murderer, an expression of such sickness and horror darkened her face that her aspect was, from that moment, never wholly free of that corrosive stain.

For a long while he spoke to no one, keeping herself to her room, where, unable to cry, she became exhausted with the emotions that fought in her to find some natural outlet. At first there was only the sense of having been physically struck, and the pain of the wound. Her arms gave little jerks and tingled. A depression of utter blackness drowned her. She had no wish to live at all. Her breast pained her. It was as though a great fear filled the cage of her ribs, a globe of pain that grew and grew. For the first week after the crushing news she could not sleep. And then a kind of hardness entered her. Something she had never housed before. It came as a protection. She needed it. It helped her to grow bitter. She began to kill at birth all thoughts of love that were natural to her. She changed and she aged as she wandered to and fro across her solitary room. She began to see no reason why others, as well as Steerpike, should not be double-faced and merciless. She hated the world.

When Titus called to see her he was amazed at the change in her voice, and the sunken look of her eyes. He saw for the first time that she was a woman as well as being his sister.

On her side, she saw a change in him. His restlessness was as real as her disillusion. His longing for freedom as pressing as her longing for love.

But what could he do, and what could she do? The castle was round and about them, widespread and as unchartable as a dark day.

'Thank you for coming,' she said, 'but there's nothing we can talk about!'

Titus said nothing but leaned against a wall. She looked so much older. His heel began to work away at a piece of loose plaster above the skirting board until it came away.

'I can't believe he's dead,' said the boy at last.

'Who?'

'Flay, of course. And all the things he did. What about his cave? Empty for ever I suppose. Would you like to . . .'

'No,' said Fuchsia, anticipating his question. 'Not now. Not any more. I don't want to go anywhere, really. Have you seen Dr Prune?'

'Once or twice. He asked me to tell you that he'd like to see you, whenever you want. He's not very well.'

'None of us are,' said Fuchsia. 'What are you going to do? You look quite different. Was it awful, seeing what happened? But don't tell me. I don't want to dwell on it!'

'There are sentries everywhere,' said Titus.

'I know.'

'And a curfew. I have to be in my room by eight o'clock. Who's the man outside the door here?'

'I don't know his name. He's there most of the day and all night. A man in the courtyard too, under the window.'

Titus wandered to the window and looked down. 'What good is he doing there?' And then, turning about, 'They'll never catch *him*,' he said. 'He's too cunning, the bloody beast. Why can't they burn the whole place down, and him with it, and us with it, and the world with it, and finish the whole dirty business, and the rotten ritual and everything and give the green grass a chance?'

'Titus,' she said. 'Come here.' He approached her, his hands shaking.

'I love you, Titus, but I can't feel anything. I've gone dead. Even you are dead in me. I know I love you. You're the only one I love, but I can't feel anything and I don't want to. I've felt too much, I'm sick of feelings . . . I'm frightened of them.'

Titus took another step towards her. She gazed at him. A year ago they would have kissed. They had needed each other's love. Now, they needed it even more but something had gone wrong. A space had formed between them, and they had no bridge.

But he gripped her arm for a moment before walking quickly to the door and disappearing from her sight.

SIXTY-THREE

THE Day of the Bright Carvings was at hand. The Carvers had put the final touches to their creations. The expectancy in the castle was as acute as it was possible for it to be, when at the same time the larger and more horrible awareness that Steerpike might at any moment strike again, took up the larger part of their minds. For the skewbald man had struck four times within the last eight days with accuracy, a small pebble being found, in every case, near the fractured heads of the newly-slain, or lodged in the bone above the eyes. These killings, so wicked in their want of purpose, took place in such widely separated districts as to give no clue as to where the haunt of the homicide might be. His deadly catapult had spread a clammy terror through Gormenghast.

But in spite of this preponderant fear, the imminence of the traditional day of carvings had brought a certain excitement of a less terrible kind to the hearts of the denizens. They turned with relief to this age-old ceremony as though to something on which they could rely – something that had happened every year since they could remember anything at all. They turned to tradition as a child turns to its mother.

The long courtyard where the ceremony was to be held had been scrubbed and double scrubbed. The clanking of buckets, the swilling and hissing of water, the sound of scouring had echoed along the attenuate yard, sunrise after sunrise, for a week past. The high southern wall in particular was immaculate. The scaffolding to which the scrubbers had clung like monkeys while they ferreted among the rough stones, scraping at the interstices and sluicing every vestige of accumulated dust from niche and crack, had been removed. It sailed away, this wall, in a dwindling perspective of gleaming stone – and five feet from the ground along its entire length the Carvers' shelf protruded. The solid shelf or buttress was of so handsome a breadth that even the largest of the coloured carvings stood comfortably upon it. It had already been whitewashed in preparation for the great day, as had also the wall above it, to the height of a dozen feet. What plants and creepers had forced their way through the stones during the past year, were cut down, as usual, flush with the stones.

It was into this courtyard so unnaturally lustrated that the Carvers from the Outer Dwellings were to pour like a dark and ragged tide, bearing their heavy wooden carvings in their arms or upon their shoulders, or when the works were too weighty for a man to sustain he would be aided by his family – the children running alongside, barefooted, their black hair in their eyes, their shrill excited voices jabbing the heavy air as though with stilettos.

For the air was full of an oppressive weight. What breath there was moved hotly on its way as though it were fanned by the mouldering wings of huge and sickly birds.

The Steerpike terror had been still further intensified by these stifling conditions, and the ceremony of the Bright Carvings was for this reason all the more eagerly anticipated, for it was a relief for the mind and spirit to be able to turn to something the only purpose of which was beauty.

But, for all the consummate craft and rhythmic loveliness of the carvings there was no love lost between their jealous authors. The inter-family rivalries, the ancient wrongs, a hundred bitter quarrels, were all remembered at this annual ceremony. Old wounds were reopened or kept green. Beauty and bitterness existed side by side. Old claw-like hands, cracked with long years of thankless toil, would hold aloft a delicate bird of wood, its wings, as thin as paper, spread for flight, its breast afire with a crimson stain.

On the penultimate evening all was ready. The Poet, now fully established as Master of Ritual, had made his final tour of inspection with the Countess. On the following morning the gates in the Outer Wall were opened and the Bright Carvers began the three miles trail to the Carvers' Courtyard.

From then onwards the day blossomed like a rose, with its hundred blooms and its thousand thorns. Grey Gormenghast became blood-shot, became glutted with gold, became chill with blues as various as the blue of the flowers, and the waters became stained with evergreen from the softest olive to veridian, became rich with all the ochres; flamed and smouldered, shuddered with the hues of earth and air.

And holding these solid figures in their arms were the dark and irritable mendicants. By afternoon the long stone shelf had been loaded with its coloured forms, its birds, its beasts, its fantasies, its giant grasshoppers, its reptiles and its rhythms of leaf and flower; its hundred heads that turned upon their necks, that dropped or were raised more proudly from the shoulders than any living head of flesh and blood.

There they stood in a long burning line with their shadows behind them on the southern wall. From all these carvings three were to be chosen as the most original and perfect and these three would be added to those that were displayed in the unfrequented Hall of the Bright Carvings. The rest were to be burned that same evening.

The judging was a long and scrupulous affair. The carvers would eye the judges from a distance as they squatted about the courtyard in families, or leaned against the opposite wall. Hour after hour the fateful business proceeded – the only sound being the shouting and crying of the scores of urchins. At about six o'clock the long tables were carried out by the castle servants and placed end to end in three long lines. These tables were then loaded with loaves, and bowls of thick soup.

When dusk began to fall the judging was all but completed. The sky had become overcast and an unusual darkness brooded over the scene. The air had become intolerably close. The children had ceased to run about, although in other years they had sported tirelessly until midnight. But now they sat near their mothers in a formidable silence. To lift an arm was to become tired and to sweat profusely. Many faces were turned to the sky where the world of cloud was gathering together its gloomy continents, tier behind tier like the foliage of some fabulous cedar.

As a minor Titus was not directly involved in the actual choice of the 'Three', but his technical approval had to be obtained when the decisions were finally made. He had wandered restlessly up and down the line of the exhibits, threading his way through the crowds, which parted deferentially at his approach. The weight of the iron chain about his neck and the stone that was strapped to his forehead became almost too much to bear. He had seen Fuchsia but had lost her again in the crowds.

'There's going to be an almighty storm, my boy,' said a voice at his shoulder. 'By all that's torrential, there most certainly is!'

It was Prunesquallor.

'Feels like it, Doctor Prune,' said Titus.

'And looks like it, my young stalker of felons!'

Titus turned his gaze to the sky. It seemed to have gone mad. It bulged and shifted itself as though it were not moved by any breeze or current of the air, but only through its own foul impulses.

It was a foul sky, and it was growing. It was accumulating filth from the hot slums of hell. Titus turned his eyes from its indescribable menace and faced the doctor again. His face was gleaming with sweat. 'Have you seen Fuchsia?' he said.

'I saw her,' answered Titus. 'But I lost her again. She is somewhere here.'

The Doctor lifted his head high and stared about him, his Adam's apple very angular, his teeth flashing, but in a smile that Titus could see was empty.

'I wish you would see her, Doctor Prune . . . she looks awful, suddenly.'

'I will certainly see her, Titus, and as soon as I can.'

At that moment a messenger approached. Titus was wanted by the judges.

'Away with you,' cried the doctor in this new voice that had lost its ring. 'Away with you, young fellow!'

'Good-bye, doctor.'

SIXTY-FOUR

THAT night, upon the balcony, his mother sat upon his right hand like an enormous stranger, and the Poet upon his left, an alien figure. Below him was a vast field of upturned faces. Away ahead of him and far beyond the reach of the great bonfire's radiance the Mountain was just visible against the dark sky.

The moment was approaching when he must call for the three successful carvers to come forward and for him to draw up the carvings from below with a cord and to place them in full sight of the crowd.

The flames of the bonfire around which the multitude was congregated streamed up into the sky. Its insatiable heat had already reduced a hundred dreams to ashes.

As he watched, a glorious tiger, its snarling head bent back along its spine, and its four feet close together beneath its belly, was flung through the air, by one of the twelve hereditary 'vandals'. The flames appeared to flick out their arms to receive it, and then they curled about it and began to eat.

His longing to escape came upon him with a sudden and elemental force. He hated this gross wastage that was going on below him. The heat of the evening made him sick. The nearness of his mother and of the abstracted Poet disquieted him. His eyes moved to Gormenghast Mountain. What lay beyond? Was there another land . . .? Another world? Another kind of life?

If he should leave the castle! The very notion of it made him shake with a mixture of fear and excitement. His thought was so revolutionary that he glanced at his mother's back to see whether she had heard his mind at work.

If he should leave Gormenghast? He was unable to hazard a guess as to what such a thought implied. He knew of no other place. He had thought before, of Escape. Escape as an abstract idea. But he had never thought seriously of where he would escape to, or of how he would live in some place where he would be unknown.

And a seditious fear that he was in reality of no consequence came over him. That Gormenghast was of no consequence and that to be an earl and the son of Sepulchrave, a direct descendant of the blood line – was something of only local interest. The idea was appalling.

He raised his head and gazed across the thousands of faces below him. He nodded his head in a kind of pompous approval as yet another carving was tossed into the great bonfire. He counted a score of towers to his left. 'All mine . . .' he said, but the words sounded emptily in his head when suddenly something happened which blew his terror and his hope sky-high, which filled him with a joy too huge for him to contain, which took him and shook him out of his indecisions, and swept him into a land of hectic and cruel brilliance, of black glades, and of a magic insupportable.

For, as he was watching, something happened with great rapidity. A coal black raven, its head cocked, its every feather exquisitely chiselled, its claws gripping a wrinkled branch, was about to be thrown into the flames when, as Titus watched, in a half-dream, a ripple in the silent, heat-heavy crowd, showed where a single figure was threading its way with an unusual speed. The hereditary 'vandal' had hold of the wooden raven by its head and swung back his hand. The bonfire leapt and crackled and lit his face. The arm came forward; the fingers loosed their grip; that raven sailed up in the air, turning over and over and began to fall towards the fire when, as unforeseen and rapid as the course of a dream, there leapt from the body of the fire-lit crowds something that, with a mixture of grace and savagery quite indescribable, snatched at the height of its leap the raven from the air, and holding it above its head continued without a pause or break in the superb rhythm of its flight, and apparently floating over an ivy-covered wall disappeared into the night. For more than a minute there was no movement at all. A dreadful embarrassment held the witnesses immobile as though with a vice. The individual shock that each sustained was heightened by the stunned condition of the mass. Something unthinkable had been done, something so flagrant that the anger that was so soon to show itself was for the moment held back as though by a wall of embarrassment.

Such violation of a hallowed ceremony was unprecedented.

The Countess was one of the first to stir. For the first time since Steerpike's escape she was moved by a tremendous anger that had no connexion with the skewbald rebel. She rose to her feet and with her big hands gripping the balustrade stared into the night. The congested clouds hung with a terrible nearness and an increasing weight. The air sweated. The crowds began to mutter and to move like bees in a hive.

Isolated cries of rage from below the balcony sounded close, raw and horrible.

What was the death of a few hierophants at Steerpike's hand compared with the stabbing of the castle's very heart? The heart of Gormenghast was not its garrison – its transient denizens, but that invisible thing that had been wounded in their sight. As the cries rose and the swollen clouds pressed down, Titus, the last to move, turned his eyes to his mother's with a sidelong sweep. Sick with excitement he rose gradually to his feet.

He alone, of all who had been so fundamentally affected by the profane insult to tradition, was affected for a reason of his own. The shock he had suffered was unique. He had not been drawn into the

maelstrom of the general shock. He was alone in his unique excitement. At the first sight of that mercurial creature he was transported in a flash to an earlier day, a day which he had no longer believed in, and had relegated to the world of dreams; to a day when among the spectral oak-woods he had seen, or had thought he had seen, an air-borne figure with its small head turned away. It was so long ago. It had become no more than a fume of his mind – a vapour.

But it was she. There was no doubting that it had all been true. He had seen her before, when lost among the oakwood she had floated past like a leaf. And now again! Taller, of course, as he was taller. But no less fleet, no less uncanny.

He remembered how the momentary sight of her had awakened in him an awareness of liberty. But now! How much more so! The heat was terrible in the air, but his spine was icy with excitement.

He looked about him again, with an air of cunning quite out of character. Everything was as it was. His mother was still beside him, her big hands on the balustrade. The bonfire roared and spat red embers into the dark and stifling air. Someone in the crowd was shouting, '*The Thing! The Thing!*' and another voice with dreadful regularity cried 'Stone her! stone her!' But Titus heard nothing of this. Moving gradually backwards step by step, he turned at last and in a few quick paces was in the room behind the balcony.

Then he began to run, his every step a crime. Through midnight corridors in any one of which the skewbald Steerpike might well have been lurking, he sped. His jaw ached with fear and excitement. His clothes stuck to his back and thighs. Turning and turning, sometimes losing himself, and sometimes colliding with the rough walls, he came at last to a flight of broad shallow steps that ran out into the open. A mile away to his right the light of the bonfire was reflected on the bulging clouds that hung above it like the ghostly bolsters of some beldam's bed.

Ahead of him, Gormenghast Mountain and the widespread slopes of Gormenghast forest were hidden from his vision in the night, but he ran to them as a migratory bird flies blindly through the darkness to the country that it needs.

SIXTY-FIVE

His sense of supreme disobedience, rather than retarding his progress through the night, gave it impetus. He could feel the angry breath of retribution on the nape of his neck as he stumbled on. There was yet time for him to return but in spite of his hammering heart it never occurred to him to do so. He was propelled forward by his imagination having been stirred to its depths by the sight of her. He had not seen her face. He had not heard her speak. But that which over the years had become a fantasy, a fantasy of dreaming trees and moss, of golden acorns and a sprig in flight, was fantasy no longer. It was here. It was now. He was running through heat and darkness towards it; to the verity of it all.

But his body was profoundly tired. The sickening heat was something to be fought against and at last when within a mile of the foothills he fell to his knees and then onto his side, where he lay soaked in perspiration, his flushed face in his arms.

But his mind did not rest. His mind was still running and stumbling along. A thousand times as he lay with his eyes closed, he saw her take the ivy-covered wall with that maddening beauty of flight; effortless, and overweeningly arrogant, her small bragging head, turned away from him, and perched so exquisitely upon the neck – the whole thing floating in his mind with a kind of aerial ease.

A hundred times he saw her as he lay and a hundred times he turned restlessly from side to side, while the sprite flew on and on and its legs like water-reeds appeared to trail in the body's wake rather than cause the earthless speed of it.

And then he heard the hoarse voice of a cannon and before the heavy, tumbling echoes that followed it had ended he was on his feet again and running dangerously through the darkness, to where the high masses of Gormenghast Mountain arose in the sightless night. It was the single explosion that was the traditional warning of danger. He knew it meant that his disappearance had not only been discovered, but that his defiance of Gormenghast had been suspected by his mother.

When the time came for the three chosen carvings to be drawn up to the balcony and to be flourished before the crowd, he was no longer there. On top of the sickening heat and the terror of the swollen sky; on top of the fear of the beast of Gormenghast and of his roving catapult – on top of the unprecedented snatching of a carving from the flames, and the sight of the 'Thing' in their midst, there was now this unimaginable offence to the castle's honour, to gall not only the hierophants but the carvers.

At first they had imagined that the young earl had fainted in the heat. This had occurred to the Poet, who with the permission of the Countess disappeared into the room at the rear of the balcony. But he found no sign of the boy. As the minutes passed the anger grew, and only the heaviness of the stifling night and the resulting weariness of the crowds prevented the indiscriminate violence that might easily have developed.

The acid of this dreadful night bit deep. Something fundamental to the life of Gormenghast had been affected and weakened.

At a time when a devil was loose and the whole energy of the place was concentrated upon his capture it was stupefying to find that the castle had been stabbed to the heart by the perfidy of its brightest symbol, the heir himself to the sacred masonry, the seventy-seventh earl.

This child of fate was climbing through the gloom; stumbling among the roots of trees, forcing his way through undergrowth, pressing fanatically onwards.

How he would find her when the sun rose over the mazes of the forest and played across the trackless expanses of Gormenghast Mountain, he had no idea. He simply believed that the power that drew him could not fail to show itself.

But a time came when he was so benighted that further progress was impossible. He was sufficiently far from the castle, sufficiently lost, to evade immediate capture. He knew that search parties were even now being organized and that the vanguard of those levies was probably already on its way. He knew also that the sending forth of a single searcher redounded in Steerpike's favour. This would not be forgiven him.

Whether his absence would be associated with the sudden appearance of the 'Thing' he could not tell. Perhaps the coincidence was all too apparent. What he did know was that the sin to cap all sins would be for any member of the castle, let alone its rightful sovereign, to have the remotest association with an Outer Dweller – for the earl of Gormenghast to go in search of a daughter of that squalid cantonment and a bastard child at that. He knew from his mother downwards to the most obscure of her menials the conception of any such happening would be equally revolting. It would be worse than shameless treachery. It would be at the same time a *defilement* of the blood line.

He knew all this. But he could do nothing. He could only pretend, if ever he were caught, that the impending storm had affected his brain. But he could not alter anything. Something more fundamental than tradition had him in its grip. If he was caught he was caught. If they imprisoned him, or held him up for public contumely then that was what he deserved. If he was disinherited he had only himself to blame. He had slapped a god across its age-old face. It was so . . . it was so . . . but as the night-heat swaddled him in a near-sleep his thoughts were not of his mother's mortification, of the castle's peril, of his treachery or of his sister's anxiety, but of a thing of fierce and shameless insolence – of a rebel like himself who gloried in it: of a rebel like a lyric in green flight.

SIXTY-SIX

HE awoke to the first crash of thunder. There was a shadowy light in the dark air that could only have come from some remote and cloud-choked sunrise. And as the thunder spoke the first of the great rain came.

The danger of it was at once apparent. This was no ordinary downpour. Even the first streaks from the sky were things that lashed and kicked the dust out of the ground with a vicious deliberation.

The air was like the air in an oven. Titus had leapt to his feet as though he had been prodded with a stick. The sky seethed and rumbled. The clouds yawned like hippopotami; deep holes or funnels, opening and closing, mouthlike, now here, now there.

He began to run again, climbing all the while through a kind of half-light. The forms of trees and rocks suddenly looming over him, forced him to turn to left and right in a sudden and jerky way, for it was not until he was upon them that they made themselves known.

His immediate object was to strike the fringe of the close-set trees of Gormenghast forest, for only beneath their boughs could he hope to shield himself from the rain. It hissed in the loose foliage about him which was no kind of shelter, even for this first flurry of the storm.

For all its initial violence there was yet no sense of hurry about the rain. It gave the impression of an endless reserve of sky-wide energy.

And as he stumbled on through the rain that spilled itself from the canopies of leaf above, a streak of lightning, like an outrider, lit up the terrain so that for a moment the world was made of nothing but wet steel.

And in that moment his eyes fled over the glittering landscape, and before the enormous gloom had settled again he had seen a pair of solitary pines on a hill of boulders, and he at once recognized the place, for one of the pines had been broken by the wind and was caught in the upper arms of its brother.

He had never climbed these pines nor stood in their shade nor heard the rustle of their needles; but they were more than familiar to him, for years ago he had stared at them every time he had emerged from the long tunnel – the tunnel that led from the Hollow Halls to within a mile of Mr Flay's cave.

When he saw the pines in the lightning-flash his heart leapt. But the darkness came down again and it was at once apparent how difficult it would be not only to arrive at the pines but to strike off from them, with confidence, towards the tunnel mouth. To arrive at the pines would yet not be to come to any place where he had stood before. In the moment that he had recognized those trees he had also realized that the rest of the dazzling panorama was unknown to him. He had taken some strange path in the darkness.

But though it might well be difficult, even with the increasing light, to know exactly in which direction to move, when at last he should come to the pines (for it would of course be impossible to see the caveward mouth of the tunnel) yet it was useless to dwell upon the difficulties, and Titus, altering his direction, struck out across the wilderness of coarse grasses that were already under water. The churned 'lake' reached upwards to his ankles. It spouted all about him. What had been fierce streaks of rain were now no longer streaks. Nor even ropes. Each one was like pump-water or a tap turned to its full. And yet there was still the dreadful closeness in the air; although the tepid water, hammering him and streaming over his body mitigated the heat.

Beyond the soaking grasslands, and the alder copses, beyond the stony and grassless foothills where the big ponds were forming; beyond the old silver-mines and the gravel quarries; beyond all these in a district of harsher country than he had so far encountered, he came at last to a group of giant rocks.

By now the light had to some extent percolated through the clouds of black water and when he climbed upon the back of the largest of the rocks he was able to see the two pines, not away to his right, as he suspected they would be, but immediately ahead of him.

But there was no need for him to approach them further. He could not have found a better look-out station than the rock on which he stood. Nor was there any need for him to strain his eyes to find features in the landscape by which he could determine the position of the tunnel's mouth. For there to the east, not a mile away, was that high line of trees that overhung the shelving masses of green-gravel, which, overgrown with every kind of vegetable life, descended step-like, to where among the valley rocks the small stream chattered, the stream which Flay had dammed, and which ran within a stone's throw of what had been the exile's cave.

With the dusky light of morning strengthening, the rain, through which it had been difficult to recognize any object, so solidly had it descended, began to lessen. There was no question of the rain wishing to rest itself; far less that the sky were running out of water. No, it was only that the clouds withdrew their claws into the black pads of the storm as a wild beast might draw in its talons for no other reason than to savour the contraction.

But still the rain came down. A body of water had been held in check, but there was no stopping the overflow. Titus no longer felt the rain. It was as though he had always lived in water.

He sat down on the rock, and like a fly in amber, was a prisoner of the morning. All about him on the flat head of the rock the rebounding rain threw up its short fierce fountains, and the hard slopes seethed with it. What was he doing here, soaked to the skin, far from his home? Why was he not frightened? Why was he not repentant and ashamed?

He sat there alone, his knees drawn up to his chin, his arms clasping his legs, how small a thing beneath those continents of gushing cloud.

He knew that it was no dream, but he had no power to override the dream-like nature of it all. The reality was in himself – in his longing to experience the terror of what he already thought of as love.

He had heard of love: he had guessed at love: he had no knowledge of love but he knew all about it. What, if not love, was the cause of all this?

The head had been turned away. The limbs had floated. But it was not the beauty. It was the sin against the world of his fathers. It was the arrogance! It was the wicked swagger of it all! It was the effrontery! It was that Gormenghast meant nothing to this elastic switch of a girl!

But it was not only that she was so much the outward expression of all he meant by the word 'Freedom', or that the physical *she* and what she symbolized had become fused into one thing – it was not only this that intoxicated Titus – it was more than an abstract excitement that set his limbs trembling when he thought of her. He lusted to touch those floating limbs. She was romance to him. She was freedom. But she was more than these. She was a thing that breathed the same air and trod the same ground, though she might have been a faun or a tigress or a moth or a fish or a hawk or a martin. Had she been any of these she would have been no more dissimilar from him than she was now. He trembled at the thought of this disparity. It was not closeness or a sameness, or any affinity or hope of it, that thrilled him. It was the difference, the *difference* that mattered; the *difference* that cried aloud.

And still the rain came down, rapid and warm from the hot air it passed through. Titus' eyes were on those trees that crowned the long hill in whose shadow was the cave. A few miles to the west, a huge blur showed where Gormenghast Mountain brooded. It was streaked with the vertical bars of the rain as though it were a beast in prison.

Titus got to his feet and made his way down the rock and all at once he felt frightened. Too much had happened to him in too short a time. It was the thought of the cave, and thence the thought of Flay and from the thought of Flay as he had first seen him in his cave then sprang the image of that faithful servant with a knife in his heart and the vile room where his Aunts lay side by side. And so the face of Steerpike swam across the lines of the rain, the terrible pattern of red and white, like the mask of some horror-dance, expanding and contracting, the shoulders very spare, very high, and for a hundred paces Titus was all but sick as he ran, and more than once he turned his head over his shoulder, and peered into the rain on either hand.

It was a long journey to the cave. Even had there been no deluge he would have made for it. He thought of it as a centre from which he could move in the wilderness and to which he could return.

But when he reached it he was hesitant to enter. The old stone mouth gaped emptily. It was no longer as he remembered it. It was a deserted place.

Above the cave the hill arose tier upon streaming tier of shelving rock, the broken ledges thick with ferns and shrubs, and even trees that leaned out fantastically into space.

Titus stared up to where the upper heights were lost in the clouds but his eyes were almost at once drawn back to the cave mouth.

His head was a little lowered and thrust forward from his shoulders in a characteristic position that suggested that he was ready to butt whatever enemy might appear. His nondescript hair was black with the rain and clung across his face in streaks and rats'-tails.

The melancholy look of the entrance had for a moment dulled his excitement at seeing the place again. He stood about a dozen feet away from the mouth, and could see through the streaks of the rain the dark, dry tunnel that led to the spacious interior.

As he stood there, hesitant, his head forwards, his rain-heavy clothes clinging to his body like seaweed, it could be seen how much the last few months had changed him. His eyes were still as clear as spring water, with that glitter of wilfulness, but a frown had made a permanent groove above them. A nest of faint and shallow lines had formed between his eyes. The boyish proportions of his face were clear evidence that he was no more than his seventeen years, but the sombre expression which had become ever more typical of him was more to be expected in a person twice his age.

This *darkness* in his face was by no means the outcome of sad or tragic experience. He had had his times of loneliness, of fear, of frustration, and of late, of horror, but equally like any other child, he had had his carefree golden days, his laughter and his excitements. He was no cowed and mournful child of misfortune. He was, if anything, too much alive. Too much aware. It was that that had forced him, in the end, to wear a mask. To scowl at his school-friends, while at the same moment his heart would be beating wildly, and his imagination racing. To scowl because, by scowling he was left alone. And when he was alone he was able to brood by the hour upon his lot, to whip himself into unhealthy and self-indulgent fits of rebellion against his heritage and against the ritual that so hampered him, and conversely he was able to sit undisturbed at his desk while his thoughts flickered to and fro across the realm of Gormenghast, marvelling, as he did so, at all that it was, and how it was his mammoth legacy.

His physical vitality had begun to find its outlet through solitary exploration of the castle and the surrounding country but it was the expeditions of his imagination, of his day dreams, that drew him further and further away from companionship.

He had been, virtually, an orphan. That his mother, deep in her heart, too deep for her own recognition, had a strange need for him, as a son of the Line, was of no value to him, for he knew nothing of it.

To be alone was nothing new to him. But to have defied his mother and his subjects as he had done this day was new, and this knowledge of his treachery made him feel, for the first time since he had escaped from the carver's balcony, lonely in the extreme. Lonely, not for his home, but lonely in the knowledge of his inward isolation.

He took a step nearer the cave. The rain, surging over his head, had so glued-down his hair that his skull showed its shape like a boulder. His slightly heavy cheek-bones, his blunt nose, his wide mouth were by no means handsome in themselves, but, held in by the oval outline of the face, they formed a kind of simple harmony that was original and pleasant to the eye.

But his habit of drawing down his eyebrows and scowling to hide his feelings was making him look more than his seventeen years, and it appeared that a young man rather than a boy was approaching the cave. Directly he had decided to wait no longer, and had passed under the rough natural archway he was startled at the freedom of his head and body from the battering of the rain. He had become so used to it that standing there in the dry dust beneath the vaulting roof of the tunnel, he felt a sudden buoyancy as though a burden had been lifted.

And now another wave of fatigue heaved up in him, and he longed for nothing so much as sleep in a dry place. The air was warm in the cave, for the rain, heavy as it was, had done nothing to relieve the heat.

He longed to lie down, in his new-found lightness of body, and with nothing pouring down upon him from above, to sleep for ever.

Now that he was inside the cave, the melancholy atmosphere of desertion had lost its potency. Perhaps he was too tired, and his emotions too blunted to be conscious any more of such subtleties.

When he came to the main, inner chamber with its ample space, its natural shelves, its luxuriating ferns he could hardly keep his eyes open. He hardly noticed that a number of small woodland animals had taken shelter and were lying upon the stone shelves, or squatting on the ferny floor, watching him with bright eyes.

Automatically he tore off his clinging clothes and stumbling to a dark corner of the cave lay down beneath the arched arms of a great fern and fell, incontinently, fast asleep.

SIXTY-SEVEN

As Titus slept the small animals were joined by a drenched fox and a few birds which perched on outcrops of rock near the doming roof. The boy was all but invisible where he lay beneath the overhang of the ferns. So deep was his sleep that the lightning that had begun to play across the sky and illumine the mouth of the cave had no effect upon him. The thunder, when it came, for all that it was louder than before was equally powerless to wake him. But it was drawing closer all the while, and the last of the bull-throated peals caused him to turn over in his sleep. By now it was afternoon but the air had darkened so that there was now less light than there was when Titus sat upon the 'look-out' rock.

The roaring and hissing of the rain was mounting steadily in volume and the noise of it upon the stones and the earth outside the mouth of the cave made all but the most violent of the thunder-peals inaudible. A hare with its ears laid along its back sat motionless with its eyes fixed upon the fox. The cave was filled with the noise of the elements, and yet there was a kind of silence there, a silence *within* the noise; the silence of stillness, for nothing moved.

When the next flash of lightning skinned the landscape, ripping its black hide off it so that there was no part of its anatomy that was not exposed to the floodlight, the reflections of that blinding illumination were fanned to and fro across the cavern walls so that the birds and beasts shone out like radiant carvings among the radiant ferns, and their shadows flew away across the walls and contracted again as though they were made of elastic: and Titus stirred beneath the archery of the giant hearts-tongue which shielded him from the momentary glare, so that he did not waken, and he could not see that at the mouth of the cave stood the 'Thing'.

SIXTY-EIGHT

I

IT was hunger that finally woke him. For a while as he lay with his eyes still closed he imagined himself to be in his room at the castle. Even when he opened his eyes and found on his right-hand side the rough wall of a rock and on his left a curtain of thick ferns he could not remember where he was. And then he became aware of a roaring sound and all at once he remembered how he had escaped from the castle and had made his way through an eternity of rain until he had come to a cave . . . to Flay's cave . . . to *this* cave in which he was now lying.

It was then that he heard something move. It was not a loud sound and it was only audible above the thrumming of the storm because of its nearness.

His first thought was that it was one of the animals, perhaps a hare, and his hunger made him cautious as he rose upon his elbow and parted the long tongue of the ferns.

But what he saw was something that made him forget his hunger as though it had never been: that made him start backwards against the rock and sent the blood rushing to his head. For it was she! But not as he remembered her. It was she! But how different!

What had his memory done to her that he should now be seeing a creature so radically at variance with the image that had filled his mind?

There she sat, the Thing, balanced upon her heels, unbelievably small, the light of a fresh fire flickering over her as she swivelled a plucked bird on a spit above the flames. All about her were scattered the feathers of a magpie. Was this the lyric swallow? The fleet-limbed hurdler?

Was this small creature who was now squatting there like a frog in the dust, and scratching her thigh with a dirty hand the size of a beech leaf, was this what had floated through his imagination in arrogant rhythms that spanned the universe?

Yes, it was she. The vision had contracted to the small and tangible proportions of the uncompromising urchin – the rarefaction had become clay.

And then she turned her head and Titus saw a face that shocked and thrilled him. All that was Gormenghast within him shuddered: shuddered and bridled up in a kind of anger. All that was rebellious in him cried with joy: with the joy of witnessing the heart of defiance. The confusion in his breast was absolute. His memory of her, of a proud and gracile creature, was now destroyed. It was no longer true. It had become trite, shallow and saccharine. Proud, she was, and vibrant in all conscience. And graceful, perhaps in flight – but not now. There was nothing graceful in the way her body, uninhibited as an animal's, crouched over the flames. This was something new and earthy.

Titus who had been in love with an arrogance and a swallow-like beauty of limb, so that he longed savagely and fearfully to clasp it was now aware of how there were these new dimensions, this dark reality of slaughtered birds, of scattered feathers, of an animal's posture and above all of an ignorant originality that was redolent in her every gesture.

Her head had turned. He had seen her face. He was staring at an *original*. It was not that the face had any unique peculiarity of proportion or feature but that it was so blatant an index of all she was.

And yet it was not through any particular mobility of the features that it conveyed the independence of her life. The line of the mouth seldom altered, save when, in devouring the roasted bird, she bit with an undue ferocity. No: the face was more mask-like than expressive. It symbolized her way of life, not her immediate thoughts. It was the colour of a robin's egg, and as closely freckled. Her hair was black and thick but she had hacked it away, a little above her shoulders. Her rounded neck was set upright upon her shoulders, and was so flexible that the liquid ease with which she turned it was reminiscent of a serpent.

It was through such motions as this, and the movements of her small shoulders and in the quickness of her fingers that she conveyed to Titus, more vividly than any expression of the features could ever do, the quality of her fanatical independence.

As he watched she tossed the bones of the magpie over her shoulder, and dipping her hand into the shadows at her side drew up, out of the darkness that she cast, the little carving of the raven. Turning it round and round in her hand she stared at it intently, but no vestige of an expression crossed her face. She placed it on the ground at her side, but the earth was uneven and it fell forwards upon its face. Without a moment's hesitation she struck it with her clenched fist as a child might strike a toy in anger, and then, rising in a smooth and single action to her feet, she flicked it out of her way with her foot so that it lay upon its side against the wall.

Upon her feet she had become another thing. It was difficult to reconcile her with the creature who had squatted by the fire. She had become a sapling. Her face was turned to where the water streamed across the cave-mouth. For a few moments she stared expressionlessly at the rain-filled opening and then she moved towards it, but at her third step she stopped and as her body tautened her head gyrated on her neck. Her shoulders had not moved, but as her head swivelled, her eyes sped around the walls of the cave. Something had disturbed her.

Her slender body was poised for instantaneous action. Again her eyes flew across the walls piercing every shadow, and then for a moment they stayed their flight and Titus could see from his dark recess that she had seen his shirt where it lay, torn and sodden, on the floor of the cave.

She turned and with a tread both light and apprehensive approached the garment that lay in a pool of its own making. She sat down on her heels at its side, and again she was a frog, an almost repellent thing. Her eyes still moved about the cave, suspiciously. For a little while they lingered upon the giant ferns that, arching over Titus, hid him in their shadows.

Swivelling her head she stared backwards to the mouth of the cave, but only for a second; for the next moment she had taken the shirt, and held it up before her. A stream of rain water slid from its folds to the floor; she crushed the cloth together and then began to wring it out with a surprising strength and then spreading it out upon the ground she gazed at it, her expressionless head upon one side like a bird's.

Titus, half numbed by his cramped position, was forced to lie back and rest his arms and straighten his leg. When he rose again upon his elbow she was no longer by the shirt but was standing at the cave-mouth. He knew that he could not stay where he was for ever. Sooner or later he must make his presence known – and he was about to get to his feet whatever the consequences when a glare of lightning showed him the Thing silhouetted against the brilliance, her backbone arched a little, her head thrown back to catch the stream of translucent rain that golden as the lightning itself was falling directly into her upturned mouth. For that split second of time she was something cut out of black paper, her head meticulous in its contour, the mouth wide open as though to drink the sky.

And then the dark came down, and he saw her appear out of the gloom and grow more visible as she approached the embers of the fire. It was evident that the shirt fascinated her, for she paused when she reached it, and stared at it now from one angle, now from another. Finally she took it up and pulling it over her head and thrusting her arms through the sleeves she stood, as though in a nightgown.

Titus, whose conception of the Thing had been flung from one side of his mind to the other, so that he hardly knew whether she was a frog, a snake, or a gazelle, was now powerless to assimilate the bizarre transfiguration that now stood within a few feet of him.

All he knew was that what he had so vividly sought was with him in the cave, had sheltered, like himself, from the storm and was now standing like a child, staring down at his shirt that fell in wet folds almost to the ankles.

And he forgot the wilderness within her. He forgot her ignorance. He forgot the raw blood and the speed. He only saw the stillness. He only saw the deceptive grace of her head as it hung forward. And seeing only this he pushed aside the ferns and rose to his feet.

II

The effect of his sudden appearance upon the Thing was so violent that Titus took a step backwards. Encumbered as she was with her new garment she leapt to the side of the cave where the floor was littered with loose stones, and all in a breath she had snatched at one and flung it with a vicious speed at Titus. He jerked his head to one side but the rough stone scraped his cheek-bone and stung him badly, the blood running down his neck.

The pain and surprise which lit his face were in contrast to her inscrutable features. But it was his body that was still, and hers that moved.

She had swarmed up the rockface on her side of the cave and was leaping from ledge to ledge in an attempt to circumscribe the rough circle of wall beneath the dome. Titus had been between her and the entrance tunnel, and she was even now springing to a position from which she could swing herself over his head and drop on the stormward side – and so away.

But Titus, just in time to realize what she was doing, retreated further down the tunnel, so that he blocked the way for her escape. But he was still in a position to observe her. Thwarted in her plan, she sprang backwards to one of the higher ledges that she had already used, and there, twelve feet above him, her head among the ferns that hung downwards from the roof, she directed her gaze upon him, her freckled face expressionless, but her head moving continuously from side to side like an adder's.

The effect of the blow on his cheek was to waken Titus out of his adulation. His temper flared out, and his fear of her lessened, not because she was not dangerous, but because she had resorted to so ordinary a means of warfare as the flinging of a stone. That was something he could understand.

Had she been able to pluck out rocks from the fern-cloaked roof she would even now be doing so, and hurling them down upon him. But even as he stared up at her with angry amazement, he felt an irrational longing for her, for what was she doing but defying, through him, the very core of Gormenghast? And it was this solitary insurrection that had first affected him with wonder and excitement. And while the stinging of his cheek-bone angered him so that he wished to shake her, strike her and subdue her, at the same time the ease with which she had flitted from ledge to perilous ledge, the long wet garment slapping on the rocks as she sped, had made him lust for her small breasts and her slender limbs. He yearned to crush and master them. And yet he was angry.

How it was that she had been able to move at all across the rockface with his shirt impeding the freedom of her legs, let alone travel so speedily, he could not tell. The long sleeves flapped about her hands, but somehow or other she had been able to flick out her fingers from the folds, time after time, to grasp the cavern outcrops.

Now, as she crouched in the upper shadows, the damp cloth clinging to her and taking the form of her narrow limbs as though it had been sculptured, Titus, watching from below, cried out suddenly in a voice that seemed not his own.

'I am your friend! Your friend! Can't you understand? I am Lord Titus! Can't you hear me?'

The face like a robin's egg stared down at him from among the ferns, but there was no reply, save what sounded like a distant hissing.

'Listen to me,' he shouted again, more loudly than before, although his heart beat wildly and the words were difficult to form.

'I have followed you. Don't you see? . . . followed you . . . O, can't you understand! I've run away . . .'

He took a step nearer the wall so that she was almost directly overhead . . .

'And I've found you! So speak to me, for God's sake, can't you? Can't you?'

He saw her mouth open above him, and at that moment she might have been a giant phantom, something too earthless to be held in by the worldly dimensions of this cave, something beyond measurement. And her open mouth gave him the answer to his question.

'*So speak*,' he shouted, 'can't you?' And this is what she could not do, for the first sound which Titus heard her utter bore no relation to human speech. Nor did the tone of it convey that he was being answered even in a language of her own. It was a sound, quite solitary and detached. It had no concern with communication. It was inward and curiously pitched.

So divorced was it, this nameless utterance from the recognized sounds of the human throat, that it left Titus in no doubt that she was incapable of civilized speech and not only this but that she had not understood a word he had said.

What could he do to show her he was not her enemy, that he had no wish to avenge himself for the blood on his cheek? The thought of his wound gave him an idea, and he immediately lowered himself to his knees, never taking his eyes off her, and felt about him for a stone, her eyes following his every movement with the concentration of a cat. He could see the tenseness of her body vibrating through the shirt. When his fingers closed upon a stone he rose to his feet, stretched out his hand with the missile displayed upon his open palm. Surely she must realize that it was now in his power to fling the thing at her. For a moment or two he showed her the stone, and then tossed it backwards over his shoulder where it clanged on the solid rock of the wall behind him.

But no expression crossed the freckled face. She had seen everything but as far as Titus could tell it had meant nothing to her. But as he stared up he became conscious that she was preparing to change her position, or to make some kind of attempt at escape. For the hundredth part of a second her eyes had flicked away as though to remind herself of the surrounding footholds and the dangerous ledges, and then again her eyes switched from his face, but this time it was to something that lay behind Titus on the other side of the cave. Quick as thought he turned his head and saw what he had forgotten all about, the two wide natural chimneys through the rock, that, twelve feet above the entrance of the cave, led to the outer air.

So that was what she would try and do. He knew that she could not reach these rounded vents from where she was, but that if she could circle the cave, she might spring from the opposite side into the upper chimney, and so, out into the open, where, no doubt, she would be able to swarm across the moss-grey walls of streaming rain.

For the rain was still pounding. It was an inevitable background to all they did. They were no longer conscious of the steady roaring, of the shouts of the thunder or of the intermittent lightning. It had become normality.

And then, from where she crouched, the Thing rose in the air, and was all at once upon a broader ledge six feet to her right. There seemed to have been no muscular effort. It was flight. But once there, she tore at Titus' shirt, hauling it over her head as though she were freeing herself of a sail, but somehow it had become entangled about her, during her leap, and, blinded for a moment by its folds across her face, she had, in a momentary panic, shifted her foothold and, misjudging the area of the ledge, she had overbalanced in the darkness and, with a muffled cry, had toppled from the height.

Involuntarily, as she had leapt to the broader shelf of rock, Titus had moved after her, as though drawn by the magic of her mobility, so that as she overbalanced he was within a few feet of where she would have struck the floor. But before she had fallen more than her own length he was stationed beneath her, his knees flexed, his hands raised, his fingers spread, his head thrown back.

But what he caught was so unsubstantial that he fell with it to the floor from the very shock of its lightness. His legs weakened beneath him with surprise, as though they had been cheated of the weight, however slight, that they were prepared to sustain. He had caught at a feather and it had struck him down. But his arms closed about the sprite that struggled in the cold wet linen, and Titus gripped her with an angry strength, the full weight of his body lying across hers, for they had rolled over one another and he had forced her under.

He could not see her face; it was closely shrouded in the wet linen, but the shape of it was there as her head tossed to and fro; it was like the head of sea-blurred marble long drowned beneath innumerable tides, save where a ridge of cloth was stretched across the forehead and took the shape of the temples. Titus, his body and his imagination fused in a throbbing lust, gripping her even more savagely than before with his right arm, tore at the shirt with his left until her face was free.

And it was so small that he began to cry. It was a robin's egg, and his whole body weakened as the first wild virgin kiss that trembled on his lips for release died out. He laid his cheek along hers. She had ceased to move. His tears ran. He could feel her cheek grow wet with them. He raised his head. He had become far away and he knew that there would be no climax. He was sick with a kind of glory.

Her head was turned to one side upon the ground and her eyes were fixed upon something. Her body had become rigid. For a moment it had melted and was like a stream in his arms, but now it was frozen once more, like ice.

Slowly he turned his head, and there was Fuchsia, the rain water streaming from her to the ground, her drenched hair hanging snake-like over her face, and her face in her hand.

III

All of a sudden Titus knew that he was lying alone. The sleeve of the shirt was clenched in his hands but the Thing had gone.

He had forgotten there was any other world. A world in which he had a sister and a mother, in which he was an earl. He had forgotten Gormenghast.

And then he heard the shrill scream of derision which he was never to forget. He leapt to his feet and ran dizzily to the door of the cave. There he saw her standing in the downpour, knee deep in water, naked as the rain itself. The lightning was playing continuously now, lighting her as though she were a thing of fire herself, now flickering across her in a yellow half light.

As he stared a kind of ecstasy filled him. He had no sense of losing her – but only the blind and vaunting pride that he had held her in his arms; that naked creature that was now crying again, derisively in a language of her own.

It was finality. Titus knew in his bones that he could expect no more than this. His teeth had met in the dark core of life. He watched her almost with indifference – for it was all in the past – and even the present was nothing to the pride of his memory.

But when, out of the heart of the storm that searing flash of flame broke loose, and ripping a path across the dazzled floods, burned up the 'Thing' as though she had been a dry leaf in its path, and when Titus knew that the world was without her for ever, then something fled in him – something fled away – or was burned away even as she had been burned away. Something had died as though it had never been.

At seventeen he stepped into another country. It was his youth that had died away. His boyhood was something for remembrance only. He had become a man.

He turned and retraced his steps to where Fuchsia leaned against the wall. They could not speak.

How pitifully human she was. When he parted the long locks that straggled over her face and saw how defenceless she was, and when she pushed his hand away with the tired disillusion of a woman twice her age, then he realized his own strength.

At a time when he should have been broken by the scene he had just witnessed – by the death of his imagination – he found himself to be emptied of distress. He was himself. He was free for the first time. He had learned that there were other ways of life from the ways of his great home. He had completed an experience. He had emptied the bright goblet of romance; at a single gulp he had emptied it. The glass of it lay scattered on the floor. But with the beauty and the ugliness, the ice and the fire of it on his tongue and in his blood he could begin again.

The Thing was dead . . . dead . . . lightning had killed her, but had Fuchsia not been there he would have shouted with happiness for he had grown up.

IV

It was a long time before a word was exchanged. They sat exhausted
side by side. Fuchsia had been persuaded to take off her long red dress,
and Titus had wrung it out and it was now spread before the fire he had
re-kindled. He longed to leave the cave. It was now so much dead rock.
It was over and done with. But Fuchsia, sick with exhaustion, was in no
state to start the return journey for an hour or more.

While he moved about the cave, Titus caught sight of some dead
birds on a ledge of rock but his hunger had never returned.

Then he heard Fuchsia's voice, very low and heavy.

'I thought perhaps you'd be here. I am better now. We must go back.
The flood is rising.'

Titus walked quickly to the door of the cave. It was true. They were
in danger. Far from lessening the rain was heavier than ever with
formidable massings of cloud.

He returned quickly to her side.

'I told them you had lost your memory,' she said. 'I told them you
had been like this before. You must say the same. We'll part near the
Castle. Come on.'

She got to her feet and pulled her damp red dress over her head. Her
heart was raw with disappointment. Her fear had been for Titus' safety
and she had risked her neck for him, but her hopes had been that he
would be proud of her. To struggle all that way, and to find him
with . . . the 'Thing'!

Clinging fiercely and painfully to her pride, she swore to herself that
she would never ask him – would never speak of her. She had thought
that there was no one so close to him as herself – or that if there was, he
would tell her. She knew that she was only his sister but she had had a
blind faith that even though she had defied him over Steerpike, yet she
was more necessary to him than Steerpike had ever been to her.

Titus was gazing at her as he tucked the torn and fateful shirt into his
trousers.

'She is dead, Fuchsia.'

She lifted her head.

'Who?' she murmured.

'The wild girl.'

'The . . . wild . . . girl . . . ? So soon?'

'The lightning.'

Fuchsia turned to the cave-mouth and began to move towards the
storm.

'Oh God,' she whispered as though to herself. 'Is there nothing but
death and beastliness?' and then, not turning as she spoke, but raising

her voice. 'Don't tell me, Titus. Don't tell me anything. I would rather know nothing. You live your life and I'll live mine.'

Titus joined her at the mouth of the cave. It was a frightening sight that lay before them. The landscape was filling up with water. There was not a moment to lose.

'There's only one hope,' said Titus.

'I know,' said Fuchsia. 'The tunnel.'

They stepped forward together and received the weight of the cascading sky. Thereafter their journey was a nightmare of water. Time after time they saved one another in the treacherous flood as they waded towards the entrance of the long underground passage. A hundred incidents befell them. Their feet were caught in underwater creepers; they stumbled over submerged bushes, the limbs of trees fell headlong into the water at their sides, and all but struck or drowned them. At times they were forced to return and make long detours where the water was too deep, or too marshy. When they came to the high bank on the hill they were all but drowned. But the tunnel was there and although the water had begun to pour down its black throat yet their relief at seeing it was such that they involuntarily clasped each other. For a fleeting moment the years rolled back and they were brother and sister again in a world of no heartburn.

They had forgotten that the tunnel was so long; so inky dark, so full of vegetable beastliness, of hampering roots, and foul decay. As they neared the castle the water became deeper; for on every side of Gormenghast the landscape shelved gradually downward, the wide-spread mazes of rambling masonry lying at the centre in a measureless basin.

When eventually they were able to stand upright and emerged from the tunnel, and began to wade along the corridors that led to the Hollow Halls, the water was up to their waists.

Their progress was maddeningly slow. Step by step they forced their way through the heavy element, the inky water curling at their waist. Sometimes they would climb steps and would be able to rest for a while, at the top of a flight, but they could not stay for long, for all the while the water was rising. It was a mercy that Titus had become familiar with the one route that took them by degrees to that point behind the giant carving where, so long ago, he had escaped from Barquentine to lose himself in those watery lanes that they were now so slowly wading through.

It came at last: the halt behind the statue. Titus was in front and he worked his way around the base of the carving and cautiously leaning forward, peered to left and right along the dusky corridor. It was deserted and no wonder. Here as elsewhere the water lay like a dark and slowly moving carpet. It was obvious that the flood had poured in on every side and that the ground level of Gormenghast had been evacuated. His dormitory was upon the floor above, and Fuchsia's room was likewise above flood level. Fuchsia was by now beside him, and they were about to step forward through the water and proceed along their separate paths to their rooms when they heard the sound of a splash, and Titus dragged his sister back. The sound was repeated and repeated again in a regular beat, and then as it grew louder, they saw a glimmer on the water as a soft red light began to approach from the west.

Holding their breath they waited and a moment later they saw the flat nose of a punt or narrow raft slide into their line of vision. An oldish man sat upon a low seat at its centre. He held in either hand a short pole and these were dipped simultaneously on either side of his craft. They had not far to submerge before they struck the stone beneath and the punt was propelled forward in a smooth and unhurried manner. At the bows was a red lantern. Across the stern lay a firearm, its hammer cocked.

Both Fuchsia and Titus had seen the man before. He was one of the many watchmen or sentries who had been detailed to patrol these lower corridors. Evidently neither the storm nor Titus' disappearance had caused any relaxation in the daylong, nightlong search for the skewbald beast.

Directly the light of his lantern and its red reflection had grown small in the distance the brother and sister waded to the nearest of the great stairways.

As they climbed they became aware, even before they had reached the stairhead of the first of the spreading storeys, that a great change had come about. For looking up they saw, out-topping the stone banisters, high piles of books and furniture, of hangings and crockery, of crate on crate of smaller objects, of carpets and swords, so that the landing was like a great warehouse or emporium.

And lying across tables, or slouched over chairs, in every kind of attitude of fatigue were numbers of exhausted men. There were few lanterns still alight, but no one seemed awake, and nothing moved.

Tip-toeing past the sleepers, and leaving trails of water behind them as they went, Titus and Fuchsia came at last to a junction of the two corridors. There was no time for them to linger or to talk but they stood still for a moment and looked at one another.

'This is where we part,' said Fuchsia. 'Don't forget what I told you. You lost your memory and found yourself in the woods. I never found you. We never saw each other.'

'I won't forget,' said Titus.

They turned from each other and, following their diverging paths, disappeared into the darkness.

SIXTY-NINE

THERE was no one alive in Gormenghast who could remember a storm in any way comparable to this black and endless deluge that, flooding the surrounding country, and mounting with every passing minute, was already lapping at the landings of the first storey.

The thunder was continuous. The lightning went on and off as though a child were playing with a switch. On the vast expanse of water, the heavy branches of riven trees floated and tossed like monsters. The fish of Gormenghast river swam out in every direction, and could be seen steering through the castle's lowest windows.

Where high ground or an isolated rock or a watch tower broke the surface, these features were crowded with small animals of all kinds, that huddled together in heterogeneous masses, and took no notice of one another. By far the vastest of these natural sanctuaries was, of course, Gormenghast Mountain which had become an island of dramatic beauty, the thick forest trees hanging out of the water at its base, its streaming skull flickering balefully with the reflection of the vibratory lightning.

By far the greatest proportion of the animals still alive were congregated upon its slopes, and the sky above it, violent and inhospitable as it was, was never free of birds that wheeled and cried.

The other great sanctuary was the castle itself towards whose walls the tired foxes swam, the hares beside them, the rats in their wake, the badgers, martins, otters and other woodland and river creatures.

From all the quarters of the compass they converged, their heads alone visible above the surface, their breath coming quick and fast, their shining eyes fixed on the castle walls.

This gaunt asylum, like the Mountain (that faced it across the rain-lashed lakes, that were so soon to form an inland sea), had become an island. Gormenghast was marooned.

As soon as it became evident to the inhabitants that it was no ordinary storm that had broken upon them and that the outer ramifications of the castle were already threatened and were liable to be isolated from the main mass, and that the outbuildings, in particular the stables and all structures of wood, were in peril of being washed away, instructions were given for the evacuation of the remote districts, for the immediate recall of the Bright Carvers, and for the driving of all livestock from the stables to within the walls. Bands of men and boys were dispatched for the bringing in and the salvaging of carts, ploughs and all kinds of farm equipment. All this, along with the carriages and harnessings of the horses, was temporarily housed in the armoury on the east side of one of the inner quadrangles. The cattle and the horses were herded into the great stone refectory, the beasts being segregated by means of improvised barriers made largely from the storm-snapped boughs of trees that were piling up continuously beneath the southern windows.

The Outer Dwellers, already smarting with the insult of the broken Ceremony, were in no mood to return to the castle, but when the rain began to loosen the very foundation of the encampments, they were forced to take advantage of the order they had received, and to make a sullen exodus from their ancient home.

The magnanimity that was shown them in their time of peril, far from being appreciated, still further embittered them. At a time when they had no other work than to withdraw themselves and to brood over the vile insult they had sustained at the hands of the House of Groan, they were forced to accept the hospitality of its figurehead. Carrying their infants and their few belongings over their shoulders, a horde of sodden malcontents drew in upon the castle, the dark water gurgling about their knees.

An extensive peninsula of the castle, a thing of rough unpointed masonry, a mile or more in length and several storeys high, had been given over to the Carvers. There they staked their claims, upon the mouldering floorboards, each family circumscribing their 'sites' in thick lines drawn with lumps of chalky plaster.

In this congested atmosphere their bitterness flourished, and unable to vent their spleen on Gormenghast, the great abstract, they turned upon one another. Old scores were remembered and a kind of *badness* filled the long sullen promontory. Floor above floor was rancour. Their homes of clay were gone. They had become something which they would never have admitted in the days when they lived in open squalor *beyond* the castle walls – they had become a dependency.

From their windows they could see the dark rain pouring. With every day that passed the sky seemed thicker, and fouler in the sagging horror of its black and glutted belly. From the upper halls at the far and straggling limit of the promontory, the prisoners, for so they were in everything but name, were able to obtain a view of Gormenghast Mountain. With the first light of dawn, or by lightning flashes during the night, they noted how the flood had climbed its flanks. The horizontal branch of a far tree, or a peculiarity of some rock-face near the water's edge would be taken as a reference point, and it became their morbid interest to gauge how high and at what speed the flood was rising.

And then a kind of relief came to them – not from any outside source but through the foresight of an old carver, and this relief to their frustration took the form of boatbuilding. It was not carving in the creative sense in which they excelled, but it was carving. Directly the idea was launched, it sent forth its ripples that spread from one end of the peninsula to the other.

That they had been unable to carve had been as galling as the insult they had swallowed. Their rasps and chisels, saws and mallets had been the first things that they had gathered together when all hope of remaining in their hovels had disappeared. But they had been unable to carry with them the heavy timber or the jarl roots which they had always used. Now, however, their former media would be useless. Something of a very different nature was needed for the construction of boats or rafts or dug-outs, and it was not long before the redundant beams that spanned the ceilings, the panels from the inner walls, the doors themselves and where possible the joists and floor-boards began to disappear. The competition among the families to build up within their chalk-marked sites a pile of board and timber, was deadly and humourless, and was only to be compared with the subsequent rivalry to build not only the most navigable and watertight craft but the most original and beautiful.

They asked for no permission; they acted spontaneously, ripping away, or prising apart floor-board and panel; they climbed for hours among filthy rafters and sawed through solid pine and timbers of black oak; they stole by night and they denied their thefts by day; they kept watch and set forth on expeditions; they argued over the safety of the floors; over which timbers were dangerous to move and which were ornamental. Great gaps appeared in the floors through which the ragged children flung filth and dust upon the heads of the carvers on the floor below. The lives of the Outer Dwellers had become almost normal again. Bitterness was their bread and rivalry their wine.

And the boats began to take shape, and hammering filled the air, as in the semi-darkness, with the rain lashing through the windows and the thunder rolling, a thousand forms of craft grew into beauty.

Meanwhile in the main body of the castle there was little time for any other activity than that of moving upwards, eternally upwards, the multitudinous effects of Gormenghast.

The second floor was by now untenable. The flood, finding its own level within the honeycombed interiors, had become more than a threat to property. A growing number of the less agile or intelligent had already been trapped and drowned; doors being unopenable by reason of the weight of pressing water or directions being lost among the unfamiliar waterways.

There were few who were not engaged upon the back-breaking business of forcing a world of belongings up the scores of stairways.

The cattle so necessary to the survival of the marooned had changed their quarters time after time. Driving them up the broadest flights it had been difficult to control their panic. The stout banisters had given way like matchsticks – iron railings had been bent by the pressing weight of the climbing herds; masonry had been loosened, a huge stone lion at the head of a stairway falling down the well of the stairs, four cows and a heifer following it to their deaths in the cold water below.

The horses were led up one by one, their hooves pawing at the treads of the stairs, their nostrils distended, the whites of their eyes shining in the gloom.

A dozen men were kept busy all day shifting the loads of hay up to the upper halls. The carts and ploughs had had to be abandoned as had a heavy and irreplaceable inventory of machines and bulk of every description.

On every floor an abandoned conglomeration was left behind, for the climbing water to despoil. The armoury was a red pond of rust. A score of libraries were swamps of pulp. There were pictures floating down long corridors, or being lifted gradually from their hooks. The crevices in wood or brick and tiny caves between the stones of the innumerable walls had been swilled free of the complexity of insect life. Where generations of lizards had lived in secrecy there was only water now. Water that rose like terror, inch by clammy inch.

The kitchens had been moved to the highest of the suitable areas. The gathering together and transporting of the thousand and one things necessary to the feeding of the castle had been itself an epic undertaking. As also, in another way, had been the frantic packing and dragging from the Central Library of the traditional manuscripts, the sacred laws of Ritual and the thousands of ancient volumes of reference but for which the complex machinery of the castle's life could never be revived. These heavy crates of sacrosanct and yellowing papers were dragged at once to the high attics and a couple of sentries were posted before them.

As every landing filled with salvage, the exhausted men, their shirts stuck to their backs, their brows shining like candlewax, from the sweat that poured into their eyes, cursed the storm, cursed the water, cursed the day they were born. It seemed to have gone on for ever, this shouldering of giant cases up tortuous stairs; of straining upon ropes, only to hear them snap and the burden crash headlong down the flights they had won so dearly; the aching of their bodies and thighs; this ghastly fatigue. There was no end to it; to the mechanics of gear and rigging; to a hundred extempore inventions; to the levering and the cranking; to the winding of home-made pulleys; to the gradual raising of stock and metal; of fuel, grist and treasure; of vintage and hoards of miscellaneous lumber. From storehouse, depository, vault and ware-house, from magazine, dump and coffer, from granary and arsenal; from the splendid rooms of bygone days where the great 'pieces' mouldered; from the private rooms of countless officers; from the communal halls and the dormitories of the hierophants – from all these places everything went up, the furniture, the chattels, the works of vanity and the works of art; from the enormous tables of carved oak, to the least of silver bracelets.

But all this was not without organization. Behind it all there was a brain at work. A brain that had been drowsing since girlhood – that had been for so long a time unfocused that it had taken no less a thing than Steerpike's rebellion to make it yawn and stretch itself. It was now fully awake. It belonged to the Countess.

It was she who had given the first orders; who had called in the Bright Carvers; who had, with a great map of the central district of Gormenghast spread before her, remained seated at a table at one of the central landings, and, co-ordinating the multifarious activities of salvage and resettlement, had given her subjects no time to think of the peril they were in but only of their immediate duties.

From where she sat she could see the last of the removals from the landing below. The water had reached to about the fifth tread of this upper staircase. She stared down at the four men who were struggling with a long blackish chest. As it moved water poured out of it. Step by step it was hoisted up the wide flight. The lapping water was choked with floating objects. Every floor had delivered to the flood its quota of things lost, forgotten or worthless, the lower regions lifting their buoyant chattels inch by inch to loftier waterways where, joined by fresh flotillas, newly launched, the heterogeneous flotsam grew and grew.

For a few moments the Countess eyed the dark water in the well of the stairs before turning to a group of runners, who were stationed before her.

As she turned to face them a fresh messenger arrived panting. He had been to check the rumours that had reached the central castle of how the Bright Carvers were engaged upon boatbuilding and had all but gutted the promontory.

'Well?' she said, staring at the runner.

'It is true, your ladyship. They are building boats.'

'Ah,' said the Countess. 'What else?'

'They ask for awnings, your ladyship.'

'Awnings. Why?'

'The lower storeys have been flooded out, as here. They have been forced to launch their boats, unfinished, through the windows. They have no protection from the rain. The upper storeys refused them entry. They are already overcrowded.'

'What kind of boats?'

'All shapes, your ladyship. Excellently made.'

She propped her chin on her big hand. 'Report to the Master of the

Rough Hangings. Have him send all the canvas that has been salvaged. Inform the Carvers their craft may be requisitioned in emergency. They must make all the vessels they can. Send me the Custodian of the River Boats. We have some craft of our own, have we not?'

'I believe so, your ladyship. But not many.'

'Next messenger!' said the Countess.

An old man came forward. 'Well?' she said.

'I see no break in the storm,' he said. 'On the contrary . . .'

'Good,' said the Countess.

At this remark every eye was turned to her. At first they did not trust their hearing. Turning to each other the score or so of officials and messengers who surrounded her could see, however, that none of them had misheard. They were all equally perplexed. She had spoken softly, heavily, hardly above a whisper. 'Good', she had said. It was as though they had overheard some private thought.

'Is the leader of the Heavy Rescue here?'

'Yes, your ladyship.' A tired and bearded figure came forward.

'Rest your men.'

'Yes, your ladyship. They need it.'

'We all need it. What of it? The waters are rising. You have your list of priorities?'

'Yes.'

'Have the leaders of every section made their working copies?'

'They have.'

'In six hours' time the flood will be at our feet. In two hours' time all hands are to be woken. There is no possibility of the night being spent on this level. The Chequered Stairway is the widest. You have my order of priority; livestock, carcasses, corn; and so on, have you not?'

'Certainly, your ladyship.'

'Are the cats comfortable?'

'They have the run of the twelve blue attics.'

'Ah . . . and then . . .' her voice tailed away.

'Your ladyship?'

'. . . And then, gentlemen, we shall begin. The mounting water draws us all together. Is that so, gentlemen?'

They bowed their perplexed assent.

'With every hour less rooms are tenable. We are driven up, are we not, into a confine. Tell me, gentlemen, can traitors live in air and feed on it? Can they chew the cloud? Or swallow the thunder or fill their bellies with lightning?'

The gentlemen shook their heads and eyed one another.

'Or can they live beneath the surface of the water like the pike I see below me in the darkness? No. He is like us, gentlemen. Are the sentries posted as usual? Is the kitchen guarded?'

'It is, your ladyship.'

'Enough! We are squandering the time. Give orders that there are two hours' sleep. You will leave me.'

She got to her feet as her audience retired to propagate her instructions and leaned over the heavy balustrade that surrounded the stairhead. The water had risen half the height of a tread since she had heard of the Carvers' boats. She leaned there, like something over life size, her heavy arms folded on the balustrade, a lock of her dark red hair hanging over her wide, pale brow as she stared over and down to where the black water brooded in the well of the stairs.

SEVENTY

WHEN the Countess had heard of Titus' return to the castle, she had summoned him at once and had heard from him of how the heat had overpowered him, and of how he had lost his memory and, after he knew not how long a time, had found himself alone on the outskirts of Gormenghast forest.

As Titus had recounted these falsehoods she had stared at him but made no comment, save, after a long pause, to ask him, whether on his return he had seen Fuchsia.

'I say on your *return*' (she had added), 'as on your *outward* journey you were in no state to recognize anyone. Is that so?'

'Yes, Mother.'

'And did you see her, when you were returning, or after you returned?'

'No.'

'I will have your story circulated throughout the castle. Within an hour the Carvers will be informed of your loss of memory. Your oblivion was ill-timed. You may go now.'

SEVENTY-ONE

For little short of a fortnight the rain continued unabated; so great a proportion of the castle was now under water that in spite of the rain it was necessary for encampments to be formed upon the suitable roofs which were approached through attic hatchways. The congestion in the upper zones was appalling.

The first of the commandeered flotillas had been paddled across the deep water from the carvers' promontory. On their return journey across the roofs and upper floors the carvers were permitted to take with them what loose timber they could carry.

The Countess had a broad and handsome craft. It was designed for oarsmen and had an ample space for her at the stern to sit and steer with comfort.

The carvers had been supplied with tar and great drums of paint, and this solid boat was decorated with devices of red, black and gold. Its bows rose out of the water with a slow and massive grace and terminated in a carved head that resembled a bird of prey, its throat of sculptured feathers and its bald forehead a dusky scarlet, its eyes yellow and petalled like the heads of sunflowers, its curved beak black and sinister. This idea of a figurehead had been almost universally adopted by the carvers. As much care had been lavished in this way as upon the structure and the safety of the boats.

One day Titus was informed that a special craft had been created for him, and that it awaited him in a southern corridor. He went at once and alone to where it lay floating. At any other time Titus would have cried with joy to receive the slim and silver creature of the waterways, so exquisitely balanced on the flood; to have been allowed to step from the waterlogged and immovable table that was half afloat on the castle's seventh floor – to step into this canoe, which, unlike any he had ever seen in his picture books when a child, seemed eager to be away, at the dip of a paddle.

As it was he loved it; but with heartburn. It seemed to remind him of all he vaguely longed for. It reminded him of the days when he hardly knew himself to be an earl; when to have no father and no affection from his mother seemed normal enough; when he had seen no violence; no death; no decay. Of days when there was no Steerpike at large like a foul shadow that darkened everything and kept the nerves on edge; and more than this, the slight canoe beneath him reminded him of the days when he knew nothing of the terrible antithesis within him – the tearing in two directions of his heart and head – the divided loyalties

– the growing and feverish longing to escape from all that was meant by Gormenghast, and the ineradicable, irrational pride in his lineage, and the love, as deep as the hate, which he felt, unwittingly, for the least of the cold stones of his loveless home.

What else was it that brought the tears to his eyes as he took the paddle that was handed down to him, and dipped its blue blade in the sullen water? It was his memory of something that had fled as surely as his boyhood had fled; something that was as swift and slight and tameless as he knew this craft would be. It was his memory of the Thing.

He dipped his blade. A craftsman's masterpiece cock'd, as it were, her sweet and tapering head, whispered a curve of silver to the north, and slipping through a dusky gallery, leapt at the quickening of his paddle-stroke. Ahead of him, at the hinge of perspective, far away, a point of light, the water half way up its distant frames, sped towards him, as, skimming the flood of a black corridor, he drew, with every stroke, the nearer to the cold and rain-churned sea.

And all the time his heart was crying, and the exhilaration and the beauty of it all were the agents of his pain. Swiftly as he sped he could not outstrip his body or his mind. The paddles dipped and the craft flew but could not leave his haunted heart behind. It flew with him on the sepulchral water.

And then, as he neared the all-but flood-filled window he realized for the first time how dangerously close was its upper lintel to the surface. The light from without had strengthened considerably during the last hour and the reflection of the square of light had been so strong as to have given Titus the impression that the entire area of light, the reflections included, was an opening through which he could pass. But now he saw that he had only the top half of the bright square through which to skim. Flying towards it he fell back suddenly, and lying with his head below the level of the sides and with his eyes shut he heard the faintest of gritty whispers as, shooting the window, the delicate prow of the vessel grated the lintel.

Suddenly the sky was wide above him. An inland sea was ahead of him. A steady rain was pouring down, but compared with the long deluge they had grown to accept as normal, it seemed that he was afloat in good weather. He allowed the canoe to slacken speed of its own and when it had come to a bobbing standstill he turned her about with a stroke and there ahead of him the upper massives of his kingdom broke the surface. Great islands of sheer rock weather-pock'd with countless windows, like caves or the eyries of sea-eagles. Archipelagos or towers, gaunt-fisted things, with knuckled summits – and other towers so broken at their heads as to resemble pulpits, high and sinister; black rostrums for the tutelage of evil.

And then a qualm, empty cold and ringing, as though he was himself a hollow bell stirred in his bowels like a clapper. An exquisite sense of loneliness grew beneath his ribs, like a bubble of expanding glass.

The rain had ceased to fall. The agitated water had become silent, motionless. It had taken on a dark translucence. Afloat upon a yawning element he gazed down to where, far below him, trees grew, to where familiar roads wound in and out, to where the fish swam over walnut trees and strangest of all to the winding bed of Gormenghast river, so full of water that it had none of its own.

What had all this that filled his eyes with amazement and pleasure, what had it all to do with the despoiling flood, the wreck of treasures, the death of many, the haunt of Steerpike who, driven slowly upwards, was hiding even now? Was this where Fuchsia lived? And the Doctor and the Countess, his own mother, who, it seemed, after trying to approach him had drawn away again?

In a state of overwrought melancholy he began to slide forward over the still waters, dipping his paddle every now and again. A dull light from the sky played over the water that streamed in sheets from gutterless roofs.

As he neared the isles of Gormenghast, he saw away to the north, the carvers' navy like scattered jewels on the slate-grey flood. Immediately ahead of him, as he proceeded, was the wall through one of the windows of which he had so dangerously skimmed. What was left of the window and of those on either side was now submerged and Titus knew that yet another floor of the central castle had by now been abandoned.

This wall, which formed the blunt nose of a long stone headland, had a counterpart a mile to the east. Between these two a vast and sombre bay lay stretched, with not a break in its surface. As with its twin, this second headland had no windows open at flood level. The water had a good twelve feet to climb before the next tier of casements could be entered or affected. But turning his eyes to the base, or curve of the great bay – to where (had it been in reality a bay) the sands might well have stretched, Titus could see that the far windows in that line of cliffs, no larger in his sight than grains of rice, were, unlike those of the headlands, far from regular.

Those walls, covered with ivy, were in many ways peculiar. Stone stairs climbed up and down their outer sides and led to openings. The windows, as he had already observed, appeared to be sprinkled over the green façades of the cliff with an indiscriminate and wayward profluence that gave no clue as to how the inner structures held together.

It was towards this base of the 'bay' that Titus now began to paddle, the limpid flood as chill as death beneath him, with all its rain-drowned marvels.

SEVENTY-TWO

It seemed to Titus a deserted place, a fastness of no life – rank with ivy, dumb with its toothless mouths, blind with its lidless eyes.

He drew in to the base of the abandoned walls where a flight of steps rose slanting out of the depths of the water, and, climbing alongside the wet green wall of ivy, rose to a balcony forty feet above his head – a stone affair surrounded by an iron railing decoratively wrought but so corroded with rust, that it only waited the tap of a stick to send it crumbling to the water.

As Titus stepped from his craft on to the stone steps at water level, and kneeling, lifted it dripping from the water and laid it carefully along the length of a stone tread, for he had no painter, he became conscious of a distinct malevolence. It was as though the great walls were watching his every move.

He pushed his brown hair back from his forehead and lifted his head so that he faced the towering masonry. His eyebrows were drawn together, his eyes were narrowed, his trembling chin was thrust aggressively forward. There was no sound but the dripping of the rain from the acres of ivy.

Unpleasant as was this sense of being under observation, he fought back the panic that might so easily have developed and, more to prove to himself that he was not afraid of mere stone and ivy rather than because he really wished to mount the stairway and discover what lay within the melancholy walls, he began to climb the slippery steps that led to the balcony. And as he began his ascent, the face that had been watching him disappeared from the small window close to the summit of the lowering wall. But only for a moment, for it reappeared so suddenly again at another opening that it was difficult to believe that it could be the same face that now stared down to where the steps slid under the water and where Titus' canoe lay 'beached'. But there could be no doubt of it. No two faces could either be so identical of blemish, nor so cruelly similar. The dark red eyes were fixed upon the little craft. They had watched his approach across the 'bay'. They noted how light, rapid and manoeuvrable it was, how it had answered to the merest whim of its rider.

He turned his eyes from the craft to Titus, who by now, having climbed a dozen steps was within a couple more of being immediately below the heavy block of stone which Steerpike had loosened, and which he had half a mind to send hurtling down upon the youth below.

But he knew that the death of the Earl, much as it would have gratified him, would not in fact materially advance his chance of escape. Had it been certain that the stone would strike his lordship dead, he would have had no hesitation in satisfying what had now become a lust for killing. But were the stone to miss its prey and splinter on the steps far below, then not only would Titus have every right to imagine that he had been ambushed – and who would ambush the Earl save he himself – but also a more immediate dislocation of his plans would result. For there was little doubt that Titus on recovering from his shock would not dare to continue with his upward climb, but would return immediately to his craft. And it was this boat that Steerpike was after. To be able to move at speed through the tortuous waterways of the castle would double his mobility.

Driven from haunt to haunt, from hiding place to hiding place by the rising water, his operations conditioned always by the necessity of his being within striking range of the stores and larders, it had in the narrowing zone of manoeuvre become imperative for him to be able to travel with equal speed and silence over both land and water. For days he had starved when the mobile kitchens were so positioned in a curve of the spacious west wing that it was impossible for him, guarded as they were, to plunder.

But they had moved, since then, at least three times, and now, with the possibility of the rain having stopped for good, it was his savage hope that they had found a fixity in that high sub-attic room above which in a barricaded and all but lightless loft he had established his headquarters. In the ceiling of this murky refuge a trap door opened upon a sloping roof of slates, where swathes of creeper bandaged it from sight. But it was the hatch in the floor below him which, when lifted with a tender and secret care more usually associated with the handling of sucklings, that gave him access to the most pressing of his needs: for below him lay the stores. In the small hours, when it became necessary he would lower himself inch by noiseless inch on a long rope. The sack he brought down with him he would fill with the least perishable provisions. A dozen or more of the staff would be asleep on the floor, but the sentries were naturally posted on the *outer* side of the three doors and were no bother to him.

But this was not his only hide-out. He knew that sooner or later the floods would fall. The kitchens would again become nomadic. It was impossible to tell in which direction the life of the castle would sway as on its slowly downward journey it trod upon the wet heels of the subsiding water.

The spreading roofs themselves furnished him with seven secret strongholds. The attics and the three dry floors below provided for at least four as safe, in their varying ways, as his garret above the kitchen. And now that the flood had stayed at the same level for three days, a few feet above the majority of the landings of the ninth floor, it had become possible for him to prepare in advance a number of aqueous asylums.

But how much simpler and safer it would be for him were he able to reconnoitre the high canals in such a craft as he now saw below him.

No. He could not afford to send the rough stone hurtling down. There was more than a chance of his failure to slay. The acute temptation to crush at a single blow that life out of the heir to Gormenghast – and leave nothing more than brick and stone behind – the intoxicating temptation to take the risk and to do this, was hard to resist.

But before all else came his own survival, and if by so much as an iota he deviated in any way from what he considered to be his final advantage then the end would surely come if not now, then very soon. For he knew he was walking on a razor's edge. He gloried in it. He had slid into the skin of a solitary Satan as though he had never enjoyed the flourish of language, the delights of civil power. It was war, now. Naked and bloody. The simplicity of the situation appealed to him. The world closed in upon him, its weapons drawn, eager for his death. And it was for him to outwit the world. It was the simplest and most fundamental of all games.

But his face was not the face of a thing at play. Or even of the Steerpike of a few years back – at play; or even of sin at play, for something new had happened to it. The terrible pattern that made of it a map, the white of the sea, the red, the continents and spattered islands, was hardly noticeable now. For it was the eyes that drew away the attention from all else.

For all the characteristic cunning and agility of his brain, he was no longer living in the same world that he lived in before he murdered Flay. Something had altered. It was his mind. His brain was the same but his mind was different. He was no longer a criminal because he chose to be. He had no longer the choice. He lived now among the abstractions. His brain dealt with where he would hide and what he would do if certain contingencies arose, but his mind floated above all this in a red ether. And the reflection of his mind burned through his eyes, filling the pupils with a grizzly bloodlight.

As he stared down like a bird of prey from its window'd crag, his brain saw, far below him a canoe. It saw Titus standing on the stone balcony. It saw him turn and after a moment's hesitation enter the rotting halls and disappear from view.

But his mind saw nothing of all this. His mind was engaged in a warfare of the gods. His mind paced outwards over no-man's-land, over the fields of the slain, paced to the rhythm of the blood's red bugles. To be alone and evil! To be a god at bay. What was more absolute.

Three minutes had passed since the Earl had disappeared into the maw of the building below him. Steerpike had given him time to move well into the fastness before he took action. There had been the chance of the sudden reappearance of the youth, for the lower halls were dark and sinister. But he had not reappeared, and the time was now ripe for Steerpike to make his leap. The descent was of a sickening duration. The blood hammered in the murderer's head. His stomach turned over and for a while he lost consciousness. When his reflection, flying upwards from the depths to meet him was shattered at the surface, and as the spume of water rose like a fountain, Steerpike's body, far below the surface, continued its descent until, at last, as his feet touched lightly upon the submerged head of a weather-cock, he began to rise again to the surface.

The disturbed water had become quite smooth again.

Dazed with the effort of the long fall, sick with swallowed water and with painful lungs, yet it was only a moment or two before he had struck out for the stone stairway.

When he reached it and climbed the few steps to where the canoe lay quietly upon her side, he wasted not a moment in setting her upon the water. Boarding her nimbly he grasped the paddle that lay within and with the first half-dozen strokes was speeding beneath the ivy-covered walls towards one of the few windows which coincided with the water level.

It was of course necessary for Steerpike to make immediately for cover. The great bay ahead was a death trap, where, were a fish to raise its head above the surface it would be seen at once!

At any moment the young Earl might return. It was for him to skid unseen through the first of the flood windows leaving no trace. As Steerpike sped rapidly over the water he had, as far as possible, kept his head turned back over his shoulders for the possible reappearance of the earl. Were he to be seen it would be necessary for him to make his way at once to one of his hiding places. There would be no possibility of his being overtaken, but to be sighted would, for many reasons, be unfortunate. He had no wish for the castle to know he could travel by water – nor that he roamed so far afield as to these frowning headlands; the sentries might well be reinforced, the vigilance sharpened.

So far he had been fortunate. He had survived his fall. His enemy had been out of earshot when he had splashed into the water; he had sighted a window through which he would pass with ease and behind the dark jaw of which he could remain until darkness descended.

For a few minutes at a time, as he slipped along the base of the dark walls he was forced to turn his head, to correct the course of the canoe, but for the most part his eyes were fixed upon the empty balcony to which at any moment his enemy might return.

It was when he had but three or four lengths of his canoe to go, before he turned her into the castle that, concentrating upon a faultless entry, he was unable to see that Titus had stepped out upon the open balcony.

He could not see that on immediately discovering the disappearance of his boat, Titus had started forward and had then swept his eyes across the bay until they had come to rest upon the only moving object – the far canoe as it began its curve into the cliff. Without a thought Titus drew backwards into the doorway around which he now peered, his body shaking with excitement. Even at that distance there was no mistaking the hunched shoulders of the marauder. It was well that he had stepped backwards so quickly, for as the canoe took its curve and straightening out, slid rapidly at the castle, as though to crash its delicate prow against its flank, Steerpike, certain of a perfect entry, returned his attention to the distant balcony, and as he noted its emptiness he disappeared into the wall like a snake into a rock.

SEVENTY-THREE

THE Doctor was exhausted; his eyes red with lack of sleep, his features wasted and drawn. His skill was in unending demand. The flood had gathered in its wake a hundred subsidiary disasters.

In a long attic room which became known as the hospital, the improvised beds were not only filled with cases of fracture and accident of every description, but with the victims of exhaustion, and of various sicknesses resulting from the dank and unhealthy conditions.

He was now upon his way to a typical accident. The news had been brought to him of yet another case of broken bones. A man had fallen apparently while trying to carry a heavy crate up a slippery stairway, its treads swimming in rain water. On reaching the place the Doctor found that it was a clean break of the femur. The man was lifted onto the professional raft at the spacious centre of which the Doctor could apply his splints or perform whatever temporary operation was necessary, while at the same time his orderly at the rear propelled them back in the direction of the hospital.

Dipping his long pole with excellent regularity the orderly would send the raft sliding steadily along the corridors. On this particular occasion as the raft, when about half way to its goal, crept gingerly through a wooden arch somewhat narrow and difficult of manoeuvre, and came out into what must have once been a ballroom, for in one of its hexagonal corners the upper levels of an ornate platform emerged above the surface, suggesting that an orchestra once filled the place

with music – as the raft edged itself out of the restricted passageway
and floated forward into all this wealth of space, Doctor Prunesquallor
sank back against the rolled up mattress he kept towards the stern of
the raft. At his feet lay the man he had been attending, his trouser torn
open from heel to hip; his thigh in a splint. The white bandages, bound
with a beautiful and firm deliberation, were reflected in the ballroom
water.

The Doctor shut his eyes. He hardly knew what was happening about
him. His head swam; but when he heard his raft being hailed by some
kind of dugout that was being paddled in his direction from the far end
of the ballroom he raised an eyelid.

It was indeed a dugout that was drawing closer, a long, absurd affair,
obviously made by the men who were now manning it, for the Carvers
would never have allowed such an object to leave their workshops. At
its stern, with his hand on the tiller, was Perch-Prism, who was
obviously in command. His black-gowned crew, using their mortar-
boards as paddles, sat in varying degrees of dejection, one behind the
other. They disliked not being able to face the way they were going, and
resented Perch-Prism's captaincy and consequent control over their
watery progress. However, Bellgrove had appointed Perch-Prism to his
post and given orders (which he had never dreamed would be carried
out) that his staff should help patrol the waterways. Schooling, of
course, had become impossible, and the pupils, now that the rain had
stopped, spent most of their time leaping and diving from the
battlements, the turrets, the flying buttresses, the tops of towers, from
any and every vantage point, into the deep clear water where they
swam like a plague of frogs in and out of windows and over the wide
breast of the flood, their shrill screams sounding from near and far.

And so the staff were free of scholastic duties. They had little to do
but yearn for the old days, and to chaff one another until the chaff
became acrimonious and a morose and tacit silence had fallen upon
them and none of them had anything original left to say about the flood.

Opus Fluke, the stern oar, brooded darkly over the armchair that the
flood had swallowed – the armchair which he had inhabited for over
forty years – the filthy, mouldering, hideous and most necessary support
of his existence, the famous 'Fluke's cradle' of the Common Room – it
had gone for ever.

Behind him in the dugout sat Flannelcat, a poor oarsman if ever
there was one. For Flannelcat to be glum and speechless was nothing
new. If Fluke brooded on the death of an armchair, Flannelcat brooded
on the death of all things and had done so for as long as anyone could
remember. He had always been ineffectual and a misery to himself and
others, and so, having plumbed the depths for so long, this flood was a
mere nothing to him.

Mulefire, the most difficult of the crew for Perch-Prism to control, sat like a hulk of stupid, bull-necked irritability, immediately behind the miserable Flannelcat, who looked to be in perpetual danger of being bitten in the back of the neck by Mulefire's tomb-stone teeth, and of being lifted out of his seat and slung away across the ballroom water. Behind Mulefire sat Cutflower; he was the last of them all to admit that silence was the best thing that could happen to them. Chatter was lifeblood – and it was a mere shadow of the one time vapid but ebullient wag who sat now staring at Mulefire's heavily muscled back.

There were only two other members to this crew: Shred and Swivell. No doubt the rest of the staff had got hold of boats from somewhere, or, like these gentlemen, had constructed something themselves, or even ignored Bellgrove's ruling, and kept to the upper floors.

Shred and Swivell dipping their mortarboards in the glassy surface were of course the nearest to the approaching raft. Swivell, the bow 'oar', turning his ageing face to see who it was that Perch-Prism was hailing, upset for a few moments the balance of the dugout which listed dangerously to the port side.

'Now then! Now then!' shouted Perch-Prism from the stern. 'Are you trying to capsize us, sir?'

'Nonsense,' shouted Swivell, colouring, for he hated being reprimanded over the seven heads of his colleagues. He knew that he had behaved in an utterly unworthy way, for a bow oar, but 'Nonsense' he shouted again.

'We will not discuss the matter now sir, if you please!' said Perch-Prism, dropping the lids over his small black and eloquent eyes, and half turning away his head so that the underside of his porcine nose caught what light there was reflected from the water.

'I would have thought it were enough that you had endangered your colleagues. But no. You wish to justify yourself, like all men of science. Tomorrow you and Cutflower will change places.'

'Oh Lord! la!' said Cutflower, testily. 'I'm comfy where I am, la!'

Perch-Prism was about to let the ungracious Cutflower into a secret or two on the nature of mutiny when the Doctor came alongside.

'Good morning, Doctor,' said Perch-Prism.

The Doctor, starting out of an uneasy sleep, for even after he had heard Perch-Prism's shout across the water he had been unable to keep his eyes open, forced himself upright on the raft and turned his tired eyes upon the dugout.

'Did somebody say something?' cried he, with a valiant effort at jocularity, though his limbs felt like lead and there was a fire in the top of his head.

'Did I hear a voice across the brine? Well, well, it's you, Perch-Prism, by all that's irregular! How are you, admiral?'

But even as the Doctor was flashing one of his Smiles along the length of the dugout, like a dental broadside, he fell back upon the mattress, and the orderly with the long pole, taking no notice of Perch-Prism and the rest, gave a great shove against the ballroom floor and the raft swam forward and away from the Professors in the direction of the hospital, where, he hoped, he could persuade the Doctor to lie down for an hour or two irrespective of the maimed and distressed, the dead and the dying.

SEVENTY-FOUR

IRMA had not spared herself over the furnishing of her home. A great deal of work, a great deal of thought – and, in her opinion, a great deal of taste – had been lavished upon it. The colour scheme had been carefully considered. There was not a discordant note in the whole place. It was so tasteful, in fact, that Bellgrove never felt at home. It gave him a sense of inferiority and he hated the powder-blue curtains and the dove-grey carpets, as though it were *their* fault that Irma had chosen them. But this meant little to her. She knew that he as a mere man would know nothing of 'artistic' matters. She had expressed herself, as women will, in a smug broadside of pastel shades. Nothing clashed because nothing had the strength to clash; everything murmured of safety among the hues; all was refinement.

But the vandal water came and the work and the thought and the taste and the refinement, O where was it now? It was too much! It was too much! That all the love she had lavished was drowned beneath the mean, beastly, stupid, unnecessary rain, that this thing, this *thing*, this useless, brainless element called rain, should turn her artistry to filth and pulp!

'I hate nature,' she cried. 'I hate it, the rotten beast . . .'

'Tut, tut,' muttered Bellgrove as he lolled in a hammock and stared up at one of the beams in the roof. (They had been assigned a small loft where they were able to be miserable in comparative comfort.) 'You can't talk about nature like that, my ignorant child. Good gracious, no! Dammit, I should think not.'

'Nature,' cried Irma scornfully. 'Do you think *I'm* frightened of it! Let it do what it likes!'

'You're a piece of nature yourself,' said Bellgrove after a pause.

'Don't be stupid, you . . . you . . .' Irma could not continue.

'All right, what *am* I then?' murmured Bellgrove. 'Why don't you say what's in your empty little woman's mind? Why don't you call me an old man like you do when you're angry with something else? If you're not nature, or a bit of it, what the hell are you?'

'I'm a *woman*,' screamed his wife, her eyes filling with tears. 'And my home is under . . . under . . . the *vile* . . . rain-water . . .'

With a great effort Mr Bellgrove worked his emaciated legs over the side of the hammock and when they touched the floor, rose shakily to his feet and shambled uncertainly in his wife's direction. He was very conscious of doing a noble action. He had been very comfortable in the hammock; he knew that there was a very slender chance of his chivalry being appreciated, but that was life. One had to do certain things to keep up one's spiritual status, but apart from that, her terrible outburst had unnerved him. He had to do *something*. Why did she have to make such an unpleasant noise about it all? Her voice went through his head like a knife.

But oh it had been pathetic too: railing against Nature. How maddeningly ignorant she was. As though nature should have turned back when it reached as far as her boudoir. As though a flood would whisper to itself, 'Sh . . . sh . . . sh . . . less noise . . . less . . . noise . . . this is Irma's room . . . lavender and ivory you know . . . lavender and ivory' – Tut-tut-tut, what a wife to be saddled with in all conscience . . . and yet . . . and yet . . . was it only pity that drew him to her? He did not know.

He sat down by her side beneath a small top window, and he put his long, loose arm about her. She shuddered a moment and then stiffened again. But she did not ask him to remove his arm.

In the small loft with the great castle beneath them like a gigantic body with its arteries filled with water, they sat there side by side, and stared at where a piece of plaster had fallen from the opposite wall, and had left a small grey pattern the shape of a heart.

SEVENTY-FIVE

IT was not that Fuchsia did not struggle against her mounting melancholia. But the black moods closing in on her ever more frequently were becoming too much for her.

The emotional, loving, moody child had had small chance of developing into a happy woman. Had she as a girl been naturally joyous yet all that had befallen her must surely have driven away the bright birds, one by one, from her breast. As it was, made of a more sombre clay, capable of deep happiness, but more easily drawn to the dark than the light, Fuchsia was even more open to the cruel winds of circumstances which appeared to have singled her out for particular punishment.

Her need for love had never been fulfilled; her love for others had never been suspected, or wanted. Rich as a dusky orchard, she had never been discovered. Her green boughs had been spread, but no travellers came and rested in their shade nor tasted the sweet fruit.

With her mind for ever turning to the past, Fuchsia could see nothing but the ill-starred progress of a girl who was, in spite of her title and all it implied, of little consequence in the eyes of the castle, a purposeless misfit of a child, hapless and solitary. Her deepest loves had been for her old nurse Nannie Slagg, for her brother, for the Doctor, and in a strange way for Flay. Nannie Slagg and Flay were both dead; Titus had changed. They loved one another still but a wall of cloud lay between them, something that neither had the power to dispel.

There was still Dr Prune. But he had been so heavily overworked since the flood that she had not seen him. The desire to see the last of her true friends had weakened with every black depression. When she most needed the counsel and love of the Doctor, who would have left the world bleeding to help her, it was then that she froze within herself and locking herself away, became ill with the failure of her life, the frustration of her womanhood, and tossing and turning in her improvised bedroom twelve feet above the flood, conceived, for the first time, the idea of suicide.

What was the darkest of the causes for so terrible a thought it is hard to know. Her lack of love; her lack of a father or a real mother? Her loneliness. The ghastly disillusion when Steerpike was unmasked, and the horror of her having been fondled by a homicide. The growing sense of her own inferiority in everything but rank. There were many causes, any one of which might have been alone sufficient to undermine the will of tougher natures than Fuchsia's.

When the first concept of oblivion flickered through her mind, she raised her head from her arms. She was shocked and she was frightened. But she was excited also.

She walked unsteadily to the window. Her thought had taken her into a realm of possibility so vast, awe-inspiring, final and noiseless that her knees felt weak and she glanced over her shoulder although she knew herself to be alone in her room with the door locked against the world.

When she reached the window she stared out across the water, but nothing that she saw affected her thought or made any kind of visual impression on her.

All she knew was that she felt weak, that she was not reading about all this in a tragic book but that it was true. It was true that she was standing at a window and that she had thought of killing herself. She clutched her hands together over her heart and a fleeting memory of how a young man had suddenly appeared at another window many years ago and had left a rose behind him on her table, passed through her mind and was gone.

It was all true. It wasn't any story. But she could still pretend. She would pretend that she was the sort of person who would not only think of killing herself so that the pain in her heart should be gone for ever, but be the kind of person who would know how to do it, and be brave enough.

And as she pondered, she slid moment by moment even deeper into a world of make-believe, as though she were once more the imaginative girl of many years ago, aloft in her secret life. She had become somebody else. She was someone who was young and beautiful and brave as a lioness. What would such a person do? Why, such a person would stand upon the window sill above this water. And . . . she . . . would . . . and as the child in her was playing the oldest game in the world, her body, following the course of her imagination, had climbed to the sill of the window where it stood with its back to the room.

For how long she would have stood there had she not been jerked back into a sudden consciousness of the world – by the sound of someone knocking upon the door of her room, it is impossible to know, but starting at the sound and finding herself dangerously balanced upon a narrow sill above the deep water, she trembled uncontrollably, and in trying to turn without sufficient thought or care, she slipped and clutching at the face of the wall at her side found nothing to grasp, so that she fell, striking her dark head on the sill as she passed, and was already unconscious before the water received her, and drowned her at its ease.

SEVENTY-SIX

Now that the flood had reached its height it was vital that not a moment should be lost in combing the regions in which Steerpike might be lurking – in surrounding them with cordons of picked men who, converging inwards to the centre of each chosen district, by land and water, should, theoretically, sooner or later, close upon the beast. And now above all was the time to throw in every man. The Countess had circled areas of the Gormenghast map with a thick blue pencil. Captains of Search had been given their instructions. Not a cranny was to be left unscoured – not a drain unprobed. It would be difficult enough, with the flood at its present level to run to earth so sly a quarry, yet with every day that passed the chances of Steerpike's capture would recede even further – would recede as the flood receded, for as one floor after another began to open up its labyrinthian ways, so the fugitive in the multiplying warrens, would burrow ever deeper into darkness.

It would of course be slow and gradual this going-down of the flood, but the Countess was fiercely conscious of how time was the salient factor: how never again would she have Steerpike within so close a net. Even for the flood to leave a single floor would be for a hundred vistas to spread out on every side with all their countless alleys of wet stone. There was no time to be lost.

As it was the theatre of manoeuvre – the three dry topmost floors and the wet 'floor of boats' (where the coloured craft of the carvers sped to and fro, or lay careening beneath great mantelpieces, or tied up to the banisters of forgotten stairways, cast their rich reflections in the dark water) – these theatres of manoeuvre – the three dry levels and the one wet, were not the only areas which had to be considered in the drawing up of the Master Plan. The Countess also had to remember the isolated outcrops of the castle. Luckily most of the widely scattered and virtually endless ramifications of the main structure of Gormenghast were under water, and consequently of no use to the fugitive. But there were a number of towers to which the young man might well have swum. And there was also Gormenghast Mountain.

As far as this latter was concerned, the Countess was not apprehensive of his having escaped there, not merely because she had checked the boats each evening, and was satisfied that there had been no thefts, but

because a string of boats, like coloured beads was at her orders in perpetual rotation around the castle summits, and would have cut him off by day or night.

The core of her strategy hinged upon the fact that the young man must eat. As for drink, he had a wet world brimming at his mouth.

That he might already be dead from accident or from starvation was ruled out by the body that on this very day had been discovered floating face downwards alongside an upturned coracle. The man had been no more than a few hours dead. A pebble was lodged in his forehead.

The headquarters of the Countess was now in a long, narrow room that lay immediately and somewhat centrally above the 'floor of boats'.

There she received all messages: gave all orders: prepared her plans: studied the various maps and gave instructions for new ones to be rapidly prepared of the unplotted districts so that she should have as powerful a grasp upon the smallest details as she had upon the comprehensive sweep of her master-plan.

Her preparations completed she rose from the table at which she had been sitting, and pursing her lips at the goldfinch on her shoulder she was about to move with that characteristically heavy and ruthless deliberation towards the door when a panting messenger ran up to her.

'Well?' she said. 'What is it?'

'Lord Titus, my lady . . . he's . . .'

'He's what?' she turned her head sharply.

'He's here.'

'Where?'

'Outside the door, your ladyship. He says he has important news for you.'

The Countess moved at once to the door and opening it, found Titus sitting upon the floor, his head between his knees, his sodden clothes in rags, his legs and arms bruised and scratched, and his hair grey with grime.

He did not look up. He had not the strength. He had collapsed. In a confused way he knew where he was, for he had been straining his muscles with long and hazardous climbs, struggling shoulder deep through flooded passageways, crawling giddily over slanting roofs, intent upon one thing – to reach this door under which he had slumped. The door of his mother's room.

After a little time he opened his eyes. His mother was kneeling heavily at his side. What was she doing there? He shut his eyes again. Perhaps he was dreaming. Someone was saying in a far away voice 'Where is that brandy?' and then, a little later, he felt himself being raised, the cold rim of a glass at his lips.

When he next opened his eyes he knew exactly where he was and why he was there.

'Mother!' he said.

'What is it?' Her voice was quite colourless.

'I've seen him.'

'Who?'

'Steerpike.'

The Countess stiffened at his side. It was as though something more of ice than of flesh was kneeling beside him.

'No!' she said at last. 'Why should I believe you?'

'It is true,' said Titus.

She bent over him and taking his shoulders in her powerful hands, forced them with a deceptive tenderness to and fro, as though to ease some turmoil in her heart. He could feel through the gentle grasp of her fingers the murderous strength of her arms.

At last she said, 'Where? Where did you see him?'

'I could take you there . . . northwards.'

'How long ago?'

'Hours . . . hours . . . he went through a window . . . in my boat . . . he stole it.'

'Did he see you?'

'No.'

'Are you sure of that?'

'Yes.'

'Northwards you say. Beyond the Blackstone Quarter?'

'Far beyond. Nearer the Stone Dogshead and the Angel's Buttress.'

'No!' cried the Countess in so loud and husky a voice that Titus drew back on his elbow. She turned to him.

'Then we have him.' Her eyes were narrowed. 'Did you not have to crawl across the Coupée – the high knife-edge? How else could you have returned?'

'I did,' said Titus. 'That is how I came.'

'From the North Headstones?'

'Is that what it is called, Mother?'

'It is. You have been in the North Headstones beyond Gory and the Silver Mines. I know where you've been. You've been to the Twin Fingers where Little Sark begins and the Bluff narrows. Between the Twins would be water now. Am I right?'

'There's what looks like a bay,' said Titus. 'If that's what you mean.'

'The district will be ringed at once! And on every level!'

She rose ponderously to her feet, and turning to one of the men – 'Have the Search Captains called immediately. Take up the boy. Couch him. Feed him. Give him dry clothes. Give him sleep. He will not have long to rest. All craft will patrol the Headstones night and day. All search parties will be mustered and concentrated to the south side of the Coupée neck. Send out all messengers. We start in one hour from now.'

She turned to look down at Titus who had risen to one knee. When he was on his feet he faced his mother.

She said to him:

'Get some sleep. You have done well. Gormenghast will be avenged. The castle's heart is sound. You have surprised me.'

'I did not do it for Gormenghast,' said Titus.

'No?'

'No, Mother.'

'Then for whom or for what?'

'It was an accident,' said Titus, his heart hammering. 'I happened to be there.' He knew he should hold his tongue. He knew that he was talking a forbidden language. He trembled with excitement of telling the dangerous truth. He could not stop. 'I am glad it's through me he's been sighted,' he said, 'but it wasn't for the safety or the honour of Gormenghast that I've come to you. No, though because of me he'll be surrounded. I cannot think of my duty any more. Not in that way. I hate him for *other* reasons.'

The silence was thick and terrible – and then at last her millstone words. '*What . . . reasons?*' There was something so cold and merciless in her voice that Titus blanched. He had spoken as he had never dared to speak before. He had stepped beyond the recognized border. He had breathed the air of an unmentionable world.

Again the cold, inhuman voice:

'*What reasons?*'

He was altogether exhausted but suddenly out of his physical weakness another wave of nervous moral strength floated up in him. He had not planned to come out into the open, or to give any hint to his mother of his secret rebellion and he knew that he could never have voiced his thoughts had he *planned* to do so but finding now that he had shown himself in the colours of a traitor, he flushed, and lifting his head he shouted:

'I will tell you!'

His filthy hair fell over his eyes. His eyes blazed with an upsurge of defiance, as though a dozen pent up years had at last found outlet. He had gone so far that there was no return. His mother stood before him like a monument. He saw her great outline through the blur of his weakness and his passion. She made no movement at all.

'I will tell you! My reasons were for this. Laugh if you like! He stole my boat! He hurt Fuchsia. He killed Flay. He frightened me. I do not care if it was rebellion against the Stones – most of all it was theft, cruelty and murder. What do I care for the symbolism of it all? What do I care if the castle's heart is sound or not? I don't want to be sound anyway! Anybody can be sound if they're always doing what they're told. I want to live! Can't you see? Oh, can't you see? I want to be myself, and become what I make myself, a person, a real live person and not a symbol any more. That is my reason! He must be caught and slain. He killed Flay. He hurt my sister. He stole my boat. Isn't that enough? To hell with Gormenghast.'

In the unbearable silence the Countess and those present could hear the sound of someone approaching rapidly.

But it was an eternity before the footsteps came to rest and a distraught figure stood before the Countess and waited with head bowed and trembling hands for permission to give his message. Dragging her gaze from the face of her son she turned at last to the messenger.

'Well,' she whispered, 'what is it, man?'

He raised his head. For a few seconds he could not speak. His lips were apart but no sound came, and his jaws shook. In his eyes was such a light that caused Titus to move towards him with sudden fear.

'Not Fuchsia! Not Fuchsia!' he cried with a ghastly knowledge, even as he framed the words, that something had happened to her.

The man, still facing the Countess, said, 'The Lady Fuchsia is drowned.'

At these words something happened to Titus. Something quite unpredictable. He now knew what he must do. He knew what he was. He had no fear left. The death of his sister like the last nail to be driven into his make-up had completed him, as a structure is completed, and becomes ready for use while the sound of the last hammer blow still echoes in the ears.

The death of the Thing had seen the last of his boyhood.

When the lightning killed her he had become a man. The elasticity of childhood had gone. His brain and body had become wound up, like a spring. But the death of Fuchsia had touched the spring. He was now no longer just a man. He was that rarer thing, a man in motion. The wound-up spring of his being recoiled. He was on his way.

And the agent of his purpose was his anger. A blind white rage had transformed him. His egotistic outburst, dramatic enough, and danger-ous enough on its own account, was nothing to the fierce loosening of his tongue, that like a vent for the uprush of his rage and grief, amazed his mother, the messenger and the officers who had only known him as a reserved and moody figurehead.

Fuchsia dead! Fuchsia, his dark sister – his dear sister.

'Oh God in Heaven, *where?*' he cried. 'Where was she found. Where is she now. Where? Where? I must go to her.'

He turned to his mother. 'It is the skewbald beast,' he said. 'He has killed her. He has killed your daughter. Who else would kill her?

Or touch a hair of her head, O braver than *you* ever knew, who never loved her. Oh, God, Mother, get your captains posted. Every weapon'd man. My tiredness has gone. I will come at once. I know the window. It is not yet dark. We can surround him. But by boat, Mother. That is the quickest way. There is no need for the North Headstones. Send out the boats. Every one. I *saw* him, Mother, the killer of my sister.'

He turned again to the bearer of the shattering news.

'Where is she now?'

'A special room has been prepared by the Doctor near the hospital. He is with her.'

And then the voice of the Countess, low and deep. She was speaking to the Head Officer present.

'The Carvers must be informed that they are needed, and every watertight boat finished or unfinished. All boats already in the castle to be drawn up alongside the west wall. All weapons to be distributed at once,' and then, to the messenger who had spoken of where Fuchsia lay, 'Lead the way.'

The Countess and Titus followed the man. No word was spoken until they were within a stone's throw of the hospital, when the Countess without turning to Titus said:

'If it were not that you were ill . . .'

'I am not ill,' said Titus, interrupting.

'Very well, then,' said the Countess. 'It is upon your head.'

'I welcome it,' said Titus.

While he could feel no fear, he was at the same time surprised at his own audacity. But it was so small an emotion compared with the hollow ache with which the knowledge of Fuchsia's death had filled him. To be brave among the living – what was that compared with the bonfire of his rage against Steerpike at whose door he laid the responsibility for Fuchsia's death? And the tides of the loneliness that had surged over him, drowned him in seas that knew no fear of the living, even of a mother such as his own.

When the door was opened they saw the tall thin figure of Dr Prunesquallor standing at an open window, his hands behind his back, very still and unnaturally upright. It was a small room with low rafters and bare boards on the floor, but it was meticulously clean. It was obvious that it had been freshly scrubbed and washed, boards, walls and ceiling.

Against the wall to the left was a stretcher supported at either end upon wooden boxes. On the stretcher lay Fuchsia, a sheet drawn up to her shoulders, her eyes closed. It seemed hardly her.

The Doctor turned. He did not seem to recognize either Titus or the Countess. He stared through them, only touching Titus' arm in a gentle way as he passed, for he had no sooner seen the mother and the brother of his favourite child than he had begun to move to the door.

His cheeks were wet, and his glasses had become so blurred that he stumbled when he reached the door, and could not find the handle. Titus opened the door for him and for a moment caught a glimpse of his friend in the corridor outside as he removed his glasses and began to wipe them with his silk handkerchief, his head bowed, his weak eyes peering at the spectacles in his hand with that kind of concentration that is grief.

Left together in the room the mother and son stood side by side in worlds of their own. Had they not both been moved it might well have been embarrassing. Neither knew nor cared what was going on in the breast of the other.

The face of the Countess showed nothing, but once she drew the corner of the sheet up a little further over Fuchsia's shoulder, with an infinite gentleness, as though she feared her child might feel the cold and so must take the risk of waking her.

SEVENTY-SEVEN

KNOWING that he had several hours to wait before it would be dark enough for him to venture forth, Steerpike had dropped off to sleep in the canoe. As he slept the canoe began to bob gently on the inky water a few feet from where the flood swam through the window entrance. This entrance, seen from the inside of the 'cavern', was like a square of light. But the breast of the great bay, which, from the dark interior of Steerpike's refuge, appeared luminous was, in reality, as the moments passed, drawing across its nakedness shawl after shawl of shadow.

When Steerpike had slid from the outer world, and through the brimming window, seven hours earlier, he had of course been able to see exactly what kind of a room he had entered. The light striking through the window had glanced upwards off the water and lit the interior.

His first reaction had been one of intense irritation for there were no corridors leading from the room and no stairways to the floor above. The doors had been closed when the flood had filled the room so that they were immovable with the weight of water. Had the inner doors been open he might have slid through their upper airways into ampler quarters. But no. The place was virtually a cave – a cave with a few mouldering pictures hanging precariously a few inches above high-water mark.

As such he suspected it from the first. It was no more than a trap. But to paddle out of its mouth and across the open water seemed to him more dangerous than to remain where he was for the few hours that remained before darkness fell.

A breeze was stirring the surface of the wide freshwater bay, blowing from the direction of the mountain and a kind of gooseflesh covered the surface of the water. These ripples began to move into the cave, one after another and the canoe rocked with a gentle side-to-side motion.

On either side of the 'bay' the two identical headlands, with their long lines of windows, had become silhouetted against the dusk.

Between them the ruffled waters faced the sky with an unusual agitation – a shuffling backwards and forwards of its surface which, though by no means dangerous in itself either to the smallest craft or even to a swimmer, was nevertheless peculiar and menacing.

Within a minute the breathless quiet of the evening had become something very different. The hush of dusk, the trance of stonegrey light was broken. There was no break in the silence but the air, the water, the castle and the darkness were in conclave.

A chill breath from the lungs of this conspiracy, stealing across the goose-flesh water must have moved into the cave-like chamber where Steerpike slept, for he sat up suddenly in his canoe and turning his face at once to the window, the small hairs rose along his spine and his mouth became the mouth of a wolf, for as the blood shone behind the lenses of his eyes, his thin and colourless lips parted in a snarl that extended like an open gash a mask of wax.

As his brain raced, he plucked at the paddle and whisked the boat to within a few feet of the window, where, in absolute darkness himself he could command a view of the bay.

What he had seen had been the reflections only of what he now stared at in their entirety – for from where the canoe had been stationed the upper section of the window had been hidden by a hanging sail of wallpaper. What he had seen had been the reflections of a string of lights. What he now saw were the lanterns, where they burned at the bows of a hundred boats. They were strung out in a half-circle that even as he watched was drawing in his direction thick as fire-flies.

But worse than all this was a kind of light upon the water immediately outside the window. Not a strong light, but more than he could account for by the last of the day. Nor was it natural in colour. There was something of green in the faint haze from which he now turned his eyes again. For with every moment the boats were narrowing the distance between themselves and the castle walls.

Whether or not there were other interpretations of the spectacle before him it was not for him at this critical moment to give them the shadow of a thought. It was for him to assume the bloodiest and the worst.

It was for him to suppose that they were not only ranged across the bay in search of *him* – that they knew he was in hiding somewhere close at hand between the twin headlands – but more than this, that they knew the very window through which he had passed. He must assume that he had been seen as he entered this trap and that not only were his pursuers fanned out across the water and eager for his blood, but the cold sheen upon the water immediately ahead of him was cast from lanterns or torches that were even now burning from the window above his head.

Whether or not his only hope was to slip out of the cave and, risking a fusillade from the window above, make all speed across the waters of the bay before the approaching boats not only closed their ranks as they converged, but made the cave-mouth livid with the concentration of their lights – whether he should do this, and by so doing and gaining speed in the dusk, fly like a swallow across the face of the bay and swerving to and fro as only this canoe had power to do – hope to pierce the lanterned ring, and so, running his boat alongside one or other of the creepered headlands, climb the coarse foliage of the walls – whether he should do this or not, it was now, in any event, too late – for a brilliant yellow light was shining outside the window and danced on the choppy water.

A pair of heavy castle-craft, somewhat the shape of barges, creeping in along the lapping walls, from either side of Steerpike's window, were the cause of the yellow light which the murderer had observed to his horror as it danced upon the water, for these heavy boats bristled with torches; sparks flew over the flood and died hissing upon its surface. The scene about the opening of the cave had been transformed from one of dark and anonymous withdrawal to a firelit stage of water, upon which every eye was turned. The stone supports of the window, weather-scarred and ancient as they were had become things of purest gold, and their reflections plunged into the black water as though to ignite it. The stones that surrounded the windows were lit with equal brilliance. Only the mouth of the room, with the firelit water running through and into the swallowing blackness of the throat beyond, broke the glow. For there was something more than black about the intensity of that rough square of darkness.

It was not for these barges to do more than to remain with their square noses in line with the stone edges of the window. It was for them to make the place as bright as day. It was for the arc of lanterned boats to close in and to form the thickset audience, armed and impenetrable.

But those that manned the barges and held the torches aloft, and those that rowed or paddled the hundreds of boats that were now within a stone's throw of the 'cave' were not the only witnesses.

High above the entrances to Steerpike's retreat the scores of irregularly positioned windows were no longer gaping emptily as when Titus stared up at them from the canoe and felt the chill of that forsaken place. They were no longer empty. At every window there was a face: and every face directed downwards to where the illuminated waves rose and fell to such an extent that the shadows of the men upon the barges leapt up and down the firelit walls, and the sound of splashing could be heard below them as combers of rainwater ran and broke upon the castle walls.

The wind was making, and certain of the boats that formed the chain found it difficult to keep in position. Only the watchers from above were unaffected by the worsening weather. A formidable contingent had travelled by land. There were few who had been that way before and none who had travelled so far afield as the Coupée and the Headstones of Little Sark, within the last five years.

The Countess had journeyed by water but it had been necessary for Titus to travel overland at the head of the leading phalanx, for it was no easy itinerary with the dusk falling and the innumerable choices to be made at the junctures of passages and roof tops. With his return journey fresh in his mind he had no choice but to put his knowledge at the disposal of the many hundreds whose duty it would be to scour the Headstones. But he was in no condition to make that long journey again on the same day, without assistance. While the officials were casting about for some appropriate conveyance Titus remembered the chair on poles in which he was carried, blindfolded, on his tenth birthday. A runner was despatched for this, and some time later the 'land army' moved to the north with Titus leaning back in his 'mountain chair', a jug of water in the wooden well at his feet, a flask of brandy in his hand and a loaf of bread and a bag of raisins on the seat beside him. At different times during the journey, when crossing from one roof to another or when climbing difficult stairways, he would descend from the chair and continue on foot – but for most of the way it was possible for him to lean back in the chair, his muscles relaxed, merely giving fierce instructions to the Captain of the land searchers when occasion arose. A dark anger was gaining strength in him.

What had passed through his mind as he moved through the evening air? A hundred thoughts and shadows of a hundred more. But among all these were those giant themes that over-shadowed all else and were continually shouldering themselves back into his consciousness, and making his heart at their every return break out afresh with painful hammering. Within so short a time – within the last few hours – he had thrice been through an emotional turmoil for which he was in no way prepared.

Out of nowhere, suddenly, the first sight of the elusive Steerpike. Out of nowhere, suddenly, the news of Fuchsia's death. Out of nowhere, and suddenly, the uprush of his rebellion – the danger of it, the shock of it for all about him, the excitement of it, and the thrill of finding himself free of duplicity – a traitor if they liked, but a man who had torn away the brambles from his clothes, the ivy from his limbs, the bindweed from his brain.

Yet had he? Was it possible at a single jerk to wrench himself free of his responsibility to the home of his fathers?

As his bearers threaded their way through the upper stories he was sure that he was free. When Steerpike had been dragged like a water-rat from his lair and slain – what then would there be for him to stay for in this only world he knew? Rather would he die upon its borders, wherever they might be, than rot among the rites. Fuchsia was dead. Everything was dead. The Thing was dead and the world had died. He had outgrown his kingdom.

But behind all this, behind his stumbling thoughts, was this growing anger, an anger such as he had never known before. On the face of it, it might seem that the rage that was eating him was absurd. And the rational part of Titus might have admitted that this was so. For his rage was not that Fuchsia had died and as he thought at Steerpike's hand, nor that he had been thwarted in his love for the Thing by the arbitrary lightning flash – it was not, in his conscious mind, either of these that caused him to tremble with eagerness to close with the skewbald man, and if he could to kill him.

No, it was because Steerpike had stolen his canoe, his own canoe – so light, so slight: so fleet upon the flood.

What he did not guess was that the canoe was neither more nor less than the *Thing*. Deep in the chaos of his heart and his imagination – at the core of his dreamworld it was so – the Canoe had become, perhaps had already been when he had first sent her skimming beneath him into the freedom of an outer world, the very centre of Gormenghast forest, the Thing herself.

But more than this. For another reason also. A reason of no symbolism: no darkened origin: a reason clear-cut and real as the dagger in his belt.

He saw in the canoe, now lost to the murderer, the perfect vehicle for sudden and silent attack – in other words for the avenging of his sister. He had lost his *weapon*.

Had Titus thought sufficiently he would have realized that Steerpike could not have killed her, for he could not possibly have been so far to the north as the Headstones so soon after Fuchsia's fall. But his brain was not working in that way. Steerpike had killed his sister. And Steerpike had stolen his canoe.

When at long last the roof-top army had reached the ultimate battlements and saw below them the black waters of the 'bay', lookouts were posted and given instructions to inform their captains directly the first lights appeared around the nose of the south headland. Meanwhile the hordes which covered the near-by roofs were gradually drawn down by skylights, vents and hatches until they were absorbed into a deserted and melancholy wilderness of room upon room, hall upon hall, a wilderness that had yawned so emptily and for so many years until Steerpike had begun his explorations.

The torches were lit. It seemed that the advantage of being able to tell at once whether a room were empty or not out-weighed the warning that the light would give the fugitive. Nevertheless the work was slow. At last and about the time that the four possible floors had been proved as empty as tongueless bells, a message came down that lights had been seen across the bay.

At once every window of the West walls became filled with heads, and sure enough the necklace of coloured sparks which Steerpike had seen through the mouth of his flood-room was strung across the darkness.

That no sign of Steerpike had been found in the scores of upper rooms more than suggested that he was still within his lair at water level. Titus had at once descended to the lowest of the unflooded floors, and leaning through a window, roughly at the centre of the façade, he was able, by reaching out dangerously, with his hand gripping an ivy branch, to recognize the very window through which Steerpike had sped into the castle.

Now that the light had appeared on the bay there was no time to lose for it was possible that if Steerpike was below, and saw them, he would make a dash for it. In the meantime Titus and the three captains who were with him turned back through the room and gaining the corridor behind, ran for a matter of sixty or seventy feet before they turned again into one of the west rooms and, on reaching its window and looking down, found that they were almost immediately above the flooded window.

There was no sign of him on the bay. As far as they could judge they gauged him to be directly below the room to their right which they could see through a connecting door, a largish, square-ish room covered with a layer of dust as soft as velvet.

'If he's below there and it were necessary, my lord, we could cut through to him from above . . .' and the man began to make his way into the room in question.

'No! No!' whispered Titus fiercely. 'He may hear your footsteps. Come back.'

'The boats aren't near enough,' said another man. 'I doubt he can get further into the castle. The water's only four foot from the window top. Sooner or later the doors will all be water jammed. Quite right, my lord. We must be silent.'

'Then *be* silent,' said Titus, and in spite of his anger, the heady wine of autocracy tasted sweet upon his tongue – sweet and dangerous – for he was only now learning that he had power over others, not only through the influence of his birthright but through a native authority that was being wielded for the first time – and all this he knew to be dangerous, for as it grew, this bullying would taste ever sweeter and fiercer and the naked cry of freedom would become faint and the Thing who had taught him freedom would become no more than a memory.

It was while the boats approached and converged and before the castle barges had stationed themselves on either side of the window with their effulgence, and while there was a comparative darkness still brooding upon the water outside the mouth of his lair, that Steerpike decided that he would rather remain for the moment where he was and fight the whole world if necessary with the knowledge that he could not be attacked from the rear, than skim from his retreat only to find himself surrounded in the 'bay'. It was no easy choice and it is possible that he had not truly made it, before the barge lights flared – but in all events he stayed where he was, and turning his canoe about he made another turn of his dark room. It was then that the sudden yellow light flared cruelly outside the window and stayed – as though a curtain had gone up and the drama had begun. Even as he started at the light, he knew that his enemies could not know for *certain* that he was in this watery room. They could not possibly know for instance that the inner doors of the room were shut and impassable. They could not be absolutely certain that, although he had been seen passing through the window, he had not passed out again. But how, if ever, to make use of their uncertainty, he had, for the moment, no idea.

There was nothing but the empty picture-hung walls and the water; nothing in the room to help him. And then, for the first time he thought of the ceiling. He looked up and saw that there was but a single layer of floorboards laid across rotting joists. He cursed himself for his delay and immediately began to balance himself upright in his canoe beneath a crumbling patch in the ceiling. As he reached upwards to obtain a grip upon the joists, preparatory to striking, he heard the terrifying sound of footsteps above him and the floorboards trembled within a few inches of his head.

In a moment he had dropped back into the canoe that was now rocking appreciably. The freshening wind was sending sheets of water scurrying through the window across the comparatively even surface of the emprisoned flood.

He was cut off from above and from every side. His eyes were constantly upon the brilliant yellow square of water immediately outside the window. All at once a wave rather heavier than its forerunners sent its spray leaping up to the height of the window top and the wave itself smacked spitefully at the stone supports. The dark room had become full of the slapping sound of imprisoned water. Not loud but cold and cruel – and then all at once Steerpike heard another sound – the first of the returning rain. With the sound of its hissing a kind of hope came to him.

It was not that he had lost hope. He had had none. He had not thought in those terms. He had so concentrated upon what he should do, second by second, that he had not envisaged that there might be a moment when all was lost. He had, furthermore, an overweening pride that saw in this concentration of the castle's forces a tribute to himself. This was no part of the ritual of Gormenghast. This was something original.

The unwitting pageantry of the lantern-lit boats was unique. It had not been thought out or dictated. There had been no rehearsal. It was necessitated. It was necessitated by their fear of him. But mixed with his vanity and pride was a fear of his own. Not a fear of the men who were closing in upon him, but of fire. It was the sight of the torches that stretched his face into that vulpine snarl – that whetted his evil cunning. The memory of his near-death when he and Barquentine had been wrapped together in a single flame had so festered within him, had so affected his brain that at the approach of a flame madness grew very near.

At any moment he would see, beyond the window, the gold of the rain-spattered waves broken by the bows of a boat – or perhaps of several boats without an inch between them. Or perhaps a voice would hail him and order him forth.

The lanterned craft were now close enough for their crews to be recognizable by the light of the multi-coloured flames that burned across the rough water.

Again he heard the footsteps above and again he turned up his red eyes to the rotten planks. As he did so he kept his balance with difficulty for the waves were now by no means easy to ride.

As his gaze returned from the ceiling he saw something for the first time. It was a ledge, fortuitously formed by the protruding lintel of the window.

At once he knew it as his immediate perch. He had hopes of a returning storm and of the scattering abroad of the flotilla that rose and fell in the mounting waves.

But if a storm were to develop then there would be even less time to spare before his enemies made their first move. Time was on no one's side, neither theirs nor his. They would be entering at any moment.

But it was no easy task to reach this ledge above the window, where the shadows were at their deepest. He stood in the bows of the slight canoe so that its stern rose high out of the water. One of his hands clasped a joist of the low roof above his head and the other felt along the lintel's upper edge in search of a grip. All this time it was necessary for him to keep the canoe flush against the wall, while the swell in the cave lifted it up and down.

It was vital that the canoe were kept from dancing forward on a wave so that its bows protruded across the square of the window and into the line of vision of those without. It was a hideous exertion, stretched as he was at an angle, his hands upon the ledge and ceiling, his feet together in the volatile prow of the canoe, the water dashing to and fro, lifting and falling, the thin spray everywhere.

Luckily for him he had obtained by now a firm grip with his right hand, for his fingers had found a deep crack in the uneven stone of the protruding lintel. It was not the height of this shelf that made him wonder whether he would ever reach it with the rest of his body, for, standing as he was in the canoe, it was only a foot above his head. It was the synchronization of the various things he had to do before he could find himself crouched above the window, with the canoe beside him that was so desperately difficult.

But he was as tenacious as a ferret and slowly, by infinitesimal degrees he withdrew his right leg from the canoe and prised his knee against the inside edge of the stone upright. The canoe was still standing practically on its head by reason of the pressure of his left foot in the bows. So vertical had she become that he was able with a kind of febrile genius of his own to let go of the joist above his head and with this same left hand to lift the canoe clean out of the water. He was now left with both his arms engaged – one in holding him where he was and the other in holding the canoe away from the light. He was suffering with his right knee prised as it was against the upright of the window. The other leg dangled like a dead thing.

For a little while he remained as he was, the sweat pouring over his piebald face, his muscles shrieking for release from so ghastly a strain. For this period he had no doubt that there was no end to this save that of dropping like a dead fly from a wall – dropping into the water below, where, bobbing in the golden torch light below the lintel, he would be picked up by the nearest of his enemies.

But at the height of his pain he began to pull at the entire weight of his body, to pull at it with his single hand whose crooked finger shook in the lintel crack. Inch by inch, moaning to himself as though he were a baby, or a sick dog, he drew the deadweight of his body up until, twisting over a little on one side, he was able to bring his other leg into play. But he could find no kind of irregularity in the stone upright for the questing toe of his shoe.

He rolled his eye in a frenzy of despair. Again he thought he was dropping into the water. But as his eye rolled it had, half-consciously, become aware of a great rusty nail leaning out horizontally from the shadowy joist. It shrivelled and it swelled out, this nail, as he turned his eyes to it again with a blurred conception floating in his mind that he could not at once decipher. But what his thoughts could not define, his arm put into practice. He watched it raise itself, this left arm of his; he watched it lift the canoe gradually until the bows were above his head and then, as a man might hang his hat upon a peg, he hung his craft upon the rusty nail. Now that his left hand was free he was able to get a second purchase upon the lintel crack, and to draw himself upwards with a comparative lack of pain until he was kneeling on all fours upon the twelve-inch protuberance of the heavy lintel.

Where there had been so emphatic a division between the black waves within the room and the yellow waves that tossed beyond the window, there was no longer so sharp a demarcation. The tongues of golden water slithered further into the room and the black tongues flickered out less freely into the outer radiance.

Steerpike was now lying along the shelf face downwards a few feet above the water. He was lowering his head gradually over the window's upper and northerly corner. A few dead strands of creeper that struggled across the outside wall and blurred to some extent the stone angle provided him with a kind of screen through which it was his intention to gain some knowledge of his enemies' intentions.

Lowering his head inch by inch he suddenly saw them. A solid wall of boats not twelve feet away surrounded the entrance. They rose and subsided on a dangerous swell. The rain flew down, thin but vicious, slanting across the wet and torchlit faces.

They were armed, not as he had imagined they would be, with firearms but with long knives, and at once he remembered the death-law of the place which decreed that, where possible, all homicides should die in a way as closely resembling the death of their victims as possible. It was obvious that his slaughter of Flay had precipitated the choice of weapons.

The torchlight flamed on the slippery steel. The noses of the boats wedged themselves even closer about the window's mouth.

Steerpike raised himself and sat back on his haunches. The light in the cave had grown. It was like a gold twilight. He glanced at the hanging canoe. Then he began deliberately, but rapidly to take from his various pockets those few objects that were always on his person.

The knife and the catapult he placed side by side, as carefully and neatly as a housewife arranging a mantelpiece. Most of his ammunition he left in his pocket, but a dozen pebbles were formed up like soldiers in three straight rows.

Then he took a small mirror and comb, and by the dull golden light that had crept into the cave, he arranged his hair.

When this was completed to his satisfaction, he lowered his head again over the corner of the lintel and saw how the thickset boats had made between them something like a solid wall that heaved as it hemmed him in beyond all possibility of escape. Over this solid mass, crowded with men, a smaller boat was being carried and even as he watched, was set down upon the turbulent water on the near side, so that its bows were within a few feet of the window-mouth.

And then he noticed with a start that the two castle barges were nosing their way closer to one another across the window so that his means of exit to the outside world had become a mere passageway.

With the closing in of the barges, a number of the torches that they carried were now able to send their glow directly through the window, so that Steerpike found the surface of the water in the room below him was dancing with such brilliance that were he not immediately above the window he would have been fully exposed to view.

But he also noticed that the surface brilliance had robbed the water of its translucency. There was no sense of the walls continuing down below the water level. It might well have been a solid floor of gold that heaved like an earthquake and reflected its effulgence across the walls and ceiling. He lifted his catapult from beside him and raising it to his mouth he pursed his thin, merciless lips and kissed it as a withered spinster might kiss a spaniel's nose. He slid a pebble into the soft leather of the pouch, and as he waited for the bows of a boat to appear below him, or for a voice to hail him, a great wave lifted through the window and swirling around the room like a mad thing poured out again leaving a whirlpool at the centre of the room. At the same moment he heard a clamour of voices without, and shouts of warning for the backwash had swept over the sides of several of the rocking boats. And at the same moment, as his weapon lay in his hand and the threatening water swirled below him, another thing happened. Behind the sound of the water; behind the sound of the voices outside the window, there was another sound, a sound that made itself apparent, not through its volume or stridency, but through its persistence. It was the sound of sawing. Someone in the room above had worked some sharp instrument through a rotten piece of the floor – quite silently, for Steerpike had heard nothing, and now the end of a saw protruded through the ceiling into Steerpike's room, and was working rapidly up and down.

Steerpike's attention had been so concentrated upon what was

happening outside the window where the small exploratory boat had
¹ een set upon the water, a few feet away, that he had neither ears nor
eyes for what was happening above him.

But in a lull of the waves and the shouting he had suddenly heard it,
the deliberate triding of a saw, and looking up he could see the jag-
edged thing, shining in the water-reflected light, as though it were of
gold, while it plunged and withdrew, plunged and withdrew at the
centre of the ceiling.

SEVENTY-EIGHT

I

TITUS, as the minutes had passed had grown more and more restless.
It was not that the preparation for the storming of the flooded room had
not been proceeding swiftly and well, but that far from his anger fading,
it was gaining more and more of a grip on him.

Two images kept floating before his eyes, one of a creature, slender
and tameless; a creature who, defying him, defying Gormenghast,
defying the tempest, was yet innocent as air or the lightning that killed
her, and the other of a small empty room with his sister lying alone
upon a stretcher, harrowingly human, her eyes closed. And nothing
else mattered to him but that these two should be avenged – that he
should strike.

And so he had not remained at the window overlooking the bright
and heaving water. He had left the room and descended an outer
staircase, and had boarded one of the boats, for now that Steerpike's
'cave' was so closely ringed there were scores of craft that bobbed
uselessly to and fro on the waves. He ordered the oarsmen to land him
where the inner circle of boats was forming an unbroken arc around the
window's mouth. He made his way over the heaving floor of boats until
he was facing the window and peering along the water's surface he
could see the room, filled with its bright reflections, so clearly, that a
picture hanging on its far wall was perfectly visible.

But the Countess had taken the opposite course – and though they
did not see each other they must have crossed in the amber light, for as
Titus peered into the flooded room, his mother was climbing the outer
staircase. She had also conceived the idea of cutting through the roof
immediately above the window, for she could see that it would be
difficult for anyone to enter Steerpike's trap without great danger to

himself. It was true that the room looked empty but it had been of course impossible for her to know what lay within the shadows of the *nearest* corners or against the near walls that flanked the window.

And it would be there that Steerpike would crouch, were he in the room at all.

And so she thought of the room above. When she reached it and saw that what she had planned was already being put into practice, she moved to the window and looked down. The rain which had stopped for a little had returned and a steady, slanting stream was pouring itself against the walls, so that, before she had been a minute at the window she was soaked to the skin. After a little time she turned her head to the left and stared along the adjacent wall. It reached away in wet perspective. She turned her head upwards, and the stone acres rose dripping into the night. But the great façade was anything but blank; for from every window there was a head thrust forth. And every head in the glow of the torchlight was of the colour of the walls from which it protruded, so that it seemed that the watchers were of stone, like gargoyles, each face directed to the brilliant barge-light that weltered on the waves outside the 'cave'.

But as the Countess continued to stare at 'carvings' that studded the walls to the left, a kind of subtraction came into play. It was as though embarrassment spread itself across the stone surfaces. One by one the heads withdrew until there was nothing to the left of the Countess but the emptiness of the streaming walls.

And then she turned her head the other way, where, in reverse, the scores of heads protruded and shone with the torchlit rain – until, like their counterparts, they also one by one, withdrew themselves.

The Countess turned her eyes again to the scene immediately below her and the numberless wet faces were drawn forth at once, as though by suction, from the castle walls, or in the way that the heads of turtles issue from their shells.

The small craft which had been carried over the back of the boat-cordon was now within a foot of the window. A man sat within and wielded a powerful paddle. A black leather hat, with a broad brim shielded his eyes from the rain. Between his teeth he gripped a long dirk.

It was no easy task for him, this approach through the window, between the flanking barges. The small skiff rolled dangerously, shipping the gold water over her side. The wind was now something that could be heard whining across the bay.

All at once Titus called out to the man to return.

'Let me go first,' he cried. 'Come back you *man*. Let *me* have your dagger.' The face of his sister swam across the window. The Thing danced on the bright water like a sprite and he bared his teeth.

'Let *me* kill him! Let *me* kill him!' he cried again, losing in that moment his last four years of growth, for he had become like a child, hysterical with the intensity of his imagination – and for a moment the boatman wavered, his head over his shoulder, but a voice from the wall above roared out.

'No! by the blood of love! Hold the boy down!'

Two men held Titus firmly, for he had made as though to plunge into the water.

'Quiet, my lord,' said the voice of one of the men who held him. 'He may not be there.'

'Why not?' shouted Titus, struggling. 'I saw him, didn't I? Let go of me! Do you know who I am? Let go of me!'

II

Steerpike was as motionless as the lintel on which he crouched. Only his eyes moved to and fro, to and fro, from the saw that cut its circular path through the boards above him to the radiant water below him, where at any moment the nose of the skiff might appear. He had heard the roar of the Countess' 'No!' sounding from above, and knew that when the ceiling had been cut through she would be one of the first to peer down for him – and there was no doubt that they would have a perfect view of him where he crouched in the reflected light.

To split each forehead open as it appeared at the gap of the ceiling – to leave his pebbles half protruding like the most eloquent of tombstones in the foreheads of his foes – this might very well be what he would do, but he knew that his enemies had yet no proof positive that he was there. Directly the work of his lethal catapult became evident it would only be a matter of time before his capture.

It was obvious that he could do nothing to stop the regular progress of the man with the saw. Three quarters of a circle had been completed in the rotten planks. Pieces of wood had fallen already into the swirling water.

All depended upon the appearance of the skiff. Within a minute there would be a great round eye in the woodwork above him. Even as he itched for the boat, its bows appeared, bucking like a horse, and then, suddenly, as it leapt forward again, there below him, close enough to touch, was the broad-brimmed hat of the oarsman with the dirk in his mouth.

III

The Countess, satisfied that there was no longer any danger of Titus leaping into the water, returned to where the man with the saw was resting his arm before the last dozen plunges and withdrawals of the hot and grinding blade.

'The first to put his face through the hole is likely to receive a pebble in his head. You have no doubt of this, gentlemen.' She spoke slowly. Her hands were on her hips. Her head was held high. Her bosom heaved with a slow sea-like rhythm. She was consumed with the passion of the chase, but her face showed nothing. She was intent upon the death of a traitor.

But what of Titus? The upheaval of his emotions, the bitterness of his tone; his lack of love for her – all this was, whether she wished it or not, mixed up with the cornering of Steerpike. It was no pure and naked contest between the House of Groan and a treacherous rebel, for the seventy-seventh Earl was, by his own confession, something perilously near a traitor himself.

She returned to the window and as she did so, Steerpike in the room below, changing his plan completely with the dawn of a fresh idea, thrust his catapult back in his pocket and grasping his knife got gradually and noiselessly to his feet, where he poised himself, his head and shoulders bent forward by the proximity of the roof.

The figure in the boat, who had volunteered for this hazardous mission, far from being able to keep his eyes skinned for the enemy, was unable to concentrate upon anything else but the control of the skiff, which with the waves that were now breaking upon the outer wall and sending their surges through the window, had made the flood-room into a wall of tossing water.

Nevertheless, the time came when, with a deceptive lull in the riot of trapped waves, the boatman swung his head over his shoulder, and was able for the first time to focus his eyes upon the window end of the room. At once he saw Steerpike, his face lit from below.

Directly the man saw him he let forth a gasp of excited terror. He was no chicken-heart, having volunteered to enter the cave alone, and he was now prepared to fight as he had never fought before, but there was something so terrible in the poised over-hanging aspect of the young man that it turned his bowels to water. For the moment, the volunteer was out of range of anything but the thrown knife – and it was his intention to put his lips to the whistle which hung by a cord around his neck, and warn them of the discovery of Steerpike by the single blast which had been agreed upon, when he found himself being swung forward on the crest of a wave that had entered a moment before and was following the walls as though to swill the 'cave' out. He strained at the paddle but there was no holding back the skiff, and within a matter of moments, he found himself slithering along the western side and into the shadowy corner of the 'seaward' wall.

As the boat, running forward and striking its nose upon the stones at Steerpike's side, was about to make for the window below him, Steerpike sprang outwards, and to the left, and fell with a stunning force, for all his lightness, upon the volunteer. There was no time for any struggle, the knife running between the ribs and through the man's heart three times within as many seconds.

As Steerpike delivered the third of the lightning stabs, the sweat pouring off his face like wet blood in the reflected torch light, he turned his small hot eyes to the ceiling and found that the saw was within an inch of completing the circle. In another moment he would be exposed to the view of the Countess and the searchers.

The corpse was beside him in the boat, which at the impact of his jumping body had shipped a bucket or two of water. Perhaps it was this that slowed her upon her swirling course. Whatever it was, Steerpike was able to jam his foot against a support of the adjacent window and grasping the paddle to force the boat against the weakening sweep of water, until the last of the whirl had poured itself to 'sea' again through the window. In the few seconds of respite as he bobbed in the comparative darkness of the outer corner he plucked the broad-brimmed hat of leather from the corpse's head and thrust it on his own. Then he ripped the coat off the limp and heavy body and got into it at once. There was no time for more . . . A sound of hammering above told him that the circle of floorboards was being knocked through. He caught the corpse beneath its knees and under its arms and with a supreme effort toppled it over the side where it sank beneath the restless surge.

It was now up to him to control the skiff, for he wanted not only to keep it from capsizing but to station it below the hole in the ceiling. As he plunged the heavy paddle into the water and forced the skiff to the centre of the room, the circle of wood fell out of the ceiling and a new light from above made a great pool of radiance at the watery centre of Steerpike's lair.

But Steerpike did not look up. He fought like a demon to keep his boat immediately below the lamplit circle – and then he began to call in a husky voice which, if it was nothing like his victim's, was certainly nothing like his own.

'My lady!' he called.

'What's that?' muttered the Countess in the room above.

A man edged his way towards the opening.

Again the voice from below. 'Ahoy there! Is the Countess there!'

'It's the volunteer,' cried the man who had gone so far as to peer over the rim of the circular hole. 'It's the volunteer, lady! He's immediately below.'

'What does he say?' cried the Countess in a hollow voice, for a black fear tugged at her heart.

'What does he *say*, man! For the love of the stones!'

And then she took a step forward so that she could see the broad-brimmed hat and the heavy coat twelve feet below her. She was about to call down to the figure, although the Volunteer made no move to raise his head, but it was his voice that broke the silence. For there *was* a kind of silence, although the rain hissed, and the wind blew, and the waves slapped against the walls. There was a tension which over-rode the natural sounds. And a terror that the grizzly fowl had flown.

The voice came up from under the rim of the hat.

'Tell her ladyship there's nothing here! Only a room full of water. There's no way out but the window. The doors are water-jammed. Nothing but water, tell her. Nowhere to hide an eyelash! He's gone, if ever he *was* here, which I doubt.'

The Countess went down on her knees as though she was going to pray. Her heart had gone dead in her. This was the moment, if ever there was one, for an enemy of Gormenghast to be caught and slain. Now, with the eyes of the world focused upon his capture and his punishment. And yet the man had cried 'Only a room full of water'.

But something in her would not have it that so great a preparation, so formidable a massing of the castle's strength should prove abortive – and more than this, there was something in her, at a deeper level, that refused to believe that the certainty, the quite irrational certainty that this was the day of vengeance, was but her wishfulness.

She lowered herself to her elbows and dropped her head below the level of the floor.

At the first glance it was desperately true. There was nowhere to hide. The walls were blank, save for a few mouldering pictures. The floor was nothing but water. She turned to the man below.

It was true that it was difficult for him to contend with the restless swell of the waves in the cave, but at the same time it seemed odd that this volunteer made no effort to dart a single glance towards the roof where he knew his audience lay and watched expectantly.

She had seen him step into his boat some time earlier and paddle his way between the barges. She had gazed down from the window, the rain striking her face, and had wondered what he would find. She had had no doubt that Steerpike would be waiting for him. It was this certainty which still lingered in spite of the emptiness below which prompted her to stare again at the man who had found nothing but water.

When it struck her that he was of slighter build than she had thought her notion brought no suspicion in its trail. But her eyes, which had left the volunteer again and were following the curve of the wall, now came to rest on something which she had previously missed. The shadows were darker to the right of the single window and she had failed to detect that there was something hanging from the ceiling. At first she could make nothing of it, save that it appeared to be suspended from a joist and that it was about six feet in length, but gradually, as her eyes became used to the peculiar vibrations of the reflected light, and as now one part and now another of the object became illuminated by a glancing beam, so she became at last aware that she was looking at Titus' canoe . . . the canoe which Steerpike had stolen . . . and in which he had entered this very room. Then where was he? The room was empty of life, empty of everything save the water, the canoe and the volunteer. And there was no way to escape on foot and no reason why he should have wished to do so with so slight and safe a vessel at his command. Whatever the cause of Steerpike's disappearance, why should the canoe be hanging from the ceiling?

When she turned her eyes back to the broad-brimmed hat below her and noted the shoulders beneath it, and saw the nervous strength and agility with which the man handled the boat, she was affected by the first shadow of a suspicion that this volunteer below her had altered in some subtle and curious way from the solid boatman she had seen from the window. But her suspicion was so tenuous that she had no grasp upon its implications. Yet that a kind of disturbance, a kind of suspicion, had been aroused, however vague, was enough for her to draw a deep breath and then, in a voice of such power and volume that the figure below her started at the sound –

'Volunteer!' she roared.

The man beneath her appeared to be in such trouble with his boat that it was impossible for him to keep her from shipping water and to look up at the Countess at the same time.

'My Lady?' he cried up, wielding his paddle feverishly, as though to keep immediately below her, 'Yes, My Lady?'

'Are you blind?' came the voice from the ceiling. 'Have your eyes rotted in your head?' What could she mean by that? Had she seen . . .? 'Why have you made no report on it?' boomed the voice. 'Have you not seen it?'

'Very . . . difficult . . . keep afloat, My Lady, let alone . . .'

'The *canoe*, man! Does it mean nothing to you that the traitor's boat is hanging from the ceiling? Let me see your –'

But at that moment a fresh surge swept through the window below and twisted Steerpike's boat about as though it had been a leaf, and as it rotated the wash and swell of the water turned it so far over upon its side that as it was carried away from the centre of the flooded room the

Countess saw a flash of white and scarlet beneath the broad-brimmed hat and at almost the same moment her eyes were attracted away from their prize, for an empty face appeared out of the waves immediately below her; for a moment it bobbed about like a loaf of bread and then it sank again.

The world had gone dead in her, and then with almost unbelievable rapidity the two faces, appearing one after another, had transformed her gloom, her brooding spleen, her hungry malice, her disappointment into a sudden over-riding vigour of brain and body. Her anger fell like a whip lash upon the waters below. She had seen, within a moment of each other, the skewbald traitor and the volunteer.

Why the boat was hanging from the ceiling, and a score of other questions were no longer of the remotest interest. They were entirely academic. Nothing mattered at all save the death of the man in the broad-brimmed hat.

For a moment she thought that she would bluff him, for it was unlikely that he had seen the head appear out of the waves, or knew that she had glimpsed his mottled face. But this was no time for games of bluff and blarney – no time to spin it out. It was true that she might have given secret orders to the outer boats to enter the cave in force and to take him at a moment when he was diverted from his scrutiny of the window by some object being thrown into the water from above, but all such niceties were not relevant to her mood, which was for quick and final slaughter in the name of the Stones.

IV

Titus had ceased to struggle and was only waiting for the moment when the two louts, who (no doubt with the most loyal intentions) were saving him from himself, relaxed for a moment and gave him the opportunity to jerk himself clear of them.

They had him by his coat and collar, on either side. His hands which were free had crept gradually together across his chest and he had secretly undone all but one of the jacket buttons.

The scores of boatmen, dizzy with the rising and falling of the water, and drenched with the rain, and tired with the eternal rekindling of the torches, had been unable to understand what was happening within the flooded 'cave', or in the room above it. They had heard voices and a few excited shouts but had no idea of the true situation.

But suddenly, the Countess herself appeared at the window and her resonant voice bored its way through the wind and rain.

'All boatmen will attend! There will be no fumbling! The Volunteer is dead. The traitor who is now wearing his hat and coat is immediately below the window, in the room you are surrounding.'

She paused, and wiped the rain off her face with the flat of her hand, and then her voice again, louder than ever –

'The four central boats will be sculled by their stern oars. Three armed men will be on the bows of each boat. These boats will move forward when I lift my hand. He will be brought out dead. Draw your knives.'

As these last words were thrust out into the storm the excitement was so great and there was such pressing forward of all the men and boats that it was with difficulty that the four central boats of the cordon freed themselves from one another and manoeuvred into line.

It was then that Titus, noticing how his captors had loosened their grip upon him as they stared spellbound at the window of the fateful room, wrenched himself forward and slipped his arms suddenly out of the sleeves of his jacket, and dodging through a group of boatmen dived into the water, leaving his empty coat behind him, in their hands.

He had had no sleep for many hours. He had had little to eat. He was living upon the raw end of his nerves, as a fanatic will walk upon spikes. A fever had started. His eyes had become big and hot. His nondescript hair was plastered over his forehead like seaweed. His teeth chattered. He burned and froze alternately. He had no fear. It was not that he was brave. It was that fear had been left somewhere behind. It had been mislaid. And fear can be wise and intelligent. Titus had no wisdom at this moment and no sense of self-preservation. No sense of anything at all except a hunger for finality. All his heartburn had been laid, unfairly for the most part, at Steerpike's door – as had been his sister's death and the death of his Passion, the mercurial sprite.

As he swam he gloried. The torchlit water closed over him, and broke away again in yellow flakes. He rose and subsided on the flood, his arms thrashing at the waves. All that the sky had emptied from its maw, the giant reservoirs, broke at his brow. He gloried.

His fever mounted. As he grew weaker he grew fiercer. Perhaps he was in a dream. Perhaps it was all a delusion – the heads at a thousand windows – the boats tossing like gold beetles at the foot of the midnight heights; the flooded window that yawned for blood and drama, the upper window where his mother loomed, her red hair smouldering, her face like marble.

Perhaps he was swimming to his death. It didn't matter. He knew that what he was doing was what he must do. He had no option. His whole life had been a time of waiting. For this. For this moment. For all it was and all it would mean.

Who was it that swam within him, whose limbs were his limbs and whose heart was his heart? Who was he – what was he, as he battled through bright waters? Was he the Earl of Gormenghast? The seventy-seventh lord? The son of Sepulchrave? The son of Gertrude? The son of the Lady at the window? The brother of Fuchsia? Ah yes, he was that. He was the brother of the girl with the white sheet to her chin and her black hair spread across the snow-white pillow. He was this. But he was no brother of her *ladyship* – but only of the drowned girl. And he was no one's figurehead. He was only himself. Someone who might have been a fish of the water, a star, or a leaf or a stone. He was Titus, perhaps, if words were needed – but he was no more than that – oh no, not Gormenghast, not the seventy-seventh, not the House of Groan, but a heart in a body that swam through space and time.

The Countess had seen him from her window but there was nothing she could do. He was not making for the cave-mouth, where the boats were already filling the narrow entrance, but for one of those outer stairways that rose out of the water at irregular intervals along the castle's face.

But she had not time to wait and follow his progress. Three swimmers were already in the water and giving chase. Now that she had seen the first of the boats entering the cave-mouth she turned back from the window and returned to the centre of the room where a group of officers was gathered about the huge spy-hole. As she approached them, a tall man who had been kneeling above the opening fell backwards with a crimson chin. Four of his teeth had been broken off and these with a small pebble rattled together in his mouth while his head shook with pain. The others drew away at once from the dangerous opening.

As they did so Titus entered the room, leaving a trail of water at every step. It was obvious that he was ill with fever and exhaustion, and ungovernable with the fire of it. His naturally pale skin was flushed. His peculiarities of body appeared to be strangely accentuated.

The sense of scale, which he had inherited from his mother – that effect of being larger than he really was, of being over-size, was now peculiarly in evidence. It was as though it were not just that Titus Groan had entered, but that his abstract, a prototype had come through the door, and that the floodwater that dripped from his clothes was somehow spilled in heroic measure.

The rather bluntish cast of his face was even blunter and plainer. The lower lip, trembling with excitement, hung open like a child's. But his pale eyes, so often sullen in their withdrawal, were now not only bright with the fever but with a lust of revenge – no lovely sight – and were icy at the same time with a determination to prove himself a man.

He had seen his private world break up. He had seen characters in action. It was now for him to take the limelight. Was he the Earl of Gormenghast? Was he the seventy-seventh? No, by the lightning that killed her! He was the First – a man upon a crag with the torchlight of the world upon him! He was all here – there was nothing missing, brains, heart and sentience – an individual in his own right – a thing of legs and arms, of loins, head, eyes and teeth.

He walked sightlessly to the window. He made no sign to his mother. He was her traitor. Let her watch him, then! Let her watch him, then!

He had known, ever since he slipped from his coat and dived into the water, the radiant purpose of the single mind. He had no room in his system for fear. He knew that it was only for him to fall upon this symbol of all things tyrannical – Steerpike the cold and cerebral beast – for him to be fulfilled. His medium was a short and slippery knife. He had bound a rag about its handle. He stood at the window, clasping the ledge with both hands, and stared out at the fantastic torch-lit scene. The rain had stopped, and the wind that had been so boisterous had dropped with remarkable suddenness. In the high north-east the moon disengaged itself of a smothering cloud.

A kind of ashen light spread itself over Gormenghast, and a silence came down over the bay which was only broken by the slapping of the water against the walls, for although the wind had ceased the flood had not subsided.

Titus could not have said why he was standing there. Perhaps it was because he was as near as he could be to the fugitive – the flood-entrance being denied him, and the circular opening guarded. From where he was, free of his captors, he could at least be close to the man he wished to kill. And yet it was more than this. He knew that his would be no spectator's rôle. He knew somehow or other that the human hounds, armed as they were, would be no match for so sly an animal as the one they had at bay. He could not believe that mere numbers could deal with so lithe and ingenious a fiend.

None of this had been consciously argued within his head. He was in no state to rationalize anything. As he knew it was for him to escape and to swim to the steps, so he knew that it was for him to enter this room and to stand at this window.

v

All at once there was a terrible cry from below, and then another. Steerpike, who had had no alternative but to bring his skiff to the back of the room as the first of the four boats nosed her way through the window, had stretched and loosened his deadly elastic, twice, in quick succession. His next three deliveries were aimed at the torches that were stuck in iron rings along the sides of the first boat, and two of these were sent hurtling into the water where they hissed and sank.

These three pebbles were the last of his ammunition save for those which he had left behind him on the lintel above the window.

He had his knife, but he knew that he could only throw it once. His enemies were countless. It was better for him to keep it as a dagger than to throw it away, and to waste it upon the death of some cipher.

By now his enemies were very close – the length of an oar away. The nearest man was hanging lifeless over the side. The two cries that had been heard were from the men towards the stern who had received a stone apiece in the ribs and the cheek-bone. There had been no cry from the first man who was hanging over the stern like a sack of flour and trailing a hairy hand in the water, as his journey from this world to the next had been so rapid as to allow him no time for remonstrance.

With no pebbles left Steerpike tossed his catapult away and following it with his body was all at once deep in the water and swimming beneath the keels of the boats. He had dived steeply and was quite certain that he could not be seen from above, for he had noticed how although there were reflections upon the water there was no sign of anything tangible *beneath* the surface.

The only one in the first boat who was in a condition to shout, lost no time about informing the world. In a voice that sounded more relieved than anything else, although the man had tried to hide his emotions, 'He's dived!' he shouted. 'He's under the boats! Watch the window, there, third boat! Watch the window!'

Steerpike slithered rapidly through the inky darkness. He knew that he must get as far as he could before rising to the air for breath. But like Titus he was deadly tired.

When he reached the window, the air was half gone from his lungs. He could feel the stone support with his left hand. The keel of the third boat was just above his head and to the right. For a moment he rested and lifted his head to it, and then shoving himself away he passed through the lower half of the window, grazing its rough stone sill, and then turning sharply to his left slid along the wall. Six feet above the darkness in which he swam, the sheen of the surface water lapped the wall beneath the Countess' window.

He remembered, of course, that one of the two barges was immediately above him. He was swimming beneath a wooden monster, its catwalks bristling with torches – its blunt nose crowded with men.

What he did not know as he rose to draw breath, his lungs all but bursting, was whether between the side of the long barge and the wall that towered above it, there would be room for his head to rise above the surface.

He had never seen these castle barges before and had no idea whether their sides rose vertically out of the water, or whether they swelled slightly outwards. If the latter, there was a chance of his being able to be hidden by the convexity, which, reaching out as far as the wall, would leave a long roofed-in ditch where for a little while at least he could breathe and be hidden.

As he rose he felt for the wall. His fingers were spread out and ready for the touch of the rough stones; and it was with a shock that they made contact, not with stone but with a matted, fibrous, tough subaqueous blanket of that luxuriant wall-ivy which covered so great an area of the castle's face. He had forgotten how, as he had skimmed to the fateful flood-room in the stolen canoe he had noticed the ivy with its long tentacles, and how the face of the castle had appeared not only mutilated and pocked with sockets of where once the glass eyes glittered, but was covered with these climbing rashes of black growth.

As he clawed at the underwater branches he continued to rise, and all at once his head struck upon the hull of the barge where it bulged out to the wall.

It was then that he knew that he was nearer death than he had ever been. Nearer than when he was caught in the burning arms of the dead Barquentine. Nearer than when he had climbed to Fuchsia's secret attic. For he had no more breath than for a few excruciating seconds. His way was blocked above him. The side of the barge, in swelling outwards made contact with the wall below the surface and blocked his upward path. There was no pocket of air. It was solid water. But even as a great hammer of desperation beat at his temples he turned to the ivy. To drag himself up by its outer branches would simply take him to the long narrow water-filled roof. But how deep was it, this labyrinthine under-water shuffle of saturated midnight; of endless leaves, of hairy arms and fingers?

With what remained of his strength he fought it. He fought the ivy. He tore at the scales of its throat. He pulled himself *into* it. He tore at its ligaments, he broke its small water-logged bones; he forced its ribs apart and as they strained to return to their ancient curves he fought his way through them. And as he grappled and pulled his way inwards, something inside him and very far away was saying, 'You have not reached the wall . . . you have not reached the wall . . .'

But neither had he reached the air – and then at a moment when, unable to hold his breath any longer, he took his first inevitable draught of water.

The world had gone black, but with a kind of reflex, his arms and legs fought onwards for a few seconds longer, and then with his head thrown back he collapsed, his body supported by the network of the ivy boughs about him.

It was some while before he opened his eyes to find that only the mask of his face was above water. He was in a kind of vertical forest – an undergrowth that stood upon its end. He found that he was doing nothing to support himself. He was cradled. He was a fly in a drowned web. But the last spasms of his upward straining body had taken his face above the water.

Slowly he turned his eyes. He was but a few inches above the level of the barge's catwalk. He could see nothing of the barge itself, but through gaps in the ivy the torches shone like jewels, and so he lay in the arms of the giant creeper and heard a voice from above:

'All boats will stand out from the cave-mouth. A line will be formed across the bay immediately. Light every torch aboard, every lantern, every stick! Ropes will be passed beneath the keel of every boat! This man could hide in a rudder. By the powers, he has more life in him than the lot of you . . .'

Her voice, in the complete silence that had followed the withdrawal of the squall, sounded like cannon fire.

'Great hell, he is no merman! He has no tail or fins! He must breathe! He must breathe!'

The boats moved out with much splashing of oars and paddles, and the two barges wallowing in the still water were shoved away from the wall. But while the various craft moved into the open bay and began to form a line sufficiently far out as to be beyond the range of any under-water swimmer, Titus, standing beside his mother at the window, hardly knowing that she was there or that the boats had moved, for all the commotion and for all the violence and volume of his mother's orders, had his eyes focused, fanatically, upon something almost immediately below him. What his eyes were fixed upon seemed innocent enough, and no one but Titus in his febrile state would have continued to scrutinize a small area of ivy a foot above the surface of the water. It was no different from any other section that might be chosen at random from the great blanket of leaves. But Titus, who, before his mother's arrival at the window beside him, had been rocking in a kind of dizzy sickness to and fro had, as the accumulated effect of his rising fever and physical exhaustion began to reach a final stage, seen a movement that he could not understand – a movement that was not a part of his dizziness.

It was a sharp and emphatic commotion among the ivy leaves. The water and the boats and the world were swaying. Everything was swaying. But this disturbance of the ivy was not a part of this great drift of illness. It was not inside his head. It was taking place in the world below him – a world that had become as silent and motionless as a sheet of glass.

His heartbeat quickened with a leaping guess.

And out of his guess, out of his weakness, a kind of power climbed through him like sap. Not the power of Gormenghast, or the pride of lineage. These were but dead-sea fruit. But the power of the imagination's pride. He, Titus, the traitor, was about to prove his existence, spurred by his anger, spurred by the romanticism of his nature which cried not now for paper boats, or marbles, or the monsters on their stilts, or the mountain cave, or the Thing afloat among the golden oaks, or anything but vengeance and sudden death and the knowledge that he was not watching any more, but living at the core of drama.

His mother stood at his shoulder. Behind her a group of officers obtained the best view that they could of the scene without. He must make no mistake. At a slip or a sign a dozen hands would grab him.

He slipped his knife into his belt, his hand shaking as though it were blue with cold. Then he rested his hands upon the window-sill again and as he did so he stole a glance over his shoulder. His mother stood with her arms folded. She stared at the scene before her with a merciless intensity. The men behind him were dangerously close but were gazing past him to where the boats were forming a single line.

And then, almost before he had decided to do so, he gathered his strength together and half vaulting, half tumbling himself over the sill, fell the first half dozen feet through the loose outer fringes of the ivy, before he snatched at the stems and, checking the momentum of his descent, found that he was at last hanging from branches that had ceased to break.

He had noted that the small, suspicious area of ivy for which he was making was directly below the window from which he had vaulted (and which was now filled with startled faces), directly below, and at water level. He could hear his name being called and orders being shouted across the 'bay' for a boat to be brought up immediately, but they were sounds from another world.

And yet, while this sense of being far removed from what he was doing held him suspended in a world of dreams he was, at the same time, drawn down the ivy-wall as though by a magnet. Within the blur of weakness and remoteness was a core of vivid impulse, an immediate purpose.

He hardly knew what his body was doing. His arms and legs and hands seemed to be making their own decisions. He followed them downwards through the leaves.

But Steerpike, who had had to alter his position when an unbearable cramp had affected his left leg and shoulder, and who had hoped that a careful stretching of his limbs would in no way affect the stillness of the outermost leaves, had by now heard the noise of branches breaking above him, and knew that the results of his movement were dire indeed. After so desperately fought a battle for refuge from his pursuers, it was indeed a malicious fate that saw to it that he should so soon be discovered.

He had of course no idea that it was the young earl who was

descending upon him. His eyes were fixed upon the dark tangle of
fibrous arms above his face. It was obvious that whosoever it was would
not make his descent through the body of the ivy, close to the wall. To
do this would be to move at a snail's pace, and to battle all the way with
the heaviest branches. His pursuer would slide down the outer foliage
and probably burrow wall-wards when a little above and out of reach
of him.

And this is what Titus intended, for when he was about five feet
above the water he came to a stop and waited a little to regain his
breath.

The moon which was now high in the sky had to some extent made
the torches redundant. The bosom of the bay was leprous. The ivy
leaves reflected a glossy light. The faces at the windows were both
blanched and wooden.

For a moment he wondered whether Steerpike had moved, had
climbed from where a foot above the water he had seen the tell-tale ivy
come to life and shiver, and whether he, Titus, was even now within a
few inches of his foe, and in mortal peril. It seemed strange at that
instant that no daggered hand arose out of the leaves and stabbed him
where he hung. But nothing happened. The silence was accentuated
rather than lessened by the sound of distant oars rising and falling in
the bay.

Then, with his left hand gripping some interior stem, he forced away
the swathes before his face and peered into the heart of the foliage
where the branches shone like a network of white and twisted bones at
the inrush of the moonbeams.

There was but one course for him. To burrow in as deeply as he
could, and then to descend in the gloom until he found his foe. The
moonlight was now so strong that a kind of deep twilight had taken the
place of the rayless midnight among the leaves. Only at the deeply-
hidden face of the wall itself was the darkness complete. If Titus could
reach as far inward as the wall and work his way down it might be
possible to see, before he reached the level of the flood, some shape that
was not the shape of ivy branch or leaf – some curve or angle that
loomed among the leaves – perhaps an elbow, or a knee, or the bulge
of a forehead . . .

VI

The murderer had not moved. Why *should* he move? There was little to
choose between one cradle of ivy and another. What was there to be
gained by any temporary evasion? Where could he escape to, anyway?
The patch of ivy was a mere seventy feet in breadth. It was only a

matter of time before his capture. But time when it is short is very sweet and very precious. He would stay where he was. He would indulge himself – would taste the peculiar quality of near-death on the tongue – would loll above the waters of Lethe.

It was not that he had lost his will to live. It was that his brain was so exact and cold a thing that when it told him that his life, for this reason, and for that reason, was within a few hours of its end, he had no faculties wherewith to combat its logic. Below him was the water in which he could not breathe. To the north was the water through which to swim was immediate capture. To move to his left or right would bring him to the margins of the ivy. To climb would bring him to the scores of windows in every one of which there was a face.

Whoever it was who was crawling towards him down the wall had presumably informed the world of his purpose, or had been given orders to come to grips. Someone had seen a movement in the ivy.

But it was strange that, as far as he could hear, there was only *one* boat approaching. The rise and fall of the two oars were distant but perfectly distinct; why was not the whole flotilla on its way towards him?

As he drew his knife to and fro across his forearm some dust fell through the twisted stems above him and then a branch broke with a crack that seemed within a yard of his head.

But it was not *immediately* above him, this noise. It appeared to come from deeper in the ivy, from somewhere between himself and the wall.

For him to move would be to make a sound. He was curled up like an emaciated child in a cot of twigs. But with his right hand gripping the dagger at his left shoulder, he was prepared at any instant to make an upward stab.

His small, close-set eyes smouldered with an unnatural concentration in the darkness, but it was not their natural colour, extraordinary as that was, that showed in the gloom, but something more terrible. It was as though the red blood in his brain, or behind his eyes, was reflected in the lenses. His lips, thin as a prude's, had fused into a single bloodless thread.

And now he began to experience again, but with even greater intensity, those sensations that affected him when, with the skeletons of the titled sisters at his feet, he had strutted about their relics as though in the grip of some primordial power.

This sensation was something so utterly alien to the frigid nature of his conscious brain that he had no means of understanding what was happening within him at this deeper level, far less of warding off the urge to *show himself.* For an arrogant wave had entered him and drowned his brain in black, fantastic water.

His passion to remain in secret had gone. What was left of vigour in his body craved to strut and posture.

He no longer wanted to kill his foe in darkness and in silence. His lust was to stand naked upon the moonlit stage, with his arms stretched high, and his fingers spread, and with the warm fresh blood that soaked them sliding down his wrists, spiralling his arms and steaming in the cold night air – to suddenly drop his hands like talons to his breast and tear it open to expose a heart like a black vegetable – and then, upon the crest of self-exposure, and the sweet glory of wickedness, to create some gesture of supreme defiance, lewd and rare; and then with the towers of Gormenghast about him, cheat the castle of its jealous right and die of his own evil in the moonbeams.

There was nothing left, no, of the brain that would have scorned all this. The brilliant Steerpike had become a cloud of crimson. He wallowed in the dawn of the globe.

Ignoring all precautions, he wrenched the boughs about him, and every window heard the sound, as they cracked in the silence with reports like gunfire. The lenses of his eyes were like red-hot pinheads.

He tore away the thick ivy stems, and cleared a cave, within the masses of the foliage, stamping and descending with his feet until they found purchase a foot beneath the water. His left hand gripped a solid arm of the parasite, as hairy as a dog's leg.

The knife was ready for the strike. He had thrown back his head. In the darkness of the leaves above him he heard a sound. It was a kind of cry or gasp – and then, a great bush of branches fell in a crackling heap – fell, as it were, down the black chimney which Steerpike's sudden violence had created – fell with gathering speed with Titus riding upon its back.

As Titus fell he saw the two red points of light below him. He saw them through the tangle of the broken ivy.

Fear had a few moments earlier suddenly come to him, for his brain had cleared – as in a hot sky of continuous cloud, an area, no bigger than one's thumbnail will clear, and show the sky. And with this momentary clearance of his brain from the fumes of fever and fatigue, came the fear of Steerpike and darkness and death.

But directly the branches broke below him as he hung in the twisted night, and directly he fell, the fear left him again. He said to himself, 'I am falling. I am moving very fast. I will soon be on top of him. Then I will kill him if I can.'

The knife in his hand was quite steady as he fell: and when he crashed his way through the branches which had come to a thick and watery halt at the congested surface of the flood he saw it shine in his hand like a splinter of glass in a penetrating ray of the moon. But only for the fraction of a fleeting instant did he see that thin blade of steel for, as he had fallen he had been shovelled outwards into the moonlight so that suddenly another object as brilliant as the thin blade held his eyes, a thing with eyes like beads of blood, and a forehead like a ball of lard – a thing whose mouth, thin as a thread, was opening and as it opened was curling up its corners so that no other note could possibly have come from such a cavity as the note that now rang across the flood-bay that climbed the ancient walls and turned the silent audience to stone – a note from the first dawn, the high-pitched overweening cry of a fighting cock.

But even as this blast of arrogance vibrated through the night, and the crowing echoes rang through the hollow rooms and wandered to and fro, and thinly died – Titus struck.

He could see nothing of the body into which his small knife plunged. Only the head, with its distended mouth and its grizzly blood-lit eyes, was visible. But he struck the darkness under the head, and his fist was suddenly wet and warm.

What had happened to Steerpike that he should have been the first to receive a blow – and a blow so mortal? He had recognized the earl, who like himself had been lit by the moonbeams. That the Lord of Gormenghast should have been delivered into his hands at this great moment and be his for the killing, had so appealed to his sense of fitness that the urge to crow had become irresistible.

He had swung full circle. He had given himself up to the crowding forces. He, the rationalist, the self-contained!

And so, in a paroxysm of self-indulgence – or perhaps in the grip of some elemental agency over which he had no power, he had denied his brain, and he had lost the one and only moment of time in which to strike before his enemy.

But at the rip of the knife in his chest all vision left him. He was again Steerpike. He was Steerpike wounded, and bleeding fast, but not yet dead. Snarling with pain he stabbed, but as he stabbed Titus fell in a faint and the knife cut a path across the cheek – not deep but long and bloody. The sharp pain of it cleared the boy's mind for a fraction of time and he thrust again into the darkness below his face. The world began to spin and he was spinning with it and he heard again, very far away the sound of crowing, and then opening his eyes he saw his fist at his enemy's breast, for the lozenge of moonlight had spread across them both, and he knew that he had no strength to withdraw the knife from between the ribs of a body arched like a bow, in the thick leaves. Then Titus stared at the face, as a child who cannot tell the time will stare at the face of a clock in wonder and perplexity, for it was nothing any more – it was just a thing, narrow and pale, with an open mouth and small, lacklustre eyes. They were turned up.

Steerpike was dead.

When Titus saw that this was indeed so, he collapsed at the knees and then slumped forward out of the ivy and fell face downwards into the open water. At once a cry broke out from a hundred watchers, and his mother, framed by the window overhead, leaned forward and her lips moved a little as she stared down at her son.

She and the watchers from the windows all about her and above her had, of course, seen nothing but the commotion of the ivy leaves at the foot of the walls. Titus had disappeared from the air and had burrowed into the thick and glossy growth, its every heart-shaped leaf had glinted in the moonlight. For long seconds at a time the agitation of the leaves had ceased. And then they had begun again, until suddenly they had seen a fresh disturbance and realized that there were two figures under the ivy.

And when Steerpike had thrown his secrecy away and when Titus had fallen through the chimney of leaves, and while they had exchanged blows, the sound of their struggle and the breaking of branches and the splash and gurgle of the water as their legs moved under the surface – all these noises had sounded across the bay with peculiar clarity. The flotillas, in the meantime, unheard by the protagonists, had once again advanced upon the castle and were now very close to the wall. The captains had expected fresh orders on arriving beneath the walls, but the Countess, immobile in the moonlight, filled up her window like a carving, her hand on the sill, her gaze directed downwards, with motionless concentration. But it was the cry of the cock, triumphant, terrible, that broke the atrophy and when, a little later, Titus fell forward out of the ivy and the blood from his cheek darkened the water about his head, she sent forth a great cry, thinking him dead, and she beat her fist upon the stone sill.

A dozen boats lunged forward to lift his body from the flood, but the boat which had been the first to leave the flotilla some while earlier and whose oars both Titus and Steerpike had heard was in advance of the rest, and was soon alongside the body. Titus was lifted aboard, but directly he had been laid at the bottom of the boat, he startled the awe-struck audience by rising, as it seemed, from the dead, for he stood up, and pointing to that part of the wall from which he had fallen, he ordered the boatmen to pull in.

For a moment the men hesitated, glancing up at the Countess, but they received no help from her. A kind of beauty had taken possession of her big, blunt features. That look which she reserved, unknowingly, for a bird with a broken wing, or a thirsty animal, was now bent upon the scene below her. The ice had been melted out of her eyes.

She turned to those behind her in the room. 'Go away,' she said. 'There are other rooms.'

When she turned back she saw that her son was standing in the bows, and that he was looking up at her. One side of his face was wet with blood. His eyes shone strangely. It seemed that he wished to be sure that she was there above him and was able to see exactly what was happening. For as the body of Steerpike was hauled aboard by the boatmen, he glanced at it and then at her again before a black faint overtook him and his mother's face whirled in an arc, and he fell forward into the boat as though into a trench of darkness.

SEVENTY-NINE

THERE was no more rain. The washed air was indescribably sweet. A kind of natural peace, almost a thing of the mind, a kind of reverie, descended upon Gormenghast – descended, it seemed, with the sunbeams by day, and the moonbeams after dark.

By infinitesimal degrees, moment by golden moment, hour by hour, day by day, and month by month the great flood-waters fell. The extensive roofscapes, the slates and stony uplands, the long and slanting sky-fields, and the sloping altitudes, dried out in the sun. It shone every day, turning the waters, that were once so grey and grim, into a smooth and slumbering expanse over whose blue depths the white clouds floated idly.

But *within* the castle, as the flood subsided and the water drained away from the upper levels, it could be seen how great was the destruction that the flood had caused. Beyond the windows the water lay innocently, basking, as though butter would not melt in its soft blue mouth, but at the same time the filthy slime lay a foot deep across great tracts of storeys newly drained. Foul rivulets of water oozed out of windows. From the floors lately submerged the tops of objects began to appear, and all was covered with grey slime. It began to be apparent that the shovelling away of the accumulated sediment, the swilling and scouring of the castle, when at long last, if ever, it stood on dry land again, would stretch away into the future.

The feverish months of hauling up the stairways of Gormenghast all that was now congesting the upper storeys would be nothing to this regenerative labour that lay before the hierophants.

The fact that at some remote date the castle was likely to be cleaner than it had been for a millennium held little attraction for those who had never thought of the place in terms of cleanliness – had never imagined it could be anything but what it was.

That the flood had once threatened their very existence was forgotten.

It was the labour that lay ahead that was appalling. And yet, the calm that had settled over Gormenghast had soothed away the rawness. Time lay ahead – soft and immeasurable. The work would be endless but it would not be frantic. The flood was descending. It had caused havoc, ruin, death, but it was descending. It was leaving behind it rooms full of mud and a thousand miscellaneous objects, sogged and broken; but it was descending.

Steerpike was dead. The fear of his whistling pebbles was no more. The multitudes moved without fear across the flat roofs. The kitchen boys and the urchins of the castle dived from the windows and sported across the water, climbing the outcrops as they appeared above the surface, a hundred battling at a time to gain some island tower – new-risen from the blue.

Titus had become a legend; a living symbol of revenge. The long scar across his face was the envy of the castle's youth, the pride of his mother – and his own secret glory.

The doctor had kept him in his bed for a month. His fever had mounted dangerously. For a week of high delirium the doctor fought for his life and hardly left his bedside. His mother sat in a corner of the room, motionless as a mountain. When at last he became conscious of what was happening around him and his forehead was cool again his mother withdrew. She had no idea what to say to him.

The descent of the waters continued at its own unhurried pace. The rooftops had become the castle's habitat. The long flat summit of the western massives had now, after three centuries of neglect become a favourite promenade. There, the crowds would wander after sundown when their work was over, or lean upon the turrets to watch the sun sink over the flood. The roofs had come into their own. There, throughout the day, the traditional life of the place was, as far as possible, continued. The great Tomes of Procedure had been saved from the wreckage, and the Poet, now Master of Ceremonies, was ceaselessly at work. Extensive areas had been covered with shanties and huts of every description. The various strata of Gormenghast had been gradually drawn to such quarters as best suited their rank and occupation.

More and more of Gormenghast Mountain became visible. The high and jagged cone grew bigger every day. At sunrise with the thin beams slanting across it and lighting the trees and rocks and ferns, it was an island mad with birdsong. Noon brought the silence: the sun slid gently over the blue sky and was reflected in the water.

It was as though all that had happened over the last decade, all the violence, the intrigue, the passion, the love, the hate and the fear had need of rest and that now, with Steerpike dead, the castle was able at last to close its eyes for a while and enjoy the listlessness of convalescence.

EIGHTY

Day after day, night after night, this strange tranquillity swam through the realm. But it was the spirit that rested; not the body. There was no end to the coming and going, to the sheer manual labour and to all the innumerable activities that hinged upon the re-conditioning of the castle.

The tops of trees had begun to appear with all but their strongest branches broken. Fresh shapes of masonry lifted their heads above the surface. Expeditions were made to Gormenghast Mountain from whose slopes the castle could be seen to be recovering its familiar shape.

There, on the rocky slopes, not more than three hundred feet from the claw-like summit. Fuchsia had been buried on the day following Steerpike's death.

She had been rowed by six men across the motionless flood in the most magnificent of the Carvers' boats, a massive construction, with a sculptured prow.

The traditional catacomb of the Groan family, with its effigies of local stone had been fathoms under water and there had been no alternative but to bury the daughter of the Line, with all pomp, in the only earth available.

The Doctor, who had not dared to leave the young earl in his illness, had been unable to attend the ceremony.

The grave had been hacked out of the stony earth upon a sloping site, chosen by the Countess. She had battled her way to and fro across the dangerous ground in search of a place worthy to be her daughter's resting place.

From this location the castle could be seen heaving across the skyline like the sheer sea-wall of a continent; a seaboard nibbled with countless coves and bitten deep with shadowy embayments. A continent, off whose shores the crowding islands lay; islands of every shape that towers can be; and archipelagos; and isthmuses and bluffs; and stark peninsulas of wandering stone – an inexhaustible panorama whose every detail was mirrored in the breathless flood below.

By the time that Titus had to a great extent recovered not only from the horror of the night, but from the effects of the nervous exhaustion that followed, a year had passed and Gormenghast was once again visible from top to bottom.

But it was dank and foul. It was no place to live in. After dark there was illness in every breath. Animals had been drowned in its corridors; a thousand things had decayed. The place was noxious. Only by day the swarms of the workmen, toiling indefatigably, kept the place inhabited.

The roofs had by now been deserted, and a gigantic encampment was spread abroad across the grounds and escarpments that surrounded the castle; a kind of shanty town had arisen, where huts, cabins, shacks and improvised constructions of great ingenuity made from mud, branches, strips of canvas, and all kinds of odd pieces of iron and stone from the castle, shouldered one another in a fantastic conglomeration.

And there, while the work proceeded, ever towards one end, that part of Gormenghast that was made of flesh and blood lived cheek by jowl.

The weather was almost monotonously beautiful. The winter was mild. A little rain came every few weeks, in the spring corn was grown on the higher and less water-logged slopes. Above the encircling encampments the great masonry wasted.

But while the 'drying out' of its myriad compartments and interstices proceeded and while this sense of peace lay over the scene, Titus, in contradiction to the prevailing atmosphere, grew, as his recovery became more complete, more and more restless.

What did he want with all this softness of gold light? This sense of peace? Why was he waking every day to the monotony of the eternal encampment; the eternal castle and the eternal ritual?

For the Poet was taking his work to heart. His high order of intelligence which had up till now been concentrated upon the creation of dazzling, if incomprehensible, structures of verbiage, was now able to deploy itself in a way which, if almost as incomprehensible, was at the same time of more value to the castle. The Poetry of Ritual had gripped him and his long wedge-shaped face was never without a speculative twist of the muscles – as though he were for ever turning over some fresh and absorbing variant of the problem of Ceremony and the human element.

This was as it should be. The Master of Ritual was, after all, the keystone of the castle's life. But as the months passed Titus realized that he must choose between being a symbol, for ever toeing the immemorial line, or turn traitor in his mother's eyes and in the eyes of the castle. His days were full of meaningless ceremonies whose sacredness appeared to be in inverse ratio to their comprehensibility or usefulness.

And all the time he was the apple of the castle's eye. He could do no wrong – and there was honey to be tasted on the tongue, when the hierophants drew back from the rocky paths to let him pass and the children screamed his name excitedly from their shacks, or stared in big-eyed wonder at the avenger.

Steerpike had become an almost legendary monster – but here, alive and breathing, was the young earl who had fought him in the ivy. Here was the dragon-slayer.

But even this became monotonous. The honey tasted sickly in his mouth. His mother had nothing to say to him. She had become even more withdrawn. Her pride in the courage he had shown had emptied her of words. She had reverted to the heavy and formidable figure, with her white cats for ever within range of her whistle and the wild birds upon her massive shoulders.

She had risen to an occasion. The uprooting of Steerpike and the salvaging of the flooded castle.

Now she drew back into herself.

Her brain began to go to sleep again. She had lost interest in it and the things that it could do. It had been brought forth like a machine from the darkness and set in motion – and it had proved itself to be measured and powerful, like the progress of an army on the march. But it now chose to halt. It chose to sleep again. Her white cats and her wild birds had taken the place of the abstract values. She no longer reasoned. She no longer believed that Titus had meant what he had said. She connected it with his delirium. It was impossible to believe that he could have known that his words were heresy. He had craved for a kind of freedom disconnected from the life of his ancient home – his heritage – his birthright. What could that mean? She relapsed into a state of self-imposed darkness, lit only by green eyes and the bright backs of birds.

But Titus could no longer bear to think of the life that lay ahead of him with its dead repetitions, its moribund ceremonies. With every day that passed he grew more restless. He was like something caged. Some animal that longs to test itself; to try its own strength.

For Titus had discovered himself. The 'Thing', when she had died in the storm had killed his boyhood. The death of Flay had seasoned him. The drowning of Fuchsia had left a crater beneath his ribs. His victory over Steerpike had given him a kind of touchstone to his own courage.

The world that he pictured beyond the secret skyline – the world of nowhere and everywhere was necessarily based upon Gormenghast. But he knew that there would be a difference; and that there could be no other place exactly like his home. It was this difference that he longed for. There would be other rivers; and other mountains; other forests and other skies.

He was hungry for all this. He was hungry to test himself. To travel, not as an Earl but as a stranger with no more shelter than his naked name.

And he would be free. Free of his loyalties. Free of his home. Free of the maddening forms and ceremonies. Free to become something more than the last of the great Line. His longing to escape had been fanned

by his passion for the 'Thing'. Without her he would have never dared
to do more than dream of insurrection. She had shown him by her
independence how it was only fear that held people together. The fear
of being alone and the fear of being different. Her unearthly arrogance
and self-sufficiency had exploded at the very centre of his conventions.
From the moment when he knew for certain that she was no figment of
his fancy, but a creature of Gormenghast Forest, he had been haunted.
He was still haunted. Haunted by the thought of this other kind of
world which was able to exist without Gormenghast.

One evening, in the late spring, he climbed the slopes of
Gormenghast Mountain and stood by his sister's grave. But he did not
remain there for long, gazing down at the small silent mound. He
could only think what all men would have thought; that it was pitiful
that one so vivid and full of love and breath should be rotting in
darkness. To brood upon it would only be to call up horrors.

A light wind was blowing and the green hair of the grass was combed
out all one way from the brow of the mound. A faint coral-coloured
light filled the evening, and, like the rocks and the ferns about his feet,
his face was lit with it.

His somewhat lank, pale brown hair was blown across his eyes
which, when he lifted them from the mound and fixed them upon the
towered massings of the castle, began to glitter with a strange
excitement.

Fuchsia had left. She had finished with Gormenghast. She was in
some other climate. The 'Thing' was dead. She also had taught him, by
the least twist of her body in mid-air, that the castle was not all. Had
he not been shown how wide was life? He was ready.

He stood there quite silently, but his fists were clenched and he
pressed them against one another, knuckle to knuckle, as though to
fight down the excitement that was accumulating in his breast.

His broad, rather pallid face was not that of any romantic youth. It
was, in a way, very ordinary. He had no perfect feature. Everything
seemed a little too big and subtly uneven. His lower lip was thrust a
fraction forward of the upper and they were parted so that his teeth
were just visible. His pale eyes, a stoneish blue with a hint of dim and
sullen purple, were alone peculiar and even striking in their present
animation.

His loose-limbed body, rather heavy, but strong and agile, was bent
a little forward at the shoulders, with a kind of shrug. As a storm
gathers its clouds together, so in his chest he felt a *gathering* as his
thoughts fell into place and led one way, and his pulse-beat, as though
underlining his will to rebel, throbbed at his wrists.

And all the while the sweet air swam about him, innocent, delicate,
and a single cloud, like a slender hand floated over the castle as though

to bless the towers. A rabbit emerged from the shadows of a fern and sat quite still upon a rock. Some insects sang thinly in the air, and suddenly close at hand a cricket scraped away on a single bowstring.

It seemed a strangely gentle atmosphere to surround the turmoil in Titus' heart and mind.

He knew now that to postpone his act of treachery would make it no easier. What was he waiting for? No time would ever come when an atmosphere of sympathy, welling as it were out of the castle, would help him on his way, would say 'Now is the Time to go'. Not a stone of the castle would own him from the moment he turned his back.

He descended the slopes, threading the trees of the foothills and came at last to the marshland paths and then after crossing the escarpment, approached the gate in the outer walls.

It was when he saw the great walls looming above him that he began to run.

He ran as though to obey an order. And this was so, though he knew nothing of it. He ran in the acknowledgement of a law as old as the laws of his home. The law of flesh and blood. The law of longing. The law of change. The law of youth. The law that separates the generations, that draws the child from his mother, the boy from his father, the youth from both.

And it was the law of quest. The law that few obey for lack of valour. The craving of the young for the unknown and all that lies beyond the tenuous skyline.

He ran, in the simple faith that in his disobedience was his inmost proof. He was no callow novice; no flighty child of some romance of sugar. He had no sweet tooth. He had killed and had felt the wide world rustle open from the ribs and the touch of death had set his hair on end.

He ran because his decision had been made. It had been made for him by the convergence of half-forgotten motives, of desires and reasons, of varied yet congruous impulses. And the convergence of all these to a focus point of *action*.

It was this that made him run as though to keep pace with his brain and his excitement.

He knew that he could not now turn back save in the very teeth of his integrity. His breath came quick and fast, and all at once he was among the shacks.

The sun was now upon the rim of the skyline. The rose-red light had deepened. The great encampment wore a strange beauty. A populace meandered through the wandering lanes and turned at his approach and made a path for him. The ragged children cried out his name, and ran to tell their mothers that they had seen the scar. Titus, drawn back suddenly into the world of reality, came to a halt. For some time he remained with his hands on his knees and his head dropped forward and then when he had regained his breath and had wiped the sweat from his brow, he walked rapidly to that part of the cantonment where a stockade had been built to surround the long shanty where the Countess lived.

Before he entered the stockade through the clumsy iron gate he motioned to some passing youths.

'You will find the Master of the Stables,' he said, in his mother's peremptory manner. 'He should be with the horses in the west enclosure. Tell him to saddle the mare. He will know her. The grey mare with a white foot. He will bring her to the Tower of Flints. I will be there shortly.'

The youths touched their brows and disappeared into the gathering dusk. The moon was beginning to float up and from behind a broken tower.

As Titus was about to push open the iron gate he paused, turned on his heel, and set off into the heart of a town of looted floor-boards. But he had no need to advance as far as the Professors' quarters nor to turn east to where the Doctor's hospital lifted its raw woodwork to the rising moon. For there ahead of him, and walking in his direction along the foot-worn track was the Headmaster, his wife and his brother-in-law, the Doctor.

They did not see him until he was close upon them. He knew they would wish to talk to him, but he knew he would not be able to make conversation, or even listen to them. He was out of key with normality. And so, before they knew what had happened, he reached out and simultaneously gripped the Doctor and the old Professor by their hands, and then releasing them he bowed a little awkwardly to Irma, before he turned on his heel and, to their amazement, began to walk rapidly away until he was lost to their sight in the thick of the dusk.

When he reached the stockade he made no pause but entered and told the man who stood outside the door of the long shanty to announce him.

He saw her at once as he entered. She was sitting at a table, a candle before her, and was gazing expressionlessly at a picture book.

'Mother.'

She looked up slowly.

'Well?' she said.

'I am going.'

She said nothing.

'Good-bye.'

She got heavily to her feet and raising the candle and bringing it towards him she held it close to his face and fixed her eyes on his – and then, lifting her other hand, she traced the line of his scar very gently with her forefinger.

'Going where?' she said at last.

'I am leaving,' said Titus. 'I am leaving Gormenghast. I cannot explain. I do not want to talk. I came to tell you and that is all. Goodbye, Mother.'

He turned and walked quickly to the door. He longed with his whole soul to be able to pass through and into the night without another word being spoken. He knew she was unable to grasp so terrible a confession of perfidy. But out of the silence, that hung at his shoulder blades, he heard her voice. It was not loud. It was not hurried.

'There is nowhere else,' it said. 'You will only tread a circle, Titus Groan. There's not a road, not a track, but it will lead you home. For everything comes to Gormenghast.'

He shut the door. The moonlight flowed across the cold encampment. It shone on the roofs of the castle and lit the high claw of the Mountain.

When he came to the Tower of Flints his mare was waiting. He mounted, shook the reins, and moved away at once through the inky shadows that lay beneath the walls.

After a long while he came out into the brilliant light of the hunter's moon and sometime later he realized that unless he turned about in his saddle there was no cause for him to see his home again. At his back the castle climbed into the night. Before him there was spread a great terrain.

He brushed a few strands of hair away from his eyes, and jogged the grey mare to a trot and then into a canter, and finally with a moonlit wilderness before him, to a gallop.

And so, exulting as the moonlit rocks fled by him, exulting as the tears streamed over his face – with his eyes fixed excitedly upon the blurred horizon – and the battering of the hoof-beats loud in his ears, Titus rode out of his world.

TITUS ALONE

FOR MAEVE

ONE

To north, south, east or west, turning at will, it was not long before his landmarks fled him. Gone was the outline of his mountainous home. Gone that torn world of towers. Gone the grey lichen; gone the black ivy. Gone was the labyrinth that fed his dreams. Gone ritual, his marrow and his bane. Gone boyhood. Gone.

It was no more than a memory now; a slur of the tide; a reverie, or the sound of a key, turning.

From the gold shores to the cold shores: through regions thighbone-deep in sumptuous dust: through lands as harsh as metal, he made his way. Sometimes his footsteps were inaudible. Sometimes they clanged on stone. Sometimes an eagle watched him from a rock. Sometimes a lamb.

Where is he now? Titus the Abdicator? Come out of the shadows, traitor, and stand upon the wild brink of my brain!

He cannot know, wherever he may be, that through the worm-pocked doors and fractured walls, through windows bursted, gaping, soft with rot, a storm is pouring into Gormenghast. It scours the flagstones; churns the sullen moat; prises the long beams from their crumbling joists; and howls! He cannot know, as every moment passes, the multifarious action of his home.

A rocking-horse, festooned with spiders' rigging, sways where there's no one in a gusty loft.

He cannot know that as he turns his head, three armies of black ants, in battle order, are passing now like shades across the spines of a great library.

Has he forgotten where the breastplates burn like blood within the eyelids, and great domes reverberate to the coughing of a rat?

He only knows that he has left behind him, on the far side of the skyline, something inordinate; something brutal; something tender; something half real; something half dream; half of his heart; half of himself.

And all the while the far hyena laughter.

TWO

THE sun sank with a sob and darkness waded in from all horizons so that the sky contracted and there was no more light left in the world, when, at this very moment of annihilation, the moon, as though she had been waiting for her cue, sailed up the night.

Hardly knowing what he was doing, young Titus moored his small craft to the branch of a riverside tree and stumbled ashore. The margins of the river were husky with rushes, a great militia whose contagious whisperings suggested discontent, and with this sound in his ears he dragged his way through the reeds, his feet sinking ankle-deep in ooze.

It was his hazy plan to take advantage of the rising ground that was heaping itself up upon the right bank, and to climb its nearest spur, in order to gain a picture of what lay ahead of him, for he had lost his way.

But when he had fought his way up-hill through the vegetation, and by the time he had fallen in a series of mishaps and had added to the long tears in his clothes, so that it was a wonder that they held together at all – by this time, though he found himself at the crown of a blunt grass hill, he had no eyes for the landscape, but fell to the ground at the foot of what appeared to be a great boulder that swayed; but it was Titus who was swaying, and who fell exhausted with fatigue and hunger.

There he lay, curled up, and vulnerable it seemed in his sleep, and lovable also as are all sleepers by reason of their helplessness; their arms thrown wide, their heads turned to some curious angle that moves the heart.

But the wise are careful in their compassion, for sleep can be like snow on a harsh rock and melt away at the first fleck of sentience.

And so it was with Titus. Turning over to relieve his tingling arm he saw the moon and he hated it; hated its vile hypocrisy of light; hated its fatuous face; hated it with so real a revulsion that he spat at it and shouted, 'Liar!'

And then again, and not so far away, came the hyena laughter.

THREE

WITHIN a span of Titus's foot, a beetle, minute and heraldic, reflected the moonbeams from its glossy back. Its shadow, three times as long as itself, skirted a pebble and then climbed a grassblade.

Titus rose to his knees, the aftermath of a dream remaining like remorse, though he could remember nothing of it save that it was Gormenghast again. He picked up a stick and began to draw in the dust with the point of it, and the moonlight was so fierce that every line he drew was like a narrow trench filled up with ink.

Seeing that he had drawn a kind of tower he felt involuntarily in a pocket for that small knuckle of flint which he carried with him, as though to prove to himself that his boyhood was real, and that the Tower of Flints still stood as it had stood for centuries, out-topping all the masonry of his ancient home.

He lifted his head and his gaze wandered for the first time from all that was immediately at hand, wandered away to the north, across great phosphorescent slopes of oak and ilex until it came to rest upon a city.

It was a city asleep and deathly silent in the emptiness of the night and Titus rose to his feet and trembled as he saw it, not only with the cold but with astonishment that while he had slept, and while he had drawn the marks in the dust, and while he had watched the beetle, this city should have been there all the time and that a turn of his head might have filled his eyes with the domes and spires of silver; with shimmering slums; with parks and arches and a threading river. And all upon the flanks of a great mountain, hoary with forests.

But as he stared at the high slopes of the city his feelings were not those of a child or a youth, nor of an adult with romantic leanings. His responses were no longer clear and simple, for he had been through much since he had escaped from Ritual, and he was no longer child or youth, but by reason of his knowledge of tragedy, violence and the sense of his own perfidy, he was far more than these, though less than *man*.

Kneeling there he seemed most lost. Lost in the bright grey night. Lost in his separation. Lost in a swath of space in which the city lay like one-thing, secure in its cohesion, a great moonbathed creature that throbbed in its sleep as from a single pulse.

FOUR

GETTING to his feet, Titus began to walk, not across the hills in the direction of the city, but down a steep decline to the river where his boat lay moored, and there in the dark of the wet flags he found her tethered and whispering at the water-line.

But as he stooped to slip the painter, two figures, drawing apart the tall rushes, stepped forward towards him, and the rushes closed behind them like a curtain. The sudden appearance of these men sent his heart careering and before he knew well what he was doing he had sprung into the air with a long backward bound and in another moment had half fallen into his boat, which pitched and rocked as though to throw him out.

They wore some kind of martial uniform, these two, though it was difficult to see the form it took, for their heads and bodies were striped with the shadows of the flags and streaked with slats of radiance. One of the heads was entirely moonlit save for an inch-thick striation which ran down the forehead and over one eye, which was drowned in the dark of it, then over the cheekbone and down to the man's long jaw.

The other figure had no face at all; it was part of the annihilating darkness. But his chest was aflame with limegreen fabric and one foot was like a thing of phosphorus.

On seeing Titus struggling with his long bow-oar they made no sound but stepped at once and without hesitation into the river and waded into the deepening bed, until only their plumed heads remained above the surface of the unreflecting water; and their heads appeared to Titus, even in the extremity of his escape, to be detached and floating on the surface as though they could be slid to and fro as kings and knights are slid across a chessboard.

This was not the first time that Titus had been suddenly accosted in regions as apparently remote. He had escaped before, and now, as his boat danced away on the water, he remembered how it was always the same – the sudden appearance, the leap of evasion, and the strange following silence as his would-be captors dwindled away into the distance, to vanish . . . but not for ever.

FIVE

HE had seen, asleep in the bright grey air, a city, and he put aside the memories of his deserted home, and of his mother and the cry of a deserter in his heart; and for all his hunger and fatigue he grinned, for he was young as twenty years allowed, and as old as it could make him.

He grinned again, but lurched as he did so, and without realizing what he was doing he fell upon his side in a dead faint, and his grin lost focus and blurred his lips and the oar fell away from his grasp.

SIX

OF the bulk of the night he knew nothing; nothing of how his small boat twisted and turned; nothing of the city as it slid towards him. Nothing of the great trees that flanked the river on either side, with their marmoreal roots that coiled in and out of the water and shone wetly in the moonlight; nothing of how, in the half-darkness where the water-steps shelve to the stream, a humpbacked man turned from untangling a miserable net, and seeing an apparently empty boat bearing down upon him, stern first, splattered his way through the water and grabbed at the rowlocks and then, with amazement, at the boy, and dragged him from his moon-bright cradle so that the craft sped onward down the broad stream.

Titus knew nothing of all this; nor of how the man who had saved him stared blankly at the ragged vagrant beneath him on the shelving water-steps, for that is where he had laid the heap of weariness.

Had the old man bent down his head to listen he might have heard a faraway sound, and seen the trembling of Titus's lips, for the boy was muttering to himself:

'Wake up, you bloody city . . . bang your bells!
I'm on my way to eat you!'

SEVEN

THE city was indeed beginning to turn in its sleep, and out of the half-darkness figures began to appear along the waterfront; some on foot hugging themselves in the cold; some in ramshackle mule-drawn carriages, the great beasts flaring their nostrils at the sharp air, their harsh bones stretching the coarse hide at hip and shoulder, their eyes evil and their breath sour.

And there were some, for the most part the old and the worn, who evolved out of the shades like beings spun from darkness. They made their way to the river in wheel-barrows, pushed by their sons and their sons' sons; or in carts, or donkey wagons. All with their nets or fishing-lines, the wheels rattling on the cobbled waterfront while the dawn strengthened; and a long shadowy car approached with a screech out of the gloom. Its bonnet was the colour of blood. Its water was boiling. It snorted like a horse and shook itself as though it were alive.

The driver, a great, gaunt, rudder-nosed man, square-jawed, long-limbed, and muscular, appeared to be unaware of the condition of his car or of the danger to himself or to the conglomeration of characters who lay tangled among their nets in the rotting 'stern' of the dire machine.

He lay, rather than sat, his head below the level of his knees, his feet resting lazily on the clutch and the brake, and then, as though the snorting of a distant jackass were his clue, he rolled out of the driver's seat and on to his feet at the side of the hissing car, where he stretched himself, flinging his arms so wide apart in doing so that he appeared for a moment like some oracle, directing the sun and moon to keep their distance.

Why he should trouble so often to bring his car at dawn to the water-steps and so benefit whatever beggars wished to climb into the mouldering stern, it is not easy to fathom, for he was eminently a man of small compassion, a hurtful man, brazen and loveless, who would have no one beside him in the front of the car, save occasionally an old mandrill.

Nor did he fish. Nor had he any desire to watch the sun rising. He merely loomed out of the night-old shadows and lit an old black pipe, while the cold and hungry began to pour towards the bank of the river, a dark mass, as the first fleck of blood appeared on the skyline.

And it was while he stood this particular morning, with arms akimbo, and while he watched the boats being pushed out and the dark foam parting at the blunt prows, that he saw, kneeling on the water-steps, the humpbacked man with a youth lying prostrate below him.

EIGHT

THE old hunchback was obviously at a loss to know what to do with this sudden visitant from nowhere. The way he had clawed at Titus and dragged him from the sliding boat might well have suggested that he was, for all his age, a man of rapid wit and action. But no. What he had done was something which never afterwards failed to amaze him and amaze his friends, for they knew him to be clumsy and ignorant. And so, reverting to type, now the danger was over, he knelt and stared at Titus helplessly.

The torches further down the stream had been lit and the river was ruddy with reflected light. The cormorants, released from their wicker-work cages, slid into the water and dived. A mule, silhouetted against the torchlight, lifted its head and bared its disgusting teeth.

Muzzlehatch, the owner of the car, had wandered over to the

hunchback and the youth and was now bending over Titus, not with any gentleness or concern, so it seemed, but with an air of detachment – proud, even in the face of another's plight.

'Into the chariot with it,' he muttered. 'What it *is* I have no idea, but it has a pulse.'

Muzzlehatch removed his finger and thumb from Titus's wrist and pointed to his long vibrating car with a massive index-finger.

Two beggars, pushing forward through the crowd that now surrounded the prostrate Titus, elbowed the old man out of their way and lifted the young Earl of Gormenghast, as ragged a creature as themselves, as though he were a sack of gravel, and shuffling to the car they laid him in the stern of the indescribable vehicle – that chaos of mildewed leather, sodden leaves, old cages, broken springs, rust and general squalor.

Muzzlehatch, following them with long, slow, arrogant strides, had reached about half-way to his diabolical car when a pelt of darkness shifted in the sky and the scarlet rim of an enormous sun began to cut its way up as though with a razor's edge, and immediately the boats and their crews and the cormoranteers and their bottle-necked birds, and the rushes and the muddy bank and the mules and the vehicles and the nets and the spears and the river itself, became ribbed and flecked with flame.

But Muzzlehatch had no eye for all this and it was well for Titus that this was so, for on turning his head from the daybreak as though it were about as interesting as an old sock, he saw, by the light of what he was dismissing, two men approaching smoothly and rapidly, with helmets on their identical heads and scrolls of parchment in their hands.

Muzzlehatch lifted his eyebrows so that his somewhat louring forehead became rucked up like the crumpled leather at the back of his car. Turning his eyes to the machine, as though to judge how far it was away, he continued walking towards it with a barely perceptible lengthening of his stride.

The two men who were approaching seemed to be not so much walking as gliding, so smoothly they advanced, and those fishers who were still left upon the cobbled waterfront parted at their approach, for they made their way unswervingly to where Titus lay.

How they could know that he was in the car at all is hard to conceive; but know it they did, and with helmets glittering in the dawn rays they bore down upon him with ghastly deliberation.

NINE

It was then that Titus roused himself and lifted his face from his arms and saw nothing but the flush of the dawn sky above him and the profuse scattering of the stars.

What use were *they?* His stomach cried with hunger and he shook with the cold. He raised himself upon one elbow and moistened his lips. His wet clothes clung to him like seaweed. The acrid smell of the mouldering leather began to force itself upon his consciousness, and then, as though to offer him something different by way of a change, he found himself staring into the face of a large rudder-nosed man who at the next moment had vaulted into the front seat, where he slid into an all but horizontal position. Lying at this angle he began to press a number of buttons, each one of which, replying to his prodding finger, helped to create a tumult quite vile upon the eardrums. At the height of this cacophony the car backfired with such violence that a dog turned over in its sleep four miles away, and then, with an upheaval that lifted the bonnet of the car and brought it down again with a crash of metal, the wild thing shook itself as though bent upon its own destruction, shook itself, roared, and leapt forward and away down tortuous alleys still wet and black with the night shadows.

Street after street flew at them as they sped through the waking town; flew at them and broke apart at the prow-like bonnet. The streets, the houses, rushed by on either side, and Titus, clinging to an old brass railing, gasped at the air that ran into his lungs like icy water.

It was all that Titus could do to persuade himself that the impetuous vehicle was, in fact, being driven at all, for he could see nothing of the driver. It seemed that the car had an existence of its own and was making its own decisions. What Titus *could* see was that instead of a normal mascot, this stranger who was driving him (though why or where he did not know) had fixed along the brass cap of the radiator the sun-bleached skull of a crocodile. The cold air whistled between its teeth and the long crown of its skull was flushed with sunrise.

For now the sun was clear of the horizon, and as the world flew past, it climbed, so that for the first time Titus became aware of the nature of the city into which he had drifted like a dead branch.

A voice roared past his ears, 'Hold tight, you pauper!' and the sound flew away into the cold air as the car swerved in a sickening loop, and then again and again as the walls reared up before them, only to stream away in a high torrent of stone; and then, at last, diving beneath a low arch, the car, turning and slowing as it turned, came to rest in a walled-in courtyard.

The courtyard was cobbled and in between the cobbles the grass flourished.

TEN

AROUND three sides of the yard the walls of a massive stone-built building blocked the dawn away, save in one place where the slanting rays ran through a high eastern window and out of an even higher western window to end their journey in a pool of radiance upon a cold slate roof.

Ignorant of its setting and of the prodigious length of its shadow; ignorant that its drab little breast glowed in the sunrise, a sparrow pecked at its tinted wing. It was as though an urchin, scratching himself, absorbed in what he was doing, had become transfigured.

Meanwhile Muzzlehatch had rolled out of the driver's seat and lashed the car, as though it were an animal, to the mulberry tree which grew in the centre of the yard.

Then he meandered with long, lazy, loose-jointed strides towards the dark north-western corner of the yard and whistled between his teeth with the penetration of a steam whistle. A face appeared at a window above his head. And then another. And then another. There was then a great rattling to be heard of feet upon stairs, and the jangling of a bell, and behind these noises a further noise, more continuous and more diverse, for there was about it the suggestion of beasts and birds; of a howling and a coughing and a screaming and a kind of hooting sound, but all of it in the distance and afar from the foreground noises, the feet loud upon the stairs and the jangling of a near-by bell.

Then out of the shadows that hung like black water against the walls of the great building a group of servants broke from the house and ran towards their master, who had returned to his car.

Titus was sitting up, with his face drawn, and as he sat there facing the huge Muzzlehatch, he became, without thought, without cognizance, irrationally savage, for at the back of his mind was an earlier time when for all the horror and the turmoil and the repetitive idiocy of his immemorial home, he was in his own right the Lord of a Domain.

The hunger burned in his stomach but there was another burn, the heartburn of the displaced; the unrecognized; the unrecognizable.

Why did they not know of him? What right had any man to touch him? To whirl him away on four mouldering wheels? To abduct him and to force him to his courtyard? To lean over him and stare at him with eyebrows raised? What right had anyone to save him? He was no child! He had known horror. He had fought, and he had killed. He had lost his sister and his father and the long man Flay, loyal as the stones of Gormenghast. And he had held an elf in his arms and seen her struck by lightning to a cinder, when the sky fell in and the world reeled. He was no child . . . no child . . . no child at all, and rising shakily to his feet he stood swaying in his weakness as he swung his fist at Muzzlehatch's face – a vast face that seemed to disintegrate before him, only to clear again . . . only to dissolve.

His fist was caught in the capacious paw of the rudder-nosed man, who signed to his servants to carry Titus to a low room where the walls from floor to ceiling were lined with glass cases, where, beautifully pinned to sheets of cork, a thousand moths spread out their wings in a great gesture of crucifixion.

It was in this room that Titus was given a bowl of soup which, in his weakness, he kept spilling, until the spoon was taken from him, and a small man with a chip out of his ear fed him gently as he lay, half-reclined, on a long wicker chair. Even before he was half-way through his bowl of soup he fell back on the cushions, and was within a moment or two drawn incontinently into the void of a deep sleep.

ELEVEN

WHEN he awoke the room was full of light. A blanket was up to his chin. On a barrel by his side was his only possession, an egg-shaped flint from the Tower of Gormenghast.

The chip-eared man came in.

'Hullo there, you ruffian,' he said. 'Are you awake?'

Titus nodded his head.

'Never known a scarecrow to sleep so long.'

'*How* long?' said Titus, raising himself on one elbow.

'Nineteen hours,' said the man. 'Here's your breakfast.' He deposited a loaded tray at the side of the couch and then he turned away, but stopped at the door.

'What's your name, boy?' he said.

'Titus Groan.'

'And where d'you come from?'

'Gormenghast.'

'*That's* the word. *That's* the word indeed. "Gormenghast." If you said it once you said it twenty times.'

'What! In my sleep?'

'In your sleep. Over and over. Where is it, boy? This place. This Gormenghast.'

'I don't know,' said Titus.

'Ah,' said the little man with the chip out of his ear, and he squinted at Titus sideways from under his eyebrows. 'You don't know, don't you? That's peculiar, now. But eat your breakfast. You must be hollow as a kettledrum.'

Titus sat up and began to eat, and as he ate he reached for the flint and moved his hand over its familiar contours. It was his only anchor. It was, for him, in microcosm, his home.

And while he gripped it, not in weakness or sentiment but for the sake of its density, and proof of its presence, and while the midday sunlight sifted itself to and fro across the room, a dreadful sound erupted in the courtyard and the open door of his room was all at once darkened, not by the chip-eared man but, more effectively, by the hindquarters of an enormous mule.

TWELVE

TITUS, sitting bolt upright, stared incredulously at the rear of this great bristling beast whose tail was mercilessly thrashing its own body. A group of improbable muscles seldom brought into play started, now here, now there, across its shuddering rump. It fought *in situ* with something on the other side of the door until it forced its way inch by inch out into the courtyard again, taking a great piece of the wall with it. And all the time the hideous, sickening sound of hate; for there is something stirred up in the breasts of mules and camels when they have the scent of one another which darkens the imagination.

Jumping to his feet, Titus crossed the room and gazed with awe at the antagonists. He was no stranger to violence, but there was something peculiarly horrible about this duel. There they were, not thirty feet away, locked in deadly grapple, a conflict without scale.

In that camel were all the camels that had ever been. Blind with a hatred far beyond its own power to invent, it fought a world of mules; of mules that since the dawn of time have bared their teeth at their intrinsic foe.

What a setting was that cobbled yard, now warm and golden in the sunlight, the gutter of the building thronged with sparrows; the mulberry tree basking in the sunbeams, its leaves hanging quietly while the two beasts fought to kill.

By now the courtyard was agog with servants and there were shouts and countershouts and then a horrible quiet, for it could be seen that the mule's teeth had met in the camel's throat. Then came a wheeze like the sound of a tide sucked out of a cave; a shuffle of shingle, and the rattle of pebbles.

And yet that bite that would have killed a score of men appeared to be no more than an incident in this battle, for now it was the mule who lay beneath the weight of its enemy, and suffered great pain, for its jaw had been broken by a slam of the hoof and a paralysing butt of the head.

Sickened but thrilled, Titus took a step into the courtyard, and the first thing he saw was Muzzlehatch. This gentleman was giving orders with a peculiar detachment, mindless that he was stark naked except for a fireman's helmet. A number of servants were unwinding an old but powerful-looking hose, one end of which had already been screwed into a vast brass hydrant. The other end was gurgling and spluttering in Muzzlehatch's arms.

Its nozzle trained at the double-creature, the hose-pipe squirmed and jumped like a conger, and suddenly a long, flexible jet of ice-cold water leapt across the quadrangle.

This white jet, like a knife, pierced here and there, until, as though the bonfire of their hatred had been doused, the camel and the mule, relaxing their grips, got slowly to their feet, bleeding horribly, a cloud of animal heat rising around them.

Then every eye was turned to Muzzlehatch, who took off his brass helmet and placed it over his heart.

As though this were not peculiar enough, Titus was next to witness how Muzzlehatch ordered his servants to turn off the water, to seat themselves on the floor of the wet courtyard, and to keep silent, and all by the language of his expressive eyebrows alone. Then, more peculiar still, he was surprised to hear the naked man address the shuddering beasts from whose backs great clouds of steam were rising.

'My atavistic, my inordinate friends,' whispered Muzzlehatch in a voice like sandpaper, 'I know full well that when you smell one another, then you grow restless, then you grow thoughtless, then you go . . . too far. I concede the ripe condition of your blood; the darkness of your native anger; the gulches of your ire. But listen to me with those ears of yours and fix your eyes upon me. Whatever your temptation, whatever your primordial hankering, yet' (he addressed the camel), 'yet you have no excuse in the world grown sick of excuses. It was not for you to charge the iron rails of your cage, nor, having broken them down, to vent your spleen upon this mule of ours. And it was not for you,' (he addressed the mule), 'to seek this rough-and-tumble nor to scream with such unholy lust for battle. I will have no more of it, my friends! Let this be trouble enough. What, after all, have you done for me? Very little, if anything. But I – I have fed you on fruit and onions, scraped your backs with bill-hooks, cleaned out your cages with pearl-handled spades, and kept you safe from the carnivores and the bow-legged eagle. O, the ingratitude! Unregenerate and vile! So you broke loose on me, did you – and *reverted*!'

The two beasts began to shuffle to and fro, one on its hassock-sized pads and the other on its horny hooves.

'Back to your cages with you! Or by the yellow light in your wicked eyes I will have you shaved and salted.' He pointed to the archway through which they had fought their way into the courtyard – an archway that linked the yard in which they stood to the twelve square acres where animals of all kinds paced their narrow dens or squatted on long branches in the sun.

THIRTEEN

THE camel and the mule lowered their terrible heads and began their way back to the arch, through which they shuffled side by side.

What was going on in those two skulls? Perhaps some kind of pleasure that after so many years of incarceration they had at last been able to vent their ancient malice, and plunge their teeth into the enemy. Perhaps, also, they felt some kind of pleasure in sensing the bitterness they were arousing in the breasts of the other animals.

They stepped out of the tunnel, or long archway, on the southern side, and were at once in full view of at least a score of cages.

The sunlight lay like a gold gauze over the zoo. The bars of the cages were like rods of gold, and the animals and birds were flattened by the bright slanting rays, so that they seemed cut out of coloured cardboard or from the pages of some book of beasts.

Every head was turned towards the wicked pair; heads furred and heads naked; heads with beaks and heads with horns; heads with scales and heads with plumes. They were all turned, and being so, made not the slightest movement.

But the camel and the mule were anything but embarrassed. They had tasted freedom and they had tasted blood, and it was with a quite indescribable arrogance that they swaggered towards the cages, their thick, blue lips curled back over their disgusting teeth; their nostrils dilated and their eyes yellow with pride.

If hatred could have killed them they would have expired a hundred times on the way to their cages. The silence was like breath held at the ribs.

And then it broke, for a shrill scream pierced the air like a splinter, and the monkey, whose voice it was, shook the bars of its cage with hands and feet in an access of jealousy so that the iron rattled as the scream went on and on and on, while other voices joined it and reverberated through the prisons so that every kind of animal became a part of bedlam.

The tropics burned and broke in ancient loins. Phantom lianas sagged and dripped with poison. The jungle howled and every howl howled back.

FOURTEEN

Titus followed a group of servants through the archway and into the open on the other side where the din became all but unbearable.

Not fifty feet from where he stood was Muzzlehatch astride a mottled stag, a creature as powerful and gaunt as its rider. He was grasping the beast's antlers in one hand, and with the other he was gesticulating to some men who were already, under his guidance, beginning to mend the buckled cages, at the back of which sat the miscreants licking their wounds and grinning horribly.

Very gradually the noise subsided and Muzzlehatch, turning from the scene, saw Titus, and with a peremptory gesture beckoned him. But Titus, who had been about to greet the intellectual ruffian who sat astride the stag like some ravaged god, stayed where he was, for he saw no reason why he should obey, like a dog to the whistle.

Seeing how the young vagrant made no response Muzzlehatch grinned, and turning the stag about he made to pass his guest as though he were not there, when Titus, remembering how his host-of-one-night had saved him from capture and had fed him and slept him, lifted his hand as though to halt the stag. Staring at the stag-rider, Titus realized that he had never really seen that face before, for he was no longer tired nor were his eyes blurred, and the head had come into a startling focus – a focus that seemed to enlarge rather than contract, a head of great scale with its crop of black hair, its nose like a rudder, and its eyes all broken up with little flecks and lights, like diamonds or fractured glass, and its mouth, wide, tough, lipless, almost blasphemously mobile, for no one with such a mouth could pray aloud to any god at all, for the mouth was wrong for prayer. This head was like a challenge or a threat to all decent citizens.

Titus was about to thank this Muzzlehatch, but on gazing at the craggy face he saw that his thanks would find no answer, and it was Muzzlehatch himself who volunteered the information that he considered Titus to be a soft and rancid egg if he imagined that he, Muzzlehatch, had ever lifted a finger to help anyone in his life, let alone a bunch of rags out of the river.

If he had helped Titus it was only to amuse himself and to pass the time, for life can be a bore without action, which in its turn can be a bore without danger.

'Besides,' he continued, gazing over Titus's shoulder at a distant baboon, 'I dislike the police. I dislike their feet. I dislike that whiff of leather, oil and fur, camphor and blood. I dislike officials, who are nothing, my dear boy, but the pip-headed, trash-bellied putrid scrannel of earth. Out of darkness it is born.'

'What is?' said Titus.

'There is no point in erecting a structure,' said Muzzlehatch, taking no notice of Titus's question, 'unless someone else pulls it down. There is no value in a rule until it is broken. There is nothing in life unless there is death at the back of it. Death, dear boy, leaning over the edge of the world and grinning like a boneyard.'

He swung his gaze from the distant baboon and pulled back the antlers of the mottled stag until the creature's head pointed at the sky. Then he stared at Titus.

'Don't burden me with gratitude, dear boy. I have no time for –'

'Don't bother,' said Titus. 'I will never thank you.'

'Then go,' said Muzzlehatch.

The blood ran into Titus's face and his eyes shone.

'Who do you think you are talking to?' he whispered.

Muzzlehatch looked up sharply. 'Well,' he said, 'who *am* I talking to? Your eyes blaze like the eyes of a beggar – or of a lord.'

'Why not?' said Titus. 'That is what I am.'

FIFTEEN

HE made his way back through the tunnel and across the quadrangle and so out of the grounds until he came to a spider's web of tortuous lanes, and walking on and on, found himself at last upon a wide stone highway.

From there he saw the river far below and smoke rising in rosy plumes from countless chimneys.

But Titus turned his back on the vista and, as he climbed, two long cars, side by side, flashed by without a sound. There could have been no more than an inch of space between them as they sped.

At the back of the cars, one in each, and very upright, sat two dark, be-jewelled, deep-bosomed women who had no eyes for the flying landscape but smiled at each other with unhealthy concentration.

Far behind in the wake of the cars and farther with every passing moment, a small ugly black dog with its legs far too short for its body, tore with a ridiculous concentration of purpose down the centre of the long winding road.

As Titus climbed and as the trees closed in on either side, he wondered at a change that had come over him. The remorse that had filled him lately with so black a cloud had spent itself and there was a ripple in his blood and a spring in his step. He knew himself to be a deserter; a traitor to his birthright, the 'shame' of Gormenghast. He knew how he had wounded the castle, wounded the very stones of his

home; wounded his mother . . . all this he knew in his head, but it did not affect him.

He could only see now the truth of it – that he could never turn back the pages.

He was Lord Titus, Seventy-Seventh Lord of Gormenghast, but he was also a limb of life, a sprig, an adventurer, ready for love or hate; ready to use his wits in a foreign world; ready for anything.

This was what lay beyond those far horizons. This was the pith of it. New cities and new mountains; new rivers and new creatures. New men and new women.

But then a shadow came over his face. How was it that they were so self-sufficient, those women in their cars, or Muzzlehatch with his zoo – having no knowledge of Gormenghast, which was of course the heart of everything?

He climbed on, his shadow climbing beside him on the beautiful white stone of which the road was built, until he had almost reached a dividing of the highway, the eastern arm, an aisle of great oaks, and the western . . . but Titus was not able to fix his attention upon the trees nor upon anything else, for moving out of the shade into the sunlight, with a dreadful unhurried pace, were the two tall figures, identical in every way, their helmets casting a deep shade across their eyes, their bodies moving smoothly across the ground.

SIXTEEN

WITHOUT waiting for any orders from the brain a demon in his feet had already carried Titus deep into the flanking trees, and through the great park-like forest he ran and ran and ran, turning now this way and now that way until one would say he was irrevocably lost, were it not that he was always so.

But when, having fallen exhausted, he got to his knees and parted some branches, he found himself gazing at the very road from which he had fled. But there was no one there and after some while he walked out boldly and stood in the centre of the road as though to say, 'Do your worst.' But nothing happened except that what Titus had taken to be an old thorn bush got to its feet and shambled its way towards him, its shadow like a crab on the white stone highway. When it had come so close to Titus that he could have touched it with an outstretched foot the thorn bush spoke.

'I am a beggar,' it said, and the soft grit of its dreadful voice sent Titus's heart into his mouth. 'That is why I am stretching out my withered arm. Do you see it? Eh? Would you call it beautiful with that claw at the end of it – can you see it?'

The beggar stared at Titus through the red circles of his eyelids, and alternately shook his old knuckly fist and opened it out with the palm upwards.

The palm of that hand was like the delta of some foul dried-up river. At its centre was a kind of callus or horny disc, a tell-tale shape that argued the receipt and passage of many coins.

'What do you want?' said Titus. 'I have no money for you. I thought you were a thorn bush.'

'I'll *thorn* you!' said the beggar. 'How dare you refuse me! Me! An emperor! Dog! Whelp! Cur! Empty your gold into my sacred throat.'

'Sacred throat! What does he mean by that?' thought Titus, but only for a moment, for suddenly the beggar was no longer there but was twenty feet away and was staring down the white highway looking more like a thorn bush than ever. One of his arms, like a branch, was crook'd so that the claw at the end of it was conveniently cupped at the ear.

Then Titus heard it – the distant whirring sound of a fast machine, and a moment later a yellow car the shape of a shark sped from the south.

It seemed that the cantankerous old mendicant was about to be run down, for he stood on the crown of the road with his arms out like a scarecrow, but the yellow shark swerved past him, and as it did so a coin was tossed into the air by the driver, or by the shape that could only *be* the driver, for there was nothing else at the wheel but something in a sheet.

It was gone as quietly as it had arrived and Titus turned his face to the beggar, who had retrieved the coin. Seeing that he was being scrutinized the beggar leered at Titus and threw out his tongue like the mildewed tongue of a boot. Then to Titus's amazement the foul old man swung back his head and, dropping the silver coin into his mouth, swallowed it at a gulp.

'Tell me, you dirty old man,' said Titus softly, for a kind of hot anger filled him and a desire to squash the creature beneath his feet, 'why do you eat money?' And Titus picked up a rock from beside the road.

'Whelp!' said the beggar at last. 'Do you think I'd *waste* my wealth? Coins are too big, you dog, to sidle through me. Too small to kill me. Too heavy to be lost! I am a beggar.'

'You are a travesty,' said Titus, 'and when you die the earth will breathe again.'

Titus dropped the heavy stone he had lifted in anger, and with not a backward glance made for the right-hand fork where, with a prodigious sigh, an avenue of cedars inhaled him, as though he were a gnat.

SEVENTEEN

TREE after tree slid by to the pace of his footsteps. In the gloom of the cedars his heart was happy. Happy in the chill of the tunnel. Happy in the danger of it all. Happy to remember his own childhood and how he had acquitted himself in a tract of ivy. Happy in spite of the helmeted spies, though they awoke within him a dark alarm.

He had lived on his wits for what seemed so long a while that he was very different now from the youth who had ridden away.

It had seemed that the avenue was endless, but suddenly and unexpectedly the last of the cedars floated away behind him as though from a laying-on of hands, and the wide sky looked down, and there before him was the first of the *structures*.

He had heard of them but had not expected anything quite so far removed from the buildings he had known, let alone the architecture of Gormenghast.

The first to catch his eye was a pale-green edifice, very elegant, but so simple in design that Titus's gaze could find no resting place upon its slippery surface.

Next to this building was a copper dome the shape of an igloo but ninety feet in height, with a tapering mast, spider-frail and glinting in the sunlight. An ugly crow was sitting on the cross-tree and fouling from time to time the bright dome beneath.

Titus sat down by the side of the road and frowned. He had been born and bred to the assumption that buildings were ancient by nature, and were and always had been in the process of crumbling away. The white dust lolling between the gaping bricks; the worm in the wood. The weed dislodging the stone; corrosion and mildew; the crumbling patina; the fading shades; the beauty of decay.

Unable to remain seated, for his curiosity was stronger than his longing to rest, he got to his feet and, wondering why there was no one about, began to make his way to whatever lay beyond the dome, for the buildings curved away as though to obscure some great circle or arena. And indeed it was something of this kind that broke upon his view as he rounded the dome, and he came to a halt through sheer amazement;

for it was *vast*. Vast as a grey desert, its marble surface glowing with a dull opaque light. The only thing that could be said to break the emptiness was the reflection of the structures that surrounded it.

The farthest away of these buildings, in other words those that fanned out in a glittering arc on the opposite side of the arena, were, to Titus's gaze, no larger than stamps, thorns, nails, acorns, or tiny crystals, save for one gigantic edifice out-topping all the rest, which was like an azure match-box on its end.

EIGHTEEN

HAD Titus come across a world of dragons he could hardly have been more amazed than by these fantasies of glass and metal; and he turned himself about more than once as though it were possible to catch a last glimpse of the tortuous, poverty-stricken town he had left behind him, but the district of Muzzlehatch was hidden away by a fold in the hills, and the ruins of Gormenghast were afloat in a haze of time and space.

And yet, though his eyes shone with the thrill of his discovery, he suffered at the same time a pang of resentment – a resentment that this alien realm should be able to exist in a world that appeared to have no reference to his home and which seemed, in fact, supremely self-sufficient. A region that had never heard of Fuchsia and her death, nor of her father, the melancholy earl, nor of his mother the countess with her strange liquid whistle that brought wild birds to her from distant spinneys.

Were they coeval; were they simultaneous? These worlds; these realms – could they *both* be true? Were there no bridges? Was there no common land? Did the same sun shine upon them? Had they the constellations of the night in common?

When the storm came down upon these crystal structures, and the sky was black with rain, what of Gormenghast? Was Gormenghast dry? And when the thunder growled in his ancient home was there never any echo hereabouts?

What of the rivers? Were they separate? Was there no tributary, even, to feel its way into another world?

Where lay the long horizons? Where throbbed the frontiers? O terrible division! The near and the far. The night and the day. The yes and the no.

A VOICE. 'O Titus, can't you remember?'
TITUS. 'I can remember everything except . . .'

VOICE. 'Except . . . ?'

TITUS. 'Except the way.'

VOICE. 'The way where?'

TITUS. 'The way home.'

VOICE. 'Home?'

TITUS. 'Home. Home where the dust gathers and the legends are. But I have lost my bearings.'

VOICE. 'You have the sun and the North Star.'

TITUS. 'But is it the same sun? And are the stars the stars of Gormenghast?'

He looked up and was surprised to find himself alone. His hands were cold with sweat, and the dread of being lost and having no proof of his own identity filled him with a sudden stabbing terror.

He looked about him at this sheer and foreign land, and then, all in a breath, something fled across the sky. It made no sound other than the slither of a finger across a slate, though it seemed to have passed as close as a scythe.

By now it was settling, a speck of crimson on the far side of the marble desert where the furthest mansions glinted. It had seemed to have no wings but an incredible purpose and beauty, like a stiletto or a needle, and as Titus fixed his eyes upon the building in whose shadow it lay, he thought he could see not one, but a swarm.

And this was so. Not only was there already quite a fleet of fish-shaped, needle-shaped, knife-shaped, shark-shaped, splinter-shaped devices, but all kinds of land-machines of curious design.

NINETEEN

BEFORE him lay stretched the grey marble, a thousand acres of it, with its margins filled with the reflections of the mansions.

To walk alone across it, in view of all the distant windows, terraces, and roof-gardens was to proclaim arrogance, naked and culpable. But this is what he did, and when he had been walking for some while a small green dart detached itself from the planes on the far side of the arena and sped towards him, its glass-green belly skimming the marble, and an instant later it was upon him, only to veer at the last moment and sing away into the stratosphere, only to plunge, only to circle Titus's head in narrowing gyres, only to return like a whippet of the air to the black mansion.

Bewildered, startled as he was, Titus began to laugh, though his laughter was not altogether without a touch of hysteria.

This exquisite beast of the air; this wingless swallow; this aerial leopard; this fish of the water-sky; this threader of moonbeams; this dandy of the dawn; this metal play-boy; this wanderer in black spaces; this flash in the night; this drinker of its own speed; this godlike child of a diseased brain – what did it do?

What did it do but act like any other petty snooper, prying upon man and child, sucking information as a bat sucks blood; amoral; mindless; sent out on empty missions, acting as its maker would act, its narrow-headed maker – so that its beauty was a thing on its own, beautiful only because its function shapes it so; and having no heart it becomes fatuous – a fatuous reflection of a fatuous concept – so that it is incongruous, or gobbles incongruity to such an outlandish degree that laughter is the only way out.

And so Titus laughed, and as he laughed, high-pitched and uncontrolled (for at the back of it all he was scared and little relished the idea of being singled out, pin-pointed, and examined by a mechanical brain), while he laughed, he began at the same time to run, for there was something ominous in the air, ominous and ludicrous – something that told him that to stay any longer on this marble tract was to court trouble, to be held a vagrant, a spy, or a madman.

Indeed the sky was beginning to fill with every shape of craft, and little clusters of people were spreading out across the arena like a stain.

TWENTY

SEEN from above Titus must have appeared very small as he ran on and on. Seen from above, it could also be realized how isolated in the wide world was the arena with its bright circumference of crystal buildings: how bizarre and ingenious it was, and how unrelated it was to the bone-white, cave-pocked, barren mountains, the fever-swamps and jungles to the south, the thirsty lands, the hungry cities, and the tracts beyond of the wolf and the outlaw.

It was when Titus was within a hundred yards of the olive palace, and as the princes of maintenance turned or paused in their work to stare at the ragged youth, that a gun boomed, and for a few minutes there was a complete silence, for everyone stopped talking and the engines were shut off in every craft.

This gun-boom had come just in time, for had it been delayed a moment longer Titus must surely have been grabbed and questioned. Two men, halted in their tracks by the detonation, drew back their lips from their teeth and scowled with frustration, their hands halted in mid-air.

On every side of him were faces; faces for the most part turned towards him. Malignant faces, speculative faces, empty faces, ingenuous faces – faces of all kinds. It was quite obvious that he would never pass unnoticed. From being lost and obscure he was the focus of attention. Now, as they posed at every angle, as stiff as scarecrows caught in the full flight of living, their half-way gestures frozen – now was his time to escape.

He had no idea of the significance which was presumably attached to the firing of the cannon. As it was he was served well by his own ignorance and with a pounding heart he ran like a deer, dodging this way and that way through the crowd until he came to the most majestic of the palaces. Racing up the shallow glass pavements and into the weird and lucent gloom of the great halls, it was not long before he had left the custom-shackled hierophants behind him. It is true that there was a great number of persons scattered about the floor of the building who stared at Titus whenever he came into their range of vision. They could not turn their heads to follow him, nor even their eyes because the cannon had boomed, but when he passed across their vision they knew at once he was not one of them and that he had no right to be in the olive palace. And then as he ran on and on the cannon boomed again and at once Titus knew that the world was after him, for the air became torn with cries and counter-cries, and suddenly four men turned a corner of the long glass corridor, their reflections in the glazed floor as detailed and as crisp as their true selves.

'There he goes,' cried a voice. 'There go the rags!' But when they reached the spot where Titus had halted for a moment they found he was indeed gone and all they had to stare at were the closed doors of a lift shaft.

Titus, who had found himself cornered, had turned to the vast, purring, topaz-studded lift not knowing exactly what it was. That its elegant jaws should have been open and ready was his salvation. He sprang inside and the gates, drawing themselves together, closed as though they ran through butter.

The interior of the lift was like an underwater grotto, filled with subdued lights. Something hazy and voluptuous seemed to hover in the air. But Titus was in no mood for subtleties. He was a fugitive. And then he saw that wavering in his underwater world were rows of ivory buttons, each button carved into some flower, face, or skull.

He could hear the sound of footsteps running and angry voices outside the door and he jabbed indiscriminately among the buttons, and immediately soaring through floor after floor in a whirl of steel the lift all at once inhaled its own speed and the doors slid open of their own accord.

How quiet it was and cool. There was no furniture, only a single palm tree growing out of the floor. A small red parrot sat on one of the upper branches and pecked itself. When it saw Titus it cocked its head on one side and then with great rapidity it kept repeating, 'Bloody corker told me so!' This phrase was reiterated a dozen times at least before the bird continued pecking at its wing.

There were four doors in this cool upper hall. Three led to corridors but the last one, when Titus opened it, let in the sky. There, before and slightly below him, lay spread the roof.

TWENTY-ONE

No one found him all that sun-scorched evening and when the twilight came and the shadows withered he was able to steal to and fro across the wide glass roofscape and see what was going on in the rooms below.

For the most part the glass was too thick for Titus to see more than a blur of coloured shapes and shadows but he came at last to an open skylight through which he could see without obstruction a scene of great diversity and splendour.

To say a party was in progress would be a mean and cheese-paring way of putting it. The long sitting-room or salon, no more than twelve or fifteen feet below him, was in the throes of it. Life, of a kind, was in spate.

Music leaped from the long room and swarmed out of the skylight while Titus lay on his stomach on the warm glass roof, his eyes wide with conjecture. The sunken sun had left behind it a dim red weight of air. The stars were growing fiercer every moment, when the music suddenly ended in a string of notes like coloured bubbles and to take their place a hundred tongues began to wag at once.

Titus half closed his eyes at the effulgence of a forest of candles, the sparkle of glass and mirrors, and the leaping reflections of light from polished wood and silver. It was so close to him that had he coughed a dozen faces would, for all the noise in the room, have turned at once to the skylight and discovered him. It was like nothing else he had seen, and even from the first glimpse, it appeared as much like a gathering of creatures, of birds and beasts and flowers, as a gathering of humans.

They were all there. The giraffe-men and the hippopotamus-men.

The serpent-ladies and the heron-ladies. The aspens and the oaks: the thistles and the ferns – the beetles and the moths – the crocodiles and the parrots: the tigers and the lambs: vultures with pearls around their necks and bison in tails.

But this was only for a flash, for as Titus, drawing a deep breath, stared again, the distortions, the extremes, appeared to crumble, to slip away from the surge of heads below him, and he was again among his own species.

Titus could feel the heat rising from the long dazzling room so close below him – yet distant as a rainbow. The hot air as it rose was impregnated with scent; a dozen of the most expensive perfumes were fighting for survival. Everything was fighting for survival – with lungs, and credulity.

There were limbs and heads and bodies everywhere: and there were *faces*! There were the foreground faces; the middle distance faces; and the faces far away. And in the irregular gaps *between* the faces were *parts* of faces, and halves and quarters at every tilt and angle.

This panorama in depth was on the move, whole heads turning, now here, now there, while all the while a counterpoint of tadpole quickness, something in the nature of a widespread agitation, was going on, because, for every head or body that changed its position in space there would be a hundred flickering eyelids; a hundred fluttering lips, a fluctuating arabesque of hands. The whole effect had something in the nature of foliage about it, as when green breezes flirt in poplar trees.

Commanding as was Titus's view of the human sea below him, yet however hard he tried he could not discover who the hosts might be. Presumably an hour or two earlier when even a deep breath was possible without adding to the discomfort of some shoulder or adjacent bosom – presumably the ornate flunkey (now pinned against a marble statue) had announced the names of the guests as they arrived; but all that was over. The flunkey, whose head, much to his embarrassment, was wedged between the ample breasts of the marble statue, could no longer even see the door through which the guests arrived, let alone draw breath enough to announce them.

Titus, watching from above, marvelled at the spectacle and while he lay there on the roof, a half-moon above him, with its chill and greenish light, and the warm glow of the party below him, was able not only to take in the diversity of the guests but, in regard to those who stood immediately below him, to overhear their conversation . . .

TWENTY-TWO

'THANK heavens it's all over now.'

'What is?'

'My youth. It took too long and got in my way.'

'In your *way* Mr Thirst? How do you mean?'

'It went on for so *long*,' said Thirst. 'I had about thirty years of it. You know what I mean. Experiment, experiment, experiment. And now . . .'

'Ah!' whispered someone.

'I used to write poems,' said Thirst, a pale man. He made as if to place his hands upon the shoulder of his confidant, but the crush was too great. 'It passed the time away.'

'Poems,' said a pontifical voice from just behind their shoulders, '. . . should make time stand *still*.'

The pale man, who had jumped a little, merely muttered, 'Mine didn't,' before he turned to observe the gentleman who had interpolated. The stranger's face was quite inexpressive and it was hard to believe that he had opened his mouth. But now there was another tongue at large.

'Talking of poems,' it said, and it belonged to a dark, cadaverous, over-distinguished nostril-flaring man with a long blue jaw and chronic eyestrain, 'reminds me of a poem.'

'I wonder why,' said Thirst irritably, for he had been on the brink of expansion.

The man with eyestrain took no notice of the remark.

'The poem which I am reminded of is one which I wrote myself.'

A bald man knitted his brows; the pontifical gentleman lit a cigar, his face as expressionless as ever; and a lady, the lobes of whose ears had been ruined by the weight of two gigantic sapphires, half opened her mouth with an inane smirk of anticipation.

The dark man with eyestrain folded his hands before him.

'It didn't come off,' he said, '– although it had *something* –' (he twisted his lips). 'Sixty-four stanzas in fact.' (He raised his eyes.) '– Yes, yes – it was very, very long and ambitious – but it didn't come off. And why . . . ?'

He paused, not because he wanted any suggestions, but in order to take a deep, meditative breath.

'I will tell you why, my friends. It didn't come off because you see, it was *verse* all the time.'

'*Blank* verse?' inquired the lady, whose head was bent forward by the weight of the sapphires. She was eager to be helpful. 'Was it *blank* verse?'

'It went like this,' said the dark man, unclasping his hands before him and clasping them behind him, and at the same time placing the heel of his left shoe immediately in front of the toe of his right shoe so that the two feet formed a single and unbroken line of leather. 'It went like this.' He lifted his head. 'But do not forget it is *not* Poetry – except perhaps for three *singing* lines at the outside.'

'Well, for the love of Parnassus – let's *have* it,' broke in the petulant voice of Mr Thirst who, finding his thunder stolen, was no longer interested in good manners.

'A-l-t-h-o-u-g-h,' mused the man with the long blue jaw, who seemed to consider other people's time and patience as inexhaustible commodities like air, or water, 'a-l-t-h-o-u-g-h,' (he lingered over the word like a nurse over a sick child), 'there *were* those who said the whole thing *sang*; who hailed it as the purest poetry of our generation – "incandescent stuff" as one gentleman put it – but there you are – there you are – how is one to tell?'

'Ah,' whispered a voice of curds and whey. And a man with gold teeth turned his eyes to the lady with the sapphires, and they exchanged the arch expression of those who find themselves, however unworthily, to be witnesses at an historic moment.

'Quiet please,' said the poet. 'And listen carefully.'

A mule at prayer! Ignore him: turn to me
Until the gold contraption of our love
Rattles its seven biscuit boxes, and the sea
Withdraws its combers from the rhubarb-grove.

This is no place for maudlin-headed fays
To smirk behind their mushrooms! 't is a shore
For gaping daemons: it is such a place,
As I, my love, have long been looking for.

Here, where the rhubarb-grove into the wave
Throws down its rueful image, we can fly
Our kites of love, above the sandy grave,
Of those long lost in ambiguity.

For love is ripest in a rhubarb-grove
Where weird reflections glimmer through the dawn:
O vivid essence vegetably wove
Of hues that die, the moment they are born.

Lost in the venal void our dreams deflate
By easy stages through green atmosphere:
Imagination's bright balloon is late,
Like the blue whale, in coming up for air.

It is not known what genus of the wild
Black plums of thought best wrinkle, twitch and flow
Into sweet wisdom's prune – for in the mild
Orchards of love there is no need to know.

What use to cry for Capricorn? it sails
Across the heart's red atlas: it is found
Only within the ribs, where all the tails
The tempest has are whisking it around.

No time for tears: it is enough, today,
That we, meandering these granular shores
Should watch the ponderous billows at their play
Like midnight beasts with garlands in their jaws . . .

It was obvious that the poem was still in its early stages. The novelty of seeing so distinguished-looking a man behave in a manner so blatant, so self-centred, so withdrawn at one and the same time had intrigued Titus so keenly that he had outlasted at least thirty guests since the poem started. The lady with the sapphires and Mr Thirst had long since edged away, but a floating population surrounded the poet who had become sightless as he declaimed, and it would have been all the same to him if he had been alone in the room.

Titus turned his head away, his brain jumping in his skull with words and images.

TWENTY-THREE

Now that the poem was gone, and gone with it the poet, for truly he seemed to follow in the wake of something greater than himself, Titus became aware of a strange condition, a quality of flux, an agitation; a weaving or a *threading* motion – and then, all at once, one of those tidal movements that occur from time to time at crowded parties, began to manifest itself. There is nothing that can be done about them. They move to a rhythm of their own.

The first sensation perceived by the guest was that he or she was off-balance. There was a lot of elbow-jogging and spirit-spilling. As the pressure increased a kind of delicate stampeding began. Apologies broke loose on every side. Those by the walls were seriously crushed, while those in the centre leaned across one another at intimate angles. Tiny, idiotic footsteps were taken by everyone as the crowd began to surge meaninglessly, uncontrollably, round and round the room. Those who were talking together at one moment saw no sign of one another a few seconds later, for underwater currents and cross-eddies took their toll.

And yet the guests were still arriving. They entered through the doorway, were caught up in the scented air, wavered like ghosts and, hovering for a moment on the coiling fumes, were drawn into the slow but invincible maelstrom.

Titus, who had not been able to foresee what was about to happen, was now able to appreciate in retrospect the actions of a couple of old roués whom he had observed a few minutes earlier, seated by the refreshment table.

Long versed in the vicissitudes of party phenomena, they had put down their glasses and, leaning back, as it were, in the arms of the current, had given themselves up to the flow, and were now to be seen conversing at an incredible angle as they circled the room, their feet no longer touching the floor.

By the time some balance was restored it was nearly midnight, and there was a general pulling down of cuffs, straightening of garments, fingering of coifs and toupees, a straightening of ties, a scrutiny of mouths and eyebrows and a general state of salvage.

TWENTY-FOUR

AND so, by a whim of chance, yet another group of guests stood there beneath him. Some had limped and some had slipped away. Some had been boisterous: some had been aloof.

This particular group were neither and both, as the off-shoots of their brain-play merited. Tall guests they were, and witless that through the accident of their height and slenderness they were creating between them a grove – a human grove. They turned, this group, this grove of guests, turned as a newcomer, moving sideways an inch at a time, joined them. He was short, thick and sapless, and was most inappropriate in that lofty copse, where he gave the appearance of being pollarded.

One of this group, a slender creature, thin as a switch, swathed in black, her hair as black as her dress and her eyes as black as her hair, turned to the newcomer.

'Do join us,' she said. 'Do talk to us. We need your steady brain. We are so pitifully emotional. *Such* babies.'

'Well I would hardly –'

'Be quiet, Leonard. You have been talking quite enough,' said the slender, doe-eyed Mrs Grass to her fourth husband. 'It is Mr Acreblade or nothing. Come along dear Mr Acreblade. There . . . we are . . . there . . . we are.'

The sapless Mr Acreblade thrust his jaw forward, a sight to be wondered at, for even when relaxed his chin gave the impression of a battering ram; something to prod with; in fact a *weapon*.

'Dear Mrs Grass,' he said, 'you are always so unaccountably kind.'

The attenuate Mr Spill had been beckoning a waiter, but now he suddenly crouched down so that his ear was level with Acreblade's mouth. He did not face Mr Acreblade as he crouched there, but swivelling his eyes to their eastern extremes, he obtained a very good view of Acreblade's profile.

'I'm a bit deaf,' he said. 'Will you repeat yourself? Did you say "unaccountably kind"? How droll.'

'Don't be a bore,' said Mrs Grass.

Mr Spill rose to his full working height, which might have been even more impressive were his shoulders not so bent.

'Dear lady,' he said. 'If I am a bore, who made me so?'

'Well who *did* darling?'

'It's a long story –'

'Then we'll skip it, shall we?'

She turned herself slowly, swivelling on her pelvis until her small conical breasts, directed at Mr Kestrel, were for all the world like some kind of delicious *threat*. Her husband, Mr Grass, who had seen this manoeuvre at least a hundred times, yawned horribly.

'Tell me,' said Mrs Grass, as she let loose upon Mr Kestrel a fresh broadside of naked eroticism, 'tell me, dear Mr Acreblade, all about *yourself*.'

Mr Acreblade, not really enjoying being addressed in this off-hand manner by Mrs Grass, turned to her husband.

'Your wife is very special. Very rare. Conducive to speculation. She talks to me through the back of her head, staring at Kestrel the while.'

'But that is as it should be!' cried Kestrel, his eyes swimming over with excitement, 'for life must be various, incongruous, vile and electric. Life must be ruthless and as full of love as may be found in a jaguar's fang.'

'I like the way you talk, young man,' said Grass, 'but I don't know *what* you're saying.'

'What are you mumbling about?' said the lofty Spill, bending one of his arms like the branch of a tree and cupping his ear with a bunch of twigs.

'You are somewhat divine,' whispered Kestrel, addressing Mrs Grass.

'I think I spoke to you, dear,' said Mrs Grass over her shoulder to Mr Acreblade.

'Your wife is talking to me again,' said Acreblade to Mr Grass. 'Let's hear what she has to say.'

'You talk about my wife in a very peculiar way,' said Grass. 'Does she annoy you?'

'She would if I lived with her,' said Acreblade. 'What about you?'

'O, but my dear chap, how naïve you are! Being *married* to her I seldom *see* her. What is the point of getting married if one is always bumping into one's wife? One might as well not be married. Oh no dear fellow, she does what she wants. It is quite a coincidence that we found each other here tonight. You see? And we enjoy it – it's like first love all over again without the heartache – without the *heart* in fact. Cold love's the loveliest love of all. So clear, so crisp, so empty. In short, so civilized.'

'You are out of a legend,' said Kestrel, in a voice that was so muffled with passion that Mrs Grass was quite unaware that she had been addressed.

'I'm as hot as a boiled turnip,' said Mr Spill.

'But tell me, you horrid man, how do I feel?' cried Mrs Grass as she saw a newcomer, lacerating her beauty with the edge of her voice. 'I'm looking so well these days, even my husband said so, and you know what husbands are.'

'I have no idea what they *are*,' said the fox-like man newly arrived at her elbow, 'but you must tell me. What are they? I only know what they become . . . and perhaps . . . what drove them to it.'

'Oh, but you are *clever*. Wickedly clever. But you must tell me all. How *am* I, darling?'

The fox-like man (a narrow-chested creature with reddish hair above his ears, a very sharp nose and a brain far too large for him to manage with comfort) replied:

'You are feeling, my dear Mrs Grass, in need of something sweet. Sugar, bad music, or something of that kind might do for a start.'

The black-eyed creature, her lips half open, her teeth shining like pearls, her eyes fixed with excited animation on the foxy face before her, clasped her delicate hands together at her conical breasts.

'You're quite right! O, but *quite*!' she said breathlessly. 'So absolutely and miraculously *right*, you brilliant, *brilliant* little man; something sweet is what I *need*!'

Meanwhile Mr Acreblade was making room for a long-faced character dressed in a lion's pelt. Over his head and shoulders was a black mane.

'Isn't it a bit hot in there?' said young Kestrel.

'I am in agony,' said the man in the tawny skin.

'Then why?' said Mrs Grass.

'I thought it was Fancy Dress,' said the skin, 'but I mustn't complain. Everyone has been most kind.'

'That doesn't help the heat you're generating in there,' said Mr Acreblade. 'Why don't you just whip it off?'

'It's all I have on,' said the lion's pelt.

'How delicious,' cried Mrs Grass, 'you thrill me utterly. Who are you?'

'But my *dear*,' said the lion, looking at Mrs Grass, 'surely you . . .'

'What is it, O King of Beasts?'

'Can't you remember me?'

'Your nose seems to ring a bell,' said Mrs Grass.

Mr Spill lowered his head out of the clouds of smoke. Then he swivelled it until it lay alongside Mr Kestrel. 'What did she say?' he asked.

'She's worth a million,' said Kestrel. 'Lively, luscious, what a plaything!'

'Plaything?' said Mr Spill. 'How do you mean?'

'You wouldn't understand,' said Kestrel.

The lion scratched himself with a certain charm. Then he addressed Mrs Grass.

'So my nose rings a bell – is that all? Have you forgotten me? *Me!* Your one-time Harry?'

'Harry? What . . . my . . . ?'

'Yes, your Second. Way back in time. We were married, you remember, in Tyson Street.'

'Lovebird!' cried Mrs Grass. 'So we *were*. But take that foul mane off and let me see you. Where have you been all these years?'

'In the wilderness,' said the lion, tossing back his mane, and twitching it over his shoulder.

'What sort of wilderness, darling? Moral? Spiritual? O but tell us about it!' Mrs Grass reached forward with her breasts and clenched her little fists at her sides, which attitude she imagined would have appeal. She was not far wrong, and young Kestrel took a step to the left which put him close behind her.

'I believe you said "wilderness",' said Kestrel. 'Tell me, how wild *is* it? Or isn't it? One is so at the mercy of words. And would you say, sir, that what is wilderness for one might be a field of corn to another with little streams and bushes?'

'What sort of bushes?' said the elongated Mr Spill.

'What does that matter?' said Kestrel.

'*Everything* matters,' said Mr Spill. '*Everything*. That is part of the pattern. The world is bedevilled by people thinking that some things matter and some things don't. Everything is of equal importance. The

wheel must be complete. And the stars. They *look* small. But are they?
No. They are large. Some are very large. Why, I remember –'

'Mr Kestrel,' said Mrs Grass.

'Yes, my dear lady?'

'You have a vile habit, dear.'

'What is it, for heaven's sake? Tell me about it that I may crush it.'

'You are too *close*, my pet. But *too* close. We have our little areas you
know. Like the home waters, dear, or fishing rights. Don't trespass,
dear. Withdraw a little. You know what I mean, don't you? Privacy is
so important.'

Young Kestrel turned the colour of a boiled lobster and retreated
from Mrs Grass who, turning her head to him, by way of forgiveness
switched on a light in her face, or so it seemed to Kestrel, a light that
inflamed the air about them with a smile like an eruption. This had the
effect of drawing the dazzled Kestrel back to her side, where he stayed,
bathing himself in her beauty.

'Cosy again,' she whispered.

Kestrel nodded his head and trembled with excitement until Mr
Grass, forcing his way through a wall of guests, brought his foot down
sharply upon Kestrel's instep. With a gasp of pain, young Kestrel
turned for sympathy to the peerless lady at his side, only to find that her
radiant smile was now directed at her own husband where it remained
for a few moments before she turned her back on them both and,
switching off the current, she gazed across the room with an aspect
quite drained of animation.

'On the other hand,' said the tall Spill, addressing the man in the
lion's pelt, 'there is something in the young man's question. This
wilderness of yours. Will you tell us more about it?'

'But oh! But do!' rang out the voice of Mrs Grass, as she gripped the
lion's pelt cruelly.

'When I say "wilderness",' said the lion, 'I only speak of the heart.
It is Mr Acreblade that you should ask. His wasteland is the very earth
itself.'

'Ah me, that Wasteland,' said Acreblade, jutting out his chin,
'knuckled with ferrous mountains. Peopled with termites, jackals, and
to the north-west – hermits.'

'And what were *you* doing out there?' said Mr Spill.

'I shadowed a suspect. A youth not known in these parts. He
stumbled ahead of me in the sandstorm, a vague shape. Sometimes
I lost him altogether. Sometimes I all but found myself beside him,
and was forced to retreat a little way. Sometimes I heard his singing,
mad, wild inconsequential songs. Sometimes he shouted out as
though he were delirious – words that sounded like "Fuchsia",
"Flay" and other names. Sometimes he cried out "Mother!" and

once he fell on his knees and cried, "Gormenghast, Gormenghast, come back to me again!"

'It was not for me to arrest him – but to follow him, for my superiors informed me his papers were not in order, or even in *existence*.

'But on the second evening the dust rose up more terribly than ever, and as it rose it blinded me so that I lost him in a red and gritty cloud. I could not find him, and I never found him again.'

'Darling.'

'What is it?'

'Look at Gumshaw.'

'Why?'

'His polished pate reflects a brace of candles.'

'Not from where I am.'

'No?'

'No. But look – to the left of centre I see a tiny image, one might almost say of a boy's face, were it not that faces are unlikely things to grow on ceilings.'

'Dreams. One always comes back to dreams.'

'But the silver whip RK 2053722220 – the moon circles, first of the new –'

'Yes, I know all about that.'

'But love was nowhere near.'

'The sky was smothered with planes. Some of them, though pilotless, were bleeding.'

'Ah, Mr Flax, how is your son?'

'He died last Wednesday.'

'Forgive me, I am so sorry.'

'Are you? I'm not. I never liked him. But mark you – an excellent swimmer. He was captain of his school.'

'This heat is horrible.'

'Ah, Lady Crowgather, let me present the Duke of Crowgather; but perhaps you have met already?'

'Many times. Where are the cucumber sandwiches?'

'Allow me –'

'Oh I beg your pardon. I mistook your foot for a tortoise. What is happening?'

'No, indeed, I do not like it.'

'Art should be artless, not heartless.'

'I am a great one for beauty.'

'Beauty, that obsolete word.'

'You beg the question, Professor Salvage.'

'I beg nothing. Not even your pardon. I do not even beg to differ. I differ without begging, and would rather beg from an ancient, rib-staring, sightless groveller at the foot of a column than beg from you, sir. The truth is not in you, and your feet smell.'

'Take that . . . and that,' muttered the insultee, tearing off one button after another from his opponent's jacket.

'What fun we do have,' said the button-loser, standing on tip-toe and kissing his friend's chin: 'Parties would be unbearable without abuse, so don't go away Harold. You sicken me. What is that?'

'It is only Marblecrust making his bird noises.'

'Yes, but . . .'

'Always, somehow . . .'

'O no . . . no . . . and yet I like it.'

'And so the young man escaped me without knowing,' said Acreblade, 'and judging by the hardship he must have undergone he must surely be somewhere in the City . . . where else could he be? Has he stolen a plane? Has he fled down the . . . ?'

TWENTY-FIVE

THEN came the stroke of midnight, and for a few moments gooseflesh ran up every leg in Lady Cusp-Canine's party, swarmed up the thighs and mustered its hideous forces at the base of every backbone, sending forth grisly outriders throughout the lumbar landscape. Then up the spine itself, coiling like lethal ivy, fanning out, eventually, from the cervicals, draping like icy muslin across the breasts and belly. Midnight. As the last cold crash resounds, Titus, alone on the rooftop, easing the cramp in his arm, shifting the weight of his elbow, smashes suddenly the skylight and with no time to recover, falls through the glass roof in a shower of splinters.

TWENTY-SIX

IT was very lucky for all concerned that no one was seriously hurt. Titus himself was cut in a few places but the wounds were superficial and as far as the actual fall was concerned, he was particularly fortunate in that a dome-shouldered, snowball-breasted lady was immediately below him as he fell.

They capsized together, and lay for a moment alongside one another on the thickly carpeted floor. All about them glittered fragments of broken glass, but for Juno, lying at Titus's side, and for the others who had been affected by his sudden appearance in mid-air and later on the floor, the overriding sensation was not pain but shock.

For there was something that was shocking in more than one sense in the almost biblical visitation of a youth in rags.

Titus withdrew his face, which had been crushed against a naked shoulder, and got dizzily to his feet, and as he did so he saw that the lady's eyes were fixed upon him. Even in her horizontal position she was superb. Her dignity was unimpaired. When Titus reached down to her with his hand to help her she touched his finger-tips and rose at once and with no apparent effort to her feet, which were small and very beautiful. Between these little feet of hers and her noble, Roman head, lay, as though between the poles, a golden world of spices.

Someone bent over the boy. It was the Fox.

'Who the devil are you?' he said.

'What does that matter?' said Juno. 'Keep your distance. He is bleeding . . . Isn't that enough?' and with quite indescribable *élan* she tore a strip from her dress and began to bind up Titus's hand, which was bleeding steadily.

'You are very kind,' said Titus.

Juno softly shook her head from side to side, and a little smile evolved out of the corner of her generous lips.

'I must have startled you,' said Titus.

'It was a rapid introduction,' said Juno. She arched one of her eyebrows. It rose like a raven's wing.

TWENTY-SEVEN

'DID you hear what he said?' snarled a vile voice. ' "*I must have startled you.*" Why, you mongrel-pup, you might have killed the lady!'

An angry buzz of voices suddenly began and scores of faces raised themselves to the shattered skylight. At the same time a nearby section of the crowd, which until a few moments ago had appeared to be full of friendly flippancy, was now wearing a very different aspect.

'Which one of you,' said Titus, whose face had gone white, 'which one of you called me a mongrel-pup?' In the pocket of his ragged trousers his hand clenched the knuckle of flint from the high towers of Gormenghast.

'Who was it?' he yelled, for all at once rage boiled up in him, and jumping forward he caught the nearest figure by the throat. But no sooner had he done so than he was himself hauled back to his position at Juno's side. Then Titus saw before him the back of a great angular man, on whose shoulder sat a small ape. This figure whose proportions were unmistakably those of Muzzlehatch now moved very slowly along the half-circle of angry faces and as he did so he smiled with a smile that had no love in it. It was a wide smile. It was a lipless smile. It was made up of nothing but anatomy.

Muzzlehatch stretched out his big arm: his hand hovered and then took hold of the man who had insulted Titus, picked him up and raised him through the hot and coiling air to the level of his shoulder, where he was received by the ape who kissed him upon the back of his neck in such a way that the poor man collapsed in a dead faint, and then, since the ape had already lost interest in him, he slid to the carpeted floor.

Muzzlehatch turned to the gaping circle of faces and whispered 'Little children. Listen to Oracle. Because Oracle loves you,' and Muzzlehatch drew a wicked-looking penknife from his pocket, flicked it open and began to strop it upon the ball of his thumb.

'He is not pleased with you. Not so much because you have done anything wicked but because your Soul smells – your collective *Soul* – your little dried-up turd of a Soul. Is it not so? Little Ones?'

The ape began to scratch itself with slow relish and its eyelids trembled.

'So you would *menace* him, would you?' said Muzzlehatch. 'Menace him with your dirty little brains, and horrid little noises. And you, ladies, with your false bosoms and ignorant mouths. You also have menaced him?'

There was a good deal of shuffling and coughing; and those who were able to do so without being seen began to retreat into the crowded body of the room.

'Little children,' he went on, the blade of his knife moving to and fro across his thumb, 'pick up your colleague from the floor and learn from him to keep your hands off this pip-squeak of a boy.'

'He is no pip-squeak,' said Acreblade. 'That is the youth I have been trailing. He escaped me. He crossed the wilderness. He has no passport. He is wanted. Come here, young man.'

There was a hush that spread all over the room.

'What nonsense,' said a deep voice at last. It was Juno. 'He is my friend. As for the wilderness – good Heavens – you misconstrue the rags. He is in fancy dress.'

'Move aside, madam. I have a warrant for his arrest as a vagrant; an alien; an undesirable.'

Then he moved forward, did this Acreblade, out of the crowd of guests, forward towards where Titus, Juno, Muzzlehatch and the ape waited silently.

'Beautiful policeman,' said Muzzlehatch. 'You are exceeding your duty. This is a party – or it was – but you are making something vile out of it.'

Muzzlehatch worked his shoulders to and fro and shut his eyes.

'Don't you ever have a holiday from crime? Do you never pick up the world as a child picks up a crystal globe – a thing of many colours? Do you never love this ridiculous world of ours? The wicked and the good of it? The thieves and angels of it? The all of it? Throbbing, dear policeman, in your hand? And knowing how all this is inevitably so, and that without the dark of life you would be out on your ear? Yet see how you take it. Passports, visas, identification papers – does all this mean so much to your official mind that you must needs bring the filthy stink of it to a party? Open up the gates of your brain then, policeman dear, and let a small sprat through.'

'He is my friend,' said Juno again, in a voice as ripe and deep as some underwater grotto, some foliage of the sea-bed. 'He is in fancy dress. He is as nothing to you. What was it you said? "Across the wilderness?" Oh ha ha ha ha ha,' and Juno, having received a cue from Muzzlehatch, moved forward and in a moment had blocked Mr Acreblade's vision, and as she did this she saw away to her left, their heads a little above the heads of the crowd, two men in helmets who appeared to slide rather than walk. To Juno they were merely two of the guests and meant nothing more, but when Muzzlehatch saw them he gripped Titus by the arm just above the elbow and made for the door, leaving behind him a channel among the guests like the channel left on a field of ripe corn where a file of children has followed its leader.

Inspector Acreblade was trying very hard to follow them but every time he turned or made a few steps his passage was blocked by the generous Juno, a lady with such a superb carriage and such noble proportions, that to push past her was out of the question.

'Please allow me –' he said. 'I must follow them at once.'

'But your tie, you cannot go about like that. Let me adjust it for you. No . . . no . . . don't move. Th-ere we are . . . There . . . we . . . are . . .'

TWENTY-EIGHT

MEANWHILE Titus and Muzzlehatch were turning to left and right at
will, for the place was honeycombed with rooms and corridors.

Muzzlehatch, as he ran, a few feet ahead of Titus, looked like some
kind of war-horse, with his great rough head thrown back, and his chest
forward.

He did not look round to see whether Titus could keep up with his
trampling pace. With his dark-red rudder of a nose pointing to the
ceiling he galloped on with the small ape, now wide awake, clinging to
his shoulder, its topaz-coloured eyes fixed upon Titus, a few feet behind.
Every now and again it cried out only to cling the tighter to its master's
neck as though frightened of its own voice.

Covering the ground at speed Muzzlehatch retained a monumental
self-assurance – almost a dignity. It was not mere flight. It was a thing
in itself, as a dance must be, a dance of ritual.

'Are you there?' he suddenly muttered over his shoulder. 'Eh? Are
you there? Young Rag'n'bone! Fetch up alongside.'

'I'm here,' panted Titus. 'But how much longer?'

Muzzlehatch took no notice but pranced around a corner to the left
and then left again, and right, and left again, and then gradually
slackening pace they ambled at last into a dimly-lit hall surrounded by
seven doors. Opening one at random the fugitives found themselves in
an empty room.

TWENTY-NINE

MUZZLEHATCH and Titus stood still for a few moments until their eyes
became adjusted to the darkness.

Then they saw, at the far end of the apartment, a dull grey rectangle
that stood on end in the darkness. It was the night.

There were no stars and the moon was on the other side of the
building. Somewhere far below they could hear the whisper of a plane
as it took off. All at once it came into view, a slim, wingless thing,
sliding through the night, seemingly unhurried, save that suddenly,
where was it?

Titus and Muzzlehatch stood at the window and for a long while neither of them spoke. At last Titus turned to the dimly outlined shape of his companion.

'What are you doing here?' he said. 'You seem out of place.'

'God's geese! You startled me,' said Muzzlehatch, raising his hand as though to guard himself from attack. 'I'd forgotten you were here. I was brooding, boy. Than which there is no richer pastime. It muffles one with rotting plumes. It gives forth sullen music. It is the smell of home.'

'Home?' said Titus.

'Home,' said Muzzlehatch. He took out a pipe from his pocket, and filled it with a great fistful of tobacco; lit it, drew at it; filled his lungs with acrid fumes, and exhaled them, while the bowl burned in the darkness like a wound.

'You ask me why I am here – here among an alien people. It is a good question. Almost as good as for me to ask you the same thing. But don't tell me, dear boy, not yet. I would rather guess.'

'I know nothing about you,' said Titus. 'You are someone to me who appears, and disappears. A rough man: a shadow-man: a creature who plucks me out of danger. Who are you? Tell me . . . You do not seem to be part of this – this glassy region.'

'It is not glassy where I come from, boy. Have you forgotten the slums that crawl up to my courtyard? Have you forgotten the crowds by the river? Have you forgotten the stink?'

'I remember the stink of your car,' said Titus, '– sharp as acid; thick as gruel.'

'She's a bitch,' said Muzzlehatch, '– and smells like one.'

'I am ignorant of you,' said Titus. 'You with your acres of great cages, your savage cats; your wolves and your birds of prey. I have seen them, but they tell me little. What are you thinking of? Why do you flaunt this monkey on your shoulder as though it were a foreign flag – some emblem of defiance? I have no more access to your brain than I have to this little skull,' and Titus fumbling in the dark stroked the small ape with his forefinger. Then he stared at the darkness, part of which was Muzzlehatch. The night seemed thicker than ever.

'Are you still there?' said Titus.

It was twelve long seconds before Muzzlehatch replied.

'I am. I am still here, or some of me is. The rest of me is leaning on the rails of a ship. The air is full of spices and the deep salt water shines with phosphorus. I am alone on deck and there is no one else to see the moon float out of a cloud so that a string of palms is lit like a procession. I can see the dark-white surf as it beats upon the shore; and I see, and I remember, how a figure ran along the strip of moonlit sand, with his arms raised high above his head, and his shadow ran beside him and jerked as it sped, for the beach was uneven; and then the moon slid into the clouds again and the world went black.'

'Who was he?' said Titus.

'How should I know?' said Muzzlehatch. 'It might have been anyone. It might have been me.'

'Why are you telling me all this?' said Titus.

'I am not telling *you* anything. I am telling myself. My voice, strident to others, is music to me.'

'You have a rough manner,' said Titus. 'But you have saved me twice. Why are you helping me?'

'I have no idea,' said Muzzlehatch. 'There must be something wrong with my brain.'

THIRTY

ALTHOUGH there was no sound, yet the opening of the door produced a change in the room behind them; a change sufficient to awake in Titus and his companion an awareness of which their conscious minds knew nothing.

No, not the breath of a sound; not a flicker of light. Yet the black room at their backs was alive.

Muzzlehatch and Titus had turned at the same time and as far as they knew they turned for no more reason than to ease a muscle.

In fact they hardly knew that they *had* turned. They could see very little of the night-filled room, but when a moment later a lady stepped forward, she brought with her a little light from the hall beyond. It was not much of an illumination but it was strong enough to show Titus and his companion that immediately to their left was a striped couch and on the other side of the room, down-stage as it were, supposing the night to be the auditorium, was a tall screen.

At the sight of the door opening Muzzlehatch plucked the small ape from Titus's shoulder and muzzling it with his right hand and holding its four feet together in his left, he moved silently through the shadows until he was hidden behind the tall screen. Titus, with no ape to deal with, was beside him in a moment.

Then came the click and the room was immediately filled with coral-coloured light. The lady who had opened the door stepped forward without a sound. Daintily, for all her weight, she moved to the centre of the room, where she cocked her head on one side as though waiting for something peculiar to happen. Then she sat down on the striped couch, crossing her splendid legs with a hiss of silk.

'He must be hungry,' she whispered, 'the roof-swarmer, the skylight-burster . . . the ragged boy from nowhere. He must be very hungry and very lost. Where would he be, I wonder? Behind that screen for instance, with his friend, the wicked Muzzlehatch?' There was a rather silly silence.

THIRTY-ONE

WHILE sitting there Juno had opened a hamper which she had filled at the party before following the boy and Muzzlehatch.

'Are you hungry?' said Juno, as they emerged.

'Very hungry,' said Titus.

'Then eat,' said Juno.

'O my sweet flame! My mulcted one. What are you thinking of?' asked Muzzlehatch, but in a voice so bored that it was almost an insult. 'Can you imagine how I found him, love-pot?'

'Who?' said Juno.

'This boy,' said Muzzlehatch. 'This ravenous boy.'

'Tell me.'

'Washed up, he was,' said Muzzlehatch, '– at dawn. Ain't that poetic? There he lay, stranded on the water-steps – sprawled out like a dead fish. So I drove him home. Why? Because I had never seen anything so unlikely. Next day I shoo'd him off. He was no part of me. No part of my absurd life, and away he went, a creature out of nowhere, redundant as a candle in the sun. Quite laughable – a thing to be forgotten – but what *happens?*'

'I'm listening,' said Juno.

'I'll tell you,' continued Muzzlehatch. 'He takes it upon himself to fall through a skylight and bears to the ground one of the few women who ever interested me. O yes. I saw it all. His head lay sidelong on your splendid bosom and for a little while he was Lord of that tropical ravine between your midnight breasts: that home of moss and verdure: that sumptuous cleft. But enough of this. I am too old for gulches. How did you find us? What with our twistings and turnings and doubling back – we should by rights have shaken off the devil himself – but then you wander in as though you'd been a-riding on my tail. How did you find me?'

'I will tell you, Muzzle-dove, how I found you. There was nothing miraculous about it. My intuition is as non-existent as the smell of marble. It was the boy who gave you both away. His feet were wet and still are. They left a glister down the corridors.'

'A glister, what's a glister?' said Muzzlehatch.

'It's what his wet feet left behind them – the merest film. I had only to follow it. Where are your shoes, pilgrim-child?'

'My shoes?' said Titus, with a chicken bone in his hand. 'Why, somewhere in the river, I suppose.'

'Well then; now that you've found us, Juno, my love-trap – what do you want of us? Alone or separately? I, after all, though unpopular, am no fugitive. So there's no need for me to hide. But young Titus here (Lord of somewhere or other – with an altogether most unlikely name) – he, we must admit, is on the run. Why, I'm not quite sure. As for myself, there is nothing I want more than to wash my two hands of both of you. One reason is the way you haven't my marrow. I yell for nothing but solitude, Juno, and the beasts I brood on. Another is this young man – the Earl of Gorgon-paste or whatever he calls himself – I must wash my hands of him also, for I have no desire to be involved with yet another human being – especially one in the shape of an enigma. Life is too brief for such diversions and I cannot bring myself to scrape up any interest in the problems of his breast.'

The small ape on Muzzlehatch's shoulder nodded its head and then began to fish about in the depth of its master's hair; its wrinkled, yet delicate, fingers probing here and there were as tender yet as inquisitive as any lover's.

'You're almost as rude as I was hungry,' said Titus. 'As for the workings of my heart, and my lineage, you are as ignorant as that monkey on your shoulder. As far as I am concerned you will remain so. But get me out of here. It is a swine of a building and smells like a hospital. You have been good to me, Mr Marrow-patch, but I long to see the last of you. Where can I go, where can I hide?'

'You must come with me,' said Juno. 'You must have clean clothes, food, and shelter.' She turned her splendid head to Muzzlehatch. 'How are we going to leave without being seen?'

'One move at a time,' said Muzzlehatch. 'Our first is to find the nearest lift-shaft. The whole place ought to be asleep by now.' He strode to the door and, opening it quietly, discovered a young man bent double. He had been given no time to rise from the keyhole, let alone escape.

'But my dearest essence of stoat –' said Muzzlehatch, gradually drawing the man forward into the room by his lemon-yellow lapels (for he was a flunkey of the household '– you are most welcome. Now, Juno dear, take Gorgon-paste with you and lean with him over the balustrade and stare down into the darkness. It will not be for long.'

Titus and Juno, obeying his curiously authoritative voice, for it had power however ridiculous its burden, heard a peculiar shuffling sound, and then a moment later – 'Now then, Gorgonblast, leave the lovely lady in charge of the night and come here.'

Titus turned and saw that the flunkey was practically naked. Muzzlehatch had stripped him as an autumn tree is stripped of its gold leaves.

'Off with your rags and into the livery,' said Muzzlehatch to Titus. He turned to the flunkey. 'I do hope you're not too chilly. I have nothing against you, friend, but I have no option. This young gentleman must escape, you see.'

'Hurry, now, "Gorgon",' he shouted. 'I have the car waiting and she is restless.'

He did not know that as he spoke the first strands of dawn were threading their way through the low clouds and lighting not only the few aeroplanes that shone like spectres, but also that monstrous creature, Muzzlehatch's car. Naked as the flunkey, naked in the early sunbeams, it was like an oath, or a jeer, its nose directed at the elegant planes; its shape, its colour, its skeleton, its tendons, its skull, its muscles of leather – its low and rakish belly, and its general air of blood and mutiny on the high seas. There she waited far below the room where her captain stood.

'Change clothes,' said Muzzlehatch. 'We can't wait all night for you.'

Something began to burn in Titus's stomach. He could feel the blood draining from his face.

'So you can't wait all night for me,' he said in a voice he hardly recognized as his own. 'Muzzlehatch, the zoo-man, is in a hurry. But does he know who he is talking to? Do you?'

'What is it, Titus?' said Juno, who had turned from the window at the sound of his voice.

'What is it?' cried Titus. 'I will tell you, madam. It is this bully's ignorance. Does he know who I am?'

'How can we know about you, dear, if you won't tell us? There, there, stop shaking.'

'He wants to run away,' said Muzzlehatch. 'But you don't want to be jailed, do you now? Eh? You want to get free of this building, surely.'

'Not with *your* help,' shouted Titus, though he knew as he shouted that he was being mean. He looked up at the big cross-hatched face with its proud rudder of a nose and the living light in its eye and a flicker of recognition seemed to pass between them. But it was too late.

'Then to hell with you, child,' said Muzzlehatch.

'I will take him,' said Juno.

'No,' said Muzzlehatch. 'Let him go. He must learn.'

'Learn, be damned!' said Titus, all the pent-up emotion breaking through. 'What do you know of life, of violence and guile? Of madmen and subterfuge and treachery? My treachery. My hands have been sticky with blood. I have loved and I have killed in my kingdom.'

'Kingdom?' said Juno. 'Your *kingdom*?'

A kind of fearful love brimmed in her eyes. 'I will take care of you,' she said.

'No,' said Muzzlehatch, 'let him find his way. He will never forgive you if you take him now. Let him be a man, Juno dear – or what he thinks to be a man. Don't suck his blood, dear. Don't pounce too soon. Remember how you killed our love with spices – eh? My pretty vampire.'

Titus, white with indecision, for to him Juno and Muzzlehatch seemed to talk a private language, took a step nearer to the smiling man who had turned his head across his shoulder so that the little ape was able to rest its furry cheek along its master's.

'Did you call this lady a vampire?' he whispered.

Muzzlehatch nodded his smiling head slowly.

'That is so,' he said.

'He meant nothing,' said Juno. 'Titus! O, darling . . . O . . .'

For Titus had whipped out his fist with such speed that it was a wonder it did not find its mark. This it failed to do, for Muzzlehatch, catching Titus's fist as though it were a flung stone, held it in a vice and then, with no apparent effort, propelled Titus slowly to the doorway, through which he pushed the boy before closing the door and turning the key.

For a few minutes Titus, shocked at his own impotence, beat upon the door, yelling 'Let me in, you coward! Let me in! Let me in!' until the noise he made brought servants from all quarters of the great mansion of olive-green glass.

While they took Titus away struggling and shouting, Muzzlehatch held Juno firmly by her elbow, for she longed to be with the sudden young man dressed half in rags and half in livery, but she said nothing as she strained against the grip of her one-time lover.

THIRTY-TWO

THE day broke wild and shaggy. What light there was seeped into the great glass buildings as though ashamed. All but a fraction of the guests who had attended the Cusp-Canines' party lay like fossils in their separate beds, or, for various sunken causes, tossed and turned in seas of dream.

Of those who were awake and on their feet, at least half were servants of the House. It was from among these few that a posse of retainers (on hearing the shindy) converged upon the room, switching on lights as they ran, until they found Titus striking upon the outside of the door.

It was no good for him to struggle. Their clumsy hands caught hold of him and hustled him away and down seven flights into the servants' quarters. There he was kept prisoner for the best part of the day, the time being punctuated by visits from the Law and the Police and towards evening by some kind of a brain-specialist who gazed at Titus for minutes on end from under his eyebrows and asked peculiar questions which Titus took no trouble to answer, for he was very tired.

Lady Cusp-Canine herself appeared for one fleeting minute. She had not been down to the kitchens for thirty years and was accompanied by an Inspector, who kept his head tilted on one side as he talked to her Ladyship while keeping his eyes on the captive. The effect of this was to suggest that Titus was some kind of caged animal.

'An enigma,' said the Inspector.

'I don't agree,' said Lady Cusp-Canine. 'He is only a boy.'

'Ah,' said the Inspector.

'And I like his face, too,' said Lady Cusp-Canine.

'Ah,' said the Inspector.

'He has splendid eyes.'

'But has he splendid habits, your Ladyship?'

'I don't know,' said Lady Cusp-Canine. 'Why? Have you?'

The Inspector shrugged his shoulders.

'There is nothing to shrug about,' said Lady Cusp-Canine. 'Nothing at all. Where is my Chef?'

This gentleman had been hovering at her side ever since she had entered the kitchen. He now presented himself.

'Madam?'

'Have you fed the boy?'

'Yes, my Lady.'

'Have you given him the best? The most nutritious? Have you given him a breakfast to remember?'

'Not yet, your Ladyship.'

'Then what are you waiting for!' Her voice rose. 'He is hungry. He is despondent, he is young!'

'Yes, your Ladyship.'

'Don't say "yes" to me!' She rose on tip-toe to her full height, which did not take her long for she was minute. 'Feed him and let him go,' and with that she skimmed across the room on tiny septuagenarian feet, her plumed hat swaying dangerously among the loins and briskets.

THIRTY-THREE

MEANWHILE, the powerful Muzzlehatch had escorted Juno out of the building and had helped her into his hideous car. It was his intention to take her to her house above the river and then to race for home, for even Muzzlehatch was weary. But, as usual when he was at the wheel, whatever plans had been formulated were soon to be no more than chaff in the wind, and within half a minute of his starting he had changed his mind and was now heading for that wide and sandy stretch of the river where the banks shelved gently into the shallow water.

The sky was no longer very dark, though one or two stars were still to be seen, when Muzzlehatch, having taken a long and quite unnecessary curve to the west, careered off the road and, turning left and right to avoid the juniper bushes that littered the upper banks, swept all of a sudden into the shallows of the broad stream. Once in the water he accelerated and great arcs of brine spurted from the wheels to port and starboard.

As for Juno, she leaned forward a little; her elbow rested on the door of the car, and her face lay sideways in the gloved palm of her hand. As far as could be seen she was quite oblivious of the speed of the car, let alone the spray: nor did she take any notice of Muzzlehatch, who, in his favourite position, was practically lying on the floor of the machine, one eye above the 'bulwarks' from whence came forth a sort of song:

> 'I have my price: it's rather high –
> (About the level of your eye),
> But if you're nice to me, I'll try
> To lower it for you –
> To lower it; to lower it;
> Upon the kind of rope they knit
> From yellow grass and purple hay
> When knitting is taboo –'

A touch of the wheel and the car sped deeper into the river so that the water was not far from brimming over, but another movement brought her out again while the steam hissed like a thousand cats.

'Some knit them pearl,' roared Muzzlehatch,

> 'Some knit them plain –
> Some knit their brows of pearl in vain
> Some are so plain they try again
> To tease the wool of love!
> But ah! the palms of yesterday –
> There's not a soul from yesterday
> Who's worth the dreaming of – they say –
> Who's worth the dreaming of . . .'

As Muzzlehatch's voice wandered off the sun began to rise out of the river.

'Have you finished?' said Juno. Her eyes were half closed.

'I have given my *all*,' said Muzzlehatch.

'Then listen please!' – her eyes were a little wider but their expression was still faraway.

'What is it, Juno love?'

'I am thinking of that boy. What will they do to him?'

'They'll find him difficult,' said Muzzlehatch, 'very difficult. Rather like a form of me. It is more a case of what will he do to *them*. But why? Has he set a sparrow twittering in your breast? Or woken up a predatory condor?'

But there was no reply, for at that moment he drew up at the front door of Juno's house, with a great cry of metal. It was a tall building, dusty pink in colour, and was backed by a small hill or knoll surmounted by a marble man. Immediately behind the knoll was a loop of the river. On either side of Juno's house were two somewhat similar houses but these were forsaken. The windows were smashed. The doors were gone and the rooms let in the rain.

But Juno's house was in perfect repair and when the door was opened by a servant in a yellow gown it was possible to see how daringly yet carefully the hall was furnished. Lit up in the darkness, it presented a colour scheme of ivory, ash, and coral red.

'Are you coming in?' said Juno. 'Do mushrooms tempt you – or plovers' eggs? Or coffee?'

'No my love!'

'As you wish.'

They sat without moving for a little while.

'Where do you think the boy is?' she said at last.

'I have no idea,' said Muzzlehatch.

Juno climbed out of the car. It was like a faultless disembarkation. Whatever she did had style.

'Good night then,' she said, 'and sweet dreams.'

Muzzlehatch gazed at her as she made her way through the dark garden to the lighted hall. Her shadow cast by the light reached out behind her, almost to the car, and as she moved away step by long smooth step, Muzzlehatch felt a twitch of the heart, for it seemed that he saw in the slow leisure of her stride something, at the moment, that he was loth to forgo.

It was as if those faraway days when they were lovers came flooding back, image upon image, shade upon shade, unsolicited, unbidden, each one challenging the strength of the dykes which they had built against one another. For they knew that beyond the dykes heaved the great seas of sentiment on whose bosom they had lost their way.

How often had he stared at her in anger or in boisterous love! How often had he admired her. How often had he seen her leave him, but never quite like this. The light from the hall where the servant stood came flooding across the garden and Juno was a silhouette against the lighted entrance. From the full, rounded, and bell-shaped hips which swayed imperceptibly as she moved, arose the column of her almost military back; and from her shoulders sprang her neck, perfectly cylindrical, surmounted by her classic head.

As Muzzlehatch gazed at her he seemed to see, in some strange way, himself. He saw her as his failure – and he knew himself to be hers. For they had each received all that the other could provide. What had gone wrong? Was it that they need no longer try because they could see through one another? What was the trouble? A hundred things. His unfaithfulness; his egotism; his eternal play-acting; his gigantic pride; his lack of tenderness; his deafening exuberance; his selfishness.

But she had run out of love; or it had been battered out of her. Only a friendship remained: ambient and unbreakable.

So it was strange, this twitch of the heart, strange that he should follow her with his eyes; strange that he should turn the car about so slowly, and it was strange also (when he arrived in the courtyard of his home) to see how ruminative was the look upon his face as he tied his car to the mulberry tree.

THIRTY-FOUR

In the late afternoon of the next day they took Titus and they put him in a cell. It was a small place with a barred window to the south-west.

When Titus entered the cell this rectangle was filled with a golden light. The black bars that divided the window into a dozen upright sections were silhouetted against the sunset.

In one corner there was a rough trestle bed with a dark-red blanket spread over it. Taking up most of the space in the middle of the cell was a table that stood up on three legs only, for the stone floor was uneven. On the table were a few candles, a box of matches, and a cup of water. By the side of the table stood a chair, a flimsy-looking thing which someone had once started to paint: but they (whoever they may have been) had grown tired of the work so that the chair was piebald black and yellow.

As Titus stood there taking in the features of the room the jailer closed the door behind him and he heard the key turn in the lock. But the sunbeams were there, the low, slanting beams of honey-coloured light; they flooded through the bars and gave a kind of welcome to the prisoner – so that he made, without a pause, for the big window, where, holding an iron bar with either hand, he stared across a landscape.

It seemed it was transfigured. So ethereal was the light that great cedars floated upon it and hilltops seemed to wander through the gold.

In the far distance Titus could see what looked like the incrustation of a city, and as though the sun were striking it obliquely there came the golden flash of windows, now here, now there, like sparks from a flint.

Suddenly, out of the gilded evening a bird flew directly towards the window where Titus stood staring through the bars. It approached rapidly, looping its airborne way, was all at once standing on the window-ledge.

By the way its head moved rapidly to and fro upon its neck it seemed it was looking for something. It was evident that the last occupant of the cell had shared his crumbs with the piebald bird – but today there were no crumbs and the magpie at last began to peck at its feathers as though in lieu of better fare.

Then out of the golden atmosphere: out of the stones of the cell: out of the cedars: out of a flutter of the magpie's wing, came a long waft of memory so that images swam up before his eyes and he saw, more vividly than the sunset or the forested hills, the long coruscated outline of Gormenghast and the stones of his home where the lizards lazed, and there, blotting out all else, his mother as he had last seen her at the door of the shanty, the great dripping castle drawn up like a back-cloth behind her.

'You will come back,' she had said. 'All roads lead back to Gormenghast'; and he yearned suddenly for his home, for the bad of it no less than for the good of it – yearned for the smell of it and the taste of the bitter ivy. ·

Titus turned from the window as though to dispel the nostalgia, but the mere movement of his body through space was no help to him, and he sat down on the edge of the bed.

From far below the window came the fluting of a blackbird; the golden light had begun to darken and he became conscious of a loneliness he had never felt before.

He leaned forward pressing the tightened muscles below his ribs and then began to rock back and forth, like a pendulum. So regular was the rocking that it would seem that no assuagement of grief could result from so mechanical a rhythm.

But there was a kind of comfort to be had, for while his brain wept, his body went on swaying.

An aching to be once again in the land from which he grew gave him no rest. There is no calm for those who are uprooted. They are wanderers, homesick and defiant. Love itself is helpless to heal them though the dust rises with every footfall – drifts down the corridors – settles on branch or cornice – each breath an inhalation from the past so that the lungs, like a miner's, are dark with bygone times.

Whatever they eat, whatever they drink, is never the bread of home or the corn of their own valleys. It is never the wine of their own vineyards. It is a foreign brew.

So Titus rocked himself in grief's cradle to and fro, to and fro, while the cell darkened, and at some time during the night he fell asleep.

THIRTY-FIVE

WHAT was it? He sat bolt upright and stared about him. It was very cold but it was not this that woke him. It was a little sound. He could hear it now quite clearly. It came from within a few feet of where he sat. It was a kind of tapping, but it did not seem to come from the wall. It came from beneath the bed.

Then it stopped for a little and when it returned it seemed as though it bore some kind of message, for there was a pattern or rhythm in it:

something that sounded like a question. 'Tap – Tap . . . Tap – Tap – Tap. Are . . . yóu . . . thére . . . ? Are . . . yóu . . . thére . . . ?'

This tapping, sinister as it was, had the effect, at least, of turning Titus's mind from the almost unbearable nostalgia that had oppressed it.

Edging himself silently from the flimsy bed, he stood beside it, his heart beating, and then he lifted it bodily from where it stood and set it down in the centre of the cell.

Remembering the candles on the table, he fumbled for one, lit it, and then tip-toed back to where the bed had stood, and then moved the small flame to and fro along the flagstones. As he did so the tapping started again.

'Are . . . yóu . . . thére . . . ?' it seemed to say – 'Are . . . yóu . . . thére . . . ?'

Titus knelt down and shone the candle flame full upon the stone from immediately below which the tapping appeared to proceed.

It seemed quite ordinary, at first, this flagstone, but under scrutiny Titus could see that the thin fissure that surrounded it was sharper and deeper than was the case with the adjacent stones. The candlelight showed up what the daylight would have hidden.

Again the knocking started and Titus, taking the knuckle of flint from his pocket, waited for the next lull. Then, with a trembling hand, he struck the stone slab twice.

For a moment there was no reply and then the answer came – 'One . . . two . . .'

It was a brisk 'one – two', quite unlike the tentative tapping which had preceded it.

It was as though, whoever or whatever stood or lay or crawled beneath the flagstone, the *mood* of the enigma had changed. The 'being', whatever it was, had gained in confidence.

What happened next was stranger and more fearful. Something more startling than the tapping had taken its place. This time it was the eyes that were assailed. What did they see that made his whole body shake? Peering at the candle-lit flagstone below him, he saw it move.

Titus jumped back from the oscillating stone, and, lifting his candle high in the air, he looked about him wildly for some kind of weapon. His eyes returned to the stone which was now an inch above the ground.

From where Titus stood in the centre of the cell he could not see that the stone was supported by a pair of hands that trembled with its weight. All he saw was a part of the floor rising up with a kind of slow purpose.

Woken out of his sleep to find himself in a prison – and then to hear a knocking in the darkness – and then to be faced with something phantasmagoric – a stone, apparently alive, raising itself in secret in order to survey the supine vaults – all this and the depth of his homesickness – what could all this lead to but a lightness in the head? But this lightness, though it all but brought a kind of mad laughter in its train, did not prevent him seeing in the half-painted chair a possible weapon. Grabbing it, with his eyes fixed upon the flagstone, he wrenched the chair to pieces, this way and that, until he had pulled free from the skeleton one of its front legs. With this in his hand he began to laugh silently as he crept towards his enemy, the stone.

But as he crept forward he saw before the flagstone, which was by now five inches up in the air, two thick grey wrists.

They were trembling with the weight of the stone slab, and as Titus watched, his eyes wide with conjecture, he saw the thick slab begin to tilt and edge itself over the adjacent stone until, by degrees, the whole weight was transferred and there was a square hole in the floor.

The thick grey hands had withdrawn, taking their fingers with them – but a moment later something arose to take their place. It was the head of a man.

THIRTY-SIX

LITTLE did he know – this riser-out-of-flagstones – that his head was that of a batter'd god – nor that with such a visage, he was, when he spoke, undermining his own grandeur, for no voice could be tremendous enough for such a face.

'Be not startled,' he whined, and his accents were as soft as dough. 'All is well; all is lovely; all is as it should be. Accept me. That is all I ask you. Accept me. Old Crime they call me. They *will* have their little jokes. Dear boys, they are. Ha ha! That I have come to you through a hole in the floor is nothing. Put down that chair-leg, friend.'

'What do you want?' said Titus.

'Listen to him,' replied the soft voice. ' "What do you want?" he says. I want nothing, dear child. Nothing but friendship. Sweet friendship. That is why I have come to see you. To initiate you. One must help the helpless, mustn't one? And pour out balm, you know: and bathe all kinds of bruises.'

'I wish to hell you had left me alone,' said Titus savagely. 'You can keep your balm.'

'Now is that *nice*?' said Old Crime. 'Is that *kind*? But I understand. You are not used to it: are you? It takes some time to love the Honeycomb.'

Titus stared at the leonine head.

The voice had robbed it of all grandeur, and he placed the chair leg on the table within reach.

'The Honeycomb? What's that?' said Titus at last. The man had been staring at him intently.

'It is the name we give, dear boy, to what some would call a prison. But we know better. To us it is a world within a world – and *I* should know, shouldn't I? I've been here all my life – or nearly all. For the first few years I lived in luxury. There were tiger-skins on the scented floorboards of our houses: and golden cutlery and golden plates. Money was like the sands of the sea. For I come from a great line. You have probably heard of us. We are the oldest family in the world – we are the originals.' He edged forward, out of the hole.

'Do you think that because I am here, in the Honeycomb, I am missing anything? Do you think I am jealous of my family? Do you think I miss the golden plates and the tiger-skins? No! Nor the reflections in the polished floor. I have found my luxury *here*. This is my joy. To be a prisoner in the Honeycomb. So, my dear child, be not startled. I came to tell you there's a friend below you. You can always tap to me. Tap out your thoughts. Tap out your joys and sorrows. Tap out your love. We will grow old together.'

Titus turned his face sharply. What did he mean, this vile, unhealthy creature.

'Leave me alone,' cried Titus, '– leave me alone!'

The man from the cell below stared at Titus. Then he began to tremble.

'This used to be *my* cell,' he said. 'Years and years ago. I was a fire-raiser. "Arson" they called it. I did so love a fire. The flames make up for everything.

'Bring on the rats and mice! Bring on my skinning-knife. Bring on the New Boys.'

He moved a step towards Titus, who, in his turn, moved a little nearer to the chair-leg weapon.

'This is a good cell. I had it once,' whined Old Crime. 'I made something out of it, I can tell you. I learned the nature of it. I was sad to leave it. This window is the finest in the prison. But who cares about it now? Where are the frescoes gone? My yellow frescoes. Drawings, you understand. Drawings of fairies. Now they have been covered up and nothing is left of all my work. Not a trace.'

He lifted his proud head and but for the shortness of his legs he might well have been Isaiah.

'Put that chair-leg on the table, boy. Forget yourself. Eat up your crumbs.'

Titus looked down at the old lag and the craggy grandeur of his upturned face.

'You've come to the right place,' said Old Crime. 'Away from the filthy thing called Life. Join us, dear boy. You would be an asset. My friends are unique. Grow old with us.'

'You talk too much,' said Titus.

The man from below stretched out his strong arm slowly. His right hand fastened upon Titus's biceps and as it tightened Titus could feel an evil strength, a sense that Old Crime's power was limitless and that, had he wanted to, he could have torn the arm away with ease.

As it was he brought Titus to his side with a single pull, and far back in the sham nobility of his countenance Titus could see two little fires no bigger than pin-heads burning.

'I was going to do so much for you,' said the man from below. 'I was going to introduce you to my colleagues. I was going to show you all the escape routes – should you want them – I was going to tell you about my poetry and where the harlots prowl. After all one mustn't become ill, must we? That wouldn't do at all.

'But you have told me I talk too much, so I will do something quite different and crack your skull like an egg-shell.'

All in a breath the dreadful man let go of Titus, wheeled in his tracks, and lifting the table above his head he flung it, with all the force he could command, at Titus. But he was too late, for all his speed. Directly Titus saw the man reach for the table he sprang to one side, and the heavy piece of furniture crashed against the wall at his back.

Turning now upon the massive-chested and muscular creature, he was surprised to hear the sound of sobbing. His adversary was now upon his knees, his huge archaic face buried in his hands.

Not knowing what to do, Titus re-lit one of the candles which had been on the table and then sat down on his trestle bed, the only piece of furniture left in the cell that hadn't been smashed.

'Why did you have to say it? Why did you have to? O why? Why?' sobbed the man.

'O God,' said Titus to himself, 'what have I done?'

'So I talk too much? O God, I talk too much.'

A shadow passed over Old Crime's face. At the same moment there was a heavy sound of feet beyond the door and then after a rattling of keys the sound of one turning in the lock. Old Crime was by this time on the move and by the time the door began to open he had disappeared down the hole in the floor.

Hardly knowing what he was doing, Titus dragged the trestle bed over the hole and then lay down on it as the door opened.

A warder came in with a torch. He flashed it around the cell, the beam of light lingering on the broken table, the broken chair, and the supposedly sleeping boy.

Four strides took him to Titus, whom he pulled from his bed only to beat him back again with a vicious clout on the head.

'Let that last you till the morning, you bloody whelp!' shouted the warder. 'I'll teach you to keep your temper! I'll teach you to smash things.' He glowered at Titus. 'Who were you talking to?' he shouted, but Titus, being half stunned, could hardly answer.

In the very early morning when he awoke he thought it had all been a dream. But the dream was so vivid that he could not refrain from rolling to the floor and peering in the half-darkness beneath the trestle bed.

It had been no dream, for there it was, that heavy slab of stone, and he immediately began to shift it inch by inch and it fell into its former place. But just before the hole was finally closed he heard the old man's voice, soft as gruel, in the darkness below.

'Grow old with me . . .' it said. 'Grow old with me.'

THIRTY-SEVEN

A DIM light shone above his Worship's head. In the hollow of the Court someone could be heard sharpening a pencil. A chair creaked, and Titus, standing upright at the bar, began to bang his hands together, for it was a bitter cold morning.

'Who is applauding what?' said the Magistrate, recovering from a reverie. 'Have I said something profound?'

'No, not at all, your Worship,' said the large, pock-marked Clerk of the Court. 'That is, sir, you made no remark.'

'Silence can be profound, Mr Drugg. Very much so.'

'Yes, your Worship.'

'What *was* it then?'

'It was the young man, your Worship; clapping his hands, to warm them, I imagine.'

'Ah, yes. The young man. Which young man? Where is he?'

'In the dock, your Worship.'

The Magistrate, frowning a little, pushed his wig to one side and then drew it back again.

'I seem to know his face,' said the Magistrate.

'Quite so, your Worship,' said Mr Drugg. 'This prisoner has been before you several times.'

'That accounts for it,' said the Magistrate. 'And what has he been up to now?'

'If I may remind your Worship,' said the large pock-marked Clerk of the Court, not without a note of peevishness in his voice, '– you were dealing with this case only this morning.'

'And so I was. It is returning to me. I have always had an excellent memory. Think of a Magistrate with no memory.'

'I am thinking of it, your Worship,' said Mr Drugg as, with a gesture of irritation, he thumbed through a sheaf of irrelevant papers.

'Vagrancy. Wasn't *that* it, Mr Drugg?'

'It *was*,' said the Clerk of the Court. 'Vagrancy, damage, and trespass' – and he turned his big greyish-coloured face to Titus and lifted a corner of his top lip away from his teeth like a dog. And then, as though upon their own volition, his hands slid down into the depths of his trouser pockets as though two foxes had all of a sudden gone to earth. A smothered sound of keys and coins being jangled together gave the momentary impression that there was about Mr Drugg something frisky, something of the playboy. But this impression was gone as soon as it was born. There was nothing in Mr Drugg's dark, heavy features, nothing about his stance, nothing about his voice to give colour to the thought. Only the noise of coins.

But the jangling, half smothered as it was, reminded Titus of something half forgotten, a dreadful, yet intimate music; of a cold kingdom; of bolts and flag-stoned corridors; of intricate gates of corroded iron; of flints and visors and the beaks of birds.

' "Vagrancy", "damage", and "trespass",' repeated the Magistrate, 'yes, yes, I remember. Fell through someone else's roof. Was that it?'

'Exactly, sir,' said the Clerk of the Court.

'No visible means of support?'

'That is so, your Worship.'

'Homeless?'

'Yes, and no, your Worship,' said the Clerk. 'He talks of –'

'Yes, yes, yes, yes. I have it now. A trying case and a trying young man – I had begun to tire, I remember, of his obscurity.'

The Magistrate leaned forward on his elbows and rested his long, bony chin upon the knuckles of his interlocked fingers.

'This is the fourth time that I have had you before me at the bar, and as far as I can judge, the whole thing has been a waste of time to the Court and nothing but a nuisance to myself. Your answers, when they have been forthcoming, have been either idiotic, nebulous, or fantastic. This cannot be allowed to go on. Your youth is no excuse. Do you like stamps?'

'Stamps, your Worship?'

'Do you collect them?'

'No.'

'A pity. I have a rare collection rotting daily. Now listen to me. You have already spent a week in prison – but it is not your vagrancy that troubles me. That is straightforward, though culpable. It is that you are rootless and obtuse. It seems you have some knowledge hidden from us. Your ways are curious, your terms are meaningless. I will ask you once again. What is this Gormenghast? What does it mean?'

Titus turned his face to the Bench. If ever there was a man to be trusted, his Worship was that man.

Ancient, wrinkled, like a tortoise, but with eyes as candid as grey glass.

But Titus made no answer, only brushing his forehead with the sleeve of his coat.

'Have you heard his Worship's question?' said a voice at his side. It was Mr Drugg.

'I do not know,' said Titus, 'what is meant by such a question. You might just as well ask me what is this hand of mine? What does it mean?' And he raised it in the air with the fingers spread out like a starfish. 'Or what is this leg?' And he stood on one foot in the box and shook the other as though it were loose. 'Forgive me, your Worship, I cannot understand.'

'It is a *place*, your Worship,' said the Clerk of the Court. 'The prisoner has insisted that it is a *place*.'

'Yes, yes,' said the Magistrate. 'But where is it? Is it north, south, east or west, young man? Help *me* to help *you*. I take it you do not want to spend the rest of your life sleeping on the roofs of foreign towns. What is it, boy? What is the matter with you?'

A ray of light slid through a high window of the Courtroom and hit the back of Mr Drugg's short neck as though it were revealing something of mystical significance. Mr Drugg drew back his head and the light moved forward and settled on his ear. Titus watched it as he spoke.

'I would tell you, if I could, sir,' he said. 'I only know that I have lost my way. It is not that I want to return to my home – I do not; it is that even if I wished to do so I could not. It is not that I have travelled very far; it is that I have lost my bearings, sir.'

'Did you run away, young man?'

'I rode away,' said Titus.

'From . . . Gormenghast?'

'Yes, your Worship.'

'Leaving your mother . . . ?'

'Yes.'

'And your father . . . ?'

'No, not my father . . .'

'Ah . . . is he dead, my boy?'

'Yes, your Worship. He was eaten by owls.'

The Magistrate raised an eyebrow and began to write upon a piece of paper.

THIRTY-EIGHT

THIS note, which was obviously intended for some important person, probably someone in charge of the local Asylum, or home for delinquent youths – this note fell foul of the Magistrate's intentions, and after being dropped and trodden on, was recovered and passed from hand to hand until it came to rest for a little while in the wrinkled paw of a half-wit, who eventually, after trying to read it, made a dart out of it, and set it sailing out of the shadows and into a less murky quarter of the Court.

A little behind the half-wit was a figure almost completely lost in the shadows. In his pocket lay curled a salamander. His eyes were closed and his nose, like a large rudder, pointed at the ceiling.

On his left sat Mrs Grass with a hat like a yellow cabbage. She had made several attempts to whisper in Muzzlehatch's ear, but had received no response.

Some distance to the left of these two sat half a dozen strong men, husky and very upright. They had followed the proceedings with strict, if frowning, attention. In their view the Magistrate was being too lenient. After all the young man in the dock had proved himself no gentleman. One had only to look at his clothes. Apart from this, the way he had broken into Lady Cusp-Canine's party was unforgivable.

Lady Cusp-Canine sat with her little chin propped up by her little index finger. Her hat, unlike Mrs Grass's cabbage-like creation, was black as night and rather like a crow's nest. From under the multiform brim of twigs her little made-up face was mushroom-white save where her mouth was like a small red wound. Her head remained motionless but her small, black, button eyes darted here and there so that nothing should be missed.

Very little *was*, when she was around, and it was she who first saw the dart soar out of the gloom at the back of the Court and take a long leisurely half-circle through the dim air.

The Magistrate, his eyelids dropping heavily over his innocent eyeballs, began to slip forward in his high chair until he assumed the kind of position that reminded one of Muzzlehatch at the wheel of his car. But there the similarity ended, for the fact that they had both, even now, closed their eyes meant little. What was important was that the Magistrate was half asleep while Muzzlehatch was very wide awake.

He had noticed, in spite of his seeming torpor, that in an alcove, half hidden by a pillar, were two figures who sat very still and very upright; with an elasticity of articulation; an imperceptible vibrance of the spine. They were upright to the point of unnaturalness. They did not move. Even the plumes on their helmets were motionless, and were in every way identical.

He, Muzzlehatch, had also picked out Inspector Acreblade (a pleasant change from the tall enigmas), for there could be nothing more earthy than the Inspector, who believed in nothing so much as his hound-like job, the spoor and gristle of it: the dry bones of his trade. Within his head there was always a quarry. Ugly or beautiful; a quarry. High morals took no part in his career. He was a hunter and that was all. His aggressive chin prodded the air. His stocky frame had about it something dauntless.

Muzzlehatch watched him through eyelids that were no more than a thread apart. There were not many people in Court that were *not* being watched by Muzzlehatch. In fact there was only one. She sat quite still and unobserved in the shade of a pillar and watched Titus as he stood in the dock, the Magistrate looming above him, like some kind of a cloud. His forgetful face was quite invisible but the crown of his wig was illumined by the lamp that hung above his head. And as Juno stared, she frowned a little and the frown was as much an expression of kindness as the warm quizzical smile that usually hovered on her lips.

THIRTY-NINE

WHAT was it about this stripling at the bar? Why did he touch her so? Why was she frightened for him? 'My father is dead,' he had answered. 'He was eaten by owls.'

A group of elderly men, their legs and arms draped around the backs and elbow-rests of pew-like settees, made between them a noisy corner. The Clerk of the Court had brought them to order more than once but their age had made them impervious to criticism, their old jaws rattling on without a break.

At that moment the paper dart began to loop downward in a gracile curve so that the central figure of the elderly group – the poet himself – jumped to his feet and cried out 'Armageddon!' in so loud a voice that the Magistrate opened his eyes.

'What's this!' he muttered, the dart trailing across his line of vision. There was no answer, for at that moment the rain came down. At first it had been the merest patter; but then it had thickened into a throbbing of water, only to give way after a little while to a protracted *hissing*.

This hissing filled the whole Court. The very stones hissed and with the rain came a premature darkness which thickened the already murky Court.

'More candles!' someone cried. 'More lanterns! Brands and torches, electricity, gas and glow-worms!'

By now it was impossible to recognize anyone save by their silhouettes, for what lights had begun to appear were sucked in by the quenching effect of the darkness.

It was then that someone pulled down a small emergency lever at the back of the Court, and the whole place was jerked into a spasm of naked brilliance.

For a while the Magistrate, the Clerk, the witnesses, the public, sat blinded. Scores of eyelids closed: scores of pupils began to contract. And everything was changed save for the roaring of the rain upon the roof. While this noise made it impossible to be *heard*, yet every detail had become important to the *eye*.

There was nothing mysterious left; all was made naked. The Magistrate had never before suffered such excruciating limelight. The very essence of his vocation was 'removedness'; how could he be 'removed' with the harsh unscrupulous light revealing him as a *particular* man? He was a symbol. He was the Law. He was Justice. He was the wig he wore. Once the wig was gone then he was gone with it. He became a little man among little men. A little man with rather weak eyes; that they were blue and candid argued a quality of magnanimity, when in Court; but they became irritatingly weak and empty directly he removed his wig and returned to his home. But now the unnatural light was upon him, cold and merciless: the kind of light by which vile deeds are done.

With this fierce radiance on his face it was not hard for him to imagine that *he* was the prisoner.

He opened his mouth to speak but not a word could be heard, for the rain was thrashing the roof.

The gaggle of old men, now that their voices were drowned, had gone into their shells, their old tortoise faces turned from the violence of the light.

Following Titus's gaze, Muzzlehatch could see that he was staring at the Helmeted Pair and that the Helmeted Pair were staring at Titus. The young man's hands were shaking on the rail of the bar.

One of the group of six had picked up the paper dart and smoothed it out with the flat of his big insensitive hand. He frowned as he read

and then shot a glance at the young man at the bar. Spill, the tall deaf gentleman, was peering over the man's shoulder. His deafness made him wonder at the lack of conversation in the Court. He could not know that a black sky was crashing down upon the roof nor that the light flooding the walnut-panelled Court was so incongruously coinciding with the black downpour of the outer world.

But he could read, and what he read caused him to dart a glance at Titus, who, turning his head at last from the Helmeted Pair, saw Muzzlehatch. The blinding light had plucked him from the shadows. What was he doing? He was making some kind of sign. Then Titus saw Juno, and for a moment he felt a kind of warmth both for and *from* her. Then he saw Spill and Kestrel. Then he saw Mrs Grass and then the poet.

Everything was horribly close and vivid. Muzzlehatch, looking about nine foot high, had reached the middle of the Court, and choosing the right moment he relieved the man of the crinkled note.

As he read, the rain slackened, and by the time he had finished, the black sky, as though it were a solid, had moved away, all in one piece, and could be heard trundling away into another region.

There was a hush in the Court until an anonymous voice cried out – 'Switch off this fiendish light!'

This peremptory order was obeyed by someone equally anonymous, and the lanterns and the lamps came into their own again: the shadows spread themselves. The Magistrate leaned forward.

'What are you reading, my friend?' he said to Muzzlehatch. 'If the furrow between your eyes spells anything, I should guess it spells news.'

'Why, yes, your Worship, why, yes, indeed. Dire news,' said Muzzlehatch.

'That scrap of paper in your hands,' continued the Magistrate, 'looks remarkably like a note I handed down to my Clerk, creased though it is and filthy as it has become. Would it be?'

'It would,' said Muzzlehatch, 'and it _is_. But you are wrong; he isn't. No more than I am.'

'No?'

'No!'

'Isn't what?'

'Can you not remember what you wrote, your Worship?'

'Remind me.'

Muzzlehatch, instead of reading out the contents of the note, slouched up to the Magistrate's bench and handed him the grubby paper.

'This is what you wrote,' he said. 'It is not for the public. Nor for the young prisoner.'

'No?' said the Magistrate.

'No,' said Muzzlehatch.

'Let me see . . . Let me see . . .' said the Magistrate, pursing his mouth as he took the note from Muzzlehatch and read to himself.

Ref.: No. 1721536217

My dear Filby,

I have before me a young man, a vagrant, a trespasser, a quite peculiar youth, hailing from Gorgonblast, or some such improbable place, and bound for nowhere. By name he admits to 'Titus', and sometimes to 'Groan', though whether Groan is his real name or an invention it is hard to say.

It is quite clear in my mind that this young man is suffering from delusions of grandeur and should be kept under close observation – in other words, Filby, my dear old chap, the boy, to put it bluntly, is _dotty_. Have you room for him? He can, of course, pay nothing, but he may be of interest to you and even find a place in the treatise you are working on. What was it you were calling it? 'Among the Emperors'?

O dear, what it is to be a Magistrate! Sometimes I wonder what it is all about. The human heart is too much. Things go too far. They become unhealthy. But I'd rather be me than you. You are in the entrails of it all. I asked the young man if his father were alive. 'No,' he said, '*he was eaten by owls*.' What do you make of that? I will have him sent over. How is your neuritis? Let me hear from you, old man.

Yours ever,
Willy.

The Magistrate looked up from his note and stared at the boy. 'That seems to cover it,' he said. 'And yet . . . you look all right. I wish I could help you. I will try once more – because I may be wrong.'

'In what way?' said Titus; his eyes were fixed on Acreblade, who had changed his seat in the Court and was now very close indeed.

'What is wrong with me, your Worship? Why do you peer at me like that?' said Titus. 'I am lost – that is all.'

The Magistrate leaned forward. 'Tell me, Titus – tell me about your home. You have told us of your father's death. What of your mother?'

'She was a woman.'

This answer raised a guffaw in the Court.

'Silence,' shouted the Clerk of the Court.

'I would not like to feel that you are showing contempt of Court,' said the Magistrate, 'but if this goes on any longer I will have to pass you on to Mr Acreblade. Is your mother alive?'

'Yes, your Worship,' said Titus, 'unless she has died.'

'When did you last see her?'

'Long ago.'

'Were you not happy with her? – You have told us that you ran away from home.'

'I would like to see her again,' said Titus. 'I did not see very much of her; she was too vast for me. But I did not flee from *her*.'

'What *did* you flee from?'

'From my duty.'

'Your duty?'

'Yes, your Worship.'

'What kind of duty?'

'My hereditary duty. I have told you. I am the last of the Line. I have betrayed my birthright. I have betrayed my home. I have run like a rat from Gormenghast. God have mercy on me.

'What do you want of me? I am sick of it all! Sick of being followed. What have I done wrong – save to myself? So my papers are out of order, are they? So is my brain and heart. One day I'll do some shadowing myself!'

Titus, his hands gripping the sides of the box, turned his full face to the Magistrate.

'Why was I put in jail, your Worship,' he whispered, 'as though

I were a criminal? Me! Seventy-Seventh Earl and heir to that name.'

'Gormenghast,' murmured the Magistrate. 'Tell us more, dear boy.'

'What can I tell you? It spreads in all directions. There is no end to it. Yet it seems to me now to have boundaries. It has the sunlight and the moonlight on its walls just like this country. There are rats and moths – and herons. It has bells that chime. It has forests and it has lakes and it is full of people.'

'What kind of people, dear boy?'

'They had two legs each, your Worship, and when they sang they opened their mouths and when they cried the water fell out of their eyes. Forgive me, your Worship, I do not wish to be facetious. But what can I say? I am in a foreign city; in a foreign land; let me go free. I could not bear that prison any more.

'Gormenghast was a kind of jail. A place of ritual. But suddenly and under my breath I had to say good-bye.'

'Yes, my boy. Please go on.'

'There had been a flood, your Worship. A great flood. So that the castle seemed to float upon it. When the sun at last came out the whole place dripped and shone . . . I had a horse, your Worship . . . I dug my heels into her flank and I galloped into perdition. I wanted to *know*, you see.'

'What did you want to know, my young friend?'

'I wanted to know,' said Titus, 'whether there was any other place.'

'Any other place . . . ?'

'Yes.'

'Have you written to your mother?'

'I have written to her. But every time my letters are returned. Address unknown.'

'What was this address?'

'I have only one address,' said Titus.

'It is odd that you should have recovered your letters.'

'Why?' said Titus.

'Because your name is hardly probable. Now is it?'

'It is my name,' said Titus.

'What, Titus Groan, Seventy-Seventh Lord?'

'Why not?'

'It is unlikely. That sort of title belongs to another age. Do you dream at night? Have you lapses of memory? Are you a poet? Or is it all, in fact, an elaborate joke?'

'A joke? O God!' said Titus.

So passionate was his outcry that the Court fell silent. That was not the voice of a hoaxer. It was the voice of someone quite convinced of his own truth – the truth in his head.

FORTY

MUZZLEHATCH watched the boy and wondered why he had felt a compulsion to attend the Court. Why should he be interested in the comings and goings of this young vagabond? He had never from the first supposed the boy to be insane: though there were some in the Court who were convinced that Titus was mad as a bird, and had come for no other reason than to indulge a morbid curiosity.

No; Muzzlehatch had attended the Court because, although he would never have admitted it, he had become interested in the fate and future of the enigmatic creature he had found half drowned on the water-steps. That he *was* interested annoyed him for he knew, as he sat there, that his small brown bear would be pining for him and that every one of his animals was at that moment peering through the bars, fretful for his approach.

While such thoughts were in his head, a voice broke the stillness of the Court, asking permission to address the Magistrate.

Wearily, his Worship nodded his head, and then seeing who it was who had addressed him, he sat up and adjusted his wig. For it was Juno.

'Let me take him,' she said, her eloquent and engulfing eyes fixed upon his Worship's face. 'He is alone and resentful. Perhaps I could find out how best he could be helped. In the meantime, your Worship, he is hungry, travel-stained, and tired.'

'I object, your Worship,' said Inspector Acreblade. 'All that this lady says is true. But he is here on account of serious infringement of the Law. We cannot afford to be sentimental.'

'Why not?' said the Magistrate. 'His sins are not serious.'

He turned to her with a note almost of excitement in his tired old voice. 'Do you wish to be responsible,' he said, 'both to me and for him?'

'I take full responsibility,' said Juno.

'And you will keep in touch with me?'

'Certainly, your Worship – but there's another thing.'

'What is that, madam?'

'The young man's attitude. I will not take him with me unless he wishes it. Indeed I *cannot*.'

The Magistrate turned to Titus and was about to speak when he seemed to change his mind. He returned his gaze to her.

'Are you married, madam?'

'I am not,' said Juno.

There was a pause before the Magistrate spoke again.

'Young man,' he said, 'this lady has offered to act as your guardian until you are well again . . . what do you say?'

All that was weak in Titus rose like oil to the surface of deep water. 'Thank you,' he said. 'Thank you, madam. Thank you.'

FORTY-ONE

At first what was it but an apprehension sweet as far bird-song – a tremulous thing – an awareness that fate had thrown them together; a world had been brought into being – had been discovered? A world, a universe over whose boundaries and into whose forests they had not dared to venture. A world to be glimpsed, not from some crest of the imagination, but through simple words, empty in themselves as air, and sentences quite colourless and void; save that they set their pulses racing.

Theirs was a small talk – that evoked the measureless avenues of the night, and the green glades of noonday. When they said 'Hullo!' new stars appeared in the sky; when they laughed, this wild world split its sides, though what was so funny neither of them knew. It was a game of the fantastic senses; febrile; tender, tip-tilted. They would lean on the window-sill of Juno's beautiful room and gaze for hours on end at the far hills where the trees and buildings were so close together, so interwoven, that it was impossible to say whether it was a city in a forest or a forest in a city. There they leaned in the golden light, sometimes happy to talk – sometimes basking in a miraculous silence.

Was Titus in love with his guardian, and was she in love with him? How could it be otherwise? Before either of them had formed the remotest knowledge of one another's characters, they were already, after a few days, trembling at the sound of each other's footsteps.

But at night, when she lay awake, she cursed her age. She was forty. A little more than twice as old as Titus. Next to others of her age, or even younger, she still appeared unparalleled, with a head like a female warrior in a legend – but with Titus beside her she had no choice but to come to terms with nature, and she felt an angry and mutinous pain in her bosom. She thought of Muzzlehatch and how he had swept her off her feet twenty years earlier and of their voyagings to outlandish islands, and of how his ebullience became maddening and of how they were equally strong-headed, equally wilful, and of how their travels together became an agony for them both, for they broke against one another like waves breaking against headlands.

But with Titus it was so different. Titus from nowhere – a youth with an air about him: carrying over his shoulders a private world like a cloak, and from whose lips fell such strange tales of his boyhood days, that she was drawn to the very outskirts of that shadowland. 'Perhaps,' she thought, 'I am in love with something as mysterious and elusive as a ghost. A ghost never to be held at the breast. Something that will always melt away.'

And then she would remember how happy they sometimes were; and how every day they leaned on the sill together, not touching one another, but tasting the rarest fruit of all – the sharp fruit of suspense.

But there were also times when she cried out in the darkness biting her lips – cried out against the substance of her age: for it was *now* that she should be young; *now* above all other times, with the wisdom in her, the wisdom that was frittered away in her 'teens', set aside in her twenties, now, lying there, palpable and with forty summers gone. She clenched her hands together. What good was wisdom; what good was anything when the fawn is fled from the grove?

'God!' she whispered. '– Where is the youth that I *feel*?' And then she would heave a long shuddering sigh and toss her head on the pillow and gather her strength together and laugh; for she was, in her own way, undefeatable.

She lifted herself on her elbow, taking deep draughts of the night air.

'He needs me,' she would mutter in a kind of golden growl. 'It is for me to give him joy – to give him direction – to give him love. Let the world say what it likes – he is my mission. I will be always at his side. He may not know it, but I will be there. In body or in spirit always, near him when he most needs me. My child from Gormenghast. My Titus Groan.'

And then, at that moment, the light across her features would darken, and a shadow of doubt would take its place – for who was this youth? What was he? Why was he? What was it about him? Who were those people he spoke of? This inner world? Those memories? Were they true? Was he a liar – a cunning child? Some kind of wild misfit? Or was he mad? No! No! It couldn't be. It mustn't be.

FORTY-TWO

It was now four months since Titus first set foot in Juno's house. A watery light filled the sky. There were voices in the distance. A rustle of leaves – an acorn falling – the barking of a distant hound.

Juno leaned her superb, tropical head against the window in her sitting-room and gazed at the falling leaves or to speak more truly, she gazed *through* them, as they fell, fluttering and twisting, for her mind was elsewhere. Behind her in her elegant room a fire burned and cast a red glow across the marble cheek of a small head on a pedestal.

Then, all at once, there he was! A creature far from marble, waving to her from the statue'd garden, and the sight of him swept cogitation from her face as though a web were snatched from her features.

Seeing this happen, this change in her aspect, and the movement of her marvellous bosom, young Titus experienced, all in a flash, a number of simultaneous emotions. A pang of greed, green-carnal to the quick, sang, rang like a bell, his scrotum tightening; skedaddled through his loins and qualming tissues and began to burn like ice, the trembling fig on fire. And yet at the same time there was an aloofness in him – even a kind of suspicion, a perversity quite uncalled for. Something that Juno had always felt was there – something she feared beyond failure; this thing she could not compass with her arms.

Yet even worse than this, there was mixed up in him a pity for her. Pity that punctures love. She had given him everything, and he pitied her for it. He did not know that this was lethal and infinitely sad.

And there was the fear in him of being caught – caught in the generous folds of her love – her helpless love: fierce and loyal.

They gazed at one another. Juno with a quite incredible tenderness, something not easily associated with a lady in the height of fashion, and Titus with his greed returning as he watched her, flung out his arms in a wild, expansive gesture, quite false; quite melodramatic; and he knew it to be so, and so did she; but it was right at the moment, for his lust was real enough and lust is an arrogant and haughty beast and far from subtle.

So quickly did they flow one into another, these sensations of pity, physical greed, revulsion, excitement and tenderness, that they became blurred in an overriding impetus, a desire to hold all this in his outflung arms; to bring the total of their relationship to a burning focus. To bring it all to an *end*. That was the sadness of it. Not to create the deed that should set glory in motion but to bring glory to an end – to stab sweet love: to stab it to death. To be free of it.

None of this was in his mind. It was far away, in another pocket of his being. What was important, now, with her eyes bent upon him, and the shadow of a branch trembling across her breast, was the immemorial game of love: no less a game for being grave. No less grave for being wild. Grave as a great green sky. Grave as a surgeon's knife.

'So you thought you'd come back, my wicked one. Where have you been?'

'In hell,' said Titus. 'Swigging blood and munching scorpions.'

'That must have been great fun, my darling.'

'Not so,' said Titus, 'hell is overrated.'

'But you escaped?'

'I caught a plane. The slenderest thing you ever saw. A million years slid by in half a minute. I sliced the sky in half. And all for what?'

'Well . . . what?'

'To batten on you.'

'What of the slender plane?'

'I pressed a button and away she flew.'

'Is that good or bad?'

'It is very good. We don't want to be watched, *do* we? Machines are so inquisitive. You're rather far away. May I come up?'

'Of course, or you'll disjoint yourself.'

'Stay, stay where you are. Don't go – I'm on my way,' and with a mad and curious tilt of the head he disappeared from the statue'd garden and a few minutes later Juno could hear his feet on the stairs.

He was no longer entangled in a maze of moods. Whatever was happening to his subconscious, it made no attempt to break surface. His mind fell asleep. His wits fell awake. His cock trembled like a harp-string.

As he flung open the door of her room he saw her at once; proud, monumental, relaxed; one elbow on the mantelpiece, a smile on her lips, an eyebrow raised a little. His eyes were so fixed upon her that it was not surprising that he tripped up on a footstool that stood directly in his path, and trying to recover his balance tripped again and fell headlong.

Before he could recover she was already sitting on the floor beside him.

'This is your second time to crash at my feet. Have you hurt yourself, darling? Is it symbolic?' said Juno.

'Bound to be,' said Titus – 'absolutely *bound* to be.'

Had he known her less well this absurd fall might well have distracted him from his somewhat unoriginal purpose, but with Juno hovering above him and smelling like Paradise, his passion, far from being quenched, took on a strange quality – something ridiculous and lovable – so that to laugh became a part of their tenderness.

When Juno laughed the process began like a child's gurgle.

As for Titus he shouted his laughter.

It was the death-knell of false sentiment and of any cliché, or recognized behaviour. This was a thing of their own invention. A new compound.

A spasm caught hold of him. It sidled across his diaphragm and skidded through his entrails. It shot up like a rocket to the back of his throat; it radiated into separate turnings. It converged again, and capsized through him, cart-wheeled into a land of near-lunacy, where Juno joined him. What they were laughing at they had no idea, which is more shattering than a world of wit.

Titus, turning over with a shout, flung out his hand and a moment later found it resting upon Juno's thigh, and suddenly his laughter left him, and hers also, so that she rose to her feet and when he had done so also they put their arms around one another and they wandered away to the doorway and up the stairs and along a corridor and into a room whose walls were filled with books and pictures, suffused with the light of the autumn sun.

There was a sense of peace in this remote room, with the long shafts of sunlight a-swim with motes. Without any form of untidiness, this library was strangely informal. There was the remoteness of a ship at sea – a removal from normal life about it, as though it had never been put together by carpenters and masons, but was a projection of Juno's mind.

'Why?' said Titus.

'Why what, my sweet?'

'This unexpected room?'

'You like it?'

'Of course, but why the secrecy?'

'Secrecy?'

'I never knew it existed.'

'It doesn't really, not when it's empty. It only comes to life when we are in it.'

'Too glib, my sweet.'

'Brute.'

'Yes; but don't look sad. Who lit the fire? And don't say the goblins, will you?'

'I will never mention goblins again. I lit it.'

'How sure you are of me!'

'Not really. I feel a nearness, that's all. Something holds us together. In spite of our ages. In spite of everything.'

'O, age doesn't matter,' said Titus, taking hold of her arms.

'Thank you,' said Juno. A wry little smile came to her lips and then withered away. Her sculptured head remained. The lovely room grew soft with evening light as Juno and Titus slid from their clothes, and, trembling, sank to the floor together and began to drown.

The firelight flickered and grew dim; danced and died again. Their bodies sent one shadow through the room. It swarmed across the carpet; climbed a wall of books, and shook with joy across the solemn ceiling.

FORTY-THREE

A LONG while later when the moon had risen and while Juno and Titus were asleep in each other's arms by the dying fire, Muzzlehatch, in roguish mood, having found no answer to his knocking, had climbed the chestnut tree whose high branches brushed the library window, and had, at great risk to life and limb, made a lateral leap in the dark and had landed on the window-sill of Juno's room, catching hold, as he did so, of the open frame.

More by luck than skill he had managed to keep his balance and in doing so had made no noise at all save for the swish of the returning leaves and a faint rattle of the window-sash.

For some while now, he had seen little of Juno. It is true that for a few days following the unforeseen twinge of heart, when he had watched her move away from him down the drive of her home, he had seen something of her; he had realized that the past can never be recaptured, even if he had wished it, and he turned his life away from her, as a man turns his back upon his own youth.

Why then this visitation late at night to his one-time love? Why was he standing on the sill, blocking out the moon and staring at the embers of the fire? Because he longed to talk. To talk like a torrent. To put into words the scores of strange ideas that had been clamouring for release; clamouring to set his tongue on fire. All day he had longed for it.

The morning, afternoon and evening had been spent in moving from cage to cage in his inordinate zoo.

But love them as he did, he was not with his animals tonight. He wanted something else. He wanted words, and in his wish, he realized as the sun went down, was the image of the only person in the wide world at the foot of whose bed he could sit; bolt upright, his head held very high, his jaw thrust forward, his face alight with an endless sequence of ideas. Who else but Juno?

He had thought he had had from her all that she had to give. They had grown tired of each other. They knew too much about each other;

but now, quite unexpectedly, he needed her again. There were the stars to talk about, and the fishes of the sea. There were demons and there were the wisps of down that cling to the breasts of the seraphim. There were old clothes to ponder and terrible diseases. There were the flying missiles and the weird workings of the heart. There was *all . . . all* to be chosen from. It was talking for its own mad, golden sake.

So Muzzlehatch, ignoring his ancient car, chose from his animals a great smelling llama; saddled it and cantered from his courtyard and away across the hills to Juno's house, singing as he went.

He had no wish to disturb the other sleepers, but, as there was no reply to the pebbles he flung up at her window he was forced to knock upon the door. As this bore no results, and as he had no intention of bashing his way in, or of prising a window open, he decided to climb the chestnut tree whose branches fingered the windows on the second floor. He tethered the llama to the foot of the chestnut and began to climb and eventually to make the jump.

Standing on the sill, with a thirty-foot drop below him, he continued to stare for some while at the glow of embers in the grate, before he climbed carefully at last over the sash and down into the darkness of the room.

He had been in this room before, several times, but long ago, and it seemed very different tonight. He knew that Juno's bedroom was immediately below and he started to make for the shadowy door.

He grinned to think what a surprise it would be for her. She was wonderful in the way she took surprises. She never *looked* surprised. She just looked happy to see you – almost as though she had been waiting for you. Waking out of a deep sleep she had often surprised Muzzlehatch by turning her head to him and smiling with almost unbearable sweetness before she had even opened her eyes. It was this that he wished to see again before the burning words came tumbling out.

It was when he was but a few steps from the door that he heard the first sound. With a reflex stemming from far earlier times his hand moved immediately to his hip pocket. But there was no revolver there and he brought back his empty hand to his side. He had swung in his tracks at the sound and he faced the last few vermilion embers in the grate.

What he had heard exactly he did not know, but it might have been a sigh. Or it might have been the leaves of the tree at the window except that the sound seemed to have come from near the fireplace.

And then it came again: this time it was a voice.

'Sweet love . . . O, sweet, sweet love . . .'

The words were so soft that had they not been whispered in the profound silence of the night they would never have been heard.

Muzzlehatch, motionless in the seemingly haunted room, waited for several long minutes, but there were no more words and no sound save for a long sigh like the sigh of the sea.

Moving silently forward and a little to the right Muzzlehatch became almost immediately aware of a blot of darkness more intense than the surrounding shades and he bent forward with his hands raised as though ready for action.

What kind of a creature would lie on the floor and whisper? What kind of monster was luring him forward?

And then there was a movement in the darkness by the dulling embers and then silence again and no more stirrings.

The moon broke free of the clouds and shone into the library, lighting up a wall of books – lighting up four pictures: lighting up a patch of carpet and the sleeping heads of Juno and the boy.

Walking with slow, silent strides to the window; climbing through; jumping for the chestnut tree; lowering himself branch by branch; slipping and bruising his knee; reaching the ground; untying the llama and riding home – all this was a dream. The reality was in himself – a dull and sombre pain.

FORTY-FOUR

THE days moved by in a long, sweet sequence of light and air. Each day an original thing. Yet behind all this there was something else. Something ominous. Juno had noticed it. Her lover was restless.

'Titus!'

His name sprang up the stairs to where he lay.

'Titus!'

Was it an echo, or a second cry? Whichever one it was it failed to wake him. There was no movement – save in his dream, where, tumbling from a tower, a skewbald beast fell headlong.

The voice was twelve treads closer.

'Titus! My sweet!'

His eyelid moved but the dream fought on for life, the blotched beast plunging and wheeling through sky after sky.

The voice had reached the landing –

'My mad one! My bad one! Where are you, poppet?'

Through the curtained windows of the bedroom, a flight of sunbeams, traversing the warm, dark air, forced a pool of light on the pillow. And beside that pool of light, in the ash-grey, linen shadow, his head lay, as

a boulder might lie, or a heavy book might lie; motionless; undecipherable – a foreign language.

The voice was in the doorway; a cloud moved over the sun; and the
sunbeams died from the pillow.

But the rich voice was still a part of his dream, though his eyes were
open. It was blended with that rush of images and sounds which
swarmed and expanded as the creature of his nightmare, falling at
length into a lake of pale rainwater, vanished in a spurt of steam.

And as it sank, fathom by darkening fathom, a great host of heads,
foreign yet familiar, arose from the deep and bobbed upon the water –
and a hundred strange yet reminiscent voices began to call across the
waves until from horizon to horizon he was filled with a great turbulence
of sight and sound.

Then, suddenly, his eyes were wide open –

Where was he?

The empty darkness of the wall which faced him gave him no answer.
He touched it with his hand.

Who was he? There was no knowing. He shut his eyes again. In a few
moments there was no noise at all, and then the scuffling sound of a
bird in the ivy outside the tall window recalled the world that was
outside himself – something apart from this frightful zoneless nullity.

As he lifted himself up on one elbow, his memory returning in small
waves, he could not know that a figure filled the doorway of his room
– not so much in bulk as in the intensity of her presence – filled it as a
tigress fills the opening of her cave.

And like a tigress she was striped: yellow and black: and because of
the dark shadows behind her, only the yellow bands were visible, so
that she appeared to be cut in pieces by the horizontal sweeps of a
sword. And so she was like some demonstration of magic – a 'severed
woman' – quite extraordinary and wonderful to see. But there was no
one to see her, for Titus had his back to her.

And Titus could not see that her hat, plumed and piratical, sprouted
as naturally from her head as the green fronds from the masthead of a
date-palm.

She raised her hand to her breast. Not nervously; but with a kind of
tense and tender purpose.

Propped upon his elbow with his back to her, his aloneness touched
her sharply. It was wrong that he should be so single; so contained, so
little merged into her own existence.

He was an island surrounded by deep water. There was no isthmus
leading to her bounty; no causeway to her continent of love.

There are times when the air that floats between mortals becomes, in
its stillness and silence, as cruel as the edge of a scythe.

'O Titus! Titus, my darling!' she cried. 'What are you thinking of?'

He did not turn his head immediately, although at the first sound of her voice he was instantaneously aware of his surroundings. He knew that he was being watched – that Juno was very close indeed.

When at last he turned, she took a step towards the bed and she smiled with genuine pleasure to see his face. It was not a particularly striking face. With the best will in the world it could not be said that the brow or the chin or the nose or the cheek bones were *chiselled*. Rather, it seemed, the features of his head had, like the blurred irregularities of a boulder, been blunted by the wash of many tides. Youth and time were indissolubly fused.

She smiled to see the disarray of his brown hair and the lift of his eyebrows and the half-smile on his lips that seemed to have no more pigment in them than the warm sandy colour of his skin.

Only his eyes denied to his head the absolute simplicity of a monochrome. They were the colour of smoke.

'What a time of day to sleep!' said Juno, seating herself on the edge of the bed.

She took a mirror from her bag and bared her teeth for a moment as she scrutinized the line of her top lip, as though it were not hers but something which she might or might not purchase. It was perfectly drawn – a single sweep of carmine.

She put her mirror away and stretched her strong arms. The yellow stripes of her costume gleamed in a midday dusk.

'What a time to sleep!' she repeated. 'Were you *so* anxious to escape, my chicken-child? So determined to evade me that you sneak upstairs and waste a summer afternoon? But you know you are free in my house to do exactly what you please, don't you? To live as you please, how you please, where you please, you know this don't you, my spoiled one?'

'Yes,' said Titus, 'I remember you saying so.'

'And you will, won't you?'

'O yes, I will,' said Titus, 'I will.'

'Darling, you look so adorable.'

Titus took a deep breath. How sumptuous, how monumental and enormous she was as she sat there close to him, her wonderful hat almost touching, so it seemed, the ceiling. Her scent hung in the air between them. Her soft, yet strong white hand lay on his knee – but something was wrong – or lost; because his thoughts were of how his responses to her magnetism grew vaguer and something had changed or was changing with every passing day and he could only think of how he longed to be alone again in this great tree-filled city of the river – alone to wander listless through the sunbeams.

FORTY-FIVE

'You are a strange young man,' said Juno. 'I can't quite make you out. Sometimes I wonder why I take so much trouble over you, dear. But then of course I know, a moment later, that I have no choice. Now have I? You touch me so, my cruel one. You know it, don't you?'

'You say I do,' said Titus '– though *why* God only knows.'

'Fishing?' said Juno. 'Fishing again? Shall I tell you what I mean?'

'Not now,' said Titus, '*please*.'

'Am I boring you? Just tell me if I am. Always tell me. And if you are angry with me, don't hide it. Just shout at me. I will understand. I want you to be yourself – only yourself. That's how you flower best. O my mad one! My bad one!'

The plume of her hat swayed in the golden darkness. Her proud black eyes shone wetly.

'You have done so much for me,' said Titus. 'Don't think I am callous. But perhaps I must go. You give me too much. It makes me ill.'

There was a sudden silence as though the house had stopped breathing.

'Where could you go? You do not belong outside. You are my own, my discovery, my . . . my . . . can't you understand, I love you darling. I know I'm twice your – O Titus, I adore you. You are my mystery.'

Outside her window the sun shone fiercely on the honey-coloured stone of the tall house. The wall fell featurelessly down to a swift river.

On the other side of the house was the great quadrangle of prawn-coloured bricks and the hideous moss-covered statues of naked athletes and broken horses.

'There is nothing I can say,' said Titus.

'Of course there is nothing you can say. I understand. Some things can never be expressed. They lie too deep.'

She rose from beside him and turning away, tossed her proud handsome head. Her eyes were shut.

Something fell and struck the floor with a faint sound. It was her right earring, and she knew that the proud flinging gesture of her head had dislodged it, but she also knew that this was not the moment to pay any attention to so trivial a disturbance. Her eyes remained shut and her nostrils remained dilated.

Her hands came slowly together and then she lifted them to her up-flung chin.

'Titus,' she said, and her voice was little more than a whisper, a whisper less affected than one would expect to emerge from a lady in the stance she was adopting, with the plumes of her hat reaching down between her shoulder blades.

'Yes,' said Titus, 'What is it?'

'I am losing you, Titus. You are dissolving away. What is it I am doing wrong?'

At a bound Titus was off the bed and with his hands grasping her elbows had turned her about so that they faced one another in the warm dust of the high room. And then his heart grew sick, for he saw that her cheeks were wet and there in the wetness that wandered down her cheek a stain from her lashes appeared to float and thinly spread so that her heart became naked to him.

'Juno! Juno! This is too much for me. I cannot bear it.'

'There is no need to, Titus – please turn your head away.'

But Titus, taking no notice, held her closer than ever while her cheek-bones swam with tears. But her voice was steady.

'Leave me, Titus. I would rather be alone,' she said.

'I will never forget you,' said Titus, his hands trembling. 'But I must go. Our love is too intense. I am a coward. I cannot take it. I am selfish but not ungrateful. Forgive me, Juno – and say good-bye.'

But Juno, directly he released her, turned from him and, walking to the window, took out a mirror from her handbag.

'Good-bye,' said Titus.

Again there was no reply.

The blood rushed into the boy's head, and hardly knowing what he was doing he ran from the room and down the stairs and out into a winter afternoon.

FORTY-SIX

So Titus fled from Juno. Out of the garden and down the riverside road he kept on running. A sense of both shame and liberation filled him as he ran. Shame that he had deserted his mistress after all the kindness and love she had showered on him; and liberation in finding himself alone, with no one to weigh him down with affection.

But after a little while, his sense of aloneness was not altogether pleasurable. He was aware that something was missing. Something that he had half forgotten during his stay at Juno's house. It was nothing to do with Juno. It was a feeling that in leaving her he had once again to face the problem of his own identity. He was a part of something bigger than himself. He was a chip of stone, but where was the mountain from which it had broken away? He was the leaf but where was the tree? Where was his home? Where was his home?

Hardly knowing where he was going, he found after a long while that he was drawing near to that network of streets that surrounded Muzzlehatch's house and zoo; but before he reached that tortuous quarter he became aware of something else.

The road down which he stumbled was long and straight with high, windowless walls. The lines of perspective converged not many degrees from the skyline.

There was no one ahead of him in spite of the length of the road, but it seemed that he was no longer alone. Something had joined him. He turned as he ran, and at first saw nothing, for he had focused his eyes upon the distance. Then all at once he halted, for he became aware of something floating beside him, at the height of his shoulders.

It was a sphere no bigger than the clenched fist of a child, and was composed of some transparent substance, so pellucid that it was only visible in certain lights, so that it seemed to come and go.

Dumbfounded, Titus drew aside from the centre of the road until he could feel the northern wall at his back. For a few moments he leaned there seeing no sign of the glassy sphere, until suddenly, there it was again, hovering above him.

This time as Titus watched it he could see that it was filled with glittering wires, an incredible filigree like frost on a pane; and then as a cloud moved over the sun, and a dim, sullen light filled the windowless street, the little hovering globe began to throb with a strange light like a glow-worm.

At first, Titus had been more amazed than frightened by the mobile globe which had appeared out of nowhere, and followed or seemed to follow every movement he made; but then fear began to make his legs feel weak, for he realized that he was being watched not by the globe itself, for the globe was only an agent, but by some remote informer who was at this very moment receiving messages. It was this that turned Titus's fear into anger, and he swung back his arms as though to strike the elusive thing which hovered like a bird of paradise.

At the moment that Titus raised his hand, the sun came out again, and the little glittering globe with its coloured entrails of exquisite wire slid out of range, and hovered again as though it were an eyeball watching every move.

Then, as though restless, it sped, revolving on its axis, to the far end of the street where it turned about immediately and sang its way back to where it hung again five feet from Titus, who, fishing his knuckle of flint from his pocket, slung it at the hovering ball, which broke in a cascade of dazzling splinters, and as it broke there was a kind of gasp, as though the globe had given up its silvery ghost . . . as though it had a sentience of its own, or a state of perfection so acute that it entered, for the split second, the land of the living.

Leaving the broken thing behind him he began to run again. Fear had returned, and it was not until he found himself in Muzzlehatch's courtyard that he came to a halt.

FORTY-SEVEN

LONG before Titus could see Muzzlehatch he could hear him. That great rusty voice of his was enough to split the ear-drums of a deaf-mute. It thudded through the house, stamping itself upstairs and down again, in and out of half-deserted rooms and through the open windows so that the beasts and the birds lifted up their heads, or tilted them upon one side as though to savour the echoes.

Muzzlehatch lay stretched at length upon a low couch, and gazed directly down through the lower panes of a wide french window on the third floor. It gave him an unimpeded view of the long line of cages below him, where his animals lay drowsing in the pale sun-light.

This was a favourite room and a favourite view of his. On the floor at his side were books and bottles. His small ape sat at the far end of the couch. It had wrapped itself up in a piece of cloth and gazed sadly at its master, who had only a few moments ago been mouthing a black dirge of his own concoction.

Suddenly the small ape sprang to its feet and swung its long arms to and fro in a strangely jointless way, for it had heard a foot on the stairs two floors beneath.

Muzzlehatch lifted himself on to one elbow and listened. At first he could hear nothing, but then he also became aware of footsteps.

At last the door opened and an old bearded servant put his head around the corner.

'Well, well,' said Muzzlehatch. 'By the grey fibres of the xadnos tree, you look splendid, my friend. Your beard has never looked more authentic. What do you want?'

'There is a young man here sir, who would like to see you.'

'Really? What appallingly low taste. That can only be young Titus.'

'Yes, it's me,' said Titus, taking a step into the room. 'Can I come in?'

'Of course you can, sweet rebus. Should I be getting to my palsied feet? What with you in a suit like migraine, and a spotted tie, and

co-respondent shoes, you humble me. But swish as a willow-switch
you look indeed! There's been some scissor flashing, not a
doubt.'

'Can I sit down?'

'Sit down, of course you can. The whole floor is yours. Now then,'
muttered Muzzlehatch, as the ape leapt upon his shoulder, 'mind my
bloody eyes, boy, I'll be needing them later,' and then, turning to
Titus –

'Well, what do you want?' he said.

'I want to talk,' said Titus.

'What about, boy?'

Titus looked up. The huge, craggy head was tilted on one side. The
light coming through the window surrounded it with a kind of frosty
nimbus. Remote and baleful, it put Titus in mind of the inordinate
moon with its pits and craters. It was a domain of leather, rock and
bone.

'What about, boy?' he said again.

'First of all, my fear,' said Titus. 'Believe me, sir, I didn't like it.'

'What are you talking about?'

'I am afraid of the globe. It followed me until I broke it. And when
I broke it, it sighed. And I forgot my flint. And without my flint I am
lost . . . even more lost than before. For I have nothing else to prove
where I come from, or that I ever had a native land. And the proof of
it is only proof for me. It is no proof of anything to anyone but me. I
have nothing to hold in my hand. Nothing to convince myself that it is
not a dream. Nothing to prove my actuality. Nothing to prove that we
are talking together here, in this room of yours. Nothing to prove my
hands, nothing to prove my voice. And the globe! That intellectual
globe! Why was it following me? What did it want? Was it spying on
me? Is it magic, or is it science? Will they know who broke it? Will they
be after me?'

'Have a brandy,' said Muzzlehatch.

Titus nodded his head.

'Have you seen them, Mr Muzzlehatch? What are they?'

'Just toys, boy, just toys. They can be simple as an infant's rattle, or
complex as the brain of man. Toys, toys, toys, to be played with. As for
the one you chose to smash, number LKZoo572 ARG 39 576
Aij9843K2532 if I remember rightly, I have already read about it and
how it is reputed to be almost human. Not quite, but *almost*. So *THAT*
is what has happened? You have broken something quite hideously
efficient. You have blasphemed against the spirit of the age. You have
shattered the very spear-head of advancement. Having committed this
reactionary crime, you come to me. Me! This being so, let me peer out
of the window. It is always well to be watchful. These globes have

origins. Somewhere or other there's a backroom boy, his soul working in the primordial dark of a diseased yet sixty horse-power brain.'

'There's something else, Mr Muzzlehatch.'

'I'm sure there is. In fact there is everything else.'

'You belittle me,' said Titus, turning suddenly upon him, 'by your way of talking. It is serious to me.'

'Everything is serious or not according to the colour of one's brain.'

'My brain is black,' said Titus, 'if that's a colour.'

'Well? Spit it out. The core of it.'

'I have deserted Juno.'

'Deserted her?'

'Yes.'

'It had to happen. She is too good for males.'

'I thought you would hate me.'

'Hate you? Why?'

'Well, sir, wasn't she your . . . your . . .'

'She was my everything. But like the damned creature that I inescapably am, I swapped her for the freedom of my limbs. For solitude which I eat as though it were food. And if you like, for animals. I have erred. Why? Because I long for her and am too proud to admit it. So she slipped away from me like a ship on the ebb tide.'

'I loved her too,' said Titus: 'If you can believe it.'

'To be sure you did, my pretty cutlet. And you still do. But you are young and prickly: passionate and callow: so you deserted her.'

'Oh God!' said Titus. 'Talk sir, with fewer words. I am sick of language.'

'I will try to,' said Muzzlehatch. 'Habits are hard to break.'

'Oh, sir, have I hurt your feelings?'

Muzzlehatch turned away and stared through the window. Almost immediately below him, he could see, through the bars of a domed roof, a family of leopards.

'Hurt my feelings! Ha ha! Ha ha! I am a kind of crocodile on end. I have no feelings. As for you. Get on with life. Eat it up. Travel. Make journeys in your mind. Make journeys on your feet. To prison with you in a filthy garb! To glory with you in a golden car! Revel in loneliness. This is only a city. This is no place to halt.'

Muzzlehatch was still turned away.

'What of the castle that you talk about – that crepuscular myth? Would you return after so short a journey? No, you must go on. Juno is part of your journey. So am I. Wade on, child. Before you lie the hills, and their reflections. Listen! Did you hear that?'

'What?' said Titus.

Muzzlehatch did not trouble to answer as he raised himself on one elbow, and peered out of the window.

There away to the east, he saw a column of scientists marching, and almost at the same moment the beasts of the zoo began to lift their heads, and stare all in the same direction.

'What is it?' said Titus.

Muzzlehatch again took no notice, but this time Titus did not wait for an answer, but moved to the window, and stared down, with Muzzlehatch, cheek by cheek, at the panorama spread out below him.

Then came the music: the sound of trumpets as from another world: the distant throbbing of the drums; and then, shattering the distance, the raw immoderate yell of a lion.

'They are after us,' said Muzzlehatch. 'They are after our guts.'

'Why?' said Titus. 'What have I done?'

'You have only destroyed a miracle,' said Muzzlehatch. 'Who knows how pregnant with possibilities that globe could be? Why, you dunderhead, a thing like that could wipe out half the world. Now, they'll have to start again. You were observed. They were on their toes. Perhaps they found your flint. Perhaps they have seen us together. Perhaps this . . . perhaps that. One thing is certain. You must disappear. Come here.'

Titus frowned, and then straightened himself. Then he took a step towards the big man.

'Have you heard of the Under-River?' asked Muzzlehatch.

Titus shook his head.

'This badge will take you there.' Muzzlehatch folded back his cuff, and tore away a bit of fabric from the lining. On the small cloth badge was printed the sign

'What is that supposed to mean?' said Titus.

'Keep quiet. Time is on the slide. The drums are twice as loud. Listen.'

'I can hear them. What do they want? What about your . . . ?'

'My animals? Let them but try to touch them. I'll loose the white gorilla on the sods. Put away the badge, my dear. Never lose it. It will take you down.'

'Down?' said Titus.

'Down. Down into an order of darkness. Waste no time.'

'I don't understand,' said Titus.

'This is no time for comprehension. This is a great moment for the legs.'

Then suddenly a screaming of monkeys filled the room, and even Muzzlehatch with his stentorian throat was forced to raise his voice to a shout.

'Down the stairs with you, and into the wine cellars. Turn left immediately at the foot of the flight, and mind the nails on the hand-rail. Left again, and you will see ahead of you, dimly, a tunnel, vaulted and hung with filthy webs as thick as blankets. Press on for an hour at least. Go carefully. Beware of the ground at your feet. It is littered with the relics of another age. There is a stillness down there that is not to be dwelt upon. Here, cram these in your pockets.'

Muzzlehatch strode across the room, and pulling open a drawer in an old cabinet he took a fistful of candles.

'Where are we? Ah yes. Listen. By now you will be under the city at the northern end, and the darkness will be intense. The walls of the tunnel will be closing in. There will not be much room above your head. You will have to move doubled up. Easier for you than for me. Are you listening? If not, I'll blast you, child. This is no game.'

'O sir,' said Titus, 'that is why I cannot keep still. Listen to the trumpets! Listen to the beasts!'

'Listen to me instead! You have your candle raised; but in place of hollow darkness you have before you a gate. At the foot of the gate is a black dish, upside down. Underneath it you will find a key. It may not be the key to your miserable life, but it will open the gate for you. Once through, and you have before you a long, narrow gradient that stretches at average pace for forty minutes. If you whisper the world sighs and sighs again. If you shout the earth reverberates.'

'Oh sir,' said Titus, 'don't be poetic, I can't bear it. The zoo is going mad. And the scientists . . . the scientists . . .'

'Fugger the scientists!' said Muzzlehatch. 'Now listen like a fox. I said a gradient. I said echoes. But now another thing. The sound of water . . .'

'Water,' said Titus, 'I'm damned if I'll drown.'

'Pull your miserable self together, Lord Titus Groan. You will come, inevitably, to where suddenly, on turning a corner, there is a noise above you, like distant thunder, for you will be under the river itself . . . the same river that brought you to the city months ago. Ahead of you

will spread a half-lit field of flagstones, at the far end of which you will
see the glow of a green lantern. This lantern is set upon a table. Seated
at this table, his face reflecting the light, you will see a man. Show him
the badge I have given you. He will scrutinize it through a glass, then
look up at you with an eye as yellow as lemon peel, whistle softly
through a gap in his teeth until a child comes trotting through the
shadows and beckons you to follow to the north.'

FORTY-EIGHT

FOR all the noise of water overhead, there was silence also. For all the
murk there were the shreds of light. For all the jostling and squalor,
there were also the great spaces and a profound withdrawal.

Long fleets of tables were like rafts with legs, or like a market, for
there were figures seated at these tables with crates and sacks before
them or at their sides or heaped together upon the damp ground . . . a
sodden and pathetic salvage, telling of other days in other lands. Days
when hope's bubble, bobbing in their breasts, forgot, or had not heard
of dissolution. Days of bravado. Gold days and green days. Days half
forgotten. Days with a dew upon them. And here they were, the
hundreds of them, at their stalls, awaiting, or so it seemed, the hour
that never came, the hour for the market to open and the bells to ring.
But there was no merchandise. Nothing to buy or sell. What they had
left was what they meant to keep. There was also something of a
dreadful ward, for throughout the dripping halls that led in all directions
there were beds and berths of every description, pallets, litters and
mattresses of straw.

But there were no doctors and there was no authority: and the sick
were free to leap among the shadows and soar with their own fever.
And the hale were free to spend their days in bed, curled up like cats,
or at full stretch, rigid as men in armour.

A world of sound and silence stitched together. A habitation under
the earth . . . under the river: a kingdom of the outcasts; the fugitives;
the failures; the mendicants; the plotters; a secret world with a roof that
leaked eternally, so that wide skirts of water reflected the beds and the
tables, and the denizens who leaned against pit-props or pillars, and
who long ago had been forced to form themselves into ragged groups so
that it seemed that the dark scene was seismic and had thrown up
islands of wood and iron. All was reflected here in the dim glazes. If a
hand moved, or a head was flung back, or if anyone stumbled the

reflection stumbled with him, or gestured in the depths of the sheen. It did not seem to brighten but rather to intensify the darkness that there were hundreds of lamps and that many of them were reflected in the 'lakes'. It was so vast a district that there were of necessity deep swaths of darkness hanging beyond reach of brand or lantern, dire volumes at whose centres the air was thick with dark, and smelt of desolation. The candles guttered even at the verge of these deadly pockets, guttered and failed as though from a failure of the candle's nerve.

A wilderness of tables, beds and benches. The stoves and curious ranges. The figures moving by at various levels, with various distinctness, some silhouetted, sharp and edged like insects, some pale and luminous against the gloom. And the 'lakes' changing their very nature: now ankle-deep, the clear water showing the pocked and cheesy bricks beneath and then, a moment later, at a shift of the head, revealing a world in so profound and so meticulous an inversion as to swallow up the eye that gazed upon it and drag it down, out-fathoming invention.

And overhead the eternal roar of the river: a voice, a turmoil, a lunatic wrestling of waters, whose muffled reverberations were a background to all that ever happened in the Under-River.

To those ignorant of extreme poverty and of its degradations; of pursuit and the attendant horrors; of the crazed extremes of love and hate; for those ignorant of such, there was no cause to suffer such a place. It was enough for the great city to know and to have heard of it by echo or by rumour and to maintain a tacit silence as dreadful as it was accepted. Whether it was through shame or fear or a determination to ignore, or even to disbelieve what they knew to be true, it was, for whatever reason, an unheard of thing for the outrageous place to be mentioned by those who, being less desperate, were able to live out their lives in either of the two great cities that faced one another across the river.

And so the halls and tunnels of the cold sub-river life where it throbbed beneath the angry water were, to the populace on the opposing banks, in the nature of a bad dream, both too bizarre to be taken seriously, yet horrid enough to speculate upon, only to recoil, only to speculate again, and recoil again, and tear the clinging cobwebs from the brain.

What were the thoughts of those who lived and slept in the fastness beneath the water? Were these thieves and broken poets, these fugitives affected by some stigma; were they jealous or afraid of the world? How had they all foregathered in this crepuscular region? What had they so much in common that they needed each other's presences? Nothing but hope. Hope like a wavering marsh-light: hope like a pale sun: hope like a floating leaf.

All at once and very close a harsh and unexpected noise of metal being sharpened was in horrid contrast to the soft drip . . . drip . . . drip . . . of water from above.

Far away there was an angry sound that broke into fragments that echoed for a while in hollow dungeons.

Somewhere, someone was adjusting the shutter of a lantern so that for a little while a shaft of light played erratically to and fro across the darkness, picking out groups of figures at varying distances, groups like hummocks of varying sizes, some pyramidal, some irregular, each with a life and shape of its own.

Before the door of the lantern was finally fastened the thread of light had come to rest upon a group of them. For a long while they had been silent; beneath the light the colour of a bruise. It hung above them, casting the kind of glow that suggested crime. Even the kindest smile appeared ghastly.

FORTY-NINE

MR CRABCALF lay upon a trestle bed, his brow creased with hours of semi-thought: his flat and speculative face was directed at the dark yet glistening ceiling where the moisture collected and hung in beads that grew and grew like fruit, and fell, when water-ripe, to the ground.

What did he see among the overhead shadows? Some, in his place, must surely have seen battle or the great jaws of carnivores or landscapes of infinite mystery and invention complete with bridges and deep chasms, forests and craters. But Crabcalf saw none of these. He saw nothing in the shadows but great profiles of himself, one after the other.

He lay quietly, his arms outside the thick red blanket that covered him. To his left sat Slingshott on the edge of a crate, his knees drawn up to his chin, his long jaw resting on his kneecap. He wore a woollen cap, and like Mr Crabcalf had lapsed for the while into silence.

At the foot of the bed, crouched like a condor over its young, was Carrow cooking a meal over a stove, and stirring what looked like a mass of horrible green fibre in a wide-necked pot. As he stirred he whistled between his teeth. The sound of this meditative occupation could be heard for a minute or two, echoing faintly in far quarters before a hundred other sounds slid back to hush it.

Mr Crabcalf was propped up, not against pillows or a bolster of straw, but by books; and every book was the same book with its dark grey spine. There at his back, banked up like a wall of bricks, were the so-called 'remainders' of an epic, long ago written, long ago forgotten, except by its author, for his lifework lay at his shoulder blades.

Out of the five hundred copies printed thirty years ago by a publisher long since bankrupt, only twelve copies had been sold.

Around his bed, three hundred identical volumes were erected . . . like walls or ramparts, protecting him from – what? There was also a cache beneath the bed that gathered dust and silver-fish.

He lay with his past beside him, beneath him, and at his head: his past, five hundred times repeated, covered with dust and silver-fish. His head, like Jacob's on the famous stone, rested against the volumes of lost breath. The ladder from his miserable bed reached up to heaven. But there were no angels.

FIFTY

'WHAT on earth are you doing?' said Crabcalf in a deep voice (a voice so very much more impressive than anything it ever had to say). 'I have seen some pretty revolting things in my time, but the meal that you are preparing, Mr Carrow, is the most nauseating affair that I ever remember.'

Mr Carrow hardly troubled to look up. It was all part of the day. There would have been something missing if Crabcalf had forgotten to insult his crouching and angular friend, who went on stirring the contents of a copper bowl.

'How many of us have you killed in your time, I wonder?' muttered Crabcalf, allowing his head to fall back on the pillow of books, so that a little whiff of dust rose into the lamplight, new heavens being formed, new constellations, as the motes wavered.

'Eh? Eh? How many have you sent to their deathbeds through hapless poisoning?'

Even Crabcalf was apt to become tired of his own heavy banter, and he shut his eyes. Carrow as usual made no answer. But Crabcalf was content. Even more than most he felt a great need for companionship, and he spoke only to prove to himself that his friendships were real.

Carrow knew all about this, and from time to time he turned his hawk-like features towards the one-time poet and lifted the dry corner of his lipless mouth in a dry smile. This arid salutation meant much to Crabcalf. It was part of the day.

'O, Carrow,' murmured the recumbent Crabcalf, 'your desiccation is like juice to me. I love you better than a ship's biscuit. You have no

green emotions. You are dry, my dear Carrow: so dry, you pucker me.
Never desert me, old friend.'

Carrow turned his eyes to the bed, but never ceased in his stirring of
the grey broth.

'You are talkative today,' he said. 'Don't overdo it.'

The third of the trio, Slingshott, rose to his feet.

'I don't know about you,' he said, addressing the space halfway
between Carrow and Crabcalf, 'but speaking for myself I'm hand in
hand with grief.'

'You always are,' said Crabcalf. 'At this time of day. And so am I. It
is the eternal problem. Is one to be hungry, or is one to eat old Carrow's
gruel?'

'No, no, I'm not talking about food,' said Slingshott. 'It's worse than
that. You see, I lost my wife. I left her behind. *Was* I wrong?' He lifted
his face to the dripping ceiling. No one answered.

'When I escaped from the merciless mines,' he said, folding his arms.
'When the days and the nights were salt, and my lips were cracked and
split with it, and the taste of that vile chemical was like knives in my
mouth and a white death more terrible than any darkness of the
spirit . . . when . . . I escaped I swore . . .'

'That whatever happened you would never again complain of
anything whatever, for nothing could be as terrible as the mines,' said
Crabcalf.

'Why, how do you know all this? Who has been . . . ?'

'We have all heard it many times before. You tell us too often,' said
Carrow.

'It is always in my head, and I forget.'

'But you escaped. Why fret about your deliverance?'

'I am so happy that they cannot take me. O never let them take me
to the salt mines. There was a time when I collected eggs: and
butterflies . . . and moths . . .'

'I am growing hungry,' said Crabcalf.

'I used to dread the nights I spent alone: but after a while, when for
various reasons I was forced to quit the house, and had to spend my
evenings with the others, I looked back upon those solitary evenings as
times of excitement. It has always been my longing to be alone again
and drink the silence.'

'I wouldn't care to live *alone* in this place,' said Crabcalf.

'It's not a nice place, that is very true,' said Slingshott, 'but I have
been living here for twelve years and it is my only home.'

'Home,' said Carrow. 'What does that mean? I have heard the word
somewhere. Wait . . . it is coming back . . .' He had ceased to stir the
bowl. 'Yes, it is coming back . . .' (His voice was sharp and crisp.)

'Well, let's have it then,' said Crabcalf.

'I'll tell you,' said Carrow. 'Home is a room dappled with firelight: there are pictures and books. And when the rain sighs, and the acorns fall, there are patterns of leaves against the drawn curtains. Home is where I was safe. Home is what I fled from. Who mentioned home? Who mentioned home?'

The tight-lipped Carrow, who prided himself on his control and who loathed emotionalism, sprang to his feet in a fury of self-disgust, and stumbling away, upset the grey soup so that it spread itself sluggishly beneath Crabcalf's bed.

This disturbance caused two passers-by to stop and stare. They had heard Carrow's outburst.

One of the two men cocked his scorbutic head on one side like a bird and then nudged his companion with such zest as to fracture one of the smaller ribs.

'You have hurt me bad, you have,' growled his comrade.

'Forget it!' said his irritating friend. He turned his gaze to where Crabcalf and Slingshott sat with frowns like birds' nests on their brows.

Slingshott got to his feet and took a few paces towards the newcomers. Then he lifted his face to the dark ceiling.

'When I escaped from the merciless mines,' he said, 'when the days and the nights were salt, and my lips were cracked and split with it and the taste of that damn chemical . . .'

'Yes, old man, we know all about that,' said Crabcalf. 'Sit down and keep quiet. Now let me ask these two gentlemen whether they are interested in literature.'

The taller of the two, a long-limbed, crop-headed man with a grass-green handkerchief, rose to tiptoe.

'Interested!' he cried. 'I'm practically literature myself. But surely you know that? After all, my family is not exactly devoid of lustre. We are patrons, as you know, of the arts, and have been so for hundreds of years. In fact, it is doubtful whether the literature of our time could come into being without the inspired guidance of the Foux-Foux family. Think of the great works that would never have been born without the patronage of my grandfather. Think of the works of Morzch in general, and of his masterpiece "Pssss" in particular: and think how my mother nursed him back out of chaos to the limpid vision of . . .'

'Oh, shut up,' said a voice. 'You and your family make me sick.'

It was Crabcalf who, surrounded and walled in by the hundreds of unsold copies of his ill-fated novel, felt that he if anyone should be the judge not only of literature, but of all that went on behind the sordid scenes.

'Foux-Foux indeed,' he continued. 'Why you and your family are nothing but jackals of art.'

'Well really,' said Foux-Foux. 'That's hardly fair, you know. We cannot all be creative, but the Foux-Foux family have always . . .'

'Who's your friend?' said Crabcalf, interrupting. 'Is he a jackal too? Never mind. Carrow has flown. He helped me in his day to kill emotion. But now he vanishes on an up-draught of the stuff. He has failed me. I need a cynic for a friend, old man. A cynic to steady me. Sit down, indeed. Is your friend a Foux-Foux too? I soften, as you see. I can't make enemies: not for long. It is only when I look at my books that I get angry. After all, that's where my heart's blood is. But who reads them? Who cares about them? Answer me that!'

Slingshott rose to his feet, as though it were he who had been addressed.

'I left my wife behind,' he said. 'On the fringe of the ice-cap. Did I do right?' He brought his heel down to the wet brick floor with a click and a spurt of spray.

But as no one was watching him his posture faded out. He turned and addressed the author.

'Shall I continue with the broth?' he said.

'Yes, if that's what it is,' said Crabcalf. 'By all means do. As for you, gentlemen, join us . . . eat with us . . . suffer acute bellyache with us . . . and then, if needs be, die with us as friends.'

FIFTY-ONE

At that very moment, with Crabcalf about to expand . . . Carrow gone . . . Slingshott about to dilate upon the salt mines, and Foux-Foux on the point of withdrawing a long eating-knife from his belt, and his friend about to stir what was left of the sluggish grey fibre in the pot . . . at that very moment there was a pause, a silence, and in the pregnant heart of that silence another sound could be heard, the quick muffled fly-away thudding of hounds' feet.

The sound came from the black and hollow land that spread to the south in a honeycomb of under-river masonry: the sound grew louder.

'Here they come again,' said Crabcalf. 'What dandy boys they are, and no mistake.'

The others made no reply, but remained motionless, waiting for the appearance of the hounds.

'It is later than I thought,' said Foux-Foux . . . 'but look, look . . .'

But there was nothing to see. It was only the shifting of a long shadow and a glimmer across the saturated bricks. The hounds were still a league or more away.

Why were these men with their heads cocked upon one side so anxious to see the entrance of the hounds? Why were they so intent?

It was always like this in the Under-River, for the days and nights could be so unbearably monotonous: so long: so featureless, that whenever anything really happened, even when it was expected, the darkness appeared to be momentarily pierced, as though by a thought in a dead skull, and the most trivial happening took on prodigious proportions.

But now, as other figures emerged out of the semi-darkness, there appeared out of the shadowy south seven loping hounds.

They were exceptionally lean, their ribs showing, but were by no means ill. Their heads were held high as though to remind the world of a proud lineage, and their teeth were bared as a reminder of something less noble. Their tongues lolled out of the sides of their mouths. Their skulls were chiselled. They panted as they passed: their nostrils dilated; their eyes shone. There were seven of them, and now they were gone, even the sound of them, and the night welled up again.

Where are they now, those hot-breath'd lopers? They have veered away through colonnades a-drip. They have reached a lake four inches deep and a mile across where their feet splash in the shallow, sombre water. The spray surrounds them as they gallop in a pack so tight, that it seems they are one creature.

On the far side of the broad-skirted water-sheen the floor rose a little, and the ground was comparatively dry. Here, pranked across the lamp-lit slope were small communities similar to the group that had for its recumbent centre the bedridden Crabcalf. Similar, but different, for in every head are disparate dreams.

And so, at speed, threading the groups lit here and there with lamps, the dog-pack all of a sudden and seemingly with no warning doubled its speed until it reached a district where there was more light than is common beneath the river. Scores of lamps hung from nails in the great props or stood on ledge or shelf, and it was beneath a circle of these that the hounds drew up and lifted their heads to the dripping ceiling, and gave one single simultaneous howl. At the sound of this a tall spare man with a minute fleshless head, like the head of a bird, came out of the lamp-stained gloom, his white apron stained with blood, for in his arms he held seven hunks of crimson horse-flesh. As he approached them, the hounds quivered.

But he did not give them to the dogs at once. He lifted the dripping things above his head, where they shone with a ghostly, almost luminous red. Then forming his mouth into a perfect circle he hooted, and in the silence the echoes replied, and it was at the sound of the fourth echo that he tossed the crimson steaks high into the air. The hounds, taking their turn, one after the other, leaped at the falling meat, gripped it between their teeth, and then, turning in their tracks, galloped, with their heads held high, across the great sheet of water where they disappeared into the wet darkness.

The man with the bird-like head wiped his hand on his apron'd hips and plunged his long arms up to the elbows in a tub of tepid water. Beyond the tub, twenty feet to the west was a wall, covered with rank ferns, and in this wall was an arched doorway. On the other side of this door was a room lit by six lamps.

FIFTY-TWO

HERE, in this fern-hung chamber, set about with cracked and broken mirrors to reflect the light of the lamps, are a group of characters. Some lie reclined upon mildewed couches: some sit upright on wickerwork chairs: some are gathered about a central table.

They are talking in a desultory way, but when they hear the bird-headed man begin his hooting, the sound of their conversation subsides. They have heard it a thousand times and are blunted to the strangeness of it, yet they listen as though every time were the first.

At one end of a rotting couch, with his great bearded chin propped up by knuckly fists, sits an ancient man. At the other end sits his equally ancient wife with her feet tucked up beneath her. The three of them (man, wife, and couch) present a picture of venerable decrepitude.

The ancient man sits very still, occasionally lifting his hand and staring at something that is crawling across his wrist.

His wife is busier than this, for here, there and everywhere run endless threads of coloured wool, until it seems she is festooned with it. The old lady, whose eyes are sore and red, has long since given up any idea of knitting but spends her time in trying to disentangle the knots in the wool. There were days, long ago, when she knew what she was making, and yet earlier days, when she was actually known by the clickety-clack of her needles. They had been a part, a tiny part of the Under-River.

But not so, now. Entanglement, for her, is everything. Occasionally she looks up and catches her husband's eye, and they exchange smiles, pathetically sweet. Her little mouth moves, as though it is forming a word; but it is no word but a movement of her withered lips. For his part, there is no seeing through the long, hairy fog of his beard; no mouth is locatable . . . but all his love finds outlet through his eyes. He takes no part in the disentangling, knowing that this is her only joy, and that the knots and interweavings must outlive her.

But tonight, at the sound of the hooting she lifts her head from her work.

'Dear Jonah,' she says. 'Are you there?'

'Of course I am, my love. What is it?' says the old man.

'My mind was roving back to a time . . . a time . . . almost before I . . . almost as though . . . what was it I used to do? I can't remember . . . I can't remember at all . . .'

'To be sure, my squirrel; it was a long while ago.'

'One thing I *do* remember, Jonah, dear, though whether we were together . . . oh but we *must* have been. For we ran away, didn't we, and floated like two feathers from our foes? How beautiful we were, Jonah, my own, and you rode with me beside you into the forest . . . are you listening, dearest?'

'Of course, of course . . .'

'You were my prince.'

'Yes, my little squirrel, that is so.'

'I am tired, Jonah . . . tired.'

'Lean back, my dear.' He tries to sit forward so that he can touch her, but is forced to desist, for the movement has brought with it a jab of pain.

One of the four men, who are playing cards on the marble table, turns round at the sound of a little gasp, but cannot make out where the sound comes from. He turns back to a perusal of his hand. Another to have heard the sound, is an all-but-naked infant who crawls towards the rotting couple dragging its left leg after it, as though it were some kind of dead and worthless attachment.

When the infant reaches the couch where the old couple sit silent again, it stares at them in turn with a concentration that would have been embarrassing in a grown-up. There it heaves itself up and keeps its balance by grasping the edge of the couch. In the eyes of the ragged infant there seems to be an innocence quite moving to behold. A final innocence that has survived in spite of a world of evil.

Or was it, as some might think, mere emptiness? A sky-blue vacancy? Would it be too cynical to believe that the little child was without a thought in its head and without a flicker of light in its soul? For otherwise why should the infant turn on, at the most sentimental moment, his tiny waterworks, and flick an arc of gold across the gloom?

Having piddled with an incongruous mixture of nonchalance and solemnity the infant catches sight of a spoon shining in the shadows beneath the couch and dropping to his little naked haunches he rights himself and crawls in search of treasure. He is the essence of purpose. His minute appendage is forgotten: it dangles like a slug. He has lost interest in it. The spoon is *all*.

But the dangler's done its worst . . . in all innocence, and in all ignorance, for it has saturated a phalanx of warrior ants who, little guessing that a cloudburst was imminent, were making their way across difficult country.

FIFTY-THREE

THE child, and now the father and mother, refugees from the Iron Coast, sit opposite one another at the table. The father plays his cards with a mere fraction of his brain. The rest of it, a scythe-like instrument, is far away in realms of white equations.

His wife, a heavy-jaw'd woman, scowls at him out of habit. As usual he has won enough token money to correspond to a dozen fortunes. But there is no money down here in the Under-River, nor anywhere else for them, as far as she can see. Everything has gone wrong. Her uncle had been a general long ago; and her brother had been presented to a duke. But what was that to them now? They were real men. But her husband was only a brain. They should never have tried to escape from the Iron Coast. They should never have married, and as for their son . . . he would have been better unborn. She turns her heavy-jaw-boned head to her husband. How aloof he seems: how sexless!

She rises to her feet. 'Are you a man?' she shouts.

'Delicious query!' cries a voice, like a cracked bell. ' "Are you a man?" she says. What fun! What roguery! Well, Mr Zed? Are you?'

The brilliant, articulate, white-eyelashed Mr Zed turns his eyes to his wife and sees nothing but $Tx\frac{1}{4} \ p\frac{3}{4} = \frac{1}{2} - prx\frac{1}{4}$ (inverted). Then he turns them on the willowy man with the cracked voice, and he realizes all in an instant that his last three years of constructive thought have been wasted. His premises have failed him. He had been assuming that Space was intrinsically modelled.

Realizing that this gentleman is way over the horizon, Crack-Bell tosses his hair from his forehead, laughs like a carillon, gesticulates freely to his partners across the table, in such a way as to say 'O, isn't it marvellous?'

But his partner, the sober Carter sees nothing marvellous about it, and leans back in his chair with his eyes half-closed. He is a massive, thoughtful man, not given to extravagance either in thought or deed.

He keeps his partner under observation, for Crack-Bell is apt to become too much of a good thing.

Yes, Crack-Bell is happy. Life to him is a case of 'now' and nothing but 'now'. He forgets the past as soon as it has happened and he ignores the whole concept of a future. But he is full of the sliding moment. He has a habit of shaking his head, not because he disagrees with anything, but through the sheer spice of living. He tosses it to and fro, and sends the locks cavorting.

'He's a card he is, that husband of yours,' cries Crack-Bell leaning across the table and tapping Mrs Zed on her freckle-mottled wrist. 'He's an undeniable one, eh? Eh? Eh? But oh so *dark* . . . Why don't he laugh and play?'

'I hate men,' says Mrs Zed. 'You included.'

FIFTY-FOUR

'JONAH dear, are you all right?' said the old, old lady.

'Of course I am. What is it squirrel?' The old man smoothed his beard.

'I must have dropped off to sleep.'

'I wondered . . . I wondered . . .'

'I dreamed a dream,' said the old lady.

'What was it about?'

'I don't remember . . . something about the sun.'

'The sun?'

'The great round sun that warmed us long ago.'

'Yes, I remember it.'

'And the rays of it? The long, sweet rays . . .'

'Where were we then . . . ?'

'Somewhere in the south of the world.'

The old lady pursed her lips. Her eyes were very tired. Her hands went on and on with their disentangling of the wool, and the old man watched her as though she were of all things the most lovely.

FIFTY-FIVE

'HA, ha, ha, ha, ha, ha, ha, ha, ha, ha, ha, ha!' cried Crack-Bell, throwing his head back and laughing like crockery.

'Steady on,' said Sober-Carter, the heavy man. 'You would do well to keep quiet. Life may be hilarious to you, but They are on your trail.'

'But I haven't got a trail,' said Crack-Bell. 'It petered out long ago. Don't let's think about it. I am happy in half-light. I have always loved the damp. I can't help it. It suits me. Ha, ha!'

'That laugh of yours,' said Carter, 'will be the death of you, one day.'

'Not it,' said Crack-Bell. 'I'm as safe down here as a fig in a fog. To hell with the fourth dimension. It's *now* that matters!' He tossed a mop of hair out of his eyes and, turning on a gay heel he pointed to a figure in the shades. 'Look at her,' he cried, 'why don't she move? Why don't she laugh and sing?'

The shadow was a girl. She stood motionless. Her huge black eyes suggested illness. A man came through the door. Looking to neither right nor left he made for the dark girl where she stood.

She gazed expressionlessly over the shoulder of the man as he approached her with long, spindly strides. It seemed as though, knowing his features as she did, his high flinty cheekbones, his pale skin, his glinting eyes, his cleft chin, she saw no reason to focus her sight. When he reached her, he stood aggressively, like a mantis, his knee bent a little, his long-fingered hands clasped together in a bunch of bones.

'How much longer?' she said.

'Soon. Soon.'

'Soon? What sort of word is that? Soon! Ten hours? Ten days? Ten years? Did you find the Tunnel?'

Veil turned his eyes from her, and rested them for a moment on each of the others in turn.

'What did you find?' repeated the girl, still looking over his shoulder.

'Quiet, curse you!' said the man Veil, raising his arm.

The Black Rose stood unflinchingly upright, but with all the coil and re-coil of the flesh gone out of her. She had been through too much, and all resilience had gone. She stood there, upright but broken. Three revolutions had rocked over her. She had heard the screaming. Sometimes she did not know whether it was herself or someone else who screamed. The cry of children who have lost their mother.

One night they took her naked from her bed. They shot her lover. They left him in a pool of blood. They took her to a prison camp, and then her beauty began to thicken and to leave her.

Then she had seen him: Veil, one of the guards. A tall and spindly figure, with a lipless mouth, and eyes like beads of glass. He tempted her to run away with him. At first she believed this to be a ruse, but as time elapsed the Black Rose realized that he had other plans in life, and was determined to escape the camp. It was part of his plan to have a decoy with him.

So they escaped, he from the cramping life of official cruelty; she from the pain of whips and burning stubs.

Then came their wanderings. Then came a time of cruelty worse than behind the barbed wire. Then came her degradation. Seven times she tried to escape. But he always found her. Veil. The man with the small head.

FIFTY-SIX

ONE day he slew a beggar as though he were so much pork, and stole from his blood-stained pocket the secret sign of the Under-River. The police were in the next street. He crouched with the Black Rose in the lee of a statue, and when the moon dipped behind a cloud he dragged her to the river-side. There in the deep shadows he found at last what he was looking for, an entrance to the secret tunnel; for with a cunning mixture of guile and fortune he had learned much in the camp.

But that was a year ago. A year of semi-darkness. And now she stood there silently in the small room, very upright, her eyes staring into space.

For the first time the Black Rose turned her head to the man standing before her.

'I'd almost rather be a slave again,' she whispered, 'than have this kind of freedom. Why do you follow me? I am losing my life. What have you found?'

Yet again the man cast his eyes about the small, silent assembly, before he turned once more to the girl. From where she stood she could only see the man in silhouette.

'Tell me,' said the Black Rose. Her voice, as it had been throughout, was almost meaninglessly flat. 'Have you found it? The tunnel?'

The bony man rubbed his hands together with a sound like sandpaper. Then he nodded his small head.

'A mile away. No more. Its entrance dense with ferns. Out of them came a boy. Come close to me; I do not care to be overheard. You remember the whip?'

'The whip? Why do you ask me that?'

Before answering, the silhouette took hold of the Black Rose, and a few seconds later they were out of the lamp-lit chamber. Turning left and left again they came to a corner of stones, like the corner of a street. A streak of light fell across the wet floor. Her arms were rigid in his vice-like grip.

'Now we can talk,' he said.

'Let go my arm, or I will scream for God.'

'He never helped you. Have you forgotten?'

'Forgotten what, you skull? you filthy stalk-head! I have forgotten nothing. I can remember all your dirty games. And the stench of your fingers.'

'Can you remember the whip at Kar and the hunger? How I gave you extra bread! Yes, and fed you through the bars. And how you barked for more.'

'O slime of the slime-pit!'

'I could see for all your coupling, your indiscriminate whoredom that you had been splendid once. I could see why you were given such a name. Black Rose. You were famous. You were desirable. But when revolution came your beauty counted for nothing. And so they whipped you, and they broke your pride. You grew thinner and thinner. Your limbs became tubes. Your head was shaved. You did not look like a woman. You were more like a . . .'

'I do not want to think of that again . . . leave me alone.'

'Do you remember what you promised me?'

'No.'

'And then how I saved you again; and helped you to escape?'

'No! No! No!'

'Do you remember how you prayed to me for mercy? You prayed on your knees, your cropped head bent as at an execution. And mercy I gave you, didn't I?'

'Yes, oh yes.'

'In exchange, as you promised, for your body.'

'No!'

'Escape with me or rot in lamplight.'

Again he grasped her savagely, so that she cried out in agony. But there was at the same time another sound that went unheard . . . the sound of light footsteps.

'Lift up your head! Why all this nicety? You are a whore.'

'I am no whore, you festering length of bone. I would as much have you touch me as a running sore.'

Then the man with the small skull-like head lifted his fist, and struck her across the mouth. It was a mouth that had once been soft and red: lovely to look upon: thrilling to kiss. But now it seemed to have no shape, for the blood ran all over it. In jerking back her head she struck it on the wall at her back, and immediately her eyes closed with sickness; those eyes of hers, those irises, as black, it seemed, as their pupils so that they merged and became like a great wide well that swallowed what they gazed upon. But before they closed a kind of ghost appeared to hover in the eyes. It was no reflection, but a terrible and mournful thing . . . the ghost of unbearable disillusion.

The footsteps had stopped at the sound of her cry, but now, as she began to sink to her knees a figure began to run, his steps sounding louder and louder every moment.

The small-skull'd man with his long spindly limbs, cocked his head on one side and ran his tongue to and fro along his fleshless lips with a deliberate stropping motion. This tongue was like the tongue of a boot, as long, as broad, and as thin.

Then as though he had come to a decision he picked the Black Rose up in his arms and took a dozen steps to where the darkness was thickest, and there he dropped her as though she were a sack, to the ground. But as he turned to retrace his steps, he saw that someone was waiting for him.

FIFTY-SEVEN

FOR as long as a man can hold his breath, there was no sound; not one. Their eyes were fixed upon one another, until at last the voice of Veil broke the wet silence.

'Who are you?' he said, 'and what do you want?'

He drew back his leather lips as he spoke, but the newcomer instead of answering took a step forward, and peered through the gloom on every side as though he were looking for something.

'I questioned you I think! Who are you? You do not belong here. This is not your quarter. You are trespassing. Get to the north with you or I will . . .'

'I heard a cry,' said Titus. 'What was it?'

'A cry? There are always cries.'

'What are you doing here in the dark? What are you hiding?'

'Hiding, you pup? Hiding? Who are you to cross-question me? By God, who are you anyway? Where do you come from?'

'Why?'

The mantis man was suddenly upon the youth and though he did not actually *touch* Titus, at any point, yet he seemed to encircle and to threaten with his nails, his joints, his teeth, and with his sour and horrible breathing.

'I will ask you again,' said the man. 'Where do you come from?'

Titus, his eyes narrowed, his fists clenched, felt his mouth go suddenly dry.

'You wouldn't understand,' he whispered.

At this Mr Veil threw back his bony head to laugh. The sound was intolerably cold and cruel.

The man was deadly enough without his laugh but with it he became deadly in another way. For there was no humour in it. It was a noise that came out of a hole in the man's face. A sound that left Titus under no illusion as to the man's intrinsic evil. His body, limbs and organs and even his head could hardly be said to be any fault of his, for this was the way in which he had been made; but his laughter was of his own making.

As the blood ran into Titus's face there was a movement in the darkness, and the boy turned his head at once.

'Who's there?' he cried, and as he cried, the thin man Veil took a spidery step towards him.

'Come back, pup!'

The menace in the voice was so horrible that Titus jumped ahead into the darkness, and immediately his foot struck something that yielded, and at the same time there was a sob from immediately below him.

As he knelt down he could see the faint pattern of a human face in the gloom. The eyes were open.

'Who are you?' whispered Titus. 'What has happened to you?'

'No . . . no,' said the voice.

'Raise your head,' said Titus, but as he began to lift the vague body, a hand fixed its fingers, like pincers, into his shoulder, and with one movement, not only jerked Titus to his feet, but sent him spinning against the wall, where a slant of pale, wet light illuminated his face.

Written across his young features was something not so young; something as ancient as the stones of his home. Something uncompromising. The gaze of civility was torn from his face as the shrouding flesh can be torn from the bone. A primordial love for his birth-place, a love which survived and grew, for all that he had left his home, for all that he was a traitor, burned in him with a ferocity that he could not understand. All he knew was that as he stared at the spider-man, he, Titus, began to age. A cloud had passed over his heart. He was not so much in the thick of an adventure as alone with something that smelt of death.

Where Titus leaned against the wall the cold brick ran with moisture. It ran through his hair and spread out over his brows and cheekbones.

It gathered about his lips and chin and then fell to the ground in a string of water-beads.

His heart pounded. His hands and knees shook, and then, out of the gloom the Black Rose re-appeared.

'No, no, no! Keep to the darkness, whoever you are!'

At these words the Black Rose swayed, and sank again to the floor, and then with a great effort she raised herself on her elbow and whispered, 'Kill the beast.'

The spider had turned his small, bony head in her direction and in an instant Titus (with no weapons to slice or stab, and with no scruples, for he knew that within a minute he would be fighting for his life) brought up his knee with all the force he could muster. As he did this the spider leaned forward so that the full force of the blow was driven immediately below the ribs; but the only sound to be heard was that of a rush of air as it sped hissing from between his jaws. This was the only sound. He made no kind of groan: he merely brought his hands together, the fingers making a kind of grid to protect the solar-plexus, as he bent himself double.

This was Titus's moment. He stumbled his way to the Black Rose: lifted her, and panting as he ran, he made for a blur of light which seemed to hang in the air some distance to the west where the wet floor, the walls and the ceiling were suffused with a vaporous, slug-coloured glow.

As he ran he saw (although he hardly knew he had seen it) a family move by, then stop, and draw itself together, and stare: then came another group and then another, as though the very walls exuded them. Figures of all kinds, from all directions. They saw the boy stumbling with his burden, and paused.

Veil, meanwhile, had all but recovered from the knee-stab, and was following Titus with merciless deliberation. But for all the speed of his spindly legs he was not in time to see Titus kneel down and lay the Black Rose on the ground where a shadow cast by a hoary pyramid of decomposing books hid her from view.

Immediately he had done this he turned about on his heel and saw his foe. He also saw how great a crowd had congregated. An alarm had been sounded. An alarm that had no need of words or voices. Something that travelled from region to region until the air was filled as though with a soundless sound like a giant bellowing behind a sound-proof wall of glass, or the yelling of a chordless throat.

FIFTY-EIGHT

So the grey arena formed itself and the crowd grew, while the domed ceiling of the dark place dripped, and the lamps were re-filled and some held candles, some torches, while others had brought mirrors to reflect the light, until the whole place swam like a miasma.

Were his shoulder not hurting from the grip it had sustained Titus might well have wondered whether he was asleep and dreaming.

Around him, tier upon tier (for the centre of the arena was appreciably lower than the margin, and there was about the place almost the feeling of a dark circus) were standing or were seated the failures of earth. The beggars, the harlots, the cheats, the refugees, the scatterlings, the wasters, the loafers, the bohemians, the black sheep, the chaff, the poets, the riff-raff, the small fry, the misfits, the conversationalists, the human oysters, the vermin, the innocent, the snobs and the men of straw, the pariahs, the outcasts, rag-pickers, the rascals, the rakehells, the fallen angels, the sad-dogs, the castaways, the prodigals, the defaulters, the dreamers and the scum of the earth.

Not one of the great conclave of the displaced had ever seen Titus before. Each one supposed this ignorance of the young man to be peculiar to himself, for the population was so dense and so far-flung.

As for Veil, there were many who knew his face: they recognized that horrible spidery walk; that bullet head; that lipless mouth. There was about him something indestructible; as though his body were made of a substance that did not understand the sensation of pain.

As he advanced, a hush as palpable as any sound descended and lay thick in the air. Even the most flippant and insensitive of the characters took on another colour. Knowing no reason for the conflict they trembled, nevertheless, to see the distance narrow between the two.

How the news of the impending battle had reached the outlying districts and brought back, almost on the wings of the returning echoes, such a multitude, it is hard to understand. But there was now no part of the Under-River ignorant of the scene.

Head after head in long lines, thick and multitudinous and cohesive as grains of honey-coloured sugar, each grain a face, the audience sat or stood without a movement.

To shift the gaze from any one of the faces was to lose it forever. It was a delirium of heads: an endless profligacy. There was no end to it. The inventiveness of it was so rapid, various, profluent. Each movement sank away, sank with a smouldering fist-feel of raw plunder: sank into nullity.

And all was lit by the lamps; reflected by the mirrors. A shallow pool of water at the centre of the circle reflected the long cross beams; reflected a paddling rat as it climbed a high slippery prop, reflected the glint of its teeth and the stiffness of its ghastly tail.

Somewhere in the heart of this sat Slingshott. For a little while he had forgotten to be sorry for himself, so vivid was the plight of the youth.

His hands were clasped together in the depths of his pockets as he stared down into the wet ring. Within a few feet (though they had lost sight of one another) crouched Carrow. Biting his knuckles he kept his eyes fixed upon Titus, and wondered what, without a weapon, the youth could do.

Thirty to forty feet away from Carrow and Slingshott stood Sober-Carter, and on the far side of the open space the old couple, Jonah and his 'squirrel' grasped one another's hands.

Crack-Bell, usually so irritatingly cheerful, sat with his shoulders hunched up rather like some kind of cold bird. His face had sagged: his mouth hung open. He clasped his hands, and for all that he had no part in the conflict they were cold and moist, and his pulse uneven.

Crabcalf, imprisoned by his books, had been carried to the arena in his bed. This bed, on being lifted from the floor had disclosed a rectangle of deep and sumptuous dust.

In the silence was the voice of the river, a muted sound, all but inaudible, yet ubiquitous and dangerous as the ocean. It was not so much a sound as a warning of the world above.

FIFTY-NINE

Titus had come to a halt in the centre of the 'ring', and had then turned his face to his foe, the execrable Veil. He had little hope, for the man appeared to be composed of nothing but bone and whipcord, and he remembered how quick had been the creature's recovery from the stomach-jab. It was not just that Titus was frightened: he was also awed by what he saw approaching; this Thing of scarecrow proportions: this Thing that seemed larger than life.

It was as though he were faced with a machine: something without a nervous system, heart, kidney, or any other vulnerable organ.

His clothes were black and clung to him as though they were wet, and this accentuated the length of his bones. About his skeleton waist he wore a wide leather belt; the brass of the buckle twinkled in the firelight.

As he drew close to Titus, the boy saw that he had contracted his mouth so that his lips, which were thin enough on their own account, were now no more than a thread of bloodless cotton. This in its turn had tightened the skin above, so that the cheekbones stood out like small rocks. The eyes glinted from between the eyelids, and the effect was that of a concentration fierce enough to argue insanity.

For a moment only, this concentration slackened, and in that moment he swept his eyes across the terraced hordes: but there was no sign of Black Rose. As he returned his gaze to Titus he lifted his face and saw the great beams that swept across the dim and upper air: he saw the high props, green and slimy with moss, and as his eyes travelled down the rotting pillar he saw the rat.

Now, with a corner of his gaze fixed upon Titus, and with the rat in the tail of his other eye, the spiderman moved unexpectedly, and with a sidling motion, to the left, until he was within reaching distance of the sweating pillar.

A kind of indrawn gasp of relief came from the surrounding audience. Any unforeseen action was preferable to the ineluctable drawing together of the incongruous pair.

But this relief was short lived, for something worse than the horror of the silence brought every one of them to his feet, as with a movement too quick to follow, like the flick of a cobra's tongue, or the spurt of a squid's tentacle, Veil shot out his long left arm and plucked the crouching rat from where it lurked, and crunched with his long fingers the life out of the creature. There had been a scream and then a silence more terrible, for Veil had turned upon Titus.

'And now, you,' he said.

As Titus bent down to be sick, Veil tossed the dead animal in his direction. It fell a few paces from him with a thud. Without knowing what he was doing Titus, in a fever of fear and hatred, tore away a piece of his own shirt, folded it, and dropping on to his knees, spread it over the lifeless rodent.

Then as he knelt, he saw a shadow move and he jumped back with a cry for Veil was all but upon him. Not only this but there was a knife in his hand.

SIXTY

BLACK ROSE on the far side of the ring had seen the flash of Veil's knife. She knew he kept it whetted like a razor. She saw that the young man had no weapon, and gathering her strength together she cried out, 'Give him your knives . . . your knives! The beast will kill him.'

As though the assemblage had come out of some nightmare or trance, a hundred hands slid into a hundred belts and then for a dozen seconds the air was alight with steel, the great place echoing with the clang of metal and stone. Weapons of all kinds lay scattered like stars across the floor. Some on dry ground, and some gleaming in the pools of water.

But there was one, a long, slender weapon, half-way between a knife and a sword, which, because it hurtled past Titus's head and fell with a splash some distance from Veil, forced him immediately into action. Turning, he ran to where it lay, and as he plucked it out of the shallow water, he gave a great laugh, not of joy, but of relief that he could hold something tight in his grasp, something with an edge, something fiercer, keener and more deadly than his bare hands.

Two-handed at the hilt he held it before him like a brand. The water was over his ankles, and to the minutest detail he was mirrored upside down.

Now that Veil was so close to Titus that a mere ten feet divided them it might have been thought that someone out of the great assembly would have raced to the young man's rescue. But not a finger stirred. The brigands no less than the weaklings stared at the scene in a kind of universal trance. They watched but they could not move.

The mantis-man drew closer, and as he did so, Titus drew back a pace. He was shaking with fear. Veil's face seemed to expose itself as though it were vile as a sore: it swam before his eyes like the shiftings of the grey slime of the pit. It was indecent. Indecent not for reason of its ugliness, or even the cruelty that was part of it, but in the way that it was a perpetual reminder of death.

For an instant there rushed through Titus's mind an understanding. For a moment he lost his hatred. He abhorred nothing. The man had been born with his bones and his bowels. He could not help them. He had been born with a skull so shaped that only evil could inhabit it.

But the thought flashed and fell away for Titus had no time for anything but to remain alive.

SIXTY-ONE

WHAT is it threads the inflamed brain of the one-time killer? Fear? No, not so much as would fill the socket of a fly's eye. Remorse? He has never heard of it. It is loyalty that fills him, as he lifts his long right arm. Loyalty to the child, the long scab-legged child, who tore the wings off sparrows long ago. Loyalty to his aloneness. Loyalty to his own evil, for only through this evil has he climbed the foul stairways to the lofts of hell. Had he wished to do so, he could never have withdrawn from the conflict, for to do so would have been to have denied Satan the suzerainty of pain.

Titus had lifted his sword high in the air, and at that instant, his enemy slung his blade in the direction of the youth. It ran through the air with the speed of a stone from a sling and struck Titus's sword immediately below the handle, and sent it hurtling from his grasp.

The force of this had Titus on his back. It was as though he himself had been struck. His arms and empty hands shook and buzzed with the shock.

As he lay there he saw two things. The first thing he saw was that Veil had picked up a couple of knives from the wet ground, and was coming towards him, his neck and head craned forward, like a hen's when it runs for food, his dagger'd fists uplifted to the level of his ears. For a moment as Titus gazed spellbound the mean mouth opened and the purplish tongue sped from one corner to the other. Titus stared, all initiative, all power drained out of him, but even as he lay sprawling helplessly something moved in the tail of his eye, something above his head so that for an involuntary second he found himself staring wide-lidded at a long slippery beam, a beam that seemed to float across the semi-darkness.

But what Titus saw, and what set his pulses racing, was not the beam itself, but something that crawled along it: something massive yet absolutely silent: something that moved inexorably forward inch by inch. What it was he could not quite make out. All he could tell was that it was heavy, agile and alive.

But Mr Veil, the breaker of lives, observing how Titus had, for a fraction of a second, lifted his eyes to the shadows above, stopped for a moment his advance upon the spreadeagled youth and turned his face to the rafters. What he saw at that moment was something that brought forth from the very entrails of the vast audience, an intake of terrified breath, for the figure, huge it seemed in that wavering light, rose to its feet upon the beam, and a moment later leaped into space.

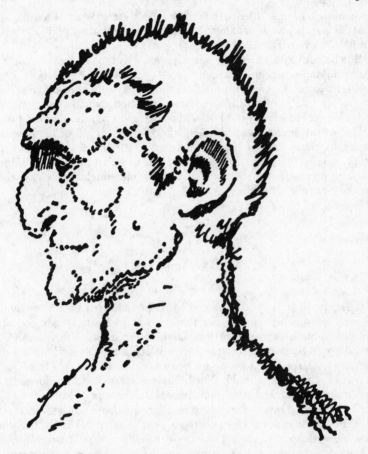

There was no computing the weight and speed of Muzzlehatch as he crushed the 'Mantis' to the slippery ground. The victim's face had been lifted so that the jaw, the clavicles, the shoulder blades and five ribs were the first to go down like dead sticks in a storm.

And yet he made no sound, this devil, this 'Mantis', this Mr Veil. Crushed and prostrate, he rose again, and to Titus's horror it seemed as though the features of his face had all changed places.

It could also be seen that there was damage to his limbs. In trying to move away he was forced to trail a broken leg which followed him like something tied to his hip: a length of driftwood. All he could do was to hop away from Muzzlehatch with that assortment of features clustered upon his neck like a horrible nest.

But he did not go far. Titus, Muzzlehatch and the great awestruck audience realized suddenly that the knives were still in his hands, and that his hands and arms alone had escaped the destruction. There, in his fists, they sparkled.

But he could no longer see his enemies. His face had capsized. Yet his brain had not been damaged.

'Black Rose!' he cried into the dreadful silence. 'Take your last look at me,' and he plunged the two knives, through the ribs, in the region of his heart. He left them there, withdrawing his hands from the hilts.

Out of the silence that followed, the horrible sound of his laughter began to grow, and as it grew in volume, the blood poured out the quicker, until there came the moment when, with a final convulsion of his long bones, he fell upon his dislocated, meaningless face, twitched for the last time, and died.

SIXTY-TWO

Titus got to his feet and turned to Muzzlehatch. He saw at once by the distant look in his friend's eye that he was in no talking mood. He seemed to have forgotten the long shattered man at his feet, and to be brooding on some other matter. When Black Rose came stumbling up, her hands clasped, he took no notice of her. She turned to Titus.

At once, Titus drew back. Not because she repelled him, for even in the drawn and sunken condition she was in, she was still beautiful. But now, she had no option but to arouse pity: she could not help it. It was a beauty to beware of. Her enormous eyes so often big with fear were now big with hope . . . and Titus knew that he must get away. He could see at once that she was predatory. She did not know it, but she was.

'She goes through hell,' muttered Titus. 'She wades in it, and the thicker and deeper it is, the more I long to escape. Grief can be boring.' Titus was immediately sickened by his own words. They tasted foul on the tongue.

He turned to her and was held again by the gaping tragedy of her eyes. Whatever she said could be nothing but mere corroboration. It could merely repeat or embroider the reality of her eloquent eyes. The trembling of her hands, and the wetness of her cheekbones. These and other signs were redundant. He knew that were he to let fall the smallest seed of kindness, then that seed would inevitably grow into some kind of weird relationship. A smile might set the avalanche moving.

'I can't, I can't,' he thought. 'I can't sustain her. I can't comfort her. I can't love her. Her suffering is far too clear to see. There is no veil across it: no mystery: no romance. Nothing but a factual pain, like the pain of a nagging tooth.'

Again he turned his eyes to her as though to verify what he had been thinking, and at once he was ashamed.

She had become emptied. Pain had emptied her. There was nothing left. What could he do?

He turned to Muzzlehatch: there was something about him that baffled the boy. For the first time it seemed as though his friend had a weakness: some vulnerable spot. Somebody or something had searched it out. As Titus watched, and as Black Rose stood with her eyes fixed upon him, Muzzlehatch turned to the great crowd.

He had heard without knowing it the first murmur, and he now became aware of a widespread stirring, as gradually the crowd began to crumble, grain by grain, making its way to the arena, gradually as though a great hill of sugar were on the move.

But what was more important, the incredulous population appeared to be drifting in the direction of the three. Within a minute, they (the Black Rose, Titus and Muzzlehatch) would, if they stayed where they were, be caught up in an insufferable press.

Before them, inexorably, came spilling out the tide. The tide of the unwanted, the dispossessed: the dross of the Under-River. Among them came Crabcalf and the bird-headed man who fed the hounds; came the old man, and his squirrel: came Crack-Bell: came Sober-Carter.

There was no time to lose. 'This way,' said Muzzlehatch, and Titus with the Black Rose clinging to his arm hurried after him, as the gaunt man strode into a blanket of darkness. Not a lantern burned: not a candle even. Only by the sound of his footsteps was Titus able to keep contact with his friend.

After what seemed an hour or more, they turned to the south. He seemed to have eyes like a cat's, this silent Muzzlehatch; for dark as it was, he never faltered.

Then, after yet an hour or more of walking, this time with the Black Rose slung over his shoulders, Muzzlehatch at last came to a long flight of steps. As they climbed, they became aware, momently, of a percolation of faint light, and then, all at once, of a small white opening in the darkness, the size of a coin. When at last they reached it, they found it to be an entrance, or for themselves an egress. They had reached one of the secret mouths of the under-river world, and Titus was amazed to see, on wriggling himself out into the air, that they were in the silent heart of a forest.

SIXTY-THREE

THEY had to wait until dark before they dared to venture to Juno's house. What else could they do with the Black Rose but take her there? As they waited the tension became almost unbearable. Nobody spoke. Muzzlehatch's eyes had a far-away look, which Titus had seldom seen before.

It was a rocky place, and over the rocks the trees spread out their branches. At last Titus walked over to where Muzzlehatch lay on his back on a great grey stone. Black Rose followed him with her eyes.

'I can't bear this any longer,' said Titus, 'what in hell is it? Why are you so different? Is it because . . . ?'

'Boy,' said Muzzlehatch, 'I will tell you. It will keep you quiet.' He paused for a long while. Then he said, 'My animals are dead.'

At the end of the forest silence that followed, Titus knelt down beside his friend. All he could say was, 'What happened?'

'The dedicated men,' said Muzzlehatch, 'sometimes known as scientists: they were after me. Someone is always after me. As usual I escaped them. I know many ways of disappearing. But what use are they now, my dear chap? My animals are dead.'

'But . . .'

'Baffled because they could not find me . . . no, not even with their latest device, that is no bigger than a needle, and threads a keyhole with the speed of light . . . baffled, I say, they turned from hunting me, and killed my animals.'

'How?'

Muzzlehatch rose to his feet on the rock, and lifting his arm caught hold of a thick branch that hung above him, and broke it off. A muscle in his jawbone ticked endlessly like a clock.

'Some kind of ray, it was,' he said at last. 'Some kind of ray. A pretty notion, prettily executed.'

'And yet you had the heart to rescue me,' said Titus, 'from the thin man.'

'Did I?' muttered Muzzlehatch. 'I was in a dream. Think no more of it. I had no choice but to make for the Under-River. The scientists were converging. They were after you, boy: they were after us both.'

'But you remembered me,' said Titus. 'You crawled along the beam.'

'Did I? Good! And so I crushed him? I was far away . . . I was among my creatures. I saw them die . . . I saw them roll over. I heard their breath blow bleakly from their ribs. I saw my zoo become an abattoir.'

My creatures! Vital as fire. Sensuous and terrible. There they lay. There they lay – for ever and ever.'

He turned his face to Titus. The abstracted look had gone and in its place was something as cold and pitiless as ice.

SIXTY-FOUR

CURSING the moon, for it was full, Titus and his two companions were forced to make a long detour, and to keep as far as possible in the shadows that skirted the woods, or lay beneath the walls of the city. To have taken the shorter path across the moonlit woods would have invited trouble.

As they made their way, their pace conditioned by the weary steps of the Black Rose, Titus, perhaps for reason of his supreme indebtedness to Muzzlehatch felt an almost ungovernable desire to shake this from him as though he were a ponderous weight. He longed for isolation, and in his longing he recognized that same canker of selfishness that had made itself manifest in his attitude towards the Black Rose in her pain.

What kind of brute was he? Was he destined to destroy both love and friendship? What of Juno? Had he not the courage or the loyalty to hold fast to his friends? Or the courage to speak up? Perhaps not. He had, after all, deserted his home.

Forcing himself to frame the words, he turned his head to Muzzlehatch. 'I want to get away from you,' he said. 'From you and everyone. I want to start again, when but for you, I would be dead! Is this vile of me? I cannot help it. You are too vast and craggy. Your features are the mountains of the moon. Lions and tigers lie bleeding in your brain. Revenge is in your belly. You are too vast and remote. Your predicament burns. It makes me hanker for release. I am too near you. I long to be alone. What shall I do?'

'Do what you like, boy,' said Muzzlehatch, 'skedaddle to the pole, for all I care, or scorch your bottom on the red equator. As for this lady? She is ill. *Ill*, you numbskull! Ill as they take them on this side of breath.'

The Black Rose turned to Muzzlehatch, and her pupils gaped like well-heads.

'He wants to get away from me, too,' she said. 'He is disgusted by my poverty. I wish you could have seen me years ago, when I was young and fair.'

'You are still beautiful,' said Titus.

'I don't care, any more,' said the Black Rose. 'It no longer matters. All I want is to lie down quietly forever, on linen. Oh God, white linen, before I die.'

'You shall have your linen,' said Muzzlehatch. 'White as a seraph's underwing. We're not far away.'

'Where are you taking me?'

'To a home by a river, where you can rest.'

'But Veil will find me.'

'Veil is dead,' said Titus. 'Dead as dead.'

'His ghost will strike me then. His ghost will twist my arm.'

'Ghosts are fools,' said Muzzlehatch, 'and much overrated. Juno will care for you. As for this young Titus Groan: he can do as he pleases. If I were in his shoes I would cut adrift and vanish. The world is wide. Follow your instinct and get rid of us. That was why you left your so-called Gormenghast, wasn't it? Eh? To find out what lay beyond the skyline. Eh? And as you once said . . .'

'I think you said, "your so-called Gormenghast". God damn you for that phrase. For *you* to say it! You! For you to be a thing of disbelief! *You*! You've been a kind of God to me. A rough-hewn God. I hated you at times, but mostly I loved you. I have told you of my home; of my family; of our ritual; of my childhood; of the flood; of Fuchsia, of Steerpike and how I killed him; of my escape. Do you think I have invented it all? Do you think I have been deceiving you? You have failed me. Let me go!'

'What are you waiting for?' said Muzzlehatch, turning his back on the boy. His heart was pounding.

Titus stamped his foot with anger, but he did not move away. A moment later, the Black Rose began to give at the knees, but Muzzlehatch was in time to catch her up in his powerful arms, as though she were a tattered doll.

They had come to an open space, and stopped where the shadows ended.

'Do you see that cloud?' said Muzzlehatch, in a curiously loud voice. 'The one like a curled-up cat. No, there, you chicken, beyond that green dome. Can't you see it? With the moon on its back.'

'What about it?' said Titus in an irritable whisper.

'That is your direction,' said Muzzlehatch. 'Make for it. Then on and beyond for a month's march, and you will be in comparative freedom. Freedom from the swarms of pilotless planes: freedom from bureaucracy: freedom from the police. And freedom of movement. It is largely unexplored. They are ill-equipped. No squadron for the water, sea, or sky. It is as it should be. A region where no one can remember who is in power. But there are forests like the Garden of Eden where you can lie on your belly and write bad verse. There will be nymphs for your ravishing, and flutes for your delectation. A land where youths lean backwards in their tracks, and piss the moon, as though to put it out.'

'I am tired of your words,' said Titus.

'I use them as a kind of lattice-work,' said Muzzlehatch. 'They hide me away from me . . . let alone from you. Words can be tiresome as a swarm of insects. They can prick and buzz! Words can be no more than a series of farts; or on the other hand they can be adamantine, obdurate, inviolable, stone upon stone. Rather like your "so-called Gormenghast" (you notice that I use the same phrase again. The phrase that makes you cross?). For although you have learned, it seems, the art of making enemies (and this is indeed good for the soul), yet you are blind, deaf, and dumb when it comes to another language. Stark: dry: unequivocal: and cryptic: a thing of crusts and water. If you ask for flattery . . . Remember this in your travels. Now go . . . for God's sake . . . GO!'

Titus lifted his eyes to his companion. Then he took three steps towards him. The scar on his cheekbone shone like silk in the moonlight.

'Mr Muzzlehatch,' he said.

'What is it, boy?'

'I grieve for you.'

'Grieve for this broken creature,' said Muzzlehatch. 'She is the weak of the world.'

Out of the silence came the far-away voice of the Black Rose. 'Linen,' it cried in a voice both peevish and beautiful. 'Linen . . . white linen.'

'She is as hot as fever can make her,' muttered Muzzlehatch. 'It is like holding embers in my arms. But there is Juno for a refuge, and a cat for your bearing; and beyond, to the world's end.

'The sleeping cat,' he muttered with a catch in his throat, 'did you ever see it . . . my little civet? They silenced him with all the rest. He moved like a wave of the sea. Next to my wolves, I loved him, Titus child. You have never seen such eyes.'

'Hit me,' cried Titus. 'I've been a dog to you.'

'Globules to that!' said Muzzlehatch. 'It's time the Black Rose was in Juno's hands.'

'Ah, Juno; give her my love,' said Titus.

'Why?' said Muzzlehatch. 'You've only just retracted it! That's no way to treat a lady. By hell it ain't. Giving your love; taking your love; secreting it; exposing it . . . as though it were a game of hide and seek.'

'But you have been in love with her yourself and have lost her. And now *you* are returning to her again.'

'True,' said Muzzlehatch. 'Touché, indeed. She has, after all, a haze about her. She is an orchard . . . a golden thing is Juno. Generous as the milky way, or the source of a great river. What would you say? Is she not wonderful?'

Titus turned his head quickly to the sky.

'Wonderful? She *must* have been.'

'Must she?' said Muzzlehatch.

There was a curious silence, and in this silence a cloud began to pass over the moon. It was not a large cloud so that there was little time to waste, and in the half-darkness the two friends moved away from one another, and began to hurry into the darkness as though they needed it, one in the direction of Juno's home, the Black Rose in his arms, and the other moving rapidly to the north.

But before they became lost to one another in the final murk Titus stopped and looked back. The cloud had passed and he could see Muzzlehatch standing at the corner of the sleeping square. His shadow, and the shadow of the Black Rose in his arms, lay at his feet, and it was as though he was standing in a pool of black water. His head, rock-like, was bent over the poor frail creature in his arms. Then Titus saw him turn on his heel, and walk with long strides, his shadow skimming the ground beneath him, and then the moon disappeared and the silence was as intense as ever.

In this thick silence, the boy waited: for what he did not know: he just waited while a great unhappiness filled him; only to be dispersed, immediately, for a far-away voice cried out in the darkness:

'Hullo there, Titus Groan! Prop up your chin, boy! We'll meet again; no doubt of it – one day.'

'Why not!' cried Titus. 'Thank you forever . . .'

But the silence was broken by Muzzlehatch with another great shout, 'Farewell, Titus . . . Farewell, my cocky boy! Farewell . . . farewell.'

SIXTY-FIVE

AT first there was no sign of a head but after a while an acute observer might have concentrated his attention more and more upon a particular congestion of branches, and eventually discovered, deep in the interplay of leaf or tendril, a line that could be one thing only . . . the profile of Juno.

She had been sitting in her vine-arbour for a long while, hardly moving. Her servants had called her, but she had not heard them: or if she had, she made no response.

Three days ago her one-time lover, Muzzlehatch, had been hidden in her attic. Now, he was gone again. The wraith he had brought with him had been washed and put to bed, but had died the moment her head had touched the snowy pillow.

There had been the funeral; there had been questions to answer. Her lovely house had been filled by a swarm of officials, including Acreblade, the detective. Where was Titus? he had asked. Where was Muzzlehatch? She shook her head for hour after hour.

Now she sat immobile in her arbour, and her bosom ached. She was seeing herself as a girl. She was remembering the gallant days. The days when the young men longed for her: risking their leaping lives for her: daring one another to swing among the high cedar branches in the dark grove near her home, and others to swim the barbarous bay when the lightning flashed above it. And those who were not so young, but whose wit and suavity beguiled her . . . the gentlemen in their forties, hiding their love away from public view, nursing it like a wound or a bruise, only to burst the stronger out of darkness.

And the elderly for whom she was the unobtainable, a will-o'-the-wisp, a marsh-light, waking their lust to life, or waking something rarer, a chaos of poetry, the scent of a rose.

Before her, through the vine leaves was a daisy'd slope that led down to a high box hedge, clipped into peacocks, heraldic against the sky. And the sky itself to which she now lifted her gaze, was filled with little clouds.

It was a favourite place of Juno's, this tangled arbour, and she had many a time found solace in its seclusion. But today was different from all other times, for a remote sense of being imprisoned by the interwoven branches began to trouble her, though she had no idea what it was that she was feeling.

Nor did she ever know for her body, working independently from the brain, rose and moved out of the arbour like a ship leaving harbour.

Now she was on the daisy'd lawn: now she was leaving the shear'd box behind: now she was meandering into pastures where dragonflies hovered and darted.

On and on she wandered, hardly taking in her surroundings, until she came to the dark cedar grove. She had not noticed it approaching for her eyes were all but sightless as she moved. But when she was within a short distance of the dark grove she found the verge of a wide glaze of dew.

Now fully awake, she stared into the depths and saw, inverted, a haunt of her girlhood – the almost legendary cedar grove.

Her first sensation was that she was upside down: but this belief was shattered when she raised her head. But before she raised it she saw someone lounging, upside-down on the underside of a great cedar-bough and defying, as he did so, the law of gravity. But when Juno raised her head and tried to locate the man on his branch, it was not so easy. At first she could see nothing but the green terraces of foliage, but suddenly she saw the man again. He was nearer to where she stood than she had expected.

Directly the man realized he had been noticed he dropped to the ground and bowed, his dark red hair falling over his eyes like a mop.

'What are you doing in my cedar grove?' she said.

'Trespassing,' said the man.

Juno shielded her eyes and gazed steadily at the man – with his dark red hair and his boxer's nose.

'Well, "trespasser": what do you want?' she said at last. 'Is this a favourite haunt of yours or am I being ambushed?'

'You are being ambushed. If I have startled you, I am profoundly sorry. I would not have you startled. No, not by so much as an ant on your wrist, or the buzz of a bee.'

'I see,' said Juno.

'But I have waited for the devil of a long while,' said the man, screwing up his forehead, 'Great Heaven, I have indeed.'

'Who have you waited for?' said Juno.

'For this moment,' said the man.

Juno lifted an eyebrow.

'I have waited for you to be deserted. And alone. As you are now.'

'What has my life to do with you?' said Juno.

'Everything and nothing,' said the tousled man. 'It is your own of course. So is your unhappiness. Titus is gone. Muzzlehatch is gone. Not for ever perhaps, but for a long while. Your house by the river, fine as it is, is now a place of echoes and of shades.'

Juno joined her hands together at her breast. There was something in his voice that belied his mop of dark red hair and general air of brigandage. It was deep, husky – and unbelievably gentle.

'Who are you?' she said at last, 'and what do you know of Titus?'

'My name is of no account. As for Titus, I know very little. Very little. But enough. Enough to know that he left the city out of hunger.'

'Hunger?'

'The hunger to be always somewhere else. This and the pull of his home, or what he thinks of as his ancestral home (if he ever had one). I have seen him in this cedar grove, alone. Beating the great branches with his fists. Beating the boughs as though to let his soul out.'

The Trespasser stepped forward for the first time, his feet breaking the mirror of green dew.

'You cannot sit and wait for either of them. Neither for Titus nor for Muzzlehatch. You have a life of your own, lady. Something that starts from now. I have watched you long before this Titus ever came upon the scene. I watched you from the shadows. Were it not that "Muzzle" whipped your heart away, I would have trailed you to the ends of the earth. But you loved him. And you loved Titus. As for me, now, you can see I'm no ladies' man – I'm a rough and ready one – but give me half a hint and I'll companion you. Companion you until the doors swing open – door after door from dawn till dusk and each fresh day will be a new invention!

'If you want me I will be here, somewhere among these cedars.'

He turned upon his heel, walked quickly away, and a few moments later he was lost in the forest and all that was left of him by way of proof were his footsteps like black smudges in the dazzling dew.

SIXTY-SIX

So Juno returned to her home, and it was true that it had already become a place of echoes, shadows, voices; moments of pause and suspense; moments of vague suffering or dwindling laughter, where the staircase curved from sight; moments of acute nostalgia where she stood all unwittingly at a window in a haze of stars; or of sweetness hardly to be borne when the shadow of Titus came between her and the sun as it rose through the slanting rain.

And while she lay stretched upon her bed one silent afternoon her hands behind her head, her eyes closed, her thoughts following one another in a sad cavalcade, Muzzlehatch, by now a hundred miles from Juno, was sitting at a rickety, three-legged table in another shaft of the same hot, ambient sun.

To right and left of him lay stretched the straggling street. Street? It was more of a track, for in keeping with everything else within Muzzlehatch's range of vision, it was half-finished and forsaken. Abandoned projects littered the land. Never reaching completion, it is never doomed. This gimcrack village that might have been a township ten times over. It had never had a past, nor could ever have a future. But it was full of happenings. The sliding moment blossomed febrile at one extreme and, at the other, was thick with human sleep. Bells rang, and were quickly stifled.

Children and dogs squatted hip-bone deep in the white dust. Elaborate trenches that were once the foundation of envisaged theatres, markets or churches, had become, for the children of this place, a battleground beyond the dreams of normal childhood.

The day was drowsy. It was a day of tacit somnolence. To work on such a day would be an insult to the sun.

The coffee tables curved away to the north, and to the south, as rickety a line of perspective as can well be imagined, and at these tables sat groups of multifarious face, frame and gesture. Yet there was a common denominator that strung these groups together. Of all the outspread company there was not one member who did not look as though he had just got out of bed.

Some had shoes, but no shirts; others had no shoes but wore hats of endless variety, at endless angles. Bygone headgear, bygone capes and jerkins and nightgowns drawn together at the waist with leather belts. In this company Muzzlehatch was very much at home, and sat at a table beneath a half-finished monument.

Hundreds of sparrows twittered and flapped their wings in the dust, the boldest of them hopping about on the coffee tables where the traditional handleless coffee cups and saucers gleamed vermilion in the sun.

Muzzlehatch was not alone at his table. Apart from a dozen sparrows, which he brushed clear of the table top from time to time, with the back of his hand, as though he were brushing away crumbs . . . apart from these there was a crowd of human stragglers. A crowd divided loosely into three. The first of these segregations loitered about the person of Muzzlehatch himself, for they had never seen a man so relaxed, or so indifferent to their stares; a man so sprawled in his chair, and at such an indolent state of supreme collapse.

Masters as they were in the art of doing nothing, they had seen, nevertheless, nothing in their lives to compare with the scale on which this huge vagrant deported himself. He was, it seemed, a symbol of all that they unconsciously believed in and they stared at him, as though at a prototype of themselves.

They noted that great rudder of a nose: that arrogant head. But they had no notion that it was filled with a ghost. The ghost of Juno. And so it was his gaze was far away.

Next to Muzzlehatch, as magnet in the soft, hot light, was his car. The same, recalcitrant, hot-blooded beast. As was his custom he had tied her up, for she was apt at unforeseeable moments to leap a yard or so in a kind of reflex, the water bubbling in her rusty guts. Today he had for bollard the unfinished monument half-erected to some all but forgotten anarchist. And there she stood lash'd and twitching. The very personification of irritability.

The third of the three centres of interest was at the back of the car, where Muzzlehatch's small ape lay asleep in the sun. No one hereabouts had ever seen an ape before and it was with the wildest speculation, not without fear, that they boggled at the creature.

This animal had become, since the tragedy, a companion closer than ever, and had indeed become a symbol of all he had lost. Not only this but it kept doubly alive in a bitter region of the mind, the memory of that ghastly holocaust when the cages buckled, and his birds and animals cried out for the last time.

Who would have guessed that behind the formidable brow of his, which appeared to be made of some kind of rock, there lay so strange a mixture of memories and thoughts? For he lay sprawling in such a way as to suggest that nothing whatever was taking place in his head. Yet there, in the cerebral gloom, held in by the meridian of the skull, his Juno wandered in the cedar grove: his Titus moving by night, sleeping by day, made his way . . . where . . . ? His ape lay coiled asleep, with one eye open, and scratched his ear. The silence droned like a bee in the heart of a flower.

The small ape gazers: the car gazers: and those that peered from short range at Muzzlehatch himself now turned their united attention to the lounging stranger; for Muzzlehatch, gripping the sides of his chair, all but bursting it, levered himself into an upright position.

Then, very slowly, he tilted back his head, until his face was level with the sky. But his eyes, as though to prove that they were not to be gainsaid by the angle of the face that lodged them, were downward cast, their line of vision grazing like a scythe the pale field of hair that made of his cheekbone, what would be for a gnat, a barley field.

Yet what he saw was not the scene before him with all its detail, but a memory of other days, no less vivid, no less real.

He saw, afloat, as it were, in the whorls of his boyhood, a string of irrelevant images; the days before he had ever heard of Juno, let alone a hundred others. Days flamboyant; days at large, and days in hiding, when he lay stretched on his back upon the high rocks, or lolled in glades until he took their colour; his arrogant nose, like a rudder, pointing at the sky. And as he lounged there, leaning precariously backwards in his chair, surrounded by a horde of ragged gapers, as might well have unnerved friend Satan himself, an old voice cried . . .

'Buy up the sunset! Buy it up! Buy it up! Buy . . . buy . . . buy. A copper for a seat, sirs. A copper for the view.' The croaking of the voice seemed to hack its way out of the arid throat of the ticket vendor, a diminutive figure dressed in nondescript black. His head protruded out of his torn collar much as the head of the tortoise protrudes from its shell, the throat unwrinkling, the eyes like beads, or pips of jet.

SIXTY-SEVEN

BETWEEN each strangulated cry the old man turned his head, and spat, swivelled his eyes, threw back his little bony head and barked at the sky like a dog.

'Buy it! Buy it! A seat for the sunset. Take your pick of 'em! every one. They say it will be coral, green and grey. Twenty coppers! Only twenty coppers.'

Threading his way through the tables, it was not long before he came upon Muzzlehatch. The old man paused, his jaws apart, but no sound came for some little while, so sharply was his attention taken by the sight of a new face at the tables.

The shadows of leaves and branches lay upon the table like grey lace and moved imperceptibly to and fro. The delicate shadow of an acacia frond fluctuated as it lay like a living thing upon Muzzlehatch's bony brow.

At last the old ticket vendor closed his jaws and then started again.

'A seat for the sunset, coral, green and grey. Two coppers for the standing! Three coppers for the sitting! A copper in the trees. The sunset at your bloody doorstep, friends! Buy it up! Buy! Buy! Buy!'

As Muzzlehatch stared through half-closed eyes at the old man the silence came down again, warm and thick with the sweetness of death in it.

At last Muzzlehatch muttered softly, 'What does he mean, in the name of mortality and all her brood . . . what does he mean?'

There was no answer. The silence settled down again, and seemed appalled at the notion that anyone could be ignorant of what the old man meant.

'Coral, green and grey,' continued Muzzlehatch as though mumbling to himself. 'Are these the colours of the sky tonight? Do you *pay*, my dears, to see the sunset? Ain't the sunset free? Good God, ain't even the *sunset* free?'

'It's all we have,' said a voice, 'that, and the dawn.'

'You can't trust the dawn,' said another, with such pathos that it seemed he held a personal grudge against tinted atmosphere.

The ticket seller leaned over and peered at Muzzlehatch from closer range.

'Free, did you say?' he said. 'How could it be free? With colours like the jewelled breasts of queens. Free indeed! Isn't there nothing sacred? Buy a chair, Mr Giant, and see it comfortable – they say there may be strokes of puce as well, and curdled salmon in the upper ranges. All for a copper! Buy! Buy! Buy! Thank you, sir, thank you. For you, the *cedar benches*, sir. Hell, bless you.'

'What happens if the wind decides to veer?' said Muzzlehatch. 'What happens to your green and coral, then? Do I get my coppers back? What if it rains? Eh? What if it pours?'

Someone spat at Muzzlehatch, but he took no notice beyond smiling at the man with such a curious angle of the lips that the spitter felt his spine grow cold as death.

'Tonight there is no wind,' said a third voice. 'A puff or two. The green will be like glass. Maybe a slaughtered tiger will float southwards. Maybe his wounds will drip across the sky . . . but no . . .'

'No! Not tonight! Not tonight! Green, coral, grey.'

'I have seen sunsets black like soot, awash in the western spaces, stirred with cats' blood. I have seen sunsets like a flock of roses: drifting they were . . . their pretty bums afloat. And once I saw the nipple of a queen . . . the sun it was . . . as pink as . . .'

SIXTY-EIGHT

LATER that evening, Muzzlehatch and the small ape shook themselves free of the gaping crowd and drove the car, slowly at the tail of a ragged cavalcade that, winding this way and that, finally disappeared into a birdless forest. On the other side of these woods lay stretched a grass terrace, if such a word can be used to describe the rank earthwork upon whose western side the land dropped sheer away for a thousand feet to where the tops of miniature trees, no longer than lashes, hovered in the evening mist.

When the two of them had reached the terrace with its swathing vistas spreading like sections of the globe itself away and away into a great hush of silence and distance mixed, as though to form a new element, they left their car, and took their seats on one of the cedar benches. These benches, forming a long line, from north to south, were placed within a few feet of the edge of the precipice. Indeed there were those whose legs were on the long side and whose feet, as a result, hung loosely over the edge of the terrifying drop.

The small ape must have sensed something of the danger for it stayed no more than a few moments before leaping from its seat on to Muzzlehatch's lap, where it made faces at the sunset.

No one noticed this. And no one noticed Muzzlehatch's strong-fingered hand as it caressed the little ape beneath its jaw. All the attention and interest these ragged people had lavished upon the stranger and his ape was now a thing of the past. Every face was tinted with an omnipresent hue. Every eye was the eye of a connoisseur. A hush as of the world ceasing to breathe came down upon the company, and Muzzlehatch tossed his head in the silence, for something had touched him; some inner thing that he could not understand. An irritant . . . a catch of the heat . . . a bubble of air in a vast aorta . . . for he found himself, all of a sudden, spellbound by what he saw above him. A coloured circus caught in a whirl of air had disintegrated and in its place a thousand animals of cloud streamed through the west.

At the backs of the watchers, and very close stood up the flanks of the high woods lit up by the evening sun, save where the shadows of the watchers were ranged against it. Before the watchers and below them the faraway valley had drawn across itself another veil of cold. Above, the sunset-watchers saw the beasts: all with their streaming manes, whatever the species: great whales no less than lions with their manes; tigers no less than fawns.

The sky was animals from north to south. Beasts of the earth and air, lifting their heads to cry . . . to howl . . . to scream, but they had no voices, and their jaws remained apart, gulping the fast air.

And it was then that Muzzlehatch rose to his feet. His face was dark with a sudden pain, a pain he was only half able to understand.

He stood at his full height in the spellbound silence, his whole body trembling. For some while, his eyes were fixed upon the sky where the animals changed shape before his gaze, melting from species to species but always with the manes propelling them.

A few feet to Muzzlehatch's side a great dusty bush of juniper clung on the verge of the precipice. One step took Muzzlehatch to this solitary object and he wrenched it free of the earth, and raising it above his head, slung it out into the emptiness of the air where it fell and went on falling.

Now every head was turned to him. Every head from near or far away: they all turned. When they saw him there, standing trembling, they could not understand that he was looking through these animals of clouds to another time and another place: to a zoo of flesh and blood. Nor did they know that the gaunt visitor was feeling for the first time the utmost agony of their death. Beast after beast of the upper air recalled some most particular one of feather, scale or claw, some most particular one of beauty or of strength . . . some symbol of the unutterable wilds.

They had been his joy in a world gone joyless. Now they were not even mouldering, these beasts of his. Nor were they turned into ash, nor any part of earth. Science had eliminated them, and there was no trace.

His brindled heron with its broken foot: where was he now? And the lemur, five months gone, yet with so wistful a face, and a jaw so full of needles. O liquidation! And for every one his own particular story. For each the divers capture: and as the cloudscape thronged itself with figures: with humps: with fins: with horns, and his mind with the images of mortality, so he trembled the more, for Muzzlehatch knew that the time had come for him to return to the scene of supreme wickedness, foul play, and death. For it was there that they lived or partly lived in cells, sealed from the light of day.

The small ape began to cry with a thin, sad, far-away sound and its master shifted it from one shoulder to the other.

Dazed by the enormity of his loss, he had for a time refused to believe; despite all evidence; had refused to consider the brutal reality of such a thing. But all the while a dreadful seed was gathering itself together beneath his ribs and on his tongue was a taste quite indescribably horrible.

But the moment came, when despite the nightmare of it all, he realized that his life, as he knew it, had snapped in half. He was no longer balanced or entire. There had been a time when he was lord of the fauna. Muzzlehatch, in his house by the mulberry tree, supremely at large among the iron cages. And there was the second, the present Muzzlehatch, vague yet menacing, lord of nothing.

Yet in this nothing, and ever since, though he did not know it, so obscure was the ghastly growth in his brain, there had been growing an implacable substance: an inner predicament from which he had no right, no wish to escape the disgusting world itself across whose body he must now retrace his way into the camp of the enemy.

And then it broke out like an asp from its shell . . . a venomous creature, growing larger every moment as the vile scene took shape.

The clouds were gone, and the prophesied colours hung in the air like sheets. He turned his back on the sky and stared up at the trees that towered above the overgrown terrace. And as he did so his hatred oozed out of him and everything clarified. The chaos of his belated anger became congealed into a carbuncle. There was no longer any need for ferocity, or the brandishing of bushes. Were he able to, he would have restored the juniper to its precipitous perch. And when he turned back his big head to the silent lines of beggars his face was quite expression-less.

'Have any of you,' he bellowed, 'seen Gormenghast?'

The heads of the sunset-gazers made no movement. Their bodies remained half turned to him. Their eyes were fixed upon the biggest man they had ever seen. Not a sound came from the long, long lines of throats.

'Forget your bloody clouds,' he cried again. 'Have you seen a boy . . .

lord of a region? Have any strangers passed this way before?' He tossed his big head. 'Am I the only one?'

No sound but the faint rustling of leaves in the forest behind him. An unhappy silence, an ugly, fatuous silence. In this silence, Muzzlehatch's temper rose again. His loved zoo, dead by the hand of science, sprang before his eyes. Titus lost. Everything lost, except to find the lost realm of Gormenghast. And then to guide young Titus to his home. But why? And what to prove? Only to prove the boy was not a madman. A madman? He strode to the forest verge, his head in his hands, then raised his eyes, and pondered on the bulk and weight of his crazy car. He released the brake, and brought her to life, so that she sobbed, like a child pleading. He turned her to the precipice, and with a great heave sent her running upon her way. As she ran, the small ape leaped from his shoulders to the driver's seat, and riding her like a little horseman plunged down the abyss.

Ape gone. Car gone. All gone?

Muzzlehatch felt nothing; only a sense of incredulity that a fragment of his life should be so vividly hung up before him like a picture on the wall of the dark sky. He felt no anguish. All he could feel was a sense of liberation. What burdens had he left upon him, and within him? Nothing but love and vengeance.

These two precluded suicide, though for a moment the lines of watchers stared as Muzzlehatch stood looking down, his feet within an inch or two of the swallowing edge. Suddenly, turning his back upon the precipice and the shadowy congregation he made his way on foot into the birdless forest, and as he strode on and on in the tracks of his out-bound journey, retracing his route, he sang in the knowledge that he would come in the course of time to a region he had left where the scientists worked, like drones, to the glory of science and in praise of death.

Were Titus to have seen him now and noted the wry smile on the face of his friend and the unusual light in his eye, he would surely have been afraid.

SIXTY-NINE

MEANWHILE Titus, whose journeyings in search of his home and of himself had taken him through many climates, was now at rest in a cool grey house in the quiet of whose protecting walls he lay in fever.

His face, vivid and animate for all its stillness, lay half submerged in the white pillow. His eyes were shut: his cheeks flushed and his forehead hot and wet. The room about him was high, green, dusky and silent. The blinds were drawn and a sense of an underwater world wavered through the room.

Beyond the windows lay stretched a great park, in whose south-east corner a lake (for all its distance) stabbed the eye with a wild dazzle of water. Beyond the lake, almost on the horizon, arose a factory. It took the sky in its stride, its outline cruising across a hundred degrees, a masterpiece of design. Of all this Titus knew nothing, for his room was his world.

Nor did he know that sitting at the foot of his bed with her eyebrows raised was the scientist's daughter.

It was well for Titus that he was unable to see her through the hot haze of his fever. For hers was a presence not easily forgotten. Her body was exquisite. Her face indescribably quizzical. She was a modern. She had a new kind of beauty. Everything about her face was perfect in itself, yet curiously (from the normal point of view) misplaced. Her eyes were large and stormy grey, but were set a thought too far apart; yet not so far as to be immediately recognized. Her cheekbones were taut and beautifully carved, and her nose, straight as it was, yet gave the impression of verging, now on the retroussé side, now on the aquiline. As for the curl of her lips, it was like a creature half asleep, something that like a chameleon could change its colour (if not at will, at any rate at a minute's notice). Her mouth, today, was the colour of lilac blossom, very pale. When she spoke, her pale lips drew themselves back from her small white teeth, and allowed a word or two to wander like a petal that is blown listlessly away. Her chin was rounded like the smaller end of a hen's egg, and in profile it seemed deliciously small and vulnerable. Her head was balanced upon her neck, and her neck on her shoulders like a balancing act, and the bizarre diversity of her features, incongruous in themselves, came together and fused into a face quite irresistible.

From far below were cries and counter-cries, for the house was full of guests.

'Cheeta,' they shouted, 'where are you? We're going riding.'

'Then go!' said Cheeta, between her pretty teeth.

Great blond men were draped over the banisters, two floors below.

'Come on, Cheeta,' they yelled. 'We've got your pony ready.'

'Then shoot the brute,' she muttered.

She turned her head from Titus for a moment, and all her features, orientated thus, provoked a new relationship . . . another beauty.

'Leave her alone,' cried the young ladies, who knew that with Cheeta alongside there would be no fun for them. 'She doesn't want to come . . . she *told* us so,' they squealed.

Nor did she. She sat quite upright, her eyes fixed upon the young man.

SEVENTY

HE had been found lying asleep in an outhouse several days previously by one of the servants on his midnight round. His clothing was drenched, and he was shivering and babbling to himself. The servant, amazed, had been on his way to his master, but had been stopped in his tracks by Cheeta on her way to bed. Being asked why he was running, the servant told Miss Cheeta of the trespasser and together they made their way to the outhouse and there he was, to be sure, curled up and shuddering.

For a long while, she had done nothing but stare at the profile of the young man. It was, taken all in all, a young face, even a boyish face, but there had been something else about it not easy to understand. It was a face that had looked out on many a scene. It was as though the gauze of youth had been plucked away to discover something rougher, something nearer the bone. It seemed that a sort of shade passed to and fro over his face; an emanation of all he had been. In short, his face had the substance out of which his life was composed. It was nothing to do with the shadowy hollow beneath his cheekbones or the minute hieroglyphics that surrounded his eyes; it was to her as though his face was his life . . .

But also, she had felt something else. An instantaneous attraction.

'Say nothing of this,' she had said, 'do you understand? Nothing. Unless you wish to be dismissed.'

'Yes, madam.'

'Can you lift him?'

'I think so, madam.'

'Try.'

With difficulty he had raised Titus in his arms and together the three of them made their midnight journey to the green room at the end of the east wing. There, in this remote corner of the house, they laid him on a bed.

'That will be all,' said the scientist's daughter.

SEVENTY-ONE

THREE days had passed since that night when she had tended him. One would have thought that he must surely have opened his eyes if only because of his nearness to her peculiar beauty, but no, his eyes remained shut, or if not, then they *saw* nothing.

With an efficiency almost unattractive in a woman so compelling, she dealt with the situation, as though she were doing no more than pencilling her eyebrows.

It is true that on the second day of her patient's fever she was amazed at the farrago of his outpourings, for he had struggled in bed and cried out again and again, in a language made almost foreign by the number of places and of people; words she had never heard of, with one out-topping all . . . Gormenghast.

'Gormenghast.' That was the core and gist of it. At first Cheeta could make nothing of it, but gradually in between the feverish repetition of the word, were names and phrases that slowly fell into place and made for her some kind of picture.

Cheeta, the sophisticate, found herself, as she listened, drawn into a zone, a layer of people and happenings, that twisted about, inverted themselves, moved in spirals, yet were nevertheless consistent within their own confines. From the cold centre of elegance and a life of scheduled pleasure she was now being shown the gulches of a barbarous region. A world of capture and escape. Of violence and fear. Of love and hate. Yet above all, of an underlying calm. A calm built upon a rock-like certainty and belief in some immemorial tradition.

Here, tossing and sweating on the bed below her, lay a fragment, so it seemed, of a great tradition: for all the outward movement utterly still in the confidence of its own hereditary truth. Cheeta, for the first time in her life, felt in the presence of blood so much bluer than her own. She ran her little tongue along her lips.

There he lay in the dusk of the green room, while the voices of the house below him rang faintly down the corridors, and the riding horses stamped in their impatience.

'*Can you hear me . . . O can you hear me . . . Can you . . . ?*'
'*Is that my son . . . ? Where are you . . . child?*'
'*Where are you, mother . . . ?*'
'*Where I always am . . .*'
'*At your high window, mother, a-swarm with birds?*'
'*Where else?*'

'*Can no one tell me . . . ?*'

'*Tell you what . . . ?*'

'*Where in the world I am . . .*'

'*Not easily . . . not easily.*'

'*You were never easy with your sums, young man. Never.*'

'*O fold me in the foul folds of your gown, O Mr Bellgrove, sir.*'

'*Why did you do it, boy? Why did you run away?*'

'*Why did you . . . ?*'

'*Why . . . why . . . ?*'

'*Why . . . ?*'

'*Listen . . . listen . . .*'

'*Why are your shoulders turned away from me?*'

'*The birds are perched upon her head like leaves.*'

'*And the cats like a white tide?*'

'*The cats are loyal in a traitors' world.*'

'*Steerpike . . . ?*'

'*O no!*'

'*Barquentine . . . ?*'

'*O no!*'

'*I cannot stand it . . . O my doctor dear.*'

'*I have missed you, Titus . . . O very much so . . . by all that abdicates you take the cake.*'

'*But where have you gone to . . . love?*'

'*Why did you do it . . . why?*'

'*Why did you?*'

'*Why . . . why . . . ?*'

'*Why . . .*'

'*Your father . . . and your sister and now . . . you . . .*'

'*Fuchsia . . . Fuchsia . . .*'

'*What was that?*'

'*I heard nothing.*'

'*O Dr Prune . . . I love you, Dr Prune . . .*'

'*I heard a footfall.*'

'*I heard a cry.*'

'*Ahoy there, Urchin! Titus the flyblown . . .*'

'*Hell how you've wandered! Who were you talking to?*'

'*Who was it, Titus?*'

'*You wouldn't understand. He is different.*'

'*He drinks the red sky for his evening wine. He loved her.*'

'*Juno?*'

'*Juno.*'

'*He saved my life. He saved it many times.*'

'*Enough. Cut out the woman in you with a jack-knife.*'

'*God save the sweetness of your iron heart.*'

'So they all died . . . all . . . fish, flesh and fowl.'

'Ha ha ha ha ha! They were only caged-up creatures after all. Look at that lion. That's all it is. Four legs . . . two ears . . . one nose . . . one belly.'

'But they killed the zoo! Muzzlehatch's zoo! Plumes; horns; and beaks compounded all together. A slice of living over. The lion's mane, clotted with blood, creaking as it crumbles.'

'I love you, child. Where are you? Am I worrying you?'

'He's been away so long.'

'So long . . . What were you doing in that part of the world that you could get so wet with the rain?'

'I was lost. I have always been lost; Fuchsia and I were always lost. Lost in our great house where the lizards crawled and the weeds made their way up the stairs and blossomed on the landings. Who is that? Why don't you open the door? Why do you keep fidgeting? Have you not the courage to open the door? Are you afraid of wood? Don't worry, I can see you through the door. Don't worry. Your name is Acreblade. King of the police. I hate your face. It is made of tin-tacks. Your arms are fixed with nails . . . but Juno is with me. The castle is afloat. Steerpike my enemy swims under water, a dagger between his teeth. Yet I killed him. I killed him dead.

'Come here and we will dance together on the battlements. The turrets are white with bird-lime. It is like phosphorus. Join hands with me, Muzzlehatch, and Juno, loveliest of all, and step out into space. We will not fall alone for as we pass window after window, a score of heads will bob along beside us, grinning like ten-to-three. Veil and the Black Rose: Cusp-Canine and the Grasses . . . and close to me, all the way as we fell, was the head of Fuchsia; her black hair in my eyes, but I could not wait for there was the Thing to seek. The Thing. She lived in the bole of a tree. The walls were honeycombs and the bole droned, but never a bee would sting us. She leapt from branch to branch until the schoolmasters came, Bellgrove, Cutflower, and the rest; their mortar-boards slanting through the shadows. Dig a great pit for them: sing to them. Make flower fairies out of hollyhocks. Throw down the bean-pods like dove-green canoes. That ought to keep them happy through the winter. Happy? Happy? Ha, ha, ha, ha, ha. The owls are on their way from Gormenghast. Ha, ha, ha! The ravenous owls . . . the owls . . . the little owls.'

SEVENTY-TWO

When Titus saw her first he imagined her to be yet another of the crowding images, but as he continued to stare at her he knew that this was no face in the clouds.

She had not seen him open his eyes, and so Titus was afforded the opportunity of watching, for a moment or two, the ice in her features. When she turned her head and saw him staring at her she made no effort to soften her expression, knowing that he had taken her unawares. Instead, she stared at Titus in return, until the moment came when, as though they had been playing the game of staring-one-another-out, she made as though she could keep her features set no longer and the ice melted away and her face broke into an expression that was a mixture of the sophisticated, the bizarre, and the exquisite.

'You win,' she said. Her voice was as light and as listless as thistledown.

'Who are you?' said Titus.

'It doesn't matter,' she said. 'As long as I know who you are . . . or does it?'

'Who am I then?'

'Lord Titus of Gormenghast, Seventy-Seventh Earl.' The words fluttered like autumn leaves.

Titus shut his eyes.

'Thank God,' he said.

'For what?' said Cheeta.

'For knowing. I'd grown to almost doubt the bloody place. Where am I? My body's on fire.'

'The worst is over,' said Cheeta.

'Is it? What kind of worst?'

'The search. Drink this and lie back.'

'What a face you have,' said Titus. 'It's paradise on edge. Who are you? Eh? Don't answer, I know it all. You are a woman! That's what you are. So let me suck your breasts, like little apples, and play upon your nipples with my tongue.'

'You are obviously feeling better,' said the scientist's daughter.

SEVENTY-THREE

ONE morning, not very long after he had fully recovered from his fever, Titus rose early, and dressed himself with a kind of gaiety. It was a sensation somewhat foreign to his heart. There had been a time, and not so long ago, when a whim of ludicrous thought could bend him double; when he could laugh at everything and anything as though it were nothing . . . for all the darkness of his early days. But now it seemed had come a time when there was more darkness than light.

But a time had been reached in his life when he found himself laughing in a different kind of way and at different things. He no longer yelled his laughter. He no longer shouted his joy. Something had left him.

Yet on this particular morning, something of his younger self seemed to be with him as he rolled out of bed and on to his feet. An inexplicable bubble; a twinge of joy.

As he let fly the blinds, and disclosed a landscape, he screwed up his face with pleasure, stretched his arms and legs. Yet there was nothing for him to be so pleased about. In fact it was more the other way. He was entangled. He had made new enemies. He had compromised himself irremediably with Cheeta who was dangerous as black water.

Yet this morning Titus was happy. It was as though nothing could touch him. As though he bore a charmed life. Almost as though he lived in another dimension, un-enterable to others, so that he could risk anything, dare everything. Just as he had revelled in his shame and felt no fear on that day when he lay recovering from his fever . . . so now he was in a world equally on his side.

So he ran down the elegant stairs this early morning, and galloped to the stables as though he were himself one of the ponies. In a few moments she was saddled and away . . . the grey mare, away to the lake in whose motionless expanse lay the reflection of the factory.

Out of the slender, tapering chimneys arose, like incense, thin columns of green smoke. Beyond these chimneys the dawn sky lay like an expanse of crumpled linen. As she galloped, the lake growing closer and closer with each stride, he did not know that there was someone following him. Someone else had woken early. Someone else had been to the stables, saddled a pony and raced away. Had Titus turned his head he would have seen as lovely a sight as could be encountered. For the scientist's daughter could ride like a leaf in the wind.

When Titus reached the shore of the lake he made no effort to rein in his grey, who, plunging ever deeper into the lake, sent up great spurts of water, so that the perfect reflection of the factory was set in motion, wave following wave, until there was no part of the lake that was not rippled.

From the motionless building there came a kind of rumour; an endless impalpable sound that, had it been translated into a world of odours, might have been likened to the smell of death: a kind of sweet decay.

When the water had climbed to the throat of the grey horse, and had all but brought the animal to a standstill, Titus lifted his head, and in the softness of the dawn he heard for the first time the full, vile softness of the sound.

Yet, for all this it looked anything but mysterious and Titus ran his eye along the great façade, as though it were the flank of a colossal liner, alive with countless portholes.

Letting his eye dwell for a moment on a particular window, he gave a start of surprise, for in its minute centre was a face; a face that stared out across the lake. It was no larger than the head of a pin.

Turning his eyes on the next of the windows, he saw, as before, a minute face. A chill ran up his spine and he shut his eyes, but this did not help him, for the soft, sick, sound seemed louder in his ears, and the far musty smell of death filled his nostrils. He opened his eyes again. Every window was filled with a face, and every face was staring at him, and most dreadful of all else, every face was the same.

It was then that from far away there came the faint sound of a whistle. At the sound of it the thousands of windows were suddenly emptied of their heads.

All the joy had gone from the day. Something ghastly had taken its place. He turned the grey horse round slowly, and came face to face with Cheeta. Whether it was because her image followed so hard upon that of the factory so that it became tainted in his mind, or whether for some more obscure cause, one cannot tell, but for one reason or another, he was instantaneously sickened at the sight of her. His joy was now finally gone. There was no adventure in his bones. All about him the dawn was like a sickness. He sat on horseback, between an evil edifice, and someone who seemed to think that to be exquisite was enough. Why was she curling the upper petal of her mouth? Could she not smell the foul air? Could she not hear the beastliness of that slow regurgitation?

'So it's you,' he said at last.

'It's me,' said Cheeta, 'why not?'

'Why do you follow me?'

'I can't imagine,' answered Cheeta, in so laconic a voice, that Titus was forced to smile in spite of himself.

'I think I hate you,' he said. 'I don't quite know why. I also hate that stinking factory. Did your father build it – this edifice?'

'They say so,' said Cheeta. 'But then they say anything, don't they?'

'Who?' said Titus.

'Ask me another, darling. And don't go scampering off. After all I love you all I dare.'

'All you dare! That is very good.'

'It is indeed *very* good, when you think of the fools I have sent packing.'

Titus turned his head to her, nauseated by the self-sufficiency in her voice, but directly he focused his gaze upon her his armour began to crack, and he saw her this time in the way he had first seen her, as something infinitely desirable. That he abhorred her brain seemed almost to add to his lust for her body.

Perched aloft her horse, she was there it seemed for the taking. It was for her to remain exactly as she was, her profile motionless against the sky; small, delicate and perhaps vicious. Titus did not *know*. He could only sense it.

'As for you,' she said. 'You're different, aren't you? You can behave yourself.'

The smugness of this remark was almost too much, but before Titus could say a word, she had flicked her reins, and trotted out of the hem of the lake.

Titus followed her, and when they were on dry ground, she called to him.

'Come along, Titus Groan. I know you think you hate me. So try and catch me. Chase me, you villain.'

Her eyes shone with a new light, her body trim as the last word in virgins. Her little riding-habit beautifully cut and moulded as though for a doll. Her tiny body horribly wise, horribly irritating. But O how desirable! Her face lit up as though with an inner light, so clear and radiant was her complexion.

'Chase me,' she cried again, but it was the strangest cry . . . a cry that seemed to be directed at no one, a distant, floating sound.

With her listless voice in his head, the factory was forgotten and Titus, taking up the challenge, was in a few moments in hot pursuit.

Around them on three sides were distant mountains, with their crests shining wanly in the dawn's rays.

Set against these mountains, like stage properties, glimmering in the low beams were a number of houses, one of which was the property of Cheeta's father, the scientist. To the south of this house was a great airfield, shimmering; a base for all kinds of aircraft. To the south again was a belt of trees from the dark interior of which came the intermittent cries of forest creatures.

All this was on the skyline. Far away from Cheeta as she sped, irrational, irritating, a flying virgin, with her lipstick gleaming with a wet, pink light on her half-open mouth; her hair bobbing like a living animal as she rode to the rhythm of the horse's stride.

As Titus thundered in pursuit, he suddenly felt foolish. Normally he would have brushed the feeling to one side, but today it was different. It was not that he cared about behaving foolishly. That was in key with the rest of his nature, and he would have ignored or retained the whim, according to his mood. No. This was something more peculiar. There was something incurably obvious about it all. Something puerile. They were riding on the wings of a cliché. Man pursues woman at dawn! Man has got to consummate his lust! Woman gallops like mad on the rim of the near future. And rich! As rich as her father's factory can make her. And he? He is heir to a kingdom. But where is it? Where is it?

To his left was a small copse and Titus made for it, throwing the reins across the horse's neck. Immediately he reached the limes he knelt down with an acid smile on his lips, thinking he had evaded her, and her designs. He shut his eyes, but only for a moment, for the air became full of a perfume both dry and fresh, and opening his eyes again he found himself looking up at the scientist's daughter.

SEVENTY-FOUR

HE started to his feet.

'O hell!' he cried. 'Do you have to keep on hopping out of nothing? Like that damn' Phoenix bird. Half blood, half ashes. I don't like it. I'm tired of it. Tired of opening my eyes to find odd women peering at me from a great height. How did you get here? How did you know? I thought I'd slipped you.'

Cheeta ignored his questions.

'Did you say "women"?' she whispered. Her voice was like dry leaves in a tree.

'I did,' said Titus. 'There was Juno.'

'I am not interested in Juno,' said Cheeta. 'I've heard all about her . . . too often.'

'You have?'

'I have.'

'How foolish of me,' said Titus, curling his lip. 'Great God, you must have plundered my subconscious. Entrails 'n all. What'll you do with such a foul cargo? How far did I go? What did I tell you? Of how I raped her in a bed of parsley?'

'Who?' said the scientist's daughter.

'My great grand-dam. The one with pointed teeth.'

'Now that,' said Cheeta, 'I *don't* remember!'

'Your face,' said Titus, 'is quite wonderful. But it spells disaster. To have you would be like holding a time bomb. Not that you mean to be dangerous. Oh no! But your features carry a danger of their own. You cannot help it, nor can they.'

Cheeta stared at her companion for a long time. At last she said . . .

'What is it, Titus, that isolates us? You seem to do all you can to belittle our friendship. You are so very difficult. I could be happy talking to you, hour after hour, but you are never serious, never.

Heaven knows, I am no talker. But a word here and there would be something. All you seem to think of is either to make love to me, or to be facetious.'

'I know what you mean,' said Titus. 'I know *exactly* what you mean.'

'Then . . . why . . . ?'

'It is more difficult than I can tell you. I have to form a barrier against you. A barrier of foolery. I cannot. I *must* not take it seriously, this land of yours, this land of factories, this *you*. I have been here long enough to know it is not for me. You are no help with your peculiar wealth and beauty. It leads nowhere. It keeps me like a dancing bear on the end of a rope. Ah . . . you are a rare one. You spend your time with me, showing me off to your father. But why? Why? To shock him and his friends. You throw off your suitors one by one, and leave them hopping mad. This jealousy whipped up is like a stink. What is it?'

Titus, reaching out for her hand as she stood above him, pulled her down to the ground.

'Careful,' she said. Her eyebrows were raised as she lay beside him.

A dragonfly cruised above them with a thin vibration of transparent wings, and then the silence settled again.

'Take your hand away,' said Cheeta. 'I don't like it. To be touched makes me sick. You understand, don't you?'

'No, I bloody well don't,' said Titus, jumping to his feet. 'You're as cold as meat.'

'Do you mean that it has always been my body and only my body that has attracted you? Do you mean that there is no other reason why you should want to be near me?'

Her voice took on a new tone. It was dry and remote but it carried with it an edge.

'The strange thing is,' she said, 'that I should love you. You. A young man who has harboured nothing but lust for me. An enigmatic creature from somewhere that is not to be found in an atlas. Can't you understand? You are my mystery. Sex would spoil it. There's nothing mysterious about sex. It is your mind that matters, and your stories, Titus, and the way you are different from any other man I have ever seen. But you are cruel, Titus, cruel.'

'Then the sooner I'm gone, the better,' he shouted, and as he swung round upon her, he found himself closer than he imagined himself to be, for he was staring down at a little face, bizarre, utterly feminine, and delicious. His arms were at once about her, and he drew her to him. There was no response. As for her head it was turned away so that he could not kiss her.

'Hello, hello!' he shouted, letting her go. 'This is the end.'

He let her go and she at once began to brush her riding clothes.

'I'm finished with you,' said Titus. 'Finished with your marvellous face and your warped brain. Go back to your clutch of virgins and forget me as I shall forget you.'

'You *beast*,' she cried. 'You ungrateful *beast*. Am I nothing in myself that you desert me? Is coupling so important? There are a million lovers making love in a million ways, but there is only one of me.' Her hands trembled. 'You have disappointed me. You're cheap. You're shoddy. You're weak. You're probably mad. You and your Gormenghast! You make me sick.'

'I make myself sick,' said Titus.

'I'm glad,' said the scientist's daughter, 'long may you remain so.'

Now that Cheeta knew that she was in no way loved by Titus, the harshness that had crept into her voice was transferring itself to her thoughts. Never before in her life had she been thwarted. There was not one of all her panting admirers who had ever dared to talk to her in the way that Titus had talked. They were prepared to wait a hundred years for a smile from those lips of hers, or the lift of an eyebrow. She stared at him now, as though for the first time, and she hated him. In some peculiar way she had been humbled by him, although it was Titus who had been stopped short in his advances. The harshness that had crept into her voice and mind was turning into native cunning. She had given herself to him in every way short of the actual act of love and she had been flouted; brushed aside.

What did she care whether or not he was Lord of Gormenghast? Whether he was sane or deranged? All she knew was that something miraculous had been snatched from her grasp, and that she would stop at nothing short of absolute revenge.

SEVENTY-FIVE

THE violent death of Veil in the Under-River was cause for endless speculation and wonderment, not for a day or two, but for months on end. Who was the boy who had made so miraculous an escape? Who was the rangy stranger who had saved him? (There were some to be sure who had seen Muzzlehatch from time to time over the last decade, but even to those he was more of a ghost than a reality and the stories that were told of him were all but legends.)

There were those who remembered Muzzlehatch on the run, and how the dripping gates had opened to him with as great a sigh as ever haunted the dream of a melancholic.

Here, long ago, in his enormous hideout he would sing until the bells gave in, or sit for hours brooding, like a monarch, sometimes covered in brambles, or daubed with earth according to the country through which he had been stealing. And there was the time, on a never-to-be-forgotten day, when he was seen immaculately clad from head to toe, striding down a seemingly endless corridor, complete with a top hat on his head, a cane in his hand (which he twirled like a juggler) and an air of indescribable hauteur.

But for the most part he was known for the shameful negligence with which he kept his garments.

But he never lived there, with the denizens. The Under-River was a refuge and nothing more to him, and so he was as much a mystery to them as to the sophisticates who lived in the great houses above the river banks.

But where had they disappeared to, these two figures, the gaunt and self-sufficient Muzzlehatch, and the young man he saved? How could they ever know, these self-incarcerated rebels; these thieves and refugees? Yet they talked of little else but the flight and where they might be. Their talk was nothing but conjecture, and could get them nowhere, yet it provided almost a reason for living. For all, except three. Three, and a most unlikely three. It seems that they had been awakened in their different ways, by the horror of the ghastly incident. They were shocked, but they did not remain so. All they wanted now was to escape, at any risk, from the thronged emptiness of the place.

Superficially unadventurous, yet restless to quit that saturated morgue: superficially inactive yet ready now to take the risk of escape. For the police were after all three.

Crabcalf, with his pale pushed-in face and his general air of martyrdom. Self-centred, if not to the point of megalomania, then very near it. What of the fact that he was bed-ridden? And what of the heavy 'remainder' of identical volumes that had once propped up his pillow and surrounded his bed for so many years?

His bed, thanks to his friend Slingshott, and one or two others, had been exchanged for an upright chair on wheels. On the back of this chair was hung a great sack. It was filled with his books, and a great weight it was. Poor Slingshott, whose duty it was to push the chair, books, Crabcalf and all, from district to district, found little pleasure in the occupation. Not only had Slingshott the lowest opinion of Literature as a whole, he had even more a distaste for this particular book in so far as it was repeated so many times, and every time a strain upon the heart.

But though it was a long book and heavy, in spite of Crabcalf having jettisoned the bulk of it, and though it was duplicated scores of times, yet Slingshott never dreamed of rebellion, or queried his rights. He knew that without Crabcalf he would be lost.

As for Crabcalf, he was so absorbed in shallow speculations, that the fact that Slingshott was in any way suffering never occurred to him.

To be sure he heard from time to time the sound of wailing, but it might just as well been the scraping together of branches for all he knew or cared.

SEVENTY-SIX

IT was on a moonless, starless night that they escaped from the Under-River and headed north by east. Within a month they were on foreign soil.

It was under a bald hill that they picked up Crack-Bell as planned. He was, for all his idiocy, the only one of the three who had any money. Not much, as they soon found out, but enough to last them for a month or two. This money was transferred to Crabcalf's pocket, where, as he said, it would be safer. When it came to money Crabcalf's vagueness seemed to desert him.

Crack-Bell had no objections. Nothing happened. He had been rich. Now he was poor. What did it matter? His laugh was as shrill, as penetrating as it always was. His smile just as fatuous. His responses just as quick. Compared with his two companions, Crack-Bell was intensely alive, like a monkey.

'Here we are,' he cried. 'Bang in the middle of somewhere. Don't ask me where, but somewhere. Ha, ha, ha.' His crockery laughter rattled down the hill in broken pieces.

'Mr Crabcalf, sir,' said Slingshott.

'Yes?' said Crabcalf, raising an eyebrow. 'What do you want this time? Another rest, I suppose.'

'We have covered a lot of heavy ground today,' said Slingshott, 'and I am tired. Indeed I am. It reminds me of those . . .'

'Years in the salt mines. Yes, yes. We know all about them,' said Crabcalf. 'And would you care to be a little more careful with my volumes? You handle that sack as though it were full of potatoes.'

'If I may get a tiny word in edgeways,' trilled Crack-Bell. 'I would put it like this . . .'

'Unstrap my volumes,' said Crabcalf. 'All of them. Dust them down with a dry cloth. Then count them.'

'When I was in the mines you know, I had time to think . . .' said Slingshott, obeying Crabcalf mechanically.

'Oh la! And did you then? And what did you think of? Women? Women! Ha, ha, ha. Women. Ha, ha, ha, ha.'

'Oh no. Oh no indeed. I know nothing of women,' said Slingshott.

'Did you hear that, Crabcalf? What an extraordinary statement to have made. It is like saying "I know nothing of the moon".'

'Well, what *do* you know of it?' said Crabcalf.

'As much as I know of *you*, my dear fellow. The moon is arid. And so are you. But what does all this matter? We are alive. We are at large. To hell with the moon. It's a coward anyway. Only comes out at night! Ha, ha, ha, ha!'

'The moon figures in my book,' said Crabcalf. 'I can't remember quite where . . . but it figures quite a lot. I talk, or rather, I dilate you know, on the change that has come over the moon. Ever since Molusk circled it, it has been quite a different thing. It has lost its mystery. Are you listening, Slingshott?'

'Yes, and no,' said Slingshott. 'I was really thinking about our next encampment. It was different in the mines. There was no . . .'

'Forget the mines,' said Crabcalf. 'And mind your clumsy elbow on my manuscript. Oh my friends, my friends, is it nothing that we have escaped from that pernicious place? That we are all three together as we had planned? That we are here at peace on the lee side of a bald hill?'

'Yet even here one cannot help remembering that beastly grapple. It quite turns me up,' said Slingshott.

'Oh my. It was a scrap indeed! Bones, muscles, tendons, organs, 'n all sorts, scattered this way and that, but what does it matter now? The evening is fine; there are two stars. Life is ahead of us . . . or some of it is. Ha! ha! ha!'

'Yes, yes, yes. I know all about that Crack-Bell, but I can't help wondering . . .'

'Wondering?'

'Yes, about that boy. He sticks in my mind,' said Slingshott.

'I didn't see much of him. I was some way down the hill. But from what I saw, and from what I know of life, I should say he was well reared.'

'Well reared! Ha, ha, ha, ha, ha! That's very spicy.'

'Spicy! You fool! Do you think I've spent my life in the Under-River? I was a valet once.'

Slingshott rose to his feet.

'The dew is rising,' he said. 'I must build the fire. As for the young man, I would give much to see him.'

'Obviously,' said Crabcalf. 'He had an air about him. Yet, why should we want to . . . ?'

'To see him?' cried Crack-Bell. 'Why should we? Oh la! He and his
crocodile friend. Oh la! What food for conjecture.'

'Leave that to me,' said Crabcalf. 'I have a head like a compass, and
a nose like a bloodhound. For you dear Slingshott, the encampments
and the care of the volumes . . . Crack-Bell, for forage and the wringing
of hens' necks. Oh my dear, how neatly and fleetly you move when the
moon gloats on farms and the yards are black and silver. How neatly
and fleetly you stalk the livestock. If ever we catch up with the boy we
will have wine and turkey.'

'I don't drink,' said Slingshott.

'Hush!'

'What is it?'

'Did you not hear the laughter?'

'Sh . . . sh . . .'

SEVENTY-SEVEN

THERE was a sound; and their heads turned together to the west flank
of the bald hill.

Came slithering through the dusk the entrail gobblers: the belly-
brained, agog for carrion. The jackals and the foxes. What are they
digging for? The scrabbling of their horn-grey nails proceeds. Their
eyes start like jellies. Their ears, the twitching spades of playing-cards.
Ahoy! scavengers! The moon's retching.

As Slingshott, Crack-Bell and Crabcalf crouched trembling (for at
first it might have been anything, so curiously repellent was the noise)
another kind of sound caused them to turn their heads again, and this
time it was towards the sky.

Out of the blind space, sunless and terrible, like coloured gnats
emerging from the night, a squadron of lime-green needles, peeling at
speed, made for the earth.

The jackals lifted their vile muzzles. Slingshott, Crabcalf, and Crack-
Bell lifted theirs.

There was no time for fear or understanding. They were gone no
sooner than they appeared. But, fast as they travelled, there was
something more than speed for its own sake. *It seemed they were looking for
someone.*

The jackals and the foxes returned to their carcase on the other side
of the bald hill, and in doing so they were unable to see the helmeted

figures, who now stood against the sky like tall carvings, identical in every particular.

They wore a kind of armour, yet were free to move with absolute ease. When one of them took a step forward, the other took a similar step at the same moment. When one of them shielded his huge hollow eyes from the moon, his companion followed suit.

Had they been guiding those soundless aerial darts? It did not seem so, for their heads were bowed a little.

Around their column-like necks were tiny boxes, suspended from metal threads. What were they? Could it be that they were receiving messages from some remote headquarters? But no! Surely not. They were not the sort of mortals to obey. Their silence in itself was hostile and proud.

Only once did they turn their gaze upon the three vagrants, and in that double gaze was such a world of scorn that Crabcalf and his two trembling pards felt an icy blast against their bodies. It was not for them that the helmeted pair were searching.

Then came a growl as the teeth of one of the jackals met in the centre of some dead brute's intestines, and at that sound the tall pair turned upon their heels, and moved away with a strange and gliding action that was more terrible than any strut or stride.

Now *they* were gone the jackals followed suit, for nothing was left on the bones of the poor dead beast. Like a canopy the countless flies hung over the skeleton as though to form a veil or shawl of mourning.

The three from the Under-River climbed at last to the crest of the hill, and saw spread out in the moonlight, on every side, a lunar landscape, infinitely brittle. But they were in no mood for pulchritude.

'No sleep for us tonight,' said Crabcalf. 'I don't like the place one little bit. My thighs are as wet as turbots.'

The other two agreed that it was no place for sleep, though it fell upon Slingshott, as always, to push the wheeled chair up and down the slopes of this horrible terrain, with not only Crabcalf on board, but his 'remainder' of sixty-one volumes.

Crack-Bell (who, over and above the blanching effect of the moon on his face was, in his own right, as white as a sheet) walked a little behind the other two, and in an attempt to appear courageous, whistled an air both shrill and out of key.

SEVENTY-EIGHT

AND so they moved in a single file across the white landscape, and encountered no sign of a living creature. Crabcalf was seated in his high-backed chair on wheels; his sack of identical books in his lap. Slingshott, his retainer, pushed his master, laboriously, down narrow defiles, along cold ridges, across deserts of shale. As for Crack-Bell, he had long ago given up whistling, saving his breath for the thankless task of hauling an old cooking stove, some camping gear, and a stolen turkey. Staggering along in the rear of this three-piece cavalcade, with nothing but a cold night ahead, Crack-Bell, by his very nature, could not help the irritating grin that hovered over the lower regions of his face, nor the mad twinkle in his empty eyes. 'Life is good,' they seemed to say . . . 'Life is very good.'

Had it not been that he took up the rearguard station his facial fatuities must surely have maddened his two companions. As it was, he trudged along unseen.

SEVENTY-NINE

SHE sat motionlessly at her peerless mirror, gazing not *at*, but *through* herself, for her meditation was deep and bitter, and her eyes had lost their sense of sight. Had she been aware of her own reflection and freed her eyes of the veil that lay like a cataract across them, she would have seen, first of all, the unnatural rigidity of her body, and she would have relaxed not only the muscles of her spine, but those of her face.

For there was, in spite of her beauty, something macabre about her head; something she would certainly have attempted to disguise had she known it permeated her features. But she knew nothing of this, and so she sat there, bolt upright, staring, with her eyes out of focus, while the blank reflections of her orbs stared back.

The stillness was horrible, especially when, like something palpable, it coagulated and seemed almost to drown the only authentic sound, that of a dry leaf as it fluttered from time to time against the glass of a distant window.

The very atmosphere of Cheeta's dressing-room was in itself enough to chill the blood, so austere and loveless it was. And yet, although it

sent a vile chill up the spine, it was not, on that account, a place of ugliness. On the contrary, it was majestic in its proportions and superb in its economy.

The floor, to begin with, was spread from corner to distant corner with a tundra of white camel skins, pale as white sand and soft as wool.

The walls were hung with tapestries that glowed with a sullen, prawn-coloured luminosity . . . a system of concealed lighting that gave the impression that the muted light was not so much falling upon the tapestries, as emerging from them. As though they were themselves effulgent, and burned their lives away.

EIGHTY

NOT so many years ago she had cried out, 'Oh how I hate you all.' The elders shook their heads. 'What does she mean?' they said. 'Has she not everything that money can buy? Is she not the scientist's daughter?'

But she was restless, was Cheeta. Would she care for this? Would she care for that? No. Would she accept the Greeziorthspis Tapestries? She would accept them.

They were bought for her, thus denuding a small country of its only treasure.

So here they hung in the great room that was designed to take them, lovelier than ever, burning away in dusty pinks and golds, but with no one to see them, for Cheeta had deserted what was once her joy.

They had gone dead on her; or she on them. The unicorns leapt unseen. The crags that blushed in the sun's rays, meant nothing now. The perilous combers were now no longer perilous.

The floor of camel-hair; the walls of tapestry; the dressing-table. It was carved from a single hunk of granite. Upon its surface were laid out, as usual, the articles of her toilet.

The surface of the black granite was peerlessly smooth, yet thrillingly uneven to the palm of the hand, appearing to bulge, or sway, and the reflections of the various instruments were as sharp as the instruments themselves, yet wavered. For all the multiplicity of her toilet, the coloured objects took up the merest fraction of the surface. To right and left of them, the granite fanned out in adamantine yet sumptuous undulations.

But Cheeta who sat upright on the camel-hair seat of her chair was today in no frame of mind to run the palms of her hands in silent and sensuous delight. Something had happened to her. Something that had never happened before. She knew now for the first time that she was unnecessary. Titus Groan had found that he could do without her.

Beneath the rigidity of her small, slender, military spine was a writhing serpent. Beyond the blankness of her seemingly dead eyes was a world of febrile horror, for she now knew that she hated him. Hated his self-sufficiency. Hated a quality that he had, which she lacked. She lifted her glazed eyes to the sky beyond the mirror. It swam with little clouds, and her sight cleared at last, and her eyelids fell.

Her thoughts like scales began to shed themselves until there was an absolute nothingness in her head, a nothingness made necessary, for the intensity of her dark thoughts had been horrible and could not be kept up forever, short of madness.

Beyond the mirror, scissoring its way across the sky, was her father's pride. The latest of all his factories. Even as she watched, a plume of smoke spiralled its way out of one of the chimneys.

Rigid as herself in her agony, her implements were drawn up in battle array. A militant array of eccentrics; instruments of beauty; coloured like the rainbow; shining like steel or wax; the unguent vases carved in alabaster; the Kohl; the nard.

The fragrance from the onyx and the porphyry pots, the elusive aromatic spikenard . . . olive and almond and the sesame oil. The powdery perfumes, ground for her alone; rose, almond, quince. The rouges, the spices and the gums. The eyebrow pencils, and the coloured eyeline; mascara and the powder brush. The eyebrow tweezers and the eyelash curlers. The tissues, the crêpes and several little sponges. Each in its place before the perfect mirror.

Then there was a sound. At first it was so faint it was impossible to make out what was being said, or whether indeed it was her voice at all. Had it not been that there was no one else in the room one would not have guessed the sound to come from such pretty lips as Cheeta's. But now the sound grew louder and louder until she beat upon her granite dressing-table with her minute fists and called out, 'Beast, beast, beast! Go back to your filthy den. Go back to your Gormenghast!' and rising to her feet she swept the granite table with her arm so that everything that had been set out so beautifully was sent hurtling through the air to smash itself and waste itself upon the white camel skins of the carpet and the dusky red of the tapestries.

EIGHTY-ONE

OUT of the bitterness that was now a part of her, like an allergy, *something* had begun to arise to the surface of her conscious mind; something that might be likened to a sea monster rising from the depths of the ocean; scaled and repulsive. At first she did not know or feel any kind of contraction, but gradually as the days went by, the nebulous ponderings began to find focus. Something harsher took their place until she realized that what she craved was the knowledge not just of *how* to *hurt* but *when*. So that at last, a fortnight after her argument with Titus, she realized that she was actively plotting the downfall of the boy, and that her whole being was diverted to that end.

In sweeping her make-up to the floor she had swept away all that was blurred in her mind and passion. This left her not only more venomous but icy-headed, so that when she next saw Titus her behaviour was the very heart of poise.

EIGHTY-TWO

'Is that the boy?' asked Cheeta's father, the merest wisp of a man.

'Yes, father, that is he.' His voice had been utterly empty. His presence was a kind of subtraction. He was nondescript to the point of embarrassment. Only his cranium was positive – a lard-coloured hummock.

His features, if described piecemeal, would amount to nothing, and it was hard to believe that the same blood ran through Cheeta's body. Yet there was something – an emanation that linked the father and daughter. A kind of atmosphere that was entirely their own; although their features had no part in it. For he was *nothing*: a creature of solitary intellect, unaware of the fact that, humanly speaking, he was a kind of vacuum for all that there was genius in his skull. He thought of nothing but his factory.

Cheeta, following his gaze, could see Titus quite clearly.

'Pull up,' she said, in a voice as laconic as a gull's.

Her father touched a button, and at once the car sighed to a halt.

At the far end of an overhung carriage-way was Titus, apparently talking to himself, but just as Cheeta and her father were about to suppose that he had lost his senses, three beggars emerged out of the distant tangle of leaves, at Titus's side.

This group of four had apparently not heard or seen the approach of the car.

The long drive was dappled with soft autumnal light.

'We have been following you,' said Crack-Bell. 'Ha, ha, ha! In and out of your footsteps as you might say.'

'Following me? What for? I don't even know you,' said Titus.

'Don't you remember, young man?' said Crabcalf. 'In the Under-River? When Muzzlehatch saved you?'

'Yes, yes,' said Titus, 'but I don't remember *you*. There were thousands of you . . . and besides . . . have you seen him?'

'Muzzlehatch?'

'Muzzlehatch.'

'Not so,' said Slingshott.

There was a pause.

'My dear boy,' said Crack-Bell –

'Yes?' said Titus.

'How elegant you are. Just as I used to be. You were a beggar when we saw you last. Like us, you were. Ha, ha, ha! A mouldering mendicant. But look at you now. O la la!'

'Shut up,' said Titus.

He stared at them again. Three failures. Pompous as only failures can be.

'What do you want with me?' said Titus. 'I have nothing to give you.'

'You have everything,' said Crabcalf. 'That's why we follow you. You are different, my lord.'

'Who called me that?' whispered Titus. 'How did you know?'

'But everybody knows,' cried Crack-Bell, in a voice that carried to where Cheeta and her father watched every move.

'How did you know where to find me?'

'We have kept our ears to the ground, and our eyes skinned, and we used what wits God gave us.'

'After all you have been watched. You are not unknown.'

'Unknown!' cried Crack-Bell. 'Ha, ha, ha! That's good!'

'What's in the sack?' said Titus, turning away.

'My lifework,' said Crabcalf. 'Books, scores of them, but every one the same.' He lifted his head in pride, and tossed it to and fro. 'These are my "remainders". They are my centre. Please take one, my lord. Take one with you back to Gormenghast. Look. I will dip for you.'

Crabcalf, brushing Slingshott aside from the wheel-chair tore open the sack, and plunging his arm down its throat, drew forth a copy from the darkness. He took a pace towards Titus, and offered him the enigmatic volume.

'What's it about?' said Titus.

'Everything,' said Crabcalf. 'Everything I know of life and death.'

'I'm not much of a reader,' said Titus.

'There's no hurry,' said Crabcalf. 'Read it at your leisure.'

'Thanks very much,' said Titus. He turned over a few pages at random. 'There are poems too, are there?'

'Interlarded,' said Crabcalf. 'That is very true; there are poems *interlarded*. Shall I read you one . . . my lord?'

'Well . . .'

'Ah, here we are . . . mm . . . mm. A thought . . . just a passing thought. Where are we? Are you ready, sir?'

'Is it very long?' said Titus.

'It is very short,' said Crabcalf, shutting his eyes. 'It goes thus . . .

'How fly the birds of heaven save by their wings?
How tread the stags, those huge and hairy kings
Save by their feet? How do the fishes turn
In their wet purlieus where the mermaids yearn
Save by their tails? How does the plantain sprout
Save by that root it cannot do without?'

Crabcalf opened his eyes. 'Do you see what I mean?' he said.

'What is your name?' said Titus.

'Crabcalf.'

'And your friends?'

'Crack-Bell and Slingshott.'

'You escaped from the Under-River?'

'We did.'

'And have you been searching for me a long while?'

'We have.'

'For what reason?'

'Because you need us. You see . . . we believe you to be what you say you are.'

'What do I say I am?'

The three took a simultaneous step forward. They lifted their rugged faces to the leaves above them and spoke together . . .

'You are Titus, the Seventy-Seventh Earl of Groan, and Lord of Gormenghast. So help us God.'

'We are your bodyguard,' said Slingshott in a voice so weak and fatuous that the very tone of it negated whatever confidence the words were intended to convey.

'I do not want a bodyguard,' said Titus. 'Thank you all the same.'

'That is what I used to say when I was a young man,' said Slingshott. 'I thought as you did . . . that to be *alone* was everything. That is before they sent me to the salt mines . . . since then, I . . .'

'Forgive me,' said Titus, 'but I cannot stay. I appreciate your selflessness in searching for me, and your idea of protecting me from this and that . . . but no. I am, or I'm *becoming*, one of those damnable selfish so-and-sos, forever biting at the hand that feeds them.'

'We will follow you, nevertheless,' said Crack-Bell. 'We will be, if you like, out of sight. We have no pretensions. We are not easily dissuaded.'

'And there will be others,' said Slingshott. 'Men of spleen and lads of high romance. As time goes on, you'll have an army, my lord. An invisible army. Ready eternally for the note.'

'What note?' said Titus.

'This one of course,' cried Crack-Bell, pursing his lips and expelling a note as shrill as a curlew's. 'The danger note. Ha, ha, ha, ha! Oh no.

You needn't fear a thing. Your viewless army will be with you, everywhere, save in your sight.'

'Leave me!' cried Titus. 'Go! You are over-reaching yourselves. There is only one thing you can do for me.'

For a while the three sat glumly, staring at Titus. Then Crabcalf said . . .

'What is it we can do?'

'Scour the world for Muzzlehatch. Bring news of him, or bring the man himself. Do that, and you can share my wanderings. But for now, please G O, G O, G O!'

EIGHTY-THREE

THE three from the Under-River melted into the woods, and Titus was left alone, or so he thought. He broke and re-broke a small branch in his hands, and then turned away and began to retrace his steps in the direction of the scientist's daughter. It was then that he suddenly saw her.

A few minutes earlier Cheeta had stepped from the car, and her father had turned it about and slid silently away, so that Titus and Cheeta found themselves drawing closer to one another with every step they took.

Anyone standing half-way between the approaching figures would have seen, as he turned his head this way and that, how similar were their backgrounds; for the tree-walled avenue was flecked with gold and green, and Cheeta and Titus were themselves flecked also, and floated, it almost seemed, on the slanting rays of the low sun.

Their past which made them what they were and nothing else, moved with them, adding at each footfall a new accretion. Two figures: two creatures: two humans: two worlds of loneliness. Their lives up to this moment contrasted, and what was amorphous became like a heavy boulder in their breasts.

Yet in Cheeta's bearing, as she moved down the avenue, there was no sign of passion or of the ice in her heart and Titus could only marvel at the way she moved, inevitably, smoothly, like the approach of a phantom.

The merest shred she was: slender as an eyelash, erect as a little soldier. But O the danger of it! To fill her clay with something that leaps higher and throws its wild and flickering shadow further than the blood's wisdom knows. How dangerous, how desperate and how explosive for such a little vessel.

As for Titus, she held him steadily in her eye. She saw it all and at once, his somewhat arrogant, loose-jointed walk, his way of tossing his nondescript hair out of his eyes, his bloody-mindedness, implicit in the slouch of his shoulders, and that general air of detachment which had been so great a stumbling block to the young ladies in his past, who saw no fun in the way he could become abstracted at the oddest moments. That was the irritating thing about him. He could not force a feeling, or bring himself to love. His love was always elsewhere. His thoughts were fastidious. Only his body was indiscriminate.

Behind him, whenever he stood, or slept, were the legions of Gormenghast . . . tier upon cloudy tier, with the owls calling through the rain, and the ringing of the rust-red bells.

EIGHTY-FOUR

WHEN Cheeta and Titus came abreast, they stopped dead, for the idea of cutting one another would have been ludicrously dramatic. In any event, as far as Cheeta was concerned, there was never any question of letting the young man go by like a cloud, never to return. She was not finished with him. She had hardly started. She recognized in the sliding moments, a quality that set this day apart from others. It was a febrile day, not to be gainsaid; a day, perhaps of insight and heightened apprehension.

And yet at the same time there was, in spite of the tension, a feeling in both of them that there was nothing new in what was happening; that they had shared in years gone by, an identical situation, and that there was no escape from the fate that overhung them.

'Thank you for stopping,' said Cheeta, in her slow and listless way. (Titus was always reminded when she spoke of dry leaves rustling.)

'What else could I do?' said Titus. 'After all, we know each other.'

'Do you think so?' said Cheeta. 'Perhaps that would be a good reason to *avoid* one another.'

'Perhaps,' said Titus. The avenue hummed with silence.

'Who were they?' said Cheeta at last. The three short syllables of her question drifted away one by one.

'Who do you mean?' said Titus. 'I'm in no mood for riddles.'

'The three beggars.'

'Oh them! Old friends of mine.'

'Friends?' whispered Cheeta, as though to herself. 'What are they doing in Father's grounds?'

'They came to save me,' said Titus.

'From what?'

'From myself I suppose. And from women. They are wise. Wise men are the beggars. They think you are too luscious for me. Ha, ha, ha, ha! But I told them not to worry. I told them you were frozen at the very tap-root. That your sex is bolted from the inside; that you are as prim as the mantis, that gobbles up the heads of her admirers. Love's so disgusting, isn't it?'

Had Titus not been ranting with his head thrown back, he might for a split second have seen, between the narrowing eyelids of the scientist's daughter, a fleck of terrible light.

But he did not see it. All he saw when he looked down at her was something rare and flawless, as a rose or a bird.

The eyes that had blazed for a moment were now as luminous with love as the eyes of a monkey-eating eagle.

'And yet you said you loved me. That is the spice of it.'

'Of course I love you,' said Cheeta, throwing the words away like dead petals. 'Of course I do, and I always will. That is why you must go.' She drew her pencilled eyebrows together, and at once became another creature, a creature in every way as unique and bizarre as before. She turned her head away, and there she was again, or was she someone else?

'Because I love you, Titus; so much, I can hardly bear it.'

'Then tell me something,' said Titus in so casual a voice that it was all that Cheeta could do to control a spurt of rage, which, had she given vent to it, might have ruined her carefully laid plans. For above all Titus must not be allowed to leave as he intended on the evening of this very day.

'What is it you want to ask me?' She drew herself close to him.

'Your father . . .'

'What about him?'

'Why does he dress like a mute? Why is he so dreary? What's in his factory? Why is his brow like a melon? Are you sure he *is* your father? Whose are those faces that I saw? Thousands of them, and all of them the same, staring like waxworks? What was that stink that crept across the lake? What is it he's making there? For, by God, the very look of the place turns me up. Why is it surrounded by guards?'

'I never asked him. Why should I?' said Cheeta.

'Has he not told you anything at all? And what about your mother?'

'She's . . . What's that?'

There was a faint sound of footsteps, and they drew into the hem of the woods together, and were only just in time, for as they moved, two figures lifted their heads in perfect yet unaffected unison, and slid over the soft turf. On their heads they wore helmets that smouldered in the low rays of the sun.

As they passed, there was yet another sound, apart from the whisper of their feet on the grass. Titus (whose heart was thudding, for he recognized the enigmatic pair) was able for the first time to hear yet *another* noise. It was a low and horrible hissing. It seemed as though a deep-seated anger had at last found vent for itself through the teeth of these identical figures. Their faces showed no sign of excitement. Their bodies were as unhurried as ever. They had control of every muscle. But they could do nothing about the tell-tale hissing which argued so palpably the anger, the ferment and the pain that was twisted up inside them.

They passed by, and the hissing died away, and all that could be seen were the sunbeams glancing from their studded helmets.

As soon as they were far enough away, the fauna of the woods crept out from their hiding places in the boles of trees, or in among the roots and burrows, clustered together on the dappled ride, their private enmities forgotten as they stared at the retreating figures.

'Who were they?'

'Were?' said Titus. 'They're in the present tense, God help me.'

'Who *are* they, then?'

'They sleuth me. I must *go*.'

Cheeta turned to look at him. 'Not yet,' she said.

'At once,' said Titus.

'Impossible,' said Cheeta. 'All is ready.'

The shadow of a leaf trembled on her cheekbones. Her eyes were huge; as though they were sunk for one purpose only . . . to drown the unwary . . . to gulp him down to where the wet ferns drip . . . a world away; down, down into the cold. She hated him because she could not love him. He was unattainable. His love was somewhere else, where dust blossomed.

Cheeta bit her pretty lips. In her head was malice, like a growth. In her heart was a kind of yearning, because passion was not part of her life. Even as she stared she could see the lust in his eyes; that stupid male lust that cheapened everything.

Titus leant forward suddenly, and caught her lower lip between his own.

'You are almost without substance,' he said, 'save for the bits of you that you call your body. I'm off.' As he raised his head he ran his tongue along her throat, and cupped her perfect little breast in his left hand. 'I'm away,' he whispered. 'Away for good.'

'You cannot go,' she said. 'Everything is ready . . . for you.'

'Me? What do you mean? Everything is ready for what?'

'Take your hand away.' She turned at the sound of her own words so that Titus could not see an expression pass across her face. It was lethal.

'They will all be there,' she said.

'Who, in God's name?'

'Your friends. Your early friends.'

'Who? Who? What early friends?'

'That would be telling, wouldn't it?'

There was something sickening about the way this glib childish phrase was delivered in that same laconic drawl. 'But it is all for you.'

'*What* is? O jumping hell!'

'I'll tell you,' said Cheeta, 'and then you'll have no option. It's only one night, and there's only a little time to wait for it. A night in your honour. A farewell party. A feast. Something for you to remember as long as you live.'

'I don't want a party,' said Titus. 'I want . . .'

'I know,' said Cheeta. 'I do indeed know. You are eager to forget me. To forget that I found you destitute and nursed you back to health. You have forgotten all this. What did you do for me, except be horrible to my friends? Now you are strong again, you think you'll go. But there is one thing that you must not forget, and that is that I worship you.'

'Spare me that,' said Titus.

'Yes, worship you, my darling.'

'I am going to be sick,' said Titus.

'Why should you not be? I am also sick. To the very roots of myself. But can I help it? Can I? When I love you without hope?'

Mixed with her loathing of what she was saying was a shred of truth, that, small as it was, was yet enough to make her hands tremble, like the wings of humming-birds.

'You cannot desert me, Titus. Not now, when all is prepared for you. We will laugh and sing, and drink and dance, and go mad with all that one night can give us.'

'Why?'

'Because a chapter will be over. Let us end it in a flourish. Let us end it not with a full stop, dead as death, but with an exclamation mark . . . a leaping thing.'

'Or a question mark?' said Titus.

'No. All questions will be over. There will be only the facts. The mean, sharp, brittle facts, like the wild bits of bone, and us, the two of us, riding the human storm. I know you cannot stand it any longer. This house of my father's. This way of living. But let me have one last night with you, Titus; not in some dusky arbour where all the ritual of love drags out for hours, and there is nothing new; but in the bright invention of the night, our egos naked and our wits on fire.'

Titus, who had never heard her say so much in so short a time, turned to her.

'Our star has been unlucky,' she said. 'We were doomed from the beginning. We were born in different worlds. You with your dreams . . .'

'My dreams?' cried Titus. 'I have no dreams! O God! I have no dreams! It is you who are unreal. You and your father and your factory.'

'I will be real for you, Titus. I will be real on that night, when the world pours through the halls. Let us drain it dry at a gulp and then turn our backs on one another, forever. Titus, oh Titus, come to the barbecue. *Your* barbecue. Tell me that you'll be there. If for no other reason than that I would follow your tousled head to the ends of the earth.'

Titus pulled her towards him gently, and she became like a doll in his arms, tiny, exquisite, fragrant, infinitely rare.

'I will be there,' he whispered, 'never fear.'

The great dreaming trees of the ride stretched away into the distance, sighing; and as he held her to him a spasm passed across her perfect features.

EIGHTY-FIVE

WHEN at last they parted, Cheeta making her way down the aisle of oak trees, and Titus slanting obliquely through the body of the forest, the three vagrants, Crack-Bell, Slingshott, and Crabcalf got to their feet, and followed at once, and were now no more than forty feet from their quarry.

It was no easy task for them to keep track of him, for Crabcalf's books weighed heavily.

As they stole through the shadows they were halted by a sound. At first the three vagrants were unable to locate it; they stared all about them. Sometimes the noise came from here, sometimes from there. It was not the kind of noise they understood, although the three of them were quick in the ways of the woods, and could decipher a hundred sounds, from the rubbing together of branches to the voice of a shrew.

And then, all at once, the three heads turned simultaneously in the same direction, the direction of Titus, and they realized that he was muttering to himself.

Crouching down together, they saw him, ringed by leaves. He was wandering listlessly in the half-darkness and, as they watched, they saw him press his head against the hard bole of a tree. As he pressed his head he whispered passionately to himself, and then he raised his voice and cried out to the whole forest . . .

'O traitor! Traitor! What is it all about? Where can I find me? Where is the road home? Who are these people? What are these happenings? Who is this Cheeta, this Muzzlehatch? I don't belong. All I want is the smell of home, and the breath of the castle in my lungs. Give me some proof of me! Give me the death of Steerpike; the nettles; give me the corridors. Give me my mother! Give me my sister's grave. Give me the nest; give me my secrets back . . . for this is foreign soil. O give me back the kingdom in my head.'

EIGHTY-SIX

JUNO has left her house by the river. She has left the town once haunted by Muzzlehatch. She is driving in a fast car along the rim of a valley. Her quiet companion sits beside her. He looks like a brigand. A hank of dark red hair blows to and fro across his forehead.

'It is an odd thing,' says Juno, 'that I still don't know your name. And somehow or other I don't want to. So I must call you something of my own invention.'

'You do that,' says Juno's companion, in a gentle growl of such depth and cultivation that it is hard to believe that it could ever issue from so piratical a head.

'What shall it be?'

'Ah, there I can't help you.'

'No?'

'No.'

'Then I must help myself. I think I will call you my "Anchor",' says Juno. 'You give me so deep a sense of safety.'

Turning to look at him she takes a corner at unnecessary speed, all but overturning the car.

'Your driving is unique,' says Anchor. 'But I cannot say it gives me confidence. We will change places.'

Juno draws in to the side of the road. The car is like a swordfish. Beyond it the long erratic line of the amethyst-coloured mountains. The sky overhanging everything is cloudless save for a wisp way down in the far south.

'How glad I am that you waited for me,' says Juno. 'All those long years in the cedar grove.'

'Ah,' says the Anchor.

'You saved me from being a sentimental old bore. I can just see myself with my tear-stained face pressed against the window-panes . . .

weeping for the days long gone. Thank you, Mr Anchor, for showing me the way. The past is over. My home is a memory. I will never see it again. For look, I have these sunbeams and these colours. A new life lies ahead.'

'Do not expect too much,' says the Anchor. 'The sun can be snuffed without warning.'

'I know, I know. Perhaps I am being too simple.'

'No,' says the Anchor. 'That is hardly the word for an uprooting. Shall we go on?'

'Let us stay a little longer. It is so lovely here. Then drive. Drive like the wind . . . into another country.'

There is a long silence. They are completely relaxed; their heads thrown back. Around them lies the coloured country. The golden cornfields; the amethyst mountains.

'Anchor, my friend,' says Juno in a whisper.

'Yes, what is it?'

His face is in profile. Juno has never seen a face so completely relaxed, and without strain.

'I am so happy,' says Juno, 'although there is so much to be sad about. It will take its turn, I suppose . . . the sadness. But *now* . . . in this very *now*. I am floating with love.'

'Love?'

'Love. Love for everything. Love for those purple hills; love for your rusty forelock.'

She sinks back against the cushions and closes her eyes, and as she does so the Anchor turns his lolling head in her direction. She is indeed handsome with a handsomeness beyond the scope of her wisdom. Majestic beyond the range of her knowledge.

'The world goes by,' says Juno, 'and we go with it. Yet I feel young today; young in spite of everything. In spite of my mistakes. In spite of my age.' She turns to the Anchor . . . 'I'm over forty,' she whispers. 'Oh my dear friend, I'm over forty!'

'So am I,' says the Anchor.

'What shall we do?' says Juno. She clutches his forearm with her jewelled hands, and squeezes him.

'There is nothing we can do, except live.'

'Is that why you thought I should leave my home? My possessions? My memories? Everything? Is that why?'

'I have told you so.'

'Yes, yes. Tell me again.'

'We are beginning. Incongruous as we are. You with your mellow beauty that out-glows a hundred damsels, and me with . . .'

'With what?'

'With a kind of happiness.'

Juno turns to him but she says nothing. The only movement comes from the black silk at her bosom where a great ruby rises and sinks like a buoy on a midnight bay.

At last Juno says, 'The sunlight's lovelier than it's ever been, because we have decided to begin. We will pass the days together as they pass. But . . . Oh . . .'

'What is it?'

'It's Titus.'

'What about him?'

'He is gone. Gone. I disappointed him.'

The Anchor moving with a kind of slow, lazy deliberation takes his place at the wheel. But before the swordfish whips away he says . . .

'I thought it was the *future* we were after.'

'But O, but O, it *is*,' cries Juno. 'Oh my dear Anchor, it is indeed.'

'Then let us catch it by its tail and fly!'

Juno, her face radiant, leans forward in the padded swordfish, and away they go, soundless save for the breath of their own speed.

EIGHTY-SEVEN

SHAMBLING his way from the west, came Muzzlehatch. Once upon a time there was no shambling in his gait or in his mind. Now it was different. The arrogance was still there, redolent in every gesture, but added to it was something more bizarre. The rangy body was now a butt for boys to copy. His rangy mind played tricks with him. He moved as though oblivious of the world. And so he was, save for one particular. Just as Titus ached for Gormenghast, ached to embrace its crumbling walls, so Muzzlehatch had set himself the task of discovering the centre of destruction.

Always his brain returned to that mere experiment; the liquidation of his zoo. There was no shape in all that surrounded him, whether branch or boulder, but revived in him the memory of one or other of his beloved creatures. Their death had quickened in him something which he had never felt in early days; the slow-burning, unquenchable lust for revenge.

Somewhere he would find it; the ghastly hive of horror; a hive whose honey was the grey and ultimate slime of the pit. Day after day he slouched from dawn until dusk. Day after day he turned this way and that.

It was as though his obsession had in some strange manner directed his feet. It was as though it followed a path known only to itself.

EIGHTY-EIGHT

OUT of the fermentations of her brain; out of the chronic hatred she bore him, Cheeta, the virgin, slick as a needle to the outward eye, foul in the inward, had at last conceived a way to bring young Titus to the dust; a way to hurt him.

That there was some part of her which could not do without him, she refused to believe. What might once upon a time have turned to some sort of love, was now an abhorrence. How could a wisp contain such a gall as this? She smarted beneath the humiliation of his obvious boredom . . . his casual evasion. What did he want from her? The act and nothing else? Her tiny figure trembled with detestation.

Yet her voice was as listless as ever. Her words wandered away. She was all sophistication; desirable, intelligent, remote. Who could have told that joined in deadly grapple beneath her ribs were the powers of fear and evil?

Out of all this, and because of this, she had framed a plan; a terrible and twisted thing, that proved, if it did nothing else, the quality of her inventive brain.

A cold fever of concentration propelled her. It was a state more readily associated with a man's than with a woman's mentality. And yet, a sexless thing, it was more dreadful than either.

She had told Titus of the farewell party she was preparing in his honour. She had pleaded with him; she had made her eyes to shine; her lips to pout; her breasts to tremble. Bludgeoned by sex he had said he would be there. Very well, then, her decks were cleared for action. Hers was the flying start; the initiative; the act of surprise; the choice of weapons.

But to put her plan into action necessitated the co-operation of a hundred or more of their guests, besides scores of workmen. The activity was prodigious, yet secret. There was co-operation, yet no one knew they were co-operating; or if they did, who, where, why, or in what way. They only knew their own particular roles.

She had in some magnetic way convinced each particular man and woman that he or she was at the centre of the whole affair. She had flattered them grotesquely, from the lowest to the highest; and such were the varieties of her approach, that no dupe among them but found her orders unique.

At the back of it all was a nebulous, accumulative foreboding; a gathering together in the cumulus sky; a mounting excitement in the heart of secrecy; a thing like a honeycomb which Cheeta alone apprehended in its entirety, for she was no drone, but author and soul of the hive. The insects, though they worked themselves to death, saw nothing but their own particular cells.

Even Cheeta's enigmatic father, the wisp, with his dreadful skull the colour of lard, knew nothing except that on the fateful night it was for him to take his place in some charade.

It might be thought that with everyone seemingly working at cross purposes it was merely a matter of time before the whole intricate structure irrevocably collapsed. But Cheeta, moving from one end of the domain to the other, so synchronized the activities of the guests and workmen (carpenters, masons, electricians, steeple-jacks, and so on) that, unknown to themselves, they and their work began to coalesce.

What was it all about? Nothing of its kind had ever happened before. Speculation was outlandish. It knew no end. Fabrication grew out of fabrication. To every inquiry there was one reply from Cheeta.

'If I should tell you, there'd be no surprise.'

To those prickly young men who saw no reason why so much expenditure and attention should be lavished upon Titus Groan, she winked in such a way as to suggest a conspiracy between her critics and herself.

Here, there and everywhere she flitted like a shadow; leaving behind her instructions, now in this room, now in that, now in the great timber-yard; now in the kitchen; now where the seamstresses were huddled like bats; or in the private homes of her friends.

But a great deal of her time was spent elsewhere.

From then on, Titus was shadowed unknowingly, wherever he went.

But those who shadowed him were in their turn shadowed, by Crabcalf, Slingshott and Crack-Bell.

Full of old crimes, they had learned the value of silence, and if a branch stirred or a twig snapped one can be sure that none of these gentlemen was responsible.

EIGHTY-NINE

CHEETA, when she had first conceived her plan, had assumed that her party would take place in the great studio that covered the whole of the top floor of her father's mansion. It was a studio indeed, lovely in its lighting, bland in its floorboards, vast in its perspectives (the easel no larger than a ninepin when seen from the door, reared up like a tall insect).

But it was wrong, fatally wrong, for it had an air about it . . . almost of that kind of innocence that nothing can eradicate. Innocence was no part of Cheeta's plan.

Yet there was no other room in the building, large though it was, that suited her purpose. She had flirted with the idea of knocking down a long wall in the southern wing which would have opened up a long and ponderous hall; but there again, the 'feel' would have been wrong; as was the longest of the twelve high barns, those rotting structures on the northern boundaries.

As the days went by, the situation became more and more peculiar. It was not that there was any slackening of vitality among the friends and labourers; rather that the sight of scores upon scores of seemingly incongruous objects under construction inflamed the general speculation to an almost unbearable degree.

And then, one overcast morning as Cheeta was about to make a tour of the workshops, she stopped suddenly dead, as though she had been struck. Something she had seen or heard had wakened a memory. All in a flash came the answer.

It had been a long time ago, when Cheeta was a mere child, that an expedition had been mounted, the main purpose of which had been to establish the exact boundaries of that great tract of land, as yet but vaguely charted, that lay, a shadowy enigma, to the south-west.

This excursion proved to be abortive, for the area covered was treacherous marshland, along whose sluggish flanks great trees knelt down to drink.

Young as she had been, yet Cheeta, by a superb imitation of hysteria, eventually forced her parents to allow her to join the expedition. The extra responsibility involved in having to take a child on such a mission was maddening, to put it at its mildest, and there were those on the return journey who were openly against the intractable child, and fully believed their failure to be due to her presence.

But this was long ago, and had been all but forgotten: all save for one thing, and this itself had been smothered away in her unconscious mind until now. Like something long subdued, it had broken free and leapt out of the shadows of her mind in devastating clarity.

It was hard for Cheeta, all at once, to be sure whether it was a valid memory of something that was really there, a hundred miles from her home, or whether it was a startling dream, for she had no recollection of the finding of the place, nor of leaving it. But she was not long in doubt. Image after image returned to her as she stood, the pupils of her eyes dilated. There could be no doubt about it. She saw it with a mounting vividness. *The Black House.*

There in that setting of immemorial oaks, threaded by that broad, fast, knee-deep river . . . there surely, where the masonry was crusty with age, was the setting above all settings for the Party.

It was now for Cheeta to discover someone who had been there on that faraway day. Someone who could find the place again.

Driving her fastest car, she was soon at the gates of the factory. At once she was surrounded by a dozen men in overalls. Their faces were all the same. One of them opened his mouth. The very act was obscene.

'Miss Cheeta?' he said in a curiously thin voice, like a reed.

'That's it,' said Cheeta. 'Put me through to my father.'

'Of course . . . of course,' said the face.

'And hurry,' said Cheeta.

They led her to a reception room. The ceiling was matted with crimson wires. There was a black glass table of unnatural length, and at the far end of the room the wall was monopolized by an opaque screen like a cod's eye.

Eleven men stood in a row while their leader pressed a button.

'What's the peculiar smell?' said Cheeta.

'Top secret,' said the eleven men.

'Miss Cheeta,' said the twelfth man. 'I am putting you through.'

After a moment or two an enormous face appeared on the opaque screen. It filled the wall.

'Miss Cheeta?' it said.

'Shrivel yourself,' said Cheeta. 'You're too big.'

'Ha, ha, ha!' said the huge face. 'I keep forgetting.'

The face contracted, and went on contracting. 'Is that better?' it said.

'More or less,' said Cheeta. 'I must see Father.'

'Your father is at a conference,' said the image on the screen. It was still over life-size, and a small fly landing on his huge dome of a forehead appeared the size of a grape.

'Do you know who I am?' said Cheeta in her faraway voice.

'But of course . . . of . . .'

'Then stir yourself.'

The face disappeared, and Cheeta was left alone.

After a moment she wandered to the wall that faced the cod's-eye screen, and played delicately across a long row of coloured levers that were as pretty as toys. So innocent they looked that she pressed one forward, and at once there was a scream.

'No, no, no!' came the voice. 'I want to *live*.'

'But you are very poor and very ill,' said another voice, with the consistency of porridge. 'You're unhappy. You told me so.'

'No, no, no! I want to *live*. I want to *live*. Give me a little longer.'

Cheeta switched the lever and sat down at the black table.

As she sat there, very upright, her eyes closed, she did not know that she was being watched. When at last she raised her head she was annoyed to see her mother.

'You!' she said. 'What are you doing here?'

'It's absorbing, you know,' said Cheeta's mother. 'Daddy lets me watch.'

'I wondered where you got to every day,' muttered her daughter. 'What on earth do you do here?'

'Fascinating,' said the scientist's wife, who never seemed to answer anything.

A big arm came across the screen and thrust her aside. It was followed by a shoulder and a head. The father's face suddenly swam towards Cheeta. His eyes flickered to and fro to see if anything had been altered. Then they rested on his daughter.

'What do you want, my dear?'

'Tell me first,' said Cheeta, 'where are you? Are we near each other?'

'O dear no,' said the scientist. 'We're a long way apart.'

'How long would it take me to . . .'

'You can't come here,' said the scientist, with a note almost of alarm in his voice. 'No one comes here.'

'But I want to talk to you. It's urgent.'

'I will be home for dinner. Can't you wait until then?'

'No,' said Cheeta, 'I can't. Now listen. Are you listening?'

'Yes.'

'Twenty years ago, when I was six, an expedition set out to plot out territory in the south-west. We found ourselves bogged down and had to give up. On our return journey we came unexpectedly upon a ruin. Do you remember?'

'Yes, I remember.'

'I am questioning you in secrecy, father.'

'Yes.'

'I must go there today.'

'No!'

'Yes. But who will guide me?'

There was a long silence.

'Do you mean to have the party *there*?'

'Exactly.'

'Oh no . . . no . . .'

'Oh yes. But how to *find* him. Who was he? The man who led the expedition long ago? Is he alive?'

'He is an old man now.'

'Where does he live? There is no time to waste. The party is close upon us. Oh hurry father. Hurry!'

'He lives,' said the scientist, 'where the Two Rivers join.'

Cheeta left him at once, and he was glad, for Cheeta was the only thing he feared.

Little did he know that someone more to be feared was making his way, all unknowing, in the direction of the factory. A figure with a wild light in his eyes, a five day growth on his chin, and a nose like a rudder.

NINETY

IT was not long before Cheeta ran the old man to ground, and a tough old bird he proved to be. She asked him at once whether he remembered the expedition, and in particular the unhealthy night that the party spent at the Black House.

'Yes, yes. Of course I do. What about it eh?'

'You must take me there. At once,' said Cheeta, recoiling inwardly, for his age was palpable.

'Why should I?' he said.

'You will be paid . . . *well* paid. We'll go by helicopter.'

'What's *that*?' said the septuagenarian.

'We'll fly,' said Cheeta, 'and find it from above.'

'Ah,' said the old man.

'The Black House . . . you understand?' said Cheeta.

'Yes, I heard you. The Black House. South-sou'east. Follow the knee-deep river. Aha! Then west into the territory of the wild dogs. How much?' he said, and he shook his dirty grey hair.

'Come now,' said Cheeta. 'We'll talk of that later.'

But it was not enough for the dirty old man, the one-time explorer. He asked a hundred questions; sometimes of the airborne flight, or of the machine, but for the most part of the financial side which seemed to be his chief interest.

Finally everything was settled and within two hours they were on their way, skimming the tree-tops.

Beneath them was little to be seen but great seas of foliage.

NINETY-ONE

TITUS, drowsy in the arms of a village girl, a rosy, golden thing, opened one eye as they lay together on the banks of a loquacious river, for he had heard through the ripples another sound. At first he could see nothing, but lifting his head he was surprised to see a yellow aircraft passing behind the leaves of the overhanging trees. Close as it was, Titus was yet unable to see who was piloting the machine, and as for the village maiden, she neither knew nor cared.

NINETY-TWO

THE weather was perfect, and the helicopter floated without the least hindrance over the tree-tops. For a long while there was silence aboard, but at last Cheeta, the pilot, turned to look at her companion. There was something foul in the way his dirtiness was being carried aloft, through the pure air. What made it worse was the way he stared at her.

'If you keep looking at me,' she said, 'we may miss the landmarks. What should we be looking for now?'

'Your legs,' said the old man. 'They'd go down very nice, with onion sauce.' He leered at her, and then all at once cried out in a hoarse voice; 'The shallow river! Alter her course to south'd.'

Three long cobalt-blue mountains had hoisted themselves above the horizon and what with the sunlight bathing the foliage below them, and dancing down the river, it was a scene so tranquil that the sudden chill that rose, as though on an updraught from below, was horrible in its unexpectedness. It seemed that the cold in the air was directed against them, and at the same moment, on looking down as though to see the cause of the cold, Cheeta cried out involuntarily . . .

'The Black House! Look! Look! There below us.'

Hovering as they descended; descending as they hovered, the ill-matched pair were now no more than weather-cock high above the ruin . . . for so it was . . . though known (time out of mind), as the Black House.

Very little of the roof was left, and none of the inner walls, but Cheeta, gazing down, recalled immediately the vast interior of the building.

It had an atmosphere about it that was unutterably mournful; a quality that could not be wholly accounted for by the fact that the place was mouldering horribly; that the floor was soft with moss; or that the walls were lost in ferns. There was something more than this that gave the Black House its air of deadly darkness; a darkness that owed nothing to the night, and seemed to dye the day.

'I'm bringing her in,' said Cheeta, and as they came down to make a perfect landing in a grey carpet of nettles, a small fox pricked its ears, and loped away, and as though taking their cue, a murmuration of starlings rose in a dense cloud which coiled its way up, up into the sky.

The old man, finding himself on terra firma, made no immediate effort to get to his feet, but stretched out his withered arms and legs, as though he was a ragged windmill, and then, prising himself to his feet . . .

'Hey you!' he cried. 'Now that you're in it, what do you *want* with it? An armful of bloody nettles?'

Cheeta took no notice, but made her way, quick and light as a bird, to and fro across what might have been the shell of an abbey, for there was a heap of masonry that might or might not have been some kind of altar, sacred or profane.

As Cheeta flickered to and fro over the moss and fallen leaves, with the pale sun above her and the surrounding forest breathing gently to itself, she was taking note of every kind of thing. To her it was second nature to remember anything that might prove to her advantage, and so today it was a case of absorbing into her brain and being, not only the exact lie of the land; not only the orientation and the proportions and the scale of this bizarre setting, but also the exits and entrances that were to fill with figures unforeseen.

Meanwhile, the old man, unabashed, made water in a feeble arc.

'Hey, you,' he shouted in that gritty voice of his, 'where is it then?'

'Where is what?' whispered Cheeta. It was obvious from her tone of voice that her mind was elsewhere.

'The treasure. That's what we've come for, ain't it? The treasure of the Black House.'

'Never heard of it,' said Cheeta.

A flush of anger spread itself over the old man's face so that the hot hue became reflected in the white of the beard.

'Never heard of it?' he cried. 'Why you . . .'

'Any more abuse from you,' said Cheeta in a voice quite horrible in its listlessness, 'and I will leave you here. *Here*, among a thousand rotting things.'

The old man snarled.

'Get into your seat,' said Cheeta. 'If you touch me, I will have you whipped.'

The return journey was a race against darkness, for Cheeta had remained longer than she had meant in the Black House. Now, sailing over the varying landscape that slid below them, she had time to make her calculations.

For instance, there was the problem of how the workmen, and later on, the guests, were to find their way through long neglected woodlands, swamps and valleys. Here and there, it is true, there were signs of ancient roads, but these could not be relied upon, as they were apt at any moment to go underground or lose themselves beneath the swamp or sand.

This problem was largely solved (in theory) by Cheeta, as she floated down the sky; for her idea was to have several scores of men dropped at regular intervals in a long line reaching from the known boundaries to the tundra of the south-east, and the forests of the Black House.

At a given time it was for these scores of isolated men to ignite the great stacks of timber that they had been collecting all day long. With the smoke from these great bonfires to guide him, the least intelligent voyager to the Black House would surely be able to make his way without difficulty, and in any fashion he chose, whether by air or on land.

The workmen, thought Cheeta, as she perused the landscape, must have at least three days' start, and must return before the first of the guests. They must work to plan and in silence, not one of them knowing the business of his neighbour.

They must come in every kind of vehicle, from great vans loaded with the most unlikely contents, to pony traps: from long cars to wheelbarrows.

At dawn, on the day of the Party . . . there must be sounded across the land the voice of a gong. And Cheeta would have been prepared to stake a fortune that anyone near Titus at the time of the gong-boom, would see a shadow cross his face . . . almost as though he were reminded of another world: a world he had deserted.

NINETY-THREE

FOR all her skill and speed, a time had come when it was impossible for Cheeta to be everywhere at the same time (a characteristic for which she was famous), and within a matter of minutes, she had stepped out of the helicopter and was on her way to the 'Making Shops', and within a few minutes more she was in rapid conversation with the more responsible of the 'makers'.

It was now impossible to carry on without a delegation of duties, for time was hard at their heels. Some part of the secrecy must inevitably be made less stringent for, unless the curtain were raised a little, there would be danger of chaos. As it was it was almost too late. For all the power that Cheeta held in her tiny, bow-string body, there was yet a murmur of discontent in the Workshops that grew louder every day.

Even among the gentry there were murmurings; and Cheeta was forced to take a couple of them into her confidence.

Apart from this there was her father. He had at last been partially won over.

'It won't be long, father.'

'I don't like it,' said the hollow wisp.

'You must do as you're told, mustn't you? Is your costume ready? And your mask?'

A fly settled on the horrible egg-shaped head. Twitching the skin of his cranium into a minor convulsion he dislodged the creature, and by the time he was able to answer, his daughter was no longer with him. Cheeta had no time to waste.

NINETY-FOUR

At a muster of the executive, which numbered nine souls including Cheeta (if she can be called a soul) and which had among its numbers representatives of all social grades, it was agreed that everybody should be kept in suspense as to where the party should take place; the chosen nine alone being in some kind of mental half-light.

These nine alone were bribed. These nine alone had some kind of inkling as to what was being made in the shops, the barns, the warehouses, and the private houses.

Yet there was rancour among the nine. It is true that compared with the horde they were privileged, but compared with Cheeta they were in outer darkness, fobbed off with bits and pieces of knowledge; knowing only that out of the miscellaneous chaos, some kind of mammoth invention was at work in Cheeta's brain.

NINETY-FIVE

'I'VE got a feeling,' said Juno, 'that all is not well with Titus. I dreamed of him last night. He was in danger.'

'He's been in danger most of his life,' said the Anchor. 'I don't think he'd know what to do with himself if he wasn't.'

'Do you believe in him?' said Juno, after a long pause. 'I've never asked you before. I've always feared the answer, I suppose.'

Anchor raised his eyes, and studied the ceiling of a private lounge on the ninety-ninth floor. Then he leaned back against an indigo cushion. Juno stood by a window. She was as regal as ever. The fullness under her chin, and the tiny crow's-feet around her eyes in no way impaired her grandeur. The room was full of a pale blue light which gave a strange glint to the Anchor's mop of red hair. Far away there was a murmuring sound like the sound of the sea.

'Do I believe in him?' queried the Anchor. 'What does that mean? I believe in his existence. Just as I believe that you are shaking. Are you ill?'

Juno turned round and faced him. 'I am not ill,' she whispered, 'but I will be if you don't answer my question. You know what I mean.'

'His castle and his lineage? Is that what worries you?'

'He's such a boy! Such a golden boy! He was always sweet with me. How is it he could lie to me, and to everyone? What do you feel at the sound of that strange word?'

'Gormenghast?'

'Yes, Gormenghast. Oh, Anchor my dear. I have such a pain in my heart.'

Anchor rose to his feet in one quiet movement and moved with a faintly rolling gait towards her. But he did not touch her.

'He is not mad,' he said. 'Whatever else he is, he is not mad. If he were mad then it would be better for madness to thrive in the world. No. *Inventive* perhaps. He may be for all we know the last word in the realms of imagery, supposition, hypothesis, conjecture, surmise, and all that is clothed in the wild webs of his imagination. But mad? No.'

Anchor looked at her with a wry smile on his lips.

'Then you *don't* believe him, for all your long words,' cried Juno. 'You think he's a liar! Oh my dear Anchor, what has come over me? I feel so frightened.'

'It was your dream,' said Anchor. 'What was it about?'

'I saw him,' whispered Juno at last, 'staggering with a castle on his back. Tall towers were intertwined with locks of dark red hair. He cried out as he stumbled . . . "Forgive me! Forgive me!" Behind him floated eyes. Nothing but eyes! Swarms of them. They sang as they floated through the air at his side, their pupils expanding or contracting according to the notes they were singing. It was horrible. They were so intent, you see. Like hounds about to tear a fox apart. Yet they sang all the while, so that it was sometimes difficult to hear the voice of Titus calling out, "Forgive me. For pity's sake, forgive me".'

Juno turned to the Anchor.

'You see, he *is* in danger. Why else should I dream? We must not rest until we find him.'

She turned her head up to his.

'It isn't love any more,' she said, 'as it used to be. I have lost my jealousy and my bitterness. Nothing of this is any longer a part of me. I want Titus for another reason . . . just as I want Muzzlehatch and others I have cared for in the past. The past. Yes, that is it. I need my past again. Without it I am nothing. I bob like a cork on deep water. Perhaps I am not brave enough. Perhaps I am frightened. We thought that we could start our lives again. But all this time I brood upon what's gone. The haze has settled like a golden dust. O my dear friend. My dear Anchor. Where are they? What shall I do?'

'We will away and find them. We'll lay their ghosts, my dear. When shall we start?'

'Now,' said Juno.

Anchor got to his feet.

'*Now it is,*' he said.

NINETY-SIX

He only knew he was aloft and airborne: that no one answered him when he spoke: that he appeared to be moving: that there was a soft buzz of machinery: that the night air was gentle and balmy: that there were occasional voices from far below, and that there was someone near him, sharing the same machine, who refused to talk.

His hands were carefully tied behind him, so that he should suffer no pain: yet they were firm enough to prevent his escape. So it was with the silk scarf across his eyes. It had been carefully adjusted so that Titus should feel no inconvenience, save that of being sightless.

That he was in such a predicament at all was something to wonder at. Indeed if it were not that Titus was apt to throw in his lot with any hair-brained scheme, he would by now be yelling for release.

He had no sense of fear, for it had been explained to him that, this being the night of the party, he must expect anything. And he must believe that to make it a night of all nights, one element alone was paramount, and that element was the element of surprise. Without it, all would be stillborn, and die before its first wild breath was drawn.

It was for him, at a future moment, to have the silk scarf plucked from his eyes to behold the light of a great bonfire, a hundred bright inventions.

It was for him to await the quintessential instant and to let it flower. Under the star-flecked sky, under the sighing of the leaves and ferns, there lay the Black House. Here was a setting for a dark splendour, a dripping of the night dew. Here was the forlorn decay of centuries, which, were Titus to set his eyes upon it, could not fail to remind him of the dark clime he had thought to toss off like a cloak from his shoulders, but which he now knew he had no power to divest.

Without surprise, all else was doomed to falter, as Cheeta well knew. It mattered not how brilliant the concept, how marvellous the spectacle, all, all would be lost unless the boy, Titus, suffered the supreme degradation.

It was not for nothing that Cheeta had sat at the end of his bed hour after hour, while he raved or whispered in his fever. Over and over again she heard the same names repeated; the same scenes enacted. She knew to the last inch whom he loathed and whom he loved. She knew almost as though it were a map before her eyes, the winding core of Gormenghast. She knew who had died. She knew who were still alive. She knew of those who had stood by Gormenghast. She knew of an *Abdicator*.

Let him have his surprise. His golden treat. His fantastic party for which no expense was enough. This will be a 'Farewell' never to be forgotten.

Cheeta had whispered . . . 'It will burn like a torch in the night. The forest will recoil at the sound of it.'

At a weak moment, all in the heat of it, when his brain and senses contradicted one another, and a gap appeared in his armour, he had said, 'Yes.'

'Yes,' that he would agree to it . . . the idea of going to an unknown district, blindfolded, for the sake of the secret.

And now he was aloft in the evening air, sailing he knew not where, to his Farewell party. Had his eyes been free of the silk scarf he would have seen that he was supported in mid-air by a beautiful white balloon like a giant whale, tinted in the light.

Above the balloon, high up in the sky, were flocks of aircraft of all colours, shapes and sizes.

Below him, flying in formation, were craft like golden darts, and far,

far below these, he would have seen, in the north, a great tract of shimmering marshland reaching away to the horizon.

To the south in the forest land he would have caught sight of smoke from the bonfire which gave them their direction.

But he could see nothing of all this – nothing of the play of light upon the silky marshes nor how the shadows of the various aircraft cruised slowly over the tree-tops.

Nor could he see his companion. She sat there, a few feet out of his reach, very upright, tiny and supremely efficient, her hands on the controls.

The workmen were gone from the scene. They had toiled like slaves. Rough country had been cleared for the helicopters, and all types of aircraft to land. The heavy carts were filled with weary men.

The great crater of the Black House that had until recently yawned to the moon was now filled with something other than its mood. Its emptiness gone, it listened as though it had the power of hearing.

There had, in all conscience, been enough to hear. For the last week or more, the forest had echoed to the sound of hammering, sawing and the shouts of foresters.

Close enough to observe without being seen, yet far enough in danger's name, the scores of small forest animals, squirrels, badgers, mice, shrews, weasels, foxes and birds of every feather, their tribal feuds forgotten, sat silent, their eyes following every movement, their ears pricked. Little knowing that between them they were forming a scattered circle of flesh and blood, they drew their breath into their lungs and stared at the shell of the Black House. The shell and the strange things that filled it.

As the hours passed, this living circumference grew in depth, until the time came when a day of silence settled down upon the district, and in this silence could be heard the breathing of the fauna like the sound of the sea.

Mystified by the silence (for the day had come for the workmen to leave, and the socialites had not yet arrived), they stared (these scores of eyes) at the Black House, which now presented to the world a face so unlikely that it was a long time before the animals and the birds broke silence.

NINETY-SEVEN

CASTING their wicked shadows, two wild cats broke free at last, from the trance that had descended upon the scores of spellbound creatures, and with almost unbelievable stealth crept forward cheek to cheek.

Watched by silent miscellaneous hordes, they slid their feline way from the listening forest and came at last to the northern wall of the Black House.

For a long time they stayed there, sitting upright, hidden by a wealth of ferns, only their heads showing. It seemed they ran on oil, those loveless heads, so fluidly they turned from side to side.

At last they jumped together as though from a mutual impulse, and found themselves on a broad moss-covered ledge. They had made this jump many times before but not until now had they looked down from their old vantage point upon so unbelievable a metamorphosis.

Everything was changed and yet nothing had changed. For a moment their eyes met. It was a glance of such exquisite subtlety that a shudder of chill pleasure ran down their spines.

The change was entire. Nothing was as it was before. There was a throne where once was a mound of green masonry. There were old crusty suits of armour hanging on the walls. There were lanterns and great carpets and tables knee-deep in hemlock. There was no end to the change.

And yet it was the same in so far as the mood swamped everything. A mood of unutterable desolation that no amount of change could alter.

The two cats, conscious that they were the focus of all eyes, grew progressively bolder until slipping down an ivy-faced wall, they positively grinned with their entire bodies and sprang into the air with a mixture of excitement and anger. Excitement that there were new worlds to conquer, and anger that their secret paths were gone for ever, and the green abodes and favourite haunts were gone. The overgrown ruin which these two had taken for granted as part of their lives, ever since, like little balls of spleen, they nuzzled and fought for the warmth of their mother's belly . . . this ruin was now, suddenly, another thing, a thing to be assimilated and explored. A world of new sensations . . . a world that had once rung with echoes, but which now gave no response, its emptiness departed.

Where was the long shelf gone: the long worn dusty shelf, festooned with hart's tongue? It had disappeared, and what stood in its place had never felt the impress of a wild cat's body.

In its place were towering shapes, impossible to understand. As their courage strengthened, the wild cats began to run hither and thither with excitement, yet never losing their poise as they ran, their heads held high in the air in such a sentient and lordly way as to suggest a kind of vibrant wisdom.

What were these great swags of material? What was this intricate canopy of bone-white branches that hung from the roof and over their heads? Was it the ribs of a great whale?

The two cats growing bolder began to behave in a very peculiar way, not only leaping from vantage-point to vantage-point in a weird game of follow-my-leader, but wriggling their ductile bodies into every conceivable position. Sometimes they ran alone along an aisle of hoary carpet: sometimes they clung to one another and fought as though in earnest, only to break off suddenly, as though by common assent, so that one or other might scratch its ear with a hind foot.

And still there was no movement from the ring of watching creatures, until, without warning, a fox suddenly trotted out of the periphery, leapt through a window in one of the walls, and running to the centre of the Black House sat down on an expensive rug, lifted his sharp yellow face, and barked.

This acted like a tocsin, and hundreds of woodland creatures rose to their feet, and a minute later were down in the arena.

But they were not there for long, for immediately after the two cats had arched their backs and snarled at the fox and all the other invaders, something else occurred which sent the birds and beasts back into their hiding places.

The sky above the Black House was, of a sudden, filled with coloured lights. The vanguard of the airborne flotilla was dropping earthwards.

NINETY-EIGHT

DELICATELY stepping from their various machines, the glittering beauties and the glittering horrors, arrayed like humming birds, passed in and out of the shadows with their escorts, their tongues flickering, their eyes dilated with conjecture, for this was something never known before . . . the flight by night. The overhanging forests; the sense of exquisite fear; the suspense and the thrill of the unknown; the pools of dark; the pools of brilliance; the fluttering breath drawn in and exhaled with a shudder of relief; relief in every breast that it was not alone, though the stars shone down out of the cold and the small snakes lurked among the ruins.

As each dazzling influx tiptoed through the mouldering doorways of the Black House, their heads involuntarily turned to the central fire; a careful structure composed of juniper branches which when alight, as now, threw up a scented smoke.

'Oh my darling,' said a voice out of the darkness.

'What is it?' said a voice out of the light.

'This is the throb of it. Where are you?'

'Here, at your dappled side.'

'O Ursula!'

'What is it?'

'To think it is all for that boy!'

'O no! It is for us. It is for our delectation. It is for the green light on your bosom . . . and the diamonds in my ears. It is bloom. It is brilliance.'

'It is primal, darling. Primal.'

Another voice broke in. . .

'It is a place for frogs.'

'Yes, yes, but we're ahead.'

'Ahead of what?'

'The avant-garde. Look at us. If we are not the soul of chic, who is?'

Another voice, a man's; a poor affair. 'This is double pneumonia,' it wheezed.

'For heaven's sake be careful of that carpet. It sucked my shoe off,' said his friend.

With every moment that passed, the crowd thickened. For the most part guests made for the juniper fire. Their scores of faces flickered and leapt to the whim of the flames.

Were it not Cheeta's party there would undoubtedly have been many more than ready to criticize the lavish display . . . the heterodoxy of the whole affair would have rankled. As it was, the discomfort of the Black House was more than made up for by the occasion. For that is what it was.

The babble of voices rose, as the guests multiplied. Yet there were many young adventurers who, tired of staring into the flames almost as much as having to listen to the shrill tongues of their partners, had begun to leave the warmth in order to explore the outer reaches of the ruin. There they came across bizarre formations reaching high into the night.

Here, as they moved, and there, as they moved, they came upon peculiar structures hard to understand. But there was nothing hard to fathom about the dusky table, dim-lit by candles, where a great ice-cake glimmered, with 'Titus, Farewell' sculpted in its flanks. Behind the cake, there arose tier upon tier, the Banquet, in half-light. A hundred goblets twinkled, and the napkins rose as though in flight.

Six mirrors reflecting one another across the sullen reaches of the Black House focused their light upon something which appeared to contradict itself, for, looked at from *one* angle, it appeared to resemble a small tower, yet from another it seemed more like a pulpit, or a throne.

Whatever it might be, there was no doubt that it was of some importance, for posted at its corners were four flunkeys who were almost abnormally zealous in keeping any odd guest who had strayed that far, from coming too close.

Meanwhile there was something happening, something – if not *of* the Farewell Party, yet close to it. Something that strode!

NINETY-NINE

HE was not entirely cut out to pattern, this strider. Barbaric to the eye, his silhouette more like something made of ropes and bones, he was nevertheless instantly recognizable as Muzzlehatch.

A little behind him, as he approached were the three one-time Under-River characters. Peculiar as they were, they paled into nothingness beside their eccentric leader whose every movement was a kind of stab in the bosom of the orthodox world.

They had searched for, and found, more by luck than wisdom (though they knew the country well), this Muzzlehatch, and had forced him to rest his long wild bones, and to shut for an hour his haunted eyes.

What they *had* hoped to do (Crabcalf and the rest) was to find Muzzlehatch, and warn him of Titus's danger. For they had come to the conclusion that some black force had been unearthed, and that Titus was in real peril.

But what they *found*, when at last they tracked him down, was not the Muzzlehatch they knew, but a man of the wilds. Of the wilds within himself and the wilds without. Not only this, but a man who had but recently been deep into the steel heart of the enemy: a man with a mission half complete. One eye had closed in satisfaction. The other burned like an ember.

Little by little, they drew out his story. Of how he came upon the factory and knew at once that he was at the door of hell. The door he had been searching for. Of how by bluff and guile, and later by force, he had found and forced his way into a less frequented district of this great place where he began to be sickened by the scent of death.

They listened carefully, the three followers, but for all their concentration they could barely make out what he was saying. Had their interpretation of his words been pooled and sifted so that it was possible to evoke a summary of all he whispered (for he was too tired to speak) then in the broadest way he told the three who hovered above him, of the identical faces: of how he slid down endless belts of translucent skin; and how, as he slid, a great hand in a glove of shining black rubber reached out for him so that Muzzlehatch was forced to haul at the creature; to haul it aboard upon the moving belt; a vile thing to touch it was and shrouded in white from head to toe; a thing that lashed out, but could not escape from Muzzlehatch's clench, and fell back at last, dead.

It seems that Muzzlehatch had ripped away the dead man's working-shroud before that cipher slid into a glass tunnel, and then, clad in white, had escaped from the belt and the empty hall, and loping away, had soon found himself in another kind of district altogether.

Strange as it seems (when it is remembered how horrible and multifarious are the ways of modern death), yet it is true that a jack-knife at the ribs can cause as terrible a sensation as any lurking gas or lethal ray. His knife was at the ready, and it was very sharp, but before he had any chance to use it, the light turned from a clear cool grey to a murky crimson and at the same moment the entire floor of the factory, like the floor of a lift began to descend.

So much could the three vagrants understand, but then began a long period of confused muttering which, try as they would they could not decipher. It was obvious that they were missing much, for the gaunt man's arms kept beating the ground as he fought to recover from his terrible experience.

At times the intensity grew less and his words came back again like creatures from their lairs, but almost at once the 'three' became aware of how, in spite of the increasing volubility, it spelt no certainty, for their master began more and more to drift away into an almost private language.

But this much they *did* discover. He must have waited almost to distraction; waited for the one opportunity when at the supreme moment he could single out a hierophant, and with his jack-knife in that creature's back, demand to be taken to the *centre*.

It came at last. The victim almost sick with fear leading Muzzlehatch down corridor after corridor. And all the time the gaunt man repeated . . .

'To the centre!'

'Yes,' said the frightened voice. 'Yes . . . yes.'

'To the centre! Is that where you're taking me?'

'Yes, yes. To the centre of it all.'

'Is that where he hides himself?'

'Yes, yes . . .'

As they proceeded, white hordes of faces flowed by like a tide. Then silence and emptiness took over.

ONE HUNDRED

Titus, where are you? Are your eyes still bandaged? Are your arms still tied behind you?

Through a gap in the forest the night looked down upon the roofless shell of the Black House studded with fires and jewels. And above the gap, floating away forever from the branches was a small grass-green balloon, lit faintly on its underside. It must have come adrift from its tree-top mooring. Sitting upright on the upper crown of the truant balloon was a rat. It had climbed a tree to investigate the floating craft; and then, courage mounting, it had climbed to the shadowy top of the globe, never thinking that the mooring cord was about to snap. But snap it did, and away it went, this small balloon, away into the wilds of the mind. And all the while the little rat sat there, helpless in its global sovereignty.

ONE HUNDRED AND ONE

TITUS was no longer in any mood for collaboration, party or no party. Up to an hour or so ago, he had been willing enough to join in what was supposed to be an elaborate game in his honour; but he was beginning to feel otherwise. Now that his feet were on terra firma he began to hanker for release. His blindness had gone on for too long.

'Undo my bloody eyes,' he cried, but there was no reply until a voice whispered . . .

'Be patient, my lord.'

Titus, who was now being led forward to the great door of the Black House came to a halt. He turned to where the voice had come from.

'Did you say "my lord"?'

'Naturally, your lordship.'

'Undo these scarves at once. Where are you?'

'Here, my lord.'

'Why are you waiting? Set me free!'

Then out of the darkness came Cheeta's voice, dry and crisp as an autumn leaf.

'O Titus dear; has it been *very* irksome?'

A group of sophisticates edging up behind Cheeta echoed her . . .

'Has it been *very* irksome?'

'It won't be long now, my love, before . . .'

'Before *what?*' shouted Titus. 'Why can't you set me free?'

'It is not in my hands, my darling.'

Again the echo from the voices, '. . . my hands, my darling.'

Cheeta watched him with her eyes half closed.

'You promised me, didn't you,' she said, 'that you would make no fuss? That you would walk quietly to the place of your appointment. That you would take three paces up and then turn about. That then, and only then, would the scarf be unknotted, and your eyes be freed. That is the moment of surprise.'

'The best surprise you could give me would be to rip these rags off! O lord of lords! How did I get mixed up in it all? Where are you? Yes, you in your midget body. O God for help! What's all the shouting for?'

Cheeta, whose hand had been raised in a signal, now dropped it again and the shouting died away.

'They want to see you,' said Cheeta. 'They are excited.'

'*Me?*' queried Titus. 'Why *me?*'

'Are you not Titus, the Seventy-Seventh Lord of Gormenghast?'

'Am I? By heaven I don't feel like it; not with you about.'

'He must be tired to be so *very* rude,' said a treacly voice.

'He doesn't know what he's doing,' said another.

'Gormenghast indeed!' said a third, with a titter. 'The whole thing's improbable you know.'

Cheeta's high heel came down like a hammer on the instep of the last speaker. 'My dear,' she said, as though to distract attention from his cry, 'those who have waited so long for the Party are drawing together. Everything is drawing together. And you will be our focus. A lord! A veritable lord!'

'Hell gripe all bleeding lords. Give me my home!' he cried.

The crowds were closing in, for there was something in the air; a chill; a menace; a horrible darkness that seemed to sweat itself out of the walls and the floor of the place. In the shuffling that followed the comparative silence, there was an undertone, almost of apprehension, unformulated as yet in their conscious minds, yet real in the prickle of their nerves. The banqueteers forsook their scented alcoves, and men of all stations withdrew from the outlying sectors, and drawn by an invisible agent, they drew ever closer to the roofless centre of the Black House.

It was not only these who were on the move. Cheeta had ordered a cluster of her personal friends to follow her (excluding her father, for he was in the forgotten room, where sat the star performers, biting their nails).

The band, with an imposing array of instruments swayed forward through the gloom, while Titus was borne forward on a human wave, struggling as he went.

It was a part of Cheeta's plan that Titus should suffer acute alarm, not to say fear, and her delicate mouth (pursed like a tiny vermilion bud) registered a certain satisfaction as to the way things were going. For she was bent on his discomfiture and shame, and even more. Now was the time for Titus to climb the three steps to the throne . . . and he stumbled as he climbed. Now was the time for him to turn about; and now, for his wrists to be freed, and for the scarf to be plucked from his eyes and for Cheeta to cry . . . 'Now!'

And now it was, for her voice, like a voice in a dungeon, awoke a string of echoes. Everything happened in the same split second. The scarves were whipped from Titus's wrists and eyes. The band crashed into dreadful martial music. Titus sat down upon a throne. He could see nothing except the vague blur of the juniper fire. The crowds surged forward as lamps blazed out of the surrounding tree-tops. Everything took on another colour . . . another radiance. A clock struck midnight. The moon came out and so did the first of the apparitions.

ONE HUNDRED AND TWO

UNDER a light to strangle infants by, the great and horrible flower opened its bulbous petals one by one: a flower whose roots drew sustenance from the grey slime of the pit, and whose vile scent obscured the delicacy of the juniper. This flower was evil, and its bloom satanic, and though it was invisible its manifestations were on every side.

It was not the intrinsic and permanent mood of the Black House, although this alone was frightening enough, with the fungi like plates on the walls, and the sweat of the stones; it was not only this, but was this combined with the sense of a great conspiracy: a conspiracy of darkness, and decay: and yet of a diabolical ingenuity also; a setting against which the characters played out their parts in floodlight, as when predestined creatures are caught in a concentration of light so that they cannot move.

Then came Cheeta's voice again, and this time it seemed to Titus that there was an edge to it he had never heard before.

'Flood in the heliotrope.' At this obscure demand the whole scene shuddered into another world of light; a weird and purplish suffusion, and for the first time, Titus, sitting bolt upright on his throne, felt a kind of palpable fear he had never experienced before.

Titus who had killed Steerpike in a war in deep ivy . . . Titus who had been lost in the underground tunnels of Gormenghast now trembled in the face of the unknown. He turned his head, but he could see no sign of Cheeta. Only a great throng of heliotrope heads . . . a world of watchers who stood as though waiting for him to stand and speak.

But where were the heads he knew? Apart from Cheeta, where was her father, the nondescript man with no hair?

It seemed they formed a kind of foreign terrain, as though of all that multitude there was not one who did not know him, yet for Titus there was not one to recognize.

About him, beyond the crowd, the walls were draped with flags. The flags that he half remembered. Torn flags; flags out of limbo. What was he doing here? What, O dearest God, was he doing? What were these shadows? What were these echoes? Where was a friend to grip him by the shoulder? Where was Muzzlehatch? Where was his friend? What was that sound like the purring of the tide? What was it that was purring if not cats?

The voice of Cheeta rose again. It was harsher with every order. The light changed and yet another mood more sinister than ever settled down upon the place, changing the quality of everything down to the least minutiae; down to the smallest frond in acid green.

Titus, his hands trembling, turned his face from the crowd, meaning to rise from the insufferable throne directly his dizziness passed by. Not only did he turn his face but his body also, for the faked green world before him was revolting to the soul.

Having turned he saw what he might never have seen, for perched along the back of the throne were seven owls, and at the same moment that he saw them there came a long-drawn hoot. It came from beyond the throne both near and far away, but as for the birds themselves they were filled with straw. Beyond the owls the darkness was lit and intersected by a filigree of webs as green as flame.

Titus, who was about to have risen to his feet, remained immobile as he stared at the brilliant mesh, and as he stared another wave of fear took hold of him.

Something, somehow, when he saw the owls, began cutting at his heart. At first there had been a quickening of excitement; he knew not why . . . a kind of thrill . . . of remembrance or of re-discovery. Was he returning to a realm he could understand? Had he travelled through time or space or both to reach this recrudescence of times gone by? Was he dreaming?

But this did not last long, this quickening of hope. He had not been asleep. He had not dreamed.

The only time he had dreamed was in his fever. It was then that he gave himself unwittingly to Cheeta's mercy.

Powerless to find satisfaction, though brilliant in her power to organize, Cheeta began to issue orders to a small group of the élite. These gentlemen turned at once to their work, which was to clear a passage from the throne, to where, in a dark hall, there lurked the Twelve.

And then, all at once she was beside him, her inscrutable little head staring up at him. Her perfect mouth quivering as though she wished to be kissed.

'You have been so quiet and so patient,' she said. 'It is almost as though you were alive. I have brought your toys, you see. I haven't forgotten anything. Look, Titus . . . look at the floor. It is covered with rusty chains. Look at the coloured roots . . . and see . . . O Titus, see the foliage of the trees. Was Gormenghast forest ever so green as these bright branches?'

Titus tried to rise to his feet, but a sickness lay over his heart like a weight.

She lifted her head again as a creature might do as it harkened. But the voice was no longer merely husky; it was grit . . .

'Let in the night,' she cried, in this new voice.

And so the viridian died and the moon came into its own, and a hundred forest creatures crept up to the walls of the Black House, forgetting the horrible colours that had so recently appalled them.

And yet there was a quality about this lunar scene which was more terrible than ever. They were no longer figures in a play. There was no longer any artifice. The stage had vanished. They were no longer actors in a drama of strange light. They were themselves.

'This is what we planned for you darling! The light no man can alter. Sit still. Why is your face so drawn? Why is it melting? After all, you've got your surprise to come. The secret's on its way. What's that?'

'A message, madam, from the look-out tree.'

'What does he want? Speak up at once!'

'A great beggar with a group behind him.'

'What of it?'

'We thought . . .'

'Leave me!'

The break in Cheeta's monologue had brought Titus to his feet. What had she said to him, that his fear should be redoubled? That terror; not of Cheeta herself nor of any human being, but of doubt. The *doubt* of his own existence; for where was he? Alone. That's where he was. Alone with nothing to touch. Even the flint from the tall tower was lost. What was there left to guide him? What did Cheeta mean when she said, 'It is almost as though you were alive'? What did she mean when she said, 'I have brought you toys to play with'? What was it that was breaking through the walls of his mind? She had said he was melting. What of the owls? And the purring of the cats? The white cats.

Whatever may have happened to his world one thing was sure: mixed with his homesickness was something else: the beginning beneath his ribs of a conflagration. Whether or not his home was true or false, existent or nonexistent, there was no time for metaphysics. 'Let them tell me later,' he thought to himself, 'whether I am dead or not; sane or not; now is the time for action.' Action. Yes, but what form should it take? He could jump from his throne, but what good would that be? There she was below him, but he no longer wished to see her. It seemed she had some power when he looked at her; some power to weaken and confuse him.

Yet he must not forget that this party was in his honour. Were the symbols that cluttered the floor of the Black House supposed to be a happy reminder of his home, or were the owls and throne and the tin crown there to taunt him?

Here he stood like a dummy while his limbs ached for action. He was no longer dizzy. He waited for the moment to advance into the heart of it all, and to do something, good or bad. As long as it was *something*.

But the expression in her eyes was no longer glazed with a deceptive love. The veil had been lifted or drawn aside, and malice, unequivocal and naked, had taken its place. For she hated him so; and hated him all the more when she realized that he was not so easily made to suffer. Yet superficially all had gone well for her. The young man was obviously in a state of grievous bewilderment, for all the affectation of his stance and the contemptuous tilt of his head. He was thus through fear. But the fear was not great enough yet to break him. Nor was it meant to. That was to come, and in assurance of this, she all but lost herself for the moment in a deadly orgy of anticipation. For it was soon to happen: and all Cheeta could do was to clench her tiny hands together at her breast.

A spasm caught hold of her face and for an instant she was no longer Cheeta, the invincible, the impeccable; the exquisite midget, but something foul. The twitch or spasm, short as had been its duration, had fixed itself so fiercely that long after her face had returned to normal it was there . . . that beastly image . . . as vivid as ever. What had taken a split moment now spread itself so that it seemed to Titus that her face had been there forever; with that extraordinary contortion of her facial muscles which turned a gelid beauty into something fiendish. Something almost ludicrous.

But what no one expected, least of all Titus or Cheeta herself, was that it should be on the ludicrous and not the terrifying that Titus should fix his attention.

Added to this there was another element that tipped the balance in favour of all that can become uncontrolled; for the spectacle of the sprite with her face turned up to his awoke the image of a dog sitting back on its haunches, waiting to be fed.

The icy Cheeta and the face that she unwittingly let loose were so at variance as to be comic. Horribly, inappropriately comic.

Such a sensation can become too powerful for the human body. It is as easy to control as a sliding avalanche. It takes a sacrosanct convention and snaps it in half as though it were a stick. It lifts up some holy relic and throws it at the sun. It is laughter. Laughter when it stamps its feet; when it sets the bells jangling in the next town. Laughter with the pips of Eden in it.

Out of his fear and apprehension something green and incredibly young took hold of Titus and sidled across his entrails. It shot up to the breast-bone: it radiated into separate turnings: it converged again, and, capsizing through him in an icy heat, cartwheeled through his loins, only to climb again, leaving no inch of his weakening body unaffected. Titus was half away. But his face was rigid and he made no sound: not a catch of the breath or a tilt of the lip. There was no penultimate stage of choking, or a visible fight for composure. It came with extraordinary suddenness, the release of pressure: and he made no effort once he had started to laugh, to check himself. He heard his voice soar clean out of register. He followed it. He yelled to and fro to himself as though he were two people calling to one another across a valley. In another moment, in a seismic access, he tore the stuffed owls from their perch. He dropped them to the ground. He could hold them no longer. He gripped his sides with his hands and staggered back into the throne.

Opening one eye as his body ached with a fresh gale of uncontrollable laughter he saw her face before him, and on that instant he was no longer the great belly-roarer: the cracker of goblets, the eye-streaming, arm-dangling, cataleptic wreck of a thing half over the throne, and all but crazed with the delirium of another world: he was suddenly turned to stone, for in her face he read pure evil.

Yet listen to the sweetness of her voice. The words like leaves, are fluttering from the tree. The eyes can no longer pretend. Only the tongue. She fixed him with her black eyes.

'Did you hear that?' she said.

Titus never having seen such an expression of loathing on any woman's face before, answered in a voice as flat as waste-land.

'Did I hear what?'

'Someone laughing,' she said. 'I would have thought it would have wakened you.'

'I heard the laughter too,' said another voice. 'But *he* was asleep.'

'Yes,' said another. 'Asleep in the throne.'

'What? Titus Groan, Lord of the Tracts, and heir to Gormenghast?'

'The same. A heavy sleeper!'

'See how he stares at us!'

'He is bewildered.'

'He needs his mother!'

'Of course, of course!'

'How lucky he is!'

'Why so?'

'Because she's on her way.'

'Red hair, white cats, 'n all?'

'Exactly.'

Cheeta, furious, had had to change her plans. Just as she was about to bring on the phantoms, and by so doing, derange once and for all the boy's bewildered mind.

And so, with a sweet smile to those at her side, she began again to create an atmosphere most conducive to madness.

It was at this moment that, without knowing what he was doing, he picked up the flimsy throne with both hands and dashed it to the ground. The silence was palpable.

At last there came a voice. It was not hers.

'He came to us when he was lost, poor child. Lost, or so he thought. But he was no more lost than a homester on the wing. He searches for his home but he has never left it, for this is Gormenghast. It is all about him.'

'No!' cried Titus. 'No!'

'See how he cries. He is upset, poor thing. He does not realize how much we love him.'

A hundred voices, like an incantation, repeated the words '. . . how much we love him.'

'He thinks that to move about is to change places. He does not realize that he is treading water.'

And the voices echoed '. . . treading water.'

Then Cheeta's voice again.

'Yet this is our farewell. A farewell from his old self to his new. How splendid! To tear one's throne up by the roots, and fling it to the floor. What was it after all but a symbol? We have too many symbols. We wade in symbols. We are sick of them. It is a pity about your brain.'

Titus wheeled upon her. 'My brain,' he cried, 'what's wrong with my brain?'

'It is on the turn,' said Cheeta.

'Yes, yes,' came the chorus from the shadows. 'That's what has happened. His brain is on the turn!'

And then the authoritative voice rose again beyond the juniper fire.

'His head is no longer anything but an emblem. His heart is a cipher. He is a mere token. But we love him, don't we?'

'Oh yes, we love him, don't we?' came the chorus.

'But he's so confused. He thinks he's lost his home.'

'. . . and his sister, Fuchsia.'

'. . . and the Doctor.'

'. . . and his mother.'

At this moment, hard upon the mention of his mother's name, Titus, turning a deathly colour, sprang outward from the debris.

ONE HUNDRED AND THREE

I<small>T</small> might have been Cheeta: but it was not. She had made a sign, and in making it she had moved back a little to obtain a clearer view of the entrance to the forgotten room. Who it was that suffered the agonizing jab in the region of the heart will never be known; but that ornate gentleman collapsed upon the pave-stones of the aisle receiving, as

though he were a scapegoat, the fury which Titus, at that moment, would gladly have meted out to all.

Panting, the sweat glistening on his face he suddenly found himself gripped by the elbow. Two men, one on either side, held him. Struggling to free himself he saw, as though through the haze of his anger, that they were the same tall, smooth, ubiquitous helmeted figures who had trailed him for so long.

They backed him up the steps to where the throne once stood, when suddenly, as he struggled and tossed his head, he saw for an instant something in the corner of his eye that caused his heart to stop beating. The helmeted figures loosened their grip upon his arms.

ONE HUNDRED AND FOUR

SOMETHING was emerging from the forgotten room. Something of great bulk and swathing. It moved with exaggerated grandeur, trailing a length of dusty, moth-eaten fustian, and over all else was spattered the constellations of ubiquitous bird-lime. The shoulders of her once black gown were like white mounds, and upon these mounds were perched every kind of bird. As for the phantom's hair (a most unnatural red), even this was a perch for little birds.

As the Lady moved on with a prodigious authority, one of the birds fell off her shoulder, and broke as it hit the floor.

Again the laughter. The horrible laughter. It sounded like the mirth of hell, hot and derisive.

Were there a 'Gormenghast', then surely this mockery of his mother must humble and torture him, reminding him of his Abdication, and of all the ritual he so loved and loathed. If, on the other hand there were no such place, and the whole thing a concoction of his mind, then, mortified by this exposure of his secret love, the boy would surely break.

'Where is he? Where is my son?' came the voice of the voluminous impostor. It was slow and thick as gravel. 'Where is my only son?'

The creature adjusted its shawl with a twitch.

'Come here, my love, and be punished. It is I. Your mother. Gertrude of Gormenghast.'

Titus was able to see in a flash that the monster was leading another travesty into the half-light. At that excruciating moment, Cheeta heard what Titus also heard; a shrill whistling. It was not that the sound of the whistle in itself puzzled her, but the fact that there should be anyone at all *beyond* the walls. It was not part of her plan.

Although he could not at first recall the meaning of the whistle, yet Titus felt some kind of remote affinity with the whistler. While this had been going on, there was at the same instant much else to be seen.

What of the monstrous insult to his mother? As far as *that* was concerned, his passion for revenge burned fiercely.

The guests, now lit by torchlight, were beginning, under orders, to sort themselves into a great circle. There they stood on the loose, grassy floor, craning their necks like hens to see what it was that followed on the heels of something preternaturally evil.

ONE HUNDRED AND FIVE

WHAT Titus could *not* see was the interior of the forgotten room where a dozen ill-tempered monstrosities had been incarcerated. But now there was a stir in the dungeon: the entrance had cleared itself of its first huge character, and close behind her, walking like a duck, was a wicked caricature of Titus's sister. She wore a tattered dress of diabolical crimson. Her dark dishevelled hair reached to her knees, and when she turned her face to the assemblage there were few who did not catch their breath. Her face was blotched with black and sticky tears, and her cheeks were hectic and raw. She slouched behind her huge mother, but came to a halt as they were about to enter the torch-lit circle, for she stared pathetically this way and that, and then stood grotesquely on her toes as though she were looking for someone. After a few moments she flung her head back so that her black tresses all but touched the ground. Now, with her blotched face turned pitifully to the sky she opened her mouth in a round empty 'O' and bayed the moon. Here was madness complete. Here was matter for revenge. It took hold of Titus and it shook him, so that he wrenched this way and that against the grip of the helmeted figures.

So strange and terrible was what he saw that he froze within the grip of his captors. Something began to give way in his brain. Something lost faith in itself.

'Where is my son?' came the soft gravel throat, and this time his mother turned her face to his, and he saw her.

In contrast to Fuchsia's raddled, hectic, tear-drenched face was his mother's. It was a slab of marble over which false locks of carrot-coloured hair cascaded. This monster spoke, though there was little to be seen in the way of a mouth. Her face was like a great, flat boulder that had been washed and worn smooth by a thousand tides.

With the blank slab out-facing him, Titus let out a cry of his own; an inward cry of desolation.

'That is my boy,' came the gravel voice. 'Did you not hear him? That was the very accent of the Groans. How grievous, yet how rare that he should have died. What is it like to be dead, my wandering child?'

'Dead?' whispered Titus. 'Dead? No! No!'

It was then that Fuchsia made her gawky way across the rough circle, the perimeter of which was thick with faces.

'Dear brother,' she said, when she reached the broken throne. 'Dear brother, you can trust *me*, surely?'

She turned her face to Titus.

'It's no use pretending; and you're *not* alone. I drowned myself, you know. We have death in common. Have you forgotten? Forgotten how I sank beneath the frog-spawn waters of the moat? Is it not glorious to be dead together? I, in my way. You in yours?'

She shook herself and clouds of dust drifted away. Meanwhile Cheeta suddenly appeared at Titus's side.

'Let his lordship go,' she said to the captors. 'Let him play. Let him play.'

'Let him play,' came the chorus.

'Let him play,' whispered Cheeta. 'Let him make believe that he's alive again.'

ONE HUNDRED AND SIX

THE helmeted figures let go their grip upon his arms.

'We have brought your mother and your sister back again. Who else would you like?'

Titus turned his head to her and saw in her eyes the extent of her bitterness. Why had he been so singled out? What had he done? Was the fact that he had never loved her for herself but only out of lust, was this so dire a thing?

The darkness seemed to concentrate itself. The torchlight burned fitfully, and a thin sprinkling of rain came drifting out of the night.

'We are bringing your family together,' whispered Cheeta. 'They have been too long in Gormenghast. It is for you to greet them, and to bring them into the ring. See how they wait for you. They need you. For did you not desert them? Did you not abdicate? That is why they are here. For one reason only. To forgive you. To forgive your treachery. See how their eyes shine with love.'

While she was speaking, three major things took place. The first (at Cheeta's instigation) was that a channel was rapidly cleared from the steps of the throne to the ring itself, so that Titus should be able to make his way without hindrance into the heart of the circle.

The second thing was the recurrence of that shrill and reminiscent whistle that Cheeta and Titus had heard some time before. This time it was nearer.

The third was that into the ring, fresh monsters began to arrive.

The forgotten room disgorged them, one by one. There were the aunts, the identical twins, whose faces were lit in such a way that they appeared to be floating in space. The length of their necks; their horribly quill-like noses; the emptiness of their gaze; all this was bad enough, without those dreadful words which they uttered in a flat monotone over and over again.

'Burn . . . burn . . . burn . . .'

There was Sepulchrave, moving as though in a trance, his tired soul in his eyes, and books beneath his arms. All about were his chains of office, iron and gold. On his head he wore the rust-red crown of the Groans. He took deep sighs with every step; as though each one was the last. Bent forward as though his sorrow weighed him down he mourned with every gesture. As he moved into the centre of the ring he trailed behind him a long line of feathers, while out of his tragic mouth the sound of hooting wandered.

More and more it was becoming a horrible charade. Everything that Cheeta had heard during those bouts of fever when Titus lay and poured out his past, all this had been stored up in her capacious memory.

One of them after another reared or loomed, pranced or took mournful steps; cried, howled or was silent.

A thin wiry creature with high deformed shoulders and a skewbald face leapt to and fro as though trying to get rid of his energy.

On seeing him Titus had recoiled, not out of fear, but out of amazement; for he and Steerpike, long ago, had fought to the death. Knowing that all this was a kind of cruel charade, did not seem to help for in the inmost haunts of the imagination he felt the impact.

Who else was there in the rough ring towards which Titus was involuntarily moving? There was the attenuate Doctor with his whinnying laughter. As Titus looked at him he saw, not the bizarre travesty that faced him with its affected gait and voice, but the original Doctor. The Doctor he loved so much.

When he had reached the ring and was about to enter it he closed his eyes in an effort to free himself of the sight of these monsters, for they reminded him most cruelly of those faraway days when their prototypes were real indeed. But no sooner had he closed his eyes than he heard a third whistle. This time the shrill note was closer than before. So close in fact that it caused Titus not only to open his eyes again, but to look about him, and as he did so he heard once more that reedy note.

ONE HUNDRED AND SEVEN

WHEN Titus saw the three of them, Slingshott, Crabcalf and Crack-Bell, his heart leaped. Their bizarre, outlandish faces fought for his sanity as a doctor fights for the life of his patient. But by not so much as a flicker of an eyelash did they betray the fact that they were Titus's friends.

But now he had allies, though how they could help he could not tell. Their three heads remained quite still throughout the commotion. Not looking at him but *through* him, as though like gun dogs they were directing Titus to turn his gaze to where, leaning against a fern-covered wall as rough as himself lolled Muzzlehatch.

As for Cheeta, she was scrutinizing her quarry, waiting for the moment of collapse; tasting the sweet and sour of the whole affair, when suddenly Titus swung his head away with a bout of nausea. She in her turn, followed his gaze and saw a figure who in no way fitted into her plans.

Directly Titus saw him, he began to stumble in his direction, though of course he could not hope to break through the human walls of the ring.

With Titus's eyes upon him and Cheeta's also, it was not long before an ever-growing number of guests became aware of Muzzlehatch, who leaned so casually in the shadow of the fern-hung wall.

ONE HUNDRED AND EIGHT

As the moments passed, less and less attention was paid to the mockers in the ring, and Cheeta, realizing that her plan was miscarrying, turned a face of concentrated fury upon this tall and enigmatic alien.

By now, according to plan, the cause of her heartburn and enmity, Titus, should have been in the last throes of subjugation.

With practically every head turned to the almost legendary Muzzlehatch, a curious silence fell upon the scene. Even the soughing of the leaves in the surrounding forest had died away.

When Titus saw his old friend he could not withhold a cry. . . . 'Help me for pity's sake.'

Muzzlehatch appeared to take no notice of his cry. He was staring in turn at the apparitions, but at last his eyes came to rest upon one in particular. This nondescript figure crept in and out of the ring as though it were in search of something important. But whatever it was the glinting eye of Muzzlehatch followed it everywhere. At last the figure came to rest, his bald head shimmering, and Muzzlehatch was no longer in doubt of the man's identity. The creature was both repulsive and nondescript, in a way that chilled the blood.

Titus again cried out for Muzzlehatch, and again there was no reply. Yet there he stood, leaning in half-light, well within earshot. What was the matter with his old friend? Why, after all this time was he being ignored? Titus beat his fists together. Surely in finding one another again there should have been aroused some kind of emotion? But no. As far as could be seen Muzzlehatch made no response. There he lounged in the shadows of the ferny pillar, a creature who might easily be taken for a mendicant, were it not that there was no beggar alive who could look so ragged and yet, at the same time, so like a king.

Had Titus, or had anyone approached him *too* closely, he or they would have seen a lethal light in the gaunt man's eyes. It was no more than a glint, a fleck of fire. Yet, this fleck, a dangerous thing, was not directed at anyone in particular; nor did it come and go. It was a constant. Something that had become a part of him as an arm or leg might be. It seemed by his attitude that Muzzlehatch might be staying there forever, so seemingly listless was his pose. But this illusion was short-lived although it seemed as though the congregation had stood there watching him for hours. They had never before seen anything like it. A giant festooned with rags.

And then, gradually (for it took a longish while for everyone to transfer their gaze from the magnetic interloper to the object of his scrutiny), gradually and finally there was not one of the assemblage who was not staring at the polished head of Cheeta's father.

One could not help but think of death, so visible was the skull beneath the stretched skin. There was at length only one pair of eyes that were not fixed upon the head; and those eyes belonged to the man himself.

Then, quite gradually Muzzlehatch yawned, stretching his arms to their extremities, as though to touch the sky. He took a pace forward, and then, at last, he spoke, yet not with his *voice* but more eloquently, with a great scarred index-finger like a crook.

ONE HUNDRED AND NINE

CHEETA's father, realizing that he had no choice but to obey (for there was something terrible and compelling about Muzzlehatch, with the crumbs of fire in his eyes) began to make his way willy-nilly in the direction of the great vagrant. And still there was no noise in all the world.

Then, suddenly, like something released, Titus beat his fists together, as a man might beat upon a door to let out his soul. Not a head turned at the sound, and the silence surged back and filled the shell of the Black House. But although there was no physical movement save for the progress of the bald man, there passed over the ground a shudder and a chill, where there was no breeze blowing, like the breath of a cold fresco, dank and rotting, filled with figures, so was this nocturnal array equally silent; when all at once, the ring of heads closed in upon the protagonists, and at the same time the two protagonists closed in on one another.

Muzzlehatch had dropped his index finger, and was approaching the scientist at a speed deliberately slow. Two worlds were approaching one another.

What of Cheeta? Where in this forest of legs could she be with her beautiful little face contorted and discoloured? Everything had gone wrong. What had been an ordered plan was nothing now but a humiliating chaos. She had been almost forgotten. She had become lost in a world of limbs. She had, more by instinct than knowledge, been making her way to where she last saw Titus, for to lose him would be for her like losing her revenge.

But she was not the only malcontent. In his own way, Titus was as fierce as she. The grisly charade had left him full of hatred. Not only this; there was Muzzlehatch too. His old friend. Why was he so silent and so deaf to his cries?

In an access of frustration he elbowed his way to the outskirts of the ring, and then, free at last, he ran at Muzzlehatch as though to endanger him.

But when Titus was close enough to strike out in his anger at the great figure, he stopped short in his tracks, for he saw what it was that had subjugated the bald man. It was the embers in the eyes of his friend.

This was not the Muzzlehatch he used to know. This was something quite different. A solitary who had no friends, nor needed any: for he was obsessed.

When Titus closed in upon Muzzlehatch in the semi-darkness he could see all this. He could see the embers, and his anger melted out of him. He could see at a glance how Muzzlehatch was bent upon death: that he was deranged. What was it then, in spite of this horror, that drew Titus to him? For Muzzlehatch had as yet taken no notice of him. What was it that urged Titus forward until he blocked the torn man's view of Cheeta's father? It was a kind of love.

'My old friend,' said Titus, very softly. 'Look at me, only look at me. Have you forgotten?'

At long last, Muzzlehatch turned his gaze upon Titus, who was now within arm's reach.

'Who is it? Let go my lemurs, boy.'

His face looked as though it were carved out of grey wood.

'Listen,' said the wanderer. 'You remind me of a friend I used to know. His name was Titus. He used to say he lived in a castle. He had a scar across his cheekbones. Ah yes, Titus Groan, Lord of the Tracts.'

'That man is me!' cried Titus in his desperation.

'Boom!' said Muzzlehatch, in a voice as abstracted as the night air. 'It won't be long now. Boom!'

Titus stared at him, and Cheeta also, through a gap in the crowd. He was shaking violently.

'Give me a clue, for God's sake. What are these "boom"s of yours? What is it that *won't be long*?' said Titus.

By now the scientist was only a few paces from Muzzlehatch, as though propelled slowly forward by an unseen force.

Yet it was not only the scientist who was inexorably on the move. The crowds, inch by inch, began to shuffle in little steps; their heads closed in upon the protagonists.

Were it not that all eyes were transfixed on the sight of the three, someone would by now have noticed Juno and Anchor.

ONE HUNDRED AND TEN

No one had noticed their arrival. A great bell pounded in Juno's bosom. Her eyes were fixed on Titus. She trembled. A rush of memories filled her. She longed to run to him and to draw him to her. But Anchor restrained her, his hand holding her trembling elbow.

Unlike Juno, the Anchor, with his mop of red-black hair, stood by her with all the sang-froid in the world. He seemed to have come into his own.

He watched every move and then led Juno away to an inky alcove. She was not to stir until he called for her. He returned to the centre of potential violence. He saw a creature break loose from a wall of legs. It was as slender as a switch. A great blood-coloured stone winked at her breast as though it spelled out some secret code. But it was her face that chilled him. It was terrible because it had given up trying. It no longer *cared*. All femininity had gone out of it. The features had become merely physical additions to the head. The face had died behind them. It was an empty place through which the winds could blow, now hot, now cold, from hell or heaven.

As for the phlegmatic Anchor, he had noted the long line of aeroplanes that glimmered in the half-darkness. There, if nowhere else, was their escape route.

Now he was ready. Now, before the evening closed in, he must strike when the moment came. Strike when? He had not long to wait for an answer.

Cheeta had by now seen not only Titus, but her father also. She had stopped as a bird stops in the middle of a run; for it was with amazement that she found herself so close to the huge stranger, who was even now picking her father up by the nape of his neck as a dog might lift a rat.

ONE HUNDRED AND ELEVEN

EVERYTHING seemed to be happening together. The light shifted like a gauze across the scene, almost as though the moon was making a return journey. Then something shone in the darkness. Something of metal, for there was no other substance that could throw out so strong a glint into the night air.

Titus, his gaze distracted for a moment by these flashes of light, turned his head away from Cheeta and her suspended father, and discovered, at last, what he was looking for. And while he watched, the leaping bonfire sent out a more than usually brilliant tongue, and this tongue, though it was far away, was strong enough to draw out of the darkness an expressionless face, and then another. Now they were gone again, though the light went on flashing above them. Plunged in their caves, their faces were no more, though their crests were alive with light. The helmeted men. Even without their helmets they would be tall. But with them, they stood head and shoulders above the crowd.

A shudder passed through Titus's body. He saw the crowds draw themselves apart so that the 'helmets' could pass through. He heard the assembly call out for them to deal with Muzzlehatch.

'Take him away,' they cried. 'Who is he? What does he want? He is frightening the ladies.'

Yet not one of that crowd, save for the 'helmets' themselves, and Cheeta, who was trembling in a diabolical rage; not one dared to take a step alone.

As for Muzzlehatch; his arm was outstretched and the scientist was still dangling at the end of it. This was the man whom he intended to slay. But now that he had the bald creature at arm's length, he could not feel the hatred so strongly.

Titus was appalled at the scene. Appalled at the vileness of it. Appalled that anyone should have thought out such an idea as to mock his family in such a way. Appalled and frightened. He turned his head and saw her, and his blood ran cold.

Revenge filled up her system, and battled with itself in her miniature bosom. Titus had scorned her. And now there was the ragged man as well, for he was holding up her family to scorn. And now Juno, whom she saw out of the tail of her eye. Her hair rose at the nape. There was no forgetting so far as Cheeta was concerned. This was the Juno of his early days. This was she; his one-time mistress.

ONE HUNDRED AND TWELVE

THE bonfire of juniper branches had been replenished, and again a yellow tongue of fire had fled up into the sky. Its light lit up the nearest of the trees with a wan illumination. The scent of the juniper filled the air. It was the only pleasant thing about the night. But no one noticed.

The animals and the birds, unable to go to sleep, watched from whatever vantage point they could cling to. There was among them an understanding that they left one another alone, until dawn, so that the birds of prey sat side by side with doves and owls, the foxes with the mice.

From where he stood, Titus could see, as though on a stage, the protagonists. Time seemed to draw to a close. The world had lost interest in itself and its positionings. They stood between the coil and the recoil. It was too much. Yet there was no alternative either of the heart or of the head. He could not leave Muzzlehatch. He loved the man. Yes, even now, though the flecks of red burned in his arrogant eyes. Sensing the widespread derangement all about him, Titus was becoming fearful for his own sanity. Yet there is loyalty in dreams, and beauty in madness, and he could not turn from the shaggy side of his friend. Nor could the scores of guests do anything. They were spellbound.

Now Muzzlehatch's boulder-like rolling of his own voice was repeated, and then immediately followed by a voice that did not seem his own. Something muted: something more menacing took its place.

'That was a long time ago,' said Muzzlehatch, 'when I lived another kind of life. I wandered through the dawn and back again. I ate the world up like a serpent devouring itself, tail first. Now I am inside out. The lions roared for me. They roared down my bloodstream. But, as they are dead, their roaring comes to nothing, for you, Bladder-head, have stopped their hearts from beating, and now it's about time for me to stop yours.'

Muzzlehatch was not looking at the living bundle at the end of his arm. He was looking through it. Then he dropped his hand and trailed the scientist in the dust.

'So I went for a stroll, and what a stroll it was! It took me to a factory at last. And there I met your friends and your machines, and all that caused the great death of my beasts. O God, my coloured beasts, my burning fauna. And there I lit the blue fuse at the centre. It can't be long to wait. Boom!'

Muzzlehatch looked about him.

'Well, well, well,' he said. 'What a pretty lot we have here! By heaven, Titus boy, the air is full of damnation. Look at 'em. D'you know 'em? Ha, ha! God's liver, if it ain't the "Helmeteers". How they do tread on our tails.'

'Sir,' said Anchor, moving up. 'Let me relieve you of the scientist. Even an arm like yours must tire at times.'

'Who are you?' said Muzzlehatch, leaving his arm where it was, like a signpost, for he had lifted it again.

'Does that matter?' said Anchor.

'Matter! Ha, that's ripe,' said Muzzlehatch. 'Ripe as your copper-coloured mane. How is it you have jumped from the ranks to join us?'

'We have a lady in common,' said Anchor.

'Who would that be?' said Muzzlehatch. 'Queen of the mermaids?'

'Do I look it?' It was Juno who, against Anchor's instructions, had crept out of the alcove, and now stood at his side.

'O Titus, my most dear!' She ran towards him.

At the sight of Juno, the air became electric and through this atmosphere a figure darted, rapid as a weasel. It was Cheeta.

So *this* was Juno; *this*, the billowy whore. Cheeta bit her under-lip until the blood ran over her chin.

She had long ago dismissed from her mind any thought of her own attractions. They had ceased to be of any interest to her, for something a thousand times more important filled her vision as a pit can be filled with fumes. But as the venomous midget slid with a dreadful intensity of purpose towards Juno, her rival, she was brought to an incongruous halt by an explosion.

Not only was Cheeta halted in her progress at the sound of the reverberation, but each in their own way found himself or herself rooted to the floor of the Black House; Juno, Anchor, Titus, and Muzzlehatch himself, the 'Helmets', the Three, and a hundred guests. And more than this. The birds and the beasts of the surrounding forests, they also froze along the boughs, until simultaneously taking wing a great volume of birds arose like a fog into the night, thickening the air, and quenching the moon. Where they had perched in their thousands the twigs and boughs lifted themselves a little in the bird-made darkness.

Seeing the others glued to the ground, Cheeta struggled against her own inability to close with them and to fight with the only weapons she possessed; two rows of sharp little teeth and ten finger nails. She had turned from Titus to Juno as the first of her enemies to dispatch, but like them, her head was turned in the direction of the sound, and she could not twist it back.

That her father, the greatest scientist in the world was hanging upside down from the outstretched arm of some kind of brigand did not, in itself, inflame or impress upon her passions, for there was no space left in her tiny tremulous body for such an emotion to find foothold. She could not feel for him. She was consumed already.

The first to speak was Anchor.

'What would that be?' he said. Even as he spoke a light appeared in the sky in the direction of the sound.

'That would be the death of many men,' said Muzzlehatch. 'That would be the last roar of the golden fauna: the red of the world's blood: doom is one step closer. It was the fuse that did it. The blue fuse. My dear man,' he said, turning to Anchor, 'only look at the sky.'

Sure enough it was taking on a life of its own. Unhealthy as a neglected sore, skeins of transparent fabric wavered across the night sky, peeling off, one after another to reveal yet fouler tissues in a fouler empyrean.

Then the crowd raised its voice, and demanded that it be set free from the ghastly charade that was taking place before its eyes.

But when Muzzlehatch approached them they drew back, for there was something incalculable about the smile that turned his face into something to be avoided.

They all drew back a pace or two, except for the helmeted pair. These two, holding their ground, leaned forward on the air. Now that they were so close it could be seen that their heads were like skulls, beautiful, as though chiselled. What skin they had was stretched tight as silk. There was a sheen over their heads, almost a luminosity. Nor did they speak from those thin mouths of theirs. Nor could they. Only the crowds spoke, while their clothes grew damp as the night fell, despoiling the exquisite gowns, and blackening their hems with dew. So with the medallioned chests of their tongue-tied escorts.

'I ask you sir, again. What was that noise? Was it thunder?' said Anchor, knowing full well that it was not. He watched the gaunt man while he spoke but he also watched Titus; and Cheeta. He watched the helmeted men who menaced Muzzlehatch. He watched everything. His eyes, in contrast to the shock of red hair, were grey as pools.

But above all he watched Juno. All eyes had by now been turned away from the direction of the sound and of the sick sky also, and formed between them a pattern in the darkness, and at the same moment the first twinge of sunrise in the forested east.

Juno, her eyes filled with tears, took hold of Titus by the arm at a moment when he longed from the bottom of his soul to get away, to leave for ever. But he did not by an iota tense or withdraw his arm from her, or do anything to hurt her. Yet Juno let go her hand from his arm, and it fell like a weight to her side.

He gazed at her, almost as though she belonged to another world, and his lips, though they formed a smile, had no life in them. Here they stood side by side, these two, with the loveliest section of their past in common. Yet they appeared to have lost their way. All this was in a flash, and the Anchor took it in.

He also took in something of another kind. The impersonal embers in Muzzlehatch's eyes appeared to have been fanned into life. The small, dull red light had now begun to oscillate to and fro across the pupils.

But in contrast to this grisly phenomenon, was the control he exercised over his own voice. It was perfectly audible though a little more than a whisper. Coming from the great rudder-nosed man it was a double weapon.

'It was not thunder,' he said. 'Thunder is purposeless. But this was the very backbone of purpose. There was no explosion for explosion's sake.'

Taking advantage of the fact that Muzzlehatch was engaged in his own oratory, Anchor moved around him, unseen, until he stood a little behind Titus, for from this position he was able to command a view of Cheeta and Juno at the same time.

The air was bristling, for they had seen one another. Without her knowing it, the initial advantage lay with Juno, for Cheeta's ferocity was almost equally divided between her and Titus.

The whole travesty had been planned as something to humiliate Titus. She had been to all lengths to insure its success; yet now it was over, and she stood among the wreckage, her little body vibrating like a bow-string.

'Dismantle them!' she screamed, for she saw out-topping the crowd, the battered masks, the hanks of hair; the Countess breaking in half, dusty and ludicrous; the sawdust; and the paint.

ONE HUNDRED AND FOURTEEN

'TAKE those things down!' she screamed, standing on tiptoe, for she saw in the tail of her eye, a great wavering, semi-human bulk, that was even now as she watched it, breaking in half and turning as it collapsed, to show the long filthy hanks of hair, the mask with its dreadful pallor, lit by the flooding of the dawn, sink to the floor. Down came the others, that had so recently been the symbols of mockery and scorn. Some with their grease-paint dripping; the dusty remnants of blotched sawdust.

All at once a woman screamed, and as though this were a signal for release, a general cacophony broke out and a number of ladies grew hysterical, striking out at their husbands or their lovers.

Muzzlehatch, whose peroration had been interrupted, merely cocked an eye at the crowd, and then stared fixedly and for a long time at what was still dangling at the end of his arm. After a while he remembered what it was.

'I was going to kill you,' said Muzzlehatch, 'in the way you kill a rabbit. A sharp stroke at the nape of the neck, delivered with the edge of the hand. I was even going to throttle you, but that seemed too good for you. Then there was the idea of drowning you in a bucket, but all these things were too good for you. You would not appreciate them. But I'll have to do something about you, won't I? Do you think your daughter wants you? Has she a birthday coming? No? Then I'll take a chance, my little cockroach. Only *look* at her. Dishevelled and wicked. Look how she pines for him. Why, you'd take his nut for an onion. I must be rude after all, my sweet dangler, for you killed my animals. Ah, how they slid in their hey-day. How they meandered; how they skidded or leapt in their abandon. Lord, how they cocked their heads. Dear heaven! How they cocked their heads!

'Once there were islands all a-sprout with palms: and coral reefs and sands as white as milk. What is there now but a vast shambles of the heart? Filth, squalor, and a world of little men.'

At the same moment that Muzzlehatch drew breath, Cheeta was seen to speed across the last few steps that divided her from Titus, like an evil thing borne on an evil draught.

Had it not been that with an unexpected agility, Juno leapt in front of Titus, he might well have had his face cut over and over by Cheeta's long green nails.

Thwarted in her passion to leave her marks on Titus's face, she howled in an access of evil as tears churned down her cheeks in channels of make-up.

For, no longer than it takes to tell it, Anchor had dragged both Titus and Juno out of reach of the malignant dart. Trembling, she stood and waited the next move, rising and falling on her tiny feet.

The dawn was now beginning to pick out the leaves from the trees of the surrounding forests and glowed softly on the helmets of the agents.

But Titus did not want to be hidden away behind the stalwart Anchor. He was grateful but angry that he should have been plucked backwards. As for Juno who had disobeyed Anchor – she was doing it again. For she also had no wish to remain in the shadow of her friend. They were too restless, too on edge to stand still. Seeing what was happening, Anchor merely shrugged his shoulders.

'The time has come,' said Muzzlehatch, 'to do whatever it was we set out to do. This is the time for flight. This is the time for bastards like myself to put an end to it all. What if my eyes are sore and red? What if they burn my sockets up? I've bathed in the straits of Actapon with phosphorus in the water, and my limbs like fish. Who cares about that now? Do you?' he said, tossing the bundle who was Cheeta's father, from one huge hand to another. 'Do you? Tell me honestly.'

Muzzlehatch bent down and put his ear to the bundle. 'It's beastly,' he said, 'and it's alive.' Muzzlehatch tossed the little scientist to his daughter, who had no option but to catch him.

He whimpered a little as Cheeta then let him fall to the floor. Getting to his feet, his face was a map of terror.

'I must go back to my work,' he said in that thin voice that sent a chill down the spines of all his workmen.

'It's no good going *there*,' said Muzzlehatch. 'It has exploded. Can you not hear the reverberations? Can you not see how ghastly is the dawn? There's a lot of ash in the air.'

'Exploded? No! . . . No! . . . It was all I had; my science, *all* that I had.'

'And she was a lovely girl, I'm told,' said Muzzlehatch.

Cheeta's father, too frightened to answer, now began to turn in the direction of the foul light that was still angry in the sky. 'Let me go,' he cried, though no one was touching him. 'O God! My formula!' he cried. 'My formula.' He began to run.

On and on he ran, over the walls and into the dawn shadows. Immediately upon his words came a thick and curious laughter. It was Muzzlehatch. His eyes were like two red-hot pennies. While the echoes of Muzzlehatch rang out, Cheeta had manoeuvred herself so that she was again within striking distance of Titus, who, now that he was some way from Anchor, had turned for a moment to stare about him at the gaping throng.

It was at that moment, with his head averted, that Cheeta struck, breaking her nails as one might crunch sea-shells. The warm blood ran profusely down his neck. At once Juno was upon her.

How she could have moved with such speed it was impossible to say. But when she leapt forward and lifted her arm to strike, Juno recoiled from touching the febrile thing, for there was something horrible in the discrepancy in their sizes, and something pitiful about Cheeta's small bedraggled face spotted with blood, however evil.

But that was where the compunction ended, and Juno, trembling as much as her antagonist, was about to be grabbed by Anchor, when the shrillest scream of all tore its way through the body of the sunrise like a knife through tissue; and immediately upon this vent from Cheeta's lungs, the little creature turned upon them all and spat. This was the once exquisite Cheeta, the queen of ice; the orchid; brilliant of brain and limb. Now with her dignity departed forever, she bared her teeth.

What was she to do? She darted her glance along the half circle. She saw how Juno was attending to Titus's wounds as well as she could. Between them and herself, stood Anchor. She looked about her wildly, and saw how the light in Muzzlehatch's eyes was directed upon her, and how there was no love in them; and how she was irrevocably alone.

She returned her gaze to Titus.

'I hate you!' she cried. 'I hate all that you think you are. I hate your Gormenghast. I will always hate it. If it were true I'd hate it even more. I'm glad your neck is bleeding. You beast! Bloody beast!'

She turned and ran from them crying out words that none of them could understand . . . ran like a shred of darkness; ran and ran; until only those with the keenest sight could see her as she fled into the deep shadows of the most easterly of the forests. But though she was soon too far away for even the best of eyes, yet her voice carried all the way, until only a far, thin screaming could be heard, and after that no more.

ONE HUNDRED AND FIFTEEN

MUZZLEHATCH turned his great hewn face to the sky.

'Come here Titus. I am suddenly remembering you. What's the matter? Do you always go round with blood all over you, like a butcher's shop?'

'Leave him alone, Muzzle dear. He's very sick indeed,' said Juno.

But they were not destined for any slackening of the pressure. Cheeta had gone it is true, and her father also, but danger was now from another quarter. The crowd was beginning to surge towards them. There were cries of anger, for they were very afraid. Everything had gone wrong. They were cold. They were lost. They were hungry. And Cheeta, the centre of it all, had forsaken them. Who could they turn to? In their lost condition, they could do little else but fling abuse at the shadowy figures, and it was only after a particularly ugly bout that a thick voice called out . . .

'And look at them,' it cried. 'Look at that fool in a bandage. Seventy-Seventh Earl! Ha! ha! There's Gormenghast for you. Why don't you come and prove yourself, my lord?'

Why this particular remark should have got under Muzzle-hatch's skin, it is hard to fathom, but it did, and he stalked to the border of the crowd in order to annihilate the man. In order to do so he passed, swaggering in his rags, between the two inscrutable Helmeteers. As he did so there was a kind of hush as they slid aside to let him through. Then, as though it had all been premeditated, they turned and, bringing out their long-bladed knives, they stabbed Muzzlehatch in the back.

He did not die all at once, though the blades were long. He did not make a sound except for a catch in his breath. The red had gone out of his eyes, and in its place was a prodigious sanity. 'Where's Titus?' he said. 'Bring the young ruffian here.'

There was no need to tell Titus what to do. He flung himself at Muzzlehatch, yet with tenderness, for all his passion, and he clasped his old friend with his hand.

'Hey! hey!' whispered Muzzlehatch. 'Don't squeeze out what's left of me, my dear.'

'Oh my dear Muzzle . . . my dear friend.'

'Don't overdo it,' whispered Muzzlehatch, as he began to sag at the knees. 'Mustn't get morbid . . . eh? . . . eh? . . . Where is your hand, boy?'

What had been diffused throughout the sunrise, had now contracted to a focus. What was atmospheric had become almost solid. As they looked at one another, they saw what some see under the influence of drugs, a peculiar nearness, and a vividness hardly to be borne.

ONE HUNDRED AND SIXTEEN

JUNO, though knowing herself to be an outsider, in spite of her devotion to them both, yet had no power to keep away from her one-time lover, and it is strange that they needed Muzzlehatch at this last moment more than vengeance. Vengeance was to come, and Anchor was on his way to dispense it.

By now the sun was clear of the eastern forests, and every shape of form and colour would have shone clearly were it not for the omnipresent veil of the foul orange tint, that bastard hue, that was neither red nor yellow, but wavered on the brink of both. The only thing that burned with decision was Anchor.

Within a few strides he was beside them. The Helmeted Men. They were wiping their long steel blades upon the dock leaves that grew profusely on the floor of the Black House. For a moment his stomach turned with revulsion, for there was no expression on their faces. During the moment, too short to be called a pause, Anchor averted his gaze, and he saw on the other side of the two 'Helmets', the three characters from the Under-River.

Anchor knew nothing of these three, but he was not left long in doubt as to their intentions. Clumsy in movement, yet working in a crude unison they took the helmeted murderers from behind, snatching their long knives and pinning their arms to their sides. Yet the more they squeezed and pinioned them the stronger the sinister couple grew, and it was only when their helmets fell to the ground that a supernatural strength deserted them, and they were at once overpowered and slain by their own weapons.

Then a great hush came down upon the Black House, and over the wide and tragic scene. Titus could, only with difficulty, help the gaunt man down to his knees, inch by inch. Never for an instant did he cease from the fighting: never for a moment did he murmur. His head was held high; his back was straight as a soldier's as he slowly sank. With one hand he gripped Titus by the forearm as hard as he could. But the youth could hardly feel it.

'Something of a holocaust, ain't it,' he whispered. 'God bless you and your Gormenghast, my boy.'

Then came another voice. It was Juno.

'Let me see you. Let me kneel beside you,' she said.

But already it was too late. Something had fled from the sunlit bulk on the floor. Muzzlehatch had gone. He had heeled over. His arrogant head lay upon its side, and Juno closed his eyes.

Then Titus stood up. At first he saw nothing, and then it was the swaying of the crowd. He saw a face . . . white as a sheet: an enormity. It was too big for a human visage. It was surrounded by crude locks of carrot-coloured hair, and there were stuffed birds perched upon the dusty shoulders. It was the last of the monstrosities to fall, Titus's mother. Turning from Muzzlehatch's side, Titus, with his eyes fixed upon this pasteboard travesty began to shake, for it reminded him of his own treachery when he left her; and the castle, his heritage.

But he was weak from loss of blood, and there came over him an absolute emptiness. It seemed that nothing mattered any more, so that when Anchor slung him over his shoulder, it was without any kind of argument. Titus had lost all his strength. Again there were cries from the congregation, which were stifled as soon as begun, for an owl the size of a large cat lolled through the air above the Black House, only to return to make sure whether what it had seen was true.

What did it see? It saw the dwindling of the juniper fire. It saw a long corpse lying by itself. Its head was turned on one side. It saw a dormouse under a bunch of couch-grass. It saw the glint of up-turned helmets, and a little to the west, their one-time owners. There they lay, sprawled across one another.

It saw Titus's bandages and Anchor's red hair in the foul morning light. It saw a bangle glinting on Juno's wrist. It saw the living and it saw the dead.

ONE HUNDRED AND SEVENTEEN

Owl or no owl, it was essential to get Juno and Titus out of this sickening place, where in the full, if beastly light of the risen sun, objects that appeared mysterious and even magnificent during the night appeared now to be tawdry; cheap; a rag-and-bone shop.

Had Anchor been alone he would have experienced no great difficulty in making an escape from what was fast becoming an angry crowd. For he could handle most aircraft and had already selected one.

But Titus was weak with loss of blood, and Juno was trembling, as though she was standing in icy water.

As for Muzzlehatch, sprawled as though to take the curve of the world; what could be done about him? That heavy body. Those prodigious limbs. Even were he to have been alive he would have had great difficulty in manoeuvring himself into the aircraft, built like a flying fish.

But now, a dead-weight with his muscles stiffening, how much more difficult!

It was then that the three vagrants ran from the crowd, Crack-Bell, Crabcalf and Slingshott. They had seen it all, and knew just as well as Anchor knew that their only hope was to jettison the dead giant and make for the planes where they stood in long lines under the cedar branches.

'Muzzlehatch; where is he?' whispered Titus. 'Where is he?'

'We cannot take him,' said Anchor. 'We must leave him where he lies. Come, Titus.'

But it was a little while (in spite of Anchor's peremptory command) before Juno could tear herself from what had been so much a part of her life. She bent down and kissed the cold craggy forehead.

Then at Anchor's second shout they left him in the pitiless sunshine, and stumbled towards the voice.

The noise of the crowd had become menacing. Was *this* Cheeta's party? The men were furious; the women tired and vicious. Their clothes were ruined. Was it not natural for the company to wish to revenge itself on something or other? What better than the remaining three?

But they had not reckoned with the men from the Under-River who, seeing how dangerously Titus and the others were placed, barred the obvious exits to the outside world.

But first they let slip through their fingers Juno, Titus and Anchor, and at that moment there began a most outrageous din. Those with a reputation as gentlemen were now forced to think otherwise for there was a great deal of scuffling and cursing before they had all fought their way out of the Black House, and into the open, where they began to mill around. Chivalry had apparently lost itself in a swarm of knees and elbows.

The Three were old campaigners and directly they saw how they had created sufficient chaos, they lost themselves in the irritable crowd.

The sky, curdled as it was, had now begun to look less ominous. A clearer, fresher stain was in the sky.

The vagrants, Crabcalf and the rest, joining up as planned in a rendezvous of branches, sat among the leaves like huge grey fowl.

Then Crabcalf lifted his head and whistled. It was the signal for Titus that all was clear as far as the making of their way was concerned, to where the long line of aircraft lay like frigates at anchor.

ONE HUNDRED AND EIGHTEEN

How beautiful they looked, those dire machines, each of a different colour, each with a different shape. Yet all of them with this in common; that speed was the gist of them.

Though it seemed to Juno, Anchor and Titus that they had been stumbling for ever, it was no more than eight or so minutes before they saw her: a lemon-yellow creature the shape of a tipcat.

As they began to clamber aboard, they could hear the angry voices growing louder every moment, and it was indeed a near thing, for as they rose into the air the first of the forsaken crowd came running into view.

But Muzzlehatch? What of that vast collapse? What of that structure? There it lay so still in the sunlight. What of the way his head lolled over in absolute death? What could they do about it? There was nothing they could do.

The machine rose into the air, and as it rose they saw him dwindle. Now he was the size of a bird: now of an insect on the bright earth. Now he was gone. Gone? Had they forsaken him? Had they lost him forever? Lost him, where he lay, depth below depth, as though fathomed under water; Muzzlehatch . . . silence forever with him; one arm flung out.

For a long while, as the aircraft rose, and moved at the same time into the south, they took no heed of one another; each of them bemused: each in a wilderness of their own.

Anchor, perhaps, his fingers moving mechanically across the controls, was less far from reality than Titus or Juno, by reason of his watchfulness, but even he was hardly normal, and there was upon his face a shadow that Juno had not seen before.

From time to time, as they sped through the upper atmosphere, and while the world unveiled itself, valley by valley, range by range, ocean by ocean, city by city, it seemed that the earth wandered through his skull . . . a cosmos in the bone; a universe lit by a hundred lights and thronged by shapes and shadows; alive with endless threads of circumstance . . . action and event. All futility: disordered; with no end and no beginning.

ONE HUNDRED AND NINETEEN

JUNO was motionless. Her profile was like that of an antique coin. A fullness under the chin; her nose straight and short; her face floated it seemed, unattached against the sky. A planet lit a cheekbone and revealed a tear. It hung there. It could not roll. The sweet down of her cheekbone held it where it was.

As Titus turned and saw her, he recoiled from her pathos. He could not bear it. He saw in her a criticism of his own defection. He suddenly hated himself for such a thought and he half rose from his seat in an agony of confusion. He loathed his own existence. He hated the unnatural from whose platter he had supped too often. The face of Muzzlehatch grew large in his mind. It filled him. It spread deeper. It filled the coloured plane. It filled the heavens. Then came a voice to join it. Was it *Muzzlehatch* with his eyes half closed upon his rocky cheekbone?

Titus shook his head to free his brain. Anchor glanced at the young man and tossed a hank of red hair from his eyes. Then he stared again at Titus.

'Where are we going?' he said at last. But there was no reply.

ONE HUNDRED AND TWENTY

THE darkness fell and the little craft sped on like an insect in the void. Time seemed to be a meaningless thing; but dawn came at last, its breast a wilderness of feathers.

The red-headed pilot seemed to be slumped over the controls but every now and again he shook himself and adjusted some device. All about him were the intricate entrails of the yellow machine; a creature terrible in its speed; lethal in its line; multitudinous in its secrets; an equation of metal.

Juno was fast asleep with her head on Titus's shoulders. He sat in stony silence while the slim plane whistled through the air.

Suddenly he sat forward in his seat, and clenched his hands. A dark flush covered his brow. It was as though he had only just heard Anchor's question.

'Did someone ask where we were going? Or am I dreaming? Perhaps it is all a figment of my brain.'

'What is the matter, Titus?' said Juno, lifting her head.

'What is the matter? Is that what you said? So *you* don't know either? Neither of you know. Is that it? Have we no destination? We are *moving*, that is all; from one sky to the next. Is that what you think? Or am I mad? I have drowned my birthplace with rant until its name stinks to heaven. Gormenghast! O Gormenghast! How can I prove you?'

Titus banged his head down upon his knees over and over again.

'Dear God! Dear God!' he muttered. 'Don't make me mad.'

'You are no more mad than I am,' said Anchor. 'Or than any other creature who is lost.'

But Titus went on banging his head on his knees.

'Oh Titus,' cried Juno. 'We will search until we find your heart's home. Have I ever doubted you?'

'It is your *pity* for me. Your damnable *pity*,' cried Titus. 'You do not believe. You are gentle, but you do not believe. Oh God, it is your terrible, ignorant pity. Don't you see it is the grey towers that I want? It is my Doctor; it is Bellgrove. If I shout will she hear me? Turn off the engine, Mr Anchor, and I will call her out of the air.' Juno and Anchor exchanged glances, and the engine was switched off. The slithering silence filled them. Titus raised his head to cry, but no sound came. Only within himself could he hear a faraway voice calling out. . . . 'Mother . . . mother . . . mother . . . mother . . . where are you? Where . . . are . . . you? Where . . . are . . . you?'

ONE HUNDRED AND TWENTY-ONE

NEVER knowing where they were, for they could see nothing but alien hills and a great unheard-of sea, yet, nevertheless, they had no option but to cruise ever deeper into the unknown.

They took it in turn to guide the sleek machine, and it was well that Titus took his share of the responsibility. To some extent it kept him from brooding.

Yet even then his mind was half aware. Childhood and rebellion . . . disobedience and defiance; the journey; the adventures and now a youth no longer – but the *man*.

'Good-bye, my friend. Look after her. She is all heart.'

Before Anchor and Juno knew what was happening he pressed a

button, and was a second or two later alone, falling through the wilds of space, his parachute opening like a flower above him.

Gradually the dark silk tent filled up with air, and he swayed as he descended through the darkness, for it was night again. He gave himself up to the sensation of seemingly endless descent.

For a little while he forgot his loneliness, which was strange, for what could have been a lonelier setting than the night through which, suspended, he gradually fell? There was nothing for his feet to touch and it was right for him to be, for the time, so out of touch in every kind of sense. And so it was with composure that he felt and saw the bats surround him.

Now lay the land below him. A vast charcoal drawing of mountains and forests. There was no habitation to be seen, nor anything human, yet the stark geology and the crowding heads of the forest trees were redolent of almost human shapes. It was among the branches of a forest tree that Titus eventually subsided, and he lay there for a little while unharmed, like a child in a cradle.

When he had freed himself of his harness, and had cut away the deflated silk, he lowered himself branch by branch, and by the time he had reached the forest floor the sunshine was threading its way through the trees.

Now he was really alone and in making for the east he had no better reason than that it was out of there that the sunbeams were pouring.

Hungry, weary, he made his solitary way, eating roots and berries and drinking from the streams. Month followed month until one day, as he wandered through the lonely void, his heart jumped into his throat.

ONE HUNDRED AND TWENTY-TWO

WHY had he stopped to stare at the shape of a rock, as though it were in any way unusual? There it stood, perfectly normal, a great lichened boulder of a thing, pock-marked by time, its northern side somewhat swollen like the sail of a ship. Why was he staring at it as though struck by recognition?

As his eyes raced over the triturated surface of this dead yet evocative thing he took a step backwards. It was as though he was being warned.

There was no getting away from it. He had seen this rock before. He had stood upon its back, a 'king of the castle', in his childhood. He now remembered the long scar, a saw-toothed fissure down its crusty flank.

He knew that if he scaled it now and stood, once again, as in the old days, a 'king of the castle', he would see the very towers of Gormenghast.

That was why he trembled. The long indented outline of his home was blocked away from his sight by the mere proximity of a boulder. It was, for no reason he could see, a challenge.

A flood of memories returned; and as they spread and inter-spread and deepened, another part of his brain was wide aware of closer manifestations. The recognized existence, the very *proof* of the stone, there before him, not twenty feet away, argued the no less real existence of a cave that yawned at his right hand. A cave where an infinity ago he had struggled with a nymph.

At first he did not dare to turn his head, but the moment had come when he must do so, and *there it was* at last, away behind his right shoulder, and he knew for very proof that he was in his own domain once more. He was standing on Gormenghast Mountain.

As he rose to his feet a fox trotted out of the cave. A crow coughed in a nearby spinney and a gun boomed. It boomed again. It boomed seven times.

There it lay behind the boulder; the immemorial ritual of his home. It was the dawn salvo. It boomed for him, for the seventy-seventh Earl, Titus Groan, Lord of Gormenghast, *wherever* he might be.

There burned the ritual; all he had lost; all he had searched for. The concrete *fact* of it. The proof of his own sanity and love.

'O God! It's true! It's true! I am not mad! I am not mad!' he cried.

Gormenghast, his home. He could feel it. He could almost *see* it. He had only to skirt the base of the great rock or climb its crusty crown, for his eyes to become filled with towers. There was a taste in the air of iron. There was a quickening it seemed of the very stones and of the bridgeless spaces. What was he waiting for?

It would have been possible, had he wished it, to have reached the mouth of the cave without a glimpse of his Home. Indeed he took a step or two towards the cave-mouth. But again a sense of impending danger held back his feet, and a moment later he heard his own voice saying . . .

'No . . . no . . . not now! It is not possible . . . now.'

His heart beat out more rapidly, for something was growing . . . some kind of knowledge. A thrill of the brain. A synthesis. For Titus was recognizing in a flash of retrospect that a new phase of which he was only half aware, had been reached. It was a sense of maturity, almost of fulfilment. He had no longer any need for home, for he carried his Gormenghast within him. All that he sought was jostling within himself. He had grown up. What a boy had set out to seek a man had found, found by the act of living.

There he stood: Titus Groan, and he turned upon his heel so that the great boulder was never seen by him ever again. Nor was the cave: nor was the castle that lay beyond, for Titus, as though shaking off his past from his shoulders like a heavy cape began to run down the far side of the mountain, not by the track by which he had ascended, but by another that he had never known before.

With every pace he drew away from Gormenghast Mountain, and from everything that belonged to his home.

CRITICAL ASSESSMENTS

CRITICAL ASSESSMENTS

Introduced, selected, and edited by G. Peter Winnington

INTRODUCTION:
THE CRITICAL RECEPTION OF
MERVYN PEAKE'S TITUS BOOKS*

G. Peter Winnington

> I predict for Titus a smallish but fervant public,
> composed of those whose imaginations are comple-
> mentary to Mr. Peake's. Such a public will probably
> renew itself, and probably enlarge, with each genera-
> tion; for which reason I hope the book may always
> be kept in print.

ELIZABETH BOWEN,
in the *Tatler & Bystander*,
April 3, 1946, pp. 23 & 28.

WHEN *Titus Groan* was published in book-hungry Britain at the
end of March 1946, it was generally well received—with reservations. Mervyn Peake was already known as a poet and illustrator;
many reviewers compared his novel with his previous work, and
found it less successful. For the novelist Howard Spring, *Titus
Groan* was 'full of the macabre power that makes Mr. Peake's
drawings notable. But [he] has not yet learned how to apply this
power effectively to the writing of fiction' (*Country Life*, December
6, 1946, p. 1108). The anonymous reviewer in the *Times Literary
Supplement* expressed similar reservations: 'Mr. Peake's distinctive
talent, as in his poetry, painting, and book illustration, should not
go unrecognized. Yet the impression he leaves is not quite that of
a novelist (March 23, 1946, p. 137). Several reviewers regretted
the absence of illustrations; Peake had wanted to illustrate his
book, but his publisher turned down the idea on the grounds that
this would have placed the novel in a different category. (The
drawings in the present edition were added in the late 1960s.)

Placing *Titus Groan* in a category remains a problem, which
explains the ambivalence of many of the reviews. Much depended

---

G. Peter Winnington is the editor of *Peake Studies*; he lectures in modern English
literature at the University of Lausanne, Switzerland.
*I insist on calling them "the Titus books" because Peake did not conceive of
them as a trilogy, but as an open-ended series, with Gormenghast providing the
setting for only the first two volumes.

on the reviewers' attitudes towards the 'grotesque', the 'fantastic' and the 'Gothic'. A few, like Kate O'Brien, were openly dismissive: 'bad, tautological prose... a large, haphazard, Gothic mess' (*Spectator*, no. 176, March 29, 1946, pp. 332 & 334); others, like the celebrated novelist and short-story writer, Elizabeth Bowen (already quoted above), were more enthusiastic: '*Titus Groan* defies classification: it certainly is not a novel; it would be found strong meat as a fairy-tale. Let us call it a sport of literature (for literature, I, for one, do find it to be)—one of those works of pure, violent, self-sufficient imagination that are from time to time thrown out.'

On balance, the reviewers were largely positive, with some lengthy eulogies in major periodicals. Herbert Reed said, 'I do not think I have ever so much enjoyed a novel sent to me for review' (*New Statesman and Nation*, May 4, 1946, p. 323). Peake's friend Maurice Collis devoted a page of *Time and Tide* (April 13, 1946, p. 354) to a serious assessment of the book; and R.G.G. Price (in the *New English Review*, vol. 12, no. 6, June 1946, pp. 592—93) concluded rhetorically: 'Grandiloquent? Thank Heavens. Verbose? Why not, if the words are good ones? Interesting and effective? Certainly.'

By this time, a few articles had appeared on Peake, but they were mostly profiles of him as an illustrator. The exception was a perceptive little article by Quentin Crisp, which is reprinted as a preface to the Overlook paperback edition of *Gormenghast*. Then known only for his eccentric appearance and profession as an artists' model, Crisp had made Peake's acquaintance several years before; in particular he had persuaded him to illustrate Crisp's literary oddity, a limerick sequence called *All This and Bevin Too*, which was published as a stapled brochure in 1943 and remains a delightful period piece.

When it came to the publication of *Titus Groan* in America, Peake was dismayed to find that the publisher had added the subtitle, 'A Gothic novel' to the cover and title-page of the book; this inevitably colored the reviews. *Titus Groan* came out late in 1946 after a flourish of advance publicity, as in the *New York Herald Tribune*: 'Just as we were struggling with *William Blake* by Mark Schorer, Will Cuppy came in and asked out of a clear sky: "What is that new novel about a character named Ug or Awk, but not by Vardis Fisher?" We knew right away he meant *Titus Groane* [sic] by Mervyn Peake' (September 1, 1946).

It left many reviewers puzzled, and they sought in vain for a meaning in the work: 'He would be a brave man indeed who offhand would attempt to determine the meaning of the story,' commented John Cournos, beating a retreat in the *New York Sun* (November 5, 1946). 'An allegory it may well be. But of what?' wondered Orville Prescott in the *New York Times* (November 8, 1946); he felt that the 'dark jewels of *Titus Groan* are buried deep and must be dug for through masses of slag and dirt.' Thomas Sugrue was equally perturbed by it: 'Perhaps *Titus Groan* is meant to represent a dream. Perhaps it is surrealistic. Perhaps it is just a dull book, without humor, without vitality, yet tumbling on for a dreadfully long time' (*New York Herald Tribune*, November 24, 1946). The *New Yorker* concluded that 'readers who look for hidden meanings may find themselves wondering whether Mr. Peake has done anything more solemn than produce a work of extraordinary imagination while having himself a very fine time' (November 16, 1946).

Difficulties of classification again proved a handicap to success, and praise was often overshadowed by such comments as 'it is almost impossible to classify' (*Call Bulletin*, San Francisco, December 7, 1946), and 'a flight of allegorical fantasy that defies classification' (Beloit *News*, Wisconsin, December 5, 1946, repeated in the Burbank, California, *Review*, January 8, 1947).

Overall, however, American reviewers were quite as favorable as the British. 'With all its defects,' concluded Hermes Nye in the Dallas, Texas, *Times Herald*, 'this remains a book for the man who relishes the fantastic, the puckish and the beautiful' (December 8, 1946). Writers again proved to be Peake's most sympathetic readers. August Derleth informed subscribers to the Milwaukee *Journal* that 'this novel offers rich reward to anyone who exercises the patience and imagination to stay with it' (November 17, 1946), and the celebrated novelist Robertson Davies, writing in the Peterborough (Canada) *Examiner* as Samuel Marchbanks, concluded: 'it is an astonishing work of art.... It has been condemned as unhealthy and absurd, but in my opinion it is neither, but a very fine book, well removed from the beaten path of contemporary fiction. I recommend it highly' (December 10, 1947).

During the three following years, Peake lived on the Channel Island of Sark; there he completed *Gormenghast* which was published in September 1950 to critical acclaim. 'No novel involving any comparable effort of imagination and fancy, of will-power and word-power, has appeared in English since the war,' wrote Emyr Humphreys in *Time & Tide* (October 21, 1950, pp. 1065-66), and R.G.G. Price, who had already been captivated by *Titus Groan*, called *Gormenghast* 'the finest imaginative feat in the English novel since *Ulysses*,' although he then spoiled the compliment by adding, 'even though *Ulysses* is of course still much the greater book' (*Punch*,

November 22, 1950, p. 507). By this time, readers had begun to appreciate that in Peake's work the story is less important than the telling. Several reviewers emphasized the escapist nature of his fiction: 'a holiday in the land of a dream' (Lionel Hale in *The Observer*, September 17, 1950) and 'as a complete holiday from reality, it is a country that will bear a third visit' (*Liverpool Daily Post*, October 3, 1950), which boded well for *Titus Alone*. The following year, Peake received the Heinemann Prize from the Royal Society for *Gormenghast* and his collection of poems, *The Glassblowers* (also 1950). But there was no American edition of *Gormenghast* until 1967.

During the 1950s, Peake found it increasingly difficult to maintain his position as an author and illustrator. On the one hand, his style and sense of humor were increasingly at variance with the spirit of the age, which led to the relative failure of his light-hearted novel, *Mr. Pye*, in 1953, and the complete flop of his verse play, *The Wit to Woo*, staged briefly at the Arts Theatre Club in 1957. On the other hand, his health was declining to the point where he could no longer hold his pen or enunciate his words clearly; whether it was Parkinson's disease or (as a contemporary doctor put it with brutal brevity to Peake's wife, Maeve) 'premature senility', it was to render him unable to work by the early 60s and kill him before the end of the decade.

His publisher encouraged him by commissioning his novella about Titus, "Boy in Darkness", for a volume called *Sometime, Never*, which contained stories by William Golding and John Wyndham. Published in 1956, it later became a successful paperback, winning a Nebula Award, and drawing welcome attention to Peake's work. But that was in the 1960s.

In 1958, Maeve assembled a version of *Titus Alone* from Peake's various manuscript drafts and submitted it for publication. In response to her request for suggestions, the publisher proposed a number of cuts to avoid, in particular, 'the direct allegory of the scientist and his death ray' (letter from Maurice Temple-Smith to Peake, July 29, 1958, printed in 'Editing *Titus Alone*', *Peake Studies*, Vol. 1, No. 4, Summer 1990, p. 20). But Peake was beyond making revisions himself; with a heavy heart, Maeve blindly followed the suggestions. 'I can clearly recall the script coming back to me with what I had intended simply as pointers to the author accepted as if they were the final version of the book, ready for publication' (letter from Maurice Temple-Smith to GPW, printed in *Peake Studies*, 1:4, pp. 26-27).

When the book was published at the end of October 1959, the reviewers' praise was qualified with terms that damned it at the same time, and sales were poor indeed. 'The remarkable thing is that so intensely subjective an experience can be communicated at all. Even when one is confused by the private symbols, one accepts their reality for the author, and re-reading may give one deeper understanding' (John Davenport in *The Observer*, November 1, 1959). 'Mr. Peake must be allowed a monstrous fertility of invention, a genuine feeling for the magnificence of the macabre, but the air of Gormenghast and the surrounding country is difficult to breathe' (*The Times Weekly Review*, November 5, 1959, p. 10). 'Nonetheless, this book is a fine a piece of fine writing—if you can take it—as we are likely to see for a long time' (*Times Literary Supplement*, November 13, 1959). However, a phrase in R.G.G. Price's review in *Punch* (November 18, 1959) pointed the way things were to move: 'Mr. Peake has created a new genre:' he wrote, 'gothic fairy tales without fairies.'

During the last decade of his life, Peake continued to write, but his texts were disconnected and his handwriting almost illegible. From these years two fragments have been salvaged: his attempts at a fourth Titus book, reproduced here (pages 347-352) under Maeve's title, 'Titus Awakes', and the story of Foot-Fruit and his dog, of which three manuscript pages were reproduced in *New Worlds* (No. 187, February 1969), alongside fiction by J.G. Ballard, Thomas Pynchon, John T. Sladek, Norman Spinrad, and D.M. Thomas.

Nineteen sixty can now be seen to be the turning point in the history of Peake's reputation, for that summer appeared the first of Michael Moorcock's articles on Peake, and the first scholarly assessment of his work. Having read the Titus books, and gone to visit their author, Michael Moorcock (then only 21) became Peake's champion, and promoted his work whenever he could in the science fiction magazines that he edited. On the academic front, there was an article in the *Chicago Review* (vol. 14, summer 1960, pp. 74-81): 'The Walls of Gormenghast: an introduction to the novels of Mervyn Peake' by the Scottish poet, translator and university lecturer (later professor) Edwin Morgan. Starting from the position that 'Poetry has to be periodically brought down to earth; the novel has to be periodically lifted off,' he claimed that Peake's work possesses 'a narrative energy and descriptive brilliance not commonly found among more conventional novelists today.' This was followed up, in 1964, by an article in the *Cambridge Review* by Michael Wood, who was the first to compare Peake's work with Kafka's as 'a world which can really be discussed only in its own terms—the reverse of an allegory' (May 23, 1964, pp. 440 & 443).

Then in the mid-60s came the meteoric rise to popularity of Tolkien's three-volume *Lord of the Rings*, and suddenly fantasy literature was back in favor. In 1967, a new American publisher, Weybright & Talley, hoping they had found another instant cult classic, brought out a fine uniform edition of Peake's Titus books, enriched with sketches from the manuscripts, and called it 'the Gormenghast trilogy'. The reception was decidedly mixed, largely because of the explicit comparisons the publishers made with Tolkien—and admirers of the one are not necessarily admirers of the other; in fact, 'they are night and day' (H.A.K. in the Boston *Globe*, November 19, 1967). Stephen J. Laut, S.J., set the tone in *Best Sellers* (November 1, 1967, p. 305) by calling the books 'a quasi-chivalric adventure' in a 'pseudo-medieval setting.' 'Could the whole thing simply be a gigantic put-on?' he wondered, and unearthed all the negative phrases from the American reviews of *Titus Groan*, including his favorite, 'baroque nonsense.' All because 'Peake is no Tolkien, nor a T.H. White, nor even a Malory.' He was echoed by 'a long and very sad groan' from Dick Adler in *Book World*, January 7, 1968 (p. 4), and by: 'maybe it just wasn't our hogshead of tea' from Aurora Gardner Simms (in the *Library Journal*, December 1, 1967, pp. 4434-5), for she found it 'dreadfully long and slow.'

There were, however, more appreciative readers; in a widely syndicated piece, Beverly Friend, a teacher in English at the University of Illinois, Chicago Circle, claimed that 'although [Peake's work] is not completely without flaws—needless scenes and characters—it can stand with the best that has been done in the English language: in theme, in method, and in scope' (*Chicago Daily News*, January 6, 1968). Writing in the *National Observer* (Washington D.C.), Robert Ostermann concluded that the books 'are, in short, a triumph. . . . The trilogy will be read and reread as a treasure by those who so regard *Don Quixote* or *The Divine Comedy*. Reckless comparisons? Not for this eccentric, poetic masterpiece' (December 11, 1967).

A three-volume paperback edition came out from Ballantine on October 28, 1968, less than a month before Peake's death. Compared with the reactions to the hardback edition, the reviews were harsh: *Publishers' Weekly* was 'too overcome by ennui to discover just what this trilogy was to be all about' (September 16, 1968, p. 72), and Robert Armstrong decided that 'anyone who is left on the edge of his chair after finishing a chapter or book has a posture problem' (Minneapolis *Tribune*, October 27, 1968). Yet this edition remained in print throughout the 1970s.

In Britain, the publication of new, illustrated, hardback editions of the Titus books was spaced over several years: while *Titus Groan* (with the introduction by Anthony Burgess printed in this Overlook edition) and *Gormenghast* came out in January and December 1968, *Titus Alone* did not appear until June 1970. They were welcomed with diminishing praise, starting with Paul Green's review in the *New Statesman*: 'Titus Groan . . . is a magnificent exception to any literary pigeon-holing . . . Underneath the superficially farcical and grotesque aspects of the novel there is a pagan grandeur and sense of desolation which is as meaningful as any allegorical or sociological interpretation' (January 26, 1968, pp. 114-15). And on the same day, Henry Tube ended his long review in the *Spectator* with the conclusion that we must see Peake, the writer and illustrator, 'not as a man with two talents, but as a genius with two nibs' (pp. 105-6). On February 15, Hilary Spurling devoted much of her 850-word review in the *Financial Times* to an extended comparison with Kafka: 'what is interesting is that Peake and Kafka use such similar, often identical, means for exactly opposite ends.'

Without the help of an Introduction by Burgess, *Gormenghast* met with more tepid praise, along with some frankly hostile comments, like Oswald Blakeston's outburst in *Books & Bookmen*: 'I can't see any real reason for critics to inflate this whole castle which is already too big for its boots' (February 1969, p. 14). Even R.G.G. Price found himself tempering his previous judgements: 'The trilogy is a freak, though a brilliant one, not a great novel. . . . On the other hand, it is more than a somber *jeu d'esprit*' (*Punch*, January 1, 1969).

The second British edition of *Titus Alone* introduced a new version of the text put together by Langdon Jones. He reinstated passages from the manuscripts that had been dropped from the first edition; they 'principally affect Chapters 24 (an entirely new episode), 77, 89, and from Chapters 99 to the end where the original published text has been considerably built up' (from the 'Publisher's Note' at the beginning of the edition). Some scholars are critical of Langdon Jones's work—see, in particular, Tanya Gardiner-Scott's book, *Mervyn Peake: the evolution of a dark romantic* (New York: Peter Lang, 1989), chapter III—but 'any attempt to reconstruct Mervyn Peake's original text of *Titus Alone* must fail because there never was such a thing' (Maurice Temple-Smith in *Peake Studies*, 1:4, p. 27).

Simultaneous with the hardback editions, paperback editions were brought out in Britain by Penguin in their series of Modern Classics and, despite the absence of really favorable reviews, they have fulfilled Elizabeth Bowen's hopes by remaining available in

Britain in paperback ever since. The only change came with the
King Penguin (U.K.) editions of 1980-81, for which I provided
limited corrections (see 'Editing Peake' in *The Mervyn Peake Review*, No. 13, Autumn 1981, pp. 2-7); all subsequent editions,
including this one from Overlook, follow these amended texts.
And I should point out that this edition of *Titus Alone* is the first
independent appearance in the United States of the text revised by
Langdon Jones. It also appeared in Overlook's omnibus edition of
the Titus books in July 1988.

Within two years of Peake's death, his Titus books were all in
print, in Britain and America, in both hardback and paperback,
and his widow, Maeve Gilmore, had published her moving memoir, *A World Away*. Then there was a major exhibition of his work
at the National Book League, London, in January 1972. The
world began to take notice; more thoughtful articles started to
appear, ranging from an appreciation of the man and his work by
Marcus Crouch in *The Junior Bookshelf* (December 1968, pp. 346-49)
to scholarly studies like 'Gids voor Gormenghast' by Professor
Herman Servotte of the Catholic University of Louvain, Belgium
(in *Dietsche Warand en Belfort*, no. 116, 1971, Englished as 'Guide
for Gormenghast' in *The Mervyn Peake Review*, No. 3, Autumn
1976, pp. 5-9). This was followed by Hugh Brogan's sensitive
assessment of his work, 'The Gutters of Gormenghast', in the
Cambridge Review in 1973, by John Batchelor's 'biographical and
critical exploration' in 1974 and, in 1976, by John Watney's
official biography. Thus Peake's reputation became more firmly
established and, by the end of the decade, reference works were at
last including Peake among the significant writers and illustrators
of the post-war period.

In 1975 an international Mervyn Peake Society was founded,
based in England and issuing *The Mervyn Peake Review*. For ten
years, the *MPR* provided a forum for discussion and critical
debate of Peake's work, and several of the articles reprinted here
first appeared in its pages. Since 1988, this need has been answered
by an independent periodical, *Peake Studies*, which appears twice a
year.

The essays reprinted on the following pages approach the Titus
books from several angles. First I have chosen a personal glimpse
of Mervyn Peake by Louise Collis, daughter of Maurice Collis.
Then come three general articles on Peake and his work, beginning with the piece by Hugh Brogan already mentioned above,
which places Peake among the neo-Romantics of the 1940s and
suggests that his 'word-pictures' enabled him to write what he
could not paint. Both Hugh Brogan and Ronald Binns (whose

essay comes next) point to Peake's affinity with *Treasure Island*, an adventure story that he knew almost by heart and that he illustrated at the height of his career. Binns goes further than Brogan in situating Peake as a poet in relation to his time and, as a novelist, to romance. The most notable essay to date is by Joseph Sanders, whose elevated debate of Peake's work argues that *Titus Groan* and *Gormenghast* 'contain a richness of detail, a grasp of psychology, and a depth of human concern that mark a great work,' while *Titus Alone* remains flawed because uncompleted. Yet the overall opus constitutes a 'successfully humanistic conception of contemporary man.'

The next group of articles (also printed in chronological order) analyses themes and aspects of *Titus Groan* and *Gormenghast*. We begin with Cristiano Rafanelli on Titus and the Thing; Bruce Hunt on *Titus Groan* and *Gormenghast* as *Bildungsroman*, and Margaret Ochocki on them as fairytale. My own essay makes use of the manuscripts to discuss how Peake handles the relationship between Fuchsia and Steerpike, and in a previously unpublished article Ann Yeoman approaches Steerpike from a Jungian standpoint.

Finally I have chosen three articles devoted to *Titus Alone*, as the most problematic of Peake's novels. Colin Greenland's and Laurence Bristow-Smith's articles, written and published simultaneously, neatly counterpoint each other. Tanya Gardiner-Scott's essay is a first attempt to approach Peake from the point of view of gender studies.

In the articles, page references to the present Overlook edition have been added *in italics*; the editions for reference and their abbreviated titles are:

WORKS BY PEAKE

G   *Gormenghast*, second English edition, London: Eyre & Spottiswoode, 1968, and Penguin, 1969. Articles subsequent to 1982 refer to the corrected King Penguin edition (1982), the Overlook hardback edition (1982), the Methuen (1985) and Mandarin (1989) paperback editions, which all have the the the same pagination.

PP   *Peake's Progress*, edited by Maeve Gilmore. London: Allen Lane, 1978; New York: Overlook Press, 1981. There is a corrected edition of this volume (Penguin U.K., 1981).

TA   *Titus Alone*, second, revised, English edition, London: Eyre & Spottiswoode, 1970, and Penguin 1970. Articles subsequent to 1981 refer to the corrected King Penguin edition (1981), the Overlook hardback edition (1982), the Methuen (1985) and Mandarin (1989) paperback editions, which all have the the same pagination.

TG *Titus Groan*, second English edition, London: Eyre & Spottiswoode, 1968, and Penguin, 1968. Articles subsequent to 1981 refer to the corrected King Penguin edition (1981), the Overlook hardback edition (1982), the Methuen (1985) and Mandarin (1989) paperback editions, which all have the the same pagination.

OTHER WORKS

BATCHELOR   *Mervyn Peake: a biographical and critical exploration* by John Batchelor. London: Duckworth, 1974 (paperback 1977).

GILMORE   *A World Away: a memoir of Mervyn Peake* by Maeve Gilmore. London: Gollancz, 1970.

MANLOVE   *Modern Fantasy: five studies* by C. N. Manlove. Cambridge: Cambridge University Press, 1975 (paperback 1978).

WATNEY   *Mervyn Peake* by John Watney. London: Michael Joseph, 1976.

MEMORIES OF MERVYN PEAKE

Louise Collis

THERE can be few more tragic histories in twentieth-century literature and art than that of Mervyn Peake. Superbly gifted as a
novelist, poet, draughtsman, painter; handsome, exuberant, magnetically charming, he was, in his middle age, reduced to a
dribbling idiot by a virulent form of Parkinsonianism.

* * * * *

I first met him in the summer of 1942. My father, Maurice
Collis, had seen some of his work at various exhibitions and had
written enthusiastically about it, especially his line drawings which
were so accomplished and utterly unlike anyone else's in their
humor, their poetic fantasy and, on occasion, their sinister shades.
He liked Mervyn personally and believed that he would have a
brilliant future.

One summer day he appeared at our address. Although in
every way polite, courteous, agreeable, he struck one immediately
as a wild, free spirit, utterly untameable. He was very handsome:
quite tall, thin, with black hair, a large intellectual forehead, a
pronounced nose, eyes rather sunken and of a peculiarly deep
and resonant blue. Above all, his entire person was imbued with
an urgent vitality.

During the afternoon, we went boating. As we rowed lazily
through the fields and woods, he recounted the plot and
ramifications—these were not fully worked out—of *Titus Groan*.
He spoke eloquently, with great animation, summoning up on the
greenish water of the Thames the towers and battlements, the
secret rooms and passages, the ghostly and monstrous inhabitants
of the castle of his imagination, Gormenghast. One saw it as
clearly as a mirage.

Maurice and Mervyn became fast friends after this. They had
much in common: a great sense of the ridiculous, for one thing;
and a healthy disrespect for authority for another. They often
met at a Chelsea café, or pub, depending on the time of day.
Once, as they were proceeding jovially down the King's Road, a
sudden gust of wind snatched a handful of manuscript poems

from Mervyn's grasp and scattered them over the traffic. They raised an outcry and everyone in the vicinity chased the dancing sheets amongst the cars and buses. All were safely restored to the author, who was enabled to continue reading:

> The paper is breathless
> Under the hand
> And the pencil is poised
> Like a warlock's wand.

'The poet cries his ghostly manifesto upon the world,' he added, wiping the paper, 'and who cares when the wind lets it drop in the dirt?' It was an extravagant day.

Besides his poems, Mervyn was now (the late forties) engaged on his second novel, *Gormenghast*. He had illustrated a number of books, mostly for children, and made hundreds of other drawings. In fact, he could never stop drawing. All his manuscripts were fully illustrated, although the publishers refused to include them, on the grounds of expense. His most casual letters, and even those addressed to bank managers, were embellished. These multitudinous activities had also to be combined with a certain minimum of teaching, sufficient to keep the family finances tottering from month to month. While fully appreciated by persons whose opinion was well worth having, as the reviews showed, his works brought in a miserable amount of hard cash.

In the early fifties, he was living sparsely in Wallington in south London, a most depressing neighborhood, unless one should happen to be a missionary.... Mervyn looked strained and tired. He was finishing his third novel, *Mr. Pye*, of which he had financial hopes, subsequently dashed. He was also in continual negotiation about a play, *The Wit To Woo*. Several famous people in the theatrical world nibbled at it, off and on, regularly raising and dashing his expectations: for weeks he would be convinced that his fortune was made and all his troubles and anxieties evaporated in a cloud of euphoria; then the great ones turned their attention in another direction. He wrote and rewrote the text. This went on for years. Finally in 1957, it was produced at the Arts Theater. The first night audience consisting mainly of friends, applauded generously, though with private reservations. Mervyn, however, suspected nothing. The next morning, he bought all the papers and settled down in Sloane Square for an enjoyable read. The reviews were savage. Everything went black before his eyes. He staggered home. He collapsed.

It now became apparent that something very bad was happening to him. For quite a while, he had been subject to passing tremors in his hands which interrupted his drawing and shook his writing. Strange fits of restlessness made him wander about aimlessly. He found it difficult to concentrate at times, as his later writing demonstrated: the vitality had gone out of it. These symptoms could no longer be put down to the effects of overwork and nervous strain on a highly excitable temperament. He had an operation that stopped the tremors, but nothing could save his mind. This brilliant intellect began steadily crumbling into imbecility. The day came when his lectures at the art college were so incoherent that he could not be kept on. He struggled to write, but it was all gibberish. He still drew in a shaky manner, often isolated figures in dunce's caps.

An exhibition of his drawings was arranged at a gallery in Portobello Road in 1963. The private view was full of artists and writers, for everyone had known and liked him in happier times. Sales were quite encouraging. He was very dim by now, bent, shrunken, pale, half conscious. Although he did not fully know who he was, or where he was, he shuffled about with a faint smile, as if he had a vague idea that the party was connected with himself in some complimentary way. He indicated a desire for drinks and cigarettes which were given to him and rescued as they fell from his hands. He whispered odd remarks.

I last saw him in 1966. Having become too difficult for his wife to manage at home—he required supervision twenty-four hours a day—he was in a psychiatric hospital. They brought him out to us in the garden, a total ruin of a man. Yet, as he stumbled to a bench and sat down, he still had the remains of his old charm, less magnetic, but poignant and moving to an unbearable degree. His voice was scarcely audible, but he somehow gave us to understand that while he could not talk, he would like us to converse and he would listen. So we spoke lightly of this and that, touching on his works and on mutual friends. He smiled occasionally, as if from a long way off. Then he got to his feet and it seemed he wished to show us the rest of the garden which was large and rather wooded. He took my arm and we progressed slowly towards the furthest clump of trees. He did not want to turn back to the hospital building, murmuring, 'On a little, on', whenever we stopped. But time came to an end. Two male nurses appeared. As they led him off, he turned and raised his hand in a feeble salute and said, quite distinctly, 'See you again soon'. The whole of his torment was in that last yearning look he gave us. Eighteen months later he was dead, aged 57.

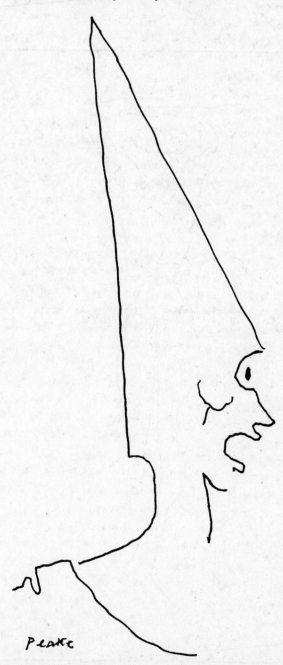

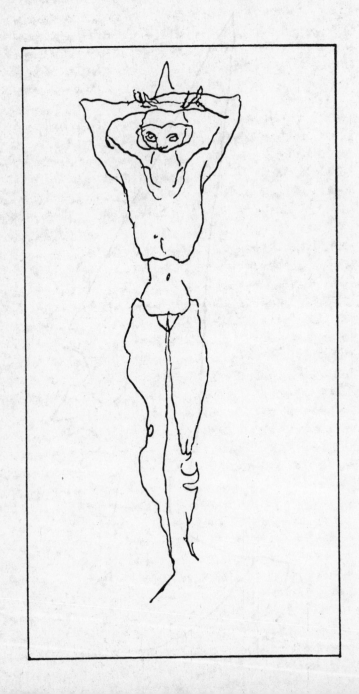

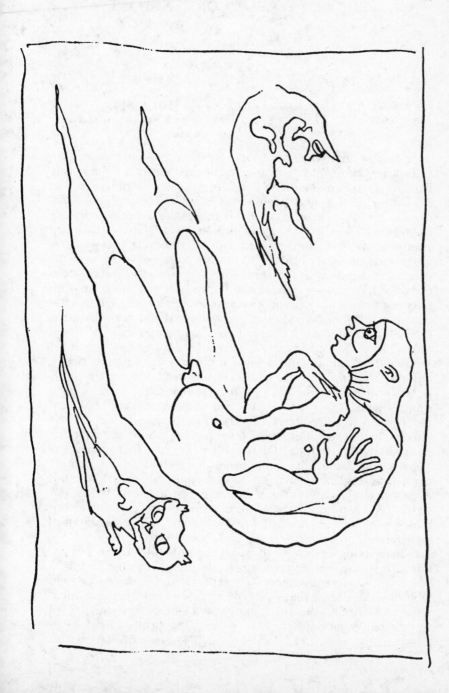

THE GUTTERS OF GORMENGHAST

Hugh Brogan

How I used to toy with that Tiger Life
—OSCAR WILDE

THE first edition of *Titus Groan* (1946) carried the words 'In Complete Conformity with the Authorized Economy Standards' like a triumphant banner. The author and the designer thus hurled a challenge at a mean, defeatist world—'see what, in spite of you, we have done.' Eyre & Spottiswoode, experienced Bible publishers, and the Glaswegian printers, Maclehose & Co., had risen spendidly to the first demands of the great fantasy. How gorgeously the heavy black print fills the page; how ceaselessly the elegant decorations at the beginning and end of chapters—even the page numerals—reinforce the impression that this is no ordinary book. Still, after twenty-five years, it retains a special smell— one that will, for anybody that remembers them, bring back the forties as nothing else can, for it was a common smell of books then. The artist-author was congratulated by Matthew Smith for sending Titus into the world without pictures (see Gilmore, p. 65), but the master illustrator's hand made itself felt on the dust-jacket, and in the tiny drawing on the title-page: variants on a single theme, the two designs both show a sad and evil bird perched on a stone image of the iron crown and chain of the Groans, in a grey wilderness of cross-hatching. Slim and light, for all its four hundred and thirty-eight pages, the first edition sits easy in one hand. By comparison the second edition (1968), printed in England, nearly a hundred pages fatter, is coarse and commonplace, in spite of the drawings rescued from the manuscript. Its forerunner remains unique (for a cool reception meant that, typographically, even the first edition of *Gormenghast* had to be a retreat, and the first *Titus Alone* was mediocre).

It may seem perverse to insist on the physical form of a book, but in this case it is only fitting. In the first place, the look of a new work can greatly affect its reception, and it was in its rich, biblical-sinister guise that *Titus Groan* made its unforgettable initial impact. Secondly, the ostentatious mock-humble obedience to 'authorized economy standards' places *Titus* firmly where it belongs: in the war-ruined forties. It is a joyous exploitation and

defiance of a dangerous world, like the contemporaneous paintings of Graham Sutherland, John Piper, Keith Vaughan, and the
rest of Mervyn Peake's generation. They all flouted economy
standards in the books they conceived and illustrated in what we
now label a 'neo-romantic' vein. It was a phase of English painting, rather than a school, and most of its surviving exponents have
left it behind; but Peake, in part because of his early illness and
death, can be almost wholly identified with it. His Belsen drawings
have a place alongside Henry Moore's 'Underground in Wartime'
series. What sets him apart is the fact that his chief monument is a
work of prose fiction. What unites him with his peers is the
nervous, frightening, elegant line which he and they had at
command. What identified him with neo-romanticism was his
profound instinct to seek an escape from our oppressive existence
of news and bills to a place where he could pour out his work
unimpeded—an actual place, such as Sark; a place of the mind,
such as Gormenghast. The interpretation of *Titus* requires equally
that we never lose our sense of Peake as a draughtsman, and as a
child of his time.[1]

It was not a time which readily accepted him. From one point of
view, the sad story of his life (so movingly set down by his widow
in *A World Away*) is the painful record of an endless struggle
between an exceptionally gifted and sensitive man and a world to
which he could give much, but which wanted from him little or
nothing. In spite of the enthusiasm of Graham Greene, John
Betjeman and others, *Titus Groan* went into only two impressions
in its author's lifetime. His other books were either remaindered
or forgotten, until, by word of mouth, his reputation began to
spread out from the faithful few. Even the great sets of illustrations did not earn him a good living, or win him the fame he
deserved. And he had the defects of his qualities. The very intensity
and intelligence of his inner life meant that he was often as
helpless as a child when the outer world had to be mastered. Life
can be a great joy to such men, but it is never easy (one thinks of
Mozart). And it dealt Peake crushing blows. In the second World
War his unimaginative country tried to make a private soldier of
him, but succeeded only in bringing on a nervous breakdown.
Peace was only a respite: within ten years he was struggling
heroically but in vain against the form of Parkinson's disease
which first silenced and then killed him, not before he had had to
endure damnable suffering at the hands of the doctors, and watch
the slow destruction of his powers.

His art, then, and especially the triple fantasy of the Titus books
can easily be seen simply as a romantic protest against the condi-

tions of his primary world. But this is probably a mistake, at least as far as *Titus Groan* and *Gormenghast* are concerned (*Titus Alone* is evidently a special case).[2] The hostile pressure of circumstances forced on the work of creation: *Titus Groan* was begun as a distraction from the miseries of basic training in the Gunners. It was, perhaps, a substitute for the drawings that Peake would have produced had the authorities been sensible enough to take Augustus John's advice and appoint him an Official War Artist. It quickly became more important to its author than anything else that was happening to him. Yet no one reading it is likely to feel that it owes its existence, in any but this accidental sense, to escapism. It is far too unsentimental, funny, urbane and cruel. It teems with wit and fancy. It is ebullient expression of a superbly brave and healthy spirit, one that could trifle gaily with madness, loneliness and obsession. Mervyn Peake, one feels, must have created anyway, and circumstances only explain why he created this particular thing at that particular time—rather as the war explains what Henry Moore and his subjects were doing in the Underground. In Peake's case the war explains, at any rate in part, why he was writing a novel, instead of the excellent poems that had previously satisfied him. It does not explain the idiosyncrasies of his talent.

For instance, the leisured pace of the Titus books can seem unendurable. Yet the author knew just what he was about. If even the murderous duel between Swelter and Flay is presented in slow motion, it is because he was ready to sacrifice many conventional virtues to achieve his unique purpose. In 1946 or thereabouts he jotted down the following points:

1) No initial conception of plot.
2) The characters 'took their way'.
3) On the qui vive which writing for opportunities for the imagination to take its own course—as long as that course didn't hurt the mood of the book.
4) Hard to make the characters talk on the same scale that they look.
5) The scale of the book—its slow pace—& its fantasy give me the chance to say practically anything, or make the characters *do* practically anything—a kind of pantechnicum.
6) A third was cut out. Typed five times—each copy blackened.[3]

This means, I take it, that his prime intention was what any reader is likely to have supposed. He wanted above all to create a secondary world in which his volcanic fancy could have complete freedom. Imagination was to take its own course; every tendril was to be allowed to uncoil, 'as long as that course didn't hurt the mood of the book.' And if the resulting rich, slow chronicle is, for some, sometimes difficult to read, it is no more so than the works of Proust, Joyce (a city, where Peake is a castle) or Flann O'Brien, the almost exact contemporary (1911-1966) who is the only writer (in his *Third Policeman*) that Mervyn Peake at all resembles. Like these other moderns, Peake exacts his own sort of attention from his readers. He knows that the easy is often the enemy of the excellent.

But neither the pressure of circumstances nor the common wish to create a realm where his fantasy was sovereign explain why his imagination made the particular demands that it did. Tolkien (to name the obvious parallel) equally created a world of his own, yet to say that is only to point to the vast gulf between Gormenghast and Middle-earth. The air is different on each side. Still, there is one important likeness, which hints perhaps at the true roots of great fantasy.

Tolkien, everyone knows, invented a language and then a world to explain and enrich it. Obviously he could not have done either successfully had he not been extraordinarily gifted, both as a philologist and as a teller of tales. Similarly, Peake was a writer born, but the fact that he was a painter too gives his writing its unique quality. Middle-earth was created to assist philology; Gormenghast to help an artist.

He had visions that could not be expressed fully, anything like fully, by his drawing, brilliant and passionately individual though it was. The visions needed to be expressed with a fullness and a visual precision that could only with great difficulty be combined. Film could be no use, for it entails its own conventions, above all the photographic ones (this must be said, however trite) which are death to the artist accustomed to controlling by his own style the representation of reality: a chair painted by Van Gogh looks as unlike a photograph as it does a chair by Cézanne. And no series of drawings, however brilliant and numerous, could convey the thought and action that the artist craved. Words were the only answer. For only in prose could such a vision as the tormented battlements of Gormenghast be realized in all its complexity of mood, morals and aspect; only through prose could the artist create a world that was exactly his, to be apprehended and accepted as we accept the vision in a painting—say, a painting by the elder Breughel.

But if words were as much his tools as pen and pencil, his eyes were the supreme instrument. For instance:

On August days Fuchsia from her window in the attic could see him far below standing at times upon a short ladder, and sometimes when the boughs were low enough, upon the grass, his long body and little legs foreshortened and his cowl over his fine head hiding his features; and diminutive as he appeared from that immense height, she could make out that he was polishing the apples into mirror-like gloss as they hung from the boughs, bending forward to breathe upon them and then with silk cloth rubbing them until she could see the glint upon their crimson skins—even from the height of her eyrie in the shadowy loft.

(*TG*, p. 100, 76)

This is indeed like a direction for a shot in a film script, but no film could direct our attention so firmly to the details the artist wants us to notice—the foreshortening, the immense distance of air between Fuchsia and the gardener, the cloth of silk, the glint on the apples; and although the scene could be made into a drawing or painting as it stands, still it would only be one such. *Titus Groan* contains thousands, possibly tens of thousands, of pictures. The labour of drawing them all would be unthinkable, when words can convey them so precisely, so economically; and no drawing could enable us to see through Fuchsia's eyes, or achieve similar effects. No, at the time that he started *Titus*, words were Peake's richest visual medium. Literally, he painted with them. We must look at his book as at a painting—realize that it freshly is what the tired old cliché, 'a word-picture', means.

It is, by any standards, an exceedingly odd picture, however brilliant the handling. In the centre of the canvas stands the castle, Gormenghast—as enormous, we gather, as Versailles combined with the Louvre, the Escorial and Windsor, then doubled or trebled. No one can know it all. A vast grey maze of towers, roofs, walls, walks, yards and gardens, its inhabitants, though numerous, are too few to inhabit more than a portion of its extraordinary chaos. It is unutterably ancient—seventy-six generations old. The castle-dwellers make sense of this waste of space and time by obeying the ritual that has grown up over the millennia; a ritual in itself irksome and meaningless, but providing, in the absence of law and religion, a framework giving security, dignity and purpose to life. The castle is really ruled by the Master of Ritual, for the nominal chief, the Earl of Groan, in the name of whose glory all must be done, is in fact the ritual's chief executant, and thus the chief victim of its ridiculous demands, which are laid before him by the Master—such things as ascending and descending the Tower of Flints three times by the stone staircase, 'leaving on each occasion a glass of wine on a box of wormwood placed there for the purpose on a blue turret.' Gormenghast is not merely the castle, it is an idol, a way of life, and the Masters of Ritual inexorably exact from the Earls, as from all lesser inhabitants, slavish compliance with the necessities of maintaining Gormenghast in being for ever.

But Gormenghast is still also a castle, full of strange corners for the word-painter, and stranger inhabitants—Rottcodd, guardian of the Hall of the Bright Carvings, Swelter, the evil chef who rules over the great kitchens, Pentecost the gardener, already described, Cora and Clarice, Earl Sepulchrave's idiot sisters, who take their breakfast at a table placed on the gigantic horizontal trunk of a dread tree stretching from its roots within the castle wall hundreds of feet along and above thin air. Peake commands the infinite leisure he needs: time is space, and he fills in every corner. Beyond the vast outer wall he shows us the mud huts of the outsiders, the great jarl-forest and, behind and above all, Gormenghast Mountain. Across its huge shoulder we can just catch a glimpse of distance, and then we reach the picture-frame.... It took the artist two large volumes to fill the canvas that the frame encloses.

The picture itself is, in turn, only a frame, or a stage, for the actions of the characters, which are, as the notes quoted above indicate, the center of Peake's imaginative, as distinct from his technical, concern and inspiration. I must turn to the meaning of their drama; but first it is worth making a few other points about the place of this technical experiment in Peake's entire *oeuvre*.

Maeve Gilmore remarks: 'above all things that he did he wished to be a painter, and I think it was perhaps the medium in which he was least sure' (Gilmore, p. 64). Her judgement must be right, yet it suggests a problem: why did Peake, sure in everything else, falter in this? An answer may perhaps be hazarded in the light of two manifestos which Maeve Gilmore quotes elsewhere. In 1949 he wrote:

This is the problem of the artist—to discover his language. It is a life-long search, for when the idiom is found it has then to be developed and sharpened. But worse than no style is a mannerism—a formula for producing *effects*, the fruit of suicide.[4]

Mervyn Peake, I suggest, never abandoned, but never solved (except possibly towards the end of his career) his problem of language as a painter, and it was an early stage of his quest which tumbled Gormenghast out of him. Only a painter could have conceived it or carried it out, in words or any other medium; but though the Titus books gave vent to his second talent, they were not the answer to his difficulty—they were almost an evasion of it.

Perhaps the trouble was that we must have something to say before we can master any language, and Peake for long found nothing suitable to say in paint. Maeve Gilmore tells us 'he had a habit of painting over his canvases so that any which were not sold were completely metamorphosized (sic), and the shapes beneath became the shapes to dominate the new painting' (Gilmore, p. 64). This is scarcely the way masterpieces are achieved, and Gormenghast could not serve as a safety-valve for ever. But there is reason to think that by the early fifties he had found his way forward. He writes to his wife from Ireland,

To canalize my chaos. To pour it out through the gutters of Gormenghast. To make not only tremendous stories in paint that approximate to the visual images in Gormenghast, but to create arabesques, abstracts, of thrilling colour, worlds on their own, landscapes and roofscapes and skyscrapes [sic] peopled with hierophants and lords—the fantastic and the grotesque, and to use paint as though it were meat and drink.

To restore to painting the giant groupings of the old masters— Tintoretto, Goya, Velasquez.

To make studies and cartoons for each canvas. To find myself by ploughing headlong into a genre, and by so doing to evolve a way of painting ANYTHING, from an angel to an apple.

To incorporate within the canvases, that in themselves would be masterly and original, still lifes, or boys or buildings, and skies based on perception.   (Gilmore, p. 107)

Still the same reaching out for freedom. This manifesto is one of those memoranda that we often make in an attempt to clarify the first gropings of an idea to ourselves; no doubt it contains some wishful thinking, some problems unresolved. It seems to confirm that the first two Titus books were written in a rush of inspiration, and that only afterwards did their author begin to ask himself what he had been doing, and why. More important, it shows that his gift was still moving forward, and suggests what he had learned about it from the years in his castle. It is deeply deplorable that this development, like all others, was cut off by his illness.

The resort to literary fantasy, then, must be seen, in Peake's case, as at least in part an attempt to resolve certain creative problems arising from the nature of his talent, and as such it is of great interest. Any lover of the Titus books, however, would protest at a suggestion that that was all. To complete the sketch of their significance, I must turn from questions of form to questions of content.

An antithetical pattern instantly becomes obvious. Against the

Reprinted with permission from *Cambridge Review*, November 23, 1973, Vol. 95, No. 2217, pp. 38-42.
For the illustration that should face one of the pages of this article:
From *Treasure Island* (1949), p. [89].

inert mass of the mouldering castle, Peake sets an ant-hill of characters moving. Against the iron rule of ritual he raises up rebellion. He counters the static, pictorial presentation with a rapid melodramatic narrative: in *Titus Groan* are five deaths by violence, in *Gormenghast* six (if we count poor Fuchsia's drowning, and overlook the minor victims of Steerpike). Partly it is a matter of artistic necessity: the books would be intolerable if nothing ever happened. Chiefly the abundance of farcical, violent or eerie incident arises because of the artist's vision. As we have seen, he wanted 'a kind of pantechnicon' in which to set his imagination and his characters free—him to say, them to do 'practically anything'. The result was his gallery of grotesque, horrifying, oddly touching, and occasionally beautiful, human creations, and the tumult of their actions.

They fall into two antithetical groups. One comprises the bulk of the population of Gormenghast (and, in *Titus Alone*, the far world beyond the castle). The other group consists of two only, Steerpike and Titus; or rather, of one, for in essence they are single: the solitary boy, carving out his destiny for himself; the great rebel against Gormenghast. It matters little, for a critic's purpose, that they are enemies; Steerpike is brilliant and malevolent, while Titus is ordinary in everything except the intensity of his revolt. Both express symbolically the author's deepest attitudes.

The figure of the boy alone haunted Mervyn Peake. He knew *Treasure Island* by heart, and, as the illustration on the facing page shows, could exploit its situations to feed his private myth. Is the boy shown Titus or Jim Hawkins? That the myth is independent of the myth of Gormenghast is proved by *Titus Alone*, by the terrifying novella *Boy in Darkness*, and above all by the projected *Titus 4*, which was to take the former Earl among 'Snows Mountains Islands Rivers Archipelagos Forests Lagoons' 'Pirates Mermaids Dreamers Decadents Athletes Invalids Blood-Sportsmen' (Gilmore, p. 106) *et cetera* in what would apparently have been a sustained *critique* of modern life. It is even possible to guess that the myth had something to do with Peake's achievement as illustrator of the *Ancient Mariner* and *Alice*, for both Carroll and Coleridge show us a soul at odds with a bafflingly alien world. It is true that Mervyn Peake himself was as unlike Alice as he was unlike Steerpike or turbulent Titus; but his instinct as man and writer was, like theirs, to question, to venture on, to break with the past and try always something new—which is, according to W. H. Auden (in *Forwords and Afterwords* (London, 1973), pp. 433-4), the mark of a major artist. And yet, like Alice, Titus and the Ancient Mariner, there was a part of him which, lonely, longed for home.

It was the weaker, secondary side of his nature, no doubt; but he could never have created the agony of Titus, exile and traitor, without it, or got his readers' sympathy.

For a writer's obsessions, if he is to succeed in interesting his public, must be of general appeal; and it is clear that Peake's myth of the lonely boy can touch us all. From one point of view it is the latest realization of the romantic myth of the artist, and thus Peake's vista of his own taste, as is suggested by his words,

With the wealth, skill, daring, vision of many centuries at one's back, yet one is ultimately quite alone. For it is one's ambition to create one's *own* world in a style germane to its substance, and to people it with its native forms and denizens that never were before, yet have their roots in one's experience.

(*Drawings* 1949, p. 11)

It is almost an allegory of that process of growing up and moving on that we call maturity. It can be seen as a passionate protest against that stubborn despair which every sensitive person must from time to time have detected at the root of things. It suggests another myth. Gormenghast is not the only castle in English literature—the most important play in the language inhabits one.

How much *Hamlet* owes to its setting is best demonstrated by the small shock of disappointment that an Englishman must suffer when first he sees the actual Elsinore. That agreeable palace, smiling on the flat shore of a flat sea, cannot, even in winter, be the haunted hold that Shakespeare writes of. No other of his plays exploits the unity of place so thoroughly. To Prospero, no doubt, his island is a prison, but it is a much more agreeable one than Denmark. And *Hamlet* offers no escape, unlike *The Tempest*. A full ship's complement sails for Naples, while all who leave Elsinore only do so to return, and the spectator never gets farther than a furlong or two from its walls, when burying Ophelia. Shakespeare no doubt planned this claustrophobic effect.

The likeness to the themes of Gormenghast is striking: castle as prison—murders—madness—revenge—above all, the alienated heir. The comparison points up an important difference. Hamlet is one of the greatest creations in literature because his personality is fascinating, and is fully set out. Titus is a shadow by his side. Yet Hamlet too owes much of his power to the fact that the embodiment of his problem, the rotten state, the prison, the evil with which he struggles, is the sinister, mysterious castle. Even his human adversaries are, like himself, sentenced for ever to Elsinore. No wonder they turn and rend each other.

The same holds true of Gormenghast. It accounts, if not for Peake's inspiration, at any rate for part of our response. But there is at least one other crucial difference. Unlike Elsinore, the castle of Gormenghast is a symbol and a world into which the maker poured, as its very matter, all his power, all his intelligence, all his rejoicing in life. It was a creation of love, and when Titus rejects it (as he does at every instant from the age of two) he seems to be rejecting love—all that goes with the ideas of family, friends, home, and country. He is also rejecting the emblem of Peake's achievements in art, and through it, perhaps, all art. We feel, in Titus's wrath, his creator's determination to break new ground, to go on. Consequently the Titus books as we have them depict a real drama, a clash of two rights; art brings the clash distressingly alive, not least by showing Titus himself as torn between their claims. Then, at the very end of *Titus Alone*, we are told that

What a boy had set out to seek a man had found, found by the act of living.

There he stood: Titus Groan, and he turned upon his heel so that the great boulder was never seen by him ever again. Nor was the cave: nor was the castle that lay beyond...

This is the moment to which the books have inexorably tended; it is a moment that must pain every reader, for it is a moment of real choice; and readers will always decide for themselves whether Titus did right or not. Many, arguing that Titus is repudiating, not just the outgrown childhood from which he first fled, but a place and people that have legitimate claims on him, will say he was wrong; others, remembering how essentially Gormenghast is a dead hand, will say he was right. Either way, we must examine our motives.

And thus, at the very end of his work, Mervyn Peake forces us to know ourselves. Fantasy comes full circle, and what may have begun for artist and public alike as a high-spirited escapade brings them at last face to face with one near and cruel aspect of the reality of all our lives.

Notes

1 The occasional over-ripeness of his prose, for example the opening page of *Gormenghast*, is the one 'period' element in his work: it reminds me of the habitual overstatement of some of the

neo-romantic artists and is very much the sort of language they used when commenting on their work.

2 So much so that it requires an article to itself; it stands appreciably apart from the Gormenghast books in several respects, though it is a legitimate sequel to them, and indeed necessary to their completion.

3 Printed here by permission of Maeve Gilmore, whose kindness to me over the preparation of this essay has been invaluable. I have scrupulously reproduced Mervyn Peake's slips of the pen, though in point 3 'which' ought surely to be 'when'.

4 *Drawings by Mervyn Peake* (London: Grey Walls Press, 1949), p. 10. Hereafter cited as *Drawings* 1949.

SITUATING GORMENGHAST

Ronald Binns

I

MERVYN PEAKE's fiction never achieved best-seller status in his own lifetime, and yet since his death in 1968 the three novels which comprise his Gormenghast trilogy—*Titus Groan* (1946), *Gormenghast* (1950), and *Titus Alone* (1959)—have become massively popular, triggering a Peake revival. His poetry, his books for children, his one other novel, *Mr. Pye* (1953), and his paintings and drawings, have been recovered from obscurity and marketed by publishers keen to cash in on his current popularity.

A creatively restless man, Peake's central achievement remains the trilogy; without it he would probably only be half-remembered as a minor poet of the forties, or as a brilliant book illustrator. Despite the popularity of his work, however, Peake's trilogy has attracted little academic recognition. It belongs to no obvious tradition, lacks an ordered structure, is occasionally careless in detail, and breaks in two after the second volume, at the point where Titus Groan abandons Gormenghast for a picaresque journey through a quite different, more futuristic world. Peake's language is narcotically rich, spilling over with adjectives, sometimes to the point of self-indulgence. The springboard of his imagination is his talent for bizarre characterization, but the plotting which binds his strange creatures together against the vast static tableau landscapes (loosely called Gothic, but only tenuously deriving from the traditional Gothic novel) appears largely haphazard, unmoving in any exploration of psychological or moral dilemma. Gormenghast remains truly *sui generis*, yet oddly English, both in its characterization (which clearly owes a great deal to Dickens) and in the nature of the sluggish, unchanging aristocratic castle society it portrays (though there is no specific attempt at allegory).

An important part of Peake's productivity went into creating for children (*Captain Slaughterboard Drops Anchor, Letters From a Lost Uncle, A Book of Nonsense*), and the Gormenghast trilogy is powerfully charged for adolescent readers. Titus Groan is only twenty when the third volume ends, and in its own way the trilogy forms a *Bildungsroman*, reworking in a heightened form of pure myth the ordeals of a youth endeavoring to break free from the grip of his family. It's also significant that Peake really only achieved substantial popularity towards the end of the sixties, at a time much more disposed to works of fantasy, and when various cultural myths of innocence and anti-rationalism were predominant.

Leslie Fiedler, pointing to the division between fiction as entertainment and fiction as high art invoked by Henry James, has argued that perhaps Stevenson's 'A humble remonstrance' to James's 'The art of fiction' was right after all, 'having reached a time when *Treasure Island* seems somehow more to the point and the heart's delight than, say, *The Princess Casamassima*'.[1] The problem with the argument that fiction should shed the weighty moral imperatives of the social novel and delight instead in fabulation and fun is that as literature becomes divorced from social experience it increasingly runs the risk of seeming merely trivial. The deterioration of the Gormenghast trilogy and of Peake's own career seems to stem from precisely this tension, with the novelist laboring painfully to make fantasy fiction true to his own disturbing experiences in war-shattered Europe. Likewise Fiedler's essay itself seems culturally dated in emphasis, for in the seventies it is surely James's novel that finds a new relevance. In contrast *Treasure Island* accommodates a set of ideological positions (religious smugness, the squire as the repository of social value, humble servants who know their place, social authority as fixed and perfect, death as a casual element in a great adventure) of the kind which became untenable after 1914. By coincidence *Treasure Island* was one of Peake's favorite books, and though his trilogy has often been appropriated as a similar kind of light escapism, to understand it we need to look beyond its status as an hermetic fiction, as fantasy, and instead situate its meaning in relation to the period in which Peake wrote and to the writer's own experiences.

II

In the poem 'Is there no love can link us?' published in his first collection *Shapes and Sounds* (1941), Peake considered his relationship as a writer to the victims of the developing world war:

> Is there no thread to bind us—I and he
> Who is dying now, this instant as I write
> And may be cold before this line's complete?

The poem concludes pessimistically that there is none at all, except a connection in time:

> There is no other link. Only this sliding
> Second we share: this desperate edge of now.

But to be connected only in time is scarcely to be connected at all, and in another poem 'The two fraternities' Peake asserts that the 'doomed' companionship of the living is more horrible than 'death's brotherhood'. The poems are slight, but that Peake in the period when these poems were written (1939-41) should have been considering his position as a writer and puzzling over ideas of human fraternity is surprising. John Watney's useful though rather brief biography gives us the picture of a writer who almost always endeavored to retreat from the world rather than engage with it.[2] For a novelist born in 1911, this is unusual. In the thirties no young or unestablished writer could afford to ignore the question of the writer's role in society or towards international politics. Even apolitical, introspective writers were affected by this prevailing cultural mood—Samuel Beckett contributed to *Authors Take Sides on the Spanish Civil War*, Malcolm Lowry wrote about the impending fascist apocalypse in 'June 30th, 1934!' But even these two writers had something in common with the then more prominent members of 'the Auden generation'—a university education. Mervyn Peake, however, had not. Having decided to become a painter he went to art school, and in the first half of the decade, while his contemporaries anguished over fascism, unemployment and poverty, Peake adopted a languid Bohemian lifestyle. During 1934-5 Peake retreated to the remote island of Sark, to join an artist's colony. His attitude of apparent indifference to the major issues of the time must have been sympathetically reinforced by the art student he later married, Maeve Gilmore, a girl from a well-off family with little patience for politics or intellectuals. Apart from one slightly curious incident when he traveled off to stay among unemployed miners in the Rhondda Valley, Peake's career seems to have been atypical of the period; indeed, his first book and only publication during the decade was an illustrated story for children, *Captain Slaughterboard Drops Anchor*, published by *Country Life* in 1939. It's ironic, therefore, that just at the moment when disillusion and withdrawal affected many writers upon the signing of the Hitler-Stalin pact, Peake began to turn his attention outwards.

The language of *Shapes and Sounds* makes it clear that Peake, temperamentally inclined to the Gothic and the fantastic, was influenced by the ideas and practice of the 'New Apocalypse' school. His style is indulgent and archaic, full of references to angels, centaurs, skulls, battlements, coffins, doom, hemlock, 'autumn grief', 'dagger'd roses', and so on. This is *Grand Guignol*—war imagined from a distance, not war experienced. There is, however, a counter-pull within the collection, where the writer goes outside the enclosed world of his imagination and finds inspiration in bored youths hanging around the streets, in miners, people in a dancehall, a group of people singing hymns in public, a hunchback. These encounters are, though, muffled and romanticized, hampered by Peake's inability to forge a distinctive style, and perhaps also by his inability to empathize with the psychology of others. He does seem to have found it difficult to understand other people as rounded individuals, and in his drawings and prose Peake appears happiest with caricature, with a retreat into pure imagination which permitted a delighted or obsessive exploitation of the weird and the grotesque. This grasp of detail but not of psychology is half-admitted by the writer himself: 'If I could see, not surfaces / but could express / What lies beneath the skin...'[3] Though moved by human suffering, Peake failed to understand its causes. His historical perspective remained apocalyptic: events piled up, horribly and meaninglessly, and he personified History as 'that witless chronicler'.[4]

In *Enemies of Promise* (1938) Cyril Connolly forecast that writers in the future would be 'required to live within their imagination's income', which is precisely what 'New Apocalypse' writers failed to do. Forties poets notoriously failed to develop, and Peake, who during the rest of his life published only two more slim volumes of verse, anticipated several of his more prominent contemporaries in abandoning verse for prose.[5] The poetry remains important, however, for the tensions and contradictions it reveals in Peake's make-up as a writer, and which were to erupt to the surface after 1945—the contrary pulls of a yearning for solidarity existing alongside a mandarin disdain for political engagement, a hazy compassion for humanity matched by a monk-like retreat from society wherever possible, and the contradiction between the enchantments of fantasy and the claims of the real world.

III

The first draft of *Titus Groan* seems to have been written very quickly between 1940 and 1942. It was later revised stylistically but the plot remained intact. In prose Peake had at last found the best medium for his pictorial imagination, though it seems he only began to conceive of further Titus Groan novels after completing the first volume. His imagination had piled up a fantastic world, yet after five hundred pages his hero was only fifteen months old. The titles of the first two volumes seem in fact oddly misplaced, for it is *Titus Groan* which established the gigantic, decaying world of Gormenghast, and *Gormenghast* which concentrates on Titus's adolescence and initiation into manhood. Perhaps the example of *Tristram Shandy* was in his mind as Peake built up his fictional world with a provocative slowness, and with the nominal hero virtually absent. Much of the first volume is concerned with lavish description of the decaying world of the castle and its environs, together with the dramatization of a range of weird and eccentric characters who have only a marginal relationship to the plot.

Titus Groan is prefaced by an epigraph taken from Bunyan's 'Author's apology' which precedes *The Pilgrim's Progress*: 'Dost thou love picking meat? Or would'st thou see / A man in the clouds and have him speak to thee?' Whereas Bunyan is nervously apologetic about using something as potentially sinful as a fiction for his Puritan myth-making, Peake makes the distinction between sensual pleasure and the cerebral delights of the imagination almost dissolve, since his language is characterized by excess, lushness, a sensual delight in playing with language. Peake's vocabulary is often exclusive: 'calid', 'crapulous', 'abactinal', 'palliasse', 'polliniferous', 'liana', 'expectoration', 'daedal', 'screaked', 'osseous', 'moil', 'triturated', and 'swart' are some of the obscure words the writer delightedly scatters through the text. What is disturbing about *Titus Groan*, however, is not so much the density of the language, or what Anthony Burgess has described as the 'almost paranoiac' attention to detail,[6] but the grotesque angles of the narrative viewpoint.

Swelter's left rump bled magnificently. There was, in point of fact, an island growing gradually—a red island that had seeped through to the white vastness of his cloth rear. The island was changing its contours momentarily, but as the echo of Swelter's scream subsided, it very much resembled in its main outline the inverted wing of an angel.... That he bled profusely could prove little. There was blood in him to revitalize an anemic army, with enough left over to cool the guns. Placed end to end his blood vessels might have coiled up the Tower of Flints and half way down again like a Virginia creeper—a vampire's home from home.[7]

This passage begins with the language of a sports commentator, and then lingers, with a perception that manages to be both detached from what is happening (blood gushing from a wound) and sensuously appreciative of aesthetic pattern. Then from a neutral statement Peake shifts to a grotesque, monstrous image of plenitude; a burlesque of a familiar kind of journalistic technique used to translate a fact into everyday terms; punctuated by a final mock-Gothic flourish. Peake's stylistic range is surprisingly broad, admitting widely diverse elements, and the overall feeling of grotesquerie is heightened by the way in which the characters often seem reminiscent of cartoon figures, possessed of absurdly elastic anatomies.

Two revealing passages of authorial commentary help to explain some of the strange features and angles of Peake's text:

There is a love that equals in its power the love of man for woman and reaches inwards as deeply. It is the love of a man or of a woman for their world. For the world of their centre where their lives burn genuinely and with a free flame.

This realization that grown-ups did not necessarily know any more than children was something against which [Fuchsia] had fought.[8]

'The great stone island of the Groans',[9] like the world of *Treasure Island*, does endorse the idea that the world of the imagination is equal to male-female relationships, and that the knowledge of adults is no more developed than that of children. Gormenghast is a world of solitaries and of introspection: the Countess with her birds and cats, the Earl in his library, Fuchsia day-dreaming in her attic. Titus's ill-matched parents scarcely ever meet, and the others—Flay, Swelter, Sourdust, Barquetine, Nanny Slagg and Steerpike—are each solitaries. The only domestic life that exists, that of Prunesquallor and Irma, is one of sour pantomime. The castle is inhabited by two classes, an aristocracy and their faithful servants, all arrested in their development, fixated on empty and absurd rituals. Many of these geriatric figures are, like Lawrence's Clifford Chatterley, symbolically crippled in one way or another. Only the Dwellers, the serfs who cluster around the castle walls, possess a natural sexuality, and it's significant that Peake, who evidently endorses the dreams and values of adolescent innocence, has great difficulty in evoking the affair of Keda and Rantel except in terms of lurid melodrama (Batchelor rightly notes the unsatisfactory dialogue and 'dramatic feebleness' of this part of the novel).[10] Peake also gives short shrift to the Dwellers' taste of adult life. At the ripe age of nineteen they suddenly wither, becoming old and wrinkled.

By calling his villain Steerpike, Peake signals his indebtedness to Dickens' mellow and nostalgic portrait of adolescence, *David Copperfield*, though the former swiftly sheds any similarities with the dashing and irresponsible Steerforth and comes much more to resemble the furtive and malicious Uriah Heep. The analogy is an odd one, however, for though the inspiration of Dickens's characterization is clear, Peake leaves his characters arrested in adolescence. None of them learn Copperfield's painful lesson— the error of his infatuation with his 'girl-wife' Dora, and the need for a mature companion in life, an equal, like Agnes.

Peake is nearer the mark with the two Shakespeare plays which he seems to hint have something in common with the lurid and distorted world of Gormenghast. Titus Groan perhaps derives his name from *Titus Andronicus* with all its melodramatic horrors, while his mother's name, Gertrude, immediately suggests *Hamlet*, another enclosed, suffocating castle world. Gormenghast seems to pun on 'gore' and 'ghastly', while 'groan' recurs throughout Shakespeare with a sexual double meaning. Peake's visionary world certainly contains the neurotic and murderous elements of the latter play, and the violence and uncertainty of tone of the former. As a flight of the imagination *Titus Groan* takes us a long way from Stevenson's commendation of the 'clean, open-air adventure'[11] which romance provides. Disturbing undertones of madness, perversity and violence permeate the text. Sourdust is burnt to death; Keda commits suicide; Lord Sepulchrave goes mad and is eaten alive by owls: Swelter's ear is chopped off. Murder is described in terms of sexual climax; strange images of mutilation intrude into the text at incongruous moments.

Gormenghast is a world transformed from tranquility and unchanging ritual to one of disturbance and tension. Though represented as a separate world, feudal and pre-industrial, twentieth-century phrases and concepts appear discreetly in the text: Peake talks of sociologists. Steerpike decides that Barquentine is 'to be liquidated'[12]—an expression new to George Orwell as late as 1938.[13] There are a range of questions we might ask about the absences in Gormenghast (producers, police, politics) but Peake never invites them. The density of the description is so lavish, the canvas so broad, that the gaps and ambiguities are all but invisible. As in a Shakespeare history play, Gormenghast is a kingdom legitimized by the forces of nature, and when Steerpike rebels he violates a mystical order that makes his doom inevitable.

The final two paragraphs of the novel capture something of this authoritative but mystifying rhetoric which Peake deploys when considering the fortunes of Gormenghast:

Through honeycombs of stone would now be wandering the passions in their clay. There would be tears and there would be strange laughter. Fierce births and deaths beneath umbrageous ceilings. And dreams, and violence, and disenchantment.

And there shall be a flame-green daybreak soon. And love itself will cry for insurrection! For tomorrow is also a day—and Titus has entered his stonghold.

As a conclusion this is not very satisfying. Peake originally planned to end *Titus Groan* with the word 'Nevertheless'—a word suggesting a continuation, but also some kind of qualification or negation of what has previously happened. His endeavor to close the narrative with a vague suggestion of panoramic, romantic destinies in the offing is over-conventional. As Roger Bromley has pointed out, traditional escapist popular fiction always ends in foreclosure, in a prescriptive conclusion where fantasy is endorsed and consciousness is 'bricked in'.[14] *Titus Groan*, however, differs from popular romance through its structural contradictions. Expectations are raised, only to be comically deflated or left in suspension. Titus Groan rebels against his imposed role as heir to the throne and pushes the regalia of Lordship into the lake. Fuchsia's future is left in doubt, her sexual exploitation by Steerpike an unanswered possibility. Marriage and family life (the holy grail of popular romance) is rendered as grotesque and absurd. Peake's characters retreat from the meaningless rituals of the castle into solipsism, yet their private worlds are corrupt, perverse or puerile. In the fate of the seventy-sixth Earl the apparently hermetic world of Gormenghast is itself brought into question: 'His sensitive mind had ceased to function, for it had played so long in a world of abstract philosophies that this other world of practical and sudden action had deranged its structure.'[15] *Titus Groan* ends, like the outcome of the war in Europe when Peake finished his first draft of the novel, unresolved, a tangle of sinister questions and unanswered possibilities.

Until 1945 Peake had led a very sheltered life, but suddenly, rather late in the day, he was employed as a war artist. He travelled across Germany and witnessed at first hand the sufferings of displaced nationals and the horrors of the concentration camp at Belsen. This last experience seems to have been traumatic, and one from which Peake never recovered.[16] His brief, disturbing 'London fantasy', which meditates on loss and failure ('The talents that never bore fruit or even flowered; the forgotten talents; the murdered talents...') possibly registers some of the pain and confusion he felt in the face of such atrocities. The closing paragraph of the Fantasy, a vision of faces in a London street, returns us to the perspectives of his earlier poems:

Beneath the electric glare; in fog; in downpour; in sunlight; in wind; at sunrise or at dusk there is no end. Each desperate moment, clutching Entirety, sinks with a smouldering fistful of raw plunder; sinks into nullity while time slides on, and the heads move by and are huge, as they nod; huge as they turn and stare: huge as the heads of mammoths.[17]

As in 'Is there no love can bind us?' reality is reduced to a succession of desperate, unrelated moments; the perceiver is overwhelmed. London is seen from the viewpoint of a pictorial artist, but also from that of a child. Human beings transform into objects, grotesque, threatening and huge. The notion of artistic possibility as 'plunder' seems oddly childish in conception (a word which conjures up Peake's fondness for *Treasure Island* once again). The reference to mammoths suggests that the world is in the grip of an ice age; the syntax hurries us on to a final notion of apocalypse. Peake was certainly disturbed by his inability to feel for the suffering victims of the war. His poem 'The consumptive, Belsen 1945' expresses his anguish at being merely a detached observer. After Belsen, Peake was no longer at home in the world: his poem 'Suddenly, walking along the open road' describes a frightening sense of alienation suddenly overwhelming him in a tranquil English landscape, and pictures the world as merely a toy, 'A marble spinning through the universe'.

Gormenghast, written between 1946 and 1949, seems both to retreat from and engage with the Belsen experience. The first half of the novel, up to chapter thirty-seven, is relatively mellow, with the focus on Titus's school-days and the headmaster's comic pursuit of Irma Prunesquallor. Initially Peake seems to have shut out his awareness of the contemporary world and indulged in a certain amount of autobiographical reverie with his nostalgic treatment of Titus's schoolboy adventures, which softens the tone of the novel. Bellgrove's courtship of Irma, climaxing in a ludicrous romantic evening involving hot-water-bottle false breasts that slip, is pure pantomime and likewise draws attention away from the darker undercurrents of the trilogy. Only in the second half of the novel does the tone darken as Steerpike's murderous quest for power reaches its end—though even here the plot retains a boys' adventure book dimension, featuring what is really a gigantic game of hide and seek.

This second volume is more conventional in its plot, but Peake gives it a peculiarly modern twist at the end. Instead of reclaiming his kingdom after defeating Steerpike in the traditional way,

Titus, now seventeen, spurns it and departs for all time from the enclosed world of Gormenghast, unhoused, a perpetual refugee. This unexpected ending seems significant as an expression of the novelist's wavering attitudes to the claims of pure fantasy and the real world that lies outside the imagination.

Although many of the characters old and new remain solitaries, *Gormenghast* contains a shift in emphasis from the previous volume by dealing with three pairs of relationships: the comic farce of Irma and the headmaster, Steerpike's sinister pursuit of Fuchsia, and Titus's infatuation with 'the Thing'. Steerpike's planned seduction is frustrated at the last moment, and Fuchsia is left to her lonely day-dreams. Peake's view of her isolation seems implicitly a critique of the world of Gormenghast itself. Cut off from society Fuchsia, a child imprisoned in a woman's body, is left with her withered fantasies. The dreamed-of prince never comes except in Steerpike's deformed and malignant figure (mutilated by fire, like Charlotte Brontë's Mr. Rochester), and Ophelia-like she drowns.

Titus's relationship is more complex. There are incestuous over-tones in his attraction towards his foster-sister, the mysterious and ethereal 'Thing'. Her sexual identity remains indeterminate for some time, and when she is revealed as female it's in a curiously sexless way. When Titus traps her he discovers that she is dumb, and he attempts to rape her (this is the closest that Peake ever comes to actually mimicking *Titus Andronicus*). Whether or not the rape is successful is ambiguous; Peake's language at this point is contradictory, and he shies away from plain statement. Titus's escapade nevertheless involves 'the death of his imagination',[18] which makes the opposition between adolescent romance and adult sexuality finally explicit. The 'Thing' is conveniently killed by lightning; thereafter all that is left for the guilty Titus to do is destroy Steerpike and depart into another world, a fallen man.

Peake's work in the fifties perpetuated the elements of uncertainty and lack of direction in his career. He quickly wrote a third novel, *Mr. Pye* (1953), hoping to produce a bestseller. Peake sadly misjudged the mood of the times; *Lucky Jim* and *Hurry on Down* were the successes of that year, besides which his own novel was merely a slight, whimsical piece—fancy, rather than imagination. The characterization is shallow and lacks the full-blooded zest of the caricature-creatures of Gormenghast. The dilemma that Mr. Pye, a thumb-sucking, eccentric evangelist, constantly invoking God as 'the Great Pal', is faced with—wings sprouting from his back one day, horns from his brow the next—is grotesque and disturbing rather than comic. A greater disaster for Peake was the failure of his play *The Wit to Woo* in 1957. Though given a West

End première, his brand of whimsy and fantasy, written in iambic pentameters, failed miserably in a London still recovering from the shock of *Waiting for Godot* and *Look Back in Anger*, both staged in the previous year. Drama was not a form in which Peake seemed likely to distinguish himself.

Among the debris of Peake's abortive and abandoned projects from the fifties appear two important fictions: *Titus Alone* and the novella *Boy in Darkness*, commissioned for a science-fiction anthology. This last work remains an astonishing *tour-de-force* and, though usually overlooked, properly belongs with any consideration of the trilogy. The Boy, fourteen years old, and clearly Titus, runs away from his castle home, crosses a strange river, and arrives in a waste land denuded of all life except for the nightmarish figures of a hyena, a goat and a lamb. As the Boy journeys deeper across this terrifying landscape of men transformed into animals, to encounter the source of all bestiality and evil, the atmosphere is reminiscent of a tale by the Brothers Grimm crossed with 'Childe Roland to the dark tower came' and *The Island of Dr. Moreau*—though at another level perhaps it expresses Peake's version of his own stunned trip across ruined Europe which culminated in the nightmare of Belsen.

Unusually for Peake the narrative is written in short, breathless sentences. There is no humor to soften the horror of this world, and the terse, economic presentation marvelously builds up a chilling atmosphere of suspense. The impact of the piece is deepened by Peake's provocative inversion of traditional cultural associations: whiteness symbolizes evil, and the lamb, emblem of Christ, is made to represent ultimate evil. Perhaps *Boy in Darkness* expresses Peake's final despair and incomprehension at the course of history, which in the past he had so easily and glibly apostrophized. The only dissatisfying feature of this dazzling novella is the perfunctory ease with which the Boy outwits the monstrously cunning Lamb and destroys it; the victory over evil seems rather artificially tacked on.

'There comes a time when the brain, flashing through constellations of conjecture, is in danger of losing itself in worlds from which there is no return', Peake commented in *Boy in Darkness*.[19] Before the progress of mental illness necessitated permanent hospitalization, Peake did manage largely to complete *Titus Alone*. The chapters are much shorter, and the world that Titus, now twenty, discovers outside Gormenghast, is radically different to anything previously experienced in his homeland. Gormenghast conjured up an ancient, feudal world, and evil contained itself in the single figure of Steerpike. By contrast, in the unidentified world of *Titus Alone* we get a vision of the future, more science fiction than Gothic romance, more urban and contemporary than the temporally and geographically remote society of Gormenghast. Titus enters a world of cars, slums, police, prostitution, prisons, courts and asylums, at the heart of which lies the sinister factory, a place of death and evil, surrounded by the stench of burning bodies. This last feature, together with the dying girl, Black Rose, reveals that Belsen still preyed on Peake's mind, though it's worth noting the ambivalence of Titus's response to the suffering girl: "I can't sustain her. I can't comfort her. I can't love her. Her suffering is far too clear to see. There is no veil across it: no mystery: no romance. Nothing but a factual pain, like the pain of a nagging tooth."[20] This seems to be Peake speaking as much as Titus, expressing his anguish at a world which had cruelly violated the fancies of his tranquil earlier life. A realistic portrayal of Belsen was outside the scope of his imagination; instead he placed his memories of the camp inside the larger, despairing vision of a futuristic, highly technological totalitarian society.

The characterization in *Titus Alone* is impoverished in comparison with the earlier two volumes of the trilogy. Muzzlehatch reincarnates Flay, and the beautiful, demonic Cheeta is reminiscent, more than just in name, of the cunning beast-humans of *Boy in Darkness*. It seems significant that the other main character, Juno, the first woman whom Titus has a sexual relationship with, should turn out to be a kind of mother-substitute, twice his age and at the other extreme from the wispy 'Thing'. The final scene in the novel serves as a reminder of the theme of repressed or displaced sexuality which runs through the trilogy. At the end a vast, foul explosion (perhaps Peake had the atom bomb in mind) obliterates the factory. Titus survives and flees, returning one day, by accident, to the very edge of his domain, arriving back at the cave where his attempted rape of the 'Thing' expelled him for ever from the world of imagination and romance. At the close of the trilogy the outcast Titus, unlike David Copperfield, has still not met a woman who is his equal. He seems doomed to perpetual solitude; as Fiedler puts it, for this kind of romance protagonist 'it is hard to imagine a real acceptance of adult life and sexuality, hard to conceive of anything but continuing fight or self-destruction'.[21] From Peake's sketchy jottings for a fourth volume it seems, indeed, that he merely envisaged further picaresque adventure, further flight. But if Titus is still in some ways a child at the end of *Titus Alone* he is nevertheless a particularly twentieth-century figure: unhoused, a refugee whose responses are 'no longer clear and simple', a youth whose burden of knowledge is one of 'tragedy, violence and the sense of his own perfidy'.[22]

In 1958 Peake wrote to his wife from the hospital, 'I have almost lost my identity... I will never write about mad people again... It has done something to me. I have played too much around the edge of madness',[23] and it's significant that the macabre climax of *Titus Alone* involves a battle for identity, more exhausting and perilous than the clean-cut boyish heroics of the final victory over Steerpike. Cheeta maliciously arranges an elaborate masque for Titus, gambling that by confronting him with the figures from his past, assembled in the form of grotesque puppets, she will succeed in toppling him into madness. For once Titus is unable to save himself, and only the fortuitous intervention of Muzzlehatch spares him. It's odd that a mere representation of the past should be sufficient to threaten Titus's sanity, and there's a sense that the materials of the trilogy were themselves feeding on their creator, who channelled his own crisis back into the novel. Whereas Titus narrowly escapes with his personality intact, Peake, tragically, didn't. The last glimpse of his hero's world which he gave us before falling silent and spending the long last years of his life in a mental hospital, is far removed from the ordered, balanced world of Gormenghast with which the trilogy began: 'All futility: disordered: with no end and no beginning.'[24] Through the Gormenghast trilogy we can, then, trace the gradual collapse of Peake's epic vision as the tension between the exploration of fantasy for its own sake and the truth of his own experience in the real, social world became too great for him to bear.

Notes

1   Leslie A. Fiedler, 'Cross the border—close that gap: post-modernism' in *American Literature Since 1900*, ed. Marcus Cunliffe (London, 1975), p. 350.

2   John Watney, *Mervyn Peake* (London, 1976). Other biographical information is available in Gilmore and Batchelor. As yet none of Peake's correspondence has been published, except for extracts quoted in Mrs. Peake's memoir. This is a pity, since Peake seems to have been exceptionally reticent about his work, and the image of the happy family man who led a blameless and uneventful life seems jarringly at odds with the neurotic and disturbed elements in his prose. A much fuller biography is needed, ideally, perhaps, a psycho-biography. Peake himself began writing an autobiography in the "fifties but quickly abandoned it; it would have been entitled, aptly, *Chinese Puzzle*. Mark Spilka, in *Dickens and Kafka* (London, 1963), makes the interesting suggestion that the grotesque, the failure to portray character except in terms of distortion, is a result of a mother-fixation. Oddly enough Peake's outburst of energy in starting *Titus Groan* followed his mother's death in the autumn of 1939.

3   'If I could see, not surfaces' in *Shapes and Sounds* (London, 1941;
    1974).
4   From 'Victims' in *Mervyn Peake*: Selected Poems (London, 1972).
5   Peake's failure to develop as a poet is embarrassingly illustrated by
    two of his later wartime poems, 'A reverie of bone'—long, archaic,
    and representative of the New Apocalypse at its windiest worst—and
    the more interesting 'The Glassblowers', which luridly romanticises
    the labor of glass-blowers making inhabitants of a magic cave full of
    fire-flutes, jugglers spinning fire, warlocks, wizardry, alchemy and
    other rhetorical bric-a-brac which takes us far from the real world of
    wages, hours, and labor conditions.
6   Introduction to *Titus Groan*.
7   *TG*, pp. 434-35 (*340-41*).
8   *TG*, pp. 77 (*58*) and 270 (*210*).
9   *TG*, pp. 414 (*324*).
10 Batchelor, p. 70.
11 R. L. Stevenson, *Memories and Portraits* (London, 1912), p. 153.
12 *G*, p. 163 (*129*).
13 See George Orwell, *Homage to Catalonia* (Harmondsworth, 1977), p.
    189.
14 Roger Bromley, 'Natural boundaries: the social function of popular
    fiction', *Red Letters*, No. 7, pp. 34-60
15 *TG*, p. 318 (*248*).
16 Peake's companion on the German trip has recently published his
    account, which adds little to what is already known but confirms the
    novelist's reticence about the incident. See Tom Pocock, 'Dreams and
    nightmares' , *The Times*, 5 August 1978, p. 5.
17 Maeve Gilmore and Shelagh Johnson (eds.), *Mervyn Peake— Writings
    and Drawings* (London, 1974), p. 78.
18 *G*, p. 424 (*339*).
19 *Boy in Darkness*, (London, 1956) p. 215.
20 *TA*, p. 140 (*110-11*).
21 Leslie A. Fieldler, *Love and Death in the American Novel* (London,
    1970), p. 321.
22 *TA*, p. 12 (*3*).
23 Gilmore, p. 128.
24 *TA*, p. 258 (*208*).

Since this article was written *Peake's Progress: Selected Writings and Drawings of Mervyn Peake*, edited by Maeve Gilmore, with an Introduction by John Watney, has been published (Allen Lane, £8.50). It adds nothing of any importance to the Peake canon, but does usefully collect together most of the writer's fugitive pieces: more poems and drawings, stories, including *Boy in Darkness*, a radio-play version of *Mr. Pye*, the text of *The Wit to Woo*, the 'Notes for a projected autobiography', and very brief early drafts of *Captain Slaughterboard* and *Titus Groan*.

"THE PASSIONS IN THEIR CLAY": MERVYN PEAKE'S TITUS STORIES

Joseph L. Sanders

DURING Mervyn Peake's life, his writing received just enough critical and financial encouragement to keep him trying, never enough to give him any assurance that a substantial number of people cared about what he wrote. That has changed. Today Peake's fiction, especially the works concerned with Titus Groan, have been republished, widely distributed in paperback, and, most importantly, admired by an increasing number of serious readers. We do care, and we are now trying sympathetically to understand what it is about Peake that impresses us.

One problem Peake faced is the still-persistent prejudice against fantasy as mere escapism. This is the attitude that Emyr Humphrys expresses in an early review dismissing Peake's novel *Gormenghast* as "an over-grown fairy tale, without any discernible moral, having no more connection with the reality of living than the Hunting of the Snark."[1] Actually, the reverse is true in the Titus stories. Through his depiction of fantastic forces that emerge out of the stories' settings—and the characters' development as they react to that setting— Peake presents a realistic picture of human life. The best way to appreciate this is through a detailed survey of setting and character development in the three novels and one novella Peake wrote about Titus Groan. Seeing Peake's intent and accomplishment more clearly should help us make a fairer evaluation of the Titus stories.[2]

First, however, we should get clear what manner of fantasy Peake's stories *are*. At first glance the Titus stories appear to have little kinship with a fantasy novel like Tolkien's *The Lord of the Rings*, filled with monsters, wizards and magic rings. Yet the real purpose of fantastic elements in Tolkien's story is to extend human desires and fears far beyond their normal range. Magic and monsters objectify human passions that disrupt the natural order. In Tolkien's fantasy, fears take physical shape and desires become supernaturally achievable. In *The Lord of the Rings*, the Ring represents a common wish, the craving to master all knowledge and power, while the creatures and wizards show alternative ways to achieve that goal by brute force or study. Tolkien views life as a terrible struggle between desires and moral impulses, which one cannot understand let alone direct but in the midst of which he must trust in divine benevolence and hope for final victory. By accepting healthy tradition and trying to submit to the purposes that tradition offers, one can at least haltingly participate in satisfying action.

Peake's type of fantasy also moves outside normal setting and familiar devices to present his conception of the human condition. It works, however, from a quite different viewpoint in a quite different manner. Peake does not accept the orthodox religious tradition that undergirds Tolkien's fiction. Furthermore, he does not believe that true power can be trapped in a ring, diagrammed by a sage, or seized by violence. In fact the systematic study of supernatural power, in religion or magic, is impossible; Peake not only rejects any particular religion but denies that man can gain any benefit from using a religious/ethical tradition as an aid to understanding. Thus, though forces beyond human comprehension sometimes are at work in Peake's stories, they resist easy labeling. The supernatural empathy between Titus and Keda's child, in *Titus Groan* and *Gormenghast*, is one such fantastic element. The mysterious certainty that guides Keda through the last month of her life may be another. However, clairvoyance or other violations of familiar natural order are very rare in these first two books; the major fantastic element is found not in the action's foreground but in its background. The action in these first two books takes place in or near Gormenghast—an immense castle, self-sufficient and completely cut off from contact with any outside society. At one point, the "evening star" appears in the night sky, suggesting that Gormenghast is located on this Earth.[3] Elsewhere, however, it is revealed that Gormenghast must have been totally isolated in its wilderness for at least 368 years (*TG*, p. 295,230). Gormenghast appears to have no real counterpart in past or present, and it is difficult to imagine the castle as part of a future that would leave it so undisturbed. It exists in its own world, one similar to the real world but not part of it.

Gormenghast's unnatural existence allows Peake to examine the human condition from a fresh perspective. At the same time, lack of overtly fantastic forces in Gormenghast reflects Peake's attitude toward the basis of responsible action. In *Titus Groan* and *Gormenghast*, there are no easy magical tools by which one can manipulate Gormenghast's power, but on the other hand the characters actually need not fear such a power's violent intervention in their lives. In a completely different setting, 'Boy in Darkness' uses many more elements that are overtly fantastic: *Titus Alone*, set in still another part of Peake's special world, uses others. However, in these works, too, characters lack full control over themselves and cannot pledge allegiance to some superhuman source of control; at the same time, still, they need not be controlled by tradition or ritual. Although most characters are not aware of it, because the human passions that went into their society's creation are hidden by the aura of revered mystery, they are free. No "god" appears directly or indirectly in the Titus stories. Instead, men worship a set of physical objects and the tradition associated with them. Peake believes that man's desires and fears created the setting and the tradition that envelopes it. He pictures man as the source of all meaning and all delusion, and shows one particular young man, Titus, becoming aware of himself in those terms and rousing himself to fight free of tradition and the settings that enforce it.

Peake's few direct comments about his practice of writing show his concern with a tradition-bound setting and the people living in it. In his description of the writing of *Titus Groan*, called "How a Romantic Novel Was Evolved," Peake states that his book grew randomly from some idle jottings, "a page of nonsensical conversation between two pompous half-wits."[4] Peake's remarks stress the importance of characters in the story's evolution, and printed with his essay are several pen and ink sketches of important characters that Peake says he drew to help "visualize the characters and to imagine what sort of things they would say" ("Romantic Novel," p. 80). But Peake's essay is only about 300 words long; the rest of "How a Romantic Novel Was Evolved" consists of five excerpts from *Titus Groan*. One is the conversation between Titus' aunts, the Twins, that roughly fits Peake's description of the doodlings with which it began. Three other excerpts, however, show characters acting instead of talking— and acting, always, in close relation to Gormenghast, an indication of how the castle, not the characters, dominated the stories.

It seems appropriate though to examine some of Peake's descriptions of Gormenghast and its surroundings, to see how characters are able to react to that setting.

At first, like the characters, the reader is likely to be overwhelmed by the castle's physical presence. The castle can be seen from as many angles, in as many ways as any real place. It is a mass of stones, a heap of walls and towers above an eruption of hovels: "mean dwellings that swarmed like an epidemic around its outer walls.... Over their irregular roofs would fall throughout the seasons, the shadows of time-eaten buttresses, of broken and lofty turrets, and, most enormous of all, the shadow of the Tower of Flints. This tower, patched unevenly with black ivy, arose like a mutilated finger from among the fists of knuckled masonry and pointed blasphemously at heaven. At night the owls made it an echoing throat; by day it stood voiceless and cast its long shadow" (*TG*, p. 159). Again, seen from a distance in summer, Gormenghast is a sprawled bulk in the dust: "It lay inert, like a sick thing. Its limbs spread. It took the shape of what it smothered. The masonry sweated and was horribly silent. The chestnuts whitened with dust and hung their myriads of great hands with every wrist broken" (*TG*, p. 413, *323-24*).

Peake's vivid descriptions convince the reader of Gormenghast's physical existence. The stories swim in such descriptions, all useful in the story and striking in themselves. Early in *Titus Groan*, for example, Steerpike escapes from a locked room to the castle roof and climbs about, trying to find a way back inside to safety; the episode lets Peake show the terrific size of Gormenghast, but it also gives him a chance to present vivid, fascinating sights like the following: "He had seen a tower with a stone hollow in its summit. This shallow basin sloped down from the copestones that surrounded the tower and was half filled with rainwater. In the circle of water whose glittering had caught his eye, for to him it appeared about the size of a coin, he could see that something white was swimming. As far as he could guess it was a horse. As he watched he noticed that there was something swimming by its side, something smaller, which must have been the foal, white like its parent" (*TG*, p. 138, *106-107*).

These passages are not only vivid descriptions; they are integral parts of the story's argument. In its first appearance before the reader Gormenghast seems to challenge "heaven" and thus the natural order of life, making an obscene gesture of defiance. But its proud egotism is countered by details that suggest failure. In the second description, the castle is presented in terms developing the earlier description's suggestion of sickness, mutilation and defeat underlying Gormenghast's pretensions. The third quotation also shows that things are happening at Gormenghast outside the inhabitants' knowledge or control. This time the disruption actually looks healthy and vital—but Steerpike's own response shows the meagerness of his vision, and this is important to the story because the way a man uses his senses reveals his potential for development. One sign of Steerpike's failure to become more fully human is his desire to force all the marvelous things he sees from atop Gormenghast to work towards his personal profit. Although he sees clearly, Steerpike sees everything either as a useful tool or as worthless trash. Since the scene he views cannot benefit him, he dismisses it from his mind. On the other hand, one sign of Titus' potential for human growth is his sudden ability to see objects as themselves, as he sits in the castle schoolroom:

> it had been the color of the ink, the peculiar dark and musty blue of the ink in its sunken bowl in the corner of his desk, which had induced his eyes to wander over the few objects grouped below him. The ink was blue, dark, musty, dirtyish, deep as cruel water at night; what were the other colors? Titus was surprised at the richness, the variety. He had only seen his thumb-marked books as things to read or to avoid reading: as things that got lost: things full of figures or maps. Now he saw them as colored rectangles of pale, washed out blue or laurel green, with small windows cut in them where, on the naked whiteness of the first page, he had scripted his name....
>
> He even saw his own hand as a colored thing before he realized it was a part of him: the ochre color of his wrist, the black of his sleeve....[5]

In still another way Peake's descriptions express his attitude toward man's predicament. Though concrete, they are extremely incomplete. Peake concentrates on rendering flashes of vision or parts of a scene thrown suddenly into dramatic highlight. Here, for example, is a panorama of Gormenghast and the surrounding country:

> Three shafts of the rising sun, splintering through the murk, appeared to set fire to the earth where they struck it. The bright impact of the nearest beam exposed a tangle of branches which clawed in a craze of radiance, microscopically perfect and adrift in darkness.
>
> The second of these floodlit islands appeared to float immediately *above* the first, for the sky and earth were a single curtain of darkness. In reality it was as far away again, but hanging as it did gave no sense of distance.
>
> At its northern extremity there grew from the waspgold earth certain forms like eruptions of masonry rather than spires and buttresses of natural rock. The sunshaft had uncovered a mere finger of some habitation which, widening as it entered the surrounding darkness to the North, became a fist of stones, which in its turn, heaving through wrist and forearm to an elbow like a smashed honeycomb, climbed through darkness to a gaunt, time-eaten shoulder only to expand again and again into a mountainous body of timeless towers.
>
> But of all this nothing was visible but the bright and splintered tip of a stone finger.
>
> The third "island" was the shape of a heart. A coruscating heart of tares on fire.

To the dark edge of this third light a horse was moving. It appeared no bigger than a fly. Astride its back was Titus. (*G*, p. 96, *73-74*).

This fragmentary vividness works directly to Peake's advantage, since it permits him to suggest that the things he describes so vividly are parts of a vast and shadowy whole; the many objects left undescribed are thus attached to particular things that dazzle a reader's senses. This corresponds to the way one normally sees things. Naturally Titus cannot see every object in the schoolroom, simultaneously, with the same rich vividness. Intense vision cannot register whole scenes; it must focus on a few objects, to explore them in detail. At its keenest, sight perceives fragments of the whole.

This recognition amplifies something we noticed earlier. Fragmentary description is appropriate because so many of the things described *are* fragments. In the passages quoted above, Gormenghast is described in adjectives like "broken," "mutilated," "smashed," "time-eaten" and "splintered." *Titus Groan* opens with a description of the Tower of Flints, "patched" only by ivy and inhabited by owls. It is a visual symbol of defiance, self-will—and defeat. Furthermore, in *Titus Groan*, Peake thus describes in detail one wing of the castle:

Most of these buildings had about them the rough-hewn and oppressive weights of masonry that characterized the main volume of Gormenghast, although they varied considerably in every other way, one having at its summit an enormous stone carving of a lion's head, which held between its jaws the limp corpse of a man on whose body was chiselled the words: *"He was an enemy of Groan"*; alongside this structure was a rectangular area of some length entirely filled with pillars set so closely together that it was difficult for a man to squeeze between them. Over them, at the height of about forty feet, was a perfectly flat roof of stone slabs blanketed with ivy. This structure could never have served any practical purpose....

There were many examples of an eccentric notion translated into architecture in the spine of buildings that spread eastwards over the undulating ground between the heavy walls of conifer, but for the most part they were built for some specific purpose, as a pavilion, for entertainments, or as an observatory, or a museum. Some in the form of halls with galleries round three sides had been intended for concerts or dancing. One had obviously been an aviary for though derelict, the branches that had long ago been fastened across the high central hall of the building were still hanging by rusty chains, and about the floor were strewn the broken remains of drinking cups for the birds; wire netting, red with rust, straggled across the floor among rank weeds that had taken root. (*TG*, pp. 203-204, *156-57*)

Much of Gormenghast now is deserted and falling into ruin. Even as it was built, however, the castle was designed piecemeal, conceived in fragments. Just as the eye can see only parts of any scene fully, the mind also can comprehend any project only partially, and, when it tried to grasp too much, is defeated eventually by nature, time, and its own vanity—the desire to believe that it has triumphed. The House of Groan proclaims its victory in the midst of confusion and decay. Most of the inhabitants of Gormenghast register the presence of the Tower and the other structures without really perceiving their import. Though they use what they see in different ways, Steerpike and Titus are apart from this general blindness. And their clear sight permits them to shape the story's action because they can act in ways inconceivable to the other people in Gormenghast.

Clearly, the other characters are only hazily conscious of reality, and thus largely are unable to act effectively. For example, the Countess avoids the most pleasant and attractive room in the castle precisely *because* "there were no shadows lurking in the corners"; she prefers "those parts of the castle where the lights and the shadows were on the move and where there was no such clarity" (*TG*, p. 98, 75). This craving for indistinctness is analogous to the Countess' mental retreat from the world around her, which separates her from husband, daughter and son, and from which she rouses only when Gormenghast's gloomy tradition is threatened.

The Countess is not alone in such willful semi-blindness; most of the other characters also are grotesquely incomplete in their understanding of themselves and their world. But where Gormenghast's physical incompleteness suggests Peake's understanding of human limitations, man's inability to see objects as wholes, the onesideness of the characters shows not simply their natural limitations but also the way Gormenghast has narrowed and warped them. The pretentions associated with the place have produced an immense body of ritual whose effects almost invariably are negative. Peake believes that ethical religious tradition is based not on some supernatural manifestation but on one man's own desire to evade consciousness, of his lack of ultimate knowledge and control by *claiming* allegiance with supernatural intelligence and power. Responding to the tendency of thought to meander in unforeseeable ways and to collapse into chaos, the rulers of Gormenghast have accumulated a body of ritual to hold their own fragments of meaning together. By labeling certain actions significant, ritual occupies and secures the minds of its adherents. But the process is circular. Ritual depends upon ritual for significance. No modifications, no freshly relevant meanings can be permitted. And the people who are most formed by ritual lack even the knowledge that there is any other way to see life; they have no way even to become conscious that they have been distorted.

For Peake, tradition embodies the most stultifying of human impulses—the will to dominate, to see the world remade in terms of self—its failure hidden only by its own self-sanctified mysteriousness. Tradition promises a share in the delight of dominating nature. In return a man must surrender his individual self to the greater self. The worshiper feels himself a part of a power that fits his deepest urges (though he is not created in *its* image, as the tradition states), within which he can follow any desire as long as he consciously frames his actions in traditional images. But the worshiper is thus prevented from developing his individual self. Such tradition can show a man only a distorted, deadening image of himself. Yet, as in Gormenghast, most people accept a role determined by tradition in preference to developing themselves freely. They are willing to imagine no other existence.

Most of the people who live in Gormenghast cling firmly to the castle's tradition. Lord Sepulchrave, Titus' father, holds off his chronic melancholia by complete absorption in ritual: "The many duties, which to another might have become irksome and appeared fatuous, were to his Lordship a relief and a relative escape form himself" (*TG*, p. 205, *159*). Even when the day's routine is over, he secludes himself in the castle library, escaping into his books. He encounters his wife only on ceremonial occasions (*TG*, p. 204, *159*). In short, his intellect, crouched under the sheltering ritual, does him no good.

By the same token, it is because of ritual that his wife's vitality is able to express itself only with inarticulate creatures. She accepts all the physical demands of ritual by divorcing her mind from the human life of the castle. In a reverie, she plans to teach Titus the same survival technique when he is older: "I [will] tell him about the skies' birds and how he can keep his head quite clear of the duties he must perform day after day until he dies here as his fathers have done and be buried in the sepulchre of the Groans and he must learn the secret of silence and go his own way among the birds and the white cats and all the animals so that he is not aware of men" (*TG*, 399, *312-13*).

Titus' older sister, Fuchsia, is less successful at finding a "safe" outlet for her energy. Early in the novel she is seen dreaming vaguely of a friend from outside her world and its ritual (*TG*, pp. 145-46, *112-13*). Yet Fuchsia *is* part of Gormenghast, too, as she perceives when Steerpike approaches her: "behind him she saw something which by contrast with the alien, incalculable figure before her, was close and real. It was something which she understood, something which she could never do without, or be without, for it seemed as though it were her own self, her own body, at which she gazed and which lay so intimately upon the skyline. Gormenghast, the long, notched outline of her home" (*TG*, p. 273, *213*). And after her father's disappearance, Fuchsia recognizes "that she was no longer free, no longer just Fuchsia, but of the blood" (*TG*, p. 459, *359*). Her character is not transformed, her role as Lady Fuchsia only adding to the tangle of purposes and feelings that ensnares her, but she is at last firmly caught within the trap of Gormenghast. Her instincts still pull her toward freedom, but the only thing Gormenghast offers her is the cold-blooded artificer, Steerpike, who recognizes Fuchsia's imaginative nature and plays on it to gain her trust (*TG*, p. 274, *214*).

Some other main characters' accommodations to Gormenghast reveal why Fuchsia, and Titus, in his turn, are repelled by a life guided by ritual. Flay has devoted his life to the castle's oppressive tradition, denying his emotions any spontaneous expression. After he is banished from the castle, when the Countess sees him throw one of her cats into Steerpike's face, he discovers that he can enjoy another kind of life: "his love of this woodland glade he had selected grew with the development of a woodland instinct which must have been latent in his blood" (*TG*, pp. 442, *346*); despite this, however, he keeps as close to Gormenghast as possible, worshiping the *idea* of the ritual going on within the walls.

Dr. Prunesquallor, on the other hand, impresses the reader by his spontaneous sympathy for Fuchsia, as much as by his bizarre mannerisms. He is the only character who can be depended upon to respond generously and effectively to the needs of people around him. His sound impulses are further shown as he muses over whether or not to ask Steerpike's aid in caring for the deranged Sepulchrave: "I will bear him in mind and dispense with him if I can but a brain is a brain and he has one and it may be necessary to borrow it at short notice but no no I will not by all that's instinctive I will not and that settles it" (*TG*, p. 394, *309*). Yet, Prunesquallor is trapped too: "although the Doctor, with a mind of his own, had positively heterodox opinion regarding certain aspects of the castle's life ... yet it was *of* the place and was a freak only in that his mind worked in a wide way, relating and correlating his thoughts so that his conclusions were often clear and accurate and nothing short of heresy" (*TG*, p. 470, *368*).

The Twins share a mindless devotion to order that is symbolized in their dearest possession—the Room of Roots. Steerpike, having flattered his way into their confidence, is astonished at the Room, which is filled with the dead, carefully handpainted roots of a tree that still clings to the wall outside the Twins' apartment; they imagine that birds will flock to "those roots whose colors most nearly approximated to their own plumage, or if they preferred it to nest among roots whose hue was complimentary to their own" (*TG*, p. 252, *196*). But in addition to reflecting the system's foolishness, the Twins show its viciousness as they dream of the power that tradition owes them so that they would be able to "make people do things" (*TG*, p. 111, *85*). Even after Steerpike has made them his dupes by promising them power, each of the Twins muses, "one day perhaps I will banish Steerpike when he's done everything for us...because he isn't really of good stock like us and ought to be a servant" (*TG*, p. 392, *307*).

All these characters see life in terms of tradition and let their lives be ruled by ritual. Gormenghast's ritual does nothing positive for them. At best, it gives them a neutral refuge from personal difficulties, but more often it encourages weakness, by overwhelming individual needs with its oppressive, indecipherable "values." For that very reason, however, the characters find it more comfortable to cling to the dead framework of ritual than to fight free. They neglect the problems whose solution might cost them real effort, and thus real pain, in favor of playing safe, mind-numbing games. And so they see everything in terms of Gormenghast. They cannot question its importance, because to do so would be to doubt the way they have spent their lives, the way they *see* life. Instead they cling to their duties and the wisps of power associated with those duties.

Steerpike is the only character in *Titus Groan* who realizes that power might be seized despite ritualistic prohibitions. At first glance, Steerpike appears to be the most sympathetic character in the book; he seems to be simply a young man who wants to escape from the brutal life of a kitchen servant. Steerpike displays intelligence and courage, for example, as he climbs from the room in which Flay had locked him to the roof of Gormenghast. But, as already noted, Steerpike uses his abilities chiefly to stock his mind with knowledge about immediately useful information: "a passion to accumulate knowledge of any and every kind consumed him; but only as a means to an end. He must know all things, for only so might he have, when situations arose in the future, a full pack of cards to play from" (*TG*, pp. 224, *174*). Significantly, what he studies while Dr. Prunesquallor's servant is the concoction of poisons.

In fact, Steerpike tries to exert too much control over the

incomprehensible forces of life—as a result of which he ultimately loses all control. Steerpike is sympathetic only to a point. He sacrifices vision and understanding as he pursues his goal. When necessary Steerpike can simulate emotion, but his real passions are held in check by cunning (*TG*, p. 156, *121*). His ruling passion is a desire for power. Like the Twins, he understands that power is the ability to compel a person to do something; unlike the Twins, he understands how to gain power in Gormenghast. But he does not realize the personal effects of that effort. Because he keeps his true self so much enslaved, he may actually be the character *most* enthralled by the proud, ultimately self-destructive spirit of Gormenghast.

Above all, Steerpike realizes that the power of his personal influence is not enough. He needs to command the power of ritual. After the castle ritualist dies in the library fire set by the Twins at Steerpike's command, Steerpike attaches himself to Barquentine, the new ritualist. Again he files for his future use the knowledge he gains: "it was in his mind to find himself on Barquentine's decease the leading if not the sole authority in matters of ritual and observance. In any event, the subject fascinated him. It was potential" (*TG*, p. 484, *380*).

For the baby boy Titus Groan, too, the future appears to be utterly determined by ritual. Lord Sepulchrave charges Titus' nurse "to instill into his veins, from the very first, a love for his birthplace and his heritage, and a respect for all the written and unwritten laws of the place of his fathers" (*TG*, p. 228-29, *178*). As we have seen, the best life the Countess can imagine for Titus is one of mechanical obedience to ritual, with his real concern elsewhere. Later, at the Earling ceremony, Barquentine tries to seal Titus' future by intoning the formula stating that Titus "will forever hold in sacred trust the castle of his fathers and the domain adhering thereto.... That he will observe its sacred rites, honor its crest, and in due time instill into the first male of his loins, reverence for its every stone until among his fathers he has added, in the tomb, his link to the unending chain of Groans" (*TG*, p. 493, *386*).

Even as a baby, however, Titus does not fit the role intended for him. As he looks up at Keda, his wet nurse, Titus' face shows that he is part of an older tradition than Gormenghast's: "there was the history of man in his face. A fragment from the enormous rock of mankind. A leaf from the forest of man's passion and man's knowledge and man's pain" (*TG*, p. 115, *88*). During the Earling, Titus instinctively rebels against ritual, refusing to hold the symbolic object (*TG*, p. 495, *387*). At the end of the ceremony,

Titus further violates Barquentine's commands: "while the concluding words were being cried in a black anger...Titus had sunk
to his knees and had begun to crawl to the raft's edge with a stone
in one hand and ivy branch in the other. And then, to the horror
of all, had dropped the sacrosanct symbols into the depths of the
lake" (*TG*, p. 496, *388*).

It could be said that Titus simply is behaving like a normal baby.
However, Peake takes the opportunity to link Titus to uncontrolled,
illogical, nonverbal forces of which the other characters repress
awareness. In the midst of Titus' spontaneous rebellion, he utters
a cry that is answered by Keda's baby (*TG*, pp. 496-97, *389*). For
some time Peake has suggested a supernatural sympathy existing
between the Thing and Titus (cf. *TG*, p 411, *322*). The link thus
symbolized will be very important in Titus' development, since in
Titus Groan, Keda performs the only complete act of rebellion,
representing the overwhelming but unreasoning power of instinct.
Wandering purposelessly, after her lovers kill each other, Keda
feels a baby growing within her. But as she listens to a bird's cry,
she realizes there is a way to find freedom from pain: "'It is over!'
screamed the beaked voice. 'It is only for the child that you are
waiting. All else fulfilled, and then there is no longer any need'"
(*TG*, p. 356, *278*). She lives only to deliver her child; then she is
free to die. Keda's child, thus, represents pure, vital freedom, in
conception and development. Yet it is clear that this freedom is of
a particular kind—impulsive and heedless, echoing the cry of a
bird rather than answering a human communication. Titus is
instinctively drawn toward the Thing's freedom; later, he will have
to see whether it can satisfy his whole self. We should note,
however, that in *Titus Groan* the only other person who gives
himself up to such a mood is the insane Lord Sepulchrave who,
after his library is burned, seeks to submerge himself in another
kind of life by imagining himself one of the owls in the Tower of
Flints. They eat him alive (*TG*, p. 440, *345*).

Titus Groan ends as Steerpike wriggles his way toward the
center of power and as Titus shows signs of possessing an individual will. The story obviously is unfinished; rather a sense of
impending change disturbs the inhabitants of the castle: "through
honeycombs of stone would now be wandering the passions in
their clay. There would be tears and there would be strange
laughter. Fierce births and deaths beneath umbrageous ceilings.
And dreams, and violence, and disenchantment. And there shall
be flame-green daybreak soon. And love itself shall cry for insurrection!" (*TG*, p. 505-506, *396*).

At the beginning of *Gormenghast*, seven years have passed.

Relatively little has changed. The Twins have fled from their official apartment, at Steerpike's command, and are concealed in a deserted wing of the castle, still hungering for power. Outside the castle walls, Flay has adapted thoroughly to life in the woods but still identifies with the House of Groan (*G*, p. 287, *228*). The Countess and Dr. Prunesquallor are only beginning to be troubled by still unfocused suspicions of Steerpike; she is awakening to the hint of Gormenghast's ritual (*G*, p. 27, *18*), and he is beginning to concentrate his considerable intellect because of a feeling that the people he loves are in danger (*G*, pp. 41-43, *29-31*). Fuchsia is still not quite a mature woman, though no longer a child. She feels drawn to both Titus and Steerpike—to Titus because of his rebellious attitude, to Steerpike because of his "vitality and air of secrecy" (*G*, p. 24, *16*). Titus is seven years older, still torn by conflicting demands of blood and ritual (*G*, p. *1,1*). Steerpike is stronger.

Most of *Gormenghast* is taken up with the development of these two young men—and the castle's response.

Steerpike appears quite secure at first. He has concealed his viciousness and is entrenched as Barquentine's assistant. Yet Steerpike cannot be content with the power that comes from administering ritual. He must keep the Twins to perform for him and must indulge himself in random exercise of power. As several teachers cross one of the courtyards, for example, an object hurtles downward and strikes one of them on the wrist; high above, "Steerpike . . . raised his eyebrows at the sound of the cry so far below him, and piously closing his eyes he kissed his catapult" (*G*, p. 213, *169*). Power is satisfying only when it can be used at will, and Steerpike is growing tired of waiting to display his power.

He is also tired of concealing his true self; the desire to scream his personal defiance of Gormenghast is eroding his rigid self-control. The combination of fatigue and impatience undoes him. In planning Barquentine's murder, Steerpike is so eager to show Barquentine his superiority that he underestimates the ritualist. Set afire, Barquentine still manages to seize Steerpike, and the two burn together. As they struggle, Steerpike forces himself to act purposefully despite the pain. He succeeds. Yet he is changed. Besides the burns that scar his face, Steerpike has suffered injury to his self-confidence: "His poise had been so shattered that a change had come about—a change that he knew nothing of, for his logical mind was able to reassure him" (*G*, p. 282, *224*). He is unaware of any alteration as he continues with the same plans for his future, while entrenching himself in the job of ritualist: "His miscalculation over Barquentine's murder had been unforgivable and he did not forgive himself. It was not so much what had happened to his body that galled him, but that he should ever have blundered. His mind, always compassionless, was now an icicle—sharp, lucent and frigid. From now onward he had no other purpose than to hold the castle even more tightly in the scalded palm of his hand" (*G*, p. 303-304, *241*). Before murdering Barquentine, Steerpike was anxious for power; now, holding practical power over Gormenghast, he cannot understand that his hold on himself has been dangerously weakened even as he resolves to control himself even more tightly.

Steerpike soon commits more serious mistakes. As interpreter of the ritual, he plans to dispose of Titus by sending him on ceremonial missions via crumbling stairs or deliberately weakened catwalks (*G*, p. 349, *278*). At the same time, he decides to woo Fuchsia, to seal his power by marrying the only other heir to Gormenghast. By playing on her sympathy for his injury and her admiration for his courage, Steerpike leads Fuchsia to accept him as a closer—and ever more secret—friend. Fuchsia is unable to analyze Steerpike: "unlike this new companion, this man of the dusk, whose every sentence, every thought, every action was ulterior, she lived in the moment of excitement, savoring the taste of an experience that was enough in itself. She had no instinct of self-preservation" (*G*, p. 344, *275*). Steerpike carefully imitates love, even painstakingly decorating a room where they meet in the evenings. Yet Steerpike's role is shattered before the romance is consummated. Flay has crept back into the castle and hides in a deserted section, watching secretly over the young Groans. His warning whisper, "'Be careful, my lady'," halts Fuchsia outside the private room (*G*, p. 351, *280*) and Steerpike, when he finds her standing there in plain sight, pushes her inside with the exclamation "'Fool'" (*G*, p. 351, *280*). Humiliated, Fuchsia withdraws from him: "She was shocked and resentful—but less resentful, for those first moments, than hurt. She had also become, without her knowing it, *Lady Fuchsia* (echoing Flay's warning). Her blood had risen in her—the blood of her Line" (*G*, p. 352, *281*). Although she can be fooled into missing sight of some things, she cannot doubt what she once has seen.

However, Fuchsia does agree to one further meeting, and Steerpike makes cold-blooded plans: he will seduce or rape her, holding the threat of exposure above her from then on. He realizes that he must act immediately. Yet he feels a terrible tension, apparently sourceless, but overwhelming. After consciously surveying every aspect of his plan, he still is impelled to fill what he perceives as a hole in his knowledge: "his brainwork was done.

His plans were complete. And yet there was one loose end. Not in the logic of his brain, but in spite of it—a loose end that he wished to tuck away. What his brain had proved his eyes were witless of. It was his eyes that needed confirmation" (*G*, p. 368, *294*). The "one loose end" refers to the Twins, who have rebelled against Steerpike and whom he has left locked in their rooms to die. Actually, as the preceding quotation shows, the matter—the Twins' death—is connected with a non-rational part of Steerpike's character. The "confirmation" is important not to the mechanics of Steerpike's plans but to his sense of himself as all-knowning and all-powerful. He is not conscious of *why* he acts as he does, but the impulse is too powerful to resist: "Steerpike was aware...that he was behaving strangely. He could have stopped himself at any moment. But to have stopped himself would have been to have stopped a valve—to have bottled up something which would have clamored for release.... He was watching himself, but only so that he should miss nothing. He was the vehicle through which the gods were working. The dim primordial gods of power and blood" (*G*, pp. 381, *303*). In the Twins' apartment, unaware that Flay, Titus and Prunesquallor have followed him, he releases his confined self and begins to dance and to "strut like a cockerel about the bodies of the women he had imprisoned, humiliated, and starved to death" (*G*, p. 381, *304*). After glorying in his defiance, Steerpike rests, emotionally satisfied but still consciously afraid of this newly-discovered part of himself: "In looking back and seeing himself strutting like a cock about their bodies, he realized that he had been close to lunacy. This was the first time that any such thought had entered his head, and to dismiss it he crowed like a cock. He was not afraid of strutting; he had known what he was doing; to prove it he would crow and crow again. Not that he wished to do so, but to prove that he could stop whenever he wanted, and start when he wished to, and be all the while in complete control of himself, for there was no madness in him" (*G*, pp. 383, *305*). The natural desire to escape the brutal life of a kitchen servant has, under the rigid control Steerpike has cultivated to circumvent Gormenghast's ritual, evolved into vicious, selfish hatred of everything around him. While Steerpike consciously has tried to save himself, that self has degenerated into something murderous and uncontrollable. So Steerpike turns back to business: "He was himself again, or perhaps he had ceased to be himself" (*G*, 384, *306*). He has chosen an attractive appearance—or appearances—to gain domination over everyone in Gormenghast. He has seen *himself* as an ice-cold, purely rational manipulator. But the emotions he has denied still exist, though in grotesque, distorted forms. They steadily have gathered force to escape Steerpike's conscious control.

Consequently when he realizes that he has been found out, Steerpike immediately discards his careful schemes and is half glad to be openly himself: "A red cloud filled his head. His body shuddered with a kind of lust... for an unbridled evil. It was the glory of knowing himself to be pitted, openly, against the big battalions" (*G*, p. 385, *307*) Rushing from the room, Steerpike flees, "turning left and right like a wild creature as he made his way ever deeper into a nether empire" (*G*, p. 386, *308*). Finally driven out of his hiding place by the flood that engulfs Gormenghast, Steerpike is trapped by a search party led by Titus. His self-control almost completely gone, Steerpike scarcely can master himself enough to devise a new hiding place in the ivy matted on the castle wall:

he began to experience again, but with even greater intensity those sensations that had affected him when, with the skeletons of the titled sisters at his feet, he had strutted about their relics as though in the grip of some primoridan [sic] power. This sensation was something so utterly alien to the frigid nature of his conscious brain that he had no means of understanding what was happening within himself at this deeper level, far less of warding off the urge to show himself....

He no longer wanted to kill his foe in darkness and in silence. his lust was to stand naked upon the moonlit stage, with his arms stretched high, and his fingers spread, and with the warm fresh blood that soaked them sliding down his wrists, spiralling his arms and steaming in the cold night air—to suddenly drop his arms like talons to his breast and tear it open to expose a heart like a black vegetable—and then, upon the crest of self-exposure, and the sweet glory of wickedness, to create some gesture of supreme defiance, lewd and rare....

There was nothing left, no, of the brain that would have scorned all this. The brilliant Steerpike had become a cloud of crimson (*G*, pp. 496-97, *397-98*).

Finally, as Titus drives at him through the ivy, Steerpike delays defending himself to utter a cry of defiance, and Titus' knife rips the life out of him (*G*, p. 499, *399*).

Steerpike *uses* Gormenghast's tradition for his own ends, but by conforming to that tradition he denies his individual personality a chance to grow freely. His death shows the futile, self-destructive attempt to seize control. Yet Steerpike excites grudgingly sympathy—at least—as well as horror, because he represents a submerged side of normal character. Despite his monstrous actions and more monstrous plans, he develops consistently with his first appearance as a young man trying to escape an intolerable future, in a situation where the rules can only repress people who wish to live in their own way, to satisfy themselves.

That description, of course, could apply to Titus as well. In fact though Steerpike and Titus become bitter enemies in the course of the story, they resemble each other very much in some ways. In the eyes of Gormenghast, heresy (echoing Satan's act of rebellion against Divine Law) is the ultimate sin. Both young men are either secretly or potentially guilty of this crime. Steerpike is specifically compared to Satan several times and Titus, too, indulges in rebellious "devilment" (*G*, pp. 15, 7 & 19, *11*). These comparisons between Steerpike and Satan increase the reader's horror of Steerpike, but they carefully stop short of full religious force. Thus the reader is shocked at Steerpike's *mode* of rebelling: however, Peake does not label rebellion itself as evil. Steerpike's rebellion is not so much against Gormenghast as against his prescribed place in the castle. Actually, his plan to improve his position unconsciously echoes the self-delusion of the men who built Gormenghast, imagining they could see life whole and master it. Beyond this, Steerpike's and Titus' attitudes differ, and thus so do the actions of which they are capable. Titus treats servants as convenient devices (*G*, p. 19, *11*): Steerpike, though, considers *all* people merely tools. Titus is not aware of his own shortsightedness, but Steerpike sees very clearly what his actions do to people. Titus wants to have power over himself, and he pays little attention to most people; Steerpike must control others to feed his hunger for power. Thus Steerpike turns inward, taking his pleasure in exercising absolute power over the Twins in their gloomy warren: "He had led them gradually, and by easy and cunning steps, from humiliation to humiliation, until the distorted satisfaction he experienced in this way had become little short of necessity to him" (*G*, p. 48, *35*). Titus turns outward, exploring the castle alone for his pure delight. Titus lives for himself. Steerpike lives against others.

Titus' development presents an alternative response to the tyranny of a tradition-bound, purposeless future. Titus feels this need dimly at the beginning of *Gormenghast*, but he is still unable to articulate it clearly. As in *Titus Groan*, ritual tries to create love of Gormenghast in Titus, but Titus is instinctively repelled by that kind of life. Even as a boy, he wants at least to "pretend . . . to be free" (*G*, p. 98, *75*).

Titus is attracted by the world outside Gormenghast, because there he can escape the restrictions of his official role. When he does find a secret way out of the castle, he experiences real solitude for the first time. However, unfamiliar with this freedom from restraint, Titus is uneasy: "now, what he had loved he loathed.... For it was as though he were being drawn towards some dangerous place or person, and that he had no power to hold himself back" (*G*, p. 132, *103*). He does not know what to do with himself. But he catches sight of another human figure, springing so freely through the forest that it seems to be flying. He cannot believe that such a creature really can exist, it is so close to his deepest longing (*G*, p. 133, *104*). Actually, it is Keda's child, now called the Thing, who lives alone in the forest. As in *Titus Groan*, Titus immediately responds to the kind of freedom the Thing represents, an important part of his nature is in tune with hers.

Yet, as with Steerpike, the two show differences as well as similarities. Despite Titus' intuitive supernatural link to the Thing, Peake is careful to describe the Thing *as* a thing, presented through images suggesting the unthinking, nonhuman order of nature: "as the light quickened the creature moved in its sleep. The eyes opened. They were clear and green as sea stones and were set in a face that was colored and freckled like a robin's egg" (*G*, p. 178, *141*). By contrast, Titus cannot simply reflect the world around him, he must think about it (*G*, p 187, *148*). Titus cannot repress his instincts—and does not try very hard—but he is not overwhelmed by them. Instead, he tries to understand what he feels and act on the basis of that understanding.

Titus' problem is that, since he is a young boy, his powerful feelings have little experience to support them. His picture of himself naturally is confused. Moreover, his feelings seem to pull in several directions. He wishes to be free of Gormenghast at the same time that he rejoices in possessing it. But he does not want Gormenghast to possess *him*. He cannot accept the narrow role set up for him, either as a matter of course or as a calculated maneuver. His instinct of self-preservation is too strong to compromise. Thus he is repelled by the whole mechanical ritual of Gormenghast (*G*, pp. 169-70, *134-35*), and when Steerpike winks at him, Titus is sickened: "beyond his knowledge, beyond his power of reason, a revulsion took hold of him and he recoiled from that wink like flesh from the touch of a toad" (*G*, p. 147, *116*). After accidentally insulting Steerpike, Titus refuses to apologize because he realizes that "he had cried 'shut-up' to the arch symbol of all the authority and repression which he loathed" (*G*, p. 310, *247*). He faints, but he does not submit. For Titus instinctively hates the power Steerpike serves and the devious compromise that gives him a grip on that power.

As a complement to his hatred of Steerpike, his attraction to the Thing pushes Titus toward maturity. His growth is not simple, though. Defiance of everything around him does not in itself help Titus find any new way to live. Separated from the Thing, after Steerpike is outlawed, Titus drifts. His emotions seem to lack object. He feels that all things are equally vulgar. Instead, in this mood of total rejection, he performs his ritual duties earnestly because they give his life some value, however flimsy. The Thing shakes him out of this fearful lethargy when she interrupts a castle ceremony to steal a carving that she desires. The violation of ritual stabs at the castle's heart—and Titus, "sick with excite-ment" (*G*, p. 403, *322*), feels a powerful emotion he had almost forgotten. He violates the ceremony himself, running after the Thing, drawn by "something more fundamental than tradition" (*G*, p. 407, *325*). He loves the Thing for what she represents: "it was that Gormenghast meant nothing to his [sic] elastic switch of a girl! . . . She was freedom" (*G*, pp 411, *358*).

This section of *Gormenghast* troubles some critics who have difficulty figuring out what to make of the Thing.[6] Is she a character? Is she a symbol? What *is* she? In fact she can be both. Fantasy does give a writer exactly this opportunity to identify a character with an abstract principle. Two things must be accom-plished, however, if the writer is to avoid sterile allegory. First, the action must be physically convincing. We have seen how Peake's gift for visual detail accomplishes this. Secondly, the action must ring true psychologically. Even if we cannot always account "realistically" for all aspects of a character's personality, we must be convinced of the emotional plausibility of what we see. In this case, Titus—unwillingly shaped by Gormenghast and its values— reaches out toward the Thing—unknowingly produced by free nature. Whatever made her what she is and whatever made her represent all she does to Titus, the real question is whether Peake can sustain our sense of vivid, surprising growth or whether he will let the story lapse into a neat, orderly puppet show.

Considering Peake's earlier description of Gormenghast's folly, the latter course clearly is closed to him. Yet he also recognizes the essential human need to find *some* place to stand amid the rush of chaotic events. The difficulty is that each individual must find his own place.

This is what Titus begins to discover. When he finds the Thing squatting in a cave and eating a freshly killed magpie, Titus glories in her freedom from any tradition, her animal originality. Yet he also discovers the limits of such total freedom when he tries to talk to her: "the first sound which Titus heard her utter bore no relation to human speech. Nor did the tone of it convey that he was being answered even in a language of her own. It was a sound, quite solitary and detached. It had no concern with communication.... So divorced was it, this nameless utterance from the recognized sounds of the human throat, that it left Titus in no doubt that she was incapable of civilized speech and not only this but that she had not understood a word he had said" (*G*, p. 421, *336-37*). The Thing's death by lightning, a moment later, confirms Titus' discovery that he must live without his dream of purely non-rational, instinctive freedom. The Thing is as free as a perfect animal, but Titus recognizes that he is a human being. At the same time, however, he does not fall back into negation. Rather, at seventeen, Titus puts childhood behind him: "He was himself.... He had learned that there were other ways of life from the ways of his great home.... He had emptied the bright goblet of romance.... The glass of it lay scattered on the floor. But with the beauty and ugliness, the ice and fire of it on his tongue and in his blood he could begin again" (*G*, p. 424, *338-39*).

The next necessary step in Titus' development is the public declaration of his independence from Gormenghast. During the flood, after he watches Steerpike steal his canoe, Titus rushes to the Countess with the news of Steerpike's new hiding place. But all the reasons Titus blurts out for hating Steerpike are personal: "'He stole my boat! He hurt Fuchsia. He killed Flay. He frightened me. I do not care if it was rebellion against the Stones—most of it was theft, cruelty and murder.... He must be caught and slain. He killed Flay. He hurt my sister. He stole my boat. Isn't that enough? To hell with Gormenghast'" (*G*, p. 459, *367-68*).

Having begun to discover who he is and to verbalize that sense of self, Titus must test himself in action. Yet the motion still is not as clearly directed as it might appear. Leading the party that traps Steerpike, Titus tastes the sweetness of his *own* power to command others, to make them do as he wishes though he recognizes that such power is dangerous, "for it grew, this bullying would taste ever sweeter and fiercer and the naked cry of freedom would become no more than a memory" (*G*, pp. 469, *376*).

At this time, Titus' thoughts revert to the Thing much more than the situation demands. He remembers her again as the trap draws tighter around Steerpike: "Two images kept floating before his eyes, one of a creature, slender and tameless; a creature who, defying him, defying Gormenghast, defying the tempest, was yet innocent as air or the lightning that killed her, and the other of a small empty room with his sister lying alone upon a stretcher, harrowingly human, her eyes closed [Fuchsia has drowned]. And

nothing else mattered to him but that these two should be avenged—
that he should strike" (*G*, p. 476, *381*).

Titus' blaming Fuchsia's death on Steerpike is not altogether
unjust. It is Fuchsia's growing melancholia, following her discovery of Steerpike's evil, that leads her to stand poised at her
window, though she actually falls into the water by accident. But
Steerpike does not even know the Thing exists and certainly is not
responsible for her death. The connection found by Titus exists at
a pre-rational level, and actually is based on the similarity between
the two young men. Both, on their separate levels, are trapped in
an unyielding, unfeeling social order. They both are too alive to
submit. Steerpike acts in a way that Titus cannot, by exploiting his
feigned submission to gain power. But Titus is not immune to the
temptation to possess Gormenghast. Even after the Thing's death,
he is torn between accepting or rejecting his role as lord of
Gormenghast. Just as Steerpike attracts as well as repels the
reader, the course of action Steerpike represents must attract
Titus even while it repels him.[7]

Ritual is one possible guide for Titus's life, and the adults
around him have submitted to ritual in one degree or another.
Looking at the people close to his own age, Titus can observe
three alternative ways of life, models of selfhood. Steerpike is
adept but two-faced and vicious; the Thing is healthily unrestrained but nonhuman; Fuchsia, although she seems to possess
the greatest capacity for growth because of her clear insights, is
too romantic to develop her understanding of what she sees and
lacks an instinct of self-preservation. No individual offers a fully
developed and attractive alternative to submission to the laws of
Gormenghast. Titus must grow through and past these failed
courses of action. He must learn what he can from them, then
discard them. Only after they are dead to him (figuratively—or
literally) can he find his own course. Thus Titus' thoughts link the
Thing, Fuchsia and Steerpike—because he needs Steerpike's death
in the same way he had needed the others' without admitting it to
himself.

Just before he spies Steerpike in the ivy and dives at him, Titus'
real desire is not simply revenge for the death of the object of his
romantic imagination, or for the death of the sister who mixed
romanticism and realism as a way of life. Rather, Titus has built a
new maturity: "a kind of power climbed through him like sap. Not
the power of Gormenghast, or the pride of lineage . . . but vengeance and sudden death and the knowledge that he was not
watching any more, but living at the core of drama" (*G*, p. 493,
395). Thus the components of Titus' rage show that he has

learned all he can by his fascination with the alien Thing, his sympathetic pity for Fuchsia, and his hatred for Steerpike. He no longer needs to delay in uncertainty. As he acts now against Steerpike, directing the searchers, he feels at once a focus for all of life and also "only himself."

And now, with Steerpike dead, Titus can act on his feeling that he has outgrown Gormenghast, and his hunger for a setting outside Gormenghast's categories. In so doing, he is not actually free, but is following "a law as old as the laws of his home. The law of flesh and blood. The law of longing. The law of change. The law of youth" (*G*, p. 508, *407*). Earlier, Peake has stressed Titus' membership in the human race and thus his being subject to needs and pressures more basic than the demands of Gormenghast's ritual. Actually, in Titus and all the other characters, passion is the root of every action. Emotion cannot be repressed indefinitely without it exploding, as in Steerpike's life, in behavior more aberrant than any open display could have been. Even directing emotion through accepted channels tends to warp the individual, making him fit only for a constricted life. Judging from the failure of the characters who deny themselves in sincere or feigned service to ritual, it appears that emotion should be allowed to develop freely, to take its rightful share of command of human actions with the intellect. Thus, as he struggles to discover himself, Titus may behave selfishly and meanly, viewed from the perspective of ritual. The reader may even find Titus as unsympathetic, at times, as he finds Steerpike. But according to Peake, Titus still is doing the only thing that can help him find meaningful freedom. He has thought and doubted long enough: now he must act according to his own feelings.

The kind of action Titus must take—and the kind of world in which he must be able to act—are sketched in the remaining two works in the series. Before turning to them, however, I should repeat that these first two novels, *Titus Groan* and *Gormenghast*, form a unit by themselves. At the end of *Gormenghast* the situation set up in *Titus Groan* has developed to a conclusion. It is not simply that many of the characters are dead: Titus has broken away from Gormenghast to find a new life. A phase of his growth is over; a dramatic movement is complete. These two books contain a richness of detail, a convincing grasp of psychology, and a depth of human concern that mark a great work. The vividness with which Gormenghast is described, the careful presentation of characters—and in particular of Titus' passionate groping toward a true sense of himself—all work with Peake's thorough presentation of his thesis concerning individual freedom versus tradition. I believe *Titus Groan* and *Gormenghast* form a unified, successful whole.

Peake's next work dealing with Titus, the novelette "Boy in Darkness," was commissioned by Peake's publishers for a collection of three original stories, *Sometime, Never.* Although "Boy in Darkness" could fit chronologically somewhere in the middle of *Gormenghast*, it represents a major step toward the world shown in *Titus Alone*. Apparently Peake was preparing himself to write another major novel to carry Titus forward into another stage of development.

In "Boy in Darkness," Titus is just fourteen years old, still imprisoned within the castle's ritual. He already knows that he hates "the eternal round of deadly symbolism,"[8] and on the night of his fourteenth birthday he instinctively seizes the chance to escape. His flight takes him into a nightmarish country outside the castle. There, captured by two grossly ugly, semi-human creatures, the Goat and the Hyena, Titus is carried toward their master, the Lamb—in the person of whom Peake simultaneously attacks religion and science.

The religious implications of the Lamb are first apparent. The Lamb lives alone, blind, in an underground apartment lit by candles and carpeted in blood-red (cf. Revelation 7:14, 12:11). His face is "angelically white" (cf. 1 Peter 1:19), and his hands move "in a strangely parsonic way" ("Boy," pp. 189-190). the Lamb is, of course, a traditional religious symbol of innocence and purity; Christ is described as "the Lamb of God" (John 1:29). In Peake's story, too, the Goat mumbles to himself that the Lamb "'is the heart of life and love, and that is true because he *tells* us so'" ("Boy," p. 174). So the Goat and the Hyena treat the Lamb with religious awe, as they pray to him: "O thou by whom we live and breathe and are!" ("Boy," p. 209; cf. Revelation, 5:13). Their awe is justified; though he did not create them in the first place, the Lamb *has* made them what they are. Specifically, the Lamb has changed the natures of all living things, shaping them to resemble the beasts they are most like spiritually. With the change they have died except for the Goat and the Hyena who have survived because of "their coarseness of soul and fibre" ("Boy," p. 201). Most recent to die was the Lion, who "only an age ago, had collapsed in a mockery of power.... It was a great and terrible fall: yet it was merciful, for, under the macabre aegis of the dazzling Lamb, the one time king of beasts was brought to degradation" ("Boy," pp. 201-202). Thus the Lamb has ironically fulfilled an image from popular religion, by making the lion lie down with the lamb.[9] Now, as he surveys Titus, Lamb's hand flutter "like little white doves" ("Boy," p. 213), another symbol of spiritual virtue. While the boy sleeps, the Lamb waits, lusting to change his nature too, but with "his hands together, as though in prayer" ("Boy," p. 216).

The host of specifically religious suggestions and images, in a story that until now has been devoid of such concern, suggests very strongly that Peake is here referring to the Christian religion as a debasing influence.[10] Peake's treatment of Gormenghast's ritual shows that he dislikes any system of values imposed on the individual from outside, offering him nothing directly relevant for himself and encouraging him in whatever weakness he possesses. So, here, the Lamb can break down but not build; despite his worshipper's praise, he does not really understand how to keep his creatures alive. Still the Lamb glories in his power. True, in changing men he has destroyed them, denying them freedom to develop for themselves; to the Lamb, however, that is incidental to his own gratification.

In addition to religion, however, Peake attacks modern technology. However different faith in religion and faith in science appear, they can function in the same way for their believers. When religion is employed systematically to manipulate and nullify human beings, it functions as a science for the priests who operate it; by the same token, when science gives man the satisfaction of godlike control over human beings, it serves a religious purpose for him. The country beneath which the Lamb lives is littered with the waste and debris of science and industry. Underground, also, is a dead wilderness of metal: "there had been a time when these deserted solitudes were alive with hope, excitement and conjecture on how the world was to be changed. But that was far beyond the skyline. All that was left was a kind of shipwreck. A shipwreck of metal... vistas of forgotten metal; moribund, stiff in a thousand attitudes of mortality; with not a rat, not a mouse, not a bat, not a spider. Only the Lamb" ("Boy," p. 190). The Lamb belongs in this setting. He, too, like those who worked in metal and stone, thrives on change, though like that of the others it is a sterile, ego-directed change only. He hungers excitedly for more living things to alter according to his desires.

Like the ritualists in Gormenghast, the Lamb frees the faithful from the responsibility of being individual human beings. Many of Peake's characters seem to desire no more. In *Gormenghast*, for example, Bellgrove the schoolmaster gives up the masterful role that had so impressed Irma Prunesquallor, because "there was no joy in will-power" (*G*, p. 340, 271). It is easier to drift, to let decisions be made by other people, by momentary pressures and, above all, by ritual rules. In "Boy in Darkness," the Lamb represents the tempting and horrifying surrender of self, this time as part of a specifically religious ritual. And, of course, the Lamb hates human beings, and his purpose in changing them is to destroy them. His only real pleasure is in the destruction of another living will, as the final proof of his power.

Facing the Lamb, Titus saves himself by using his strength of personality and his intelligence. Symbolically, when he attacks the Lamb, Titus reveals religion's physical and intellectual hollowness: Titus' sword "split the [Lamb's] head into two pieces which fell down on either side. There was no blood, or anything to be seen in the nature of a brain" ("Boy," p. 224). Titus evidently loses the memory of his experience, while returning to Gormenghast. Yet that experience may become part of him subconsciously, to give him strength for his later development.[11]

Titus Alone was written during a very difficult period for Peake. Describing his purpose, in a letter to his wife, Peake says he wishes "to canalize my chaos. To pour it out through the gutters of Gormenghast" (quoted in Gilmore, p. 107). But chaos was gaining on him. Maeve Gilmore, Peake's widow, describes his appalling nervous deterioration and the increasing difficulty he experienced in concentrating—and even in the physical activity of writing (Gilmore, p. 115).

In addition Peake faced a major test of his creative power in this final book, since Titus now must struggle toward greater maturity. As part of the escape from Gormenghast, Peake evidently had decided to let Titus find his way in what Gilmore calls "a world which was probably closer to this one [than Gormenghast] and yet alien" (Gilmore, p. 120). With his flight from Gormenghast, Titus has ceased to be a boy; to become a man he must find his way in a setting that adult readers can at least half-recognize, confronting a tradition that stems more directly from modern life.

The society into which Titus wanders is technologically advanced.[12] But its proud achievements are supported by the factories "where the scientists worked, like drones, to the glory of science and in praise of death" (*TA*, p. 159, *126*). This is both figuratively and literally true. Traditional religion does not appear in *Titus Alone*, for it has been replaced by faith in the development of technology, of the conscious intellect by itself. As Muzzlehatch comments on Titus' destroying a robot spy-device: "'You have broken something quiet hideously efficient. You have blasphemed against the spirit of the age'" (*TA*, p. 106, *82*). Like all who surrender themselves to this new faith, however, Cheeta's father is a distorted grotesque: "His presence was a kind of subtraction.... For he was *nothing*: a creature of solitary intellect, unaware of the fact that humanly speaking, he was a kind of vacuum" (*TA*, pp. 184-185, *148*). When his factory is destroyed, he collapses with the cry, "'It is all I had; my science, *all* that I had'" (*TA*, p. 251, *203*).

The idea of technological superiority is not potent enough to unify people as well as does Gormenghast's tradition. However, because faith in technology is based on the same impulse to escape from personal freedom and doubt by asserting an objective principle over the self (the assertion made over the same volatile mixture of thought and passion) the society resembles Gormenghast—a heap of fragments, thronged with grotesques. The society in *Titus Alone* is unlike Gormenghast, however, in several specific ways. The society contains unexplained lapses, incongruous pockets of confused, frustrated activity like the Under River, which corresponds to a contemporary ghetto. But because the society is less cohesive, its inhabitants must enforce unity more feverishly. While the Grey Scrubbers in *Titus Groan* looked alike, here not only the workers but the police, symbols of state authority, are "identical in every way" (*TA*, p. 29, *18*). Finally, the society of *Titus Alone* has less ability to sustain an appearance of health. Though Gormenghast is crumbling insensibly with age, Titus' new surroundings are willfully festering; the noise made by the factory belonging to Cheeta's father is "an endless impalpable sound that, had it been translated into a world of odors, might have been likened to the smell of death: a kind of sweet decay" (*TA*, p. 167, *133*). This new society is more incoherent, more intolerant of deviation, and even more dangerous to Titus' spirit than Gormenghast.

He becomes aware of this danger only gradually. Primarily he is trying to cut loose from his past and become an independent person. Titus is aided toward maturity by Muzzlehatch, zookeeper and renegade. Muzzlehatch is like Titus in the richness of his vision and his love of the world. The way Muzzlehatch adapts things to fit his dreams, however, stems from his being so intensely alive. Even his car has acquired a personality, become almost a living thing (*TA*, p. 61, *45*). Unlike the Lamb, Muzzlehatch makes things *more*, rather than less than they are, because he can love the world's variety. Muzzlehatch helps Titus because he recognizes that the young man is like him in hating the regimented society—in fact, Muzzlehatch comments that Titus is "'rather like a form of me'" (*TA*, p. 65, *49*).

Unlike Muzzlehatch, however, Titus barely can keep his sense of identity intact. He is unable to settle into a relationship with any of the people who help him, because he is afraid they can only help him to love in their ways. He does not yet know what his way is, but until he finds out he must maintain himself independent. Juno, for example, saves Titus from imprisonment by taking him into her custody. But Titus accepts her offer only out of weakness (*TA*, p. 88, *68*). For Juno intends, in the most generous way possible, to possess Titus and give him *her* sense of direction. Subconsciously recognizing this, he resolves to seduce her and thus "to bring the total of their relationship to a burning focus. To bring it all to an *end*" (*TA*, p. 91, *70*). And so he moves on, feeling a mixture of "shame and liberation" (*TA*, p. 102, *79*), to return to the search for an independent identity.

Early in the story, despite his desire for freedom, Titus still pictures himself as a lost fragment of Gormenghast. Followed by a floating, metal spy-sphere, Titus shatters the machine with the chunk of the Tower of Flints he has carried with him (*TA*, p. 103, *80*), but later realizes that he has lost all physical proof of his past (*TA*, p. 105, *82*). Muzzlehatch, however, advises him: "'Get on with life. Eat it up.... What of the castle you talk about—that crepuscular myth? Would you return after so short a journey? No, you must go on. Juno is part of your journey. So am I. Wade on child'" (*TA*, p. 107, *83*).

Titus does begin to age, and to act, as he wades on into the Under River, the haven for criminals and outcasts. There he helps the Black Rose, pathetic slave of Veil, escape from her master. But Titus still is not able to love or be loved, though even he is repelled by his desire to flee from the Black Rose's need; "'Grief can be boring.' Titus was immediately sickened by his own words. They tasted foul on the tongue" (*TA*, p. 139, *110*). Just so, Titus is forced to run away again from his gratitude to Muzzlehatch. He exclaims, to the man who has just saved him again, "'I am too near you. I long to be alone. What shall I do?'" (*TA*, p. 143, *113*). Muzzlehatch replies. "'The world is wide. Follow your instinct and get rid of us'" (*TA*, p. 144, *114*).

The next person Titus falls in with, however, is not to be cast off easily—or understanding enough to wish Titus well when he must leave her. She is Cheeta, whom Peake describes as a "modern" beauty, perfect in each detail but distorted as a whole (*TA*, p. 160, *127*). To Cheeta, who is so much a part of the modern world and its ritual, Titus is a mystery that she can neither solve nor dismiss. On his part, besides his usual reluctance to form an interdependent relationship with anyone else, Titus feels subtly repelled by Cheeta and disgusted by the factory her father owns (*TA*, p. 168, *134*). But Cheeta, feeling that she is being robbed of "something miraculous" when Titus decides to leave her (*TA*, p. 173, *138*), vows revenge.

In fact, the thing that makes Titus so mysterious to Cheeta is the very thing that makes her hate him—the independent identity that strengthened itself until Cheeta can see Titus in the same way that once *he* had seen citizens of the society: "she hated him. Hated his self-sufficiency" (*TA*, p. 183, *146*). True, Titus' extreme form of self-sufficiency is unappealing to Cheeta, to most readers, and even to Titus at least part of the time; however, it is necessary to him in this period of his growth. At this stage, his only satisfying relationship is with a village maiden, described as "a rosy, golden thing" (*TA*, p. 206, *166*). By keeping himself thus free of entanglements, while exploring experience, Titus gains understanding of the possibilities of experience and thus gains strength.

But although Titus is stronger, he does not *feel* secure yet. He always feels "the legions of Gormenghast" pressing close behind him, and he cries to the world around him, "'Give me some proof of me!'" (*TA*, p. 195, *157*). Cheeta attacks him on this point, by ordering built a distorted replica of Gormenghast in order to humiliate Titus, or drive him insane by destroying his belief in himself. She plans well. Tricked into this setting, Titus is struck by "terror; not of Cheeta herself or of any human being, but of doubt. The doubt of his own existence" (*TA*, pp. 227-228, *184*).

Muzzlehatch arrives just in time to break the mood and save Titus once more. In doing all this Muzzlehatch represents more than a handy *deus ex machina*; he is exhibiting a facet of maturity that Titus has not yet attained. Titus has been so busy maintaining himself that he has found no time to develop relationships with others. As he reels under Cheeta's attack, though, he asks: "Why had he been so singled out? What had he done? Was the fact that he had never loved her for herself but only out of lust, was this so dire a thing?" (*TA*, p. 236, *190*). However defensively, Titus' questioning of himself suggests both an awareness of responsibility and a glimpse of personal failure. In the story's context, though, the question is difficult. Cheeta's hatred of Titus is perverted and vile; Titus' aloofness is a necessary phase of his development. But beyond the stage in which Titus finds himself, of self definition by unrestrained experience, Muzzlehatch has learned that he cannot live by himself. At the beginning of *Titus Alone*, he loves the animals in his zoo, but even then he finds that they are not enough: "he wanted something else. He wanted words" (*TA*, p. 95, *73*). After his zoo is destroyed by the police because he has helped Titus, Muzzlehatch first flees, broken in spirit, then returns because of a desire to revenge himself by destroying the factory belonging to Cheeta's father—and because of an urge to help Titus. Their relationship has become a kind of love and Muzzlehatch has come to realize that meaning comes not only from the self but from the relationship of the self to others.

Titus has not come that far yet, but he may be on the way. He is essentially like Muzzlehatch, and he has passed through this difficult period without becoming corrupt. Titus' restraint from human involvement is not viciousness, and it need not be a permanent condition. At the very end of the book, wandering again in wilderness, Titus realizes he is near Gormenghast. If he wishes, he can look at the castle again to reinforce his identity; he can even enter it and return to his inherited role. He refuses: "He had no longer any need for home, for he carried his Gormenghast within him. All that he sought was jostling within himself. He had grown up" (*TA*, pp. 262-263, *212*). He is at the end of a period of doubt and defensiveness, ready to begin self-assured exploration.

As it stands, *Titus Alone* is as unfinished as *Titus Groan* would be if it were considered by itself. I have analyzed what I take to be Peake's intent to make Titus' maintenance of himself the foundation for later human connections. The change has not yet been worked out fully in *Titus Alone*. Instead the book's short chapters and choppy writing further emphasize Titus' confusion. By this time, however, Peake was unable to develop his thoughts fully, and only notes survive for the fourth book of the series (Gilmore, p. 106).

Because Peake's illness probably affected the writing of *Titus Alone* and because the series is itself a developing and in complete structure, it is difficult to evaluate Peake's books about Titus as a finished work. Perhaps a fairer question is whether or not the stories accurately represent man's sense of himself as an unfinished, growing being. I believe that they do. The Titus series is overwhelmingly concerned with Becoming, rather than with fallen man's unchangeable state of Being, and shows great faith in the individual's ability to *become* a stable, free individual. Peake offers no moral judgements of a young person's actions as he matures. For Peake, the weight of moral standards comes from their being part of a tradition, and any tradition lies outside the individual's potential and needs. Thus adherence to a morality impedes development of the whole self and denies real maturity. Titus' values are based on what works or fails for him, what pleases him or makes him feel shame. Man lives, Peake shows us, in a fantastic world, unfathomable by any mind; therefore, one cannot rely on outside teaching, but must throw himself headlong into life, transcending any limiting scheme. Titus lives through a series of vivid experiences, developing through them in a convincing manner. Titus grows beyond the limits of his tradition to become a freeminded, sympathetic man.

As a presentation of this idea, Peake's work is very impressive. In particular, his first novels—*Titus Groan* and *Gormenghast*—form a vivid and convincing unit. Even in their unfinished state, Peake's stories of Titus Groan deserve their popularity for their successfully humanistic conception of contemporary man. It is unfortunate that physical illness kept Peake from continuing his depiction of Titus' development. But there is joy and wonder in what he completed.

Notes

1. *"Gormenghast," Time and Tide* 31 (Oct. 21, 1950), 1065.
2. We face two major problems in setting up an analysis of the Titus stories. One concerns the overall form of Peake's work. *Titus Groan* (1946), *Gormenghast* (1950), and *Titus Alone* (1959), can be considered a trilogy, with "Boy in Darkness" (1956) an outlying fragment. Actually in commenting on the effects of the nervous disease that left Peake steadily less able to work or think connectedly, Peake's widow says that *Titus Alone* is only "the last book in what was called a trilogy, but which would never have ended if nature in her aggressive way had not taken possession of all that made him a unique person" (Gilmore, p. 105). I intend to examine Peake's work in its natural units, rather than in divisions artificially imposed by his illness. *Titus Groan* and *Gormenghast* form one such unit. Not only did the writing of another novel, *Mr. Pye* (1953), intervene between *Gormenghast* and the two later works, but *Titus Groan* and *Gormenghast* form a whole by themselves. These first two novels stick closely to the same setting and center on the same characters and issues, *Gormenghast* actually beginning with a synopsis of the first novel. Years pass before Peake returns to Titus, in "Boy in Darkness" and *Titus Alone*, and both the setting of the story and the focus of Peake's concern have undergone striking changes.

    Peake's illness is the source of the second problem. As his widow says above, illness impaired Peake's ability to develop the design of the Titus stories. In addition, Peake's handwriting deteriorated severely. Thus *Titus Alone* offers severe textual problems, the manuscript being extremely uncertain and semi-legible as well. Both published versions required editorial choice and guesswork (in addition to Gilmore, see Batchelor, pp. 114-123, for a description of how both published versions differ from Peake's manuscript; see also Langdon Jones' note on his labors in preparing the second edition of *Titus Alone* [London: Eyrie & Spottiswoode,

1970], pp. 7-8). Thereafter, this essay will use the second, fuller
edition of *Titus Alone* as its text.

3. *TG*, p. 358 (280).

4. In *A New Romantic Anthology*, ed. Stefan Schimanski and Henry
    Treece (Norfolk: New Directions, 1949), p. 80. Hereafter referred
    to as "Romantic Novel."

5. *Gormenghast*, pp. 83-84 (63).

6. In the study cited above, for example, John Batchelor first states
    that "the 'Thing'...is to be seen as the embodiment of the entire
    natural world. Her death creates a disharmony in the universe,
    which then mourns her with a flood which engulfs the castle" (p.
    96), but later calls her "a false goddess who deserves death by
    thunderbolt, although this is also a pathetic, and therefore mor-
    ally exalting death" (p. 99). The scene is especially perplexing
    when one remembers that the Thing is killed by a bolt of lightning—
    surely another "natural" force. Batchelor attributes this disconti-
    nuity to inconsistent characterization; "why," he asks, "should the
    spirit of nature slaughter a missel-thrush?" (p. 98). The answer
    must be that "the spirit of nature" can do *anything*. Nature does
    not have to fit our sense of decorum. The desire for consistency—as
    is the desire for a pretty, literally denatured existence—is charac-
    teristic of Gormenghast, not of the world around it. And we have
    seen what hollow pretension and folly that desire leads to.

7. C.N. Manlove also observes that Titus and Steerpike are very
    much alike (*Modern Fantasy: Five Studies*, p. 246); unfortunately
    Manlove uses this perception to question Titus' motives in rejecting
    Gormenghast. Manlove looks for clearly comprehensible purpose,
    not appreciating how Titus is trying to work his way through a
    tangle of contradictory desires. (In a later essay, Manlove attacks
    the characterization of Steerpike also, stating that his keeping the
    Twins alive so long is "without explanation" ["A World in Frag-
    ments: Peake and the Titus Books," *The Mervyn Peake Review*,
    Autumn, 1980, p. 12]. Again, Manlove wants to oversimplify,
    missing the implication that it is the very rigidness of Steerpike's
    self-control in public that forces him to keep someone hidden
    whom he can humiliate and manipulate.)

8. (London: Eyrie & Spottiswoode, 1956), p. 159.

9. The image does not come directly from the Bible. There, in
    Isaiah 11:6, "The wolf...shall dwell with the lamb, and the
    leopard shall lie down with the kid, and the calf and the young
    lion and the fatling together...." However, the notion of the lion
    and lamb, in particular, lying down together has become a part of
    popular Christian imagery all the way down to Christmas cards.

10. Although Peake was the son of a Congregational medical mission-
    ary, he did not participate in formal religion himself. Also Peake's
    widow refers to the problems they experienced in gaining her
    traditionally Catholic parents' permission to marry, and she quotes
    from a poem published in Peake's last collection of poetry: "How

foreign to the spirit's early beauty/and to the amoral integrity of the mind/and to all those whose reserve of living is lovely? Are the tired Creeds that can be so unkind" (Gilmore, p. 25).

11. Edwin Morgan suggests as much in "The Walls of Gormenghast—An Introduction to the Novels of Mervyn Peake," *Chicago Review*, 14 (1960), 76.

12. Some space exploration has been accomplished, a situation common to science fiction at the time Peake wrote (cf. chapters 18 and 19).

TITUS AND THE THING
IN *GORMENGHAST*

Cristiano Rafanelli

IT is very difficult to select a chapter as the most representative—i.e. in a certain way, paradigmatic—of a whole novel, but it seems to me that in *Gormenghast* chapter 68 fulfils this difficult role most aptly. This chapter is centered on one of the most important moments of the novel: the meeting between Titus and the Thing. Peake himself seems to be aware of this importance, since it takes him several chapters—63 to 68—to prepare the reader for the events he describes. In fact it could be said that through chapters 63—the preparation for the "Day of the Bright Carvings"—to 67 included, Peake is writing a kind of *crescendo*, starting from hints at an imminent downpour ("There's going to be an almighty storm, my boy," says Dr. Prunesquallor to Titus in chapter 63), progressing with Titus's escape to Gormenghast forest—his sheltering in a cave because of the heavy rain and his falling asleep (chapters 64-66), and culminating with the words that end chapter 67: "... he could not see that at the mouth of the cave stood the 'Thing'" (*GG*, p. 415, *332*).

This sentence is full of promise: it suddenly introduces the Thing into the scene, and gives us to understand that something very important, something decisive, is going to happen. The structure of the sentence also helps to give us this impression: the Thing—occupying the very last place in the sentence and in the chapter—is strongly pointed out, and the verbal expression "stood" suggests the image of a statue. The reader realizes that the novel is at a turning point, and his expectations are at their highest when he starts reading chapter 68.

Peake does not disappoint him. At the beginning of the chapter he creates a very particular situation. The atmosphere is quiet for the present, but the tension accumulated in the preceding chapters tells the reader that a new *crescendo*, even mightier than the previous one, is starting.

The chapter is divided into four numbered parts, each corresponding to a precise situation. The first shows Titus observing the Thing from his hiding point; the tone is quiet and almost lyrical; meditation and observation prevail. The second part—full of action and movement—describes the reaction of the Thing to Titus's appearance and their embrace. In the third—the shortest and the most poetic—we witness the death of the Thing, and Titus's farewell to his boyhood. The fourth part is a kind of *coda*; it narrates Titus and Fuchsia's return to the castle.

The four parts are not rigidly separated. Even if each is characterized by an atmosphere of its own, a gradual change in tone and atmosphere takes place towards the end of every section, culminating in an event which helps the narration to glide into a new situation—the premise to what will happen in the next part.

In the first section, for instance, Titus is a spectator and the Thing is acting. This scene suggests the image of the hidden lover observing the object of his unreciprocated love, even if the impression it leaves on Titus is not quite so pleasant. To return to the analysis of the structure: the gradual change mentioned above begins on page 418 (*334*): Titus "knew that he could not stay where he was for ever. Sooner or later he must make his presence known..." This sentence prepares us for a change of situation, and the style also changes, becoming slowly more pressing. Particularly, if we analyze the last five lines, we can divide the six sentences into two groups—the first three being in antithesis to the second three, each group being characterized by a kind of polysyndetic rhythm, since the same word is iterated at the beginning of each sentence. This iteration attains the effect of giving the narration a quicker pace, and of easing the transition to the next part.

Let us consider the last five lines more closely:

a   *And he forgot* the wilderness within her.
b   *He forgot* her ignorance.
c   *He forgot* the raw blood and the speed.
d   *He only saw* the stillness.
e   *He only saw* the deceptive grace of her head as it hung forward.
f   *And seeing only* this he pushed aside the ferns and rose to his feet.

(p. 419, *335*, my italics)

The reader will notice how perfectly framed this passage is. The first three elements—*a, b, c*—belong to the past, to the contents of the first section, being characterized by a verb—"to forget"—which has in itself a flavor of past things. The second three—*d, e, f*—belong to the present, because the verb used—"to see"—implies a present action. *f* is the direct link between the first and the second part of the chapter: by pushing aside the ferns, Titus comes out of the wings and joins the Thing on the stage of action, ceasing to be a mere hidden spectator. It is interesting to notice that *a* and *f* are perfectly symmetrical, since each of them begins with an "and".

The second part is, we have said, full of movement and action, but towards the end, when Titus is holding the Thing in his arms, Peake slackens the pace, to focus our attention on a very important moment of Titus's existence: his first sexual experience. Theatrically speaking, we could say that after the struggle in the limelight, the whole stage is now in darkness, except for a little spot of light framing the two protagonists lying on the floor. It is here, when Titus tears "at the shirt with his left [arm] until her face [is] free" from the garment (p. 423, *338*), that the tension reaches its highest point. The progressive mounting of the tone, started at the beginning of the chapter, culminates here, "as the first wild virgin kiss that trembled on his lips for release died out" (p. 423, *338*). Exactly at the end of the second part—i.e., half way through the chapter—the drama reaches its climax. Then, with the introduction of a new character, Fuchsia, we pass not only to part three but to an important change of situation as well. Titus's attention is distracted by Fuchsia's arrival, and the Thing frees herself from his grip. She goes out of the cave into the storm, and is killed by a flash of lightning. This is the other great event in the chapter, but, while the moment of Titus's embrace with the Thing was placed at the apex of a situation of extreme tension, the episode of the death of the Thing is expressed in more intimate and poetic terms. On page 424 (*339*), we read: "As he stared [at the Thing naked under the rain] a kind of ecstasy filled him. He had no sense of losing her—but only the blind and vaunting pride that he had held her in his arms..."

The physical climax has already been reached, and Titus feels satisfied. "Titus knew in his bones that he could expect no more than this" (p. 424, *339*). "But when...that searing flash of flame...burned up the 'Thing'...and when Titus knew that the world was without her for ever, then something fled in him...At seventeen he stepped into another country. It was his youth that had died away. His boyhood was something for remembrance only. He had become a man" (p. 424, *339*).

Here we reach the inner, emotional climax of the chapter, which is tightly linked with the other high point: the Thing dies, and Titus becomes a man after having the first sexual experience of his life. It is very significant that, at the end of section three, Titus begins to realize his personal situation in the new terms of his manhood with a concrete act: "When he parted the long locks

that straggled over her face . . . then he realized his own strength"
(p. 424, *339*).

The moments for dreaming, for illusion, for imagination have
died with the Thing. In the fourth section of the chapter a new
situation, real, concrete and dangerous—embodied by the trip
back under the storm—begins.

* * * *

We are now at the core of the book—perhaps even of the whole
trilogy. *Titus Groan* had described the setting of Titus's life;
Gormenghast, up to this point, had shown Titus in his longing to
be a different creature from what his inheritance imposed. Here,
by means of this major experience, he starts on his way towards
freedom—the freedom he will experience in *Titus Alone*.

The Thing plays a very important part in his evolution and
growth. She attracts him out of the castle when he is only a child.
She becomes the object of his first love experience. She dies and
takes away with her his boyhood. In these terms the Thing seems
to take on the features of a symbol—a symbol of adolescence, and
nothing more. But it is not so. She is a complex character, with a
life of her own, not a mere device to be put aside when it is no
longer useful. She is, first of all, a real creature, with all the needs
of every other human—or animal—being. Besides, it is interesting
to read a few notes from the end of volume one of the manuscript
quoted by John Batchelor, in which the Thing is called "Leaf";
"The Leaf is killed in storm. Titus returns through downpour.
The Universe weeps" (Batchelor, pp. 95-6).

It seems that the universe weeps because of her death, and we
are tempted to see the Thing as an embodiment of the natural
world, as Mr. Batchelor points out in his book on page 96.
Another important aspect of the Thing is that she forms a kind of
link between the world of the forest—green, natural and lively—
and the grey, unreal, closed world of the castle. She is in fact the
daughter of Keda, one of the Outer Dwellers, but lives in the
forest on her own. Finally, we must not forget that she is Titus's
foster-sister, since Keda had been his wet-nurse.

But, most of all, it is the particular quality of Peake's talent as
narrator that prevents his characters from becoming symbols, and
the whole story from becoming an allegory. Peake's way of writing
makes the symbol become narration; reality and fantasy are mixed
together, and we cannot—we must not—say which is which. Take,
for instance, the events narrated in the chapter we are dealing
with. Everything could be read as an allegory—Titus's boyhood

being taken away by the death of the Thing. And surely, if we summarized, in these terms, the contents of this or of any other chapter to someone who had never read Peake, it would sound extremely allegorical to him. But when we read we never gain this impression. It is only when we reflect on what we have read that questions begin to appear in our minds. When we return to the page, we are so engrossed by the narration that all such questions disappear.

Let us consider the situation of the first part of the chapter. Titus is observing an indefinite creature—just a "thing"—which at certain moments looks like a sprite, or an elf, and at others a little girl. We would not believe a word of what the writer is telling us, if he did not place this extremely fantastical situation in a very solid and realistic setting: a cave, with "rough walls of rock", and with torrential rain streaming down outside. Everything is real, concrete, tangible. The Thing herself, at times, is described as a very real being: she is squatting on the ground, eating a bird she has plucked. But when she moves, she becomes mysterious and uncanny again: "How it was that she had been able to move at all across the rockface with his shirt impeding the freedom of her legs, let alone travel so speedily, he could not tell" (p. 420, *336*). And more: "He saw her mouth open above him and at that moment she might have been a giant phantom, something too earthless to be held in by the worldly dimensions of this cave, something beyond measurement. And her open mouth gave him the answer to his question" (p. 421, *336*).

With this last sentence, we return to the field of reality. An important characteristic of Peake's art is *his continuous passing from reality to unreality, and vice versa*, so that we never realize whether it is a dream or not. This constant fluctuation between natural and unnatural, between real and unreal in the character of the Thing is epitomized when Titus succeeds in seizing her in his arms, "but what he caught was so unsubstantial that he fell with it to the floor from the very shock of its lightness ... He had caught at a feather and it had struck him down" (pp. 422-3, *338*). The Thing is concrete and real because Titus can clasp her, but at the same time she is so light, so "unsubstantial" that we are puzzled once more, and we think she is superhuman.

In fact, the situation itself is puzzling: a man making love with a sprite! and yet, while reading, we never doubt that everything really takes place, so much can the writer's talent carry us into this world of a concrete evanescence. The figure of the Thing, half way between the fabulous and the real, reminds us of another

great creation of literary imagination, the "hippogriff", the creature described by Ariosto in his *Orlando Furioso*:

> Non e finto il destrier ma naturale,
> c̆huna giumenta generò da un grifo,
> (Canto 4, stanza 18)

of which a rough translation would read:

> It is not false, the steed, but natural,
> that a mare and a griffin begot.

The comparison between Peake and Ariosto is suggested by the
fact that in both writers the fabulous is explained in natural terms.
The hippogriff is a fabulous animal, but nevertheless real, since
Ruggero (a character in the poem) takes long journeys on its back.
The Thing is a superhuman creature, but human at the same
time, because Titus clasps her and feels sexually attracted to her.
We could define this aspect of Peake's art—as also of Ariosto's as
"natural-marvellous" (*naturale-meraviglioso*).

Before chapter 68, the Thing had always appeared to Titus as
something inconsistent and aerial, with the exception of when, in
chapter 64, she is no longer "a fume of his mind, a vapor' (p.
403, *323*), but a creature "with a mixture of grace and savagery
quite indescribable' (p. 402, *321*). In chapter 68, Titus observes
her more closely and the impression he receives is by no means
pleasant. She is no longer a "lyric swallow", but is "squatting there
like a frog in the dust" (p. 416, *332*). Titus notices with disappointment that "the rarefaction had become clay" (p. 416, *332*).
Titus's reaction, portrayed by Peake with remarkable psychological precision, is the disappointment of every adolescent facing the
reality of life. What before was ideal becomes suddenly brutal,
often disagreeable and different from what we expected. "His
memory of her, of a proud and gracile creature, was now
destroyed.... This was something new and earthy" (p. 416, *333*).
It is this last adjective, denoting concreteness, banality if you like,
that defines the nature of Titus's bitter discovery. But in other
passages, as we have seen, the Thing retains her fabulous, uncanny
features, and a certain beauty linked with the grace of her flight:
"The ease with which she had flitted from ledge to perilous
ledge... had made him lust for her small breasts and her slender
limbs" (p. 420, *336*).

When Titus is wounded by the Thing he is angry, but excited at the same time, "for what was she doing but defying, through him, the very core of Gormenghast?" (p. 420, *336*). This co-existence of "grace and savagery" in the figure of the Thing is therefore very important, because it communicates a double stimulus to Titus: to love and rebellion. John Batchelor has not well caught this double aspect of the Thing in the latter part of the novel. He writes that at the beginning the Thing is "gentle, wise and altruistic", but, "in the latter part Peake simply changes his mind, perhaps because the figure refused to develop or because her spirituality had become insipid" (Batchelor, p. 99). We have seen, on the contrary, that her change is perfectly in tune with Titus's evolution and with the development of the story.

Lack of space prevents me from pointing out other interesting aspects of this chapter, but we must do justice to a remarkable side of Peake's talent: his use of language. The chapter is rich in fine passages and beautiful images. Just one instance: the Thing silhouetted against the brilliance of the lightning, "the mouth wide open as though to drink the sky" (p. 418, *334*). This is effective and highly poetic. It is a plastic image of the kind we often meet with in Peake. He liked portraying his characters in plastic postures, as though he were sketching a painting or a drawing. His original vocation for painting and drawing was always with him, and we can well say that often he painted with words, creating those "arabesques", those "tremendous stories" that he spoke of in a letter sent to his wife from Ireland.

The writer would like to express his gratitude to Maeve Gilmore for her kindness in answering his questions and making useful suggestions.

FUCHSIA AND STEERPIKE:
MOOD AND FORM

G. Peter Winnington

WHEN Mervyn Peake wrote *Titus Groan*, he knew what mood he wanted to create and he worked to achieve it, but he let the precise *form* of the book come by itself; he had no preconceived idea of how the plot was to develop. Consequently, the correlates of time and space in which the action takes place are riddled with inconsistency. On the other hand, those elements which go to make up the mood of the book, in particular the choice of words and images, hang together perfectly. To demonstrate one small aspect of this, I shall examine the language Peake used to describe the meetings between Fuchsia and Steerpike in *Titus Groan* and *Gormenghast*.

First of all, let's consider the plot and the lack of detailed advance planning. Peake's notes show that, right from the start, Fuchsia was destined to meet a tragic end that would closely involve Steerpike. But for nine years, Peake was undecided as to the manner of her death. In October 1940, when he had written about a hundred pages of *Titus Groan* (Steerpike was still locked up, and the christening scene was still to be completed), Peake thought that Steerpike should kill Fuchsia. On December 13 the same year, he wondered, "Does she commit suicide or is she killed by Steerpike?" (From the manuscripts at University College, London, Box 1, Notebook iii, hereafter abbreviated thus: MS 1.iii. I have silently corrected Peake's spelling, but left the punctuation unchanged.) He imagines "a terrible scene" in which she strikes him for suggesting that they should marry. "Thinking she has killed him [she] goes through a mental agony, revisits her attic and burns her treasures? & is burned with them. Has taken poison from [Steerpike's] purloined bottles.????" (MS1.iii)

Even when *Gormenghast* was well advanced in July 1949, we find Peake still wondering,"??Does Steerpike give Fuchsia a child and she kills him and finding herself pregnant—kills herself" (MS 3.iv). As he developed the idea of the flood, the possibility of her drowning occurred to him: "Fuchsia climbs to her attic, either slips on stairs or leaps from her attic window having tied a great weight around her body" (MS 3.iv). And so he came to write that

MEETINGS BETWEEN FUCHSIA AND STEERPIKE

1. *TG*, pp. 153-5, *119-21*. Escaping from the kitchens, Steerpike climbs over the roofs of Gormenghast and reaches Fuchsia's attic, where she discovers him.

2. *TG*, pp. 273-8, *213-17*. Steerpike forces his company on Fuchsia during one of her country walks; seeking to shelter in a cave from a sudden rainstorm, Fuchsia falls and Steerpike goes for help.

3. *TG*, pp. 285, *223* & 290-2, *227-29*. Steerpike waylays Fuchsia a few days later and expounds his views on equality.

4. *TG*, pp. 318-19, *248-49*. To escape from the burning library, Fuchsia climbs to a window and finds herself face to face with Steerpike, who is staging the rescue.

5. *TG*, pp. 339-41, *265-66*. At the burial of Sourdust, they face each other across the grave and afterwards walk together.

6. *TG*, pp. 374, *292-93*. Lord Groan goes mad; Fuchsia is sent to fetch Steerpike and she collides with him at the corner of a staircase.

7. *G*, pp. 23-25, *15-16*. "His Infernal Slyness, the Arch-fluke Steerpike" visits Fuchsia in her bedroom by climbing down a rope. He leaves a rosebud on her dressing table.

8. *G*, pp. 193-5, *153-54*. Steerpike contrives to meet Fuchsia at Nannie Slagg's grave.

9. *G*, pp. 343-5, *274-75*. Here several meetings are telescoped. Peake describes the evolution of Fuchsia's feelings for Steerpike.

10. *G*, pp. 351-7, *280-84*. The last rendezvous when Steerpike calls her a fool for lighting a candle at his door.

poignant death scene which Mr. Batchelor summarizes so heartlessly (and inaccurately): "Fuchsia drowns herself by leaping from a window" (Batchelor, p. 70). It's important to get the details right: after Steerpike has been unmasked, Fuchsia's discovery of his true nature her to lapse into a state of melancholy—a predisposition for which she inherited from her father. At the height of the flood, she conceives the idea of suicide and, playing a game rather than acting deliberately, she climbs onto the windowsill. Her reverie is interrupted by a knock on the door of her room. "Starting at the sound and finding herself dangerously balanced upon a narrow sill above the deep water, she trembled uncontrollably, and in trying to turn without sufficient thought or care, she slipped and clutching at the face of the wall at her side found nothing to grasp. so that she fell, striking her dark head on the sill as she passed, and was already unconscious before the water received her, and drowned her at its ease" (*G* p. 454, *363*).

Although her death is accidental, Steerpike is partially responsible for it, as the main cause of her depression. It seems so appropriate, so tragically inevitable, almost predictable. This impression derives not from the action, but from other elements which we can examine in the meetings between Fuchsia and Steerpike. (For the sake of convenience, I have listed these meetings separately and will refer to them by number.)

The first meeting is particularly revealing in this respect. As Fuchsia approaches her attic room, Steerpike lies on the floor, pretending to be in a faint. In the "deathly stillness", he can hear Fuchsia's heart beating (*TG*, p. 153, *119*). The fatal nature of the encounter is underlined remorselessly in the next sentence: "For the first few moments, Fuchsia had remained inert, her spirit dead to what she saw before her. As with those who on hearing of the death of their lover are numb to the agony that must later wrack them, so she for those first few moments stood incomprehensive and stared with empty eyes" (p. 153, *119*). Later we are told that she does not know whether he is "recovering or dying" (p. 154, *119*); the idea of his dying in her room is appalling to her (p. 155, *120*). In another writer's work, this would point to Steerpike's death. For Peake, it is rather the "aura" of death that surrounds their relationship.

This first meeting takes place in semi-darkness, lighted only by the single candle Fuchsia holds. In contrast to this darkness, there is the fire of emotion that flares up within her, prefiguring her brief love for Steerpike, and echoing "the agony that must later wrack" her: "As she stood there it was as though within her a bonfire had been lighted. It grew until it reached the zenith of its power and died away, but undestroyable among the ashes lay the ache of a wound for which there was no balm" (p. 154, *119*). Peake also used the sunflower (pp. 155-6, *120-21*) to underline this image of the "burning passion" that ends in death.

These elements of death, darkness and fire form a leitmotiv to the subsequent meetings between Fuchsia and Steerpike. Two of them (numbers 5 and 8) take place beside graves; in the eighth, "they were using for their pillow the narrow grassy grave-mound of her old nurse" (*G*, p. 195, *154*); the third is set against the "death-throes" of a sunset (*TG*, p. 292, *228*); in the seventh, evocation of their second meeting causes the atmosphere to become "deathly silent" (*G*, p. 24, *282*) and at their final meeting, Fuchsia's eyes "appeared quite dead" (*G*, p. 353, *282*).

Death and darkness are clearly connected in this context, as in the "death-throes" of the sunset. The meetings almost invariably take place in twilight, or involve a progression towards shadow. In fact, a general movement towards greater darkness may be observed, culminating in the "depression of utter blackness [that] drowned" Fuchsia (*G*, p. 395, *315*). A few instances:

Meeting 2: hardly have they met when they find that "the

autumn sunlight had given way to a fast tattered sky" (*TG*, p. 274, *214*). Soon, rain is falling "in a mass of darkness". The recesses of the cave in which they shelter are "in deep darkness" but they remain "in the dull light near the shielded entrance" (p. 277, *216*). Just as they refrain from going into the deeper darkness of the cave, so do their hands, which are close together, abstain from making contact (cf. meeting 9).

Meeting 3: Steerpike's disquisition on equality opens as they pass "into the light of the sinking sun" (*TG*, p. 291, *227*); when it ends, "they walked on in silence, and by the time they had reached the castle night had descended" (p. 293, *229*).

Meeting 5: the conversation takes place as "they were treading into the shadow of a tower" (*TG*, p. 341, *266*).

Meeting 7: although this is a daylight meeting, Fuchsia's room "darkened, for half the light from her window was suddenly obscured by the miraculous appearance of the young man with high shoulders" (*G*, p. 23, *14*). By the time he has left, a few minutes later, "the sky had darkened" (p. 25, *16*).

Meeting 8: in the dramatic parting that follows their fall onto Nannie Slagg's grave, Fuchsia "bounded like a wild thing into the darkness" (*G*, p. 195, *154*).

Meeting 9: here the terms are more general; Steerpike is her "man of the dusk"; "their hands met involuntarily in the darkness" (both p. 344, *275*).

The last meeting is the darkest of all: Steerpike extinguishes Fuchsia's candle and thrusts her into his unlighted room. The darkness towards which they progress is synonymous with the fatal character of their relationship; it also reflects Fuchsia's melancholy nature, "more easily drawn to the dark than the light" (*G*, p. 452, *362*), and helps to explain, in metaphorical terms, how she is attracted to Steerpike.

He, who so detests love, cold-bloodedly kindles her love for him, and it flares up, as in the bonfire image of the first meeting. At the height of the blaze, when Steerpike is planning to seduce her, Fuchsia comes to her midnight rendezvous, "her pupils dilated in the darkness" (p. 350, *279*) and commits the error of lighting a candle at Steerpike's door. "It was but a few moments before his swift, narrow, high-shouldered form was upon her and had snatched the candle from her hand and crushed out flame. In another moment his key had been turned in the lock and she had been hustled through the door. He locked it from the inside, in the darkness, but he had already whispered fiercely "Fool." With that word the world turned over. Everything changed" (p. 351, *280*).

Out goes the fire. Her love is extinguished. "She turned on her heel, in the darkened room, and before he had lit the lamp, 'Let me out of here,' she said" (*G*, p. 353, *281*). The literal and the metaphorical planes work together to emphasize the abrupt transition. "There you were, like a bonfire," says Steerpike (p. 354, *283*), echoing the simile used to describe their first meeting (when Fuchsia also had a candle in her hand). Now, even the gift of a monkey cannot rekindle her passion: "What would once have inflamed her with excitement, left her now, at this paralyzing moment, quite frozen" (p. 353, *282*). And "undestroyable among the ashes lay the ache of a wound for which there was no balm" (*TG*, p. 154, *119*).

I have neglected the intervening references to fire in favor of the striking bonfire simile. But we cannot pass over the most memorable fire of all, when Steerpike burns down the library. The chapter ends with Fuchsia's glimpse of Steerpike through the window she is about to break: "As Fuchsia began to swing her arm at the high window she focused her eyes upon it and found herself staring at a face—a face framed with darkness within a few feet of her own. It sweated firelight, the crimson shadows shifting across it as the flames leapt in the room below. Only the eyes repelled the lurid air. Close-set as nostrils they were not so much eyes as narrow tunnels through which the Night was pouring" (*TG*, p. 319, *249*). Notice how the fire is on Fuchsia's side of course, and is "repelled" by Steerpike's eyes. The capitalized "Night" is something of a surprise, for Peake rarely uses such devices. Within the context of this relationship, however, its use at this point becomes eloquent, as though Fuchsia had glimpsed her fate. And her reaction provides corroboration: "As Fuchsia recognized the head of Steerpike, the rod fell from her outstretched arm, her weakened hand loosed its grasp upon the shelf and she fell backwards into space, the dark hair of her head reaching below her as she fell, her body curving backwards as though she had been struck" (p. 319, *249*).

This fall closely resembles her final fall with which I began, except that in her fall to her death, she hits her head against the windowsill. We may be reminded here of how the birthday breakfast is punctuated by the sound of Fuchsia's head hitting the table. It is in this way that, as I said earlier, Fuchsia's death seems appropriate and tragically inevitable. Despite his lack of planning, Peake had prepared his readers for it throughout the two books: all the elements of the death scene are rehearsed in her meetings with Steerpike, so that although he is absent on that occasion, he is present in the associations we have learned to make.

At the first meeting, as Fuchsia suspiciously scrutinizes the prostrate body on her attic floor, "a blob of the hot wax [of her candle] fell across her wrist and she started as though she had been struck" (*TG*, p. 154, *119*). She needs a candlestick, but dare not take her eyes off Steerpike, so she retreats, backwards: "Before reaching the wall, however, the calf of her leg came into unexpected contact with the edge of the couch, and she sat down very suddenly upon it as though she had been tapped behind the knees" (p. 154, *119*).

Fuchsia is naturally a clumsy girl, and in the presence of Steerpike she seems even to lose her sense of balance. The second meeting illustrates this perfectly. "As she began the short, steep descent she turned for an instant to see whether Steerpike had kept pace with her, and as she turned, her feet slipped away from under her on the slithery surface of an oblique slab, and she came crashing to the ground, striking the side of her face, her shoulders and shin with a force that for the moment stunned her" (*TG*, pp. 275-6, *215*).

Beside Nannie Slagg's grave, Steerpike provokes Fuchsia by carelessly tossing away his carefully prepared wreath of roses, and she responds by burying her nails in his cheeks. Then "a tide of remorse filled her" and "she stumbled towards him [with] her arms outstretched. Quick as an adder he was in her arms—but even at that moment they fell, tripping each other up on the rough ground—fell, their arms about one another" (*G*,. p. 194, *154*).

Fuchsia lives intensely in her imagination, so that when she is abruptly recalled to the outer world, she jumps nervously. Steerpike's lightning visit by rope to her room (meeting 7) is prefaced by a tableau of Fuchsia at her window. "Then she moved, suddenly turning about at a sound behind her and found Mrs. Slagg looking up at her" (*G*, p. 21, *13*). Steerpike's arrival provokes a similarly brusque reaction: "Before Fuchsia had had a moment to ponder how any human being could appear on her window-sill a hundred feet above the ground—let alone recognize the silhouette— she snatched a hairbrush from the table before her and brandished it behind her head in readiness for she knew not what" (p. 23, *14-15*).

The last meeting sees her jump in a similar manner. As she stands before Steerpikes door, there comes the disembodied voice of Flay, who is concealed on a ledge above the doorway: "Fuchsia had started at the sound as at the touch of a red iron" (*G*, p. 351, *280*). And with this simile we return to fire images.

Within the limited scope of this article, from which I have excluded all other references to fire, death and darkness, I hope I have shown how consistent was the working of Peake's imagination. Time and again, the compete evolution of the relationship between Fuchsia and Steerpike is mirrored in a single meeting: Fuchsia's initial suspicion and reticence are craftily transformed by Steerpike into sympathy and confidence, which are then shattered by some unforeseeable event or tactless remark, whereupon her feelings swing back towards horror and disgust.

What is particularly striking is the contrast between Peake's groping for the plot and his sureness of touch in describing this relationship. We know that Peake made many alterations to his books between first draft and published text, yet a study of the manuscripts shows that the passages I have quoted here come through from first to last, untouched. In fact, many passages show no hesitation, even in the initial writing—no recasting of sentences, no juggling with adjectives and no crossing out. Peake knew precisely what he was doing here, and in this way he works subtly on the readers expectations. Therein lies the mastery, and the mystery, of Mervyn Peake.

I should like to thank Maeve Gilmore for her kind permission to quote from Mervyn Peake's manuscripts. GPW

GORMENGHAST: PSYCHOLOGY OF THE BILDUNGSROMAN

Bruce Hunt

GORMENGHAST, that spacious warehouse of dreams, contains more than is visible through any one of its myriad windows. The critic may crawl the length of its crenellated backbone, pausing like Steerpike in attempts to ascertain the dimensions of the beast, and still fail to pass beyond his own abstractions. No one has yet managed to "totalize" Gormenghast. That particular critical feat must await its competent thaumaturge, and until his or her inevitable arrival we must be content with projecting into the arena the widest range of readings that can be mustered. Our mastermind will need a broom. A polymath, indeed, might fit the post best, for judging by even the present range of readings, Peake's super-critic will need the ability to synthesize rather than the ability to promote one point of view to the exclusion of all others as pre-texts or reductions.

The psychological basis of my own contribution here does, I admit, entail a reduction: but then I do not see my reading as central or final to the process of criticizing the Gormenghast trilogy (I decline for now the struggle over definition which promises to be both endless and fruitless). The psychology is, I believe, valid on its own terms despite the onslaughts of other schools for whom co-existence is logically or ideologically inconceivable. Provided it is not used as a tool of obscurantism it can certainly be of use in the study of literature.

The concept of the *Bildungsroman*, my second starting point, is a debatable one: the word itself is perhaps used rather too often and too loosely, both by myself and by others. It does however indicate the primary object of this study, which is the chain of events, present throughout the trilogy but most clearly in evidence in *Gormenghast*, that deals with Titus's growth from childhood to apparent maturity. The pattern constituted by this selection from the plot has much in common with the traditional shape of the *Bildungsroman*. But "*Bildungsroman*" is more than a simple descriptive term. In its outward aspect, in the incidents which are seen to form the character of the protagonist, the *Bildunsroman* may usually be taken as a mediated but fairly close representation

of socio-cultural systems of belief and knowledge, with the learning and development of the protagonist appearing as a commentary on the external world and on the protagonist's relation to it.
However, there seems to be, in the common structure which
defines the *Bildungsroman*, an inner meaning that may benefit
from a psychological explanation (and, I suspect, from a cyber-
netic one too). The universal experience of growth is at the root
of the *Bildungsroman* genre. All such novels exist partly in order
to embody it, albeit in a displaced form and on their own imaginative terms. It is not difficult to recognize elements of initiation
rituals and so-called primitive myths and symbols in any *Bildungsroman*, and this invites a consideration, at least, of the implications of the extended symbolic and indeed religious dimensions of
such works. Rituals, myths, and symbols do of course exist as social
institutions, as the word "religious" implies, but it is with the
psychology of the individual in its existential or phenomenological
aspect that I am concerned here.

Despite the wide range and complexity of actual *Bildungsromane*,
inevitable when one considers the socially mimetic aspect of the
genre, it is quite possible to abstract and describe the inner order
common to them all in general and, I hope, not trivially schematic
terms. To do this I must use a recognizable vocabulary and the
Jungian model of individuation, based as it is on observation of a
wide range of pertinent phenomena, is both adequate and appropriate, although it is of course limited in other, ideological,
directions. According to this model, each individual is faced with
the task of achieving psychic wholeness, the process being in some
ways analogous to physical development. The psyche must differentiate itself from the continuum of infantile consciousness, especially surmounting the inevitable tendency towards partial self-denial.
Eventually (and this chronology is of course an abstraction) the
conscious psyche establishes contact, by means of symbolic encounter, with the unconscious mind, and integrates conscious behavior with the inmost regulative processes of the mind. It is a
process of finding identity, and as such shares with its religious
equivalents the right to self-validation, beyond the range of ana-
lytic discourse. And, whether conceived in Jungian terms or not, it
is the root-experience of the *Bildungsroman*, and perhaps of all
literary forms of the quest myth.

The world of Gormenghast, despite the brilliance and clarity of
Peake's verbal creation of tactile and visual realities, exists outside
of ordinary space and time: its space-time is *mythic*, its action is,
on the whole, that of *idealized romance* (within which we can
discern the subordinate elements of *Bildungsroman*, political and

social allegory and satire, comedy, farce, tragedy, and no doubt others, so encyclopaedic is the whole), and many of its meanings are to be found in a *symbolic* reading. In the following discussion I shall examine a series of incidents in their dual significance as "real" and symbolic actions, stressing in particular the latter mode of interpretation.

Titus is seven at the beginning of *Gormenghast*. His first appearance is on his pony, and his first action is one of disobedience. He tastes "sharp fruits," he experiences a "sudden itch for rebellion." Apart from the Christening and the deliberately symbolic moment at the end of *Titus Groan*, when the infant drops stone and ivy, "sacrosanct symbols" (*TG*, p. 496,*388*), into the lake, and establishes a magical contact with his foster-sister, as a rainbow curves over Gormenghast and the Thing's voice fills the universe, Titus has done little to assert his individuality. Here, at age seven, he is "old enough to sense his uniqueness" as heir to the Earldom, and is also "conscious of always being watched" (*G*, p. 19, *11*). The incident itself is tiny, but already we see external events counterpointed by forces from within. Peake does not make any explicit connexion, feeling it sufficient to juxtapose the two.

The next incident I select is Titus's classroom reverie (*G*, ch. 14). Too long to quote, the reverie is essentially an experience of initiation. Titus begins to follow thoughts and pictures through his mind for the *first* time (*G*, p. 83, *62*). Peake regales us with a feast of color, form, texture, thought, and feeling as the reverie develops to its climax. Titus sees—he does not merely fantasize—a pirate, "the central buccaneer, a great salt-water lord" (*G*, p. 85, *65*), whose eye looms into Titus's vision until he can see nothing else:

There was nothing else in the great world but this—globe. It *was* the world, and suddenly like the world it rolled. And as it rolled it grew yet again, until there was nothing but the pupil, filling the consciousness; and in that midnight pupil Titus saw the reflection of himself peering forward.

(*GG*, p. 86, *65*)

I observe in passing that such passages only work because Peake uses language symbolically and magically, for my main purpose is to show that here outer and inner worlds intermingle to mark Titus's growth. An essential part of Titus's growth is that he should break through the deadening forms of castle life to that which is alive and quickening. In this reverie the outer world of shape and color is transformed by aesthetic perception into an inner world of meaningful imagination. This is a crucial step.

Titus henceforth uses this very power of transformation to effect his liberation and further growth. When he sees "himself peering forward" he signals awareness of the ineluctable future.

In a world whose very existence depends on the symbolic rather than the simply denotational force of words, it is not surprising to find specific symbols operating in a coherent semantic scheme. This is the case throughout the Gormenghast trilogy. Castle, mountain, cave, lake, river, forest, labyrinth, city, underworld: these are the features of a symbolic landscape rather then the reproductions of a lifelike one, for despite their sensory vibrancy they are the visualizations of *ideas*. But I must assume this rather than prove it, for there is no space here to enumerate the instances of symbolic function or to correlate particular symbols with external systems. Nor is this entirely necessary, for all the decisive symbols are so strongly stressed in the text that it would be superfluous to try and verify their non-textual meaning, and willful to deny their existence.

Titus's moments of growth may be envisioned, as they are often indeed staged, as excursions or sorties from castle life into new experience followed by return to the first state, which is of course progressively modified as the story proceeds. Chapter 15 introduces Gormenghast Mountain into Titus's experience:

The mountain's head shone in a great vacancy of light. It held within its ugly contour either everything or nothing at all. It awakened the imagination by its peculiar emptiness.

And from it came the voice again.
"Do you dare? Do you dare?"

(*GG*, p. 97, 74-75)

In the dominant symbolic scheme, to put the matter briefly, the castle is death, matter, mother, childhood consciousness and repression, the moribund self; the mountain, its Geminian counterpart, is life, spirit, father, self-awakening, wholeness. Titus, the questing ego, uses his magical imagination to create the situations that free him. Here, he rides up the mountain, which is shining down to him through the mist, and then looks back over the mist at the castle. It is a timeless moment: "It seemed that the heart of the world had ceased to beat." The castle appears as a skull, its ivy and flags likened to the fluttering long hair of a corpse, "teeth-like" windows running along its brow. The "baleful" mist is dispersed, "the day was warm and young, and Titus was on the slopes of Gormenghast Mountain" (*G*, pp. 101, 102, 77, 78). From this position, this association of himself with the external forces of

life, Titus gains the strength to penetrate, and the word is apt, the
alluring labyrinth of the green and gold forest between the twin
peaks of castle and mountain: "Titus, wrenching two boughs
apart, thrust himself forward and wriggled into the green darkness" (*G*, p. 130, *102*). This part of the natural world is a
threshold of transformation. Peake fuses sexual and psychological
symbolism with traditional iconography (green and gold as the
colors of idyllic innocence), Titus enters this labyrinthine and
formally abstract theater of the unconscious, abandoning his coat
(traditionally a symbol of personality), and begins to "fly" through
a dream reality. As delight turns to fear we realize the transformation has begun. He plunges towards the center of the forest—and
sees the Thing for the first time. But she is registered as part of
the dream: "Titus was by now convinced that he was asleep: that
he was running through the deep of a dream: that his fear was
nightmare: that what he had just seen was no more than an
apparition" (*G*, p. 132, *103*), and he passes her by. The image/idea
remains though, and as Titus returns from the dream world he
brings it with him, first admitting her reality, then using it to
expand his own consciousness. Peake allows no ambiguity as to
what this signifies:

Something for which he had unconsciously pined had shown either itself
or its emblem in the gold oak woods.... What was it that cried to him?
What was it that this shred, this floating shred of life, expressed? For in the
air with which it had moved through space was a quality for which Titus
unknowingly hungered.... He had seen something which lived a life of
its own: which had no respect for the ancient lords of Gormenghast.... He
beat his fist into the palm of his other hand.... The glimpse of a world, of
an unformulated world, where human life could be lived by other rules
than those of Gormenghast, had shaken him.

(*GG*, pp. 133-4, *104-105*)

Once again, the events of the external world, representing as
usual real incidents in Titus's physical passage from childhood to
maturity, are transformed by the mind into a symbolic operation,
a magical and stately ballet whose dancers, abstract and ideal, act
out a universal drama, an "immortal mime" (*G*, p. 130, *102*), to
apply Peake's own description of these happenings.

   Passing over the parallel labyrinthine experience of chapter 26,
in which Titus breaks free from the oppression of the moribund
castle, again both literally and symbolically, I come to Titus's final
and decisive encounter with the Thing, examined interestingly in
Cristiano Rafanelli's article "Titus and the Thing in Gormenghast,"
reprinted on page 289.

Rafanelli's treatment certainly reveals the importance of this episode, indeed overestimating it at one point: Titus does not start on his way towards freedom in this chapter, but as I have shown, much earlier, in fact in *Titus Groan*. But Rafanelli does not discuss the wider context of the incident—Titus's previous encounters with the Thing and her subsequent function in his consciousness. I cannot here go into the antecedents of the Thing in much detail. She is Keda's daughter and Titus's foster-sister. A careful reading of Keda's story will reveal her importance as the Thing's mother: the Thing is in fact the child of passion, suffering, and sacrifice, not human—she exhibits no human qualities, indeed their absence is made clear—but a perfectly conceived animal figure, a mediator to the unconscious, enticing yet dangerous, ethereal yet ferocious. Only the admission of a symbolic function such as I have described can account for the Thing's power over Titus and consequent importance in the story. Titus's rage to possess her sexually is really a projection, an emotional correlative to the psychic need to assimilate her, to draw her meaning into himself where she can act as the animating center of his growing consciousness. Notice that at the moment of embrace, the Thing recedes into abstraction as far as Peake can take her:

He could not see her face ... it was like the head of sea-blurred marble long drowned beneath innumerable tides ... his body and his imagination fused in a throbbing lust ... his whole body weakened.... She had ceased to move. His tears ran.... He had become far away and he knew that there would be no climax.

(GG, p. 423, *338*)

Of course Titus cannot consummate his desire, for the Thing is a part of himself, related to him through a common mother. The Jungian theory of incest, be it noted, is that it symbolizes the longing for union with the essence of one's own self, for individuation.

Following her death, the Thing becomes central to Titus's inner world, whereas before she has been a magnetically attractive external pole. This is achieved through the device of Titus's canoe. Unconsciously the two are identified in his mind:

What he did not guess was that the canoe was neither more nor less than the *Thing*. Deep in the chaos of his heart and his imagination—at the core of his dreamworld it was so—the Canoe had become, perhaps had already been when he had first sent her skimming beneath him into the freedom of an outer world, the very center of Gormenghast forest, the Thing herself.

(*GG*, pp. 467-8, *374*)

Notice how the sexual reference is retained in the phrase "skimming beneath him into ... freedom," and in the direct recall of the forest experience.

And what of Steerpike? This complex and intriguing character—vibrant, lucid, cerebral, demonic—enacts separate though related dramas in *Titus Groan* and *Gormenghast*. He is, first, the usurper, the killer of the earl/king, the heartless and soulless symbol of the self ruled by ritual, "the ghastly ritual, that denies the spirit" (*G*, p. 150, *118*). Second, he is Titus's shadow, the mimic, the fake, the "cold cerebral beast" (*G*, p. 488, *391*), the demonic creature who, as he struts over his victims, is the agent of "dim primordial gods of power and blood" (*G*, p. 381, *303*), destroyed by the very forces he has tried to repress. As the shadow of Titus (who is impulsive, intuitive, emotional, sensitive, and imaginative—all that Steerpike is not) he, like the Thing, must somehow be assimilated into Titus's growing consciousness. Peake achieves this by turning Titus into a hero of mythic dimensions, a transformation that is natural to the mythos of romance and whose psychological purpose is twofold: deliverance from the infantile world and mastery of the shadow by violent destruction (not the same as repressive denial).

To be such a hero is dangerous, since it may lead to a distorted identification of the true self with what is in fact a limited role. Titus's errors of self-perception deserve separate study, but I wish to note one here: "He had emptied the bright goblet of romance; at a single gulp he had emptied it" (*G*, p. 424, *339*). This is simply wrong, for despite the death of the Thing, Titus's encounter with Steerpike, which is the climax for the romance structure, is still to come. But before tracing the consequences of this misidentification we should examine Titus's confrontation with Steerpike. Titus has intuitively discovered Steerpike's wherebouts, and prepares to attack him; from the inspiration of the guess,

a kind of power climbed through him like sap. Not the power of Gormenghast, or the pride of lineage. These were but dead-sea fruit. But the power of the imagination's pride. He, Titus, the traitor, was about to prove his existence, spurred by his anger, spurred by the romanticism of his nature which cried not now for paper boats, or marbles, or the monsters on their stilts, or the mountain cave, or the Thing afloat among the golden oaks, or anything but vengeance and sudden death and the knowledge that he was not watching any more, but living at the core of drama.

(*GG*, p. 493, 394-35).

All the decisive incidents of Titus's growth are here named and recalled, then rejected as the paramount need for vengeance and death conducts Titus to the center of the drama—not life, but drama. This is a fine perception by Peake, for the pattern enacted here, whose full complexity I have only suggested, is indeed *given*, like the text of a play, and Titus's story is but a single performance of it. Peake's awareness of this can be seen elsewhere, at the beginning of *Gormenghast*, when he explains Titus's coming rebellion as a ritual—a law—"more compelling than ever man devised" (*G*, p. 7, *1*) and at the end, when he decides to leave the castle:

He ran in the acknowledgement of a law as old as the laws of his home. The law of flesh and blood. The law of longing. The law of change. The law of youth. . . .
    And it was the law of quest. The law that few obey for lack of valor. The craving of the young for the unknown and all that lies beyond the tenuous skyline.

(*GG*, p. 508, *407*)

But inherent in Titus's triumph as the hero of romance, the "dragonslayer" who has destroyed Steerpike, the "almost legendary monster" (*G*, p. 505, *405*), is a crippling weakness. If a continuity is assumed between *Gormenghast* and *Titus Alone* it is difficult to explain the startling change in Titus's personality, from heroic confidence to confused shame and anxiety. I suggest that Titus has experienced dissociation from his true self, as a consequence of over-identification with his self-image as hero, which was appropriate only in the situations of Gormenghast. In *Titus Alone* we see Titus undergoing ordeal by experience. Again Peake constructs a world of symbolic landscapes and characters, thus freeing the archetypes from the restraints of social verisimilitude (the city as labyrinth is a feature of many *Bildungsromane*, but seldom does the ideal image inform the presentation as it does in Peake). Only after certain successful moral realizations and symbolic operations can Titus recover his Gormenghast-self and find the freedom of identity. Those who claim that the plan for a fourth *Titus* book destroys the notion of a trilogy miss, in my opinion, the dramatic unity of the three existing volumes. To be sure, more adventures could have been written, but I feel from looking at the plan (see Watney, p. 225) that a picaresque chronicle, vivid but desultory, would have been the probable result.

I have attempted to select for discussion the incidents that most clearly reveal the course of Titus's development in *Bildungsroman* fashion. From childhood to final adjustment Titus crosses a series of experiential thresholds, slowly mastering both the difficulties of his external situation and the taxing obstructions and challenges inherent in the processes of psychic growth. I have stressed mainly the inward shape of the story, not because I do not value the vitality of the action as it is, but because it has not yet received its critical due, and because, after all, it suggests something of real value. The story of Titus—and obviously the adventure action, by my reading, is not contingent but decisive in that it releases the meanings of Peake's symbolic universe—is not vaguely life-giving. It invites, and through its stylistic and dramatic artistry, secures, the reader's assent to a distinct version of ethical and psychological reality.

GORMENGHAST:
FAIRYTALE GONE WRONG?

Margaret Ochocki

Tzvetan Todorov's study, *The Fantastic*, has brought the subject of literary genre to the foreground of modern criticism. In his book, Todorov proposed that the genre generally (and sometimes loosely) termed *fantasy* actually consists of a number of closely related but distinctly recognizable modes or sub-genres. However, few of the subsequent studies of fantasy literature that attempt an estimation of Peake have considered the overall modal nature of his work, preferring to assess the subject matter, with its social and political metaphors. While it may be a specious endeavor to 'pigeon-hole' Peake for posterity—for the author himself made no attempt to categorize his works beyond using the careless term *romance*—the generic nature of Peake's fantasy is nevertheless pertinent because it remains undefined. The Gothic label has been loudly disclaimed, but it still appears in the blurb of the Penguin *Gormenghast*. It was William Hazlitt who, in 1820, first described a particular literary style as 'Gothic and grotesque', thus clearly linking the two terms. What is considered 'Gothic' in Peake's work is often simply grotesque. However, more recently, and perhaps more significantly in Peake's case, the Gothic has been theoretically linked with a very different generic term: *fairytale*.

Jan B. Gordon, writing of the seemingly contradictory nature of nineteenth-century fantasy (in *Aspects of Alice*, ed. R. Phillips, Gollancz, 1972) has suggested that the fairytale and the Gothic tale are 'the reverse sides of the same coin'. Although he did not elaborate the point, there seems every logical reason why this should be true. On a psychological level, Gothic fantasy is based upon man's primitive fears revisited, fairytale upon childhood's intuitive sense exploited. Possible common ground between the consciousness of the primitive and the child was suggested by Freud in his study, *The Uncanny* (1919). On a literary level, the German forests that gave birth to the fairytale were also the birthplace of the darker tales of E. T. A. Hoffmann, who created his fantasy world out of a nightmarish perversion of those fairy-tale images—*The Sandman* is a case in point—which were his legacy long before they became familiar to the British child. Fairytale

and Gothic, which diverged under the respective influences of
Grimm and Hoffmann, both present an image of the fantastic. In
the Gothic tale, the fantastic element is fearful, irrational and
emotive, with little in the way of moderation, the narrative being
totally subjective. Conversely, fairytale fantasy is wise and coherent, a world in miniature whose symbolism reflects the real world
in its various moods and, by its stylized format of heroes and
villains, demonstrates that evil may be challenged and overcome.
The fears that are celebrated in the Gothic are subjugated in the
fairytale. These differentiae are crucial and one would expect
them to be plainly marked. However, this is not always the case.
   Consider these two extracts: fairytale or Gothic?

There was [in the masked guests] much of the beautiful, much of the
wanton, much of the bizarre, something of the terrible, and not a little of
that which might have excited disgust. To and fro in the seven rooms
there stalked, in fact, a multitude of dreams [which] writhed in and
about, taking hue from the rooms and causing the wild music of the
orchestra to seem as the echo of their steps.

All at once, with such a shiver as when one is suddenly conscious of the
presence of another in a room where he has, for hours, considered
himself alone [I saw] a dark figure.... On and on it came, with a speedy
approach but delayed arrival; till, at last...it...rushed up to me and
passed me into the cottage....I turned and looked, but saw nothing.
Then with a feeling that there was yet something behind me, I looked
round over my shoulder; and there, on the ground, lay a black shadow
the size of a man....

Although one may be forgiven for deducing the opposite, the first
extract is from Poe's Gothic masterpiece, *The Masque of the Red
Death* (1839), and the second from MacDonald's allegorical fairytale, *Phantastes* (1858). The first affects the familiar stylized world
of royalty and splendid occasions, the symbolism of masks and the
invocation of the magical number seven. Much of the disturbing
effect of Poe's twilight world clearly derives from the fairytale
device's inherent power—or more precisely, the implied horror of
fairytale 'gone wrong'. Furthermore, while the Gothic mode may
be simply fairytale disguised, fairytale may just as surely degenerate into Gothic. Wearied by Victorian gloom, mentally jaded by
the contemplation of science and industrialism, MacDonald carried into his fairytale realm his own morbid and melancholic
preoccupations, which inclined him towards images of decadence
and death. These underlying personal elements contaminate the

simple charm of fairytale, making it comparable with the Gothic.

Apparently, fairytale and Gothic's common symbolic structure and shared evocation of imaginative and instinctive forces can give rise to an equivocal medium, the critical factor being the degree of oscillation between the imagination's lighter and darker persuasions. The fact that Peake's Gormenghast world has been alternately described as pertaining to the world of childhood and to the Gothic underlines this very point. If Gormenghast, for all its darker aspects, recalls childhood (and notably Peake's own, via imagery borrowed from China), then this alone should work to defuse the Gothic element. On the other hand, if Peake's fantasy is not Gothic, might it not be considered a modern equivalent of fairytale, not actual but disguised? Fairytale which has been— quite literally—'adult-erated'?

Many of the characteristics of Gormenghast fly in the face of conventional Gothic. The castle certainly contains every recognizable stimulus of Gothic expressed in 'all the possible combinations of ruins, ivy and owls' (as Kenneth Clark once put it). However, while Gothicisms abound, 'the madness'—a favorite Gothic theme—'is illusory and control never falters' (Anthony Burgess in his introduction to *TG*, p. 13, 5). In this, as in other matters, we are reminded of an affinity with fairytale. The castle is not a world of spirits and unfortunately-plagued Christians as conventional Gothic demands. *Gormenghast*, it is true, opens with a presentation of the key characters of *Titus Groan* in the form of ghosts wandering through the dusty corridors, but this is merely a device to give a synopsis of the first book. 'The very lack of ghosts in the deserted halls and chambers' (*G*, p. 50, 36), has an obvious explanation: the apparitions our fancy would supply are embodied in the residents themselves. Their grotesqueness is not irrational, but essential. Birds nest happily in Gertrude's hair. These are the projections of fairytale, and beyond Gormenghast, as Titus will discover when he attempts to leave, its self-sown sons and daughters cannot survive.

Steerpike apparently recognizes the equivocal nature of his dark surroundings and exploits it where he can. He woos Fuchsia by assuming hypocritical fairytale guises (*TG*, pp. 157-9, *122-24*). He tricks the slow-witted Twins by tempting them with the promise of 'wondrous' apartments and 'golden thrones' where they might 'sit aloft like...two purple queens' (*TG*, p. 344, *269*). He assumes such images will have an unquestioned appeal.

The all-governing Ritual demands an abundance of fairytale devices:

it was required of [the Earl] to ascend and descend the Tower of Flints
three times by the stone staircase, leaving on each occasion a glass of wine
on a box of wormwood placed there for the purpose on a blue turret.

(*TG*, p. 329, 257)

The Ritual is demerited fairytale, for its symbolism is forgotten
and senseless, but its hollow props fool many less gullible than the
Twins.

There is certainly a brooding evil present in Gormenghast,
precipitated by the arrival of Steerpike, and there is also violence
and fear. But the inhabitants of the castle fear for their bodies;
the inhabitants of Gothic novels fear for their souls. While gruesome enough and a common occurrence, death here has little
sting, for it is generally conveyed in so impersonal and stylized a
manner that it seems hardly disturbing at all. Some deaths even
have a sort of ghastly gaiety. The demise of Deadyawn might have
taken place in the mythical realm, alongside other unfortunates
who are danced to death in magic shoes or who, like Rumpelstiltskin,
split themselves in two with rage:

He descended from somewhere near the ceiling like a visitor from
another planet.... their hearing was appalled by the sound of a skull
being crushed like an egg—for... the Headmaster, in descending absolutely
vertically, struck the floor with the top of his cranium, and remained
upside down, in a horrible state of balance, having stiffened with a form
of premature *rigor mortis*.   (*G*, pp. 112-3, 87)

Anthony Burgess has described Gormenghast as a world of 'the
closed imagination' (*TG*, Introduction). The Gothic realm, while
apparently situated principally in man's unconscious, is a reaction
against normality which must maintain bridges to the real world
in order to achieve its effect. In Gormenghast, clearly, the laws of
nature do not always apply. The self-governing isolation of the
Gormenghast world, like Tolkien's Middle Earth, make it in this
respect also more worthy of comparison with the enclosed realm
of fairytale. The rambling Gothic vastness of the castle is largely
deceptive. Its very creation seems like a fairytale, based on the
almost mythical nature of Peake's childhood memories of a civilization which appeared to the grown man 'like the glimpses of
some half forgotten story in a book...a long lost book....they
seem far away, those days' (*PP*, pp. 472-3). Once upon a time?

Similarly, the timeless quality of Gormenghast is not merely that
of Gothic, and not only of childhood, but that of a fairytale.
Cautiously preserved, it is a microcosm which while appearing to

decay will never (one senses) perish completely, and within its own context remains wise and coherent as fairytale should. To maintain this environment the inhabitants must adhere to the rituals, which are as the deeds of fairytale; this done, the potential horror of Gormenghast's monstrous Gothic body is perpetuated, yet held at bay. Much of the attendant detail of Peake's fantasy world seemingly derives from the constant and critical modification of fairytale and Gothic elements—and there undoubtedly are some of the latter.

The Gothic tale concerns itself with the negation of ideals. Within Gormenghast (as Gertrude constantly impresses upon Titus) ideals are high, even unreasonably so. It is Steerpike, about whom there is something that 'set[s] him apart from the life of the place—something subtly foreign [and] ulterior' (*G*, p. 266, *211*), who truly introduces the Gothic to Gormenghast, for he works to destroy its idealized structure. By introducing contrary and personally-motivated elements into this self-existing realm, Steerpike gradually contaminates Gormenghast just as George MacDonald contaminated his fairytale world of *Phantastes*. His action is, implicitly, a crime against Gormenghast's indigenous nature and, as if sensing the crystal clouding, the environment reacts to its tainter as if to an 'illness' (*G*, p. 267, *212*). As the microcosm attempts to readjust itself, the natural elements of air and land, to the confusion of its dream-bound inhabitants, become progressively unbalanced in a way that has 'more than a material explanation' (*G*, p. 262, *208*). This increasingly hostile environment finally facilitates Steerpike's death, so that 'the heart of Gormenghast, purged, [may] beat again unthreatened' (*G*, p. 363, *290*). However, prior to this achievement, Steerpike's treachery claims a casualty which not only shocks the reader but appears to initiate a change in the condition of Peake's fantasy.

Poor Fuchsia, Gormenghast's tarnished fairytale princess, who is 'in a sense, ugly of face, but with how small a twist might she not suddenly have become beautiful' (*TG*, p. 51, *38*), finally finds the growing tension of her circumstances too much to bear. She yearns for her childhood world of make-believe, where the trappings of fairytale still held sway. However, her return to imaginative romance ends with her fall from a high window similar to that at which, years before, Steerpike 'had suddenly appeared...and had left a rose behind him on her table' (*G*, p. 453, *363*). Although it is shocking, Fuchsia's death retains some of the terrible beauty of fairytale. Her death transforms her from a hopeless and forgotten Rapunzel into an enigmatic sleeping beauty, the inhabit-ant of 'some other climate' (*G*, 507, *406*). It is little wonder that, to Titus and the others still trapped on the dark side of the glass, the body on the stretcher seems 'hardly her' (*G*, p. 462, *369*).

The loss of Peake's most sympathetic character precipitates those darker aspects of the fantasy which have been accumulating throughout the latter half of *Gormenghast*. The death of the 'princess' ends the dream. The 'madness' of Gormenghast—now concentrated in the increasingly unbalanced Steerpike—is no longer illusory, and the control Burgess associated with *Titus Groan* certainly seems to falter. What began as a calculated struggle for civil power has become, in Steerpike, an irrational 'lust for killing' (*G*, p. 442, *354*). Titus himself now becomes 'dangerous' (*G*, p. 460, *368*). His hatred of Steerpike has provoked in him 'a blind white rage' (ibid) which 'caused him to tremble with eagerness . . . to kill' (*G*, p. 467, *374*). He is not inspired, as fairytale logic would demand, by what is considered 'right'—the re-establishment of castle discipline—but by personal grievance: 'He stole my boat! He hurt Fuchsia. He killed Flay. He frightened me. I do not care if it was rebellion against the Stones' (*G*, p. 459, *367*).

Beneath the weight of these dark and unhealthy passions which sometimes veer perilously towards melodrama, the remaining fairytale structures rapidly crumble. The final chapters of *Gormenghast* do, in a very real sense, degenerate into something approaching the Gothic. Steerpike's death, when it comes, is not a fairytale death:

[Titus] could see nothing of the body into which his small knife plunged. Only the head with its distended mouth and its grisly blood-lit eyes, was visible. But . . . his fist was suddenly wet and warm. . . . and he thrust again into the darkness. . . . Then Titus stared at the face [and the] small, lack-lustre eyes. They were turned up.   (*G*, pp. 498-9, *399*)

However, Steerpike's elimination does not restore the castle's former order, for Titus's determination to renounce Gormenghast's ideology and become 'a real live person' (*G*, p. 459, *368*) proves just as damaging as Steerpike's violation of it. It is Titus who finally negates the fairytale, when he voices the ultimate perfidy: 'What do I care for the symbolism of it all?' (*G*, p. 459, *367*) The changed mentality at the close of *Gormenghast* leads naturally into *Titus Alone*. Gormenghast's atmosphere was always something ambiguous, 'something brutal; something tender; something half real; something half dream' (*TA*, pp. 9-10, *1*), but *Titus Alone* is the reverse of Gordon's metaphorical coin, with the Gothic face plainly uppermost. Here may be found real horror. The factory where Cheeta's father works and whose only product is death is an image which comes not from Peake's childhood but from a visit to Belsen. The madness of *Titus Alone* is a more fearful prospect than the theatrical lunacy of Lord Sepulchrave, who squats upon his mantelpiece believing himself an owl. Here is a glimpse of Peake's own despair at a time of real illness and mental instability. The threshold of true Gothic is crossed, not in *Titus Groan* or *Gormenghast*, but in *Titus Alone*.

THE CRY OF A FIGHTING COCK:
NOTES ON STEERPIKE AND RITUAL
IN *GORMENGHAST*

Ann Yeoman

IN chapter 2 of *Gormenghast*, Peake's omniscient narrator describes the ambitious young Steerpike, who has long since "dug out and flung away" his conscience from "his tough narrow breast":

High-shouldered to a degree little short of malformation, slender and adroit of limb and frame, his eyes close-set and the colour of dried blood, he is still climbing, not now across the back of Gormenghast but up the spiral staircase of its soul, bound for some pinnacle of the itching fancy—some wild, invulnerable eyrie best known to himself; where he can watch the world spread out below him, and shake exultantly his clotted wings. (*G*, 14, 7)

In this paragraph we see Steerpike as a complex amalgam of figures of evil: he is at once "little short of malformation" (we think of Stevenson's descriptions of Mr. Hyde); he has the eyes of both devil and vampire ("the colour of dried blood"); he has the power lust and drive of Faust, and the final image is that of a monstrous, demonic bird of prey dominating the world. "Born" in an inferno (the Great Kitchens are so described early in *Titus Groan*, p. 30, *21*), and from the beginning recognized by Swelter as monstrous (the Castle Cook sings his song "to a hard-hearted monshter [*sic*]"—*TG* 38, *27*), Steerpike is seen increasingly as Satanic, Faustian, vampiric and animalistic. Early in his "career," he is recognized by Dr. Prunesquallor as "A diabolically clever little monster" (*TG* 178, *138*), and in Chapter 38 of *Gormenghast*, he is described in terms which recall the initial appearance of Mary Shelley's monster to his creator in *Frankenstein*:

The sun was blocked away. For a few minutes the shadow (Steerpike) disappeared like the evil dream of some sleeper who on waking finds the substance of his nightmare standing beside his bed.... (261, *207*)

Steerpike identifies with the role of the rebel (*TG* 159, *123*) and his merciless logic teaches him that as rebel he must be "tenacious as a ferret" and subversive and deceptive as a snake. In order to seduce his victims in the manner of the serpent in the Garden of Eden, he learns to "speak their own language," be it the romantic language of Fuchsia, Dr. Prunesquallor's sophisticated repartee, or Barquentine's strict recitation of the timetables of ritual. Described most often in terms of his shadow ("It was more like the shadow of a young man . . . that moved across whiteness, than an actual body moving in space" *G*, 15, 8), Steerpike operates with the guile of the serpent, invading the secrets, vulnerability, and privacy of his potential victims through a device of "mirror glancing to mirror" (*G*, 17, 9). Steerpike's mirrors imply not the inner imaginative process of self-reflection but an attempt to so well learn the external character traits of others that he may exploit and mimic them to advantage. He gains knowledge and power through studying the surface reflection or "mirror image" of others. His concerns are material and mimetic; his advantages are won by the objective distance and unemotional clarity of vision born of his cold, calculating logic. But like Satan's Pandemonium, Steerpike's potential empire is only possible as a diabolical reflection, or "mirror image," of Gormenghast, the original; and Steerpike, also like Milton's Satan, is essentially a parodist and parasite, as is clear towards the end of *Gormenghast* when his time is running out and he echoes the lines from *Paradise Lost* in which Satan denies God's omnipotence and refuses to serve in Heaven:

[When Steerpike is cornered in the death-chamber of the Twins, his] body shuddered with a kind of lust. It was the lust for an unbridled evil. It was the glory of knowing himself to be pitted, openly, against the big battalions. Alone, loveless, vital, diabolic—a creature for whom compromise was no longer necessary, and intrigue was a dead letter. *If it was no longer possible for him to wear, one day, the legitimate crown of Gormenghast, there was still the dark and terrible domain—the subterranean labyrinth—the lairs and warrens where, monarch of darkness like Satan himself, he could wear undisputed a crown no less imperial.*   (*G*, 385-386, *307*—my emphasis)

Steerpike's vampirism is evident in his treatment of the Twins. He makes them his victims by promising them the power that is their due, he tells them, by virtue of their "blood"; and then he sucks them dry, usurping all their meagre energy for his own purposes, until they are nothing but empty skeletons. He has the power of a Svengali to mesmerize, but this is a power which is dependent upon the submission of the victim's will.

It is not difficult for Steerpike to draw the empty-headed, silly Twins into his hypnotic web, but Fuchsia presents him with more of a challenge. Whereas Steerpike's power over the Twins is covertly sexual (he tickles them with his phallic sword-stick to the point of physical helplessness—G, 47, *34*), with Fuchsia he feeds on her romantic longing for the lover who will bring her fulfillment. Peake introduces his reader to Fuchsia's emerging sexual fantasies in *Titus Groan*; significantly enough, Fuchsia is dreaming of her future lover at the same time that Steerpike is beginning his climb across the rooftops towards the window of her secret attic and his subsequent violation of that sanctuary:

He will be tall, taller than Mr. Flay, and strong like a lion and with yellow hair like a lion's, only more curly; and he will have big, strong feet because mine are big, too, but won't look so big if his are bigger; and he will be cleverer than the Doctor, and he'll wear a long black cape so that my clothes will look brighter still; and he will say: "Lady Fuchsia", and I shall say: "What is it?"   (*TG*, 146, *113*)

It is, of course, Steerpike who takes to wearing a long black cape, and Steerpike who calls her "Lady Fuchsia" in mock deference to her rank. In her own way a rebel against "the stones," Fuchsia falls in love with Steerpike because he is the epitome of difference: "She admired all that she was not. It was all so different from Gormenghast" (*G*, 351, *280*). Yet it is this difference between Fuchsia and Steerpike, more fundamental than Steerpike had anticipated, that causes their fragile relationship to shatter. Peake describes Steerpike's attempt at seduction as a work of art, but a work of art that is brittle because of the one-sided and evil nature of the lover's intent. When Steerpike calls Fuchsia "Fool":

The delicate balance of their relationship was set in violent agitation—and a dead weight came down over Fuchsia's heart.
Had the crystalline and dazzling structure which Steerpike had gradually erected, adding ornament to ornament until, balanced before her in all its beauty, it had dazzled the girl—an outward sign of his regard for her—had the exquisite structure been less exquisite, less crystalline, less perfect, then its crash upon the cold stones far beneath would never have been so final. Its substance, brittle as glass, had been scattered in a thousand fragments.   (*G*, 351-352, *280*)

The Steerpike/Fuchsia relationship is so delicate because the lovers are such extremes; their worlds, it would seem, are mutually exclusive; where they may be able to persist in conflict, they could never exist in harmony. Steerpike's is a world of shadow which takes its shape by virtue of its opposite—light. As a type of the archetypal rebel, characterized by movement and change, he can thrive only in an atmosphere of perpetual opposition, a world of inter-dependent opposites:

It was as though a shadow [Steerpike] had a heart—a heart where blood was drawn from the margins of a world of less substance than air. A world of darkness whose very existence depended upon its enemy, the light.

(G, 261, 207)

Steerpike's "every action [is] ulterior" (G, 344, 275), whereas Fuchsia's energy is usually focused in one direction: towards something or someone she can love, whether the love exists in the outside world or in the imagination. "[Fuchsia] lived in the moment of excitement, savouring the taste of an experience that was enough in itself. She had no instinct of self-preservation" (G, 344, 275). Fuchsia lives in and for the emotional intensity of the moment, unable to accommodate the rough reality of a world beyond the world of her imagination. Steerpike lives for the future—his future, or "narrative," at the expense of all others. He is, perhaps, the artisan and craftsman concerned solely with form, or artifact for its own sake; he seems to revere only objects, never people, and he abhors sentiment. And so the "artifice" of his supposed love for Fuchsia has no substance, no integrity, and is therefore too brittle to survive. Fuchsia, on the other hand, is often at a loss for the right words or "form" by which to give expression to the tumult of her emotional life, and so is more closely identified with the unself-conscious artist committed to poetic intuition (see TG, "The Attic").

So for the Twins, and for Fuchsia, Steerpike is transformed from hero and lover into murderer and villain. And despite his unchanging purpose, despite his wish to use rather than revitalize the ritual of Gormenghast, Steerpike becomes not only the agent of change but himself the victim of the change he initiates. Rather than fulfilling himself as both author and hero of his own narrative, he becomes another—albeit significant and horrific—instrument in the larger narrative of Gormenghast, its inhabitants and heir. Sensing Fuchsia's own rebellious nature, Steerpike complains to her of the tyranny of age and custom in order to gain her sympathy and win her into his power; he uses the predictability of both age and ritual to further himself, knowing that to acquire Barquentine's knowledge will render him indispensable and therefore powerful; but when he eventually cuts his way through to the "hidden centre" of Gormenghast after systematically eliminating those who stood in his way, he confronts a complexity he had not anticipated: both the implacable Countess Gertrude and the impetuous Titus—images of permanence and process, respectively.

If the ritual of Gormenghast is empty and devoid of meaning, it is evident that the "myth," or "sacred history" which we suppose must once have inspired that ritual has long since been forgotten. Peake's presentation of the "unimaginative laws" of Gormenghast that deny the spirit begs the question of what more vital myth might have imbued "the stones" with life some generations before the demise of Lord Sepulchrave and the birth of his son, the Seventy-Seventh Earl in the line of the Groans.

The consensus of most scholars of myth and ritual is that neither myth nor ritual is primary: they are interactive and interdependent. Clyde Kluckhohn, writing on a general theory of myths and rituals, argues:

Those realms of behavior and of experience which man finds beyond rational and technological control he feels are capable of manipulations through symbols. Both myth and ritual are symbolical procedures and are most closely tied together by this, as well as by other facts. The myth is a system of word symbols, whereas ritual is a system of object and act symbols. Both are symbolic processes for dealing with the same type of situation in the same affective mode. (71)

But also:

man, as a symbol-using animal, appears to feel the need not only to act but almost equally to give verbal or other symbolic "reasons" for his acts. (70)

There is, therefore, an interpretative and metaphoric function to myth as well as a symbolic function. Yet Titus finds no mythic or symbolic "reasons" for the ritual acts he is required to perform on a daily basis, and certainly it would seem that any former "mythic" basis to the society of Gormenghast, given form by the ritual to which it itself afforded significance, has evaporated. A cohesive "world view" is no longer shared by the younger inhabitants of Gormenghast, and there is division even between members of the older generation who consider themselves to be loyal to "the stones" (for example, Flay's banishment by the Countess Gertrude.)

In his article, "The Religion of Gormenghast", David Sutton argues that rather than there being no religion in the Titus books, "the true religion of Gormenghast is Gormenghast itself." He continues:

Gormenghast's society has become a personified being, a god. It is appropriate, therefore, that it should gradually acquire a devil—in the form of Steerpike.... He is a Satan figure, even down to his fear of, and torture by, fire; and his enjoyment of his evil is fitly ritualistic—as in his cockerel-like dance over the putrefied bodies of Cora and Clarice.(12-13)

Sutton argues that Peake is not an allegorist, and that therefore the narrative of *Gormenghast* cannot be reduced to a battle of Good versus Evil. Peake's characterization is far too complex to allow for such a reading. And it is complex not only in the case of Steerpike, who is at once Satanic, Faustian, hero, villain, lover, murderer and serpentine principle of energy and transformation. Gertrude is seen as synonymous with Gormenghast—the "stones"—yet she is as much a voice in tune with the outside world of nature as she is a petrifying Medusa figure, "half asleep and half aware" (*G*, 12, 5); Titus is both self-defined romantic rebel, saviour, and "king" turned traitor by the end of the second novel.

As Peake's main characters grow increasingly complex, and acquire the weight of literary, mythological and Biblical connotation (Steerpike as Faust and Satan; Gertrude as Medusa-figure and earth goddess; Titus as rebel son, etcetera), critical analysis is drawn towards the supposition that Peake is concerned with "re-mythologizing" Gormenghast. Yet, as the relationships between Peake's principal characters become more intricate, and the action more fast-paced, the narrative becomes multi-dimensional, moving away from, rather than closer to the uni-dimensional, formulaic structure of myth, away from the type of "story" that promises meaning and understanding as well as a practical resolution. If there is narrative resolution, it is a resolution in the world of profane action. The direction of Peake's narrative is not towards a revitalization of the long forgotten "myth" of the castle and the ancient line of the Groans. Steerpike is dead. The danger has passed. The Countess Gertrude stands at the end of the novel affirming that "everything comes to Gormenghast" (*G*, 510, *409*), but Titus, the future of Gormenghast, turns his back on the castle, obeying a personal "law of quest" rather than the law of convention and tradition (*G*, 508-511, *406-9*).

Despite Peake's interest in the literary and artistic image, his focus would appear to be on narrative, in the second half of *Gormenghast*, rather than on the elaboration of image for its own sake. The temporality of narrative works against the "spatial," simultaneous quality of image, yet Peake "grounds" his narrative, even when it is most concerned with action, in a series of "tableaux" to "frame" or capture in an image those stages in the metamorphosis of both Titus and Steerpike that inform the narrative movement in the first place. So the narrative does not finally "explain" or interpret Gormenghast and the passions of its principal players either to the castle's inhabitants or to Peake's readers. Such narrative expectations are frustrated. Instead of pushing towards meaning, a universal meaning that may be shared, Peake uses narrative to lead back to experience, reaffirming the primary, if personal and essentially solitary, nature of direct experience. The hopes, fears, suffering, and exhalation of Steerpike and Titus; the largely hidden terror, determination, dreams, and disillusionment of the Countess, are not shared, "public" experiences, yet they are what effect change.

Myth and ritual are essentially static. They are concerned with eternals with repetition, convention, and tradition; the mythic narrative is the story which consolidates a world view for a specific group of people in a specific time and place. According to Eric Gould, myth is the attempt to fill a gap, the inevitable gap that persists between experience and language (the description or "narrative" of experience). Gould reminds his reader that "since myth is language, it is a response to the conditions of language itself" (39), namely that language both embodies the extent of our knowledge and indicates the limits of, or gaps in, our understanding:

> The history of "what-is" becomes a summary of the scope of our inability (as much as our ability) fully to authenticate Being in language. And in the modern, I think, mythicity [Gould's term for the "nature of the mythic"] has little chance of adhering to anything more important than this lack: a knowledge of language's deconstructive talents, which is not merely nihilistic, but an attempt to account realistically for the limits of our understanding.... The incompleteness of the sign (after Saussure's well-known theory) insists that no complete meaning is possible, only a system of differences: form and meaning are never present at once; ... So we become as concerned over the play of differences and absences of meaning as we are over what Derrida has called the "metaphysics of presence."
> (40, 41)

The appropriate myth might move towards filling the widening gap in Titus's "understanding" by answering his many questions concerning his family, his heritage, and the role he is asked to play as earl of Gormenghast, but Peake does not, and cannot afford his protagonist that luxury.

As in the case of the "myth" of Gormenghast, a particular myth may over time become "fixed" and so empty itself of meaning by becoming divorced from life, the reality that it originally signified (again, the Medusa figure is a mythological equivalent of such a tendency to kill by "fixing" or turning her victim to stone.) However, Gould argues that the mythic resides at the interface of "inside" and "outside" for it is an attempt to realize the hidden, absent or dimly intuited significance (the "inside") of an experience in "fact" or story ("outside"). Myth therefore inhabits the essentially fluid margin seen as existing between conscious and unconscious, waking and dream or fantasy worlds, between inside reality and outside actualities. It may be argued, in consequence, that myth, as art, is born of the need to fill, or interpret and stabilize, our experience of the "lack"—or gap in understanding—that persists at this margin. Both art and myth, then, share a metaphoric and interpretative function, and as reality forever eludes a meaning that is absolute, this function must be seen as "process," as interpretative *act* or symbolic *proposition*, rather than as explanation with the fixity and opaqueness of an icon or idol.

As an artist Peake was individualistic and iconoclastic. His persistent image for the artist is of one who would continually break vases, break vessels, break window panes, as a symbolic prerequisite of the need to "see" and create something fresh. All but three of the carvings of the Mud-Dwellers are burnt, and these three are relegated to the Hall of Bright Carvings where, as useless icons, they become nothing more than objects for Rottcodd, the curator, to dust. Towards the end of *Gormenghast*, Peake emphasizes yet again the necessary function of the iconoclast. Without Steerpike's iconoclastic energy, no change would have occurred within the crumbling walls of Gormenghast. Without Titus's iconoclasm, the empty ritual might well have been perpetuated after the death of the rebel Steerpike. But Peake has the Poet follow Steerpike as Master of Ritual, and Titus breaks out of, rather than conforms to, the generally accepted perception of him as a hero and saviour of mythic proportion. The anticipated—or formulaic—ending to the encounter between Steerpike and Titus is thwarted. There is no resolution, there is no closure. Neither Steerpike nor Titus acts as their closest mythological precursors acted, and Gormenghast is not reaffirmed as the embodiment of all that is significant. In this way, Peake is asking his reader to look beyond the individual work of art to an intuition of the creative process which brought it into being. He asks us to look through the ponderous, opaque icon that Gormenghast has become to what it once signified—and to that which, in Titus's rebel eyes, even in its state of crumbling putrefaction, it still points: the irreducible and essentially enigmatic nature of reality.

It is process and unpredictable change that brings about Steerpike's downfall, and that also breaks the mythological mould of a battle between good and evil towards which the narrative appears to tend in the final chapters of the novel. As Peake continually illustrates, extreme positioins are untenable in the final analysis: those who survive—as those who create—are multi-dimensional rather than rigidly unidimensional. Steerpike's vulnerability is first introduced when his plans for Barquentine's death misfire.

His loss of control and the realization that he "had bungled the affair" (G, 274, *217*) distress him, and the Steerpike who is reborn out of the slimy moat after Barquentine has drowned, is an "arch contriver" who falls prey, more and more, to a side of his personality he has consciously repressed—the potential for imagination, fantasy, and the irrational:

> ...there was a *change* all the same, and when he [Steerpike] was woken an hour later by a sound in the room, and when on opening his eyes he saw a flame in the fireplace, he started upright with a cry, the sweat pouring down his face, and his bandaged hands trembling at his sides.
>
> (G, 282-283, *224*)

At the death scene of the twin aunts, Steerpike submits to an overpowering and unbridled impulse to strut like a cock around the bodies of Cora and Clarice. He is portrayed as the archetypal fiend, but Peake also indicates that Steerpike no longer knows himself: impulses are surfacing and erupting through the veneer of his rationality with a force that threatens to overwhelm because hitherto so conscientiously denied. Steerpike is no longer master in his own house:

> He was the vehicle through which the gods were working. The dim primordial gods of power and blood.   (G, 381, *303*)

Governed until now by his impeccable logic, Steerpike starts to realize, more and more, the animalistic, instinctual side of his nature. Towards the end of the fight with Titus, what betrays Steerpike is a desire that arises fromt he autonomous dream level of his psyche: he is completely overtaken by a suicide fantasy in which he sees himself, once again, in animalistic terms, in his final gesture enacting "a note from the first dawn, the high-pitched overweening cry of a fighting cock" (G, 498, *399*). Steerpike's suicide fantasy is well worth quoting in full, as it shows how he falls victim to his one-sidedness as did Sepulchrave and Fuchsia before him:

> And now he began to experience again, but with even greater intensity, those sensations that affected him when, with the skeletoins of the titled sisters at his feet, he had strutted about their relics as though in the grip of some primordian power.
>
>   This sensation was something so utterly alien to the frigid nature of his conscious brain that he had no means of understanding what was happening within him at this deeper level, far less of warding off the urge to *show*

himself. For an arrogant wave had entered him and drowned his brain in black, fantastic water.

His passion to remain in secret had gone. What was left of vigour in his body craved to strut and posture.

He no longer wanted to kill his foe in darkness and in silence. His lust was to stand naked upon the moonlit stage, with his arms stretched high, and his fingers spread, and with the warm fresh blood that soaked them sliding down his wrists, spiralling his arms and steaming in the cold night air—to suddenly drop his hands like talons to his breast and tear it open to expose a heart like a black vegetable—and then, upon the crest of self-exposure, and the sweet glory of wickedness, to create some gesture of supreme defiance, lewd and rare; and then with the towers of Gormenghast about him, cheat the castle of its jealous right and die of his own evil in the moonbeams.   (*G*, 496-497, *399-98*)

So Steerpike's ambition is sabotaged by a fantasy that springs, autonomously, from the depths of his own psyche. He is defeated by a resurgence of the "irrational inmperative," as Milan Kundera terms the archetypal, which results in that most radical transformation, death. It is something in his own nature that makes it impossible for Steerpike ever to be the idol he worked so hard to become, and to whose power he imagined the whole of Gormenghast would eventually unquestioningly yield. His final act is one of transgression, the transgression of the very fantasy of himself that had ruled his life, and in that final act he destroys both himself and the carefully-wrought image of himself.

WORKS CITED

Gould, Eric. 1981. *Mythical Intentions in Modern Literature.* Princeton: Princeton University Press.

Kluckhohn, Clyde. 1979. "Myths and Rituals: A General Theory." In *Reader in Comparative Religion: An Anthropological Approach*, ed. by William A. Lessa and Evon Z. Vogt, 66-78. 4th ed. New York: Harper and Row.

Sutton, David. 1979. "The Religion of Gormenghast: A Note." *Mervyn Peake Review* 9 (1979): 11-13.

FROM BEOWULF TO KAFKA:
MERVYN PEAKE'S *TITUS ALONE*

Colin Greenland

MERVYN PEAKE's achievement as a novelist is now generally recognized. Other critics have observed that in 1946, when *Titus Groan*, the first of the Titus books, was published, the generation that would appreciate them was hardly born. The qualities that made them odd for their time now ensure their popularity. There is still, as there always was, a Peake cult, but the taste is no longer exclusive; and even among readers who do not share it, Peake no longer suffers the reputation of being a mere English eccentric, a literary freak with the pathos of one of his own characters.

I discovered Peake when everyone else did, at the publication of the Penguin edition. In the course of ten years reading and discussing his work I have noticed an exceptional number of people who speak enthusiastically of the Titus books but soon admit they have not read all three. They have read *Titus Groan* and *Gormenghast*, perhaps more than once, and started *Titus Alone* but never finished it. It's a reaction which seems to be peculiar to Peake. I haven't found it among admirers of other fantasy and science fiction trilogies, Le Guin's or Tolkien's or Shea and Wilson's. Many English readers bought American editions of *The Sword and the Stallion* or *The Children of Dune* because they were not prepared to wait for English ones. Conversely, readers who gave up on Thomas Covenant after one or two volumes are not eager to call themselves Donaldson fans. There is a feeling that *Titus Alone* is less acceptable or plainly less good than *Titus Groan* or *Gormenghast*. A friend of mine who relished *Titus Groan* eventually returned my copy of *Titus Alone* declaring it unreadable. It is treated as a minor appendage to the major work, negligible in any assessment of the whole.

There are two qualifications that must be borne in mind. First, Peake's three books are only a trilogy because he died before he could write a fourth. No end to the series had been envisaged. 'Trilogy' suggests a neatness of organization—beginning, middle, end—which, as Maeve Gilmore has said, Peake never designed. Nor do the three give that impression of completeness. Each of them is open-ended; each last page contains an implicit—no, an explicit new beginning. The three books do not comprise a unit, though they have an essential continuity, a balanced structure, as I hope to demonstrate.

Second, we cannot forget that the meticulous craftsman who wrote *Titus Groan* was already under attack from his fatal disease when he wrote *Titus Alone*. Langdon Jones's 1970 edition of *Titus Alone* is a most faithful and coherent version, but it trembles, it wastes away, it almost falls apart. What sustains it is the very urgency of an author determined to express a vision despite the ravages of mental and physical decay.

With this in mind it is curious to read the preface to the new French translation, *Titus Errant*. André Dhôtel affirms the opinion that the book is "difficult", never saying so, but implying it by summarizing the story and insisting how logical it actually is.

The sometimes patchy appearance of this last work has often been ascribed to the fact that it was written by a man in the first stages of Parkinson's disease. *Nothing could be further from the truth.*

The shattering difference between one episode and another is proof of singular lucidity. (Peter Stap's translation, in *The Mervyn Peake Review*, No. 10, Spring 1980, p. 26)

Dhôtel's claim is a strange one. *Titus Alone* was written by a man in the first stages of Parkinson's disease. It appears "patchy" because it is patchy; otherwise there would have been no need for Langdon Jones. Under the circumstances, both medical and editorial, it could hardly be "singularly lucid"; it isn't. Dhôtel almost suggests that the irregularities of *Titus Alone* are a deliberate stylistic technique, like the fragmentations of Ballard or Vonnegut. They aren't.

Nor are they disastrous. The book does not fall to pieces. There are gaps in the fabric: abrupt and obscure transitions, and scenes whose dramatic motivation is unclear. The overall shape of the story is quite intact. The gaps are passages we may not understand, or appreciate, or believe, because the writing falls short, but there is nothing we cannot follow, though we may be as confused as Titus himself. Peake's descriptive brilliance flickers and fades through the book, but he is always explicit about the moral significance of each incident, however incomplete it remains in the reader's imagination. So what is the problem?

For the reader of all three Titus books, it may be hard to accept less after so much, just as the wavering line and empty forms of Peake's last sketches are no substitute for the density and sinuous detail of his best drawings. But for all those readers who get no further than the first page of *Titus Alone,* a major stumblingblock seems to be Muzzlehatch's outrageous car.

The epoch of *Titus Groan* and *Gormenghast* is of course undated, but as Anthony Burgess writes in his introduction,

The doomed ritual lord, the emergent hero, the castle, the hall of retainers, the mountain, the lake, the twisted trees, the strange creatures, the violent knives, the dark and the foreboding belong (however qualified by tea, muffins, tobacco and sherry wine) to a prehistoric England.

Titus could be a contemporary of Beowulf. Reading those first two volumes, we have the sensation that there is a world beyond Gormenghast, where history is flowing on, isolating the castle, but to meet a motor-car is a shock. It signals Titus's emergence from the temporal backwater straight into the mainstream of modernity. To follow him we need to make an abrupt shift of focus, and of pace. Things will now be much closer to hand and move even faster.

Peake is emphatic about the discontinuity between the castle and the world. It is the very subject of the third volume, in which Titus struggles to adjust his memory to his experience. He hates his home and has abandoned it, but it is his past and so remains in his present. As birthplace and more especially as birthright, the earldom has made him what he is. His identity crisis is precipitated by the incompatibility of the two realms. "Were they coeval; were they simultaneous? These worlds; these realms—could they *both* be true? Were there no bridges?" (*TA*, p. 32, *21*). The people among whom he wanders quite justifiably doubt his history. "'Titus Groan, Seventy-Seventh Lord?'" queries the magistrate. "'That sort of title belongs to another age.'" (*TA* p. 86, 66).

The skill of Peake's narration involves us in Titus's disturbance. Gormenghast, lavishly and minutely depicted in *Titus Groan*, with so much described and so much more suggested, looming in shadow, encloses the imagination like a Piranese dungeon. It tempts us to assent to the creed upheld by Gertrude and Sourdust, that there is nowhere else—in narrative terms, that this is the story of a separate, self-contained world, whose character is definite, however labyrinthine and compendious. But Peake's subject was not Gormenghast but Titus. He was not a Gothic writer, obsessed with his mausoleum; he was for life and youth and sunlight. The awful, fascinating grandeur of Gormenghast is presented to us on its last day, the day of the coming of Titus, and of Steerpike. Change and growth cannot be halted, time must run on. That is the whole moral of the three books. Away from the castle, Titus discovers the actual extent of the world. It is vast, so vast that Gormenghast is lost in it. "'My letters are returned. Address Unknown'" (*TA* p. 86, *66*). Similarly Peake makes us realise the extent and significance of his work by abruptly throwing open the doors to space and time. We have already appreciated the satirical aspect of Gormenghast, how it mirrors our world, in little, within limits. In *Titus Alone* the fiction reaches out to merge with it, to envelop us. There may be no bridges from the city to the castle, but from the city to London and New York and Berlin, to Belsen and Hiroshima, the roads are clearly signposted. There are cars tearing along them.

The acceleration is marked in the style. *Titus Groan* takes five hundred pages to span two years; over half of them are concerned with one day. There are innumerable passages where Peake stops the action to describe and evaluate, or winds back to lead up again with another character from another direction. In *Gormenghast* the same number of pages covers ten years. As Titus wakes up from the trance of puberty and the hunt begins, the narrative gathers speed.

Out of nowhere, suddenly, the first sight of the elusive Steerpike. Out of nowhere, suddenly, the news of Fuchsia's death. Out of nowhere, and suddenly, the uprush of his rebellion—the danger of it, the shock of it for all about him, the excitement of it, and the thrill of finding himself free of duplicity—a traitor if they liked, but a man who had torn away the brambles from his clothes, the ivy from his limbs, the bindweed from his brain.   (*G*, p. 467, *374*).

Peake's prose, elaborate and repetitive as ever, now resonates with urgency. In *Titus Alone* events move inhumanly fast, flashing past before they can be grasped: fragments of landscape and disconnected incidents, glimpses from the windows as we are hustled up and down those nameless highways. Time jumps, disappears. Readers who resist this acceleration are making a very important mistake. What they want, in effect, is more Gormenghast, though Gormenghast is the place of stagnation and living death, of the triumph of history over freedom, of ritual over desire. They are using Peake as escapist fiction, an alternative to life, not a comment upon and extension of it. The crux of the transition to *Titus Alone*, and the key to its operation as fiction, is that Peake stops allowing us to believe that his fantasy is separate from our experience. It is no longer a world away.

Titus Alone prefigures many of the concerns and techniques of the contemporary novel, not least in its relentless uncertainty.

When is Titus—in the past, the present, the future? Which is true, the castle or the city? Is the world defined by the scientists, who can see into the atom and across the globe, or by the refugees, the "displaced persons" under the river? It is not hard to see why Peake found such favour in *New Worlds* when the air resounded with the demolition of old idols and icons. Michael Moorcock, Langdon Jones and M. John Harrison all helped to champion him out of lingering obscurity. Like theirs, his fiction makes use of the conventions and tropes of popular fantasy to construct a world which is emphatically only a distortion of our own—and which insists that our own world may well be distorted already. Peake's imagination is robust, his descriptions dense and tactile with the particularity of his painter's eye. His characters, however much they would prefer to be aloof from nature and time, are gro-tesques in the satirical tradition. Moorcock has pointed out that Peake is in descent from Swift, Rabelais and Dickens, rather than the line of discreet and well-bred English fantasy from Malory through Tennyson to Tolkien. Peake made use of that tradition as of the Gothic, to inform his vision; *Titus Groan* is certainly his masterpiece, but it does not define the limits of his capability. For *Titus Alone* he made exactly the same use of science fiction. In the fifties silver skyscrapers, wingless aeroplanes, robot flying eyes and tireless android policemen were all commonplaces from the pulp era. Depicted on the screen in stories of Buck Rogers and Flash Gordon and on the comic page with Dan Dare too, they had passed into a popular currency of images familiar even to people who never read science fiction, as William Burroughs and Eduardo Paolozzi have observed. In *Titus Alone* Peake employs them as Burroughs and Paolozzi do, or as Philip K. Dick does, as images of our increasing mechanization, of the usurpation of the senses by the media, of our elimination of the natural and necessary and reliance on the artificial and arbitrary. The Titus books are a classic example of the distinction so crucial to the *New Worlds* writers, between repetition of formula and exploitation of for-mula, between the *genre* fascination with the future and fiction about that fascination. The city of Titus's exile worships the future as devoutly as Gormenghast worships the past. Peake shows each as a kind of living death, a fatal distraction from the present. Himself a fervent romantic, he presents each as a corrupt romanticism.

Brian Aldiss, David Ketterer, and others have shown the histori-cal and thematic connections between Gothicism and science fic-tion. The two characteristic mentalities are polarized in the Titus books, which tell the story of a young idealist struggling to find his position between them. *Titus Alone* bears the same attitude to science fiction as *Titus Groan* does to the Gothic, the self-conscious and calculating attitude we have muffled under the blanket term "New Wave". This fiction is as open as *genre* fiction is closed. *Titus Groan* shows the cracking of the wall, through which the present starts to seep in. *Gormenghast* tells of the flood, devastating and cleansing. *Titus Alone* takes away the wall and leaves a world scoured of landmarks. Signs and boundaries flicker ambiguously. It is not long before space and time start to melt. Its frame of reference is open: open to interpretation, to interaction with the world in which we read it. This is a condition of modernist and post-modernist writing, which recognizes that Menard's *Quixote* is not the same as Cervantes' and exploits the relationship of reader to text. *Titus Alone* is no more difficult or remote than a daily paper. Its first readers were as familiar as we are with highways and prison camps, and the various factories whose raw material is human and whose principle product is death. Death-rays may have been pretty much the monopoly of the Mekon in 1959, but in 1980 *Scientific American* reported that they had reached Russia. The slaughter of Muzzlehatch's zoo by "some kind of ray" now seems as much matter for the headlines as for the pulps. Science fiction, as I have said elsewhere, is not prediction; but it continues to offer the best equipment for exploring Wilde's provocative maxim that Nature imitates Art.

Mervyn Peake was not in the business of prediction, or even of realism, however defined. He used the properties of science fiction, as William Burroughs, Kurt Vonnegut, Angela Carter, or Doris Lessing have used them, to create a fictional space which is a distortion of our own, the distortions offering various strange reflections upon and insights into reality (however defined). The distorted landscape, the exile abroad in it, not so much on a quest as searching for the sense of his own wanderings—the pattern is central to the disrupted and alienated fiction we read and write today. In an essay I once described *Titus Alone* as "Kafkaesque": I didn't realize how close the comparison was until I reread *The Castle* recently. There are several intriguing correspondences. K's sudden, heedless, doomed love affair with Frieda is very like Titus's with Juno. The two alarming and indistinguishable "assistants", appointed to follow *K* around for reasons that are never made clear, are like another version of Titus's official, implacable pursuers. Other features also recall *The Trial*, most obviously the Honeycomb prison, "a world within a world" (*TA* p. 72, 55) whose moral and legal systems do not necessarily tally with those that operate outside, and the tenebrous courtroom with its maundering but menacing magistrate. Kafka's Castle is, in fact, quite unlike Peake's, being a small and unimpressive structure; and K, of course, is trying to get in while Titus is trying to get away, but both misfits display ambivalent emotions for their dominant edifices. The Landlady upbraids K:

"You are not from the Castle, you are not from the village, you aren't anything. Or rather, unfortunately, you are something, a stranger, a man who isn't wanted and is in everybody's way, a man who's always causing trouble...a man whose intentions are obscure..."

Couldn't that just as well be Titus Groan, the Earl, the Abdicator? Later she assures K:

"You can do what you like. Your actions may no doubt leave deep footprints in the snow out there in the courtyard, but they'll do nothing more."

"You will only tread a circle, Titus Groan." Can the individual ever be free without being lost? If he moves according to impulse, is he only going round in circles?

Titus Alone is a flawed work, perhaps best thought of as unfinished, or at least unrevised. As such, it can afford only partial satisfaction; but satisfaction is not easily obtained when those huge unanswerables are at issue. It might frustrate or disappoint a reader who requires a rigid logic of plot, like a route map at the back of the book, but it is hardly difficult to read. Such a reader is in any case ill-equipped to venture into an imagination like Peake's. The difficulty of *Titus Alone* is only that of accepting the full significance of the author's intentions. Forced to step out into the atrocious absurdity of the latter days, the escapist shares Titus's sudden feeling that, compared with this, Gormenghast was cosy.

A CRITICAL CONCLUSION:
THE END OF *TITUS ALONE*

Laurence Bristow-Smith

It would have been possible, had he wished it, to have reached the mouth
of the cave without a glimpse of his Home. Indeed he took a step or two
towards the cave-mouth. But again a sense of impending danger held
back his feet, and a moment later he heard his own voice saying...
 'No...no...not now! It is not possible...now.'
 His heart beat out more rapidly, for something was growing...some
kind of knowledge. A thrill of the brain. A synthesis. For Titus was
recognizing in a flash of retrospect that a new phase of which he was only
half aware, had been reached. It was a sense of maturity, almost of
fulfillment. He had no longer any need for home, for he carried his
Gormenghast within him. All that he sought was jostling within himself.
He had grown up. What a boy had set out to seek a man had found,
found by the act of living.
 There he stood: Titus Groan, and he turned upon his heel so that the
great boulder was never seen by him ever again. Nor was the cave: nor
was the castle that lay beyond, for Titus, as though shaking off his past
from his shoulders like a heavy cape began to run down the far side of
the mountain, not by the track by which he had ascended, but by another
that he had never known before.
 With every pace he drew away from Gormenghast Mountain, and from
everything that belonged to his home.   (*TA*, pp. 262-63, *212-13*)

  This passage, the conclusion of *Titus Alone*, is of crucial importance to all three of Mervyn Peake's 'Titus' novels. *Titus Groan* is a
vast and detailed panorama of the static, unchanging society into
which Titus is born, documenting its buildings, characters and
atmosphere, and documenting also the beginnings of Steerpike's
great challenge to its traditional way of life. *Gormenghast* charts
Titus's growth and the growth of his longing to rebel and escape
from the confines of his home. It tells how he slays Steerpike,
overcoming the greatest challenge the world of Gormenghast can
offer him and setting himself free to break away. *Titus Alone*
chronicles Titus's struggles in a world far from Gormenghast to
attain a new, independent existence, a new identity independent
of his home.

If the conclusion of *Titus Alone* fails to convince us that Titus has achieved this aim, then the whole architecture of the three books, the development of his character and the progression of his life away from Gormenghast must be substantially undermined. Yet Manlove, in his book *Modern Fantasy: Five Studies*, finds Titus's action in not returning to Gormenghast 'unacceptable, a complete and opaque denial of all that has gone before' (p. 256). Of the passage quoted above, he asks, 'What can this extraordinary conclusion mean?' (p. 255), and proceeds to challenge, individually, every part of it. This is absolutely crucial; it is towards this action and this point that the whole of *Titus Alone* has been developing. The very first paragraph of the novel tells how Titus has become lost, and at this point he ceases to be lost. One of the recurring themes of the novel has been that without proof of Gormenghast, Titus has no proof of his own identity, and here he has proof of both. All that was left unresolved after Titus's escape from the ruins of Cheeta's party is, at this point, resolved, and he is left with a simple choice—he can either return to his hereditary home or set off again in search of new adventures. He chooses the latter. If we find Titus's action, and the reasons behind it, 'unacceptable', then this must completely deny the credibility of Titus's psychological development throughout *Titus Alone* and must seriously reflect upon the development of his character in *Gormenghast*.

Why does Titus choose as he does? Peake gives the reasons quite clearly: Titus recognizes that he has reached 'a new phase' in his life (*TA*, p. 262, *212*). This is not, as Manlove suggests on page 255, an attempt to compartmentalize life in an arbitrary manner. It is rather that something which has been developing within Titus throughout his wanderings is, at this moment, recognized—hence Peake's use of the phrase 'in a flash of retrospect' (*TA*, p. 262, *212*). This new phase, which brings with it 'a sense of maturity, almost of fulfillment' (*TA*, p. 262, *212*), is of course manhood, and it comes about because, as we shall see, Titus has now established his own individual identity. It is true, as Manlove points out, that in the confused and rather nebulous passage in *Gormenghast* dealing with the effect on Titus of the death of the Thing, Peake claims that Titus 'had become a man' (*G*, p. 424, *339*; Manlove, p. 255). Yet looking back, from the vantage point of the end of the trilogy, at what followed the death of the Thing, Titus's return to the castle, his meekness before his mother (*G*, pp. 436-37, *349*), his boyish delight, albeit qualified, in his canoe (*G*, p. 438, *350-51*), his outbursts of petulance and adolescent rage (*G*, pp. 458-59, *367-68*, p. 478, *383*), and even the raw, desperate, untried nature of the courage he summons up to attack Steerpike (*G*, p. 486, *389*), it would appear to be the claim to manhood in *Gormenghast* rather than that in *Titus Alone* which deserves question and censure. In *Gormenghast*, Peake is guilty of a certain romantic naîvety, presenting Titus's transition to manhood as a moment of sudden, dramatic transformation, but in *Titus Alone* he is both more certain and more sophisticated, and the transition is presented as a gradual, time-consuming process which can only be recognized after it has taken place.

It is possible that Peake was aware of his repetition of the claim that Titus has reached manhood, and intended this second claim as a correction to the first. Peake was certainly a careless writer at times, and when he wrote *Titus Alone* the progression of his illness was impairing his ability to concentrate, but it still seems unlikely that he would unconsciously repeat himself when dealing with a matter of such importance. And this seems especially unlikely when we consider that not only has Titus returned to the exact spot where Peake first claimed that he had become a man, but that mention is also made of the particular occasion when the claim was first advanced—'a cave that yawned at his right hand. A cave where an infinity ago he had struggled with a nymph' (*TA*, p. 262, *212*).

Throughout *Titus Alone*, Peake stresses that Titus's identity is dependent upon Gormenghast, but the novel is not, as Manlove claims 'a book-long account of Titus's longing and homesickness and guilt, and of his inability to stay sane without the reality of Gormenghast' (p. 256). On the contrary, the whole point is that Titus *stays sane*—only just perhaps, and with luck, and help from Muzzlehatch, Juno and Anchor, but he stays sane. The book is an account of Titus's *survival* without Gormenghast, despite the 'longing and homesickness and guilt', which elements, while being important aspects of Titus's character, do not dominate the narrative to the extent that Manlove's statement suggests.

In *Titus Alone*, Titus undergoes, and survives, what Bruce Hunt has called 'ordeal by experience' (in '*Gormenghast:* Psychology of the *Bildungsroman*', reprinted in this book, page 303), and in doing this, 'by the act of living' (*TA*, p. 263, *212*), he establishes for himself an identity which is independent of Gormenghast. The Gormenghast which Peake says that Titus now carries 'within himself' (*TA*, p. 263, *212*) is not, as Manlove suggests (p. 255) what Titus has previously referred to as '"the kingdom in my head"' (*TA*, p. 195, *157*)—this refers to his knowledge of the existence of Gormenghast—but rather another aspect of his relationship with the castle. Up to this point, Titus has thought of Gormenghast as being the basis and the root of his identity and his character, but now he realizes that this is no longer the case. The experiences which Titus has had since leaving Gormenghast—the substance of *Titus Alone*—have changed him. He has proved that it is possible for him to survive without Gormenghast, and his character and identity are now based just as much upon this knowledge as upon the knowledge that Gormenghast exists. Thus, in the sense that Gormenghast is a metaphor for the basis of his character, Titus, with the knowledge and accumulated experience of living without Gormenghast, can be said to carry his Gormenghast 'within himself' (*TA*, p. 263, *212*). Manlove asks 'how can we accept this account as one of a final farewell' to Gormenghast? And he asks also, 'Titus has doubted Gormenghast once; what stands against his doubting it again?' (p. 256). The answer to this is clear. If Titus now carries his Gormenghast, the basis of his character, within him, then he has no further need for the physical castle, and thus no need to return there. Similarly, it no longer matters if Titus doubts the existence of Gormenghast, because the physical castle no longer has the same degree of power over his sense of his own identity.

For Titus to return to Gormenghast, as Manlove seems to want him to, would be for him to reject this new-found sense of identity, and to devalue the experiences upon which it is based. He would be reentering the world of childhood, surrendering his individual self before the symbolic identity of 77th Earl which the castle would demand him to re-assume.

Despite the fact that he often feels guilty because he has rejected the castle and betrayed his birthright, there are a number of occasions throughout the course of *Titus Alone* when Titus attempts to draw strength, or to gain the respect of others, from the fact that he is an Earl, notably when he is talking to Muzzlehatch (*TA*, p. 27, *16*; p.61, *45*) and when he is up before the magistrate (*TA*, p. 85, *65-66*). There is obviously an inherent contradiction in this—hypocrisy on the part of Titus—for he is drawing strength from a title to which he no longer has any right, which he abdicated when he left Gormenghast. He is attempting to have the best of both worlds—the freedom of the lone individual, and the respect due to an Earl. But in the world of *Titus Alone*, where, as we see at one point, any beggar can claim to be an emperor (*TA*, p. 30, *19*), Titus's claim is in any case meaningless. The note which the magistrate writes to his friend suggests that many people advance such claims, and that they are, or are regarded as, mad (*TA*, p. 84, *64*). Titus, in fact, uses his claim to be an Earl mainly as a source of personal strength, as a way of reassuring himself of his identity. At the end of *Titus Alone*, he has found a new basis for his identity which is not dependent on Gormenghast. Thus when he turns away from Gormenghast, down a track which, actually and symbolically, 'he had never known before' (*TA*, p. 263, *213*), he is rejecting not only the public and symbolic aspects of his hereditary position—which he did when he left Gormenghast in the first place—but also this personal and hypocritical use of his hereditary position. This is reflected by the fact that when Titus hears 'the dawn salvo', he knows that 'It boomed for him, for the seventy-seventh Earl, Titus Groan, Lord of Gormenghast' (*TA*, p. 262, *212*), but when he has made his decision not to return to the castle, Peake says 'There he stood: Titus Groan' (*TA*, p. 263, *212*). By not returning to the castle, then, Titus is not only demonstrating that 'He had no longer any need for his home' (*TA*, pp. 262—263, *212*), he is also coming to terms with the consequences of his much earlier decision to leave Gormenghast. And by rejecting any form of dependence, physical or mental, upon the castle, he is finally justifying his claim, first advanced many years before, to be 'Titus Groan in his own right' (*G*, p. 100, *77*).

'A BARRIER OF FOOLERY?':
THE DEPICTION OF WOMEN IN
TITUS ALONE

Tanya Gardiner-Scott

LITTLE has been written on Mervyn Peake from the point of view of gender issues. John Batchelor has commented on the lack of adult sexuality in *Titus Groan* and *Gormenghast* and he makes some insightful comments about the birth imagery in the novels (see Batchelor, pp. 79 and 83-84), but it is in *Titus Alone* that the young Titus enters the world of adult sexuality. What Peake shows us in this novel is his gender conventionality, his criticism of any model of womanhood that may be out of the ordinary, and his use of clichéd female roles.[1] Titus has escaped the Castle-Mother; now he must make his way as an adult male in unfamiliar landscapes.[2]

On the process of socialization undergone by young men, Nina Baym writes:

Not until he reaches mid-adolescence does the male connect up with other males whose primary task is socialization; but at about this time ... his lovers, and spouses become the agents of apparent socialization and domestication ... from the point of view of the young man, the only kind of women who exist are entrappers and domesticators ... these socializing women are also the locus of powerful attraction ... [which] gives urgency and depth to the protagonist's rejection of society. To do it, he must project onto the woman those attractions that he feels and cast her in the melodramatic role of temptress, antagonist, obstacle—a character whose mission in life seems to be to ensnare him and deflect him from life's important purposes of self-discovery and self-assertion.[3]

I want to argue that Peake characterizes both Juno and Cheeta from this traditionally masculine point of view. He casts his female characters in roles where they are either victims, like the Black Rose, devouring mothers, like Juno, or self-absorbed like the two lesbians—'two dark, bejewelled, deep-bosomed women who had no eyes for the flying landscape but smiled at each other with unhealthy concentration' (p. 27, *17*). Batchelor over-reacts to this passage, citing it as a 'vision of pure evil ... perverted womanhood' which 'anticipates Cheeta's role in the novel' (Batchelor, p. 126) as the evil entrapping temptress. He sees the lesbians as symbolic of the introversion of the society in which Titus finds himself, a society supremely indifferent to Gormenghast 'which was of course the heart of everything' (p. 29, *18*).

Granted, they are an effective symbol, coming as they do at the beginning of the novel, but it must be comforting to Batchelor to know that Peake was as heterosexist a writer as he is a critic in this case. There is a strong argument to be made for writing the novel from Titus' viewpoint as that young adolescent male so neatly characterized by Baym, but Peake's assumption of a complacent reader content with his encoding of the male-female power structure is disturbing, particularly in a novel which is seen as a radical departure from the world of Gormenghast (which opens up other issues). As a reader here concerned with gender issues, I will focus on Peake's characterization of Juno and Cheeta.

For a time Juno fills what little space there is for a woman in the lives of both Muzzlehatch and Titus. In the analysis provided through Muzzlehatch's third person narration, Juno and he are seen as each other's failure. All Muzzlehatch's characteristics could apply equally to Titus: 'His unfaithfulness; his egotism; his eternal play-acting; his gigantic pride, his lack of tenderness; his deafening exuberance; his selfishness' (p. 67, *50*). Titus, like Muzzlehatch, wants to be alone, unencumbered by emotional ties; both leave Juno when it suits them. But for both of them she represents security, for Titus a quasi-maternal sexuality and a refuge.

Juno's protective instincts are aroused by Titus from their first meeting. She defends him from Inspector Acreblade; she then takes him as her ward from the court, offering her home as a refuge where he can recover. She also encourages his dependence, virtually unmanning him emotionally with her cloying affection: 'All that was weak in Titus rose like oil to the surface of deep water' (p. 88, *68*). Yet their love affair is described as 'a game of the fantastic senses; febrile; tender, tiptilted' (p. 88, *68*), and she compares this new affair with that of Muzzlehatch—'how he had swept her off her feet twenty years earlier and . . . their voyagings to outlandish islands and . . . how his ebullience became maddening and . . . how they were equally strong-headed' (p. 89, *68*).

Like Muzzlehatch, king of his animals, Juno, his one-time mate and co-ruler of the heaven of their love, is described in a mixture of the piratical and the mythic, with 'her head like a female warrior in a legend' (p. 89, *68*) and a hat, 'plumed and piratical' which 'sprouted as naturally from her head as the green fronds from the masthead of a date-palm' (p. 98, *76*). She sees Titus in water images, as a long-submerged boulder, and the room in which they make love for the first time has 'long shafts of sunlight a-swim with motes' and 'the remoteness of a ship at sea' (p. 93, *72*).

She is also the woman of fashion, older, experienced and yet surprisingly tender, though she regrets her lost youth with this new opportunity—'It is for me to give him joy—to give him direction—to give him love ... My child from Gormenghast' (p. 90, 69). But whereas she and Muzzlehatch have visited islands, Titus, her 'child', [is] an island, and sometimes she doubts his sanity:

It was wrong that he should be so single, so contained, so little merged into her own existence. He was an island surrounded by deep water. There was no isthmus leading to her bounty; no causeway to her continent of love. (p. 98-99, 76)

He is not only aloof; as the relationship progresses, he pities her for having given him so much. His desire crystallizes into a subconscious urge 'to bring the total of their relationship to a burning focus. To bring it all to an [end] ... To be free of it' (p. 91, 70).

The maternal aspect of their relationship comes out more strongly in the sexual reactions between them, switching from one to the other. Juno sees Titus from the window and invites him inside. He approaches her and trips, and she literally gets down to his level in a comic parody of their first encounter and of the Garden of Eden myth:

Had he known her less well this absurd fall might well have distracted him from his somewhat unoriginal purpose, but with Juno hovering above him and smelling like Paradise, his passion, far from being quenched, took on a strange quality—something ridiculous and lovable—so that to laugh became a part of their tenderness. (pp. 92-93, 71)

Peake plays the reader along from the 'sharp fruit of suspense' (p. 89, 69) to the physiological changes as Titus becomes aroused by Juno and experiences a subconscious ambivalence towards the vulnerability of lovers. The narrator comments wryly on the sexual situation—'lust is an arrogant and haughty beast and far from subtle ... the immemorial game of love: no less a game for being grave. No less grave for being wild' (p. 91, 70-71). So much for original sin—a new compound of laughter is born, as opposed to the way Titus laughs in the Black House. From the description of the engagingly childlike laughter that they both indulge in, the language becomes almost ritualistic—reminiscent of medieval romance in rhythm and sentence structure, mimicking the intricacies of the sexual dance:

Titus, turning over with a shout, flung out his hand and a moment later found it resting on Juno's thigh, and suddenly his laughter left him, and hers also, so that she rose to her feet and when he had done so also they put their arms around one another and they wandered away to the doorway and up the stairs and along a corridor and into a room . . . (p. 93, 72)

When Juno rouses Titus from sleep, the reader is given a glimpse of him through her indulgent eyes:

It was not a particularly striking face. With the best will in the world it could not be said that the brow or the chin or the nose or the cheekbones were [chiselled]. Rather, it seemed, the features of his head had, like the blurred irregularities of a boulder, been blunted by the wash of many tides. Youth and time were indissolubly fused. She smiled to see the disarray of his brown hair and the lift of his eyebrows and the half-smile on his lips that seemed to have no more pigment in them than the warm sandy colour of his skin. Only his eyes denied to his head the absolute simplicity of a monochrome. They were the color of smoke. (p. 99, 77)

Titus is indeed submerged, in Gormenghast, and not even Juno's maternal care can salvage him. Sanders points out that she 'intends, in the most generous way possible to possess Titus and give him [her] sense of direction'.[4] Her conversation with him is a mixture of the endearments of a lover and the baby talk of a mother. Both she and Titus have an innate sense of the dramatic, as evinced by their playful posing, but, when Titus actually says he will leave, Juno is at a loss for words:

'Where could you go? You do not belong outside. You are my own, my discovery, my . . . my . . . can't you understand I love you darling. I know I'm twice your—O Titus, I adore you. You are my mystery.' (p. 101, 78)

What Muzzlehatch sees at the beginning of her association with Titus is her predatoriness, her desire to protect Titus in a gilded cage of her own making; yet here she is in genuine pain, and Titus is caught in guilt as he walks out on yet another commitment, another mother-figure; a pattern that is repeated in a different way when they leave Muzzlehatch at the end of the novel. Titus sees Juno crying and 'he recoiled from her pathos. He could not bear it. He saw in her a criticism of his own defection. He suddenly hated himself for such a thought and he half rose from his seat in an agony of confusion' (p. 258, 209). He is also repeating (in part) a pattern that he notices about her relationship with Muzzlehatch: 'But you have been in love with her yourself and have lost her. And now [you] are returning to her again' (p. 146, *114*).

Juno fulfills a traditionally, romantically female role as symbol to the men within the novel, providing a large, luxuriant femininity, a sexually appealing, quasi-maternal presence, a listening ear and an emotionality not shared by any of the other women. Her intuition about Titus as expressed through her dream (ch. 95) again conforms to this tradition, and we only see her alone briefly in her garden before the inevitable (to us) appearance of yet another male protector. Her ultimate wish is for Titus on her own terms, and Batchelor condemns her as 'indulgent, maternal, ultimately shallow' (Batchelor, p. 127).

Thus Juno is dismissed, though when Muzzlehatch asks her to help him with the Black Rose, she does so at some personal cost; when Cheeta attacks her in the Black House she does not retaliate, and she is sympathetic to Titus, even though she cannot understand his vision of Gormenghast. Finally, she is even emotionally excluded from one of the most moving scenes of the novel, Muzzlehatch's death—'though knowing herself to be an outsider, in spite of her devotion to them [Titus and Muzzlehatch] both, [she] yet had no power to keep away' (p. 253, *205*). Led by her emotions, deeply involved and then left with a legacy of affection and memories by both her lovers, she is woman as male object of desire, ideal, and inspiration. Yet these are relatively minor strands in Peake's book (pun intended!) compared to her desire to entrap Titus and make him her own.

Peake deliberately juxtaposes Juno and Cheeta, not only in terms of traits like those cited above, or by virtue of their physical contrast—Juno statuesque, Cheeta lithe, ruthless but tiny—or their attraction to the mystery of Titus Groan, but in terms of female attributes. Both are beautiful in their own way, the beauty of each symbolizing a different era: Juno the classical and Cheeta the modern, 'bizarre, utterly feminine, and delicious' (p. 172, *137*). Yet Cheeta is, as Titus puts it, 'frozen at the very taproot... bolted from the inside... prim as the mantis, that gobbles up the heads of her admirers' (p. 190, *153*). The ironic thing is that Titus can be described in the same way, though not sexually, because of his head/heart split concerning Gormenghast and his own pressing need for freedom without obligation. Juno is predatory in her own way, but she is generous, if possessive, as opposed to Cheeta's more calculatingly sexual approach. Cheeta is the ultimate embodiment of what Grass propounds during the cocktail party:

'without heartache—without the *heart* in fact. Cold love's the loveliest love of all. So clear, so crisp, so empty. In short, so civilized.' (p. 45, *32*)

A parallel can be drawn between modern love and the factory, also without a heart, as Muzzlehatch discovers.

The narrator criticizes concentration in any female form; later Cheeta comes under similar sexist censure:

With an efficiency almost unattractive in a woman so compelling, she dealt with the situation, as though she were doing no more than pencil-ling her eyebrows.   (p. 162, *129*)
    A cold fever of concentration propelled her. It was a state more readily associated with a man's than with a woman's mentality. And yet, a sexless thing, it was more dreadful than either.   (p. 199, *160*)

The concentration may be sexless, but we find Peake consistently underrating his main female characters in this novel. Is it not natural that the quasi-maternal Juno will just happen to find Anchor lurking in the bushes waiting for her to notice him? The name is significant in that Juno, unlike Cheeta, needs men as anchors for her life and sense of self. How can a beautiful woman like Cheeta be so effective in what she does, not to mention frigid?

The narrator gives the reader many clues as to how to view Cheeta. She 'was a modern. She had a new kind of beauty. Everything about her was perfect in itself, yet curiously (from the normal point of view) misplaced' (p. 160, *127*). Like the two lesbians, Cheeta is a self-contained product of her society. She has all the physical advantages, but none of the emotional ones, with absent parents both absorbed in her father's scientific work. Yet there is 'an emanation that linked the father and daughter. A kind of atmosphere that was entirely their own...for he was *nothing*; a creature of solitary intellect, unaware of the fact that, humanly speaking, he was a kind of vacuum' (p. 185, *148*), like Mr. Zed in the Under River. Cheeta herself has little curiosity about the factory, which she accepts as a fact of life. Although she lives in an environment in which she lacks for nothing, with the gorgeous Greeziorthspis tapestries as emblems of the romance she is without, and many currying her favour, her possessions bring her no joy. She wants to possess Titus as another thing; he challenges her with his combination of tradition and passion. As Sanders notes, it is Titus' independence and self-sufficiency—the very qualities that destroy his relationship with Juno—that she hates, just as 'once *he* had seen citizens of the society'.

Cheeta is not only a walking definition of anti-love; she is also an anti-woman to Peake in that she wants to possess a man as object, using the sexual because she desires to assert her own independence and power. She has adopted male values to a large extent, and the struggle between her and Titus is not just another battle of the sexes; it is a battle of reversed animus and anima, where she has more animus and is much less passive than Titus.

It is because of this that she is jealous of his involvements with other women, particularly Juno, though his 'love was always elsewhere. His thoughts were fastidious. Only his body was indiscriminate' (p. 189, *152*). Whereas he wants her body, she wants his mind, and her pride is outraged that he should reject her because she will not accommodate him sexually. Both are suffering from a mind-body split, but where Titus is emotionally preoccupied, Cheeta is sexually frigid, though she does not hesitate in the least to play on the sexual sensibilities of those around her. An excellent example of this comes when she rides out by the lake and forces Titus to chase her (ch. 73). When Titus rejects her, she becomes totally obsessed with her hatred and jealousy of him:

The merest little shred she was: slender as an eyelash, erect as a little soldier. But O the danger of it! To fill her clay with something that leaps higher and throws its wild and flickering shadow further than the blood's wisdom knows. How dangerous, how desperate and how explosive for such a little vessel. (p. 189, *151*)

Again there is the sense of narrative condescension because she is female; by contrast, Muzzlehatch and the scientist are described as simply obsessed by what drives them.

Peake presents her anger as out of all proportion, as is her reaction to Titus' rejection, and her desire to hurt him becomes correspondingly huge. In human terms her motivation is credible enough, but her enactment of revenge, using her tremendous efficiency, is completely sadistic, striking at the thing for which she values Titus: his mind. She takes what she has learned from his delirious ramblings to create a parody of his beloved Gormenghast, faking passion when she invites him to her farewell 'celebration' and manipulating him as she manipulates those helping to put her plan into action:

The shadow of a leaf trembled on her cheekbones. Her eyes were huge; as though they were sunk for one purpose only...to drown the unwary...to gulp him down to where the wet ferns drip...a world away; down, down into the cold. She hated him because she could not love him. He was unattainable. His love was somewhere else, where dust blossomed. (p. 192, *154*)

The image used is reminiscent of Steerpike's battle with Titus, as well as a siren's version of the underwater imagery that frequently links Titus and Gormenghast. Cheeta lures Titus by promising, 'All questions will be over. There will only be the facts... and us... our egos naked and our wits on fire... I will be real for you' (p. 194, *155-56*).

But the reality becomes more than even she, who has engineered the whole charade, can deal with. As it progresses, Titus becomes aware of the demonic malice behind her mask of control as she watches his mental confusion, and he can see the ludicrousness of the situation too. It is Juno's protection of Titus once Cheeta has drawn his blood—in a reversal of the Fuchsia-Steerpike episode in Gormenghast, *as she is the desecrator here—that finally strips her completely:*

the shrillest scream of all tore its way through the body of the sunrise like a knife through tissue; and immediately upon this vent from Cheeta's lungs, the little creature turned upon them all and spat. This was the once exquisite Cheeta, the queen of ice; the orchid; brilliant of brain and limb. Now with her dignity departed forever, she bared her teeth... 'I hate... all that you think you are. I hate your Gormenghast. I will always hate it. If it were true, I'd hate it even more...'   (pp. 251-52, *203*)

Having failed in every goal, the destruction of Titus' 'mind... your stories... and the way you are different from any other man I have ever seen' (p. 172, *137*), she can only leave, screaming, until all that is left is the echo of her voice.

She becomes as destructive, on a human level, as the factory is; the scientists destroy Muzzlehatch's zoo, thus causing his obsession with revenge, and she tries to make Titus a non-entity by stripping him of all that makes him unique. Her attempt is as sadistic as Veil's treatment of the Black Rose; here the modern flower of evil blooms from mind to mind. Titus' initial blindness to her true nature, and his sexual confidence with her, Juno's legacy, make him an easy, even masochistic target.

Even Juno, her rival whose relationship with Titus has been at least partially fulfilling, pities her at the Black House because of 'something horrible in the discrepancy of their sizes, and something pitiful about Cheeta's bedraggled face spotted with blood, however evil' (p. 251, *203*).

The motives of both women towards Titus are clearly delineated through a combination of omniscient and third person narration. Whereas Titus is aware of his weakness in accepting Juno's offer, he seems completely unaware, until the scene in the

Black House, of Cheeta's real feelings towards him; even when he does realize her thirst for revenge, his reaction is much more masculine—'in her face he read pure evil...never having seen such an expression of loathing on any woman's face before' (p. 230, *185-86*). In his eyes, his misdemeanour, if it can be called that, is purely sexual, another example of the male reduction of the female; notice how often Titus, despite her warnings, touches Cheeta or makes sexual comments to her. For Cheeta, although the basis for her revenge is in their relationship, Gormenghast is the ultimate rival. Cheeta's links with her father in sensibility and her frigidity are too strong to be ignored, and, where Veil is seen as a sadistic killer from the start, Cheeta evolves into something monstrous—'the nebulous ponderings began to find focus. Something harsher took their place until she realized that what she craved was the knowledge not just of *how* to hurt but *when*' (p. 184, *147*). The narrator suggests the complete unveiling of the evil at the very heart of this society through its vicious parody of another one:

Yet there was a quality about this lunar scene which was more terrible than ever. They were no longer figures in a play. There was no longer any artifice. The stage had vanished. They were no longer actors in a drama of strange light. They were themselves.   (p. 227, *183*)

Another link that binds Juno and Cheeta together is Titus' laughter. There are many kinds of laughter in this novel—the frightened, nervous laughter of Titus as he is circled by the green dart (ch. 19), the lovers' laughter of Juno and Titus, and the incredulous laughter of Titus in the Black House. The narrator comments on the episode of the green dart in a way that prepares the reader for Cheeta later:

its beauty was a thing on its own, beautiful only because its function shaped it so; and having no heart it becomes fatuous—a fatuous reflection of a fatuous concept—so that it is incongruous, or gobbles incongruity to such a degree that laughter is the only way out.   (p. 34, *23*)

When Titus watches Cheeta's expectant look at the Black House, even in the midst of his mental trauma he suddenly sees her for the bitch she is (associatively speaking):

long after her face had returned to normal it was there...that beastly image...as vivid as ever...with that extraordinary contortion of her facial muscles which turned a gelid beauty into something fiendish. Something almost ludicrous...the spectacle of the sprite with her face turned up to his awoke the image of a dog sitting back on its haunches, waiting to be fed.   (p. 229, *185*)

The narrator beautifully conveys the incongruity of Titus' physiological reactions, contrasting their innocence with the personified evil around him—'Out of the fear and apprehension something green and incredibly young took hold of Titus' (p. 229, *185*). The physiological description is an expansion of that given to his laughter with Juno. The verbs used in both accounts are active— 'sidled...shot up...radiated...converged again...capsizing... cartwheeled' (pp. 93, *70* and 229, *185*), and the effect is of a mounting crescendo. Each episode of laughter stops instantly: the first when he touches Juno and the second when he sees Cheeta's glare. Whereas between Titus and Juno the laughter is a special, mutual creation, for Cheeta it serves to further fragment Titus' concept of himself:

Cheeta: 'Did you hear that?...Someone laughing...I would have thought it would have wakened you.'
Another Voice: 'I heard the laughter too...But he was asleep.'
                                                  (p. 230, *185-86*)

Here the release is shortlived and, instead of dissipating the tension, it serves to heighten it further. Cheeta, then, is a representative of the new society in which Titus finds himself. While Juno is rarely seen without Muzzlehatch, Titus, or Anchor at her side, the reader is given information about Cheeta both omnisciently and from within her own detachment (see chapters 79, 80 & 81). Muzzlehatch's obsession is a 'dreadful seed' (p. 157, *125*); Cheeta's is described in language reminiscent of the narrator's at the end of Thackeray's *Vanity Fair*: 'something had begun to rise to the surface of her conscious mind; something that might be likened to a sea monster arising from the depth of the ocean; scaled and repulsive' (p. 184, *147*).

Where Veil is like the crazed killer that Steerpike becomes, Cheeta is like the younger Steerpike, able to conjure up the impression of an emotion she does not actually possess. These three related characters are examples of Peake's variations on the characters and themes central to his art. One of his strengths is this ability to stretch the reader's perspective by the combination of similarity and difference in each portrayal.

Only in the Black House does Cheeta reveal her evil character, abandoning all she has schemed for in a cathartic quasi-exorcism, 'like a shred of darkness...until only a far thin screaming could be heard and after that no more' (p. 252, *203*). With her character,

Peake comes to an almost fairytale resolution: the outwardly beautiful but inwardly ugly midget cannot cope with her power to hurt, and ends up hurting herself more than Titus, although the price he pays in the loss of Muzzlehatch is a high one.

Thus neither the 'old style' women, as represented by Juno the classic, nor the 'modern' woman, as represented by the driven, power-hungry Cheeta (who seeks new ways of dealing with old emotions) is presented as ideal. As the destruction wrought on Muzzlehatch's zoo can be deemed an act of petty spite at the escape of Titus, so Cheeta's elaborate evil-doing can be seen purely as the childish revenge of a woman scorned, a typically masculine perspective. Perhaps this is what Peake is trying to convey when he has Titus use schoolboy slang with her (p. 193, *155*). Obviously the attempt to derange Titus is neither childish nor innocent in conception or execution. Yet for all her subterfuge and her will to hurt Titus, there is still the condescending sense of a spoiled, thwarted child throwing an adult-sized temper tantrum.

The implication, then, particularly in terms of the emotional Juno-Titus-Cheeta matrix, seems to be that, although technology has changed and developed, the human heart is as much a 'vast shambles' (p. 250, *202*) as ever. It is therefore not surprising that the only male-female love presented as totally satisfying to Titus in this new society is purely carnal (ch. 91). Because each woman represents an aspect of Titus himself, making his emotional abandonment of both inevitable, Peake's depiction of the main female characters in *Titus Alone* is, finally, traditionally phallocentric.

Notes

1. For example, in response to Titus' comment that 'the stink of your car ... [smells] sharp as acid; thick as gruel,' when they are talking about his car, Muzzlehatch remarks, 'She's a bitch ... and smells like one' (p. 56, *41*).

2. I am indebted to Professor W P Day for drawing to my attention the image of the Castle as mother-figure.

3. See Nina Baym's 'Melodramas of Beset Manhood' in *The New Feminist Criticism: essays on women and literary theory* (New York: Parthenon, 1985), p. 73.

4. See Joseph Sanders' 'The Passions in their Clay': Mervyn Peake's Titus Stories' reprinted on page 257 of this book.

TITUS AWAKES

INTRODUCTION

THE impetus to write what could perhaps be called a "biography" of Titus Groan, goes back a long way in Mervyn Peake's life, perhaps as far as his childhood in China, where, as the son of a missionary doctor he was isolated in a foreign environment.

It was not however, until early 1940 that the idea of writing a whole book about Titus finally emerged. He and his wife, Maeve would spend hours in their cottage near Arundel, Sussex discussing the plot, characters and events that would fill the book, while he awaited the inevitable call-up to the army.

When it came, he started to write *Titus Groan* in earnest, in "publishers dummies" those hard-back blank page replicas of what a book would look like that publishers gave to their sales representatives to help them sell the book.

He would send the completed copies to Maeve and she would keep them by her to be the first things to be saved, after her sons, in the event of enemy bombing.

The first book, *Titus Groan*, covers the first year of his hero's birth; the second brings Titus up to adolescence and the inevitable rebellion against parental authority. The third, *Titus Alone* records the first impressions and reactions of a young man entering the strange and often hostile surroundings of the larger world beyond his childhood recollections.

When, however, he came to writing the fourth book, Parkinson's Disease had such a grip on him that he was only able to put down with great difficulty a few sentences, in almost illegible handwriting.

It fell upon Maeve after his death, to decipher those squiggles and give us Mervyn Peake's very last writings.

She felt moved enough to write the book that Mervyn would have written, for as she once said: "He wanted to bring Titus to old age and death".

But although Maeve completed over 45,000 words of the book she entitled "World Without End" she herself died before she could complete it.

The few pages in existence are presented here under the title that Maeve thought Mervyn Peake might well himself have selected of "Titus Awakes".

In these few pages the humor, convincing fantasy and sharp descriptive awareness of the world, are still evident, and one cannot but feel saddened and cheated that the world of this fourth book was destined never to be revealed.

JOHN WATNEY

PREADVENTURE

MEANWHILE the castle rolled. Great walls collapsed, one into another sometimes with a roar of dust, sometimes with no sound.

The colours of the tracts were horrible. The vilest green. The most hideous purple. Here the foul shimmering of rotting fungi—there a tract of books alive with mice.

In every direction great vistas opened, so that Gertrude standing at the little window of a high room, would seem to command a world before her eyes, though her eyes were out of focus.

It had become a habit of hers to stand at this particular window, from which a world lay bare, a chowder of cats at her feet and her dark red hair full of nests.

Who else is there alive in this echoing world? And yet for all the collapse and the decay, the castle seemed to have no ending. There were still the endless shapes and shadows, echoing the rides of stone.

While the Countess Gertrude moved about her home, it might be thought that she was in some kind of trance, so silent she was. The only sound coming from her hair in whose deep coils the small birds twittered.

As for the cats, they swarmed about her like froth.

One day the massive Countess standing before the little window of her bedroom lifted her matriarchal head and brought her eyes into focus. The birds fell silent and the cats froze into an arabesque.

And as she approached from the west, so Prunesquallor, his head in the air, approached from the east, and as he minces he sang in a falsetto un-utterably bizarre.

'Is that you, Prunesquallor?' said the Countess, her voice travelling gruffly over the flagstones.

'Why, yes' trilled the Doctor, breaking off in his own peculiar improvisation. 'It most assuredly is.'

'Is that you, Prunesquallor?' said the Countess.

'Who else?'

'Who else,' said her voice travelling across the flagstones.

'Who else?' cried the Doctor. 'It assuredly is. At least I hope so.' And Prunesquallor patted himself here and there, and pinched himself to make sure of his own existence.

CHAPTER 1

THE DESCENT FROM
GORMENGHAST MOUNTAIN

WITH EVERY PACE he drew away from Gormenghast Mountain, and from everything that belonged to his home.

That night, while Titus lay asleep in the tall barn, a nightmare held him. Sometimes as he turned in his sleep he muttered, sometimes he spoke out loud and with extraordinary strange emphasis. His dreams thronged him. They would not let him go.

It was early. The sun had not yet risen. Outside the barn the hills and the forests were hoary with cold dew, and blotched with pools of ice.

What is he doing here, the young man, 77th Earl and Lord of Gormenghast. This surely is a cry from his home and his friends. Friends? What was left of them. As for his home, that world of fractured towers. What truth is there in its existence? What proof had he of its reality.

Sleep brought it forth in all its guises, and as he turned again, he hoisted himself on his elbow and whispered 'Musslehatch, my friend, are you gone then forever?'

The owl made no movement at the sound of his voice. Its yellow eyes stared unblinking at the sleeping intruder.

Titus fell back against the straw and immediately three creatures sidled into his brain.

The first, so nimble on his feet was Swelter, that mountain of flesh, his belly trembling at every movement with an exquisite vibration. Sweat poured down his face and bulbous throat in runnels. Drowned in his moisture, his eyes swam here no larger than pips.

In his hand he carried as though a toy, a double-headed cleaver.

At his shoulder stood something which was hard to define. It was taller than Swealter, and gave forth a sense of timber and of jagged power. But it was not this that caught the senses, but the sound of knee-joints cracking.

For a moment they beamed at one another, this dire couple in a mixture of sweat and leather—and then their mutual hatred settled in again, like a foul plant or fungi. And yet they held hands, and as they moved across the arena of Titus' brain they sang to one another. Swelter in a thin fluted voice, and Flay reminiscent of a rusty key turning in a lock.

They sang of joy, with murder in their eyes. They sang of love, with bile upon their tongues.

Those tongues. Of Swealter's it is enough to say that it protruded like a carrot. Of Flay's that it was a thing of corroded metal.

What of the third character. The lurker in the shade of Swelter's belly? Its tongue was green and fiery. A shape not easily found. It was for the main part hidden by a bush of mottled hair.

This third apparition, a newcomer to Titus' brain, remained in the shadow, a diminutive character who reached no higher than Swelter's knee-joint.

While the other two danced, their hands joined, the tiny creature was content to watch them in their foul perambulations, until loosening their grip upon one another Swealter and Flay rose to full height upon their toes and struck one another simultaneously, and Titus in his dream twisted away from them.

* * * *

From here onwards the content and the writing become too difficult to decipher.

THE TITUS BOOKS WERE NEVER ENVISAGED
AS A TRILOGY

MERVYN PEAKE's listing of possible characters and events

Snows	Fires	Affluence
Mountains	Floods	Debt
Islands	Typhoons	Society
Rivers	Doldrums	
Archipelagos	Famine	
Forests	Pestilences	
Lagoons	Poverty	
Soldiers	Monsters	Pirates
Thieves	Hypocrites	Mermaids
Actors	Madmen	Dreamers
Painters	Bankers	Decadents
Psychiatrists	Angels	Athletes
Laborers	Devils	Invalids
Eccentrics	Mendicants	Blood-Sportsmen
Lepers	Vagrants	
Lotus Eaters		
Shapes	Sounds	Colors
Echoes	Tones	Scents
Textures		

What these books would have been.

MERVYN PEAKE (1911-1968) was a playwright, painter, poet, illustrator, short story writer, and designer of theatrical costumes as well as novelist. His first book of poems, *Shapes and Sounds*, was published in 1941. He also wrote *Rhymes without Reason* (1944), *Captain Slaughterboard Drops Anchor* (1945), *The Craft of the Lead Pencil* (1946), *Letters from a Lost Uncle* (1948), *Mr. Pye* (1953), also published by Overlook, *The Wit to Woo*, a play (1957), and *The Rhyme of the Flying Bomb* (1962). In addition, he illustrated several classics including *The Rime of the Ancient Mariner, Alice in Wonderland, Treasure Island* and *The Hunting of the Snark*.